Josh + Kat

THE COMPLETE TRILOGY

USA Today and International Bestselling Author

Lauren Rowe

BOOKS BY LAUREN ROWE

Standalone Novels

Smitten

Swoon

The Reed Rivers Trilogy (to be read in order)

Bad Liar

Beautiful Liar

Beloved Liar

The Club Trilogy (to be read in order)

The Club: Obsession

The Club: Reclamation

The Club: Redemption

The Club: Culmination (A Full-Length Epilogue Book)

The Josh and Kat Trilogy (to be read in order)

Infatuation

Revelation

Consummation

The Morgan Brothers (a series of related standalones):

Hero

Captain

Ball Peen Hammer

Mister Bodyguard

ROCKSTAR

The Misadventures Series (a series of unrelated standalones):

Misadventures on the Night Shift

Misadventures of a College Girl

Misadventures on the Rebound

Standalone Psychological Thriller/Dark Comedy

Countdown to Killing Kurtis

Short Stories

The Secret Note

infatuation

USA Today and International Bestselling Author

Lauren Rowe

1

JOSH

Oh my fucking God. What's wrong with Jonas this time? I'm so worried I'm jumping out of my skin. I look out the window of the limo, wracked with the same sense of dread I always feel when Jonas calls me with that barely contained panic in his voice. Of course, I dropped everything and immediately caught the next flight to Seattle, just like I always do—but this time, unlike every other time, I don't have a clue what's happened to freak Jonas out. And that, in turn, freaks *me* out.

"Hey," I call up to the limo driver. "Can you change the channel to something a bit more mellow, please?" The song blaring in my ear is "I'm Too Sexy" by Right Said Fred, definitely not a song that's gonna calm my jangling nerves.

"How's this?" the driver says, switching to another station on the radio. The song playing now is "Mad World" by Tears for Fears.

"Yeah," I say, smirking to myself. "Leave it here. Thanks."

When I saw my brother's incoming call on my phone earlier this evening, I figured Jonas had gotten back from his trip to Belize with the "most amazing girl ever," the one and only Sarah Cruz, the magical, mystical unicorn he hacked into U Dub's server to find, sight unseen, and that he was calling to slobber all over the phone about how "amazing" she is. But the minute I heard his voice, I knew he wasn't calling to babble happily about his Belizian getaway with his new crush—I knew something was wrong. Very, very wrong.

"Are you okay? Is Sarah okay?" I asked him, my stomach twisting into knots.

"Yeah, I'm okay. The trip was incredible—Sarah's incredible," Jonas replied. But before I could exhale with any kind of relief, he said something that sent me reeling: "It's The Club, Josh. It's total bullshit—a fucking scam. I think Sarah's in danger—like, maybe *serious* danger."

What the fuck? I couldn't process what that statement could possibly mean.

Mad World, indeed.

It's been well over three hours since Jonas called and said those bizarre words, and I still haven't figured out what the fuck he meant by them. *The Club's a scam?* Well, no, it isn't, Jonas. I happen to know through my own personal experience it's one hundred percent *not* a scam. I can personally attest that I filled out my application, paid my money, and got exactly what I asked for, to the letter, in multiple cities, over the course of one very awesome and cathartic month. So what's the fucking scam?

The more likely scenario is that Jonas didn't get what he asked for because, whatever it was, it was literally impossible to deliver. Knowing him, he probably asked for something only some magical combination of the circus, the philosophy department at Yale, and *American Ninja Warrior* could have delivered. And that's what he thinks of as a *scam*? Maybe this is a wanton case of "it's not them, it's *you*."

Shit. When I told Jonas about The Club in the first place, I should have told him, "Dude, when you fill out your application, less is more. Just go for the big one or two things you're dying for and leave it at that. You can only do so much in one month, trust me—don't get too ambitious." I shake my head. Jonas is so fucking bad with women, I swear to God—and he always has been. They fall all over themselves the minute they see him, of course—everywhere he goes women practically throw their panties at him. But then he opens his fucking mouth and starts quoting fucking Plato and talking in riddles and looking like a fucking serial killer and they run away, screaming in bloody terror. (God only knows how he tricked this Sarah girl into sticking around for so long. Hell, maybe she has a thing for Plato, too, for all I know.)

But for the sake of argument, let's say The Club is some kind of scam (which it's not); how the fuck could that possibly mean this new girl of Jonas' is in some kind of danger—let alone "serious" danger? I can't wrap my brain around any of it. The only thing I can think is that Jonas must have met Sarah in The Club? But that makes no sense. When I asked Jonas about his membership not too long ago, he said he'd applied but had gotten hopelessly distracted by his quest to get laid by his mystery law student.

I'm just so fucking confused. I look out the window of the limo, listening to the song for a long minute.

Frankly, I'm really worried that all this rambling is a sign that Jonas is having some sort of psychotic break again. And if that's what's really going on, why now? As far as I know, my brother's been in full beast mode lately. I mean, shit, just last week when we negotiated the acquisition of all those rock-climbing gyms, he was in tiptop form, kicking ass and taking names like the beast he is. He was a sight to see, actually—he sure out-beasted me by a fucking mile. Of course, he couldn't stop talking about this Sarah chick the whole three days I was with him—which is so unlike him, at first I wasn't sure if he was punking me—but I didn't see that as any cause for alarm. In fact, I was happy for him.

But now, I'm wondering if his obsession with her was a sign that things weren't completely right in his head.

Actually, I was a tad bit worried when he called me in the first place, barking at me to find some random girl who'd sent him an email. (Any time Jonas gets ultra-obsessed about something, it's usually not a good sign for his mental health.) But, much to my relief and surprise, the magical, mystical Sarah Cruz turned out to be well worth his effort, a truly fantastic girl. The minute I met her during our mutual limo ride to the airport, I thought, *Now here's a girl who's gonna bring out the very best in my brother.* She's absolutely adorable. And I can certainly understand the physical attraction, too, I don't mind admitting.

So what the fuck happened in the four days between that limo ride and today that made Jonas' wheels fall off his cart?

Downtown Seattle is whizzing past me outside my car window.

I exhale and shake my head.

I'm so fucking worried right now, I can't think straight. I just wish I understood what's going on with Jonas. And The Club. And Sarah? I shake my head again. What the fuck did Jonas mean she might be in serious danger?

My phone buzzes with a text and I look down.

"Hey, Josh!" the text says. "Looooooooooooong time no see. How ya doing, baby? LOL!"

I chuckle in surprise. Now there's a name I never expected (or particularly wanted) to see on my phone again: *Jennifer LeMonde.* I admit I was dazzled by the girl's pedigree (and slamming body) when we dated for four or five months when I was twenty-three—chalk that up to youth and being stoned out of my mind half the time—but once the initial heat and the novelty of her Grammy-winning daddy and Oscar-winning mommy wore off, not to mention the weed, I quickly realized Jen was very likely the least interesting girl in the world. And that's when I decided once and for all to pull my shit together and lay off the weed and fulfill my family obligations in earnest. And I've stayed on track ever since, other than during the occasional short vacations of total debauchery I've allowed myself over the years (which I'm not sorry about, by the way). Honestly, my little sojourns into hedonism have helped me stay the course, something I've been bound and determined to do, not just for me, but for Jonas, too. I mean, let's face it, Jonas and I can't both be on the verge of a nervous breakdown at all times, and Jonas long ago called dibs on that role.

"Hey, Jen," I type. "It's been a long time. What's up?"

"Have you seen what's going on with Isabel lately? OMG!"

"Yeah. Hard to miss. Good for her. I'm thrilled for her," I type.

I'm being sincere. From what I remember of Isabel from seven years ago, she's a really sweet girl. I'm honestly thrilled all her dreams of stardom are coming true.

"The studio rented Isabel a freaking castle in San Tropez all next week to celebrate her movie opening at number one!" Jen writes. "Dude. It's literally a castle! Made me remember that time our whole group partied together in Cannes—remember that? Or, actually, come to think of it, you probably don't! LOL!!!!" She adds a whole bunch of wineglass emojis and a marijuana-leaf emoji and a smiley face wearing sunglasses. "So, anyhoo, Isabel's getting a huge group together to party in the castle in France (did I mention it's a freaking castle???!!!! OMFG!!!!) and she wanted to know if maybe you and Reed wanna join us for a mini-reunion? It'll be just like old times! LOL!" She adds what appears to be a dancing cat, a reference I'm not sure I understand.

I stare at my phone for a moment, shaking my head. I'm not even remotely tempted. "Sorry. I'm in Seattle for a family emergency," I write. "Gonna be tied up here for a while helping my brother. Plus, I'm an old man nowadays, Jen. You wouldn't even recognize me. I'm practically chasing damn kids off my lawn. Been working pretty hard building my family's business since you last saw me. But, hey, feel free to contact Reed directly to ask him if he's interested. I'll send you his number. And please tell Isabel congrats on all her success for me," I continue. "I'm genuinely thrilled for her. Just saw she won some People's Choice Award or something? Ha! Awesome. She's America's Sweetheart."

"I know! She totally is! LOL! She's blowing up! She's gonna do Jimmy Fallon in NYC when she gets back from France! OMFG! Can you believe it? She's so excited."

"Saw her face plastered on a billboard on my way to LAX today. She looks great. Tell her nice boob job, btw. Her surgeon did excellent work. Unless that's photoshop?"

"Not photoshop. The real fake deal. Brand new, actually. She'll be geeked you noticed. Did you notice her nose, too? (The polite answer is no. Haha!)"

"She looks great, top to bottom. Tell her I said so. But she was always beautiful."

"Aw, come on, Josh. You're making me remember what a sweetheart you are. I wanna see you soooooo bad! Are you sure you can't swing it? Pwetty pwease? I'll make sure you have a REALLY good time." She adds a winking emoji.

I smirk. This is patently ridiculous. Jennifer LeMonde can't possibly give a rat's ass about me, any more than I give one about her. We dated for, what, five months when we were in our early twenties. Not exactly a soul connection. Obviously, this is more about Isabel pining for Reed like she always has than about Jen and me. My guess is Isabel asked Jen to lure Reed to France by any means necessary, including using me as bait.

When I don't immediately reply to Jen's last text, she sends another one right on its heels. "What if I promise not to wear my bikini top the entire time we're there? 'When in France,' right? I remember how much you looooved my pretty titties." She adds a bikini emoji and a pair of lips. "And they're still all-natural, baby!" Winking emoji.

"Sorry. Can't. Family emergency, like I say," I write. But what I'm thinking is, *I'm thirty fucking years old, Jen. You really think I'm gonna travel halfway around the world just to see a pair of tits (even if they are, admittedly, the most perfect pair of tits I've ever seen)?*

"Bummer." Sad-face emoji. "Saw you and your brother on the cover of some magazine the other day, creamed my panties just looking at you. Talk about the Wonder Twins. Day-am. You boys should be in movies."

"Thanks."

"Well, okay. Text me if something changes. I'll be crossing my fingers you change your mind."

"Family emergency, like I say," I type. "Sorry."

"Well, if France isn't gonna work out, we'll have to get together another time really soon. I've been thinking about you a lot lately. About how much fun we used to have." She adds a lips emoji. "I'd make it worth your effort if you come see me, Josh." Another winking emoji.

I roll my eyes. Was she always this annoying? I just told the girl I've got a family emergency and that my brother needs me—and she invites me to fuck her rather than ask me if everything's okay? Not to mention I told her I've been working hard to build my family's business and she didn't ask me for any details? Par for the course, though. Our "relationship," such as it was, certainly wasn't based on anything deep.

The limo stops and I glance up from my phone. I'm in Jonas' driveway. Damn. For a second there, I'd actually forgotten where I was headed.

I exhale audibly. Whatever's waiting for me on the other side of Jonas' front door isn't gonna be good—I can feel it in my bones.

2

JOSH

The minute I walk through Jonas' front door, my brother bounds toward me like a Labrador retriever, dragging his new chew toy (Sarah) with him as he goes.

"Hey," I say, putting down my duffel bag and giving Jonas a big hug. "Well, hello, Sarah Cruz." I give her a hug, too. "Fancy meeting you here."

"Get used to it," Jonas says, obviously thrilled to be saying those words.

"So what the hell's going on?" I ask, steeling myself for whatever fucked up shit's about to come my way.

Jonas moans. "It's so fucked up, man."

My stomach twists. I sit down on the couch, readying myself. "Tell me."

Jonas sits down next to me and runs his hand through his hair, obviously getting ready to launch into some sort of monologue, but before he gets a word out, the bathroom door on the far side of the spacious room opens abruptly and a blur of golden blondeness moves into my peripheral vision. My eyes dart toward the movement—I wasn't aware there was anyone else here besides Jonas, Sarah, and me—and then I absentmindedly look back toward Jonas.

But all of a sudden, my brain processes the startling golden perfection my eyes just beheld and my eyes dart back to the astonishing figure striding toward me. Oh my fucking God. *Who the fuck is this creature?*

The girl walking toward me is literally the most spectacularly beautiful woman I've ever laid eyes on in my entire life, without exception (and this is coming from a guy who briefly dated Miss Universe and currently fucks a Victoria's Secret model whenever we both happen to be in L.A.). This girl's... oh my God. She's the precise sum of parts I'd order at the Build-a-Girl store if there were such a thing. Holy fuck. And she's headed right toward me, smiling at me like she can read my exact thoughts.

She's got to be a model. Or an actress. Of course, she is. What else could she be, looking the way she does? Shit. Damn. Fuck. Oh my God. Holy fucking Christ.

Miss Perfect sashays right up to me, without hesitation. "I'm Kat," she says, putting out her hand. "Sarah's best friend."

She's got sky-blue eyes. Her long hair is a heart-stopping shade of golden blonde—and it's obviously totally natural. And, oh my God, this can't be happening—*she's got a subtle little indentation in her chin, too—the slightest cleft.* That's always been my Achilles' heel—ever since I made out with Jessica Simpson at Reed's twenty-first birthday party so many years ago.

"Josh," I say, taking her hand. "Jonas' brother."

"I know," she says, smirking. "I read the article." She motions in the direction of the coffee table.

I glance down to see which article she's referring to, and I'm bummed to discover it's the one that made Jonas out to be some kind of deep-thinking poet with a Midas touch with investments and me out to be nothing but a giant, throbbing dick with cotton between my ears.

"I sure hope you're more complicated than that article makes you out to be," Kat says, her blue eyes sparkling.

I look at Jonas, hoping maybe he'll step in and say something to help a brother out, like, oh, I dunno, how 'bout, "Oh, that reporter was just trying to sell magazines." Or, maybe, "We thought we were doing a serious interview about Faraday & Sons and it turned into a fluff piece for *Tiger Beat*." But Jonas doesn't say a damned thing on my behalf. Of course, he doesn't, the mother-fucker. I guess now that he's got his dream girl all locked up he's content to let me twist in the wind in front of a woman who looks like mine?

"If the article is to be believed," Kat goes on, smirking at me, "Jonas is the 'enigmatic loner-investment-wunderkind' twin—and you're just the simple *playboy*."

I laugh. So this girl's not only gorgeous, she's sassy, too? Oh, how I like me a sassy woman.

"That's what the article said?" I ask, even though I know that's exactly what the article said.

"In so many words," she says, arching one of her bold eyebrows.

"Hmm," I say, returning her raised-eyebrow gesture. "Interesting. And if someone were writing a magazine article about you, what gross over-simplification would they use?"

She bites her lip. "I'd be 'a party girl with a heart of gold.'" She glances at Sarah and they share a smile.

Oh man. This girl's too much. My skin is buzzing like I've just downed a double shot of Patron. "How come I only get a one-word description—*playboy*—and you get a whole phrase?" I ask.

She shrugs. "Okay, party girl, then."

"That's two words," I say.

Kat raises her eyebrow, yet again. "In this hypothetical magazine article about me," she purrs, "they'd spell it with a hyphen."

Oh, well, fuck. My dick just stretched and yawned and said, "Do I smell coffee and doughnuts?"

She smirks. She knows she's caught a fly in her web. But then again, I'm guessing flies in her web are just par for the course for her.

"So what's going on here, Party Girl with a Hyphen?" I ask. "I take it we didn't all congregate here to party?"

"No, unfortunately," Kat says breezily. "Though, hey, we did have some of your tequila earlier, so thanks for that." Her mouth tilts up, and I have the palpable urge to kiss it. "No, I'm just here to support Sarah," she says, "and, well, I think I might be some kind of refugee in all this, too." She looks at Jonas and frowns. "Although I think maybe Jonas is being slightly overprotective having me stay here. I'm not sure yet."

"You're a *refugee* in all this?" I ask, suddenly on full alert. "What the fuck's going on, Jonas?"

Jonas grunts. "Sit down," he says.

I sit down, my stomach churning. I can't for the life of me guess what he's about to tell me. How are Sarah *and* Kat involved in whatever the fuck's going on? I can't even fathom the connection.

Jonas takes a deep breath and launches into a story that immediately makes my brain hurt. *Sarah worked for The Club? And she was Jonas' intake agent— the one who reviewed his application?* Holy shit! Well, well, well, Little Miss Sarah Cruz isn't quite the naive little law student I thought she was, after all. But, hang on, Jonas is still yammering. There's more? *Sarah emailed Jonas after reading his application? And that's when he got a boner to find her?* Oh my God. This is too much. What the fuck did little Miss Cruz say to Jonas in that email of hers? And what the hell did he say in his application that caught Sarah's attention in the first place?

Oh my God. There's even more to the story. Jonas is still talking. I can't fucking believe it. Some woman in a purple bracelet showed up to meet Jonas at a check-in before he'd ever met Sarah and—hang on, I thought Jonas said he never actually became a member of The Club—and then that same woman turned up at another guy's check-in wearing a yellow bracelet?—and Jonas knows all this because Sarah and Kat went to spy at both check-ins! Whoa, whoa, whoa. *Sarah went to spy on Jonas at a check-in with a woman in The Club?* Holy shit. And, even after that, she's nonetheless sitting here right now, looking at Jonas like he walks on water? Now that's an open-minded woman. I wonder if Kat's as open-minded as her kinky little law-student friend.

I glance at Sarah and she flashes me an endearing look that could only be described as "adorkable." I laugh out loud. Well, shit. If this girl's kinky, then I must be shy and intellectual. Oh man, Sarah's a total dork, through and through, God love her—no wonder my dork of a brother digs her.

". . . so I was thinking we could try to trace The Club through emails," Jonas is saying. "Do you still have any of the emails from when you were a member?" he asks.

Gee, thanks, Jonas. Is my brother *trying* to keep me from getting laid by the most beautiful woman I've ever seen?

I glance at Kat, my cheeks instantly turning red, and I'm surprised to find her eyes blazing at me. *Oh.* Nice. Kat's not grossed out by the revelation that I'm a past member of The Club, she's *intrigued. Lovely.*

I clear my throat. "I don't know if I kept any of their emails," I say. "It's been about seven months since my membership and I don't typically keep emails past three months."

"Shit," Jonas says. "Would have been nice to have something to trace."

Jonas goes on to explain that he and Sarah came home from Belize to find Sarah's and Kat's apartments trashed and their computers stolen—which proves, according to Jonas, that The Club will stop at nothing, including physical violence, to keep both women from divulging the supposedly indisputable fact that The Club is actually nothing more than a global prostitution ring.

I don't reply, partly because I'm simply trying to process Jonas' reasoning, but also because Kat is so fucking hot, it's hard for me to think straight in her presence.

I wonder if Kat's got a boyfriend. Please, God, don't let her have a boyfriend. Oh shit, what if she's married? I glance at her finger. No wedding ring. Thank God. Does she live here in Seattle? Yeah, she must—Jonas said she and Sarah spied on Jonas and that other guy at their check-ins in town. Huh. If Kat lives here, the odds are slim she's a model. I wonder what she does for a living, then. Does she—

Oh.

Jonas is staring at me like he expects me to say something. Shit. I have no idea what he's been saying for the past few minutes.

"Huh," I finally say, trying to look deep in thought. "Interesting."

Jonas exhales a shaky breath, clearly containing some sort of rage at my response. But what the fuck does he expect? I can't track each and every one of his ramblings under the best of circumstances, let alone when a woman like Kat is sitting fifteen feet away from me, looking at me like she's thinking about sucking my dick.

And, anyway, it's obvious to me Jonas is probably grossly misinterpreting the situation or, at the very least, overreacting to it (shocker!). Even if Sarah and Kat saw some chick wearing a yellow bracelet after she'd fucked Jonas a few nights earlier wearing a purple one, that doesn't necessarily mean the sky is falling, does it? It could simply mean some women in The Club are assigned more than one color. Why is that such a fucking revelation? Some people have extremely varied tastes, after all.

Or maybe one of Jonas' exes found out he's been dating Sarah and went ballistic, trashing Sarah's apartment in a fit of jealous rage (and then doing the same thing to Sarah's best friend's place, too)? Even if that seems like a far-fetched scenario, it's probably no crazier an idea than some hitman coming after Sarah and Kat simply because they happened to observe some woman wearing two different colored bracelets.

Jonas is glaring at me again, obviously waiting for me to say something.

I clear my throat. "Wow," I say. But he's still waiting, and so are Sarah and Kat. "I'm not sure, bro," I add. "I met some really great girls." It's a true state-ment—I honestly did meet some really great girls in The Club—but, none-theless, even as I say it, I cringe at how douche-y it sounds.

I glance at Kat and, yep, she's put off.

Oh, really? So she's intrigued when she finds out I *joined* a high-priced sex club, but put off to learn I actually *enjoyed* my short time in it? Ha! This one's a handful, I can already tell.

"How long was your membership, Josh?" Sarah asks.

"A month," I reply.

"And you... completed your entire membership period... successfully?"

Oh my God. Sarah can barely get the words out. This girl really is adorable —and, yep, clearly, there's not a kinky bone in her body. A total goody-two-shoes, through and through, which is funny considering she processed sex club applications for a living.

"Oh, yeah. Definitely," I say, looking at Kat and smiling broadly. Maybe I shouldn't smile, but I can't help it—I'm enjoying how every little thing I say about The Club pulls an animated reaction from Kat of one kind or another.

Plus, shit, I'm just being honest here: My month in The Club was fucking awesome—just what the doctor ordered after Emma ripped my heart and stuck it into a blender. Fucking yourself back to happy truly shouldn't be underrated, I gotta say—it was exactly what I needed at the time. Plus, in an unexpected twist, a handful of the women I hooked up with that month stayed with me in my hotel room for hours after we'd fucked and listened to me pour my guts out about my shattered heart. I normally never would have been such a blathering pussy-ass, of course—I'm not Jonas, for fuck's sake—but I guess there was freedom in knowing I'd never see any of those women again. And so, I let my guard down completely and let it flow—and at the end of that whirlwind month of fucking and fantasy-fulfillment and unexpected gut-spilling, I actually felt like myself again, ready to move on and stop acting like a brokenhearted little pussy.

I've never told anyone about my month in The Club, except to suggest to Jonas that he join—(if anyone needs to fuck himself to happy, it's my brother, that's for fucking sure)—but now that it's out in the open in front of Sarah and Kat (and especially Kat), I'm not gonna crawl into a hole and act like I'm embar-rassed by it. I was single. It was fun and uniquely cathartic. As far as I'm concerned, I have absolutely nothing to be ashamed of when it comes to my time in The Club. Might some of those girls have been hookers? Well, now that I think about it, sure—how else could The Club have supplied everything I asked for in my application, to the letter? But I can't believe *all* of them were straight-up hookers. Some of them might just have been looking for a very wealthy boyfriend with a big ol' dick.

"There's no way all those girls were prostitutes," I say, but even as the words come out of my mouth, I realize I don't actually believe them. The truth is, even as I filled out my application, I didn't care *how* The Club supplied what I asked for—just as long as they did. So, okay, if it turns out the women I fucked in The Club were all prostitutes, then fine, they were well worth the money, and then some. Clearly, I needed to do something to move on from Emma—and fucking my way back to beastliness with a bunch of super cool, nonjudgmental, hot-as-hell women was a helluva lot cheaper (and a lot more fun) than a month's worth of therapy. "They were super cool, all of them," I say, matter-of-factly. Fuck it.

Sarah crinkles her nose. "They were *all* super cool, huh?" she asks. "Well, Julia Roberts was 'super cool' in *Pretty Woman*, too."

I chuckle. Oh my God, I absolutely love this girl. "True," I say. I flash Jonas a look that says, "She's a cutie, bro," but his eyes are as hard as fucking flint right now.

Shit. Here we go. I know that look. It means my brother's about to lose his fucking shit.

"How many women could you possibly have gone through in a month?" Kat suddenly blurts from across the room.

Oh, hello. I lock eyes with Kat and, yup, it's written all over her gorgeous face: she wants me. Oh, fuck yes, she does. I can't help but smile as my cock begins tingling at the blatant desire on her face.

"I mean . . ." Kat says, but she doesn't continue.

I keep staring at her, making her squirm, daring her to say more and show her cards, but she doesn't.

She bites her lip.

"A couple," I finally say slowly. Oh yeah, this is gonna be fun.

Sarah lets out a little moan that wrenches my attention away from Kat's gorgeous face. "Josh, did you ever use your membership to meet a 'super cool' girl in the Seattle area?" she asks, her face darkening with anticipatory horror.

I wanna laugh at the expression on Sarah's face. Oh my God, she's so fucking cute, this woman.

I nod. "Once," I say. I scowl, but my scowl is for Sarah's benefit—mainly to match her look of obvious horror at the thought of Jonas and me having been unwitting Eskimo brothers with some random, nameless woman in Seattle. As far as I know, Jonas and I have never fucked the same woman, and I'm certainly not fond of the idea, but if it happened by sheer chance with a woman neither of us cares about or intended to pursue for something more serious than a one-night stand, it really wouldn't be the end of the fucking world.

"Brunette. Piercing blue eyes—like the bluest eyes you've ever seen—fair skin," Jonas says, rattling off the description of his Seattle girl like he's doing the

play-by-play at a Seahawks game. "C-cup. Perfect teeth. Smokin' hot body—"
He looks at Sarah apologetically. "Sorry, baby."

"It's okay." Sarah says—and, damn, it sure sounds like she means it. Well, that settles it: Sarah's totally awesome in my book. If there's one thing I can't stand, it's a jealous woman.

"No," I say. "That doesn't describe my Seattle girl." Honestly, I don't actually remember my Seattle girl specifically—my whole month in The Club is a bit of a blur—but by Jonas' description, it's abundantly clear we didn't hook up with the same woman. "When I filled out my application," I continue, glancing at Kat, "I requested only—"

I stop talking midsentence, thanks to the look on Kat's face: the girl's sitting on the edge of her seat, looking like she's literally holding her breath at whatever I'm about to say. Ha! What the fuck does Kat think I'm about to say?

That's funny. The truth is I was about to say something pretty innocuous —but obviously, the girl's imagining something pretty fucking titillating, or maybe even really fucked up. Well, far be it for me to disappoint her depraved imagination. In fact, I can plainly see by the revved-up expression on Kat's face, it's in my extreme interest to let this girl's imagination run wild.

"Thank God, bro," I say, making a big show of my relief. "That would have been just like having sex with *you*." I mock-shudder at the thought.

Jonas flashes me his usual look of annoyance. "We're totally off track here," he barks out. "The only thing that matters is that these bastards have fucked with Sarah and Kat, and we have no way of knowing whether they're done fucking with them or if they're just getting started."

I lean back on the couch and sigh. Yep. My gut tells me Jonas is overreacting to this situation, probably spurred on by somehow trying to impress Sarah. "Oh, I don't know," I say, putting my hands behind my head.

Oh shit. Oops. I just unleashed Jonas' crazy as surely as if I'd opened the door to a rabid dog's cage.

"*Sit down, Jonas*," I say emphatically, over and over, in response to Jonas' tirade, but he won't listen to me. "Let's just talk about this for a minute, rationally."

"Oh, *you're* gonna tell *me* how to be rational?" Jonas seethes. "Mr. Buys-a-Lamborghini-on-a-Fucking-Whim-When-His-Girlfriend-Breaks-Up-With-Him is gonna tell *me* to be rational?"

I roll my eyes.

Nice, Jonas. First my stupid-ass brother outs me for joining a sex club and now he's gonna give me shit for what a pussy I was after Emma drop-kicked me and cheated on me with that Ascot-wearing prick? Talk about a cheap shot.

Up 'til now I was feeling pretty entertained by my asshole-brother, maybe even sympathetic, but now I feel like throttling him. But because I'm the sane and rational twin in this fucked-up duo, I somehow manage to keep my shit together, like I always do. "I'm just saying I don't know; that's all," I say, gritting my teeth. "I'm not saying I disagree. Big difference. Just sit the fuck down for a minute. Jesus, Jonas."

But, of course, Jonas doesn't immediately shut the fuck up or calm the fuck down or do anything even remotely resembling sane rationality. Why? Because he's Jonas, which, I guess, gives him a lifelong pass to act like a fucking lunatic while I sit here holding his shit together for him, even though on any given day it takes almost all my strength to hold my own shit together, thank you very much.

It takes ten minutes of talking to Jonas like the man-child he is, but I finally get him to sit down and breathe deeply.

"Okay," I say, taking a deep breath. Jesus God, give me strength. "Let's think. What's the point in taking down the entire organization? I mean, really? Just *think* about it, logically. That sounds like an awfully big job—and maybe overkill. Think about it, Jonas. Yes, we've got to protect Sarah and Kat, of course . . ." I smile at Sarah and then at Kat. "*Of course.* And we will. I promise. But beyond that, why do we care what The Club does?"

Jonas shifts in his seat. He's considering.

That's good. I'm clearly making headway. I take another deep breath.

"Why kill a fly with a sledgehammer when a flyswatter will do?" I continue. "The Club provides a service—and very well, I might add, speaking from experience. So, yeah, maybe things aren't exactly as they appear, maybe they oversell the fantasy a bit—but so does Disneyland. I mean, you can go ride a rollercoaster anywhere, right?—but you pay ten times more to ride that same roller coaster at Disneyland. Why? Because it's got Mickey Mouse's face on it."

Jonas' eyes could cut diamonds right now.

"Maybe all these guys who join The Club want to ride a roller coaster with Mickey Mouse's face on it—and they're happy as clams to pay a shitload to do it. They don't even *want* to know they could ride the same roller coaster *without* Mickey's face on it for two bucks down the street."

I'm trying to make Jonas see another side to things, something he's never been particularly good at doing, but I've clearly just tripped yet another Jonas-landmine—I've barely gotten my last words out when the dude begins literally sputtering with outrage, so Sarah steps in to speak for him.

"Josh," Sarah says, putting her hand gently on Jonas' forearm. "Your premise is faulty. When you buy a ticket for Disneyland, you *know* you're signing up to ride a Mickey Mouse roller coaster. Not everyone signs up to ride a Mickey Mouse roller coaster when they join The Club—but that's what they give them, anyway."

Okay, now I'm completely confused. What the hell is she talking about? Why would anyone join The Club, except for the sole purpose of riding a Mickey Mouse roller coaster? That's all The Club is or could ever be—a vehicle for mainlining cotton candy—no more or less—an unhealthy but delicious diet of pure sugar to be consumed once in a blue moon for a short period of time, even though you know it's total crap for a growing boy. I mean, shit, only a fucking moron would think he could consume cotton candy as his diet's main staple, right?

I wait for Sarah to explain further but, apparently, that's all she's gonna say. She sits back down on the couch and primly folds her hands in her lap.

"What do you mean?" I ask.

Jonas exhales. "She means not everyone is totally fucked-up like you and me." He clears his throat. "Or, at least, like me—you seem to have been cured of your fuckeduppedness by that stupid book."

I burst out laughing at that one. Good times.

"She means some people are, you know, *normal,*" Jonas continues. He sits down on the couch next to Sarah and puts his arm around her, obviously displaying some sort of solidarity with her. Wow, he must really like this girl, because what he just said is the stupidest thing I've ever heard him say.

"What the fuck does that even mean?" I ask. "*Normal?*"

Jonas doesn't answer. (Of course, he doesn't—because there's no defending the idiocy of his comment.)

"Okay, fine, let's say there are *normal* people out there... Why the fuck would any *normal* person join The Club?"

"To find love," Jonas says quietly. "That's what normal people want. That's what The Club promises to the normal ones. And it's a scam."

I burst out laughing again. Oh my God, that's the funniest thing I've ever heard in my entire life. But Jonas and Sarah don't look the slightest bit amused. I glance at Kat, hoping to find one other sane person in this room besides me, and, thankfully, the Party Girl With a Hyphen doesn't disappoint—she flashes me a sexy little smirk that says she thinks Jonas and Sarah are being ridiculous, too. I match her smirk with one of my own and she flashes me a wide smile that bares her perfect, white teeth.

"It's true," Sarah says, like she's defending truth, honor and the fucking American way.

"Seriously?" I say. I take a beat to study my brother's face. But, yeah, he's dead serious. "Did *you* join The Club looking for love?" I ask. I swear to God, if he says yes, then I know for sure this adorable Sarah Cruz girl has cast a fucking spell on him. Either that, or he's truly had a psychotic break.

Jonas looks at Sarah like he's asking his master for permission to speak, and Sarah nods. Well, that answers that question—she's cast a spell on him. He kisses the back of her hand. "No, I didn't," Jonas says.

"Well, neither did I," I say, trying to ignore how pussy-whipped my brother's acting right now. "I can't imagine anyone ever would. That's pretty far-fetched—even if someone's *normal.*" I shoot an apologetic look at Sarah. Even if my brother's acting like a flop-dick right now, that's no reason for me to be disrespectful to Sarah. Obviously, she's passionate about this ridiculously naïve notion of hers. "Sorry, Sarah," I say.

Sarah nods and shoots me a half smile.

"I'm pretty sure I joined The Club because I was having some kind of mental breakdown," Jonas says softly. "*Again.*"

Whoa, whoa, whoa. I shake my head with whiplash. *No.* Those are the exact words I didn't want to hear coming out of Jonas' mouth tonight. I'm not equipped to babysit Jonas through another mental breakdown. No fucking way. I've been doing it my whole fucking life and I don't wanna do it anymore. Shit. And he seemed to be doing so well lately. What have I been missing?

"Though I didn't realize it at the time, of course," Jonas continues. He looks at Sarah. "I joined The Club because I didn't understand what was really going on with me, what I really wanted—or what I needed. I was spiraling, man."

My heart is thumping out of my chest. Shit, shit, shit. I don't know what the hell to say. I thought Jonas was kicking ass and taking names lately, I really did. Work has been better than ever—the whole company is a fucking behemoth right now, thanks primarily to Jonas and his incredible instincts for deals. And he's in the best shape of his life, too.

True, the guy's been kind of a weird hermit for a while now—obsessed with nothing but climbing and working out and finding new investment opportunities—and, true, I've often thought Jonas should get out more, maybe go to a fucking party now and again, fuck some random woman he meets in a fucking bar, for Chrissakes. But that's just not Jonas. He's always been the sensitive one, attaching a deeper meaning to everything, including sex.

Actually, I suggested Jonas join The Club for a month in the first place because I figured a little meaningless sex might do the guy a world of good, exactly the way it did for me (and he's clearly not capable of getting random pussy for himself, that's for sure, though God only knows why, given what he looks like). And now I'm finding out my poetic brother viewed joining The Club as some sort of "surrender to insanity"? Well, shit.

I run my hand through my hair, desperation descending upon me. I feel like I could cry like a baby right now, even though I haven't cried since I was ten years old. I seriously cannot do this again. I've carried my brother's sanity on my back my whole fucking life, even when I've barely been able to hold the weight of my own. And I'm tired. I cover my face with my hands for a moment, trying to pull myself together.

There's a long silence in the room.

"Well, all righty, then," Kat finally says.

I glance up at her and she smiles warmly at me.

And just like that, I regain my footing. "Holy shit, Jonas," I mumble, rubbing my hands over my face. "I'm all in when it comes to protecting Sarah and Kat, okay? Whatever it takes—you know that, right?"

"I know." Jonas exhales. "Thanks."

"I just think maybe you're overreacting about—"

"Fuck, Josh!" Jonas leaps up from the couch and glowers over me like he's about to strangle me—but I don't flinch. The dude wouldn't hurt a fucking fly and we both know it. "These motherfuckers threatened my girl and her best friend. Do you understand? They crossed the fucking line!"

I stand and open my mouth to speak, but Jonas cuts me off.

"I'm not letting them near her." He pulls Sarah up off the couch and into him. "I'm gonna protect her—which means decimating the fuck out of them. Do you understand me? *Decimating them.*"

"Whoa," I say. "Calm down." Every hair on my body is standing on end. What the fuck is happening right now? He's spiraling into some sort of panic attack and I don't fully understand why.

"I'm not gonna let it happen again, Josh," he blurts. "I couldn't survive it this time—I know I couldn't. I barely survived it before. You didn't see what I saw... the blood... it was everywhere. You weren't there." He shuts his eyes tight. "You didn't see her. I'm not gonna let it happen again. I can't do it again."

I feel like he just punched me in the teeth. Why the fuck is he saying this to me, especially in front of Sarah and Kat? I'm well aware I was sitting at a fucking football game, cheering happily, while Jonas watched our mother being fileted like a fish. No one needs to remind me of that fact.

"Jonas... Oh my God," I say.

"I thought *you'd* understand, of all people." Jonas' voice is thick with emotion. "I don't want to do this alone, but I will. I'll do whatever I have to do, don't you understand? I can't let anything happen to her. Not again. Never again."

This is insane. I can't believe Jonas is comparing this situation to what happened to our mom. Motherfucker. He's crossed a line here. He's fucking crossed a motherfucking line. "Ladies, could you give us a minute?" I say, gritting my teeth. "*Please.*"

Jonas juts his chin at me and squeezes Sarah like he's worried I might fucking attack her or something.

"Jonas," Sarah whispers, brushing her lips against his jawline. "Talk to your brother, baby. He's on your team." She touches his face. "Your brother's on your side. Just listen to him. He dropped everything to come here for you. Listen to him."

Jonas lets go of Sarah's hand, grabs her face with both hands, and kisses the hell out of her. Clearly, his kiss is a giant "fuck you" to me, but I don't understand what I've done to deserve it.

When Jonas pulls away from kissing Sarah, he looks fiercely at me, his nostrils flaring, glaring at me like he's daring me to say a fucking word. But I'm not even tempted to speak. There's nothing I could possibly say that wouldn't involve the words "crazy" and "fuck" and "you."

"One can easily forgive a child who's afraid of the dark," Jonas says, visibly trembling. "The real tragedy of life is when men are afraid of the light."

I roll my eyes. Fan-fucking-tastic. Another Plato quote from my crazy-ass brother. Fuck me. This is gonna be a long fucking night.

3

KAT

As Derek kisses my lips, he runs his fingertips along my thigh underneath my pencil skirt. I return his kiss with equal enthusiasm and run my fingers through his hair. Heck yeah, I do. Derek the ex-SEAL-bodyguard is way, *way* hotter than Kevin Costner ever was (and Kevin Costner was pretty freaking hot back in the day). I lean back onto the arm of my couch, pulling Derek's lips with me as I go and coaxing Derek's body on top of mine. Holy shitballs, this man's clearly got a hard body beneath that Men's Wearhouse suit. And that's not all that's hard about Derek, either—the bulge behind his slacks feels like it was forged in a steel factory. Good lord.

It's all I can do not to bust out singing Whitney Houston's "I Will Always Love You"—not because I will always love Derek Insert-Last-Name-Here, obviously. I only met the guy less than twenty-four hours ago, and, as far as I can tell, he's got the personality of a baseball bat. No, that iconic song is on the tip of my (extremely busy) tongue right now because *oh my effing God* I'm about to fulfill a fantasy I've had since I first witnessed a certain juggernaut of cinematic artistry at the tender age of nine.

My mom rented *The Bodyguard* from Blockbuster Video on a Friday night (plus video games for my dad and four brothers to keep them distracted while we two girls watched our movie), and by Sunday afternoon, I'd watched that damned movie at least six times from start to finish (and that was a full year before we got our first DVD player, which means I actually had to *rewind* that freaking thing every time I wanted to re-watch it, so that tells you how committed I was to Whitney and Kevin's once-in-a-lifetime love).

And all through the years since that first *Bodyguard* marathon, through puberty and high school and college, whenever I've been dumped or no one asked me to a dance or I've had PMS or gotten a crappy-ass grade in a class (that last one being a fairly common occurrence), I've watched Kevin and Whitney as a sort of therapy, I guess, kind of like digging into a cinematic pint of Ben and Jerry's.

So it's no wonder that now, as a twenty-four-year-old woman with an unapologetic sex drive and an unwavering dedication to you-only-live-once, having hot sex with my very own real-life bodyguard is right at the top of my sexual bucket list. I mean, come on. Not all sex has to be about some kind of deep soul connection—sometimes, it can simply be about making a lifelong sexual fantasy come true.

"Katherine Morgan?" Derek the Bodyguard asked yesterday when I opened the front door of my apartment and beheld his no-nonsense hotness for the first time. I leaned against the doorjamb and smiled broadly, pleasantly surprised about the gift the universe had just plopped into my lap (or, more accurately, the surprise Sarah's new boyfriend, Jonas, had just plopped into my lap).

"Yes, I'm Katherine Morgan," I replied to Derek yesterday, extending my hand and flashing him my most flirtatious smile. "But please, call me Kat." I knew a bodyguard would be coming to my house, of course—Jonas had already said as much earlier that morning—but only in my wildest dreams did I imagine he'd look like Derek.

"Miss Morgan," Derek said, seemingly impervious to my charms. "My name is Derek Something-or-Other, and I've been assigned to protect you." He looked at his phone. "By a Jonas P. Faraday?"

"Yeah. Jonas mentioned he'd be sending someone. Thanks for coming."

"I'll be watching over you during the daytime," Derek continued matter-of-factly. "And my partner, Rodney, will take the night shift." He motioned across the street. "That's Rodney over there, just so you know what he looks like."

I walked out of my apartment and peered across the street in the direction Derek was pointing—and there, sitting in a nondescript sedan, was Father Time. When Rodney saw me looking at him, he curtly waved, started his engine, and drove away, and I suppressed the urge to laugh with glee that Derek had been the one to show up on my doorstep to take the first shift.

"Come in," I purred to Derek, brushing past him into my apartment.

"Sure. Just to do a sweep of your surroundings and give you a safety de-briefing. After that, I'll keep watch from across the street to give you privacy." His tone was strictly professional—very Kevin-Costner-at-the-beginning-of-*The-Bodyguard*. Not the least bit flirtatious.

Things looked grim for my chances of singing Whitney's tune right about then—and honestly I might have dropped the whole thing if it weren't for what happened next: Derek's eyes unmistakably darted down to the curve of my breasts in my tight-fitting blouse and then down to my hips in my slim-fitting business skirt and then back up to my lips—*at which point they flickered with unmistakable desire.* And that's when I knew Mr. Professional Bodyguard maybe wasn't quite as all-business underneath that dark suit as he seemed—and that maybe, just maybe, it was only a matter of time before Derek the Body-guard would be whispering things like, "No, Kat, I can't protect you like this" and "Not on my shift" and "I was hired to protect you, not to help you shop" into my ear.

"Come in, Derek," I said, waltzing back into my apartment from the walk-way. "You wanna cup of coffee?" I asked breezily, even though coffee wasn't at all what I was thinking about.

Derek grinds his hard-on into me and kisses me, jolting me back to the delicious present on my couch. His hand skims my thigh under my skirt and I widen my legs to let him know I'm not at all shy here, big fella, that this isn't my first time at the sexy-times-rodeo and he need not be quite so respectful of my *vagina* (which I've noticed he hasn't even attempted to touch).

Derek reacts to my implicit invitation by floating his hand up toward the increasingly wet crotch of my panties. *Yes. That's right. Go for it, Bodyguard. Do it. I've got the chorus of Whitney's song all cued up for you, baby.* But, damn, his hand stops at the inside of my thigh and then trails across my hipbone and around to my ass.

Damn.

I press into him with increased enthusiasm, and—

My cell phone buzzes on the coffee table, repeatedly, with an incoming call.

Crap. I'm supposed to be at work right now, actually. I had an early break-fast meeting with a client (the owner of a new boutique) about the social media campaign I'm planning for her—and afterwards, I swung by my apartment on my way back to the office "to grab an umbrella." Or so I said. Yes, it had started to pour—this is Seattle, after all—but we have plenty of extra umbrellas and plastic ponchos at the office. What I was actually doing with the whole "I gotta grab an umbrella" ruse was creating an excuse to lure my new bodyguard (who'd been shadowing my every move all morning long) into my apartment to see if I could seduce him into seducing me.

My phone stops buzzing and I refocus my attention onto Derek's lips.

I kiss him a bit more enthusiastically and he follows my lead, running his hand over my blouse, right over my nipple. *Good. That's good. Come on, Derek. Let me be your Whitney.*

I wonder who was calling. Was that my boss? Or maybe Hannah Banana Montana Milliken? Or maybe it was Sarah, calling to tell me some new juicy tidbit about her new boyfriend (who supposedly loves her but won't say the actual words)? Or maybe, just maybe, it was the boyfriend's Hottie-McHottie-pants brother, Josh Faraday?

I smile at the thought, even as I'm kissing Derek.

Josh sure didn't try to hide his attraction to me the night before last at Jonas' house.

"Don't worry about me, guys," Josh yelled to Jonas and Sarah as Jonas barreled to his room with Sarah slung over his shoulder. "I'll just party the night away with Party Girl with a Hyphen."

"Oh no, you won't, Playboy," I shot back at him. "You'll have to find another Mickey Mouse roller coaster to ride tonight."

Of course, I was wildly attracted to him, too—who wouldn't be?—but I'm not sure how I felt about his whole "Mickey Mouse rollercoaster" analogy. And, regardless, there's nothing I love better than taking a cocky guy down a peg. It's kinda my specialty, actually.

I was trying to stun Josh into humbled silence with my little zinger, but Josh wasn't even remotely fazed. He swaggered over to me and leaned his lips right into my ear, making the hair on the nape of my neck stand up and my crotch tingle. "So that's how we're gonna play this, huh, Party Girl with a Hyphen?" he said. "We're gonna play it cool? Okay, babe, fine with me—we'll play it however you like," he whispered, his warm breath teasing my ear. "But we both know where this is headed. Mmmm." And with that, he sauntered out of the room, whistling as he went, and never looked back.

I must have stood there for a solid five minutes, my mouth hanging open and my crotch pulsing in my panties. Day-am.

My phone buzzes sharply with a voicemail on the coffee table next to my couch.

Who the heck is trying to reach me so insistently?

Derek's tongue is swirling around mine and his hard-on against my thigh is becoming urgent. Well, whoever's calling, they'll just have to wait. I press myself into Derek's erection, goading him on, and he reacts by kneading my ass with his strong hand. Hmm. That ass-kneading thing isn't really working for me, actually. There's just no finesse to it. It's like the dude's wearing freaking oven mitts. Or maybe the problem is that Derek just isn't that great a kisser?

Oh, shit, I've still gotta come up with my social media campaign for that chain of barbeque restaurants. Damn. Maybe Hannah will help me brainstorm? Yeah, I'll take her to lunch tomorrow and see if she'll pretty-please help me out. We haven't been to The Tavern in a while. They've got such great salads—

Oh, jeez. I'm thinking about salad while kissing my hot bodyguard? What the hell? Come on, Kat! Kevin Costner. Whitney Houston. Bodyguard. *Focus.*

My phone buzzes again, just once, with an incoming text. Oh jeez. Someone's really trying to reach me. I push on Derek's chest. "Hang on a minute," I say. "Lemme check my phone real quick."

Derek sits up and wipes his mouth, his eyes blazing.

I grab my phone and look at the display. The missed call was from a number I don't recognize. A "323" number. Isn't that L.A.? I peek into my texts and the new text is from that same unrecognizable number, too: "Kat, this is Josh Faraday," the text says. My heart skips a beat. "Call me immediately. Please. It's urgent that I talk to you."

Derek kisses me and kneads my ass again.

Could it be the Playboy is calling me with an "urgent" invitation to dinner? Sarah told me Josh asked for my phone number last night, intending to ask me to dinner after Jonas kicked him out of his house, but Sarah told him I was already out to dinner with my new bodyguard. Sarah said Josh looked deflated and said he was gonna hop a flight back to L.A.—but did he change his mind and stay in Seattle?

I push on Derek's chest again and sit completely upright. "Excuse me, Derek," I say, wiping my mouth with the back of my hand. "I've got to make a quick call."

Derek exhales, clearly frustrated, but I don't care. It's suddenly quite clear to me I'd rather be out on a date with Josh Faraday, world-class Mickey-Mouse-rollercoaster-rider or not, than trying to screw a bodyguard wearing oven mitts who couldn't kiss his way out of a paper bag.

I practically sprint into my bedroom and close my door behind me, my heart leaping out of my chest.

Josh Faraday. Now *there's* a guy who makes visions of blowjobs dance in my head. The minute I laid eyes on the man, I felt like I'd been struck by a sexual lightning bolt—and I'm positive he felt it, too. He didn't even try to hide it.

But I've got to be careful. Josh is obviously a player of staggering proportions, and I'm not a girl who likes to be chewed up and spit out by any man. If anyone's gonna do the chewing up and spitting out, then it's gonna be me. And I'm not so sure I could manage getting the upper hand with a seasoned player like Josh Faraday.

Every article I read about the Faraday brothers when I was snooping around in Jonas' office the other night (and there were a lot of them) made at least passing reference to Josh's oversized appreciation for beautiful women. But, of course, I would have figured that out without the benefit of those articles. One quick Google search of the guy revealed he burns through supermodels and reality TV starlets and actresses and daughters of moguls like a Weedwacker. I mean, seriously. The dude's face is plastered all over the Internet with strikingly beautiful women at black-tie events and fundraisers and concerts and parties all over the frickin' world. Jeez. I love to have fun, too, God knows I do—but I'm just a pharmacist's daughter living in Seattle and working at a PR firm. My idea of fun is going to a karaoke bar with my friends on a Saturday night—not the Cannes Film Festival with Isabel Randolph. Holy shitballs.

And the way he referred to the women in The Club as Mickey Mouse rollercoasters was kinda Douchey McDouchey-pants I gotta say. I'm certainly not one to judge anyone, guy or girl, for enjoying sex and having a whole frickin' lot of it—more power to all my horny sistren and brethren—but before I volunteer to be one of Josh Faraday's many, many rollercoasters, I'd sure like to know what I'd be getting myself into. Holy shitballs. That's an understatement.

I'd give literally *anything* to read that boy's application to The Club and find out his dirty little secrets.

But first things first: why'd he call? Well, no sense wondering. I'll just call him back and find out. And, heck, maybe as a condition to saying yes to dinner (if, indeed, that's what he's aiming for), I'll ask him to email me his Club application. Why not? It sure seems like Sarah reading Jonas' application from the get-go worked out pretty damned well for them.

I take a deep breath. Okay, yes. That's my strategy. I'll say yes to dinner *if* he sends me his application. Bold. Ballsy. Kind of obnoxious—but awesome. Yes.

I'm about to press the "call back" button next to Josh's text, when I remember his voicemail message. I'd better listen to it first before calling him back.

"Kat, this is Josh Faraday," Josh's voice says—and the tightness of his tone makes my stomach clench. That's not the tone of a man calling to ask a girl out on a date. "Please call me right away," he says. "It's urgent. Thank you."

Now I'm confused. What on earth could—

I gasp.

Sarah.

Oh my God. Was Jonas right? Was Sarah actually in grave danger, just like he predicted? I can barely breathe as I push the "call back" button on my phone.

Josh picks up my call immediately. "Kat?" he says, his voice tight.

"What happened, Josh?" I blurt. "Is it Sarah?" I sit down on the edge of my bed, swallowing hard. This is gonna be bad. This is gonna be really, really bad. I know it is. I suddenly feel like I'm gonna throw up.

Josh exhales loudly. "Sarah's been stabbed."

"No," I blurt.

"She's at the hospital now. Jonas just called me." His voice wobbles. "She was attacked in a bathroom at school."

"No." Tears instantly flood my eyes. "*Sarah.*"

"I'm trying to get a flight back to Seattle—not having any luck. I need you to get Sarah's mom and get over to the hospital as soon as possible, okay?"

"Oh my God. Oh my God. Sarah."

"Kat. Listen to my voice. I need you to get Sarah's mom and get over to the hospital as soon as possible. Can you do that for me?"

I take a deep breath and wipe my tears. "Okay."

"Good girl. I'll get there as soon as I can."

I can't control my emotions anymore. I lose myself to sobs. "Sarah. Oh my God. No."

4

KAT

There's a raging storm outside Sarah's hospital window, but the rain is no match for my tears. Oh my God, this is the worst day of my life. Sarah's my best friend. My partner in crime. My rock. We finish each other's sentences. We laugh 'til we pee. She's more than my best friend—she's my *sister*. We tell each other everything—or, at least, *I* tell Sarah everything. I'm not sure it works the other way around. But I've never cared about that because that's just Sarah. She's this weird mixture of shy and reserved and confident and insecure and hilarious and crazy all at once. There's just nobody like Sarah Cruz. She's the absolute best.

And some bastard out there *purposefully* hurt my girl? Just the thought is making me bawl all over again. How could anyone even think of hurting Sarah of all people? The girl wouldn't hurt a fly. And someone tried to *kill* her just because she figured out their stupid sex club is actually a prostitution ring? Who the fuck cares? *That's* worth killing the best girl in the world over?

I look across the hospital room at Sarah, asleep in her hospital bed. She's bandaged and hooked up to tubes and wires and monitors. She looks tiny and pale.

I just can't believe this is happening.

Sarah's mom is seated next to Sarah's bed, asleep and draped over her daughter's bed. And in the corner of the room, there's Jonas Faraday, the so-called "boyfriend" himself, sitting in a chair that looks way too small for his large body, his muscled arms crossed over his Seattle Seahawks T-shirt. The poor guy looks horribly pained, even in his sleep—distraught, I'd even say. Gazing at him right now, it's suddenly perfectly clear I've completely misjudged him. I had my doubts about his intentions toward Sarah, and I told him so, but looking at him now, he sure looks every bit the devoted and loyal boyfriend. Shit. I wish I'd been nicer to him at his house yesterday morning. The guy gave me a computer and I acted like a total bitch. Classic Kat.

I look at Sarah again and tears squirt from my eyes for the millionth time today.

Sarah always says I've got a heart of gold, but she's wrong. She's the one who cares so deeply about making the world a better place, not me. She's the one who's always thinking about helping people, not me. Compared to Sarah, I'm a downright bitch. And not just a bitch, a horribly reckless bitch. What the fuck was I thinking, trying to seduce my *bodyguard?* Jonas hired Derek to *protect* me, not fuck me. Jonas was right all along—the bad guys really were out to get Sarah and maybe me, too, and what did I do? I made the whole thing about me getting my rocks off. I'm so freaking predictable—and so freaking ashamed of myself, I feel physically ill.

But wait a minute. It takes two to tango. Derek was the one who was supposed to be a *professional*, right? How the hell did he plan to protect me while pounding me? My life was quite possibly at stake and he was macking down on me! *Oh my God.* Is my life at stake now? I feel like I'm gonna barf. I throw my hands over my face. This whole situation is crashing into me like a ton of bricks.

My phone buzzes in my purse with a text and I pull it out. *Josh Faraday.* I wipe my eyes. I feel oddly comforted seeing his name on my screen.

"Are you at the hospital?" Josh writes.

"Yeah, I'm in Sarah's room now," I reply. "The doc says Sarah lost a ton of blood and she's definitely in a lot of pain, but she's gonna be okay, thank God. She'll probably go home tomorrow. She got really lucky. The blade didn't hit anything critical."

"SO AWESOME. Huge relief. OMG. Is my brother there? He hasn't answered any of my texts or calls. I'm worried."

I look across the room at Jonas again. His face is twitching in his sleep like he's having a nightmare. Just as I'm about to look away from him, his entire body jolts like someone just leaped out from behind a bush and yelled "Boo!" Aw, poor guy. He's actually kind of breaking my heart right now.

"Yeah, he's here," I write. "He's asleep."

"When he wakes up, could you tell him I couldn't get to Seattle tonight? All flights are grounded due to weather."

As if on cue, thunder crashes outside the hospital window. "Yeah, if he wakes up while I'm still here, I'll be sure to tell him," I write.

"Thanks."

There's a long beat. Is that the end of our text-conversation? I drop my phone in my lap and stare at Sarah for another long moment, listening to the driving rain outside the window, my thoughts drifting to the thousands of times Sarah's been the best friend a girl could ever hope for.

I've just decided something. I'm done being Classic Kat. From this day forward, I'm New Kat—a responsible and levelheaded girl. A girl like Sarah.

Smart. *Careful.* A look-before-leaping kind of girl, especially when it comes to men. New Kat takes things slow. New Kat has her head on straight. New Kat doesn't just jump into the sack or throw her heart away willy-nilly. New Kat isn't tempestuous and crazy. Nope. She's just like Sarah. Well, pre-Jonas Sarah, that is. I don't know what the heck's happened to Sarah since she met Jonas—nowadays, she's acting like me. But that's beside the point.

My phone buzzes with another text. "How are you holding up, Party Girl?" Josh asks.

I take a deep breath and tap out an honest answer to the question, tears streaming down my cheeks. "Not good. The Party Girl doesn't feel at all like partying right now."

"I know what you mean. The Playboy doesn't feel at all like playing right now, either." He adds a sad face to the end of his message.

Well, as long as I'm being honest, I might as well go all in. "I've never cried so many tears in all my life, Josh," I write. And, of course, the act of writing that message makes me cry even harder. "This is the worst day of my life."

I've no sooner pressed send on that message than my phone buzzes with an incoming call from Josh.

I bolt out of my chair and into the hallway to answer. "Hi," I say softly into my phone, my cheeks suddenly hot. I don't like crying in front of men, even over the telephone. It always ignites their superhero instincts—and I'm not a girl who needs to be saved.

"When I get there," Josh says softly, his voice low and masculine, "you can cry on my shoulder all you like, Party Girl."

There's a long pause. I'm having a physical reaction to that statement, not to mention the masculine tone of his voice.

"Thanks," I finally say. "I'd like that."

There's another long pause. "So how's that bodyguard working out for you?" he finally asks. "Do you like him?"

"Do I *like* him?" I repeat, my pulse suddenly pounding in my ears. Does he suspect I was trying to get into my bodyguard's pants when he called earlier today?

Josh exhales. "I mean does he make you feel *safe?* Is he doing a good job of protecting you?"

"Oh." I exhale. "Well, actually," I say, "I've got two bodyguards—one for day, one for night. The nighttime guy is here at the hospital now—in the waiting room. I feel pretty safe with him. But I'm gonna ask for a replacement for the daytime guy."

"You don't feel safe with the daytime guy?"

"No."

"Why not?" There's a strange edge to his voice. He inhales sharply. "Did he make a pass at you, Kat?"

Holy Jealous Boyfriend, Batman—except, of course, that Josh Faraday isn't my boyfriend. We've never even been on a flippin' date.

"Shit," Josh breathes before I can reply to his initial question. "What's the bastard's name?"

"Josh," I manage to say. "No, he didn't make a pass at me." I think that's technically true—I'm the one who made a pass at Derek. "But if he had," I continue, "it wouldn't be any of your business." I let that sink in for a minute. "Derek just didn't take things seriously enough for my taste, that's all," I say evenly.

"*Derek*, huh?" Josh says, his voice edged with testosterone.

"What the hell, Josh?" I say. "You sound like a caveman. Don't worry about it. I'm asking for a new guy. Problem solved." I'm suddenly pissed. He has no claim on me. I can do what I want. "I'd better get back into the room," I say stiffly. "I came out into the hallway to take your call."

He exhales. "Listen, Kat. I don't want you being alone 'til we figure this shit out. Not for a minute. Okay? Jonas obviously had a sixth sense here—he was totally right. We've got to take this seriously."

"Yeah. Okay. Got it. Thanks. But like I said, Rodney's out in the waiting room, and I'll get a new guy tomorrow."

"You promise?"

I exhale with exasperation. I'm not sure I like this caveman crap from a guy I'm not even dating. "I'm getting a new guy because it's what I wanna do, not because you told me to do it."

"Jeez. Touchy. I'm just looking out for you."

Tears flood my eyes. "I'm sorry. I'm a wreck right now. Ignore me. I didn't mean to be bitchy. It's been a really hard day, Josh."

"Oh, I'm sorry. I know," he coos. "Of course, it has."

I sniffle into the phone. "I'm sorry."

"No worries."

We're silent for a long moment.

"Okay, well, I gotta go," I say. "I came into the hallway to take your call. If Sarah wakes up, I wanna be there."

Josh exhales. "Kat, listen . . ." But he doesn't finish the thought. "Yeah, I gotta go, too. Don't forget to tell my brother I'm stuck down in LA, but I'll get there as soon as I can. Please tell him, okay? I'm really worried about him." His voice breaks. "He's been through a lot, Kat—something like this was the last thing he needed."

"It's okay, Josh," I say softly. "Hang in there, okay?"

I hear him breathing, but he doesn't reply.

"I'm sure this is rough on you—being down there when your brother's wigging out up here."

He doesn't reply for a long beat. "Kat, you have no idea."

"Hang in there."

There's another long beat.

Josh clears his throat. "It sounds like Sarah's gonna be good as new, so crisis averted. Jonas will take her to his house tomorrow and nurse her back to health and he'll be happy as a clam. I'm sure the minute I walk through his door tomorrow, he'll kick me the fuck out again, just like he did last night."

I chuckle. "He kicked you out last night?"

"Yeah. I guess he wanted some *privacy*, if you know what I mean."

I can hear him rolling his eyes across the phone line.

"Well, from what I heard before you got to Jonas' house the other day, consider yourself lucky you didn't hear them. Yeesh."

"Really?"

"Oh my God. They sounded like they were dying in there."

He laughs. "Don't tell me any more. I make it a point not to think about my brother having sex."

I laugh, wiping the tears out of my eyes as I do.

"I've never seen Jonas like this about a girl. Ever," he says. "I actually think this might be the real thing for him."

"Really? Wow. Sarah said the same thing."

"Awesome. I'd hate for Jonas to get his heart broken. He doesn't put it out there very often. Looks like he's fallen hard for this girl."

I never thought for a minute about *Jonas* getting his heart broken—I've been too concerned about Sarah getting hers smashed to smithereens.

"Trust me, if anyone's heart's gonna get broken here, it won't be Jonas'," I say. "Sarah's all in."

"Well, good. I hope it works out for them. They're awesome together."

"Yeah, they are."

"Okay, well . . ." he says. "Hopefully, I'll get my ass back up there tomorrow on the first flight out, just in time for him to kick me out of his house again." He chuckles. "So when I'm up there with nothing to do, maybe we'll have a chance to hang out—maybe grab some dinner or drinks?"

"Maybe," I say casually, but my heart's racing. I'm sure he can hear me smiling over the phone line.

"Mmm hmm," he says. "Okay, Party Girl with a Hyphen. I forgot we're playing it cool. That's fine. We both know how this ends—but, sure, we can play it that way."

"I have no idea how this ends," I say, my crotch tingling at the flirtatious tone of his voice.

"Oh, well, then, far be it for me to spoil the ending for you." He pauses. "Well, I better go. Hang in there, Party Girl. I'll be there soon and you can cry on my shoulder all you like."

"Thanks. Maybe I'll see you soon, Playboy."

"Oh, you can count on it."

5

JOSH

"Dude, pull your head out of your ass. *Please*," I say. "She's not gonna stay at her mom's house forever."

"I'm going fucking crazy," Jonas mutters, gripping his steering wheel like a madman. "I'm about to fucking blow."

I exhale and look out the passenger window of the car, trying to collect myself. My brother is a fucking lunatic. There's no way around it. I truly thought dragging Jonas rock climbing all day would take his mind off Sarah—and, specifically, the fact that she's decided to stay at her mom's house to recuperate instead of Jonas' (and also hasn't been very communicative while she's been there, either)—but I was wrong. Dead wrong. Not only did Jonas continue obsessing about Sarah throughout our climb today, he did it while I was trapped on a fucking mountain with him with nowhere to go. Jesus Christ. If I'd known Jonas was gonna drive me nuts during our entire climb, I would have just sat on his couch, watching basketball and drinking way too much beer. At least then I could have left the room occasionally to bang my head against the wall. Or, at the very least, numbed myself with way too much alcohol.

All I wanna do right now is call Sarah and say, "Whatever's going on between you and Jonas, please just give the guy a fucking call and tell him whatever the fuck's on your mind, good or bad, because until my high-strung brother hears from you and confirms whatever it is you're thinking, he's gonna be a fucking nightmare to be around." But, obviously, I'm not gonna do that. The girl was stabbed. She's probably scared and freaked out and maybe a little bit confused right now. She's got plenty on her plate worrying about her own mental health without having to worry about Jonas' too. I've got to just let this thing take its natural course—and pray to God it goes Jonas' way. Because after everything Jonas has had to endure in his life, I really don't want his dream girl to shatter his heart, too.

"Jonas, I know it's hard for you," I say, "but you've just gotta let the girl sort her shit out. She's been through a huge trauma. She probably just needs a little break. Be patient with her."

"I don't do patient."

"No shit." I roll my eyes. "But it's only natural she'd want her mom after what she's been through. I'm sure most people with a mother would react the same way."

Jonas literally snarls at me.

I roll my eyes at him again. "Oh my fucking God. Jonas, I'm as motherless as you are. Obviously. I didn't say that to twist some knife into your heart. I'm just saying we don't know what it's like to turn to a mother in a time of crisis—but other people do. Normal people."

"But why isn't she even talking to me?" Jonas says. "I understand her wanting her mom. But something's off. I can feel it. And it's fucking killing me."

"Just give her a little space," I mumble, but my tone isn't compassionate. I've been with Jonas all fucking day. I'm all out of compassion. "Sarah wanting to be with her mother is no reflection on how she feels about you. Stop thinking everything's about you all the time. You make me want to open my car door and hurl myself onto the freeway just to get away from you."

Jonas grits his teeth as he glares out the windshield of his car. "Maybe I should drive over there?" he finally says. "Tell her how I feel?"

"No, Jonas."

He grips the steering wheel again. "Or send flowers with a note?"

"Flowers? Jesus, Jonas. *No.* Just leave her alone."

"Maybe I should, I don't know, go park my car across the street from her mom's house and sit there for a while?"

I laugh. "What the fuck? You mean like a stalker?"

"No, not like a *stalker*. Like a *boyfriend*."

"Like a... Ha!" I can't control my laughter. "That's your idea of what a boyfriend does? You're gonna go be John Cusack in *Say Anything* with the beat box over your head, standing in the rain?"

"John Cusack didn't stand in the rain."

"Sure he did."

"No."

"Well, either way," I say. "That'd be totally stalker-ish. It was stalker-ish when John Cusack did it in the first place. I don't know why everyone thinks that was so fucking romantic. It was just *weird*. Fucking desperate. Women hate desperate."

Someone cuts Jonas off and he honks his horn. "Motherfucker." There's a long pause. "Well, I can relate," he says.

"To what?"

"To John Cusack." He exhales. "I'm desperate."

I shake my head. What the fuck am I gonna do about my fucking brother? He doesn't say a word about any particular woman since Amanda, not a fucking word, and now he won't shut the fuck up about this one? I can't decide whether I like hermit-Jonas or desperately-in-love Jonas better. "You sent a couple bodyguards over to her mom's house, right?"

"Yeah."

"Well, then. She's safe. That's all that matters. Leave her alone."

Jonas sighs audibly. "But if I drive over there, she might at least notice me sitting out there. And then she'd know I'm thinking about her."

I can't help but chuckle. I've never in my life met someone like my brother. Probably a genius IQ, no exaggeration. He's easily twice as smart as I am. Triple as smart. And yet he's so fucking stupid he makes me want to wring his neck at least a hundred times a day. "What would be the point of you sitting there in your car, watching the house, Jonas? Explain this to me."

Now it's Jonas rolling his eyes at me like I'm a complete moron. "Because then maybe she'd come out."

I laugh. "And then what?"

He shakes his head but doesn't answer me.

"Dude, Sarah's healing from being stabbed multiple times and having her head busted wide open like a walnut. And you want the poor girl to hobble outside in her little nightgown and fuzzy socks and pat you on the head and say 'Good, doggie'?"

"I didn't... No. I just . . ." His anguish is palpable.

"You know what she'd *really* say? She'd say, 'Gosh, Jonas. Ever thought of sending a *text*?'"

He grumbles. "Okay, so what if I—"

"Jonas, *no*. Stop. No stalking. No calling. No flowers. No boom box. No luring the poor girl across the street in her nightgown and slippers. Do you want to push this girl away forever?"

His face flashes with earnest concern. "No. Of course not. Quite the opposite."

"Do you want her to think you're a total pussy?"

He clenches his jaw. "No."

I shake my head. "Then just give her some fucking space. Please. Just listen to me. When am I ever wrong about women?"

He opens his mouth and then closes it.

"The answer is 'Never.' *I'm never wrong.* I'm some sort of woman-whisperer, dude—trust me. You want a woman to want you? Then you gotta know when to leave her the fuck alone. Just chill the fuck out and give the girl some time to figure her shit out. I guarantee you, if you back off and let Sarah take things at her own pace, let her figure out what she's feeling and what she needs, she's gonna call you and say, 'Come get me, Jonas. I want you.' Mark my words, bro."

"But what if I just—"

"No! Just let her call you when she's ready to talk. And in between, send her a few texts to let her know you're thinking about her—nothing too heavy. She's probably all doped up on pain meds and feeling like shit and sleeping most of the time, anyway. And her mom's probably bringing her homemade chicken tortilla soup or whatever. You can't compete with that magical-mom shit, bro. No one can. That's why everyone says, 'There's nothing like a mother's love.' I realize we don't know what the fuck they're talking about, but the rest of the world does. I'll bet you a thousand bucks if you listen to me and give her some space, she's gonna call you within three days and say, 'Come get me.'"

Jonas grunts. "Why would I take that bet? I'd be betting against myself."

We've arrived at Jonas' house, thank God. I've never wanted to get out of a car more in my entire life. Jonas pulls into his driveway and kills the engine on his car. He turns to look at me, his eyes blazing. "Josh, you don't understand."

"I think I do."

"No. I have something really important I need to tell her. Right away. Something she needs to understand."

"Whatever it is, it'll have to wait."

He shakes his head furiously. "Josh, listen to me. I need to tell her something—something I've never said to any other girl—even Amanda." He swallows hard. *"The most important thing there is to say.* I'm gonna say it to Sarah."

I can't believe my ears. My brother's gonna tell this girl he *loves* her? Wow, he's never even said those words to me. Jesus, I'm light years ahead of Jonas in my emotional evolution, and I've only said those words to one girl in my entire life. (And it didn't work out so well.)

"Wow, Jonas," I begin to say, but he cuts me off.

"So don't fucking tell me to be *patient*," he roars, out of nowhere. He abruptly gets out of his car, slams his car door like he's trying to tip the car onto its side with me in it, and stalks toward his house.

I watch Jonas as he marches away, imagining myself hurling Chinese stars into his back. Oh my fucking God. I can't take it anymore. I'm trying to be compassionate with this motherfucker. Just like I've tried to be my entire fucking life. But it's hard to be compassionate with a guy when he's a total and complete dick.

6

JOSH

Oh, yeah. So good. *Yes.* I pump my shaft with increased intensity as the steaming hot water of the shower rains down on me. I can't stop imagining her face, her unbelievable face. Oh my God. She's a gift from God, created just for me. Those eyes. Those gorgeous blue eyes. That subtle little cleft in her chin. I imagine myself pressing the tip of my cock into that little cleft in her chin right before sliding my full length into her sassy little mouth.

Oh God. I can barely breathe. I'm about to blow. I'm so close. I work myself even more furiously. My cock feels like a rocket about to lift off. Oh fuck. Yes. It's beginning to ripple.

And her lips. They're perfect, just like everything else about her. I imagine those lips wrapped around my hard cock, sliding up and down, devouring me. I run my finger over my wet tip, imagining it's her swirling tongue.

"Oh shit," I say out loud. I open my mouth wide and a blast of hot water floods it. My knees are buckling. I'm twitching. I'd pay a million dollars if my hand could be her warm mouth right now—two million if it could be her tight little pussy. The Club is full of hookers, it turns out? Fine by me. Some women are well worth the money. If Kat asked me to pay her to fuck her, I surely would. No questions asked. I'd give anything, *anything,* to see Kat looking up at me with those big blue eyes, her lips wrapped around my cock. I imagine her eyes glittering the same way they did when she found out I'd been a member of The Club. That's the look that told me the girl is up for anything—with the right guy, anyway.

I'm the right guy for you, baby. Fuck yeah, I am. You've never been fucked like this before. That's right, baby.

I fondle my balls with my free hand while my pumping hand continues working my shaft. Oh shit. My knees are buckling. This is so good. Any second now.

I picture her on top of me, riding me, her blonde hair falling down over her shoulders and cascading over her perky little tits. Erect nipples. Cleft in her chin. Blue eyes. Tight little body. Oh my God. She throws her head back. She's having an orgasm. She's screaming my name.

My skin prickles for just an instant, like I've got a chill even under the steaming hot water, and then an epic orgasm slams into me, making me spurt a massive load all over my hands. I shudder with my release and lean my head against the marble shower wall.

"Kat," I say out loud, like she's lying next to me in bed. "Oh my God."

That's the first time in a really long time I've stuck with the fantasy of one woman while jacking off. I usually start out thinking about whatever woman I've been seeing lately, whatever sex act we might have recently performed, and then, at some point, move on to that raven-haired dental assistant I always fantasize about, even though she's married and never gives me the slightest whiff of a come-on, or the college professor I used to fuck during office hours during my second year at UCLA, or, occasionally, the platinum-blonde Swiss foreign exchange student in high school who de-virginized me when I was a wee little freshman, the one who taught me exactly where to touch her and how to get her off. And then, right at climax, without fail, whether I like it or not, my brain inevitably slams me with Emma's angelic face, the face that fooled me for so long into thinking she was The One.

Hot water is gushing down my back.

"Kat," I say again, reliving the vision of her riding me, her face awash in ecstasy.

She's the most gorgeous girl I've ever seen.

Holy shit.

I want this girl.

I want her bad.

And I'm stuck here with my goddamned brother.

7

JOSH

When I enter the family room after my shower, Jonas is nowhere to be found, which is good because, after his little tantrum in the car, I still feel like punching him in his pretty face. I grab a beer from the fridge, plop myself down on Jonas' pristine white couch, and turn on the basketball game.

Shit. I should be with the Party Girl with a Hyphen right now, pouring on the charm, making her realize this story's ending is inevitable—not babysitting my high-maintenance brother. But I can't leave him right now, especially to go chase a girl (even if that girl happens to be a particularly gorgeous one). He's just too wound up. I'd never forgive myself if he lost his shit completely and did something stupid.

I take a giant swig of my beer. Seriously, though. I don't blame Jonas for freaking out about Sarah, despite what I said to him before. What the fuck's going on with her? Is she fucking with him? I mean, in theory I understand why Sarah opted to stay with her mom instead of recuperating at her temperamental boyfriend's house. Jonas isn't exactly anyone's first choice as a relaxation buddy. But why has Sarah been so fucking non-communicative with the poor guy while she's resting up? Is she doing what I always do—keeping the other person guessing? If so, why? He's obviously waiting with bated breath to hear from her —she must know that. And yet she's not calling him back? She's just been engaging in superficial text conversations with the poor guy, tearing a page right out of my book. I hate to admit it, but things don't look good for my brother's chance at a happy ending here.

I shake my head and exhale. Please, God, let this girl call him and tell him she wants him, once and for all. Please, God, let her do the equivalent of holding a boom box over her fucking head. Because if Jonas shatters again, then it's gonna be me who'll have to pick up his infinite pieces—again. And at some point, there's not gonna be enough superglue in the world to hold that mother-fucker together anymore.

I take another long swig of my beer.

Well, shit. I should just call Sarah for him and ask her what the fuck's going on. I down the rest of my beer. Hell yeah. That's exactly what I should do. Nobody fucks with my brother. She seems like the coolest girl in the world, I must admit—but right now she's fucking with him. No doubt about it. And that's not cool.

No. Obviously, I can't do that. She's not fucking with him. I'm just being an idiot. She was stabbed. She's being hunted by a global crime syndicate. Jesus. Maybe placating Jonas' feelings isn't high on her priority list right now.

Poor Jonas. My stomach twists. What the fuck am I gonna do with him?

I run my hand through my hair, my stomach twisting into knots. I exhale loudly.

Well, I gotta do something.

A smile dances on my lips. Maybe I should try to get some inside informa-tion from her hot best friend? Now there's a call I certainly don't mind making.

I pull out my phone and I'm assaulted with a naked selfie from Bridgette, her legs spread-eagle, her fingers shoved up her hairless crotch, a huge smile on her face. The note accompanying the photo reads, "Come and get it, Faraday!"

I roll my eyes. What the fuck have I been doing, messing around with Brid-gette? She's stunning to look at, but she's such a fucking train wreck, it's not even worth it.

"Your waxer missed a spot," I text to her in reply.

Her reply is immediate. "Ha, ha. Are you gonna come hit this or not?"

"Not. I'm in Seattle with my brother. Family emergency."

"Oh damn," she writes. "I was in the mood for some huge Faraday peen. I don't always do peen, but when I do, I make it huge Faraday peen."

"The most interesting woman in the world," I write, though it's the furthest thing from the truth.

"I guess I'll have to find some other huge peen to satisfy me, then," Brid-gette writes.

"Good luck with that. Once a girl's had Huge Faraday Peen, no other peen shall do."

"Well, then, I guess I'll just have to get me some pussy. You know I'm a big believer in affirmative action."

"Whatever floats your boat, Bridge. Enjoy."

"So when will you be back in LA?"

"A couple days at least," I write. "Just depends on how long my brother needs me." Of course, I have no desire to fuck Bridgette when I get back to LA, whenever that happens to be. I've long since lost interest. But we're so rarely in the same city at the same time, given both of our travel schedules, I've never felt the need to make a formal declaration of my lack of interest.

"Okay. See ya around," she writes. "Say hi to your big dick for me."

I stare at my phone for a long minute. Really? That's it? *'Say hi to your big dick'?* I tell the woman I've got a family emergency and that the length of my stay in Seattle depends on how long my brother needs me and she doesn't even ask me what's up? Or if my brother's okay? Well, that's Bridgette for you in a nutshell: a sociopathic narcissist, through and through.

I'm done. I should have done this a long time ago. I've spiraled into total douchebaggery since Emma, and I'm fucking sick of myself.

"Hey, Bridgette," I type. "I'm gonna take a break from meaningless booty calls and sociopathic narcissism for a while. Well, forever, actually. It's been super fun. Thanks for the memories. Best of luck." I press send. A total dick move, but I don't care. She's not even gonna ask me if everything's okay with my family? Didn't I just tell her I'm in Seattle for a fucking family emergency? Jonas is literally my only family, other than my uncle, and she knows it—I told her about Jonas once when she told me about her sister going into rehab—and she's not even gonna ask me if he's okay?

"Sure thing," she writes back immediately. "I'm going to Milan next week and then to Barbados for a shoot. I'll text you next time I'm in LA, just in case you change your mind, which we both know you will. *Küsse,* Faraday."

I'm tempted to write something like, "Erase me from your contacts," but I refrain. I'll just leave it. I said what needed to be said. And it felt pretty damned good, too. I just turned down one of the most objectively beautiful women in the entire world. (Well, physically, anyway—I think her heart is filled with battery acid.) That's got to be a sign I'm headed in a new, healthier direction.

There's a clattering noise in the kitchen and I look up. Jonas is freshly showered, doing something in the kitchen, looking like a bull in a china shop. "I'm making myself some kale-apple-beet-spinach-carrot juice," he shouts at me. "You want some?"

I hold up my beer. "No, I've got my vitamins right here, bro, thanks."

He doesn't reply.

I feel electrified. I should have told Bridgette I wasn't interested in her a long time ago. It's time to clean up my act. My little vacation in The Club was perfectly understandable, and I'm not at all sorry about it, but after that, I just kept going in vacation-mode in my real life, too. I don't need to see a shrink to figure out I've been wallowing in self-pity since Emma, afraid to get back in the dating pool with real women. But it's been almost a fucking year since Emma kicked me in the teeth and then didn't even have the courtesy to break up with me officially before running off with that ascot-wearing cocksucker. It's seriously time for me to move on and stop acting like a douche. That's it. No more mainlining cotton candy for me—it's time for me to start feasting on some meat and potatoes again.

"Hey, you know what?" I call to Jonas. "Yeah, gimme some kale-apple-whatever-whatever juice. Sounds great, bro."

I swig my beer, letting my mind wander. Today marks a new era for me. No more women who are only in it for courtside seats at Lakers games or backstage passes to concerts—women who don't even ask me if I'm okay when I've had a family fucking emergency.

Kat's beautiful face flickers across my mind, but I force myself not to think about her. This isn't about Kat in particular. This is about me checking back into reality. Moving on. Getting my personal life back on track. This is about me getting off the Douche Train.

I tap out a text. "Hey, Party Girl with a Hyphen. I've got a quick question for you."

She answers immediately. "Hey, Playboy. Did you make it back up to Seattle okay? How are you doing? Is Jonas hanging in there?"

Well, holy shit. After my text exchange with Bridgette, Kat's genuine interest in how we're doing feels like a thunderbolt cracking the sky. Is this just a coincidence or a sign from God?

"Jonas is a fucking wreck," I reply. "A total asshole to be around. That's why I'm texting you, actually. Do you know if Sarah's been avoiding Jonas?"

"Not to my knowledge. Why do you ask?"

"It seems like she's giving him the cold shoulder, maybe—but, of course, she's also recently been stabbed by a hitman, so it could be that. But, seriously, Sarah hasn't asked to see Jonas since she left the hospital. That seems a bit odd. I'm worried he's about to get crushed. He's really, really into her, Kat—like, seriously out of his mind for this girl."

"I'll see if I can get some info," Kat writes. "But Sarah's my best friend, so it's not a lock I'll be able to tell you whatever I find out."

"I understand. But I'm kinda desperate for any little crumb you can feed me. Any intel you could throw my way would be greatly appreciated. I'd owe you one."

"Well, I will say this—as far as I know, Sarah's absolutely crazy about Jonas."

"Good to hear."

"So how are you doing, Playboy?" Kat writes. "Are you okay? Must be hard trying to keep Jonas on track all the time. From what I saw at Jonas' house, you have your work cut out for you."

Yeah, there's no question about it: this text exchange with Kat is a sign from God. I can't remember the last time a woman asked me sincerely how I'm doing.

"Thanks for asking," I write. "I'm okay. I just decided to stop being a total douche so I'm doing pretty good."

Jonas sits down next to me on the couch and hands me a juice concoction that looks like it was squeezed out of an alien.

"Thanks," I say.

He doesn't reply, but instead turns up the volume on the basketball game.

"You've decided to stop being a douche? So you were a douche and now you're magically not one anymore?" Kat writes.

"Correct," I write.

"Any particular thing that's inspired your decision to make douchebaggery a thing of the past?"

"Nope. Just had to be done."

"Hey, you wanna start working on our business plan?" Jonas asks, swatting my thigh. "I've got a thousand ideas."

"When the game's over," I say to Jonas. "There's only ten more minutes left." I look at my phone again. "Hey, can you talk rather than text?" I type to Kat, suddenly yearning to hear her voice.

"Not right now. I'm just now leaving a client meeting with my boss. We're heading back to the office in her car."

"What do you do?"

"I work at a PR firm. We just met with a client about a social media campaign for a chain of barbeque restaurants."

"How'd it go?"

"Good. They loved everything I came up with, except for my proposed slogan. (Damn it!) But I'm gonna work on it with this awesome girl from my office when I get back to the office. No worries."

"Hey, I've got a great slogan you can use. My gift to you."

"Awesome. I'll take any help I can get. Hit me."

"I've got your pulled pork right here, baby!"

"LOL. OMG. That's actually kind of brillz. This chain is all about being brash and blue-collar and funny. They might actually like it."

"Oh no. That wasn't my slogan idea. That was just me trying to sweet talk you, PG. The slogan idea is this: 'Hey, if you like barbeque, then we'd appreciate it if you'd eat at our restaurant. Thank you.' What do you think? Pure genius, right?"

"OMG. I'm literally laughing out loud right now in my boss' car. You're a PR whiz, PB."

"I've got all kinds of mad skillz, PG. I'm a wise and powerful man; you should know that up front."

"And a total douche—oh, wait, except that you're not now. Scratch that." She attaches a winking emoji.

"Exactly. You only live once, right? Best not to waste valuable time being a total douche."

"Hey! I say that ALL THE TIME," she writes.

"You say 'best not to waste valuable time being a total douche' all the time?"

"Haha. No. I say, 'You only live once.'"

"So do I. YOLO. It's kind of my thing."

"Oh, God, no! Not YOLO. Don't say YOLO! Oh, the humanity!"

"Douchey?"

"Yes. Don't do it!"

"What about 'go big or go home.' Can I say that? Because I say that all the time, too," I write.

"Yes. And you may also say, 'I can sleep when I'm dead.' Those are fine. Just not YOLO," she writes.

"What about 'Work hard, play hard'? I say that one all the time, too."

"You like spiffy little catchphrases, huh?"

"Hey, at least I'm not running around quoting Plato all the time."

"What's wrong with Plato?" she writes.

"Hang around my crazy-ass brother for a day and you'll see."

"LOL. Okay."

"Oh, I just thought of another one I say all the time. 'Under-promise and over-perform.'"

"Oh, words to live by," she writes.

"I do. Religiously."

"Interesting."

"So is that it?" I write. "I can say all that stuff, just not YOLO?"

"Correct. Just not YOLO. EVER. Though you CAN say the actual words 'you only live once.' Just not 'YOLO.'"

"So many fucking rules. Jesus."

"Dude, I don't make the rules. I just enforce them."

I laugh out loud.

"And for God's sake don't get a YOLO tattoo!" she writes. "Promise me!"

I burst out laughing. "I make no such promise."

"Don't do it!"

"How about a YOLO tattoo on my ass? Can I do that?"

"LOL! The absolute worst possible scenario! DO NOT DO IT! TOTALLY AGAINST THE RULES!!!!"

I can't stop laughing. "There's something you really should know about me, PG: I like breaking rules."

"Do what you must, but you've been warned. A YOLO tattoo is social suicide."

I laugh again. "Okay. Good to know. So what other really uncool things should I avoid like the plague besides a YOLO tattoo on my ass? Help an old man out."

"How old are you?"

"Thirty," I write.

"Holy shitballs! Where's your walker?"

"How old are you?"

"Twenty-four."

"Aw, just a kitten."

"Meow."

"This is good. I need help from a whippersnapper like yourself to keep me in the cool. What else should I absolutely avoid, according to these rules of yours?

"Not MY rules. They're just THE rules."

"Okay. What else is against THE rules?"

"A barbed-wire tattoo around your bicep fo shizzles. Don't do it."

I laugh to myself. I couldn't agree more with that one. "Okay," I write. "I promise I won't get that no matter how drunk I am."

"And don't get a tribal band around your bicep, either, unless you're from the Islands. Are you an Islander, Josh?"

"Nope. Duly noted."

"Or dragon. Cliché."

I laugh. "Really?"

"Yup. And God help you if you get a girlfriend's name tattooed onto your arm. Just ask Johnny Depp. He had to get 'Winona Forever' lasered to 'Wino Forever.' Lasers are painful, Josh. Not good. Don't do it."

"Yeah, I could see how that could be a bit of an oops."

"A little gold hoop in your left ear. Don't do it."

"Jesus. The Rules are as long as my fucking arm. Anything else?"

"Nope. Avoid all that redonkulousness and you'll be super cool."

"So you're allowed to use the word redonkulousness and I can't say YOLO?"

"Correct. Again, let me repeat. I do not make THE rules. I merely enforce them."

I laugh out loud again.

"Whoa, did you see that?" Jonas says, swatting my knee.

I look up and catch the instant replay of a smooth-as-silk pass and dunk on TV.

"Sweet," I say. But I don't care about the game right now. I'm having too much fun playing with a certain little kitten. I look back at my phone.

"Hey, my boss is about to get off her phone call, so I better go," she writes.

"Josh," Jonas says. "Game's over. You ready to do some Climb & Conquer?"

"I gotta go, too," I write. "My captor has summoned me. Hey, you've still got those bodyguards around the clock, right?"

"Yeah."

"Good. Stay safe. Have a good one, PG."

"You, too, PB. Have fun with your captor."

"Thanks. He's always an adventure, for sure."

"Who are you texting with?" Jonas asks.

I look up. Jonas has already opened his laptop. He's staring at me.

"Just a girl."

Jonas gives me a knowing look. "No sexting when you're sitting on a couch with me. Ew."

"Fuck you. Come on. Climb & Conquer, baby. Let's do this. I'm chomping at the bit to get our baby launched, put out the press release. Hey, when are we gonna tell Uncle William we're both leaving the company, by the way?"

"Soon," Jonas says. "I just gotta figure some shit out first. With both of us leaving . . ." He lets out an anxious breath. "I don't want Uncle William to feel like we're deserting him."

"I know, but it is what it is. I'll be seeing him next week at the board meeting," I say. "Why don't I tell him then?"

"No, just wait," Jonas says. "Lemme figure out the game plan first, get my strategy into place, write the press release. I really wanna tell him in person together."

Jonas looks so wracked with anxiety, I don't have the heart to argue with him. "Okay, bro, whatever you say." I pat his cheek. "No worries. But I really should go to that meeting, regardless. Are you gonna be okay if I leave and go to New York next week?"

"Of course. You don't have to babysit me. I'm a grown-ass man."

"I know."

There's a long pause.

"But thanks for babysitting me," Jonas finally says. He exhales. "Thanks for coming when I called."

"I always will."

We smile at each other.

"Okay, Climb & Conquer," Jonas says. "Our baby. Let's figure out how to give her legs."

"And then wings." I rub my hands together. "It's gonna be fucking awesome, bro."

"Fuck yeah, it is. I've got the whole thing planned in my head. Now to flesh it out and make it real."

Jonas launches into an animated monologue about his vision for our new company, but as excited as I am about the whole thing, my mind keeps wandering. I keep thinking about Kat, her golden blonde hair swooshing across her naked shoulders, those big blue eyes of hers staring at me as she rides me. Or sucks me off. Or as I fuck her nice and slow, my hands cupping her breasts. Shit. Just thinking about her is making me hard again.

"Hey, are you listening to a word I'm saying?" Jonas asks. "I'm bursting at the seams to tell you this stuff and your eyes are glazed over."

"Sorry. Got distracted. I'm totally listening now. Shoot."

Jonas looks at me sideways. "Does this have anything to do with whoever you were texting a minute ago?"

"I can neither confirm nor deny," I say. "But if it *does*, it's because she's so fucking hot, no mortal man could resist her."

Jonas laughs. "You're talking about Kat, aren't you? She's exactly your type, man."

I grin broadly. "Never mind. Come on," I say, rubbing my hands together. "Climb & Conquer. Let's do this shit. I've never been more excited about anything in my entire life."

8

KAT

My phone beeps loudly with an incoming text. Shoot. I thought I'd turned off the ringer when Cameron and I sat down at our table. I reach into my purse. *Oh.* My stomach fills with butterflies—it's a text from Josh Faraday. My eyes dart across the spacious restaurant, just in time to see Cameron slip into the men's restroom. I look back down at my phone, grinning like a fool.

"Free at last, free at last, thank God almighty, I'm free at last!" Josh's text says.

I chuckle and tap out a quick reply. "What happened?"

"Can I get a 'fuck yeah!' from the gorgeous blonde in the front row?"

"Who me?"

"Yeah you! Do you see another gorgeous blonde in the front row?"

I laugh out loud. "Fuck yeah!" I type. "What am I 'fuck yeahing' about?"

"Sarah just called Jonas and asked him to 'bring her home.' Jonas just flew out of here like a bat out of hell to get her!"

"Fuck yeah!" I type. I can't wipe the huge grin off my face. I look across the restaurant again, toward the bathrooms, but there's no sign of Cameron yet. I steal a quick glance toward the bar area and lock eyes with my bodyguard Rodney. He nods and I smile.

"Jonas kicked me out the minute Sarah called, the ungrateful bastard," Josh writes. "Thank God! Because now I'm freeeeeeeeeeeee!"

My phone buzzes with an incoming text from Sarah.

"Jonas is coming to get me!" Sarah writes. "Woohooooooooo!"

"Woohoooooooooooooooooo!" I type.

"Woo fucking hooooooooo!" Josh replies immediately.

Oops. I'd meant that last woohoo for Sarah. "Woohoo!" I type again, this time to Sarah. "So happy for you, girlio! Are you feeling better?"

"A million times better," Sarah writes. "I think I was depressed. Or high on painkillers? Or both. But I feel like me again. Woot! Can't wait to see Jonas. I've been going through Jonas withdrawals."

"Go get him, honey. I'm actually on a date with Cameron right now. Remember him from the sports bar when we spied on Mr. Yellow?"

"OMG! Kat! You mean the baseball player guy? Kerzoinks! Hottie! Those eyes! That smile! That jawline! Gah!"

"I know. I gotta go. He's in the bathroom."

"Okay, I gotta go, too. Jonas will be here any minute. I'll call you tomorrow. Have fun with Mr. Razor Commercial. Bwahahahahahaa."

"I will. Have fun with Thor. Bwahahahahahaaaaa. I love you, girl."

"I love you, too." She sends me a string of bright red hearts and I return them, relief and elation flooding me. *Sarah's back.*

I go back to the thread with Josh. "Sarah just texted me," I write. "She's doing a happy dance about Jonas. Woohoo!"

"Just in time. Jonas was seriously about to lose his mind. I had to talk him down from standing outside Sarah's window with a fucking boom box ten different times."

"Haha! Sarah would have loved that," I write.

"Why the hell do girls love that movie?"

"Because it's romantic."

"It's lame."

"ROMANTIC."

"By any chance do you have a VAGINA?"

"Why, yes, I DO."

"Well, then, that explains why you don't know that movie is LAME."

I laugh out loud. "ROMANTIC."

"No. Standing outside a girl's window holding a boom box isn't ROMAN-TIC. It's LAME," Josh writes.

I scoff at my phone. "By any chance do you have a PENIS?"

"Why, yes, I DO."

"Well, then that explains why you don't know that movie is ROMANTIC."

"It's not romantic. It's DESPERATE."

"Sometimes love can feel DESPERATE," I write. "And why are we writing selected words in ALL CAPS?"

Cameron slips into his chair across the table from me and I abruptly put my phone down on the table.

"Sorry I took so long," Cameron says. "There's a kid over there celebrating a birthday so I stopped to say hi and sign an autograph."

"That's so sweet, Cameron. No worries. I was actually texting with my friend Sarah." That statement's not technically a lie, is it? Even though I've fudged the timeline a wee bit?

"Oh, how's she feeling?"

"Much better."

"Good."

He picks up his menu. "Have you decided what you're gonna order?"

"Not yet," I say. "I haven't even looked at the menu yet. Sorry."

"No worries."

My phone vibrates with an incoming text, but I exercise superhuman strength and leave it sitting on the table next to me.

"I'm really glad we were finally able to get together, Kat."

"Me, too. Thank you for being persistent. Sorry I had to cancel on you."

He shoots me a sparkling smile. "*Twice.*"

"Twice. Yeah. So sorry about that."

As bad luck would have it, I cancelled on Cameron the first time because my place had been broken into by The Club, and the second was because Sarah had been attacked.

"All's well that ends well. We're here now. But I must admit I was beginning to wonder if your dad is Tony Soprano or something."

I laugh. "I don't blame you for wondering."

He laughs. "Glad we're here now."

"Me, too."

I bite my lip.

What the hell is wrong with me? Cameron is gorgeous. And charming. And charismatic. And he just made a cute joke about my dad being a mob boss, for crying out loud. That was funny, right? *And I like funny.* So why am I not feeling this? I felt it when I met him in that sports bar (just before Sarah dragged me out of there after Stacy the Bitch read her the riot act in the bathroom).

Cameron purses his lips as he studies the menu.

He's a total catch. I just need to get my head in the game. I look at my menu. "So what looks good to you tonight?" I ask.

"You mean besides you?"

I smile, but I'm forcing it. All I want to do right now is read whatever text is sitting on my phone from Josh Faraday.

A waiter approaches the table.

"Hello, folks," he says. "How are we doing this evening?"

"Great," Cameron says. "How are you?"

With Cameron's attention diverted to the waiter, I quickly pick up my phone and sneak a peek.

"Well, I used all caps for the word VAGINA because that word is most definitely all-caps worthy. How it spiraled out of control from there, I have no idea. I think we should STOP. So, hey, PG. I'M IN THE MOOD TO CELE-BRATE!" Josh's last text says. "Let me take you to my favorite restaurant in

Seattle. They make the best MARTINIS in the city. You'll SCREAM WITH PLEASURE. Oh, and you'll like the MARTINIS, too. Snicker."

My stomach somersaults. Oh my God. Of all the nights for Josh Faraday to ask me out. This can't be happening.

"And for you, miss?" the waiter asks.

I look up from my phone. The waiter is looking at me, his eyebrows raised. My eyes drift to Cameron's face. He's looking at me expectantly.

"What would you like to drink, miss?" the waiter prompts.

"Uh. Yes. Thank you." I clear my throat. "A dirty martini, Grey Goose, two olives, please. Thank you."

"Great. I'll get your drinks and come back for your food order."

"Thanks," Cameron says.

The waiter walks away and Cameron picks up his menu again.

"What are you drinking?" I ask. "I didn't hear your order."

"Just water. I don't drink," he says.

"Oh," I say. "I didn't realize. I can cancel my martini if—"

He laughs. "No worries. I'm used to it."

"You don't drink because you're sober, or . . .?"

"I don't drink during the season."

I'm relieved. "How long is the season?"

"Including spring training and post-season, if you're lucky, about eight months."

What the fuck? The guy doesn't drink for eight months of the year? "Good lord," I say. "No drinking for eight whole months? It's like you're pregnant once a year." I shudder with mock horror. Or maybe it's just straight-up horror, actually. That sounds like a fate worse than death to me.

"Yeah, pretty much."

"Do you get weird cravings, too—like for pickles and ice cream?"

He laughs. "Thankfully, no."

"I really wouldn't knock drinking as part of a healthy lifestyle," I say. "Vodka comes from potatoes. Potatoes are vegetables. Hence, vodka is a vegetable." I snort.

Cameron grins politely, but he doesn't laugh. He looks back down at his menu. "I'm thinking the surf and turf. You?"

Ooph. Brutal. Where's our chemistry? Is it hanging out with Waldo? I feel like I'm pulling teeth here. Surely, Cameron must feel the same way. "Yeah, surf and turf sounds good," I say. Oh my God, my phone is calling to me like a siren. I've got to respond to Josh's invitation. "Hey, you know what, Cameron? I'm so sorry, but I just need to finish something . . ." I motion to my phone. "I'll be quick. I promise."

"Okay," he says tentatively.

"Sarah again," I say.

"Oh, yeah, take your time." By the compassionate tone of his voice, it's obvious he thinks being there for my best-friend-Sarah-who-was-stabbed-in-a-bathroom is something admirable. And, bitch that I am, I'm happy to let him think it if it means I can get away with texting Josh for a little bit longer.

"I'll just be a minute. And then I'm all yours."

He flashes me a beaming smile. "I like the sound of that."

"I'm really sorry, PB," I text to Josh quickly, my heart pounding. "I'd love to celebrate your freedom with you with the best martini in Seattle, but I just sat down for dinner. Can I take a rain check?"

"HOLY FUCK PUT YOUR FORK DOWN!" he immediately replies. "I'M COMING TO GET YOU RIGHT NOW! Where are you?"

I bite my lip to keep myself from giggling. "No can do. I've already ordered," I write.

"Well, then, that's an easy one. How about I join you? Are you with friends? Make sure you order whatever you want. Dinner's on me."

My stomach twists. Shit. I stare at my phone for a long beat, trying to decide how to word my reply. "I'm not with friends," I write. "I'm on a date." I press the send button, wincing. But I can't figure out another way to phrase it.

"NOOOOO!" he replies immediately.

I bite my lip again, but it's no use. A giggle escapes my mouth. I glance up at Cameron. He's studying his menu intently.

"It's a first date," I reply. "We were supposed to go out the night I met you at Jonas', actually. And then it got rescheduled and we were supposed to go out the night Sarah was attacked. And now we're here. Finally."

"Kat, the universe clearly doesn't want you to date this guy. Get up and leave now! What do you need the universe to do before you start listening— send a fucking bus crashing into the restaurant?"

I laugh out loud.

Before I can reply, Josh sends another message. "Tell him you have to leave. I'll send a car for you right now. It'll be there in five minutes. Tell him NOW."

I make a face at my phone. On what planet would I ever ditch Cameron like that? I'm a bitch, but I'm not that big a bitch. That might be how things happen in movies (and, admittedly, in one of the many fantasy-pornos that plays inside my head) but that's not how nice people in real life act. "I'm not gonna do that," I write to Josh. "Cameron's a nice guy. And I've already cancelled on him twice."

"So what. He deserved it. He's a tool."

"He's not a tool. Far from it."

"Yes, he is. Obviously."

"He's not."

"Yes, he is. You wanna know how I know?"

"Enlighten me."

"Because you're on a date with him and you're more interested in texting me."

I smile broadly. *Touché*, Playboy.

"Ergo, he's a tool," Josh writes.

JOSH & KAT: THE COMPLETE TRILOGY 47

I shouldn't do it—I know I shouldn't—but I can't help myself. "He's not a tool. He's a professional baseball player."

"Oh, really?"

"Really," I text.

"Oh. Minor or major league?"

"Major."

"Bah. He's probably some benchwarmer, Kat, trying to impress you. He's some utility player or relief pitcher who sits around waiting for someone to pull a hamstring so he can get in the game. That's why he said 'professional baseball player' instead of saying his team or his position."

"Well, a boy in the restaurant just asked him for his autograph. Do kids ask for autographs from players who sit on the bench?"

"No," he writes. "Not usually."

I smirk.

"Is he on the Mariners?"

"I don't know. I didn't ask."

"The guy says he's a professional baseball player and you don't ask him for what team?"

"No, I just said, 'That's cool.' I was playing it cool, acting like I didn't care. That's a bit of a strategy of mine with guys, if you must know. A girl should never seem too eager, especially with a pro athlete." I attach a winking emoji.

"Ah, clever. The ol' 'I don't give a shit you're a major league ball player' strategy. Clever. Works every time, I'm sure."

"Well, it certainly worked this time, anyway."

"Grrrrrrrrrrrrrrrr."

"LOL."

"Well, does he live in Seattle?" Josh texts.

"Why are we talking about my date?" I write.

"I need to know what I'm dealing with. Does he live in Seattle?"

"I'm pretty sure he does. His phone number is 206."

"What's his name?"

"Cameron."

"CAMERON?"

"Correct."

"Oh Jesus. Motherfucking fuck. Does he have dark hair? About six foot two? Looks like an ad for aftershave?"

"Yeah! That's him. That's what Sarah said! She said he looks like an ad for razors."

"Motherfucker! That's because he IS an ad for razors. Literally! He's Cameron Schultz, Kat! Goddammit!"

"Yeah! Schultz! That's his last name. Now I remember. You know him?"

"No, I don't know him personally. I know who he is because he's a fucking ALL-STAR! Kat, you're on a date with the fucking shortstop for the Mariners!"

"Oh. That's cool. Haha! Maybe I should have asked more questions."

"Kat, this is my worst nightmare right now. You know that, right? I literally had this very nightmare last night," Josh writes.

"Why is this your nightmare?"

"You know why. But I'm not gonna feed your ego and say it. I can play the 'I don't give a shit' game, too. It doesn't just work on professional ball players, it also works on gorgeous women who are used to men falling all over them."

"Okay, well, as long as neither of us gives a shit, I guess I'll go, then. I'm on a date with an All-star baseball player, in case you didn't know."

"WAIT! No. I take it back. I GIVE A SHIT! I'm coming to get you. Where are you?"

I giggle. "Screw you, dude. I'm having fun. I'm on a date with Cameron Fucking Schulz. I'm sure he's about to re-enact his latest razor commercial for me. Sexy!"

"Put your fork down. My Party Girl with a Hyphen's not allowed on a date with Cameron Fucking Schultz. Hell no. Especially when I'm in the mood to celebrate my freedom. Tonight's MY night, Party Girl, not that dickweed's. Tell him to step the fuck aside and let a real man show you a good time."

Those butterflies in my stomach just turned into bald eagles. I can't think what to say in reply, so I just stare at my phone, freaking out.

"Kat, tell him you've had a family emergency. Or that you feel sick. I don't fucking care what you say. Just end the date. I'm coming right now. THIS IS MY FUCKING NIGHT AND YOU'RE MY GODDAMNED PARTY GIRL WITH A HYPHEN!"

My entire body feels electrified. "OMG. You're nuts. No."

Cameron clears his throat and I look up from my phone. Oh crap. Cameron's staring at me intently. My cheeks blaze with sudden heat.

"I'm sorry, Cameron," I say. "I'm being rude—absolutely horrible." I put my phone down. But then I pick it right back up. "I'm... Lemme just... I just need to say goodbye."

"No worries. She needs you. I understand. You're worth the wait." His eyes darken.

"Thank you," I say, blushing. "Just a minute more, I promise. And then I'm all yours."

He picks up his water, salutes me, and winks. "I'm gonna hold you to that."

"Please do," I say, but my voice lacks its usual flirtatiousness. I bury my nose in my phone again. "Careful, Josh. You're gonna make me sleep with Cameron just to spite you."

"NOT FUNNY, KAT."

"I'm not being funny. I've never slept with a pro athlete before. It's on my list."

I've no sooner pressed send on that last text when my phone buzzes with an incoming call from Josh.

I decline the call and put my phone back on the table, smiling at Cameron.

"Sorry about that," I breathe. The phone buzzes with another incoming call and I decline it again. "She's just really needy right now," I say, despicably spiraling into full-blown, pathological deception. "Post traumatic stress or something, poor thing." Oh my God, I'm morally bankrupt. Heinous. Reprehensible.

Turned-on.

"Why don't you just go give her a quick call?" Cameron suggests. "Make sure everything's okay. And then we'll start fresh, you and me."

I nod. "Yeah, good idea. Thanks. As long as you don't mind." My phone buzzes with another incoming call and I decline it. "I'm just gonna step out front, real quick, call her, see if everything's okay, and then I'll put my phone away for the rest of the night. I promise."

The waiter comes to the table with my martini and sets it in front of me. "Are we ready to order?"

My phone buzzes with another call and I decline it.

"I don't think we're ready to order yet—" Cameron begins.

"No, no, I'm ready," I say. "I'll only be gone a minute, I promise."

He smiles at me.

I quickly place my order with the waiter, take a huge swig of my martini, and then another, and sprint outside, gripping my phone with white knuckles as I go. I'm scum right now. A lying, deceitful, insincere piece of shit. But I can't help it. I feel like a junkie hankering for her next fix—and Josh Faraday is most definitely my next fix.

The chilly night air feels like a slap to my face—which is good. Maybe it'll slap some sense into me. I'm being an absolute nightmare right now. A female-asshole, which is a massive step above bitch. Oh my God, I need to stop this. I'm on a date with Cameron. He's hot. He's a professional athlete. He's sweet—like a Boy Scout. Jeez, the man's pursued me through *two* cancellations of our dinner date. I've got to go back in there and give him my undivided attention. He deserves that much. And I will. Just as soon as I talk to Josh for a teensy-weensy second.

I press the button to call Josh.

"Oh my fucking God!" Josh shouts in my ear the minute the call connects. "Just the *thought* of you sleeping with Cameron Fucking Schultz is turning me into my goddamned brother. I'm coming to get you. Tell me where you are. You're not allowed to be on a date!"

I laugh. "Oh, please. I've seen your Instagram account, Josh. You're not exactly a monk."

"Don't believe everything you see. I just got propositioned by a bisexual supermodel the other day *and I turned her down.*"

I laugh. "Well, give the man a medal."

"Tell me where you are."

"No."

He's silent for a long beat. I can practically hear his gears turning. "Are you gonna turn this guy down or what?" he finally asks, his voice intense.

"Wouldn't you like to know?"

"Oh my fucking—"

"Josh, you're assuming he's gonna make me some kind of offer. There might not be anything to turn down."

"Ha! Kat, gimme a fucking break. Of course, the guy's gonna make you an offer."

"Not 'of course.' We might not hit it off. You never know."

"Kat, Jesus. Don't act like you don't know you're literally the most gorgeous girl on planet earth. You're physical perfection and any man who meets you is gonna want to sleep with you and he's gonna pull out all the stops to seduce you."

I'm speechless. He just said things that would rock any girl's world—and he said them like he was rattling off state capitals.

"So, are you gonna turn him down or not?"

"You think I'm the most gorgeous girl on planet earth?" I ask, my mouth still hanging open.

He exhales with exasperation, like I'm asking a stupid question. "Of course. You're insanity—a fantasy come to life. You must know that."

My heart is suddenly pounding in my ears.

"You're drop-dead gorgeous," he continues, his voice shifting from matter-of-fact to something distinctly sexual. "Anyone who sees you is gonna want you. It's fucking primal. Anyone would want you."

"Anyone?" I ask, clearly asking if that word includes Josh.

"*Anyone.* Jesus, Kat. *Of course.* That little cleft in your chin?" He makes a sound like I just licked his dick. "I've got a hard-on just thinking about it. God help me if I ever get to touch it, I'm gonna lose my fucking mind."

I swallow hard.

"And on top of all that, you're funny and sassy, too. You're the whole package, Kat. A fucking eleven."

Holy shitballs, I wanna have sex with this man. If we were alone right now, my clothes would already be off and my legs spread. A thought pings my brain like a pebble against a window: *What did you ask for in your application to The Club, Josh Faraday?*

"So, where are you?" Josh says softly, like he's luring a rescue puppy with a hunk of sausage. "I wanna celebrate my newfound freedom tonight with my Party Girl with a Hyphen and I won't take no for an answer."

I can barely breathe. "I can't, Josh," I finally say. "I'm not gonna do that to Cameron. I'm a bitch, but I'm not that big a bitch. We'll celebrate tomorrow."

"Aw, come on, Kat. If you're willing to meet me tomorrow night, that means you already know you're not gonna be on a date with Cameron Schulz tomorrow night, which means you already know you're not gonna sleep with him *tonight*, which means there's no point in going through the motions with him anymore. Under the circumstances, the kind and efficient thing to do, therefore, is to stop wasting everyone's time and come hang out with the guy you actually want to sleep with tonight. It's the kindest thing you could possibly do, Kat—don't you wanna be a kind person?"

"And you're assuming the guy I actually want to sleep with is you?"

"Of course. It's no big secret."

I scoff. "You're awfully cocky."

"No, I'm *confident*—and with very good reason."

Oh man, that last comment sent a shiver down my spine. "I wouldn't be so confident, if I were you," I say. "I haven't spent five uninterrupted minutes with Cameron, thanks to you—with a little time, we might really hit it off. You never know. Maybe I *will* be sleeping with him tomorrow night. Hell, maybe I'll throw caution to the wind and sleep with him tonight."

Josh's voice shifts to something animalistic. "*Kat, fuck that shit right now. I'm the sane twin compared to my brother, but I'm still a fucking Faraday—you can't say that fucking shit to me. Do you understand me?*"

Oh, his voice is so fucking sexy right now, I'm wetting the cotton crotch of my undies.

His voice turns into a low, intense growl. "You like torturing me. Is that it? It gets you off?"

I'm so freaking wet. Oh my God, I want him. "Yeah, actually. It does."

"Oh my fucking God," he replies. "Go back in there and tell him you've got to go. Tell him you got a better offer from a man who's gonna make you scream tonight."

My heart is racing. The cool air on my face is doing nothing to calm my raging arousal right now.

"Come on, Kat. Do it now. Right now. I've got such a big fucking hard-on for you right now—and I know exactly how to use it."

"You'd make me scream, huh?"

"Oh yeah. You bet. All night long, baby."

"Coming from a guy who joined a sex club, I'm not sure if that's good or bad. Would you make me scream your name or scream for the police?"

He laughs. "You'll just have to roll the dice and find out, baby. Either way, you'll thank me."

I let out a shaky breath and shift my weight. I feel like every drop of blood and fluid in my body has flooded into my crotch all at once.

"You know how this story ends every bit as much as I do, Party Girl," he coos. "Let's cut out the middle bullshit and get to the good stuff. Because, trust me, the good stuff is really, really good."

"I don't have any idea how this story ends."

"Yes, you do."

"No, I don't."

"Well, I do. And, believe me, it's *so fucking good* it's gonna make you drip down your thighs."

My clit flutters. So, it turns out Josh Faraday's a dirty-talker, huh? He just gets better and better. I take a deep breath. "It's gonna be that good, huh?"

"So. Fucking. Good. Oh my God. Best you ever had."

If I weren't on a public sidewalk right now, my fingers would already be inside my panties. "What'd you ask for in your application, Josh?" I purr.

He exhales. "You'll just have to roll the dice and find out, Party Girl. Come on, Kat. YOLO. I've got a boner the size of the Space Needle for you right now. I jacked off in the shower yesterday, thinking about you. Don't make me do it again tonight. What a waste of an epic boner. Come on."

Oh man, he's making me so aroused, I can't think straight. "What'd you write in your application, Josh?" I ask. "Tell me and maybe I'll tell Cameron I feel a migraine coming on."

"I don't negotiate with terrorists," he says. "Just tell me where you are."

I laugh, even though I don't want to do it.

"YOLO, Kat," he whispers like he's trying to put me into a trance. "YOOOOOLO."

I laugh again and shake my head, bringing myself to my senses. "Are you gonna tell me what you asked for in your application or not?"

"Not. You just have to roll the dice. That's half the fun of fucking someone new. Come on."

I'm pissed as hell he won't tell me. Didn't I just say I'd ditch Cameron if he told me? That'd be an exceedingly bitchy, heartless thing to do to the guy—and I'm still willing to do it *for him*—even though Cameron is a goddamned Major League baseball player, too. Well, now I'm pissed.

"Come on, Kat. *YOLO*," Josh coos, clearly still thinking he's got a chance of getting what he wants.

"Nope. I'm not gonna be a total bitch to Cameron. And I'm not gonna sleep with you without knowing what I'm getting myself into. So forget it."

"Tell him you've gotta go. Right now."

"No. We've already ordered our food—really expensive, nice food. Surf and turf."

"Wow. Big spender."

"Stop it. He's nice—a really sweet guy. He doesn't even drink."

Josh bursts out laughing. "What? Oh my God. He just gets better and better."

I'm smiling so big, my cheeks hurt.

Oh man, Josh is laughing his ass off like I've just said the funniest thing in the world. "Fun guy," he finally chokes out. "Oh yeah, you're having a blast, Party Girl." He laughs again. "No wonder you're talking to me instead of sitting with him. You couldn't get away from him fast enough."

"A guy doesn't have to drink to be fun. I think it's awesome Cameron doesn't drink—it shows he's got discipline."

"Pfft," Josh scoffs. "No, you don't think it's awesome. You were mortified when he told you, admit it."

I audibly shrug. He's right, of course. But wild horses couldn't make me admit that to him right now. "Why don't we just see each other tomorrow night?" I purr.

Josh exhales. "I can't. I'm headed to New York tomorrow on the early flight on business. And then I gotta be in LA for a couple days on a deal. I won't be able to get back to Seattle for at least a week."

I make an "oh well" sound. In all honesty, I'm wildly disappointed, but I'm not gonna let him know that. "Well, then, I guess we'll be seeing each other in a week or so," I say primly. "If ever."

He makes an exasperated noise.

"Assuming you've sent me your application to The Club by then, of course," I add. "Since that's a required prerequisite of me going out with you."

He makes a scoffing sound.

I ignore him. "Oh, *and* assuming I'm not impregnated by Cameron Schulz by then—which is entirely possible."

Josh makes a caveman roar that shocks the hell out of me. "Fuck this, Kat!" he booms. *"Tell that boring, sober motherfucker to fuck off right now.* I mean it. No more bullshit. I'm coming to get you. Tell me where you are."

I can only imagine how shocked my face looks right now. I must look like that emoji with wide eyes. I didn't expect that kind of volcanic reaction. Jeez. It came out of nowhere. He always seems so laid back. I open my mouth, but nothing comes out.

"Are you there?" Josh barks.

"Yeah."

"Enough with the bullshit, Kat. Playtime's over. You don't wanna be with Cameron Fucking Schulz tonight and you know it. You wanna be with *me.* Now tell me where you are because I'm coming to get you."

Kerzoinks, as Sarah would say. Sounds like he's got something of a jealous streak. Ha! Well, he's in for a rude awakening. Because Kat Morgan doesn't do jealous-boyfriend bullshit. Ever. Wait. What am I thinking? Josh isn't even my boyfriend! We're not even dating! Why would he think, even for a minute, he's in any position to tell me what to do?

"Hmm," I say calmly, like he just asked me for directions to the nearest gas station. "I don't think so, Playboy. Caveman shit doesn't really work with me, you ought to know."

He's either fuming or coming on the other end of the line—I'm not sure which. By the noise he just made, it could be either.

"You know what *I* think's gonna happen right now? I'm gonna hang up the phone and go back into the restaurant and have a nice meal with a very sweet guy who politely asked me out to a very nice restaurant, and rescheduled *twice* despite his very busy schedule, and who's treated me with nothing but respect all night long—and who, it turns out, happens to be the starting shortstop for the Mariners. Who knew?"

Josh makes another raging caveman noise. "Kat. I'm not kidding. Stop fucking around and tell him—"

"So I guess I'll see you soon, whenever you're in Seattle next—*if* I'm not already desperately in love with Cameron Schulz and carrying his love child by then."

"*Kat.*"

"What?"

"Fuck."

I don't reply.

"Come on," he says. "Stop it."

He's clearly used to getting whatever he wants, when he wants it.

"Travel safe, Josh. I really do hope to see you soon."

"*Kat.*"

I'm about to hang up, but his tone is so emphatic, I feel compelled to stay on the line. "*What?*"

He exhales. There's a long beat as he collects himself. "YOLO, Kat," he says earnestly.

I bite my lip. Oh, he's good. He's really good. A giggle escapes my mouth, even though I don't want it to.

Oh man. I want him. He's one hundred percent right. But I've got a problem. I make it a rule never to sleep with a man on a first date if I'm interested in him as potential boyfriend-material. It's a rule I *never* break. I'm not quite sure if all my interactions with Josh add up to the equivalent of a first date or not, but I don't want to risk it. But, regardless of my stupid rule (because if ever there was a time to break my rule, it's now, with Josh), if Josh is leaving on a flight to New York first thing tomorrow, then tonight's not our night, anyway. Something tells me when I finally get to take a big ol' bite out of this particular man's ass—and I'm not being figurative there—I'm gonna wanna go back for seconds and thirds and fourths and fifths. I exhale a long, shaky breath. It's been so freaking long since I've felt even a glimmer of what I'm feeling right now, I don't want to fuck it up by being Classic Kat.

"I gotta go, Playboy," I say. I exhale again and my tone shifts to complete sincerity. "Josh, seriously. It'd be too heartless, even for me, to blow off Cameron after how sweet he's been to me. I can be a bitch, you should be warned, but not that big a bitch."

Josh is silent on the line for a long beat. "Shit," he finally says. "Okay. Then. Fuck. I guess I'll see you next week, then."

"I'm looking forward to it."

He exhales with resignation.

"Hey, make sure you get my email address from Sarah in the meantime."

"Why?"

"So you can send me your Club application. It's required reading before I'll go out with you."

He audibly rolls his eyes. "Not gonna happen."

I laugh. "You're used to getting whatever you want, when you want it, aren't you?"

"Damn straight."

"Well, guess what? *So am I.*"

He laughs. "Mmm hmm. Well, sucks to be you, Party Girl. I guess you've finally met your match."

"Mmm hmm. We'll see."

He chuckles. "We'll see."

"Travel safe, Josh," I say earnestly. "I gotta go have dinner with *Cameron Schulz,* the shortstop for the Mariners." I wait a beat, but he doesn't reply. "I hope to see you soon, Josh," I add sincerely.

"Tell Cameron his batting average sucks dick right now and that whiff at the plate last night against the Yankees was a fucking embarrassment."

"I'll be sure not to tell him you said so."

"Bye, Kat."

"Bye, Josh. I'll look forward to your email with your application attached."

"Not a fucking chance, Party Girl. Not a fucking chance in hell."

I laugh. "We'll see about that."

"Yeah, good luck with that."

"I don't need luck. I've got you right where I want you, Playboy."

"Mmm hmm. I think it's the other way around."

"That's what I *want* you to think."

He laughs. "Sure thing, PG. Keep telling yourself that. Bye, Kat."

"Bye, Josh."

I hang up and turn off my phone. For a long beat, I stand in the chilly night air, staring at the traffic whizzing by on the street, my crotch throbbing mercilessly and my heart leaping out of my chest. He's right. He's got me right where he wants me—not the other way around—just like every other woman he burns through, I'm sure. Clearly, the man has his pick of every bisexual supermodel and starlet in Hollywood, and I can see why. Well, maybe I'm the first woman who's gonna teach this Playboy that not all women will say "how high" when a rich, handsome, charismatic studmuffin like Josh Faraday commands, "Jump."

After a moment, a wide smile spreads across my devious, bitchy, turned-on, intrigued, conniving little face. If Josh wants me, he's gonna have to work for it —something he's clearly not used to doing. I'm dying to read his frickin' application, that's true, but at this point, that stupid application is more than just an application to a sex club. *It's a brass ring.* If this is gonna be a battle of wills, then I'm gonna be the one who wins it.

My smile widens.

Kat Morgan knows two things in this life: men and PR. And, by God, when it comes to Josh Faraday, victory will be mine. Along with his supremely bitable ass.

9

KAT

"Hey!" I shout, knocking on the door of Jonas and Sarah's hotel suite. "Vegas, baby!" I begin pounding maniacally on the door like I'm the Energizer Bunny on speed, which is actually a perfect analogy because I feel high with excitement—out of my mind with unbridled glee. I'm in the Promised Land, baby! My own personal Mecca! And on Jonas' generous dime, no less. Ha! My hotel room is freaking spectacular—I could never in a million years afford to stay in a hotel like this on my own—plus, as Josh would say, I'm free at last, I'm free at last, thank God almighty, I'm *finally* free at last of my round-the-clock bodyguards (with Jonas' permission). Who knew having two grumpy old guys trail your every move for a week and a half could become so freaking suffocating? No wonder Whitney finally fucked Kevin—she just needed to de-stress from having some grouchy guy following her around twenty-four-seven.

And the most exciting thing of all? Sarah's finally feeling back to her old self again, and then some. When Sarah called yesterday to say, "Pack your bags for Vegas, Kitty Kat—we're going *Ocean's Eleven* on The Club's motherfucking ass!" I practically peed my pants.

"I'm in!" I shrieked (even though I had absolutely no idea how I could possibly contribute a damned thing to going *Ocean's Eleven* on The Club's motherfucking ass).

"Woot!" Sarah replied.

"Woot!" I shouted back.

"Will it be just you, me, and Jonas?" I asked, trying to sound breezy and nonchalant.

"Who else would be joining us?" Sarah asked coyly.

"Oh, I dunno," I answered. "No one in particular. Just wondering."

Sarah laughed. "Well, a certain *hacker* will be joining us, if that's who you're referring to," Sarah said, teasing me.

"Oh, that's good," I said. "Yeah, we'll definitely need one of those."

"Mmm hmm," Sarah said. "Fo shizzle pops."

There was a very, very long beat, during which I held my breath and bit the inside of my cheek with anticipation until Sarah burst out laughing.

"Oh, Kitty Kat. Of course, the Playboy's gonna be there, too. Wherever Jonas goes, Josh goes, too—that's something as reliable as gravity."

I exhaled like I'd just surfaced from being held forcibly underwater.

I hate to admit it, but I've been going out of my mind thinking about Josh this whole week while he's been in New York—I can't remember the last time my Rabbit's gotten this much action in a single week.

Thankfully, Josh has made it clear he's been thinking about me, too, though he's obviously playing his cards close to his vest, the smooth bastard. On the one hand, he's sent multiple texts this past week, just enough to let me know he's thinking about me, but, on the other hand, his texts say absolutely nothing. No teasing. No innuendo. No semi-inappropriate photos. Not even any questions about Cameron Fucking Schulz. And, notably, no reference whatsoever to his application, despite my explicit demands for it. Just the occasional, "Hey, Party Girl" and "Whatcha doing, hot stuff?" or "Did you have a nice dream about me last night, PG?"

Of course, I know Josh's game—I've played it a time or two (or three) myself: he's forcing me to make the first move—breaking me down, making me question his interest. Bush league. He clearly doesn't understand whom he's dealing with here.

Well, two can play the "I don't give a shit" game. Hmmph. All week, I've answered each and every one of Josh's texts with pleasant but brief and noncommittal bullshit. "Hey yourself," I've replied. Or "Oh, nothing, just looking for something interesting to read—hint hint," or, on occasion, "None of your freaking beeswax, PB." If Josh thinks I'm gonna chase him like every other girl obviously does, he's sadly mistaken. And so, to put it mildly, our recent communications have been textually unsatisfying—while subtextually dripping with heat—and the whole situation is making me want to jump his freaking bones.

Bastard.

I continue pounding on Jonas and Sarah's door, my excitement about to boil over.

"Hey!" I shout again. "Vegasssssss!"

The door to Jonas and Sarah's room opens abruptly and Sarah's beaming face greets me.

"Woohoo!" I shriek, throwing my arms around her.

Sarah clutches me like her life depends on it and the two of us jump up and down, screaming, for a solid minute. When we finally unravel our bodies, I enter the spacious suite, instantly in awe.

"Wow," I say, marveling at the splendor of our surroundings. Wall-to-wall marble floors. Sleek leather and glass furniture. Light fixtures that look like works of art. And, the *coup de grace*, floor-to-ceiling windows overlooking The Strip.

"Wow, Jonas," I say. "You really knocked yourself out. I bet, like, rock stars and Prince Harry stay in this place, especially with that private elevator to get up here. It's amazing."

Jonas is standing by the fully stocked bar, looking hella hot in his jeans and tight T-shirt, if I do say so. "I wanted to show my precious baby an extra good time," Jonas says, "seeing as how this is her first trip to Sin City."

My precious baby? I glance at Sarah and she's positively giddy. Is it possible the manwhore has changed his manwhoring ways at the magic touch of the right woman? I've read about that mythical phenomenon in fairytales, but I've never seen it happen in real life—or, at least, it's never happened to me.

"Oh, Jonas," Sarah coos, blushing. "You're so sweet."

Jonas' face bursts with immediate color. Aw, he's absolutely adorable right now. I just wanna pinch his cheeks. I can plainly see why Sarah's so smitten with him—this boy's a puppy!—I don't know why I didn't see it before.

"Thank you for paying for my flight, Jonas," I say, smiling. "And my room."

"You're welcome. You got checked in okay?"

"Yes, thank you."

Sarah flashes an adorable smile at Jonas and he returns it.

Oh good lord, these two are smitten. "Did you see this view?" I say, grabbing Sarah's hand and pulling her to the floor-to-ceiling windows at the far end of the room. "Just wait 'til you see The Strip at night. The lights are gonna blow you away." I sigh. "God, I love Vegas."

"I've seen The Strip in movies," Sarah says, "but I bet it's really cool in person."

I glance at the bar and spy a bottle of my favorite champagne chilling on ice. "Oh, champagne!" I squeal. This day just keeps getting better and better.

"I'll get you a glass," Jonas says, moving gracefully toward the bar.

There's a loud knock at the door to the suite. "Open up, you beast!"

Oh my God. Every hair on my body stands on end. *He's here.* Shit. I wish I'd checked my makeup before heading up to Jonas and Sarah's room. Gah. "Do I look okay?" I whisper to Sarah. I bare my teeth. "Do I have anything in my teeth?"

Sarah grins broadly. "You look perfect," she says. "He'll be putty in your hands."

Jonas opens the door and there he is, the Playboy himself, dressed in a designer suit perfectly tailored to his muscled frame, standing next to a much smaller, kind of nerdy-looking guy in a V-neck T-shirt and goatee.

Holy shitballs. My chest constricts at the sight of Josh's utter deliciousness. Was he always this hot?

I've ogled countless photos of Josh on the Internet since I first met him at

Jonas' house two weeks ago, but absolutely no two-dimensional simulation of the man comes even close to capturing his magnetism. He's oozing raw masculinity, even in that expensive suit. In fact, the sophistication of his clothes somehow emphasizes the brute swagger hiding underneath the fabric. Oh my fucking God. This man is sex on a designer stick.

"You ready?" Sarah whispers.

I nod. "Let's do it."

She grabs my hand and we bounce happily over to the guys.

Oh shit, I'm trembling. What the hell's gotten into me? I never act this way. I feel like a schoolgirl with a crush.

"Hey, Party Girl with a Hyphen," Josh says, his eyes sparkling wickedly.

"Well, hey yourself, Playboy," I say, sounding remarkably collected, I must say. "It's a crazy, fucked up world when a Playboy and a Party Girl cross paths in *Vegas*, huh?" He bursts out laughing and I join him. "It's good to see you again," I say. Wow, I sound like I hardly give a shit. Sometimes I amaze even myself.

Josh wraps me in a huge hug and kisses me on both cheeks and I practically melt into his strong arms. Oh my God, his cologne is divine. Was he wearing that cologne the first night I met him? It's deadly.

I kiss him softly on the cheek and the sensation of his skin under my lips makes my skin sizzle and pop.

He puts his hand on my cheek and brings his lips to my ear. "You look gorgeous, Party Girl," he whispers.

"Uh," I say. Oh my God. I can't even think. Is it possible he's gotten even *better-looking* than he was two weeks ago?

Josh grins. "You ready to find out how this story ends, Party Girl?" He rubs his thumb along my cheek.

Before I can reply, the hipster guy standing next to Josh makes a weird noise, like a horse rejecting a saddle, and I suddenly realize I haven't introduced myself. I train my full attention on the hipster-nerd-guy and extend my hand, ignoring the fact that my cheek is still tingling where Josh just touched me. "Hi, I'm Katherine Morgan," I say. "But everyone calls me Kat."

"Oh. Huh. Hi. See. I'm ... Nice... fleb beet you."

"What?" I laugh.

"Hennessey. But... calls... Henn. Me. Calls. Henn. Everyone. Me."

Jonas bursts out laughing from behind me and the hipster guy's face turns beet red. Oh my gosh, this hacker dude's the most adorable human I've ever met. I'm already in deep, irreversible like with him. Without even thinking about it, I wrap him in a huge hug and kiss his cheek. He looks like he could break into beat poetry at any given moment. Adorbs! I want to take him home and put him in a rhinestone jacket and feed him treats. "I'm so excited to meet you, Henn," I say. I kiss him on the cheek again and his face turns the color of a vine-ripened tomato.

"Kat, stop treating Henn like a Chihuahua," Sarah says. "Henn, tell her to stop assaulting you."

I laugh and release the poor guy. "Sorry, Henn," I say. "I'm impulsive. I should have warned you. Sometimes, I just can't control myself." I glance at Josh on that last comment and his eyebrows drift up, every so slightly.

Henn nods and mumbles something adorably incoherent.

"Time for alcohol!!" Josh booms. "I always say, 'If a guy doesn't drink, he must be a total fucking tool.' Or, at the very least, he's just fucking *boring*." He shoots me a smart-ass grin and strides to the bar. "Don't you agree, Kat?"

I twist my mouth, trying desperately not to smile. "Not necessarily," I say. "Sometimes, it just means a guy is *disciplined*."

Josh scoffs. He refills my champagne glass and then Sarah's and grabs three beers from the fridge. "Oh yeah," he says, snapping his fingers like he's just remembered something important. He opens the first of the bottles and hands it to Jonas. "I've also heard from several *extremely* reliable sources that guys who don't drink also make limp-dick-shitty-ass lovers."

"Really?" Henn asks.

"Yup."

"Well, jeez," Henn says. "Hand me a beer, then. *Pronto*. And a couple shots."

Josh hands Henn a beer, his eyes still trained on me, his expression clearly saying, "Don't fuck with me, little girl—you're out of your depths."

I look away. Holy shitballs, Josh Faraday is sexy as hell.

The five of us move to the black leather couches in the sitting area and make ourselves comfortable—and I gotta say when Josh Faraday makes himself comfortable, it's a sight to behold: he leans back, spreads his strong legs, and unapologetically adjusts his dick in his pants.

"I'm shocked you splurged on this place, bro," Josh says, glancing around the room. "So un-Jonas-like of you."

"Would you stop telling me what's Jonas- or un-Jonas-like of me already? Apparently, you have no idea what I'm like."

Josh laughs. "Apparently not."

I bite my lip. *Sexy man. Sexy man. Sexy man.* I can't think straight.

Henn opens the browser on his computer and logs into some application-program-thing.

"Okay, folks. I've got an update on the Oksana sitch you had me working on."

"Fantastic," Jonas says, rubbing his hands together.

We all crowd around Henn's laptop—and when I bend over to get a good look at Henn's screen, Josh rests his hand on the small of my back. Oh my God, his touch is drawing every ounce of blood from my brain into the three square inches of flesh under his palm. Holy Hotness, Batman, I can barely process what Henn's saying right now. It seems to be something about someone named Oksana Belenko.

"Sounds like an Olympic ice skater, doesn't she?" Henn says, but I'm barely listening. Josh's hand has moved from the small of my back to the curve of my hip. Holy shitballs. Nuclear energy is wafting off Josh's body just a few inches from mine.

"Boom shakalaka," Henn says, showing us something on his screen.

"See? Fucking genius," Josh says. His hand returns to the small of my back, where it begins making little swirling motions.

"You sure that's our girl?" Sarah asks.

Henn explains why he's sure he's got the right Oksana.

"So that means we've got a confirmed physical address?" Sarah asks.

"Yep."

"Wow," Sarah says. She pauses, the gears apparently turning inside her head. "So it sounds like Oksana supplies the girls for The Club—" She looks at Josh. "Or, if you'd prefer, the Mickey Mouse roller coasters."

Sarah and I simultaneously burst out laughing and Josh straightens up, abruptly removing his swirling hand from my back.

"It was an *analogy*," he says, looking genuinely annoyed.

"We know, Joshie, we know," Sarah says, winking at him. "But it's still funny." She looks at me and makes a ridiculously cute cartoon-face and I burst out laughing again. God, I love Sarah. Relief floods me yet again to have her safe and sound.

"Yeah, Oksana's like this frickin' old-school *madam*," Henn says. "Probably not the brains behind all the tech stuff."

"She's probably got a business partner who handles the tech side of things," Jonas says.

"Definitely," Henn agrees. "And whoever that person is, he or she knows exactly what the hell they're doing. Because there's no finding these guys by accident. And even then," Henn continues, sipping his beer, "their storefront is just a shell. Their real shit's gotta be buried way down in the Deep Web. And that's a scary place."

"What's the Deep Web?" I ask.

Henn grins broadly at me.

"Is that a stupid question?" I ask, blushing.

"Oh no, not stupid at all. I'm just so used to hanging out with computer geeks all day long, I forget normal people don't know about this stuff." He smiles at me again. "I'm glad you don't know what it is. It means you're probably a well-adjusted, happy person."

I laugh. "I am, as a matter of fact."

"I can tell," Henn says. "Happiness is a very attractive quality in a person."

"Thank you," I say. My eyes flicker to Josh and I'm shocked to see he's already staring at me—looking at me like he wants to fuck my brains out, actually. My skin sizzles and pops, yet again.

Josh clears his throat. "So, guys, before Henn launches into The Grand

Story of the Deep Web, how about we all do a shot of Patron? We're in Vegas, after all—when in Rome."

"Sounds like a fabulous idea to me," I say. "Do we have Patron in the bar?"

"Of course," Jonas says. "I made sure of it. My brother is nothing if not predictable."

Josh strides purposefully behind the bar, grace in motion, flashing me a come-hither stare as he goes.

I feel like he's pulling me on a string. "I'll help you out, Playboy," I blurt, bounding over to the bar.

"Why, thanks, Party Girl," Josh says.

I stand next to him in the bar and lean into him, involuntarily drawn to his sheer physicality. He leans his muscled body into mine and whispers softly in my ear. "You ready to cut the middle bullshit yet, Party Girl—see how this story ends?"

"That depends. Are you ready to give me your application?"

He laughs. "I told you—I don't negotiate with terrorists."

"Well, then. I guess not."

10

JOSH

"You're freaking me out, Henn," Kat says.

She's responding to Henn—he's just finished explaining the difference between the Surface Web (the "Internet we all know and love" where anyone can "Google a sushi restaurant") and the Deep Web (the "ink-black waters below the surface" where "jihadists and drug warlords and fucking human traffickers" operate)—and it's obvious from Kat's facial expression she's completely horrified by what she's just heard.

"How have I never heard of this before?" Kat asks. "Have you heard about this, Sarah?"

Sarah shakes her head, exactly the way Goofy would. I can't help but chuckle at the sight of her. The more I get to know this girl, the more I love her. She's smart and sweet and a total ass-kicker, on the one hand, and yet the dorkiest, goofiest girl I've ever met on the other. I don't think I've met anyone quite like her before—and I've especially never met anyone better suited for my brother.

"Kinda freaks you out when you hear about it for the first time, huh?" Henn says.

"Totally," Kat agrees. "It reminds me of when I found out there are trillions of invisible microbes on my skin at all times."

"Please don't talk about that whole microbes-on-your-skin thing," I say. "That always creeps me out."

Kat bursts out laughing and I join her. It's easy to laugh when Kat does—the girl laughs like a dude.

Henn continues his tutorial, explaining in detail how he only uses his hacking-superpowers for good. "I leave no trace, take nothing, do no harm," Henn says, "unless I'm being paid to leave a trace, take something, do harm, of course. But I only do that kind of thing when I'm positive I work for the good guys."

"But how do you know you're working for the good guys?" Jonas asks, clearly skeptical. "Everyone thinks their cause is righteous. Hence, the concept of war."

I'm about to jump in and defend Henn, but he clearly doesn't need my help.

"Well, yes, of course." Henn looks right at Kat and flashes what I imagine he's hoping is a charming smile. "But let me show you how I tell the good guys from the bad guys." He looks right at Sarah. "Sarah, are you a good guy or a bad guy?"

"A good guy," Sarah says.

"And there you go."

Sarah shrugs like it makes perfect sense. "And there you go," she says.

Jonas is clearly not impressed. "But who would ever say they're one of the bad guys? Who would even *think* that about themselves? People are brilliant at justifying their actions to themselves—trust me, I should know."

"Well, *yeah*," Henn concedes. "But I don't always *believe* people when they say they're one of the good guys. In fact, I rarely do. If I *believe* them, the way I just believed Miss Cruz here, then that's good enough for me."

"Aw, you believe me, Henn?" Sarah asks.

"I do. Indubitably."

"Why, thank you."

"Of course."

"Sometimes, it's a no-brainer," Henn continues. "Like when a job comes from Josh, for example, I always know I'm fighting for truth and justice and the American way, no questions asked. Because a guy can set his moral compass to Josh—he's *always* one of the good guys, through and through."

Thank you, Henn.

Now *here's* a guy who's got a brother's back, unlike Jonas. I glare at my stupid brother, sending him a nonverbal "fuck you" for the way he let me twist in the wind in front of Kat the other day—but Jonas is too engrossed in staring at Sarah like a lovesick puppy to notice me.

"Thanks, man," I say to Henn.

"Just speaking the truth," Henn replies.

"Well, well, well," Kat says, arching that bold eyebrow of hers. "It turns out the Playboy's a good guy, after all—Mickey Mouse roller coasters notwithstanding."

I smile broadly.

She bites her lip.

Oh man, I can't wait to fuck this gorgeous woman. It's gonna be so fucking good.

"So, Henn," Jonas says. "If The Club lives in the Deep Web, how the fuck do we find them and take them down?"

Henn proceeds to explain his strategy for implanting malware onto Oksana Belenko's computer. In essence, Sarah's got to pay a personal visit to "the pimpstress extraordinaire," as he calls her, obtain her email address, and then send Oksana an infected email on the spot, which Oksana's got to open in Sarah's presence. Sounds kind of hairy to me, actually—I agree completely when my brother insists on accompanying Sarah on her mission.

"But they think I'm *playing* you, remember?" Sarah protests in a huff. "Why on earth would I bring you with me if I'm *scamming* you?"

"I don't know," Jonas says, crossing his monstrous arms over his chest. "Use that big-ass brain of yours to come up with something they'll believe."

Sarah sighs in frustration.

"It's non-negotiable, Sarah. We're doing this together or we're not doing it at all."

Sarah huffs. "Why would I bring you to meet her? It makes no sense."

Jonas looks at me, obviously inviting me to come up with a suggestion, but I've got nothing.

"They think I'm *playing* you," Sarah says slowly, like she's thinking out loud. "Why would I bring you with me?"

"I don't know, but it's non-negotiable."

"I heard you the first time, Lord-God-Master." Sarah crosses her arms over her chest. After a moment, she picks up her champagne flute and ambles to the floor-to-ceiling windows on the other side of the room. Nighttime has descended on the city while we've been talking and The Strip's dazzling display of neon lights is sprawled out before us.

"Wow," Sarah says, staring out at the expanse of lights. "It's beautiful."

We all get up and take in the view alongside her, drinks in hand.

"Let's take a photo, Sarah," Kat says. The two girls smile for a selfie on Kat's phone, followed by Jonas and Sarah, at Kat's urging.

"You two look good together," Kat says to Jonas. "*Really* good together."

At Kat's words, Jonas looks like a fucking kitten being stroked. Aw, Jonas. Shit. It's times like this I remember my brother's gone his whole life without a single person other than me telling him how fucking awesome he is.

"Don't post those pics anywhere, Kat," Henn warns. "We don't want the bad guys knowing we're on their turf."

"I won't post them; don't worry. I just want to remember being here in Vegas with my best friend for her first time." Kat wraps Sarah in a warm hug. "Thank God you're okay. I was so worried about you. I love you so much."

"I love you, too." Sarah says, nuzzling into Kat's blonde hair.

I can't take my eyes off Kat and Sarah right now—especially Kat. Yeah, she's gorgeous, but I already knew that. Yeah, she's sassy as hell. But, watching the way she's so tenderly kissing and hugging Sarah, it's suddenly dawning on me she might also be... dare I say it... *sweet?* Huh.

Sarah whips her head up and gasps. "I've got it," she says.

"You've got what?" Kat asks, brushing Sarah's dark hair out of her face.

Sarah disengages from Kat, suddenly animated with an idea. "We use their *greed* against them."

"That's my girl," Jonas says. "I knew you'd think of something."

Sarah leaps over to Jonas and throws her arms around his neck, something she seems to do a lot, I've noticed. "This is gonna work."

"Of course, it will," Jonas says. "We're an unstoppable team."

Henn looks at his watch. "Okay, get your plan figured out and we'll launch first thing tomorrow. I'm gonna work all night on my malware. I want to make sure whatever we send them is ironclad." He grabs his laptop, clearly excited to get to work.

"Well," Kat says, her hands on her hips. "While Henn's hard at work cooking up a fancy virus, I guess the rest of us will have to find *something* to do in Las Vegas. Hmm." She taps her finger on her temple like she's solving an algebra problem. "What on earth could we possibly do in *Las Vegas*?" She raises her eyebrow at me, clearly inviting me to provide a suggested solution to the riddle.

"You like to gamble, Kat?" I ask.

Her face lights up. "I love it."

How did I know she was gonna say that? "What's your game?"

"Blackjack."

"Lame," I say.

"Excuse me?"

"The real fun is craps."

"I've never played," she says. "It seems complicated."

"Nah, it's easy. I'll spot you a grand and teach you how to play."

Her eyes pop out of her head. "I'm not gonna take your money."

I love that she just said that—I can't remember the last time a woman said anything even remotely like that to me, actually—but, of course, it's out of the question.

"No, you've got to roll the dice for me, Party Girl," I say matter-of-factly. "You've got first-timer's luck *and* lady luck on your side, and they only let you roll when you've got a bet on the table."

"Well, then, I'll bet my own money."

She tosses her golden hair behind her shoulder in what appears to be a misplaced gesture of defiance. Oh God, she's such a sexy little thing.

"Kat," Jonas says. "Let my brother pay for your fun."

Thank you, Jonas.

Finally, for the first time ever, my brother has actually stepped in to help me with a woman. I open my mouth to thank him for his unexpected assistance, but the fucker keeps talking.

"There's nothing Josh Faraday loves more than throwing his hard-earned money away on mindless entertainment," Jonas adds.

I laugh. I knew it was too good to last. "*That's* your idea of helping me, bro?"

Jonas shrugs.

"You'd be doing me a favor, Kat," I say, turning away from my useless brother and fixing my eyes on Kat's ridiculously beautiful face. "Betting on a first-time roller is the dream of every craps player—it's as exciting as it gets. *And I love excitement.*"

Kat grins and bites her lip, her eyes blazing. "Okay, Playboy," she says. "I'm in. You had me at 'excitement.'"

Ooooooooooh, I like this girl. My skin is beginning to tingle.

"But we're all going out together, right?" she asks, looking at Sarah.

"Of course," Sarah says.

"Where should we take these lovely ladies to dinner?" Jonas asks me.

My dick is beginning to tingle along with the rest of me. "It just so happens I know the perfect place," I say.

"Of course you do," Jonas replies.

"Do you ladies think you can handle a night out with the Faraday brothers?" I ask, but the only lady I'm looking at is Kat.

Sarah and Kat squeal with excitement, and Sarah throws her arms around Jonas' neck for the hundredth time today. "Thank you, Jonas."

I stride over to Kat. "Hey," I say softly.

"Hey," she replies, her blue eyes blazing at me.

"You ready to earn that nickname of yours, Party Girl with a Hyphen?"

Her eyes flicker at me. "I was born ready, Playboy."

I hold her gaze for a long beat. She truly is the most spectacularly gorgeous woman I've ever beheld. I have the sudden, irresistible urge to kiss her. I lean in, slowly.

"Just as soon as you resend me that email that must have gotten lost," she says, pressing on my chest and halting my forward progress. "The damned thing must have gone into my spam folder when you sent it earlier this week."

"Gosh, Kat," I say. "I didn't send you an email this week."

"No?"

"Nope."

"Why not?"

"Because I don't have a *vagina.*"

"Oh, really? Huh. That's too bad."

"It's too bad I don't have a *vagina?*"

She smirks. "It's too bad you didn't send me that email. I was really looking forward to reading it."

I smile at her. She might be the most gorgeous creature I've ever beheld, but she's also the most stubborn. Jesus God. "You're not gonna get what you want this time, no matter how sexy you are," I say. "So you can stop banging your head against the wall. Wouldn't want you to bruise that pretty forehead of yours."

"You obviously don't know me at all. I don't back down," she says. "I only get more determined."

"There's a first time for everything."

She squints at me. "We'll see."

"I guess so."

She stares me down. When I don't look away, her cheeks flush. She clears her throat. "Why don't you ask Henn to come with us to dinner?" she says. "Since we're obviously just gonna have a friendly dinner and nothing more, the more the merrier, right?"

"Great idea," I say. "Henn, you wanna join us for dinner?" I call to him sharply, but I don't take my eyes off her. My cock is rock hard. I'd pay any amount of money to have her sitting on it right now.

Henn doesn't reply.

"Yo, Henn?" I call to him, devouring Kat with my eyes. "You wanna join us for dinner, man?"

"Oh, Josh," Henn says. "How many times do I have to tell you? You can wine and dine me all you like, but you're never gonna get me into bed."

Kat chuckles.

I step close to her and brush her cheekbone with my fingertip, and she abruptly stops laughing.

She parts her lips and lifts her face like she wants me to kiss her. My cock is straining for her.

I lean down and brush my lips as close as humanly possible to hers without actually making contact. "Laugh it up, Party Girl," I whisper. "But Henn's not the one I'm gonna wine and dine and get into bed tonight." I pull back from her face and wink.

11

JOSH

"Hard four!" the dealer yells.

"Woohoo!" Kat shrieks.

"You're on fi-yah, sistah!" Sarah shouts. She shakes her ass into Jonas' crotch, and he gropes her ass and hips.

The dealer pushes a stack of chips at Kat and she leans over the craps table to collect them—which, of course, gives me the perfect opportunity to ogle her backside. Jesus. That sequined mini-dress of hers is barely longer than a men's dress-shirt, and holy shit, she's working it *hard*. Endless, toned legs. Sky-high heels. Long, tousled blonde hair cascading down her back. And a tight little ass to cap it all off. In summary, the girl is smoking hot. Gorgeous. Sexy. Beautiful. I can't come up with enough praise to do her justice. She's physical perfection.

An old dude in a Hawaiian shirt on the other side of Kat leans into her shoulder. "What number ya feeling, Blondie?"

Kat picks up the dice. "I'm not sure," she answers. "I'm just gonna bet the pass line this time—I'm not getting a vibe."

"Oh, I'm feeling a six for sure," Sarah says confidently, wiggling her ass into Jonas' crotch again. "I'm feeling hella *sixy* right now, baby."

Jonas presses himself into Sarah and wraps his arms around her. "Oh, my precious baby's feeling *sixy*, is she?"

"Yes, sir, baby-sir," she says. "Sixy as hell."

Jonas throws a couple thousand bucks in chips onto the table. "On six," he says to the dealer, his free hand running up and down Sarah's torso. "Always bet on Sarah Cruz."

"Hard or easy six?" Hawaiian Shirt Guy asks Sarah, clearly hanging on her every word.

"Easy," she answers.

Jonas nibbles her neck and pulls her hips into him forcefully. Jesus. Who the fuck is my brother right now? I've never seen him act like this with a woman, ever. He's acting like... *me*.

"Oh my," Sarah says, laughing. "Easy six... and hard... *Jonas*."

Jonas bursts out laughing.

Kat and I look at each other, grimacing.

"I don't know whether to swoon or barf," Kat whispers to me and I chuckle.

"I'm definitely leaning toward 'barf,'" I reply.

"Easy six," Hawaiian Shirt Guy yells to the dealer, jumping on the Sarah-train.

"Me, too," I say, throwing a couple orange chips onto the table. "And for the lady, too," I add, throwing a thousand-dollar chip to the dealer for Kat.

"Josh, no. You already gave me plenty of gambling money. I'll use the money you gave me."

"Nah, put that away, PG. I've got a feeling—trust me."

In a sudden flurry, every other guy at the table follows suit, throwing their chips onto six, all of them betting on Sarah's intuition.

Kat picks up the dice. "Jeez, talk about pressure," she mutters. She tosses the dice onto the table.

Easy eight.

Everyone at the table cheers. It's not a six, true, but it's not crapping out, either, which means we're all still alive.

The dealer quickly distributes winnings on the roll.

"Bets?" the dealer invites.

"Yeah, add this to my six," I say to the dealer, tossing yet another pumpkin to him. "Plus another one for the lady," I say, tossing yet another orange thousand-dollar chip onto the table.

Kat looks at me with wide eyes. "No, Josh. *Stop*. No more."

I wink. "Humor me," I say. "I have a feeling."

Kat presses her lips together, but she doesn't argue. She holds the dice out to Sarah.

"*Vaya con dios*," Sarah says with solemnity. She blows on them.

"Come on, Blondie," Hawaiian Shirt Guy says. "Roll us a six."

Kat rolls. *Five.* Everyone at the table cheers. We're still alive.

"Add this to the lady's bet on the six," I say, throwing the dealer another orange. "And put this on mine." I throw him three more orange chips.

Kat takes a deep breath, blows on the dice, and rolls again. *Jackpot.*

The entire table erupts. Kat and Sarah leap into each other's arms, jumping up and down, while Jonas and I look on, laughing hysterically and shaking our heads.

When Kat disengages from Sarah, she sees the mammoth stack of chips headed her way from the dealer. "Oh my effing God," she says, her face suddenly turning to ash. She scoops up her winnings with shaking hands, suddenly looking like she's gonna puke. "I've gotta stop rolling now," she says, her voice tight. "That's it for me."

"You can't stop," I say. "Your roll's not finished."

"I can't... I've gotta stop. I can't gamble anymore. Oh my God."

"Good call, Kitty Kat," Sarah says. "Quit while you're ahead. Speaking of which." She turns around, puts her arms around Jonas' neck for the millionth time tonight, and whispers something into his ear.

Jonas' entire body jolts. He abruptly pushes all his chips over to Kat's already mammoth stack, grabs Sarah's hand, and yanks her away from the table like he's pulling a blowup doll. "See you guys later," he calls out over his shoulder.

"See you, bro," I shout. "Have fun."

And just like that, the lovebirds disappear into the crowded casino.

"Wait, Jonas!" Kat yells. "Your chips!" But he's long gone. "Jonas gave me his chips," Kat says, her eyes wide. "Oh my God. He gave me his chips."

"Because he wanted you to have them."

"But that's got to be—" She does a cursory count of the chips in front of her. "Holy shitballs! Almost fifteen thousand bucks! Plus what I won on that last roll, thanks to your extra bets—oh my effing God. I've got like twenty thousand bucks here, Josh."

"Congratulations."

"But . . ."

"Kat, whatever Sarah said to Jonas to make him shove those chips at you was obviously far more enticing to him than any amount of money."

Kat's mouth is hanging open. Obviously, this is a life-changing amount of money for the girl.

"Take it, Kat. You just made everyone at this table a crapload of money, including me. That's how Vegas works, baby. You earned it."

The dealer shoves the dice at Kat. "Still your roll, miss," he says.

She shakes her head. "You roll for a while, Josh. I'll just watch." She plops a tall stack of orange chips in front of me on the ledge of the table.

"What's this?" I ask.

"The money you gave me to gamble with at the beginning, plus the oranges you just threw onto the six for me."

"Come on, Blondie. It's still your roll," Hawaiian Shirt Guy says, clearly getting annoyed.

"Josh, I can't." She looks at me for help, her face tight.

"She's done," I say forcefully—even though I know it's unthinkable for a hot roller to quit mid-roll. Hawaiian Shirt Guy starts protesting, but I glare at him, making him shut his fucking mouth. I tip the dealers a thousand each and scoop up my chips. "Come on, Blondie," I say, staring down Hawaiian Shirt Guy. "Let's go celebrate our good fortune."

We begin walking toward the cashier, our hands overflowing with our bounty.

"I can't keep all this," Kat says. "This is an insane amount of money."

"Don't overthink it."

She holds out her chips. "Really, I can't. Take it before I give in to temptation."

I tilt my head at her. "You got a car payment?" I ask.

She nods.

"Will this pay off the loan?"

She snorts. "And then some."

"Then that settles it. It would be fiscally irresponsible for you *not* to accept this money. Don't be fiscally irresponsible, Kat."

She looks unsure.

I chuckle. "Seriously, Kat. That's chump change to Jonas, and you just made me a ton of money. See?" I hold out my chips to prove it. "I'm *rich!*"

She purses her lips. "Well... are you gonna expect something in return?"

"Nope. No strings attached."

Surprisingly, her face flashes with disappointment, not relief.

Interesting.

"Although, of course," I quickly add, "I *do* expect to get something from you tonight—something that's gonna be so fucking awesome, you're gonna thank me profusely and beg me to do it again and again. But you're gonna give it to me because you wanna do it so fucking bad, it hurts—not because you're paying me back for a few stupid gambling chips."

12

KAT

"Whatcha drinking?" Josh asks me when the bartender approaches us for our order.

"A dirty martini. Grey goose. Two olives," I say.

"I like your style, Kat." He smiles at the bartender. "Make it two—plus two shots of Gran Patron, please."

When the bartender leaves, Josh turns a heated gaze on me. "Jesus, Kat. You're so fucking beautiful, you're causing me pain."

"Wow. Thank you. You're so fucking beautiful, you're pissing me off."

He laughs. "You're so fucking beautiful, you make me wanna punch a wall."

"Well, you're so fucking beautiful, you make me wanna hurl all over you."

"Wow. Really?"

"Yup."

"Damn. I must be *really* fucking beautiful."

"Or I've got a particularly weak stomach," I say. "Which, actually, I do."

He pauses briefly. "You really are fucking beautiful, Kat." He reaches out, slowly, like he's not sure if I'm gonna stop him or not, and gently touches the tip of his finger to my chin.

I close my eyes. "Holy Who-Knew-a Chin-Could-Be-an-Erogenous-Zone, Batman," I say.

One side of his mouth hitches up. "I've wanted to touch this little cleft in your chin since the minute I first laid eyes on you," he says, his voice low and intense.

I take a deep breath. My flesh feels hot under his fingertip.

His hand migrates to my cheek. He pulls me toward him.

I stiffen, halting my forward progress. "What'd you ask for in your application, Josh?" I whisper.

He leans back sharply. "Seriously?"

I nod.

"Fuck. You're the most stubborn woman in the entire fucking world."

I shrug. "I warned you. I only get more determined."

The bartender puts our drinks in front of us and Josh raises his shot glass.

"To you, Kat. May you soon realize the folly of your ways and stop being so fucking stubborn."

"Thank you, Josh. And to you, as well." I raise my glass. "May you soon realize I never back down so you might as well give me what I want now so we can move quickly to the inevitable conclusion of this ridiculous showdown."

We clink our shots and down them.

"You don't really give a shit what's in my application, do you?" he asks. "You just wanna *win*."

"Sure, I care. I'm absolutely dying to know. And now that you're being so secretive about it, I wanna know even more." I wag my finger at him. "You should have used reverse psychology on me, Josh. I might have dropped the whole thing if you hadn't been so freaking weird about it."

He scowls. "I'm not being weird about it. It's just... not *relevant*."

I exhale. "What if sleeping with you means waking up in a dog collar, chained to a donkey? That seems like something I should know."

A wide grin spreads across his face.

"Why are you smiling like that?"

"Because you just tacitly admitted you want to sleep with me. Otherwise you wouldn't care if I like donkeys and dog collars."

I scowl at him. "Okay, how about this? I don't need to see the actual application. Just tell me verbally what you said in it. That's my final offer."

"Oh, that's your 'final offer,' huh? You think you're running this negotiation?" He takes a long sip of his drink. "Nope. I don't negotiate with terrorists. Ever."

I throw up my hands. "You're really frustrating, you know that? The harder you fight me on it, the more I wanna know."

"And you gotta know before you'll even *kiss* me now? Not just before you *fuck* me?"

"Correct. The stakes have officially risen."

He exhales with exasperation. "Lame. Just one kiss, Kat. You don't need an application to give me a simple kiss."

"It won't be a simple kiss."

"It won't be a simple kiss," he concedes, nodding. "That's true. Because after one kiss, you're gonna wanna fuck me." He grins. "You won't be able to control yourself."

I roll my eyes, though he's undoubtedly right: if I kiss this man, it's gonna take a grand total of forty-three seconds before I jump his bones. I know it as surely as I know my own name.

"Your demand is patently unfair, you know," he continues. "Because *you* don't have an application to give to *me*. You're asking me to bare my perverted soul to you without getting anything in return. Sex doesn't count because you want it as much as I do."

"Fine, then. I'll lay my perverted soul bare to you, too. I've got nothing to hide. Ask me anything you want—right here and now."

He motions to the bartender. "Another couple shots, please. Gran Patron. Limes. Thanks."

"I'm serious," I say. "I'll show you how truth and honesty works. Let 'er rip."

"Okay." He sits back, assessing me with smoldering eyes. "Admit you're soaking your panties for me right now."

I shift in my seat. "No."

"No, you won't admit it—or no, you're not soaking your panties for me?"

"No, I'm *not* soaking my panties for you."

"Bullshit. It's written all over your face. You're soaking them clean through." He rolls his eyes. "I thought you were gonna model truth and honesty for me. Ha! You're so full of shit." He swigs the last of his drink.

I lean forward and grin. "I'm not full of shit. I'm telling the God's truth. I'm not soaking my panties for you—*because I'm not wearing any panties*."

13

JOSH

Oh fuck. She's the devil.

My dick is doing fucking jumping jacks in my pants.

I can't breathe.

What the fuck is wrong with this woman? Is she insane? Her dress is barely longer than a fucking T-shirt. Is she trying to give the entire world an unimpeded peek at her pussy? All of a sudden, I can't remove my eyes from her crotch or stop imagining what's hiding just beyond the sequined hem of her itty-bitty dress.

She re-crosses her toned, bare thighs and flips her blonde hair, and I tear my eyes away from her lap.

"Do you always go commando?" I ask. But then I roll my eyes at myself. *That's* my lame response? Who the fuck am I right now—*Jonas?*

"No," she says, laughing. "I typically wear underpants. A teeny-tiny G-string, to be exact." She blows me a kiss and winks.

Oh, she's a fucking sadist.

"That's what I was wearing tonight, actually—a teeny, tiny, black lace G-string—mmmm—but I took it off in the bathroom right before we sat down at the bar." She opens her beaded clutch purse and pulls out a tiny black swatch of lace. "Looks like you're not the only one who likes a little *excitement,* Playboy." She winks again.

Holy fuck. My pulse is suddenly pounding in my ears. I lean forward, right into her gorgeous face.

"Goddammit, Kat. That's it." I pull out my credit card and throw it onto the bar. "This bullshit competition is over. Get up. I'm taking you upstairs right now."

She laughs and doesn't move a muscle. "Great. Can't wait to read your application before we get started."

"Kat. *No.*"

"I've told you my terms, Playboy—and I'm prepared to do *anything* I have to do to get what I want." She whirls her undies around on her finger. "*Anything at all.*"

I exhale, exasperated. "Dude, you're a freaking suicide bomber, you know that? You want me as much as I want you—but you're willing to blow yourself to smithereens in order to *win.*"

She re-crosses her legs, yet again. "Gosh, is it breezy in here? Wow. It feels kinda breezy in here." She mock-shivers and lets out a sexy growl. "God, I wish I had an application to a sex club to keep me warm right now. Brr."

"You're evil," I say, my voice low and intense. "Pure fucking evil. You're a fucking *jihadist.*"

She smiles broadly. "Oh, I like that word. I *am.*" She laughs. "Oh, God. I really am."

My cock is throbbing. "Half the fun of being with someone new is not knowing what you're getting yourself into in advance. Maybe you wake up chained to a donkey; maybe you don't. It's like opening a present on Christmas. You don't get to ask, 'What's in the box?' before you rip into it—you just rip into it, baby."

She shrugs and re-crosses her legs, yet again. "Interesting theory. Let's agree to disagree."

"I feel like you're licking my balls and punching them at the same time," I say.

She bursts out laughing. "Oh my God. You're hilarious."

"And you're demonic."

"I am. I really am."

"Obviously."

She shrugs. "Sorry. I can't help it. It's the way I am. I have four brothers. You show weakness with four brothers, you're dead."

"You have *four* brothers?"

She nods. "You'd be shocked what I've had to do to survive and thrive in a house with four guys. Holding off on kissing you 'til I get my way, even though all I wanna do right now is kiss the hell out of you—including sucking on that delectable lower lip of yours, by the way, mmm, that's a sexy lower lip—is freaking child's play. So give up now because I *will* get what I want. Just ask my brothers. *I always win.*"

I'm rendered speechless for a moment. "Well, joke's on you because I also grew up with four brothers," I finally manage to say. "All of them contained in the sole person of Jonas Faraday. You'd be shocked what I've had to do to survive and thrive in a house with a brother with four personalities. Holding off on kissing you 'til I get my way, even though all I wanna do right now is kiss the hell out of you—including biting that goddamned lower lip of yours and doing unmentionable things to that goddamned cleft in your chin—is freaking child's play."

She parts her lips but doesn't speak.

"Do I give off a Jeffrey Dahmer vibe or something?" I ask, leaning forward into her personal space.

"Not at all." She leans back and sips her drink. "Maybe that's why I'm so damned curious. Your seeming normalcy makes me wonder even more why a guy like you felt the need to join a sex club."

"I didn't *need* to join a sex club—any more than I *need* to go to Tahiti or Monaco."

"Or Disneyland," she adds, snickering.

I roll my eyes. "Or Disneyland. Correct. Joining The Club was a *vacation*." I sip my drink calmly. "Which means it's soundly in the realm of 'none of your fucking business.' I don't owe you a play-by-play of my vacations. And, news flash, I'm not gonna let you run my credit report or call my ex-girlfriends, either."

She takes another long sip of her drink. "Oh, that's a great idea about calling your ex-girlfriends, Playboy. I didn't think of that. You can email me their contact information along with your application."

I smirk. "You do realize, in theory, you could wake up gagged and chained to a donkey after fucking any guy, right? The fact that I joined The Club doesn't make me any more or less a pervert-weirdo-serial-killer-donkey-fucker than the average guy."

"Maybe, maybe not. I'll know for sure after I read your application. And by the way, I didn't say anything about waking up *gagged*. You just added that part." She raises one of her eyebrows at me.

I feel my cheeks blazing, despite my best efforts to keep a neutral face.

"Sarah sure enjoyed reading Jonas' application," she says. "Maybe I'll like yours as much as she liked his."

"Ah, so that's what this is about. Jonas and Sarah."

She shrugs, but her body language tells me I've hit the nail on the head.

"But Jonas didn't *willingly* give Sarah his application, you might recall—he sent it to an anonymous intake agent. If Jonas had met Sarah in real life the way I've met you, he never would have given her his fucking application, not in a million years, I guarantee it. Sarah only had it because Jonas had no choice in the matter—and she misappropriated it for her personal use." I sip my drink slowly. "Shame on her."

"But that's my whole point. Jonas wouldn't normally have given it to her—and yet that's exactly why they clicked so hard and fast. All cards on the table. Nothing to hide. No way to hold back, even if they wanted to. I think there's something to that kind of forced honesty."

Oh, she's good, but I'm not gonna fall for her manipulations. "Sure you wanna try it—it's a one-way street. No downside for you."

We sip our drinks again, eying each other.

"Yeah, but most likely a *huge* upside for you," she says. "Think about it like that."

She makes an excellent point, I must admit. But I'd never tell her that. "Did Sarah show you Jonas' application, by any chance?" I ask.

"No. She wouldn't even summarize it verbally for me. And she wouldn't tell me what she wrote to him in response, either."

"Yeah, neither would Jonas. Not a word."

"Damn. I'm dying to know."

"Me, too."

"Well, whatever they said to each other, it sure seems to have worked out well for them." She looks earnest. "It seems like maybe they're on to something with all that... forced honesty."

Well, shit. If I knew she was right—if I knew participating in some sort of bizarre honesty-game would turn out to be some sort of unparalleled aphrodisiac, I'd be all in. I really would. But I don't know if she's right. For all I know, my application could easily have the opposite effect than she's anticipating. It could make her run away, screaming. And, regardless, at this point, I'm probably doomed no matter what it might say. She's pinning so much expectation on the damned thing, it can't possibly live up to whatever kinkfest she's imagining it to be. No matter what it says, it's gonna be anticlimactic now.

And, more importantly, is it gonna open up an entire dialogue I have no intention of having? What I wrote in my application is a fucking time capsule— a moment in time I have no desire to revisit or fucking explain. My stomach twists. Yeah, it's settled. No matter what, I'm *not* gonna give this goddamned terrorist my fucking application.

"Do you usually practice 'complete honesty' with guys before you'll even *kiss* them?" I ask.

"No. I can't remember ever practicing 'complete honesty' with a guy, period," she replies. "Have you ever practiced complete honesty with a woman?"

"Complete?"

"Yeah."

"No. I came very close once. It didn't work out very well."

She twists her mouth.

"But enough about that." I drain my drink. "I don't negotiate with terrorists, like I said. So make your unreasonable demands all night long if you want— you're not getting what you want."

She exhales. "I tell you what. Just *tell* me what your stupid application says —and we'll call it a day. Tell me and then kiss me and then... who knows what might happen next?" She looks at me suggestively.

"Nope."

Her pucker turns to a pout.

"I don't negotiate with terrorists."

"So you keep saying."

"You don't even care about my stupid application. You're just trying to *win*."

"I could say the same thing about you. At least I'm being reasonable."

"You're being reasonable?"

"Yes. I backed down from my original demand and said you could just *tell* me what's in it. *And* I've offered to answer any questions honestly tonight. But you? You're just sticking to your guns, not budging an inch."

"All right. Show me how it's done." I lean forward, my eyes blazing. "Play the honesty-game."

"Fine. Ask me anything."

"Admit Cameron Fucking Schulz bored you to fucking tears."

She twists her mouth—and then she nods.

I laugh. "*I knew it.*"

"I went back into the restaurant after we talked and after two minutes with the guy I wanted to gouge my eyes out."

"Hey, maybe I like this honesty-game, after all." I chuckle. "So how'd he take it when you turned him down?" I ask, picking up my drink gleefully.

I'm expecting her to laugh with me or at least break into a wide smile. But she doesn't. Instead, she furrows her brow, takes a long sip of her drink, and levels me with an unflinching gaze. "I didn't turn him down."

14

JOSH

She continues staring at me, her blue eyes sparkling with defiance.

"You *fucked* Cameron Schulz?" I blurt.

Her cheeks flush. "Back at his place." She maintains my gaze, her eyes blazing. "He has a very nice house, bee tee dubs. Just what you'd expect of a professional baseball player."

I don't know whether to cry or scream. Or charter an airplane to Seattle and kick Cameron Fucking Schulz's ass. Oh my fucking God. I glance around the bar, my heart racing, clenching and unclenching my fists.

She fishes a crunchie thing out of the bowl in front of us and pops it into her mouth. "And I'm not sorry or ashamed about it. He was sweet and I got to check off one of my fantasies. (I'm big on fantasies, bee tee dubs. It's kinda my *thing*.) So, yeah, I count the entire experience as a win-win."

I open and shut my mouth like a fish on a line.

"News flash, Playboy. Not all sex has to be deep and meaningful. Even for the members of the species with *vaginas*."

I'm still speechless.

She drains her drink.

"What fantasy did you get to check off?" I finally say. Oh my God, I feel physically ill just saying the words.

"Well, gosh, that's kind of a personal question." She laughs. "But since we're being completely *honest* and all, I'll tell you. One of my all-time fantasies has always been to have sex with a professional athlete—though admittedly, in a manner much more exciting than it went down with Cameron." She pops another crunchie into her mouth. "I slept with a guy on the football team in college who was drafted by the Lions his senior year, but he went pro *after* I slept with him so I don't think that counts as having sex with a pro athlete. Do you think it does?" She pops another crunchie thing into her mouth and washes it down with her martini.

I press my lips together, incapable of saying a goddamned thing. I'm feeling a strange mixture of arousal and rage and complete repulsion.

"Oh, please," she finally says. "You think sex *always* has to be something deep and meaningful and profound? Pffft."

I make a face.

"Well, then. Why should it be any different for me? Just because I have a *vagina?*"

I lean back in my chair. "So you say. I'm not sure I believe it."

She laughs.

"Just tell me right now, Kat. Do you really have a vagina? Because I swear to fucking God, if you're hiding a dick and balls under there, I'm gonna lose my fucking shit."

She laughs. "I'm not a dude. I promise."

"Because you're acting like a dude right now."

"Nope. Rest assured, I do indeed have a *vagina* and ovaries and fallopian tubes. Oh, and boobs, too, which I've been told multiple times are 'absolutely perfect,' bee tee dubs. But I can certainly understand your confusion about my genitalia, because I'm actually an *honorary* dude, probably from growing up with four brothers and all."

I can't formulate a response. My head is reeling.

"And, to be clear, I don't have *only* meaningless sex. I absolutely love mean-ingful sex, too, but I'm not hung up about it either way. I do what I want—oh, and I'm very *selective*. I'm just saying when I *do* have meaningless sex, it's because I want to do it—and, therefore, I'm not at all sorry or ashamed about it. My choice."

I mull that over.

"So I take it you've never had meaningless sex, then?" she asks. "That's so sweet."

"This is a really bizarre conversation. Excuse me," I say to the bartender. "Two more shots of Patron, please."

"Have you ever wished you could have meaningless sex, Josh?" she persists.

I roll my eyes. "I've had meaningless sex, Kat."

"But it was somehow supposed to be simultaneously meaning*ful* for the woman you were screwing, is that it?"

"No. Of course, not."

"Well, there you go. Works both ways. Have you ever had *meaningful* sex?"

"Of course. I strongly prefer it, actually. But I find it's much, much harder to come by."

She nods. "I agree. I prefer it, too—and, yes, it's much, *much* harder to come by."

We stare at each other for a long beat.

The bartender places our shots in front of us.

"To you, Kat—to the honorary dude who's blowing my mind right now."

"To you, Josh—to the playboy who's maybe not quite as much of a playboy as I originally thought."

We knock back our shots.

"Whew," she says. "I can't feel my toes."

"So do you possess any other dude-like qualities besides unapologetically engaging in meaningless sex with sports stars?" I ask.

"Well, my brothers say I laugh like a dude, but I don't know about that."

"You do. Totally."

"I hardly ever cry."

"Okay. That's a plus."

"I'm not easily offended, but when I am, watch the fuck out, because I've got a fucking temper, motherfucker, and I will cut you."

"Whoa. Good to know. Anything else?"

"Well, I can burp the alphabet. And I don't flinch when men fart around me—the sound of men farting is just white noise to me at this point, like a sound machine that lulls me to sleep."

I laugh. "Wow."

"Yup."

"What about girlie stuff? Tell me some of that stuff so I don't start imagining you hiding a dick and balls under there."

"Well, let's start with the biggest girlie thing of all: I have a *vagina*."

"That's definitely a biggie. Glad to hear it."

"Oh, and here's something. I like saying the word *vagina*. Vagina, vagina, vagina. I say it a lot. *Vagina*."

"Actually, I think that's another dude thing. Vagina, vagina, vagina. See? I like saying it, too. *Vagina*."

"Or maybe that's a *girlie* thing about *you*."

"Hmm. I never thought of it that way. *Vagina*. Hmm. I dunno. You may be right."

"Have you noticed people never say that word?" she says. "Why is that?"

"Because they're pussies," I reply.

She laughs.

"What else?" I ask. "Tell me something really girlie about you that'll prove you've got a *vagina* under there, once and for all."

"Okay. Well, I'm a sucker for sequins and fringe."

"You and Neil Diamond. That proves nothing."

She laughs. "Good point. You're right. Okay. Let's see. Pink is my favorite color." She looks up at the ceiling, thinking. "I love getting pedicures and doing yoga and drinking white wine. Oh, and eating cupcakes. That's all pretty girlie."

"Especially if you do all of it while wearing sequins and fringe," I say.

She laughs. "I have Hello Kitty sheets on my bed. And I'm not talking about my childhood room at my parents' house. I currently have Hello Kitty sheets on my bed in my apartment."

"Whoa."

"Kitty Kat," she says by way of explanation. She winks.

"I figured."

"Let's see. Well, my all-time favorite movie is *The Bodyguard*. My close second after that is *Pretty Woman*. And the bronze goes to *Magic Mike*."

"Okay, okay. That's it," I say, holding up my hands. "I need nothing further. I'm now one hundred percent convinced you've got a *vagina*."

"Whew. What a relief. I was beginning to worry my dick was really, really tiny."

I laugh.

We sit and stare at each other for a long moment. I'd pay an inordinate amount of money to know what she's thinking right now. Right after paying an inordinate amount of money to fuck her.

"You said sleeping with a pro athlete is *one* of your fantasies?" I say.

"Correct. Well, it *was*." She snickers and makes a "check mark" motion with her finger in the air.

I grimace.

She laughs. "But, actually, my pro-athlete fantasy is a bit more elaborate than what I did with Cameron. And it involves an NFL player, actually—not a baseball star—so maybe that checkmark was a wee bit premature."

"Wow. Your fantasy is pretty specific, huh?"

She nods. "MVP of the Super Bowl, to be exact—in the locker room after the big game."

"Interesting. Are all your fantasies that specific?"

She nods. "You have no idea."

"You've got a lot of fantasies?" I ask.

"I do. Lots and lots." She sips her drink.

I'm finding it a bit hard to breathe. "All of them *specific?*"

"Most of them."

"Tell me some of them," I say. I can feel my cheeks blazing.

She leans forward. "I'll tell you *all* of them—*just as soon as you tell me what you wrote in your application.*"

I smile. "Here we go again. No."

She exhales. "Okay, then. No fantasies for you." She licks her lips. "Too bad. You would have liked them."

I squint at her.

"Answer a question for me, Josh."

"Maybe. Maybe not." I sip my drink.

"Did you sleep with someone while you were in New York?"

I choke on my drink. Jesus. This woman's gonna be the death of me.

Under any other circumstances, I'd lie right now. But after what she told me about Cameron, that's obviously not an option.

I take a long, deep breath. "Yeah."

Her eyes light up. "*I knew it*. Such a hypocrite."

"I'm not a hypocrite. I slept with a girl I used to know a long time ago. We both just happened to be in New York at the same time, by sheer coincidence. Completely meaningless."

She smiles. "Ah. Blast-from-your-past sex—definitely *not* a fantasy of mine." She shudders. "That can be dangerous."

"Dangerous? How so?"

"It can bring up old feelings—and usually only for *one* person, which is *never* good." She shudders again.

I scoff. "There were no old feelings to bring up. We dated for, like, four months seven years ago, and I don't think we had sober sex more than twice."

She purses her lips. "How'd you guys wind up hooking up after all this time?"

I exhale. "It's a long story."

"I've got time."

I have no desire to tell this story. I exhale and run my hand through my hair.

"Come on, Playboy. Spill it."

I roll my eyes. "My good friend Reed happened to be in New York last week because one of his bands was doing *Saturday Night Live*. Coincidentally, Reed's ex-girlfriend Isabel and her best friend—the girl in question—had just come back from a week in France and stopped in New York so Isabel could do this TV interview thing. The girls figured out Reed and I were both in New York by total coincidence—thank you, Instagram—so they invited us to go to the show taping with them. After the show, we all went out for dinner and drinks and I... got... shit-faced... and made an impulsive and extremely stupid decision." I feel sick. I wouldn't normally be saying a word of this to anyone, let alone a woman I'm interested in sleeping with. Why am I saying all this?

Kat sips her drink quietly. "So your friend Reed's in a band?"

"That's what you want to know after everything I just said? You wanna know if my friend Reed's in a band?"

She shrugs. "To start with, yeah."

"No, Reed's not in a band—he owns a record label. He also co-owns a dance club here in Vegas. Maybe I'll take you there tonight."

"Oh, I'd love that. I *love* to dance. Who's the band that played on *Saturday Night Live*?"

I pause. "That's really what you're curious about? You're not gonna ask me about *her*?"

"Oh, I'm getting there, trust me. I'm just playing it cool."

I laugh. "Ah, stealing a page out of my book."

"It's a good page."

"Red Card Riot."

"*That's* the band on your friend's label? Wow. I love them."

"Yeah, they're awesome."

She screeches the chorus from Red Card Riot's monster rock hit, "Shaynee."

"Great song," I say.

"Have you met them?" she asks.

"No, the guys in the band didn't come out with us in New York. I think they had some groupies to 'meet and greet.'"

"I'm sure they did. They're huge right now—your friend Reed must be thrilled."

"Yeah. He's always had quite the knack for spotting talent. A bit of a Midas touch."

She takes a sip of her drink and then levels me with an unflinching gaze. "So do you plan to see her again?"

"Okay, here we go."

"I told you I'd get to it."

"And you did."

She pauses. "So do you plan to see her?"

"No." I snort. "Never. Like I said. It was completely meaningless."

She chews the inside of her mouth.

"Do you plan to see Mr. Baseball again?" I ask, my heart pounding.

"No."

"Really?"

"Really."

"He wants to see *you* again, though, right?"

She nods.

"You're not gonna say yes when he asks?"

"He's already asked twice. And I've already said no both times." She presses her lips together. "I told him very clearly it wasn't gonna work out. I was nice about it, but clear."

I make a caveman sound.

"What does that grunt mean?"

"It means I'm plotting his murder in my head."

"Why? He didn't do anything wrong."

I grunt again.

She smiles. "You're *jealous*?"

"Of course, I'm jealous. Fuck yeah, I am."

"But I just told you I'm not gonna see him again."

"So what. I can't get a certain visual out of my head and it's making me crazy."

Her smile broadens.

"You like that I'm jealous?"

She thinks for a minute. "Usually, I'd say no—that I hate jealous bullshit. But, yeah, I'm liking it." She bites her lip. "So does Miss Blast from Your Past wanna see you again?"

I nod. "She seems to think we've got some sort of... *soul connection.*" I make a face. "But I've already told her it's not gonna happen."

"Hmmph."

"What does that mean? Are you *jealous* of Miss Blast from My Past?"

"Honestly?"

"Of course. Isn't that what we're doing here—playing the honesty-game 'til we both wanna bang our heads against a wall?"

She laughs. "Um... I'm more like *envious*, I think, but, no, not *jealous*. I don't get jealous when I'm not in a relationship." She glares at me, clearly telling me my jealousy about Cameron Schulz is premature. "Now, if you were my *boyfriend* and I found out you'd fucked another woman, then, yes, I'd be so jealous I'd burn your fucking house down. And then I'd cut off your balls, roast them over the burning embers of your house, smash them between two graham crackers with a Hershey bar and make testicle-s'mores out of them, which I would then gobble up as I stood over your writhing, whimpering body on the ground."

Holy shit. I'm so shocked, I can't even laugh. But Kat does—in fact, she belly laughs and throws back her head, completely enthralled with herself.

"And do you wanna know *why* I'd burn your house down and make myself s'mores out of your balls, my dearest Josh?"

I shake my head. "I'm too scared of you to even venture a guess."

"Because if you were my *boyfriend*, I would never, ever cheat on you, I can promise you that on a stack of bibles. *Never.* I've never cheated and I never will. And here's why: because I never agree to be someone's *girlfriend* unless I'm one hundred percent willing to give the guy my whole heart. And as the relationship progresses, if I'm feeling like cheating, then I don't stay. It's scorched earth maybe, but a man never, ever has to wonder where my feelings stand." She picks up her drink. "It also means that, if you were my boyfriend and you cheated on me, then you'd undoubtedly be breaking my heart."

I place my palm on my chest, steadying myself. I look down at the bar, collecting myself. This girl just knocked the wind out of me.

"But since you and I aren't even dating, then, no, I'm not *jealous.*" She takes a long sip of her drink. "Because I can't justify getting jealous when a man's not mine to begin with."

"I've never met anyone like you, Kat," I manage to say.

"Thank you," she says. "I've never met anyone like you, either."

"You're like some bizarre, undiscovered species of fish that washes ashore after a nuclear disaster and freaks everyone the fuck out," I say.

She laughs. "Wow. That's your idea of a compliment?"

"I'm normally much smoother than this, I assure you. You bring out the Jonas in me."

She laughs. "Jonas seems pretty damned smooth, actually."

"Not usually. Just with Sarah all of a sudden. She brings out the Josh Faraday in him, I guess."

She grins and I can't help smiling back at her like a fucking dope.

There's a very long beat, during which we're smiling at each other, not saying a damned thing. Finally, Kat bites her lip and touches my hand, sending electricity throughout my entire body.

"For God's sake, Playboy," she purrs, "just tell me what's in your application so we can get this show on the road. Please?" She squeezes my hand and licks her lips. "I'm suddenly feeling extremely... *impatient*."

Oh man, she's good. She's very, very good. But she's also shit out of luck. There's no fucking way I'm giving this girl my application. Period. And certainly not in exchange for the honor of fucking her. Hell no, when she finally fucks me, it's gonna be for no other reason than she's dying for it, not because I gave her some stupid application.

I drain the rest of my drink. "Nope." I clap my hands together. "Getting this show on the road is entirely up to you, Party Girl. All you have to do is kiss me, just once, and then I'll know you've conceded your demands and have finally decided to find out the good old-fashioned way if I'm gonna chain you to a donkey or not."

She smirks. "No, no, no, my dearest Playboy; you've got it backwards. What's actually gonna happen is *you're* gonna kiss *me*—thereby signaling to *me* you agree to my demands and will give me what I want."

We stare each other down.

"I'm not gonna give you my application, Kat. It's none of your fucking business."

"Oh, I think you are."

"Nope."

She puckers. "I'm a really good kisser, Playboy." She raises an eyebrow. "At least, that's what Cameron Schulz said."

I squint at her. "You're evil."

"I am."

I motion to the bartender. "Check, please." I glare at her for a long beat. She looks so fucking sure of herself—and so fucking hot, I doubt this girl's experienced disappointment once in her entire life. "Okay, Party Girl," I say. "The time for chitchat is over. I'm not gonna give you what you want—which means you're not gonna fuck me." I make a sad face and she matches it. "So I guess that means there's only one thing left for us to do," I continue.

"And what would that be?"

"Dance, of course."

Her face lights up. "Oh, I *love* to dance."

"Well, of course, you do. You're the *Party Girl With a Hyphen*, for fuck's sake."

She grins.

"It's time for you to earn that nickname of yours, babe." I touch the cleft in her chin one more time and then put out my hand. "Let's go, baby. Time to paint Sin City red."

15

KAT

Josh slams the taxi door shut and we bound toward "the hottest dance club in Vegas," hand in hand. A line of immaculately dressed people waiting to get into the club wraps around the side of the building and down the block, but, apparently, lines don't apply to Josh Faraday—because he grabs my hand and pulls me past the throngs of people and straight to the front doors.

"Hey, Barry," Josh says to a very, very large black man standing at the front door of the club.

The man beams a huge smile at Josh. "Joshua Faraday," he says, bumping fists with Josh. "I didn't know you were coming out tonight."

"Yeah, it was super last minute. Is Reed in town, by any chance?"

"Yeah, he just flew in this afternoon. Have you texted him?"

"A few minutes ago, but he hasn't responded yet. Will you let him know I'm here? We'll hang out by the downstairs bar for a bit so he can find us." Josh motions to me. "Oh, sorry. Barry, this is my lovely date for the evening, Kat."

"Hello there, Kat," Barry says in his deep voice. He puts out his hand and I take it.

"Nice to meet you, Barry," I say.

"Careful, Barry. Don't look her in the eyes. She'll hypnotize you with that fucking gorgeous face and try to trick you into telling her your darkest secrets."

I look at Josh, flabbergasted, but Josh and Barry are laughing easily together.

"I dunno, Josh. Seems like there are much worse things that could happen to a guy than getting royally fucked over by this one here."

"Amen, brother," Josh says.

"Uh . . ." I say, at a loss for words. I think Barry just complimented me, but I'm not sure if "thank you" is an appropriate reply.

Before I can figure out what to say, Barry opens the velvet rope and motions for us to pass into the club. "Have fun, kids. Go easy on him, Kat. He's a good guy." He chuckles. "I'll tell Reed you're here."

The minute Josh and I enter the club, I slip into some sort of hedonism-induced coma. I've been to my share of nightclubs, but I've never seen a temple to pure excess quite like this. Almost-nude women "bathe" throughout the club in clear Plexiglas bathtubs filled with flower petals; lithe, rippling acrobats in skin-tight bodysuits hang from the ceiling on trapeze swings, twisting and gyrating like the performers Josh and I saw earlier tonight with Jonas and Sarah at *Cirque Du Soleil*; seizure-inducing lights and lasers are bouncing around every square inch of the place; and screens scattered throughout the club flash shocking pornographic images in rapid-fire succession, so fast my brain isn't sure what my eyes just witnessed. It's sheer spectacle. Obscenity. Titillation to the extreme. *And I love it.*

Josh pulls me to a long, sparkling bar and flags down the bartender.

"Martini?" he shouts into my ear above the thumping music.

"Shots!" I yell. "So we can get onto the dance floor right away."

"Good idea!" Josh shouts back and turns toward the bar.

Oh man, I'm ready to dance. Even standing here at the bar, my body's already begun involuntarily herking and jerking to the bass-heavy beat.

A phenomenally good-looking guy in a suit sidles up to Josh and taps him on the shoulder. Josh turns toward the unidentified tap and, when he sees the guy, his entire face lights up. The two men hug with what looks like extreme affection and as they break apart the guy kisses Josh on his cheek with a giant, enthusiastic swak.

Josh motions to me, talking into the guy's ear, and Mr. Handsome smiles and waves at me, though I can't hear a thing above the thumping music.

Josh leans into my ear. "Reed's part-owner of this club."

"Nice to meet you Reed," I say, but it's clear he can't hear me. He just smiles and waves again. Wow. He's a really, really good-looking man. I lick my lips. I guess hotties travel in packs. *The Brotherhood of the Traveling Hottie McHottie-pants,* I think, making myself laugh.

The bartender places the shots in front of us on the bar, and Josh distributes them among the three of us.

Josh leans into Reed's ear and says something and they both burst out laughing. Reed nods and slaps Josh's back.

Damn, I wish I had superhuman hearing right now. But all I can hear is the blaring music. Appropriately, the song playing right now is "I Can't Feel My Face" by The Weekend, a song about a guy who, of course, can't feel his face, presumably because he's drunk or high. On what, though, it's not clear. Booze? Lust? Whichever it is (or both), I'm right there with him. Fo shizzle-pops.

Josh and Reed are still talking in each other's ears and laughing, so I begin dancing in place to the music, marveling at just how little I can feel my face. Or toes. Or brain. I'm verging on drunk, actually. And it feels hella good.

"Thanks, bro," I hear Josh say. "I owe you one."

"You bet."

Josh turns his gaze on me and smiles like a wolf. He leans into my ear and snakes his arm around my waist.

"You still going commando?" he asks, right in my ear. His hand migrates down to my ass.

"I guess you'll have to find out for yourself," I say. "Right after you kiss me and concede to my terrorist demands," I say.

He laughs. "You mean after *you* kiss *me* and give up your fucking *jihad*."

I shake my head and retract my lips completely into my mouth, signaling my lips are unkissable until he gives me what I want.

He laughs and grabs my hand. "Come on, Madame Terrorist. It's time to dance."

16

KAT

Holy hell.

If dancing is any indication whatsoever of a man's sexual prowess, then Josh Faraday is a sex god. Oh my God, the way he swivels and rocks those hips makes me yearn for him to grind them just like that on top of me while wearing nothing but a cocky smile. Holy shitballs. This man can *move*.

The song playing is "Want To Want Me" by Jason Derulo and Josh knows every word. He's singing the song to me, serenading me—and with so much charm and swagger, I can't help but laugh with glee. I can't remember having this much fun dancing with a guy—with my girlfriends, sure. But with a guy? A *hot* guy? No. Usually, when I'm dancing with a really hot guy, I'm so concerned about coming off as sexy and desirable to him, I forget to just let loose and have fun. But Josh makes it impossible to feel anything but totally uninhibited. Oh my God, I'm laughing too much to even try to be sexy. I throw my hands above my head and wiggle my hips and giggle uncontrollably, mirroring Josh's confident movement, and he laughs his ass off at every little thing I do. And the crazy thing is, having fun like this is making me so wet, I'm worried I'm gonna drip down my bare thigh in this shorty-short dress.

As the song reaches its conclusion, Josh looks up toward the balcony and locks eyes with Reed. He gives Reed a thumbs up and Reed returns the gesture. When Josh's eyes dart back to me, he levels me with a smile that makes me feel like he's planning to put me in an oven with some onions and potatoes.

The song abruptly changes to a hip-hop song I don't know. But, clearly, Josh does—because as the rapper begins spitting out lyrics, Josh mouths every single word along with him. Oh my God, Josh is freaking hilarious right now. He's thugging out to the song, going all in, shaking his ass and owning it. Oh man, I've never seen a concoction of maleness quite like this before. He's raw and smooth and funny and hot and goofy all at the same time. He's redefining sexy for me, right here and now. He's just... wow.

I listen intently to the lyrics of the song, trying to plumb the depths of my dance-club memories, but nope, I don't recognize it. I pull out my phone, activate my Shazam app—and just when the song title displays on my phone— "Kiss Me" by Lil Wayne—Josh begins singing along to the chorus. "Kiss me," Josh raps, grinding his hips like he's auditioning for *Magic Mike*. "Kiss me."

I laugh. What a sneaky little bastard. And a hilarious one.

He inches closer and closer to me, still rapping and grinding his hips ferociously, until, suddenly, and with great dramatic flair, he grabs me, pulls me into him, and grinds his body into mine with enthusiastic thrusts to the beat of the music. "Kiss me," he says to me, his lips on my ear, his intoxicating cologne wafting into my nostrils. His strong hands encircle my waist and grip my back as he presses his undulating body into mine. His lips migrate to my cheek, where they trail the length of my jawbone. His tongue laps at my neck.

Oh muh guh. Playtime's over. Shit just got real.

His hard-on presses into me, thrusting, grinding, making my knees weak— and, holy shitballs, there's no mistaking the size of that hard bulge, even through the man's pants. Good lord. Josh doesn't need to chain me to a donkey —he's got it covered on his own.

He parts my legs with his thigh and grinds his hard dick right into my clit, over and over, still rapping and groping me as he does.

I throw my head back.

Yes.

My clit ignites inside my panties. I'm beginning to warp and ache. My skin is beginning to prickle.

"Kiss me," he says into my ear, gyrating his body against mine. Oh my God. He's taking my breath away.

His mouth skims my ear and lands on my cheek and then my neck. I run my fingers into his hair, pressing my breasts into the hardness of his chest and my crotch into the bulge of his pelvis. Oh God. He nuzzles the tip of his nose against mine, teasing me. His lips are an inch away from mine, skimming, teasing, hovering as close as humanly possible without actually making contact, his erection continuing to grind into me as his mouth taunts me.

The song is thumping in my ears.

The lights on the dance floor are entrancing me.

My body is moving in time with his.

He smells so frickin' good, I wanna ingest him.

I feel dizzy.

Weak.

Frenzied.

I lift my leg and encircle his hip with it, aching to take him inside me. He shifts position and presses himself even more feverishly against me, sending his hard-on right up against the exact spot that makes me burst into flames.

Yeeeeeeeeooooowwwwwwww. *Yes.* Right there. I press into him harder, moaning, and he rubs that hard bulge ferociously against me, still rapping the words to the song.

His hand navigates under the hem of my dress and brushes against my bare ass cheek, causing goose bumps to erupt all over my body.

Without the slightest hesitation, he fingers my ass crack, presumably trying to figure out if I'm wearing a G-string, and when he finds the string, he slides his fingers all the way down it, down, down, down, and then forward, straight to the crotch, where his fingers begin exuberantly stroking the soft, extremely wet fabric of my panties.

My knees buckle and he holds me up, his fingers continuing to stroke. He kisses my ear and then my neck, yet again, rapping into my ear. "Kiss me," he purrs.

His lips migrate to mine and hover, yet again, just over my lips, inviting me to bridge the gap and slip my tongue into his mouth—inviting me to lay my weapon down.

But I don't.

"Terrorist," he breathes.

Without warning, his fingers slip underneath the fabric of my G-string and plunge right into my wetness.

Holy fuckburgers.

I cry out in surprise and extreme pleasure, pressing myself into his fingers and gyrating to the pulsing music.

"You're so fucking hot," he whispers in my ear. "Stop torturing me."

I don't reply, but he can plainly feel how badly I want him, too. I'm absolutely dripping for him.

I moan loudly right into his ear and lick his cheek, and his body responds against mine with obvious excitement. I run my hands through his hair, grinding myself into his fingers like I'm riding on top of a big, hard cock. I inhale sharply. I can't breathe. My body is warping. "Oh God, here it comes," I say into his ear. "A big one. Oh God. Josh, yeah. Don't stop. Just like that."

A huge orgasm slams into me and I stiffen in his arms, my loud moans swallowed by the blaring music as my body clenches around his fingers, over and over.

"Oh shit," he says. "Yeah, baby. Do it."

When the clenching and warping and rippling stops, I can barely stand. I nuzzle my face into his neck and he holds me close, supporting my entire body weight in his arms. He presses his body into mine as he holds me, and our bodies sway together to the loud, thumping music.

A new song begins. "In Da Club" by 50 Cent.

He suddenly pulls back from me and puts his hands on my face. His chest is rising and falling sharply. His gaze is intense.

By the look on his face, I'd guess he's trying to decide if fucking me counts as losing the bet. Or, at least, that's what I'm trying to figure out. Did we decide *kissing* or *fucking* ends our stalemate? I can't remember now.

Sweaty bodies are bouncing and swaying all around us on the dance floor, but we're standing stock still, looking at each other, trembling with pent-up desire. I tilt my face up to his and close my eyes, inviting him to swoop in and kiss me already. But he doesn't take the bait.

"*Fuck*," he says.

I open my eyes.

He's glaring at me like he's enraged at me.

He releases my face, grabs my hand, and begins dragging me across the packed dance floor. It takes effort to snake through the sea of bouncing people, but finally we're off the dance floor, working our way through the crowded club. The restrooms are in sight—but there are long lines of people waiting to get into both sets. Is that where he was intending to take me? Or was he headed to the exit? Or maybe to the bar? Any of these destinations is equally possible, given our current location in the club.

He stops walking.

"Fuck," he says, gripping my hand. He looks up at the ceiling for a brief moment, apparently gathering himself. "Goddammit."

50 Cent raps his famous line about being into *sex* rather than *lovemaking* and I can't help but sing along at the appropriate moment.

Josh chuckles. "You're hell on wheels, Kat. Jesus Christ."

Out of nowhere, Reed appears next to us, swatting Josh on his shoulder. "Hey, man."

"Oh, hey, bro." Josh glances at me, a wistful smile on his lips. "Thanks for the song."

"Did it work?" Reed looks at me. "Did you kiss him?"

I shake my head. "Nope."

"*No?* Uh oh. Are you losing your touch, Faraday? I thought it was a fool-proof plan."

"Hell no, I'm not losing my touch. I'm wise and powerful; you know that. This woman's not normal. She's made of fucking steel or something—the most stubborn woman alive."

"Oh, she's *stubborn*, huh?" Reed says. "So she's the female version of you?"

Josh laughs. "Hey, maybe that explains why I find her so goddamned attractive." He squeezes my hand.

Reed laughs. "So, hey, man, there's someone I want you to meet." He looks over his shoulder, zeroes in on some guy across the room, and motions to him. "I just signed this amazing guy to the label—a rapper-singer-songwriter-multi-instrumentalist. Oh my God, he's so fucking incredible, man, I'm crapping myself that we got him. A year from now, mark my words, he's gonna be the biggest thing in music."

A blonde guy with tattoos walks up with a beautiful, dark-haired girl on his arm.

"Guys, this is Will Riley—'2Real'—one of the most talented songwriters and performers you're ever gonna meet, no exaggeration—and his girlfriend, Carmen."

"Aw, thanks, Reed," Will says. "Hey, guys."

Carmen smiles sweetly and waves at us in greeting—and she instantly reminds me of Sarah.

"This is my buddy, Josh Faraday, and his apparently *stubborn* friend, Kat."

"Hey, Josh," Will says. "Hey, Stubborn Kat. That sounds like a character from a comic strip—like some sort of bad *Garfield* rip-off."

Josh laughs. "Oh no! Stubborn Kat won't get off the couch and it's already noon."

"Damn it, Stubborn Kat! She won't chase the ball of yarn," I add. "No matter how many times you throw it for her."

"Chase a mouse?" Reed says. "Hell no. Stubborn Kat just painted her claws."

"Damn that, Stubborn Kat," Josh adds.

"Stubborn Kat won't do *anything* you want her to do—as *usual*. Aw, gosh, Stubborn Kat!" Will says.

We all laugh hysterically.

"So, hey, guys," Reed says, "I'm throwing a little party in the penthouse suite right now. The guys in Red Card Riot just got into town for their show at the Garden Arena tomorrow night, and they're ready to blow off some steam tonight. Plus, we're celebrating Will coming on board. You two wanna join the party?"

Josh looks at me for confirmation and I nod furiously.

"Yeah, absolutely."

"Hey, isn't Henn in town with you?"

"Yeah."

"Well, call that little fucker and tell him to join us."

"I doubt he'll come. He's working on an important job tonight."

"Well, shit, man." Reed looks at his watch. "It's almost two. Call him and see if he's done for the night. It's not a raging party 'til Peter Hennessey breaks out his dance moves."

Both guys laugh hysterically.

"Oh man," Josh says, shaking his head. "One of the simple pleasures in life. I'll call that little fucker right now."

17

KAT

W hen Josh and I walk through the door of Reed's penthouse suite, along with Reed, Will, and Carmen, we join a raging party already in progress in the most magnificent hotel suite I could ever imagine. The interior is fit for a sheik—twice the size of Jonas and Sarah's suite—plus, French doors at the far side of the massive main room reveal a private terrace and swimming pool outside.

I glance around, my heart racing. Insanely attractive people are milling around, lounging, laughing, swigging drinks, smoking pot, making out—and I'd say half of them are at least vaguely recognizable to me from my near-constant consumption of celebrity gossip.

Reed motions to two young guys on the couch smoking pot—a strawberry blondie with piercings and tattoos and a dark-haired hottie with striking, cobalt blue eyes—and they stride over to Reed and bro-hug him.

"Hey, man," the dark-haired hottie says to Reed, hugging him.

"How was Dallas?" Reed asks.

"Fucking awesome," dark-haired-hottie says. "Great crowd. It still gives me chills every time an entire arena sings along to a song I wrote." He grins adorably.

Reed pats his cheek. "Get used to it, Baby Dino. Where are the other guys?"

"Around here somewhere. Probably passed out. It's been a long-ass day."

Reed addresses our small group. "Everyone, this is Dean Masterson and C-Bomb from Red Card Riot. RCR is playing tomorrow night at the MGM Grand—lemme know if any of you want tickets to the show."

Will and Carmen instantly leap at the offer, thanking Reed profusely, while I jump up and down, tugging on Josh's arm.

Josh laughs at my exuberance. "Looks like Kat's in for sure. But I'm not sure what the fuck we've got going on tomorrow night—I'm in town for this thing with my brother." Josh looks at Will and Carmen. "If it turns out I can't go, can Kat go with you guys?"

Oh. It didn't occur to me we might be tied up tomorrow night with our mission to take down The Club, whatever the heck that means. "Oh, no, Josh, that's okay," I mumble. "I wouldn't go without you."

"Of course, you would. You can't miss seeing RCR—and from the VIP section, no less."

"Fuck the VIP section," Reed says. "I'll take you backstage, Kat. You can watch the show from there."

"Really?" I say. "Wow."

"Thanks, man," Josh says.

"No problem, bro. Just text me when you know who's going tomorrow," Reed says. "Jonas, Henn, whoever's in your group. Just lemme know. Speaking of which, where's Henn? I miss that little fucker."

"I called him. He's still working," Josh says. "He said he might be able to break free tomorrow night, depending on how the work thing goes. It's all really up in the air."

"Okay, lemme know. So, Dean," Reed says to the dark-haired hottie, "2Real's been writing songs for his debut album. Wait 'til you hear what this guy writes. Fucking brilliant. Game-changing. I'm not exaggerating. You're gonna wanna get in on this. I was thinking you two might set up a writing sesh when you're back in L.A. after the tour? I have a feeling if you guys lock yourselves into a room together for a day, a number one hit's gonna come out of it."

"Sure," Dean says. "I'd love to."

"Sick," Will says, his face bursting with excitement. "Looking forward to it."

The two guys exchange numbers.

"You guys just did *SNL*, right?" Will asks.

"Yeah. Last week. Surreal," Dean says.

"Were you shitting your pants the whole time?"

Dean laughs. "Totally."

Everyone laughs.

"I'd totally shit my pants, too, no doubt about it," Will says.

"Well, then, you'd better invest in some fucking Depends, 2Real," Reed says. "Because you'll be doing *SNL* one of these days, too—sooner rather than later, I predict."

Will pulls Carmen into him. "That'd be so fucking insane." His face is on fire.

"There's no doubt in my mind," Carmen says, nuzzling into him.

Josh begins chatting comfortably with the RCR boys and Will about music and the tour, but I'm completely mute. It's totally out of character for me, but I can't seem to think of anything witty to say, so I figure I'd better not talk at all. How did I get here? Red Card Riot's hit "Shaynee" was playing in the taxi on the way to Reed's club, and now two members of the band are standing here, swigging beers and chatting amiably with Josh about their show in Dallas earlier tonight? It takes a lot to make me speechless, but, by God, I am.

Josh puts his arm around me. "Are you okay, PG?"

"Yeah. Why?"

"You're awfully quiet."

"I'm just... stunned."

He laughs. "How 'bout a drink?"

I nod, though I'm already feeling extremely buzzed, truth be told.

"A martini?"

I shake my head. "Surprise me," I say. "I love surprises."

He winks. "My kinda girl."

After Josh leaves, I unabashedly eavesdrop on Will's conversation with Dean and C-Bomb. They're talking about their musical influences with incredible passion. God, I wish my youngest brother, Dax, were here. Listening to these guys talk would be his dream come true.

After a moment, my eyes drift to Carmen and I notice she looks a little bit lost.

I move to her and put my arm around her shoulder. "Hey, Carmen. Is this party as overwhelming to you as it is to me?"

Carmen twists her mouth adorably. "I feel like a deer in headlights," she admits. "It wasn't too long ago I was watching Will perform at a local club for fifty people."

"Have you and Will been together a long time?"

She nods. "About two years. What about you and Josh?"

"Oh, we're not a couple. This is just our first night out."

"Seriously? Wow. I would have guessed you've been together forever."

I laugh. "That's funny."

I glance across the suite at Josh—he's deep in concentration, making some sort of complicated concoction at the bar—and my skin buzzes at the mere sight of him.

Carmen rests her cheek on my shoulder in the most adorably affectionate way, making me think of Sarah again.

"Carmen, you remind me so much of my best friend, Sarah, it's uncanny."

"I do?"

I nod. "She's the best. Gorgeous, funny, super-duper smart. Weird." I laugh. "The sweetest girl you'll ever meet."

"Well, thanks. It sounds like you've just given me a huge compliment."

"Definitely."

Josh returns with two glasses and hands me a red-colored drink.

"What is it?" I ask, sniffing it. "You looked like you were busy building an atomic bomb over there."

"It's an original creation. I call it a Kiss," he says, a cocky grin spreading across his face.

"Oh, really? I've never had one of those—at least not from you," I say.

"I figured you were dying to taste a Kiss from me, though." He winks. "So I decided to make your dreams come true."

I smirk. "Gee, thanks. What's exactly in a Kiss from Josh Faraday?"

"All sorts of stuff to make your toes tingle and your face go numb. Try it."

I take a long, slow sip. "Whoa, it's strong," I say. "And delicious. Kinda curls my toes, actually."

"That about sums up a Kiss from Josh Faraday: toe-curling."

I motion to his cup. "Is that what you're having, too?"

"No, I made myself something totally different—I call it The Terrorist." He takes a sip from his cup. "It really socks a punch. Honestly, it'll probably knock me off my feet—might even be the death of me. But something tells me it's gonna be well worth the pain."

18

———

KAT

After downing two Kisses from Josh Faraday, I've suddenly got a freaking fantabulous idea. "Let's go for a swim, Joshie Woshie."

"Yessssssssssssss, Kitty Kat," he says. Without hesitation, he rips off his jacket and begins unzipping his pants while I frenetically pull my mini-dress over my head and kick off my shoes.

I throw my dress over the back of a lounge chair, adrenaline coursing through my veins (along with the booze), and stand with my hands on my hips like Wonder Woman in front of Josh, wearing nothing but a G-string, belly ring, black-lace push-up bra, and a smile. "Hey, Playboy," I coo. I wink and pucker my lips at him.

He stops what he's doing and freezes, his eyes fixed on me. "Whoa."

I shake my ass, honk my boobs like they're horns on the handlebars of a little girl's bike, and cannonball into the pool with a humongous splash. When my face breaks the surface of the water, I'm treated to the hilarious vision of Josh furiously kicking off his shoes and peeling off his pants like they're on fire.

"Come on, Playboy," I catcall to him. "That's as fast as you can move, you pansy-ass?"

There's a huge splashing noise to my right. And then another. And another. Sounds like I've started a trend. I glance toward the splashing—it's two guys and a girl I recognize from a sitcom—and then my eyes drift back to Josh. He's just now in the process of removing his button-down shirt... to reveal... holy motherfucking shit on a fucking stick. Wow. Holy Washboard Abs, Batman. Holy Pecs. Holy Biceps. Holy Hot Damn. Josh Faraday is unexpectedly a freaking god among men.

Good lord. I knew I felt hard muscles underneath his designer suit when we were dirty dancing. And I knew the dude regularly climbs rocks and mountains with his brother. But I never could have predicted... *this*—this walking temple of masculine perfection. For the love of all things holy, Cameron Fucking Schulz is a professional athlete and his body doesn't hold a freaking candle to Josh's. Josh is a living sculpture. Ripped and perfectly proportioned. Lean in all the right places and buffed out where it counts. Holy hell.

And speaking of buffed out where it counts, Jesus Christ, those little white briefs can't hide the extremely large package he's got between his legs. Holy hell, I'm swooning.

And on top of all that, oh my God, as if all that goodness weren't enough to hurtle a woman into instant orgasm, the man is absolutely riddled with the sexiest tattoos I've ever seen, too. How the hell did I not know he was covered in ink until now? His chest is emblazoned boldly with the swirling word "GRACE," and the word "OVERCOME" is inked across his lower abs, right above the waistband of his tighty-whities. When he pivots to throw his shirt onto a nearby chair, a tattoo I can't make out flashes quickly on his left side—I think I saw a tree? And when he turns the other way, oh my God, to top it all off, there's a fire-breathing dragon covering his right bicep.

A dragon?

Oh, jeez.

I'm pretty sure I told Josh dragons are top of the list of "social suicide" tattoos, along with YOLO and barbed wire and girlfriend tattoos. Why the hell did I say all that? I was just talking out my butt—babbling off the top of my head. Sometimes I'm too snarky for my own good.

Well, damn, just one look at him and it's obvious my made-up rules were meant to be broken. This boy could sport a YOLO tattoo framed by barbed wire wrapped around a fire-breathing dragon's neck and stamped with an ex-girlfriend's name and he'd make it all look sexy as hell. Hot daaaaaaaa-yam, this is a sexy man. My skin's bursting into scorching flames just looking at him, even though I'm standing in cool water up to my chest.

Josh grins at me from the ledge of the pool, obviously enjoying the expression on my face. "Why are you looking at me like that, Kat?" He pats his rock-hard abs and snaps the waist of his briefs playfully, just below his "OVER-COME" tattoo. "Haven't you ever seen a guy in his undies before?"

There's a rippling commotion just behind him and a loud squeal, but I'm too fixated on Josh's exquisite body to take my eyes off him. Fuck the bet. Fuck the application. I'm gonna have drunken sex with this gorgeous man right now and come like a freight train. Right fucking now. In the bathroom. Or in one of the back bedrooms of the suite. Or, hell, right here in this goddamned swimming pool, if need be. Hell yeah. That's the plan. We'll just pretend we're hugging and cuddling in the water and all these drunk, high people around us will never effing know I'm having the orgasm of my life.

"Josh Faraday, you better get your gorgeous ass—" I begin, but I stop.

Holy shitballs.

Isabel Randolph just waltzed right up to the edge of the pool! Oh my God.

She's even more beautiful in person than on the big screen. I feel faint. How is this my life right now?

"Reed!" Isabel says, waving happily toward the swimming pool, her eyes focused immediately to my right.

I glance to my side and Reed's standing just a few feet away from me in the pool, holding a drink. When did he get into the pool? And, hey, he looks mighty fine, I must say.

"Hey, Isabel, you came," Reed replies, smiling broadly. "Awesome to see you."

"Wouldn't have missed it. Hey, Josh," Isabel says, turning her attention to Josh a couple feet away from her on the ledge of the pool. She kisses him on both cheeks and then unabashedly looks him up and down. "Wow. You're looking awfully... *fit*."

Josh opens his mouth to reply, but before he can say a damned word, his face pales like he's seen a freaking ghost.

"Josh Faraday," a blonde woman says, emerging from the milling crowd and sauntering toward him and Isabel. "I had no idea you'd be here." She squeals. "I don't see you for seven long years, and now, out of nowhere, I get to see you *twice* in two weeks—*and both times without a stitch of clothes on?*" She giggles gleefully. "I guess there's a God, after all."

19

JOSH

I feel physically ill.

I look at Kat in the pool and her face is a mixture of rage and... well, no, nothing else. Just rage. Shit. I look at Reed in the pool and he grimaces at me like I just got pounded in the face with a sledgehammer.

Jen takes another step forward, advancing on me like she's gonna hug me, so I do the only thing my drunken brain can come up with to save myself: I cannonball into the pool.

The minute I emerge from my splash-landing—or is it a crash-landing?—I throw my hands up at Reed. "What the fuck, man?" I ask, my voice low but intense.

Reed throws his hands up in mimicry of my posture. "You didn't tell me you were gonna be in Vegas this week, Faraday—how the fuck was I supposed to know?" he says, matching my energetic whisper. "I invited Isabel to the RCR concert when we saw her last week in New York. You should have told me then you were gonna be in Vegas if you didn't want to see—"

"I didn't know I'd be here—it came up last minute. Why didn't you at least tell me Jen was coming tonight? Jesus, Reed. Help a brother out."

"I didn't even know Jen was coming—I didn't even know *Isabel* was coming. She said she'd *try,* and that's the last I heard." He lowers his voice to barely above a whisper. "And I sure as fuck didn't know she'd bring *Jen,* man." Reed glances furtively at Kat.

"Fuck," I say. "Not good, man."

"It's your own damned fault," Reed says. "Play with crazy, you're gonna get crazy-burned."

I turn to Kat, ready to apologize or assure her or laugh with her—hell if I know where her head is at right now—and the expression on her face makes it clear she's pissed (though about what, I'm not sure).

"Kat, listen," I begin. "I—"

There's a loud splashing noise right behind me. Jesus, no. I wheel around, hoping my gut is wrong. But it's not wrong, unfortunately—Jen just jumped into the pool in her bra and underpants, giggling and squealing like she's auditioning for *Girls Gone Wild*.

I grunt in frustration and lunge over to Kat. "Kat, I'm not even *remotely* interested in her. I told you that—"

"Josh!" Jen says wading up to me, her jaw-dropping tits on bodacious display in her see-through electric-blue bra. "Isabel didn't tell me you were coming to see RCR, too. *Awesome*." She puts her hand on my arm and leans into me like she's gonna kiss me.

I jerk my arm and lurch back from her violently, toward Kat.

"Jen, I'm here with someone." I motion to Kat. "I'm on a date."

Jen's face instantly turns to ice. "Oh." She clenches her jaw. She blatantly looks Kat up and down. "So are you gonna introduce me to your *date*? Unless, of course, you don't know her name?"

I feel physically sick. "No need to be—"

"Actually, he doesn't know my name," Kat spits at Jen. "He hasn't asked me for it and I haven't supplied it, despite the fact that we were just about to fuck in this pool." She glares at me sideways and then flashes a sweet smile at Jen. "I'm Kat." She puts out her hand.

Jen takes Kat's hand like she's picking up trash from the side of the road. "Jen." Jen looks Kat up and down again. "A Vegas girl, I presume?" Her nostrils flare. "When in Rome, I guess, huh, Josh? Charming."

Kat turns her demonic eyes on me, full-force. "Oh, so your name is *Josh*, is it? Did I hear that right? Or did she call you *Jess*?"

I don't reply. Well, not with my vocal chords. My dick certainly seems to be replying, loud and clear. Yeah, my dick's always had a thing for crazy, it's true—not to mention a perfect pair of tits. Not to mention *two* perfect pairs of tits, all of them glistening wet and covered in barely-there see-through bras.

Kat stares Jen down, smiling the whole time. "You know what, Jen? I think you just saved me from doing something really *dumb*." She's spitting nails through that beauty-queen smile of hers. "This guy here—Josh or Jess, whatever his name is—won't stop talking about some woman he banged in New York last week."

Jen's face lights up. What the fuck is Kat doing to me right now? Is she clinically insane?

"Yeah, he keeps going on and on about how this New York girl was a horrible fuck, that the whole thing was totally meaningless to him, how he was so fucking shitfaced drunk he doesn't even remember it—'oh, it was such a *huge* mistake, blah, blah, blah'—she was such a fucking airhead'—I mean, how chicken-shit is that? Why the hell did he bang that poor girl if she was such a horror show? What a fucking douche."

Jen's brief elation from a moment ago is long gone. Now she looks like she was just whacked across the face with a two-by-four.

This is one of the most uncomfortable moments of my life. Jen looks like she's gonna cry—which makes me feel like the biggest prick on the planet—and Kat, the demon-queen herself, is glaring at me like she's readying her blow-torch, a Hershey bar, some graham crackers, and a very sharp knife.

"And here I was stupidly about to give the guy more of the same," Kat continues, on a roll. "Just some meaningless, shitfaced sex he won't even remember tomorrow. Ha! Well, fuck that shit."

Without warning, Kat heaves herself out of the pool and glowers at Jen from the ledge, her incredible body dripping wet and on full, glorious display.

"He's all yours, Jen. Maybe you'll have more luck than the poor girl he burned through in New York last week—whoever the hell she was." She flashes me a rage-filled smile. "Bye-bye, Jess. Or Josh. Whatever your name is. Have fun in Vegas, asshole—when in Rome." With that, she struts over to the nearby lounge chair, grabs her sparkling dress, and waltzes toward the open French doors leading back into the suite.

A man has never leaped out of a swimming pool so fucking fast in his entire life.

"Kat," I yell after her. "Wait."

But she doesn't wait. Hell no, she doesn't, because she's a goddamned terrorist. She marches straight through the French doors, into the suite, and toward the front doors, her incredible ass-cheeks shuddering with each ground-quaking march of her long, toned legs. On her way to the front door, she makes a pit stop at C-Bomb sitting on the couch. She bends over and whispers something to him, her tits falling out of her bra and into his face as she does. I'm just about to leap across the room and tackle him when he nods and hands her his drink—which looks to be straight whiskey or Scotch. She throws the whole drink back in one fluid motion and hands the empty glass back to him. "Thanks, son, I owe you one," she says, patting him on the head.

"Any time," he says, smirking and looking right at her chest.

"Kat," I say, my blood pounding in my ears.

She completely ignores me. She puffs out her fucking incredible chest and marches haughtily toward the front door of the suite, her ass-cheeks bouncing with each determined stomp.

Jesus Christ. This woman is gonna be the death of me.

"Kat, wait," I say, running to catch up to her. But she ignores me again. Jesus, the girl's having a *bona fide* tantrum—but she's so fucking hot while she's doing it, I truly don't mind.

"Kat, what the fuck are you doing?" I call to her.

She swings open the heavy front door of the suite and marches right through it, toward the private elevator at the end of a long hallway, her sequined dress in her hand, her wet body glistening under the hallway lights.

"*Kat*," I say, making my way through the doors. She's halfway down the hall. "Wait. I'm coming with you and I can't go down there in my fucking underwear."

She stops on a dime.

Oh, *that's* what made her finally stop? Another peek at my nearly naked body? Well, good to know.

She whips around to look at me, and, instantly, her gaze falls right on my dick. My very, very hard dick.

Her mouth drops open. "Wow," she says, her eyes not wavering from my crotch.

I look down. My soaking wet briefs are completely see-through. I might as well be completely naked right now.

She opens her mouth and closes it again. "Wow," she says again, her eyes fixated on my hard-on beneath my see-through briefs.

My dick twitches under her gaze and hardens even more. "Just stay put," I say. "Okay? I'm gonna get my clothes from inside and come right back. I'm coming with you."

"No," she says, her hand on her hip. "Fuck that shit."

I laugh. "Fuck *what* shit? What the fuck does that mean?" I ask.

"Did you see how she talked to me? 'A Vegas girl, I presume?' Ha! I'm not gonna stay here and get treated like scum on the bottom of her fucking shoe." She whips back around and marches toward the elevator at the end of the hall again.

"Kat, *wait*. You're drunk. You can't go alone."

"Yes, I can."

"You don't even have your fucking shoes."

She stops short and looks down at her feet like she truly had no idea she's shoe-less. "Well, hmmph. I don't need no stinkin' shoes."

I laugh. She's so fucking adorable. "You said you never get jealous," I say. "What happened to that, hmm? 'I never get jealous unless the guy is mine in the first place.' Remember that?"

"Yeah, well." She sniffs the air and wobbles in place. "I guess I changed my motherfucking mind. So sue me, fucker."

I laugh. "Nice language."

"Girls can't say fuck? Fuck, fuck, fuck."

I laugh again. "Kat, you're acting fucking crazy."

Her face changes from pissed to hurt on a dime. "Why'd you fuck *her* of all people, Josh?" She wipes her eyes. "She's so *mean*. So... snooty. What were you thinking?"

"What was I *thinking*?" I shrug. "Not a whole lot."

"Why'd you fuck such a mean, mean girl? I hate mean girls."

I'm utterly confused. "You want me to have meaningless sex with only nice girls?"

She ignores me. "And why'd you let her keep thinking you were interested in her after New York, huh? She obviously thought there was some sort of open invitation afterwards."

"No. I told her I wasn't interested."

"No, you didn't. No frickin' way. Or if you did, you didn't make it clear enough. Total douche move, Josh Faraday."

"What are you talking about? What's a total douche move?"

She waggles her finger at me. "I should have known with that whole 'Mickey Mouse roller coaster' thing. *Douchey.* I should have listened to my Scooby Doo senses."

"What the *fuck* are you talking about? It's douche-y that I had sex with Jen?"

"No. That you had sex with a girl who obviously wants a relationship and then left her hanging. *That's* douche-y."

"Oh, and I assume you sat Cameron Schulz down right after you fucked him and told him he has zero chance with you?"

"Well, not then and there, no. I'm not *that* heartless. But, yeah, I told him later when he called, very clearly, that I wasn't feeling it. But maybe, now that I think about it, that was a mistake on my part. Maybe I should have said yes when he asked to see me again because a) he's not a douche, and b) I don't know if I've mentioned this but *he's the shortstop for the goddamned Mariners!*"

I roll my eyes. "Gimme a fucking break. You'd rather scratch your eyes out than go out with that tool again—unless, of course, you suddenly have a huge craving for Shirley Temples."

"Maybe I do," she seethes. "Maybe that's exactly what I want right now, come to think about it—a nice, sweet guy who actually *respects* women and doesn't fuck any mean bitch who happens to have a great rack—and, did I mention?—who happens to be the shortstop for the goddamned fucking Mariners!"

"I respect women," I say lamely.

"Maybe this is exactly the wake-up call I needed," she huffs. She waves her arms at me in a bizarre little frenzy like she's a magician on meth trying to make me disappear, and then she turns back around and begins stomping away from me again.

"*Goddammit, Kat,*" I say. "Stop."

She stops and whirls around, glaring at me.

"What are we fighting about?" I ask earnestly. "I'm totally confused."

She doesn't reply. She whirls away from me, *again,* and saunters away, once again mesmerizing me with the stomping motion of her incredible ass.

"Kat," I bellow. "You're a fucking train wreck. Chill the fuck out and listen to me."

She turns back around to face me and crosses her arms over her spectacular chest. "*What?*"

I know we're supposedly in the middle of a heated conversation right now—maybe even a fight—about *what* I'm not entirely sure because I can't figure out exactly what I've done wrong and why she's reacting this way—but the truth is I can't stop looking at her insane body. It's as gorgeous as her face. She's perfection from the top of her head to the bottom of her feet. Jesus. She's not an eleven like I previously thought—she's a fucking *twenty*—*way* hotter than Bridgette, and Bridgette's a fucking supermodel, for fuck's sake.

"*What?*" Kat repeats, tapping her toe.

I swallow hard. "You were gonna fuck me in the pool?"

"What?" She scoffs. "*No.* You wish."

"You told Jen we were just about to fuck in the pool."

She rolls her eyes. "I just *said* that to piss off your nasty little bitch of a fuck buddy. I'd never be just another ride on your freaking 'Mickey Mouse roller coaster.' Hell no. I'm officially done with that. Starting now." Those perfect tits of hers are rising and falling sharply with her rage. Fuck, she's turning me on so much, I can't think straight.

"What the fuck are you so pissed about?" I ask. "I told you I fucked Jen in New York and you didn't give a shit. I didn't know she was gonna be here tonight—I wasn't the one who invited her. So what the fuck's made you so goddamned mad?"

She presses her lips together, her cheeks rising with color.

I chuckle. "Oh man." I smile broadly, realization descending upon me. "You're so *jealous,* you can't see straight," I say. "Miss I'd-Only-Be-Jealous-If-You-Were-My-Boyfriend is so fucking jealous, she's about to explode." I take a cautious step toward her and she takes a step back like a skittish pony. "Aw, come on, Party Girl. Tell the truth. You're jealous as shit." I smirk. "Come on, babe. We're telling the truth tonight, remember—we're playing the honesty-game?"

"Well, one of us is, anyway," she says, taking another step back. "And one of us is full of shit. I'll leave it to you to decide which of us is which."

I laugh. "You're insane right now. Certifiably insane." I bite my lip. "But I guess that's what jealousy will do to a woman, huh?"

She scowls.

"You were totally gonna fuck me in the pool just now, and you know it."

She shakes her head, but her eyes tell me I'm right.

"You wanna talk about who's full of shit? You don't give a shit about my stupid application—that's all an act. All you care about is feeling my hard cock deep inside you—nice and deep, making you come like I did in the club, only even harder." I take another slow step toward her, and to my surprise, she doesn't back up this time. Oh shit, her nipples are hard little pebbles behind her skimpy lace bra. "Aw, poor little Party Girl," I coo at her. "You wanna fuck me so bad, just thinking about my hard cock inside you is making you drip down your thigh." I point.

She jerks her head down to look between her thighs. "*No.* That's just water from the pool, you sicko."

I laugh. "Oh no, it's not. It's your juices. You're dripping wet for me, aching for me so bad it hurts."

"Screw you," she mutters. She wheels around and marches emphatically down the hallway toward the private elevator, throwing her sequined dress over her head as she goes. She gets tangled in her dress briefly while it's over her head and walks smack into the wall with a loud thud.

I grimace for her. "Ouch. You okay, babe?"

She bounces off the wall and wobbles for a moment in place and then yanks her dress firmly over her head and onto her tight little frame. "I'm *fine*," she says emphatically. She pulls her wet hair out from the back of her dress and smooths her dress over her hips, her face the picture of pure defiance.

I laugh. She's so fucking cute right now, she's killing me.

"It's not funny," she huffs.

"I'm going back into Reed's suite to get my clothes and your shoes and purse and then we're going back to our hotel and we're gonna fuck."

Her lips part with surprise.

"No more terrorist bullshit," I say firmly. "No more demanding my fucking application. I'm gonna fuck you and make you come so hard, you're gonna cry. If you think you're dripping down your thigh now, just wait 'til I get through with you." I begin to turn cautiously away from her, not sure if my skittish pony is gonna stay or run, and she bangs the call button for the elevator, flashing me blazing eyes.

"Don't do it, Kat," I say. "*Wait here.*"

"You're not my boyfriend—and I'm obviously not your girlfriend any more than *Jen* is. And, yes, I *do* demand your application before you can do a goddamned thing to me—even *kiss* me. So there." She sticks out her tongue.

"Real mature," I say, my heart suddenly pounding. Shit. She can't really be serious about going down to the casino floor without me, can she? "I mean it, Kat. Stay here. I can't go down there like this." I motion to my wet briefs.

"Hmmph."

The doors to the private elevator open and she glares at me, her eyes on fire.

"Kat. I can't go down into the casino wearing nothing but wet underwear and a hard dick. Don't go."

She sticks her tongue out again.

I roll my eyes. "Kat, I promised Jonas I wouldn't leave your side tonight. Please stop acting like a fucking toddler."

She steps inside the elevator, smirking. "Sucks to be you. Hopefully, your crazy-ass brother won't beat your ass too hard for breaking your promise to him." She waves. "*Ciao, motherfucker.*"

"Kat. *Stop.* Don't you dare fucking leave me right now."

Her pout turns into a diabolical smile. "'Don't you dare'? Ha! Just a tip, *Jess*," she says. "Never use that threat with me—it'll backfire every freaking time." The doors begin closing. "I *hate* that, Jess. I really do." She waves as the doors close on her smug face and, just like that, she's gone.

"Goddammit, Stubborn Kat!" I scream out loud in the empty hallway. I make a long, exasperated sound like a pot about to boil, and then I turn and sprint back into Reed's suite (which isn't a pleasant thing to do with a raging hard-on, I gotta say), muttering words like "terrorist" and "fucking" and "crazy" and "bullshit" and "so fucking hot I wanna punch a goddamned wall" to myself as I go.

20

KAT

O h shit. Why did I just do that? What came over me? I never get jealous, ever, unless I'm in a committed relationship—and even then it's an extremely rare emotion for me to feel. And here I was, ready to rip that bitch's pretty little head off and cut off Josh's balls and smash them between two graham crackers. Am I just ugly drunk? That's gotta be it. Why do I care who Josh slept with last week? I did the exact same thing, didn't I?

No, I didn't. I didn't sleep with the meanest little *bitch* in the whole, wide world and then *obviously* leave the door open for her afterwards to think there was even a snowball's chance in hell for more of the same. Jen looked awfully happy to see Josh—when she saw him, she certainly didn't look like she thought she'd been rejected by him a few days before.

My head is reeling. I can only assume my brain has short-circuited from sexual frustration and seething jealousy. And who could blame me after what I witnessed tonight? Goddammit, Josh is literally the hottest man I've ever laid eyes on, by far. Jesus Christ, I had no idea what he was hiding under his suit. I practically climaxed at the sight of him standing in that damned hallway with that ridiculous dick of his. Oh my God, I could see every detail of it, every ridge and bulge—the tip, the shaft, his balls, that little vein—all of it as plain as day under the wet fabric of his briefs. Good lord, he'd gag me with that thing. Maybe even kill me. But what a way to go. My clit is throbbing mercilessly just thinking about it. If I had my vibrator right now, it'd take me less than a minute to give myself the biggest orgasm of my life.

The elevator arrives at the lobby floor and the doors open onto the hotel's bustling casino. Wow, it's closing in on dawn and this place is still jumping.

What the hell is happening to me right now? I feel completely out of control. Like, literally *insane*. I can't even remember half of what I just said to

Josh in that hallway. Why the hell did I rip into him like that? I honestly didn't care when he told me about his New York screw earlier tonight—I *really* didn't—but I suppose *hearing* about her and *seeing* her are two different things. When he told me about fucking some faceless blast from his past, I didn't have to stare at her perfect boobs and tiny waist and get hit with her snooty I'm-better-than-you-rich-bitch glare. And I didn't have to imagine Josh thrusting his enormous dick into her petite little body and ripping her in two or pressing his magnificent muscles and tattooed skin against her, making her scream his name.

A repulsive image suddenly flickers across my brain: Josh naked with a gigantic hard-on and *Jen,* not me, down on her knees, taking his enormous dick into her mouth. Oh my God, I'm gonna barf. That should be me, goddammit! I throw my hands over my face, stuffing back tears. *That should be me.*

Why am I reacting like this? Josh isn't my boyfriend. Whatever I've been starting to feel about him, I'd better back it the fuck up and cool my jets. This guy's not even remotely interested in having a committed relationship, not with me or anyone. And, frankly, neither am I. I'm single and loving it. Hell yeah, I am. *Loving it!*

There's a craps table a few feet away so I drift over to it like a drunk driver following headlights on the freeway, my bare feet shuffling along the dirty casino carpet as I walk. I peek over at the game just in time to see a handsome gray-haired man roll a seven and crap out.

My eyes are burning. There's a lump in my throat.

I think I might have just embarrassed myself in that hallway.

I acted like a toddler.

Not to mention a terrorist, just like Josh said—a jealous, pissy, bitchy little terrorist. And a mean girl. That's right, I said it. I was every bit as mean to that bitch as she was to me in the first place. Maybe even meaner. Right now she's probably crying to her bestie—*Isabel Effing Randolph, for crying out loud!*—about how she doesn't understand what Josh could possibly see in a mean bitch like me.

And she's right. But that bitch started it, goddammit! '*Charming, Josh,*' she said, looking me up and down. Who could blame me for tearing into her? If Sarah were here she'd tell me what I did was justifiable bitchicide.

I just can't understand what Josh ever saw in a girl like that. Is he *really* that shallow? I'm not exactly an endless reservoir of deep thoughts, I'll admit, but I'm not human plankton like that girl. And, even more importantly, I'm *nice.* Or, okay, I'm not *mean* (not normally, anyway)—although, okay, yes, I have a bit of a bitchy streak, a wee bit of a temper—and it certainly came out tonight. But I'm not flat-out *mean* (not usually). Sarah always says I have a heart of gold, doesn't she? And Sarah's a fantastic judge of character.

Seriously, if Josh is interested in a girl like Jen, even for one night, just because she has an incredible body—which, holy hell, she sure does, oh my effing God, that was quite a body on her—then he truly must be the diehard

playboy I pegged him for right from the start. And that thought makes me feel...
What does it make me feel? I can't identify it.

Rejected.

Yeah. That's it. I feel rejected more than anything else—even more than
jealous.

And that's just plain stupid.

But I can't help it.

All night long—or, actually, even before coming to Vegas—I've been feeling
like Josh and I have some sort of special connection, something with potential
to turn into something serious. Something maybe even beautiful. And now I
can't help thinking that's exactly what Jen thought she had with Josh, too.
Maybe Josh makes every girl feel like girlfriend-material, simply because he's so
damned gorgeous and charming? Jen was clearly clueless about the way Josh
really felt about her—am I equally clueless, too?

The shooter at the craps table rolls a nine, and everyone breathes a sigh of
relief.

Goddammit, why don't I have my purse or phone? Or at least my effing
shoes? Classic Kat. I cross my arms in a huff and wobble in place with the
effort.

Shit. I feel kinda bad for how hard I punched that mean girl in the teeth,
even though she was a total bitch. Did I really have to go *quite* that nuclear on
her ass? Couldn't I maybe have just thrown a cherry bomb at her? Or maybe
even, like, a dart? I put some horrible words into Josh's mouth—words that probably shattered her heart, if, indeed, she's got one buried underneath those spectacular breasts.

Jeez. Maybe I don't have a heart of gold, after all, no matter what Sarah
says.

I wipe my eyes. They're suddenly burning like crazy. I can't seem to
swallow that huge lump in my throat. Maybe I'm just a bitch through and
through.

"Kat."

I turn around. It's Josh, holding my shoes and purse and looking incredibly
relieved to see me.

Without even thinking about it, I throw my arms around his neck and
squeeze—and he encircles me in his strong arms.

He kisses me on the cheek. And then the ear. And then the neck. I brush
my lips against his jawline, aching for him to kiss me like I've never been kissed
before.

But he doesn't.

He pushes a large swath of wet hair off my cheek. "What the fuck is wrong
with you? You went fucking psycho on me."

I shake my head.

"Come on, Kat. Talking lets the feelings out."

"I'm just drunk," I say, squeezing him with all my might. "Ignore me—I'm not acting like myself. Just, please, forget this ever happened. I'm not mean, I swear."

"Forget this ever happened? Highly unlikely," he says. "A man doesn't soon forget the sight of a bare ass like yours marching down a hallway." He nuzzles his nose into mine but, again, he doesn't kiss me, not that I can blame him.

I kiss his cheek. And then his ear.

He shudders at the touch of my lips.

"Josh," I whisper, my heart aching. I want him so bad, it hurts.

After a moment, Josh pulls back from me and looks deep into my eyes, rubbing my cheeks with his thumbs. "I guess this settles it, huh?—you really *do* have a vagina."

I smile. "That wasn't clear to you when you stuck your fingers inside it on the dance floor?"

"Could have been smoke and mirrors—you never know." He pushes more wet hair off my face. "You just kicked Jen's ass so fucking hard. Oh my God. You absolutely decimated that girl."

"I should have warned you—I've got a bit of a temper."

"You did warn me. I just didn't realize you meant you were a trained fucking assassin. *Jesus.*"

"I shouldn't have done that to her. She's a bitch, but she didn't deserve that. It's just that I was just so effing—"

"*Jealous,*" he says, finishing my sentence for me. "Just so effing *jealous.*"

I exhale and nod. "Yeah."

He holds my face in his hands. "Well, you're in luck. Because I happen to be a sick fuck and I thoroughly enjoyed watching you go batshit crazy with jealousy over me."

"You did?"

"Oh yeah," he says. "It gave me a raging hard-on, you might have noticed."

I grin. "Oh, you had a hard-on? Hmm. I didn't notice."

He laughs. "Or maybe I just had a raging hard-on from ogling your smokin' hot body. Jesus, Kat. You're fucking incredible."

"You're pretty incredible yourself," I say.

There's a long beat.

"You still sticking with your stupid jihad?" he asks. "Or are you ready to let me take you back to our hotel and make all your dreams come true?"

"*Jihad,*" I say, swallowing hard. Damn, it pains me to say that. I wish he could understand what I'm really saying to him. At this point, it's not about his application anymore. *I want him.* And I won't settle for getting anything less than of all of him now.

Josh looks genuinely disappointed. "It's not fair, you know. You don't have an application to give me in return."

"If I did, I'd give it to you," I say.

He mulls that over for a moment. "I thought you only get jealous with boyfriends."

Something in the way he just said that makes my heart race. "It was the truth when I said it. I'm sorry. This has never happened to me before."

He touches the cleft in my chin for a long moment and I close my eyes at his sensuous touch.

After a moment, he removes his finger and slowly licks the indentation in my chin with a languid flicker of his tongue.

My knees buckle and my clit zings. I stick out my tongue, yearning for his warm tongue to intertwine with mine, but he pulls back. I let out a shaky breath. Holy shitballs, that was sexy.

"You hungry?" he asks softly. "Suicide-bombing can really work up an appetite."

I shift my weight. Blood is flooding into my crotch. "Yeah, I'm starving."

He looks at his watch. "We're supposed to meet up with our *Ocean's Eleven* crew in just a few hours—no sense sleeping before then, right? Let's go back to our hotel and grab some breakfast, maybe gamble a little—we can crash after we meet with everyone."

"Yeah, sounds good. 'Sleep when you're dead,' right?"

"'Go big or go home,'" he says, smirking.

"YOLO."

Josh touches the cleft in my chin again, his sapphire eyes sparkling at me. "That's right, baby—you only live once. So don't fuck it up." He pauses, his eyes looking deeply into mine. "What am I gonna do with you, Kat?" he whispers. "Huh? You're a goddamned runaway train."

I shrug and wipe my eyes. "I know. I'm off the tracks."

He exhales softly and slips his hand in mine. "Come on, Madame Terrorist. Let's get you back to the hotel and get some food into you before you pass out—or, God forbid, injure some more innocent bystanders."

21

JOSH

Kat's drunk but beautiful head is resting on my shoulder as we sit in the back of the taxi, heading to our hotel. I grab her hand and look out the window at the pre-dawn zombies shuffling down The Strip. My eyelids are beginning to feel heavy. My head is beginning to pound. And yet I feel like I'm walking on air, sitting here next to Kat, holding her hand.

"Who's Grace?" Kat suddenly asks.

"What?"

"The tattoo on your chest. You've got the dragon on you arm, so I can only assume the tattoo on your chest is the ever-regrettable ex-girlfriend-tattoo."

"'Grace' isn't a person," I answer smoothly, like I always do. I don't give a shit how "honest" I said I'd be with her—I don't bare my soul about that particular tattoo to anyone, and certainly not to a woman I'm interested in. If Emma taught me anything, it's that laying myself completely bare to a woman is a colossally bad idea. "It's a reference to the phrase, 'But for the grace of God go I,'" I continue. "It's just a simple way of reminding myself to be humble and not take anything for granted—something I regularly need to be reminded of, it seems."

She absorbs that for a moment. "No ex-girlfriend tattoo anywhere?"

"Nope."

"You've got ex-girlfriends, though, right?"

"Sure."

"Anything that lasted more than a month?"

I scoff. "My longest relationship lasted three years."

"Wow. What was her name?"

"Why?"

"Just curious."

"Emma."

She squints. "You don't have a current girlfriend, right?"

"I already told you I fucked Jen in New York last week. I wouldn't have done that if I had a current girlfriend—and I most certainly wouldn't be sitting here with you."

She smiles. "Just checking."

I squeeze her hand. "I'm not a cheater," I say.

She nods. "Good to know." She touches the tips of my fingers. "Okay, so no to girlfriend tattoos; yes to dragons. How about YOLO wrapped in barbed wire?"

"Oh, great idea for my next drunken mistake."

She laughs. "Please don't."

"What do you care? You're not the one who's gonna have to look at it for the rest of your life."

There's an awkward pause. That came out kinda weird. Shit. Now I feel like I should say, "Unless, of course, it turns out you *are* the one who's gonna have to look at it for the rest of your life." But then that would be an even weirder thing to say. Shit. I look out the car window, my mind racing. When it comes to Kat, I keep finding myself saying shit I shouldn't say and having thoughts I never, ever have.

"So what's the deal with the dragon on your arm?" she asks, thankfully filling the awkward silence.

I clear my throat. "Ah. That was my very first drunken tattoo, though certainly not my last. I'm kinda known for drunken tattoos, actually. It's sort of a thing with me and my friends."

She laughs. "Can't wait to see your collection up close some time."

"Oh, you will."

My heart is pounding in my ears.

"So what's the deal with the dragon?" she asks.

"Ah, the dragon. I'd love to tell you I got it for some profound and intellectual reason—dragons have all sorts of meaning and symbolism, especially in Asia—but since you and I have agreed to play the honesty-game, I'll tell you the truth: I stumbled into a tattoo parlor in Bangkok, drunk and high as a kite, and thought, 'Dude. A dragon would be so rad.'"

She laughs.

"Reed got a tattoo that night, too—but not a dragon. His is way, way cooler than mine, actually—which isn't surprising, since he's way cooler than me."

"Reed was in Bangkok with you?"

"Yeah. After my first year of college, I traveled the whole summer with Jonas, all over the place, and for a short bit of our trip, some of my buddies joined us."

"You like to travel?" she asks.

"I love it. You?"

"I haven't done a lot of it, but I've loved it when I've gotten the chance. My parents took the whole family to Mexico for their anniversary when I was a teenager. And then we went on a Caribbean cruise for Christmas a couple years later. That was super fun."

I make a face.

"You don't like the Caribbean?"

"I don't like cruises—unless, you know, you're talking about a private yacht. That's the only way to travel by sea."

She scoffs. "Oh, well. Who doesn't demand a private yacht when traveling by sea? Duh."

I cringe.

"It's not like I have stock in a cruise line or anything," she sniffs. "I was just saying I was happy to get to go somewhere out of the country, that's all, like most normal people would be. And, by the way, my dad's a pharmacist and my mom has her own little interior designer company, so it was a really big deal for them to take five kids on a week-long cruise."

I feel my cheeks burning. "I'm sorry," I say. "That was really snobby and out-of-touch of me to say. Sometimes my inner douchebag oozes out. Please forgive me."

But she's not done with me yet. "I guess you better get another tattoo to remind yourself to be humble, huh? Because the 'Grace' one doesn't seem to be doing the trick."

There's a really long pause, during which I feel like my tongue is literally tied into knots along with my stomach. She looks out the window of the cab, apparently gathering herself, her cheeks bursting with color, and I stare at her profile, marveling at her beauty. How is it possible she keeps getting more and more attractive to me? Usually, a beautiful woman like Kat becomes less and less physically attractive the more I get to know her. I mean, with someone like Kat, you'd think there'd be only one way to go from here, right? But, nope, I'm more and more drawn to her with each passing minute.

"I'm sorry," I say earnestly. "I'm a total douchebag sometimes. I know this about myself. Please always call me on it. So few people in my life do."

"Oh, I will."

"Obviously."

"What's that supposed to mean?"

"Exactly what you think it means: that you will *obviously* call me on my shit. No more, no less. That's all it means."

"Oh. Yeah, well, that's true. I will."

"Jesus. You're insane."

"Sorry," she says. "I can't even blame you for being out of touch, honestly. I mean, how are you supposed to know what's normal? Just look at your effing shoes, for crying out loud. How much did those things cost?"

I look down at my shoes.

"More than a thousand bucks?" she asks.

I flash her an annoyed look.

"I thought so." She shakes her head. "You never stood a chance."

"Again, you lick my balls and punch 'em at the same time."

She laughs.

For a moment, we look out the window at the rat-haired horror shows dragging their sorry asses down The Strip in the pre-dawn light.

"Oh, look at that poor girl," I say pointing to a young woman who unintentionally looks like an extra in the *Thriller* video.

"Poor baby," Kat says. "Doing the Walk of Shame in *Vegas* is like reaching the Super Bowl in the sport." She shakes her head. "I've done the walk of shame a time or two myself—but never in *Vegas*. I've got my *standards*, for crying out loud."

I laugh.

"To be honest, it always pisses me off that people say women are doing a 'walk of shame,' but they never say that about guys. I mean it takes two to tango, right?"

"Absolutely." I look out the window. "I've definitely done my share of shame-walking." I scoff. "I've done my share of everything, actually. I was a bit out of control for a while."

"But not anymore?"

"Not anymore."

"Was The Club part of your out-of-control phase?" she asks.

Goddammit. I hate that she knows about The Club. There's no other circumstance in which a woman I'm interested in would know about that. "No," I say. "The Club was just a short vacation from my adult responsibilities. I did that *way* after my out-of-control phase. It was just a blip. No more or less."

"And now it's over—the blip, I mean?"

"Yeah, now it's over."

"Until the next blip."

I don't reply—but she's pegged me right. Surely, another blip's coming at some point. When your brother is Jonas—and you're his only lifeline—losing your shit for more than a blip here or there just isn't an option.

"Tell me the story of why you got your 'grace' tattoo," she says. "Were you drunk and high in Thailand for that one, too?"

I look out the window of the cab. "No, I got that particular tattoo in L.A. when I was stone-cold sober," I say. "I was twenty-three and recently out of school—it took me a little while to graduate—and I decided it was time to stop throwing my life away on total and complete bullshit and start living a life that my..." I swallow hard. "That *I* could be proud of." I shrug. "I decided to start living up to my name. So I decided to open a satellite office of Faraday & Sons and stop destroying myself, and the rest is history."

"And did you?"

"Yeah, I opened the L.A. office about the time Jonas took over the main Seattle office."

"No, I mean, did you stop destroying yourself? Did you start living a life you could be proud of?"

"Oh." I run my hand through my hair. "Mostly. A few slip-ups now and again over the years." I look into her gorgeous blue eyes. "But, yeah. By and large."

Another long pause.

"Isn't Thailand one of those countries where they could put you in jail and throw away the key if you get caught with drugs?"

"Yeah. Why?"

"You said you were drunk and high as a kite in Thailand."

"Oh. Yeah. Well. I thought I was invincible back then. Or maybe I didn't care if I wasn't. Actually, it's funny you say that. I've got a pretty hairy story about that night. I'll tell it to you some time, maybe."

There's a long beat.

"Josh, I know what happened to your parents," she says. "Sarah told me. I'm really sorry."

I'm stunned. I had no idea Kat knew about my parents. What the fuck? She knows about The Club *and* my parents? Fuck.

"It was a long time ago," I respond stiffly.

She doesn't press me, thankfully, but she's clearly looking at me with sympathy in her eyes. Shit. I don't have any desire to be the Poor Little Rich Boy in anyone's eyes, least of all Kat's.

"No worries," I add. I squeeze her hand to reassure her and she squeezes back.

Our taxi pulls up in front of our hotel and I help Kat out of the car. She's pretty wobbly.

"You okay?" I ask, holding her arm.

"I'm fan-fucking-tastic. Just a little car sick, I think. I'll be fine once I eat something."

We walk toward the front doors of our mammoth hotel.

"Do you need to put on some dry undies before we eat? My briefs are still wet—I think my dick is getting chafed."

"Oh, well, we don't want that," she says. "Yeah, I could use a change, too. Let's run up to our rooms and meet at that Americana restaurant on the far side of the casino in fifteen."

"You aren't gonna pass out on your bed and not come back down, are you?" I ask.

"Not a chance. I'm the Party Girl, remember? I'm a machine."

"Atta girl," I say. "But I'd better walk you up to your room, just to make sure you get there safely."

"You mean so you can have *sex* with me," she says coyly, batting her eyelashes. "I know your game, Playboy."

"Kat, I'm not gonna fuck you for the first time at six in the morning after a long-ass night of partying when you're obviously drunk off your ass and, no offense, look like road kill."

She scowls at me.

"Oh, wait, scratch all that. I forgot we're playing the honesty-game here. The truth is I'd totally fuck you, despite all that, for sure—but I'm most definitely *not* gonna fuck you 'til you've dropped your ridiculous demands."

She makes a "good luck with that" face.

"Hey, you're the one who made The Rules, PG. I'm merely enforcing them."

She pauses, considering something. "Well, how about this? What if we fuck without any kissing?" she asks. "Would that be a loophole?"

I laugh. The woman's trying to find a loophole from her own bullshit? Clearly, she's a heartbeat away from caving completely. "You're not in any shape to negotiate on the bet, PG. You made your demands, and now you have to live with them. The only way out now is to concede. There's no middle ground."

She scowls yet again.

I suppress the urge to laugh out loud at her expression. She's such a bull-shitter, this girl. She wants me so bad, she's about to pull her hair out. Time to turn up the heat.

"Plus, I happen to like kissing when I fuck," I say nonchalantly. "I like it a lot. Every variety of it."

She stops walking abruptly and puts her arms out like she's trying to balance herself on a log.

Oh man, she's drunk. Her eyes are half-mast. Her hair's matted against her head. Her eye makeup is smudged. And she's still fucking gorgeous.

"Look, here's the thing you're obviously not getting about me, Party Girl: I've been exercising superhuman patience my whole fucking life. You think you're gonna wear me down? *Nothing* fucking wears me down—I've got the patience of a fucking saint. I've been the fixer my whole life—and nothing ruffles me. As far as I'm concerned, there's a time and place for everything— including fucking the one and only Party Girl with a Hyphen—and until the right time for that bit of awesomeness presents itself, I'll just wait and be patient, let you drip down your thighs 'til you're begging me for it."

She's speechless.

I can't suppress my laughter anymore. She's too fucking cute. "Come on, PG. Let me get you to your room to change." I grab her limp arm and usher her toward the hotel again, but after three more steps, she stops short and hunches over.

"Kat?"

She nods and puts her hand to her mouth. "Yeah. I'm fine." She takes two more steps and stops again, grabbing her stomach.

"Kat?" I grab her shoulders? "Are you okay?"

"I'm fine. I think I just need to—"

Without warning, she bends over and barfs—all over the sidewalk—and all over my two-thousand-dollar shoes.

22

KAT

I slowly open my eyes. I don't feel great, but it definitely could have been a *lot* worse. When Josh brought me to my room after I barfed all over him, he helped me shower—in my bra and undies, I noticed—ordered me chicken noodle soup from room service, and made me drink a bunch of Gatorade and take four Ibuprofen before finally tucking me into bed. I have to admit, I kinda swooned at how attentive and sweet he was, even through my queasiness.

I look at the clock. Three o'clock. Wow, I slept a full seven hours. I grab my phone and look at my emails. Damn. I've got two messages from my boss, attaching documents that require my attention. Obviously, I'm gonna have to head back to Seattle soon or risk losing my job. My work is piling up and I've already used up all my vacation days this year. Hmm. Maybe there's a way for me to finagle this.

I forward my boss's email to my co-worker Hannah, asking her if maybe she's willing to help a sistah out?

Hannah's email reply is immediate. "Of course, baby. I got you. Any time."

"Thanks, baby. You know I'll return the favor."

"You've helped me with a thousand pitches, girl. And I still owe you big time for helping me with the politician who sent the dick pic to the teenager."

"You don't owe me a damned thing," I write. "And if you do, then helping me with this pitch puts you way ahead, for sure."

"Where are you? Still in Vegas?" Hannah writes.

"Yeah. And currently hung over. Partied all night. You won't believe who I partied with."

"Who?"

"RED CARD RIOT!"

"WTF!!!!!! Are you serious?"

"Serious. LMFAO," I write.

"Cray," Hannah writes.

"Probs going to their concert tonight, too. And watching from backstage!!!!!"

"No way! Double cray. Are they hot?"

"Totes. But really young. Just wee little baybays."

"Oooooh, you could do the Mrs. Robinson thing. That'd be hot."

"That's not one of my fantasies, actually. But, trust me, I've got plenty of others."

"Oh, I know you do. LOL," Hannah writes.

"Thanks again, girl. You're a great friend."

"Takes one to know one. Speaking of which, say hi to Sarah. How's she feeling?"

"She's great. Breaking news: she's in luuuuuurve."

"Awesome! With that guy she went to Belize with?"

"Yup. And he's in luuuuuuuurve with her, too."

"Aw." Hanna attaches a heart emoji. "I'm jelly." She attaches a green-faced emoji.

"Me, too." I exhale wistfully. "Okay, gotta go," I write. "Just woke up. Gotta get some food in this sad-sack body."

"By all means. Partying requires fuel. Have fun."

"Thanks again for the assist."

"No worries. Have an extra drink for me. Or two or three."

"Thanks, Hannah Banana Montana Milliken."

"LOL. Any time, Kitty Kat."

"Meow."

"Mwah."

Phew. Catastrophe averted. At least for now. I have no doubt Hannah will style me—the woman's damn good at PR—and that ought to buy me at least a little time. But, clearly, I can't stay out here in Las Vegas forever. Sooner or later, the jig's gonna be up. I just wish I knew how long Operation *Ocean's Eleven* was going to last (and what my part in it might be).

I scour the rest of my emails. Nothing important. I move on to my texts.

There's a text from Sarah. "Hey, Kitty Kat. What happened with you and Josh last night? Did you have fun? Winky winky boom boom? Jonas and I are heading out to Henderson to meet Oksana the Pimpstress right now. Kerzoinks! I just pissed my pants a little bit writing that. Okay, well, just wanted to check in and say hi and get all the juicy deets about last night. You're probably sleeping, knowing you. Hope you didn't barf, girl. But if you did, I hope you didn't barf on Josh. But if you did, I hope Josh held your hair for you, since I wasn't there to do it like usual. See you later when we get back. IF WE GET BACK." She attaches a scared-face emoji. "If I don't come back, just know I loved you with all my heart and soul. Oh, and, just in case, I hereby bequeath you my One Direction albums."

I tap out my reply. "Hey, girl. Just woke up. Yes, I barfed. Yes, Josh held my hair. He showered me and Gatoraded me, too, and then put me to bed." I attach a blushing emoji. "Don't say 'IF we get back.' NOT FUNNY. I love you, too, with all my heart and soul, and then some. It's probably too late for you to get this now, but be super-duper careful with the pimpstress. Don't leave Jonas' side. See you when you get back. Can't wait to hear all about it." I attach an ear emoji. "And I don't want your stinkin' 1D albums, you tweener. If I did, though, does this mean you're 'bequeathing me' (WTF??) your entire laptop? Sorry to look a gift horse in the mouth, but I'm not sure I know how to extract the digital files off your laptop. Heehee. Love you, girl. Meow. Xoxo."

My next text is from Josh from an hour ago. "You up yet, PG?"

I type a reply. "Hi, PB. Just woke up."

His reply is instantaneous. "You feeling like death warmed over?"

"No, I feel pretty fab. Can you talk?"

My phone rings. "Hey," his smooth voice says. I hear slot machines ringing and people cheering in the background.

"Thanks for putting me to bed and taking such good care of me. Sorry I barfed on your fancy shoes."

"I hated those shoes anyway. Total douchebag-shoes."

"I was thinking of getting something to eat before Jonas and Sarah get back from meeting the Pimpstress Extraordinaire. Do you know if they're back yet?"

"Not yet. I saw them before they left. They were both wearing matching platinum bracelets engraved with each other's names."

"What? Oh my God."

"You should have seen them, Kat. Seriously, they can't get enough of each other. They're pretty cute."

My heart flips over in my chest. "Wow. Good for them."

There's a long beat.

Josh clears his throat. "So did you get any sleep?"

"A ton. How about you?"

"A couple hours at most. Henn and I are down in the casino playing craps, waiting for Jonas and Sarah to come back."

"Okay, I'll get dressed and come on down."

"No. I don't want you walking around alone. Text me when you're ready to come down here."

"Will do."

I jump in the shower and wash my hair and lather my body from head to toe. And when I'm done with the functional aspects of my shower, I grab the showerhead and stick it between my legs, positioning the strong stream of water right on my clit. My body's reaction to the vibrating water is extreme and instantaneous. Whoa, oh yeah, I'm ready to go.

I close my eyes and begin touching myself, trying to duplicate the precise way Josh touched me when we "danced" at Reed's club. God, that was hot. So *fucking* hot.

Oh, I'm already pulsing like crazy.

My fingers massage and rub, working round and round.

I imagine the ridges and ripples of Josh's abs, the incredible muscles on his arms, that tight "V" on either side of his lower pelvis, his tattoos, and, the crowning glory, that incredible hard-on I saw hiding beneath his wet briefs.

Oh, I'm especially sensitive to touch right now. Getting myself off today is gonna be as easy as falling off a greasy log.

I begin moaning softly.

Oh, I'm right on the cusp.

I imagine the outline of Josh's hard dick in his wet briefs, and then I fantasize about it sliding inside me, thrusting in and out of me, over and over.

His lips are on mine, devouring me. His hands are touching my naked body. He's whispering in my ear, calling me his Party Girl with a Hyphen.

Oh yeah. My skin is beginning to prickle like I've got a chill, always a deliciously disorienting sensation under hot steaming water.

I imagine the cocky expression on Josh's face when he accused me of dripping down my thigh with desire for him—*which I was.* Oh, God, yes, I was.

I'm rocked with a massive orgasm that makes my insides twist and shudder.

"Fuck," I blurt. "Oh my God."

Pleasure is vibrating between my legs and throughout my abdomen.

Oh boy. That was a nice one.

I return the showerhead to its holder and lean into the shower wall for a moment.

I've never wanted a man this much in all my life.

Damn.

What have I done? How the hell am I gonna get myself out of this pickle I've created? Never in a million years did I think it would take this long to wear Josh down. I figured he'd throw me some nominal, flirtatious resistance and then give me what I want, the way all other men do, to be perfectly honest. *Goddammit.* I feel like stomping my foot in frustration.

I get out of the shower and dry off with one of the thick, white towels on the nearby shelf and quickly check my texts again—I stayed in the shower longer than I intended to—and, oopsies, there's a group text from Jonas, telling Henn, Josh and me to meet him and Sarah up in his suite in ten minutes. Oh, crap. I better get a move on.

I quickly dial Josh. He picks right up.

"Did you see Jonas' text?" I ask.

"Yeah, I just got it a minute ago. Henn and I are on our way to your room to get you. We don't want you walking up to their suite alone. See you in five."

23

———

JOSH

I t's official. Sarah Fucking Cruz is the biggest badass I've ever met. She took a naked selfie in the bad guys' bathroom and emailed it to them right then and there? She must have ice in her veins. Ha! Well, I guess Kat's not the only terrorist in our group. Holy shit.

"And then," Sarah continues, beaming, "*both* of them opened my email right on the spot."

"Now *that's* the way to do it, Sarah Cruz! Who's the fucking genius now?" Henn shouts, scrambling to his laptop.

I glance over at Jonas in the far corner, intending to share a look of celebration with him, but his jaw is clenched and his eyes are blue chips of granite.

"Bingo," Henn says after a brief moment of studying his screen. "You did it, Sarah. We're in. I've got Oksana's computer and that guy's phone. Holy shit. Jackpot."

"She's a fucking assassin," I whisper to Kat.

"Birds of a feather flock together." She winks.

I chuckle.

"Oh my God," Henn says, staring intently at his computer screen. "The bastard forwarded your email to another computer and opened your photo there, too." He makes a sound of extreme joy. "Brilliant, Sarah." He clicks a button on his keyboard and, all of a sudden, his cheeks suddenly turn bright red.

"So, Henn?" Sarah asks, her cheeks flushing every bit as much as Henn's.

Henn jerks his head up from his screen, his cheeks blazing. "Yes?"

"So now what?" Sarah asks.

"Well, um," Henn says. He swallows hard. Oh yeah, my boy's definitely been thrown for a loop by something on his screen. Henn clears his throat. "I'll snoop around both computers and this Max guy's phone and see what I can find. And then we wait for them to hopefully access their mainframe and bank accounts. I imagine we won't have to wait too long."

"Can you delete that photo?" Jonas asks, his voice tight. "Can you find it and erase it everywhere?"

"Um, sure, no problem," Henn says quickly, his face turning an even darker shade of red. "I can delete it right now, if you want me to. I've got total access."

Oh, well, that answers that question: Henn's looking at the selfie Sarah sent to Oksana and Max. Ha! Poor Henn never did know how to keep a poker face.

"Yeah, but if you delete that photo off their computers now, won't that tip them off?" Kat asks.

"Yeah," Henn says. "If that photo magically disappears, this Max dude is gonna know something's up for sure—and if he designed their tech like he says, then he's a badass motherfucker of epic proportions and we don't want to do anything to tip him off."

"Well, then, don't delete it. I don't want to give them any reason whatsoever to be suspicious," Sarah says. She juts her chin at Jonas.

"I agree," Henn says. He winces at Jonas like he's expecting to get punched.

Jonas exhales and crosses his arms over his chest, his brand new engraved bracelet gleaming on his wrist. Oh man, he's in full serial-killer mode right now, though I don't understand why. What did he expect Sarah to do? It was do or die time and she *did*. If she were my girl, I'd be kissing her from head to toe right now, telling her she's a fucking genius. Seriously, my brother is the dumbest (smartest) guy I know.

"God, Sarah," Kat says, laughing. "First the solo-boob shot and now this. You're quite the exhibitionist, aren't you?"

"A 'boob shot?'" I ask. "Oh my goodness, tell us more, Sarah Cruz."

Sarah blushes. "Just a little sexting with this really hot guy I met online." She looks at Jonas, but he remains stone-faced. "A hot guy who *used* to have a sense of humor," she continues. "It's no big deal—all the kids are doing it these days."

Jesus. My brother's being a total prick. I gotta help this poor girl out. "And all the politicians," I add.

"And athletes," Henn says.

"And housewives," Kat adds.

"And grandmas," I say.

"And some priests, too," Henn adds, and everyone (except Jonas) laughs.

Kat beams a smile at me and I wink back at her.

"Sarah, you picked the perfect bait for your email," Kat says, swigging from a water bottle. "No matter how smart or powerful or rich a guy might be, he's got the same Kryptonite as every other man throughout history." She raises one eyebrow at me. "*Naked boobs.*"

I return the eyebrow-raise. "Are we really that simple?" I ask.

"Yes," Kat says. "You really are."

I laugh.

"Never underestimate the power of porn," Henn says.

"That's catchy," Kat says. "The porn industry should adopt that for a bill-board campaign."

"I don't think the porn industry needs help with their marketing," Henn says.

I look over at Jonas again, hoping he's eased up on the psycho-killer bullshit, but he's still channeling Ted Bundy over there. Shit. Poor Sarah. A woman's got to be superhuman to put up with my fucking brother, I swear to God—or maybe just a masochist.

"That was really quick thinking on your feet, Sarah," I say. "You went in there hoping to harpoon a baby whale, and you wound up landing Moby Dick. Great job." I raise my eyebrows pointedly at Jonas. "Right, bro? *Aren't you proud of her?*" I say.

Jonas scowls at me, the bastard.

"I was scared; I'm not gonna lie," Sarah says. "My hands were shaking like crazy the whole time I was in there. But there was no way I was gonna leave that building without implanting that virus, no matter what. There was too much at stake."

"You're such a badass, Sarah," Kat says.

Jonas exhales and uncrosses his arms and Sarah shoots him a look that says, "Screw you, motherfucker." Ah, well, maybe little Miss Sarah Cruz is gonna be able to handle my brother, after all.

"Hey, guys," Henn says, engrossed with something on his screen. "Holy shit. Oksana's going into her bank account right now—that Henderson Bank we were scouting out before?" He stares at the screen for another ten seconds. "Sha-zam. She just typed in her password. Ha! I got it." He shakes his head. "Oh man, I love technology."

"So what do we do?" Sarah asks.

"We wait a few minutes for her to log off, and then we go in and snoop around."

"Sounds like the perfect time for me to fill drink orders," I say, heading to the bar. "Party Girl with a Hyphen?"

"Club soda, please."

"You sure you don't want a little hair of the dog?"

She shakes her head, grimacing. "I'm sure."

Damn, she's cute. "I'll join you. My liver could probably use a little break."

"We're really not living up to our nicknames, you know," she says.

"I won't tell if you won't."

I get everyone else's drink orders, and just as I'm passing a glass of champagne to Sarah, Henn calls us over to his computer screen. "She's logged off," he announces. "Let's go in."

We all gather around Henn's computer, bursting with anticipation.

"Well, she's already deposited your checks—one hundred eighty thousand big ones," Henn says. "I bet that boils your blood, huh, Jonas?"

Jonas grunts.

"And she just transferred half of it into her savings account. Hmm," Henn says, sounding perplexed.

"What?" Sarah asks, her eyes bugging out.

"Even after today's deposit, Oksana's got only about half a million total in these two accounts." He furrows his brow.

"Hmm," I say.

"Hmm, indeed," Henn agrees. "Chump change. These must be Oksana's personal accounts—definitely not The Club's main accounts."

"Damn," Sarah says. "So how do we find the big money?"

Jonas walks away from the group to the other side of the room, apparently mulling things over.

"We just have to wait for them to log into their main bank accounts," Henn says. "It could be five minutes, five hours, five days—who knows?"

I glance at Kat and something's made her visibly anxious all of a sudden, though I have no idea what it was.

"But I guarantee they'll lead us there sooner or later," Henn continues. "And in the meantime, I'll take a nice, long gander around their files and data, make copies of everything, see if there's anything of interest. Oh, and I'll listen to Max's voicemails, too. That's so cool you got Max's phone, Sarah." He sips his beer. "Dang, there's a lot to do."

I exhale loudly, drawing everyone's attention, including Kat's. "Well, it looks like poor Henn's gonna be working through the night again, going through all this stuff." I pull out my phone, intending to text Reed about those RCR tickets. "What do you say, Party Girl with a Hyphen—you wanna paint Sin City red with me again?"

"I'd actually like to help Henn, if that's okay," Kat says.

I'm blown away. She'd rather stay here and help Henn with his hacking shit than watch the RCR concert from backstage?

"I'm kind of excited about all this. I have a strong motivation to want to bury these guys," she adds. She looks at Sarah and her facial expression bursts with protectiveness. "Would that be okay with you, Henn? Or would I be in your way?"

My heart is racing and my skin is buzzing. I wouldn't have predicted Kat turning down backstage tickets at the Garden Arena to help Henn hack into The Club—not in a million years.

"No, that'd be awesome," Henn says. "But only if you really want to. I mean Josh and Jonas are *paying* me to do this, so . . ."

"Could you use my help, too?" I ask.

Henn's face lights up. "Yeah. That'd be great."

"Okay, then. I'll order us room service and the three of us will get to work."

"Make that the four of us," Sarah says. "I'll stick around and help, too. I'm pretty motivated to bury these guys, too."

We all look at Jonas. Obviously, this is his cue to say, "Me, too." Or better yet, "No, baby, lemme take you out to celebrate how you kicked the bad guys' asses today." But Jonas doesn't say either of those things. Of course not. Because he's an imbecile—a socially inept imbecile. Instead, my stupid serial-killer-moron of a dumbshit-brother just stands in the corner, silently sipping his beer. Well, I guess I'll just have to give the fucker a little push.

"Nah," I say. "You two kids should go out and *celebrate*." I look at Jonas pointedly. "Or stay *in* and celebrate, whatever floats your boat. Either way, *definitely celebrate*—you both kicked ass today."

Jonas' eyes flicker with sudden understanding of what I'm trying to tell him. He looks at Sarah, but he's already blown it—she's looking away, gritting her teeth. Oh shit. She looks like she's ready to join Kat in roasting some testicle s'mores.

I grin at Sarah, trying to charm her into forgiving my stupid brother. "The three of us will move our party down to my suite and let you two crazy kids swing on the chandeliers up here."

Jonas takes a long, slow sip of his beer, staring at Sarah—and she's flashing him the most adorable look of defiance I've ever seen. Well, actually, she's flashing him the *second* most adorable look of defiance I've ever seen—the first being the look Kat flashed me last night when she stood in that hallway in her skimpy undies, dripping wet, absolutely crazed with jealousy, banging on the call button for the elevator.

Jonas drains his beer and puts the bottle down—a good start—but then the moron doesn't cross the room and take Sarah into his arms. *Dumbshit.* Does he have fucking eyes? Or half a brain? Clearly, that's all Sarah wants him to do—take her into his arms and give her a kiss. I always say, when it comes to women, especially an angry one, just about any problem can be solved with a fucking awesome kiss.

Jonas crosses his arms over his chest and stares at Sarah.

I lean into Kat. "I feel like I'm watching Wimbledon."

She nods. "I think it's Jonas' serve."

I snicker.

"What do you say, baby?" Jonas finally says. I nod enthusiastically. Definitely a good start.

But Sarah doesn't reply. She juts her chin at him, her eyes on fire. She's such a cutie, I don't know how he's resisting her right now.

"You up for a little celebration tonight?" Jonas asks.

I hold my breath. How could she possibly resist him? He's clearly at least trying to turn on the charm. But Sarah shrugs and looks away.

"Why doesn't he just walk over to her and *kiss* her?" Kat whispers to me.

"Maybe she's told him kissing is off limits—maybe she's a fucking terrorist on a jihad," I whisper back.

Kat scoffs. "Or maybe she's just a frickin' *genius*."

"Or maybe she's painted herself into a corner she doesn't know how to get herself out of," I say.

Kat grunts.

"I think we should celebrate," Jonas says.

Sarah shrugs again. Oh man, she's holding firm.

"She definitely learned that stonewalling thing from her best friend," I whisper.

"Hmmph."

"Aw, come on, baby," Jonas says, grinning at Sarah. "You wanna have a little fun?"

"There it is," I whisper. "Game, set, match."

"Not so fast," Kat whispers. "Not gonna be that easy."

"Twenty bucks says she lays down her weapon right here."

"You're on. She'll hold out for at *least* two more asks. Trust me."

"*Maybe*," Sarah says.

"See?" I whisper. "He's got her."

Kat puts up a finger, as if to say, "Wait for it."

"And maybe *not*," Sarah adds, pursing her lips.

Kat puts out her hand. "Pay up."

Jonas mocks Sarah's pout. "What if I said *please?*"

"Double or nothing?" I whisper. "Next ask."

"You're on, fool," Kat replies.

Sarah's trying to suppress a smile. "Then I'd say *possibly*."

"Ha!" I whisper. "Pay up."

Kat puts up her finger.

"But not *probably*," Sarah says.

"Fuck," I say.

Kat puts out her palm again and I lay forty bucks in it, rolling my eyes.

"What if I said pretty please?" Jonas asks, smiling broadly.

"Double or nothing again?" Kat whispers.

I shake my head and Kat giggles.

Sarah shrugs again.

"Jesus. Glad I didn't make another bet," I whisper. "She's as stubborn as you."

"What if I said pretty please *and* that we can do whatever you want, anything at all, you name it?" Jonas asks.

"Okay, whoa. I think he's overdoing it," I whisper to Kat.

She giggles. "No, he's doing the bare minimum."

"*Anything at all?*" Sarah asks.

"Don't do it," I whisper to Kat.

"He will," Kat says.

"*Anything at all*," Jonas confirms.

Kat giggles. "Sucker."

"Pussy," I say.

"But sweet," she responds.

Sarah touches the platinum bracelet on her wrist. "You'll be at my mercy completely?"

Jonas squints and bites his lip, considering.

"Don't do it," I whisper.

"He will."

Jonas still hasn't replied.

"Hang tough, man," I whisper. "Fight the good fight."

"He's toast," Kat replies.

"Stand strong," I whisper.

"He's a goner."

"Well? Will you be at my mercy or not?" Sarah prods him. "What do you say?"

"He says yes," Kat says.

"Definitely," I agree.

"Hmm." Jonas walks slowly toward Sarah like she's pulling him on a string. "What do I say?" he says softly. When he reaches Sarah, he takes her face in his hands and whispers to her, but I can't make out what he's saying. Clearly, whatever it is, he's saying it with passion.

"Really, you should owe me at least a hundred bucks," Kat whispers. "Are you always this stupid, or just when it comes to women?"

"How was I supposed to know Sarah's a terrorist like you?"

"Who do you think taught her all her tricks?" Kat says.

We both giggle.

Jonas and Sarah are whispering to each other and kissing like they're the only two people in the room.

"Hey, PG," I say, leaning into Kat. "Why'd you look like you were gonna have a stroke when Henn said it might take five days before he's able to crack The Club's system?"

She waves me off. "Oh nothing."

"Tell me. You looked like you were gonna throw up right then."

"Which isn't an unusual look for me, unfortunately." She shoots me an adorable smile. "Sorry about your shoes again."

I chuckle. "No worries. What's going on?"

She rolls her eyes. "I just, you know, I've got a job. Bills to pay. I don't have enough vacation days to cover me staying in Vegas that much longer. If it takes five days for us to complete this 'mission,' whatever the heck it is, I'll probably have to quit my job. Or maybe take an unpaid leave, if they'll let me, I dunno. But it's okay. Wild horses couldn't drag me away if Sarah needs me here. It's a no-brainer. Don't worry about it."

24

KAT

By the time the second round of room service arrives at Josh's suite, Henn, Josh, and I have been extracting and analyzing information off the bad guys' computers and phone for almost five hours straight.

"Woot!" I squeal when the room service guy spreads the plates of goodies on a glass table in the middle of the suite. "Now this is my idea of heaven on earth."

We all gather around the table, drooling at the decadent food in front of us.

"Yummalicious," I say, rubbing my hands together with glee. "Everything looks so tantalizing, it's hard to decide where to start."

"That's exactly what women say when they throw themselves at me," Henn says. "*Where. To. Start?*"

I laugh.

Henn considers the various plates of dessert in front of him. "It's a no-brainer—chocolate cake is the clear entry-point."

"Careful. Chocolate cake is a gateway drug," Josh says.

"I'll risk it," Henn says.

"I like the way you think, Henn. YOLO, right?" I shoot Josh a wink and he smiles.

"Slide that plate between us, Kitty Kat," Henn says. "We'll share."

I hand Henn a fork and slide the cake plate between us. "Josh? You wanna succumb to death by chocolate with us?"

"Nah, I'm a cheesecake man, through and through. Send that bad boy down here."

Henn slides the cheesecake across the table toward Josh.

"Hey, Josh, shoot that apple pie over to papa," Henn says, a huge bite of chocolate cake stuffed in his mouth.

"Here you go, papa," Josh says.

"Oh no, did they forget the ice cream?" I ask. "Please, God, no."

"It's right here," Henn says, shoving the bowl of ice cream at me. "Save your prayers for world hunger or curing cancer."

"Or Seahawks games," Josh adds.

I laugh.

When our eating frenzy has slowed down a bit, we lean back in our chairs, patting our stomachs.

"That hit the spot," I say. "Thinking so hard really works up an appetite. Who knew?"

Henn laughs.

"I don't know how you do it day after day, Henn," I say. "Just a few hours of thinking hard and my brain hurts."

"It's not thinking hard for Henn. Like I keep saying, he's a fucking genius," Josh says.

"Thanks, man."

"So what's next, boss?" Josh asks.

"We send all the data we've extracted through translation software and hope whatever comes out the other side leads us to our next rabbits to chase."

"How long 'til you crack into their system, you think?" Josh asks.

"There's no way to know for sure, but I'm guessing just a couple days. Maybe four or five, outside."

My stomach turns over and my chest tightens. Damn. I'm definitely gonna have a problem keeping my job if this takes much longer than another day or two. I glance up at Josh and he's staring at me intently. I half-smile at him, but I'm suddenly wracked with anxiety.

"I tell you one thing, though," Henn says. "Having you guys helping me out tonight sure sped things up a ton. Probably shaved a couple days off."

"It was amazing watching you work," I say.

"Yeah, that's what all the pretty girls say, Kitty Kat."

I laugh. "I'm sure they do, Henny."

"Actually, no, they don't. That was humor borne of pain."

"That's all humor is," Josh says. "The flipside of pain."

"Hey, no deep conversations allowed here," I say. "Only superficial banter, please. And cake."

"Amen," Josh says. "No argument from me."

"Henn, I can't imagine why girls aren't tackling you to the ground as you walk down the sidewalk," I say. "You're obviously the total package."

"Why, thank you."

"Which means whatever's not working for you can be traced to whatever you're doing or *not* doing to get their attention. What's your go-to move to close the deal, if you know what I mean?"

"No, I don't know what you mean. That's the problem. *I have no idea what you mean.*"

I shoot a worried look at Josh. "The patient is flatlining, doctor. We need the crash cart."

Josh laughs. "He's too nice—that's the problem," Josh says. "Just dick it up a little bit, Henn, and women will be elbowing each other in the earholes to get to you, I guarantee you."

"*Dick it up*'?" I repeat.

"Absolutely. There's a time and place for nice and sensitive and sweet—and a time and place for dicking it up. And something tells me Henn needs to introduce more dick into his repertoire."

"*That's* your advice for attracting women? 'Dick it up'?"

"Absolutely." He winks at Henn. "Trust me, man. Just throw a big ol' steaming pile of 'I don't give a fuck' on every woman who crosses your path for the next month, and you'll have to beat the babes off with a stick."

"Sorry, Josh," Henn says. "No offense, but your advice is utterly worthless to me. When *you* dick it up, I'm sure women wanna birth your babies—but if I were to dick it up even a little bit, women would just call me a dick and walk away."

"That's not true, man," Josh says. "When it comes to women, certain things are tried and true, no matter who you are."

I sit back in my chair, smirking at Josh. "Please, oh wise and powerful one, tell us *more* nuggets of wisdom about how any man, no matter who he is, can bag a babe."

"I'd be glad to. Well, for one thing, women *think* they wanna be chased— that's what all the movies and books tell 'em they want—but they don't. Not really."

"We *don't*?" I ask. "Huh. Fascinating."

"It's true. You chase a woman too hard, she thinks you're desperate—and women *can't stand desperate*." He grins at me. "That's rule number one. If you do the equivalent of driving to her house and holding a boom box over your head, you might as well hand her your dick and balls in a Ziplock baggie, too, 'cause you're not gonna need 'em any more." He leans back, looking at me with smoldering eyes. "You always gotta leave her wondering, keep her guessing—at least a little bit." He winks at me. "That's how to keep her wanting more."

I lean forward, my eyes locked on his. "Oh, so, for instance, if a guy's got a business trip to New York for a whole freaking week, then he should just text brief messages to a woman like, 'Hey' and 'What's up?'—just enough to let the babe feel like he's thinking about her but brief and superficial enough to keep her wondering if he's even interested at all?"

Josh grins broadly. "*Exactly.* Let her wonder if you give a shit or not. Keep her off-balance. And then just sit back and watch her eat out of the palm of your hand the next time she sees you."

"Hardly," I say.

"Dude. What the fuck are you two talking about?" Henn asks.

Josh ignores him. "But you have to be wary. Because she's a demon spawn and she'll start fucking with you—doing shit like demanding to see something you've never shown *anyone,* something that's none of her fucking business—all while acting like what she's asking for is perfectly reasonable and that *you're* the crazy one if you say no."

"Interesting. Maybe she's not playing head games, though—ever think of that? Maybe you're reading the situation wrong, completely misunderstanding her motivations."

"No, that's just bullshit justification for sociopathic behavior."

"*Sociopathic?*"

"Borderline."

"Wow."

"The bottom line is that she's just a goddamned terrorist—which means that on principle alone, you must never, ever *give in to her unreasonable demands.* You just gotta keep your eye on the prize—the big picture—and stay strong."

"What the fuck are you two talking about?" Henn asks.

"And the big picture is . . .?" I ask, completely ignoring Henn. "Pray tell?"

"You don't know?"

I shake my head. "No, I don't."

"Well, if you haven't figured it out by now, then I can't help you."

I squint at Josh. "So that's the sum total of your advice on how to bag a babe, huh? Dick it up, dig in your heels, don't act desperate, and keep your eye on the prize?"

"Yeah, pretty much. That and *always* wear cologne. Women are highly sensory creatures. You gotta overwhelm all their senses—sight, sound, smell, touch. It's primal." One side of his mouth tilts up.

"Okay, this I understand," Henn says. "Wear cologne. That's something I can actually do."

"Well, as long as it's the *right* cologne, yes," I say. "Wear the wrong cologne, and you're sunk. The wrong cologne is worse than no cologne at all."

That cocky grin isn't going anywhere. "Oh really? Well, what about mine, for instance? Right or wrong?"

I hate to give him the satisfaction, but the truth is the truth. "Very, very *right.*" I say. I inhale deeply as if I'm taking in his scent from across the table.

Josh barks the name of his cologne at Henn. "Write that down, man. You heard the woman—she likes my cologne *a lot.*" He licks his lips, assessing me. "Actually, you know what, Henn? If you're gonna get advice on how to bag a babe from anyone, you should get it from Kat. She's probably the world's foremost expert."

I narrow my eyes. What does that mean? Did he just call me a slut? Or does he think I'm bisexual? "No, I think Josh has lots and lots more experience bagging *babes* than me."

Josh rolls his eyes. "Testy, testy. Jeez. What I mean is that you're a babe, so best to ask you. Actually, you're the best of both worlds. You've got a *vagina* (so

I'm told—I'm still not sure I believe it) *and* you've got four brothers, too. So as a woman *and* an honorary dude, you can give our beloved Henny the female *and* male perspectives on babe-baggery. Shit, with those credentials, you could probably teach a Learning Annex seminar on the subject, maybe even a twelve-week course."

I smile broadly. "Thank you for recognizing my expertise."

Josh nods. "Plus, you're demonic as hell. If he's gonna learn the ropes, best if he learns from an instructor who blows shit up, rather than one who plays by the rules. No one ever learned a damned thing from following The Rules. Ever. Am I right?"

I shoot him my most demonic look. "Well, actually, yeah, we're definitely in agreement about that."

Josh grins.

"Well, all right, then." I turn my attention to Henn, popping up from my chair. "Get up, Henny. We're gonna role-play." I let my eyes drift suggestively to Josh. "One of my very favorite things to do, actually." I wink.

The smoldering look on Josh's face tells me he understands my meaning just fine.

"Come on, Henn. Get up."

Henn stands warily.

"Okay. We're at a bar. You see me from across the room. You're interested in me. Go."

"*Go?*"

"Yeah, go. Do what you'd normally do when you see a babe at a bar."

"You want me to do what I usually do when I see a really pretty girl at a bar?"

"Correct."

Henn shrugs, beelines to the front door of the suite, opens the door, and leaves the room. Josh and I look at each other and burst out laughing. After a beat, there's a soft knock at the front door and Josh strides to it, still laughing.

"Thanks," Henn says, re-entering the room. "Damn door locked behind me."

I'm laughing so hard, I'm crying. "Oh, Henny, you're hilare."

"I think maybe my strategy needs a little fine-tuning," Henn says.

"Just a little," I agree. "Okay, so approach me. Come on. Pretend I'm a girl you're interested in."

"Well, that's not hard to do," he mutters.

"Come on. Just be yourself."

Henn stares at me for a long minute and then throws up his hands. "I have no fucking idea what to do." He plops himself into a chair.

"Don't overthink it. The truth is, it doesn't actually matter what you say to a woman—it's all in your attitude. You know how in public speaking, they say to imagine your audience naked?"

"Yeah. You're saying I should imagine you naked? Oops. Too late. I just did." His face turns bright red. "Confession time: that wasn't the first time I've done that. Sorry."

I laugh. "No, no, no. Don't imagine the babe naked—you'll get too flustered. Instead, just imagine your dick is so big, it drags on the ground." I glance at Josh pointedly and he shoots me a naughty smile.

"Do you have any advice that's a bit more *concrete* than that?" Henn asks. "Imagining my dick is dragging on the ground seems a bit *esoteric*."

I laugh. "Okay, I've got a great rule of thumb for you," I say. "Every time you open your mouth to talk to a woman you're interested in—a *babe* you wanna bag—ask yourself this question: 'Is what I'm about to say more or less likely to get me a blowjob?' If the answer is yes, then say it—but if the answer is no, then shut the fuck up."

Josh bursts out laughing.

"Whoa," Henn says.

"Words to live by," Josh says. "Did one of your brothers come up with that little gem?"

"No. That's all me."

"Damn," Josh says. "I think we just discovered who of the three of us is the *real* fucking genius. *Damn*."

"If all men knew that one simple rule," I continue, "the world would be a much happier place."

"Fuck yeah," Josh agrees. "For everyone." He spreads his legs and reaches under the table, presumably adjusting his dick in his pants. "What other tips you got, Madame Professor? I must admit, I'm finding your lesson plan highly educational."

"That's it. I'm done talking. Now it's time for Henny to learn through *doing*. Come on, Henny. Get up. It's role-play time."

Henn scowls at me.

"Oh, come on. This is for your own good. Try to pick me up, using all the advice I just gave you."

Henn grimaces.

"Get up. Come on," I say.

Henn begrudgingly stands.

"Okay. We're in a bar. I'm a babe you're interested in bagging. *Go*."

"Bars aren't really my thing, actually. I have a lot more success at places like, you know, Starbucks. Gimme a woman with a laptop in Starbucks, preferably a cute little brunette with glasses, and I'm Don Juan."

"Okay. Fine. We're in Starbucks. I've got a laptop. *Go*."

"Brown hair and glasses?"

"You bet. Now *go*."

"Well, is your laptop a Mac or a PC?"

I make a face. "Whichever. That's not important. *Go*."

"Not *important*? Are you *mad*?"

"Okay, fine." I roll my eyes. "A Mac. Now, *go*."

"Can you be more specific, please? What model? A Mac Book Pro? Or a Mac Book Air? And how many gigabytes of memory?"

"Holy Filibuster, Batman!" I shout.

Josh laughs.

"No more stalling, Henn," I say. "Come on. *Goooooooooo*."

"*Fine*." He closes his eyes briefly, and when he opens them, he's clearly got his Casanova face on. "Um. Oh, hi there, pretty brunette lady with glasses. I'm Hennessy. I was wondering, is your name 'Wi Fi' by any chance?"

I make a face. "Is my name '*Wi Fi*'?" I ask, not comprehending his meaning.

"Yeah, because I really feel a *connection* to you."

We all laugh together.

"I told you, I have no idea," Henn says, smiling shyly. "The initial approach is the hardest thing for me."

"You just have to act like it's a foregone conclusion," Josh says. "Make her think it's her lucky day you've graced her with your attention."

I roll my eyes. "Oh, this I gotta see. Show us how you do it, Playboy."

"Oh, you wanna see how I do it, huh?"

"Hell yeah. Razzle-dazzle us, Playboy."

He smirks. "You sure you can handle it?"

"Pretty sure."

"Okay, I'll show you the Playboy razzle-dazzle, but I gotta warn you, even in role-play, it's gonna make you wanna sleep with me."

"I'll risk it."

"Just sayin'—you've been warned."

"I'll risk it," I say again.

"I think you should sign a waiver first."

I roll my eyes. "Just give it to me already."

"That's exactly what you'll say after I show you the Playboy razzle-dazzle."

I laugh. "We'll see about that. Come on."

"Fine. But we're at a bar, not Starbucks. At least let me play on my home turf."

"Okay," I say. "We're at a bar. *Go*."

Josh slowly gets up from his chair and sidles up to me, taking his sweet time.

"Hey, beautiful," he says smoothly. "I'm Josh." He puts out his hand.

I take his hand. "Hi, I'm Kat."

He leans into me, close enough for me to get a whiff of his cologne, and my knees instantly go weak.

He whispers softly into my ear. "What are you drinking, Kat?"

My clit zings. "A mojito," I choke out.

He turns to Henn. "Hey, bartender, another mojito for the gorgeous lady with the sexy little cleft in her chin." He looks at me and levels me with a dark blue smolder that makes my clit pound like a jackhammer. "You ready to get out of here, sweetheart? Because I'm in the mood to make you feel so fucking good," he whispers, almost inaudibly, skimming his hand down my arm. "Before you answer, you should know: I've got a huge dick and I know exactly how to use it to make you scream. All you need to decide is whether you wanna have the night of your life."

There's a long beat during which I feel warm wetness literally ooze into the crotch of my panties.

"What do you say, honey? You ready to go?"

I nod.

"Let's go."

He holds out his hand and I take it.

All of a sudden, I want one thing: for Josh to pull me out the door and straight to my room. But, instead, Josh releases my hand and turns to Henn, smiling.

"Badah-bing-badah-boom," he says. "Easy peasy. Now you try it. Just like that."

"Ummmmmmmm," Henn says. "Could you be serious, please? I actually wanna know what you do, no kidding around."

"I wasn't kidding around. That's what I do."

Henn laughs. "Come on, Josh."

Josh whips his attention onto me. "Kat, in all seriousness—would that have worked on you if I did it just like that?"

"In all seriousness?" I say. Oh man, my heart is racing out of my chest. "*Hell yes.*"

"See?" Josh says. He shrugs. "Success with babe-baggery is all about confidence. Everything else is secondary." He sits back down, a cocky grin on his face. "Thank you, Kat." He winks. "You're excellent at role-play—not surprisingly."

I sit back down, flustered.

"It always boils down to confidence," Josh says. "Am I right, Madame Professor?"

"Yeah," I say, struggling to regain my composure. Oh shit. There's a deep, dull ache in my abdomen that won't go away. I clear my throat. "But don't forget, Josh, getting the babe hooked on the line is only the first step—then you've actually got to be able to *deliver* on all that bravado or else you're sunk." I shoot Josh a smart-ass look that, hopefully, says, "You're full of shit."

Josh's eyes are brimming with confidence. "Well, duh. It goes without saying a guy's gotta be able to deliver on everything he promises—that's where true confidence comes from, being able to walk the walk." He winks. "'Under-promise and over-perform,' I always say. And believe me, I just under-promised on what I can perform."

Oh holy hell. I can't breathe.

"So let's start simple, then," Josh says to Henn. "The first step is being able to kiss a woman like a boss. For women, kissing is everything—you gotta be able to curl her toes, man. From there, all good things will come to you.

Kiss a woman right, she'll be begging you for more. Am I right, Madame Professor?"

I shoot Josh a pointed look. "Yep. No doubt about it. Begging."

Josh bites his lip.

"Well, no sweat, guys. Because I happen to be a fantastic kisser."

"Really?" I ask, surprised.

"Yup."

"*Fantastic?*"

"Well, okay, maybe not *fantastic*. But pretty damned good."

"What's your technique?"

"My *technique?* Well, I can't *describe* it. It's a show-me-don't-tell-me kind of thing."

"Well, you gotta give me something to work with here, Henny. How else am I gonna be able to give you feedback?"

"I can't describe it," Henn says, shrugging his shoulders. "You'll just have to trust me."

"Try explaining it to me, Henn," I say. "Josh is right—that first kiss can make or break you—lead you to the Promised Land or sink you like a stone." I flash Josh a smart-ass look. "You gotta get it right."

Josh squints at me. "Yeah, Kat's right. But that's only because women some-times place ridiculous importance on what should be a simple kiss—irrational, ridiculous, stupid importance—when they should just chill out and go with the flow and stop acting like a fucking terrorist."

"Jesus, Josh," Henn says.

Josh's eyes are locked with mine. I squint at him, and he returns the gesture.

"Why don't you just *show* her, bro?" Josh says, still looking at me. "That's the simplest way for us to approach this."

My face involuntarily morphs into a "what the fuck" look.

"You don't mind, do you, Kat?" Josh asks evenly.

"You mean... you want me to . . .?" Henn asks.

"Yeah, why not?" Josh says. "Unless, of course, Kat's gonna require you to reveal all your secrets in order to kiss her?"

I narrow my eyes at Josh and then whip my head to look at Henn. "I think it's a great idea for you to kiss me. How else are we gonna know if you've got the right technique?"

Henn's face is bright red. "I don't think this is such a good idea, guys."

"Why the fuck not?" I say. I look at Josh with defiance. "It's just for instruc-tional purposes, right? No big deal." Josh isn't really gonna let me kiss another man in his presence, is he—even if it's just Henn? Even if it's just for "instruc-tional purposes"?

"I agree," Josh says, clenching his jaw.

I open my mouth, horrified. What the *fuck?* He's gotta be bluffing.

"The woman obviously places a shit-ton of importance on kissing," Josh continues. "So I'm sure her feedback will be invaluable to you." His eyes are searing holes into my flesh.

There's no way he's gonna let me go through with this, right?

"No, it's too weird," Henn says. "I mean, you two guys are a couple... right?"

"Josh and me?" I say through gritted teeth. "Noooo. Josh and I haven't even kissed—and we've mutually decided we're not going to. Ever. We just don't see eye to eye on certain things."

Josh swallows hard, his eyes burning. "Kat's right. We're never going to kiss because she's a fucking terrorist who takes some sort of sick pleasure in holding men hostage for ransom she has no business demanding."

"What am I missing here?" Henn asks. "What's going on with you two?"

"Nothing's going on, like I said. Josh and I are just friends—friends who don't tell each other everything, and therefore don't kiss."

Henn looks confused. "You require someone to tell you 'everything' just to *kiss* you? What does that mean?"

"Nothing. Not *everything*. Just certain things." I clear my throat. "Things I'd tell if the situation were reversed."

Henn and Josh exchange a look.

I look down, color rising in my cheeks. Is Josh really gonna watch me kiss another man?

"Go ahead, Henn," Josh says. "*YOLO.*"

I swivel my head up to look at Josh. He looks like he wants to kill me right now—right after he fucks the living hell out of me.

Well, if he's not gonna stop me, then I'm not gonna stop me, either.

Is Josh really not gonna stop me?

I look at Josh. He's glaring at me. I look at Henn. He looks utterly confused.

"Okay, Henn," I say. "Gimme your best kiss. I'll critique you from the field. And, Josh, you watch closely from the nose-bleed seats so you can give Henn your feedback, too."

Josh doesn't reply.

"Did you hear me, Josh? I want you to watch Henn kiss me—watch *closely.*"

"I heard you, Madame Terrorist."

Henn looks at Josh, seemingly for permission.

"Go ahead," Josh says. "Kiss her. She's all yours." He exhales and leans back in his chair, crossing his arms over his chest.

He's really not gonna stop me? Goddammit! I feel like stomping my feet, I'm so mad. Doesn't he realize this whole thing's not about his stupid application anymore? We're way beyond that now. Now it's about something more—something bigger.

"Kat?" Henn asks. "Are you okay?"

I wipe my eyes, emotion threatening. I don't look at Josh—I can't. I'm afraid if I do, my eyes will betray every last thought bouncing around in my head. I want him. I want him so bad, I'm aching. But I want all of him. Not just his lips or his very large dick. I want to know what's hiding beneath his Happy Josh mask. "Yeah, I'm fine. Let's do this," I say.

"You're sure you're cool with it?" Henn asks me.

"Yeah. I'm sure." I stand. "I can't think of a single reason not to."

I can feel Josh's eyes on me, but I don't look at him.

Henn stands slowly.

"And you're cool, Josh?"

"Yup."

My chest is tight. I still can't look at Josh. "Okay," I say. "Gimme your top-of-the-line smooch, Henny. Hit me with your best shot."

Henn takes a slow step toward me. "You're sure?"

"I'm sure." I put my finger up. "Just for instructional purposes, though."

"Yeah, I know." Henn exhales. "Should I go brush my teeth first? Have a mint?"

"Did you eat onions or garlic recently?"

"No. Chocolate cake, apple pie, cheesecake, ice cream. Oh, and tiramisu."

"We're good, then."

He exhales and shakes out his arms. "Whew. Okay."

Henn takes another step toward me. And then another. But then he stops. He glances at Josh—but since I can't bring myself to look at Josh's face right now, I have no idea what Henn is seeing over there. Whatever it is, Henn obviously feels emboldened by it, because he turns back to me and takes another step, bridging the final gap between our bodies.

Henn cups my face gently in his palms and leans forward.

I close my eyes and, within half a second, Henn's soft, warm lips meet mine, gently at first—as if he's introducing himself to me—and after a few seconds, coax my mouth open with surprising confidence and skill. He slides his tongue into my mouth, instantly leading my tongue into a sensuous, languid, swirling motion—until, after one last flicker of his tongue, his lips guide mine closed and he retreats.

Henn's lips leave mine. Kiss over.

Holy shitballs.

I open my eyes to find Henn staring at me, his eyes wide and face red.

I glance at Josh, my cheeks suddenly blazing with heat, and my breath catches at the ferocious expression on his face. I don't know Josh well enough to understand exactly what emotion he's telegraphing right now—is that anger, arousal, jealousy... or something else? Whatever it is, it's clear to me the man is feeling something fueled by a shit-ton of testosterone.

"I... That was... um . . ." I stammer. "Wow, Henn." I swallow hard. "I don't think you need... any... instruction whatsoever."

25

JOSH

Jesus Christ. Enough, already. When will this torturous kiss between Henn and Kat end? *Enough*. Well, now I know: I'm dealing with a fucking monster. A gorgeous, twisted, evil, sexy fucking monster. I didn't think she'd actually go *through* with it. What the fuck is she thinking? Poor Henn's never gonna recover from this goddamned kiss. I'm only watching it, and she's scarring me for life.

After what seems like forever, Henn and Kat *finally* break away from their kiss, and Kat's eyes instantly dart to me. I steel myself, expecting her to smile like the vicious shark she is—like the prehistoric *killing* machine she is—but the look on her face absolutely floors me. Her eyes aren't blazing with smart-ass defiance, no—they're glistening with something else... *Hurt.*

Henn hasn't stopped staring at Kat since they broke apart from their kiss, even though she's looking at me. Jesus, the poor guy looks like he just stumbled out of a hookah lounge.

Clearly, I've got to say something to smooth things out here, even though I'm literally trembling in my seat with adrenaline.

"Awesome, Henn," I say. "You nailed it man—or should I say *her*?"

Kat's face contorts into unbridled disgust.

Henn fidgets and takes a step back.

"I watched your technique carefully, man," I continue breezily, "looking for any chink in your armor. But I couldn't find a damned thing to critique. *You* should be giving *me* pointers, man."

"Yeah, you slayed it, Henn," Kat adds, her voice tight. Her mouth smiles, but her eyes don't. "All I've got is praise, baby."

I stand abruptly. "Well, I think I'm gonna hit the sack. I'm pretty wiped."

Kat stands. "Me, too. Unless you still need some more help, Henn?"

"No, I'm good. I can take it from here." He looks at his watch and clears his throat. "Wow, it's almost three. I'm gonna get another Americano and start going through the first batch of stuff that's been processed through translation software." He looks at his three laptops sprawled on the table. "Should I move my shit to my room and work there?"

"Nah, no worries. Stay put. I'm just gonna crash. Gimme your room key, man. I'll crash in your room." My eyes flicker briefly to Kat to get a read on her —to see if maybe she's toying with the idea of letting me "crash" in her room for the night—and I'm met with blue eyes of steel. My eyes dart back to Henn. "What's your room number again, man?"

"1836."

"Okay, well, nighty night, man." I slide Henn's key-card into my pocket. "Don't drink too many Americanos. That shit'll kill you." I start moving toward the front door of the suite. "Come on, Kat. I'll walk you to your room."

"No need."

"I promised Jonas I wouldn't leave you alone while we're here in Vegas, unless you're safely in your room."

She clenches her jaw. "Well, we wouldn't want you to break a promise to Jonas, would we?"

"Thanks again for all the help tonight, guys," Henn says. "You cut my workload down by hours."

"Any time, bro. We're all in this together."

Kat hugs Henn and kisses him on the cheek. "You're amazing, Henn—a fucking genius."

"So I've been told."

"And thanks for the kiss," she says. "I know it was for instructional purposes only, but it was a really, really lovely kiss."

"Really?"

"Yeah. One for the memory book."

"Hang on a sec, Kat," I say. I quickly gather my toiletries and a change of clothes from the bedroom and stuff everything into a small duffel bag. "Okay. See you in the morning, Henn. Do you need anything from your room?"

"No. I'll call down to the front desk for a toothbrush. I'm fine."

"Okay. Good night, man."

I silently guide Kat through the front door of the suite.

"It's all fun and games 'til someone gets hurt," I mutter the second the door closes behind us.

"I couldn't agree more," she says, gritting her teeth.

"Didn't look like you gave a shit about someone getting hurt a minute ago," I reply.

She whips around to face me, her eyes blazing. "What the *fuck* is wrong with you?" she asks.

"I could say the same thing to you. Are you a complete sociopath?"

"What? You're the one who offered me up like I was a wench at a pirate-bride auction."

"Ha! I didn't think you'd actually *do* it. I hope you're happy now. You've ruined that boy."

"*I've* ruined him? You're the one who threw me at him! And now you're all pissy because I did exactly what you told me to do?" she seethes. "Who's the sociopath now?"

I throw up my hands in frustration.

"It looks like I'm not the only one who's a suicide bomber, huh?" she says. "Looks like you're willing to blow yourself up to win every bit as much as I am."

She's right about that. Fuck. I'm a fucking suicide bomber, goddammit. What's happening to me? Kat's driving me certifiably insane.

Wordlessly, I grab her arm and pull her to the elevators—I'm gonna drag her to her room and ditch her sorry ass there, let her think about what she just did to poor Henn—what she just did to me, goddammit—but when the doors open, something overtakes me. This woman makes me fucking crazy. I can't get enough of her, even when she pisses me off.

I pull her inside the elevator, drop my duffel bag, and slam her against the fucking wall, pressing my hard-on into her and kissing her neck.

She moans loudly. "Yes," she breathes.

"Stop torturing me," I say, groping her breasts. "No more fucking games."

She throws her head back and lifts her leg around my waist, guiding my hard-on into her crotch. I grind into her, pinning her hands above her head, licking and kissing her face, her ears, her chin—but not her lips. Fuck no, not her lips. There's no fucking way.

The doors open. We're on her floor. I pick up the duffel and drag her out of the elevator roughly and into the hallway, but we don't make it more than a few steps before I'm attacking her again. Goddamn this woman. I pin her to the wall again, just outside the elevator, and unbutton her jeans, sliding my hand inside her pants. She cries out as my fingers slide into her pussy. Oh God, she's so wet. My dick is throbbing mercilessly. I can't stand this anymore. I've got to have her. "You're evil," I say, sliding my fingers in and out of her. "You're so fucking evil."

She moans loudly as my fingers fuck her furiously.

She begins pawing at the front of my jeans, trying to unbutton my fly.

"I've got to have you," I growl. "Fuck this shit, Kat. Come on."

"Yes," she says. "Do it. Come on."

The nearby elevator dings.

I pull my hand out of her pants and leap back from her, shaking with my arousal, and a small group of forty-something women tumble out of the elevator, laughing hysterically.

"Which way?" I mumble. "I forget your room number."

She points. "2715."

I grab her arm and yank her toward her room, my cock throbbing, my nostrils flaring. "No more bullshit. I'm fucking you right now. This is over right now."

"Why didn't you stop me?" she asks as I drag her down the hallway.

"Because I didn't think you were gonna actually go through with it."

"I thought for sure you were gonna stop me."

We've reached her room. "Gimme your key. I'm fucking you right now."

She exhales. Something in her eyes has shifted. "No, wait." She swallows hard. "Why didn't you stop me?" Her eyes are glistening with obvious hurt. "I thought you wouldn't be able to stand seeing another man kiss me—even Henn."

My heart squeezes. She looks authentically hurt.

"Kat," I say, shocked at the genuine emotion on her face.

"I thought you'd stop me." She wipes her watering eyes.

Oh, shit. I've fucked up here, haven't I? I've really fucked up.

"I just..." I begin, my head reeling. "I thought we were in a... battle to the death... I was... just trying to force your hand."

Why does she look like she's about to cry?

Kat wipes her eyes again. "I'm tired of battling to the death, Josh," she says softly, exhaling. "Or maybe I'm just plain tired." She motions to her room. "You wanna fuck me, but you don't wanna take off your mask. Sorry, but I'm not interested."

I'm speechless.

She exhales a long breath. "I'm just gonna get some sleep tonight. I'm totally sleep deprived."

"What? No. Let me come in with you."

"Why? What's the point?" Her blue eyes have steeled over. "Thanks for walking me to my room." She turns to swipe her key-card in the lock.

"Kat, wait." I grab her arm.

She freezes.

My pulse is pounding in my ears. How did we go from attacking each other in the elevator to this? What just happened?

"I'm sorry, Kat," I say. "I... thought you'd back down. I was just... I didn't understand. I didn't know it would hurt your feelings."

She stares at me, apparently waiting for me to continue.

But I don't. I don't know what else to say.

"I think I just need a short break from the game—or maybe I just need a little sleep. Either way, I just wanna crash."

"Kat, wait," I say, squeezing her arm gently. "Let me come in. Talk to me."

She shakes her head. "Why won't you just tell me what's in your application? How bad can it really be? I'm clearly not Snow White—I'm sure I'll understand. What's the big deal at this point?"

I don't reply.

"Is it S&M, Josh? Is that what you're into? Because I wouldn't care."

"Just, please. Enough. Stop pushing for this. It's gonna backfire. Trust me. It's gonna backfire and we won't be able to stuff that genie back into the bottle."

"But if I give in now where would we go from there?" She wipes her eyes again. "I admit I've fucked this up. Okay? I've taken it too far, created a no-win situation—I admit that." Her eyes water. "But it is what it is. And now I can't figure out an endgame besides seeing it through to the bitter end. If I don't insist on it now, then it'll always be this big 'thing' between us. I'll always wonder what the hell you're hiding from me."

I swallow hard. "It's not that big a deal, okay? It's really not. It's just that I don't talk about certain things," I say softly. "I'm not always Happy Josh, okay? I'm not always what I seem. And you reading that application would force me to spill my guts to you in a way... I'm not willing to do."

She twists her mouth. "I never spill my guts, either, Josh. I hate spilling my guts, believe me. But if I had an application, I'd give it to you," she says softly. "I really would, Josh. I'd spill my guts to you, if the situation were reversed."

"Easy for you to say. The situation's not reversed."

"But if it were, I'd tell you my secrets." Her lip is trembling.

I can't formulate a reply. She's breaking my heart. I don't understand what's happening. I haven't even kissed this goddamned girl and I feel like she's got a stranglehold on my fucking heart.

I shake my head, at a loss. I'm stuck between a rock and a hard place. She says if she gives in and quits the battle, she'd never trust me? But it works the same way on my end, doesn't it? If I tuck my dick and balls between my legs and give her what she wants, if I act like a pussy-whipped little puss who can be manipulated into doing puppy tricks for her, where the fuck could we possibly go from there? We'd be doomed.

"I'm not gonna give it to you," I say evenly. "If you wanna get with me, then get with me. If you don't, then don't. That application shouldn't have anything to do with it, either way."

Her eyes are unreadable to me. She sighs. "I think maybe we should just concentrate on saving the world for a bit, okay? Things have gotten out of control. That's my fault, not yours. I'm sorry about that." Her eyes suddenly flood with tears. "I think we should just take a break on battling to the death for a while—concentrate on saving the world."

"Kat. Wait. Let me come in. Not to fuck you. Just to be with you. Just to sleep next to you."

"Josh, we're obviously two suicide bombers on opposing missions—both of us stubborn as hell. We're not a good combination." She opens her door. "Thanks for walking me to my room. I appreciate it." She slips inside her room, and her voice travels through the gap in the door, just before it closes. "I'm sorry, Josh. Good night."

26

KAT

"Well, to summarize," Henn begins, "we're dealing with some big shit here, fellas. Like, oh my fucking God." He cracks a huge smile. "Totally awesome."

We're all gathered around the table in the early afternoon light of Jonas and Sarah's suite to hear the latest on what Henn's uncovered about The Club—much of it, apparently, after Josh and I left the suite last night around 3:00 a.m.

Josh slipped into our meeting after me, looking groggy and bleary-eyed, and took a seat at the table next to me, nodding curtly as he sat down, his face tight and his eyes unreadable.

"Just tell me—were you able to get into The Club's system?" Jonas asks Henn.

"No, not yet. Wherever it is, it's buried deep, deep, deep in the web, way deep. But I'm getting close. I've got lots of breadcrumbs to follow. I'm hot on their trail, fellas. And very pretty ladies." He smiles at me and winks at Sarah.

"You should have seen how Henn figures things out," I say, pointedly not looking at Josh to my left. "He's a techno-Sherlock Holmes."

"The man's a fucking genius," Josh adds. He puts his right arm across the back of my chair as he speaks, but I lean forward in my chair to avoid letting his arm cradle my back. Just one touch and I'll melt. And I don't feel like melting right now.

Josh exhales with frustration, but I don't look at him.

"What do we know so far?" Jonas asks.

Henn launches into telling Jonas and Sarah what he (and Josh and I) discovered last night: namely, that The Club's operations are way bigger than any of us expected.

"What about a member list? Any luck on that?" Sarah asks.

My phone buzzes with an incoming text and I take a quick peek. Shoot. It's from my boss. This isn't gonna be good. I've been putting her off for days.

I open the message:

"Kat!" my boss writes. "Wow, wow, wow! Just got the signed contract and full retainer from this new client of yours! Holy crap! Biggest up-front retainer we've ever landed, by far. I know you're in meetings all day on your new account (!), but call me ASAP. I want to hear all the details. If you need me to fly to Las Vegas to help you with *anything* just say the word. Fantastic work! Of course, take as long as you need out there. Just check in occasionally to give me an update so we can manage our workload internally. Keep up the great work! We'll drink champagne when you get back!"

I keep reading and re-reading the email, not comprehending what my eyes are seeing and feeling like I've slipped into some sort of gap in the space-time continuum. Did I take acid and not remember? Have I been roofied? What the *hell* is she talking about?

I look at Josh, but he's listening intently to whatever Henn's saying.

"The identity of that über VIP guy seems like something we'd better nail down," Henn is saying. "His emails are double encrypted, but I cracked an email from Oksana to Max forwarding one of the über VIP guy's emails—and the guy said shit like 'my security personnel will post outside the door.' He's got security personnel? And they 'post' outside doors? Like, who the fuck says that?"

"A rock star?" Sarah suggests. "Guys like that always have bodyguards."

"No," Henn says. "Not based on what I've seen."

"Yeah, I know plenty of rock stars with bodyguards—and they don't talk like that," Josh says.

"I'll keep working on it," Henn says. "Okay, so are you guys ready for your minds to be officially blown?"

"You mean there's *more*?" Sarah asks.

"Oh yeah. The next part is what makes this so much fun." Henn looks at me. "I figured this next part out right after you left last night."

I look at the group apologetically. "I finally had to get some sleep."

"That's what happens when you don't subsist on a diet of caffeine and nicotine," Henn says.

"Did you leave to get some sleep, too?" Jonas asks Josh, flashing him a knowing look.

"Yeah, I couldn't keep up with Henn, either," Josh says. "I think I left around the time Kat left." He glances at me, his eyes full of apology. "Maybe just a little bit later."

It suddenly hits me like a thunderbolt: *Josh.* Whatever my boss was just babbling about in her email, it was Josh's doing.

I ask Henn a question absentmindedly, requesting clarification on something, but my mind is shifting into frenetic overdrive. There's no doubt in my mind: Josh contacted my boss and requested my personal "PR services" out here in Las Vegas.

"Oh my God," Josh mumbles in response to something Henn just said, his entire body stiffening next to me. He pulls his hand away from the back of my chair and rubs his eyes like he's blown away by something. Uh oh. I wasn't paying attention. What did I just miss?

"What?" I ask, my stomach twisting with dread.

"They're funding the Ukrainian separatists," Josh answers, his face draining of color.

I don't have the faintest idea what the hell that means.

"Which means Oksana's funding Putin through the back door," Jonas adds, as if that would make things clearer for me.

But it doesn't. Ukrainian separatists? Putin? Who's Putin? That sounds familiar, but I forget. Wait, isn't he that Russian guy? Obviously, I just missed something major when my brain was fixated on my boss' email.

"You guys, break it down for me," I say. "Sorry."

"Okay, back in the day, there was the U.S.S.R., right?" Jonas says. "Then it got broken up into all these pieces—Russia and Ukraine and the Baltic states. Well, now Putin wants to put all the pieces of mother Russia back together again, to resurrect the former empire—and he wants the diamond of his new Soviet Union to be Ukraine."

"And is Ukraine down with that plan?" I ask, wishing I'd paid more attention in my political science class in college. I honestly don't even know exactly where Ukraine is, to be honest.

"No, not the official government," Jonas says. "But there's a faction within Ukraine—the *separatists*—and they want to *separate* from their government and go along with Putin's reunification plan. So the separatists have waged armed conflicts with their own government, funded by the Russians."

Jonas and Josh exchange a look of extreme anxiety.

"Holy shitballs," I say softly, even though, honestly, I'm still not one hundred percent sure I get it. Whatever's happening, though, it's obviously holy-shitballs-worthy.

"Yeah, most definitely," Henn says. "Well said."

"We've got to find out who Mr. Bigwig VIP is," Jonas blurts. "We need to know who all the heavy hitters are. You said congressmen are involved in this shit, right?"

"Yup," Henn says.

"That could be really, really bad," Josh says, his body stiff and tight next to mine. His face looks ashen.

"Seriously. 'Oh, hi, constituents. Please re-elect me,'" Henn says, putting on his best congressman-voice. "'I added more police to our streets, got a library built, and voted to increase the minimum wage. Oh, *and* I paid a whole bunch of money to a Ukrainian prostitution and weapons ring to fund the reunification of the Soviet Union. Can I count on your vote during the next election?'"

Oooooh, I totally get it now. Leave it to Henn to explain things in terms I can easily understand. Ooph. Holy shitballs, indeed. This is a big deal.

"This is too big for us to handle on our own," Sarah declares emphatically. "We've got to hand this over to the FBI." Her eyes widen. "Or the CIA? I don't even know which one. I mean, jeez, I'm a first-year law student at U Dub." She shakes her head. "This is like, a matter of international significance—and that's not even an exaggeration."

Henn talks for a while, explaining how he plans to obtain the bad guys' passwords and banking information, all with the goal of uncovering data we can use to convince the good guys to take immediate action—and, suddenly, I feel like a round hole in a square peg. What the heckity-heck am I doing here? How can I possibly help with all this? I know what value everyone else in this room brings to our *Ocean's Eleven* crew, but what on earth is my role?

When Henn finishes talking, Sarah leaps out of her chair like a woman possessed.

"Henn, I'm your new best friend," she says.

She explains she's gonna write a kick-ass report with supporting documentation which we'll submit to the authorities and we all agree enthusiastically with her plan.

"Kat," Sarah says sharply at the end of her passionate speech, her eyes like lasers.

"Yes, ma'am." My heart's beating out of my chest. My brain is in overload. I keep thinking "Holy shitballs" on an endless loop.

"For each and every criminal count, I'm gonna need a piece of supporting evidence—something to show them we're not making this stuff up," Sarah says, looking at me. She's in full ass-kicking mode now. "I'll tell you exactly what kind of thing I'm looking for, and then you'll go digging through whatever Henn's been able to find so far to get it for me. You'll be my research assistant."

"I can do that," I say, my stomach churning. But what I'm thinking is, "*Holy shitballs.*"

"That's good," Jonas says. "And Josh and I will powwow and figure out our best strategy for the hand-off. I agree—we're going to have to turn this over to *someone*—but to whom? That's the question. If we put it in the wrong hands, we might just buy ourselves an even bigger enemy than The Club."

"What does that mean?" I ask, the hairs on my arms standing up.

"It sounds like there are plenty of powerful people on that client list who wouldn't want this scandal to see the light of day," Jonas says.

Josh puts his arm around my shoulders and I lean into him, shaking. This whole thing is making my head spin and my stomach churn. "Holy shitballs," I say under my breath.

"It's all gonna come down to the money," Jonas says. "Money talks."

"I agree," Josh says, pulling me into him.

"Henn, that's top priority, okay?" Jonas says. "Track the money. Get access to it."

"Roger," Henn says. "Shouldn't take me more than a couple days."

"We can do this," Sarah says. "Look at the talent in this room. We don't need no stinkin' George Clooney and Brad Pitt and Matt Damon."

"Yeah, but I sure wish we had that Chinese acrobat guy," Henn says. "He was cool."

Finally, someone in this room who speaks my freaking language.

"The one they stuffed into the little box?" I ask. "I loved him."

Henn beams a smile at me that instantly calms my raging nerves. "Yeah, he was rad."

"Yen. Wasn't that his name?"

"Oh *yeah*. Good memory, Kat." He taps his temple. "Brains *and* beauty."

I return his beaming smile. Thank God for Henny.

"Hey, guys, sorry to interrupt your profound musings, but I'm kind of getting tunnel vision here," Sarah says. "There's a lot to do and I wanna get started right away."

"Sure thing," I say (even though I'm thinking "holy shitballs"). "Whatever you need, boss."

"Hey, Sarah," Henn says. "One more thing. What do you wanna do about Dr. Evil's text to you?"

Sarah's face turns bright red.

"I'm monitoring his phone, remember?" Henn says, motioning to his laptop. "'I'm not a patient man.' What was *that* all about?"

27

KAT

Sarah sputters and stammers for a moment, clearly incapable of responding to Henn's question, so Jonas grabs her hand and speaks for her, telling the group about how Max demanded a "freebie" from Sarah yesterday at The Club's offices and then followed up with a creepy-skeevy text demanding she come through.

"What should I do?" Sarah asks the group, obviously wracked with anxiety. "Ignore him? Answer him? Hide?"

"Ignore him and hide," Jonas says firmly. "I don't want you saying a fucking thing to that motherfucker."

"I agree," Josh says, clenching his jaw. "Ignore him and hide."

Finally, something I know a shit-ton about. *Men.*

"No," I say emphatically, straightening up in my chair. "*Answer* him and hide. Ignoring him will piss him off, and we don't want to piss that guy off. We want to keep him calm and confident and predictable."

There's a brief silence while everyone mulls over what I've just said.

"Dr. Evil's real boner isn't for Sarah—it's for Jonas," I continue.

"Jesus, Kat," Jonas says, grimacing. "Please don't say it that way."

I can feel Josh's eyes trained on me, and suddenly, I feel emboldened. I might not be the sharpest knife in the drawer when it comes to braniac stuff like hacking and world politics and legal research and figuring out how to take down a global crime syndicate, but when it comes to men and PR, I'm flippin' Einstein, peeps.

"Not *sexually*," I say. "He's got an *alpha-male* boner for you, Jonas. This is all about a beta silverback wanting to knock off the obvious alpha. He wants what you've got so he can *win.* Hence, his Jonas-boner."

"For Chrissakes, *please* stop saying that," Jonas says.

"So how should I reply to him, then?" Sarah asks.

"We have to keep him off your back and convince him you're motivated solely by greed and absolutely *not* by loyalty to Jonas," I say. "The more he thinks your interests are the same as his, the safer you'll be. You've got to keep him trusting you. If you ignore him, he'll start getting paranoid."

Sarah looks at Jonas and he nods like he's in agreement with everything I've said—and when I glance at Josh, he nods encouragingly, a smile dancing on his lips—so I forge ahead. "Tell Max not to text—Jonas is monitoring your phone," I say, "and he's just on the cusp of giving you another humongous check. That way, you play right into his egomania and also appeal to his greed. No matter how much he wants his little freebie to satisfy his Jonas-boner—"

"Okay, Kat, that's enough," Jonas cautions.

"—he won't insist on it at the risk of sabotaging the scam. We'll just make Jonas out to be the bad guy and let Sarah sound like she's doing her best to manage him and keep the money rolling in."

Everyone's staring at me, but no one's saying a word.

I glance at Josh again and the look on his face right now is unmistakable: I've surprised him.

I shrug. "What? There are two things I know well in this life—PR and men."

Josh laughs a full-throated laugh and beams a heart-stopping smile at me, quite obviously thoroughly impressed.

"Nice," Henn says, grinning broadly at me.

"Hey, I might be *dumb*," I say, "but I'm not *blonde*."

Everyone laughs and so do I—but the way Josh is laughing and smiling is making me do more than laugh; it's making me sizzle and pop like Rice Krispies in milk.

Josh grabs my hand and squeezes it, his eyes blazing at me. "Does everyone agree with Kat on this? Because I most certainly do."

Everyone expresses enthusiastic agreement with everything I've said, and I feel myself swell with pride.

Josh leans into my ear, still squeezing my hand. "I do believe this little fishy just went for a swim in the river." He kisses the top of my hand.

I look at him quizzically and he smiles broadly.

"Trust me, I won't," Sarah is saying in response to something Jonas just said. "Now that I know that creep's out there watching me, I have no desire to leave the suite ever again. I've got to hunker down and write my report, anyway. This is going to be a huge job." Sarah shakes her head. "This is so crazy."

"It's totally insane," Henn agrees, exhaling happily. "Isn't it *awesome*?"

Henn and Sarah begin chatting about their strategy for gathering the mountain of data and documents Sarah needs for her report and my attention drifts to Josh. He's staring right at me, his eyes smoldering.

"Hey, Josh," I whisper. "Can I talk to you for a minute over there?"

"My pleasure."

We move to a sitting area in the corner of the suite, away from the rest of the group.

"What's up, Party Girl with a Hyphen?" Josh asks. He leans back in his chair, making himself comfortable.

"I got a really interesting email from my boss a little while ago," I say.

"Oh yeah?" he asks. "What'd it say?"

"It seems I've somehow managed to secure a huge new account for my firm —an account I've apparently been working on while I've been here in Vegas, all while getting shitfaced and barfing on your shoes—an account that's so big and important and *lucrative* my boss told me to 'stay in Vegas as long as needed.'"

"Wow. Sounds like a big account. Congratulations."

"What did you do, Josh?"

He bites his lip. "Not a whole lot. I just picked up the phone and called a friend, that's all."

"Josh, what's going on?"

He smiles broadly. "It seems one of the owners of the hottest nightclub in Las Vegas, a good friend of mine—a guy named Reed?—remember him?—well, Reed met you the other night and you two got to talking and you wound up blowing him away with a thousand amazing ideas for raising the visibility and branding for his club. And now, understandably, he wants *you* personally, and only *you*, to work on a massive PR campaign for his club all month. He's redoing *all* the branding, at your suggestion, which is a huge job. Of course, he understands what a major inconvenience it is, having your personal, undivided attention for so long all the way out here in Vegas, so he was very happy to pay a ridiculous premium for your exclusive services—up front."

I'm speechless.

"Pretty straightforward." He beams a huge smile at me.

"But... is there an actual campaign? Something I actually have to *do* in exchange for this payment?"

"Well, there's no actual PR campaign," he says. "But, yes, you have to *do* something in exchange for the payment. Of course."

I raise an eyebrow. "And what would that be?" I feel heat rising in my cheeks.

"Well, *obviously*, you've gotta help us topple the Evil Empire and save the world." He shrugs. "You're a fucking PR-genius, Kat. If I didn't already know that about you, you sure proved it in spades a minute ago."

I blush.

He puts his hand on my knee and leans forward like he's gonna kiss me, and my breathing catches in my throat. He leans closer, his eyes burning, and I close my eyes, bracing myself for his warm lips against mine. But, nope. No kiss. Instead, I feel the sensation of his fingertip pressing lightly against the cleft in my chin.

I open my eyes.

His blue eyes have darkened.

"We all need you here, Kat—you just proved that. And speaking for myself personally, I have no desire to save the world without my Party Girl with a Hyphen by my side."

28

KAT

For hours and hours, Sarah and I have worked alongside Henn, gathering and assembling evidence for Sarah's report while Josh and Jonas have worked tirelessly on the other side of the room, researching, analyzing, and formulating the big-picture strategy for whatever the heck we're finally gonna do with the report when it's done.

"Dudes, I'm turning into a pumpkin," Henn finally declares, his face the picture of total exhaustion. "I can't uncross my eyes."

"Go crash, Henny," Sarah says. "You've already given us plenty of stuff to work with for the rest of the night."

"I won't sleep too long. There's still an ass-load worth of shit to do. I just need a power nap."

"Hey, Americanos and Red Bulls can only stave off the physical needs of the human body for so long," Sarah says.

"I'll see you pretty ladies later." He stumbles away, bleary-eyed.

"What about you, Kitty Kat?" Sarah asks. "You need a break?"

"Hell no," I answer. "I'm an evidence-assembling machine. Just give me another task and I'm on it."

"Coolio Iglesias," Sarah says. "Let's turn on some music—that always helps me get my second wind." She flips through her music library on her laptop. "Oh, *yes*. My girl, Audra Mae—now there's a voice that inspires greatness." She presses play on a song and a freaking hurricane of a female voice blasts me and jolts me back awake.

"Who's this?" I ask. "Oh my God. She's incredible."

"Audra Mae and the Almighty Sound," Sarah says. "'The Real Thing.'"

"Holy shitballs," I say. "I'm gonna make this my ringtone. I've got goose bumps."

We listen to the song all the way through, and when it ends, I want to hear it again.

"Play it on a loop, Sarah," I say. "I'm already addicted. Gah!"

"Right? I know. She sings right from her soul." She glances at Josh and Jonas across the room, their noses buried in Jonas' laptop. "Hey, how are you boys doing over there? You've been going nonstop for hours."

"Just coming up with a foolproof plan to fuck the bad guys up the ass, baby," Jonas mutters, typing something on his keyboard.

"Jonas, your eyes are bugging out of your head—maybe you should take a short break—like, go work out or something?" Sarah says.

"There's no time for that," Jonas says, not taking his eyes off his screen. "I'm on a mission from God here, baby."

Sarah begins to say something more, but Jonas cuts her off.

"Because I love my baby more than life itself."

Sarah takes in a sharp breath. "Holy crappola," she whispers.

"Holy shitballs," I reply, my heart racing vicariously for her. "Is that the first time?"

She shakes her head. "No, but definitely the first time in front of other people."

"Aw." I grab her hand. "Our little boy is growing up."

Sarah smiles broadly. "That gorgeous man never ceases to surprise me."

"I could say the same thing about that gorgeous man's brother," I say.

I stare at Josh for a long beat. He's wearing jeans and a T-shirt today, a rarity for the ever-fashionable Playboy, and he looks hot as freaking hell. Jesus God, everything about that man—from his taut muscles to the slight wave of his dark hair to his sly smile, even the dragon on his bicep peeking out from his short sleeve—is drawing me to him uncontrollably.

But, damn, he's stubborn. And guarded, too—deceptively so. He comes off as so open and easygoing, but he's hiding darkness under there, I can feel it. I try to imagine Josh fucking me in a bunny suit, but that doesn't ring true. More than likely, he's into S&M, right? He's gotta be some kind of a dom—into whips and chains and butt plugs. I imagine myself calling him "master" in a doggie collar and my clit pulses. I could work with that. Or, whoa, wait, maybe he's a *sub?* Holy Not What I'm Hoping For, Batman. Not at all. That's the thing—it could be *anything.* It's killing me not knowing.

"Kat?" Sarah says.

"Sorry," I say. "Got distracted."

Sarah gives me a document and asks me to scour it for any references to international money transfers.

"Sure thing," I say. But the words on the page are beginning to blur. My head is bobbing on my neck like I'm a drowsy truck driver. I didn't even study this hard in college, for crying out loud.

For the hundredth time tonight, I glance over at Josh across the room. He's engaged in an animated conversation with Jonas about... What the heck are those two jabbering about now?—I strain to listen over the music on Sarah's laptop—oh, which NFL quarterback is the greatest of all time. Well, that's an easy one: *Joe Montana*. Everyone knows that. Duh. Surely, my dad, mom, and three out of four of my brothers would say the same thing.

"It's a no-brainer," Josh says. "*Joe Montana*."

I smile broadly to myself. Josh would fit right in with my family.

"That's the conventional answer," Jonas says. "But I'd argue Peyton Manning has recently overtaken the top spot."

I roll my eyes. Well, that's plain ridiculous.

"No way," Josh says from across the room. "That's fucking ridiculous."

I smile to myself again. Great minds think alike.

Jonas keeps arguing his (ridiculous) position until, suddenly, without warning, Josh reaches up, midsentence, and flicks Jonas' forehead with his index finger.

Jonas abruptly stops talking and puts his hand on his forehead. "*Ow.*"

For a short beat, it's not clear if Jonas is gonna throttle Josh or laugh uncontrollably, but then Jonas' features contort into unmistakable amusement and he lets out a belly laugh, causing Josh to burst out laughing, too. All tension averted, Josh leans back, spreads his legs, and shifts his dick in his pants.

"Dumbshit," Josh mutters, shaking his head.

Jonas chuckles.

"*Peyton Manning.*"

"Sorry," Jonas says, still laughing.

"You should be, bro—you fucking should be."

The boys laugh together a bit more and then finally refocus their attention on Jonas' laptop.

My jaw is hanging open.

My chest is tight.

My pulse is pounding in my ears.

I can't take my eyes off Josh, though all he's doing is staring at a laptop.

Audra Mae is singing from Sarah's laptop into my ear, and suddenly, I realize her lyrics were written for me—for this moment. *I want Josh.* And I'm coming for him, just like Audra Mae is coming for her man in the song.

Josh had better watch the fuck out.

Forget what I said about wanting to take a break from our battle to the death. That was before this moment—before Josh correctly named Joe Montana as the all-time best NFL quarterback of all time. Before Josh defended his (correct) position with a perfectly timed forehead-flick, expertly diffusing potential tension with humor. Before he shifted his donkey-dick in his pants for the umpteenth time, making my crotch burn and my pulse race. Before Audra Mae and the Almighty Sound entered the room and belted out my own feelings into my ear. And, most of all, that was before Josh Faraday paid some ungodly amount of money to my boss so I can continue saving the world here in Las Vegas with him *and* keep my job in Seattle, too. *"And speaking for myself personally, I have no desire to save the world without my Party Girl with a Hyphen by my side,"* Josh said. Holy hell, I get goose bumps just thinking about him saying those words to me.

I want him. I want him. I want him.

And not just sexually, either—I'm way past simply wanting to bang Josh now (though God knows I want to bang him more than I want to breathe). I want Josh to be *mine*—in every conceivable way. I want his body. I want his heart. I want his soul. *And, goddammit, I want his secrets, too.*

Josh says I've been demanding something from him that I can't or won't give him in return? Well, he's got a point about that, actually. But what if I *did* unexpectedly have something to give him in return for his secrets? What if I had secrets of my own to give him—and what if I turned the tables on him and gave them to him *first*?

"If I had an application, I'd give it to you," I told Josh last night outside my room after the Henn-kissing debacle.

"Easy for you to say," Josh replied. *"You don't have one."*

But what if I *did*? That would change everything, wouldn't it?

"Hey, Sarah," I whisper, leaning into her shoulder.

"Hmm?"

"Do you happen to have a copy of an old Club application lying around?"

Sarah pauses what she's doing and looks up. "Um. No, all the applications I had were on my laptop that got stolen."

"And Henn hasn't been able to access member applications yet?"

"Not yet." She puts down the document she's reading with sudden emphasis and looks at me like I've suggested we try to sneak up on the President of the United States and give him a wedgie. "Katherine Morgan, even if we *could* get our hands on Josh's application, you absolutely can't read it without his permission."

I roll my eyes. "I know that. Jeez. Gimme some credit."

Sarah's looking at me like she doesn't buy a word of my bullshit.

I pause. "Okay, yes, I'd read that effing application in a heartbeat if I could get my grubby little hands on it," I say.

Sarah laughs. "I know."

"But I'm not trying to get Josh's application through Henn—I wanna get it directly from Josh. And to do that, I need to see the questions he answered—the questions everyone answers when applying to The Club."

Sarah presses her lips together. "Why?"

I ignore her question. "Do you remember the questions?"

"They're burned into my gray matter for eternity. *Why* do you want them?"

"Would you email them to me, exactly the way they're worded on a standard application?"

Sarah smirks. "Are you by any chance planning to write *answers* to these questions, my dearest friend?"

A smile spreads across my face. "Why, yes, that is the plan, my lovely, darling friend."

"Oh my, my, my. Are you gonna apply to the *Josh Faraday Club,* by any chance?" She shoots me a naughty smile.

"Ooooh, I like that, Sarah. Why, *yes,* I do believe I am," I say slowly, my skin tingling.

"Did Josh *ask* you to apply to his club?"

"No. He has no idea. This is gonna be a surprise—or more like a *blindside.*" I glance furtively across the room at Josh. He and Jonas are chatting calmly about something on Jonas' laptop. "This is gonna be a diabolical tactic to get two suicide bombers to finally lay down their bombs and make nice—very, very *nice.*"

"Well, I'm sure it'll work like gangbusters. The day Kat Morgan can't get a man to bend to her mighty will, the rest of us might as well crawl into bunkers and await the End of Days."

"I'm not so sure this time, to be honest. Josh is the hardest nut to crack I've ever encountered. The Most Stubborn Man in the World."

"So he's the male version of you, then?"

I nod slowly, not taking my eyes off Josh across the room.

Sarah laughs. "Well, that's a scary combination. Definitely sounds *explosive.*"

"That's what we are—even against our mutual interests." I begin to say something more but wind up yawning, instead.

"Aw, honey, you better get some sleep," Sarah says. "You look like you're gonna pass out."

"Yeah, I'm about to fall over."

I get up and stretch.

"Oh, are you heading out, Kat?" Josh asks, his head whipping up from his work.

"Yeah," I say. "I've gotta get some sleep—I'm about to crash and burn."

"I'll walk you to your room. Hold on just a sec." He turns to confer with Jonas about something.

"Enjoy getting blown to bits, girl," Sarah whispers. "*Ka-boom.*"

"Nah. There are no explosions on the agenda tonight," I say. "Tonight, I'm gonna get good and rested so I can write my application to The Josh Faraday Club first thing tomorrow."

Sarah smiles at me suggestively. "I'll send you those questions ASAP."

"Thanks. I appreciate it. I'm gonna start working on my 'application' the minute I wake up."

Sarah doesn't reply. Something across the room has grabbed her attention. I glance across the room. Oh. Correction. *Someone* has grabbed Sarah's attention. Oh my, that's quite a look Jonas is giving Sarah right now—it's downright primal.

"I'll send those questions to you as soon as I can, Kitty Kat," Sarah says absently, not taking her eyes off her smoldering boyfriend. "Something tells me my hunky monkey boyfriend is gonna distract me from writing those questions for you for at least the next few hours."

29

JOSH

My phone beeps with an incoming text, waking me from a dead sleep. Jesus. Is it night or day? My body clock is totally fucked up.

I grab my phone and check the screen with one eye. Shit. *Jennifer LeMonde.*

"Hey, Josh," Jen's text says. "I'm still waiting on that phone call you promised me. I'm available now."

Fuck. When I sprinted back into Reed's suite the other night to grab my clothes and Kat's stuff, I practically bowled Jen over.

"Did you really say all that stuff about me?" Jen asked, marching behind me in a huff as I grabbed my clothes off a nearby lounge chair. "You think I'm an 'airhead'?"

"No, I don't think you're an airhead," I said, even though I think she's an airhead. "I'm sorry, Jen," I continued. "I'd love to explain everything to you, but I've gotta run right now. I'll call you later. I never called you an airhead, I swear. Kat put words into my mouth."

"Wait," Jen said as I gathered my clothes up, frantic about where Kat might have stumbled off to with no shoes, purse or phone, wandering around all by herself in a fucking casino at the break of dawn. "I need to talk to you."

"I'll call you later, Jen. I promise," I said. "But right now I gotta go."

"Do you promise to call me?" Jen asked.

"Yeah."

And then I promptly didn't call her. Because I've been busy. And obsessed with Kat. And because... I'm... a dick.

Fuck.

I press the button to place a call to Jen, despite the fact that every fiber in my body revolts against the idea.

She picks up immediately. "Hi," Jen says stiffly. "So nice to finally hear from you."

"Hi, Jen," I say. "I'm sorry I didn't call sooner. I've been really busy."

"Mmm hmm. You still in Vegas?"

"Yeah. You?"

"I'm at the airport now. Heading to New York. My mom's got a show opening tomorrow night."

"You mean on Broadway?"

"Yeah."

"I didn't know your mom did live theatre."

"She doesn't. This is her first time. She's shitting a brick."

"Well, I hope she breaks a leg. How was the RCR concert the other night?"

"Great." She exhales. "So did you say all that stuff about me or not?"

"No."

"None of it?"

"Well, I said we had meaningless sex, which we did, as I'm sure you'll agree." I pause, waiting for her to agree, but she doesn't. "Jen," I continue, flustered, "Kat knew I was with you in New York when she said all that shit. She was just mind-fucking you for the purpose of fucking with me."

There's a beat.

"Well, then, she's an even bigger bitch than I thought," Jen says coldly.

"Yeah, she tore you a new one, for sure. I'm sorry about that. Kat can be pretty intense. She was just jealous."

"Why'd you tell her about our night in New York in the first place? I take it you didn't just meet her in Las Vegas?"

"Yeah, I met her before."

"Is she your girlfriend?"

"No, she's not my girlfriend. It's kinda hard to explain what she is."

Jen snickers. "Well, it's interesting you told her about me. That wasn't very nice of you." I can hear her smiling across the phone line. "No wonder she was jealous."

Shit. This is totally backfiring on me.

Jen's voice shifts into full flirt mode. "So, hey, enough about The Jealous Bitch. Why don't you come to New York with me? I'll take you to the premier of my mom's show and to the after-party and—"

I take a deep breath. "Jen, no. That's what I'm calling to tell you. I thought we were on the same page last week in New York—both of us just having some meaningless, drunken fun. I'm sorry if you were up for something different than that." I clear my throat, suddenly extremely uncomfortable. "I should have been clearer with you, Jen. I'm not looking for a relationship. I'm sorry if I... misled you."

Oh my God. I'm suddenly realizing something: Kat might have had a point the other night when she called me a douche. It's distinctly possible I didn't make my intentions clear enough to Jen last week—even though I could plainly see the girl was way more into me than any casual hook-up ought to be. And, if I'm really digging deep into the honesty bin, I probably left things way too open-ended with Jen, just like Kat said I did, simply because I didn't want to hurt her feelings... or... actually, because I didn't want to deal with her feelings at all.

"Josh," Jen says. "I'm not looking for anything *deep* from you. Let's just hang out and see if—"

My phone buzzes with an incoming text and I pull back to see who it's from.

"*I hit the motherlode,*" Henn writes. "*All hands on deck!*"

"Oh, shit. I gotta go, Jen," I blurt, pressing the phone back into my ear. "Something really important just came up. Sorry. Gotta go."

"What?"

"Look, Jen, I'm sorry about the other night at the party. Kat's got a bit of a temper, it turns out." The image of Kat stomping like a toddler down the hallway, dripping wet, barefoot, her incredible ass-cheeks hanging out of her black G-string, pops into my mind. "She put words into my mouth. I absolutely didn't call you an airhead. That's what I wanted to tell you—and also that I'm not at all interested in a relationship. I'm sorry to cut this short, but I really gotta go."

30

KAT

I take a deep breath. I've got a full flock of butterflies flapping around in my stomach. Our *Ocean's Eleven* crew is scheduled to meet at ten to head over to the Las Vegas branch of the FBI, Sarah's report in hand, and by God, I'm determined to give Josh my application before then. I take another deep breath, turn up the volume on the Audra Mae and the Almighty Sound song I'm now officially addicted to ("The Real Thing"), thanks to Sarah, and place my hands on my keyboard. Here goes nothing.

"The following is my application to The Josh Faraday Club," I type onto my screen. "All answers will be one hundred percent honest. (And bee tee dubs, some of this stuff is kind of personal, so please keep it in confidence.)"

Name?

"Katherine Ulla Morgan," I write. "But everyone just calls me Kat." I take a deep breath. I never tell anyone about this. I can't believe I'm writing this. "I'm named after my dad's mother Katherine and my mom's Swedish grandmother Ulla. Pretty name, huh? *Katherine Ulla Morgan.* Yeah, it's pretty until you realize my initials spell 'KUM.' Let me repeat that, in case you're not understanding the full implication: my initials spell the word 'KUM' *and I have four brothers.* Which means that, in addition to being called Kat and Kitty Kat my whole life, I've also been called charming things like... wait for it... Kum Shot, Jizz, Splooge, Pecker-Snot, Man-Yogurt, Dick-Spit, Schlong-Juice, Jerk-Sauce, and, oh, so many more clever and classy things only boys would ever dream up.

"The only one of my brothers who's never joined in on the semen-infused nicknaming is my oldest brother, Colby—and I'm pretty sure I know why. As family lore goes, my clueless mother had originally wanted to give Baby Colby her grandfather's name as his middle name, but thanks to a family tradition on my dad's side (whereby the first-born son is given the middle name of Edwin),

Colby narrowly escaped being named Colby *Ulysses* Morgan. And so, perhaps in adherence to the philosophy 'But for the grace of God go I'—a philosophy you've expressed a strong affinity for, too—Colby's always stuck to calling me 'Kumquat.' (As a side note, my second oldest brother Ryan ultimately wound up with the dreaded 'Ulysses' moniker as his middle name, but being called 'RUM' and 'Bacardi' and... wait for it... 'Captain Morgan' hasn't exactly scarred him for life.)

"So, there you have it. I'm KUM. What you choose to do with the truth about my name is entirely up to you. But be warned: if you're suddenly feeling an irresistible urge to call me Cream-of-Sum-Yung-Guy or Baby-Gravy or Protein-Milkshake, you won't be the first. There's literally no semen-related name you could sling at me that I haven't already been called a hundred times in the 'comfort' of my own home or in the hallways of middle school (where, for three long years, we were most unfortunately required to mark our full initials onto the hem of our P. E. shorts).

"Beginning in high school (when I thankfully was no longer required to display 'KUM' on my P. E. shorts anymore), I started lying and saying my middle name is Ella. And to this day, I never tell anyone the truth about my middle name, just in case they're apt to put two and two together and start calling me Nut-Butter or Trouser-Juice or Man-Chowder or Spunk.

"Why, you might wonder, am I telling *you* of all people my KUM-tastic secret after all this time? I'm not entirely sure. All I know is that, judging by the way Sarah and Jonas have benefitted from playing the honesty-game right from the start, I'm eager to give the game a whirl, too. With you."

Age?

"24," I type.

Provide a brief physical description of yourself.

I stare at my computer screen for a moment. Josh is already quite familiar with almost every square inch of me—I mean, jeez, the man has seen me throw a tantrum in my underwear and shoved his fingers up my wahoo on a dance floor. But, still, I might as well answer the question.

"I have blonde hair, blue eyes, and a VAGINA," I write, giggling to myself.

With this application, you will be required to submit three recent photographs of yourself to your intake agent. Please include the following: one headshot, one full-body shot revealing your physique, and one shot wearing something you'd typically wear out in a public location. These photographs shall be maintained under the strictest confidentiality.

I pull out my phone and take a selfie-headshot, crossing my eyes and puckering my lips. Next, I strip off my clothes and stand in front of the full-length mirror in my hotel room and snap a quick shot of myself in my bra and undies—a sight he's already well acquainted with. And, for my last required shot—"something I'd typically wear in a public location"—I throw on my sequined dress from the other night, kneel at the toilet and pretend to be barfing into it while holding my phone above my head and snapping a photo.

"I'm attaching all three required photos with this application," I write. "Enjoy!"

Please sign the enclosed waiver describing the requisite background check, medical physical, and blood test, which you must complete as a condition of membership.

"If you want to do background and credit checks on me, knock yourself out. But if you don't want to expend the effort, let me tell you exactly what you'd find out: I've never been convicted of a crime (though I've broken the law a time or two and not gotten caught, heehee); I've got two credit cards, one of which is maxed out (and which I'm planning to pay off with my craps winnings); I'm paid up and current on my rent at my apartment; I'm one payment behind on my car loan (which I'm also going to pay off with my gambling winnings); and I've been employed at the same PR firm for almost two years.

"The last time I checked, my credit score was around 660, which is decent but not stupendous. It's possible it's gone down slightly recently because of that missed car payment. I swear to God, I'm normally really responsible when it comes to paying my bills, I really am, but when my place was trashed by The Club, there were several things I needed to replace and I just didn't have enough cash to go around for all that stuff plus my car payment, too. I was planning to make a double payment this month (because I'm supposed to get a raise when I hit my two-year anniversary at work), but now, thanks to you and Jonas (and some lucky dice!), I can pay off the whole car loan in one fell swoop. (Thank you so much!)

"You know, writing this makes me realize I haven't adequately thanked you for that craps money. I think I was just sort of stunned and also maybe a little uncomfortable with how easily I took it from you. I probably shouldn't have said yes so fast, if at all, but I couldn't stop myself. Not having a car payment or that Visa bill hanging over my head every month is going to be so effing amazing, I can't begin to tell you. So thank you again, very, very much. I'm really grateful. And thank you also for arranging everything so I could stay here in Las Vegas to save the world with our *Ocean's Eleven* crew *and* keep my job. Your generosity is truly mindboggling, Josh. I've never met anyone with such a big and generous heart. The way you take care of everyone around you, including me, is admirable and beyond attractive and sexy. I want you to know I'm grateful and blown away by your incredible thoughtfulness. Thank you.

"Okay, back to the application. What would you learn about me if you called my ex-boyfriends? Well, probably that I'm a wee bit crazy (sorry!), overly dramatic at times (sorry again!), and stubborn (news flash!). But I can also be bighearted, especially with the people I care about, devoted to my friends and family, funny, and outlandishly serious about having fun. (I think maybe I've got a little Jekyll and Hyde thing going on?)

"You'd also find out I've had only three serious boyfriends in my life—one in high school and two in college. Besides those three 'serious' boyfriends, I've also had other 'relationships' that have lasted anywhere from one night to, oh, about three or four months maximum, but, for purposes of this application, I'm only gonna bother telling you about the three boys I've cared enough about to bring them home to meet my family:

"My first serious boyfriend was in high school—a guy named Kade. Kade was two years older than me and oh man did I love, love, loooooooooooooove him. Holy shitballs, I loved that boy. I used to write 'Kat + Kade' on all my notebooks and practice writing my signature using his last name. Kade was the star quarterback on my high school's football team, and when he went away to college on a scholarship, he decided he needed to have the 'full college experience,' which, roughly translated, meant he didn't want to be tied down by having a sixteen-year-old girlfriend pining for him back home. Of course, my adult self realizes that was absolutely the best decision for both of us, but at the time I didn't think my heart would survive the horrible pain.

"My second serious boyfriend was Nate. I met him at a fraternity party in college. He was sweet and funny and completely in love with me from day one. He was also smart and athletic and a truly good person. He wanted to become a doctor and work with Doctors Without Borders, not even kidding. And on top of all that, the boy was objectively perfect-looking, too (one of those can't-find-a-bad-angle types). Plus, he was head over heels in love with me, which I found an attractive trait in a boyfriend. Oh my God, how Nate worshipped me. He always talked about how the second he saw me, he just *knew* we were meant for each other. 'It was love at first sight,' he would always tell people, and I always wondered if he noticed I never said, 'For me, too.'

"The truth was I didn't love Nate the way he loved me, and I knew it in my bones. I never felt that thunderbolt he felt when he saw me, though I was physically attracted to him (because, like I say, he was objectively gorgeous). Maybe I should have listened to my gut and cut ties with Nate sooner, but I was young and I kept thinking the passion would come. It had to, right? Nate was perfect in every way. And sure enough, as time went by, I loved him more and more. I truly adored him for the wonderful guy he was, how funny he was, how endlessly thoughtful and sweet and good. But I never, ever fell in love with Nate. And I knew it. I didn't practice writing my name using his last name. I never ached for him when we were apart—hell, I didn't even *think* about him when we were apart, to be perfectly honest. I never got butterflies when we held hands or kissed or had sex, though all were exceedingly pleasant. And I most certainly didn't feel an ounce of jealousy at the thought of him with another girl. Not an ounce. And yet Nate made it abundantly clear he lived to make me smile, yearned to touch me every chance he got, dreamed about me, and for sure envisioned me as his future wife.

"Why didn't I feel what Nate felt for me? To this day, I have no fucking idea. But for a long time, I truly thought things would change and I'd come to my senses and fall head over heels. 'When you like a flower, you pick it,' my mom always says. 'When you love a flower, you water it and let it grow.' So I figured I'd just keep watering our flower and soon my feelings would morph and ignite into the kind of life-or-death passion I'd always dreamed of experiencing. But they didn't. I guess some things just can't be forced, no matter how much you water them.

"Finally, about a year into our relationship, I was at a party with friends where I met a guy who made my panties burst into flames in a way I'd never felt with Nate, not even once. Honestly, the guy took my breath away with just a glance. It was like he'd cast a spell on me and my lady-parts. I'd never experienced full-body lust like that before. I didn't know my body was even capable of getting that dripping wet—and that was just from *looking* at the guy. I could only imagine what would happen if I actually got to touch him.

"It took all my self-restraint not to cheat on Nate that very night (because believe me, my *vagina* desperately wanted to do it), but I didn't. Instead, I nutted up and sat Nate down the next morning and I broke it off with him as gently as I could (and then went out and banged the shit out of that hot guy from the party four nights later on our second date).

"To say I broke Nate's heart is an understatement. Even as I'm writing this, I'm crying at the memory of the look on his face when I told him I wasn't in love with him. To this day, I've never felt more like a shitty person than when I told that beautiful, sweet, loving boy I didn't want to be his girlfriend anymore for no other reason than 'I dunno why.'

"Now and again, I'll get an occasional email from Nate, asking me how I'm doing, if I'm happy, asking if I'm married, and I always feel like crying when I have to reply honestly to him, 'I'm really great, Nate. Still single. How are you?' I know he's hoping one of these times I'll write, 'I was an idiot. Please take me back.' But I'm never even remotely tempted to write those words. And, honestly, I hate myself for it.

"I tried to be in love with Nate. I really did. But, apparently, passion isn't something you can force. If it were, I swear I'd be passionately in love with that boy to this very day—because he so deserved that.

"My third serious boyfriend was the one who shattered my heart into a million tiny pieces. Garrett Bennett. Or as I like to refer to him, The Asshole.

"I met Garrett on the first day of my junior year. I was walking to class with Sarah when Garrett beelined right to me from across a large lawn and asked me out, saying I was the most beautiful girl he'd ever seen and if I didn't say yes to a date, I'd ruin his life. Well, to say my panties were wet at the sight of him is an understatement. The boy had an animal magnetism I'd never encountered before. So, of course, I said hell yes.

"On our first date, Garrett took me to a really nice restaurant, the nicest restaurant I'd ever been to, actually. Not the burgers and fries I'd been expecting. As it turned out, his dad was a senator and his mom some sort of philanthropist-lady who organized trips to Africa through her church. And the dude played on the freaking golf team at our school. (Who *does* that?) He seemed sort of fancy to me, but in a good way.

"But it wasn't his swankiness that made me like him that night. Our conversation flowed easily and I laughed a lot. He was hysterically funny. (And did I mention he made my panties wet?) Actually, wait, let me amend the statement that he was hysterically funny. I'm not really sure if that's true, in retrospect. The guy could have recited the phone book that night and I would have giggled like a fucking idiot. I was just instantly smitten. It was Nate, but in reverse. In fact, more than once during dinner, I thought, *So this is what Nate felt!* If you'd asked me that night, 'Do you believe in love at first sight?', I would have shrieked, 'Yes!'

"So, anyway, when Garrett asked me to come back to his place after dinner, I said *yes, yes, yes*. I'd only intended to make out with him, to tell you the truth, because honestly, up until then, I'd never had first-date sex or even a one-night stand. (Even that guy I banged after breaking up with Nate lasted two months.) Plus, Garrett had made a few comments during dinner that made it clear he'd come from an extremely conservative religious background, unlike me (organized religion is pretty much nonexistent in my household—as long as I'm dumping my entire life's story on you, might as well hit you with religion, too), so I didn't think first-date sex would be in the cards with a guy like that. But one thing led to another and another, pretty damned quickly, actually, and soon, Garrett and I were at his place having headboard-banging sex like nothing I'd ever experienced before.

"This kind of sex was a revelation to me. Before Garrett, I'd never had such uninhibited, wild sex. Even sex with the after-Nate guy wasn't nearly as explosive as sex with Garrett Bennett. Our chemistry was off the freaking charts. I felt like I could be as wild as I wanted to be with him, like there were no limits —and that opened up a whole new side to myself I didn't even know existed. I'd been giving myself orgasms for years before then, and I'd had orgasms during oral with guys, but this was the first time I had orgasms during sex with a guy— during actual intercourse—and it was like, wow, wow, wow, wow.

"I was immediately addicted, as you can probably imagine. I could never get enough. I wanted more, more, more, every chance I got. And so, from that day forward, for the better part of the next seven months, I banged Garrett as much as possible, which wasn't as much as I would have liked (because, as he kept telling me, golf is an extremely time-consuming sport, especially for someone trying to go pro).

"But suffice it to say we had a ton of sex. But we also had lots and lots of conversations, too, mostly in bed, during which I told him pretty much every honest thought I had about anything and everything, never holding back. For some reason, the uninhibited sex made me feel uninhibited in all ways, like I could tell Garrett anything. No topic was off limits, and I just babbled and babbled.

"In some very big ways, it was obvious Garrett and I came from strikingly different backgrounds and families, but it didn't matter. I just always felt like Garrett totally "got" me and secretly saw the world the way I did, despite his parents' expectations about what and who he was 'supposed' to be.

"Honestly, I felt like I'd met my perfect match—my soul mate, if you will (a phrase I've since banished from my vocabulary). We never said 'I love you' to each other, because Garrett made it obvious he didn't feel comfortable with saying 'trite' words like that—but that was fine with me. I knew in my heart how we both felt—so I didn't need to hear the stupid, trite words.

"About six months into our relationship, I invited Garrett to meet my family and, much to my thrill, he said yes. I was super nervous about it because Garrett meeting my family was a pretty big deal to me, but, much to my relief, everyone in my family wound up loving him to pieces. Well, everyone except my oldest brother Colby, who despised Garrett almost instantly. 'What the fuck is wrong with you, Kumquat?' he said. 'Can't you see he's using you?'

"I couldn't believe my ears. I felt completely offended and hurt, like Colby was telling me I wasn't good enough for a guy like Garrett from a fancy family with a senator-dad. 'No, honey,' Colby said. 'He's a loser—not even close to good enough for you. He's completely full of shit.' Well, I lost it. I told Colby I was gonna marry Garrett one day and it's too bad he wouldn't be invited to my wedding and until he learned to say something nice about my future husband he could just forget he had a fucking sister. (Full disclosure: I'm sort of overly dramatic sometimes when I get mad.) Colby said, 'Don't worry, Kumquat, I'll be there to pick up your pieces when he breaks your heart.'

"I was pissed as hell at Colby, especially since everyone else loved Garrett the way I did. But Colby's comments did make me wonder why Garrett never brought me home to meet his family. But Garrett just kept finding excuses, telling me his dad (the senator) was traveling, or his mom was getting a facelift or bringing school supplies to underprivileged youth in Guatemala or some other rich-person-helping-the-world thing like that—and it just never worked out.

"Finally, about eight months into our relationship, I was supposed to go to a concert with Sarah for her birthday, but she came down with the stomach flu. So I decided to use the opportunity to give Garrett a sexy surprise at his apartment.

"When Garrett opened his apartment door, I clutched my trench coat, intending to rip it open and flash him my birthday suit underneath, when I glimpsed a beautiful brunette over his shoulder inside his apartment. She was sitting at a candlelit table-for-two, a vase of red roses at its center—something Garrett had never once set up for me. Even from a distance, I could see a large, sparkling cross around her neck. And when she moved her hand to her mouth in surprise, something twinkled brightly on her finger in the candlelight.

"Instantly, every doubt and concern I'd stuffed down and reasoned away for months—and every single word Colby had said to me—came slamming into me full-force. In a flash, I knew that pretty, demure girl in Garrett's apartment was his girlfriend—and maybe even his fiancée if I was reading that flash on her hand correctly—and I knew with every fiber of my being that he'd already said those three little 'trite' words to her, the ones I'd longed to hear him say to me. Motherfucker.

"When I tore out of there, sobbing, Garrett followed me, explaining to the back of my head that Maggie's father was some lah-de-dah über-wealthy businessman who'd invented air freight or some shit like that and she was a really sweet girl from his church back home and well-connected and, he said with utmost reverence, *Maggie was saving herself for marriage.* At that last statement, I whirled around to face Garrett, my mouth hanging open, my heart shattering. 'Are you calling me a slut?' I asked. He didn't reply, which was reply enough. 'I thought you *loved* me,' I said, wiping away the hot tears streaming down my cheeks. 'I thought you wanted to marry me one day.' And do you know what that motherfucker did? He chuckled at the thought of marrying me. And then he said, 'Come on, Kat, you're a great girl—super fun—*but you're just not marriage material.*'"

I sit and stare at the screen for a minute, tears streaming down my cheeks. Man, those words from Garrett still cut me to the core. I wipe my tears and place my fingers on my keyboard again, but I can't see well enough to type yet. I can't believe I'm letting The Asshole get to me, even to this day. But I can't help it. The pain of getting blindsided like that never fully goes away, I guess.

"I've never told anyone (except Sarah) what The Asshole said to me that night," I finally type. "I've always been too embarrassed and ashamed, I guess. I didn't even tell Colby what Garrett said. All I told him was, 'You were right.'

"And yet now I'm telling you," I write. "Why? Honestly, I don't fucking know."

I have to stop typing for another minute. I'm too emotional. Why the hell am I baring my obviously pathetic soul to Josh like this? Is getting his stupid application really this frickin' important to me?

No, it's not. I don't care about his application right now. Writing this to Josh isn't about me getting his stupid application anymore. This is about something much bigger than that.

I wipe my eyes again. I'm veering way off track here. Have I even answered this particular question yet? I'm not sure. I re-read the question at the top of the page again. Oh yes.

"So that's pretty much the story of my ex-boyfriends," I write. "Besides those three guys, I've dated plenty of guys for a few months here or there and had sex with a truckload besides that, as I've mentioned, but no one serious enough to bring home."

I glance up at the question I'm supposedly answering again. Oh, yes. Okay.

"As far as blood tests," I write, "I'll submit to any kind of testing you require (as long as it doesn't involve math). But in the interest of saving time, let me just tell you what the testing would reveal: I'm clean. About two months ago, when I went in to get a new prescription of birth control pills, I got tested. And even though I'm on the pill, I insist on condoms every single time I have sex, no exceptions, unless I'm in a committed relationship and the guy's been tested.

(But, hey, like I say, if you require formal medical testing before my application can be approved, then I'll sign or do whatever you request.)"

Sexual orientation? Please choose from the following options: Straight, homosexual, bisexual, pansexual, other?

"Straight. But in the interest of full disclosure, I should inform you I made out with a girl during my senior year in college. It's a long story that can be summarized as follows: Truth or Dare combined with Ecstasy combined with a pervy boyfriend (hers) can lead a girl to do anything once. I can honestly say the experience didn't cause me to question my sexual orientation whatsoever. In fact, it wasn't nearly as hot as it sounds, I'm sorry to say. But, regardless, I'm definitely straight."

Do any of your sexual fantasies include violence of any nature? If so, please describe in detail.

I sit and think. Well, jeez. I have lots and lots of fantasies, for sure, some of them pretty darn elaborate, but do any of them involve actual *violence*? No.

I place my hands on the keyboard and begin typing. "I have lots and lots of fantasies—it's kind of a *thing* with me," I write. "And not a single one of them involves actual violence. However, a couple of my fantasies involve the *threat* of violence, but only as a backdrop to setting the scene. For instance, I've got a bodyguard fantasy that only makes sense if there are bad guys coming to get me, or else why the heck do I have a bodyguard? (And to answer the question that's just popped into your head, no, I didn't have sex with any of the bodyguards Jonas hired to protect me from The Club.)"

I smirk to myself. Sure, I *almost* had sex with Derek the Bodyguard, but Josh doesn't need to know that.

I begin typing again.

"The threat of violence is also prevalent in another one of my fantasies, one in which I'm held captive by a sex-slave-master. The sex-slave master absconds with me one night and forces me to be his slave, but he never actually hurts me. And, also, in regards to violence, a second sex-slave-master comes to steal me away from the first, but my original captor fights the other bad guy to the death and protects me (which kinda turns this scenario into yet another bodyguard fantasy, doesn't it?)."

I stare at my screen. Holy What the Fuck Am I Doing, Batman? I can't write all this shit to Josh. He's gonna think I'm a freaking loon, which I am. I've never told anyone about the elaborate, imaginary pornos bouncing around in my head. What if Josh reads all this and decides I'm too much of a freak? Or worse, that, based on this stuff, we're not sexually compatible? That would be pretty soul crushing.

I let my fingers hover over my keyboard again, trying to decide what to do.

Fuck it. Better to be completely honest and get rejected for who I really am than to hide myself and make him like me. Like my new favorite singer, Audra Mae, said in her powerful song, better to be The Real Thing, for better or worse.

Are you a current practitioner of BDSM and/or does BDSM interest you? If so, describe in explicit detail.

"I am not a current practitioner of BDSM," I write. "As I've described above, the idea of being tied up as part of my 'captive' fantasy interests me—although, I should tell you, I'm not turned on by the idea of being physically harmed in any way."

Shit. I hope that last part's not a deal-breaker with Josh. Goddamn, I wish I knew what Josh wrote in his freaking application.

Payment and Membership Terms. Please choose from the following options: One Year Membership, $250,000 USD; Monthly Membership, $30,000 USD. All payments are non-refundable. No exceptions.

"I'd like a one-month membership, please," I write. "I don't have $30,000 to pay you for your services, unfortunately—but, hopefully, you'll find it in your heart to waive your membership fee (or maybe accept services in lieu of payment, heehee?)."

Please provide a detailed explanation about what compelled you to seek membership in The (Josh Faraday) Club.

"I wanna get in your pants."

I chuckle to myself. That'd be funny if I left it at that. But I'm not going for funny. I'm going for full-scale nuclear decimation of this man.

"Remember how you accused me of dripping down my thigh in that hallway after Reed's party?" I write. "And remember how I scoffed and said it was just pool water trickling down my leg? Well, I lied. I *was* dripping down my thigh for you, just like you said. Before witnessing your muscled, tattooed body in that hallway, I was already quite fond of masturbation, I must admit—but ever since I saw you in that hallway, Josh, I've taken self-love to an art form. I want you so badly I'm in pain, desperate to feel your hard-on sliding deep inside me.

"But I'm not gonna give in to my desire for you without seeing your mother-fucking application first. Why? Because it's not about the application anymore, Josh. It's about something bigger than that. I don't want Happy Josh. I want Real Josh. And I'm willing to show you the real Katherine Ulla Morgan to get him.

Please provide a detailed statement regarding your sexual preferences. To maximize your experience in The Club, please be as explicit, detailed, and honest as possible. Please do not self-censor, in any fashion.

"Well, I feel like I've already answered this one. I want to read your application, word for word, without censorship of any kind, and then I want you to do whatever freaky things you've asked for in your application to me, exactly as described. I want to be your Mickey Mouse roller coaster, Josh—and I want you to be mine. Come on, Josh. *YOLO.* I've told you my secrets. Now it's time for you to tell me yours."

31

JOSH

"We really need to talk to your boss," Jonas says to the FBI agent sitting across the table from us.

"Yeah, well, that's not gonna happen. I'm who you get."

"I'm Jonas Faraday," Jonas says smoothly. "And this is my brother, Josh."

I nod at the guy.

"We run Faraday & Sons in Seattle, L.A. and New York," Jonas continues. "We'd like to talk to the head of this office."

The kid shrugs. "I'm the only one available to talk to you, sir. Sorry."

"How long have you been an agent?" Kat asks.

The guy shifts his attention to Kat in all her blonde glory and his entire demeanor detours from "stop wasting my time, bastard" to "I'd love to help in any way I can."

"Four months," he replies, his mouth relaxing into a semi-smile.

"Did you go to Quantico for training like they show in the movies?" Kat asks.

"Yeah."

"Wow. That's cool. So what's your assignment? All I know about the FBI is what I saw in *Silence of the Lambs*." Oh my God, Kat's in full terrorist mode. I can't help but smirk in admiration.

The agent's smile broadens. "Well, new agents are assigned to run background checks for the first year, mostly. And, of course, I'm the lucky guy who gets to talk to all the nice people such as yourselves who come in off the streets of Las Vegas to report the crime of the century."

"Everyone's gotta start somewhere," Kat says breezily. She leans forward like she's telling a dirty secret. "So here's the thing, Agent Sheffield. I've come here today off the streets of Las Vegas to report the crime of the century."

He laughs.

Kat's face turns serious. "Actually, I'm not kidding. I'm here to report the crime of the century."

He props his hand under his chin, obviously enthralled by the mere sight of her, as any man would be. "What's your name?"

"Katherine Morgan. But you can call me Kat."

"Kat," he repeats. "I tell you what. You guys file your report with me and I promise I'll take a long look at it within the next two weeks—maybe even a week. And, if I see something there, I'll most certainly investigate further."

"Thank you, Special Agent Sheffield," Kat says, biting her lip seductively. "I really appreciate that." She bats her eyelashes. "What's your first name?"

"Eric."

"*Special Agent Eric*," she purrs. "The thing is, this is an urgent matter—this is a career-making kind of case for an agent such as yourself, I swear to God."

Holy shit. I feel like standing up and slow-clapping right now. She's blatantly flirting to get Eric to read Sarah's report—anyone could see that, even him—and yet, she's so damned gorgeous and charming and unapologetic in her sensuality, he obviously doesn't care if he's being used.

"Henn," Sarah interjects. "Will you please play Special Agent Sheffield that voicemail we have cued up?"

"Yes, ma'am." Henn presses a button on his computer and a gruff male voice speaking Ukrainian fills the room.

"Yuri Navolska," Sarah says. "About a minute after leaving that message, he sliced the external jugular vein in my neck and stabbed me in the ribcage, causing me to fall back and crack my skull on a sink ledge."

I've suddenly got chills over my entire body, imagining that violence being inflicted on poor Sarah. I glance at Jonas and he's clenching his jaw.

"If you need to see the scars on my head and torso, I'll show you," Sarah continues.

"No, that's okay. I believe you."

"Please," Kat pleads. "These guys tried to kill my best friend. Just give us a couple hours of your time."

Agent Eric sighs. "You've got more voicemails besides this one?"

"Several," Henn says. "About all kinds of nasty stuff. Maksim Belenko's a really bad dude—prostitution, weapons, drugs, money laundering."

"Okay," Eric says. He nods definitively. "Let's dig in. We'll go through the report together, page by page, and if it's everything you say it is, I'll take this to my boss today."

Kat leaps up from her chair and gives Eric a big hug while Sarah and Henn take seats on either side of Agent Eric, their determination and excitement apparent.

I watch Kat for a long beat.

She's obviously incredible to look at, but, watching her right now, it's clear she's much more than a gorgeous face (and slamming body). She's a fucking force of nature. Smart as hell. Brilliant at reading people. Savvy. The most determined woman I've ever met. Which reminds me, what the hell is the email she sent me before we left for the FBI offices? God only knows what that little terrorist is up to now.

"I sent you an email, Playboy," Kat said coyly about twenty minutes before we left our hotel. "Read it when you can."

"Sure thing, PG," I said.

But just then, Jonas asked me to research something about the jurisdiction of the DEA, and I got completely sidetracked.

I guess now would be a good time to read it, whatever it is—Sarah, Henn, Jonas, and Kat are busy talking about Sarah's report, and I certainly don't have anything to contribute to their conversation, eye candy that I am.

I quickly pull my laptop from its case and click into my email inbox. I scroll for a moment until I find Kat's email from two hours ago. The subject line says, "*Please read this.*" There's no text in the body of the message, just a Word document and three photo files attached. I click on Kat's attached Word document and instantly have a fucking heart attack, followed immediately by a fucking boner.

"*The following is my application to The Josh Faraday Club,*" the document says. "*All answers will be one hundred percent honest. (And, bee tee dubs, some of this stuff is kind of personal, so please keep it in confidence.)*"

"Oh my God," I blurt. I look up. Sarah, Henn, Jonas and Eric are absorbed in Sarah's report—but Kat's looking right at me, looking like she's holding her breath.

She knows I'm reading it.

I feel my face turn completely red.

Kat smiles a wicked smile, motions to my computer like she's saying, "Get back to work, asshole," and then slowly, ever so slowly, returns her attention to the group.

I look back down at my screen, my heart beating out of my chest, and continue to read:

"*. . . my initials spell KUM… Kum Shot, Jizz, Splooge, Pecker-Snot, Man-Yogurt, Dick-Spit, Jizz, Schlong-Juice, Jerk-Sauce,*" she writes, and I put my hand over my mouth to keep from bursting out laughing.

"*. . . I have blonde hair, blue eyes, and a VAGINA,*" she writes.

This time, I laugh out loud. I can't stop myself.

I look up at Kat, chuckling. She's already been watching me intently, biting the tip of her finger nervously. I shake my head at her, nonverbally calling her evil. She nods, a smart-ass expression on her face.

"*. . . I'm attaching all three required photos with this application. Enjoy!*"

I click into her first attached image. A silly headshot. She's making a fishy-face and crossing her eyes, and yet, even making this ridiculous face, she's gorgeous as hell.

Photo number two. Jesus Christ. The body that mesmerized me the other night when it was stomping down that hallway, dripping wet.

I glance up at her.

Her chest is rising and falling visibly, mirroring mine.

I look back at my screen. Photo number three: something she'd 'typically wear out in public.' I click on the image and laugh out loud again. She's pretending to pray to the porcelain gods, wearing her sparkly dress from the other night.

Jesus Christ.

She truly is the female version of me. Anything for a laugh.

What the fuck am I gonna do about this girl? It suddenly dawns on me, full-force: I'm powerless to resist her. I've been thinking all along I've got the upper hand with her, but I've been kidding myself. At the end of the day, she's gonna get whatever she wants, eventually, from me and anyone else—no one could possibly resist her—and I know it. It's inevitable. She's fucking gravity. Death. Taxes. I feel like I'm hurtling in slow motion toward a brick wall, but I can't stop myself.

I look down at my screen again and continue reading, my pulse pounding in my ears.

Aw, shit. My heart breaks for this Nate guy.

I keep reading.

And reading.

Motherfucker.

Garrett Bennett.

I grit my teeth. I feel the vein in my neck bulging. I wanna kill this fucker. I wanna hunt him down and rip him limb from limb. What kind of motherfucking asshole does that to a girl—any girl?—but especially one as awesome as Kat? He called my girl a slut? Said she's not 'marriage material' just because she likes sex a whole lot? He's the one who taught her how to like it so much, after all, didn't he?—and he certainly reaped the benefits of her newfound sexual prowess. And then he turned it around on her and burned her at the stake for it? I feel literally homicidal right now, I really do. Having a live wire in the bedroom is every guy's fantasy, and this guy made Kat feel like shit about it? If that motherfucker were here right now, I think it's safe to say I'd be going to prison for what I'd do to him on federal property.

I keep reading, my blood boiling, my heart clanging in my ears.

"I want to read your application, word for word, without censorship of any kind, and then I want you to do whatever freaky things you've asked for in your application to me, exactly as described. I want to be your Mickey Mouse roller coaster, Josh—and I want you to be mine. Come on, Josh. YOLO. I've told you my secrets. Now it's time for you to tell me yours."

Holy fucking shit.

"So what do you want me to do?" Agent Eric asks, thumbing through the exhibit log.

"We want a meeting in D.C. within the next two days with power players at the FBI, CIA, and Secret Service," Jonas says.

They continue talking, but I can't follow their conversation. The words on my computer screen are calling to me like a siren—drawing me in like a drug.

I read the entire application again from start to finish, my mind racing, my heart variously racing and breaking, my blood boiling, and, most of all, my cock throbbing the whole time. And when I'm done reading it for the third time, I close my eyes, trying to figure out what the fuck to do. I've never wanted a woman so much in all my life. She's a force of a nature. How am I supposed to resist a fucking tornado? A tsunami? An earthquake? I can't.

"You're not bullshitting me? You can do it?" Agent Eric asks Henn.

"We can do it," Henn says.

"Then I'll vouch for you with my boss," Eric says. "I'll do everything in my power."

I breathe deeply, trying to control my racing thoughts and hard dick. What the fuck am I gonna do? I gotta give her my application, don't I? Shit. Yeah, I do. I wouldn't have believed it possible, but I'm gonna do it. There's no other logical conclusion to this story. The woman just bared her entire soul to me, not just her sexual history. If I don't at least give her my stupid application in return, then I truly am the sociopath she accused me of being. Not to mention a fucking pussy. And an asshole.

"Hey, Agent Sheffield," Sarah says. "I've got a favor to ask of you. You do background checks, right?"

"Yeah," Eric replies. "Every day."

I'm instantly pulled away from my thoughts about Kat. I don't recall a "favor" being part of the strategy Jonas and I cooked up for today's meeting. What the fuck is Sarah talking about?

"I'd like you to find two people for me," Sarah continues.

I look at Jonas as if to say, "What the fuck is she talking about?" and he shakes his head, totally at a loss.

"This isn't a demand," Sarah continues. "It's just a personal favor. But it's really important."

I look at Kat and shoot her the same "What the fuck is she talking about?" look I just flashed Jonas. Kat shrugs, clearly as in the dark as the rest of us.

"Who are the two people?" Eric asks.

"The first is a woman named Mariela from Venezuela."

32

JOSH

The room warps and buckles. Did Sarah just say she wants Agent Eric to find *Mariela from Venezuela?* My brain can't process what I'm hearing.

I look at Jonas. His face looks exactly the way I feel: blindsided.

If Jonas has told Sarah about Mariela, then he's surely told her about Mom, too. Does that mean he's told her *everything?*

"I don't know her last name," Sarah continues calmly, "but she worked for Joseph and Grace Faraday in Seattle during the years from...I'm guessing 1984 to around 1991."

What the fuck is happening right now? I feel like Sarah just punched me in the balls. I glance at Jonas again. He's got his hands over his face. Good idea. I do the same.

"In 1991, Grace Faraday was murdered in her home . . ." Sarah continues, and the minute she says Mom's name this second time, I suddenly realize she just revealed the true meaning of my "Grace" tattoo to Kat.

I steal a quick look at Kat, and her eyes tell me she's already put two and two together. *She knows.* Oh, fuck. I seriously can't do this. Enough with the honesty-game. It's too much. I put my hands over my face again. I'm shaking.

"Hang on," Eric says. "Could you repeat all that?"

Sarah repeats everything again slowly, including Mom's name, yet again, just in case Kat didn't catch it the first two times. "Grace Faraday," Sarah says. "She was murdered in her home... We need you to find *Mariela*—and if she's not alive, then her children."

"Okay. That sounds doable," Agent Eric says.

Am I hearing that right? This FBI guy is gonna track down Mariela?

I look across the room at Jonas. He looks like he's in total shock.

"Awesome, Eric," Sarah says. "Thank you. And there's one more woman, too. I don't know her first name—but her maiden name was *Westbrook*."

Oh Jesus Christ.

Jonas and I exchange a look of pure astonishment. This is beyond insanity. Sarah's asking the FBI guy to find Mariela *and* Miss Westbrook? Well, that settles it beyond a doubt: Jonas has told Sarah literally every little thing about his life, and therefore mine: Mom, Mariela, Miss Westbrook, Dad, The Lunacy. Holy fuck. I never thought I'd see the day. Haven't we always said no one needs to know about all that—that it's best if these things remain between us?

"Miss Westbrook was a teacher in Seattle in probably 1992," Sarah continues, "and then she married a guy in the Navy named Santorini who was later stationed in San Diego."

"What do these two women have to do with The Club?" Eric asks.

"Absolutely nothing," Sarah says. She gazes at Jonas in a way I've never seen anyone look at him before—with so much tenderness my heart stops vicariously for him. "This would be a personal favor to me," Sarah says, not taking her eyes off Jonas. "I don't have the resources to find these ladies by myself without having their full names, but I think you can do it."

"Shouldn't be a problem."

"Thank you. I'm gonna need this information as soon as possible, please."

"I'll do my best."

I can't stop staring at Sarah—at the way she's looking at Jonas. I've never seen anyone look at him like that. Shit, I've never seen anyone look at *me* like that.

My eyes are burning. I've suddenly got a lump in my throat. Holy shit. What's happening to me right now? I'm about to lose complete control. I swallow hard and steal a quick look at Kat. Her eyes are glistening and her face is red.

I cover my face with my hands again, too overwhelmed to look at her anymore. I can't process this. It's too much.

I honestly never thought Jonas would find a woman he'd tell about Mom and Dad and The Lunacy, too. And I certainly never thought, if he did, that woman would nonetheless look at him like Sarah's looking at Jonas right now. I swallow hard, forcing my emotions down again. I'm so happy for my brother right now, and so fucking relieved for myself, I feel like crying, which is a fucking crazy thought. Holy shit. Jonas is gonna be happy. Sarah loves him, warts and all. I swallow hard again. This is fucking incredible.

But wait.

My joy for my brother is suddenly derailed by an overwhelming sense of panic for myself.

Kat.

She knows too much. She knows things I never tell anyone—things I don't want her to know. In the taxi after Reed's party, Kat already told me she knows about my parents, thanks to Jonas telling Sarah. "It happened a long time ago,"

I said breezily, dodging the subject like I always do. But now she knows I'm not quite as unscathed by everything as I let on—that my tattoos aren't just quippy doodles on my skin or youthful, drunken attempts at being profound. Now she knows my skin is inked with my life's greatest sorrow.

She knows.

And yet.

Kat gave me her "application" to "The Josh Faraday Club," didn't she—even though she knows I'm more scarred than I let on? She did it because she wants to see the scars, whatever they are.

"What's the name of the school where Miss Westbrook worked in Seattle, Jonas?" Sarah asks Jonas. "That might be helpful for Eric to know for his search."

There's a beat. Jonas isn't answering her. He looks like a deer in headlights.

Aw, Jonas.

"St. Francis Academy," I say, answering for my brother.

Jonas flashes me a grateful smile and I grin at him. Some things will never change.

"Okay. I'll do my best," Eric says.

"Thank you," Sarah says. She puts her arm around Jonas' back and squeezes him tightly, and he leans into her, completely at ease in her tender embrace.

"Okay," Agent Eric says. "I'll go talk to my boss right now. I'll give you guys a call later." He nods at Kat, reassuring her in particular. "I promise I'll give it my all."

"I know you will, Eric," Kat purrs. She shifts her eyes to me and leaves them there. Oh my God, she's looking at me like she sees right through me—like my invisible shield has somehow vanished and I'm laid bare for her. "*I have full faith in you,*" Kat says.

33

JOSH

"Henn, pass the ketchup," I say, but I can barely concentrate on my burger.

Our meeting at the FBI was un-fucking-believable in countless ways, not the least of which is the fact that Kat's application to The Josh Faraday Club is burning a hole in my proverbial pocket. And heart. And dick.

"You crushed it, Kat," Jonas says. "You were amazing."

"Absolutely," Sarah agrees.

Henn passes the ketchup to me. "Who's the fucking genius now?" he says. "Damn, girl." He puts his fist up and she bumps it with hers, a huge smile on her gorgeous face.

Kat fantasizes about me while masturbating?

"To Kat," Sarah says, raising her beer, and the rest of us hold up our beers in Kat's honor, too. "You're the reason Eric started taking us seriously," Sarah says. "No doubt about it."

"Aw, thanks," Kat says. "But it was definitely a team effort."

We all raise our glasses again and drink to "the team."

She wants to feel my hard-on sliding deep inside her?

I clear my throat. "So how are we gonna get the money, Henn?" I ask, pointedly not looking at Kat. Shit, I'm hard as a rock right now. If I look at her, I'm not gonna be able to stop myself from grabbing her and kissing the hell out of her right here and now, in front of everyone. "I thought you said most of those accounts are set up for in-person transfer only." Fuck. I can't stop imagining Kat masturbating.

Ever since I saw you in that hallway, she wrote, *I've taken self-love to an art form.*

I shift in my chair, trying to relieve the throbbing of my dick in my pants, but it's no use.

"They are," Henn says. "Which, obviously, means we're going to transfer the money in-person." He pauses, shooting Kat a meaningful look. "Hello, Oksana Belenko."

Kat grimaces sharply. "Oh, I dunno—" she begins.

"You'll be fine," Henn says. "I'll set you up with a passport and a driver's license—"

"I don't know if I can—" Kat says, sputtering.

"You *can*," Henn says. "Today proved that. Indubitably. Don't worry, Kitty Kat." He touches the top of her hand. "I'll hack into each account and shave thirty years off Oksana's age—they won't even question you're her for a second. And then I'll walk into each and every bank with you, right by your side."

"But will she be safe?" Sarah asks.

"I'll make sure of it," Henn says.

"So will I," I add.

At my words, Kat's eyes flicker to me and my cock hardens even more. The right thing to do is pull her aside and kiss her for the first time in private—but I'm not sure I can wait.

A waitress walks by and Kat flags her. "Double Patron shots all around, please." When the waitress leaves, Kat lets out a long exhale. "Okay, I'll do it."

"Kat, are you sure?" Sarah asks. "You don't have to do this."

"Yes, I do. This ain't no casino heist, fellas—and very pretty lady." She winks at Sarah. "This is about taking these guys down so they can't hurt you ever again, Sarah. It's a no-brainer."

Holy shit. She's blowing my mind today—first, with the FBI guy, and then with her application, and now with this. She's willing to impersonate Oksana Belenko to steal The Club's money? I wouldn't have thought it possible when we first started on this bizarre adventure, but Kat's turned out to be every bit as valuable to the team as any of us—far more valuable than me, actually.

"We'll create an offshore account," Jonas is saying to the group. "And funnel everything into it at the last possible moment."

"*Two* offshore accounts," I say pointedly. "I think we're gonna have to take a little *finder's fee* on the deal—don't you think, bro? Maybe one percent?"

A light bulb goes off on Jonas' face—as usual, my brother can read my mind.

"Fuck yeah," Jonas says. "Great idea. Yeah, five and a half mill sounds about right for our commission. Kat and Henn, you guys will each get a cool mill off the top. You've both earned it."

I nod emphatically. A million each is exactly what I'd had in mind.

"Are you *serious*?" Kat squeals. "You're gonna give me a *million* dollars?"

"You deserve it," Jonas says.

Kat squeals again and leaps up to hug Jonas, jiggling her tight little body with excitement, and then moves on to kiss Sarah full on the mouth.

Oh, Jesus. That's it. I give up. I've got to kiss this woman right now. Waiting 'til we're alone is a fucking pipe dream. Whatever she wants, yes, I'll do it. I don't fucking care anymore. She told me her shit, I'll tell her mine. I've got to have her, no matter the price.

Kat's done kissing Sarah and now it's my turn. She bends down, obviously intending to chastely kiss my cheek—but I stand abruptly, grab her face, pull her sexy little body firmly into mine, and devour her lips. My tongue slides inside her mouth and instantly leads hers into sensual movement.

Kat yelps with surprise and throws her arms around my neck, her tongue responding to my entreaties with extreme enthusiasm.

I press myself into her even harder, suddenly overcome with so much arousal, I can barely stand, and she runs her hands through my hair.

Oh, God, I'm light-headed. Every nerve ending in my body is in overload, surging with pleasure and relief. Oh, God, yes, she tastes incredible, better than I'd even imagined. And she smells fucking amazing. Our tongues swirling and intertwining feel electrically charged. Oh my fuck, if we were alone in my room the way I'd originally planned to finally kiss her, her clothes would already be off and my cock inside her. It's just that good.

But, shit, we're not alone.

Fuck.

Contrary to every primal urge coursing through my body, my lips release hers.

She pulls away from me, her lips red and her eyes smoldering.

I clutch my chest and smile at her. "I feel like I've been waiting a lifetime to do that," I say softly.

"Why the hell did you wait so long, Playboy?" Kat breathes, pressing herself into my hard-on.

"Gee, I wonder why." I press my forehead against hers, grinning broadly.

"So does this mean you're finally gonna tell me?" Kat says.

I nod. "You win," I whisper, almost inaudibly. "God help me, you little terrorist, you win."

Kat laughs and sits back down, grinning from ear to ear, a living portrait of victory, but when she sees Henn's face across the table, her face instantly falls.

"Oh, Henny. I'm sorry," she says.

Henn shakes his head. "No, it's great. You're both the best." He swallows hard. "Indubitably." He tries to smile.

"Hey, Henn—" I say.

"No, really." He waves me away. "I'm good."

But, clearly, he's not good. Not good at all.

Kat gets up from her seat next to mine and works her way around the table to Henn. She grabs his shoulders emphatically and stares into his eyes. "You're the best. I'm proud to call you my friend." She kisses him on the cheek.

But he's clearly heartbroken.

Shit.

The waitress arrives with the tequila shots Kat ordered and Sarah leads the charge on raising our drinks in the air. "To the Party Girl with a Heart of Gold and the Hacker," Sarah says, clearly trying to cheer Henn up. "A couple of *mill-ion-aires*."

"Here, here," I say.

"Yeah, well, let's not put the cart before the horse," Kat says, putting down her empty shot glass. "There's still the little matter of actually getting the money."

"Oh, we'll get it—don't you worry," Henn says.

I grab Kat's hand under the table and squeeze it and she leans into me.

"Those fuckers almost killed you, baby," Jonas is saying to Sarah. "They owe you a shitload more than three million bucks. Plus, you've been our fearless George Clooney through all this—you deserve it."

"One hundred percent," I say.

"No, I can't—"

"Sure you can," I say.

"Absolutely," Kat adds. She returns my hand-squeeze under the table and leans right into my body.

"But what about you, Josh? Don't you want some of the money?" Sarah asks.

I laugh. "Hell no."

"But you've been helping us from minute one—"

"Of course, I have. I wouldn't have it any other way." I smile at Jonas and he grins.

"Just don't make a decision about the money yet," Jonas says to Sarah. "Think about it for a little while."

Kat puts her hand on my thigh under the table and my cock twitches violently.

"*I want you so badly I'm in pain*," she wrote to me. Jesus Fucking Christ. I can't wait another minute to fuck her.

"So, Henn, how quickly do you think you can—" Sarah abruptly stops talking.

Some dude in a suit has just walked up to our table.

Sarah looks ashen.

Jonas looks like he's about to commit murder.

Oh, Jesus. Shit. This dude's got to be Max—the creep who demanded a "freebie" from Sarah. No wonder Jonas looks like he's about to kill the fucker—I wanna kill him myself. I look at Kat and her eyes are bugging out of her head.

"What do you want?" Jonas spits out, putting his arm protectively around Sarah. He looks like a rabid Doberman pinscher on a leash.

"Hello, Mr. Faraday," the guy says smoothly. "Sarah." He glances at the rest of the table for show, but it's clear he doesn't give a shit about anyone but Sarah.

"I hope you're still enjoying your stay here in Las Vegas?" the guy asks.

"What the fuck do you want?" Jonas asks.

"I had some business in the hotel—what a coincidence to run into you."

The expression on Jonas' face makes me release Kat's hand under the table, just in case I need to leap up and fight this fucker.

"Hi, Max," Sarah says, her voice shaky. "Yeah, that's one helluva coincidence. Hey, everybody, this is Max—a friend of mine. These are some friends of Jonas' who met us in Vegas to party—Jonas' brother Josh, Josh's girlfriend Kayley, and his roommate from college, Scott."

Max barely acknowledges the rest of us. "I just need to steal you for a couple minutes, Sarah." He puts his hand out like he's expecting Sarah to take it.

"No," Jonas says, pulling Sarah into him.

"Hey, guys," Sarah says to the group. "Could you all excuse us for a few minutes?"

I look at Jonas, unsure whether we should leave him and Sarah alone with this asshat or not. "Um... ," I say.

Jonas nods at me, signaling it's okay for us to go.

I flash Jonas a look asking him if he's sure, and he nods again.

"Sure," I say slowly. "Come on, Kayley. Scott. Let's go roll some dice." The three of us get up from the table and walk toward the front door of the restaurant—but just inside the front doors, we stop and watch Jonas and Sarah for a long moment, assuring ourselves they're gonna be safe if we leave, and when it seems certain the guy is here to flap his gums and nothing more, we slip outside the restaurant and enter the bustling casino.

"Whoa, that guy was exactly like I pictured him," Henn says. "Talk about Dr. Evil."

My eyes lock with Kat's. She smiles broadly at me.

"Did you see Jonas' face?" Henn asks. "That Max dude's about to become hash browns, man."

I can't wait another minute. I grab Kat's hand and pull her toward the elevators on the far side of the casino.

"Hey, boss," Henn says behind me. "The craps tables are this way, man."

"You're gonna have to play on your own for a little while, Henn," I say over my shoulder.

"Oh," I hear Henn say behind me. "Gotcha." He sounds crestfallen. And I'm intellectually sorry about that, I really am—because I love that fucking genius like a brother—but right now, the only thing I care about is finally getting to experience the motherfucking force of nature that is Katherine Ulla Morgan from the inside-out.

"Are you taking me to read your application?" Kat whispers, clutching my hand.

I don't reply. We've reached the elevators and I bang on the call button. Now that I've kissed her, I'm about to explode with my pent-up sexual desire. I'm a dam about to break.

"Are you taking me to read your application?" Kat repeats, her voice barely controlled excitement.

I turn to face her. "No. I'm taking you to my room where I'm going to fuck the living shit out of you," I say evenly. "And *then* I'll give you my goddamned motherfucking application."

She clamps her lips together, shocked.

I grunt with frustration and lean in to whisper into her ear. "And I swear to God, you little terrorist, you better not say another goddamned fucking word about that motherfucking application until after I'm through fucking you. You'll get what you want, I swear to fucking God, because it's clear to me now you're as inevitable as goddamned gravity, but first things first I'm gonna get inside that tight little body of yours and fuck you 'til you're screaming my name."

34

KAT

The elevator arrives and Josh pulls me inside, his chest heaving, his eyes blazing. An orchestral version of "Take on Me" by A-ha greets us in the enclosed space.

The doors begin closing and Josh lunges at me, making my clit zing with anticipation—but just before the doors slide shut, a hand stops their progress and an elderly couple steps into the elevator car.

Josh leans abruptly away from me, clasps his hands in front of his crotch, and looks down at the floor of the elevator.

I straighten up, feeling light-headed and weak-kneed.

"Hello," the lady says. She's got silver hair and she's wearing a simple sundress.

"Hello," I say brightly to the woman and her husband, trying to distract attention away from Josh and his pained expression.

"Are you two having fun?" the woman asks.

"Definitely. You?"

"Oh, yes. We always have fun in Vegas. We play the slots and see a show—always a good time."

"Have you been winning?"

The lady laughs. "No."

I look at Josh. His head is bowed. His hands are still clasped in front of his pants.

"What show did you see this time?" I ask, my heart racing.

Josh shifts his weight next to me.

"Blue Man Group," the woman replies, her eyes darting to Josh and back to me. "What have you been up to, honey?"

"Oh," I say. "Nothing much. The usual Vegas stuff—a little craps, *Cirque*

Du Soleil, plotting to overthrow the evil empire and save the world, bringing a stubborn man to his knees—you know, blah, blah, blah."

The woman chuckles.

The older couple's floor dings and they step out, and the minute they're gone, Josh leans toward me aggressively, like he's gonna fuck me right here and now. But a dad with two young kids in swim gear immediately gets onto the elevator, causing Josh to step back and clasp his hands in front of his crotch again.

"We're going *up*," Josh barks out, his eyes like lasers.

"Oh, whoops, thanks," the dad says, putting his arm out to stop the elevator doors from closing. "Come on, guys, step out," the dad says, glaring at Josh. "Daddy messed up. We've gotta go *down* to get to the pool. Sorry about that, folks."

"No problem—have fun," Josh says, obviously trying to make amends for how loudly he just barked at the guy.

Wow. I've never seen Josh look more like his brother than he does in this moment. If this is how Jonas looks at Sarah on a regular basis, then it's no wonder she's suddenly been acting like a cat in heat.

The dad and his kids step off the elevator and the doors close behind them —and Josh freaking *attacks* me. His lips are on mine. His hands are all over me, exploring my breasts and ass and back. Oh lordy, he smells so fucking good. His tongue is sensual and confident, his lips utterly delicious. His hand moves confidently between my legs, under my sundress, right to the crotch of my panties, where his fingers confidently stroke me. I pull back slightly and grip the bulge in his pants as his fingers slide over the fabric covering my clit.

"Oh my God, Kat," he murmurs as I vigorously stroke the hardness under his slacks.

"I'm *dying*," I breathe, my body bursting into flames.

The elevator doors open and we tumble out together, still kissing and groping each other. We bang into the wall with a loud thud but keep going, both of us moaning and laughing at the same time as we work our way down the short hallway toward Josh's room.

"You have a condom?" I mumble into his lips. Oh my God, my body's already beginning to warp and twist from deep inside.

"Mmm hmm."

We're a frantic tumble of lips and fingers and limbs, hurtling together voraciously toward Josh's suite, until—*boom!*—our writhing bodies literally crash into a cart filled with towels and cleaning supplies right outside Josh's room.

"No," Josh growls. "No, no, no."

He grabs my hand and yanks me into his suite, a low rumble simmering in his throat—and, yep, sure enough, a maid is in the bedroom across the large suite, tucking a sheet.

"We don't need cleaning service today," Josh shouts at the poor woman across the large suite, making her freeze mid-tuck.

"Oh, I'm sorry, sir," she says. "I was just finishing up this—"

"Thank you," Josh says, his tone adamant. "You can go. *Please.*"

The maid looks flustered. "Yes, sir." She exits the bedroom and heads toward the front door.

"Thank you so much," Josh says, obviously trying to soften his tone.

"Do you want clean towels before I—"

"*Nope.* We're good. Thank you so much." He squeezes my hand.

The woman presses her lips together and beelines out the front door as fast as her short legs will carry her, obviously surmising exactly what we've barreled into Josh's hotel room to do.

"Oh my fucking God," Josh says the moment the door shuts behind the woman. He hastily reaches behind my back and unzips my dress. "I've waited my entire life to get inside you, Katherine Ulla Morgan." He kisses my neck and peels my dress off my shoulders. "Nothing's gonna stop me now—this hotel could crumble to the fucking ground and they'd find me under the rubble, my dick still hard and inside you."

I laugh.

He pulls my unzipped dress down past my torso, over my hips, to the floor, sliding his palms along my bare skin as he goes, and before I even know what's happening, my dress and bra are on the floor, his tongue is in my mouth, my nipples are rock hard, and he's backing me against a nearby table, his hard-on behind his pants grinding into my crotch.

His mouth leaves mine and devours my neck, collarbone, breasts, nipples. He bites my left nipple and sucks on it feverishly, and I throw my head back, my entire body convulsing and bursting into flames at his mouth's voracious assault. Holy shit, this feels incredible. I can't remember the last time I wanted a man this bad, if ever.

He kisses my stomach, swirling his tongue around the piercing on my belly button, and then moves on to my hips and pelvis, his lips and tongue giving me goose bumps of pure pleasure. I grab and pull feverishly at the collar of his shirt, wordlessly begging him to take off his clothes so I can press my body against his nakedness, but he ignores my implicit request, abruptly kneeling down and leveling his mouth with my crotch. "I couldn't hear you well enough when you came on the dance floor—the music was too loud. I wanna hear every little sound you make when you come."

Oh. I shudder with arousal.

He slides my G-string off my hips, his fingertips caressing my hipbones, his warm lips laying soft kisses on the flesh just below my belly button. When he suddenly and fervently pulls my pelvis into his face, my entire lower abdomen tightens sharply and begins to burn.

"So fucking gorgeous," he murmurs, his warm, wet tongue swirling around the perimeter of my crotch. I grip the table behind me, bracing myself for the delectable moment when his tongue is finally gonna land right where I want it most. Oh God, I'm desperate for him to take my throbbing clit into his mouth and suck on it like a lollipop.

He's getting closer and closer to ground zero, but he's drawing it out, teasing me, sending me into a frenzy. I prop my left thigh onto his shoulder, straining my pelvis toward him, jerking like a dog in heat. I grab his head and yank his hair and he moans into my crotch, puffing warm air onto my sensitive flesh.

Finally, after what seems like forever, his warm tongue flickers onto my clit and begins lapping at me voraciously, eliciting a sound from me like I've just placed my hand on a hot stove. I press myself into him violently, desperately, jolting, gripping the table behind me, my pelvis jerking rhythmically with the hungry movements of his lips and tongue.

"Oh, hell yeah," I breathe. "Fuck, that's good."

Oh God, I'm beginning to clench forcefully from deep inside. This is incredible. This man right here gets the job done right.

"You taste so fucking good," he growls from between my legs. "So *fucking* good."

As his mouth continues working my tip, he slides his fingers deep inside me —and that's all my body needs to release forcefully. In an instant, pleasure is slamming into me like a hurricane—I'm twisting, warping, shuddering around his fingers, all the while grasping urgently at his head between my legs. "Josh," I sputter. "Oh my God, *yes.*" I claw at him, gasping, gripping the hair on the back of his head, his ears, cheeks, neck, yanking at the fabric of his shirt—doing whatever it takes to survive the brutality of the pleasure I'm experiencing.

Josh abruptly takes my thigh off his shoulder and stands up to his full height, his eyes blazing like blue coals. He licks his glistening lips and begins slowly unbuttoning his shirt, his eyes never leaving mine. I'm dripping down my thighs with my arousal, jerking my pelvis in anticipation of the delicious fucking I'm about to take. Oh my God. My clit is vibrating with a low, insistent hum, rippling with faint aftershocks from my orgasm.

As Josh continues unbuttoning his shirt, I reach down and stroke the bulge in his pants, reveling in the delectable hardness of him against my fingertips. I can't think straight. All I can do is *want.*

He peels off his shirt and tosses it onto the floor and I'm treated to the same panty-soaking view of his muscled, tattooed torso I beheld in the hallway after Reed's party. Only this time, he's even sexier than he was to me then, if that's possible.

"Oh my God," I whisper, ogling him. "Oh my *God.*"

Josh flashes a cocky grin. "I know, but feel free to call me *Josh.*"

Even through my intense arousal, I laugh.

"Oh man, I'm gonna fuck you so hard, Party Girl," he growls. "I'm gonna fuck you *and* your fucking Hyphen, baby."

I semi-chuckle—my brain knows that was funny—but I'm too wound up to laugh. I can barely stand, I'm so frickin' aroused.

I run my hands over the "Grace" tattoo on his muscled chest, convulsing with excitement as I do, and then across his "OVERCOME" tattoo scrolling across his ripped lower abs. Oh God, I'm beginning to feel desperate for him.

He leans forward and kisses me, caressing my breast as he does, and I reach down hungrily to unfasten his pants.

I open his belt and zipper and quickly open the front of his pants.

His humongous bulge is trapped inside simple white briefs. I yank feverishly on his underwear and he pulls them off.

I look down at his naked body and convulse with pleasure at the sight of him. Holy fuckballs, he's the sexiest man alive.

Josh embraces me and I melt into his arms, shaking with excitement.

His lips are on mine, his tongue in my mouth, his hands on my back. He gropes my ass and skims his fingers inside my ass crack and I moan involuntarily. Oh God, I'm losing my fucking mind with anticipation.

"Fuck me already," I say. "*Please.*"

I pull back from him and grasp his shaft, twitching with arousal as I do—and at my eager touch, Josh grips the back of my hair, pulls my head back and leans right into my face.

"You've been torturing me—so now I'm torturing you."

He kisses me deeply, still gripping my hair, making my knees buckle.

"I like hearing you beg," he breathes. "As you should."

I'm reeling. I can't think straight. I feel like I'm losing hold of my sanity. Why won't he do it already? I've already waited far too long.

"Please," I beg.

He smiles wickedly. "Oh my God, the things I'm gonna do to you," he whispers, almost to himself. He grabs his pants off the floor, fishes into his pocket, and pulls out a foil packet. Ten seconds later, he looks up from rolling the condom onto his erection, growls, turns me around abruptly and guides my shuddering body to the nearby table.

Good lord, I can't remember the last time a man turned me on this much. I'm non-functional—his for the taking, any which way he pleases. I've quite literally never been this turned-on before.

"You want me, Kat?" he whispers into my ear, pulling my backside into him and reaching around to grope my breasts. "Because I'm gonna fuck you so hard you'll forget all about that fucking application."

"Please," I gasp.

Without warning, he slaps my ass and I yelp with surprise. "You know why I just did that?"

"Because I'm a fucking terrorist."

"That's right, baby." He growls with pleasure.

His fingers move to my crotch and massage my clit rhythmically as he glowers over me from behind.

I moan loudly. "Fuck me."

"Oh, say it again."

"Fuck me."

"Beg me for it," he growls, grinding his dick into my back and working my clit with fervor.

Oh, yeah, I'm liking this. He's good at this. "*Please*," I breathe.

"Please what?"

"*Please fuck me.*" Oh my God, he's working my clit better than any battery-operated-boyfriend ever could.

"Admit you've touched yourself just like this, dreaming about sucking my hard cock."

How'd he know that? "Yes," I breathe. "Every fucking day."

"Now beg me to fuck you one more time. And maybe I will."

Oh good lord. I'm so turned on, I'm gonna come before he's even entered me.

"Fuck me," I say between teeth gritted. This is too much. I'm going fucking insane with anticipation. "*Please* fuck me, Josh. *Please.*" I'm shuddering, trembling, dripping with arousal. My head is spinning. My clit's on fire. I can't wait another minute.

"You're gonna come for me first," he growls, his fingers working me into a frenzy.

At his words, my skin begins prickling like I've got a sudden chill. "Oh, shit," I say. "*Yes.* I'm about to come. Oh fuck. It's gonna be a big one." I grip the table. "Oh, Jesus."

He puts his lips right against my ear, his fingers still working me. "That's right," he whispers, his breath tickling my ear. "Beg me."

"Fuck me now," I gasp. "Please."

He slaps my ass again and I yelp with excitement.

"My little terrorist," he says, his voice low and taut. "I'm torturing you because you've been so, so bad."

I've never been treated this way. Men usually act like I'm their pretty, precious trophy—a prize to be won and worshipped. Nate certainly never spoke to me this way, not even once, and Garrett never said a frickin' word during sex beyond growling like a bear. Sure, occasional guys have talked dirty to me during sex, but this... this thing Josh is doing to me... this is a whole new level—and it's turning me on like crazy.

"Please," I whimper, sweat beading on my brow.

"Bad girl." He slaps my ass again and, immediately, a massive orgasm slams into me, wrenching my insides like a towel being wrung out to dry.

He growls with pleasure. "Oh my God, you're so fucking hot, baby."

He sticks his fingers deep inside me again, making me cry out at the sensation, and the next thing I know, his hard cock is finally, mercifully sliding deep inside me, deep, deep, deep inside me, filling me to the brim and then some.

Josh makes a sound of pure pleasure and that's enough to push me over the edge.

"Oh, *fuck*," I say, my body clenching forcefully around his hardness.

I'm absolutely shocked—I've never had back-to-back orgasms like this, and

I've certainly never had an orgasm triggered solely by the sensation of a man entering me, either. Holy shitballs, I'm being turned inside out.

"Fuck, oh my God. Fuck," I say as warm waves of pleasure grip me.

I lay my palms on the table in front of me, steadying myself as my body tightens and ripples and warps around Josh, this time even harder than the last time. "Oh, Jesus," I choke out. Oh my God, his cock is absolutely enormous inside me—if he misused that thing, he'd surely rip me in two. But, oh my God, no, he's not misusing it—he's using it exceptionally well. I'm clenching so furiously around his cock, I can't breathe.

Josh lets out a low moan as his dick burrows into me all the freaking way—balls deep, baby—and then he grips my hips from behind and leads my body into rhythmic movement with his.

"You're perfect," he whispers into my ear, his hands groping every inch of my body voraciously. "Jesus Fucking Christ, you're fucking incredible."

His thrusts are becoming more and more intense. I gasp with excitement and reach up over my shoulder to grab his cheek and pull him into me.

"You feel so good," he murmurs into my ear, cupping my breasts in his large hands. He kisses my neck, pinches my nipples, fucking me all the while in rhythmic thrusts. "You're so fucking wet and tight," he growls. "You feel so good."

Good God, I can't think. I'm overwhelmed with pleasure.

"You feel so fucking good," he whispers into my ear again, pumping rhythmically inside me. "You've got a magic pussy, baby."

Oh Jesus. I've never been treated like this before—never been fucked so well and with such glorious dirty-talk, too. Oh my God, I'm losing my freaking mind.

I slam myself into him as best I can on wobbly legs, moaning and grunting as I do. I'm riding his cock as hard as I can, losing complete control. I'm a rubber band about to snap. I reach down and touch the spot where his cock is sliding in and out of me, then let my fingers wander to his balls and feel them swinging and slamming to and fro against me as he thrusts. The sensation makes me shudder with pleasure.

"You're gorgeous," he whispers into my ear, his fingers working my clit as he thrusts. His free hand finds its way to my mouth and I suck voraciously on his fingers.

He makes a strangled sound. Oh, he's ramping up hard. I can feel it.

He pulls his finger out of my mouth and abruptly bends me over the table, pushing on my back and forcing my sweaty chest into the glass.

"You liked torturing me, didn't you?" he growls.

"Yes," I breathe.

He slaps my ass harder than ever and my body jerks with pleasure.

"Tell me you're sorry for what you did."

"I'm not sorry," I say.

He spanks me again.

I inhale sharply, and that hand-on-a-hot-stove sound escapes my lips again.

"Oh, yeah, that's it," Josh says, apparently already keyed into my body's cues. "Here it comes, baby. Come for me."

A couple more spanks and deep thrusts and I climax again, gasping as I do —and a moment later, Josh jerks with what seems like a massive orgasm, too.

When my body stops warping and clenching, and Josh seems to have finished coming behind me, I sprawl myself onto the table, completely spent, soaking in sweat and shaking with my exertion.

Oh my God. That was the best sex of my entire life. I never wanted it to end. And, holy shitballs, I wanna do it again as soon as humanly possible.

"Holy That Was Even Better Than I Expected, Batman," I finally say, my sweaty cheek resting against the glass table. "Daaaaaay-am."

Josh laughs and slaps my ass, hard, but I barely flinch.

"Hell yeah, it was, Batman—or, shit, wait, are you Robin?" He chuckles. "Dude, I just realized—were Batman and Robin *gay*?"

"I think they were just really, really, *really* close friends."

Josh pulls out of me and turns my limp body around to face him. "You're amazing," he says simply, looking into my eyes with surprising tenderness. "I had pretty high expectations for fucking the Party Girl with a Hyphen, I gotta admit, and it was even better than I'd fantasized."

He cups my face in his palms and kisses me—and I melt into him, returning his kiss passionately, my heart racing. For several minutes, we kiss and kiss and kiss, making up for lost time, I suppose, our mouths consuming each other voraciously, my sweaty breasts smashed into his muscled chest, my arms wrapped firmly around his neck.

"Best ever," he whispers.

"Ditto," I whisper. I don't know if he's saying this to me as a figure of speech, but I'm being literal. That was quite literally the best sex of my life. "I feel high right now," I say. "Like I could jump out a five-story building and fly."

Josh laughs. "'I am a golden god.'"

"*Almost Famous*," I quip, easily identifying the source of his quote.

Josh beams a smile at me. "We can add that to your list of dude-like qualities: 'can identify movie quotes.'"

I laugh. "Yeah, I'm pretty damned good at it, actually."

"You're good at everything," he says tenderly. He sighs and strokes my hair. "You're amazing—like a drug. I feel totally buzzed right now. Jesus."

I blush.

"I loved your application, by the way. Best gift I've ever gotten." He smirks. "And utterly diabolical of you, I must say—brilliant strategic maneuver. I couldn't resist you after that."

"So does that mean I'm a shoe-in to get approved for the Josh Faraday Club?"

"Oh, you're a shoe-in, for sure, baby. Fuck yes. But the approval process takes a bit of time, you should know, so you gotta be patient. I suggest we order some room service while we wait for round two of the review process—that motherfucker Max interrupted my burger and fries and I'm hangry as hell about it."

I laugh. "Oh, really? Is that how this is gonna go down? You're just gonna keep fucking me 'til I forget all about your application?"

"Yeah, that's pretty much the plan."

"That wasn't the deal," I say, narrowing my eyes. "The deal was you kiss me, you give me the application."

"No, the deal was I kiss you; I *fuck* you; I give you the application. I've kissed you. I've fucked you—and now I'm gonna fuck you again and again (all part of the *approval* process, baby)—and *then* I'm gonna give you my application."

A wave of anxiety floods me. "Josh, you aren't really gonna try to weasel out of giving it to me, are you?"

He flashes me a megawatt smile. "Of course not. I never go back on my word. That's something you should know about me right up front." He touches my thigh. "My promise is ironclad."

I exhale in relief.

"Don't worry, PG, the review process will continue only as long as we're in this hotel room together. Just give me this little bubble of time to fuck you without that shit hanging over my head—and when we leave this hotel room, the review process will be complete, your membership will be approved, and that stupid application will be all yours."

I make a face.

"Aw, come on, PG. I kiss you; I fuck you; I give you my application. That was the deal. Remember? You said kissing you would lead to immediate fuckery. I'm just taking you at your word."

I glare at him. I'm not sure that was the deal. But sex with Josh is so freakin' good, I'm not feeling the urge to argue with him.

"Don't fight me on it, baby, just enjoy the ride." He snickers. "YOLO, right? Wasn't that the super-cool thing you told me to say as much as possible?"

I roll my eyes.

"YOLO, Kat. YOOOOOOOLO."

With that, he pulls the condom off his dick, slaps my ass yet again, and heads into the bathroom—giving me my first ever view of his beautiful bare ass... which, much to my shock (and squealing delight), is stamped across its left cheek with four tiny, but unmistakable, letters.

35

KAT

"What the fuckity, Josh? You didn't feel the slightest urge to mention the 'YOLO' tattoo on your ass cheek when I was going on and on about how 'YOLO' tattoos are social suicide?"

We're sitting in our underwear on Josh's bed, macking down on double cheeseburgers, fries, and Moscow mules from room service, laughing hysterically and involuntarily wiggling our bodies to the beat of the disco song blaring on Josh's laptop ("You Dropped a Bomb on Me" by The Gap Band, which Josh says is now his official theme song).

"How the heck did you manage to keep quiet about your tattoo? That must have taken Herculean willpower."

"Meh, I figured it'd be best for you to find out about it exactly the way you did—by seeing my ass in all its glory after I'd fucked you." He smiles wickedly. "So much more fun than just *telling* you about it. Am I right?" He chomps a French fry.

I laugh. "Why the *hell* do you have 'YOLO' stamped on your ass cheek, Josh? It's inexcusable. Seriously, if I had any self-respect whatsoever, I'd grab my shit and go."

He laughs. "I lost a bet." He takes a big bite of his burger.

"What?" I shriek.

"I lost a bet," he mumbles, his mouth full of burger.

"Well, what was the freaking bet?"

He finishes chewing. "See, that's the thing. I don't remember exactly."

"What?" I shriek. "You got 'YOLO' tattooed onto your ass-cheek and you don't even know *why*?"

"Well, I know *why*—generally speaking. The bet was over a quote from *Happy Gilmore*. I just can't remember *which* quote we were arguing over."

I smack my forehead with my palm. "Please tell me you're kidding. You got YOLO inked onto your ass over a quote from *Happy Gilmore*?"

Josh laughs and turns off the blaring disco song. He looks at his laptop for a moment, searching for something. "Oh, this is a good one. Listen to this—Jonas turned me on to these guys." An acoustic guitar suddenly fills the room. "X Ambassadors. 'Renegades.'"

"Yeah, great song," I say. "You were about to tell me how *Happy Gilmore* led to your tragic ass-tattoo."

He shrugs. "It's embarrassing."

"All the more reason to tell me."

He rolls his eyes. "It was when I was at UCLA, when I lived in my fraternity house. A group of us used to say 'YOLO' all the time, laughing our asses off about it, thinking we totally made it up. And, hell, maybe we did, for all I know —several years later, Zac Efron got 'YOLO' tattooed on his hand and my friends and I texted each other like crazy about it, like, 'Did you see Zac Efron stole our thing, man? We came up with that years ago!' And, then Drake claimed he invented it in a song, and Reed was like, 'Yeah, that's 'cause the fucker came to my house for a fucking party and we were all saying it!'"

I laugh. "You guys started a trend."

"That's what cool kids do, baby." He winks.

"But that doesn't excuse you getting it stamped onto your ass, Josh Faraday. That's just inexcusable. Seriously."

He chuckles.

"Please explain this horrifying tragedy to me."

He laughs gleefully. "Well, like I say, 'YOLO' was kind of a thing with my friends and me, but only because we thought it was super douchey and hilarious and stupid. And one night at the house I was drinking beer with Henn and Reed and a few other guys and we were throwing out movie quotes and guessing the movie, as one does, and Henn threw out some quote from *Happy Gilmore*. I was like, 'Dude, no, you've got it wrong.' And he was like, 'No, dude, I have it exactly right.' And I was like, 'No, no, man, it's *this*.' And he was like, 'No, man, it's definitely this other thing.' And I was like, 'I love you, man, like a brother, but you're wrong as shit.' So we went around and around, both of us positive we were one-hundred-percent right, until finally Reed said, 'Okay, dudes, put your money where your mouth is. Whoever's wrong has to get 'YOLO' inked onto his ass.' Well, everyone in the room lost his shit. For some reason, that was the funniest idea we'd ever heard. So, of course, I was like, 'Hell yeah. I'm in, motherfucker.' Because the chance to saddle Henn with a fucking 'YOLO' tattoo, and on his *ass cheek* no less, for eternity, was too good to pass up. And I guess Henn was thinking the same exact thing about me, so he was like, 'Boo-fucking-yah.' So we shook on it and then Reed put on a DVD of *Happy Gilmore* and found the scene with the quote, whatever it was, and, *motherfucker*, Henn was exactly right."

For a long beat, I'm laughing too hard to speak and Josh is right there with me.

"That's just... insane," I finally choke out. "What a horrible, horrible reason to get YOLO stamped on your ass."

"Could there possibly be a good reason?"

I consider. "Yes. If Make-A-Wish called and asked you to do it for some poor kid with cancer. That's literally the only defensible reason to get a 'YOLO' tattoo anywhere on your body."

Josh laughs. "But, see, the thing is I never go back on my word—no matter what. We went out that very night to a tattoo place in Hollywood and I did it." He chuckles to himself, seemingly at a memory. "Henn and Reed were laughing so hard the whole time, they wound up on the floor of the place, sobbing like little girls."

"Well, I hope it was worth it," I say. "Because you've got that horrible thing *forever,* Josh."

He shrugs. "Meh, there's no such thing as forever. Skin's just temporary— we're all gonna die, right? Sooner or later, maybe sooner. And, yeah, it was totally worth it—in fact, it turned out to be a very good thing."

"How could a 'YOLO' tattoo on your ass possibly turn out to be a good thing?"

"Because it's a constant reminder to me of something I don't wanna forget." He considers his words for a moment. "I was so fucking sure I was right about that damned quote—and I was dead fucking wrong. So I guess that stupid tattoo reminds me not to get too cocky or comfortable in life—no matter how much I think my shit doesn't stink, I could always be dead wrong." All joviality in his demeanor is gone. He swigs his drink.

His face has turned dark. I bite the inside of my cheek, unsure how to respond.

"And, hey, either way, it's a good story, right?" he adds. He's obviously trying to lighten things up again. "So that's always a win in my book."

"Oh, yeah, it's definitely a good story," I agree. "And a very telling one, too."

"Telling? In what way?"

"About you as a person."

"Oh yeah? Pray tell—what does my YOLO ass-tattoo tell you about me as a person? Besides the fact that I'm a total dumbshit, of course."

I chuckle. "It tells me plenty of stuff—some of it kind of deep."

He raises his eyebrows. "Well, this ought to be good."

I take a long sip of my drink, gathering my thoughts. "Well, okay, they're not *all* deep and profound things—some are kind of, you know, online-profile-ish."

"Tell me all of it."

"Okay. Well, you were in a fraternity, obviously."

He nods.

"And you're fun."

"I am."

"You're a guy who'll do frickin' anything for a laugh."

He makes a face like that's patently obvious.

"You're an extremely loyal friend."

"I am. Extremely."

"You're a man of your word," I continue. "That's pretty deep and profound, I'd say."

He nods decisively. "I am most definitely a man of my word."

"Unless you've promised to give a girl your application to The Club after you kiss her."

He rolls his eyes. "Patience, little terrorist. It's coming. The review process is just a bit lengthier than you realized. Kiss, fuck, application, I told you—we're still in the 'fuck' stage of the proceedings. What else?"

I make a stern face about the application, but he looks so adorably charming, I melt. "Well, you like to party—or at least you did back then."

He holds up his drink, making it clear this observation is still accurate and I return the gesture. We clink our glasses and take giant swigs of our drinks.

"What else?" he asks.

"You like dumb comedies like *Happy Gilmore*," I reply.

He laughs. "Definitely. Oh shit. *Please* tell me you like dumb comedies. I should have mentioned that's a bit of a deal-breaker with me. No movies with subtitles, please."

"Of course, I love dumb comedies," I say. "*Duh.* I have four brothers, remember? Until I went off to college, I didn't know televisions were capable of showing anything besides dumb comedies, football, and my mom's HGTV."

Josh laughs. "I really should have asked you about your movie preferences before I fucked you. I got lucky, but it could have gone horribly wrong for me." He grins. "So what are some of your favorite dumb comedies? *Anchorman?*"

I nod enthusiastically. "'I love Scotch. Scotchy, Scotch, Scotch,'" I say, doing my best Ron Burgundy impression. "'Here it goes down—down into my belly.'"

Josh belly laughs. "'I'm kind of a big deal.'"

I giggle.

"So what's at the tippy-top of your list of favorites?" he asks.

"Well, in the modern era I'd have to say *Twenty-One Jump Street* is pretty damned high on the list."

"Ah, good one. 'Hey, hey, stop fuckin' with Korean Jesus! He ain't got time for your problems! He busy—with Korean shit!'" Josh shouts, doing his best Ice Cube impression.

I laugh hysterically. "'Chemistry's the one with the shapes and shit, right?'" I reply, doing my best stoned Channing Tatum.

"'Did you just say you have the right to *be* an attorney?'" Josh adds, laughing his ass off.

"'You *do* have the right to be an attorney, if you want to,'" I reply, and Josh laughs his ass off.

"'You have the right to... suck my dick, motherfucker!'" he says.

Oh, jeez. We're laughing so hard we can't breathe.

"Oh my God, Kat—you're a dude, through and through," Josh finally says, beaming at me. "A really, really hot dude with a tight, wet, magic pussy."

I bite my lip. Man, I love this boy's dirty mouth.

"So what about a classic?" he asks. His face is glowing.

"Hmm. I'd have to go with *Zoolander*."

He shoots me the "Blue Steel" male-model face Ben Stiller made famous in that movie.

"Blue steel!" we both shout at the same time.

"Oh my God, Josh," I say. "You're the first person I've ever seen make 'Blue Steel' look *good*."

He laughs. "So is that it? Is that everything you've figured out about me from my deep and profound 'YOLO' ass-tattoo?"

"Oh no, there's more." I look at him sideways. "You clearly have a bit of an evil streak."

"No, I don't. Not at all. We're talking about *me*, not *you*, remember?"

"Ha, ha."

"Really, though, I don't have a mean bone in my body."

"Ha! You were willing to tag poor Henn's ass for the rest of his life, for nothing but stupid yucks."

Josh looks wildly offended. "How the fuck does that make *me* evil? Henn was willing to do the exact same thing to me—and, in fact, he *did* do it to me. That makes Henn way more evil than me."

"But Henn was *right*."

"But I didn't know that. Actually, the most heinous person of all was Reed. He's the one who came up with the diabolical idea in the first place, just for his sick pleasure, the prick."

"Yeah, that was pretty evil."

There's a beat as we both sip our drinks, smiling broadly at each other. My skin is buzzing with electricity.

"What else can you tell about me, Party Girl? I like this game."

"Well, you've got an extraordinarily beautiful ass. Perhaps the most beautiful ass I've ever seen."

"Thank you. Back at you. Especially when it's stomping furiously down a hallway in nothing but a G-string."

"Oh, you liked that, did you?"

"I liked that a lot."

"I could tell." I wink. "Your wet undies were completely see-through, you may recall."

He licks his lips. "You wanted me so bad," he says, "you were losing your fucking mind—not to mention dripping down your legs."

I smirk, but I don't deny it.

"So tell me more, PG. More, more, more."

"Well..." I trail off. "Besides the fact that you have a beautiful ass?"

"Besides that. Something deep and profound."

"Okay. Well . . ." I twist my mouth. "You seem to be ... kind of... I don't know the word. I took Philosophy 101, but I forget it all. *Fatalistic?*"

"I think that's when someone believes their fate is, like, written in the stars—outside their control. Is that what you mean?"

"No. That's not it. Well, maybe, sort of."

"Because I *am* fatalistic to some degree. I think some things are beyond our control—like a brick wall you're hurtling toward whether you like it or not. Nothing you can do about it."

"Well, jeez. That's kind of a bummer."

"Not necessarily. Some brick walls feel fucking awesome when you crash into them." His eyes flicker. "Some brick walls are worth the pain."

I blush.

"What about you—do you believe in fate?"

I shake my head. "No. I believe in kicking ass."

He smirks. "So, then, what did you mean to say?"

"What is it when someone thinks nothing matters? That everything is kind of pointless in the end?"

"I think that's nihilism. I'd have to ask Jonas, though. But, of course, I'd never do that because then he'd talk my ear off about fucking philosophy for an hour and then I'd have to kill myself, which would be a major bummer."

"Oh. Well, I wouldn't have been able to come up with the word 'nihilism' if my life depended on it. I must have meant something else. I dunno."

"Is that what you think of me? That I don't think anything matters?"

"No. Of course not. I know things matter to you."

He shifts his position on the bed. "Because I definitely think some things matter. A man's word. Friends. A man's family—whatever's left of it, anyway." A shadow briefly crosses his face. "It's just that so *few* things really matter, there's no sense getting too worked up about much. Getting a stupid ass-tattoo? Who gives a shit, you know? Like I say, in the end we're all gonna die anyway, might as well just enjoy the ride and not sweat the small stuff."

"So maybe your YOLO tattoo isn't really a reminder to you not to get too cocky or comfortable, after all," I say tentatively. "Maybe, it's more something to help you remember the few things that actually matter to you."

There's a long beat.

"What about your other tattoos?" I ask, suddenly uncomfortable with the silence. I wasn't trying to get all deep—it kind of happened by accident. "Did you get your other tattoos in tribute to the few things that matter—or because we're all gonna die, anyway?"

He makes a face. "Some of each, depending on the tattoo."

"When did you get the one for your mom?" I ask.

"When I was twenty, I think."

"She died when you were seven?"

He nods.

"Why did you tell me it means 'But for the Grace of God I go' rather than telling me it's your mom's name?"

He shrugs. "I never tell people about my mom."

"Why not?"

"Why are you asking me so many questions?"

"Because I gave you my application and you still owe me yours."

He makes an annoyed face. "When I was really young, I used to tell people about her whenever anyone asked. Jonas and I had to see a therapist when we were kids and I used to just talk and talk and talk. Blah, blah, blaaaah. But when I was a teenager, I noticed every time I told people, I felt *worse*, not better. Telling people made them look at me funny—like there was something wrong with me because my mom was murdered—like, I dunno, all of a sudden, they thought every time I laughed I was full of shit. And then, after my dad died, and everything that happened with Jonas, I just shut the fuck up completely. From then on, talking about Mom just opened the floodgates to questions about my dad, which meant I'd pretty much be talking about Jonas and all his shit. And I realized I don't need anyone scrutinizing my face as I'm talking for telltale signs that I'm 'laughing through the pain.'"

I bite my lip.

He exhales. "New topic. Have you always been this way?"

"What way? Annoying?"

"No. So fucking *orgasmic*."

"Oh." I make a face like he just gave me whiplash. "Wow, that was a sudden shift in topic."

He forges right ahead. "I've never been with a woman who has orgasms so easily and often as you do." He smirks and bites into a fry. "I'm already addicted to making you come. Best game ever."

I feel a surge of pure elation, but I don't reply.

"Jesus, if I could come that many times in a row, I'd never leave my room. You must masturbate all the time."

I blush.

"Oh, come on. Cat got your tongue, Kitty Kat? You wrote me that awesome application and now you're gonna get all shy on me?"

"It's different to write all that stuff down than to talk about it, face-to-face."

"Aw, come on, PG." He shoots me an incredibly charming look. "It's just me, remember? Honesty-game. How often do you masturbate?"

I feel my cheeks blazing.

"Come on, Kat. Honesty-game, baby."

I sigh audibly. "Every day, pretty much. I try not to let a day go by without having an orgasm."

"*Nice.*"

"An orgasm a day keeps the blues away."

"I love it. When did you discover your motor runs so hot?"

My cheeks are hot. "Growing up, my brothers always talked about sex and jerking off as easily as talking about the weather. When I was, like, twelve or thirteen, I asked my oldest brother, Colby, if girls jerk off and got off, too, just like boys, and he said, 'Sure they do—of course—it's just a bit harder to tell.' He was so matter of fact about it, like it was no big deal. He made me feel like one of the guys, like it was perfectly natural and not shameful or weird. So later that day I put the showerhead between my legs and left it there on the massage setting, and within a few minutes, I had my very first orgasm. And I *loved* it. I mean, I was like, 'Oh my God, that was the best feeling ever.' So then every single time I took a shower, I just made it a habit to give myself an orgasm, along with washing my hair and shaving my legs—just a part of my routine. And soon, I was getting off twice in one shower. And then I started reading romance novels as a teen and touching myself and getting myself off... I dunno. I just got really good at it." I shrug and take a huge bite of my burger.

Josh's eyes are boring holes into my face.

"What?" I ask.

"You're incredible," he says. "The hottest woman alive. Do you have any idea how hot you are?"

"Honesty-game?" I ask.

He smirks. "Of course."

"Yeah, I think I'm pretty hot." I giggle and take a bite of a French fry.

He laughs. "Yes, you are, Madame Terrorist. Most definitely."

"Do you know how hot you are?" I ask.

"Honesty-game?"

I nod.

"Yeah, I think I'm pretty hot."

We both laugh.

"So when you masturbate, what's your weapon of choice?" he asks, swigging his drink.

"Why do you wanna know all this?"

"I'm collecting intel for future use. Plus, it's just plain turning me on."

I make a face. "Well, recently, the thing I like to use the most while touching myself is the memory of this one really hot guy with a huge dick, standing in a hallway, dripping wet in his tighty-whities, every detail of his hard-on clearly visible beneath his wet briefs."

Josh grins. "Wow, that's quite a coincidence, because, recently, I've been partial to jacking off to memories of this one incredibly hot terrorist, stomping down a hallway in her bra and G-string, her bare ass-cheeks quaking with fury as she goes."

I laugh.

"So tell me exactly how you like to masturbate. What works best for you? Lying down? Shower? Toys? Fingers?"

All of a sudden, my clit is tingling. "*Why?*"

"Because I wanna know. It'll help me get you off to know exactly what you like."

"It's hard to explain."

"Ah. Show me don't tell me?"

I nod. There's a beat. I know exactly what he wants me to say. My heart is pounding in my ears. I bite my lip. "Would you like to watch me do it some time?" I ask softly.

He nods, his eyes smoldering. "I thought you'd never ask."

My cheeks flush. I swallow hard. Why is this turning me on so much?

"But, first, tell me about it." He licks his lips. "I wanna hear you tell me."

I bite the tip of my finger. "Well, I really like to do it in the shower, with my fingers. I also have a vibe—a Rabbit. That does the trick the quickest, but sometimes I don't want quick. Sometimes I like to take my time, let it build and build until I get myself off so hard I have a backache the next day."

He exhales slowly. "This conversation is turning me the fuck on."

"I can see that." I glance down at his huge erection behind his briefs.

"Have you ever used a Sybian?" he asks.

"A what? A *Sybian?*"

He nods.

"No, I have no idea what that is."

He looks aghast. "No idea?"

I shake my head.

He takes a huge swig of his drink, clearly energized by whatever grand idea has just popped into his head. "Oh shit. You're gonna be epic on a Sybian."

"What is it?" I ask.

His eyes are absolutely blazing with excitement. His dick is rock hard in his briefs. "I'd rather show you than tell you," he says. He grabs his laptop off the nightstand, turns off the music, and begins searching the Internet for a moment. "Bingo," he says after a minute. "Oh, PG, we're gonna have some fun tonight." He smiles broadly at me. "You trust me?"

"In what context?"

He furrows his brow, obviously offended by my question. "In any context."

"I'll answer that question after I've read your application."

"Bullshit. You trust me."

I shrug. "I've been wrong before."

"You're not wrong this time."

Goose bumps erupt all over my skin. I nod.

Elation floods his face. "Excellent." He grabs his phone and punches out a phone number on his screen, evil-laughing with glee as he does. "Yeah, hey," he says into the phone. "I'm looking to rent a Sybian tonight, as soon as possible?" He pauses to let someone on the other end of the line speak. "No, tomorrow won't work—it's gotta be tonight. Right *now*. I want it delivered to my hotel room within the next thirty minutes." Josh says the name of the hotel and pauses to let the person on the other end of the line speak. "Listen, dude. I don't care if someone else reserved it. That's not my problem. I want it and I'll make you an offer you can't refuse. What's your usual rate for rental and delivery of a Sybian for one night?" He pauses. "Okay, piece of cake. I'll pay you ten times that, in cash, *if* you get it to my hotel room within the next thirty minutes." Josh smiles broadly and winks at me. "Yeah, I thought so." He repeats the name of the hotel and gives the guy his room number. "Thirty minutes or less, I'll pay ten times your usual rate. If it's here within an hour, I'll pay only five times as much," he says. "Any longer than that, I'll pay three times your usual rate, as long as it's here by midnight." He smirks. "Yeah, okay, see you soon."

When Josh hangs up the phone, I'm staring at him, dumbfounded. What the hell did I just agree to?

Josh rubs his hands together. "Oh, Party Girl. You're in for such a treat. And so am I. Shit. I can't wait to see this. I've never been with a woman who gets off like you do. This is gonna be fucking amazing."

"You've never been with a woman who gets off like me? Really?"

"Really—and, trust me, women get off with me—I've got a magic cock—but you're something special. A fucking unicorn."

"Seriously?"

"You know you are."

"No, I don't. How would I know that? I have no basis of comparison. I'm not the one who sleeps with women."

"Ha! That's right—you've only slept with *one* woman." He winks.

I roll my eyes. "I didn't *sleep* with her. I just *made out* with her."

"What, exactly, is the difference between making out and sex when there's no dick involved?"

I think for a minute. "I'm not sure. But we definitely just made out."

"Well, did you two just kiss and kind of grope each other outside your clothes?"

I blush.

"Holy shit. More than that?"

I don't reply.

"Did you go down on her?"

"*No.*"

"She went down on you?"

I blush again. "*No.* Just kissing and heavy petting. But we weren't in our clothes." I clear my throat. "Stop looking at me like that."

Josh bites his lip. "I'm not looking at you like anything. Tell me all about it."

"No."

"Honesty-game."

"Screw that. So far, the honesty-game has been me spilling my guts to you and getting nothing from you in return."

He grins. "Now you see how it feels."

I roll my eyes.

"Come on, PG. Gimme a little dirt about your lesbo-encounter. Look how hard you're making me." He motions to the bulge behind his briefs.

I feel myself blushing like crazy. "My friend was just trying to drive her boyfriend crazy. They'd had a fight and he was being an ass and she was trying to make him lose his shit. We were just being, you know, naughty, trying to get him riled up. It was pretty hot, actually. He sat there and watched us."

"Ah, so that's what turned you on, huh? Having him watch?"

My cheeks are absolutely blazing. "Yeah. I guess so."

Josh's boner is absolutely huge behind his briefs—and the look of arousal on his face is unmistakable.

"Did the boyfriend join in after a bit?"

My heart is racing. "I think I'll wait to answer that question 'til after I've seen your application. The honesty-game only gets you so much when it's a one-way street. Speaking of which, I do believe it's time you gimme that damned application."

"I kiss you; I fuck you; I give you my application—I told you. We're still in the I-fuck-you portion of our program." He lies back onto the pillows on the bed, smirking, and puts his arms behind his head—revealing tattoos on the undersides of his biceps that say "Welcome to" on one arm and "the Gun Show" on the other.

"Oh, Jesus, Josh, no," I say, rolling my eyes. "No, no, no. Those are even worse than freaking 'YOLO'!"

He laughs.

"You're hopeless." I hit my forehead with my palm. "Oh my God. What am I gonna do with you?"

He's laughing his ass off. "I told you. Drunken tattoos are kind of my *thing*. These bad boys were a dare." He flexes his bicep and kisses it.

"Josh. *No*."

"Kat. *Yes*. I had to—I had no choice. Reed 'double-dared' me, Kat. What else was I supposed to do?"

I laugh. "Holy hell. From here on out, you're gonna check with me before you even walk past a tattoo parlor. Do you understand me?"

He laughs. "Thanks, Mom."

I twist my mouth. "You're joking, but that shit wouldn't have happened if you'd had an ounce of fucking parental supervision in your life. You're just an overgrown child."

He shrugs. "Yeah, probably. I haven't had a parent since I was seventeen."

"You've never had anyone tell you to stop acting like an idiot, have you? Everyone around you just double-dares you and goads you on."

"Pretty much."

"Well, jeez." I shake my head. "Call me before you do anything else involving ink on your body. Do you hear me? You're a freakin' train wreck, Josh Faraday. You need someone to slap you occasionally."

He belly laughs. "I know—I totally do." He's beaming at me.

I roll my eyes. "That shit would so not fly in my house. My mom would have whipped you the fuck into shape. Jesus God."

He laughs.

"So what's the deal with your other tattoos? What other monstrosities am I gonna find on you?"

"No other monstrosities. Everything else is meaningful."

"What's the story of 'OVERCOME'?"

He takes a long sip of his drink. "Sorry, I don't tell anyone the truth about that one."

"No?"

He shakes his head.

"What do you say when people ask you?"

"I just say it means, you know, 'keep your chin up' or 'rise above' or some other inspirational sound-bite like that."

"But that's not true?"

"Well, yeah, it's *true*. But that's too simplistic to be the whole truth."

"What's the whole truth, then?" My heart is suddenly clanging wildly.

He looks at me with hard eyes for so long, I'm not sure if he's ever going to answer my question. "I never tell anyone the whole truth about that particular tattoo."

I bite my lip. "Well, gosh, I never tell anyone my initials spell *KUM*." I flash him my most charming smile. "*And* I never tell anyone I made out with a woman. *Or* about Garrett Asshole Bennett calling me a slut." I feel my cheeks burning. "And I *never* tell anyone about poor, sweet Nate and how I broke his heart." I frown. Even saying his name makes me feel literally sick with guilt.

Josh looks unimpressed.

"Aw, come on, Josh. I already know the truth about your 'Grace' and 'YOLO' tattoos, so why not go balls-deep and tell me about the rest of them, too?"

Josh exhales. "Yeah, but I never would have told you the true meaning of 'Grace.' Sarah spilled the beans for me, against my will."

I purse my lips. What more can I do? I can't force the guy to open up to me.

Josh takes a deep breath. "Shit." He looks up at the ceiling like he's trying to make a decision.

I wait, my skin buzzing.

Josh looks at me with sparkling eyes. "Goddamn you, Kat. I really can't resist a woman who uses the phrase 'balls-deep.'"

I grin.

He sighs audibly. "I got my 'OVERCOME' tattoo so I'd see it every single day and feel inspired to keep going, no matter how much I sometimes just wanna lie down and say 'I can't fucking do it anymore.'"

I wait again.

"You sure you wanna hear the whole fucking thing?"

I nod. "Honesty-game."

"Okay. Here it is. Honesty-game." He exhales loudly. "I got it because sometimes, it's all too much. Sometimes, I wanna just... you know... escape."

I nod, encouraging him to keep talking.

"I got it because my mom was slaughtered while I was sitting at a fucking football game with my dad. Because my poor brother was so traumatized by what he witnessed that day, he still hasn't recovered." His voice cracks.

He pauses, collecting himself.

I nod again.

"I got it because my dad killed himself by blowing his brains out, and made sure poor Jonas would find him." His voice cracks again. "I got it because my dad offed himself without saying goodbye to me or leaving me even a goddamned fucking note." He swallows hard. "I got it because Jonas drove himself off a fucking bridge that same day, and if he'd succeeded in offing himself, I would have joined him at the bottom of that bridge." He looks at me with blazing eyes.

I nod again. My skin is electrified.

"You want more? Because I got more."

I don't even hesitate in my reply. "I want it all, Josh."

His eyes are on fire. His chest is heaving. "I got it because, after the thing with my dad, my brother was in a fucking mental institution for almost a full year, totally and completely losing his shit—he didn't even look like himself, Kat. There was nothing I could do to help him. No joke I could tell to make him laugh. No words of wisdom to make it all better. So I went away to college or else I was gonna fucking kill myself, I swear to God—I was right on the verge —and I joined a fraternity and lived in the loudest, most chaotic house I could fucking find and got shit-faced half the time and high the other half and made friends who saved my fucking life. And from there on out, I've been Happy Josh all the live-long fucking day."

My heart is racing. I swallow hard.

His voice becomes low and quiet. "I got it because sometimes I get so fucking tired of being the sane brother, the one who always rises above, the one you can always count on, the *happy* one, I just lose my fucking shit, Kat. I lose it. And then I go on a bender of one kind or another until I get whatever crazy fucking shit out of my system—and then I go back to being Happy Fucking Josh just like I always am—just like Jonas needs me to be."

I swallow hard, trying to alleviate the lump in my throat.

I wait, but Josh doesn't say anything else.

He clears his throat. "Will you excuse me for a minute?" he says abruptly.

Without waiting for my reply, Josh gets off the bed, beelines to the bathroom, and disappears.

I sit for about a minute, staring at the closed door, trembling, swallowing hard.

And then a dam breaks inside me and I burst into tears.

36

KAT

For ten minutes, I sit and wait for Josh to come out of the bathroom. And in that time, I manage to regain control of my emotions. I'm calm again. My eyes are dry.

I switch the song on Josh's laptop to Audra Mae (my new favorite) singing "The River." And then, I sit and wait.

Josh comes out of the bathroom and sits back down on the bed, positioning himself exactly the way he was before he left the room.

I open my mouth to speak, but he cuts me off.

"So, PG, I have yet to discover a single tattoo on you," he says, his voice light and bright. "And, believe me, I've conducted an extremely thorough search."

I shift my position on the bed. My heart feels like it's gonna hurtle out of my chest. I put my hands over my face, collecting myself. I didn't expect him to come back in here and pretend he never said any of that stuff to me. I was steeling myself to hold back my tears while he continued pouring his heart out to me. I didn't expect him to come back in here like nothing happened.

"Ever thought of getting a tattoo?" he asks, his voice tight, his eyes pleading with me to play along.

I can't concentrate. I don't know what to do—how to react. "Um," I stutter, "I have one, actually."

"You do? Where?" His eyes are warming, reverting to the way they always look.

I pivot my body and lift my hair, revealing a tiny scorpion on the nape of my neck. "I'm a Scorpio."

"Whoa. Sexy. Can't believe I missed that. So are you into astrology? Or you just really like being a Scorpio?"

"Yeah, I love astrology. I've read a bunch of books on it."

There's a beat. His chest is rising and falling visibly. He bites his lip.

"Um, I wanna get a second one," I say, still not sure how I'm supposed to proceed here. "But I've just never been able to decide on something that would be meaningful enough—something I'd want 'til the end of time."

"Well, that's silly. There's no such thing as ''til the end of time.' Just get what you like right now. That's all we have, no matter what story we tell ourselves to make us feel better."

There's a long beat. Damn. He's kinda dark.

His eyes flicker. "I don't wanna sit here and talk about my fucking feelings all night long, okay? Just forget I ever said all that shit to you, okay? Don't ask me about it—just put it out of your head, okay? Please."

"Okay. I'm sorry."

"What are you sorry about?"

"For... I dunno. Forcing you to spill your guts if you didn't want to."

"You didn't force anything. I'm a grown-ass man." He pauses a long time. "I shouldn't have told you all that. I'm sorry."

"No need to apologize. I'm a grown-ass woman. I told you in my application—I want to know the real you. I don't want Happy Josh. I want Real Josh."

He stares at me for a long beat. "So, as far as a second tattoo for you goes, my advice is don't overthink it. My brother always thinks his ink has to make some earth-shattering statement about the meaning of life." He scoffs. "But you can waste half your life trying to be all deep and profound all the time. The bottom line is we're all gonna die—so who gives a shit if you die with 'YOLO' stamped on your ass or not?"

My stomach is somersaulting. This is not the fun-loving Josh I've come to know.

He motions to my half-eaten plate of food. "You done with that, PG?"

I nod.

He grabs the half-eaten burger off my plate and polishes it off and then clears my plate of all leftover French fries, too. "You want another drink?"

"Thanks."

He gets up and puts our empty plates on a table and then moves behind the bar, his glorious body on full, dazzling display. "So, okay," he says, opening a bottle. "Where the fuck can I find this Garrett Bennett fuckwad? Because I swear to God I wanna hunt him down and beat the fucking shit out of him."

I don't reply. He suddenly looks different to me.

"Stop looking at me like that," Josh says, his jaw pulsing. "See? This is exactly why I don't talk about any of this shit. Now you're looking at me funny. I don't like it."

"I'm not looking at you funny."

He scoffs. "This is the real me, Kat." He motions to his bare torso. "What you see is what you get—a wise and powerful man with a huge cock."

There's a long beat.

Josh clenches his jaw. "So, back to Garrett Asshole Bennett. Why do you care if that guy said you aren't 'marriage material,' Kat? He was obviously a total prick."

I swallow hard. I've never talked about Garrett Asshole Bennett with anyone. I've always been too ashamed at what an idiot I was. I open and close my mouth, struggling to find words.

"What does it matter what some total douchebag said about you?" Josh persists. He pours something into two glasses on the bar. "You're awesome, Kat. A beast. He was obviously dead wrong about you."

My heart is pounding in my ears. Did Josh just indirectly call me *marriage material*?

"It just freaks me out how utterly *clueless* I was. I was ready to give my heart to a guy who thought I was a slut."

"That reflects poorly on him—not on you. You trusted him. He took advantage of you. He was a shit. A cruel, heartless, self-loathing, small-minded, small-dicked little shit."

"It's okay. In the end, it was probably a good life lesson."

"What was the lesson?"

I consider my words. "I think Garrett Bennett is my 'YOLO' tattoo. I was one hundred percent sure of something, and I turned out to be dead wrong." I shrug, trying to come across like it's no big deal. "Good thing to remember."

He looks pained. "That douche deserves to get the shit kicked out of him," he says between gritted teeth.

There's a loud knock at the door and Josh is instantly distracted. A wide grin spreads across his face. "Oh, damn. Looks like talking about our fucking feelings will have to wait, thank God." He suddenly slaps his face—really hard —leaving a bright red mark.

"What the hell?" I gasp.

Josh chuckles and slips around the bar toward the front door, a wide smile on his striking face. "I do believe your chariot has arrived, Party Girl."

37

KAT

Josh hands the delivery guy a huge wad of cash and gleefully turns back around, a large, hefty-looking cardboard box in his arms, an evil gleam in his eye.

At the look of trepidation on my face, he laughs. "Don't worry, PG. You're gonna love it."

"What is it?"

"You'll see."

He places the box on the edge of the bed, opens the flaps, and peeks inside. "Come to papa," he says, his dick visibly hardening in his briefs.

He pulls out a tarp-looking thing and spreads it on top of the bed.

"Oh, jeez," I say. "Am I about to star in an episode of *Dexter?*"

Josh chuckles.

"Why the heck do we need a freaking *tarp?*"

"Because things can sometimes get a bit messy." He winks.

"Huh?" I say.

But Josh doesn't elaborate.

"Did you write about this machine in your application to The Club?" I ask.

He scoffs. "*No.* Don't think about that stupid application right now. Just live in the moment, Kat. Just enjoy the *ride.*" He snickers. "Literally and figuratively."

"What the fuck is this thing?"

Josh reaches into the box and pulls out a little black machine—a little half-domed box-machine, about a foot long and wide and high, attached to a black power cord and a small control box. Basically, the thing looks like a curved saddle with a power cord.

"It's an orgasm machine," Josh says simply. "It was designed to give a woman the most powerful orgasm she's ever experienced—over and over and over again—for as long as she can stand it." He places the Sybian in the middle of the bed on top of the tarp. "This baby's about to rock your world, Kitty Kat." He smiles greedily. "And, therefore, mine."

I survey the contraption for a moment, utterly fascinated. "So I sit on top of it?"

"Yeah, ride it, cowgirl."

My lower abdomen is beginning to burn and tighten with anticipation.

He points at a flesh-colored strip of prickled rubber on top of the machine, at the apex of the half dome. "This rubber strip here presses against your clit, giving you as much vibration as you can handle—I think the highest setting is something like a small jet engine or something, literally." He laughs. "And then the second stimulation is... Hang on." He reaches into the box, rummages around, and pulls out a clear bag filled with hygienically sealed, flesh-colored dildos, complete with veiny shafts and mushroom tips.

My eyes go wide. "Whoa."

"Pick whichever cock you want," he explains, holding up the bag of dildos of varying sizes. "And then it rotates inside you, hitting your G-spot over and over, while the vibration on the pad blasts your clit."

A dull ache is beginning to burn painfully in my lower abdomen. "This thing looks pretty intense."

"Yeah. It is. Are you game to try it?"

My nipples are hardening. My crotch is filling up with blood. My clit is fluttering and zinging in my panties. "Um. Yeah?"

"Excellent." He sits down on the edge of the bed, his face blazing, and pats the empty spot next to him. 'Okay, PG. Pick your dick."

I sit next to Josh on the bed and he hands me the clear bag of vacuum-sealed dildos. I look through them for a moment, studying each one carefully, my heart racing. There are several varieties to choose from, including a double-pronged dildo thing clearly intended to slide up two holes at once.

"Yeesh," I say, holding up the double-duty dildo. "This one looks interesting."

He grins. "I think you'd better start with something slightly less ambitious for your first ride at the rodeo. Maybe next time for that one."

"Yeah, definitely next time." I roll my eyes and he laughs. I rummage around again and pull out a detailed rubber finger, complete with a knuckle and nail bed. "Wowza." I hold it under Josh's chin like I'm tickling him. "Coochie coo."

Josh laughs. "That's probably a good choice, seeing as this is your first time out. Good entry-level dildo."

"Hell no, I need something more than a freakin' *finger*. I want a *cock*, man. Come on." I rummage through the bag again and finally hold up a big, fat dildo with a thick shaft and bulging tip. "How about this one?" I say.

"Whoa, that's pretty big for your first time," he says. "You sure you don't want to start a little smaller, maybe get used to the rotation first?"

"No way. I like big cock, baby."

His eyes ignite. "Oh yeah?"

"The bigger the better." I blush like a virginal schoolgirl. I'm talking a good game—but this whole situation is way outside my comfort zone. I've never done anything like this. "Have you done this before?" I ask. "I mean, you know, rented an 'orgasm machine' for someone?"

"No." He smiles like that's a stupid question. "I've seen women riding Sybians online, of course—you know, in porn and on Howard Stern or whatever—but I've never rented one for a woman—though I've always fantasized about doing it." His eyes light up. "Especially with a woman like you."

I feel my entire face turning beet red. "And what kind of woman am I again?" If he's calling me a slut, I swear to God I'm gonna—

"Hot as the fucking hinges of hell," Josh replies.

Oh. My inner voice shuts the hell up.

There's a beat.

"Ready, babe?"

My chest is tight.

Before I can reply, Josh bends down and takes my nipple into his mouth.

Instantly, my body bursts into flames. Oh God, forget the machine. I want him—I want him inside me.

But Josh pulls back. "Okay, cowgirl," he says, his eyes sparkling. "Time to ride."

I nod. My cheeks are hot.

"Go pee while I attach your dildo and get everything all set up for you."

"I don't have to pee."

"Try. You need to void your bladder completely before you get on this thing. It's gonna make you feel like you're gonna piss yourself, even though you're not. You gotta be able to relax completely for it to work its magic."

"Lovely," I say, scrunching up my face.

"Oh, it will be," he says, his blue eyes sparkling wickedly. "Trust me."

38

KAT

I come out of the bathroom.

Josh has attached the dildo to the machine, plugged the power cord into the wall, and laid the control box neatly in front of the box on the bed. He turns to look at me, his face ablaze.

"Come here, babe," he coos. He holds out his hand and I pad across the room toward him, my skin zipping and zapping with anticipation.

When I reach him, he takes my hand, pulls me into him, and begins kissing me.

"This is a big-time fantasy of mine," he says into my lips. "Thank you."

"My pleasure," I say—though my mind is reeling. I really don't know what I've gotten myself into—and whether this truly will be my "pleasure" or not. I've never let a man watch me masturbate before in any form, let alone on a machine with a jet engine.

His fingers slip inside my undies and into my wetness. "This is gonna be epic," he says, kissing my neck. He snaps the waistband of my G-string. "Take these motherfuckers off, baby."

I pull my undies down, shuddering with anticipation, and stand before him naked, my clit throbbing under his gaze.

"You're gorgeous," he says, his eyes smoldering. "You ready?"

I nod.

"Climb on, cowgirl."

"Are you gonna show me how to work the controls first?" I ask.

"Oh, no." He grins. "*You're* not gonna work the controls—*I'm* gonna work them."

"*You're* gonna work the controls?" I ask, my eyes wide. "No, I'd feel much more comfortable working them for myself."

"Nope. I gotta be in control, Kat." His jaw muscles pulse. "That way, you can lose yourself completely. No thinking required. You'll just go on the ride of your life." He strokes my hair like I'm a puppy. "I'll take care of you, babe, I promise. No worries."

"What if it's too much? Too fast? Too strong?"

"Then I'll slow it down."

There's a long beat.

"You can trust me. It'll be fucking amazing."

I exhale. "You'll be careful with me? You'll listen to whatever I say?"

"Of course." He smiles. "Always."

"Okay."

"The vibe on your clit and the rotation of the dildo run completely independently of each other, each of them on a separate control dial. So we'll start really slow—one stimulation at a time and on the lowest setting. And then we can work our way up higher and higher on the first stimulation—we'll start with the dildo—and then we'll add vibe if you're liking it—nice and slow to start, and we'll work our way up to *The Exorcism*. Whatever you can handle."

"Oh, Jesus," I say, hopping back. "No *Exorcism*."

He laughs.

"I'm serious, Josh. No *Exorcism*. Save letting me get possessed by Satan for the second date."

He chuckles.

"I'm relieved you find that funny. I still haven't read your application, you may recall. Please tell me Satanism isn't something that turns you on."

He rolls his eyes. "No, Satanism doesn't turn me on. What kind of pervert do you think I am?"

"Dude, I have no idea what kind of pervert you are. That's the whole point of me wanting to see your application."

"All in good time, PG. All in good fucking time. In the meantime, have a seat on this bad boy so we can make any necessary adjustments before we get started."

"Adjustments?"

"We have to make sure the vibe is perfectly flush with your clit when you're sitting completely upright. You don't wanna have to lean forward to get your clit stimulated, or else the dildo won't hit your G-spot at the right angle. And that's where the money is—hitting your G-Spot." He smiles devilishly. "A woman who has clit orgasms *loves* sex—but a woman who gets G-spot orgasms *can't live without it for a single fucking day.*"

I stand staring at him, speechless for a moment. I've never heard a man talk this way. I feel like, up until this moment, I've slept with a whole bunch of boys. But Josh is a real man.

Josh motions gallantly to the machine. "Your chariot awaits, m'lady. Hop on."

I can't believe I'm doing this. I'm about to let Josh watch me masturbate on a jet engine?

"Do me a favor," I say. "Take off your briefs. I wanna be able to see your hard-on while I ride."

A broad smile spreads across his face. "My pleasure." He wordlessly removes his briefs, revealing his massive hard-on. "Climb aboard, my lady," he says softly, motioning to the machine.

My crotch is aching and burning. My nipples feel like bullets. My chest is tight. "Honestly, I'd rather climb aboard your cock right now," I whisper.

His cock twitches. "All in good time. That's coming next. Now get on, babe. This is a total fantasy for me; you have no idea."

I crawl onto the bed and straddle the machine on my knees, hovering my crotch just above the tip of the huge dildo, contemplating how the hell to lower myself onto it. Now that it's positioned right at my entrance, it seems a helluva lot bigger than it did a moment ago.

"Wait. Hang on," he says.

I freeze with the dildo positioned right against my entrance.

He bounds over to a duffel bag in the corner and comes back with a condom packet and a bottle of lube. He opens the packet and lays the rolled-up condom on top of the opened wrapper on the corner of the bed—out of the way but clearly at the ready—and then he squeezes some lube into his hand and spreads a huge mess of it all over the dildo, then across the prickly rubber pad intended for my clit, and then he reaches between my legs and covers my clit and hole and lips in slickness, making me shudder and moan softly at his touch. Without missing a beat, he squirts another big glob of lube into his palm and matter-of-factly slathers his hard-on with lube.

I'm suddenly overwhelmed with sexual excitement. "Okay to sit now?" I ask, my voice tight.

"Yeah." His voice sounds as excited as the way I feel: totally turned-on.

I lower myself slowly, taking the dildo into me, and position myself gingerly into the saddle. "Whoa," I say, shifting around and getting acclimated. "This thing's *huge.*"

"You want a smaller one?"

"No, no, this is good." I take a deep breath, willing my body to relax around the rubber inside me. "Ooph. It's big, though. Just gimme a second. Damn."

"You okay?"

"Yeah. I get off the hardest when I feel totally filled up. Just give me a second to relax."

His cock twitches. "This is so fucking hot." He exhales.

I take another deep breath and my body relaxes and absorbs the dildo completely.

"Okay, I feel good," I say. "Whew."

"All right, lemme check the fit." He bends down and carefully assesses the contact point between the machine and my clit. "Yup, looks good," he says. He touches my clit gently, making me twitch. "Keep your clit perfectly flush with this rubber strip for maximum pleasure. Okay? No need to lean forward. It's all adjusted perfectly."

I'm already twitching and shuddering with anticipation. I nod.

"Sit back, Kat. The key is letting that cock hit your G-spot over and over. That's where the money's at, baby."

I sit back.

"Good. Does it feel like your clit is flush with the pad when you sit back like that?"

"Yep."

"The more upright you sit, the more G-spot stimulation you'll get—and that's what we're really going after. *G-spot*—not clit, contrary to popular belief."

I nod. "Silly rabbit, clits are for kids."

He laughs. "You're so fucking hilarious." He looks me up and down for a moment, his eyes devouring me, his erection straining.

"Um. Josh? Hello? I'm kinda sitting here with a big, fat dildo up my wahoo?"

He laughs. "Okay, PG. Here we go." He kneels in front of me on the bed, his hard-on massive, and strokes the curve of my hip for a moment, making me shudder. "I'll start with the dildo first, rotating on low, no vibe at all yet, just so you can get used to the motion inside you. Okay?"

I nod and let out a shaky breath. "Please be careful with me."

He touches my hair. "You're in good hands, baby."

I nod again.

Josh sits on the bed next to me and picks up the control box like a kid with an X-box. "You ready, babe?"

I nod.

The machine comes to life, humming loudly, and the dildo begins rotating slowly inside me, swiping repeatedly at a pinpoint location. "Oh," I say, taken aback at the sudden sensation. "Wow. That's amazing." I lean forward instinctively, trying to relieve the pressure already building inside me.

"No, don't lean forward," Josh reminds me. "You can lean back, but never forward. Go against instinct. Don't try to relieve the pressure. Push through it."

I lean back, as instructed. "Wooh," I say, the sensation making my skin prick. "Wow. That's really nice. Whoa."

A beaming smile spreads across Josh's face. "You like that, babe?"

I nod and take a deep breath, trying to steady myself.

"That's the lowest setting—just rotation, no vibration."

"Oh," I say again. "Wow. That's hitting me exactly right. It's like magic. Wow."

"This thing is engineered to do nothing but give you orgasms," Josh says. "Just tell me when you're comfortable, and I'll increase the speed of rotation a bit."

Wooh, this thing is igniting me with no clit stimulation whatsoever, just the swipe... swipe... swipe of the dildo inside me, rotating round and round, hitting my G-spot at the exact right spot with each revolution. It's amazing, really, like nothing I've felt before. So precise. I moan softly. "Oh, God, I like this," I say, my voice beginning to quaver. My skin suddenly erupts with goose bumps. There's suddenly a strange pressure in my ears.

"Wooh," I say softly. "Oh boy."

"Ready for faster?"

I take a deep breath and nod.

Josh twists a dial on the control box and the rotation inside me palpably increases in speed. Swipe, swipe, swipe, the dildo goes, quite a bit faster than before, hitting my G-spot in rapid succession with only a fraction of a second in between each swipe.

"Oh, Jesus," I say. I let out a very loud moan. The wall of my vagina contracts sharply and doesn't release. It just keeps tightening. "Ooph," I say. Something huge is building inside me. I've never felt anything quite like this before. "Holy shit," I say. I begin to lean forward, aching to relieve the pressure.

"No. Don't lean forward. *Back.*"

I lean back.

"Good. Now start humping it, babe," Josh says. "Move your hips like you're on top of me, fucking the shit out of me, trying to get yourself off."

I comply, and it's like I've been struck by lightning. My body begins squeezing and clenching fiercely, winding tighter and tighter.

"Yeah, that's it," Josh says. He's begun stroking himself with his free hand. "Oh my God. So hot. Just like that, babe."

I look at Josh, the way he's jerking himself off, the totally perverted look on his face, and my entire body bursts into a ball of flames.

I move my hips forward and back with increased enthusiasm, imagining I'm fucking him, and he growls his approval. "Nice," he says, his hand stroking his shaft fervently. "Oh, Kat. You're killing me right now. You're so fucking hot."

The movement of my hips, combined with the rotation of the dildo and the sight of Josh jacking off—and especially the look on his face—are all conspiring to turn me into something inhuman. Oh, jeez, I'm about to turn into a freaking werewolf. I'm sweating. My skin is rippling all over. My heart is leaping out of my chest.

Josh twists the dial again.

Swipe-swipe-swipe-swipe-swipe-swipe-swipe-swipe-swipe-swipe,   the machine says, a perfect frenzy of precise stimulation.

Holy shitballs. Jesus fucking Christ. Oh my God.

I make a sound like a wild boar that's just been struck by a hunter's crossbow.

"Holy shit," I gasp. The pleasure is too much to bear. I have to relieve the pressure somehow. I lean back and fondle my breasts and pinch my nipples and throw my head back, grinding my hips voraciously into the machine, growling like a maimed beast. I'm completely swept away by the outrageous sensation inside my body. I literally bite my fingers, my knuckles, grab at my hair, claw at my face, looking for relief from the painful pleasure.

"I'm pushing it higher," Josh chokes out, and the machine buzzes louder.

The dildo is raging inside me now, whacking the shit out of me from the inside. I look down, expecting to see my abdomen visibly zigging and zagging and lurching with the insane rotation of the dildo inside me, like how that alien bursts out of that guy in *Alien*, but all I see is my usual belly and pelvis.

"Oh, Jesus," I whimper.

I'm howling like a trapped animal, fucking the shit out of the machine, sweating like a pig. I'm in pain now. Horrible, brutal pain. And it feels so good.

The entirety of my skin suddenly pricks with goose bumps, exactly like I'm about to throw up—and a strange numbing feeling overtakes my feet. That's something new. What the hell is that? "Oh, shit," I say. "I'm gonna come." I roar. "Oh fuck. It's coming." I dry heave. Whoa, that's new, too.

My toes curl and I let out a weird screeching sound.

"I'm turning on the vibe now, along with the rotation," Josh whispers, his hand working his shaft furiously.

A low vibration hits my clit and, instantly, my body hurtles into some sort of a seizure, warping and clenching and twisting so violently, I feel like I'm gonna lose control of my bowels. My eyelids flutter and my eyeballs roll into the back of my head. I dry heave again.

I shriek. "Oh my fucking... *fuck!*"

My entire body wracks with the most intense orgasm of my life. It's indescribable. I feel like I'm being possessed by a fucking demon.

But rather than give me relief, Josh increases the vibration on my clit.

I can't control myself. I feel like I'm being electrocuted.

I begin releasing strangled expletives at the top of my lungs as my body is slammed by orgasm after orgasm without reprieve. Is this one long, continuous, unending climax, or multiple ones stacked one on top of each other? I can't tell. The pleasure doesn't end. My body's in some sort of trance, warping and wrenching, buckling and undulating, over and over, without relief. I feel like I'm gonna barf or burst into tears or piss all over myself. Or all of the above.

I make yet another sound I've never heard myself make before, and, all of a sudden, I feel warm fluid gushing out of me and pooling underneath me in the saddle. Was that pee? Well, if it was, I don't even care. I just keep humping the saddle furiously, shrieking, my head thrown back, sweat pouring down my face and trickling down my breasts, my body creating a loud slapping noise as my flesh pounds furiously into the wet saddle over and over.

I manage a glance at Josh and he looks enraptured.

The vibe and rotation both increase together and I shriek.

I run my hands over my face, through my hair, bite my fingers, moaning with pleasure and pain. All of a sudden, I feel Josh's lips on my hard nipples, sucking me. He's licking up the sweat off my neck, kissing me furiously.

"I want you to suck my cock," he growls.

I nod. "No. Yes, yes."

He rises to his feet on the bed, bends his legs to lower his dick to the right height for my face, and shoves his hard-on in front of my face. But instead of shoving it into my mouth, he unexpectedly stops and places his wet tip on my chin, right on my little indentation.

"Oh yeah," he says, running his hands through my hair. "Look up at me."

I can barely follow his command. I'm about to come again.

He growls. "Been wanting to do that since I first saw that little cleft in your chin."

Before I can reply, he slides his hard-on from my chin into my mouth, and I instantly begin sucking on him voraciously, moaning loudly as I do.

This is insane pleasure. My body and mouth are both filled up with cocks, my clit is vibrating, his hands are running through my hair. I swirl my tongue against the little hole at his tip, and he growls loudly, grabbing furiously at the back of my head.

My eyes roll back into my head again.

I'm dizzy.

A strange vertigo overtakes me, a kind of tunnel vision. I feel like I'm literally gonna keel over. A blast of white light bursts in front of my eyes and momentarily dances in my field of vision, as if I've just come inside after being in the brightest light and my eyes haven't yet adjusted.

I bat Josh's hand forcefully and pull my mouth off his hard-on.

"I can't," I sputter.

Josh drops down to the control box in a flash and the machine instantly stops humming. The vibration stops. The dildo stops moving.

The machine comes to a complete stop—and yet I'm still twitching and gasping like a freshly caught fish.

Without hesitation, Josh leaps behind me on the bed, roughly lifts my pelvis off the dildo, pushes me forward onto my hands and knees over the machine, and begins furiously licking and suckling my pussy from behind, lapping up the fluid that's literally dripping out of me.

I shudder and moan at the sensation of his tongue and mouth slurping and sucking and lapping at my sensitive folds and creases, at how passionately he's eating me.

"Are you on the pill?" he grunts.

"Yes. Do it."

"Are you clean?"

"Yes. Do it."

"I'm clean."

"Do it."

He plows into me without hesitation, all the way, and proceeds to fuck the motherfucking shit out of me.

I cry out with pleasure as a bone-rattling climax hurtles through me, yet again.

I'm delirious. Out of my head. Aching for him to tear me clean apart.

His fingers reach around me to my clit as he pounds me, and, all of a sudden, I'm blinded. Literally. All I can see is a white light. Then yellow. Pink. Holy shit. My abdomen twists. I feel like I'm gonna throw up. My toes curl. My skin pricks. I dry heave again.

Warm fluid suddenly gushes out of me the way it did on the machine a few minutes ago and spurts down my thighs. Oh, Jesus. I can't see. I literally can't function. I think I'm gonna black out.

Josh grips the back of my hair and comes so hard inside me, I can feel his cum shooting into me.

Holy... Something-Something, Batman. Fucking hell. I'm so fucked up right now, I can't even come up with a clever Batman quip. Fucking fucky fuck. Holy fuck. Fuck. That's about all I got. Holy Fuck, Batman. Fuck you.

Josh scoops me up into his arms from behind, kisses my neck, and fondles my sweaty breasts. I can't return his affection. I can't move. I'm an inanimate object in his arms. A floppy, spineless, sweaty blow-up doll.

I feel his lips against my ear, his hands in my sweaty hair. "You're the hottest woman alive, Katherine Ulla Morgan," he says, kissing my ear. "My fantasy in every fucking way. Holy fucking shit."

39

JOSH

Kat shifts in my arms in her sleep and I freeze.

I'm freaking out.

I never, ever have sex without a condom. Ever. It's my cardinal rule and I never break it. *Ever.* No matter the woman. No matter how hot she is. No matter how hot the sex promises to be. I didn't even go bareback with Emma, and we were together for three fucking years. What the *fuck* was I thinking doing it with Kat?

I look at Kat's sleeping face, my heart racing. What if we just made an accidental Faraday? I can't stop hearing my dad's voice, ringing in my head: "'Don't you dare let me catch either of you making an accidental Faraday with a woman unworthy of our name or I'll get the last laugh on that gold digger's ass and disown the fuck out of you faster than she can demand a paternity test.'" How many times did I endure hearing Dad say those fucking words to Jonas and me? Way too many times to count. It was his fucking mantra.

I study Kat's sleeping face again. Even asleep, even without animation to her features, she's utter perfection. That cleft in her chin slays me. Her eyebrows. Her lips.

Adrenaline floods me.

Who gives a fuck what Dad said? Kat's not a gold digger—and Dad's no longer here to disown me even if she were. So what if Kat and I fucked up and made an accidental Faraday? It's none of his fucking business, either way. And, anyway, it was well worth the fucking risk. I smile to myself. Best sex of my fucking life. In the international sport of fucking, this woman just took the gold *and* silver medals. And when I fuck her for a third time, which I plan to do as soon as she wakes up, she'll no doubt snag the bronze medal, too. The woman's got superpowers or something. She's a fucking fembot is what she is. Oh my God. That's it. *Katherine Ulla Morgan is a fucking fembot.*

I'm screwed. Doomed. I smile to myself again. But what a way to go.

Kat shifts in my arms in her sleep and I freeze again. Oh my God. I'm acting like a complete lunatic right now. A total and complete lunatic. I'm acting like fucking Jonas is what I'm doing, letting my mind run uncontrollably. I need to get a fucking grip.

Kat shifts again and a lock of her blonde hair falls into my face.

I breathe in her scent.

Damn, she smells good.

I lift the sheet up and stare at her sleeping body for a moment. I take in the curve of her breasts as she breathes in and out slowly. Her waxed pussy. Her flat belly with her sexy little belly-ring. Her long, toned legs. Her bright blue toenails. Oh my fuck, she's a drug.

I put the sheet back down and gaze at her sleeping face for the hundredth time.

She's so fucking gorgeous, I could look at her all day and never get tired of her face. Her nose. Her lips. Her cheeks. All of it, gorgeous. I can't find a single flaw with this woman. Well, physically, anyway. She's certainly flawed as hell otherwise, that's for fucking sure. First off, she's jealous as fucking hell—something I normally *hate* in a woman. But wait a second. Is that really a flaw when it comes to Kat? Because, holy shit, I kinda like that about her. It's a nice change from how Emma never gave a shit, no matter what I did or what woman practically threw herself at me right in front of her. I thought it meant Emma was somehow more evolved than the average woman, somehow *enlightened*—smarter than me. Of course, in retrospect, now I know it just meant she didn't give a shit.

But enough about Emma. I don't give a shit about her right now. I can't believe I even let my mind wander to her when I've got a woman like Kat in my bed. Speaking of which, I just thought of another flaw. She's stubborn. So fucking stubborn I want to throttle her. But, wait. I like that about her, too. I want things my way, of course—but I wanna *work* for it. Otherwise, I get bored. And there's no such thing as getting bored with Kat, is there? Jesus God, no.

And, in Kat's defense, she's not just jealous and stubborn. She's also ridiculously funny. And smart. Not a brainiac in the traditional sense, maybe, but who the fuck needs book smarts? Bah. Overrated. Just look at Jonas. Smart as hell and the biggest dumbshit I know. Kat's the kind of smart I care about: witty, clever, intuitive, and sassy. Oh God, is she ever sassy. And, on top of all that, she's got a heart of gold underneath all that gorgeousness. It's buried deep underneath a thick outer layer of evil, maybe, but it's there, for sure, buried nice and deep. The way she loves Sarah—the way she doesn't even think twice about her own safety when it comes to protecting Sarah and going after the bad guys for her... man, that shit knocks me out. And, damn, she sure does love her family, too. I've never met a girl from a happy family before. It makes her fascinating to me.

And oh my God, who am I kidding about all that shit, anyway? She could be fucking Attila the Hun from the orphanage across the street and I'd still be infatuated with her after what I just experienced. Holy motherfucking shit, can this woman fuck. I've never seen anything like her. I seriously wanna murder that Garrett Something-or-Other guy—what the fuck was his name? Slut-shaming motherfucker. He sure didn't mind Kat being a slut when he was banging her against his headboard, did he? Fucking asshole cocksucking fuck-wad. He must have a very tiny dick, that's all I can say. Asswipe.

Because this woman can suck a dick and ride a cock and come like a fucking tornado. And I don't know any man, other than that fucking douchebag, who'd even *think* of putting a woman down for any of that. Hell no.

Kat stirs again and her eyes flutter open. She smiles and my heart skips a beat.

"Hey," she says softly. "I drifted off."

"No worries. I enjoyed watching you sleep."

"Well, that's not creepy or anything."

"Let me clarify: I enjoyed lifting up the sheet and ogling your naked body while you slept."

"Oh. Okay, I feel better now." She stretches. "Wooh. Every single muscle in my body is sore. Wow. That was intense."

She puts her arms around me and I follow her lead, pulling her into me. We lie nose to nose for a long moment.

"I had some sort of *episode*," she says.

"Sure looked that way. Damn."

"Dude. I went blind. Like, lights were flashing before my eyes. I saw white, then pink, then yellow. And then everything went black. I thought I was dying or being beamed up by aliens."

"Cool."

"Weird," she says.

"Awesome," I say.

"That's never happened to me before. I think I might have had an aneurysm."

"Have you ever squirted before?"

"Is that what I did? I *squirted*? I've never heard that term before."

"You've *never* heard of squirting? Jesus, woman, have you been living under a sexual rock without access to wifi?"

She shrugs.

"Yeah. It's totally a thing. Watch some Internet porn some time, dude. It's kind of like the brass ring of porn."

"Huh."

"You don't watch *porn*?"

"No. It bores me. I like erotic novels a lot. That's my porn. I love them."

"Ah. Yet again, you prove you've got a vagina."

"Dude, if your dick sliding into a warm, tight, wet hole between my legs didn't prove that well enough, then I'm done."

"Could have been smoke and mirrors, you never know."

She laughs.

"I like your warm, tight, wet hole, by the way. I like it a lot."

"Aw, thank you." She puts her hand on her heart like she's accepting an Academy Award. "What a lovely thing to say."

I laugh.

"I kinda surmised you liked my warm, wet hole when you sucked on it like a kitten getting the last drops of milk out of a baby bottle," she adds.

"Holy shit, Kat. That was so fucking hot."

She giggles. "Best ever, fo shizzle ba dizzles."

"Best ever really?"

"Mmm hmm. That's for damn sure. Feel free to help yourself to my warm, wet hole any ol' time you like. Jesus God, that was good. Seriously, that right there was the absolute most amazing sexual experience of my life."

I'm electrified. I push my body into hers and nuzzle my nose into her cheek. "You're so fucking sexy, Kat. I feel like an addict and you're my drug."

She kisses me. "Me, too."

"And the way you rode that Sybian? That memory will stay with me for the rest of my days."

She giggles. "That machine was something else. No wonder it's big in porn."

"Yeah, but that's the thing. I've seen it a million times in porn, and it never does *that* to anyone. Not even close. Jesus. I knew you'd get off on it, but I could never have predicted *that*. It was like you got electrocuted."

"It was incredible. If I owned one of those things, I'd never leave my house."

"If you owned one of those things, *I'd* never leave your house. You wouldn't need an alarm clock. I'd sit in the corner of your room yelling, 'Wake up, Kat! It's Sybian time again!'"

She smiles, but then she pauses, apparently considering something. "I need to tell you something, Josh. I never have sex without a condom—well, unless I'm in a committed relationship and we've both been tested. I don't go without protection casually."

"I was just now freaking out about the same thing. I never do it, either."

"You're sure you're clean?" she asks.

"I'm positive. Just had my annual physical. You?"

"Yeah, I'm sure. One hundred percent. I was tested two months ago when I went on the pill, and I've used condoms every single time since then."

I exhale, totally relieved. "Okay. Well, then I think we should—" I'm interrupted by my phone ringing on my nightstand. "Hang on," I say, turning onto my back and reaching for my phone. I look at the screen. It's Jonas.

"Hey, bro," I say.

Instantly, just by the sound of Jonas' breathing across the phone line, I can tell he's agitated about something.

"Agent Eric just called," Jonas says stiffly. "The feds want a meeting with Sarah and me in Washington *tomorrow*."

"Holy shit." I sit up from Kat, my heart leaping out of my chest. "So are you and Sarah gonna catch a flight tonight?"

"Yeah, I already booked a red-eye. We're packing up now."

"Wow." I run my hand through my hair. "This is big."

"What still needs to be done before Henn can make those bank transfers?" Jonas asks.

I look at Kat. She looks anxious.

I think for a minute. "Um. Henn said he needs to take Kat's passport photo and make her an 'Oksana Belenko' passport. But he said that won't take long."

"Okay, good. I don't know how fast this thing's gonna move once Sarah and I have that meeting. You three need to be ready to make those money transfers as early as tomorrow, just in case."

"We'll be ready."

"Can you come up to my room?" Jonas asks. "I need to talk to you before I leave." He lets out a loud breath. "There's something I need to bounce off you."

"Sure thing, bro. Don't stress. Whatever it is, we'll figure it out. Let me hop in the shower and come right up. Hang on a sec." I pull the phone away from my face and address Kat. "Jonas and Sarah are leaving in an hour for the airport —they're going to D.C. to meet the feds tomorrow. You wanna head up to their room with me?"

Kat's eyes go as wide as saucers. She nods.

I put the phone back to my mouth. "Kat and I will jump in the shower and be there as soon as possible. I'll call Henn and tell him to join us, too."

"Kat's with you?"

"Yeah."

"And the two of you need to hop in the shower?"

I can't help grinning broadly. "Yep."

"I knew you two were fucking! Why have you guys been so secretive about it?"

I ignore the question. "So we'll be up there in fifteen, okay?"

"You like her?"

I look at Kat's gorgeous face. She looks anxious. "Mmm hmm," I answer.

"Awesome. Okay, see you in a few. Oh, and hey, Josh, I need to talk to you privately when you get up here—without the girls overhearing us, okay?"

"Cool. Whatever it is, we'll figure it out."

Jonas lets out a long breath. "Thanks, Josh. See you soon."

"You bet. So, hey, wait, how'd it go with Max after the rest of us left the restaurant? He was like a fucking James Bond villain with metal teeth."

"No, he's a villain from *Die Hard*."

I laugh. "*Exactly.* Oh my God, yes."

"That's what Sarah says."

"So what happened after we left?"

"Nothing. We just swung our dicks around for a bit. I called him mother-fucker like twenty times and told him not to even look at Sarah and he stomped away like a butt-hurt little baby."

"Good."

"Motherfucker."

"Pussy-ass bitch." I pause. "Hey, Jonas, now that I've seen the guy, I have a weird feeling about him—a really bad feeling. Don't underestimate him. The dude looks like he has no soul."

Jonas makes a sound of agreement. "Hence the reason I wanna talk to you privately before Sarah and I head to the airport. I'm thinking no loose ends."

"Yeah, I follow you, bro," I say. "I agree."

"I just wanna talk it through. Make sure I'm not missing anything."

"Gotcha. I'm thinking the fucker from the bathroom at U Dub, too."

Jonas' breathing hitches on the other end of the line. "You've read my mind."

"It's not hard to do. You're kind of a simpleton."

Jonas laughs. "Okay, motherfucker, stop fucking the shit out of Kat for a goddamned minute and get up here. There's a lot to talk about before Sarah and I head out."

"I'd only stop that particular activity for you, bro, just so you know."

"Good times?"

"The best of times. Oh my fucking God."

"Excellent."

"Kat and I will see you in a few."

"Okay. Call Henn."

"Will do."

I hang up with Jonas.

"What's going on?" Kat asks, her eyes bugging out.

I explain everything Jonas and I talked about (other than Jonas' desire to leave no loose ends). "So, hey, let's hop in the shower real quick and head up to their room," I say.

Kat's face ignites. "Oh, so we're gonna finally leave this room, huh?"

"Yeah, we gotta get the crew together to talk about . . ." I trail off. My heart lurches into my mouth. Oh shit. That's right. I kiss her. I fuck her. *I give her my application.* Shit. The jig is up.

"You promised you wouldn't leave this room without giving me that appli-cation," Kat says evenly.

I exhale a long, exasperated breath.

"You promised," she says.

"Yeah, I know. But Jonas and Sarah have to go to the airport within the hour and there's a ton of stuff we all need to figure out before they go. There's no time for our little game—not right now. We've gotta press the 'pause' button 'til they leave."

Kat throws up her hands in frustration. "Seriously?"

"Just 'til they leave."

She's fuming.

"Babe, we gotta save the world right now."

She exhales with exasperation. "*Fine*. Goddammit. I'll press the 'pause' button. But only because I love Sarah so much and I wanna take those assholes down as much as anyone. But the minute they leave for the airport, you're gonna give me that goddamned application."

I take a deep breath. My pulse is pounding in my ears. Shit. Things have been going so well between us. I don't want to fuck things up.

"Is it on your laptop?" she asks.

I nod.

"Email it to me right now."

I shake my head. "No way. The deal was you get to *read* it—you don't get to *have* it."

She rolls her eyes. "Then I suggest you bring your frickin' laptop with you to Jonas and Sarah's suite so you can hand it over to me the *minute* they leave."

I don't respond. I guess some part of me was hoping that, after I finally fucked her, Kat would say, "To hell with the stupid application. It doesn't matter anymore."

Kat touches my chest and goose bumps erupt on my body. "Josh, listen to me. My initials spell KUM. I grew up being called Kum Shot and Jizz. A guy I thought I *loved* turned out to have a fucking fiancée and told me I'm a slut." She smiles, but there's no mistaking the insecurity in her eyes. "Not to mention the fact that I just sucked your gigantic dick while riding an orgasm machine and then came so hard I went momentarily blind." She shoots me an adorable grin. "And you're nervous about sharing some stupid sex club application with me?" She strokes my face. "Holy Nothing Can Shock Me Now, Batman."

I close my eyes. She kisses me gently.

"Holy Give Me Some Credit, Batman," she whispers, continuing to kiss me.

I return her kiss. My dick is hardening. But, shit, there's no time. My brother's waiting. I pull away.

She puts her finger under my chin and kisses my lips gently. "Holy *YOLO*, Batman."

I smile at her. What man could resist her? I tried my mighty best, I really did, but even I couldn't pull it off. "Okay," I say. "A promise is a promise. The minute Jonas and Sarah leave, I'll hand it over. I give you my solemn word as a Faraday."

40

JOSH

The five of us have gone over Jonas and Sarah's talking points for the big meeting in Washington tomorrow, twice, and Henn has walked us through the logistics of how our very own "Oksana Belenko" is gonna get The Club's approximately five hundred fifty-four million bucks transferred out of the bad guys' twelve bank accounts. During the whole conversation, every one of us has looked on anxiously, but none more than Kat—which is understandable, considering she's the one who's gonna have to waltz into each and every bank and commit large-scale bank fraud.

I wish I could do the job for her, I really do. In fact, I've pushed Henn to come up with some way to transfer the money that doesn't rely on Kat, but he keeps telling me there's no other way: the accounts are all in Oksana's name and the majority of them require in-person transfers for amounts over a million bucks. Henn and I went around and around, but there's no alternative. We can't do it without Kat.

"Don't worry, Kitty Kat," Henn says. "I promise. It's gonna go like clockwork. I've rigged it so the banks will think you're Oksana, no questions asked, and I've also figured out a way to block the bad guys' access to the Internet on their devices during the whole time we're in the banks, just in case they try to check their accounts while we're in the middle of things."

Kat bites her lip. "Thanks, Henny."

"We'll both be right by your side," I say, taking her hand in mine. She leans into my shoulder and I kiss the top of her head. "I'll be right there with you, PG," I whisper. "Every step of the way."

"Okay, so are you three good?" Jonas asks.

"Yeah, we're good," I say. "Are you two good?"

Jonas and Sarah look at each other. "Do you have any questions, baby?" Jonas asks.

Sarah shakes her head. "No, no questions. But I do have a comment: holy crappola—I'm shitting a brick."

Jonas laughs and kisses her forehead. "No need for brick-shitting. Your report is gonna do all our talking for us."

Sarah takes a deep breath. "God help me if I wind up on some government watch-list after all this."

"Don't worry. They wouldn't be meeting us in the first place if they didn't take your report seriously."

Sarah nods and exhales.

Jonas looks at me. "Josh, can I talk to you for just a second?"

"Sure, bro."

"Do you mind, baby? I just gotta talk to Josh for a quick second, and then we'll head out."

"No worries. I'll chat with Kitty Kat."

Jonas and I get up and Sarah and Kat instantly launch into a rapid-fire conversation behind our backs.

"You two want me to join you or... ?" Henn asks us.

Jonas looks at me for my input.

I nod.

"Yeah," Jonas says. "Thanks, Henn. We could definitely use your brain."

The three of us move to a sitting area on the other side of the suite, far enough away that the girls won't overhear us.

Jonas looks nervously across the room. "There's not a lot of time, so lemme cut to the chase. I want Max and the Ukrainian Travolta dead." He clenches his jaw.

Henn doesn't seem the slightest bit surprised. "Shouldn't be hard to persuade the feds to do it for you. The feds are gonna want them dead, too."

"How do you figure?"

"Well, dude. Come on. The Secretary of Defense is one of The Club's biggest clients? Not good. They'll do whatever the fuck you ask them to do to keep that quiet and make sure this deal goes off without a hitch. Offing a couple Ukrainian separatists is a small price to bury that particular bit of information."

"'Ukrainian separatists' isn't really sexy enough," I say. "I don't think the average person watching the news understands all that."

"True," Henn says. "Good point."

"I think we need something easily digestible for the masses—something the media will pick up on and run with—something the feds can feed to them that they won't even question."

We're all silent for a beat.

"Terrorists?" I say.

"*Yes*," Henn says. "The media can spin that 'til the end of fucking time. They'll eat that shit up."

"Yeah, but *Ukrainian* terrorists? Americans don't even know where Ukraine is," I say.

"That's true." Henn says.

"*Russian* terrorists?" Jonas says.

"Yeah," Henn says. "'A Russian terrorist cell.'"

"Ha! Perfect," I say. "You're a fucking genius."

"So I've been told," Henn says.

"I like it," Jonas says, nodding. He looks deep in thought.

"It's actually eerily perfect," Henn says. "It's got all the bogey-man buzz-words at once, tied up in a neat little package. The news stations will have themselves a field day, whipping everyone into a frenzy, which means the feds will have a free pass to do whatever they need to do in plain sight—all in the name of protecting us all from a huge terrorist threat.'" Henn nods emphatically. "It's brillz."

"What if those two fuckers die in a shoot-out during a raid on the 'terrorists' compound'?" I ask. "That's pretty sexy, isn't it?"

"Perfecto," Henn says. "Maybe those two fuckers 'pulled weapons on officers' during the raid? That'd be the cleanest for the feds and best for us, too—no way to trace anything back to us. Simple. Effective. Believable. The feds save the world. We have nothing to do with it. Great mega-story for the news outlets. It's a win-win-win."

Jonas nods. "Thanks, guys." He looks emboldened. "I think that might work if I sell it right."

Henn scrunches up his face, thinking. "Lemme see if I can't get you a little insurance to help you out, big guy. Maybe I can dig up some more shit on the Secretary of Defense. Some compromising photos or whatnot. Kiddie porn on his computer. A dick pic he sent to a minor? I'm sure there's something. There's always something with these guys. A little insurance would be a good thing to have in your pocket in case the feds balk about taking those two guys out as part of the deal. "

"Thanks, Henn," Jonas says. "Yeah, insurance would be awesome."

"Cool. No problem."

"Is that everything, bro?" I ask.

Jonas looks at his watch. "Just one more quick thing. What about Oksana? Does she pull a weapon during the shoot-out or not?"

We all ponder the question for a moment, pursing our lips.

"The more people 'pulled weapons on officers' and didn't make it out alive, the less believable the whole thing is," Henn says. "Plus, women are much less likely to pull a weapon, statistically speaking. We don't wanna raise any suspicion that anything's hinky."

Jonas clenches his jaw. "Did you uncover anything whatsoever to suggest Oksana had something to do with the hit on Sarah?"

"Or maybe knew about it beforehand?" I ask, my jaw clenching in sympathy with my brother's. I want these fuckers dead every bit as much as he does.

Henn shakes his head. "Everything I've seen tells me Max ordered the hit and the Ukrainian Travolta carried it out. All evidence is that Oksana's a pimp-stress and a loyalist to mother Russia, but not a stone-cold killer. Max is the head of the snake. Indubitably."

Jonas looks deep in thought.

I touch my brother's shoulder. "I vote you be the God of the *New* Testament, Jonas—show the perfect measure of force and mercy."

Jonas runs his hands through his hair. "Fuck. I dunno." He exhales. "I'll think about it on the plane some more."

"Okay. Follow your gut." I hug him. "Be safe, bro." I kiss him on the side of his neck.

"You, too," Jonas says. He kisses my cheek. "Be careful in the banks, guys. Please."

"We will."

"Take extra good care of Kat." He looks across the room at Sarah. She's chatting and giggling happily with Kat. "My girl can't live without her."

I stare at Kat across the room, my heart suddenly bursting in my chest. "I won't let anything happen to her, bro."

"We'll keep her safe, big guy," Henn says.

Jonas hugs Henn. "You're a fucking genius, man. I can never thank you enough for all you've done."

"Hey, man. We're family now."

They slap each other's backs and when they pull apart, Jonas looks determined.

"You got this," I say. "You're a fucking beast, bro."

"Fuck yeah," Jonas says.

"Fuck yeah," I reply.

"Fuck yeah," Henn echoes. "Wow, I feel so *masculated* right now. Is this how you guys feel every fucking day? Wow."

We all laugh.

I look at my watch. "Okay, bro. You better get your ass to the airport. Keep us posted. We'll be ready all day tomorrow. Just give us the word and we'll head to the banks."

Our threesome walks over to the girls, and after the five of us have completed every possible permutation of hugging and whispered goodbyes, Jonas and Sarah waltz out the door, bags in hand and determined expressions on their faces.

"Good luck saving the world, guys!" Kat shouts to their backs.

"Holy crappolaaaaaaaaaaaa!" Sarah shouts, just as the door closes behind her.

They're gone.

Henn, Kat, and I look at each other in a shared daze for a long moment.

"Holy shitballs," Kat finally says.

"Big shit going down in little China," Henn says.

"Or little Ukraine," I add.

"Shit just got real," Henn says.

"Fo shizzle pops," Kat says.

Henn exhales, filling his cheeks with air like a blowfish. "Welp." He looks at Kat. "I guess we'd better take your photo for your Oksana passport, huh? If Jonas and Sarah call upon us to save the world tomorrow, we'd best be ready."

41

JOSH

"Okay, Kitty Kat," Henn says, his eyes bugging out. "There's nothing to stress about. I've already shaved years off Oksana's age on all the banks' systems and I'm gonna swap your photo for Oksana's on the accounts using photo identification. Tonight, I'm gonna check and recheck all the passwords and codes on every account, too, just to make sure everything goes off without a hitch tomorrow. Oh, and I'm gonna infect the bad guys' devices with malware to block their wifi at the flip of a switch too—just on the off chance they try to log into their accounts while we're in the middle of making the transfers."

"How many Americanos have you had today, Henny?" Kat asks.

"Why does everyone always ask me that?" He chuckles. "So are you ready to get your photo taken, Oksana?" He motions to the door of Jonas and Sarah's suite. "I think we should head down to the casino and look for a white wall as a background."

Kat steals a glance at me, and there's no mistaking what she's thinking about. "Sure thing," she says tentatively, still looking at me. "How long do you need me?"

"Just a few minutes. Shouldn't take long once we find a good backdrop."

"Is there any hacker-stuff you could do first, before taking my photo? Maybe for about an hour?"

"Um. Sure. I can certainly work on my malware for a while. And I've got a little research on the Secretary of Defense to do for Jonas."

"In that case, how about we split up for a bit? You guys do whatever while I stay here in the suite and do a little personal reading? It won't take too long."

"Cool," Henn says. "Actually, I could use to blow off a little steam for a bit before I get to work, if you guys don't mind. You wanna roll the dice with me, boss?"

"Yeah," I say slowly, my stomach clenching. "I gotta talk to Kat first, though. I'll catch up with you in a bit."

"Cool. See you soon. Just text me when you're ready to meet up."

The minute Henn leaves, I take Kat's face in my hands and kiss her. And then I kiss her again. And again. And again. All I wanna do is kiss her one last time before my application potentially fucks everything up—but before I know it, my clothes are off and so are hers and she's on top of me on the bed, riding me, screaming my name, humping me exactly the way she rode that Sybian—and I'm underneath her, guiding her smooth hips, groping her hot little ass, mesmerized by the way her tits are bouncing, by the little cleft in her chin, the way her blonde hair falls around her shoulders, and wondering how the fuck I'm letting myself have sex without a condom *again* (even though it feels so, so fucking good).

When we're done, we hop in the shower, neither of us speaking.

Clearly, that was a detour neither of us expected or planned. We're like fucking dynamite, the two of us. A nuclear reaction.

"You're on the pill, right?" I ask.

"Yep. Still on the pill since the last time I told you."

"Sorry. Just double-checking."

She smiles. "Sorry. Ask me as many times as you need. Yes, I'm on the pill."

"I'm sorry. My dad used to put the fear of God into me about having sex without a condom. I've never done it before. I'm just paranoid."

"You've never had sex without a condom before?"

I shake my head.

"Not even with girlfriends?"

"Never. You're my first."

I lather her up under the hot water for a moment.

"So you've literally *never* felt sex without a rubber before me? Not once?"

I shake my head again—and then I grin broadly. "It feels fucking *amazing*."

She grins broadly. "Yeah, I bet it does. Jeez, Josh. No wonder you think I'm amazing. Ha!"

I kiss her. "You are," I say. "It's not just that."

She throws her arms around me and kisses me. "God, I'm addicted to you."

"Me, too. You're a drug."

I take my sweet time in the shower with her, washing her, touching her. And then, what the fuck, why not? I get down on my knees and eat her out, too, bringing her to a climax that has her pulling on my hair like it's on fucking fire.

When we're done, we dry ourselves off with the fluffy white towels and get dressed quietly, a sense of doom descending upon me. The jig is up. There's nowhere else to run. I've got to give it to her now.

"Can I make you a drink, PG?"

"Sure. Surprise me," she says.

"My kind of girl," I reply. My voice is casual, relaxed. But it's an act. My stomach is tight. My pulse is pounding in my ears.

I bring her the drink. "An old fashioned," I say.

"Oh, you hipster." She notices my empty hands. "You didn't make one for yourself?"

"I don't wanna be here when you read my application," I say. "I'm gonna go down to the casino and meet Henn."

"Oh. Okay. Suit yourself."

There's a long pause. I stand, rooted to my spot, my hand in my pocket.

"Now would be when you *finally* give me your application, Josh," she says.

I exhale. "I know."

There's another long pause. I'm waiting for her to say, "Don't worry about it. I don't care what it says." But she doesn't. She just stares at me, smiling like a wolf.

"Okay," I finally say. I grab my laptop from the table, click into my PDF-formatted application, and lay the laptop on her lap. "Here you go, Madame Terrorist," I say. "Enjoy."

"Thank you kindly," she says.

"Text me when you're done so I can come get you. I don't want you to be alone out there—now more than ever. I didn't like the looks of that Max guy."

She nods. "I promise."

I take a deep breath. "Okay. Well. Happy reading."

"Thank you."

I linger briefly, hoping she'll say never mind. But she doesn't.

I bite the inside of my cheek for minute. "Okay, well, bye."

"Bye." She shoots me a clipped wave.

I return her wave and stride to the front door of the suite, my heart pulsing in my ears. Just before I leave, I turn back around. Kat's settling herself into her chair. She takes a swig of her old fashioned and leans into the screen, biting her lip.

The hair on the back of my neck stands up. This is it—the brick wall I've been hurtling toward without brakes since I first laid eyes on that beautiful terrorist. And now the damned wall is finally here, an inch from my fucking nose, and there's nowhere to turn.

I take a deep breath, open the door, and quietly slip into the hallway.

The door closes behind me.

I close my eyes.

Crash.

revelation

USA *Today* and International Bestselling Author

Lauren Rowe

42

KAT

The door to Jonas and Sarah's suite closes behind Josh's back and I look down at Josh's laptop, holding my breath with excitement. This is it. I can't believe I'm finally gonna read Josh's application to The Club, after all this build-up. My chest is tight. My stomach is in knots. What on earth did that man write that's made him so skittish about revealing it to me? Well, I guess there's only one way to find out:

Name?

"Joshua William Faraday," he writes. Oh, I didn't know Josh's middle name is William. For some reason, seeing his full name makes my heart flutter.

With this application, you will be required to submit three separate forms of identification. The Club maintains a strict "No Aliases Policy" for admission. You may, however, use aliases during interactions with other Club members, at your discretion.

"OK," he writes.

Age?

"29," he writes.

I stop and think. Josh is thirty. I wonder when he had his birthday? I'd love to know his zodiac sign. Damn, it sure would suck donkey balls if it turned out we were cosmically incompatible.

Provide a brief physical description of yourself.

"I'm 6'1, 190 lbs. I've got brown hair and blue eyes and tattoos on my torso and arms. I prefer not to talk about the meanings of my tattoos at length, so please tell whoever gets assigned to me not to ask about them.

"I work pretty hard at keeping fit," he continues. "I'm a big believer that a man only gets one chance at a first impression, so I try to make mine count, every time. Just to be clear: I'm not applying for membership to The Club because I have some sort of inferiority complex about my appearance (I don't) or because I can't attract women on my own (I can)."

I can't help but smile. Even when Josh is being kind of douche-y, he's sexy as hell to me.

With this application, you will be required to submit three recent photographs of yourself to your intake agent. Please include the following: one headshot, one full-body shot revealing your physique, and one shot wearing something you'd typically wear out in a public location. These photographs shall be maintained under the strictest confidentiality.

Oh, this I gotta see. I scroll down, assuming Josh's photos will be attached to the end of his application, but they're not there. I scan the top of the document, looking for some indication of where I can find his pictures—but, nope. There's nothing. Goddammit! I grab my phone.

Josh answers my call immediately. "Wow, that was fast," he says. "I'm only just now walking into the casino."

"Where are your photos?"

"My photos?"

"Yeah, the three photos you submitted with your application."

"Oh, my *photos*." He pauses. "Why do you want them? You already know exactly what I look like."

"I just want to see them."

"But you've already seen every inch of me—you've seen my YOLO'd ass, for Chrissakes." He snickers. "Not to mention my balls."

I join him in snickering. "Up close and personal."

He snickers again.

"But I still wanna see your photos."

He sighs. "How 'bout this? I'll come back up there and let you take three photos of me any which way you want. We'll have a photo shoot, just you and me, baby."

"Ooh, sounds fun—I'll definitely take a rain check on that offer. But I still wanna see the photos."

He grumbles. "But *why*?"

"Because I wanna see what photos you thought would best represent yourself to perverts in a sex club."

There's a long pause. "You're such a fucking pain in the ass, you know that? A terrorist and a colossal pain in the ass."

"I told you—I'm a *Scorpio*. We're extremely focused and we also have a disproportionate sense of entitlement. Plus, I gave you my three photos—a deal's a deal."

He laughs. "Oh my God, those photos, Kat."

"You liked them?"

"I *loved* them. The one of you in your undies was so hot—and then I practically pissed myself laughing at the one of you pretending to barf over the toilet. You're so funny."

"Thank you. You're pretty funny yourself—but funny ain't gonna get you off the hook, dude. Those photos are part of your application, which means they're part of your promise."

He grunts. "*Fine.* Are you familiar with Macs?"

"Yeah, I've got one—from your brother, actually."

"My brother gave you a Mac?"

"Yeah. To replace the one The Club stole from me."

"That was awfully nice of him—I didn't know Jonas knew how to be nice."

"Yeah. He's been super nice to me. Okay, quit stalling. Where are the photos?"

He groans. "*Fine.* Go to 'Finder' and click on 'Pictures' on the left side of the screen."

"Yep. Okay."

"And now do you see the folder..." Josh says, but I don't hear the rest of his sentence because something has caught my attention on Josh's laptop screen: a folder labeled "Sick Fuck." Well, jeez, with a name like that, the folder might as well be named "Open me, Kat!"

"Do you see it?" Josh says.

"Mmm hmm," I say, clicking on the "Sick Fuck" folder.

Oh my God. I'm looking at a bunch of photos of naked women—lots and lots of naked women—all of them blonde, all of them gorgeous, and all of them striking poses like porn stars.

"Kat? Are you still there?"

"Yeah, I'm here," I say, scrolling through the photos. There's probably close to twenty different women here. "Josh, who are all the blondes?"

"What?" he asks, his voice suddenly tight.

"The porn stars in the folder labeled 'Sick Fuck'?"

"Jesus Fucking Christ! Get out of there, Kat! That's personal!"

"Who are they?"

"I didn't give you permission to look through my private stuff. *Get the fuck out of there right now.* Jesus!"

"Oh, waah, waah. So you like porn—you're such a pervert." I laugh, but he doesn't join me. "Come on. Just tell me who they are. It's no big whoop."

"This is a total breach of trust. Absolutely inexcusable."

I ignore his outrage. It's an extremely effective tactic I've learned from observing my brothers over the years: remain calm in the face of indignation and then deny, deny, deny any and all wrongdoing until the person angry with you simply forgets what they're mad about.

"Are these photos off the Internet, or are they women you actually know?" I ask calmly.

There's a long silence. "This is total bullshit," he grumbles, but it's clear his outrage is already beginning to soften. "I want to lodge a formal complaint," he says.

I laugh. "With whom?"

"With... the Common Decency Police."

"Okay. Duly noted. Complaint lodged."

"Because you *suck*."

"Yes, I do, actually, as we both know very well. And if you ever want me to do it again, then answer my question."

Out of nowhere, his fury roars back to life. "Oh, fuck no," he bellows. "Let me set you straight about something right here and now: I do *not* tolerate any form of sexual extortion in a relationship. That's an absolute deal-breaker with me. You wanna suck my dick? Great; then suck it. You don't wanna suck it? Then don't. But don't use sex as a weapon to manipulate me. I fucking *hate* that."

My heart lurches into my throat—and not because Josh is chastising me—I don't care about that—but because Josh just said he doesn't tolerate any form of sexual extortion *in a relationship*. Are Josh and I *in a relationship?*

"Jeez," I manage to say. "Overreact much?"

"I'm not *overreacting*," Josh replies. "I absolutely *hate* that shit."

"Okay, okay. Jeez-*us*. I'm sorry. I'll never again say, 'If you want me to suck your dick, then fill-in-the-blank.' Happy?"

"Yes. Thank you. I hate that shit."

"Fine. Got it. But I must say I find your whole speech awfully ironic considering I used sexual extortion to get you to give me your application in the first place."

He pauses. "Hey, wait a minute—you *did*, didn't you? Well, that was kinda shitty of you."

"Hey, whatever works."

There's a long beat during which I'm smiling from ear to ear.

"So," I say. "You still haven't answered my question, Playboy: Who are all the blonde playmates?"

He makes a sound of frustration. "I was hoping you'd forgotten about that."

"No chance. I'm a Scorpio. We hold grudges. So who are they?"

"You don't have permission to be snooping around in that folder, Kat. Click out."

I don't reply to him—I'm too busy looking through the folder.

"Hello? Madame Terrorist? Did you hear me? Exit the folder. You're trespassing."

"Yeah, I heard you. And I would totally follow your instruction, I really would—but the thing is, I'm having somewhat of a *conundrum*."

"And what is that?"

"It's kind of like a dilemma."

"Have I done something to give you the impression I've got the vocabulary of a sixth-grader? I know what a *conundrum* is—I'm asking what is *your* conundrum, specifically?"

I seriously can't wipe the smile off my face. "Well, on the one hand," I say, "I really want to respect your request. I *really, really* do, because I'm actually a fairly nice person, despite the way I tend to behave around you, and also because I think you're probably right: it was very, very naughty of me to go through your personal stuff without permission."

"Thank you. And on the other hand?"

"Well, on the other hand, I really, really like being *naughty*."

Josh makes a sexy sound. "*Oh.* Well, that *is* quite a *conundrum.* What on earth are you gonna do about it?"

"I dunno—I haven't decided yet. Maybe I'll just look through your pervy blonde-porn-star folder while I figure it out." I scroll through the photos again, my smile hurting my cheeks. "These women all look the same, Josh," I say, still going through the photos. "Looks like you've got a *type,* huh?"

He audibly shrugs. "I like what I like."

"Who are they?"

He pauses briefly and then exhales. "They're just women I've met."

"*Met?* I'm guessing you've done more than *meet* these girls."

He doesn't reply.

"Have you *slept* with all of these women?"

"So now you're slut-shaming me?"

"No. I'm the last person in the world who would ever slut-shame anyone."

"You do realize the whole point of your application to me was to make me feel safe enough to reveal my inner-most perverted thoughts to you? You're supposed to be luring me into *emotional intimacy,* Kat."

"Oh crap. That's right. Shoot. I should have warned you: I suck at emotional intimacy. I'm working on it, though, I swear."

"You're never gonna break down my walls now," Josh says playfully.

"Damn. Oh well." I audibly shrug and he laughs. "So who took all these photos? Was it you?"

"Nope."

"No? Oh, I thought you were gonna say yes. Did you take *some* of them?"

"So we're playing a game of Perverted Twenty Questions, are we?"

"Yeah. Isn't it *fun?*"

"No."

"Come on. I've still got nineteen questions to go."

"Nineteen? Ha! More like ten. And that's generous."

"Okay ten. Did you personally take *any* of these photos?"

He exhales loudly. "Just one."

"Oh, now that's an interesting answer. Not what I expected. I thought it'd be all or nothing." I suddenly remember Sarah saying Oksana photographs every girl in The Club. "By George, I think I've got it," I say. "Are these the women you slept with in The Club?"

Josh sighs loudly. "Correct. All but two of them."

"Well, now I'm confused again. You mean all but two of these women were in The Club—or there are two Clubbers missing from this folder?"

"Your mind is a scary place, Kat. You're like Henn but in a totally different context. You're a man-hacker."

I laugh. "Thank you. Now answer the question, please."

He exhales audibly. "Every woman from The Club is there—*plus* there are two non-Clubbers in the folder, too."

"Ah. Interesting. Two bonus-women from real life. This just gets more and more intriguing. Which ones are the non-Clubbers and why'd you put them in the folder with all the Clubbers?"

"Aren't you out of questions yet?"

"Nope." I pause. "I've still got eight to go."

He scoffs.

"You personally took *one* of the non-Clubbers' photos—not *both* of them?"

"Correct."

"Hmm. So that means one of the non-Clubbers *sent* you her photo?"

"Correct. You're now officially out of questions."

"No way. I've still got at least eight left."

"Eight? You started with ten and you've asked like fifty."

"I've been asking *sub*-questions to questions, Josh—sub-questions don't count as full questions."

He grumbles.

"So, come on, which one of these pretty ladies was the one non-Clubber you personally photographed? And why'd you put her in the Sick Fuck folder with all the others?"

He pauses. "No comment."

"Aw, come on."

"You've got my application. That's what I promised you—nothing more. Perverted Twenty Questions is now officially over."

"Aw. Not fair."

"It's totally fair—and if not, then too bad. Life isn't fair."

"Just tell me why you have all these photos and then I'll drop it. I promise."

Josh exhales. "Okay, Madame Terrorist. Fine." He mutters something to himself under his breath. "I requested a specific type of girl in my application, and so The Club emailed me photos of women they'd selected for me to make sure they were exactly what I wanted. And at the end of my membership-month, I didn't know what the fuck to do with all the photos so I put them into a folder."

"And labeled it 'Sick Fuck.'"

He doesn't reply.

"And you didn't have any inkling these women were hookers before Jonas told you?"

Josh pauses. "I was pretty specific about what I wanted in my application, so I figured The Club likely made some kind of special arrangement to deliver on my wishes—but I didn't know for sure. Just because a woman is willing to meet a rich guy in a hotel room and fulfill his sick-fuck-fantasies doesn't necessarily make her a hooker, does it?"

I consider that bit of logic. "No," I finally say. "Not necessarily. Especially when he looks like you."

"Thank you. But, honestly, I really didn't care one way or the other if the women were being paid on the side—I just didn't wanna know about it. All I was trying to do was escape reality for a month—I wasn't looking for some sort of deep soul connection."

"So you asked for blondes?"

"Kat," he says softly. "You've got my application. Just read it. No more questions."

The earnest tone of his voice has thrown me. I thought we were bantering, and now, suddenly, he seems totally sincere. "Okay. I'm sorry."

"It's okay."

I wait a beat. "But can I ask one more teeny tiny itty bitty question? In the name of emotional intimacy?"

He chuckles despite himself. "What?" he asks.

"Thank you. Wow, we're *killing* the emotional intimacy thing, Josh. We're emotionally intimate beasts."

He chuckles again. "This isn't emotional intimacy, Kat—this is just plain torture."

"I'm almost positive they're one and the same thing," I say. "Though I can't be sure."

He laughs a full laugh, which I take as a good sign. "Okay, Madame Interrogator, what's your last question?"

"Do you typically only sleep with blondes—or just in The Club? And is it sex with *blondes* that makes you a sick fuck?"

He pauses for a moment. "That's two questions."

"Sorry. Couldn't help myself."

"Okay. Here's the deal: I'm gonna tell you the answer to these two questions and then this interrogation is officially done."

"Okay."

"I don't *only* sleep with blondes. I've been with women of all shapes, sizes, colors, ethnicities, and hair colors, and I've enjoyed them all. In fact, I've enjoyed them all *immensely*."

"Thanks. Little more info than I needed."

"And, no, I don't have some bizarre complex whereby I think sleeping with a beautiful blonde woman somehow transforms me into a sick fuck. Yes, I specifically requested *blondes* in The Club because The Club was about fantasy-fulfillment and escape from reality, and, call me unimaginative or trite, but when I shop at the fantasy store, at least for purposes of fulfilling the fantasies I specifically asked for in The Club, that's what I want—a classic blonde. Why? I don't know. It's just the way I'm wired—I definitely have a *type*." He makes a sound that emphatically signals he's done talking.

"Thank you," I say smoothly, scrolling through the photos again. "Yep, I'd agree you definitely have a type." I snort. "Actually, they all look just like..." I abruptly stop speaking. Holy shit.

There's a long beat.

"Yeah, Kat," Josh finally says. He lets out a loud puff of air. "They look just like *you*."

He's read my mind. I swallow hard.

"Less attractive versions of you, of course," he continues softly. "They're all wannabe-Kats. You're what my brother refers to as the 'divine original.'"

I'm tingling all over. "The *'divine original'*?" I breathe. "What's that?"

He lets out a long groan. "I can't believe I just said that. It's this Plato-thing Jonas is always babbling about. Forget I ever said it—I wanna gouge my eyes out every time my brother mentions it and now it's me who's saying it. Gah."

I press my phone into my ear, my breathing shallow. "What does it mean, Josh?" I ask softly. "Whatever it means, it's making me tingle all over."

"It just means you're the original template and everyone else is a knock-off." He lets out a long sigh. "Like, you know, you're the authentic Gucci bag and everyone else is one of those counterfeits they sell on the sidewalk in New York."

I pause, letting that sink in. I've never been to New York, actually, but his metaphor is still perfectly understandable to me. "So does that mean I make you a sick fuck more than anyone else?"

He growls with exasperation. "You don't make me a sick fuck—*no one* makes me a sick fuck. Someone I cared about once *called* me a sick fuck and I was pissed as hell about it when I named that folder, that's all. I was, you know, flipping that person the bird when I named that folder."

While Josh has been talking, I've been leafing through the photos. There's one girl I keep going back to again and again. She's not working the lens or *trying* to be sexy like the others—in fact, the woman is clearly put off by posing for the photo—and her shyness about the whole thing makes her all the more alluring. Suddenly, there's no doubt in my mind this shy girl is the non-Clubber Josh photographed himself—and, if my Scooby Doo senses are right, she's also the one who pissed him off by calling him a "sick fuck."

"What about the shy one?" I ask.

"The shy one?"

"The one who looks mortified to be posing for a naked photo? She looks pretty divine-original-ish to me. Is she the one you photographed yourself?" I swallow hard. "Is she your ex-girlfriend?"

He doesn't reply.

"Did she call you a sick fuck?"

"Click out of there, Kat," he says softly, a stiffness overtaking his tone. "Interrogation over."

My skin erupts in goose bumps. He's not kidding around. Shoot. He sounds genuinely upset.

"Okay, I'm out," I say, exiting the folder.

"I'm gonna go," he says evenly. "Happy reading."

"No, *wait*. Please, Josh. *Wait*." The angry edge in his voice has made my chest tighten. Clearly, I've pushed too hard. "I'm sorry, Josh. Sometimes I take things too far. It's a major flaw of mine."

Josh chuckles despite himself.

I bite my lip, smiling into the phone. "I'm sorry—I didn't mean any harm."

"Says the woman with a bomb strapped to her chest." He lets out a long exhale. "Just read my goddamned application, okay? I can't take it anymore. The anticipation's killing me. Just read it and make your decision already."

"My *decision*?"

He pauses. "Whether to sleep with me or not," he finally says.

"Oh yeah, that's right," I say. "Well, a girl's gotta know if she's gonna wake up chained to a goat."

"No, a *donkey*."

"Oh yeah. That's right. A girl's gotta know these things."

"You never know what might happen with me. I'm kind of a sick fuck."

"According to whom?"

He doesn't reply.

"The Shy Girl?"

He pauses. "Yeah."

"That's Emma?"

"Yup."

"Well, Josh, I haven't even read your application yet, and I can already tell you Emma was full of shit."

He lets out a yelp of surprise.

I clear my throat. "So back to the reason I called in the first place," I say. "Where are the three photos you submitted with your application?"

"Well, strangely enough, Kat, they're in a folder marked 'Club Application Photos.' Imagine that."

"Oh. Well, gosh. That makes a whole lot more sense than putting them into a folder called 'Sick Fuck.'"

Josh sighs. "Hey, can I just come up there? I thought I wanted to stay as far away as possible while you were reading my application, but all of a sudden I'd rather just sit next to you while you read it and watch your facial expressions."

My heart leaps. "Are you by any chance planning to *distract* me again, Joshua William Faraday?"

"Maybe."

I smile broadly into the phone. "Yeah, I think that's a great idea," I say. "Get your YOLO'd-ass up here, Playboy. We'll read the damned thing together, line by perverted line—and *maybe*, if you're extra nice to me, I'll let you distract me again."

I can hear his smile again.

"I'll be right there," he says.

43

KAT

The minute Josh and I hang up from our call, I scroll through his blonde-girl "Sick Fuck" folder again, this time more slowly than before. These are some spectacularly gorgeous women here—and he thinks I'm some sort of 'ideal form' of all of them? Surely, he's just flattering me. I mean, come on.

I stop scrolling.

Holy crap.

I recognize one of the women in the folder. I think she's a well-known model—like, literally on Victoria's Secret ads and the covers of fashion magazines. Yep, I'm sure of it. Her name is Bridgette something. Is she the 'bisexual supermodel' Josh said he turned down? She's gotta be the second non-Clubber in the folder.

I look at my watch. Gah. Josh should be here any minute. I click out of the "Sick Fuck" folder, intending to take a quick peek at his three photos before he arrives, but on a sudden impulse, I find myself dragging the entire "Sick Fuck" folder into the trashcan and pressing "Empty trash." Oops. My finger must have slipped.

And now back to my actual mission. I click into the folder marked "Club Application Photos" and open the first of three images. It's a headshot. Josh is smiling and looking as charismatic and confident as ever. Oh man, those eyes. I could sit and stare at them all day long. He's gorgeous.

I click on the next photo. It's classic Josh Faraday. He's in a perfectly tailored, blue designer suit, looking like an ad for Hugo Boss or cologne. Yummy.

I click on the third photo and... *ka-boom.* My ovaries explode like two little nuclear bombs. Josh is completely nude in this third shot, every inch of his ripped and muscled—*and erect*—body on full display—and, oh my fuck, the shit-eating grin on his face is so unapologetic, it instantly makes my blood boil with desire. Holy crappola, as Sarah would say, I'm short-circuiting at the sight of him.

Without even thinking about it, I click into Josh's email account, address an email to myself attaching Josh's smoking-hot-bad-boy-with-a-gigantic-boner-selfie, and press send. Zowie, as Sarah also likes to say, that sucker's definitely gonna inspire countless future orgasms.

Hey, as long as I'm sending myself stuff from Josh's computer, I figure I might as well send myself his application, too, right? That way, if he distracts me again when he gets up here, I'll be able to read it later from the comfort of my own bed.

Just as I press "send" on my second email to myself, a notification message flashes across the upper right corner of Josh's screen: he's got an email from someone named "Jennifer LeMonde" with the subject line "Hey, Cutie!"

My stomach clenches.

My lip snarls involuntarily.

Jen.

Oh, God, I shouldn't do it—I know I shouldn't. But show me a woman in my exact shoes who wouldn't read that goddamned email and I'll show you a woman with no pulse or vagina—or, at the very least, no balls.

I open the email.

"Josh!" Jennifer LeMonde writes. "OMFG! I'm so bummed you didn't come to NYC with me. My mom's show was amaaaaaaaaaazing. You would have looooooooooved it. Critics are saying she's a shoo-in for a Tony. And the party afterwards was REDONK. You should have seen the A-listers who showed up! I've attached a pic of Mom and me at the after-party. (Mom says hi, btw—she totally remembers you from that time we all stayed at our house in Aspen.)

"I wanted to send you a quick note to thank you for calling me after Reed's party. I was pretty bummed at how everything went down that night, to be honest. I'm really glad we had a chance to talk so you could clear everything up for me.

"I've been thinking about what you said and I totally understand where you're coming from. I feel the exact same way. So if you're ready to chill with someone who's not gonna explode like a fricking grenade all over you like The Jealous Bitch (can you say drama?? OMG!), then let's hang out again. I'm totally up for what you suggested. We'll just hang out and have some fun and see where it leads. No pressure. Nothing serious.

"So, anyway, next weekend is my birthday (the big 2-9!) and my mom's letting me use our house in the Hamptons to celebrate. I'm gonna invite a bunch of friends and I really want you to come. No drama. Just FUN FUN FUN! It would be the best birthday present EVER if you'd come and hang out (and hopefully make me scream again!! Heehee!).

"I know how much you like my 'pretty titties' (LOL!) so I'm attaching a special pic just for you. It's just a little something to tide you over 'til you can come see them in person (and motorboat them again if you want! LMFAO!). Thanks again for explaining everything to me when we talked. We're defo on the same page. No relationship. Nothing serious. I'm totally down with that plan. XOXOXOXO Jen."

I have never felt this capable of murder in my entire life.

Holy I Wanna Beat the Living Shit Out of Her, Batman.

And Then I Wanna Cut Off His Balls and Roast Them Over the Burning Embers of His Fucking House, Batman. And Then I Want To Eat Them In Between Two Graham Crackers.

I'm gritting my teeth so hard, they're about to crumble like shards of bleu cheese in my mouth. I'm 'The Jealous Bitch,' huh? Did Jen coin that cute little nickname for me, or did Josh help her come up with it—perhaps during their after-party phone conversation? Was that phone conversation when Josh "suggested" they get together again so he could "motorboat" Jen's "pretty titties" *again*?

Why the hell did Josh call Jen after Reed's party? He told me he wasn't the least bit interested in her. Did he rush back to his room for a little phone sex after washing the barf off his shoes and my hair and putting me to bed?

I should click out of this email, I really should—that would be the self-preserving thing to do—but instead I torture myself and click on the first photo attached to Jen's email.

I shriek.

What the holy hell? Jen's mom is *Gabrielle LeMonde*? I blink rapidly, my brain overloading. Gabrielle LeMonde is a national treasure—an icon! I've seen every one of her frickin' movies—and not just the comedies, either!—the really boring ones in which she spoke in a spot-on British accent, too! What. The. *Hell*?

Well, this sure sheds light on why Josh hooked up with Jen in the first place. If I were a twenty-three-year-old guy with a huge dick, I'd have fucked Gabrielle LeMonde's daughter too, just to be able to say I did—especially if she had a body like Jen's. And Jesus, now it makes total sense that Jen pals around with movie stars like Isabel Randolph. Good lord, Jen's entire contacts list must be a who's-who of Hollywood's young elite.

My head is spinning. I feel like I'm gonna barf. It's suddenly hitting me like a ton of bricks that Josh is literally one of the world's most eligible bachelors—like *literally*. Holy shit. Before this moment, Josh was Sarah's boyfriend's brother—his gorgeous and rich brother—his hilarious and well-dressed brother—his smoking hot and sexy brother—his brother who arranged for me to stay in Vegas *and* keep my job, too—his brother who fucked me so brilliantly, I blacked out there for a minute—but, still, just a human-brother-dude who presumably puts his pants on one leg at a time (and who presumably stows his donkey-dick in one of those pant legs before zipping up).

But now, out of nowhere, it turns out Josh is some quasi-celebrity-god among men who lives in an alternate universe populated by world-famous actresses and their spawn? And Victoria's Secret supermodels? Oh, and freaking Red Card Riot, too? What the heck? Who is this Most Interesting Man in the World who could hop a cross-country flight on a whim for no other reason than to attend the birthday party of a fuck-buddy who happens to be the daughter of Gabrielle LeMonde? Gah! Insanity.

My stomach flips over.

I'm usually a confident girl—probably more so than the average Jane, if I'm being honest—but how could I ever be so cocky as to think a guy like that would ever pick *me* out of literally *anyone* on the planet to choose from? I roll my eyes even though I'm sitting here alone. I've always had a pretty high opinion of myself, truthfully (which isn't something I usually admit out loud), but all of a sudden, in comparison to the women who populate Josh's rarified world, I feel shockingly average. Not to mention, quite possibly, really *gullible*, too. Has Josh just been selling me a line of bullshit? Does he make *every* girl feel special the way I've been feeling with him? Have I been a fool?

Oh, jeez, my eyes are filling with tears. Why do I suddenly feel like I'm standing at Garrett Bennett's door all over again, about to get annihilated? I take a deep breath to steady myself.

The healthy choice would be to click out of Jen's email right now. It's making me doubt Josh and I don't want to do that. He's been nothing but incredible toward me. Generous. Attentive. Affectionate. Passionate. I'm acting crazy right now. So what if Jen's mom is Gabrielle LeMonde? That doesn't change anything. Why is that sending me into a tailspin? I should shut Josh's laptop and stop this right now.

But I don't.

In fact, I do the opposite: I open the second picture attached to Jen's email.

Holy Oh-No-She-Didn't, Batman.

If I felt sick after seeing the picture of Jen with her movie-star mom, then I feel terminally ill after seeing this second photo.

It's a naked selfie of Jen. She's smiling broadly and pushing her "pretty titties" up toward the camera—obviously inviting Josh to "motorboat" them "again."

My eyes prick with tears. Is Jen a pathetically desperate girl who's pursuing a hot guy after he's clearly told her to get lost? Or, to the contrary, is she a girl who's merely going after a guy who slept with her and then continued *encouraging* her? Josh told me he's not interested in Jen—and yet he called her after Reed's party. Why'd he do that? And what did he "suggest" to her when they spoke? Suddenly, I don't know what's what anymore.

My heart is racing. I wipe my eyes. I never cry and I'm not gonna start now. Hell no. It's so unlike me to feel this jealous and insecure. God, I hate myself right now. I'm acting like a freak and a puss and a lunatic. I need to detach. I need to stop caring. Josh Faraday isn't my boyfriend (though I admit I want him to be), and I'm not his girlfriend. I've got no right to feel this way. The man can do what he wants.

No, he can't. He's mine, goddammit. Mine.

I slam Josh's laptop shut and set it on the table. I've got to get the hell out of here. Josh will be here any minute to "distract" me from his application and I need to pull my shit together before then—because right now I feel like I'm going to fly completely off the handle and say a million things I'm gonna regret.

I stand to leave—just as the door of the suite bursts open.

Josh bounds into the room. "Hey, Party Girl with a Hyphen," he says, holding up a condom packet playfully. "Can I interest you in a little *distraction* from your reading?"

I stalk straight past Josh toward the front door, my eyes burning and my mouth clamped shut.

"Kat?"

I march to the door and fling it open like I'm trying to take the damned thing off its hinges.

"Oh shit," Josh says. "You read my application without me?" His voice is pure anguish. "Goddammit, Kat. Lemme explain. This is exactly why I didn't want you to read that stupid thing in the first place."

44

JOSH

"**K**at, come on!" I shout at her back, but she keeps marching down the hallway toward the penthouse's private elevator, her arms swinging wildly. *Déjà fucking vu.* How many times am I gonna have to chase this goddamned terrorist down a fucking hallway? "Oh, come on, Kat. It wasn't *that* bad."

But she just keeps on marching. She pounds on the call button for the private elevator and crosses her arms, her back to me.

"You can't possibly be *this* upset. What the hell?"

She whirls around and I'm shocked to see hot tears streaming down her cheeks.

Panic floods me. My application made her *cry*? Shit. I've obviously grossly miscalculated the situation. I'm floored. "Kat," I blurt, my chest tightening. "I know everything I wrote in that application came off as douche-y and angry and fucked-up, but the truth is I was just heartbroken when I wrote all that shit." Oh God, the words are tumbling out of my mouth. "I'd just gotten out of a three-year relationship that didn't end well," I ramble, "and I won't go into detail about everything that happened, but trust me, I had some shit to work out." I take a deep breath. "I was devastated, to be perfectly honest—I felt like there was something deeply wrong with me, and..." My heart is racing. I swallow hard. "For reasons I don't wanna go into, there was no way for me to do any of that stuff I wrote about with my girlfriend. And that was okay, *of course,* because I never would have pushed her to do anything she wasn't comfortable with—*never*—but when we broke up—well, actually, when she *cheated* on me instead of doing me the courtesy of actually breaking up with me—I figured, 'Well, fuck it. YOLO. Life throws you lemons, make lemonade.' So I joined The Club and rode a month's worth of Mickey Mouse roller coasters so I could pull my shit together and move on. And I don't regret any of it because it actually worked—I totally moved on and now I'm perfectly fine." Shit. I'm rambling. I'm incoherent. I'm out of breath. Fuck. I force myself to stop talking.

Kat's tears have dried up. She's stone-faced and looking at me like I've got fingers growing out of my head.

"To be perfectly honest," I continue, even though I know I should shut the fuck up, "I didn't expect you to be so upset by what I wrote. I admit I didn't wanna give you my application, but it wasn't because I was *ashamed* of what I asked for, it was because I didn't wanna have to explain all this shit about Emma to you. I'm not ashamed about The Club, Kat. I was *single*. It was one month of my life. No one was hurt—far from it." I shift my weight. Shit, I think I'm digging myself an even deeper hole. "Frankly," I continue, deciding the best defense is a good offense, "I'm shocked you're so upset. Now that I've gotten to know you—or at least I *thought* I'd gotten to know you—I actually thought you'd be pretty understanding about everything I wrote—or, at least, about most of it." My voice cracks, despite my best efforts to sound calm and collected. I rub my forehead. "I honestly thought you'd maybe even get off on some of it."

Her eyes are wide.

The bell dings on the private elevator behind Kat's back. The doors open and then close—but, thankfully, Kat doesn't move from her spot in the hallway.

What the fuck happened to the woman who wrote me that awesome 'application' to the 'Josh Faraday Club'? The woman who felt crushed when some asshole called her a slut and said she wasn't 'marriage material'? Where's the girl who admitted she has a shitload of crazy-elaborate sexual fantasies, for fuck's sake? I thought my perverted shit would be right up her alley, I really did. And where the fuck is the incredible girl who rode a Sybian 'til she squirted and literally passed out? Because I can't imagine *that* girl reacting to my application with *tears*. I run my hand through my hair. Shit. I feel like I'm reliving that last, horrible, blindsiding conversation with Emma all over again.

"Just please tell me why you're crying," I say, trying to keep my voice from sounding panicked. "I truly thought you'd understand about my application."

"Josh," Kat begins, but then she pauses.

My stomach twists with anticipation. Here it comes. I brace myself.

"I haven't read your application," she says softly. "You've misunderstood me."

I close my eyes. Oh, how I wish I could stuff every word I just said back into my stupid goddamned mouth. I open my eyes. Shit.

"I started reading it, yes," she continues. "But then I called you when I got to the part about your three photos, and then I saw your 'Sick Fuck' folder and—oh, yeah, bee tee dubs, I permanently deleted that folder, sorry, I can be kind of impulsive sometimes." She takes a deep breath. "And then I went into your email account to send myself that naked photo of you with the gigantic boner—oh, and I also sent myself your application, too, by the way—sorry if that pisses you off, but, whatever, I am what I am—and, anyway, while I was in your email account, you got an incoming email." Her lip curls with unbridled disgust. "And *that's* what I'm crying about, Josh: the freaking *email*."

I can barely breathe. "What email?"

Her eyes water and she wipes them. "An email from Jen—your blast from the past."

The hair on my neck stands on end.

"And let me just say this," Kat says, her voice edged with barely contained rage. "If a woman is totally into you and you keep stringing her along, even though you're not into her, then at some point you're not a *playboy*, you're just a flat-out *prick*."

"*What?*"

"Unless, of course, you *are* into her and you've been peddling me a line of total bullshit this whole time—in which case, you're not just a *prick*, you're also a flat-out *liar*."

"What the *fuck* are you talking about, Kat?" I ask, dumbfounded. "What did Jen say in her email?" I pull my phone out from my pocket and frantically scroll through my inbox. And there it is—an email from Jen. I quickly read it, doing my best to see Jen's message through Kat's (batshit-crazy) eyes. "Oh, Jesus," I stammer. "No, no, no, Jen *completely* misunderstood me," I blurt. "I called to tell her I'm not interested in her—I swear to God—that's what I told her."

"Well, Jen sure seems to think you called to 'suggest' something along the lines of you 'motorboating' her 'pretty titties'—*again*." Her nostrils flare. Her face is bright red. She looks like a fucking fire-breathing dragon right now.

Shit. I look at Jen's email again, my heart racing. "Kat, no. I didn't suggest a fucking thing. I told Jen I wasn't interested in her. I said I'm not in the market for a relationship."

"Maybe you *think* that's what you said to her, but clearly you didn't. Because she clearly thinks there's still a chance for *something* with you, Josh, and when it comes to you, she'll obviously take any little crumb she can get, no matter how small and pitiful."

"Well, shit. Hang on. Lemme read it again."

"It makes me wonder if you're ever completely honest when it comes to women. Do you ever just tell it like it is? Or do you always spin things to avoid hurt feelings—or maybe to keep your motorboating-options open?"

"Hang the fuck on, Kat. Jesus fucking Christ, you demon-woman, lemme fucking look at it."

Kat presses her lips together and crosses her arms over her chest, her eyes blazing. "I don't mind a manwhore if he's honest about it—I really don't—I mean, as long as he's not running around collecting baby-mommas or STD's —*but I absolutely cannot stomach a goddamned liar*."

"Fuck, Kat. Would you shut the fuck up for a minute? Jesus, you're a fucking lunatic." I look down at my phone and read again while Kat silently fumes. "Okay, clearly there's been a huge misunderstanding," I say when I'm done reading.

"Don't forget to take a peek at the photos she sent you, too," Kat says. "They're super-duper awesome."

I'd be a fool to open those photos with Kat standing right here, I know—but I do it, anyway. Why? Because, apparently, I'm every bit the suicide-bomber she is.

I open the first photo. It's Jen and her famous mom, their cheeks pressed together.

"Yeah, so what?" I say. "Who cares if Jen's mom is—"

"Open the second photo, Josh."

I roll my eyes and open the second photo. Oh. Wow. Hello, Jen's beautiful tits. Yeah, that woman's got some gorgeous tits, I must say. But so what? I look up at Kat, ready to tell her she needs to take a chill-pill, and she's absolutely seething with jealousy. If she were a cartoon character, her skin would be green and steam would be shooting out her ears.

I stifle a grin, remembering Kat's sexy little speech about how she never, ever gets jealous. The girl is all talk. I open my mouth to speak, but before I can say a goddamned word, Kat launches into me again.

"Do you always just tell women what they want to hear, Josh? That's what I wanna know. Which leads me to the million-dollar question: Have you just been telling *me* what I wanna hear?"

My urge to smile vanishes. I throw up my hands, suddenly enraged. "Gimme a break, Kat. I've been one hundred percent honest with you and you know it."

"I'm not so sure. You keep telling me I'm 'the most beautiful woman you've ever been with' and then I see you've been with a freaking Victoria's Secret 'Angel.'"

"So?" I ask.

"So, then I know for a fact you're just blowing smoke up my butt."

"Oh my God. You're *pissed* I said you're more beautiful than a Victoria's Secret supermodel?" I take a deep breath, trying to control my rising anger. "Why are you doing this? I haven't given you shit about Cameron Schulz or any of the guys you've slept with—and it sounds like there's plenty to choose from."

Oh shit, I shouldn't have added that last bit. Ooph. The top of her head just popped off.

"Well, maybe you'd react differently if Cameron emailed me a photo of his balls and asked me to 'motorboat' them!" Her eyes bug out. "*Again!*" she shrieks.

I stifle the urge to laugh. She's pretty funny right now.

Kat's still fuming. "And you wanna know the reason *why* Cameron's not sending me goddamned dick-and-ball-pics?" she continues. "*Because I was honest and clear with him about my lack of interest.*"

"Oh, okay, sure, Kat—you're so fucking *honest* all the time. Let's talk about that cute little speech of pure fiction you made about how you never, ever get jealous unless you're in a committed relationship. Hmm? What about that?" I scoff. "So, okay, maybe I didn't get my words exactly right when I talked to Jen. But that was because I was trying to let her down easy. At least I was trying to be *nice*."

She clenches her jaw. "What does that mean? You don't think I'm nice?"

I pause. "No, I... I think you're nice—really nice. It's just that..." Why do I keep feeling like I'm digging myself a deeper hole? "It's just that, you know, you're a Scorpio," I say.

She looks at me blankly.

"God wouldn't have designed you with a stinger on your tail if he didn't want you to use it on occasion, right?"

Her mouth is hanging open.

"But that's okay. I like your stinger." Oh boy. I'm really not doing myself any favors here. Okay. Once again, the best defense is a good offense. "Jesus Christ, Kat," I say. "You're just like my fucking brother—physically perfect and you don't even know it. And you're needy just like him, too." I shake my head. "Kat, you're absolutely beautiful. I told you. I couldn't have designed you better myself. But you're also insane, apparently. You're seriously driving me crazy."

Her cheeks flush.

There's a long beat.

"I'm not usually this crazy," she says softly. She twists her mouth. "Something happens to me when I get around you." She throws up her hands. "Look, I'm being an asshole—okay? I realize that. I'm sorry." She exhales and flaps her lips together. "I tell you what. I'm gonna go downstairs and meet up with Henn and do the photo thing for my Oksana passport, okay? And while I do that, why don't you stay here and write a reply to Jen. Whatever's the truth, just tell her, once and for all, as clearly as possible."

"I'm not interested in her, Kat, like I keep saying."

She bares her teeth. "Glad to hear it. And after I do the photo thing with Henn," she says, "I'm gonna sit my butt down at a Blackjack table, drink some whiskey, and get control of myself. I'm sorry I lost it—that email just really threw me for a loop."

"Why?" I ask. "I already told you I fucked Jen. And, yeah, okay, I buried my face in her tits when I did it. So sue me." I grin. "She's got some really nice tits."

Kat presses her lips together.

"Kat, she means nothing to me, like I said. I only called her because I told her I would when I ran back into the party and practically ran her over trying to get your shoes and purse."

There's a long beat.

"I don't get why you're reacting this way," I say.

Kat looks up at the ceiling and then back at me, her face suddenly awash in emotion. "Just tell me right here and now, once and for all: are you Garrett Bennetting me?" she blurts. Tears suddenly flood her eyes and she wipes them.

"*That's* what this is all about?"

She nods.

I roll my eyes. "*No*," I say emphatically. "Of course not. I shouldn't even have to tell you that."

She wipes her eyes again. "All those women, Josh." She looks up at the ceiling like she's trying to keep tears from spilling out of her eyes. "I don't care if you're a manwhore. It's just... you can have any woman you want—anyone at all. The daughter of Gabrielle LeMonde—"

I scoff loudly, shutting her up.

"A Victoria's Secret Angel."

"A devil-woman with battery acid in her heart."

Kat bites her lip, obviously trying to suppress a smile. "Emma."

"A woman who called me a sick fuck and then promptly ran off with a dude who owns polo ponies and wears a fucking *ascot*."

There's a long beat. Kat's eyes are unreadable to me.

"I'm obviously way out of line here—just a total head case," she says. "I'm sorry." She exhales loudly. "I'm gonna go get a drink and play blackjack while you reply to Jen's email. She's a twat and a half, don't get me wrong, but even twats have feelings, too, and she deserves an honest response. Lemme just go downstairs and pull myself together for a bit, okay? I'm really sorry I'm acting so crazy."

She turns around to pound the elevator call-button, her shoulders slumped.

Fuck this shit. I'm not in the mood to write an email to *Jen* right now. There's only one thing I want to do: kiss my smokin' hot Party Girl with a Hyphen.

I bound down the hallway to Kat, my cheeks on fire, a massive lump in my throat, my dick rock hard. I grab her shoulders, whirl her around to face me, and kiss the shit out of her. "I'm not Garrett Bennetting you, Kat," I mumble into her lips. "I promise."

45

KAT

My kiss with Josh has ramped up to full-throttle-I-wanna-fuck-your-brains-out within seconds. Josh breaks away from me, his blue eyes darkening with heat, slams my body roughly into the wall, yanks my mini-skirt up, and pulls my panties down.

I throw my head back, shaking with my arousal, and it bangs sharply against the wall of the hallway. But even the pain of whacking my head feels fucking awesome right now. I'm absolutely hyperventilating with anticipation. "Josh," I breathe, shoving my hand into his open pants and grasping his erection. "I'm sorry. I'm batshit crazy."

"You really are."

I laugh.

"I'm not like him, Kat," he breathes. "I'd never do that to you."

"I know. I don't know why I'm so crazy," I say. "I'm sorry."

"It's okay—apparently, I get off on crazy."

He shoves his hand into his pocket frantically but comes up with nothing but the key card to Jonas and Sarah's suite. He tries his other pocket and again comes up with nothing. "*Fuck,*" he says. "I must have left the condom on the table in the suite."

"We don't need it," I gasp, grasping his erection with authority. "I'm on the pill. I'm clean. Just fuck me." I'm writhing against the wall, crazed by my arousal.

Without another word, he slams me against the wall like he's mugging me and plunges himself into me with shocking ferocity.

"You feel so fucking good," he says, moving his hips exactly the way he did on the dance floor the other night.

I groan and shudder with pleasure and relief.

"I love feeling your pussy against my cock with nothing between us." He bites my neck. "You've got a magic pussy, Kat."

Oh, God, I love that he's a dirty-talker.

After a few minutes of Josh's deep thrusting and heated whispers into my ear, I make my patented just-burned-my-hand-on-the-stove sound and he growls his reply, his hips moving relentlessly.

"You're always so wet for me. Oh shit. You're so fucking *wet*."

"I start dripping the minute you step within twenty feet of me," I growl.

He lets out a long, low moan that's so sexy, I convulse with excitement.

"I can't get enough of you. I've never been addicted like this."

My skin pricks all over with a sudden chill. "Oh, God," I say. "Here it comes." For an instant, I feel exactly like I'm gonna throw up. My insides are beginning to warp and twist. "Oh, shit."

"Come on, baby." He kisses my ear and gropes my breast. "Come on."

"Oh shit!" I claw at his chest and pull at his hair and devour his lips as my body explodes with painful pleasure. Oh my God, I can't get enough of this sensation. *I can't get enough of this man.*

"You're amazing," he says, his voice gruff, his thrusts turning brutal. "You feel so good."

I feel swept away. I can't even remember where I am. It's like Josh and I are flying, weightless, swirling together. I'm high on him. On his hard shaft moving in and out of me. On his scent, the taste of his voracious lips, the sound of his sensuous growls in my ear. He's completely overwhelming me in every way.

Except, wait, I think I just heard something besides Josh's growls in my ear.

"You feel so fucking good," Josh says, his hips gyrating forcefully. "So wet. So tight. Oh, fuck."

Hang on. Was that a little dinging noise? Almost like a bell?

Before my brain can answer that question with the phrase, "Yes, you dumb-shit—that was the freakin' elevator," Henn's strangled voice echoes into the hallway: "Oh my fuck. Gah!"

I freeze, instantly mortified at the sound of Henn's horrified voice, but Josh doesn't stop. To the contrary, he impales me with monster-truck force into the wall and lets out a strangled sound that quite plainly signals he's in the midst of an extremely pleasurable orgasm.

I hold my breath and close my eyes, letting the dual sensations of Josh's climax and my own wretched embarrassment about Henn stumbling upon us undulate simultaneously through me.

I hear the sound of the elevator doors closing followed by nothing but Josh panting in my ear. I open one eye and cautiously peek at Josh. He's staring at me, his face beaded with sweat, his eyes smoldering. I glance over his shoulder toward the elevator, my heart racing, my clit rippling with an aftershock. The elevator doors are closed. Josh and I are alone in the hallway. Henn's nowhere to be found.

I look at Josh again, my cheeks blazing with a strange mixture of embarrassment and arousal, my heart racing. We stare at each other for a long, silent beat, our chests heaving in synchronicity. After a moment, one side of Josh's mouth hitches up, ever so slightly, into a smirk.

"Well, that was embarrassing," he says.

And that's all it takes—we both burst into hysterical laughter.

46

KAT

"I'd love to rinse off real quick," I mumble, pulling up my G-string. "Jeez, Josh. That was a lot."

He laughs. "Sorry, not sorry." He pulls out his phone. "Lemme just text Henn and tell him we'll be down in a few. I'm sure he came up here wanting to take your passport photo."

"I'm so embarrassed."

Josh scoffs. "Eh, he'll get over it." He looks at his phone. "Oh, I've actually got a text from ol' Henny. Imagine that."

I wince. "What does it say?"

"It says, 'Where the fuck are you guys? Text me where to find you.'" Josh snickers. "Well, I guess he got his answer, huh?"

Josh taps out a reply, laughing to himself as he does.

"What are you saying to him?"

"Just that we'll be down in a few."

"Oh, good. I was worried you were—"

"*And,* that I missed his text because you and I were busy taking ol' one-eye to the optometrist."

"You did not!"

He shows me his phone. He did. In those exact words.

"*Josh!*"

He laughs. "Hey, nothing smooths out an awkward situation better than humor. Trust me, I should know. I've been smoothing out awkward situations my whole fucking life."

"Ugh. *Josh.*" I put my hands over my face.

"Kat, the man saw me fucking the shit out of you. I don't think my text will come as a huge surprise." When I don't join Josh's laughter, he nuzzles his nose into my ear. "Aw, don't worry, babe. He'll recover. Henn's got a whopper of a crush on you, for sure, but he's a big boy." He moves my hair behind my shoulder and kisses my neck. "Maybe seeing us together will help Henn move past his little crush." Josh's phone pings in his hand and he looks at it. "Henn says, 'Meet me in an hour. An eye exam should never be rushed.'" Josh laughs heartily. "See? What did I tell you? Little Henny's already bounced back."

"You're not embarrassed Henn saw us screwing the crap out of each other?"

"Well, yeah, of course, I'm embarrassed. Fucking in front of Henn isn't high on my list of things to do. But I'm not gonna lose any sleep over it. At least I was fucking an insanely gorgeous woman and not a goat. Well, not this time, anyway."

"Ha, ha. Don't make bestiality jokes, Josh—I still haven't read your perverted application. Speaking of which, how have I *still* not read your perverted application?"

"Hey, I gave it to you. I've met my obligation. If you haven't read it by now that's on you."

"How do you keep distracting me? Are you some sort of evil genius?"

"Yes, I am—the world's dumbest evil genius."

"I just realized something," I say, having a genuine epiphany. "You've been diabolically controlling me this whole time, haven't you? Controlling me while letting me think *I'm* controlling *you*."

He shrugs. "I'm wise and powerful, babe; I warned you right from the start." He shoots me a megawatt smile. "What's the rush on reading that damned thing, anyway? You said you emailed it to yourself, right?—so now you can read it whenever."

I smile. I can't believe how relaxed and easygoing Josh has become about his application—what a turnaround since we first started sparring over it.

Josh looks at his watch. "Jonas and Sarah should be landing in D.C. in about an hour—Jonas said they'd be landing around seven Washington time. So let's take a nice, long shower, let you rinse out your cooch and maybe scrub off some of that batshit-crazy you've got all over you—and then we'll meet Henn for the photo thing. By then it'll be time to touch base with Jonas and Sarah to see if they have any news about today's meeting with the feds." He pulls me to him close. "And *then* we'll grab a few hours of sleep together in my room, just me and you." He kisses my neck. "Sound good, my crazy little Party Girl with a Hyphen?"

I think my heart's gonna burst right out of my chest. "That all sounds perfect, Playboy."

47

KAT

U p 'til now, all of my naked interactions with Josh have been fast and furious. But now, in this steaming hot, post-hallway-fuckery shower, I'm finally getting the chance to slowly touch and appreciate every inch of Josh's muscled, tattooed body. And appreciate it, I do. Holy hot damn. He's gorgeous.

I squirt shower gel into my palm and eagerly run my hand over his "Grace" tattoo on his chest and then down the ruts and ridges of his abs and across his pelvis, skimming my palm between the "V" cuts in his waist and over the word "OVERCOME."

And, glory be, as I touch Josh, he returns the favor, slowly exploring every curve and crevice of my wet body with his palms and fingertips.

"You're beautiful," Josh says softly in my ear, kissing my neck. "Gorgeous."

My fingertips slide to the tattoo on the right side of his torso, behind his ribcage. Before now, I haven't paid much attention to this one. But now that I'm studying it, I'm noticing it's an intricate scene of a fish swimming in a river, shaded by an overhanging tree on a nearby riverbank.

"What's the story on this one?" I ask, touching the fish with my fingertip.

He runs his hand across my right nipple and down my side, over the curve of my hip, and down my ass cheek. "I'll give you my standard answer first," he says softly, his lips grazing my ear. "And then, I'll tell you the whole truth."

"Okay," I whisper, just before his lips find mine.

We kiss for a long time, letting the hot water pelt us as we do, our hands exploring each other as our lips and tongues intertwine.

Finally, Josh pulls away from my mouth and licks my jawline.

I shudder with pleasure. Oh, God, I can't get enough of him. I'm absolutely intoxicated with him.

"Your tattoo?" I breathe.

"Sorry, I got distracted," he says. He smiles and his eyes sparkle. "My standard answer is it's a fish because I'm a Pisces," he says, his hands skimming over my ass. "Which is true."

"You're a *Pisces*?" I say, pulling away from him in surprise.

"What? Is that bad?"

"Oh, no. It's just... " I trail off. There's no way I'm gonna explain that Pisces is the astrological sign most compatible with Scorpio. "You just seem like such a classic Pisces, that's all," I say smoothly.

"Yeah? What are the characteristics of a classic Pisces?"

I think briefly. "Compassionate, adaptable, accepting, devoted, and imaginative."

He puts his forehead on mine. "Wow, I *rock*."

I laugh. "Don't get too enamored with yourself. That was just the *good* Pisces stuff. You're also indecisive, self-pitying, lazy, and escapist."

"Oh shit." He grins. "I *suck*."

We both laugh.

He kisses me again.

"What about you, Miss Scorpio? What's the rap on you?"

"I'm loyal, passionate, resourceful, and dynamic."

He laughs and pinches my ass. "Dead-on accurate." His hands migrate up my back. "Now what's the shitty Scorpio stuff?"

I frown. "Well, *supposedly*, I'm obsessive, suspicious, manipulative, unyielding, and... *jealous*. But I think that's all a load of crap."

We both burst out laughing.

"Oh my God, that's hilarious," he says. "Maybe there's something to this astrology stuff, after all."

"It's amazing how spot-on it can be."

"So you're pretty into it?" he asks.

I shrug. "I don't manage my life based on astrology—I told you, I'm not one to think everything's fated—I'm a firm believer in kicking ass—but I do think it's crazy how accurate astrology can be regarding people's personalities and compatibility."

"When's your birthday?" he asks.

"November sixteenth. When's yours?"

"March ninth—and Jonas', too, obviously."

"Aw, that's right. I forgot Jonas is a Pisces, too. Sarah's also a Pisces." I smile wistfully. "They're Pisces-Pisces-sittin'-in-a-tree. That's so sweet."

"Two Pisces is good?"

"It's amazing. Pisces-Pisces is one of the top love compatibilities on the Zodiac. When two Pisces join together, it's a deep spiritual connection. They're both water signs, so two Pisces *meld* together completely, intertwining and becoming inseparable. They bring out the spiritual side in each other."

"What about Pisces-Scorpio?"

I can't believe Josh just asked me about our astrological love compatibility. My heart is racing. "Pisces and Scorpio are highly compatible, too—also both water signs," I say, my skin pricking with goose bumps even under the pounding hot water. "But a Scorpio-Pisces union is especially notable for its intensity and off-the-charts passion. When Pisces and Scorpio get together, it's like *ka-boom*."

His eyes flicker. "Hmm. I think maybe I'm becoming a believer in astrology."

He presses himself into me and I feel the unmistakable sensation of a hard-on jutting into my hip. I look down. *Oh, hello.* Josh has apparently fully recovered from our tryst in the hallway and he's ready to go again. Holy hell, Joshua William Faraday is a virile motherfucker.

Josh smirks and slides his fingers between my legs. "I think I'm officially addicted to making you come," he says softly. "You're my new favorite game."

I never thought I'd see the day, but I actually think I've had my limit of body-twisting orgasms for one day. But, damn, this man's definitely got a gigantic boner. Looks like there's only one thing for a girl to do: without saying a word, I kneel and take Josh's hard-on into my mouth.

I rarely give head, actually—a guy's gotta be pretty damned special to me to exert that kind of effort—but when I *do* give it, then by God, I do it right. And this time is no exception.

Technically, I already gave Josh a blowjob while I rode the Sybian, but if I'm being honest, that really wasn't my best work—I certainly didn't deliver the Katherine Morgan Ultimate Blowjob Experience the way I'd normally do, that's for sure. Of course, under the circumstances, my lackluster oral performance couldn't be helped—I defy any woman to supply a mind-blowing blowjob while having an orgasm-induced seizure on a jet engine—but now, suddenly, I feel an urgent desire to show Josh exactly what my mouth can do.

Why? Because I want him. I want him *bad*. And in my experience, there's no weapon more lethal in a woman's arsenal than giving a man the best blowjob of his life. If she can do this, she can have anything or anyone she desires. Harsh, perhaps, to state the fact so starkly. But true nonetheless.

I begin licking and sucking on Josh's shaft, and he immediately makes it clear he's an ardent fan of my work. But I'm just getting started. Because a blowjob worthy of being called a Katherine Morgan Ultimate Blowjob Experience can't be good. It can't even be great. No, a blowjob worthy of this lofty title must be nothing short of mind-blowing.

Of course, every mind-blowing blowjob starts at its inception with a can-do attitude—a girl's *really* gotta want to suck that dick—or else she truly shouldn't even bother.

To get myself in the right frame of mind to deliver oral epicness, I engage in a little *role-play*, if you will, a little mental trick that turns me on and inspires me to reach for greatness every time: I simply imagine I'm a high-priced call girl who charges a million bucks per blowjob and my only mission is to make my client say, "You're worth every fucking penny, baby." Oh man, it gets me going every time. (And if I'm turned on, I'm motivated to turn *him* on, too.)

But while a good attitude is an essential ingredient to giving a man the most intense oral experience of his life, it can only take a girl so far if she doesn't also have fantastic technique.

Through trial and tribulation, I've surmised that the most effective oral techniques ascend a "ladder of pleasure," if you will, that goes a little something like this:

Rung One. If a girl aims to give a man at least a *pleasurable* blowjob (which should be a baseline goal, or else why is she putting a cock into her mouth, for crying out loud?), then she's gotta lick and suck that guy's dick like she's got heatstroke and it's a popsicle on a summer day.

Rung Two. If a girl wants to give a man a pleasurable and highly memorable blowjob (which, again, should be every girl's goal—because sucking a man's dick and then being forgotten is definitely not something to aspire to in life), then she's gotta lick and suck that man's dick *plus* his balls *and* she's gotta do it all like she's been bitten by a rattlesnake and his dick and balls contain the antidote to the venom.

Based on conversations with friends and articles I've read in *Cosmo*, I'd venture to guess that's where most girls stop climbing the ladder of pleasure—at Rung Two.

But I'm not most girls. In fact, I'm exactly what Josh accused me of being: I'm a frickin' terrorist. If I'm gonna give head, then by God, I'm gonna make the owner of that dick and balls fall head over heels in love with me.

Which brings me to Rung Three. At rung three, a girl's gotta do all of the above, *plus* fondle every freakin' inch of his jewels and back forty and taint, including massaging his asshole (and fingering it if he seems into it); *plus* she's gotta grip his shaft like it's a life preserver and she's a woman-overboard in stormy seas. But she can't stop there. Hell no. She's also gotta suck on his tip like it's liquid chocolate. Take his balls into her mouth while pumping his shaft and swirling her tongue on his tip and licking and sucking his little hole like she's high on meth and she thinks that hole is spurting more juice.

I've just reached the third rung of the ladder on Josh.

He moans like a dying buffalo.

Clearly, he's thoroughly enjoying his Katherine Morgan Ultimate Blowjob Experience.

And, holy hell, so am I. Oh my, yes. *So am I.* In fact, I'm getting off on doing this for Josh almost as much as if he were doing the same for me between my legs. This is new. I've never felt quite this turned on before while giving head. Oh my God. I think I'm gonna come.

Oh my hell. I think it's time to identify a fourth rung on the ladder of pleasure: doing all of the above things in a hot, steamy shower with the sexiest man alive, Joshua William Faraday.

Josh releases into my mouth with a grizzly bear growl and I'm surprised to realize I'm coming too, right along with him. Wow, that's a first. A truly delectable first.

When I'm done, and Josh's hard-on has stopped jerking and rippling in my mouth, I stand up and get a long mouthful of hot water from the showerhead, loosen my jaw, and turn back to him.

His eyes are on fire. He kisses me greedily, shaking with an aftershock. "Oh my God, Kat. That was... *Thank you.*" He kisses my nipple and begins to kneel, obviously intending to return the favor.

"Hang on," I say, touching his shoulder. "I'm good."

He looks up at me, surprised.

"We've got to get downstairs to meet Henn," I say.

"But I wanna get you off, too," he says, grinning. "It's only fair."

"Oh, I came. Like a freight train. While I was swallowing."

His face ignites. "Are you serious?"

I smile and nod.

"Oh my God. You're amazing." He straightens up. "You're a unicorn, Kat. You're... oh my God." He's in a frenzy. "What planet are you from? You're amazing."

"Hey, I'll certainly take a rain check, though," I say. "When we have more time, maybe you can try to beat me at my own game." I wink. "A little competition never hurt anyone."

He smiles lasciviously. "Oh, Party Girl. You're on. I look forward to it."

48

KAT

Josh turns off the water and we step out of the shower together.

"So what's the second half of the story of your fish tattoo?" I ask.

He hands me a towel and I begin drying myself.

"Oh, yeah. Sorry. I got distracted. *Again.*" He laughs and towels himself off. "You seem to have that effect on me." He takes a deep breath. "The tattoo represents something my mom always used to say to Jonas and me." He grabs his pants off the floor of the bathroom and begins dressing. "I don't actually have a ton of coherent memories about my mom—we were pretty little when she died—but one thing I remember really clearly is she always called Jonas and me her 'little fishies'—because, you know, we're Pisces." He flashes me a huge smile. "My dad said she loved astrology. Just like you."

My heart leaps. "Oh, cool," I say, but on the inside, I'm kind of freaking out to share this similarity with his mother.

"Yeah, so my mom always said, 'Everybody's a genius, but if you judge a fishy by its ability to climb a tree, it'll live its whole life believing it's stupid.'"

"Ah," I say, scrutinizing his tattoo. "That's a pretty wise and powerful thing to say."

"She didn't make it up—I looked it up—it's a quote from Einstein. But she loved it and said it all the time."

"So your fishy is swimming along happily in the river, rather than climbing the nearby tree?"

"Wouldn't want the poor guy spending his whole life believing he's stupid."

"Of course not, especially since he's wise and powerful."

Josh finishes buckling his belt. "So tell me something, PG. Another round of the honesty-game."

"Sure."

"Did a little piece of you get turned on when Henn saw us fucking?"

"What?" I blurt, utterly appalled. "Of course not. I was absolutely mortified."

Josh silently buttons his shirt.

"Why?" I ask. "Were *you* turned on?" I zip up my miniskirt and reach for my shirt.

"No. Not at all." He finishes buttoning his shirt. "I was just curious, based on something you wrote in your application."

"Josh, it was *Henn*," I say. "I'm gonna have horrible nightmares about him stumbling upon us 'til the day I die."

We're both fully dressed. Josh grabs my hand and leads me out of the bathroom, toward the main room of the suite. "Yeah, I know. Me, too. But..." he begins tentatively. "Does the idea of *someone* watching you turn you on? Someone who's not Henn?"

My pulse has begun pounding in my ears. "Like, *who*?"

"I dunno. When you had your little lesbo-encounter in college wasn't the other girl's boyfriend watching?"

My cheeks flush. I nod.

"And did you like it?"

I've never talked about this with anyone. I clear my throat. "Yeah."

"You liked him watching?"

I nod. "The fact that her boyfriend was watching was the hottest thing about the whole thing."

Josh's face lights up.

"Well, that and, you know, the whole excitement of doing something taboo. But the actual making-out part—you know, what my friend physically did to me, what I did to her—that wasn't the real turn-on. If we'd been in private, just the two of us, it never would have happened."

"Interesting." Josh leads me to the table in the middle of the suite and sits me down. He leans over me, his hands on the arms of my chair. "And did the boyfriend join in with you two girls at some point?"

I've never told anyone about that night. My heart is racing. I nod.

"And did you like it when he did?" He leans forward slightly, leveling his blue eyes with mine.

"Um. It was just okay, to be honest. The guy was *really* into his girlfriend. So once things got going, I pretty quickly started feeling like a third wheel, and I didn't like that feeling."

He chuckles.

"At all."

He grins. "Why doesn't that surprise me?"

"I've come to realize I need to be the center of attention."

"No shit?" He flashes a cocky grin.

I try to look offended at that comment, but it's impossible. I join him in laughing.

He glides to the bar. "How about a quick drink before we meet Henn?" He looks at his watch. "We've got about twenty minutes."

"Just some water. I'm pretty wiped out."

"Water it is. So was that your only threesome, Party Girl?" he asks, busying himself behind the bar.

"Yeah. I never had the desire to do it again after that. I realized I was more turned on when her boyfriend was watching than when he actually joined in."

"Interesting," he says, mixing a drink behind the bar. "So you said in your application you have lots of fantasies. Is that one of your fantasies—someone watching you with another person?"

My cheeks are on fire. "Um, no, not really. I haven't given it much thought since then. But I guess it could be kind of fun to experience the whole thing the way my friend did—being the center of attention instead of the third wheel. I was just window dressing during the whole thing, but I suppose it might be fun to be the *window*."

He brings me my water, his eyes blazing. "Here you go," he says. He places my water on the table in front of me and sits down next to me. He places his hand on my thigh.

"What about you?" I ask, my heart thumping in my chest. "Would you be interested in... watching?"

"Just tell me where and when."

Oh shit. He misunderstood me. I was speaking hypothetically—asking him whether he has the general fantasy of watching a *hypothetical* woman he's attracted to getting it on with another woman. I wasn't specifically asking him if he wants to watch *me* with another woman.

There's a long beat as I try to figure out how best to clarify my question.

Josh takes a long sip of his drink. "But only if you were totally comfortable with it," he adds, his eyes burning.

"Is that a martini?" I ask.

"Yeah, you want one?"

"Maybe just a sip of yours."

I'm expecting him to slide his drink toward me, but, instead, he takes a long gulp of his drink, grabs my face, leans into me, and kisses me deeply, letting the delicious fluid in his mouth gush into mine.

"Holy shitballs," I say when he pulls away from my lips. "That was so freakin' hot." I laugh.

He licks his lips. "So do you think you'd be up for letting me watch you with a woman? I'd really enjoy it."

I pause. "I'm not bisexual."

He shrugs. "You don't need to be. You wouldn't have to do much to make me very happy. You could do as little or as much as you'd want. What you do isn't really the point of it for me."

He slides his martini to me, reading my mind, and I take a long sip.

"You wouldn't have to do anything that makes you even remotely uncomfortable. You'd be surprised how little it takes to make me a very happy boy."

My pulse is pounding in my ears. "I think it would depend," I say. I put down the drink.

"On what?"

"On who the other woman was."

He smiles broadly.

"In college, my friend and I were both totally weirded out afterwards and we never got back to normal," I say. "The experience pretty much ruined our friendship."

He leans forward, his eyes locked onto mine, and cups my jawline in his palm. "What if you could pick the woman? And do as little or as much as you pleased with her?"

I swallow hard. My heart is beating wildly. "It... would... be totally up to me?" I stammer.

He leans back and drops his hand from my face, his eyes ablaze. "The question wouldn't be whether the woman turns *me* on—the only question would be whether she turns *you* on. If so, that would do wonders for me."

My head is spinning. "Would you ultimately join in and have sex with both of us—or just with me?"

"What would you prefer?"

"Just with me."

"Then that's what I'd do."

"You'd have to swear not to lose control and start fucking the other woman."

He scoffs. "Kat, I'm not an animal. I don't 'lose control' and start fucking people like a dog humping a leg. I'm not some sort of sex offender."

I think my heart is medically palpitating. "Because if you started having any kind of sexual contact with the other woman, then I'd get crazy-jealous."

Josh shoots me a look that says "no shit" but he doesn't say anything.

"If we did it, it wouldn't be all about making me jealous, right? It'd be about turning me on—and, therefore, you?"

"Correct."

"Making me jealous wouldn't be some sort of secret, ulterior motive?" I feel like my heart's gonna hurtle right out of my chest. "You wouldn't tell me one thing beforehand, just to get me to do it, and then blindside me later, right?"

His face melts into total sincerity. He puts both hands on my cheeks this time and leans his forehead against mine. "Kat, I'd *never* blindside you, in any context. Sexual or otherwise."

My heart is racing so fast, I'm practically yelping for air. "Because I'd only do it if the other woman was gonna be the third wheel, not me." I can't believe I'm negotiating the terms of this. How did this conversation go from hypotheticals to actual negotiation so quickly?

"I'd respect that," he says. "One hundred percent. It'd be all about you. I wouldn't lay a finger on the other woman if you didn't want me to. Not even a pinky."

I'm having a hard time pushing air into my lungs. "That's what I'd want," I say. "Not a finger. Absolutely no contact between you and the other woman. It'd be all about me and you."

"Done." His eyes are like lit torches.

"And you'd sit and watch?"

"I would."

"Would you jack off?"

"If that's something you'd be okay with."

"Yes."

"Then, yes."

"But you wouldn't come. I'd want you to be able to fuck me. Really hard."

He shudders. "When I got to the point I couldn't stand it anymore, I'd pull you aside and tell the other woman to leave and I'd fuck the shit out of you."

I'm breathless. My skin is bursting with heat. I slide from my chair to sit on his lap and he wraps his arms around me. "Or, who knows," I purr, "maybe you'd tell her to stay and watch—see what she's missing out on?" I can't believe I just said that. This man brings out a whole new level of naughty in me.

Clearly, Josh can't believe I just said that, either. "If that's what you'd want, absolutely," he says. "Totally up to you."

I can barely breathe. "And she wouldn't be anyone either of us knows?" I say softly. "Nobody you know?"

"It'd be whoever you pick, babe. Anyone at all, as long as she tests clean. I don't give a fuck who she is. It's all about you."

My clit is throbbing so hard, it hurts. "But what if I wind up picking someone you're more attracted to than me? I'd be able to tell, and I wouldn't like it," I say.

He places his fingertip in the cleft in my chin. "That's literally impossible."

Holy fucking shit. I seriously can't breathe right now. I'm trembling. I swallow hard. "We'd do it and never see her again? Because I wouldn't want this kind of fantasy-thing to follow us into our real life."

He chuckles.

"What?"

"You just perfectly articulated why I joined The Club."

I make a face that says, "I see your point" and he smiles broadly.

"You're amazing, Kat," he says. He puts his hand under my chin and kisses me. "I think you might be perfect." He kisses me again. And then again. "You're kinda freaking me out, actually."

My head is spinning. I can't focus. I lean into him and bite his lower lip, totally aroused, and he makes a noise of surprise.

I suck on his lower lip and then pull away. "How would we find her?" I whisper, licking my lips from our kiss.

"It'd be easy to do if we set our minds to it, I'm sure."

"We'd have to be one hundred percent sure we'd never see her again. I wouldn't want some horny blonde bitch stalking you afterwards." I jerk back.

"What?" He looks concerned.

"*Jen.*"

The aroused expression on Josh's face instantly vanishes. "No, Kat. Fuck no. Anyone but Jen."

"No." I roll my eyes. "Not *Jen.* Her email, Josh—I want you to reply to Jen's email. I want you to tell her you're not interested in her. Right now. Show me."

He shakes his head and exhales, letting his lips flap together in exasperation as he does. "Way to lick me and punch me in the balls *again*, PG. Jesus Fucking Christ. Madame Terrorist returns."

"Open your laptop, Josh," I say, punching him in his shoulder. "We're gonna send that bitch an email right now and put her out of her freakin' misery —and therefore put me out of mine."

49

JOSH

"Hey, Jen," I say, enunciating the words as I type them onto the screen of my laptop. Kat's sitting on my lap, her arm around my shoulder, the side of her head against mine, staring at my screen as I type. "Thanks for your invitation to your birthday weekend," I write. I stop and look at Kat. "That okay so far, boss?"

"So far, so good," she says. "Continue."

"Why don't *you* just write it? Something tells me you're gonna rewrite the whole damned thing anyway, no matter what I say."

She laughs. "Nope. This is all you."

I roll my eyes. "Remind me why I'm doing this?"

"You mean why are you replying to Jen at all? Or why are you doing it with me looking over your shoulder?"

"Both."

"Well, you're replying to Jen because you're not a total douche and she deserves a reply. She invited you to her twenty-ninth birthday party, after all. The polite thing to do is RSVP."

I purse my lips, annoyed.

"*And* you're doing it with me looking over your shoulder because this email reply is gonna give me near-orgasmic pleasure. And you like giving me pleasure, right, baby?"

I grumble.

"Aw, poor Josh has to put on his big-boy pants. Come on. Just hit her with some compassionate honesty. The more you do it, the easier it gets. Trust me."

"I just don't like hurting people's feelings."

She scoffs. "And letting her twist in the wind is gonna hurt her feelings less than an honest email? I've been in her shoes with guys, and believe me, a girl feels like a piece of shit when a guy doesn't even give her the courtesy of a reply."

"There's a man alive who didn't give you the courtesy of a reply?"

"Mmm hmm."

"I don't believe it."

"Turned out the guy was married."

"Ooph."

"And I had absolutely no idea."

"God, men are such pricks."

She laughs. "Come on. Quit stalling. You're so damned good at distracting me."

"I already told her twice. Once in New York and then again on the phone after Reed's party. She's just deaf or dumb, I guess."

"No, you *think* you told her, but you must not have." She shrugs. "First rule of PR, Josh: failure to communicate is on the speaker, not the listener."

I let out a loud puff of air. "I was pretty damned clear both times, Kat."

"Obviously not," Kat says. "She's really into you, Josh—which means she's hearing what she wants to hear and telling you what she thinks you want to hear. You need to shut the door and turn the frickin' lock." She pauses pointedly. "Unless you don't *want* to shut the door?"

"Gimme a fucking break."

She motions to the screen. "Then, type."

I begin typing again. "I hope you have a great birthday," I write, saying the words out loud as I do. "I won't be able to join you. I'm..." I stop typing. "You're gonna rewrite all of this, aren't you?"

"Just keep going."

"Well, shit. *You* write it, for fuck's sake. What am I gonna say to the girl, 'I'm not into you? I used you for sex? I was thinking of Kat when I fucked you'?"

Kat's face lights up like the Fourth of July. "Oh, I like that." She motions to the screen. "Write that."

"I'm not gonna write *that*."

"Is it the truth?"

"Well, yeah."

"All of it?"

"Yeah."

"Even the part about you thinking of me while fucking her?"

"Of course. I already told you that."

"No, you didn't."

"Yes, I did."

"No, you didn't."

"I sure as hell did."

"No."

"Well, if I didn't, lemme tell you now. I couldn't stop thinking about you, fantasizing about you, jacking off while thinking about you—and you wouldn't leave your date with Cameron Fucking Schulz for me and I was pissed and frustrated as hell."

"Oh, well, that's something different than thinking about me while having sex with Jen."

"What? What are you talking about?"

"Saying you worked yourself up into sexual frustration by jacking off and thinking about me and *then* fucked Jen to relieve your frustration is quite different from saying you fucked her *and thought of me while doing it.* See the difference?"

I put my hand on my forehead like she's giving me a splitting headache.

"Do you see the difference?"

"Yes. I see the difference."

"Likewise, whatever you said to Jen in New York and on the phone after Reed's party wasn't the same thing as, 'I am not remotely interested in you in any way, shape or form, so leave me the hell alone.' Whatever you said to her, she interpreted to mean, 'I am not interested in a *serious relationship* with you, but I will quite happily continue to casually fuck you.'"

I close my eyes, trying to escape the torture.

"You're hilarious."

I open my eyes. "Why?"

"Because you're this big, strong, gorgeous guy with all the swagger and confidence in the world—but secretly you're kind of a puss."

"No, I'm not. Absolutely not."

"Yes, you are. You're scared of female emotion. You're scared of making a girl cry. Waaaah."

I exhale loudly. "Can we please just write the email? Seriously. I've already spent way too much of my time on this."

"This isn't about Jen. This is about you learning a *life lesson*, Playboy. Clearly, growing up without a mom, there was no one to teach you how to understand and communicate with women. You need some tutoring."

I feel instantly defensive—but quickly realize she's got a point. "You might be right about that," I say. "I've never thought about it that way."

"Of course, I'm right. I've got four brothers and a dad to teach me how to talk and think like a dude. But who do you have to teach you how to talk and think like a chick?"

I purse my lips, considering. "My personal assistant?"

"Doesn't count."

"Then no one."

"Well, don't you worry, honey. I'm here to save the day. So let's try this again." She motions to the computer screen. "Say what you really mean. Say it kindly, but say it clearly."

I grumble, but I put my hands on my keyboard. "I'm sorry if I gave you the wrong impression when we spoke the other day," I type. "I'm not interested in pursuing a relationship of any kind with you." I stop, waiting for Kat's reaction, but she's stone-faced. I continue typing again. "In New York, I truly thought we were both up for the same thing: a meaningless one-night stand. That was probably a stupid assumption by me, given our history. In fact, I was probably being insensitive by making that assumption. I should have known your feelings might be involved. But mine weren't." I pause and look at Kat. "Okay?"

She touches my cheek and assesses me with earnest eyes. "You're doing great."

I'm floored by her sudden show of tenderness. I swallow hard and turn back to my screen. But I can't think. My heart is suddenly pounding wildly.

"Go on," she says. "Just tell the truth, whatever it is."

I take a deep breath. "The truth is," I type, "I'm interested in someone else." Oh shit, my heart is racing. "Really, really interested. I don't know where things might lead with her, or if she's interested in me in return, but I'd like to find out. And that means I can't fuck it up by being a total douche and continuing to pursue something with you."

I look at Kat. Her mouth is hanging open.

She puts her hand on her heart.

"And, yeah," I continue typing, "if you think I'm talking about The Jealous Bitch, you're right. She might be a grenade that unpredictably explodes all over me, but that's what I like about her."

I'm practically panting. Holy motherfucking shit.

Before I've even turned my head to get a read on Kat's reaction, her lips are on mine and her tongue is in my mouth and my hands are on her cheeks and her arms are around my neck and we're kissing the hell out of each other. She presses herself into me and I wrap my arms around her, pulling her close, grasping at her for dear life, whispering her name into her lips.

After several minutes, my phone pings on the table and we begrudgingly pull away from each other, our faces on fire. I look at my phone. It's a text from Henn:

"Hey, dipshit. I can understand you wanting an especially thorough eye exam, considering who your optometrist is," Henn writes. "But you and Kat need to get your asses down here ASAP. Meet me on the casino floor near the elevator bank in five."

50

KAT

I crawl into bed with my laptop and sigh with happiness. Yeehaw, I'm finally gonna read Josh's application, without even the possibility of an interruption.

After Henn took my photo downstairs (after we'd finally located a simple white wall to use as a backdrop), the three of us briefly talked to Jonas, who told us the meeting with the feds is going down later today at one o'clock Washington time.

"You three need to be ready to transfer the money as early as one thirty Washington time," Jonas warned during our call. "I doubt we'll be asked to do it that quickly—I'm guessing the meeting with the feds will take hours—but you have to be at the ready, just in case."

"Sure thing, bro," Josh said. "No *problemo*."

After we hung up from our call with Jonas, I suddenly felt like I was gonna melt onto the floor with exhaustion. "I'm gonna get into my jammies, get nice and cozy in my bed, and do some *reading* before I drift off to sleep," I told Josh and Henn. "Nighty-night, boys."

"Okay, Kitty Kat," Henn said. "I've got everything I need now. See you in the morning." And off he went.

"How 'bout I come to your room with you?" Josh offered, pulling me into him.

"Nope," I said. "I'm going in alone. It's finally time for me to find out what kind of perverted-sick-fuck-goat-fucker you really are, Joshua William Faraday. No distractions."

Josh pressed himself into me. "Aw, come on, PG. I'll lie next to you in bed while you read. That way I can answer any questions you might have."

"No way, Playboy," I replied.

"I'll massage your feet while you read."

I paused, considering. I really love a good foot massage. "No," I finally said. "No more distractions. Nighty-night."

And now, here I am. Finally. Sitting in bed in my tank top and undies with my computer on my lap, a huge smile on my face and an Avicii song blaring through my speakers ("Addicted to You," featuring vocals by my new obsession, Audra Mae).

I quickly check my phone. I've been horrible about replying to texts and emails since coming to Sin City. This whole trip has been like entering some sort of Twilight-Zone-alternate-dimension. I scroll through my texts. I've got a text from my mom, asking me to call her so she can "hear my voice." No rush there. And a text from my oldest brother, Colby, (addressing me as Kumquat), asking me if I've gambled away next month's rent yet and telling me to call Mom so she can "hear my voice."

There's a text from my baby brother, Dax, (addressing me as Jizz), informing me he used the extra key to my apartment to "hang out" in my place for a few days and, oh yeah, by the way, oops, he ate all my food.

I've got a text from Hannah at work, telling me she misses her lunch buddy and asking me to call her whenever. I wince. Hannah's really picked up my slack at work while I've been gone. I owe her big-time.

I've got a text from Sarah from an hour ago, telling me she and Jonas landed in Washington D.C. and are set to meet at FBI headquarters later this afternoon. "Oh muh guh," Sarah wrote. "I'm crapping my pants. But Jonas is cool as a cucumber about the whole thing so he's keeping me sane."

I smile at that last sentence. Jonas is keeping *Sarah* sane? Gotta love those two.

"Go get 'em, girl," I reply to Sarah's text. "You're gonna blow all those fancy G-men away. The Vegas branch of our crew is standing by."

And, finally, there's a text from Josh from five minutes ago: "Hey, PG. Do me a favor and text me the minute you're done reading my application," he writes. "You don't have to tell me what you think about it. Just tell me when you've read it or else I won't be able to fall asleep."

"Will do," I reply. "I'm about to start reading now."

His reply is instantaneous. "Just keep an open mind," he writes. "Just remember when I wrote that thing, I was really upset."

"Yeah, yeah. I know. Don't sweat it, PB. How bad can it be?"

"Um... " he writes.

I've got a pit in my stomach. "I'll text you when I'm done," I write.

"Promise?"

"Promise."

I grab my laptop, find the email with Josh's application attached, snuggle into my soft, white pillows, happily listening to Avicii and Audra Mae serenade me, and begin reading:

Name?

"Joshua William Faraday," he writes. And, yet again, the sight of his full name sends a shiver down my spine. "Sexy man," I say out loud in my empty hotel room.

With this application, you will be required to submit three separate forms of identification. The Club maintains a strict "No Aliases Policy" for admission. You may, however, use aliases during interactions with other Club members, at your discretion.

"OK," he writes.

Age?

"29," he writes.

Provide a brief physical description of yourself.

I scan his full response to this question again. But this time reading Josh's words, my heart races and leaps: "I prefer not to talk about the meanings of my tattoos at length, so please tell whoever gets assigned to me not to ask about them."

A wave of excitement washes through me. If that's how Josh felt when he wrote those words, he certainly doesn't seem to feel that way now—or, at least, not when it comes to me.

With this application, you will be required to submit three recent photographs of yourself to your intake agent. Please include the following: one headshot, one full-body shot revealing your physique, and one shot wearing something you'd typically wear out in a public location. These photographs shall be maintained under the strictest confidentiality.

Just for the heck of it, I click onto Josh's naked-bad-boy-photo and stare at it for a moment. This man sends my pulse racing and my blood boiling in a way I've never felt before. Damn, boy—just like Audra Mae is singing in my ear right now—I'm absolutely addicted to him.

Please sign the enclosed waiver describing the requisite background check, medical physical, and blood test, which you must complete as a condition of membership.

"Done," he writes.

Sexual orientation? Please choose from the following options: Straight, homosexual, bisexual, pansexual, other?

"Straight," he writes.

Do any of your sexual fantasies include violence of any nature?

"Yes," he writes.

Whoa. Holy shitballs. Not what I expected. I move quickly to the next section.

If so, please describe in detail. Please note that your inclination toward or fantasies about sexual violence, if any, will not, standing alone, preclude membership. Indeed, we provide highly particularized services for members with a wide variety of proclivities. In the interest of serving your needs to the fullest extent possible, please describe any and all sexual fantasies involving violence of any nature whatsoever.

"I have a sexual fantasy in which I come to the rescue of a woman who's been bound and raped."

Whoa again.

Are you a current practitioner of BDSM and/or does BDSM interest you? If so, describe in explicit detail.

"BDSM interests me insofar as it relates to fulfilling the fantasy described above."

Payment and Membership Terms. Please choose from the following options: One Year Membership, $250,000 USD; Monthly Membership, $30,000 USD. All payments are non-refundable. No exceptions. Once you've made your selection regarding your membership plan, information for wiring the funds into an escrow account will be immediately forthcoming under separate cover. Membership fees shall be transferred automatically out of escrow to The Club upon approval of your membership.

"I'm interested in a one-month membership, administered according to my exact specifications, described below. If additional payment beyond your usual monthly fee is required for you to deliver exactly what I've asked for (below), I'm open to further negotiation of your fee. Please advise."

Oh my effing God. My heart is pounding forcefully in my ears. I can't read Josh's words fast enough.

Please provide a detailed explanation about what compelled you to seek membership in The Club.

"It's pretty simple, actually: I'm joining The Club because I'm a sick fuck. Or so I've been recently told by someone I loved and trusted with all my fucking heart. Well, I might be a sick fuck, but at least I'm not a heartless liar. I'm not the one who begged me to open up, pleaded with me to tell her the truth about my deepest desires and told me it was safe and she wouldn't judge me, and then when I finally broke down and told her everything, called me a 'sick fuck' and said there's something 'deeply wrong with me' and then cheated on me with a douchebag who wears a fucking ascot and says 'bloody hell' and rides polo ponies for fuck's sake. Motherfucking bastard asshole. After three years she couldn't give me the courtesy of breaking up with me? I had to hear she'd run off with that douche from a friend? Ha! And this was all because of shit I merely *fantasized* about doing—I hadn't even done any of it yet—and she ran away screaming (and right into that fucktard's arms)?

"For three years, I tried my damnedest to *fix* her and love her and protect her as best I could. But it turns out she was too broken to be fixed and loved and protected—or at least too broken to be fixed by a 'sick fuck' like me. Well, if I'm gonna lose the only girl I've ever loved for simply *fantasizing* about doing some crazy shit, then I might as well fucking do all of it, huh? Especially now that she's gone for good, riding off into the sunset on a fucking polo pony. Why should I suffer all the consequences of being a sick fuck without reaping all the rewards, too? So let's do this shit, motherfuckers. I'm ready, baby—as ready as a sick fuck can possibly be."

I look up from my screen, overwhelmed. Holy effing shit. My heart is beating so hard, I feel like it's going to crack me wide open from the inside-out. I take a deep breath, look back down at the screen, and continue reading.

Please provide a detailed statement regarding your sexual preferences. To maximize your experience in The Club, please be as explicit, detailed, and honest as possible. Please do not self-censor, in any fashion.

"If you were a woman telling me to be as explicit, detailed, and honest as possible and not self-censor myself in any fashion, I'd laugh in your face. But since you're some mysterious 'intake agent' at an underground sex club, and since I've got literally nothing to lose at this point, I'll do it. But here's the deal: I want absolute assurance you're gonna give me precisely what I ask for, to the letter. If after reading this you determine you can't give me exactly what I want, every fucking time, then don't approve my membership. Because, just to be clear, I don't need this club to get laid—I can do that just fine on my own with some of the world's most beautiful women. The only reason I'm applying to this club is to fulfill my 'sick fuck' fantasies, *exactly as described*. Because I don't want this shit to taint my real life.

"Before I describe what I want you to give me, let's first talk logistics—because I don't have the time or attention span to do things your usual way. The way this club was described to me by a buddy, it's my understanding you typically assign each new member a color-coded bracelet so he can hook up with like-minded women with similarly coded bracelets at bars or wherever. Well, that's not gonna work for me. I'm too busy and what I want is too specific. So what I want is for you to read this application, go through your database, and then curate compatible women for me, no color-coded bracelets or check-ins required.

"I've recently learned I'll be traveling around the country for about a month in the near future, appraising certain investment opportunities for my company. (I anticipate visiting about twelve cities over the course of one month —my exact itinerary to be finalized.) In each city of my month-long 'tour,' on each designated date (by four o' clock in the afternoon), I'll leave a room key under the name 'Emma' at the front desk of a designated five-star hotel. At precisely eight o'clock, I'll enter the reserved room to find one of two scenarios awaiting me, exactly as described below:

"Scenario One. Two willing women curated by you will be in the room, awaiting my arrival, preferably already naked. The women should expect to have sex with me and/or each other, depending on my mood and the level of my attraction to each woman. At the very least, they'll definitely perform sexual acts with each other while I watch.

"Scenario Two. When I enter the room, a blindfolded and naked woman, tied to the bed, will already be there. I will not be the one who tied the woman up—she'll already be in the required state when I arrive—which means someone besides the woman will initially need to accompany her to the room to help her get into position. By the time I arrive, that third party participant absolutely must be gone. Please note I will arrive at the room promptly at eight o'clock sharp, no earlier or later, to allow the woman and whoever's assisting her to plan the set-up accordingly.

"After I've entered the room, the woman should expect to engage in some form of sexual activity with me while she remains bound and blindfolded. The sex will be pleasurable and nonviolent. But please note we will be enacting a role-play in which the sex is nonconsensual.

"At the end of the blindfolded portion of our activities (which shall last no more than one hour at the outside), I will remove the woman's blindfold. When I do so, this will signal for purposes of our mutual role-play that I am someone entirely new, specifically someone who has newly entered the room to rescue her from the "attack" she's just endured (which, I repeat, will be pleasurable and nonviolent). I'll proceed to untie the woman and further sexual contact will likely occur at that time, at my discretion.

"A few important caveats and requirements: First, condoms will be used at all times, no exceptions. Second, there will be absolutely no violence of any nature, no exceptions. Any suggestion of violence during the rape-bondage role-play scenario will be purely theatrical and intended to enhance the role-play. Please note that words like "no" and "stop," etc. during the bondage scenario will not be heeded. If the woman feels uncomfortable or scared in any way, she must use the safe word "Sick Fuck." If she uses that phrase, I will immediately stop whatever I'm doing and take explicit instruction from her, whatever that is, including stopping, slowing down, and/or untying and releasing her.

"Third, all participating women must be extremely fit and natural blondes. This is non-negotiable.

"Fourth, at least three hours in advance of each date, each woman will leave a signed nondisclosure agreement and consent form for me at the hotel front desk (templates of both forms will be forwarded to you under separate cover once my membership is approved). The consent form shall detail the woman's understanding of and agreement to participate in all activities detailed above, especially the nonconsensual role-play, plus her understanding of the safe word and its function, and her consent to participate in all activities, without limitation. In addition, I'll also require a copy of each woman's medical testing, dated no earlier than two days before our meeting, establishing she's tested negative for pregnancy and all sexually transmitted diseases. Again, if these requirements necessitate payment beyond your usual monthly membership fee, please contact me to negotiate the increased fee. I do realize I'm asking you for services above and beyond your typical matching services, and I'm amenable to paying a premium for your individualized attention.

"Finally, if room service and/or an in-room massage is desired by my date (or dates) before I arrive at eight o'clock sharp, she/they should feel free to charge any desired expenses to the room. My primary concern is her (their) comfort and enjoyment.

"As far as which of the two scenarios is scheduled in each city on my itinerary, surprise me. As long as each scenario is represented equally over the course of the month, I'll be more than satisfied.

"So there you go. These are my sick-fuck fantasies. I wound up losing the only woman I've ever loved over them—and I hadn't even acted on any of them yet. So fuck it. Let's do this. If my fantasies are gonna ruin my life, then I should at least get to do them, don't you think?

"I look forward to hearing from you. Thank you."

I can't stop staring at my laptop screen.

I turn off the music. I need silence. I'm overwhelmed.

Holy Not What I Was Expecting, Batman.

This is a lot to take in. I feel like my brain is short-circuiting.

My head hurts.

And so does my heart.

That Emma girl really did a number on Josh, didn't she? Wow. What a bitch.

I read the entire application again, my heart racing.

Wow. It's no less overwhelming to me the second time around.

I sit and stare at the wall for ten minutes, a thousand emotions bombarding me.

My eyelids are drooping. God, I'm so damned tired, I can't think clearly. And I certainly can't formulate what I wanna say about all this to Josh just yet.

Now I understand why Josh didn't want me to read his damned application. For him, our tug-of-war over his application wasn't a game—not the way it was for me, anyway. For him, it was an act of emotional self-preservation.

No wonder he called me a terrorist.

He must have hated me for how hard I pushed.

Shit. I should have let the man have his privacy. I should have left him alone.

I grab my phone off the bed next to me and tap out a text to Josh. "I've read it," I type. "Gonna sleep now—about to keel over. Let's talk later, after I wake up."

Josh's reply is instantaneous. "Is it worse than being chained to a donkey?"

I roll my eyes. "You said I didn't have to tell you my thoughts right away—you said I only had to text that I've read it."

"Yeah, yeah, I know I said that," he writes. "And I totally meant it. But just tell me one thing now, just so I can fall asleep: What are all your thoughts about my application?"

I grin. He's so cute. "Too many thoughts all at once. I'm too sleep deprived to think. Just let me catch a couple hours of sleep and then we'll talk." I press send.

Josh's application has made me feel a thousand different emotions, all at once, but mostly, I feel a horrible pang in my heart for the rejection Josh endured at the hands of someone he loved and trusted.

I sigh. Oh, Josh. I really can't let him twist in the wind for hours while I sleep. *I* know his application doesn't change a goddamned thing between us, but *he* doesn't know that. I don't want to talk about all this in detail just yet, but I certainly don't want him to feel anxiety, either.

I pick up my phone and call him.

"Hi," Josh says, picking up my call after one ring.

"Hi."

There's a long beat as Josh waits for me to say whatever I'm calling to say. I can hear him holding his breath on his end of the line.

"All I wanna do is sleep," I say evenly. "That's all."

He still doesn't say anything.

"I don't wanna talk just yet. I really need to process exactly what I wanna say to you. Okay?"

"Okay," he says softly.

"But... I was thinking... will you come to my room and sleep with me tonight? I don't wanna be alone—I want to be with you."

He lets out a loud puff of air. "Hell yeah. I'll be right there."

51

JOSH

I'm jolted awake by a banging at the door. My eyes spring open.

I'm tangled up with Kat in her bed, in my briefs, and I've got a gigantic woody. I was having an awesome dream—a totally awesome dream about Kat. It was so blatantly symbolic, so *obvious*, I feel like slapping my subconscious for being so lacking in imagination. In my dream, Kat was giving me an incredible blowjob and Emma walked into the room. But rather than jerk out of Kat's mouth and rush to smooth things over with Emma, I just said, "Oh, hey, Emma. I'm kinda busy right now." And then I looked down at Kat, at her blue eyes looking up at me, and I smiled.

There's another loud bang at the door. "Hey, are you guys in there?"

Kat lifts her head, bleary-eyed. She looks at the clock and rubs her eyes. "Oh crap. My alarm didn't go off."

I leap out of bed and bound to the door. "Yeah, we're here," I call out.

I open the door to find Henn standing there. His eyes immediately train on my gigantic boner. "Well, good morning," Henn says cheerily, staring at my crotch. His eyes snap up to my face. "Dude," he says. "We've gotta be on-call to save the world today, remember?"

"Sorry," I mumble. "Our alarm didn't go off."

He motions to my dick. "Mmm hmm. Time to get your other head in the game, Faraday." He peeks past me into the room. "Kat?"

"Yep," she calls from inside the room. "Come on in, Henny."

I open the door wide and Henn strolls past me. He's definitely got his swagger on today—which makes sense: I suppose Henn's playing in some sort of Hacker Super Bowl today.

"Hey, Kitty Kat," Henn says. "Sorry to intrude on your optometry appointment *again*, but Jonas texted ten minutes ago, asking me to confirm all the money's still in place and we're ready to move at his signal. I told him we're good to go any time, boss, of course—and then I ran around like a chicken with my head cut off looking for you two losers. Jesus, guys. You're gonna give me gray hair, and I'm much too young and pretty for gray hair."

"Sorry," Kat and I say in unison.

"I know you guys are busy falling in love and all—"

My eyes instantly dart to Kat's face, my cheeks bursting with color, and she looks like Henn just stuck her finger into an electrical socket.

"—but we've gotta keep our eye on the job," Henn continues. "Jonas and Sarah went into their meeting with the feds a few hours ago and we've got to be ready, just in case. Once we've delivered the money, then you two can go off and do whatever the hell kind of eye exam you want, all night and day, but right now I need both of you to keep your eyes on the prize and your heads in the game."

I look down. This is exactly why I've stayed friends with Henn for so long: he's one of the few people in my life that calls me on my shit. He's right. I've been letting myself get hopelessly distracted from what we're here in Las Vegas to do.

"To be honest, the odds are low we'll be asked to make the transfers today," Henn continues, his tone much softer, "so I'm sure we're okay—Jonas is ninety-nine percent sure his meeting's gonna go 'til the end of the banking day today—but he wants us to stand by just in case. No room for error."

"You're totally right, Henn," Kat says. "We'll stop acting like complete idiots."

"Not you, Kitty Kat. Just *him*," Henn says, winking at her. "You can do no wrong, pretty lady."

Kat grins at Henn. "Hear that, Josh? You're a terrible influence on me." She laughs. "Do I have time to take a quick shower, Henny?" She sits up and the bed sheet slides off her torso—clearly revealing the outline of her nipples under her thin, white tank top.

Oh shit. I don't think she's ever looked sexier than she does right now.

"I think you'd better just throw on your clothes and be ready in five, just in case," Henn says, averting his eyes from Kat's skimpy tank top. He looks at his watch. "The minute banking hours are over here in Vegas, then we'll be off the hook 'til tomorrow morning and you can shower and all that. But, in theory, Jonas could call literally any time now so we've got to be ready to move on a dime."

"Okay," Kat says, rubbing her face. "Sorry, Henny. We'll pull our shit together and get our heads in the game from now on. Right, Josh?"

"Absolutely," I say. *Holy fuck, Kat's nipples look amazing in that tank top.* I look away, my cock tingling.

Kat picks up her phone. "Oh, I've got a text from Sarah. She says one of the guys in the meeting looks like he could stuff her into the trunk of his car and she'd never be heard from again." Kat chuckles to herself. "Oh, shoot, I've got another missed call from my friend Hannah. I should give her a quick call. She's probably got a question on this big account she's handling for me at work. Do I have time to make a quick call? Super-duper quick?" She bats her eyelashes.

Henn nods. "Yeah, really quick. But you might have to get off if Jonas calls and gives us the signal."

"Okay. Like lightning."

I can't peel my eyes off her. I've never seen her first thing in the morning before. She's turning me on. Especially after what happened last night: after reading my application, she opened her door, wordlessly hugged me, and led me to her bed; then, without a word, the two of us lay down together, our bodies pressed close, our arms wrapped around each other, and quickly drifted off to sleep.

It was such a simple interaction, but I have no idea how to put into words how much it meant to me. The woman had just read my sick-fuck fantasies and she serenely fell asleep in my arms. Whatever she plans to say to me about that application at some point in the future will be icing. The way she fell asleep in my arms last night? That was the cake.

Kat dials Hannah's number and presses the phone to her ear.

Her eyes drift to me as she waits for Hannah to pick up.

"How'd you sleep, babe?" she asks softly, the phone pressed to her ear.

My entire body buzzes. Has Kat called me 'babe' before? I don't think so. But if so, she's never said it quite like that.

"Good," I say, my skin electrifying. "You?"

"Good." She beams a smile at me. "Really, really good."

Holy shit. I feel high. With one brief and seemingly innocuous exchange, the woman just confirmed exactly what's going on inside her head: she doesn't think I'm a sick fuck.

Kat's attention is drawn to her phone. "Hi, Hannah Banana Montana Milliken," she says. "So what's up?" She listens for a minute. "Oh, no worries. Just tell them we'll do a Twitter campaign instead—that's their demographic, anyway. We'll make lemonade out of lemons. No problem. We can set up a live chat with a hashtag." She pauses. "Oh, I dunno, how 'bout hashtag-I've-got-your-pulled-pork-right-here?" She winks at me. "And then we'll select a winner," she continues. "I'd say a gift card. Yeah. That sounds good. But I can talk to them if you prefer—I'll probably be free later today to chat." She laughs. "Aw, anytime. Thanks for picking up all the slack while I've been gone."

Henn and I look at each other. The woman's a PR badass; there's no doubt about it. I love seeing her like this, kicking ass and taking names.

"Yeah, I am, as a matter of fact," Kat says into the phone, her eyes drifting to me. "Mmm hmm. Actually, yeah, he *is*." She beams a huge smile at me.

Henn rolls his eyes and shoots me a smirk.

"Funny you should ask that, Banana," Kat says, her eyes leaving me and landing on Henn. "He *does*. And he's the coolest guy you'll ever meet. Actually, he's a *fucking genius*."

Henn shifts his weight.

Kat suddenly extends her phone toward Henn. "Henn, my adorable and funny friend Hannah Millikin wants very much to say hello to you."

"To *me*?" Henn asks, his face turning red.

Kat laughs. "Yup. Come on, Henn. *YOLO*." She holds out the phone again, insisting he take it. "Hannah's the coolest girl you'll ever talk to, I promise. A total goofball. Loyal. Smart. Cute. Funny. The list goes on and on. Nothing to lose by just saying hi."

Henn waffles.

"Oh, and did I mention?" Kat says. "She got brown hair and glasses." She winks.

Henn takes the phone, his cheeks rising with color. "Well, this isn't awks or anything," he says into the phone. "Hello, Hannah Millikin. I'm Peter Hennessey—but everyone just calls me Henn." He pauses to let Hannah talk and then chuckles. "Yeah, she *did* kinda make it sound like your idea, actually." He laughs again. "She's a sneaky one, for sure." He pauses. "Um, you know, just working... I'm a computer specialist—a freelance programmer." He clears his throat and listens for a moment. "L.A., New York, Toronto, Denver—I go wherever the job takes me, and I can work from anywhere, so I travel a lot, but I mostly live in L.A. in a crappy-ass apartment. Where are you? Oh, yeah, duh. Kat just said she works with you. Yeah, sure, I get up there sometimes—I love it there. Good salmon." He pauses. "Me, too," he finally says. "Indubitably." He grins broadly at something Hannah's saying. "Yeah, I hope so. Thanks." He blushes and hands the phone back to Kat. "Here you go."

"Not so awks after all, huh?" Kat says playfully.

Henn flashes a shy smile. "Not nearly as awks as it could have been," he agrees. "She made it easy."

Kat grins and grabs the phone. "Hey, girl. Isn't he the cutest? I know, right? Sure, I'll send you a picture." She lowers her voice. "Word on the street is he's a *phenomenal* kisser, too." She beams a smile at Henn and giggles. "Yeah, I will. Okay, bye, Banana. Thanks again."

Kat puts her phone down, grins devilishly, and steeples her fingers like a cartoon villain. "Oh, my darling Henny, I have a *feeling*."

"About what?"

"About *you* and my dear friend Hannah Banana Montana Millikin. What's your sign?"

"My *sign*? Sagittarius."

Kat's face lights up. "Ah, the explorer. Well, that makes perfect sense. And super-duper perfect with Leo."

"Hannah's a Leo?" I ask.

Kat nods. "And Sag-Leo is a fabulous combo. Maybe when we're done saving the world all four of us can go out to dinner some time?"

"I'd be up for that," I say.

Henn shrugs and makes a face like he's got nothing to lose. "Um. Sure."

Kat scrolls through the photos on her phone for a moment. When she finds what she's looking for, she hands her phone to Henn. "That's Hannah," she says.

Henn looks at the phone. "Wow. She's super cute." He blushes. "Yeah, I'd totally be up for dinner. Sounds great."

"Awesome." Kat's eyes are positively sparkling. She plops her phone onto the bed next to her. "Okay, boys. I'm gonna brush my teeth and wash my face and then, *voila,* I'll be Oksana Belenko for as long needed."

With that, she hops out of bed in her itty-bitty G-string and barely-there tank top and sashays to the bathroom on her long, toned legs, her blonde hair falling down her back—completely unaware of, or not giving a shit about, the male shrapnel she's leaving behind in her glorious wake.

52

KAT

I 'm practically peeing myself with laughter.

Josh, Henn, and Reed are telling the story of how Josh wound up with "YOLO" inked onto his ass, and Will, Carmen, and I are laughing so hard, we can barely keep ourselves upright at the table.

As it turned out, Josh, Henn and I weren't called upon to make the money transfers today. At around four o' clock our time, Sarah and Jonas called to tell us we were free until eight tomorrow morning, at which time they wanted us to station ourselves outside the first bank on our agenda, ready to go at their signal. Which meant that after Josh, Henn, and I did a little shopping for clothes befitting the wealthy pimpstress Oksana Belenko, we decided to let off a little steam and have a great meal together.

"Let's call Reed," Josh suggested. "Get the band back together."

As it turned out, Reed was on his way to the airport with Will and Carmen when Josh called, but at his friend's invitation to dinner, he turned his car around. And now Josh, Henn, Reed, Will, Carmen and I are sitting together in a five-star restaurant, half-way through our amazing meal, laughing 'til tears pour down our faces.

"You *knew* I had the quote wrong the whole time?" Josh shouts at Reed, incredulous. "After ten years, this is the first time I'm hearing this part of the story."

Reed is laughing so hard, he's crying. "Of course, I knew. You were dead in the water, bro. Everyone knew it. It wasn't even close."

"Then why the hell did you goad me on like that?"

"And miss watching you to get 'YOLO' tattooed onto your ass?"

Josh can't believe his ears. "For all these years, I thought you didn't know. I thought you were being fair and impartial."

Reed shakes his head, laughing. "Hell no. I was Team Henn all the way. It served you right, bro. You were being a total dick about it."

Henn is howling with laughter. "You're demented, Reed."

"Hey, all in good fun."

"Fun for *you*, maybe," Josh says. "You're not the one with YOLO tattooed on his ass."

"Aw, bad tattoos happen to the best of us," Will says, slapping Josh on the shoulder. "Look at this." Will rolls up his sleeve and shows Josh a tattoo on his forearm—and I immediately slap my hand over my mouth at the sight of it. Oh my God, no. Will's got a *dragon* on his arm—one of the tattoos on my so-called list of no-no's.

"Oh, look, a *dragon*," Josh says, smiling, his facial expression morphing into one of pure glee. "Do you see that, Kitty Kat?"

My cheeks burst into flames. Holy crap. Why the heck did I name dragon tattoos as one of the items on my "social suicide" list? I was talking out my butt—pulling it out of thin air. Why the heck did I say that?

Josh looks at me and smirks wickedly and I shoot him a look that begs him for mercy.

"I got the heart first," Will says, oblivious to the nonverbal exchange happening between Josh and me. Will points to a prominent heart on his dragon's chest. "My ex-girlfriend and I got matching hearts."

Josh's face lights up at Will's use of the word "ex-girlfriend."

Oh no. *No.* This can't be happening.

"Oh, so you got the heart with your *girlfriend*, did you?" Josh asks Will. "Who's now your *ex*-girlfriend?"

"Yeah, I was sure we'd be together forever. But then she slept with my best friend, so I had to get the dragon to camouflage it."

The smile on Josh's face is positively merciless. "Hey, Kat. Did you catch that? Will's got *both* a dragon tattoo *and* an ex-girlfriend tattoo." Josh can barely contain his giddiness. "Imagine that."

My cheeks are on fire. Why, oh why, did I say all that stuff to Josh about prohibited tattoos? I was just being snarky. I had no idea what I was saying.

"What's so funny?" Will asks, looking confused. "Why do I feel like I'm missing the joke?"

Oh, God, please, no. This can't be happening. I cover my face with my hands.

"Are you feeling like crawling into a hole about now, PG?" Josh asks.

I nod from behind my hands and Josh hoots with laughter.

"Well, Will," Josh begins like he's teaching a lesson to a grade-schooler. "Kat here's got a very specific list of tattoos that she's decided in her infinite wisdom are *cliché* and stupid and therefore tantamount to committing 'social suicide,' as she so colorfully puts it."

"And dragons and hearts are both on Kat's list?" Will asks.

"No, not hearts, surprisingly. Just dragon and *girlfriend* tattoos." Josh chuckles happily. "Social suicide, both of them, Will, I'm sorry to inform you— but they're simply not allowed. I guess you'll have to get that shit lasered, huh?"

"Oh, shit," Will says. "Yeah, this is a catastrophe. I've got *two* prohibited tattoos? Damn that Stubborn Kat. She won't do anything you want her to do *and* she thinks your tattoos are stupid."

I'm dying. I'm physically dying. "No, Will, I..." I begin, but I can't speak. I've never been so frickin' mortified in my life.

"And guess what *else* is on Stubborn Kat's list?" Josh continues, beaming.

Will shrugs. "I dunno. Flowers? I've got flowers for my momma, too."

Josh shakes his head. "Nope. Flowers are allowed. Guess again. I'll give you a hint: it's on my ass."

The entire table erupts with laughter.

"Well, I can't blame Stubborn Kat for that one," Will says.

"Neither can I," Reed says. "She probably took one look at your ass and added it to the list."

"Oh no," Josh says, laughing. "That's the best part. Stubborn Kat came up with this list *before* she'd seen a single one of my tattoos."

The table erupts again. Everyone but me is laughing so hard, they can't breathe.

"Before?" Will says. "Oh shit. And you hadn't even *told* her about any of 'em?"

Josh is laughing too hard to speak, so he simply shakes his head.

I look at Henn, desperate for an ally, and he flashes me a sympathetic frownie-face. "Hang in there, Kitty Kat," he says above the fray.

Josh places his forehead down on the table, apparently spent from laughing so hard.

"Hey, at least you've only got *one* tattoo on the prohibited list," Will says. "I'm the loser with *two*."

I open my mouth to apologize profusely, but nothing comes out. This is the most embarrassing moment of my life.

"Oh shit, hang on," Josh says, trying to catch his breath from laughing. He raises his head from the table, and with great flourish, rolls up his sleeve to display the dragon tattoo on his beautiful, bulging bicep.

The whole table loses it again.

And I want to die. I truly want to die.

"YOLO *and* a dragon," Will says. "Tsk, tsk."

Josh wipes his eyes.

"And she said all that shit before she knew any of your tattoos? Aw, come on someone must have told her. She was just fucking with you." Will looks at me. "Please tell me you were just fucking with him, Stubborn Kat."

I shake my head, an apologetic look on my face. "I was just talking out my butt, being a total smart-ass."

Will hits his forehead with his palm. "Truth is stranger than fiction, man. This is the best story, ever."

Josh nods. "I seriously couldn't believe it. We were texting and I just stared at my screen, like 'oh my fucking God, I've hit the mother lode.'"

"Gosh darn it, Stubborn Kat," Will says, putting on his cartoon voice. "She sniffs out your stupid tattoos and nails you to the wall with 'em."

"Kinda the way some cats curl up with dying people at a nursing home," Reed says, and everyone laughs. "Why didn't you just tell her, man?" Reed asks Josh.

"No fucking way I was gonna tell her," Josh says. "I figured I'd let her find out the good old fashioned way—by seeing my ass." He winks and Reed and Will clink their glasses against Josh's.

"Atta boy," Reed says.

I'm peeking at the group from behind my hands, afraid to come out. My eyes drift to Henn again and he makes a face that tells me he feels my pain.

"Hey, Stubborn Kat," Josh says. "Why don't you tell the group *all* of your amazing rules. Enlighten us. Amaze us with what a hip whippersnapper you are."

"I believe a hip whippersnapper's actually called a '*hippersnapper*,'" Will says.

Everyone at the table (except for me) laughs. I can't stop hiding behind my hands. This is sheer pain right here.

"Aw, come on, babe. 'You don't make The Rules, you just enforce 'em.' Remember?"

I shake my head. "There's no way I'm making any declarations about what's cool and what's not in this crowd. Every man at this table could tattoo Bert and Ernie onto his forehead and make it look cool," I say.

Will picks up his napkin and rubs it forcefully against his forehead. "Well, I guess now would be the time to remove this makeup on my forehead and show you..."

Everyone laughs, yet again.

"You're not gonna enlighten us about all The Rules for Being Cool, Stubborn Kat?" Josh asks.

I shake my head.

"She's normally not so shy, I swear," he says.

"Come on, Stubborn Kat," Will says. "What else is on the list? We've got dragons, YOLO, girlfriends that didn't work out, and what? I've got two so far—I'm hoping to rack up some more points before the night is over."

I put my head on the table and bury my head with my arms. "Make it stop," I mumble.

Will laughs.

"Come on, guys," Henn says. "Make fun of me for a while, as usual. How 'bout I dance for you?"

"Oh, yeah. Let's make Henny dance—my favorite thing!" Reed says, suddenly giddy. He bangs on the table. "Dance puppet-boy, dance!"

Henn grumbles.

"We'll definitely have to hit my club after dinner."

Everyone agrees.

"But back to Kat's list," Will says. "Come on. What else is on it, Stubborn Kat? I bet I've got at least some of the stuff on the list, whatever it is."

Josh grabs my hand and kisses it. "You're not gonna tell him?"

I shake my head. "I'm never gonna say anything about anyone's tattoos ever again, as long as I live."

Josh grins and looks at Will. "Barbed wire on your bicep—or a tribal band, unless you're an Islander. Stubborn Kat was very specific about that. You got either of those, man?"

"Fuck no. I agree with Stubborn Kat on both. And yet, right now, I wish so bad I had both so I could pull up my sleeve and see the look on her face."

Everyone laughs at the thought, even me.

"Me, too," Josh says, squeezing my hand. "I never thought I'd be bummed *not* to have barbed wire."

"Hey, it's never too late, Faraday," Reed says, laughing. "We're in Vegas, after all."

"There you go again, Reed," Josh says. "Trying to get me inked with something stupid." He sips his drink. "Well, lucky for me, I'm not gonna get drunk tonight, or I'd probably do it."

"No, you wouldn't," Henn says. "Barbed wire would be too stupid even for you, Josh."

"Bite your tongue," Josh says. "There's no such thing as a tattoo that's 'too stupid' for Josh Faraday—not if you ply me with enough alcohol and double-dare me, anyway."

"Oh, we know, Mr. 'Welcome to the Gun Show,'" Reed says.

Josh, Henn, and Reed burst out laughing.

"'I double-dare you,'" Reed says, apparently re-enacting something—and all three guys laugh again, shaking their heads.

"You're a Neanderthal, Josh," Henn says.

Josh sips his drink happily. "I really am."

"I take it you've got a tattoo that says 'Welcome to the Gun Show'?" Will asks, incredulous.

Josh nods.

"On your arms, presumably?"

Josh nods again.

"Oh shit. *Horrible.* That's gotta be on Kat's list, too, right? Please tell me it is. That's gotta be double points."

Josh shakes his head. "Surprisingly, not on the list. Too horrible to even mention, I suppose. Right, Kat? Some tattoos are too stupid to make the list?"

My face is hot. "Please make it stop," I say.

Josh squeezes my hand and kisses the side of my head. "All in good fun, baby," he whispers to me. "This is how we show we like you." He squeezes my hand again.

"Well, dude, aren't you gonna show me?" Will says.

"Show him," Reed says.

Josh shrugs, unbuttons his shirt, and pulls it down off his shoulders, revealing his muscled, tattooed chest and the tops of his gorgeous arms—and the sight of him makes my crotch instantly start filling with blood.

Josh bends his arms behind his head and flexes and everyone at the table bursts into laughter at the sight of the tattoos on the undersides of his biceps.

"Welcome to... the Gun Show," Reed says, pointing out Josh's tattoos like he's Vanna White on *Wheel of Fortune*. "That was the night I learned Josh Faraday will do literally *anything* to get a laugh."

I've gone back into hiding behind my hands, partly because the sight of Josh baring his body in this restaurant is making me want to jump his bones and partly because I feel like I'm gonna barf.

"Hell yeah, I will. Life's too short. Hey, Kat. Are you gonna come out from hiding any time soon?" Josh asks. "Come on, babe, join the party. We're all friends here. Nobody's mad at you. It's all in good fun. It's just what friends *do* with friends—they torture them."

I slowly come out from under my arms like a turtle. "You guys, when I said all that stuff about prohibited tattoos and social suicide, I was just being a total and complete smart-ass. I just pulled that stuff out of thin air. I take it all back."

"Ha! Don't backtrack now, PG. Go big or go home, babe."

"No, I was totally wrong. Please, God, just let me reverse time and take it all back." I take a huge gulp of my martini.

"Come on, Stubborn Kat," Reed says. "Don't let Josh bully you into backing down from your closely held beliefs. Stay true to yourself."

I shake my head. "He's not bullying me. I don't believe any of what I said." I move my arm like I'm blessing them all. "You're all supremely cool. Forget I ever said any of it."

"How the hell did you survive with four brothers, Kat?" Josh says, spearing a vegetable on his plate. "A little bit of teasing and you back down? I expected so much more from Stubborn Kat."

"You have *four* brothers?" Will asks.

"And no sisters," Josh adds.

"Wow. That must have been fun growing up," Will says.

I nod. "Fun and hell, simultaneously—kind of like right now. Two older, two younger. They taught me to have a thick skin, for sure."

"The girl might as well have grown up in a frat house," Josh says. "She's an honorary dude. Well, usually. She's definitely acting like a girl right now." He takes a huge bite of food and grins.

I smile thinly at him.

Josh grabs my hand and kisses it again. "Well, young lady, let this be a lesson to you. I'm not only wise and powerful, I'm super cool, too—right down to my stupid tattoos." He addresses the group. "See, the thing Kat doesn't realize, is that it's the 'stupid' tattoos that are the best ones. Because mistakes, big and small, are what teach us to learn and grow."

"*Exactly*," Will says emphatically. "Even the stupid tattoos wind up being profound if you think about them like that."

"I was just being a smart-ass, Will. Please don't be offended," I offer.

"I'm not offended at all," Will says gently. "My dragon tattoo *is* kinda stupid—but the cool thing is that it's camouflage for a huge mistake." He smiles broadly at me. "That's why I love it. Every time I look at the damned thing, I'm reminded I got my heart broken into a million pieces and came out the other side a dragon." He takes a bite of his food.

Josh throws up his hands, totally enthralled. "Now see, that's what I'm talking about, bro. Every tattoo, even if it's a mistake, is a reminder of who you *were* versus who you are now. A map of your evolution as a man." He swigs his drink.

"Amen," Will says. "The body is a living canvas. It's all there: victory, failure, mistakes, lessons learned—all there for the world to see."

"You know what we should do?" Josh says to Will, slamming down his fork with sudden excitement. "We should both complete our lame-ass trifectas tonight. Together."

"Fuck yeah. Barbed wire, it is, baby," Will says. They clink drinks.

"Oh God, no, Will," Carmen says, putting her hand on Will's forearm. "Honey, no. Please."

Will laughs and takes another bite of his food. "Don't worry, Car. I'll just get it on my ass, like my boy here. A little barbed wire on my ass for you and no one else." He laughs.

"There you go," Josh says, laughing. "Genius. It's just skin, right?" He takes a bite of his steak.

"Fuck yeah," Will agrees. "I'm totally gonna do it. We're all a pile of skin and bones sooner or later. That's what gets me going every fucking day, knowing I'm running out of time."

"Amen," Josh says. "Hey, maybe I'll join you—add a little barbed wire to my dragon's neck, maybe?"

"Hey, great idea," Will says. "I'll totally add barbed wire to my dragon."

"Jesus Christ," Reed says. "Will, stop listening to Josh Faraday of all people about tattoos. Listen to him about everything else, because the guy's a fucking genius, just not about tattoos."

"Shut the fuck up," Josh says. "I'm wise and powerful about *all* things, including tattoos."

"Don't do it," Reed says to Will.

"Dude, Reed's using reverse psychology on you," Henn warns Will. "He's being the puppet master."

"No, I'm not. I'm sincerely telling *Will* not to do it," Reed says. "Although *you* should absolutely do it, Faraday. Add yet another stupid tattoo to your stupid collection."

"My collection isn't stupid," Josh says. "Didn't you hear a damned thing Will and I were just saying? Even the stupid ones are *profound,* man. We're *living canvases,* Reed. Duh. We're *artists* and *art,* all at the same time."

"Yeah, Reed. We're *living canvases,*" Will agrees with solemnity. "We're artists and art, all at the same time. We're living performance art and our tattoos are our way of flipping the bird to *mortality.*"

"That's right," Josh says emphatically. "Getting barbed wire would be like saying, 'Mortality, fuck you. You might be gunning for me, but you'll have to get through my barbed wire to get *me,* motherfucker. Raaaaah.'"

Reed rolls his eyes.

"So lemme get this straight, boss," Henn says, pursing his lips like he's considering something very serious. "You got YOLO stamped on your *ass* because you were flipping the bird to *mortality?*"

Josh laughs. "Absolutely. Now, when the Grim Reaper comes for my ass, maybe he'll see it and stop and say, 'Never mind.'"

Everyone laughs.

Carmen leans into me. "Josh is hilarious," she whispers.

I nod and bite my lip. "He sure is."

Josh swigs his drink happily. Man, he's having fun tonight.

"Okay, okay, I cannot tell a lie," Josh is saying. "I must admit, I wasn't thinking deep and profound thoughts about my mortality when I got YOLO stamped on my ass. I wasn't thinking much of anything, actually. I was just a twenty-year-old asswipe who thought he knew everything."

"Aw, don't be too hard on yourself," Reed says. "All twenty-year-old dudes are asswipes who think they know everything. I know I was."

"How old are you, Will?" I ask.

"Twenty-three," he replies. "And I don't think I know everything."

"Well, I thought I knew everything when I was twenty-three," Reed says, shaking his head. "Turns out I sure had a whole lot to learn between twenty and thirty."

"Ditto," Henn agrees. "Jesus, has it really been ten years since Josh got his stupid YOLO tat? Oh my shit, we're getting old."

"Remember when thirty sounded so old?" Reed says, looking wistful.

Josh nods. "I never thought I'd make it to thirty."

"Really?" I ask, the hair on my arms standing up. "Doesn't everyone think they're gonna live to a hundred and three?"

Josh shrugs and takes a bite of his food but doesn't reply.

I look at Josh for a long beat. When I opened my door to him last night and wordlessly took him into my arms, the look on his face was so vulnerable, it took my breath away—and, just now, that exact same expression flashed across his handsome face.

"Jeez, before we know it," Henn says. "We'll be *forty* and in the middle of our mandatory midlife crisis."

"Jesus. Who knows what fucked up shit Faraday will do then?" Reed says.

"He'll probably get himself a midlife-crisis car like a fucking Lamborghini or some shit like that. Oh, whoops. Already did that."

"He's got a *Lamborghini*?" Carmen whispers to me, her eyes wide.

I nod and she mouths, "Wow."

"Hey, might as well have the douche-car to match the douche-tattoos," Josh says, clearly not the least bit offended by Reed's jab. "Like I always say, 'Go big or go home.' Right, Kat?"

I lean into Josh and put my head on his shoulder. "I'm sorry," I whisper. "I feel like an idiot."

He kisses the top of my head. "We're just teasing you, babe," he whispers back. "It's what we do if we like you. No worries—never worry in this crowd. We're just playing."

"So how about forty, big guy?" Henn asks Josh. "Can you imagine that?"

Josh shrugs but doesn't reply. He takes a bite of his food.

"Well, I can picture all of us at forty," Henn says. "We're all exactly the same as we are now—strikingly handsome, fucking geniuses—only difference is we're married and driving minivans full of screaming kids."

Reed makes a scoffing noise. "I think your crystal ball's got a loose wire, bro —at least relating to me." He swigs his drink.

"No 'married with children' for you?" I ask Reed. But, really, I'm indirectly asking Josh—hoping maybe he'll join in the conversation. Why has he gone suddenly mute?

Reed shakes his head emphatically. "No, thanks. I'm gonna be like George Clooney. That dude's got the right idea."

"Oh, I bet even George Clooney will get married one day," Carmen says. "When he meets the right woman."

"I think so, too," I agree.

"No way," Reed says. "Not George. He'll be the last man standing."

"I'm with the girls on that one," Henn says. "When George finds the right woman, he won't wanna let her go. I'd bet anything on it."

"Oh, you'd bet *anything* on it?" Reed asks slowly, rubbing his hands together.

"Just a figure of speech," Henn says. "Don't even try your Jedi mind tricks on me."

Josh laughs.

"Hey, Carmen. Why do you say that about George?" Reed asks. "What do you see that I don't?"

Carmen shrugs. "Oh, I dunno. I don't know the guy. He just seems like a passionate person. And passionate people are always the ones who fall the hardest." She looks at Will lovingly.

Will's face is absolutely adorable right now. He leans in and kisses Carmen on the cheek.

"I agree with Carmen," Henn says. "When a man finds the right woman, it's a game-changer." He shrugs. "So I hear."

"Aw, it sounds like you're a diehard romantic, Henn," Carmen says.

"Maybe I am. All I know is I'd love to be married one day to the right girl and maybe even have a little baby. A little daughter maybe. I think that'd be really nice."

"Really?" I say. "That's so sweet, Henny." I feel myself blushing. I sneak a peek at Josh—he's sipping his drink, not saying a word—and my cheeks blaze even hotter.

"What about you two?" Henn asks, and my stomach seizes—but when I glance at Henn, ready to deflect his question, he's looking straight at Will and Carmen, not at Josh and me.

Will and Carmen look at each other for a beat. "Um," Carmen finally says. "Well, I'd love a family one day. But I think that's a loooooong way off."

Will laughs. "Good answer." He wipes his brow comically. "Phew."

I can't bring myself to look at Josh right now and I'm not sure why. My skin feels electrified. "So what about you, Will? What does your future hold, ya think?" I ask, trying to deflect attention from my hot cheeks.

"Oh, I can answer that," Reed says. "Will's gonna be a mega-superstar." He holds up his drink and everyone follows suit. "A toast. To 2Real—the next big superstar."

"Hear, hear," everyone says, clinking glasses.

Carmen leans over and kisses Will on his cheek and he smiles.

"My boy 2Real's gonna be a household name, mark my words," Reed continues.

"Thanks, Reed."

"No need to thank me, man. I'm just telling it like it is. You're a fucking genius." Reed addresses the group. "After my party the other night, Will and Dean sat down with an acoustic guitar and started messing around, and within an hour, they'd written the bones for the most badass song you've ever heard in your life. The thing's gonna be a smash hit." He snaps his fingers. "And they wrote it just like that."

"It's totally awesome," Carmen agrees. "I can't get it out of my head."

Will's eyes are sparkling with sudden animation. "Dean and I totally hit it off—brothers from another mother. We're planning to record it in L.A. next month after Red Card Riot's tour ends."

"I bet we'll wind up making it the lead single off your album," Reed says. "It's just that good."

"What's it called?" I ask. "When I hear it on the radio a year from now, I wanna remember this conversation and say, 'I knew him when.'"

"We'll probably call it 'Crash,'" Will says. "It's pretty dope, if I do say so myself. Best song I've ever written. I can't wait to get into the studio and get it down—I've got a million ideas for the instrumentation. I'm gonna do something really unexpected with it."

Reed rubs his hands together. "I smell a hit."

The waiter arrives to clear dishes and bring refills on drinks.

"What about you, Party Girl with a Hyphen?" Josh asks, breaking his long silence. "What do you see in your future?"

"Um..." I say. Josh didn't answer this question earlier, I noticed, so I'll be damned if I will. Although, if I were being honest, I'd tell him I'm beginning to see a future that includes him. "Well, I'd really like to own my own PR firm one day," I say, opting for a safe but true answer to the question.

Josh looks completely floored by my answer. "Wow," he says. "Really? That's awesome. I had no idea. 'Party Girl PR.'"

"Hey, I like it," I say.

"Well, fingers crossed, maybe you'll come into a million bucks one day soon and you can make that happen sooner than you ever imagined." He winks.

I grin broadly. Crazy as it sounds, I'd actually forgotten about the million bucks Jonas and Josh promised me if we're actually successful in transferring The Club's money tomorrow.

"Oh yeah, speaking of PR," Reed says, "thanks for all your hard work on the campaign for my club, Kat." He laughs. "Impeccable work so far."

"Thanks for being my client," I say. "Was it you who called my boss and charmed her pants off?"

"Yeah, I called her," Reed replies. "And I couldn't have been more insistent we had to have you personally. But I just picked up the phone. It was Josh who paid the bill—he's really the one to thank, not me." He winks at Josh.

I flash a huge smile at Josh. "Well, thank you both. I'm really grateful I've been able to hang out here all this time without losing my job."

"Anything for Josh," Reed says. "I can't even count all the favors this dude has done for me over the years. Josh Faraday might have douche-y tattoos and a midlife crisis car, and he might think he's one hundred percent right about *Happy Gilmore* when he's dead wrong, and he might—"

"*Okay*," Josh says emphatically. "I think she gets the point, Reed. I'm an idiot and a douche. Move on to the good stuff."

"*But*," Reed continues. "Josh Faraday is the best friend a guy could ask for and one of the best humans you'll ever meet."

"I'm not sure if I should kiss you or bitch slap you," Josh says.

Reed puckers and Josh laughs.

Quickly, Josh, Reed, and Henn launch into another snarky conversation about something or other—but I've stopped listening to them. I'm suddenly too busy gazing at Josh and thinking about how cute he is when he laughs with his friends. I'm thinking about how beautiful his blue eyes are, especially set off by the blue jacket he's wearing and in the flickering candlelight of this swanky restaurant. I'm remembering the vulnerable look on Josh's face when I opened my door to him last night, and how he melted into my arms without saying a word besides, "Kat." I'm wondering how a man can suffer so much heartbreak in his life—his mom's murder, his dad's suicide, his brother being institutionalized, his heart getting broken—and yet still manage to laugh and joke around with his friends the way he's doing right now, like he doesn't have a care in the world.

I'm thinking all these thoughts and a whole lot more as I stare at Josh in the candlelight and hold his hand in mine.

I lean my head against his muscled shoulder and take a sip of my drink with my free hand and let out a long, relaxed, happy exhale.

Yes, I'm thinking a thousand thoughts right now—and all of them about Joshua William Faraday.

The table erupts in laughter again at something Henn just said. But I'm not listening to the conversation. I turn my face and take a long whiff of Josh's cologne, and my crotch tingles.

At my movement, Josh kisses the side of my head, even as he's still engaged in conversation with the table, and my heart skips a beat.

Holy shit.

I want him.

And with each passing day, each passing minute, I seem to want Josh more and more. I want to take him home to meet my family and watch football on the couch and eat my mom's famous chili and watch my brothers make fun of him relentlessly for one thing or another. I want to make love to him in my apartment, slowly, for hours, and then drift off to sleep, and not wonder whether he'll be there when I wake up in the morning. I want to see where he lives in L.A. and sit in the passenger seat of his car, whether it's a Lamborghini or Hyundai, while he drives me to his favorite bar—whether it's a dive bar or some hot spot—and I don't want any other woman—any other *blonde*—to sit in that seat besides me.

I squeeze Josh's hand and he squeezes back.

But feeling this way about any man, especially the world's most eligible bachelor—a playboy who dates supermodels and celebrities (and who, by the way, clearly has a pervy-streak a mile long)—sure seems like an extremely precarious thing to do.

53

JOSH

"Go, Henny! Go, Henny!" Kat chants, shaking her ass, and I laugh. As we make our way down the hallway to my room, Kat's re-enacting the way Henn danced tonight on the dance floor at Reed's club, and she's doing an uncannily accurate impression.

I join her in doing "The Henn" and she practically falls over, laughing.

"Man, that white boy can dance," she says.

"Well, he *thinks* he can, anyway," I say.

"When it comes to dancing, isn't that all that matters?" she counters.

"No." I laugh. "Not at all."

She laughs.

"It's Reed's personal mission to get Henn to dance every time he sees him," I say. "Reed says watching Henn dance is his own personal happy place."

"Well, yeah. Reed made that pretty clear," Kat retorts. "'Dance, puppet-boy, dance,'" she says, imitating what Reed said to Henn all night long. She giggles. "You three together are just like my brothers—I felt right at home. And Will sure fit right in with you guys as the fourth musketeer, didn't he?"

"Love that guy."

"He reminds me of my little brother Dax."

"I'd like to meet your brothers," I say, and the minute I do, I want to stuff the words back into my mouth. Who just said that? Was that *me*? Dude. Saying you want to meet a girl's family is not a casual thing. "Maybe some day," I add.

She bites her lip. "Sure. Some day."

We've arrived at my room. I swipe the key card and motion to her to enter first. Shit. My heart is racing. I've got to watch myself. Slow my shit down. It's one thing to be feeling like this in Las Vegas, but her family's in Seattle—in real life. Who knows what the future holds when we leave the bubble of this place?

"Where should I put this?" she asks, holding up the duffel bag with her toothbrush and change of clothes we picked up from her room before coming to mine.

"Well, in the bedroom, of course," I say, grinning and she smiles broadly at me. I put her bag in my bedroom and come back out to the sitting area.

"Something to drink, Party Girl?" I ask, moving to the bar.

"Just water. I know I'm not living up to my nickname, but you're absolutely killing me."

"Water it is," I say, moving to the bar. "Your liver just sent you a thank you note."

"*Gracias, señor.*" She flops down on the couch in the sitting area. "So what were you and Will talking about on the way to Reed's club—something about you helping Will's dad with something?"

"Oh, nothing major. I'm just gonna see if I can do Will's dad a favor, make a few calls," I say, grabbing water bottles from the minibar.

"About what?"

"It's no big deal. He's worried his dad is making some bad investments with a buddy—maybe even getting conned by someone he trusts. I'm gonna snoop around and see what I can find out for him."

"Wow. That's nice of you. You seem to do a lot of favors for people," she says.

I push her blonde hair behind her shoulder. "Only for people I like a lot." I bite her shoulder and she giggles in response.

"Is that why Will got that ass-tattoo tonight—as payment for the favor you're gonna do for his dad?"

I laugh. "Hell no. He was just *inspired* by our deep and profound conversation at dinner to get the stupidest tattoo I've ever seen in my entire life, bar none."

She giggles again. "Why didn't you join him? I thought Josh Faraday's never seen a stupid tattoo he didn't like. What happened to the barbed wire you were gonna get to complete your 'social suicide' trifecta?"

"I chickened out. I guess even I've got my limits." I shrug. "Or maybe I just wasn't drunk enough."

"I swear I've never laughed so hard as when Will dropped his drawers right in front of all of us and got that ridiculous thing. He took the drunken tattoo to a whole new level tonight."

"Yeah, if getting a stupid tattoo is actually deep in a twisted sort of way, then 2Real is one incredibly profound motherfucker." I chuckle. "I should sic Jonas on the guy and watch what happens."

Kat laughs. "I'm sure they'd totally hit it off."

"No, Jonas would quote Plato to Will all night long and poor Will would be like, 'Um, can you bring back the dumb Faraday now? He was a lot more fun.'"

"You're not the dumb Faraday."

"Compared to Jonas, I sure as hell am. My brother is ridiculously brilliant—

a whiz with numbers, amazing at solving puzzles, always thinking about something deep and meaningful, unlike me. And the boy's got *vision*. My mom always called him magic."

Kat bites her lip. "You're magic, too, Josh."

I blush. "Not like Jonas. Now, don't get me started on what a complete and total dumbshit Jonas is about people and life in general," I continue, "and especially about relationships—that's a whole other story. The boy's a fucking tool. But, man, Jonas—now there's a magical beast of a dumbshit of a man."

She's listening to me intently. Damn, she's so fucking beautiful. I could sit and look at her all day, every day, and never get tired of her face. I put my fingertip over the slight cleft in her chin and she smiles shyly.

"So enough about my idiot-genius brother," I say softly. "Are you ever gonna tell me what you thought of my application? We haven't been alone for two minutes since Henn woke us up and I've been dying to hear what you think."

She presses her lips together. "You wanna hear what I think, huh?"

I nod, my stomach clenching.

"Well, first off..." She looks up at the ceiling, apparently gathering her thoughts. "Well, first, let's just get this out of the way: I don't think you're a sick fuck." She smiles. "But if you are, then I don't care."

I'm tingling all over. I thought she'd say that, based on the way she fell asleep in my arms after reading it last night, but it sure feels good to hear her say it out loud.

"Well, okay, maybe you're a teeny-tiny bit of a sick fuck," she amends, "but I *like* that about you."

My cock stretches its arms and yawns inside my pants.

"Secondly, I think that, whatever you did to those women in The Club for a month?" She levels me with her sparkling blue eyes. "I want you to do it to me, too—*exactly* the way you did it to them."

Oh shit. My cock just sat upright in bed and yelled, 'Do I smell coffee?'"

There's a long beat as I process what she just said.

She grins broadly. "I also think... as long as you're gonna show me your fantasies, without holding back, then, maybe, if you're willing... " She takes a deep breath. "Maybe I could show you mine?" Again, she bites her lip. "Because I'm actually a bit of a sick fuck myself."

My cock is now doing jumping jacks on the floor next to its bed. "I'd love that," I say, trying to keep my voice steady. "What are your fantasies? In your 'application', you mentioned a bodyguard fantasy and some sort of captive fantasy?"

She nods. "Yeah. Actually, I think the captive fantasy might be pretty consistent with your saving-the-raped-girl fantasy. We might be able to do a two-for-one there."

I shift in my seat, trying to relieve the pressure on my cock. "Just tell me what you want and I'll do it," I say.

She takes a deep breath. "Really? You want the whole thing?"

I nod. "Of course. Tell me the whole damned thing."

She beams a smile at me that stops my heart. "Okay, well, um, let's start with my captive fantasy." She looks giddy. "Well, I'm held captive by a horribly dangerous man who captured me in order to make me his sex slave. But then, after taking me—sensuously, *not* violently, by the way—he winds up falling desperately in love with me—and then after a while another bad guy comes to kidnap me, also intending to make me his sex slave, of course, and my original captor fends him off in a sword fight—"

"A *sword* fight?"

"Yeah, my fantasy kind of toggles between present day and a kind of historical-fiction-locked-in-a-dungeon kind of thing."

"Interesting."

"Anyway, when the second bad guy is finally dead, my original captor unties me and says I can go, because now he cares about me too much to keep me as his prisoner. It's like if you love something, set it free, you know? But I don't want to go—in fact, all I want to do is stay and fuck him for hours and hours—so that's what we do, only this time, without the bondage, because now it's my *choice* to stay and that's what makes it so sexy."

I'm in a daze listening to her, completely shocked.

There's a beat.

I suddenly realize she's not talking anymore.

"So, that's it," she declares, filling the silence.

"Wow," I say. "That was quite a bit more... detailed than I was expecting."

She shrugs. "I fantasize in Technicolor—what can I say?"

I laugh. "It's like a mini-porno."

"*Exactly.* Yes. A mini-porno starring *me.*"

"And you've got more of these mini-pornos bouncing around in your head?"

"Tons."

"And who are the guys who play opposite you in these pornos?"

"Well, depending on the mini-porno-fantasy, it could be any number of fantasy-guys—Channing Tatum gets cast a lot; Charlie Hunman makes appearances quite frequently; this hot married guy who works at the bank." She blushes. "But that was all before I saw you standing in that hallway in your wet briefs. Lately, there's only one star of all my imaginary-mini-pornos: Joshua William Faraday."

I smile and so does she.

"So you think my captor-fantasy would work with your saving-the-girl fantasy?" she asks. "Or is it too weird to mix and match?"

"I think that would work just fine." I shift again. My cock is throbbing in my pants. "And what about the bodyguard fantasy? Is it pretty detailed, too?"

She smiles from ear-to-ear, clearly excited by what she's about to say. "Okay, so in *this* one, I'm a world-famous singer and my life is in serious danger because some stalker is after me. So a gorgeous bodyguard has been hired to protect me—a really serious, no-nonsense kind of guy, like a former Secret Service agent. And, one night, I'm performing a concert in a beautiful, sparkly outfit, like a kind of space-age-y-looking thing? Or maybe I've got a beautiful headscarf around my head and I'm looking really somber, sitting on a chair. It just depends what song I'm performing. But either way my bodyguard gets spooked by something he sees in the crowd and he rushes onstage and swoops me up to protect me from an assassin and he literally carries me away from harm, and even though we're not supposed to do it—because my bodyguard's a true professional and takes his job really seriously—we just can't resist our off-the-charts attraction and we totally get it on."

There's a long beat before I'm able to speak without laughing. "So you're saying you've got a porno-version of *The Bodyguard* that plays inside your head?" I say evenly, trying my damnedest not to laugh.

She makes a face. "You're making fun of me? I'm telling you my deepest, darkest, hottest fantasies and you're *laughing* at me?"

I can't contain myself anymore. I burst out laughing. "No, I'm not making fun of you, I swear. I'm sorry, babe. Continue. I'm loving this."

"I've seen *The Bodyguard* like twenty times, okay? And I've always wanted to be Whitney. Stop laughing at me."

I bite my lip, trying to stop laughing. "It sounds amazing. What else?"

"Well, I'm not gonna tell you now." She crosses her arms over her chest in a huff. "You're supposed to be making me feel safe enough to disclose my inner-most thoughts, Josh—you know, luring me into some kind of *emotional intimacy* —not making me feel like a complete *weirdo*."

I laugh. "I should have warned you—I suck at emotional intimacy."

"*Obviously*," she says. But there's a gleam in her eye.

I touch her chin again. "I'm sorry, PG. Please forgive me. I'm a dick."

She pouts.

"Tell me more, babe. Tell me every last thing that turns you on. I wanna know. Don't hold back."

"No. You're just gonna laugh at me." She sticks out her lower lip.

"Never. Well, okay, I might laugh. But that doesn't mean anything. I laugh at everything. That's just who I am. I love hearing your fantasies, I swear."

"I have a lot of 'em, you know," she sniffs. "*A lot.*"

"Are they all as elaborate as the ones you just told me about?"

She considers. "Yeah, pretty much. I have an extremely active imagination."

"Come on, babe. Tell me everything. I might laugh, but only because I think you're so fucking adorable."

"I'll tell you if you answer one honesty-game question for me."

"Okay. Shoot."

"Why did Emma call you a sick fuck?"

My stomach instantly clenches.

"I don't get it," Kat continues. "Did you ask her to do something beyond what you wrote in your application? Because the stuff you wrote is kinky, sure, but not enough to make a girl call you names and run off with a guy wearing an ascot."

I exhale. "It's complicated."

There's a long beat.

"What's complicated about it?" she finally asks.

"I'd really rather talk about you and your mini-pornos. I've totally moved on from Emma. I really have."

"But I want to understand. Just answer this and I won't beat a dead horse, I promise. Did you ask her for something beyond what you wrote about in your application? Is there something else you fantasize about that you didn't write about—something you haven't told me yet? Because I want to know it all."

I shake my head. "What I put in my application is pretty much it. And it's what I told her about—well, actually, just the savior thing. I never even told her about the threesome thing. I'd planned to tell her that, too, but once I'd told her about the bondage-savior fantasy, it became clear there was no point in telling her anything else."

She twists her mouth. "But why? I don't understand. Was she really conservative or something? Was she a virgin?"

I take a long time, figuring out what to say. I breathe deeply and finally decide there's no way, other than to just say it. "Emma's sexuality was complicated." I exhale. "Everything about Emma was complicated, actually. She'd been brutally raped as a teenager and she was deeply traumatized by the experience." My stomach is turning over. "Understandably. So she needed a lot of extra tenderness... I mean, sex was just really tricky for her because she was really... you know, like I said, traumatized. So... yeah." I exhale. "I was always really patient and gentle with her and... we were together a really long time, and I wanted to try to help her, and then I just started to... you know... the reality was I started to have needs and she wasn't meeting them. And I felt really guilty about that, considering what she'd been through... But she kept pushing me to be honest with her... accusing me of wanting more than she could give me... and when I finally decided to open up and tell her everything about my past, and my mother, and about my fantasies, and I finally told her what I wanted to try, just to see if maybe the experience would maybe somehow quiet the raging voices in my head. Well, that shit didn't fly with her. In fact, nothing about me worked for her in the end. *Nothing.*" I run my hands through my hair. "I've thought about it a lot—why I was so attracted to her when we were obviously such a mismatch. Being with her was like banging my head into a brick wall, day after day. But I just wanted so badly to take care of her." I pause, thinking. "I sometimes sit and think about why the fuck I get turned on by certain things other guys probably don't. And when I analyze myself, I realize, yeah, I really *am* a sick fuck. I mean, getting off on the shit I do, when you think about what happened to my mom, it's pretty demented." I stop myself. My face is hot. I put my hands over my face, collecting myself. *Fuck.*

There's a long beat.

"I really am a sick fuck, Kat," I say simply. "I know I am. After what happened to my mom, I have no business incorporating bondage into my sexual fantasies. That's just sick. Emma was right. There's something deeply wrong with me. And telling a girl who'd been raped about it and asking her to try it with me to help me was also deeply fucked up. But what she didn't get was I was all about *saving* the girl, you understand? That's what gets me off. I just want to be the savior." I've got a lump in my throat. "Just once."

Kat nods.

I exhale. There's a goddamned lump in my throat that won't go away. "It's still sick, though," I say, pushing through my emotion. "Not to mention obvious and stupid." I swallow hard and the lump recedes. "It's some sort of twisted... I dunno. I guess I don't have the best imagination." I take a deep breath. "And, shit, I guess I should tell you something else, as long as I'm telling you the whole truth." I exhale and roll my eyes. "You might as well know just how obvious and stupid and deeply disturbed I really am."

Kat's sitting on the edge of her seat, her blue eyes fixed on me without blinking.

"My mom was blonde," I say. "Just like you. Just like Emma. Just like all the girls in my Sick Fuck folder. And she was gorgeous, too. Everyone always said she looked just like Grace Kelly."

Kat grabs my hand. "I figured."

"You did?"

She nods. "What did your dad look like?"

"Like me, pretty much. I have his dark hair." I squeeze her hand, grateful for her reassuring touch. "I look like my dad and Jonas looks like my mom."

Kat chuckles. "But you and your brother look so much alike, other than your hair."

"No, Jonas is the one who looks like my mom, and I'm the one who looks like my dad. My dad always said so. Maybe that's why my dad could never even stand to look at Jonas."

She blanches.

There's a long beat.

"If Jonas looks like your mom, then you do, too, Josh," she says softly. "Just with darker hair. You two look so much alike."

I shrug.

Kat strokes my arm with her free hand. "So. Okay. Fine. You're a sick fuck, Josh. Your mom made an indelible impression on you. You're obviously deeply traumatized by what happened to her. And you probably feel all kinds of guilt —totally misplaced, by the way—that Jonas was there and you weren't."

"But, Kat. It's pretty fucked up that all I wanna do is fuck beautiful blondes and my mom was a beautiful blonde. Emma thought that was really sick."

"Fuck Emma. You were *seven* when she died. Where else were you gonna get your idea of female beauty other than from your mom—especially if she happened to look like Grace Kelly? Growing up, that standard of beauty must have gotten reinforced for you everywhere you looked. Magazines, movies. It's everywhere."

I stare at her for a long minute, not saying anything. I'm too blown away to speak. I've never had a conversation even resembling this one before. Not even with my childhood therapists.

"Josh, the bottom line for me is that the stuff you wrote in your application turned me on." She squeezes my hand. "Look, I totally get what you're saying—and I agree you've obviously got some deep-seated issues that have influenced your sexual fantasies—you've definitely got some sort of complex relating to what happened to your mom and you're searching for some sort of therapeutic release, some sort of... what's that word?" She snaps her fingers and scrunches her face.

"Catharsis?" I offer.

"*Yes.* Catharsis. Exactly. As an adult, you're using sex as some sort of *catharsis* or redemption or whatever. Okay, I get it. But so what? We're all perverts in one way or another, if we're being honest—it's just that people are so rarely honest when it comes to what they like behind closed doors. Well, I say let the doctors figure out your diagnosis if ever you're in danger of harming someone or yourself—but until then, who cares? All I know is that you make me soak my panties every time I'm near you and when I read your application, I started dripping down my thighs."

My breath catches in my throat. "Oh," I manage to say, but it's all I can muster.

The subtlest of smirks dances on her lips. "All I know is that whatever you did to those women in The Club, I'm turned on by the idea of you doing it to me, too, exactly the way you did it to them." The smirk she's been suppressing takes over her mouth. "I want you to pretend I'm one of the women in The Club and show me exactly what you like, without treating me any differently than you treated them." She lowers her voice to barely above a whisper. "I want you to treat me like your high-priced whore."

I'm rock hard right now.

Her eyes are blazing. "Actually, that happens to be one of my top fantasies."

My heart is absolutely racing. I swallow hard. "Well, but..." I sputter. "Kat, as it turns out, the women in The Club actually were paid *hookers.* I didn't know it at the time, of course, but in retrospect, there's a very good reason they were all so 'uncannily compatible' with me and eager to please."

She makes a face like I'm saying something nonsensical.

"So," I say, feeling the need to explain myself further, "unlike them, you might have, you know... *limits.*"

Her eyes darken. "Don't piss on me. Don't crap on me. Don't hurt me. That's it."

She's taken my breath away. "I have no interest in doing any of those things," I say.

"Other than those three things, do whatever you want to me," she says. "Literally." Her eyes flicker. "In fact, I want you to."

I have never been more attracted to a woman than I am right this very minute. I clear my throat. "Please tell me you're not fucking with me right now."

"I'm not fucking with you," she says, heat rising in her cheeks. "I often fantasize I'm a high-end call-girl. It's what I imagined when I gave you that blowjob in the shower." She licks her lips. "I can't begin to tell you how much that turns me on."

My dick physically hurts, it's so hard.

"That's why I came when you did—because I was fantasizing I'd just given you your money's worth."

"Oh."

"So I guess I'm a sick fuck, too," she says. "Is that okay with you?"

I nod. "That's very okay with me."

"Good. Then let's just agree once and for all we don't give a shit if we're sick fucks. If we are, then so what. Fuck Emma. She's a bitch." Her eyes blaze. "Yeah, I said it. *Fuck her.* And fuck anyone else who has a problem with what turns us on. We're not screwing goats, right? We're gonna screw each other— and maybe one woman-to-be-named later, too." She snickers. "Fuck anyone who makes you feel ashamed of what you like, Josh, including Emma the Bitch."

I feel like I've entered an alternate universe. A fucking awesome alternate universe.

Kat smiles broadly and touches my face gently. "We'll fulfill each other's fantasies, right down the line. It'll be the honesty-game, sexual edition." She skims her fingertip over my lips. "Are you in?"

"I'm so fucking in."

She drops her hands from my face. "I should warn you, though, most of my sexual fantasies are gonna require you to role-play. You're gonna have to be all-in—assume your part."

"No problem."

"And if we're really gonna do this, then I wanna go big or go home."

"That's my motto."

"I thought YOLO was your motto."

"I have several."

"It's not the particular sex act that gets me going, it's the *scene*—the scenario. I don't care what you wanna do to me, as long as you set the right scene for me and let me lose myself."

My heart is racing. "Good to know. Name it, we'll do it. I'll make it happen for you exactly like you want it."

"But, wait. Think about it before you commit. Getting the scene the way I fantasize about it might take some planning on your part—and I can't be the one who arranges stuff. It has to happen *to* me, you know?—as if it's real. That's what's gonna let me lose myself completely. It's like *The Wizard of Oz*. I wanna see the giant, talking head of Oz the whole time—I don't wanna see the man behind the curtain."

I grin. "Babe, I've got this. Tell me all your fantasies, in detail, just like you told me the others, and I'll make 'em all come true, to the letter. I'll be your own personal Make-A-Wish Foundation."

She smiles broadly. "My own personal *Josh Faraday Club*," she corrects.

I wink at her. "Yours truly."

"Oh my God, I'm so excited." She wiggles in her seat. "When would we do this fantasy-exchange thing?"

"As soon as humanly possible," I say, my cock straining.

Her eyes are absolutely smoldering. "I wish we could start right now."

"Well, yeah, but unfortunately we gotta save the world first."

She snaps her fingers. "Damn it. Saving the world always gets in the way of acting out mini-pornos."

I laugh. "I tell you what. Right after we're done saving the world, we'll get started on our fantasy-fulfillment extravaganza that very night—right here in Vegas. We'll take a couple days to decompress, just you and me, before we have to return to our real lives for a bit. How 'bout we do my fantasies first here in Vegas and then we'll conquer yours the first chance we get in L.A.—because it sounds like yours are gonna take some advance planning."

"Sounds good," she says. "Better than good."

I breathe deeply, my body electrified. This woman's a dream come true.

"So let's talk about the whole watching-me-with-another-woman fantasy," she says. "Who's she gonna be? How are we gonna find her?"

"She can be anyone you want, as long as she's clean. Look in my sick fuck folder if you want. I'm sure Henn could track any of those ladies down."

She makes a face. "I deleted that folder."

"Oh, baby, my computer backs up daily. It's in The Cloud."

She rolls her eyes.

I laugh.

"No wonder you didn't get mad at me. And here I thought you were so Zen." She shrugs. "Well, I don't wanna do it with one of those girls. I want someone new."

"That's fine."

She looks on edge.

I cup her face in my hand. "Hey, if you're not into it, we don't have to do that one. I mean, if this were real life, I never would have told you about that whole thing in the first place."

"What do you mean 'if this were real life'? This isn't real life?"

I'm stumped. Of course, this isn't real life. This is Las Vegas. This is saving the world. This is fantasy-fulfillment. "I meant, if we were, you know, dating like usual. If you hadn't read my application. Due to the circumstances, you know stuff about me no other woman ever has."

There's an awkward silence.

"We don't have to do the thing with another woman. Seriously," I say.

She sighs. "Josh, I *want* to do it. I wanna pretend I'm just a girl in The Club and that you've paid to do whatever you did with all those girls, exactly the way you did it." She pauses. "Wait, no. Not exactly. I don't want you to touch the other woman. Not a pinky."

"I know. We already agreed to that. I wouldn't even want to touch the other girl, honestly. Not if I was with you. That'd be like macking down on canned Spaghetti O's when I've got a plate of homemade pasta right in front of me." I touch the slight cleft in her chin. "A pretty dumb thing to do."

Her cheeks flush. "But it's still gonna turn you on? Even though you've already done it with all those girls?"

"Honestly, I was pretty done with the whole thing after my month in The Club—it gets kinda old after you've done it a couple times, especially when you don't give a shit about either woman. But the thought of doing it with *you.*" I shudder with arousal at the very thought. I stroke her hair for a moment. "I've never gotten to do it with someone I'm..." I stop myself from saying anything more. I bite my lip and drop my hand from her hair. Shit.

"Someone you're what?" she asks, her interest obviously piqued. She tilts her head.

"Someone I'm..." I stop again. Nope. I really shouldn't say that to her.

"What?"

There's a long beat.

"What were you gonna say, Josh?" she asks. She weaves her fingers into mine. "Tell me."

I clear my throat. "I've never gotten to do it with someone I'm really attracted to beyond the physical," I say softly.

She smirks. "That's really sweet. Thank you. But it's not what you were about to say."

I pause. I can't say what I was gonna say. It's too much too soon.

"Someone what?" she prompts. "Come on. We're still playing the honesty-game, aren't we?"

"I've never gotten to do it with someone I'm in a relationship with," I say evenly.

There's a long silence.

Shit.

Fuck.

She's just staring at me, not saying anything, her hand interwoven in mine.

What am I doing? What am I saying? Why isn't she saying anything?

I pull my hand out of hers and run it through my hair. Goddammit. I should have just said "someone I'm dating." That would have been a safer bet. But are Kat and I even dating? I don't know what the fuck we're doing. This whole time in Vegas together has been so bizarre and concentrated and amazing—I can't make heads or tails of what we'd call what we're doing in real life.

Kat sighs and sets her jaw, apparently coming to some sort of decision.

"I think we should be exclusive," she says definitively.

My heart physically stops beating for a second. Holy fucking shit.

"At least during this fantasy-exchange thing," she adds quickly.

My stomach bursts with butterflies. My cheeks burst into flames. "Yeah, good idea," I say quickly. "I think so, too."

Her face is on fire. "Because I like not using condoms with you," she continues. "I like feeling you inside me with nothing between us. But I'm only willing to continue that way if we're exclusive."

"I agree." Now my heart is racing. Holy shit. My chest physically hurts. "Shit, I don't wanna go back to condoms, ever, as long as I live." Oh shit. What am I saying? What did I just imply?

"Good." Her cheeks flush. "Condoms are hereby banished. Gone." She clears her throat. "For as long as you want." She takes a deep breath. "You know, at least during the time while we're"—she takes another deep gulp of air—"doing our fantasy thing." She makes a weird face.

I nod, my heart still racing like a runaway train. "Agreed."

"Good," she says. "Yep. Done. Exclusive."

"Yep. We're officially exclusive as of right now. You and me."

She grins. "Okay. Good."

"Great."

"I'm all yours."

My entire body jolts at the sound of those three words. *I'm all yours,* she just said to me. Holy hot fucking damn, I've got to sit down.

"Okay," she says, almost to herself. She exhales loudly. "Cool."

"Cool," I say.

We sit and stare at each other, smiling, neither of us speaking.

I feel like my IQ just went down fifty points. My brain isn't functioning.

What exactly did we just agree to? She suggested being exclusive just for purposes of our little fantasy-fulfillment exchange. Does that mean we're not in an actual relationship—that we're some kind of exclusive fuck buddies? Because it sure feels like this girl's a helluva lot more than my fuck buddy. Fuck, I should ask her for clarification. But I'm not sure I wanna hear her answer.

I clear my throat. "So when are you gonna have your period? We should plan your trip to L.A. around that."

She grins. "I'm not. I take extended birth control pills. No period. I've got a year's worth of pills and I'm only two months in."

I smile broadly. "Excellent."

"So no break in our perverted activities will be required for the foreseeable future. Well, at least not on account of my period, anyway. Stuff like work and life will surely get in the way—and the fact that we don't live in the same city ought to throw a wrench in things, for sure."

"Why? It's less than a two-hour flight from Seattle to L.A. I can get a hard-on at ten and, if I charter a flight for you, you'll be at my house, sucking it by twelve thirty."

She bursts out laughing. "You're so gross."

"That's not gross. That's *romantic*."

She laughs. "You'd charter a flight just to get a blowjob?"

"I can't think of a better reason to charter a flight. Especially if the blowjob was gonna be from you. *Damn*."

She laughs again. "Well, okay, but what about work? Don't you have a company to run or something? Now that I think about it, how come you never seem to have to work?"

"Well, actually, I'm kinda between jobs at the moment. Not officially, but..." I lean in close to her and touch her golden hair. "Jonas and I are about to start a new business together. We haven't made a public announcement yet, so this is actually confidential, but we're both leaving Faraday & Sons to start something new."

"Wow. Really? Congratulations. What is it?"

"I can't tell you—not because I don't trust you—I do. But I promised my brother I wouldn't tell anyone about our new business before we've told our Uncle William in person—he runs Faraday & Sons with us—and I never break a promise to Jonas. Well, not to anyone—but especially not to Jonas."

Her face melts into an expression much like the one she had when she opened her hotel room door to me last night. "I can't wait to hear all about it whenever you're allowed to tell me," she says softly.

"I can't wait to tell you. If Jonas and I can pull it off the way we envision it, it's gonna be epic—well, the way *Jonas* envisions it—my brother's always the one with the big ideas—I'm just along for the ride, doing what I can to make myself useful."

She smiles and her blue eyes twinkle. "I'm sure it's gonna be amazing, whatever it is, Josh."

I pause. I was about to say something, but I suddenly forgot what it was. She's so fucking beautiful; occasionally, I lose my concentration when I look at her.

"So, hey," I say, looking at my watch. "We're meeting Henn in the lobby in about seven hours, so I think we'd better get some sleep. We'd better have our wits about us while we're saving the world tomorrow."

"Yeah, you're right. I'm a freakin' zombie right now. At some point, I'm defi-nitely gonna need a full eight hours of sleep—you're killing me, smalls."

"Eh, we can sleep when we're dead, PG. Speaking of which, how 'bout *before* we sleep, you get that hot little body of yours into my bed and let me make good on that rain check from our shower?"

"Aren't you the one who just said we need to get some sleep for tomorrow?"

I wave my hand. "I meant we need sleep *after* I give you the best orgasm of your life."

Her eyes light up. "You sure you're up to it? That rain check was for you to go for the gold."

I lean in and kiss her slowly, taking my sweet time, grasping the back of her neck firmly as I do, and she ignites under my touch. When I pull away from her, there's no mistaking the heat in her eyes.

"I'm positive," I say, leering at her. "There's no point in doing it if I don't do it phenomenally, right?"

"I couldn't agree more."

54

KAT

Josh, Henn and I are sitting in a dive bar in Henderson, Nevada, just down the street from the fifth and final bank of this morning's money-stealing tour. As far as we know, every single money-transfer went off without a hitch, exactly according to plan—but all we can do now is sit and wait to hear from Jonas to find out whether or not the feds were able to access the money.

"Just say as little as possible," Henn coached me this morning as we stood across the street from the first bank on our agenda. "Be pleasant and polite but completely *unmemorable*," he added—but then he looked me up and down and rolled his eyes. "Which is like telling LeBron James or an Oompah-Loompah not to be memorable."

"Henn, *come on*," I whined, trembling. "I'm freaking out. Just tell me exactly what to do."

"Don't freak out, Kat," Josh said, putting his muscled arm around my shoulders and giving me a squeeze. "You've got this."

"Indubitably," Henn agreed.

I rubbed my face. "Just tell me exactly what to do," I said, my voice wobbling. "Because I'd rather not go to prison for robbing a bank today."

"Well, you wouldn't go to prison for 'robbing a bank,'" Henn corrected. "You'd go to prison for multiple counts of bank fraud, grand theft larceny, identity theft, and conspiracy, probably." He snorted with laughter, but neither Josh nor I joined him.

"*Dude*," Josh said.

"Not at all funny," I added, gritting my teeth.

"Sorry," Henn said, stifling his grin. "Hacker humor. Gotta keep things light and bright or else you go a little cuckoo. But, okay, listen up. When you go in there, just think, 'I'm filthy rich and this is *my* money and I'll do whatever the fuck I want with it.' It's all in the attitude. You gotta have swagger."

"Just like baggin' a babe," Josh added, winking.

"Exactly—except, for God's sake, don't 'dick it up.'" Henn cast a snarky look at Josh. "That might work in a bar, dude, but we're in my house now."

Even through my anxiety, I couldn't help but grin.

Henn grinned. "And *never* flirt. You'll be too nervous and it'll come off as weird. Just open with a simple pleasantry to get your nerves out—maybe like, 'how's your morning going?'—and then, *boom*, launch into instructing the teller about the transfer in a clear, calm voice. Don't explain *why* you want the transfer or act apologetic—they're not doing you a favor here—it's *your* money."

"Jesus," I mumbled, putting my hands over my face. "You guys really think I can pull this off?"

"Of course," Henn said. "The trick is to *be* Oksana Belenko—not *pretend* to be Oksana Belenko."

"Wax on, wax off, Kat," Josh added reverently.

I laughed. "I know, right? Henn's totally Mr. Miyagi-ing me right now."

Henn rolled his eyes and forged ahead. "You already *look* the part—thanks to Josh's impeccable sense of style—now all you have to do is *be* the part."

I looked down at my ridiculously priced designer outfit—Prada dress, Louboutin heels, and Gucci bag—all supplied by Josh the day before during a whirlwind shopping spree. "Oksana Belenko wouldn't be caught dead in anything less than Prada," he'd insisted.

"I have to admit, being dressed like a *mill-i-on-aire* definitely makes me feel more Oksana-Belenko-ish," I said, staring at the bank across the street. I tried to smile breezily, but I couldn't do it.

Josh assessed my ashen face for a long beat. "Henn, give us a minute," he said, and without waiting for Henn's reply, he cupped my entire head in his palms like a bowling ball and kissed me full on the mouth. When he pulled away from kissing me, still holding my head firmly, he leveled me with his sapphire-blue eyes. "You've got this, Katherine Ulla Morgan," he said quietly, gazing with intensity into my eyes—and then he did the thing that's rapidly becoming my Achilles' heel: he gently touched the slight indentation in my chin.

And, just like that, my stomach stopped turning over and my jaw set.

I nodded. "Okay," I said. "Freak-out officially over."

Josh kissed my forehead. "There's my girl. Okay, Henn," he called over his shoulder. "Oksana's ready to rob a bank now."

"Yeehaw," Henn replied. "Oksanta Claus is coming to town, bitches. Let's do this."

And now here we are, an hour and a half later, all transfers completed, drinking beers and Patron shots in a seedy bar, waiting to hear from Jonas.

Just like Henn promised, the whole thing went off without a hitch (or so it seems thus far). Each and every bank believed, without a doubt, that I was the one and only *mill-i-on-aire* (many times over) Oksana Belenko—and therefore entitled to do whatever I pleased with *my* millions of dollars. Of course, I crapped my Stella McCartney panties (another gift from Josh) every single time I waltzed into yet another new bank and informed the teller of my desire to close my account—especially when a teller went to get his or her manager for "standard approvals." But, each and every time, my panty-crapping turned out to be completely wasted energy because no matter the approvals or security clearances or identification required at any particular bank, thanks to Henn, I always checked out as Oksana Belenko.

Indubitably.

Josh throws his head back, laughing at something Henn just said.

I sip my beer, still trying to get the shakes out.

"'Oksanta Claus is coming to town'?" Josh says, laughing. "Where do you come up with the shit you say, Henn?"

Henn shrugs. "I just get divine inspiration, what can I say?"

The waitress passes our table and Josh flags her. "Another round, please." He holds up an empty shot glass and shoots her a panty-melting smile.

The waitress visibly swoons. "You got it, sugar."

I bring my beer to my lips again, and my hand visibly shakes.

"You okay, Kat?" Josh asks.

"Yeah." But the truth is, I feel like I'm gonna barf—and not from the Patron. Today was insane. It's one thing to want to do something outrageously scary to help your best friend, and it's quite another to physically force yourself to actually do it while crapping your pretty undies the entire time. As I found out today, thinking about doing something brave (or tremendously stupid) and doing it are two very different things.

"Do you need—" Josh begins, but his phone rings and we all jump.

"Here we go," Henn says, rubbing his hands together.

Josh puts his phone to his ear, his eyes bugging out. "Jonas," he says evenly, and then he listens. "Oh, thank God." He addresses Henn and me. "We did it, guys. They got it all."

Henn fist-pumps the air, but all I can do is lean back in my chair, my body melting with outrageous relief.

"We're in a bar in Henderson," Josh says. He looks around and his eyes fall on a television behind the bar. "Yeah, they've got one, but it's not on." He listens for a moment and rolls his eyes. "Really? We've been sitting here wondering this whole fucking time, shitting our pants, and you didn't—" He listens again and smiles wickedly. "*Oh.* Well, then I forgive you." He snickers. "I'm sure you were. Okay, we'll turn on the TV and check it out. I'll call you right back." Josh flags the waitress. "Hey, could you turn on the TV—put it on the news?"

"Sure, sweetie." She walks over to the bartender, says something, and the TV comes on—and, literally, instantly, there's no doubt our crafty little *Oceans' Eleven* crew has hit a grand slam homerun.

"Just keep it here," Josh calls to the bartender.

On the screen, a female reporter is talking into the camera while a banner declaring "Terrorist Threat Foiled in Las Vegas" scrolls beneath her. Behind the reporter, law enforcement officers in Kevlar vests are marching in and out of a cement building, carrying boxes.

"Hey, could you turn up the sound, man?" Josh calls to the bartender.

"... being told by federal authorities the terrorist plot was 'sophisticated, imminent and massive,'" the reporter is saying.

I'm confused. They're calling The Club *terrorists*? Maybe I don't fully understand the implications of that word. The Club was plotting *terrorism*?

"... and that the terrorist organization has ties to the Russian government."

Henn chuckles. "Dude, it's like I'm a fucking ventriloquist."

"Straight from your puppeteering mouth into the reporter's," Josh replies, his eyes fixed on the screen.

I'm totally confused. What the hell are Josh and Henn talking about?

An older woman with dyed blonde hair appears on-screen being escorted into a dark sedan.

"... in this footage from earlier, we see one of the alleged terrorists being taken into custody," the reporter says.

"Is that Oksana?" I ask.

Henn nods. "Yup."

"She's a *terrorist*?" I ask dumbly.

The look that passes between Henn and Josh in reaction to my question makes me feel like I must be having a total blonde moment. What the heck am I missing here?

The reporter continues: "... the names of the two alleged terrorists killed during the raid have now been confirmed by authorities—"

"*Henn*," Josh says insistently, yanking on Henn's sleeve.

"Yeah, I know," Henn says, batting Josh's hand away like he's swatting at a fly.

"... the two men killed in a shoot-out with federal authorities at the scene were Mak-sim Be-len-ko and Yu-ri Na-vol-ska," the reporter says slowly, clearly doing her mighty best not to screw up the pronunciations of the names.

"Oh shit," Josh says, beaming, and Henn high-fives him.

"Both," Henn says.

"Fan-fucking-tastic."

What are they talking about? My brain is struggling to process. The Maksim guy who got killed is obviously that creepy Max guy who ordered the hit on Sarah and demanded a freebie from her. Well, good riddance to that bastard and may he rot in hell. But who's the other guy who died in the raid? Yuri something? Sarah mentioned a Yuri during our meeting with Agent Eric, I think—yeah, it was when Henn played that voicemail from her attacker—

I gasp. Holy shitballs. I just got it. *Both*. Henn meant that both men directly responsible for the hit on Sarah died today.

My entire body erupts in goose bumps.

Oh my God.

I don't know how Jonas did it—and what Josh and Henn had to do with it, but those two bad-guys biting the dust today doesn't seem to be a coincidence. It seems I'm not watching a news story unfold on the television screen—I'm watching a PR campaign.

"Josh," I blurt. But before I can say another word, he's standing next to me, pulling me up from my chair, and enfolding me in his muscled arms.

"We did it," he breathes into my lips. "We saved the world." With that, he kisses me with such ferocious intensity, my knees buckle.

When Josh breaks away from kissing me, he moves on to Henn, wrapping him in a massive bear hug. "Thank you," he mumbles into Henn's ear. "You're my brother for life, man."

My heart pangs at the earnest tone of Josh's voice. If I didn't realize it before now, today's victory obviously meant something deeply personal for him.

Josh's phone rings and he pulls away from Henn, rubbing his face. "Yo," he says into the phone. "Yeah, we just saw it." He presses his lips together, obviously containing his emotion. "I'm so proud of you, Jonas. You left no stone unturned." He listens. "I know. We can finally breathe again... No, no, no. Don't second-guess yourself, man. It was the perfect measure of force—like a fucking sniper." He listens for long beat. "Wow. I didn't know if they'd go for that. Fucking fantastic." He beams a smile at Henn and me. "Yeah, they're both standing right here. I'll let you tell them yourself. Hey, guys. Jonas has some exceedingly good news for you."

Josh hands the phone to Henn, a huge smile on his face, and puts his arm around me.

"Hey, big guy—congrats," Henn says into the phone. "You're welcome. I told you, I always wear a white hat." He listens and his eyes go wide. "*Tax free?* Are you kidding me? Oh my God." Henn looks at me, grinning from ear to ear. "Guess what Kitty Kat? We're each getting our million bucks completely *tax-free.*"

"*Tax free?*" I shriek—and then I promptly burst into gigantic, soggy tears.

Josh embraces me and I wrap my arms around his neck, sobbing like a kid on her first day of kindergarten.

"Looks like you'll be opening that PR firm sooner than you thought," Josh coos into my ear. He kisses my wet cheeks and then my lips. "Ssh," he says gently, stroking my back. "You did so good today, babe. You deserve every penny. You kicked ass."

Clearly, he thinks I'm crying about the money. And I am. That's a shitload of money. Holy shitballs, especially tax-free. But that's not the biggest reason I'm crying, I don't think. Mostly, I think I'm just relieved that the threat of danger to Sarah (and myself) is now, finally, blessedly, over. And I'm also sobbing with relief that I'm almost certainly not gonna get carted off to prison today—which is good, because God help me if I had to call my dad from jail. And, finally, I think I'm crying for no other reason than the fact that I *really, really* need a full eight hours of sleep. Holy Sleep Deprivation, Batman—I can't keep going like this. Even the Party Girl With a Hyphen needs to freaking *sleep* occasionally, for the love of God!

"Aw, babe, ssh," Josh coos, cradling me in his strong arms and kissing my tears. "This is great news—nothing to cry about."

But my body won't stop wracking with sobs. I squeeze Josh tighter and press myself into his broad chest with all my might.

Josh chuckles and squeezes back, kissing every inch of my salty, wet, snotty face, and whispers in my ear. "We did it, babe. It's over now." He puts his lips right against my ear. "Well, this settles it once and for all: you've definitely got a vagina."

I burst out laughing through my sobs, and he laughs with me, holding me close.

After a moment, I feel a tap on my shoulder, and when I pull my nose out of Josh's neck, Henn's holding up the phone to me. "Sarah wants to talk to you for sec."

I wipe my eyes and take the phone from Henn.

"Hi, babycakes," I say. "Congratulations."

"Kitty Kat!" Sarah shrieks. "*You're a mill-i-on-aire!*"

I laugh and wipe my eyes again. "So I've heard," I squeak out, my voice cracking. "I can't believe it."

"Aw, Kat," Sarah says, her voice breaking along with mine. "You were so brave today."

"Oh my God, Sarah, no, I wasn't brave at all," I reply. "I was totally crapping my pants the whole time."

Sarah laughs. "I can't wait to hear all about it."

"I can't wait to hear about D.C.," I reply.

"Ha! Talk about pants-crapping. Jeez. I was in the room with all those men in suits and I was so nervous, I kept imagining myself hopping on the table and tap dancing like a frog in a top hat."

"That makes no sense."

"Exactly. The whole meeting, I was like, 'fleffer fleegan geebah doobah.'" I laugh.

"But Jonas was masterful." She sighs. "Oh, Kat. He's incredible."

"Things going well with you two?" I ask.

"Amazing-incredible-never-been-happier-best-case-scenario. Gah! I'm so in love, it hurts."

I giggle.

"We're gonna need to do a good-old-fashioned sleepover when I get back so I can tell you all about it."

"Coolio. I'll bring the champagne," I say.

"Hell yeah, you will," Sarah says. "Seeing as how you're now a fancy *mill-i-on-aire*."

"Hey, aren't you a fancy *mill-i-on-aire,* too?" I ask.

Sarah giggles. "Why, yes, as a matter of fact, I am." She squeals. "I keep forgetting about that."

I roll my eyes to myself.

"Okay, I'll bring the champagne," Sarah says. "You bring the chocolate. *If* you can peel yourself away from Josh for a night, that is," she says coyly. "Have you two gone off like a nuclear bomb yet?"

"Um, yeah, pretty much," I say, my eyes drifting to Josh's face. He's watching me intently, his blue eyes sparkling.

"The good kind of nuclear bomb, I hope?" she asks.

"Is there a bad kind?"

"Uh. Yeah. There is."

"Well, it's the good kind, then. The very, very good kind." I sigh. "Oh, Sarah."

"Oh, Kat."

"So when are you coming home?"

"A couple days. We're gonna swing by New York first to visit—oh hang on." She says something obviously not intended for me. "Okay, my sweet love, hang the fuck on. Yes, I know. *Patience,* hunkster." Now she's back to me on the phone. "Jonas wants to talk to Josh again. He's a wee bit amped right now," she whispers. "He's kinda bouncing off the walls. God, he's so cute."

I laugh. "Okay. But—" My voice breaks with emotion again. "I love you, Sarah. Please just know I love you so much. I'm so frickin' relieved you're healthy and safe."

Sarah's voice instantly floods with emotion. "I love you, too, Kitty Kat. And I'm *so* frickin' relieved, too."

I hold out the phone to Josh, wiping my eyes, and he grabs it from me.

"Yo." Josh listens for a beat. "*Tonight?*" He suddenly looks stricken. "Dude, *no way.*" Josh looks at me pointedly as he listens again. "Because I have something *extremely* important to do here in Vegas tonight, that's why." He rubs his face. "Jesus Fucking Christ." He exhales. "*Fine.* But I'll come tomorrow night, not tonight... . Because I can't, that's why, motherfucker... . Because I've got something I need to do here in Vegas tonight... . So what? You head out to see him tonight and I'll come tomorrow—no big deal. *Because I've got something to do, Jonas. Chill the fuck out.*" He listens and then grins broadly. "It's none of your business what it is." He laughs. "Well, I'm not saying yes or no, but if it were that, then I think you'd agree that's something *extremely* important." Josh looks at me lasciviously, like a wolf scoping out a bunny. "Oh, bro, you have no idea."

My clit begins faintly buzzing.

Josh laughs. "It'll be fine, Jonas, trust me. When you're telling Uncle William the news, just hold up a photo of a trout and he won't even notice what you're saying." He belly laughs. "Okay. Bye. You, too. Oh, hey, Jonas?" He pauses. "I'm proud of you, man. Remember the text I sent the other day? Pretend I just sent you another one just like that." He snickers. "Sorry. I know. Fuck me." He slaps his cheek hard, making me jump back with surprise. "Yeah, I did it, cocksucker." He laughs. "Okay. See you tomorrow, bro."

Josh hangs up and looks at me mournfully. "Well, Party Girl, I've got some bad news. I gotta hop a flight to New York tomorrow morning, first thing."

"Oh," I say, the wind completely knocked out of my sails. I was really looking forward to spending a few days (and nights) alone with Josh in Vegas, just the two of us living out our sick-fuck fantasies together before being forced to leave this bizarre bubble and return to real life (and our separate cities). I don't know if this thing with Josh (whatever it is) is going to carry over into the real world or not—and if not, I don't feel ready to find that out. "Why do you have to go to New York?" I ask, trying to keep my voice from sounding too hurt.

"Jonas and I have to talk to our uncle about something important," Josh continues, "and Jonas insists we do it as soon as humanly possible." He twists his mouth. "And, unfortunately, Jonas is one hundred percent right about that. It's not something that should wait."

"I'll be heading off tomorrow, too," Henn says. "Jonas said the feds want me to meet with them in D.C. to help them sort through the database. But, hey, that still leaves us tonight to celebrate, right guys? It's not every day a guy (or girl) saves the world, huh? And especially not with his best friends."

Josh and I exchange a look. What have we been thinking? We went on and on about launching into our sick-fuck fantasy fulfillment the minute our mission was complete—but, clearly, that's a nonstarter. There's no way in hell either of us would ever let our beloved Henny celebrate this incredible victory all by his little, brilliant, quirky self. I make a face at Josh and he smiles wistfully, obviously resigned to our sudden change of plans for tonight.

"*Of course*, we're gonna celebrate, Henny," I say.

"Wouldn't have it any other way," Josh says, fist-bumping him. "And we're gonna do it in style, my man. Leave it all to me—I'm gonna make sure we have the night of our fucking lives."

Henn flashes Josh a look of appreciation and excitement that's so freaking adorable, I want to throw a little rhinestone vest on him and toss him into my brand new Gucci purse.

"Hey, I've got a brilliant idea," I say. "How 'bout we fly Hannah Banana Montana Millikin into Vegas on the next flight to celebrate with us?" I look at my watch. "There's still plenty of time to get her here in time for dinner, isn't there?"

Josh looks at his watch. "There sure is. Great idea. I suddenly feel like we need some additional staffing on that PR campaign." He winks.

"What do you think, Henny?" I ask. "You up for letting Hannah Banana Montana Millikin crash our party?"

Henn grins. "Awesome." He raises one eyebrow. "As long as you tell her to wear her glasses."

"I'll tell her," I say.

"You know," Josh begins, his wheels obviously turning. "As long as Hannah Banana Montana Milliken is gonna come all the way out here, it'd be a crying shame to send her back home tomorrow. How 'bout you two girls hang out for a few days and have some fun? We've still got Jonas and Sarah's penthouse suite —I forgot to check out of it like Jonas asked me to." He makes a face that says, *Yeah, I'm a fuck-up.* "When Henn and I leave, you and Hannah can stay a couple days in the penthouse like a couple of *mill-i-on-aires.* Have yourselves a mini-vacay, on me."

"Really?" I squeal.

"Sure. Book spa appointments, go shopping, see *Thunder from Down Under* or whatever." He laughs. "Order drinks by the pool, dine like queens, get pedicures and massages, do whatever the hell you girls wanna do for however long and I'll pick up the tab. Go crazy, all of it completely on me."

I'm trying to contain myself, but a strange noise erupts from my throat.

Josh laughs. "You've earned it, babe—you kicked ass today. We *literally* couldn't have done it without you. And there's no rush going back to Seattle, right?—you're still on my dime for the PR campaign for another couple weeks."

I'm giddy; I'm not gonna lie. But this seems too much to accept, even for me. "It's too generous," I say. "I'd love to hang out with Hannah for a few days, but I can certainly foot the bill myself, you know. If you haven't heard by now, I'm gonna be a *mill-i-on-aire.*"

Josh swats at the air. "Fuck no. You can't piss away your finder's fee money on debauchery—you're gonna need every dime for Party Girl PR, remember?" He winks. "If anyone's gonna piss away their money on debauchery, it's gonna be me. It's kinda my specialty."

I throw my arms around Josh's neck again, and for a second, I'm in serious danger of bawling again. "Thank you, Josh," I breathe.

Josh kisses my cheek and squeezes me tight. "I'll be counting the days 'til I see you again," he says softly into my ear, his voice low and sexy. "I can't wait to get started on what we talked about."

"I can't wait, either," I say into his neck, inhaling his cologne.

We break apart from our clinch and I move on to Henn, wrapping him in a tight hug. "This is gonna be the best night ever in the history of the world, Henny. You're gonna absolutely adore Hannah."

"Hey, when it comes to celebrating victory over the Evil Empire, the more the merrier, I always say."

"Well, duh," I say. "Isn't that what everyone always says after a long day of saving the world? 'The more the merrier.'"

"It's what they always say," Henn agrees.

"Tell Hannah I'll book the three o'clock flight for her on Alaska," Josh says, looking at something on his phone.

"Okay, I'll call her now. Thank you so much, Josh. She's gonna be thrilled."

Josh pulls me into him and kisses me gently. "It's my pleasure, Kat." He pushes himself into me and his erection juts against my hip. He presses his lips into my ear. "Have fun with your girlfriend—but make no mistake about it: the minute I get back from New York, you're all mine."

55

JOSH

"Excuse me, fellas," Sarah says, scooting back from the dining room table. "Gonna head to the ladies' room."

When she stands up from the table, Uncle William stands, too, which prompts Jonas and me to do the same.

Sarah smiles shyly. "Wow, so chivalrous, fellas. Golly gosh. Thank you."

The minute Sarah's left the dining room and the three of us have settled back into our chairs, Uncle William leans forward, his blue eyes fixed on Jonas. "You gonna marry this girl?" he asks.

I'm utterly shocked by the question. I mean, I know Uncle William is an old-fashioned kind of guy and all, and Sarah's obviously an incredible girl, and a perfect fit for Jonas, too, but Jonas only just met her, for fuck's sake. There's no way in hell Jonas is even *thinking* about taking a giant leap like *marriage*—

"Absolutely," Jonas answers smoothly. "As soon as humanly possible, in fact."

Uncle William chuckles and leans back in his chair. "Glad to hear it. Congratulations, son. Don't let this one get away. I loved her the minute I met her."

Jonas nods. "Me, too."

I'm in total shock right now. I knew Jonas was head over heels in love with Sarah, but I had no idea he was ready to *marry* her.

"You're sure, Jonas?" I ask.

"Never been more sure of anything in my life."

"That's awesome, bro," I say, my heart racing. "Does she know?"

"No," Jonas says, suddenly looking anxious. "Am I supposed to *ask* her if I can *ask* her?"

I laugh. "No, Jonas, you dumbshit," I say. "That's not what I meant. I'm just saying if you're gonna surprise the girl, then make sure you blow her socks off. This is the story she's gonna be telling her grandkids one day. So don't fuck it up."

Jonas nods, but I've clearly put the fear of God into him.

I lean back in my chair, my mind reeling. I can't believe it. My brother's gonna ask a girl to marry him. And not just any girl. Sarah Fucking Cruz—a badass of epic proportions. A girl who doesn't take any of his shit. A girl with a heart of pure gold.

All of a sudden, I feel an overwhelming surge of relief flooding my body. Jonas is gonna have a *wife*. Holy shit. Someone to love him forever—and someone for him to love in return. He'll finally have someone (besides me) to take care of him, to listen to him, to rein him in when his thoughts start spiraling out of control. And he'll finally have someone besides me to tell him he's a beast every fucking day of his life.

If Sarah says yes, that is.

Oh my God. I clutch my chest. Sarah Cruz had better say yes to my brother. Oh, please, God, let that woman say yes. Let her look past Jonas' fuckeduppedness and stupidity and constant Plato-izing and see what I see— the greatest guy in the whole fucking world.

"You've got to get a huge-ass ring," I blurt. "So big, it sears her fucking corneas."

Jonas nods. "Well, duh."

"You say that but you weren't already planning to do that, were you?"

"Yes, I was. I was already planning to get her a diamond so big she needs a wheelbarrow to carry it around."

Uncle William laughs. "Good boy. He's got it handled, Josh. Now leave the poor boy alone. Jonas loves her. He'll do it right."

"No, Jonas can't be trusted to do this right," I say defiantly. "If this were a business deal, sure, he'd be all over it and I wouldn't say a goddamned thing. But this is a *girl*. Left to his own devices, he'll do some crazy-ass *metaphor* that'll either scare her or bore her to tears."

Uncle William laughs and Jonas scowls at me.

"So what's your big plan for the proposal, Jonas?" I ask, crossing my arms over my chest. "Because it's got to be rock solid, man, I'm telling you—it's got to be a homerun. There's absolutely no room for failure."

Jonas runs his hand through his hair. "Jesus, you're freaking me out. I thought I had the perfect idea, and now you're making me doubt myself."

I'm practically hyperventilating. If Sarah says yes, then she'll *live* with him. In his house. *Forever.* Which means she'll always be there to keep Jonas on track and make him laugh and, most importantly, *I won't have to worry about him anymore.* Or, well, at least, not nearly as much as I currently do.

"Dude, listen to me," I say, my voice spiking with sudden urgency. "We've got to pull out all the stops—trick Sarah into saying yes."

Jonas looks indignant. "Fuck you. I don't need to *trick her*." He looks at

Uncle William, apparently hoping for a little backup, but Uncle William doesn't say anything. "Well...I've tricked her pretty well so far, haven't I?" Jonas says, and we all laugh.

Sarah enters the dining room and Jonas' entire face lights up like a bonfire.

"Hi, baby," he says.

"Hi, love," she replies, returning Jonas' goofy smile and taking her seat.

Love? Sarah called my brother 'love'? Oh my fucking God. Sarah Fucking Cruz is gonna say yes. Praise the lord—she's gonna agree to become Mrs. Faraday. If I were capable of shedding a tear, I'd surely shed one of happiness right now.

56

JOSH

Dessert and coffee are done. And for the past thirty minutes, Uncle William's been telling Sarah stories I've never heard before about his late wife, Sadie, (a raven-haired beauty who died in a car accident about a year before Jonas and I were born).

"Do you have any photos of her?" Sarah asks.

"Of course," he says. "I've got our entire wedding album upstairs."

"Oh my gosh," Sarah breathes, her cheeks flushing. "May I see it?"

"Of course. And I've got a whole bunch of pictures of Jonas and Joshua from when they were little I'll show you, too. You'll get a kick out of those."

Sarah squeals. "And do you have photos of yourself as a little boy, too, Uncle William?"

"Sure, I might be able to dig up one or two," Uncle William says, standing up from the table with Sarah. "Boys? Care to join?"

"Come with us, baby," Sarah says, holding out her hand to Jonas.

"Sure," Jonas says smoothly—shocking me for the billionth time today. He takes her hand.

I never would have predicted Jonas would say yes to voluntarily going down memory lane. As Jonas well knows, almost all of Uncle William's photos of Jonas and me as happy little kids include Dad—and normally, like me, Jonas bends over backwards to avoid seeing a photo of that bastard every bit as much as I do. But, damn, I guess up is down and right is left when my brother's in the presence of little Miss Sarah Cruz.

Uncle William looks pointedly at me and I shake my head.

"I think I'll sit on the veranda and look at the Hudson for a bit," I say.

My reply can't possibly surprise Uncle William. As far as I'm concerned, if

I never see Dad's face again, it'll be too soon for me—and Uncle William knows it.

"Okay, son," Uncle William says softly. "Katya's got the blue room in the back all ready for you. Just make yourself at home, as usual."

"Thanks," I say. "I appreciate it."

The trio walks toward the far hallway, Sarah's arm threaded into Uncle William's.

"I bet Jonas and Josh were the cutest little things," Sarah says happily.

"Oh, they were adorable little buggers," Uncle William says, just before they exit the room. "Oh my, did those boys climb every rock and tree and chair and piano. I remember this one time, I found Jonas and Joshua..."

They're gone.

I smile to myself. I so rarely see Uncle William outside of a business context. I'm not used to seeing him acting like this—so relaxed and nostalgic. I can only assume he's acting this way thanks to Sarah. Our crew's fearless leader puts everyone at ease, doesn't she? Especially my high-strung brother. She's like aloe vera on a sunburn for Jonas—a soothing balm for his soul. And anyone can see it. Uncle William obviously has.

I didn't detect even a hint of skepticism about Sarah from Uncle William, not even a whiff he thinks Sarah's a gold digger. His demeanor toward her has been one-hundred-eighty degrees from the cold way he reacted to Amanda when Jonas brought her here that one and only time—and Jonas had been with Amanda almost a year by then, I'm pretty sure. And now he brings Sarah here after a fraction of that time, and Uncle William falls all over himself to make her feel like part of the family? Wonders never cease.

I get up slowly and stretch, groaning, and then amble toward the French doors leading out to the veranda overlooking the river from on top of the world, patting my stomach as I walk. Damn, I've got to start hitting the gym like a madman when I get home. I've been a glutton this whole week in Vegas. Shit, especially now that fitness is gonna be my business, I've got to kick it up a notch, take a page out of Jonas' book. I certainly can't let my stupid brother show me up in the gym. Ha! Oh, fuck, I'm excited. I'm so fucking excited, I feel like a kid on Christmas Eve. My awesome life's about to get a whole lot more awesome. Sayonara, Faraday & Sons, I won't miss you.

I inhale deeply as the cool night air on the veranda hits my face and settle myself into one of the cushioned wicker chairs overlooking the shimmering river in the distance.

I'm just so flabbergasted at today's turn of events, I can't process. Jonas is gonna get engaged to a girl he's basically just met—and Uncle William is thrilled about the idea. Shit, Uncle William just *encouraged* Jonas to do it. I never would have predicted that in a million-trillion years. And that wasn't even the first time Uncle William shocked the hell out of me tonight: he absolutely floored me with his reaction when he found out both Jonas and I are leaving Faraday & Sons, too. I thought for sure he'd try to persuade us to stay—maybe talk about honor and obligation and how much it meant to our father to have his sons carry the mantle of Faraday & Sons. But he didn't say any of it. All he did was look both of us in the eyes and say, "I'm proud of you boys. Always follow your hearts." I swear to God, wonders never cease.

My phone vibrates in my pocket. I grab it and grin at the text message on my screen.

"Hi, Playboy!" Kat's message says. "Wanted to give you a little update on what your generous donation to the Kat and Hannah Hedonism Fund has bought you!" She adds a string of emojis: red hearts, clapping hands, a champagne bottle, a donkey and handcuffs. I laugh out loud. "We're having SO MUCH FUN!!! Thank you, thank you, thank you, my dearest, darlingest Playboy!!!! You are the most generous man in the whole wide world! And the sexiest, too!!!!!!! MEOW!" She adds a dog emoji. I don't know what the fuck that's supposed to mean, especially in light of her "meow," but I laugh anyway.

A second message comes in right on the heels of the first one. "Oops. I meant..." She adds a cat emoji. "The dog and cat were right next to each other on the emoji menu and I pressed the wrong one. The cat is me! MEOW! I'm Kitty Kat and this is you." She adds a muscled arm emoji. "Because you're so big and strong and sexy!! And together we're..." She adds an emoji of a fireworks display.

I can't wipe the smile off my face. Something tells me Kat is drunk-texting right now. And I love it. I'm about to write a reply when I get another message from her.

"And now—dooh-dooh-dooh!!!" Kat writes, followed by a trumpet emoji. "It's time for a slideshow created especially for you, my dearest, darlingest Playboy with the Heart of Gold! Here you go!"

A photo of Kat and Hannah by the pool, toasting the camera with fruity-looking drinks, hits my screen. Kat's holding up a white napkin with the message, "THANK YOU, JOSH!" scrawled across it in black ink.

There's no time to reply. Another photo lands on my screen: Kat and Hannah in fluffy white bathrobes, sitting on an overstuffed white couch, toasting the camera with what looks like ice water. They look like they're in a spa waiting room. Again, Kat's got a napkin with a message written across it: "YOU ROCK, JOSHUA WILLIAM FARADAY!"

Another photo. Kat and Hannah draped around a shirtless, greased-up, tanning-bed-muscle guy, all three of them standing under a neon sign that says "Thunder from Down Under." I laugh out loud at the expressions on the girls' faces in this shot. They're both making "O" faces. The writing on Kat's napkin this time is too lengthy and small to read, so I touch my screen and zoom in on the napkin 'til it's legible. "This man just impregnated both of us, Josh!" the napkin says. "Your money hard at work!" I burst out laughing.

If the glistening guy in the photo didn't look so completely gay, I might blanche at this note. But, what am I thinking? Probably not, actually. Kat's fucking hysterical, no matter what she does. She just kills me. And I must say,

Hannah seems to be quite the sidekick for my adorable little terrorist—a great girl through and through. Henn sure thought so when the four of us had a three-hour dinner and then went dancing last night. Talk about instant chemistry—Henn and Hannah clicked like they'd known each other for years. Same sense of humor; same quirky-hipster-cool dorkiness; and, oh my God, what a comedy duo on the dance floor those two turned out to be.

Yet another photo lands on my screen. This time it's Kat and Hannah sitting at a table in what appears to be a high-end restaurant, holding up wine goblets and a napkin that says, "To Josh Faraday, our generous benefactor!"

I can't help smiling. I can't believe this is the same girl who didn't chase me even *once* during my last trip to Manhattan a couple weeks ago. She played it so fucking cool that whole week, didn't she? Doing nothing but replying to my few, brief douchebag-texts to her, always making sure not to say a damned thing to reveal her interest in me. I knew her game, of course—since it was the same game I was playing with her—but, still, it surprised the hell out of me she could hold out so long without revealing a single crack in her hard-to-get armor.

This time, though, the woman's got no game whatsoever. And I love it. She's been peppering my inbox with adorable and affectionate texts almost nonstop since even before I boarded my flight for NYC. And I've been doing the same to her, pretty much nonstop. I can't help myself—I haven't been able to stop thinking about Kat since I kissed her goodbye early this morning and headed to the airport. Man, that was one bed I was sorry to leave.

Another photo lands on my screen. This time, the photo is Kat all by herself, alone in the same bed I left her in this morning. She's wearing her barely there white tank top and G-string—the same clothes she was wearing this morning when I kissed her goodbye. Her hair's tousled. Her eyes are half-mast and full of arousal. Man, that's the look that makes my cock tingle—the same look she gets right after she comes. I'd bet anything she took this photo right after getting herself off—and, hopefully, thinking of me while she did it.

But that's not even the best part of the photo. The best part, the thing that's making my heart pound painfully in my chest, is what Kat's napkin says this time: "Wish you were here."

"Me, too," I say aloud into the darkness of the night. In fact, there's no place I'd rather be than in bed next to Katherine Ulla Morgan. I take a deep breath, my mind smelling her phantom scent all around me. Damn. I miss her.

I touch the button on my phone to call her, my skin buzzing, my heart panging—but before the call connects, the French door behind me opens and Jonas walks onto the veranda. I quickly disconnect the call.

57

JOSH

"Hey, bro," I say to Jonas, glancing behind him to see if he's alone. He is. Good. I'm eager to talk to my brother man-to-man for a bit, just the two of us.

Jonas hands me a bottle of beer and takes the wicker chair next to mine, overlooking the moonlit river. "Uncle William's moved on to showing Sarah photos of his fly-fishing trips," Jonas says.

"Aaaah! Run away!" I say.

"As fast as my legs would carry me."

I take a sip of my beer. "That man sure can talk about fish."

"He sure can."

"Even a fish would get sick of Uncle William's stories about fish," I say. "They'd be like, 'Dude. Talk about *humans* occasionally. *Please.* You're hurting my fish-ears.'"

Jonas chuckles. "The man loves his fish."

"Do fish have ears?" I ask.

"Sort of," Jonas says. "Fish don't have *traditional* ears, but they have ear parts inside their heads that pick up sounds in the water. Functionally, they're ears, even if not technically so."

I laugh. "You're a fount of useless knowledge, Jonas Patrick Faraday."

He swigs his beer, smiling. "I really am."

There's a long beat as we both drink our beers and look out at the spectacular view of the river.

"Uncle William sure handled the news of our double-departure awfully well," I say. "He shocked the fuck out of me."

"I know. I thought it'd be like jumping off a cliff to tell him, and it was more like stepping off a curb."

"It almost seemed like he was expecting it, didn't it?"

"Totally," Jonas agrees. "I had that exact same thought."

We gaze out at the lights on the Hudson forty floors below for another long moment, drinking our beers.

"I can't wait to get started building our baby," Jonas finally says. "I have so many ideas for Climb & Conquer, my head's been going a mile a minute."

"As opposed to when?"

Jonas laughs.

"I'm pumped, too," I say, laughing. "Telling Uncle William felt like getting freed from a lifelong cage."

"That's *exactly* how I felt," Jonas says. "I feel like I'm floating."

"Me, too. *Exactly*. To Climb & Conquer," I say, holding up my beer. "And to the Faraday twins—two fucking beasts among men."

"Hear, hear," Jonas says, clinking my beer with his. "Fuck yeah."

"Fuck yeah," I agree.

"I'll finalize the press release on my flight home. We can release it on Monday."

"Awesome," I say.

"Fuck yeah," Jonas says.

"Fuck yeah."

We look out at the river for a moment, drinking our beers, each of us apparently lost in our excited thoughts.

"So Uncle William sure took to Sarah right off the bat," I say.

"Oh my God. You should have seen him when we first got here last night," Jonas says. "I kept warning Sarah before we arrived not to take it personally if Uncle William was kinda standoffish or super formal, you know?—but he acted like she was his long-lost daughter the minute he laid eyes on her. Just fell totally and completely in love with her."

I chuckle. "Just like you," I say.

Jonas grins. "Just like me."

"Congrats, by the way," I say. "She's perfect for you. I don't know how you managed to find her. She's a needle in a haystack."

Jonas beams a smile at me but doesn't reply.

"So you told her?"

Jonas looks at me funny, obviously not catching my meaning.

"The three little words?" I clarify.

"Oh." Jonas' grin broadens. "Yeah. I told her." I can tell he's blushing, even in the moonlight.

"First time ever saying it?"

"Yeah." His smile broadens yet again.

"Did it freak you out to say it?"

"Not in the slightest. It just felt good—really, *really* good."

I ponder that for a minute. "You were never tempted to say it before Sarah?"

Jonas crinkles his nose like I've said something distasteful. "No."

"Not even to Amanda?"

Jonas shrugs. "Well, I knew I was 'supposed' to say it to Amanda based on the passage of time—I knew she *wanted* me to say it to her. But, no, I was never even tempted. Did you ever say it to Emma?"

I nod. "It took me three years, but yeah."

"Three years? Wow, and here I thought I was the emotionally stunted asshole of the two of us."

I shrug and sip my beer. "Not something to say lightly."

Jonas makes a sound that tells me he agrees with my statement. "Emma's the only girl you've ever said it to?" he asks.

I nod.

"Damn. She hung in there for three fucking years, waiting for you to say it?"

I shrug. "Yeah. But we had the whole long-distance thing, you know—three years wasn't really three years if you add up the time we were actually in the same room."

"How'd it feel when you said it to her?" Jonas asks. "Did it feel good or did it freak you out?"

"Both."

"Did she say it back?"

"Yeah, she said it back—and for a brief moment in time, I felt kind of like, 'Phew. That's a relief. I'm normal.'" I shake my head. "But in retrospect, exchanging those words just lulled me into a false sense of security. Once I said them, I started thinking it was safe to say some other shit too—and, as I found out pretty damned quick, it wasn't."

I can feel Jonas' eyes on me, but he doesn't speak.

"As it turns out, saying the words doesn't make the feelings real." I pause. "It was like Emma was signing a software licensing agreement—she just scrolled to the bottom and pressed 'I agree.'"

Jonas makes a sympathetic sound.

"In fact, come to think of it, Emma didn't actually say the words back to me. She just said, 'Me, too.'"

"Ooph."

"Yeah." I pause. "Ooph."

There's a beat.

"I thought I loved her—I really did," I say. "But now that I'm watching you and Sarah, I realize I probably didn't. I mean can you really love someone if they don't love you back?"

My question is rhetorical, but Jonas answers me, anyway. "I like to think I'd love Sarah even if she didn't love me back. And yet I can't imagine I would have been *able* to love her like I do if she didn't love me. The way Sarah loves me makes me feel like it's safe to love her all the way."

There's another beat during which we both look out at the sprawling view of the river. This has to be the most unexpected conversation of my entire life.

"Emma never looked at me the way Sarah looks at you, bro," I say softly. "Not once." My heart squeezes painfully in my chest at the admission. "Seeing you and Sarah together makes me realize Emma never loved me."

Jonas makes a sympathetic noise. "Then she wasn't The One."

I swallow hard, swig my beer, and look out at the Hudson again. A light from some sort of boat is skimming slowly across the black water in the distance.

"Josh, you're better off," Jonas says. "If a woman doesn't look at you the way Sarah looks at me, then she's not worthy of you."

I nod, but I don't say anything. When the fuck did Jonas become the wise and powerful brother in this duo? The guy falls in love with the greatest girl in the world, and suddenly he's some kind of love guru?

"So, on a related topic," Jonas says, "how's it going with Kat?"

A huge smile involuntarily bursts across my face at the mere mention of Kat's name. "Good."

"You like her?"

I bite my lip, but I can't control the goofy grin that's taken over my face. "Yeah, I like her. She's a handful, though. Kinda crazy."

"Oh, well, that's good, right?—you like crazy."

"I sure do."

Jonas chuckles.

"Which is a good thing," I say, "because she's batshit crazy. And stubborn as shit. But she's also super cool and sweet and funny and smoking hot, too. A handful, like I say."

"Sounds fun."

"She's the most fun I've ever had, if you know what I mean. Oh my God, the woman's like a dude in the best possible way." I snicker despite myself. "She doesn't... hold back."

"*Excellent.*"

"I didn't even know a woman like Kat existed. She's like a whole new species of freaky-ass fish that washes to shore after a nuclear disaster."

Jonas laughs.

"That's what I told her, actually. I told her she's a freaky-ass fish."

"No, you didn't."

"Yeah, I did."

Jonas bursts out laughing. "Now there's some Valentine's Day bullshit if I ever heard it." Oh, man, he's laughing his ass off, which, in turn, makes me laugh, too. "You told her that? And here I thought *I* was the dumb Faraday twin," Jonas says, still laughing.

We laugh our asses off together for quite some time. Finally, Jonas wipes his eyes and takes a sip of his beer. "That's hilarious, Josh."

"I'm a charming son of a bitch, what can I say?"

Jonas shakes his head. "A woman like that, you better make sure you deliver what she expects—don't fuck it up."

I shoot him a look that says he's a moron. "I *can't* fuck it up—I just told you, she's like a dude. She's a slam-dunk, every time. She's amazing—a unicorn."

"Oh, ho, ho. That's what you might *think* with a girl like that. Just be careful—a unicorn will lull you into a false sense of confidence. Don't start getting lazy."

"What the fuck are you talking about?"

"If you don't know then I can't explain it to you."

"Try."

He sighs. "She's *really* good at getting herself off, right?"

I don't reply. I'm a gentleman, after all.

"So that means she doesn't actually *need* you," he continues. "You're nothing but a luxury item to her—a Lamborghini, if you will. And as you of all people should know, no one buys a Lamborghini for basic transportation. They get the Lamborghini because they want all the stupid bells and whistles (and because they're an idiot with their money)."

"What the fuck are you talking about?"

Jonas shrugs. "I'm just sayin' a girl can get dissatisfied pretty damn quick with her ridiculously expensive Lamborghini if it doesn't deliver everything that's been promised in the brochure."

My heart is racing. I don't know how it's possible, but my idiot brother is actually making a shit-ton of sense.

"So as your girl's designated Lamborghini," Jonas says, "you need to make it your sacred mission to give her everything she expects from a two-hundred-thousand-dollar car." He swigs his beer. "You gotta convince that woman she actually *needs* a goddamned Lamborghini."

Shit. He's right. "So what do I need to do?" I ask.

"You gotta be able to do stuff for her she can't do for herself. Make her come so hard, she's literally addicted to you."

"Oh, well, *that* I can do. Believe me, I know how to make a woman come hard."

"One way? Two ways?"

"All ways. Fuck off."

"Mmm hmm."

"Fuck you. I'm good."

"But are you *great*? Do you aspire to excellence every single time?"

"What the *fuck* are you talking about? Do I *aspire*...? Just to be clear, we *are* talking about fucking, right? Or is this conversation about something completely different and I've been totally confused the whole time?"

"Ah, grasshopper. Fucking is never just fucking."

I roll my eyes.

"You said she's a unicorn. I'm just saying you gotta bring your 'A' game every time with a unicorn. There are no free passes. You gotta study up—

continuously improve your skills—keep ratcheting it up for her. You can never, *ever* just 'wet your dick.'"

I cringe. "*Jonas.*"

He shrugs.

There's a beat.

"Study up?" I finally ask.

"A man catches himself a unicorn, then he best study up so he can feed her the right kind of unicorn-food."

"*What the fuck are you talking about?*"

Jonas rolls his eyes, pulls out his phone, and taps something out on it.

I lean over, trying to get a glimpse of his screen. "What are you doing?"

"I'm ordering some books for you. They'll be at your house when you get home. Read 'em before you see Kat again. You're welcome."

"Fuck you," I say.

"No, fuck *her*—with supreme devotion and expertly calibrated skill." The light from his phone illuminates the huge grin on his face. "I know you think you're the wise and powerful Faraday twin—and you *are* about most things—but about this one thing, I'm nothing short of godly. Just trust me."

"Whatever, bro," I mumble. Of course, I'm beyond excited to read whatever books Jonas just sent to my house, but I'd never tell him that. "Hey, bro, can I ask you something?"

"It's called a G-spot," Jonas says. "And it's the key to the kingdom."

"Fuck you," I say. "I know about the G-spot, fucktard. I'm not a moron."

"Of course, you do. Sorry to insult you. What's your question?"

"What I'm about to say has nothing to do with me *doubting* your connection with Sarah, okay? So don't flip out on me. Just remain calm."

"I would never, ever flip out on you, Josh. I'm nothing if not an endless reservoir of calm contemplation."

We both laugh.

"I'm just wondering..." I say. "Everything's just been so fast for you two—"

"A lot's happened in a short amount of time—we've already lived through a lifetime's worth of shit together."

"Oh, totally. I get that. I'm just wondering, you know..." I clear my throat. "How do you *know*?"

"How do I know what? How to make her come? Read the books I sent you, dumbshit." He laughs, but I don't. He tilts his head, obviously realizing I'm asking him something in earnest. "How do I know I *love* her?" he asks.

"No, not exactly. What I'm asking is different than that—bigger than that." I bite my lip, thinking. "How do you know Sarah's *The One*? How do you know she's the last woman you ever wanna be with—the last woman you ever wanna *sleep* with for the rest of your whole fucking life? How do you know you can promise Sarah *forever* and one hundred percent *mean it*?"

Jonas shrugs. "I just know. I've never been more sure of anything in my whole life."

"But *how* are you so sure? What *exactly* do you feel about Sarah that makes you so sure you don't just *love* her—because I totally get *that*—but that you *also* wanna spend the rest of your life with this *one* girl and not keep searching for some other girl who might be a teeny-tiny bit more perfect?"

Jonas sips his beer slowly, apparently pondering the question. "When you find what you're looking for, you know," he finally says. "We're the greatest love story ever told—our love is the wonder of the wise, the joy of the good, the amazement of the gods."

There's an exceptionally long pause during which I have to keep myself from rolling my eyes. "Oh, well," I say evenly. "That explains everything. Thanks." I take a long swig of my beer and look out at the river. "That reminds me, I like your new ink. In English, I notice. That's something new for you."

Jonas looks down at the tattoo newly inscribed on the outside of his left forearm and his platinum bracelet glints in the moonlight. "Thanks. Yeah, I wanted the whole world to be able to read my words and understand their meaning. It's my declaration of love for Sarah. I'm shouting about my love for her from the top of the highest mountain."

I chuckle to myself. Oh man, Kat's list of "prohibited" tattoos is the gift that just keeps on giving. "So you got a *girlfriend* tattoo, huh?" I say, trying to stifle my laughter. "So, so awesome, bro."

"Soon to be a *wife* tattoo," Jonas says proudly, his excitement palpable. "Why are you laughing, motherfucker? What's so funny?"

"I'm not laughing at you, I swear to God. Kat's got this stupid list of tattoos that she says are uncool or whatever. And girlfriend tattoos are on the list."

Jonas shrugs. "Like I've ever given two shits about being cool?" He swigs his beer, still looking out at the river. "And, anyway, it won't be a *girlfriend* tattoo for much longer." He's obviously bursting with excitement about that last statement.

"Hey, don't feel bad about having a tattoo on Kat's list—dragons and YOLO are on the list, too—both supremely uncool, it turns out," I say.

Jonas chuckles. "Well, I could have told you that."

"No, but get this: Kat came up with her list *before* she saw any of my tattoos."

Jonas bursts out laughing. "Really? Oh my God. That's pretty funny."

"Yeah, Reed and I raked her over the coals pretty good the other night at dinner, along with this hip-hop guy signed to Reed's label. Cool dude. You'd like him. He's a deep thinker, just like you. Anyway, this rapper-dude had an ex-girlfriend tattoo and a dragon." I laugh at the memory. "Kat looked like she was gonna hurl the whole dinner. So fucking funny. I think we made her pay for her sins pretty well."

"Wow, you should see your face when you're talking about Kat," Jonas says. "You *really* like her, huh?"

I can't hide my huge smile. "Yeah, bro, I like her a lot." The image of Kat in her skimpy white tank top and G-string, her eyes drunk with arousal, and her hair tousled pops into my head. "So back to my question, bro," I say. "Do you think you could, maybe, explain things in a way that's not"—I grab his forearm roughly and read his brand new tattoo—"our 'love is the joy of the good, the wonder of the wise, the amazement of the gods'? I know it's hard for you, Jonas, but can you just *try* to talk like a normal person, just once?"

Jonas swigs his beer, apparently thinking. "Okay, how about this: Sarah's holding my hand and leading me outside a dark cave toward the light that is the divine original form of myself."

I roll my eyes. "Oh, gee, thanks. That's *so* much better."

Jonas laughs. "I was just fucking with you—although that's all true, just to be clear." He laughs to himself for a good long minute. "Okay. The bottom line is that I'd rather be with Sarah than anywhere else in the world. I'd go to fucking IKEA with her if it meant being with her."

My skin suddenly erupts with goose bumps. "*Wish you were here,*" Kat's napkin said—and what thought popped into my head when I saw it? "*So do I.*"

Jonas exhales loudly. "It's just so easy with Sarah. I'm *completely* myself with her, you know? I never have to worry I'm saying the wrong thing. I've shown her everything—good, bad, ugly, silly, crazy, creepy—and she accepts it all. And she's *kind.* And nonjudgmental." He sighs happily. "And so *smart.*"

"So you told her everything?" I ask.

"*Everything.* Absolutely nothing left out. And, hey, that's reason enough right there to marry the girl. I only wanna do that shit once, man. Baring your entire soul to another person is fucking exhausting."

All of a sudden, I'm thinking about how Kat led me into her bed after reading my application and then fell asleep in my arms.

"I dunno, Josh—I just *know,*" Jonas continues. "It's really not all that complicated. For once in my life, it's not about what I think—it's about what I feel. I'll never want anyone besides Sarah, ever, 'til the end of time, and I'm sure of it. It's literally impossible for me to want someone else. Sarah's the divine original form of woman-ness. She's the ideal form of beauty—the pinnacle of perfection that all other women aspire to—the goddess and the muse—so what the fuck else could I possibly want?"

"Shit, I was totally with you until that last bit. 'The goddess and muse,' Jonas? Come on, man. What does that shit even mean?"

He shrugs. "If you don't understand it, then I can't explain it to you."

"Jonas," I say, "I'm serious, man. Please, just break it down for me. If you had to pick one thing that makes you know for sure Sarah's The One, what would it be? Not 'goddess and muse' shit, but, like, something tangible? Something concrete?"

"I can't pick only one thing. It'd be impossible."

I continue to look at him earnestly.

"But, okay, I'll try my best to dumb it down for you, Josh-Faraday style."

"Thank you. Not everyone's a fucking genius about relationships like the wise and powerful Jonas Faraday."

Jonas smiles and his eyes sparkle in the moonlight. "Sarah Cruz, *the goddess and the muse*"—he flashes me a snarky look—"makes me laugh like no other woman ever has—like no other *person* ever has, even *you*. She laughs at almost all of my jokes, even the really lame ones—and she's being totally sincere when she does." He smiles and his white teeth gleam in the moonlight. "Looking at that woman gives me a boner the size of the Space Needle, even when she's just sitting there reading one of her law books and scrunching up her nose." I can see his face suddenly light up, even in the dim light. "And on top of all that, sex with her is akin to a religious experience." He lets out a happy sigh. "If a guy needs more than all that to be eternally happy with one woman, then he's either crazier than me or just a greedy-ass motherfucker."

As if on cue, the door behind us opens and Sarah appears.

"Hey, boys," Sarah says.

"Hi, baby."

"Hi, Sarah Cruz," I say.

"*Hola,* Josh Faraday."

She sits on Jonas' lap and throws her arms around his neck. "I had to come find you." She kisses his cheek. "I started to feel lonely."

"Oh no. You were feeling lonely, baby?"

"Mmm hmm." She kisses his lips.

Jonas puts down his beer and stands, holding Sarah in his arms like he's about to cross a threshold with his bride. "Well, I know exactly what to do to cure my baby's loneliness. See you in the morning, Josh. Nice chatting with you."

With that, Jonas is gone, taking the woman of his dreams with him.

I return my gaze to the slow-moving lights on the dark river in the distance, a certain loneliness I'm well acquainted with descending upon me. Almost immediately, my thoughts turn to Kat. To the awesome photos she sent me from Las Vegas. To the way she fell asleep in my arms after reading my application. To the way she laughs like a dude—and fucks like one, too. To the long list of porno-fantasies she shared with me last night after we got back from our night out with Henn and Hannah. To the way she stomped down that hallway, soaking wet in her G-string, after Reed's party. To the way she kicked ass in each and every one of those banks. To the way she called me "babe" in front of Henn after he woke us up.

I take a long swig of my beer and stare at the dark river, Jonas' words echoing in my head: *If a guy needs more than all that to be eternally happy with one woman, then he's either crazier than me or just a greedy-ass motherfucker.*

58

KAT

I look out the window of the taxi at the driving rain pelting the car window. My phone buzzes with an incoming text and I look at the screen.

"Hey, PG," Josh's text says. "I'm about to board a flight from JFK to LAX. Just wanted to say hi real quick."

I smile at my phone. I can't believe how attentive Josh has been these past few days during his trip to New York. What a stark difference from his prior trip to New York right before Las Vegas, when he sent me crap messages all week long like, "Hey, Party Girl!" and "What's up?" Looks like Josh is ready to move past The Game Where We Pretend We Don't Give a Shit. And that's a damned good thing, because I stopped playing that game a long time ago.

"Hey there, Playboy," I type. "I was just thinking about you. I just landed at SEA from... Dang it. What's the airport code for Las Vegas? LVS?"

"LAS," Josh writes.

"Well, aren't you the airport-code guru."

"Yeah, I know them all," he writes. "My life is one giant airport code."

"LOL. (That's not an airport code, btw—that's just me laughing.)"

"Thanks for the clarification," he writes. "For a second, I thought you were flying in from Derby Field in Lovelock, Nevada."

"Wow, you really DO know your airport codes. Why have you been to Lovelock, Nevada?"

"I haven't. I only know LOL because I once read an article about funny airport codes. Other sidesplitting entries include SUX in Sioux City and OMG in Namibia."

"LOL."

"Derby Field!" he writes.

"Hey, it's an airport-code version of 'Who's on First?'" I write.

"Totally. OMG."

"Namibia!" I write.

"LOL."

"Derby Field!" I write.

"Gah!" he writes. "Make it stop."

I laugh out loud and the taxi driver's eyes in the rear view mirror glance back at me.

"Can you talk?" Josh writes. "I've got a few minutes before boarding."

"Yes, sir. Call me now."

When his call comes in, I pick up immediately, smiling broadly.

"Hi, Playboy," I coo.

"Hi, Party Girl with a Hyphen," he says. "How are you, beautiful?"

Wow, he sounds incredibly chipper. "I'm great. I'm sitting in a taxi on my way home. How are you?"

"Well, I'm bright-eyed and bushy-tailed and feeling fine as wine, thank you for asking. The world is my oyster."

"Wow. You sound extremely perky today."

"I am. Jonas and I told my uncle we're leaving Faraday & Sons the other night, and yesterday we mapped out the transition with the board of directors. I'm so excited, I'm bouncing off the walls."

"Congratulations. Does this mean you can finally tell me about what you and Jonas are planning?"

"Yeah, but I'd rather tell you in person in between kissing every inch of your naked body. It's too awesome to explain in a brief phone call." He makes a celebratory grunt. "I'm so *pumped.*"

Holy shitballs. He's acting like that "kissing-every-inch-of-your-naked-body" comment was a total throwaway, but it took my breath away. "I'm so excited for you, Josh," I breathe.

"Thanks. Can't wait to tell you about it when I see you, which *by the way,* is the reason I wanted to talk to you. When are you gonna come see me?"

"As soon as possible," I say, though the words catch in my throat. Josh and I were together in Las Vegas for only a week, after all, though it certainly felt a whole lot longer than that, and, now that I'm back in Seattle and returning to my real life, I feel unsure of where things stand between us. "So, hey, thank you so much for flying Hannah and me first class, by the way—we geeked out the whole time. It was awesome, but totally unnecessary."

"Kat, please, you can't fly *coach.*" He makes a sound like he's shuddering.

I laugh, but I'm not entirely sure he's kidding.

"It was my first time, actually," I say. "Wow, the seats are so cushy and the flight attendants are so damned *nice.*"

"That was your *first* time out of steerage? Oh, the humanity."

"Yeah. Hannah's too. She kept asking for extra peanuts just to see if they'd bring 'em."

"Well, get used to the idea of unlimited peanuts, babe—I see lots and lots of peanuts in your future."

My heart stops. What does that mean? Is he saying that, since I'm about to become a *mill-i-on-aire*, I'll be able to book first-class tickets any time I please on my own—or is he implying he'll regularly be flying me first class... *to visit him?*

"Oh, hey, guess what?" Josh says. "Henn has some 'work' in Seattle next week. What a coincidence, huh?"

"Yeah, Hannah told me. They've already got dinner plans. We're invited to join, if we can."

"Next week? Nope. If I get my way, you'll be here in L.A. next week, acting like my paid whore." He snickers.

Holy hell. Josh is positively on fire right now. This is as relaxed and easygoing as he's ever been with me.

"Speaking of which," Josh continues, "I've been thinking about how to pull off all your mini-pornos, and I think I'm gonna hit 'em out of the park."

I giggle. On our last night in Vegas, after coming back from our night-on-the-town with Henn and Hannah, and after having some freaking awesome sex, Josh and I lay in bed together and I told him chapter and verse about each and every one of the mini-pornos that regularly play inside my head. The man was so enthusiastic he even pulled out his laptop and started taking notes.

"Some of that shit's gonna be like putting on a fucking Broadway show," Josh continues, chuckling, "but I'm up for the challenge."

I cup my hand over my mouth to keep my voice from traveling to my driver.

"You don't have to enact *every* fantasy I told you about—" I begin, but Josh cuts me off.

"Oh, I'm doin' em all, PG—and I'm doing 'em *right*. Fuck yeah, I am. I've got a few things I gotta pound out at work for the next week or so," Josh continues, "but then I'm all yours, baby. So what's your calendar look like for a visit some time next week?"

"Um, I dunno," I say, heat rising in my cheeks. This conversation is overwhelming me in the best possible way. "I'll need to look at what's waiting for me on the work calendar and let you know."

"Cool. Don't keep me hanging though, or I'm gonna go all Jonas Faraday on your ass." He laughs to himself. "Oh my fucking God. I can't wait to see you and get started on our little fantasy-fulfillment exchange. It's gonna be *epic*." He lowers his voice. "Kat, I can't stop thinking about—" He abruptly stops. There's a ridiculously long pause. "It."

It? There's a long pause. That felt like a weird choice of words.

"I can't stop thinking about... *it*, either," I say slowly, but I'm not completely sure what we're talking about. Are we saying we can't stop thinking about our upcoming fantasy-fulfillment exchange? Is that the "it"?

"Oh, they're boarding my flight," Josh says quickly. "Be sure to send me a note telling me when you can come to L.A. I've still got you on the clock for my

'PR campaign,' so if it'll make it easier for you to get away from work, I'd be happy to throw some more money onto the 'campaign' and—"

"Oh, gosh, no, don't pay anything more to my firm, Josh. Once I get my finder's fee money, I'll probably be quitting, anyway, to start my own thing."

"Awesome, Kat. Wow. Just think—we'll both be birthin' babies at the exact same time. My new company with Jonas and Party Girl PR will grow up together."

"Ha! Well, our babies might be *born* at the same time, but they're definitely not gonna *grow up* together. Your baby's gonna be in a slightly different tax bracket than mine. Yours will be attending private pre-school and learning to play cello and speak Mandarin while Party Girl PR will be eating paste in the corner at the McDonald's Play Land."

Josh hoots with laughter. "God, you're funny. But, no, Kat, seriously—the size of your business doesn't matter—you'll still be an *entrepreneur*. And in my book, that makes you a fucking *beast*." He makes an exaggerated roar like a T-Rex.

I laugh. "Wow."

"Try it."

I mimic his roar.

"There you go. Feels good, doesn't it?"

"Um... Well, actually, I think my roar is a bit premature. I've got a crap-ton to figure out before I decide if I'm actually gonna do it or not."

"Why wouldn't you do it?"

"Because I don't know what the heck I'm doing. I know PR, but I don't know anything about running a business. I'm only twenty-four, for crying out loud. I'm a wee little baybay, Joshua. Waaah."

He scoffs. "I started the L.A. office of Faraday & Sons at twenty-four and I didn't know a goddamned thing. But I kicked fucking ass and took names, anyway—like the wise and powerful man I am. I learned on the job and so will you."

"Yeah, but I don't have a brother and uncle working with me in case I don't know something—it's just me, and I don't know the first thing about a million things."

"Like what?"

"Well, like whether my company should be an LLC or S-Corp or which billing software I should use. Plus, I've got to figure out a logo and website design and—oh *crap*—what if I wanna hire an actual *employee*? I don't have the first idea how to set up payroll or—"

"Whoa, slow down, High-Speed," Josh soothes. "You're stressing me the fuck out." He chuckles. "I'll help you with all that stuff. Piece of chocolate cake, little baybay."

"Josh, no, you can't help me with that stuff—I have to learn it, that's the whole point of starting my own thing."

"No, doing everything by yourself is most definitely *not* the whole point, you fool." He makes yet another scoffing noise. "The point of owning your own business is being your own boss and getting to do the thing that makes you a fucking beast—which in your case is being a PR phenom—it's definitely not setting up billing software and payroll. And, realistically, you'll probably be a one-woman operation for a while, so getting you up and running will be easy-peasy. Don't stress it, babe. I got you."

"Yeah, but I still don't know how—"

"Ssh. I tell you what I'm gonna do, baby," Josh says smoothly. "I'll line up whatever you're gonna need to get your business off the ground—an accountant, bookkeeper, IT guy, website designer, whatever. I've got all those folks sitting on my contacts list already, so just a couple of quick phone calls and, *boom*, you'll be all set."

I'm positively swooning right now. "You'd do that for me?"

"Of course, I would. I'd do anything for you, Kat."

Holy shitballs. Josh tossed out that last sentence like he was simply stating the obvious, but I'm floored. "I really didn't mean to imply I was expecting you to—"

"Oh, I know. I never thought that. I just wanna help."

"Are you sure?"

"Positive."

"You know you don't have to—"

"*Dude.* You're pissing me off. Just say 'thank you.'"

I smile into the phone. "*Thank you.* Very much."

"My pleasure."

I feel light-headed. "So does that mean you're gonna be, like, an investor?"

"No," he says quickly. "I don't want an ownership stake—I'm not making a long-term commitment here. I'm just offering to help you get your baby off the ground, that's all—no strings attached."

There's an awkward pause. He said all that a lot more emphatically than was necessary, I do believe.

"Okay," I say slowly, my heart beating wildly. Did he just tell me in code he doesn't want a long-term relationship with me?

There's a long pause.

"But, I mean, don't get me wrong," he stammers. "I'm super excited for you and I wanna help you out."

I pause, trying to decide what we're really talking about here. I feel like he just kissed me and slapped me. "Maybe I'd better figure everything out on my own, after all," I say tentatively. "But thanks for your offer, anyway."

He makes a sound of frustration. "What the fuck just happened?"

"What do you mean?"

"You were all happy and grateful and excited and then you suddenly became a chick. What suddenly crawled up your ass?"

I'm shocked. "*What crawled up my ass?*"

"Oh, Jesus. Vagina!" he shouts. "Sometimes I forget you're not just a hot-lookin' dude."

"What the hell...?" I say, bristling. *"What crawled up my ass?"*

"Bad choice of words. Sorry. It's what I'd say to a dude. Forget I said it. Listen, Kat. Here's the deal. I'm gonna help you because you're my Party Girl with a Hyphen—not because I want a stake in your company, that's all I'm saying. Okay? Don't get all freaked out and start overanalyzing everything and start looking for secret codes."

Whoa. It's like he can read my damned mind.

"I'm being above-board with you: I wanna help you. That's how I feel right now. How will I feel a few months from now? I have no idea. All I know is that right now, I wanna help you. And I wanna see you. And be with you and touch you and fuck you and lick you and fucking bite you, and I can't stop thinking about you, no matter what the fuck I do—" He abruptly stops talking.

Suddenly, there's complete silence on the line.

Wow, that was quite the rambling speech from Mr. Joshua William Faraday.

I pause a really long time, collecting myself, my hand on my heart.

He doesn't say another word.

"Okay," I finally say. "Well, then, thank you for your *short-term* and completely *uncommitted* help. I appreciate and accept it."

There's another really long beat.

Josh swallows hard on his end of the line and clears his throat. "Great. You're welcome. So what do you think about calling the company 'Party Girl with a Hyphen PR'?" he asks, clearly changing the topic of conversation. "Is that too long?" he asks.

"Is what too long?"

"The name 'Party Girl with a Hyphen PR.'"

"Oh. Yeah, definitely," I manage to reply. "And also too weird." I clear my throat. "Actually, I was thinking of calling my company 'PG PR'? Is that too boring? I'm thinking 'Party Girl PR' kinda sounds like an event planner."

"Yeah, you're totally right. Good call, PG. That's why they pay you the big bucks. 'PG PR.' I like it. Oh fuck, they're boarding my flight."

"Okay. Thanks for everything, Josh."

"My pleasure."

My pulse is pounding in my ears. "Fly safely."

"That's always the plan, babe. Oh, hey, PG. One more thing. Real quick. I sent you a little present. It should be waiting for you when you get home."

"A *present?* Oh my God, Josh, no. I still haven't thanked you enough for everything you've already done for me."

"It's just a small gift. You'll see."

"But, no, Josh, you've already done too much."

"Hey, you've done a lot for me, too. By my count, we're pretty even."

"If you're talking about all the amazing sex we've had, we're not close to even—that was all for *my* benefit, I assure you."

"Dude. I'm not paying you for sex—though sex with you is so damned good, I gladly would—especially since I know you have a raging call-girl fantasy and all." He snickers. "But no, you big dummy, I'm talking about evening the score for everything you did in Las Vegas. We all owe you big, Oksana, especially me."

"Especially *you*? How's that?"

"Because if something were to happen to Sarah, then Jonas would fall apart —which means my life would suck. So I need to guard Sarah like the crown jewels. Plus, on a personal note, I'd strongly prefer my application never get into the wrong hands, so I'm pretty relieved about the way things worked out."

Oh, I never thought about that.

He takes a deep breath. "*So*, like I said, I'd say we're pretty much even—in fact, I might very well still owe you—oh shit. Gotta run, PG. Hey, there'll be wifi on my flight, so be sure to email me when you get my gift."

"Okay, I will. Thank you again. Fly safely."

He sounds like he's running. "Oh, and don't forget to tell me when you can make it to L.A. so I can book your flight—whoa, whoa, hang on!" He's obviously shouting to someone on his end of the line. "Yeah, I'm on this flight. Thanks." He addresses me again. "Okay, PG? Email me."

"You better go, Josh—don't miss your flight."

"Yeah, I'm walking on board now. Talk to you later, Party Girl with a Hyphen. See you soon."

My stomach bursts with butterflies and my heart squeezes. "Bye-bye, Playboy with a Heart of Gold. Can't wait."

He sighs cartoonishly, like he's Lucy watching Schroeder playing piano. "Bye, Kat."

I can feel his wide smile through the phone line. I hope he can feel mine in return.

"Bye, Josh."

I hang up my phone, my mouth hanging open, my eyes as wide as freakin' saucers. For a long moment, I look out the window of the cab in a daze, staring at the rain pounding insistently on the glass. Holy crappola, as Sarah always says, that entire conversation shocked the living hell out of me. Josh acted like... I can't even finish the thought without possibly making my heart explode.

And *I* acted the exact same way toward him.

We *both* acted like...

Oh my God, both of us did, right? I wasn't imagining it, was I?

I clutch my chest. Holy My Heart's Gonna Burst Out of my Chest, Batman. I'm having trouble breathing. I take a deep, steadying breath. That conversation threw me for a loop. It was just so effing... *affectionate*. And *comfortable*. And *sweet*. (Well, except when he asked what crawled up my ass —that wasn't so sweet.) There was none of our usual cat-and-mouse thing going on—it felt like the cat had already caught its coveted mouse, long ago, and was now pinning it down and licking it from nose to tail.

I stash my phone in my purse—the Gucci bag Josh bought me during our Oksana-inspired shopping spree—and stare at the rain out the taxicab window. Holy hell, Josh's generosity knows no bounds. He's already done so much for me, and now he's gonna help me get my little company off the ground, too? I thought I'd be at least forty before I even attempted to make that particular dream come true.

The windshield wipers are going back and forth at full speed, lulling me into a kind of trance.

I don't care what Josh says—we're definitely not *even* when it comes to the two of us bestowing gifts and favors on each other. I joined our *Ocean's Eleven* crew to protect Sarah and possibly myself, too—not to mention to get a free trip to Las Vegas with my best friend. Yes, everything wound up blowing up and becoming way, way bigger than any of us had ever imagined, but still... Josh keeps doing stuff for me, *personally*, and I most definitely didn't save the world for him specifically. There's no way around it: all I've done is take, take, take from Josh, letting him give, give, give to me 'til he's blue in his ridiculously gorgeous face. And I've done absolutely nothing to deserve his generosity or express my gratitude. In fact, I'm getting perilously close to becoming a total user-abuser, if I'm not already there. But what gift can I possibly give to Josh that would come even close to everything he's already given to me?

My heart is throbbing in my ears. My chest is tight.

I already know the answer, of course. It's not a big mystery: his deepest, darkest sexual fantasies served up on a silver platter.

And that's exactly what I'm going to give him. Right down the line.

Of course, giving Josh complete sexual satisfaction, no matter what form that comes in, isn't some sort of noble or charitable pursuit on my part—ha! It will be my sublime pleasure to give Josh exactly what he desires in the bedroom, a gift to myself as much as him. Hell yeah, it will.

And it's not all the gifts and money Josh has given me that's making me feel this way, either. Nate used to shower me with gifts, too (though on a much smaller scale), and I never once physically ached for him the way I'm aching for Josh right now. I never once daydreamed about feeling Nate pushing himself deep inside me, or closed my eyes and imagined his warm tongue on my clit, or fantasized about waking up in Nate's arms and wordlessly taking his morning wood into my mouth.

I breathe deeply, arousal suddenly seeping into my panties.

I never once felt a near-desperate urge to fuck Nate any which way he likes it, literally, *any which way*, no matter how dirty or naughty it might be, or felt the urge to make his desires my own, or fantasized about sitting on his face or riding his cock 'til I'm screaming his name. And I certainly never once imagined Nate sitting at the dinner table with my family on Thanksgiving, or on the couch with my brothers, watching the Seahawks and eating my mom's famous chili.

I gasp and jerk forward in my seat, clutching my throat like I'm choking on a chicken bone. Oh my fucking shit. What am I thinking? I want to take Josh home to meet my family? I haven't taken anyone home since Garrett.

I stare at the rain battering the window of the taxicab, still clutching my throat, trying desperately to think of some logical reason why I'm feeling like a tortured, lovesick puppy that doesn't involve falling for the world's most eligible bachelor (who, in case I missed it, just told me in not-so-secret code he's not at all interested in a long-term commitment). But I can't come up with a damned thing.

I'm falling for the world's most eligible bachelor.

Oh God.

No. I need to stop feeling this way right now and get a handle on my emotions. I press both of my palms on my cheeks, willing myself to stop feeling this all-consuming ache. Infatuation is fine. Sexual attraction is fine. We'll-see-where-this-goes is perfectly fine. Really liking someone a whole lot is perfectly fine. But risking inevitable, shattering heartbreak is emphatically *not*.

Dude, I need to think rationally, with my brain, and not my lady-parts.

I'm in lust, and nothing more. Well, that and very strong like. Very, very strong like. But once I get back to work and the routine of my real life, once the neon lights and excitement of our spy-caper-porno in Las Vegas have faded for both of us and reality sets in and we remember that Josh and I live not just in different states but in different *worlds*—because I'm not a supermodel and my mom isn't a movie star with houses in the Hamptons and Aspen, for crying out loud—I'm sure my fairytale-delusions will crash down to reality without a parachute.

Indubitably.

59

KAT

When I enter my apartment, my youngest brother, Dax, is on the couch, playing his guitar and singing a song I've never heard before. When he sees me, he sets down his guitar and lopes over to me, his lean muscles taut in his tight-fitting T-shirt.

"Jizz," he says warmly, wrapping me in a big hug. "Welcome to my humble abode."

I kiss his cheek. "Hey, baby brother," I say. "Thanks for keeping my apartment safe and sound."

"It was hard work, but somebody had to do it. Was Vegas a blast?"

"Yeah, it was amazing."

"How much money did you lose?"

"Oh, not too much," I say coyly. "So, hey, was that a new song you were just playing?"

"Yeah, I was just fine-tuning it. It's not done yet."

"Play me what you've got." I lead him to the couch and we sit.

"Naw, I'll play it for you when I've got it finished."

"I won't criticize it. Just play me what you got."

His face lights up. "Well, if you insist."

I laugh. "I do."

Dax picks up his guitar and plays an up-tempo song about looking for love in the anonymous faces he passes on a busy city street—and his expressive voice and vulnerable lyrics transport me with every word and note.

"Wistful, hopeful, funny, romantic, and lonely all at the same time," I say when he's done. "I absolutely love it."

"Yeah, but you love everything I write."

"True. But that doesn't mean I'm not sincere."

He grins. "So, hey, I got your mail for you." He slides a stack of mail on the coffee table toward me.

"Oh, thanks. I never thought I'd be gone so long." I start rifling through the stack. "Bills, bills, bills. Credit card offers. Coupons. Catalogs. Doesn't look like I missed—" I look up. Oh. I'm talking to myself. Dax isn't in the room. I look back down at the stack of mail and continue sorting it.

I hear a thudding noise in the center of the room and look up just in time to see Dax straightening up from putting down a heavy-looking box. "This bad boy got delivered a couple hours ago," he says. "From someone named J.W. Faraday."

My skin pricks with goose bumps. "Oh, okay, thanks," I say, trying to sound casual—but, oh my God, the size of that box sure looks familiar. I pop up off the couch, intending to shoo Dax away, because, oh my God, if that box contains what I think it does, there'd better not be any markings on the outside to give it away.

"And, of course, I already opened the box for you, sis," Dax continues, "just to be super-duper helpful."

A weird screech of anxiety escapes my throat.

Dax chuckles. "Whoever this J.W. Faraday guy is, he's *awfully* generous—and somewhat of a perv, too, it seems."

"You *opened* it?" I blurt angrily.

"Of course, I did. I'd never make my sister open a big ol' *box* all by herself with her own two fragile hands. I'm a *gentleman*." He opens the already-cut flaps of the box with a wide smile and pulls out a humongous assortment of dildo-attachments, all packaged together in a clear plastic bag. "So many dicks to choose from, Jizz. I don't know how you'll decide." He places the dildos on my coffee table with a wide smile.

"Oh my God," I say, my cheeks burning. I can't breathe. I've never been so embarrassed in all my life. But Dax isn't done with me. He reaches inside the box, pulls out the main event, and places it carefully on the floor.

At the sight of my brand new Sybian, my face explodes with instant heat, both from excitement and embarrassment, but I force myself to remain calm. Dax might have no idea what a Sybian is, I tell myself—I'd certainly never heard of one before last week when Josh rented one for me.

"This is the first time I'm seeing a Sybian in person," Dax says, standing over it with his hands on his hips.

I throw my hands over my face, completely mortified. I can't believe my baby brother's here to witness this gift from Josh. Nightmare.

"It's really quite the feat of modern engineering," he says.

I don't reply.

Dax laughs. "So who the fuck is this guy, Jizz?"

I still don't reply.

"Aw, come on. It's just me."

As I often do, I decide my best defense is a good offense. "I can't believe you opened my personal stuff, Dax!" I yell, throwing my hands up in outrage.

But Dax completely ignores my outburst—a tactic I've seen him employ too many times to count (and a tactic I've copied and used to great success myself). In fact, he's smiling serenely at me. "I think Sybians cost like fifteen hundred bucks," he says. "Gosh, you must have done something awfully nice to J.W. Faraday to make him wanna send you such an expensive gift."

I open my mouth to yell at him, but nothing comes out. I'm so freaking embarrassed, I can't speak.

Dax bursts out laughing. "Oh, looks like I hit the nail on the head, huh? Well, whatever you did to the guy, you apparently did it very, very well." He buckles over laughing.

"You're so gross, Dax. Stop it."

But he won't stop laughing.

"Stop it."

Nope. He's thoroughly amused.

"You had absolutely no business opening that box." I march over to him in a huff and punch him in the shoulder. "Did the label on the package say 'David Jackson Morgan'? *No, it didn't.*"

He scoffs. "Close enough—it was stamped 'Personal & Confidential.' Hell, the damn thing might as well have said, 'Open me, Dax.'"

I can't help but smile broadly, even through my pissiness. That's my line, of course. Dax and I have always shared a brain.

Dax shrugs. "Seriously, a guy can't see a big ol' box sent to his *sister*, addressed to 'Katherine *Ulla* Morgan,' no less, *and* marked '*Personal & Confidential*' and not open it, for crying out loud. Gimme a break, Jizz—I'm but a man, not a saint."

My irritation is softening. Goddamn my baby brother, I can never stay mad at him for long. "Just don't tell everybody about this, okay? It's really personal."

He scoffs. "Of course not. I'd never tell any of our brothers about any of this."

I laugh. "You tell them everything, Dax, especially Keane."

"I don't tell Peen *everything*. I only tell him about my music and girls—"

"Like I said, 'everything.'"

"But I never tell him your stuff. Seriously, Jizz, I never do." His eyes are earnest. "I swear." He flashes me an adorable puppy-dog smile. "You aren't really pissed at me for opening your box, are you?"

I roll my eyes. "No," I say begrudgingly. "But never do it again."

He crosses his heart. "The next time a guy with a lord-of-the-manor name sends a big box marked 'personal & confidential' to Katherine Ulla Morgan at your apartment, and I'm here all alone when the delivery comes, I swear to God I will not open it before you get home. So who is this 'J.W. Faraday' chap?" he asks, saying Josh's name with a Queen-Elizabeth-British accent. "Sounds like a guy with a butler."

I plop down on the couch and Dax follows suit, settling himself right next to me. I grab his hand (something I've been doing ever since Mom brought him home from the hospital for the first time when I was four), and I lean my cheek against his strong shoulder.

"Joshua William Faraday," I breathe, my heart skipping a beat as I say the words.

"So you know each other's middle names, huh? Sounds serious, brah."

I don't reply. Dax is being flippant, I think—but his comment hits on the exact thing I can't stop wondering: Is this thing with Josh something serious or are we having some sort of extended fling?

"Hey, by the way," Dax says, "you'll probably wanna read this." He holds up a small sealed envelope. "It was inside the box."

I snatch the envelope from him, hyperventilating. Oh, thank God, it's still sealed.

"It pained me not to read it," Dax says. "It really did. But I figure there are some lines even I shouldn't cross, seeing as how you're my sister and all."

I tear open the envelope, pull out a typewritten note (taking great care to keep it out of Dax's line of sight), and read as fast as my eyes can manage:

"My Dearest Party Girl with a Hyphen," Josh's note says. "I hope you get lots and lots of enjoyment from your new toy. Please make use of it every day when I can't be there personally to make you scream. While you use it, I want you to imagine it's me who's fucking you, nice and slow, and whispering into your ear as I do about how amazing you feel, how dripping wet you are for me, and how much you turn me on."

Holy shitballs.

My breathing has suddenly become labored.

"Until we meet again," Josh continues in his note, "I want you to use your new toy every time you feel even the slightest bit horny or lonely. (Because even when I can't be with you in person, I'm determined to keep my hot-wired Party Girl with a Hyphen completely satisfied—wouldn't want her feeling even remotely tempted to fuck Cameron Schulz again, now would I?)

"I'm looking forward to seeing you again very soon and making each and every one of your (highly detailed) sexual fantasies come true. *Exclusively* yours, Playboy."

"Oh. My. God," I say breathlessly. My crotch is exploding with arousal in my panties and I'm panting like a Pekingese running a hundred-yard dash.

"What does it say?" Dax asks.

I press the note against my chest. "It says, 'It's none of your frickin' business, Dax Morgan.'"

"Aw, come on."

"No way."

He makes a wry face. "So what's the status with you two—are you in a relationship or... ?"

"I have no freaking idea what our status is. Whatever we're doing defies standard labeling."

"The guy sends you a fifteen-hundred-dollar gift and you don't know the status? That's a lot of money to spend on a gift for some chick you're just hanging out with."

I shrug. "It's hard to explain."

"Are you at least dating?"

I sigh. "Yeah. I think so. I mean we've both made it clear we're really into each other. But I don't know where things are headed—he gets really skittish the minute he feels like he's being penned in. But on the other hand we agreed to be exclusive."

"You're exclusive? Well, then it's way beyond dating."

I sigh. "One would think. But we're exclusive only temporarily. It's hard to explain."

"*Temporarily* exclusive? That's a new one. I gotta steal that."

"It was me who suggested it."

He flashes me a look that says, "You're an idiot."

I rub my face. "This week was just a unique set of circumstances. We were together day and night, doing this crazy thing to help Sarah, and it was this incredible, fairytale existence. It's like we were in the fantasy suite on *The Bachelor* for an entire week—and my feelings for him were so freaking intense and surreal—and now it's like the show is over and the cameras are off and it's back-to-reality time."

Dax nods.

I shake my head. "I just don't know if what we felt in Vegas will translate to real life. Plus, he lives in L.A. and travels a ton and I'm here, obviously. So, I dunno, it might be kinda tough to keep the fantasy alive."

Dax motions to the Sybian. "Looks like he's giving it the ol' college try."

I bite my lip to suppress a huge smile.

"I must say, giving you a Sybian as a gift is an interesting choice—he could have gone with shoes or a purse."

"Oh, he did. Both."

"And you still don't know if he's serious about you? I think you might be overanalyzing things here. The guy's making his feelings pretty clear."

I sigh. "I don't wanna get my hopes up."

"This is so unlike you. Why are you being so...?"

"Analytical?"

"Annoying."

I make a face. "I don't know. Josh and I are just so incredibly..." I was about to say *sexual*, but then I remember I'm talking to my little brother, not to Sarah. "*Physical*," I say, opting for a tamer word to finish my sentence. "The physical chemistry is so off the charts, it makes me wonder if I'm just in some sort of hormone-induced coma and not seeing things clearly."

"Just because you have incredible physical chemistry with the guy doesn't mean it's not serious, too," he says.

"So I've heard. But from what I've seen personally, at least as an adult, it's one or the other."

He pulls back and looks at me, stupefied. "Are you serious?" he asks.

I nod.

"Jizz, that's fucked up. How'd you get so fucked up?"

I shrug.

"You can have off-the-charts physical chemistry without it being 'serious,' for sure—and thank God for that." He snickers. "But it doesn't work the other way around: you absolutely *cannot* have something serious if you don't have physical chemistry. The fact that you think it's one or the other is so fucked up, it's pathetic. It's like you've got a... what's the word I'm looking for... that complex thing?"

I make a face. "A Madonna-whore complex?"

"Exactly. Only in reverse. What's it called when a woman thinks that about a guy?"

"A Jesus-manwhore complex?"

We both laugh.

"Yeah, I don't think society has a cute little phrase for when it's a guy."

"What about that Nate guy?" Dax asks. "You guys were pretty serious, right?"

"Serious, yes, but we were sort of blah in the physical department," I say. "At least it was blah for me."

"Ooph. I think maybe you *do* have a Madonna-whore complex when it comes to guys, sis, whatever it's called—like you somehow think the guys who turn you on the most can't possibly be boyfriend material."

I make a face. He might have a point there. Hmm.

"But that's the whole point of this grand experiment we call life—finding the serious stuff *and* the physical stuff all rolled up together into one fucking awesome person."

"How'd you get so deep at such a tender age?" I ask.

Dax grabs my hand and kisses it, a move that instantly makes me think of Josh.

"That's not even a remotely deep thing to say, sis," Dax says. "It's pretty fucking basic. I think maybe you're just particularly stupid when it comes to relationships."

I know Dax is kidding, sort of, but I think he might be on to something here —I think I might very well be particularly stupid when it comes to relationships involving me. "I think when the sex is crazy-good-off-the-charts with a guy, it makes me kinda skittish in a twisted way," I say. "Like I think things are too good to be true—and then I start shutting down emotionally to protect myself and the whole thing becomes a self-fulfilling prophecy."

Dax squeezes my hand but doesn't reply.

"The thing is, with this guy Josh, the physical part is so freaking good, he could be Jeffrey Dahmer and I'd be like, 'Oh, em, gee, Jeff, you're such a sweetheart!'"

Dax laughs.

"And that scares me. I feel like I might have a huge blind spot. But on top of that, horror of horrors, he's funny and sweet and generous, too, and he makes me feel really special." I shake my head. "I guess I'm just trying to figure out if he's really as perfect as he seems? Or if this is just too good to be true."

"Well, have you seen any chopped up body parts in his freezer?"

"No, but I haven't been to his house yet. Stay tuned."

"He lives in L.A.?"

I nod.

"What does he do?"

"He runs some sort of investment company with his brother and uncle. Other than that, he climbs rocks with his brother and parties with rock stars and supermodels. Get this: he used to date Gabrielle LeMonde's daughter."

"Seriously?"

"Yeah, and that model that's on all the Victoria's Secret commercials—Bridgette something—the blonde with the perfect body? Her, too."

"Bridgette *Schmidt*," Dax says reverently. "Oh my God. She's my top desert-island pick. Your guy dated *her*? Wow."

"Well, actually, come to think of it, I don't know if he *dated* her, but he certainly *did* her."

"Damn, who the fuck is this guy? Jesus. I guess he's a major playah-playah, huh? Maybe that's the 'not-so-perfect' thing you're afraid is lurking in the shadows of his tormented soul."

I sigh. "He's not as big a playah-playah as he sounds. I mean, don't get me wrong, he definitely likes having sex with gorgeous women—when Josh Faraday is single, he's apparently *very* single—but I don't think he's as much of a playboy as I initially thought. He had this long-term girlfriend he was really devoted to... " I shrug. "But, then again, he had a heart attack on the phone just now when he thought I was trying to pin him down to something beyond next week." I roll my eyes and lean my head back onto the back of the couch. "Aw, shit, I dunno, Dax. I need to just chill the fuck out and stop overanalyzing things. I'm acting like a chick."

"You totally are. I've never seen you act like this. You know what you need to do?" Dax says. "Tap into your inner Peen. That'll cure your chickiness right up."

"Nobody should ever tap into their inner Peen," I say. "Even Peen should stop tapping into his inner Peen."

We both have a good laugh about that.

"So why did this Faraday guy send you a fucking Sybian?" Dax asks. "Did you lose a bunch of money to him in a high-stakes poker game and now you've gotta do porn to pay off your debt?"

"He's not a porn king, Dax. Gimme some credit. He's this—I don't even know what he does, actually. Google him. His company is called Faraday & Sons—Joshua Faraday."

Dax pulls out his phone and Googles while I talk.

"It's some sort of investment thing. He travels all the time, looking at potential companies to buy—I don't even know what he does. He never talks about it."

"Oh, wow," Dax says. He's found the homepage of Faraday & Sons. "Were these guys genetically engineered by Monsanto or what? Which one is your guy?"

"The one with the dark hair. The other guy's his fraternal twin brother, Jonas—Sarah's new boyfriend, actually."

"Whoa, Sarah's dating Thor?"

"Yeah. And he adores her. I've never seen two people more into each other in all my life."

"Aw, good for her." He scrutinizes the photo for a long beat. "Well, now I can see why you're feeling a tad bit confused. I'm completely straight and I'd do him, especially if he bought me a dress and shoes and a Sybian."

I laugh.

Dax continues scrutinizing the photo. "He's exactly your type, only the best-looking version of it I've ever seen. He looks a lot like that football-player dude you dated in high school."

I shrug. "Yeah, I know. I guess I've got a type."

"What was his name again?"

"Kade."

"That's right. He looks like he could be Kade's older, better-looking brother." Dax looks up from the phone and appraises me with sympathetic eyes. "Poor, Jizz. I don't know how any woman could figure out if she had actual feelings around this guy. He must leave a wake of exploded ovaries wherever he goes."

"Exactly," I say. "I told you—the dude could keep a severed head in his fridge and I'd totally reach behind it to get myself a Diet Coke while giggling at something he just said."

Dax laughs and looks at his phone again. "Yeah, both of 'em are just stupid-good-looking. It's like God fell asleep at the 'good looking' switch and didn't move on to the next guy on the conveyor belt like he was supposed to."

"And I just spent a week with him in freaking *Las Vegas* of all places—and all expenses paid, too. No wonder I can't distinguish fantasy from reality. The whole thing was like a fairytale."

"Snow White and the Seven Sybians."

"How the hell do you even know what a Sybian is, by the way?"

He scoffs. "Dude, I'm twenty and I'm a guy," he says, as if this answers my question.

I shrug.

"Every twenty-something-year-old male in America knows what a Sybian is —it's a porn staple. Howard Stern even has one in his studio for female guests to ride. It's, like, Porn 101."

"Really? I had no idea. I'd never even heard of one 'til last week."

"Well, are you a twenty-something-year-old male?"

"Not the last time I checked."

"And do you watch a shit-ton of porn?"

"Never."

"Well, there you go. Now you know why you discovered the Sybian for the first time while watching porn with Sir J.W. Faraday."

I bite my lip. Dax has obviously misunderstood the circumstances under which Josh first acquainted me with my new toy—and, as far as I'm concerned, that's a very good thing. No one ever needs to know I rode that thing for Josh's pleasure—least of all my brother. "So, hey, that concludes the 'What Happens In Vegas Stays In Vegas' portion of our program," I say. "There's something that happened in Vegas I actually *want* to tell you about." I take a deep breath, a huge smile bursting across my face. "Guess who I partied with one crazy night while I was there?"

"Who?"

"All four members of Red Card Riot." I can barely keep from squealing.

"What?" he bellows, his face the picture of pure astonishment. "How the *fuck* did that happen?"

I tell him about that night at Reed's party, omitting certain key elements such as Jen's attendance at the party and my near-naked tantrum in the hallway (because I'm a big believer that editing one's life stories in the retelling is a girl's prerogative).

"Damn, I wish I could have been there," Dax says wistfully, shaking his head. "I would have *loved* to hang with those guys. Can you imagine what it would feel like to play for an entire *arena* of people, all of them singing along to a song you wrote?"

I shake my head, awed by the thought. "When I met them, they'd just performed on *Saturday Night Live* the prior week, and the lead-singer guy, Dean, started talking about it with this rapper guy and all I could think was, 'God, I wish Dax could hear this.'"

The look on Dax's face is so cute right now, I wanna throw him into a papoose and wear him on my back.

"You lucky bitch," he mumbles.

"It ain't no luck, son. I *make* my luck."

He laughs. "Yes, you do. Always."

"If RCR comes to Seattle, I'll totally ask Josh if his friend Reed might get us backstage—well, if Josh and I are still doing our 'temporarily-exclusive' thing by then, that is."

"Who's Reed? And why would he be able to get us backstage at a Red Card Riot concert?"

I smile. This is exactly the piece of the story I've been *dying* to tell Dax for days. "Reed's the guy who threw the party in Vegas where I met Red Card Riot."

"How does he know them?"

It's as if we choreographed this conversation in advance. "Well, let me see if I remember how he knows them," I say. "Hmm." I look up at the ceiling like I'm deep in thought. "I think Reed knows Red Card Riot because... *they're signed to his record label!*"

Dax tilts his head like he's not sure he heard me correctly.

I giggle. "Reed *owns* a record label, Dax. Like, he literally *owns it—and RCR is one of his bands.*"

Dax is looking at me like I've just proved time travel is real. "And you partied with him?" he asks, incredulous. "You partied with the owner of a record label?"

I nod, grinning from ear to ear. "*Twice.*" I hold up two fingers for emphasis.

Dax's thoughts are clearly racing. "So... oh my God. Does this Reed guy know your name or did you just sort of, you know, shake hands in a crowded bar?"

"No, we totally hung out. Had real conversations. He called me Stubborn Kat."

Dax makes a face of total confusion.

"They were all joking that Stubborn Kat is like some kind of *Garfield* rip-off. 'Oh no, Stubborn Kat ate all the curly fries and now she won't get off the couch!'" I say by way of explanation, but he still looks nonplussed. "Never mind. I just mean we totally hung out and became friends. I went to his party the first night and then out to dinner with him and his friends a second night."

Dax runs his hands through his hair, totally freaking out. "Listen to me, Jizz." His eyes are blazing. "This could be a really lucky break for me. *Fuck.* Oh my God." He bites his lip. "Do you think you could send this Reed guy my demo? Or would that make Sir J.W. Faraday feel like you're just using him to get to Reed?"

I laugh. "Um, there's no way in hell Josh would ever think I'm using him to get to Reed."

Dax's face lights up. "So you'll send him my demo?"

I sigh and shake my head solemnly. "Sorry, Dax. No. I don't feel comfortable sending Reed your demo. I'm sorry."

Dax is obviously crestfallen but trying to hide it. "It's okay," he says evenly. "Yeah, no problem. I totally understand. Sorry, I didn't mean to—"

"But only because that demo doesn't show how totally *awesome* you are!" I add brightly. "Only because we've got this one amazing chance to make an *awesome* first impression with the guy who owns Red Card Riot's record label and we're totally gonna blow him outta the water!"

He looks like I've punched him and kissed him all at once. "Yeah, but that demo's all I've got—at least for now. I'm working on it, but it's gonna be a while."

"How much do you still need?" I ask.

For as long as I can remember, Dax and his band (but mostly Dax) have been saving their pennies to record a full-length studio album of his songs with full instrumentation. But saving that kind of money—fifteen thousand bucks, he estimates, to record and produce the album exactly the way he wants it—is an awfully tall order for a group of twenty-something musicians living hand-to-mouth by playing bars and festivals.

"I had almost three thousand saved, but then my bike totally crapped out on me so I'm basically back to square one."

"So you still need about fifteen grand or so?"

"Well, we could certainly record an album for less if we cut some corners on production value. Or I guess we could just do a few songs instead of a full album—or maybe another basic demo." He puffs out his cheeks like a puffer fish, thinking. "But I really didn't wanna do another demo—been there done that—I wanted to put together a full album that showcases who we are and what we can do." He runs his hand through his hair. "Shit. Maybe I should just record a quick demo with my acoustic guitar on my iPad, just so you have something current to send to the guy before he forgets who you are—"

"Nope. We're not gonna send Reed a demo, Dax." I pull a thick envelope out of my purse and plop it onto the coffee table with a thud. "Because you're recording a full album."

"What's that?"

"Open it."

Dax opens the envelope and peeks inside. "Oh my... What the fuck is this? Did you rob a bank?"

I smirk. Oh, if only Dax knew how spot-on that comment is. I'd originally planned to use this wad of cash to pay off my credit cards and car, of course, but that was before I found out I'm gonna be a *mill-i-on-aire*.

"Where the fuck did you get this kind of cash?" Dax asks, his eyes wide.

"Playing craps," I say matter-of-factly. "That's almost twenty grand there, baby. Enough for whatever album you've been dreaming of making plus a bit extra for bells and whistles: strings, horns, a freaking choir—whatever. Or maybe PR for the album when you release it or a down payment on a new bike. *Whatever*. It's yours. Go forth and prosper."

"How the fuck did you win twenty grand playing *craps*?" Dax asks. "How is that even possible? You must have been betting, like, hundreds of bucks per roll—maybe even thousands."

"Yeah, well, Josh spotted me some gambling money and then his brother walked away from the table and gave me all his chips. So, actually, I didn't win any of this money fair and square. But Josh insisted I keep it, so whaddayagonnado?" I shrug. "And now it's yours."

"Wait a minute. The dude *gave* you *twenty* grand and you're not sure if he's *serious* about you? Are you mentally deficient?"

I wave him off. "No, trust me. You don't know Josh. Just because he's crazy-generous and he gave me an insane amount of money doesn't necessarily mean he wants a serious relationship with me. He has a warped sense of reality when it comes to money. The guy wears two-thousand-dollar shoes (which, true story, I barfed on one night). *He drives a frickin' Lamborghini, Dax.* The guy's not normal."

"Dude, I don't care how rich he is or what shoes he wears or what car he drives. If a guy gives a woman, especially a woman he's sleeping with, twenty grand, then he thinks she's one of two things: a *very* high-priced hooker or the woman of his dreams."

My heart skips a beat. Damn, my brother has a knack for hitting the nail right on the head sometimes.

Dax picks up the envelope and begins counting the hundred-dollar bills inside, shaking his head with awe as he does. When he's finally done counting, he looks up at me, his eyes glistening. "Thank you so much, Kat," he says. "I'll repay you one day, I swear to God, every last penny." His voice breaks adorably. "I'm gonna do everything in my power to make you proud of me, Kat."

I grin from ear-to-ear. It's so rare that Dax calls me Kat. With him, I'm always Jizz or sis (or Splooge or Protein Shake if he's feeling particularly silly). He must feel uniquely overcome right now to be addressing me by my real name.

"You never need to pay me back," I say. "It was never my money in the first place. And I'm already proud of you. All I want is for you to make the exact album you wanna make—no holding back."

He lurches at me and wraps me in a fervent hug. "I love you, Kat. You're my all-time favorite sister."

I laugh and kiss his cheek, my eyes stinging. "I love you, too. You're my all-time favorite baby brother."

We hold each other for a long beat.

"Now get the fuck out of my house, you mooch," I say, pulling away from our embrace and wiping my eyes. "I've got a thank-you email to write to our mutual benefactor, and then I've got a hot date with a certain piece of motor-ized machinery."

Dax laughs. "No shit, you do." He rubs his eyes. "Thanks so much, Kat. I'll never forget this as long as I live."

"I didn't do it so you'd owe me something. I did it because watching you make your dreams come true will be the same thing as making my own dream come true."

He wipes his eyes again. "I'll make you proud, sis."

"You already have."

There's a beat. We're smiling at each other like simpletons. I think this is one of the best moments of my life. Way better than if I'd received something amazing for myself.

"Now get the fuck out," I say. "You're cramping my style."

He kisses me on the cheek again, shoves his guitar into its case, scoops up his envelope full of cash, and strides toward my front door. But a few feet from the door, he stops short and looks down for a very long beat, his back still to me.

When Dax finally whirls around to face me, I'm expecting him to thank me again, or maybe say something deep and poignant—but that's not what happens.

"*You slept with Cameron Schulz?*" he blurts. "*The baseball player?*"

My eyes dart to the coffee table, searching frantically for Josh's note—but it's not where I left it. Goddammit!

Dax holds up Josh's card between his two fingers like he's holding a cigarette, a wicked smirk on his face.

"Get the fuck out of my house," I say evenly, pointing to the door.

Dax tosses the card onto my kitchen counter. "Wow, Jizz," he says smoothly. "You're my fucking hero, dude."

60

KAT

The minute the door closes behind Dax's back, I pull out my laptop from my carry-on bag, log in remotely to my firm's network, and check the shared calendar, trying to figure out when I can realistically commit to a trip to L.A. to see Josh.

Based on the workload I'm seeing on the firm's calendar, I seriously shouldn't go for at least a month. I was in Las Vegas way longer than I ever expected to be, and, based on what I'm seeing on my firm's calendar, my absence has quite obviously been felt. Dang it. If I'm gonna stay at this job, I really should take a chill pill on skipping town for a while. But am I gonna stay at this job or open my own firm in the near future? That's the million-dollar question. And if I *am* gonna start my own thing, then I suppose in good conscience I really shouldn't sit for too much longer on my company's payroll while I'm getting my own ducks in a row. Shoot. I've got some big-girl decisions to make.

I flip into my personal calendar, just to see if there's something requiring my attention here at home next week. Whoa. Today's the *eighteenth*? All this time, I've been thinking it was the seventeenth. I look up sharply from my screen. Wait. Did I miss taking a birth control pill somewhere along the line this past week?

I quickly rummage into my bag and pull out my pills. Oh crap. Yeah, I missed a day. Well, it's no wonder with the crazy hours Josh and I kept in Vegas. Who could keep track of day and night the way we were going?

Quickly, I pop one of my pills to make up for my lapse. It really shouldn't make that big a difference, right? It's just one day. In fact, I'm pretty sure the pill I missed was yesterday.

Okay, back to the calendar. It looks like I can head down to L.A. on Thursday of next week. But should I give notice at my job before I leave? Gah. I just don't know. It'd be a huge leap of faith. I'm conflicted.

I take a deep breath and click into my email account, poised to send Josh a quick email giving him my proposed dates and thanking him for his latest gift, when I think, "Hey, I should attach a photo of the Sybian to my thank-you email so Josh can see that it arrived."

I pull out my phone to snap a quick photo of the machine sitting in the middle of the room, but then I get an even better idea: "Hey, I should take a photo of *me* sitting on the Sybian, smiling happily for the camera."

One side of my mouth hitches up with an even better idea: "I should pose on the machine buck naked."

My smile widens. I'll send Josh a naked photo of myself as if I were one of the hookers in The Club.

Yes.

Surprisingly, I've never sent a man a naked-selfie before (mainly because my mom always put the fear of God into me that any naked photo I'd send, no matter how much I might trust the guy at the time, would eventually wind up on hotgirls.com after things went south in the relationship). But when it comes to Josh, I don't think for one minute he'd betray me, ever, come what may. Hey, if one of the world's top models trusts Josh with a photo of herself sticking her hand up her cooch, then surely, a non-celebrity like me can trust him, too.

I peel off my clothes, situate myself suggestively on the saddle of my new machine, raise my phone above my head, and snap a photo, giggling to myself as I do—and when I survey the resulting photo, I laugh out loud. Well, if I'm going for "treat me like one of the whores in The Club," then I've definitely succeeded with this shot.

I grab my laptop and sit on my couch, still completely nude, and begin writing an email with the photo attached:

"Dear Mr. Faraday," I write. "Thank you for your application to The Katherine Ulla Morgan Club, also known as the KUM Club, also known as the Fantasy Fulfillment Club. We have reviewed the sexual preferences you described in your application and have determined that you are, indeed, one helluva sick fuck, Mr. Faraday. But do not fret because, as it turns out, we absolutely adore sick fucks here at The KUM Club. In fact, lucky for you, our most sought-after girl at The KUM Club strongly prefers sick fucks above all other freaks and perverts—and guess what, you lucky bastard? She's a blonde!

"The fantasy-provider to whom I refer goes by many code names, including The Jealous Bitch and Madame Terrorist to name a few, but the code name she strongly prefers the most is Party Girl with a Hyphen (abbreviated herein as 'PGWH').

"As mentioned, PGWH is *by far* our most popular and coveted fantasy-provider. Wise and powerful men the world over, including sheiks, kings, politicians, and professional athletes (including Cameron Schulz, the shortstop for the Seattle Mariners!!!) clamor for this woman's valuable services. And it's no wonder: it is said PGWH can give a man a blowjob that will make him weep with joy like a newborn lamb.

"PGWH is very selective of her clients, but she has viewed your photos and determined she would be willing to bestow her remarkable talents upon you. If you desire this talented and coveted blonde woman's services (as every other wise and powerful man from around the globe does), then PGWH would be *very* excited to make your every fantasy come true. In fact, she'd like nothing better (as long as you pay her eminently reasonable fee, addressed below).

"Mr. Faraday, PGWH is the top fantasy-provider in the world. As I'm sure you can understand, a woman like that doesn't come cheap. Indeed, you'll have to pay handsomely to experience PGWH's charms: one *million* dollars per night.

"Perhaps you're thinking this price seems a tad high for one night of mind-blowing pleasure with the most sought-after call girl in the entire world (even for a *mill-i-on-aire* many times over such as yourself), but please rest assured PGWH is well worth this fee. In fact, we *guarantee* that by the end of your night with this woman, you'll declare, without the slightest reservation, 'You're worth every fucking penny, baby.'

"Considering your very specific requirements stated in your application, we've attached a photo of PGWH for your approval. We hope you'll find her to be a genuine Gucci bag among counterfeits sold on the sidewalks of New York —the 'divine original' of your blonde-girl fantasies.

"Assuming PGWH meets your approval, she's available to meet you in Los Angeles on Thursday the twenty-fifth for a long weekend. Please reply with details about your *rendezvous*, including the location of the hotel you've arranged, when and under what name she should pick up her room key, etc. (whatever types of details you supplied when arranging trysts during your month-long membership in the far inferior Mickey Mouse Roller Coaster Club).

"We cannot emphasize enough that PGWH wishes to experience what you've outlined in your application, exactly the way you've described it (because she's a high-end call girl, you might recall, and not just a woman who works at a PR firm going on a date with the hottest guy ever).

"So let's talk logistics. In your application, you requested fulfillment of two different fantasies. We are happy to inform you that, with just a few minor tweaks to your requests, PGWH is willing (and quite excited) to deliver both to you, on two separate nights of her stay in Los Angeles (which means, yes, this high-end call girl's gonna cost you a grand total of *two* million bucks). So let's talk about those minor tweaks:

"Regarding your first scenario, PGWH agrees to be part of the two-woman scenario you've requested, but she's not game for both women to be naked when you first arrive to the hotel room. She might need a little coaxing to get the show on the road, so to speak, but she's confident a little alcohol and the sight of your gorgeous, turned-on face will be all that's necessary to give her a little nudge in the right direction. In the end, your fantasies are all that matter—she very much wants to deliver them to you.

"Also regarding your two-woman scenario, as previously agreed, you may touch yourself and PGWH, but you absolutely may not touch the 'other' woman. *Breach of this rule will be deemed unforgivable by PGWH and will result in her leaving the rendezvous immediately.* (If this amounts to 'sexual extortion' we're very sorry-not-sorry. It's just super-duper important to PGWH that you honor this request and never make PGWH feel like a third wheel. She wishes to be your window, not your window dressing. This is non-negotiable. Have we mentioned one of her code names is The Jealous Bitch?)

"If the foregoing revisions to the first scenario are agreeable to you, then our next step is to identify the 'window dressing' who'll be joining you and PGWH. Since you've graciously offered that PGWH may select whomever she chooses, we're happy to inform you of PGWH's selection: supermodel Bridgette Schmidt."

I take my hands off my keyboard and stare at the screen for a long moment.

Up 'til now, this email to Josh has poured out of me in a torrent of excitement—but now, my fingers have paused without my brain telling them to do it.

Am I really up for this? It's pretty kinky. Am I really gonna like kinky as much as I think I will—or am I merely turned on by the *idea* of kinky? And, besides that, when Josh and I first started "negotiating" this particular adventure, I made a big ol' stink that the woman we selected couldn't be someone either of us knows. But now that I've had a chance to think this through, I think Bridgette the Supermodel is the ideal candidate for the job.

First off, she's gorgeous. And since I'm the one who's gonna be making out with her, that's not a small point. Second, Bridgette is bisexual, at least according to Josh, which means the odds are good this won't be her first time making out with a girl—and, hopefully, she'll be more enthusiastic about fooling around with me than my straight friend in college (because that was kind of lame in retrospect). Third—and this is a biggie—Bridgette's a huge celebrity, which means she's not gonna take secret photos and sell them to TMZ.

All these reasons are pretty persuasive to me—and yet there's an even bigger reason to select Bridgette as my co-star in this particular mini-porno: Josh said Bridgette's got "battery acid in her heart."

Well, winner, winner, chicken dinner. Give that girl a salami. Because if I'm gonna voluntarily bring a beautiful, naked, blonde woman into the bedroom with a man I want for my very own—a man I've been fantasizing about taking home to meet my family—a man who makes my claws come out and jealousy rise up from my darkest bowels when I even *think* about him with another woman—then I'm sure as hell gonna make double-damn-sure that woman's not gonna have a snowball's chance in hell of stealing my man out from under me.

I take a long, deep breath and close my eyes.

Oh my, I seem to be feeling a tad bit psychotic right now.

I take a deep breath and shake it off.

And there's another reason to select Bridgette too—a very, very good reason that might be a tad bit self-sabotaging (but, oh well, that simply can't be helped): I want to see if Josh is full of shit or not. He says I'm more beautiful than Bridgette Effing Schmidt, one of the world's most beautiful women? Well, let's see if Josh is able to walk the walk of that particular smooth-talk. Will he be able to keep his hands off Bridgette when push comes to shove? Or will he find her jaw-dropping physical beauty too powerful to resist, no matter how much he feels for me?

Obviously, I might be making a huge mistake by doing this—setting myself up for epic heartbreak. Actually, come to think of it, this might be the stupidest idea I've ever had in my entire life, possibly even dumber than the idea of surprising Garrett at his apartment wearing nothing but a trench coat. But, hey, I've got to look at the big picture here: if Josh is ultimately gonna shatter my heart, I'd rather know it now than when my heart is totally on the line.

I place my hands on my keyboard again and continue typing:

"After explaining the firm no-touch rule to Bridgette, please invite her to join us during one of the nights of PGWH's stay in Los Angeles (whichever night she can make it—we'll work around her schedule).

"And now regarding the second scenario detailed in your application, which we'll call 'Saving the Girl.' Do you think it'd be possible to combine this fantasy of yours with one of PGWH's biggest fantasies, already detailed at length for you, in which she's held captive by a dangerous man? Just let us know. During this trip, fulfillment of *your* fantasies is paramount, so if simultaneously fulfilling PGWH's fantasy would somehow lessen your pleasure, we'll be very happy to fulfill PGWH's fantasy a different time.

"Well, that's about it. We look forward to serving you, Mr. Faraday. Why? Because we here at The KUM Club sure do love a good sick fuck!"

My heart stops. Oh my God, I absolutely cannot phrase that last sentence that way. Jesus God, am I mad? Quickly, I delete the last sentence and rephrase it:

"Why? Because we here at The KUM Club sure do enjoy ourselves a good sick fuck!"

Damn. That was a close call. I'm careening out of control here. Jeez. I can't drop the 'L' word like that, even as a snarky figure of speech.

"Exclusively yours," I continue writing, "The KUM Club.

"P.S. PGWH wishes to thank you profusely for your latest extremely generous gift (in a long line of generous gifts)—even though it will surely prevent PGWH from ever leaving her house again (unless it's to see you, of course). Whenever PGWH uses your gift, rest assured she'll imagine she's getting splendidly fucked by you. Certainly, with every orgasm (and there will surely be many), she'll moan your name."

My fingers leave my keyboard. I stare at the screen, my skin electrified, my crotch burning, my heart aching. Try as I might, I simply can't keep myself from falling head-over-heels for this man. The only question now is whether he wants me the way I want him. I know Josh wants me sexually, but does he want the rest of me, too? I'm simultaneously excited and nervous to find out.

I read my email once through, take a deep breath, and press send.

61

JOSH

I slam my laptop shut.

Holy fuck.

Madame Terrorist strikes again.

I glance furtively at the guy seated next to me on the plane. He's working on his laptop, completely oblivious to the naked photo of Kat that just melted my motherfucking screen. For a long moment, I look around at the other passengers in my immediate vicinity, my heart raging, my cheeks burning, my cock twitching in my pants.

I've seen my share of naked-blonde-woman-photos before now, of course, but my body's never reacted quite like this to any of them. Holy fuck, I feel like I just mainlined a cocktail of Ecstasy and Viagra. You'd think I was thirteen and sneaking my dad's stash of porno-mags the way my body's reacting to this photo of Kat.

But it's not just Kat's tits and ass making my dick so hard—it's how much of Kat's personality comes through in the shot. There's a devilish smile on her lips that tells me she was as turned on snapping this photo as I am looking at it, and, shit, there's a glint in her eye that says, "I got you right where I want you, chump," too. The woman slays me.

I can't believe Kat gave this photo to me, no coaxing required. I had to *beg* Emma to let me snap one measly naked shot of her for my birthday last year, and now Kat's sending me this for no other reason than she likes getting me hard? She's incredible.

What did Kat say after Sarah sent that naked photo of herself to Max and Oksana? *"No matter how smart or powerful a guy might be, he's got the same Kryptonite as every other man throughout history—naked boobs."* I close my eyes for a long beat, shaking my head. God, I hate proving Kat right, I really do, just on principle—but there's no way around it: Kat's naked boobs just flat-out stripped me of whatever superpowers I might have had.

And yet her naked boobs didn't come close to slaying me the way her naked words did. I already knew she was a terrorist, but now I know she's a fucking ninja with words, too.

I made fun of Jonas pretty relentlessly for the way he went ballistic over Sarah's anonymous email, sight unseen, but now I get it. Shit, I might even owe Jonas an apology for the way I gave him shit about that. If Sarah's note was even half as clever and sexy and hot as Kat's, then it's no wonder Jonas fell so hard for—

I jerk my head up from my screen, my heart suddenly rising into my throat. Did I just compare Kat and me to Jonas and Sarah? My chest tightens. I hear my pulse in my ears.

Yeah, I did.

I close my laptop, unlatch my seatbelt, and walk quickly into the bathroom, my head reeling. Once there, I latch the door with shaking hands, splash cold water on my face and rock-hard dick (because the idea of wacking off in an airplane bathroom is too gross even for me) and then I stare at myself in the mirror.

"Just breathe," I say to myself out loud. Shit, I look like Jonas right now. "Don't overthink it, bro. Just stay in the moment. Chill the fuck out."

But the blue eyes staring back at me won't be soothed.

How do you know? I asked Jonas.

I just know, he said.

I look at myself in the mirror for another long beat, water dripping down my cheeks and off the tip of my nose.

"She's your Kryptonite, man," I finally say to my reflection. "You're totally fucked, Superman."

62

JOSH

"Checking in, sir?" the valet attendant asks as he opens my car door.

"Yeah."

"Need assistance with any bags?"

"Nope." I hold up my car keys and a one-hundred-dollar bill. "No cars parked on either side of it."

"Yes, sir." The attendant grabs my keys and the C-note out of my hand. "I'll make sure of it."

"Bring it back with no dings in the doors and I've got another hundred for you."

"Thank you, sir. You got it."

I grab the small duffel bag on my passenger seat, straighten my tie, and stride toward the front of the hotel. Holy fuck, I can't remember the last time I was this eager to see a woman. Okay, fine, I'm full of shit—I've never been this eager to see a woman, ever, and I know it.

This whole past week, even though I've been absolutely swamped with work hammering out the transition strategy for Jonas and me from Faraday & Sons, I've nonetheless managed to continuously count the minutes to seeing Kat again. When I haven't been working, the only way I've been able to prevent my mind from spiraling into some sort of Jonas-style obsession, has been to keep myself constantly busy. I've gone to the gym and worked out like a motherfucker every night this week, followed by going home to my empty house and distracting myself with one of four go-to activities (all of which I performed while lying naked in my bed): 1) strategizing about how I'm gonna deliver on Kat's crazy-ass (but awesome) fantasies; 2) reading one of the sex-books Jonas sent me (fantastic reading, I must say—I owe my brother a huge 'thank you'); 3) chatting with Kat on the phone (or on FaceTime); and 4) jerking off, an activity which, quite frequently, overlapped with activities one, two and three (but mostly activity three).

A doorman holds open the heavy glass doors of the hotel and tips his hat to me as I enter the building. "Good evening, sir. Welcome to The Four Seasons Beverly Hills."

"Thanks," I say, gliding into the expansive lobby.

Yeah, Kat and I had some pretty fucking amazing phone- and video-chat-sex this past week, that's for sure, including two separate times when she let me watch her turn herself inside-out with pleasure while riding her new toy. But we also just *talked* a whole lot, too, about anything and everything, for hours and hours every single night—and it was *awesome*.

In one conversation, Kat told me a thousand hilarious stories about her family, and I laughed 'til my stomach hurt. Damn, she's got a fierce and funny family—and, man, do they look out for each other. When I found out Kat gave her craps winnings to her little brother so he could record an album with his band, I instantly felt this weird sense of *relief* more than anything else—relief that I'll never have to explain or defend my bond with Jonas. Clearly, the girl already completely understands what it means to put someone else's needs above your own.

I reach the check-in counter in the lobby and stand in line behind an old white guy accompanied by a much younger (and absolutely beautiful) Asian woman.

"I'll be right with you," the clerk says to the couple standing in front of me in line, looking up from assisting a family of five with their check-in. I nod curtly, just in case she was directing her comment to me, too, and then let my thoughts quickly drift to Kat again.

"Michelangelo was the coolest one," Kat insisted during one of our many conversations this past week.

"How can you use the word 'cool' in reference to the Teenage Mutant Ninja Turtles?" I asked.

"Oh, come on. You know you watched them," she chided me.

"Yeah, I *watched* them," I said, laughing. "But I never thought they were *cool*."

"Honesty-game," she said.

I exhaled. "Damn, that fucking game. Okay, yes. I thought Raphael was dope."

I smile to myself at the memory and look at my watch. The woman working behind the check-in counter is still helping that goddamned family of five and the couple's three young children are bouncing off the walls.

"Jeremy?" the clerk yells over her shoulder toward an open door behind the front desk. "Are you available to assist, please? *Jeremy?*"

But Jeremy must be off smoking a bowl because no one walks through that open door. It's just the one poor clerk behind the counter, and the line is growing behind me.

As I wait, my mind drifts to Kat again, the way it has all week long. *Kat.* She's upstairs right now, soaking her panties at the thought of being treated like Julia Roberts in *Pretty Woman*. *Kat.* What the fuck? *Kat, Kat, Kat.* That's all my brain is capable of thinking about anymore. I smile to myself. *Kat.*

I broke down and told Kat every little thing about our plans for Climb & Conquer this week, even though I'd planned to tell her about it in person. I was naked in my bed, listening to her sexy voice and feeling particularly relaxed after some pretty damned good phone sex, and everything just spilled out of me. Well, not *everything*. I didn't tell her about the fact that, since Climb & Conquer will be headquartered in Seattle, I'll finally be moving back home in a couple months. I was tempted to mention it several times, but I stopped myself. I mean, shit, God only knows where things will stand between Kat and me in a couple days, let alone a couple months. Why set her up for some kind of disappointment if things don't work out? All I can do is take it a day at a time and see where things lead, right?

The family of five bounces away from the front desk and the old-guy-Asian-woman-couple in front of me steps up to the desk.

"I'm so sorry for the wait, sir," the hotel clerk says to the old guy, and then her eyes drift apologetically to me. "I'll be with you shortly, sir."

I put my hand up to signal it's all good and the clerk smiles gratefully. The minute she looks away, though, I look at my watch impatiently. Kat's in this building *right now,* wetting herself at the thought of me treating her like my whore tonight, and I'm standing here, growing gray hair. Fuck, fuck, fuck. I seriously can't wait to see Kat.

Kat.

During another conversation this week—and God only knows how we got on the topic—Kat and I talked about what we believe happens to a person's soul after death—which led to a discussion about spirituality versus religion—a topic I'd normally avoid like the plague with anyone but Jonas (that's what years of Catholic school will do to a guy). But with Kat, the whole conversation flowed easily and naturally.

"What the hell is wrong with you, Josh?" Kat blurted at one point during our discussion about spirituality, shocking the hell out of me.

"What?" I asked, worried I'd offended her with my frank honesty on the topic.

"You're not supposed to be the deep-thinking Faraday brother. Pull yourself together, Playboy—you've got a shallow rep to live up to."

"Sorry," I replied, laughing. "It won't happen again."

The old-guy-Asian-girlfriend-couple in front of me *finally* steps away from the front desk, and I step forward.

"Checking in?" the hotel clerk asks. She looks totally frazzled.

"Yes. Joshua Faraday. My guests should have already checked into the room." I hand her my identification and credit card. "I arranged in advance for my guests to access the room before my check-in."

The woman clicks her keyboard for a brief moment. "Oh, yes, *of course,* Mr. Faraday." She suddenly looks stricken. "I'm *so* sorry to have kept you waiting in line. Oh my gosh. *Please* forgive me."

"No problem," I say smoothly, flashing her a smile.

"Let me send you a complimentary bottle of champagne to your suite to make up for the delay."

"Thank you, but, no, I'd prefer no interruptions tonight."

She blushes. "Oh. Of course." She clears her throat. "Uh, looks like your guests have already checked into the suite with no problem—it's the penthouse, as you know—and all catering and amenities requested have already been sent up."

"Excellent," I say, my heart clanging with anticipation. "The bar is stocked with Gran Patron, right?"

"Um, actually, it looks like they brought *Roca* Patron to the suite. Is that acceptable to you?"

"Yes, fabulous. Either one. Thank you."

The desk clerk smiles at me and, suddenly, I'm overwhelmed with a crazy feeling of *déjà fucking vu.* How many times have I checked into a hotel while my "guests" awaited me upstairs, an odd mixture of sexual anticipation and self-loathing coursing through my veins? And yet, today feels totally different than all those other times in The Club. Today, for the first time ever, I feel only sexual *anticipation* pumping through me, not tainted whatsoever by rampant self-loathing. Because today, unlike all the times that have come before, the hottest woman alive is waiting for me upstairs, not some random hooker I don't know or give a shit about—and not only is she hot, she's sweet and funny and smart, too. *And* in a twist of awesomeness I never could have predicted (or even hoped for), the hottest woman alive doesn't give a shit if I'm a sick fuck. In fact, she actually *likes* my sick-fuckedness. It's an incredible feeling.

The clerk hands me my key-card. "Do you know how to get to the penthouse suite, Mr. Faraday?"

"I sure do," I say. "Thanks."

I head toward the elevator bank at the far end of the lobby. My heart's beating wildly. Holy shit, I'm gonna see Kat in a matter of minutes.

Kat.

I would have preferred to personally pick Kat up from the airport this afternoon and bring her to my house for our first night together, rather than meeting her here at the hotel—I hate that I haven't even had a chance to hug her and say hello to her yet, just me and her—and I told Kat as much on the phone last night. But my little terrorist insisted we jump right into fantasy-fulfillment, first thing, before seeing each other in "real life."

"First off, we don't have a choice in the matter," she said. "Bridgette's only gonna be in L.A. Thursday night, right?"

"Yeah, but we don't have to do the Bridgette thing this trip," I said. "We can do it during your next trip."

"No, we gotta do it," Kat insisted. "We're kicking off our fantasy-fulfillment extravaganza with the stuff in your application, no ifs, ands, or buts about it. So that means whenever Bridgette can fit us in, that's when we gotta do it. Plus," she continued, "I wouldn't want to come to your house the first night, anyway, babe. That wouldn't be very call-girlish, now would it?" I could practically hear her licking her lips at that last statement. "Not seeing you beforehand will make me feel even more like a call girl. It's perfect."

The elevator reaches the top floor and I practically sprint down the long hallway toward the room, grinning from ear to ear. Kat talked a good game about wanting to fulfill *my* fantasies during this trip, but it wasn't hard to figure out she was actually chomping at the bit to fulfill her own high-priced-call-girl fantasy. When I texted Kat this afternoon to find out if she'd landed safely and connected with the driver I'd sent, she sent me a reply that made me laugh out loud:

"How the heck did you get my phone number, sir? My name isn't Kat, it's Heidi Kumquat (though, in light of my profession, I never reveal my real name). I'm a world-class call girl, sir, sought after by sheiks, kings, and presidents, working under the code name Party Girl with the Hyphen. I've just landed (safely) in Los Angeles to meet a very sexy but incredibly demanding client (whom I'd very much like to thank for flying me first-class, by the way), and, yes, his driver picked me up exactly according to plan (thank you!), and now I'm headed to my client's ritzy hotel.

"Please don't text me again, sir. My client has paid a pretty penny to have my undivided attention for the whole night, starting RIGHT THIS VERY MINUTE, and he'd be positively enraged if he found out I was texting with another man during *his* purchased time. I've been bought and paid for tonight, mind, body, and soul—which means I'm duty-bound to think of absolutely nothing but fulfilling my client's sexual desires all night long, LITERALLY NO MATTER WHAT THEY ARE, and that's exactly what I'm going to do."

I must say, that was a sexy goddamned text. If there's one thing Kat Morgan knows how to do, it's turn a man on.

I've reached the door to the penthouse suite.

Oh my God, I've got so much adrenaline coursing through me, I'm shaking.

I take a deep breath and rap twice on the door to signal I'm here and coming in, exactly the way I did before entering each new hotel room during my month in The Club—and just like I said I'd do when I replied to Kat's awesome email from "The KUM Club." And then I swipe the key and open the door.

63

JOSH

When I enter the suite, I stop just inside the door, paralyzed by the incomprehensible sight of Kat and Bridgette in the same room together. Talk about two worlds colliding. My brain can't process what I'm seeing—though, apparently, my body sure can. Hello, instant hard-on.

The women are sitting in side-by-side armchairs, sipping what looks like cranberry-vodkas, giggling happily like they're longtime friends. Kat looks like a million bucks (appropriately) in the Prada dress and heels I bought her in Las Vegas, her long, toned legs crossed demurely, while Bridgette's wearing a simple black tank top, jeans, and flip-flops, her blonde hair tied into a knot on top of her gorgeous head, her legs spread like she's a dude talking football in a sports bar. Talk about two women monopolizing the entire planet's supply of physical perfection all at once. Holy motherfucking shit. Seeing these two women together would almost certainly make a weaker man stroke-out.

"Kat," I blurt, my heart leaping out of my chest. I begin crossing the room to greet her, to take her into my arms and kiss the holy motherfucking shit out of her—has it only been a week since I last saw her, because it feels like a year?—but Kat puts up her hand sharply and shoots me a smoldering look that stops me dead in my tracks.

"So nice to finally meet you, Mr. Faraday," she says smoothly.

Oh, so it's gonna be like that, huh? I come to a complete halt.

"You're even handsomer than in your photos," she purrs. She sits up straight, arches her back, and folds her hands primly in her lap.

"So are you," I say. My heart is pounding in my ears.

One side of Kat's mouth hitches up into a devious smirk, and, suddenly, I feel like a fly in a spider's web. I thought we were here to fulfill *my* sick-fuck fantasy—so why do I suddenly feel like I'm merely a pawn in fulfilling hers?

"Let me introduce you to my friend, Frieda Fucks-A-Lot," Kat says. She motions to Bridgette who takes that as her cue to pop up and waltz toward me.

Frieda Fucks-A-Lot?

"Hey there, Mr. Faraday," Bridgette coos in her clipped English, outstretching her arms to me as she approaches.

I take a step back, but Bridgette continues advancing on me. She lays her hand on my shoulder and leans forward as if to kiss my cheek and I jerk back like Bridgette's hair is on fire. I promised Kat I wouldn't lay a finger on the "window dressing" of our threesome, whoever that turned out to be, and there's no way in hell I'm gonna risk making my temperamental "window" beeline out of yet another hotel suite and stomp down yet another hallway in a jealous huff.

But my anxiety about Bridgette touching me and bringing out the terrorist in Kat is all in vain, apparently: Kat's all charm and ease on the far side of the room, throwing her head back and giggling. "Oh, come on, Mr. Faraday," she says. "You can give Frieda a little kiss on her cheek in greeting. *Of course* that's allowed."

Bridgette turns around to look at Kat and the two women break into peals of laughter.

What the hell? How'd these two become besties so fucking fast? And why the hell is Kat acting like Bridgette's in on our game? Bridgette's not a *player* in our fantasy—she's nothing but a fucking pawn.

Bridgette hugs me and kisses me on both cheeks, but when she does, I recoil at her touch. I want absolutely nothing to do with her. The only person I wanna touch right now is Kat; specifically, I wanna rip Kat's clothes off and fuck the shit out of her—it's what I've been fantasizing about doing night and day all week long—not sitting in a chair in a corner, jerking off while watching someone else touch and kiss and lick my girl. In fact, the thought of Bridgette—or *anyone*—laying a fucking finger on my Party Girl with a Hyphen makes my stomach turn over.

"Hey, asshole," Bridgette says, swatting my shoulder. "You didn't tell me your girlfriend was *this* gorgeous." She motions to Kat. "I was just telling Kat —*Heidi Kumquat*"—she giggles and Kat joins her—"if she ever wants to try modeling, she could make an absolute *killing*. Look at that bone structure! Those legs! That skin! Oh my God, she's to die for. I can't wait to take a juicy bite out of her." She licks her lips.

Kat told Bridgette she's "Heidi Kumquat" for the night? So does that mean Kat's told Bridgette *everything* about our little game? Because when I called Bridgette and invited her to our little party, I certainly didn't. I merely asked Bridgette if she'd come hang out with me and this gorgeous girl I'm seeing, maybe make out with the girl while I watched and wacked off if things were to go in that direction (something I knew would be right up Bridgette's alley)—but I certainly didn't mention Kat being my high-priced call girl. What have these two been talking about for the last few hours before my arrival?

Kat's looking at me with hard eyes, though her mouth is smiling. Jesus. She looks like she's plotting my murder. Literally.

"No, seriously, hon," Bridgette continues, sounding remarkably sincere, "I'll hook you up with a photographer-friend of mine so you can get a kick-ass portfolio together. My agent will crap her pants when she sees you—I'm sure she could get you booked solid, if that's something you're interested in."

"Aw, thanks," Kat purrs, her smoldering gaze still fixed on me. "You're a doll, Bridgette." Her eyes flash. "I mean *Frieda*." She smirks. "I've got your number—I'll definitely give you a call. Thanks so much."

What the fuck? Why did Kat and Bridgette exchange numbers? What could possibly be the point in that?

"Why aren't you sitting, Mr. Faraday?" Kat says, motioning to a chair in the corner. "Please, make yourself comfortable. Frieda and I are both excited to *entertain* you."

I don't move. My brain and body are at odds. I know my role and what I'm supposed to do—what I should be *wanting* to do—but all my body yearns to do is kiss Kat. I haven't seen her in a week and I'm physically aching for her.

Bridgette claps her hands together. "Okay, *lieblinge*, let's start the fun, hmm? You want a drink, Faraday?" She glides toward the bar. "A shot of Patron, I presume?"

Kat levels me with a smoldering stare as she speaks to Bridgette. "Great idea. Would you be a doll and pour me a shot, too? I could use a little liquid courage."

"Aw, of course, *häschen*. Don't be nervous. I'll be gentle." She flashes Kat a brazenly sexual look. "I won't bite you *too* hard." She grabs a bottle behind the bar and begins pouring.

I still haven't moved from my spot just inside the door. I'm leaping out of my skin. Why do I feel like Kat's doing this to make me jealous, rather than to turn me on? And why the fuck is it working?

"Why don't you make those shots doubles?" Kat says to Bridgette. She winks at me and begins gliding toward a couch across the room from my assigned chair, unbuttoning her dress slowly as she goes.

"You got it," Bridgette coos.

Oh shit. I feel like I'm gonna explode. I'm shaking.

I want her.

I look at Bridgette behind the bar. I have no desire to touch any part of her —and certainly no desire to watch her kiss and stroke and lick my girl, either. If anyone's gonna do any of that stuff to Kat right now, it's sure as hell gonna be me.

Fuck this shit.

I march across the room to Kat, thwarting her progress toward the couch, and before she can say or do another goddamned thing, take her into my arms and maul her. My lips are on hers, my hands in her hair, my hard-on pressed into her crotch. Without hesitation, she presses herself into me, throws her arms around my neck, and returns my kiss voraciously.

"Aw, come on—party foul," Bridgette shouts from the bar. "It took all my restraint not to make a move on your girl 'til you got here, Josh. Kat said we had to wait and I've been—"

"We'll be back," I bark, grabbing Kat's hand and pulling her forcefully toward the bedroom. "Come on, babe. Fuck this shit."

The second Kat and I are alone in the bedroom with the door closed behind us, I fucking attack her. "Oh my God," I murmur into her lips. Jesus God, I'm drowning in her—losing my equilibrium. The smell of her. The taste of her lips. I'd forgotten how addicting she is. My dick hurts. My heart is racing. I want her so bad, I'm in pain. I'm dying to taste her pussy on my tongue, feel her tight wetness surrounding my cock, hear her make the sound like I've pricked her ass with a long needle. "Oh my God, Kat. I've missed you, babe."

"I'm not Kat—I'm a hooker from The Club," she breathes into my lips, but it's clear she's so turned on, she can barely stand.

I begin unbuttoning her dress, but my fingers aren't functioning. "I'll call you whatever you want, just as long as I'm saying it while fucking you."

"What about Bridgette?"

"Fuck Bridgette. I don't want her. I want you."

"No, I mean—"

But I devour her lips and she shuts the fuck up.

I've finally got her dress unbuttoned, thank God, and I pull it down past her hips to the floor, sliding my palms along her bare skin as I push the fabric down —and the sexy sight that unexpectedly greets me makes my cock jolt: Kat's wearing a full get-up of centerfold-worthy, sheer lingerie—a push-up bra, crotchless panties, and a garter belt that skims her flat belly just below her belly ring—all of it the shade of the ocean in Tahiti.

"Incredible," I murmur, assessing the fantastical vision in front of me. "Now *that's* a high-priced call-girl, baby."

She squeals with excitement and snaps her garter belt against her hip. "You like?"

"Fuck yeah, I do—I..." I clamp my lips together. I was about to say, "Fuck yeah, I *love* it." But using that four-letter word in any context, even regarding something as harmless as Kat's lingerie, suddenly feels clunky in my mouth. "It's incredible," I say.

I unlatch Kat's stockings from her garter belt and kneel before her, slowly peeling them down her legs, kissing each inch of newly revealed flesh as I go, swirling my tongue around the smooth skin of her thighs and then working my way up to her hips, her belly, her piercing, each flicker of my tongue and kiss of my lips eliciting moans of pleasure and knee-buckles from her.

After several minutes, I brush my fingertips over the gap in her crotchless panties, and my fingers come back slick with her wetness.

"You're so wet for me," I breathe.

"I've been wet for you all week," she whispers. "I've been dying for you."

I lean in and suck on her clit and her knees buckle sharply. She grips my hair to steady herself, and I take that as my cue to penetrate her deeply with my tongue.

"Oh my God," she breathes, running her fingers through my hair. "You're so *really* good at this."

Her knees buckle again and then again, until she loses complete balance— so I rise, take her by the hand, lead her to the bed, and lay her down on her back. She's trembling with desire, physically twitching with yearning. Her blues eyes are on fire.

Slowly, I take off my jacket.

"Oh God," she breathes. She reaches down to touch herself for a brief moment but quickly pulls her hand away, her body visibly shaking.

"Don't stop," I order. "Keep touching yourself."

"But I'm gonna make myself come. I'm almost there."

"Do it."

She complies, her eyes like hot coals as her fingers work her clit.

I slowly remove my tie, watching her.

"Oh my God," she breathes, her hand between her legs.

I peel off my shirt and she gasps at the sight of me.

"I forgot how hot you are," she says. "Oh my *God.*"

I rip off my briefs, letting my cock spring free, and crawl onto the bed next to her.

I press my skin against hers, jutting my hard-on into her hip. "Make yourself come while I watch you."

She closes her eyes, exhales, and begins moving her hand more rapidly.

As she works herself, I kiss her shoulder and neck slowly. Goose bumps rise up on her skin. I tilt her head to the side and kiss the long nape of her neck.

She moans.

I continue laying kisses all over her neck, shoulders, and torso while slowly removing her pesky bra, and the minute her breasts bounce free, I take them greedily into my mouth.

She shudders.

I stroke my fingers up and down her arm several times and then let my fingers trail all the way down to hers, until my fingers are lying directly on top of hers, joining hers in pleasuring her pussy. She moans and continues working herself, my fingers fused with hers, my lips and tongue swirling over her nipples, neck, and ear.

"You been thinking about me this past week?" I mumble into her skin, working her pussy along with her.

"Every minute of every day," she chokes out.

Our fingers work her clit together as our tongues slowly dance and swirl together.

I can't take it anymore. I gently push her hand away and begin working her clit and wetness together with my fingers, using one of the fingering techniques I recently read about in one of Jonas' books, and Kat's soft moans instantly transform into full-throated groans. I gotta admit: I thought I knew it all before reading that damn book (twice), but I'll be damned if it didn't teach me a thing or two. I shift my fingers again, giving her something I've never done before, and she begins convulsing with pleasure.

She makes a tortured sound, and I slide my finger up into her ass, right against her anus, just in time to feel her body release with rhythmic waves against my fingertip.

Oh God, I'm so aroused, my cock physically hurts. I've never enjoyed giving a woman pleasure quite this much. "You know what I thought about all week long? Eating my whore's magic pussy."

Her eyes light up.

I wouldn't say I'm a man who normally obsesses about going downtown, though I've always enjoyed it (with the right woman, of course). And yet, for some reason, when it comes to Kat, I've been literally *craving* the taste of her warm pussy day and night.

I spread her legs open and her breath catches with anticipation.

"Are you ready to earn your million bucks, baby? Because this is gonna turn me on."

She nods vigorously, her eyes blazing.

I pull the fabric of Kat's crotchless undies aside and swirl my tongue around and around, but the fabric keeps getting in my way. With a loud grunt, I pull down her undies and garter belt, throw them across the room, and then resume my assault on her with even more enthusiasm, licking and kissing and sucking every inch of her pussy until she's smashing herself into my face, clutching the sheets, gripping my hair, and screaming at the top of her lungs.

"You taste so good," I say, eating her voraciously. "So fucking good."

She releases with a loud shriek, and as she does, the sensation of her flesh rippling against my mouth gets me off so hard, I lose my fucking shit. Without thinking about it, I crawl over her, place a knee on either side of her head, grip her hair (a lot harder than I should), and wordlessly plunge my cock deep into her mouth.

"Time to earn your fee, baby," I growl.

Her response is immediate and through the roof. Either she's a better actress than Gabrielle LeMonde or she's *really* getting off on getting face-fucked. Either way, she's moaning like a sheep at slaughter as her throat receives the full length of me. I respond to her enthusiasm by thrusting even harder and deeper into her warm, wet mouth, almost all the way.

She reaches up and yanks on me, pulling me into her, signaling me to go even deeper, fuck her even harder, so I do. Oh my God, she's going insane with pleasure right now and I'm hurtling toward an epic orgasm myself on a bullet train—which means, motherfucker, I truly have to stop. Yes, I agreed to treat her like my whore—and, as it turns out, I'm quite happy to do it. But I didn't jack off for an entire week on FaceTime, just to blow my load into the woman's goddamned mouth.

I grip the top of Kat's hair firmly and pull out of her mouth—and when she looks up at me, she's in a stupor.

"You're good at sucking cock, baby," I say, rubbing the tip of my cock against the cleft in her chin. "It's no wonder sheiks, kings, and presidents want you so bad."

Her eyes light up. "I like sucking your cock, baby," she says. "Let me do it again and make you come." She lowers her mouth and licks my tip, making me shudder.

"No, babe," I say. "I want my paid whore's magic pussy."

"Yes, sir."

"Say, 'Whatever you wish.'"

"Whatever you wish," she purrs.

Wordlessly, I guide her on top of me—moaning with pleasure as my cock enters her. The minute she's on my saddle, I grip her hips and guide her pelvis into enthusiastic movement.

"Josh," she cries, her tits bouncing wildly as she fucks me. "Oh my God, yes."

She's turning me on so much, I can't even think. "You feel so good," I growl, grasping her rocking hips. "Oh my God, Kat, you feel *so* fucking good."

I slide my fingers up her ass—a move that's pushed her over the edge in the past—and this time, as before, it sends her directly into an orgasm. Her entire body stiffens. Her eyes roll back into her head. Her moans and whimpers morph into shrieks.

Note to self: Kat likes ass-play.

When Kat's climax subsides, I throw her onto the bed and guide her onto her hands and knees—and then, without hesitation, spank the shit out of her 'til she's squealing and moaning and twitching, and then I grip her hips and fuck her again from this new position. I've positioned Kat this way for my benefit—doggy-style happens to be one of my favorite ways to fuck—plus, after the orgasm Kat just had, I'm figuring she's all done and it's my turn now. But after only a handful of deep thrusts, it's clear my little whore is ramping up to go off again.

Jesus, she's supernatural.

I slow down my thrusts, trying my damnedest to hang on, and she makes that sharp-intake-of-breath sound that seems to signal an impending orgasm. I'm pretty sure that particular sound means two things: one, my girl's hanging on by the barest of threads, and, two, it's time for me to yank that mother-fucking thread and watch her unravel.

I reach underneath her and grope her breasts and pinch her nipples and she jerks underneath my thrusting body like a bucking bronco. Nice. I increase the speed and depth of my thrusts and she begins whimpering. Good. I reach around and massage her clit, using one of the techniques described in my handy-dandy new book, and she wails with pleasure.

"I'm addicted to you, baby," I say, sweat dripping off my brow. "Fucking *addicted.*"

"Oh my fuck," she responds. "Jesus Christ Superstar. Motherfucker."

Clearly, she likes what I'm doing (either that or she took acid before we started fucking), but, still, she doesn't release.

I bite her shoulder. Rub her back. Kiss her neck. Grab her hair roughly. All while thrusting and groping and licking and fingering her.

"Oh my—oh jeeeeeeeeezus," she moans. *"Yes."*

She sounds like she's possessed. Why isn't she climaxing? Women are impossible to figure out, I swear to God.

Shit. I can't hang on much longer. This is too fucking good.

Oh. I suddenly know exactly what to do.

I drape myself over her back, my fingers still working her clit, my cock thrusting deep inside her, sweat dripping off my brow and onto her slick skin, and press my lips into her ear. "You're worth every fucking penny, baby," I whisper. "Every fucking penny."

Boom. She comes like I flipped on a flashlight, screaming my name as she does. Ah, my little terrorist and her imaginary pornos. They're the key to her soul. Her entire body is clenching and rippling violently around my cock. Holy fuck, I love getting this woman off. It's my new favorite game.

I grab her hips and ram myself into her as far as my cock can go, making her scream with agony or pleasure—I don't really know which (or care)—and blow my load into her like a fucking fire hose blasting a burning building.

When I finish, she collapses onto the bed in a sweaty heap, gasping, and I lie on top of her, my body covering hers, my chest heaving, sweat pouring out of me.

"Holy shitballs," she chokes out.

"Damn."

Once I've caught my breath, I sweep her hair away from the back of her sweaty neck and kiss her hidden Scorpio tattoo. "You're my new favorite hobby, babe," I say.

She giggles. "I like being your hobby."

"You're a beast." I lick the back of her neck. And then bite it. And then I run my hands all over her sweaty body, making her moan with pleasure. Jesus Christ Almighty, I just fucked the living hell out of this woman not two minutes ago and I'm already electrified at the thought of doing it again. I can't get enough of her. I've never felt addicted like this before. I bite her shoulder and she squeals.

I crawl off Kat's back and lie alongside her, pulling her close to me on the bed.

"You're a beast," I say softly, hugging her to me. "So amazing."

"So are you," she replies softly into my chest, her voice quavering.

I tip her chin up and kiss her gently. "You're the most fun I've ever had in bed, Katherine Ulla Morgan."

Her face bursts with pleasure. "Really?"

"Not even a contest. You're in a league all by yourself. The tippy-top."

She grins.

"Worth every fucking penny," I say softly.

"But you didn't get your fantasy. We were supposed to be doing your fantasies first." She runs her hand over my chest, right over my "Grace" tattoo. "You wanna regroup and do the thing with Bridgette? I'm totally willing... now." Her eyes glint with something wicked.

"Fuck Bridgette," I say. "I'm sure she already left, anyway."

"You think?"

"If not, I'll tell her to go."

She smiles broadly. "But you seemed so turned on by the idea in Vegas."

"Eh, things change. Life is fluid. You gotta roll with it. I guess it's time to scratch that motherfucker off my bucket list—at least when it comes to you."

Her blue eyes narrow sharply.

Clearly, I've said something wrong. "What are you thinking?" I ask. "You suddenly look like a chick."

She assesses me with two chickified chips of blue granite for a moment. "I'm just trying to figure out why the change of heart—*at least when it comes to me.*"

I pause. She said that last part like she was gonna bomb my embassy—but I'd said those words to her as a compliment. What the fuck am I missing?

"Just what I said," I say slowly. "When it comes to you, all bets are off. You're a game-changer."

"Oh," she says. Apparently, she likes that answer. "After what you wrote about in your application—and how turned-on you were in Vegas when we talked about you watching me—I'm surprised. What's changed?"

Kat's right. I've done a one-eighty on the subject, at least when it comes to her. I can't honestly say I'd never wanna watch two women again—but not if one of them is Kat. At least not now. But the truth is I felt literally sick about the whole arrangement the minute I walked into the hotel room tonight and saw Kat and Bridgette sitting together. I felt like I was taking a shit right where I eat. No *bueno.*

"Yeah, I was crazy-turned-on when we talked about it in Las Vegas," I admit. "But that was *before.*" I trace her lips with my fingertip.

"Before *what?*"

Damn, she's persistent. "You know," I say.

"I actually don't."

"Before this past week."

She grins from ear to ear. "What happened this past week?"

"I thought about you nonstop."

"Oh." She grins. "Well, I thought about you, too."

"And not once did I fantasize about you fucking around with another woman. The only thing I thought about on an endless loop was doing what I just did to you."

She bites her lip, but she can't hide her smile.

"The thought of sharing you with anyone makes me wanna punch a wall or break a face."

Her face lights up. "Well, gosh, that's an unexpected development. Who would have thought?"

I lean back, narrowing my eyes at her. "You really are evil."

"What?"

I shake my head at her.

"What?"

"I thought I was coming here tonight to play out my fantasy, but we were doing yours all along, weren't we? Right from the start."

She doesn't reply, but her slow blink tells me I'm right—and that I played my part perfectly.

"Evil genius," I whisper.

She grins wickedly. "I was totally prepared to do it for you, I really was—and I still will, if that's what you want. But, yeah, I do admit I like that you couldn't stand watching me with someone else—that you wanted me all to yourself."

There's a very long beat. I don't know what the fuck to say or do, so I kiss her. And then I kiss her again, my heart racing. When we part lips, I touch her face again. She's so fucking beautiful. And so fucking evil. She's perfect.

"So, hey," I say, trying to sound casual. "I think I've had enough of hotels for a while. I can count on one hand the number of times I've slept in my own bed this past month. If it's cool with you, I'd prefer to ditch this ramshackle motel and take you to my house. I wanna kiss every inch of the great Katherine Ulla Morgan in my own bed tonight."

She presses her body into mine. "Awesome. Yeah, I didn't wanna say anything, but this place really is a dump."

I laugh.

"You're sure you don't feel like you're missing out if I don't lesbo-out with Bridgette?" she asks. "Maybe we could do it on my next trip if you're still—"

"*Babe.*" I touch the cleft in her chin and she abruptly stops talking. "*No.*" I exhale a long, shaky breath. "The thought of seeing you with someone else makes me wanna break a face." Her face lights up. "And if I break a face, it's quite possible I could get punched in return. And if I get punched, I might get a mark on my pretty face." I shake my head, chastising her. "We wouldn't want that, now would we?"

She shakes her head in mimicry of my movement. "No way. Your face is much too pretty to get marked up."

"Exactly. So that means from here on out, no one touches my Party Girl With a Hyphen but *me.*"

64

KAT

"Wow, you really like black leather, huh?" I say, looking around Josh's sleek and spacious living room.

"Yeah. Makes life simple."

"Your house is spectacular. If my mom were here, she'd fall to the floor, weeping."

He looks at me funny.

"She's an interior decorator."

"Oh." He chuckles. "Yeah, I had a top designer helping me." He grabs my hand and pulls me toward floor-to-ceiling glass on the other side of the room. "Lemme show you the view. It's gonna make you say 'Holy shitballs.'"

He pulls me outside into the night air and we're met with a view of what might as well be heaven on earth.

"Holy shitballs," I say.

Josh grins. "Amazing, right?" He motions to the infinite expanse of twinkling lights and rugged hills spanning before us into the night. "This right here is why people pay an arm and a leg for houses in the Hollywood Hills. Okay, so, over there, between those two hills? The Hollywood sign is right through there —you can't really see it right now, but I'll give you binoculars in the daylight. And if you look that way, that's downtown L.A. over there."

"Amazing. No wonder you love it here."

"Oh, I don't love L.A. I love Seattle. I just *tolerate* L.A."

"Really?" I'm floored. I thought Josh loved living in La La Land with all his flashy friends. "I thought you loved living here," I say.

Josh shrugs. "Nah, L.A. definitely gets old, other than the weather—the weather never gets old." He points in a new direction. "See that house down there? That's Chris Pratt's house..."

But I can barely process what he's saying. Josh doesn't love Los Angeles? Does that mean he might be open to moving back home one day? But, whoa, whoa, whoa, what the hell is my brain doing? Josh has made it abundantly clear he's not thinking about a long-term commitment. For crying out loud, only an hour ago the dude said he was scratching the two-woman scenario off his bucket list *"at least when it comes to me"*—which means it's still on his agenda with other women, whenever (if ever?) this crazy whatever-it-is between us has run its course.

"Wow," I stammer, even though I don't know what the hell Josh was just saying. I think it was something about Joaquin Phoenix's house?

"Let me give you the rest of the tour," Josh says.

He leads me back inside and straight past his gleaming kitchen.

"Hang on," I say. "Can I see your kitchen? It looks pretty fancy-schmancy."

"Oh, it is. My designer redid the entire thing top to bottom when I moved in four years ago—we installed professional-grade everything." He flashes me a crooked grin. "But since I don't cook, it's basically just for show."

"You have a kitchen like *this* and you don't cook?"

"Yup. I'm super-smart that way."

"You don't cook *at all?*"

"Not even a little bit. I can count on one hand the number of times I've turned on this stove in four years—and at least two of those times, I was lighting a doobie."

I laugh. "Josh, this is a frickin' gourmet kitchen. Wolfgang Puck would kill for a kitchen like this."

"Yeah, I figured a gourmet kitchen would add value on resale, and I was right." He shifts his weight. "I mean, it... *will.* Add. Value. Whenever the time comes."

Josh suddenly looks like he feels sick. I don't understand the expression on his face. He's grimacing like he's in pain.

"Well, if you don't cook at all, then how do you feed yourself?"

"Um," he says. "I... uh... I go out with friends or get food delivered. Sometimes, if I'm exhausted, I just make myself a peanut butter and jelly sandwich. Speaking of which, are you hungry? I can make you a peanut butter and jelly sandwich that's so good, it'll make you come."

"Wow. That sounds like quite a PB&J."

"Oh, it is."

"I'll definitely have to take a rain check. Every girl should try an orgasm-inducing PB&J at least once. But I'm still pretty stuffed from all the food we had at the hotel. Those crab cakes really hit the spot."

"Especially after we'd worked up such an appetite." He snickers. "Good times were had by all at the ol' Four Seasons, eh?"

"Well, good times were had by two out of three of us, anyway." I join him in snickering.

Ah, that was delicious. Just as Josh predicted, Bridgette was long gone when we emerged from the bedroom, *and* she'd left a delightful text for Josh as a parting gift, too: *"Fuck you, Faraday,"* Bridgette's angry text said—and I'm purring even now remembering the gleeful expression on Josh's face when he showed it to me. *"Lose my number, motherfucker. But tell your hot girlfriend I'll happily comfort her after you've dumped her ass and broken her heart. Auf wiedersehen, arschloch. P.S. I hope she gives you herpes."*

Josh and I laughed pretty hard about Bridgette's text.

"Battery acid in her heart, indeed," I said when I read it.

"I told you," Josh said.

The only thing more enjoyable than reading that text from Bridgette was seeing the look on her face when Josh abruptly changed the plan and dragged me into the bedroom, hell-bent on keeping me all to himself. Delicious.

I'm suddenly aware Josh has been talking while I've been lost in my thoughts.

"... and since I've been home from New York," Josh is saying, "a delivery service has been bringing me gourmet meals every few days." He grabs my hand, leads me to his refrigerator, and opens the door to reveal four neatly stacked see-through containers. "Nothing but lean proteins and greens. Everything low in saturated fats; no simple carbs; all calorie counts precisely calibrated for my weight and fitness goals. All courtesy of the one and only Jonas Patrick Faraday."

"Jonas orders your meals?"

Josh rolls his eyes. "He kept giving me shit about my burgers and fries and Doritos and I was like, 'Dude, I travel too much to think about eating right all the time—leave me the fuck alone.' Next thing I knew, these meals started showing up." He chuckles. "The dude's like having a fucking wife, I swear to God—he's such a nag. I haven't eaten any of 'em yet as an act of protest."

"Is that what you think a wife does? She nags her husband about what he eats?"

"Yeah, you know, like that cliché line? 'Take my wife, please.'"

I roll my eyes. "Wives get such a bad rap."

"Well, shit, I dunno. I have no idea what a wife does—I've never actually witnessed one in its natural habitat."

"Are we talking about a human or a water buffalo?"

Josh chuckles. "Cut me some slack. My mom died when I was little; my uncle's wife died before I was born; and my best friends are either single or in what I'd call *non-permanent* relationships."

I make a face. I didn't mean to be insensitive about Josh growing up without a mom or any maternal influences. I didn't even think about that when I made my snarky comment.

"Plus," Josh adds, seemingly unfazed by my comment, "and most importantly: there were no wives on *Full House.*"

"I'm sorry, Josh," I say softly. "I didn't think. I keep forgetting."

He waves his hands like I'm totally missing his point. "Forgetting what? It is what it is. Long time ago. No worries. I'm just saying I've never witnessed an actual wife up close, that's all. I don't know what women are really like if you actually *live* with one."

I'm suddenly starkly aware of just how different my childhood was from Josh's. I can't wrap my head around how disconnected and isolating—and *masculine*—his upbringing must have been. No wonder he has no freaking idea about marriage and relationships.

"Lori Loughlin," I say.

"Huh?"

"Lori Loughlin. She played Uncle Jessie's wife in the later seasons of *Full House*."

"Oh yeah," Josh says. "I forgot about her. I kinda stopped watching by then."

"Oh. Well, she didn't nag. She was happy and funny and supportive. That's what a real wife is like."

"Really? Well, I don't remember all that. All I remember is that she was smokin' hot."

"I thought you stopped watching by then?"

"I might have caught a couple episodes." He laughs. "She was hot."

"Still is. Saw a photo of her the other day. But, anyway, that's just TV," I concede. "Uncle Jessie's wife doesn't really count as spotting an actual wife in the wild, so your point is still well taken."

"Well, tell me, then. You've observed the species, right?"

I chuckle. "Yeah, I'm pretty sure I've spotted a genuine wife scurrying in the bushes a time or two."

"Well, enlighten me. Does your mom nag the shit out of your dad or what?"

"No. Never. My mom's the coolest woman who ever lived—super happy and energetic and just sort of like, 'If you're not happy, then get yourself happy, motherfucker, and stop bitching.'"

"Does your mom actually use the words 'motherfucker' and 'bitching'?"

"No, not unless she's *really* mad—usually at Keane." I laugh. "She's much more likely to use words like 'honey' and 'complaining'—but she'd say both in a *really* 'motherfucker' *tone*."

Josh looks absolutely mesmerized right now. "Did your mom stay home with all you kids when you were little?"

"Yeah. But she always helped decorate people's houses on the side. At first it was just her friends, and then it expanded to her friends' friends. Nowadays, she's got her own little interior decorating business and she absolutely *loves* it. In her spare time she cooks the most incredible food—the best turkey chili you've ever had, oh my God—oh, and her spaghetti sauce is next level, and her lasagna is to die for. I think she wishes her ancestors came from Italy instead of Sweden." I laugh. "Oh, sorry, what was I saying? I get all excited when I talk about my mom's food."

"You were saying your mom doesn't nag your dad."

"Oh, yeah, that's right. She doesn't. She leaves him the hell alone and makes herself happy cooking incredible food and decorating people's houses and going to her exercise classes. You should see my mom with her little five-pound weights, doing her classes at the gym. She's such a little badass."

He chuckles.

"Oh, and she plays Bunco with her friends, too."

"What's Bunco?"

"It's this stupid dice game. It's basically craps with wine. But I think the dice are just an excuse to get drunk. I can't be sure of that, but that's my strong hunch."

Josh laughs. "I love your mom already."

I bite my lip. I know Josh meant that comment as a throwaway—a figure of speech—but it made my heart flutter nonetheless.

"So do you cook like your mom?"

"Not really. She's always wanted to teach me, but I'm too frickin' lazy to learn. Dax is an awesome cook, though—he's the one who always hangs out with Mom in the kitchen. And Colby cooks in the firehouse all the time, so he's pretty good, too—but he only knows how to cook in quantities for ten guys." I laugh. "Ryan's adequate—a little better than me—but he makes the best guacamole. And Keane is freakin' hopeless. The dude can't boil water."

"Well, thank God you're at least better than *Peen*," Josh says. "Or else I would have had to un-friend you."

I grin. In one of our many conversations this past week, I told Josh a bunch of stories about my brothers, including several that showcased Keane (also known as "Peen" in our family) as the beloved fuck-up of our family.

"Hey, can I get you something to drink?" Josh asks.

"Thanks. Do you have sparkling water?"

"Club soda okay?"

"Yep, same-same. Thanks."

Josh moves across his kitchen and pulls a couple glasses out of a cabinet. "Would you care for a little vodka in your club soda, Party Girl? I've got Belvedere and Absolut."

I shrug. "Why the fuck not?"

Josh laughs. "Words to live by. Which one?"

"Surprise me. I feel like living on the edge." I lean my butt against the counter.

"A girl after my own heart." He grabs a bottle of Belvedere from a low cabinet. "So what do you guys call Dax?"

"Dax is actually his nickname, a contraction of David Jackson."

"I didn't realize that. Cool." He fills the glasses with ice. "And Colby?"

"Cheese."

"Well, shit. That's not fair. You're Jizz and Kum Shot and Baby Gravy and Keane is Peen, but Colby gets to be something as G-rated as 'Cheese'?" He pours vodka into the glasses. "Not fair."

"Oh, it all evens out in the end," I say, enjoying the view of Josh's ass as he bends over to grab something from his fridge. "No one gets off easy in my family, I assure you. We all get raked over the coals somehow, just in different ways."

Josh closes his fridge, a bottle of something in his hands. "What about Ryan?"

"Ryan is RUM, Bacardi, Captain, Captain Morgan."

"Oh yeah, you said that in your application." He grins. "Ryan *Ulysses* Morgan."

"That's right." I grin. "Sometimes, when he's dressed up to go out—which he is a lot—he's 'Scion' or 'Pretty Boy.' Ry is basically you if he had a *much* bigger budget to work with."

"I like him already."

"You would, trust me. You'd love him. He's perfectly groomed and put together at all times, slays it with the ladies, charm oozing out his pores. The other guys ride him mercilessly for how pretty he is and how much he cares about his appearance. I can only imagine how much shit my brothers would give you if they ever met you."

Josh chuckles. "Well, thanks for the heads up. I'll make sure to dress down when I meet your brothers. I'll take a page out of Jonas' book and go with a T-shirt and jeans."

"Aw, come on now, Josh—don't go changin' to try to please 'em. You just do *you*, baby." I pause. I really shouldn't say what I'm thinking. But I can't help myself. "So are you thinking you might wanna meet my family one of these days?"

Josh's cheeks flush. He swallows hard. "Um. Yeah." He busies himself with our drinks again, his body language suddenly verging on robotic. "Maybe."

I laugh out loud. This man is a raging head case.

"No pressure, Josh," I say, genuinely amused by his suddenly anxious body language. The man is visibly twitching. "I brought it up just to watch you squirm. No worries." I should leave it at that. I really should. But, no. When it comes to Joshua William Faraday, I simply can't help myself. "But, um, actual-ly," I begin, trying really, really hard to sound easy-breezy-Cover-Girl. "Colby's birthday is next weekend. My mom's gonna make her famous spaghetti and Dax is gonna make carrot cake—Colby's favorite meal." I clear my throat. "Super chill. Just the fam. You'd be welcome to join us for dinner, if you... happen to be... in Seattle. But if not, then no pressure, of course." Oh shit. What am I doing? Even as the words tumble out of my mouth, I know they're a horrifically bad idea. I should know by now: Josh is perfectly fine when we're enjoying each other in the here and now, but the minute I start talking about the future, he breaks into a frickin' cold sweat. I quickly wave at the air like what I've just said is the stupidest thing I've ever said. "Actually, pretend I never said any of that," I mumble. "I'm just kidding. Again."

Josh remains focused on the drinks he's making. Notably, he doesn't turn around and say, "Don't be silly, Kat—that's a great idea!" He just continues silently mixing our drinks, his back to me.

Holy hell, this is awkward. Why did I say all that? I really should know by now that pinning Josh down to anything even remotely relating to the future is a nonstarter.

"A twist of lime?" Josh finally says, his back still facing me.

I look down at my hands, heat rising in my cheeks. After everything I just said, *that's* what Josh asks me? If I want a lime in my drink? I really should have known. I'm such an idiot.

"Um. Sure," I say. "A twist of *lime* would be *amazing*." Oh boy, that last bit came out way bitchier than I'd intended.

But Josh seems to be unfazed by my bitchiness (which seems to be par for the course with him, thankfully). He turns to face me and clears his throat. "Colby's birthday dinner sounds great," he says, his jaw muscles tight. "Thanks for the invitation. I'd love to go." He tries to smile. He's not successful, but he's trying.

My heart leaps into my mouth.

Holy I Think I Just Harpooned a Whale, Batman.

"Tell the truth," I say. "The only reason you wanna come is Dax's carrot cake."

Josh laughs. "How did you know? Yeah, I've always had a soft spot for carrot cake."

"And cheesecake," I say, remembering our scarf-out the night we helped Henn in Las Vegas.

"You remember."

"Of course. I remember everything you've told me, Josh."

There's a long beat.

"Actually, Daxy makes a great cheesecake, too. It's just as good as his carrot cake. I'll see if he'll do both."

Josh's blue eyes darken to sapphire. "No, don't. I'll bring one from a bakery. No reason to make him think I'm a pain in the ass right from the get-go." He bites his lip. "So, hey, now that I'm coming up to Seattle next weekend, how about we check off one of your fantasies while I'm there? There's one specifically I think I could pull off better in Seattle than here."

My heart is absolutely racing. "Great," I squeak out, trying not to sound as thrilled as I feel. "Sounds good." I cross my arms over my chest and quickly uncross them. Crap. I suddenly don't know what to do with my hands.

"Cool," Josh says. He turns back around to face the drinks on the counter. "Just let me know the date so I can put it on my calendar."

"Yeah, I will," I say, my heart pounding in my ears. "Colby's birthday is the fourth. Not sure if we're doing it on his actual birthday or another night. I'll let you know."

"Cool. Sounds good. Assuming I don't have a work commitment that night, of course."

"Oh, of course."

Josh lets out a long exhale and then glides across the kitchen and hands me my drink. "Here you go, Party Girl." He flashes a megawatt grin, relieved of his earlier inability to maneuver his mouth into a smile. "I added just a *touch* of cranberry to the soda for you. Hope that's okay."

"Great." I take a sip. "Yummalicious. What else is in there?"

"The tiniest splash of grapefruit juice, just to take the edge off the cranberry."

"Oh, kinda like a Sea Breeze plus soda."

"Exactly."

"I like it. Thank you." I take another sip. "Ooph. That's a strong drink."

"Go big or go home, I always say." He winks. "Come on, PG. Let's go chill out in the living room."

65

KAT

We amble out of the kitchen, drinks in hand, into the living room—and I settle myself onto the black leather couch while Josh chooses some music for our listening pleasure.

"So how long have your parents been married?" Josh asks, fiddling with his laptop.

"Thirty years this August."

He looks up from what he's doing, obviously astonished. "Wow. That's crazy."

"Yeah. Pretty crazy."

A song begins playing through Josh's sound system—a male vocalist backed by an acoustic guitar.

"What is this?" I ask, somewhat surprised by Josh's song selection. I'd have pegged him to play us something with a thumping beat.

"James Bay," he says. "'Scars.' Jonas had it on the other day when I was with him in New York and it slayed me. I bought the guy's whole album on the spot and every song is phenomenal." Josh sits down next to me and puts his hand on my thigh. "This James Bay guy sings with his soul."

"That's a great description."

Josh sips his drink and listens to the music for a moment. "So, thirty years, huh? Are your parents happily married?"

I'm shocked he's asking questions about my family. "Definitely," I say, my skin suddenly buzzing.

"Even after *thirty* years?"

"Well, I'm sure they've both wanted to murder each other more than once over the years. But, yeah, they're still totally in love. More so than ever, I think.

I like being around them—they're nice to each other. They still laugh at each other's jokes."

"Wow." He looks deep in thought.

I take a deep breath. I shouldn't ask the question rolling around in my head —I really shouldn't. But I can't help myself. "So, are you gonna be like Reed, you think? Are you gonna ride off into the sunset alone and unencumbered by messy human emotion?"

Josh looks taken aback by my question. "Uh, wow." He makes a weird face. "Is that what Reed said? I didn't interpret it quite that way." He makes a face. "But, um, yeah, I don't really envision myself getting married, if that's what you're asking."

I sip my drink. Why did I just ask him that? I really didn't need to hear him say that so starkly, even if I already knew that's what he'd say.

"I don't have anything against marriage, mind you," Josh continues. "I'm totally happy for your parents if it works for them—kind of in awe of them, actually—I just don't see the logical point of marriage as an institution," he continues. "I mean, if you wanna be with someone, be with them. If you don't, then leave. No need to get a piece of paper from the government that forces you to stay if you'd rather go."

I sip my drink quietly, listening to the music, wishing I could rewind time and un-ask the question. If I were my own life coach, I'd be slapping myself across the face right now and shouting, "Fucking idiot!"

"You disagree with me?" he asks, studying my face.

"No," I say. I sip my drink. "I most certainly do *not* disagree." I really, really should leave it at that. Definitely. That would be the wise thing to do.

"But?" he prompts.

"No 'but.' I don't disagree with you *in concept* one little bit." I sip my drink again. Damn, that's a strong drink. And, damn, I wish I hadn't asked Josh about marriage of all things, for crying out loud. I'm truly an idiot, not to mention quite possibly a masochist, too.

"*But?*" he repeats.

"But..." I say, drawing out the word. Oh hell. Keeping a lid on every frickin' thought that flashes into my head isn't my strong suit, especially when it comes to Joshua William Faraday. "*But* watching my parents through the years—the way they've stuck it out through thick and thin and how strong they are because of it—how strong our whole family is because of it—I think there's a bit more to marriage than just, you know, 'I can't leave your sorry ass because that goddamned piece of paper forces me to stay.'" My cheeks burst with color. Why am I saying all this? "But," I continue, trying to appease the shrieking voice inside my head telling me to press the eject button, "I definitely hear you —marriage certainly isn't for everyone." I clear my throat. "I'm not sure it's for me, honestly. I was just saying it's worked out well for my parents." Oh God. I wish I could jump into a time machine, go back to three minutes ago, and say, without elaboration or qualification, "Oh, I totally agree. One hundred percent."

Josh makes a face I can't interpret. "Maybe marriage *might* make sense for people who want to have kids."

There's an awkward pause. Did he just backtrack? Are we meeting in the middle? Hmm. I do believe we are. Which therefore means I should leave it at that. But, oh God, I can't. "Well, *actually*," I begin, ignoring the warning bells going off in my head, "if you think about it, marriage makes *less* sense if you've got a kid with someone."

He looks at me like I've just shouted, "Justin Bieber for President!"

"Because," I continue, pissing off my internal life coach even more, "whether or not you've got a piece of paper from the government, once you have a kid with someone, that person's gonna be in your life forever and ever, regardless. I think it's more meaningful to *choose* to be with someone just because you want to make a life with them, not because you plan to make them a vessel for your mighty spawn."

There's an awkward silence.

I seem to have rendered Josh (and myself) speechless. What the *fuck* am I doing? If I were my own life coach, I'd be throwing my hands up in disgust saying, "You're obviously completely un-coachable."

James Bay's voice fills the room for a very long moment.

"That's kind of the flipside of what my dad always used to drill into Jonas and me," Josh finally says. "He was obsessive about it, actually." He puts on a booming, paternal voice, clearly imitating his father: "'Boys, when you've got Faraday money, women will try to trap you into marriage with an 'accidental' pregnancy right and left—every goddamned time you fuck one of 'em. Don't you dare let me catch either of you *ever* making an accidental Faraday with a woman unworthy of our name or I'll get the last laugh on that gold digger's ass and disown you faster than she can demand a paternity test.'"

My jaw drops. What the fuckity fuck?

"That's why I've always been obsessive about wearing condoms," Josh continues softly. "Way before I'd ever even gotten to second base with a girl, I was already freaking out about unwittingly creating an 'accidental Faraday' with some random woman who was 'unworthy' of my name and bank account."

I clutch my stomach. I feel physically sick. What kind of father says all that to his young sons? Preaching safe sex is one thing, sure, I get that—especially when you've got a kajillion dollars to your name, I suppose—but a father conditioning his pubescent sons to think every girl out there is a gold digger and telling them he'd *disown* them if they ever knocked someone up is pretty fucked up, if you ask me. "Your dad sounds like he was a real peach," I mumble.

"Oh, you have no fucking idea," Josh says between gritted teeth.

A sudden panic rises up inside me. "Josh, I'm on the pill—you know that, right? I would never, ever do that to you—"

Josh looks ashen. "Oh, God, I know that. I didn't mean—"

"I'd never, ever try to *trick* you into anything. In fact, we can go back to using condoms, if you want, every single time—"

"Kat, please. Stop. I know you'd never try to trick or trap me. I'm sorry I said—"

"We can use condoms," I persist. I'm totally freaking out.

"Kat, please. Pretend I never said anything. I didn't mean to imply..." He takes a deep breath and shakes his head. "Jesus, my dad is the gift that keeps on giving, isn't he? Listen to me, Kat, I know you'd never do that to me. The only reason I felt comfortable enough to tell you the fucked-up shit my Dad said is because I know you'd never do that."

Oh, jeez. I've never been so relieved not to be pregnant in all my life. Last week, after losing sleep for two nights over that birth control pill I'd missed, I finally traipsed down to the all-night drug store and bought myself a pregnancy test. And when I peed on that little stick and it came back with only one little pink line, I let out the longest exhale of my life.

"I'm definitely not gestating an accidental Faraday," I say, trying to sound light and bright but obviously not succeeding. "I'm a *mill-i-on-aire* now, remember? I don't need to trap you for your stinkin' Faraday money."

Josh runs his hands through his hair. "Kat, please forgive me. I was just telling you what my dad said because... I don't even know why I said it. I certainly wasn't implying you were trying to trap me in some way or that you'd even *think* of doing that. I think I was just trying to reveal one of the many ways I'm fucked up to you—trying to explain why I might be unusually high-strung or weird about certain things." He shakes his head and exhales. "I think I was just trying to... you know... take a stab at... *emotional intimacy*." He makes a face that says, "I guess I still suck at it."

I chuckle. I can't help it. He's so frickin' cute.

Josh exhales. "The truth is I'm actually pretty fucked up, Kat. I'm just really good at hiding it."

I grab his hand. "No you're not, Josh. Not at all." I grin. "You're actually *horrible* at hiding it."

He bursts out laughing and all tension between us instantly evaporates. He grabs the back of my neck and pulls me into him for an enthusiastic kiss. "You're awesome, Kat," he mumbles into my lips. "So fucking awesome." He pulls back and looks into my eyes for a moment, his blue eyes sparkling. "I've never told anyone about all that. My dad was so fucked up, you have no idea—he said the craziest shit all the time. Sometimes, looking back, I can't figure out what shit was normal father-son stuff to say and what shit was just, like, you know, totally out of line. It all jumbles together."

"I'm glad you told me. I really like the Josh who can't hide he's fucked up."

"But your family sounds so normal. You must think I'm a ticking time bomb of crazy."

"Oh, please. My family has its crazy, too. Not necessarily in the same league as your father, but crazy nonetheless. And, hey, why would I care if you've got crazy in your family? Since I have zero desire to make a Faraday with you, I'll never have to worry about passing your crazy-genes on to my offspring."

Josh bristles. Shoot. I shouldn't have said he has crazy-genes. That was pretty insensitive, given what he's been through with his father and brother.

"You have *zero* desire to make a Faraday with me?" Josh says.

I'm astonished. *That's* what offended him?

"Not even a little bit?" he asks, shooting me a charming smile.

"Not even a little bit," I say. And it's the truth.

"Well, shit, Kat," he says, pouting. "I'm genuinely offended."

I throw my hands up. "You're *offended* I don't wanna make a baby with you? What the *fuck*? Do you have a split personality?"

"Quite possibly. I do have crazy-genes, after all." He makes a "crazy" face.

I chuckle. "I thought you'd be thrilled I don't want to make a Faraday with you."

"Well, yeah, sure, from a practical standpoint, I'm elated. But from an evolutionary standpoint, I'm deeply offended. You should be chomping at the bit to snag my fabulous genes, crazy or not. Look at me. I'm an ideal sperm donor."

I laugh. "Oh, really? You've got a pretty high opinion of yourself, huh?"

"I'm saying from an *evolutionary standpoint*. Our only purpose as a species is to reproduce. There's no other reason for existence. You're born. You reproduce. You die. That's the game of life—finding someone to give you hearty spawn so you can live eternally through them."

"Wowza." I'm speechless for a moment. "Well, I think I'm gonna have to disagree with you—it sounds to me like you're *not* as ideal a sperm-donor as you think. I'd prefer my spawn to have a father who wants them, first of all—that's always nice—plus, I'd want my spawn to inherit a little bit of humility along with their chiseled cheeks and rock-hard abs."

"No, no, no. You've got it all wrong. From an *evolutionary* standpoint, humility is completely counterproductive. Does a peacock say, 'Aw, shucks,' about the feathers on his tail? No, he's genetically engineered to *flaunt* his tail. Why? So he can attract the best peahen in the flock."

"Peahen?"

"The female version of peacock. The name for male and females together is actually 'peafowl.'"

"And you know this factoid because?"

"Because I grew up with Jonas. The dude's got so much weird shit trapped in his brain, it's bizarre."

I chuckle. "Well, I'm not a *peahen*, I'm a human. And, either way, I don't wanna make a baby with you—human, peafowl, or otherwise. Not for really reals and not as part of an evolutionary experiment. I'm too selfish. I've seen what it takes from watching my mom, and no thanks—I'm quite happy going to work and yoga classes and doing shitfaced karaoke." I shrug.

Josh squints at me, apparently disbelieving my sincerity.

I shrug. "What can I say? You can add no-baby-no-thank-you to the list of ways I'm like a dude. I'm missing the baby-gene—it's not personal to you. I don't even like going to my friends' baby showers." I shrug. "But, hey, I'm only twenty-four. Still a wee little baybay. Check back with me in ten years when my biological clock is ticking like an atomic bomb—who knows if I'll be chomping at the bit to board the baby-train then? You never know, I guess."

"Hell no," Josh says. He swigs his drink. "I won't give a shit about your ticking clock when you're *thirty-four*. Pfft. Optimal child-bearing-age is twenty-six. You'll be no good to me when you're thirty-fucking-four."

"Why the *fuck* do you know the 'optimal' child-bearing-age for a woman? You're creeping me out."

Josh laughs heartily. "Jonas. I told you, the guy knows everything. Ask him the life span of a blue whale or the average rainfall in the Amazon or how to make a cherry bomb out of paperclips and he'll know it off the top of his head. The dude's a freak." He sips his drink. "And Jonas says twenty-six is the magic number. Past that, you're just a useless sack of ovaries and fallopian tubes, baby."

I burst out laughing. People aren't supposed to talk this way. I absolutely love it.

After we finish laughing at the sheer ridiculousness of our conversation, there's a long, awkward beat. I keep waiting for him to speak, but apparently, he's waiting on me. Well, hell. I might as well call out the pink elephant sitting smack in the middle of the room.

"So does that mean you might want little Faradays one day with some trampy little twenty-six-year-old? Is that what you're saying?" I ask.

Josh clears his throat. "Actually, no. I don't know why I just said all that. I was just trying to be snarky, but it backfired. For some reason, whenever I'm with you, I say crazy shit I'd never normally say. It's like I get some sort of Kat-specific Tourette's Syndrome."

I laugh. "I know the feeling—apparently, it's a two-way syndrome."

"Actually, I've never been able to picture myself having kids—but, then again, I've never been able to picture myself more than two weeks into the future, unless you're talking about something business related, of course. Ask me to draw up a five-year business plan for Climb & Conquer, and I'm your guy; ask for year-to-year projections on a new investment, I'm on it; but try to pin me down to coffee next week, and I freak out."

"Gosh, I hadn't noticed," I say.

He ignores my sarcasm. "But, hey, same as you—check back with me in ten years. Maybe guys have a biological clock, too."

I sip my drink, trying to seem casual, but my heart is about to hurtle out of my chest and splatter against the wall. I can't believe we're having this conversation. "Guys don't have a biological clock," I say. "Men can unleash their super-sperm any ol' time, even after every single one of their ball-hairs has turned gray."

He laughs.

"And, anyway, knowing you, I'd think I should check back with you in *fifty* years, not ten. Given your extreme terror of commitment, I wouldn't want to cause you undue stress."

"Yeah," he says. "Good idea. I'll unleash my super-sperm at eighty. That way, when I go to the drugstore, I'll be able to buy diaper cream and denture cream at the same time. One-stop-shopping."

I laugh. "Awesome. You're gonna win so hard at the game of life, dude."

He laughs. "'Hey there, whippersnapper! I can't find my teeth! Let's make a baby!'"

I laugh again. "Oh, yeah, I'm sure your twenty-six-year-old tramp is gonna go weak in the knees over your eighty-year-old ball sack and wrinkled ass. Talk about a gold-digger—we both know that poor girl's gonna be looking at her watch every five minutes, just waiting for you to die."

"Well, my future gold-digging spawn-carrying twenty-six-year-old might not get weak in the knees over my saggy ball-sack, I'll grant you that, but she's gonna cream her panties over my wrinkled ass, I guarantee it. I mean, seriously, who could resist a wrinkled ass stamped with 'YOLO'?"

I burst out laughing. "Oh my God, Josh. Fifty years from now, your twenty-six-year-old spawn-carrier won't even know what YOLO stands for. By then, YOLO will be the equivalent of 'Daddy-o' or 'far out.'"

Josh puts on his "old man" voice again. "Damn kids. Back in my day, YOLO ass-tattoos were the bees' knees."

"That statement will be a bald-faced lie—I don't care how far into the future you make it."

"Aw, come on. Just wait. I'm a trendsetter, baby. Sure, the trend hasn't caught on *yet*, but it's coming, you'll see."

We share a huge smile.

"I really think we're on to something here, Kat. If I wait 'til after I'm diagnosed with dementia to have my first kid, then I can have him and forget he was ever born all in the same day."

"Brilliant. Talk about a surefire way to solve your fear of commitment." I take a long swig of my very strong drink. Wow, the vodka's really hitting me hard.

Josh blanches. "Why do you keep saying I'm afraid of commitment? You said that earlier, too. I'm not."

I don't reply. Oh shit. He looks genuinely offended. "Oh," I begin, at a loss. "I'm sorry. I thought I was saying something that's just a basic fact, like, 'Your eyes are blue.'"

"I had a girlfriend for three years, Kat," he says. "I'm not the least bit afraid of commitment."

I feel the urge to laugh out loud, so I drain my drink.

"I had a girlfriend for *three* years," Josh repeats. "I know how to commit."

Fuck it. The vodka is giving me liquid courage. "Honesty-game?" I ask.

He makes a face like he's just bitten into a lemon. "Yes?"

"You're a commitment-phobe, Josh," I say simply. "Text-book."

"No, I'm not. Absolutely not."

"Yep." I take a swig of my drink. "You are."

"A three-year relationship isn't a commitment? What's the longest relationship you've had?"

"About a year—with Nate."

"Ha! You're one to talk."

I take another swig. "This isn't about me and my horrible relationship skills." Oh wow, Josh put *a lot* of vodka into my drink, didn't he? "We're talking about *you* and yours—and the fact is you're deathly afraid of commitment in any form. Yes, you had a girlfriend for three years—and certainly that meant *something*, I'll grant you that, but it sounds like it was three years of a whole lot of nothing. I'm sorry to break it to you, but you and your girlfriend apparently never *talked* about anything real. You couldn't be yourself around her at all—and the minute you revealed who you really are, what you really want, she shamed you and ran off with Prince Harry. So, yes, you were in a relationship for three years, and, yes, it shows you have character and integrity, but it doesn't prove you're not afraid of commitment. I mean, in a way it proves your fear of commitment even more so."

"More so? Really? How do you figure?"

"Because you must have stayed with a woman like that for a reason. You must have known deep down she was every bit as incapable of emotional intimacy as you are. You liked that she never required you to reveal a goddamned honest thing about yourself in three freakin' years."

He looks shocked.

I press my lips together. Oh shit. I just dropped another one of my atomic bombs, didn't I? Oh fuck. That was harsh. Honest, but harsh.

I just can't help myself. Ever since reading Josh's application (and seeing Emma's beautiful, shy photo in Josh's Sick Fuck folder), I've had somewhat of a fixation on this Emma bitch. On the one hand, I've felt the primal urge to rip her limb from limb for hurting Josh. And, on the other hand, I've honestly been a bit obsessed with trying to figure out why the heck he stayed so long with a woman who was so obviously his total mismatch in every way (other than the fact that she's literally the most stunningly beautiful creature I've ever seen).

Josh looks floored. Pissed, I'd even say.

"Damn, that drink you made me was really, really strong," I say, my face turning hot.

Josh's jaw muscles are pulsing like crazy.

Shit. Maybe I've totally misjudged this. Maybe he can commit. Hell, maybe he was on the verge of asking Emma to marry him, for all I know. Oh, jeez, yes. Maybe that's why he now says marriage isn't in the cards for him? Is Josh just a case study of a man with a shattered heart? But, clearly, I can't ask him if he was about to propose. It's too sensitive. I opt for something slightly more innocuous. "So did you and Emma live together?"

Josh makes a face I'm not expecting, like he's embarrassed about what he's about to say. "No. It was a long-distance relationship. She lives in New York."

Oh, Sweet Jesus. Is he frickin' kidding me? "It was a *long-distance relationship?*" I boom, totally shocked.

"Yeah. So?" he says, clearly defensive. "I get out to New York all the time for work. I saw her a lot."

There's a very long silence.

Josh's face is bright red.

I'm sure mine is, too.

James Bay is singing to us about scars.

I feel like I've said way, way, way too much. My inner-bitch just came out full-force. God, I suck sometimes. "So... what's your favorite movie of all time?" I ask brightly. "If you could be anyone from *NSync other than Justin Timberlake, who would you be? Do you have a spirit animal?"

"You're not what I'd call the world's foremost expert on relationships," Josh says, his voice low and intense. "I wouldn't exactly hire you to write the definitive textbook on *How to Have a Healthy, Lasting Relationship.*"

I part my lips, speechless.

His jaw is clenched.

I squint at him for a long moment, trying to look like a badass—but then, goddammit, tears prick my eyes. "You're right," I finally say. "I pretty much suck at relationships." I wipe my eyes. "I'm sorry for saying all that stuff. I shouldn't have said it."

He twists his mouth and exhales. "If you hadn't said it, you'd still be thinking it."

I don't correct him. He's right.

He shakes his head. "I must say, you have quite a knack for *not* kissing my ass, Kat."

I smash my lips together.

"I'm not used to it," he says.

"Sorry," I say.

Josh shakes his head like he's chastising me. "No apology required."

I bite my lip.

He grazes his fingertips up the length of my arm and my skin electrifies under his touch.

"You get really sassy when you're buzzed, you know that?" he says.

I nod. My crotch is suddenly burning.

"But you know what?"

I wait.

"I *really* like sassy."

I bite my lip. My heart is racing at his simple touch.

"Did I hurt your feelings?" he asks softly. His fingers move up my arm and drift along my jawline. "When I said you're a flop-dick when it comes to relationships?"

I smile. "Oh, is that what you said? Jeez, that's a whole lot meaner than what I *thought* you said. All I thought you said was you wouldn't hire me to write some textbook."

He chuckles. His fingertips skim the length of my hairline.

"I'm not mad at you," I say softly. "I'm the opposite of mad at you."

He smiles wickedly. "Oh, yeah?"

"Yeah."

Josh touches my chin and my body ignites. He leans in and kisses me gently.

We sit and stare at each other for a moment. A legion of butterflies has unleashed inside my stomach.

His eyes drift to my empty glass. "Would you like another one, Party Girl? The night is still young."

"Yes, thank you. But not nearly as strong this time, Playboy. I wanna be fully conscious for whatever might happen next. Something tells me it's gonna be good."

He smirks. "Good idea." He stands, grabs my glass, and heads toward the kitchen—but before he turns the corner, he turns back around. "Hey, Kat. Thanks for always playing the honesty-game with me. So few people do that with me—most people just kiss my ass."

"Well, you can hardly blame 'most people,' Josh—you've got a truly kissable ass."

He grins. "Thanks to the 'YOLO' stamped on it—which, I'm telling you is gonna be all the rage one of these days, mark my words."

I laugh. "Keep telling yourself that, Playboy, if it helps you look yourself in the eye every day."

His blue eyes are positively sparkling at me right now. "Your drink is coming right up, Party Girl."

"Thanks."

"My extreme pleasure."

66

KAT

I feel myself literally swoon as Joshua William Faraday exits the living room to fetch us another round of drinks. That man is so freaking charming, and so freaking hot, and so freaking funny and adorable and sweet and generous and sexy (and I could go on and on), it's just not fair. I feel like I'm playing tennis against Roger Federer armed with nothing but a fly swatter.

I can't remember the last time I felt like this—so gooey and heart-fluttery and fairytale-believe-y and emotional. I've got to get a grip on myself, slow my shit the fuck *down*. Tap into Classic Kat for a while. Jeez. My feelings are moving too effing fast, especially considering whom I'm dealing with here.

Oh my God, I'm losing it. Falling *hard*.

This is so unlike me. I'm never the one *chasing* the guy—I'm always the one being *chased*. I'm the one who says, "I'm not sure I'm feeling it, sorry," and then *he* says, "Well, then, baby, lemme try to *convince* you." Isn't that *exactly* what Cameron said? Yep. After one date, he was ready to chase me to the ends of the earth, God knows why.

And that's the way I like it. I *like* being chased. What the hell did Josh tell Henn when he was being "Hitch" and teaching Henn to "dick it up"? I scoff out loud at the memory, even though I'm sitting here alone in this room. "Women *think* they wanna be chased," Josh said, "that's what all the movies and books tell 'em they want—but they don't. Not really. If you do the equivalent of driving to her house and holding a boom box over your head, you might as well hand her your dick and balls in a Ziplock baggie, too, 'cause you're not gonna need 'em any more."

What a big ol' bunch of bullshit. Of course, we wanna be chased. Idiot.

And, yet, here I am, aching for him, ready to hand him my whole heart and soul, aren't I? And he's the one who always pulls back.

I look up at the ceiling. What the hell have I gotten myself into with this man? Is he even capable of giving his heart to me—at least at some point? If I break down and make the depths of my feelings known to him, would he be thrilled or scared to death?

I lean back on the couch and squeeze my cheeks, pondering the situation.

Oh damn. I can't feel my face.

My gut tells me he'd be scared to fucking death. Maybe thrilled, too—but his fight or flight instinct would surely kick in. It's just too soon. A guy like him needs more time. Heck, a girl like me needs more time. Usually. I truly don't know what the fuck is happening to me. Where the hell is shallow, hedonistic, meaningless-sex-seeker Classic Kat when I need her?

As I glance around the room, lost in my thoughts, a small, framed photo on a table catches my eye. I can't make out the image from this distance, so I get up to take a closer look.

When I pick the photo up, I can see it's a faded shot of a stunningly beautiful blonde woman sitting in a wicker love seat with two tousled little boys—all three of them tanned and windswept and bursting with what appears to be authentic joy. The smiles on their glowing faces aren't canned "say cheese" grins—these people are bursting with genuine down-to-their-bones happiness. I can almost hear their ghostly peals of laughter rising up from the image.

God, it pains me to think what happened to this poor woman shortly after this photo was taken. Oh, and her poor little boys. I scrutinize the boys' faces in the photo, tears welling up in my eyes. I know Josh and Jonas are fraternal twins, but they look virtually identical in this shot. It'd be impossible to tell them apart if it weren't for Josh's slightly darker hair.

Tears blur my vision.

It kills me to think about how devastated those boys must have been when their mommy was so unexpectedly and savagely ripped from their young lives.

I wipe my eyes, but it's no use. I can't seem to stop my emotions from overflowing out of me. I take a deep breath and try to stuff my emotions down. It's suddenly hitting me full-force that the cute little boy in this picture—the one with the slightly darker hair—is standing in the next room, mixing me a drink, trying his earnest best on a daily basis to "overcome" everything he's had to endure.

Ice cubes rattle on the far side of the room and I snap my head up toward the sound.

Josh is standing at the entrance of the living room, his facial expression the same as when I opened my door to him in Las Vegas after reading his application.

His eyes dart to the photo in my hand and then back to my face.

The music swirls around us for a long moment. Finally, I hold up the photo and try to grin. "Your mom was stunning."

Josh doesn't reply.

I walk across the room with the photo and sit on the couch. "Tell me about her." I pat the couch next to me.

He looks torn.

James Bay is serenading us, singing about scars.

"Come on, Josh," I say. I pat the couch again.

He crosses the room and nestles himself onto the couch next to me, his lips pressed tightly together.

"She was beautiful," I say.

"You're her spitting image," he says softly.

I look down at the photo in my hand. Well, I can certainly see that I bear a resemblance to his mother, maybe even a striking one, but calling me her 'spitting image' is pretty far-fetched. For one thing, from what I can see from this photo, Josh's mother radiated pure kindness—a quality I'm certain I don't possess, unfortunately. Plus, her features are literally perfect. It's like she was concocted by mad scientists in some sort of government-sponsored lab. No one would ever say that about me, I don't think.

Josh takes the photo from my hand and looks down at it wistfully.

"Poor Jonas," he says.

"Poor Josh," I add.

Josh sighs like he's got the weight of the world on his shoulders. "No, I got off easy. I was at a football game with my dad when she died. Poor Jonas saw the whole fucking thing." He shakes his head mournfully. "Poor little dude was so traumatized, he didn't say a word for a year afterwards."

"*Nothing?*"

"Nothing. Literally. Not a word."

"For a whole *year?*"

"For a whole year. I did all his talking for him."

"How'd you know what to say?"

"I just knew. Later, after he'd started talking again, he told me I'd always gotten it right. It was like we shared a brain."

"What did Jonas say when he started talking again?"

Josh smiles. "We were sitting in the car with our nanny, listening to the radio, and I was singing along to a song—whatever it was, I can't remember—and after not saying a single fucking word for a *year*, my bizarre, hilarious, crazy brother said, and I quote, 'Shut the fuck up, Josh. You're singing so goddamned loud, I can't hear the fucking music.'"

I burst out laughing and Josh does, too.

"What made him talk again all of a sudden?"

"Not *what*—*who*. Jonas talked again thanks to one very special and extremely attractive woman: our third-grade teacher, Miss Westbrook. If it hadn't been for her, Jonas wouldn't be here right now, I'm sure of it. Which, of course, means neither would I."

My stomach turns over. "What do you mean 'neither would I'?"

Josh pauses a long time before speaking again, apparently choosing his words carefully. "If it weren't for Miss Westbrook, there's no doubt in my mind Jonas would have methodically figured out a way to kill himself before his thirteenth birthday. Granted, fun fact, Jonas actually *did* fling himself off a bridge when he was seventeen, right after my dad shot himself, but that's a whole other story. But if it weren't for Miss Westbrook, he would have done it much more precisely than driving off a bridge, and he would have succeeded." His eyes glisten. "And if Jonas had succeeded in killing himself when I was still a little kid, if he'd left me alone with my dad in that big house for years and years..." He shakes his head. "I wouldn't have been able to overcome it."

The image of Josh's "overcome" tattoo flickers across my mind.

"Do you think that's why you never envision yourself in the future?" I ask.

Josh looks at me blankly.

"At dinner with Reed, you said when you were twenty, you couldn't imagine yourself at thirty—and now that you're thirty, you can't picture yourself at forty. Do you think your brain has trouble imagining the future because you're subconsciously not convinced you'll have one? Because you're not sure what Jonas might... do?"

He shakes his head like I just gave him mental whiplash. "Wow." He makes a face that says "holy fuck." "Well, shit. I guess that's as good a theory as any. Whoa." He smiles. "Deep thoughts by Katherine Ulla Morgan."

I shrug. "Hey, even a broken clock is right twice a day."

"Can't we just talk about *The Teenage Mutant Ninja Turtles*? How 'bout that Raphael?"

I wince. "Sorry."

"No, no, don't apologize. I'm just kidding." He sighs. "I guess I'm just not used to talking about this stuff."

"Sorry. We don't have to."

"No, it's good. It feels good."

"Really?"

"Yeah."

I bite my lip. "So how did Miss Westbrook get Jonas to talk?"

"Well, to tell you about Miss Westbrook, I kinda have to give you a little primer on Jonas first."

"Okay," I say, leaning back. "I'm not going anywhere."

He pulls me close to him and wraps his arm around my shoulder.

"I know Jonas seems like some kind of gorilla-robot, but he's actually really sensitive. Always has been, especially when it comes to women." He shakes his head. "Like, take my mom, for instance. Even when he was little, Jonas didn't just love her, he *worshipped* her. I loved her, too, of course. With all my heart. And yet, even I could see Jonas loved her differently than I did. As far as he was concerned, Mom was *literally* an angel."

I feel the sudden urge to get even closer to him. I slide myself onto his lap and wrap my arms around his neck.

He wraps his arms around my back in reply.

"He was the same way with Mariela, too," Josh continues. "Our house-keeper before my mom died. I used to beg Jonas to come outside to climb a tree with me and he'd be like, 'No, I'm gonna clean pots with Mariela.'" Josh laughs and shakes his head at the memory. "Right after my mom died, it's a long story, but my dad blamed Mariela for my mom's death and sent her away—and Jonas just completely melted down. I guess losing them both was just too much for the little guy." Emotion threatens to overtake Josh's face. He looks down and composes himself.

"You lost them, too," I say softly, touching his arm.

Josh looks back up, his face earnest. "Yeah, but I'm not *Jonas*."

"I don't understand."

He shakes his head. "I'm *Josh*. The fixer. The closer. Life throws shit at me, I just deal with it. I solve problems. I fix things. I'm coated in Teflon, baby—shit slides right off me and doesn't leave a mark. But not Jonas. Even Mariela told me, 'Take care of your brother, Josh. You know he's the sensitive one.'"

"So you thought it was your job to take care of Jonas, even though you were so little, too?"

"It's always been my job to take care of Jonas, and it always will be. I'm sure in the womb Jonas was trying to understand the functionality of the umbilical cord or articulate the meaning of life, and I was like, 'Dude, chill the fuck out—doesn't this amniotic fluid feel *awesome*? It's like a Jacuzzi!'"

I know Josh's words are funny, but the expression on his face isn't. My heart's suddenly aching for him. I push myself even closer into him, run my hands through his hair, and kiss him gently. When we break apart, tears are streaming down my cheeks, but Josh's eyes are bone-dry.

"When was the last time you cried?" I ask softly.

He shrugs. "Probably not since I was about ten. I cried like a baby when my mom died and Mariela got sent away, and I used to cry a ton the first few years whenever Jonas got sent away. But then one day when Jonas was gone, my dad found me sitting on the grass, crying my eyes out, and he reamed me for being a 'fucking cry-baby-pussy-ass.'" He shrugs. "And that was that. I never cried again. I've come very, very close many times since then, but I've never actually shed a tear."

I'm blown away. "Not once?"

He shakes his head. "I think there might be something wrong with me."

I make a sad face.

"So, anyway, I got sidetracked. I was supposed to be telling you how Miss Westbrook got Jonas to talk, right?" He shifts his body underneath me and I'm treated to the unmistakable sensation of his hard-on poking me in the crotch.

"*Oh*," I say. "Hello."

"Hello." He grins.

"What's that for?"

"You're sitting on my lap."

"That's all it takes?"

"Apparently."

I grin at him. "That's all it takes for me, too," I say.

"I'm addicted to you," he whispers.

"I'm addicted to you," I whisper back, my heart racing.

He nuzzles his nose into mine. We kiss gently for a few minutes, listening to the music. My crotch is absolutely burning.

He pulls back. "What were we talking about?"

"Miss Westbrook."

"Oh, yeah." He lays a quick peck on my lips. "Jonas became Miss Westbrook's after-school helper, and to make a long story short, she did this crazy, amazing thing he hadn't experienced in a really long time: she was nice to him." He shrugs. "And that's pretty much it—well, and she was smoking hot, too." He grins.

"But how do you think she convinced him to speak? A year's a long time."

"I don't know exactly what she said or did to him when they were all alone in that classroom, but whatever it was, he adored her. She could have asked Jonas to fly and he would have figured out how to sprout wings." He sighs. "All I can say is it's a good thing Sarah's not some kind of evil madman bent on destroying the universe because if she were, we'd all be screwed. The boy would figure out how to do it for her."

"I think the feeling's mutual."

Josh nuzzles my nose again. "Don't tell Sarah, but Jonas is gonna pop the question."

I'm floored. *"What?"*

Josh grins broadly. "He's been sending me photos of rings this whole past week. Hang on." He rearranges me on his lap so he can grab his phone from his pocket. "See?"

I look at his screen—and sure enough, Jonas has texted Josh countless images of diamond rings, all of them bigger than my head.

"Holy Hope Diamond, Batman," I say.

Josh laughs. "Which one do you think Sarah would like the best? Jonas won't leave me alone about it."

I scroll through the images, shaking my head. "Hell, if I know. They're all freaking spectacular—oh, wait. No. *This one.* Wow." I point to a princess-cut dazzler that, for whatever reason, screams "Sarah" to me. "She's gonna totally freak out."

"Bless you." Josh grabs his phone from me and shoots off a quick text to Jonas. "You just saved me from hours of torture, Kat. Thank you."

"When's he gonna ask her?"

"In two weeks—he's taking her on a surprise trip to Greece right after her final exams."

I gasp. "He's gonna ask her in *Greece?* Oh my God." I clutch my heart. "Oh my shit, Sarah's gonna crap her pants. *Greece?*"

"You ever been there?"

"No, remember? I've only been out of the country to Mexico and on a cruise to the Caribbean. I told you about the cruise and you said the only way to travel by sea is by private yacht."

Josh laughs. "I said that? Oh my God, I'm such a douche sometimes."

I laugh.

He nuzzles my nose. "So get this, babe. Jonas is planning to make poor Sarah hike to the top of *Mount Olympus*—because, he says, she's 'the goddess and the muse'"—he chuckles happily—"and then he's gonna make her jump *off* the mountain and paraglide down to the beach—and *that's* where he's gonna ask her." He laughs heartily. "So fucking Jonas."

"But Sarah's deathly afraid of heights."

He touches my hair. "Well, sucks to be her, then. He wants to create some kind of *metaphor*."

My brain tells me I should smile and laugh, but my eyes unexpectedly fill with tears instead. Oh my God, I'm a hot mess. I cover my face with my hands. What the hell is wrong with me lately?

"Kat? What's wrong?" He looks genuinely concerned. "Why are you crying?"

I shake my head and laugh at myself through my tears. "I'm just so happy for Sarah," I say, but even as I say it, I'm not sure if this completely explains my sudden (bizarre) tears (though, of course, I am insanely happy for Sarah). "I dunno, maybe I'm just so freakin' relieved Sarah's okay—I was so worried about her when she was attacked." Another true statement—but, again, I'm not sure this is the source of my tears. "Or maybe I'm just sloppy-drunk. That was a really strong drink, Josh." I half-smile.

Or maybe finding out Jonas is gonna propose to Sarah made my heart pang for myself, if I'm being brutally honest. Maybe my heart clanged so forcefully inside my chest cavity when Josh said those words, the sensation literally brought tears to my eyes.

Josh looks at me funny for a long beat.

I feel like I've said something wrong. Or, at least something awkward. I didn't just now say my deepest thoughts out loud, did I?

After a moment, Josh grabs my face and kisses me passionately. Whoa. This is quite a kiss.

"You're a good friend," Josh whispers into my lips, his passion obviously surging all of a sudden. "I like that about you."

"Josh," I breathe. His kiss has ignited me.

He rises off the couch, taking my fluttering, swooning, aroused body with him—and I throw my arms around his neck.

"Okay, Party Girl with a Hyphen," Josh says, his eyes blazing. "Time to finish the tour of my house. Next stop: my bedroom."

"Wow. Katherine Ulla Morgan's finally gonna be in my bed," Josh says gleefully. "Glory be."

I giggle, peel off my clothes, and crawl into Josh's luxurious bed, my skin on fire. "Hurry up, Joshua William Faraday. Don't keep Katherine Ulla Morgan waiting."

"I'll be right there. Just getting some music cued up." He glances at me from across the room, his blue eyes smoldering. "Another one from James Bay. I can't get enough of this album."

As the song starts playing, Josh joins me in bed, his erection straining as he crawls over me—and in a flash, his warm skin is covering mine.

"Hey, gorgeous," he says softly, his muscles bulging as he rests his forearms on either side of my head. "Welcome to my bed."

"Thank you. It's a pleasure to be here."

The song is swirling around us, filling the room with words that seem to have been written especially for us—especially for this moment. Did Josh select this song as some sort of coded message to me—or is it just coincidental that James Bay is singing to us to "Let It Go" and reveal our truest selves to each other?

"I love it," I murmur as Josh's lips gently press into mine.

He moans his agreement into my mouth. "Me, too."

Goose bumps erupt all over my body. These words are making my heart pang.

Josh raises my arms above my head, pins my wrists together with one of his large palms, and proceeds to slowly kiss and touch his way down my arms all the way down to my mouth, where he sucks my lower lips and teases me mercilessly for a while with tender kisses, until finally leaving my mouth for my breasts. Oh God, I'm already writhing with pleasure and we're just getting started. His lips leave my breasts and trail down to my belly, where he swirls my belly ring in his mouth, and then moves on to laying soft kisses on my hip bone and pelvis.

"You smell so good," he breathes. "I'm rock hard for you."

I'm on fire.

When his lips finally move to the sensitive folds between my legs, I let out a long, low moan, already on the cusp of climax, and when his tongue finds my clit, I grip the sheet and arch my back, my body clenching and releasing forcefully.

"You're amazing, baby," he says, his mouth lapping at me. "I love the way you get off."

When my orgasm subsides, he works his way back up my body, kissing, sucking, caressing, massaging, and licking me into a frenzy.

I'm enraptured.

His face is suddenly in mine. Oh God, I could stare into those blue eyes forever. The room is spinning. He cups my cheek in his palm and presses his warm skin into the full length of my body. "I can't get enough of you, baby," he says.

"I'm addicted, Josh," I reply. "I'm totally addicted to you."

He slides his fingertips between my legs, brushing my wetness gently until I'm squirming and yelping with arousal, and I return the favor, touching him exactly the way he's touching me—*adoringly*. We kiss and kiss, caressing each other gently as we do, until both of us are trembling and making sounds of extreme arousal.

I feel transported. I can't think. I can only *want*. I wrap my legs around him, pressing my body into his. "Please," I breathe. I'm trembling with desire. "Please. I want you, Josh. Please." I'm using a phrase I've used with him before: I want you. But this time I mean it in a new way. This time, I'm telling him the bare truth: I want *him*, not just sexually. I want him to be mine in every way. I've never ached like this before. My heart hurts. "I want you, Josh," I say again. "I want you so much it hurts." Oh my God, I feel like crying, I want him to be mine so, so much.

"I'm all yours," he says. He parts my legs and slides his hardness inside me, burying his shaft deep inside me, kissing me deeply as he does, stroking my hair, sucking on my lower lip again, thrusting his body slowly in and out of mine—and all of it as "Let It Go" continues to swirl around us.

I caress his ass and dig my fingers into him and he responds by thrusting passionately into me. "Why do you always feel so fucking *good?*" he asks, his voice strained.

"Josh," I breathe. But that's all I can manage. I'm feeling too overwhelmed to say more. With each thrust of his body, each time his chest rubs against mine, each touch of his lips, my heart feels like it's physically reaching outside of my chest to join with his.

Sex with Josh has never been like this before. He's fucked my brains out many times, made me literally pass out with pleasure, but this feels different. It doesn't feel so much like he's *fucking* me, it feels more like he's... what was that word he used when he talked about the way Jonas loves? It feels like he's *worshipping* me.

I've no sooner had the thought than I'm jolted with a palpable electric current. Holy hell, it's like someone flipped a switch on our mutual circuit breaker.

"What the fuck?" Josh says softly, his body moving with mine.

Oh my God. He feels it, too?

"What *is* that?" he asks, his voice ragged.

"I don't know," I choke out.

He touches my face and kisses me, his passion spiking. "What the fuck are you doing to me?"

I shake my head and press my palm into his chest, right onto his mother's name. "I don't know."

As the song builds, so does the crazy electricity between us. It feels too big to contain, too pleasurable to bear.

Suddenly, I don't want an inch of separation between us. I want all of him. Every inch. I hitch my legs up higher around his thrusting body, as high as I can manage, trying to coax him into the farthest recesses of my body and he responds by guiding my thighs to his shoulders. And that's all it takes to send my body releasing with an orgasm so pleasurable, it makes my eyes water.

"Yeah, baby," Josh says, his passion obviously on the verge of releasing. "Oh my God. You're amazing, babe."

In one smooth movement, Josh pulls out of me and rearranges us. Suddenly, he's on his back and I'm on top of him, straddling him, riding him. His hands are all over me. His face is intense. I grab his finger off my breast and suck it voraciously.

He moans and thrusts underneath me with increased fervor.

I'm vaguely aware the music has moved on to the next song on James Bay's album. He's singing about "craving." Oh God, these words were written for us, too. I've been craving this man since the minute I laid eyes on him.

Our movement becomes heated. Josh is thrusting into me, grabbing at me, groping me, kissing me, groaning, and I'm gyrating my hips wildly on top of him, rubbing myself against his hard shaft as I do. He touches my clit and massages me—and I absolutely explode with pleasure.

"Yeah," he chokes out as my body undulates around his cock, over and over. "Get it, baby."

Right on my heels, Josh jerks underneath me, his body releasing into mine. "Oh God," he groans. "Holy fuck."

As Josh comes, I gaze at him from my perch on top of his body.

I love watching his features contort from pure pleasure. I love seeing every muscle in his body tense and tighten and then relax. My eyes drift across all the swirling ink decorating his skin—to his abs and chest, glistening with sweat.

His body is quiet now. He's all done. His blue eyes are fixed on mine. Oh, those eyes. I trace his eyebrow with my fingertip and he blinks slowly, obviously completely spent. I lean down and kiss his lips gently and then trail gentle kisses along the length of his jaw, to his ear, and then down to his neck. I inhale the scent of him and swoon. Oh my effing God, I cannot get enough of this man.

I kiss and lick his chest tattoo, each and every letter, and then I let my tongue migrate down his torso to his little fishy swimming in the river and then down to the deep ridges in his abs. I kiss every letter of his "overcome" tattoo along his waist and let my tongue explore the sharp "V" cuts above his pelvis as the song swirls around us, giving voice to what I'm feeling deep inside. After a while, my mouth finds his nipples, then his neck, his jawline, his lips. We kiss passionately for a long time until, finally, we pull away from each other and stare into each other's eyes.

My head is reeling. I've never experienced sex like this. This was something new—the perfect alignment of heart, body, mind, and soul. It took my breath away.

Josh wraps a lock of my hair around his finger and sings along softly to the last chorus of "Craving" straight to the end of the song. Another song on the album starts, and at the first chorus, it becomes clear what this new song must be called—"If You Ever Want To Be In Love."

Josh stops playing with my hair. "Excuse me for a minute, PG." He abruptly guides me off him, hops off the bed, and practically sprints toward his bathroom, leaving me in the bed alone with my mouth hanging open, listening to the rest of the song by myself.

68

JOSH

I splash cold water on my face and look at myself in the mirror. What the fuck just happened between Kat and me? I wouldn't even call what we just did *sex*. It felt more like a nuclear reaction. *Sexual fusion.* Is that a thing? Well, if not, it is now.

I stare at my reflection in the mirror.

Water is dripping off my brow and down my nose.

Holy motherfucking shit.

How many times has Kat or I said, "Sex doesn't have to be deep and meaningful"? And now, all of a sudden, I feel like going back in a time machine to each and every one of those conversations and shouting, "Yeah, but sometimes it *is*, Kat—*sometimes it is!*"

Jesus Christ. That was epic. The way her body felt around mine. Her eyes. Her lips. That electricity coursing between us. I could *feel* it. *And the music.* Oh my God. What the fuck was James Bay trying to do to me? Turn me into a blubbering pussy? I thought that James Bay album was cool when Jonas played it for me in New York, that's all—I just really liked the guy's voice. "Hey, that's cool," I said when Jonas played one of the songs for me. "Who is that?" I had no idea those songs would later provide the soundtrack of my complete and total undoing.

Holy fucking damn, that was some seriously mind-blowing sex.

Which, by the way, makes no sense at all. Ever since breaking up with Emma, all I've done is fantasize about all the kinky-ass shit I wanna do, all the ways I wanna let my inner sick-fuck run amok—and *that's* what got me off so hard?—the most straight-forward, basic kind of sex a guy can have? But, oh my fucking God, it was incredible. Kat felt so fucking good, and the music was so perfect, and that electricity came out of nowhere and rocked my world... Holy fuck. I literally had to run away from her when that last song started playing or else I was gonna turn into fucking Jonas and start calling her the 'goddess and the muse' or some shit like that.

For Chrissakes, the way I was feeling in that moment, I was on the cusp of pouring my heart out to her, on the verge of telling her a thousand things I'd never normally say. For Chrissakes, I was about to babble about my upcoming move to Seattle! "When I move to Seattle," I was about to say, "I wanna do this every night with you, babe." Those are the exact words I was on the verge of saying to her! They were on the tip of my fucking tongue—even though I'm not moving for three motherfucking months! How could I even *think* of making an implied promise like that? Sure, I'm addicted to Kat right now—*painfully* addicted—Jesus God—I feel like a fucking labradoodle fetching a stick every time I'm in her presence—but who knows how long this white-hot passion's gonna last? This thing with Kat and me is brand new, after all. At this stage in a relationship, three months from now might as well be thirty years. Things might work out—and, shit, I sure hope they do—God, I hope they do—but they might not. Like I always say: under-promise and over-deliver. That's the path to happiness and peace of mind in all things.

But, goddammit, I wanted so badly to tell her about my upcoming move to Seattle, plus a bunch of other stuff, too. I wanted to tell her how excited I am to sit down to dinner with her noisy, chaotic family, to meet her mom and dad and brothers and just sit there, watching everyone interact. I wanted to explain that it's a big fucking deal for someone like me to sit down for a birthday dinner with a real family—a *big* family—even though it's a ho-hum kind of thing for everyone else. In fact, I wanted to tell her, the whole reason I lived in my fraternity house for my first two years in college (even though the place should have been condemned) was because I craved being around noise and chaos and laughter and *people* so badly after growing up my whole goddamned life in a fucking morgue with Joseph Stalin breathing down my neck.

Oh my God, I wanted to take Kat's gorgeous face in my hands and stare into those icy-blue eyes that see right through me and tell her she blows me the fuck away, and not just in bed, but in every conceivable way—that I can't find a goddamned fucking fault with her—that even her stubbornness and jealousy and evil make me want her that much more, more than I've ever wanted any other woman, in fact. That I can't stand it when we're apart. That she's hilarious. And sweet. And honest. A force of nature. That she makes my heart physically *hurt* when she does nothing more than smile at me.

I lean forward and stare at myself in the mirror. I'm trembling. Panting. Freaking out. I need to get a grip.

I wanted to tell her I'm falling so fast and hard for her, I feel like I need a Dramamine. And a parachute. And a fucking last will and testament.

Fuck.

I stare at my blue eyes reflected back at me in the mirror.

"Pull yourself together, man," I say through gritted teeth. "Stop acting like a total puss." I nod in reply to myself, take a deep breath, and slap my cheek *hard* —and then, once I feel like I've regained control of myself, I turn around and head back into my room.

69

JOSH

When I emerge from my bathroom, there's yet another James Bay song playing—this one, thankfully, in no danger of sending me into a tailspin. Kat's sprawled naked on her stomach across my bed, looking like a wet dream, her long, toned limbs stretched across my mattress, her blonde hair unfurled across my pillow, her tight ass just begging to get spanked or bitten or fucked. Or all of the above. Jesus. I wouldn't mind being greeted with this vision every time I come out of my bathroom.

I crawl onto the bed and drape my body over hers, pressing my naked body into hers. "Hey, babe," I say softly.

She turns her head and rests her cheek on the pillow.

"Hey," she says softly. "Everything okay?"

"Mmm hmm. Everything's great." I push her hair to one side and stroke the Scorpio tattoo on the back of her neck. "How are you?"

"Good."

She squirms underneath me and I lift up, letting her turn onto her back so that we're lying nose to nose, our bodies pressed together.

"You look like you have one eye," she says, pressing her nose into mine. "One very blue and beautiful eye."

"I'm Mike Wazowski," I say.

She laughs. "Why do you know that?"

"Are you kidding me? I love *Monsters, Inc.*"

She laughs. "You never cease to surprise me."

"Mike Wazowski!" I say in the voice of Boo. "Kitty!"

"Admit it—you were stoned out of your mind when you watched that movie, weren't you?"

"*No*, as a matter of fact. I was, like, sixteen or something—still a very nice boy."

She laughs. "Sorry. Didn't mean to offend you."

I pause. "I was a very nice boy at one point, Kat—I went to see cartoon-movies in the theatre and everything."

"I'm sure you were."

I pause. "Although, in the interest of the honesty-game, I watched *Monsters, Inc.* stoned out of my mind later on DVD."

She bursts out laughing and I join her. God, I'm fucking addicted to her. I can't resist reaching out and touching her golden hair. It's the color of straw. Spun gold. Sunshine. I stroke her hair for a moment and she purrs like a cat.

"You blow me away, Kat—not just in bed. All the time. With everything you do and say."

She inhales sharply. "You blow me away, too." Her face turns bright red.

I suddenly feel like I'm on the verge of babbling every thought in my head again—all the stuff I was about to say a minute ago, before I escaped into the bathroom. Fuck me, I wanna tell her about Seattle.

"All right, babe," I say, rolling off her. "Enough talking about cartoons—we've got kinky-fuckery to talk about."

She laughs. "Nice transition."

I sit up in bed. "So here's the deal, Heidi Kumquat. When I wrote my application to The Club I was in a totally different state of mind than I am now."

She nods. This is not news to her.

I exhale. "Would you be terribly disappointed if we moved right into doing everything on your fantasy list and skipped the stuff I wrote about in my application to The Club?"

"Why?"

I shrug. "Doing that shit now just feels like trying to relive my junior prom. Now all I wanna do is go to my *senior* prom—with you."

She grins. "Aw. You're asking me to prom?"

"So you're not disappointed?" I ask. "You seemed pretty excited to be on the receiving end of all that shit in my application."

She shrugs. "Hey, if you're not feeling it, then we don't do it. And, anyway, I got to be a high-end call girl. That's what I was really jonezing for." She makes a checkmark motion in the air. "Plus, I unexpectedly got a bonus mini-porno out of it, too—watching you get all riled up at the thought of anyone but you touching me was utterly delicious." She shoots me a wicked smile.

"*I knew it.*"

She laughs a full-throated laugh.

"Diabolical," I say, smiling. "Okay, cool. It's settled. We're doing your fantasies, baby."

She squeals with pleasure.

"So this is how it's gonna work. You'll just go about your life, okay?—and sometimes shit will just start happening to you. And when it does, you'll just play along. Don't worry, you'll totally know what to do because—" I slap my hands together hard, making her flinch. "Sorry. I just had a brilliant idea. I'll be right back." I leap out of bed and race to my hallway closet, my pulse pounding in my ears. Holy fuck, this is gonna be epic. I quickly find what I'm looking for and sprint back to my bed. "Open your hand, babe." She does, and I place a poker chip in her palm. "Every time a fantasy is starting, you'll get a poker chip just like this one. That way you'll never be confused about whether a role-play is starting. You know, you won't go, 'Are you *really* a fireman? Is my house *really* burning down—or are you here to eat my pussy?'"

She laughs. "I don't have a fireman fantasy—Colby's a fireman. Too weird."

I roll my eyes. "It was just an example, babe. I know all your fantasies, remember? I took copious notes. I'm just saying the poker chip will be our secret signal so I'll never need to say, 'Hey, Kat, I'm doing a fantasy now.' That way you can just relax and enjoy the ride and play along."

"But what if there really *is* a fire—using your example—and it happens *after* you've already given me the poker chip? You'd be like, 'Fire, Kat! Fire!' And I'd be like, 'Oh, yeah, baby. I'm on *fi-yah*.'" She giggles.

"Good point," I say, laughing with her. "We should have a safe word in case we need to stop the role-play for any reason."

"Okay. How about 'overcome'? Wasn't that what you used with the women in The Club?"

I wave my hands in dismissal. I don't even want to think about those women right now. "That was *then*, babe—this is now. Our fantasy-sex-club is all about *fun*—not exorcising my fucking demons."

"Awesome," she says, her eyes blazing. "How about 'sick fuck,' then?"

"*Babe.* Did you not hear a word I just said? I'm over it. Plus, I kinda dig it when you call me a sick fuck. I wanna keep that phrase as fair game. You never know what you might scream when I'm fucking the shit out of you in a dental chair."

"Ooh." She raises an eyebrow. "We're gonna do the dentist thing?"

"Oh my God, you're a terrible listener. What'd I just say? Yes. We're gonna do *everything*."

She squeals. "Oh my God. This is gonna be *redonk*."

"So what's the safe word? It can be anything. Onomatopoeia."

She giggles. "Who's the idiot who came up with that word? Who needs so many syllables to say '*Bam!*'?"

I laugh.

"Brouhaha?" she asks.

"What the fuck? *No.* Weirdo."

She shrugs.

We sit and think.

"Peanut butter and jelly sandwich?" she offers.

I jut my lip, considering it. "Since that's the only thing I know how to make, in theory, it *could* come up."

"I truly cannot fathom how either of us would say 'peanut butter and jelly sandwich' while fucking, but okay, if you say so. How about 'rainbows and unicorns'? That'll never come out of my mouth, I guarantee you."

"Might come out of mine—you're a total unicorn, babe. I could totally imagine myself blurting that in a moment of weakness. Even if I don't say 'rainbows' along with it, it could still get confusing."

She laughs. "This shouldn't be that hard."

I sit and think for a moment. "Flesh-eating bacteria," I say.

"Hell no. You're demented to even suggest it. Come on. Dinosaur. Doorknob. Dandelion. Dungarees. Deedle-deedle-dee. Pick one."

I laugh. "No, hang on. I'm kinda digging 'flesh-eating bacteria.' I can't imagine any sexual scenario in which those words would ever come up."

"As opposed to 'dungarees' or 'dandelion'?" She rolls her eyes. "Come on, Josh. Spaghetti. Skateboard. Ballerina. Scooby Doo. Multi-vitamin. *From Justin to Kelly.* 'My Little Pony.' Hot tamale."

"Oh my God." I hoot with glee. "*From Justin to Kelly.* Winner-winner-chicken-dinner."

Kat rolls her eyes. "What? *No.* I was totally kidding. Harry Potter. Chili-cheese fries. 'Go big or go home.' Hunky dory."

"Nope. We've got our winner. *From Justin to Kelly* it is."

She twists her mouth. "You're a silly man."

I laugh.

"You totally saw that movie, didn't you?"

"Hell yeah. It was part of initiation in my fraternity. I saw it during hell-week."

She laughs. "You got *hazed* with *From Justin to Kelly*?"

I nod. "It was brutal."

She's laughing her ass off. "Oh my God."

"So, hey, babe, there's something I wanna run past you before we get started."

"Okay."

"In order to pull off some of your crazy-ass stuff, I might need to enlist a little help occasionally from third parties—not for anything sexual, obviously—never anything sexual—just in setting the stage for a scenario."

She makes a face. "Could you be more specific about how you define 'setting the stage'?"

"Not without giving things away."

There's a long beat.

"I promise you won't be embarrassed or compromised in any way," I say. "You'll always be fully dressed. I just wanna make these imaginary-pornos as close as possible to what you described to me—and occasionally I think I might need to cast an extra or two to do it."

She beams a huge smile at me.

"What?" I ask.

"You're adorable."

I scoff.

"You are."

"So is that a yes?"

She nods. "I've got a safe word, right? If I've got a problem with anything at any time, then I'll use it."

"That's right, babe. You can always count on *From Justin to Kelly* to protect you."

She rolls her eyes. "Oh, Joshua. You're a silly, silly man."

I laugh.

"And a very sweet one, too."

70

JOSH

"Why don't you shower in my bathroom while I use the shower in the guest room?" I suggest as Kat and I walk into my house. We've just come in from an awesome day of hiking and climbing rocks in Malibu and we're both covered in a thick sheen of sweat and dirt. "I'm gonna take a quick shower and answer a few work emails before we head back out."

"Okay," she says. "Sounds good."

"Feel free to use the sauna in my bathroom, if you want." I look at my watch. "We've got just under an hour before we need to leave to make our reservation. This place is impossible to get into, so we can't be late."

"Hey, you probably take longer than I do, Mr. Exfoliate and Moisturize."

"You've only got one skin, Kat," I say.

She laughs.

I show her where the towels are and leave her to get to it and then race out of my room to make a phone call in the guest room.

"Hello?" the woman on the other end of the line says.

My pulse is pounding in my ears. "Hey, Kaitlyn. This is Josh Faraday. Just calling to confirm we're still on for tonight?"

"Yeah." She exhales. "I really can't emphasize enough how much trepidation I have about this. I'm really putting my faith in Reed. He said you're a great guy and that I can trust you completely, so I'm taking a gigantic leap of faith. Please don't make me regret this."

"Oh, I know this is a huge favor—and I'm really grateful. Reed isn't steering you wrong. I'm totally trustworthy. I paid close attention at our walk-through-orientation on Tuesday, and I'll be ridiculously careful and respectful with all your stuff, just like you showed me, I promise. If I break *anything*, no matter how slightly, I'll replace it with a brand new model—and I won't touch any of the stuff you told me is off limits. Like I said, this is more for show than anything—I just wanna set the stage for her—really wow her when she opens her eyes for the first time."

Kaitlyn clicks her tongue. "Just, please. This could go horribly wrong a thousand ways."

I don't like the anxious tone in her voice. God help me if this woman does an about-face and changes her mind. "Hey, how 'bout I throw another ten grand your way, just to say thank you and put your mind at ease?"

"Whoa. Really?"

"Yeah. Maybe the price we originally agreed upon was too low. It's not like there's a market for this kind of rental. I don't want you feeling taken advantage of."

"Wow, thanks." Her voice is noticeably warmer. "Yeah, another ten grand would definitely put me at ease. Thanks. You still want me to burst in on you at ten?"

I laugh. "Hell yeah, I do. That's a critical part of my girl's fantasy. I'll time everything on my end so we'll be ready for you exactly at ten. I'll leave your plastic sword outside the door."

"Your girlfriend's got quite the imagination."

"Yeah, she does," I say, smiling to myself. I like hearing the words "your girlfriend" in reference to Kat.

"You're *sure* you wanna do the whole sword-fight-thing? I still think it's gonna be more comedic than sexy, Josh."

"Yeah, I gotta do it. My girlfriend's gonna love it."

Kaitlyn exhales. "Okay. If you insist."

"My girl's got this bizarre little script in her head. I've gotta stick to it."

"Okay," Kaitlyn says. "To each her own."

"So we're good, then?"

"Yep. We're good."

"What time can we come?"

"Any time. The place is ready for you now. I'll text the door-code to you. Oh, and I bought some brand new feather ticklers for you to use. They're on that rack I showed you to use—the one next to the harness."

"Thanks so much."

"Please don't touch anything but what I showed you."

"I won't. I promise."

She exhales audibly for the hundredth time during this short conversation. "Josh, I know we already talked about this, but it bears repeating: Don't try to push things too far. You don't have a clue what you're doing and she's a total newbie. The shock value of the place is gonna be the main thing, okay? Don't try anything other than what I explained to you or else you're gonna hurt or scare her."

"I promise. Thank you. This is just gonna be about role-play. Nothing hard-core, I promise."

"Please don't make me regret this."

"I won't."

She pauses. "So can you bring the extra money tonight? All cash?"

"Yup. No problem. I'll put it outside the door with your sword."

"Thanks. You're absolutely *sure* about that damned sword?"

"Positive. It's in the script. Gotta do it." I chuckle. "See you in a bit."

"Okay. See you soon."

71

KAT

I lean into the mirror to apply a light sheen of gloss to my lips. I scrutinize my eye shadow. Maybe I should add a little more shimmer to my—

The door to the bathroom bursts wide open.

A black-clad figure in a ski mask lunges at me.

I shriek at the top of my lungs.

But before I can move or react beyond screaming in terror, the blackened figure grabs my hand and places something in my palm. I look down, my throat burning and my hand trembling. *A poker chip.* Holy shitballs. Every single drop of blood in my body whooshes into my crotch, all at once. Is it possible to have a heart attack and orgasm at the same time?

I look back up at the menacing figure in the ski mask, but before I can react further, he wraps me into a stifling bear hug, sending the unmistakable scent of Josh's cologne into my nostrils.

"No!" I shout, wiggling and squirming in my deliciously scented attacker's arms. "Let me go!"

But the brute won't be deterred. He grabs my wrists roughly and slaps soft cuffs on them, immobilizing me with his strong arms as he does.

"No!" I shout again, trying desperately to free myself from the dreaded cuffs. "Let me go!" I squirm and writhe with all my might, but, goddammit, I can't free myself from my bindings or my attacker's strong arms. (Yay!)

"No," I choke out, even though every fiber of my body wants to yell, "Yes, yes, yes!"

I feel something slipping over the top my head and then over my eyes (soft satin!) and suddenly everything goes completely black.

"Let me go!" I yell. "Right now!"

But the horrible man—or dare I say, the *horribly* sexy man?—doesn't stop.

He lifts me completely off the ground, crushing my body against his, and, in a flash, I feel myself being carried out of the bathroom in long, delicious, cologne-infused strides.

"Please," I whimper. "Let me go."

He doesn't reply. He's carrying me in loping movements. I nuzzle my face into him and breathe in his sexy scent, my clit burning with intense arousal. This is incredible.

"Who are you? Why are you here?" I shout. Oh, God, he smells good. I'm already twitching with desire.

I hear a door opening. The sound of shoes on hard cement. There's the sound of a car door opening followed by the sensation of my body being laid down in an extremely small space. Oh fuck, no—Josh isn't putting me in the trunk of his car, is he? Oh shit.

"*From Justin to Kelly!*" I shriek.

His movement freezes.

"You're not putting me in the trunk of a car, are you?"

"No, babe," Josh's voice says soothingly. "I'm laying you down in the back-seat of my Beemer."

I exhale. "Oh, okay. Whew. I get really claustrophobic—I should have mentioned that."

"Babe, I'd never put you in the trunk of a car. You could get hurt."

I exhale. "Okay. Whew."

"*Babe.* Come on. I'll never risk your safety."

I exhale with relief again. "Okay. Good. Thank you. Proceed."

"You okay?"

"Yeah. I'm great." I grin. "This is so awesome, Josh. Oh my God. When you burst into the bathroom, I had a freaking heart attack."

He laughs. "You should have seen the look on your face. Sorry if I scared you."

"No, no, it was a good kind of scared. I loved it. My panties are already soaked—or, then again, maybe that's pee."

He laughs. "Okay, you ready to keep going now?"

"Yeah. Sorry I pulled the safe word so fast. I won't do it again."

"No, no. Use the safe word as much as you need. That's what it's for. I never want you to be scared. This is supposed to be fun."

I exhale. "Okay. Thanks."

"Don't hesitate to use it if you need it, babe."

"Okay." I shake it off. "No more breaking character. Go, baby. I'm already totally wet for you."

He makes a sexual sound. "Don't tempt me to fuck you right here—I'm rock hard." His fingertips graze my thigh and slip inside my undies and then right into me. "Oh my God," he says. "You're soaking wet." His fingers massage me for a moment, making me writhe and moan.

I spread my legs, inviting him to fuck me right here and now.

"Oh my God," he says. "What am I doing? I've got a whole thing planned, babe. Stop being evil."

His fingers retreat from me, leaving me aching and wanting more.

I hear the unmistakable sound of him licking his finger vigorously. "You taste like sugar, baby. So sweet."

My clit jolts. "Josh," I breathe. "Take me now."

"Patience, babe," he says, his voice low and sexy. "You're in for a wild ride." The car door shuts and a moment later, I hear a car engine start.

We're unmistakably on the move.

After a few minutes of driving, music suddenly blares in the car—Britney Spears, "I'm a Slave 4 U"—and I burst out laughing.

Josh's laughter joins mine.

"Hilare," I say. "You're so funny, babe."

"Hey, you didn't say *From Justin to Kelly*," Josh says. "You gotta stay in character unless you say it."

"There's no way I can stay in character if you're gonna make 'I'm a Slave 4 U' the soundtrack of my abduction into sexual slavery."

"Just to be clear, there's no other circumstance when I'd ever play this song —this song is a testament to just how far I'll go for a laugh."

"Mission accomplished," I say.

"Okay, back in character now." The song switches to "Fever" by the Black Keys.

I sigh happily. "This is so frickin' awesome."

After what seems like forever, the car stops and the engine turns off. The driver's door opens—and then the car door nearest to me—and then I'm being lifted up by strong arms and carried like a sack of potatoes, my cuffed wrists dangling down.

Josh stops walking and shifts my body weight slightly. There's a beeping sound, and then the sound of a door opening. He walks several paces and it's clear to me we're now indoors.

Josh sets me down gently onto my feet. I wobble slightly—the blackness of my blindfold is disorienting—and he grasps my forearm just above my cuffs to steady me.

"You okay?" he whispers.

I nod.

"Hang on." I sense him moving away briefly and then returning to me. He grasps my forearm again and guides my body down. "Kneel," he commands at full voice, his tone menacing. My knees are met with a soft cushion. "I saw you walking down the sidewalk last week and I had to have you," he continues in his bad-guy voice. "I've brought you to a place far from civilization where no one can hear you scream. Do as I say or else—" He stops for a long beat. "Hey, babe. *From Justin to Kelly*. I can't do this part. It's making me think about my mom. I feel sick."

My stomach drops into my toes. "Oh, I didn't even think about that. I'm so sorry. Take off my blindfold."

"No, I'll be okay as long as we skip this first part. Let's just pretend I said all the shit necessary to get you under control—that I already crushed your spirit like a sex-slave-master would and made you totally submissive to me. Okay?"

"Are you sure? We can stop."

"No, I'm good as long as we skip this first part. I don't wanna threaten you."

"Okay. No problem. But if you decide you wanna stop, just lemme know."

"Okay." He exhales. "God, I wish you could see your nipples under your dress right now. They're like little bullets. So fucking sexy."

I lick my lips.

"Hey, why don't we get some music cranking?" he says. "That'll help loosen things up. Hang on."

I remain on my knees in the blackness, my cuffed arms dangling in front of me, wondering where the hell he's taken me.

After a brief moment, an old-school funk song fills my ears.

I feel Josh's body heat next to me again. "'Thank You For Letting Me Be Myself,'" Josh says. "Sly and the Family Stone—greatest funk band ever."

I've never heard this song before, but it's definitely got a great groove—my body's already involuntarily pulsing to the beat—and I can't imagine a better song to kick off our mutual sick-fuckedness than a tune called, "Thank You For Letting Me Be Myself."

I hear the sound of Josh's fly unzipping. "Open your mouth," he grunts.

I do as I'm told and warm flesh unexpectedly whacks me in the mouth. I flinch out of surprise.

"Lick my balls," he growls softly.

I smile. That was an extremely porno-y thing to say, especially with this awesome bow-chick-a-wow-wow-music blaring around us. And that's exactly what I wanted—to star in my own porno. Hell yeah. I stick out my tongue and do as I'm told—well, as best I can, anyway—I must say, without the use of my eyes or hands to help me with my task, licking and sucking on balls feels a bit like bobbing for dangling apples—but after a few minutes, I get the *hang* of it (snicker) and really start delivering some seriously excellent ball-licking-and-sucking, if I do say so myself.

"Good," Josh says after several minutes, his voice ragged. "Congratulations. You've just earned the right to suck my cock."

My clit flutters. "Thank you, sir," I purr. I open my mouth. It's watering with anticipation. Being Josh's slave is turning me on every bit as much as I fantasized it would.

I feel the sensation of Josh's wet tip resting against the subtle cleft in my chin (surprise!), followed by his shaft sliding into my open mouth, all the way to the back of my throat—so far, my eyes bug out behind my blindfold. Holy motherfucking shitballs. Good lord, that's a lot of dick all at once.

My throat closes up and I gag.

"Relax," Josh coos, running his hands through my hair. "Take a deep breath and relax your throat."

I breathe through my nose and focus on releasing my throat muscles, and sure enough, my throat opens up and Josh's cock slides farther into me. Holy Big Dick, Batman, Josh is so far inside my throat, I can't do a damned thing but sit here like a blowup-doll. This ain't no Katherine Morgan Ultimate Blowjob Experience, folks—this is nothing but Crack Whore Blowjob. I'm just a warm hole, for crying out loud—no skill or finesse required for this job. I can't suck or lick or swirl my tongue or finger or massage or do any of my other tricks. I could be anyone, really. Anything. It's demeaning, I tell you—dehumanizing. *And I love it.*

Josh lets out a particularly sexy sound and my body begins clenching furiously in reply—but my throat is so filled up, I barely make a sound.

He's rippling in my mouth. He's gonna blow. Oh my God. This is so effing sexy.

But, nope. He doesn't come. He pulls out of my mouth, instead.

I cough and sputter, trying to calm my raging throat muscles.

I can hear Josh breathing heavily. "Since you sucked my dick so well," he says, his voice ragged, "I'm gonna reward you by taking off your blindfold now."

"Thank you, sir," I squeak out in a scratchy voice. Oh my God. My throat is throbbing.

Josh's fingers slide into my hair and then, suddenly, the blindfold is off.

"Holy shitballs," I say, looking around and blinking in the soft light. "What the... ?"

"This is my *lair*," Josh says, obviously trying (but failing) to suppress a huge grin.

Oh my effing God, we're in a *bona fide* sex-dungeon—a glittering, gleaming BDSM dungeon like nothing I've ever seen or even imagined. I knew places like this existed, but this place is... well, out of a fantasy.

It's a large, windowless room with black marble floors. The walls are painted a deep chocolate brown. Gold and crystal chandeliers hang from the ceiling, along with an eye-popping assortment of cages, harnesses, whips, chains, pulleys, racks, and other suspended contraptions I couldn't identify if my life depended on it. There's an X-shaped, padded rack in the middle of the room. A system of pulleys in the far corner next to a bunch of studded leather straps. A neatly arranged assortment of leather riding crops and feathered rods sits prominently in the middle of the room. Oh, shit, what's that spherical cage-thing hanging from the ceiling? It looks like a birdcage for a very, very large canary.

"Come with me." Josh pulls me to standing and drags me across the room to a harness-looking-rack-contraption. Wordlessly, he unlatches my soft cuffs, strips off all my clothes, and straps me into bindings, spreading my limbs out into a four-pointed star. Oh my God. I'm completely opened up in this position —his for the taking, any which way he pleases.

My body is jolting with excitement.

"Relax into the bindings," Josh says, his voice full of smooth confidence. "They'll hold your weight."

I try to let myself relax, but I can't seem to do it.

"Take a deep breath," he commands, grazing his fingers across my belly. "And then let it out slowly."

I do as I'm told and allow myself to melt into my bindings—and, I'll be damned, just like he said, my limbs are being fully supported and held into place. I'm like a fly caught in a web. Immovable. Completely at his mercy. A little sound of arousal lurches out of my throat.

Josh peels off his clothes slowly, his blue eyes smoldering at me as he does, and stands in front of me, his erection straining, his muscles tense. "Your body is mine," he says.

"Yes, sir."

He looks me up and down for a moment, smiling wickedly. "Hmm. What shall I do to my slave first?"

I shudder.

He ambles over to a nearby rack and runs his hand along a selection of implements, finally selecting a long, feathered rod from the rack. When he returns to me, he's smiling devilishly.

"I had to have you," he says. "I couldn't go another day."

He lazily drifts the tickler over my breasts, belly, and hips, culling goose bumps out of every square inch it touches. I moan. He does it again. And then again. And then he leans into me and unexpectedly sucks on my hard nipple.

When I cry out with excitement, he reaches down and plunges his fingers inside me, making me jerk and jolt in my bindings.

"Dripping wet," he says softly. "Such a good girl."

At his words, as if right on cue, I feel a glob of wetness ooze out of my crotch like thick molasses and onto my thigh.

"Oh," he says. He brings his fingers to his mouth. "Delicious."

I let out a long, steady exhale.

Josh walks slowly around to my backside and begins tickling the backs of my thighs and ass with his feather.

I let out a little moan. I can't stand this anymore. I've never wanted a man as much as I want Josh right now. I shift my hips, desperate to relieve the pressure building inside me, but it's no use. I'm about to climax. I can feel it. I'm in pain with this ache.

The feather retreats.

A warm, wet tongue licks my ass, and just when I begin melting into the delicious pleasure, I feel a sharp pain on my ass cheek—the unmistakable sensation of being bitten.

I shriek and jerk in my bindings.

He chuckles.

"Jesus," I mutter.

His tongue returns to my backside and begins exploring every inch of my ass as his fingers slide to my clit and wetness and begin working me with astonishing skill. Oh shit. I've never been touched like this before. Where'd he learn to do this? Oh my fuck. His tongue is lapping at me from behind while his fingers are *owning* me. I want to writhe, but I can't. I want to shift to relieve myself of the pressure building inside me, but I'm completely immobile.

"Fuck!" I say through gritted teeth. "Fuck, fuck. Oh my God. *Fuck.*"

My body suddenly wracks with a twisting orgasm and I jerk against my bindings like a fish out of water.

Before my orgasm ends, I feel Josh rising up behind me. There's the unmistakable sound of fluid splooging out of a bottle and then a finger sliding up my asshole. I shudder. Oh my effing God. He wraps his arms around me from behind, cleaves himself to my back, grabs ahold of my breasts with lubed palms, and slides his slick cock up my ass, eliciting a low groan from deep inside me.

"I own you," he growls into my ear, his voice strained.

I'm incapable of replying. I've tried anal before, but not like this—not when I'm completely sober (and therefore feeling every goddamned inch). Not when I'm bound and trussed like a pig on a spit in a goddamned sex dungeon. Not when the dick in question is a freaking donkey-dick, not to mention attached to the sexiest fucking slab of man I've ever seen—who just so happened to abscond with me out of a bathroom while wearing a freaking ski mask.

I moan loudly.

"I'm gonna make you come so hard," he says into my ear. "Harder than you ever have."

I groan. This is too intense. I'm not sure I can handle this. I thought I could, but it might be too much, even for a dirty little freak like me.

"Beg me for more," he whispers into my ear. "I'm not in all the way yet."

There's *more?* Holy fucking hell. This sure feels like all of him.

"Beg me," he grits out.

"More. *Please,*" I choke out, even though I'm not sure I can handle it.

He gives me what I've asked for and I inhale sharply in shock—but before I can exhale my breath, something glides inside my vagina and begins vibrating from deep inside me. Oh my fuck. My breathing is shallow. I'm like a pug with heatstroke. Oh my God. There's more. Something begins swiping at my clit like a tongue. Oh Jesus. He's using some kind of rabbit vibe on me. Oh my fuckity fuck. I let out a strangled cry. I've never been filled up like this, stimulated in every conceivable way all at once. I feel like my body's scattering in a thousand directions, all at once, exploding and melting at the same time. Too much. No more. Can't handle. Gah.

Josh pumps his donkey-dick harder inside me while the vibe does its thing.

"Oh fuck," he says, his voice ragged. "*Fuck.*"

Yeah. My thoughts exactly.

One of his hands gropes my breast and pinches my nipple so hard, I shriek, and just like that, my body spasms violently with pleasure so intense, I dry heave. Oh shit, I've never done that before. Oh God. I do it again. I'm losing complete control of my bodily functions. I feel like I'm gonna barf. Or pee. Or crap myself. Or all of the above. I've never felt this much intense pleasure all at once. My body can't handle it. It's going completely haywire. My insides are twisting violently. It's like the pleasure is literally tying me into knots. I make a strangled, gagging sound, followed by a whimper. And then another shriek. But Josh doesn't stop. In fact, he fucks me harder.

I jerk pathetically, trying to escape the clenching pleasure that's brutalizing me, but my bindings hold me firmly in place.

"No more," I yell. "I can't do it. Stop." I have never in the history of my life said these words during sex. But this extreme pleasure—or is it pain?—is just too much for me to endure. I can't function. I can't survive it. "Stop," I say. "Stop."

But Josh doesn't stop. In fact, his thrusts are becoming even deeper, if that were possible, and even more passionate.

He bites my shoulder so hard, I'm sure he's broken the skin.

I shriek again and convulse like he's electrocuted me.

"You're *mine*," he breathes.

Warm liquid suddenly (and shockingly) gushes out of me in a torrent. I convulse again and again, enraptured and tormented in equal measure, crying out for relief but getting none. I dry heave again. And then finally, mercifully, my body goes completely slack. I hang my head and a drop of sweat—or is that a tear?—falls down the tip of my nose and to the ground. Holy crap.

Josh quickly unties my wrists and I crumple into his arms, shaking and twitching.

His lips press against my ear. "Did I hurt you?"

I shake my head.

"Did it feel good?"

I nod.

He picks me up and carries me into a small bathroom with red walls and gold fixtures. He sets me down gently. "Can you hold onto the counter for a second?" he asks.

I nod.

He turns on the water in the shower and then guides me under the warm stream.

"You're sure I didn't hurt you?" he asks. "I think I got carried away."

I shake my head.

"You told me to stop, but you didn't use the safe word."

"I didn't want you to stop. I'm glad you didn't stop. Only stop if I use the safe word."

He kisses my mouth and pulls me into him gently, letting the warm water rain down on us. "You're sure you're okay?"

"It was amazing."

He washes me from head to toe, and when he's done, guides me out of the shower and dries me off. "Stay here," he commands. "I have something for you."

I nod and wait. I'm shaking like I've just run a marathon.

He's gone quite a while, it seems, and when he returns, he's fully dressed and holding up a white satin nightie. "Lift up your arms," he commands.

I do as I'm told and he slips the nightie over my head and onto my body. I'm confused as to why he's dressing me rather than keeping me naked, but I'm too fried to give it much thought.

"Come." He grabs my hand and pulls me out of the bathroom and back into the dungeon. Everything's been cleaned—there's no sign of my messy orgasm and absolutely nothing out of place. He guides me to a bed in the corner, lays me onto my back, and wordlessly secures bindings around my wrists and ankles.

"You don't have to tie me up anymore," I say, pulling against my bindings. "I won't try to escape."

"No. I can't risk losing you," he says simply.

A wave of glee washes over me. I know he's simply following my script, but those words make my skin buzz, nonetheless.

"I'm not tricking you," I coo. "I didn't run when you left me alone in the bathroom, did I? You can trust me."

He pauses, mulling that over. "No," he finally says. "I can't risk it. You're a *unicorn*." He shoots me a snarky look, obviously proud of himself for deftly inserting that little gem into our scene. "I can't risk it."

"Please."

He sets his jaw. "No. Now that I know what it's like to have you, I don't think I can live without you."

My heart stops. Was that in the script? Or did Josh say that in real life?

"What's your name?" I ask.

He makes a face like I've just asked him to spell *antideluvian*. "Um," he says, apparently pondering the question. "Joshua Faraday," he finally says.

That's not at all what I expected him to say. I thought he'd come up with some exotic sex-slave-master name like Magnusson Carmichael III. For my part, I've certainly planned a sexy name and backstory—I'm an heiress named Chantel Giodissimo—but, jeez, if Josh is going to be himself for our role-plays, then I should do the same. And, in fact, now that I'm thinking about it, it's probably better if we just "be ourselves," just like the song says.

"Hi, Joshua," I say softly. "I'm Katherine Morgan. It's nice to meet you. I sure wish we'd met under different circumstances than you breaking into my house and absconding with me."

Josh smirks. "*Absconding* with you?"

I grin. "Yeah. *Absconding*. And you gave me a freaking heart attack when you did it, by the way. Oh my God."

He flashes an adorable grin. "I'm sorry, Katherine. I didn't mean to scare you when I *absconded* with you. It's just that when I saw you walking down the sidewalk the other day, I had to have you." He glances at the clock and I follow his gaze. It's a few minutes to ten. He trains his beautiful blue eyes back on me. "Please forgive me if I scared you."

"I forgive you. You've given me intense pleasure, Joshua—pleasure I couldn't have imagined."

His beautiful eyes are smoldering at me.

"Will you untie me, Joshua?" I ask softly.

He shakes his head. "I can't. You'll run away. And if I lose you, I'll be wrecked."

My heart lurches into my throat. He sounds so earnest. I can't tell if that was Joshua Faraday the Sex-Slave-Master speaking—or Joshua William Faraday?

I open my mouth to tell him I'd be wrecked if I lost him, too, but before I can say a word, the door to the dungeon swings wide open and a slender figure wearing a ski mask bursts into the room.

I shriek in surprise and pull violently on my bindings.

"I've come to steal her away," a woman's voice says in a lackluster monotone. She holds up a plastic sword. "I saw her and I had to have her."

I look at Josh with wide-eyed astonishment and he bursts out laughing.

The masked intruder lowers her sword and shifts her weight, her body language conveying total annoyance.

"*From Justin to Kelly*," I say. "Who the heck is this poor woman, Josh?"

Josh wipes his eyes and motions to the masked figure. "Kat, this is Kaitlyn—she owns this place. Kaitlyn's one of the top Dommes in Los Angeles."

"*The* top," Kaitlyn corrects. "If I do say so myself."

"Sorry. *The* top. You can take off your mask, Kaitlyn. Oh my God. This is so fucking hilarious."

Kaitlyn removes her mask to reveal a very attractive woman, with brown hair and dark, piercing eyes, in her early forties or so.

"Hi," Kaitlyn says to me calmly. "I'm here to steal you away and make you my sex slave."

I giggle. "Nice to meet you, Kaitlyn." I jut my chin at my wrist restraint. "Sorry I can't wave hello. So you're here to fight to the death for me, huh?"

Josh is still laughing. "Oh my God, this is so ridiculous. I'm sorry, Kaitlyn, I should have listened to you."

Kaitlyn rolls her eyes.

"I'm so sorry, babe. I didn't think it would be this lame. I thought it would be fun and silly, but not *lame*."

"It's adorable. I love it. You thought of everything."

"I was originally thinking about hiring a stuntman and choreographing a whole big thing with pyrotechnics, but the logistics just seemed crazy. There would have been, like, twenty people involved, and I didn't think you'd like that."

"Good call," I say, laughing. "Embarrassing myself in front of Kaitlyn here is plenty."

Kaitlyn shrugs. "Don't be embarrassed. My whole life is about helping people fulfill their fantasies. This is a first, I admit, but, hey."

"Thank you," I say. "So what do you say we press fast-forward on the sword fight? Pretend you two have already fought and Kaitlyn lost?"

Kaitlyn nods and looks to Josh for confirmation.

"Hell no," Josh says. He reaches down next to the bed and pulls out a plastic sword to match Kaitlyn's. "We gotta have a sword fight, babe—I don't care if it's ridiculous, it's in your script. We gotta follow the script."

Kaitlyn and I exchange a look.

"Okay," she says. She begrudgingly holds up her sword. "I'm here to steal her away and make her my sex-slave."

I giggle. This is utterly ridiculous. A travesty. I absolutely love it.

Josh leaps up from the bed, on the attack. "*En guarde!*" he shouts.

For a few minutes, Josh and Kaitlyn whack each other's swords like preschoolers on a playground while Josh shouts lines from *Princess Bride*, until, finally, Kaitlyn falls into a chair with a sword shoved into her armpit and dies.

"Let this be a lesson to any man who tries to *abscond* with what's mine," Josh says, standing over Kaitlyn's body. "Fuck you, all of you. She's mine."

A ripple of pleasure zings through my body. It's ridiculous, yes—but it's freaking hot, too. The boy has put a lot of effort and thought into making my silly fantasy come to life. I can't help but swoon.

Kaitlyn opens her eyes. "So... Is that it, then?"

"Yeah. That'll do it." Josh helps her up. "Thanks again for everything, Kaitlyn. You're a trooper. Now be gone!" He laughs.

Kaitlyn shakes her head. "Have fun, you two. Now that I've seen you in action, I totally get it. You're total goofballs." She smiles for the first time since she stepped foot in the room and turns toward the door. "Be sure to turn out the lights and lock up when you go."

"Will do," Josh says. "Thanks again."

"Thank you!" I call out to Kaitlyn's back just before she slips out the door.

Josh turns to me. "How cool was that? I just had a sword fight with a real-life dominatrix."

"How'd you hook up with her?" I ask, an alarming thought beginning to creep into my head. "Is she a *friend* of yours?"

Josh rolls his eyes. "Cool your jets, Madame Terrorist. Kaitlyn's a friend of Reed's. I've never used her services." He laughs. "And to answer your next question, no, Reed's not a client of hers, either. They're just friends. Reed knows everyone in L.A.—well, anyone who's interesting." He beams a huge smile at me. "So, my sexy little sex-slave, are you ready to keep going with our porno? We've still got the third and final act to perform, you may recall: The Big Reveal."

I smile broadly. "Ooh la la. The Revelation. Yes."

"Any last words before we get back into character?"

I think for a minute. There are definitely words I'm dying to say to Josh, three little words to be exact, but I can't do it. They're magic words a girl simply can't be the first to say in a relationship.

"Nope. I'm good," I say. "Proceed."

"Quiet on the porn set!" Josh yells over his shoulder to an imaginary crew. "And... *action*." He crawls onto the bed and cups my cheek in his palm. "Are you hungry, Katherine?"

"Yes, Master Joshua. Starving."

Josh reaches down next to the bed, retrieves a small cooler, and pulls out a sandwich in a Ziplock baggie.

"Aw," I say. "*From Justin to Kelly*. You made me an orgasm-inducing peanut butter and jelly sandwich? So sweet."

"Wouldn't want my sex-slave going hungry." He grins. "I've got an apple and some chips for you, too, if you want 'em."

"You're the sweetest sex-slave-master, ever. Thank you. I was ready to eat my hand when we got back from hiking. Now I'm ready to eat both arms."

He breaks off a bite-sized piece of the sandwich and feeds it to me.

"Whoa," I say, chewing the sandwich with gusto. "You told the truth—I just came."

Josh laughs.

"Why is this sandwich so good? Did you lace it with something illegal?"

"Nope. Just organic strawberry jam."

He feeds me another bite.

"This sandwich is so frickin' good," I say, "it's giving me *Munchausen* syndrome."

Josh chuckles. "No, babe. Not *Munchausen* syndrome. That's when you poison someone slowly just so you can keep being their caretaker."

"Oh." I giggle.

He chuckles. "You're so cute."

"So what did I mean, then?"

"*Stockholm* syndrome, I think."

"Is that where someone held captive falls in love with their captor?" I ask.

"Yeah," he says.

"Okay, then, yeah. That's what I have for sure."

We both stare at each other for an awkward beat.

Oh shit. I think I just told Josh I'm in love with him.

He feeds me another bite of sandwich but doesn't say anything for a long beat.

"Water?" he finally asks, his voice tight.

"What?" My cheeks feel flushed. I just told him I love him in a clever sort of backhanded-code, didn't I?

Josh holds up the water bottle. "Thirsty?"

"Oh. Yeah. Thank you."

He holds the bottle to my lips and I take a long guzzle, my heart racing. Damn. I wish I'd told him more clearly than that, in a way that would have left no doubt. I shouldn't have been so subtle. I should have said, "This sandwich is so good, *it made me fall deeply in love with you, Joshua William Faraday.*" But I didn't. I left it vague. "Yeah, that's what I have," I said—and nothing more. Idiot. And now the moment has passed.

"Chips?" Josh asks.

"What kind?"

"Doritos." He holds up a little red bag. "Original flavor."

"Thank you."

He pops a chip into my mouth and then into his own. "Fuck you, Jonas—I eat what I want—although I must admit I feel kinda bad I'm chowing down on Doritos while gourmet meals are sitting in my fridge."

"How about we eat Jonas' food tomorrow night?" I say. "We can stay in and rent a movie."

"Awesome. Yeah, a quiet night at home with my Party Girl with a Hyphen sounds damned good. More water, babe?"

I shake my head. "I'm good. I'm done."

"You ready to keep going with the porno?"

I nod.

"Cool. I've got my entire speech ready for act three." He stows the remaining food in the cooler. "Give me my cue, babe," he says softly. "I'm gonna slay it."

I clear my throat. "Untie me, Joshua," I whisper. "I don't want to be a prisoner anymore. I need my freedom."

Josh touches my cheek tenderly. "Katherine, when I *absconded* with you, all I cared about was making you mine, through any means necessary. All I cared about was what I wanted. But now, even though I want you more than ever, I care too much about you to keep you as my prisoner anymore. Now the thing I want more than my own happiness is yours." He touches the cleft in my chin.

Holy Exploding Heart, Batman. Not To Mention Ovaries. I know Josh was merely following the loose script I babbled to him in Las Vegas, but he delivered his lines with such breathtaking sincerity, my heart seems to have lost its ability to discern fantasy from reality.

"Hang on," he says. He gets up and walks behind the bed, outside of my field of vision. I strain against my bindings. What's he doing? He's supposed to untie me now and ravage me as a free woman.

A song begins playing over the sound system and my heart stops. Holy shitballs. He's cued up "If You Ever Want To Be In Love" by James Bay—the song that made Josh literally bolt out of his bedroom when it came on last night. Oh my effing God.

Josh returns to the bed. His clothes are off and his hard-on is massive. He sits on the edge of the bed, gazing at me with smoldering eyes, and slowly begins untying me.

Holy shitballs.

The minute I'm free, he pulls my nightie and underwear off my body and guides me onto his lap and straight onto his erection. I take him into me and wrap my thighs around his waist, throw my arms around his neck, and ride him feverishly, spurred on by the song—and especially what it means that he's decided to play it for me in this magical moment.

"Don't leave me," Josh whispers, cradling me in his arms, fucking me, caressing me, kissing my face.

I'm lost in him. I gyrate my hips on top of him and smash my breasts against his muscled chest, desperately trying to press my beating heart against his.

"Josh," I breathe. I can barely push air into my lungs. I'm gasping for air, suddenly overcome by a surge of energy coursing between us.

I want him. I need him. *I love him.*

"Don't go," he says. "Stay with me."

"I'm not going anywhere," I breathe. "Oh, Josh. I'm all yours."

72

KAT

For the past kajillion hours, Josh and I have been sitting on his black leather couch, smoking weed and listening to the Black Keys (the current song is "Tighten Up") and semi-watching our favorite scenes from our favorite movies (on mute)—*Twenty-One Jump Street, Zoolander, Happy Gilmore, Anchorman, Harold and Kumar, This is the End,* and selected episodes of *Parks & Recreation,* too. And while we've availed ourselves of the aforementioned samplings of musical and comedic genius, Josh and I have also been voraciously gobbling down every single morsel of the gourmet, healthy meals supplied by Josh's ever-so-thoughtful and fitness-conscious brother.

Oh, and perhaps I should mention we've done all of the above-mentioned activities in our birthday suits.

Oh, and perhaps I should also mention "eating" Jonas' gourmet, healthy meals has actually entailed licking, nibbling, and slurping food off each other's stomachs and thighs, and out of each other's belly buttons, and, yes, okay, if you really must know, off of (or out of) each other's most sensitive places.

I take a long drag on the joint Josh offers me and blow the smoke into his face in a steady, controlled stream. Man, I'm stoned. Stoned out of my mind. Fred-Flintstoned. Emma Stoned. Sharon Stoned. Rolling Stoned. Sly Stalloned. Oh, wait, no. That last one doesn't really work. I think I meant Sly and the Family Stoned? Wasn't that the funk band Josh introduced me to yesterday in the sex dungeon? Well, in any event, let's just say tonight I've definitely become a naturalized citizen of the peaceful and munchie-eating land of Estonia. I burst out laughing.

"What?" Josh asks, his eyes glazed over.

"I dunno. It was funny, though."

"God, you're beautiful," Josh coos, obviously feeling rather Oliver Stoned himself. "I could look at your gorgeous face forever." He leans forward, grabs my face, and kisses me deeply.

"You said *forever*," I say into his lips, smiling.

"What?"

"I didn't know your mouth was capable of uttering that word."

"You must have misheard me. I don't even know that strange word. What I actually said was, '*Florebblaaaah*.'"

I roll my eyes.

Josh flashes me a goofy grin. "Aw, come on, baby. My douchebaggery is my charm."

"Mmm hmm."

He sighs audibly. "Oh, Kat, Kat, *gorgeous* Kat. Are you gonna wait for me or not, Gorgeous, Stubborn Kat?"

"Hmm? Sure, I'll wait." I grab the remote control and pause the movie, freezing Michael Cera grabbing Rihanna's ass in *This Is the End*. "Go ahead." I motion toward the bathroom.

"No, no. I don't mean wait for me to go to the *bathroom*. I wanna know if you're gonna wait for *me*?"

I stare at him for a long beat. "You mean *florebblaaahhhhh*?"

He doesn't reply.

"Dude, what are you talking about?"

He bristles. "Never mind." He grabs a bottle of Patron from the floor next to him and takes a swig.

My stomach twists. How does this man make me feel so freaking good and so flippin' insecure all at the same time? Last night in the sex dungeon, after he'd untied me, Josh made love to me so passionately, so *urgently*, I felt that crazy electricity coursing between us again—that same supernatural electricity as the prior night in Josh's bed—and I thought my heart was gonna burst with joy. But, afterwards, did we talk about what we were both so obviously feeling toward each other? Nooooope. Of course not. Because, it seems, talking about our 'fucking feelings' is off limits with Joshua William Faraday.

"You mean will I wait for you to pull your head out of your ass?" I ask.

"Yeah," Josh says without hesitation. "Exactly."

"Yeah, I'll wait. You're definitely worth the wait."

He smiles broadly. "Thank you." He hands me the bottle of tequila.

"But I won't wait three fucking years, I'm telling you that right now, moth-erfucker." I take a swig from the bottle.

"Well, how long will you wait, then?" he asks.

"I dunno. It depends."

"On what?"

"On what happens between now and then," I say.

He nods. "That's a very deep statement, Kitty Katherine." He runs his hand through his hair and I'm assaulted with the words "Welcome to" flashing me from underneath his bicep. "Hand over the tequila, babe."

I hand him the bottle and he takes a swig.

"I've never done this with a woman before," he says.

"Done what?"

Josh motions to the tequila and the half-eaten food and the TV. "Partied with a girl like she's a dude."

"You call eating vegan creamed spinach out of my cooch 'partying like a dude'?"

He bursts out laughing. "You're so fucking funny, Kum Shot. You're as funny as any of my friends. Funnier."

"Yeah, I'm hilare. And don't call me Kum Shot."

"I could do anything with you and have fun. We could go to the fucking dry cleaners and it would be fun."

"Dude, who wouldn't have fun at the dry cleaners? Those motorized racks are rad. Or here's an idea," I say. "We could go to the fish market and sing the 'Fish Heads' song. Now *that* would be fun."

"I don't know the 'Fish Heads' song."

"No? Are you kidding me?"

He shakes his head.

"Well, shit, boy, Google it now. Search 'Fish Head song YouTube.'" I lean back into the leather couch and spread my naked legs wide, surrendering completely to the chemicals coursing through my bloodstream. "You're welcome, motherfucker."

"I like it when you say motherfucker," he says.

"Motherfucker."

"Sexy."

"Come on, Joshua. Google. 'Fish Heads.' Song. YouTube."

Josh grabs his phone off the table and the moment the unmistakable vocals begin, he laughs his ass off—which, of course, makes me laugh, too.

"How did I not know about this?" Josh asks when the song ends. "Best song ever. Oh my God. When I visit you in Seattle next weekend, I'm gonna take you to Pike's Place Market just so we can sing this song at the top of our lungs."

"At the stall at the very end? Where the guys throw the fish?"

"Of course."

"Aw, that sounds like a fun date. You really know how to razzle-dazzle a girl, Playboy."

"I told you that from day one, didn't I? I said, 'Get ready for the Playboy Razzle-Dazzle.' But did you believe me? Noooooo."

"Oh, I believed you. I just *pretended* not to believe you."

"What was the point of doing that, may I ask? You knew how our story was gonna end. Why torture me?"

I shrug. "I had no idea how our story was gonna end—I still don't."

"You don't?"

"No. Do you?"

He pauses. "No, actually. I thought I did. But now I realize I only knew the ending of the first chapter—not the ending of the *story*."

"What's the ending of the first chapter?" I ask.

"We fuck like rabbits."

"Oh, that's a good ending." I exhale. "Well, if I tortured you in Vegas, then I'm not sorry. You were too frickin' cocky for your own damn good. You had to be taken down a peg."

"Ha! Liar. You were dying to get into my pants from minute one. You were like, 'Gimme your application, Playboy!' And I was like, 'I'm gonna fuck you first and *then* give it to you, Party Girl!' And you were like, 'Yippee! Yes! Please fuck me!'"

"Is that what I sound like? A chipmunk?"

"Yeah, and I sound like Mr. T. 'I pity the fool!'"

"Well, you're delusional. You were the one dying to get into *my* pants. When I kissed Henn, you practically had a stroke."

"Ooph. Totally. But the worst was thinking about you with Cameron Fucking Schulz." He grunts. "Even stoned, thinking about him fucking you makes me wanna break that guy's Captain-America-fucking-face. No one touches my Party Girl with a Hyphen but me. Fuckin' A." He swigs from his bottle again.

I bite my lip. "Wow. Sounds pretty serious, dude."

He bites his lip in mimicry of my gesture. "It just might be."

"It *might* be?" I ask coyly.

"Yeah. It *might* be."

"Can't I at least get a *probably* out of you?"

Josh makes a face that says, "Sorry, come back later."

I scrunch up my face. "You suck balls, Josh. You suck big ol' donkey balls. God, you piss me off." I grunt loudly.

"Whoa! Where'd Stubborn Kat come from all of a sudden? Don't stress me out, Stubborn Kat. This is a stress-free zone. I'm chillaxing."

I glare at him.

He flashes a toothy grin. "I'm a drifter, baby. It's part of my charm." He flexes his arm and kisses his bicep. "You know you can't get enough of me."

"Yeah. Pretty sure I can. Pretty sure I just did."

He laughs. "Aw, why you so mad all of a sudden, Stubborn Kat? What'd I do to piss you off this time?"

I grunt with exasperation. "Why the *fuck* do you even have a calendar-app on your goddamned phone, Josh? That's what I wanna know. You can't keep straight what you've got planned for the next *week*? Hmm?"

"What?" He laughs. "You're making zero sense. I have no idea what you're talking about."

I huff. "It doesn't matter. Blah, blah, blaaaaaaaaaaaaaaah."

"What are you ranting about, you nutjob?"

"Never mind. Forget it."

"Okay. Forgetting is something I'm good at." He looks around at the half-eaten trays of food around us. "You hungry again, babe?"

"Hmm. I might be able to eat a little something-something."

"Green beans? Some sort of squash-thing? What's your pleasure, Party Girl?'

"Squash *a la dick*, please," I say.

"Excellent selection." He smears himself with a trail of veggies from his tattooed chest down to his tattooed waistline and then down his dick and balls —and then he lies back, his arms behind his head, his muscles bulging, his douche-y underarm tattoos on full, douche-y-McDouche-y-pants-display, and flashes me a lascivious grin. "*Bon appetit, beau bébé.*"

Without hesitation, I lean in and lick up every morsel of food off his pecs and abs and his "Overcome" tattoo and finally work my way downtown—and I'm not even the slightest bit grossed out as I do any of it. In fact, I find the entire experience highly enjoyable. When every crevice, ridge, crease, bulge, wrinkle, and fold of him is clean as a whistle, I continue licking and sucking on his hard-on for quite some time, doing my damnedest to give him the Katherine Morgan Ultimate Blowjob Experience, but although Josh seems to be enjoying himself tremendously, he doesn't seem even close to climaxing.

"Dude. That is some serious stamina," I finally say, sitting up and loosening my jaw. "Are you made of steel?"

"Sorry, babe. I'm too stoned to come. It feels amazing, though. But, yeah, you could stick a Dyson on there and I'm not gonna blow. Sorry." He laughs and pulls me into him for a kiss. "Jesus, Kat. You're so fucking beautiful, you make me wanna punch a professional athlete."

I laugh. "You're so fucking beautiful, you make me wanna roll you in Nutella and lick you from head to toe."

"Will you please remind me to buy a huge jar of Nutella tomorrow?"

"Sure thing. As long as you remind *me* to remind *you* to buy a huge jar of Nutella tomorrow."

We laugh hysterically.

"Shit," Josh says. "I can barely remember my own name right now. I'm so fucking high."

"Your name is Joshua William Faraday and you're the sexiest man alive."

"Thank you, Katherine Ulla Morgan. You're the most gorgeous woman I've ever laid eyes on. And you're smart and sweet and funny, too. Best girl ever, ever, ever. *Florebblaaaaaaaaaaaah.*"

"Wow. Can you write my eulogy, please?"

"No, because I don't want you to die. People always seem to die around me and I hate it."

I make a sad face. "I'm sorry."

"It's okay. I'm over it. Just please don't die, Kat."

"I'm totally down for that plan—I promise to live florebblaaaaaaah."

"Cool. Let's live florebblaaaah, just you and me. We'll eat healthy, gourmet food sent to us by my dear brother and we'll fulfill each other's sick-fuck-fantasies and we'll be happy, happy, happy florebblaaaaaah."

"Okay. Cool. Where will we live and be happy, happy, happy floreb-blaaaaaah?"

"Seattle, of course. Where else?"

I sigh wistfully. "That would be amazing. I wish we both lived in Seattle so bad."

"'Twould be amazing," Josh says. "Hey, did I mention you're sweet? Because you are."

"Yep. That's what you said."

"And you're smart, too."

"Yep. That's me. Sweet and smart." I snort. "That's what everyone always says about me."

"You don't think you're sweet and smart?"

I pause. "I think I'm sweet with the people I care about, but you're not gonna hear anyone say, 'Oh, that Kat—she never says an unkind word about anyone.'"

We both laugh at the ridiculousness of anyone saying that about me.

"And I'd say I'm *witty*. Sometimes *clever*. Often *diabolical*. But, no, based on my college transcripts, not particularly *smart*."

"Fuck that shit. You're smart. Which is why your new company's gonna kick ass. Speaking of which, when are you gonna quit your job and stop waffling?"

"I dunno. It's one thing to have a faraway dream about something you *might* wanna do 'one day' and another to all of a sudden be expected to make it happen overnight." I shrug. "Maybe I'm not as *entrepreneurial* as I thought. Damn, that's a big word."

"What are you afraid of?"

I make a "duh" face. "Failure."

"Bah. Fuck failure. It's what happens right before success." He flexes and kisses his arm again. "I should know. I've failed a lot."

I purse my lips, unconvinced.

"Don't be scared. I'll help you. You can't fail with the muscle and charm of Joshua William Faraday behind you." He flexes his other arm and kisses it.

"Yeah, as long as I don't need help in, say, a *month*?"

He makes a face of pure annoyance.

"Seriously, thanks for the offer," I say. "I appreciate it. It's just a huge deci-sion—definitely not one to make while high as a kite." I pause, not remembering what I was just about to say. "This is only the fourth time I've smoked pot in my whole life. Did I tell you that? Last time was in college. I haven't done this in *florebblaaaaaah*."

"Really? A party girl like you? I'm shocked."

"Well, Sarah's the one who named me 'Party Girl with the Heart of Gold,' don't forget. Everything's relative, I guess—compared to Sarah, I'm Keith Richards."

He laughs.

"So do you smoke a lot, Playboy? You seem much more composed than I am right now—your tolerance must be pretty high."

"Nah, these days hardly ever. I've just got too much shit to do to put my brain on mental lockdown for hours on end. Back in the day, though? Oh my God. I was baked my entire first year at UCLA. I'm shocked I didn't get kicked out of school, I was such a fucking screw-up. I finally cleaned myself up that first summer, thank God—and then I had a bit of a wobble again right after graduation, before I'd figured out what the fuck to do with myself—but then I finally pulled myself together for good at twenty-four. That's when Jonas suggested I open an L.A. office of Faraday & Sons. I followed his advice and it was exactly what I needed—it gave me some purpose in my life."

"How did you pull yourself together that first summer?"

"I went to Jonas Rehab. We backpacked together through Asia and some other places that summer. Funny thing was, Jonas had just gotten out of the psych hospital, and I was supposedly on that trip to help *him*—but he's the one who helped me, by far."

"How? What'd he do?"

"He was just Jonas. There's nothing like being around Jonas Patrick Faraday and his constant 'pursuit of excellence' to make a guy realize he's a total flop-dick."

"Is that when you got your dragon tattoo? You said you got it in Bangkok, 'drunk and high as a kite.'"

"Damn, you've got a good memory."

"I remember everything you've told me."

"Yeah, it was on that trip—about a week in. Remember how in the beginning of *The Karate Kid* he starts off being a little punk? That was me the first week of my trip with Jonas. We'd been climbing all week and I was like, 'I'm sick of this wax-on-wax-off shit, man; I wanna party,' so I flew Reed and some homeys into Bangkok while I left my dorky brother to climb more rocks on his own up north." Josh shakes his head. "I was such a little prick to leave Jonas like that—such a total fucking douchebag. Inexcusable." He sighs. "So, anyway, when Jonas and I met up again a few days later in Cambodia, I knew I'd fucked up, and I just was like, 'Okay, Mr. Miyagi, I'm ready now. Teach me the art of *karate*.'"

I laugh.

"Jonas had just come from climbing all alone for days and he was this savage *beast*—just, like, oh my God, this golden god—and I looked like something the cat barfed up. I took one look at Jonas, and one look at my pitiful self, and realized it was time for me to stop being a total asswipe-douchebag-waste-of-space. And that was that. Jonas and I became this unstoppable duo—two savage beasts crushing it across three continents. The Faraday Twins. The ladies never stood a chance." He laughs.

I snicker. "Oh, I bet. I can only imagine how women across three continents soaked their panties over The Faraday Twins."

"Oh, shit, it was like stealing candy from a baby. Well, actually, not at first because Jonas was the biggest dork in the entire fucking universe." He rolls his eyes. "But, oh my fuck, even when Jonas was a total train wreck, women still practically threw themselves at the guy everywhere we went. Once, this woman was sitting next to Jonas at this bar, and when she got up to leave, she left her room key in front of him. And Jonas stood up and held up the key and shouted to her across the bar, 'Excuse me, ma'am! You forgot your room key!'" Josh buckles over laughing. "Classic Jonas. But then I started coaching him and he got way better. The trick was not letting him talk—making him the 'something shiny.' That was always our best strategy." He winks.

I laugh. "Josh, you're not exactly the 'something dull,' you know."

"Meh, I'm a good-looking guy—I'm not gonna pretend I don't know that. But Jonas is, like, supernatural. People always fall all over themselves when he walks into a room. He's just got this weird magic about him no one can resist. I think it's the fact that he's obviously so fucked up. People love that shit."

"Well, I think you're every bit as magical and fucked-up as your brother and then some."

He laughs.

"I'm serious. I swear to God, if I'd been one of the girls who encountered you and Jonas during your travels, I would have gone for *you*, hands down."

"Really?"

"Heck yeah. You've got that mischief in your eyes I can't resist. Jonas is sweet and crazy, but you're the bad boy—and I can never resist a bad boy."

"Oh yeah? I'm a bad boy, huh?" He runs his fingertips up my bare thigh.

"Oh, yeah," I say.

"Well, guess what? This bad boy's suddenly hungry again, baby. You got any sweet potatoes over there? I'm thinking about macking down on some sweet potatoes *a la pussy*."

"Oooh, sounds delish." I smear the requested food all over my pelvic bone and clit. "*Bon appetit, monsieur*."

Josh leans down and laps up the mashed potatoes off my pelvis, making me writhe, and then he devours my clit like a starving man on a Snickers bar. It feels insanely awesome, but there's just no way I'm gonna reach orgasm.

After a while, Josh sits up from between my legs and stares at me. "Nothing?"

I shake my head. "Feels fantastic, but I can't get there. Too stoned."

He leans back. "Well, at least we look good, huh, PG?"

"Damn straight, we do, PB." I flex my bicep and kiss it.

Josh laughs. "Okay, it's official," he says. "This sucks. No more weed for you. It's been fun and all, super-duper fun, you're hilarious—but it's now abundantly clear I'm the idiot who turned a Ferrari into a fucking lawnmower. I should be taken into the woods and shot for doing that."

I shrug. "You didn't do it. I'm the one who sucked on the joint."

"No, I'm the one who pulled it out and said, 'Hey, PG, ya wanna?' But I've officially learned my lesson. From here on out, I'll never do anything ever again to keep my beautiful Ferrari from hitting top racing speeds like she was built to do."

I sigh. "Probably for the best. But we had fun, though, didn't we?"

"Fuck yeah, we did. Good times were had by all." He smirks. "So, hey, PG, whaddaya say we take a shower and clean all the spinach and sweet potato out of your cooch and then roll around naked in my bed for a while? I wanna see if I can get my little Ferrari's engine revving to full-throttle again, against all odds."

"Sounds fun."

"Everything's fun with you, babe." He kisses the top of my hand, pulls me up, and leads me toward his bedroom like a rag doll. He lets out a long, happy sigh. "Another fantasy checked off the list," he mutters softly, seemingly to himself. He makes a sloppy checkmark with his finger in the air.

"We just fulfilled a fantasy?"

"Fuck yeah, we did. The very best one."

"What was it?"

Josh beams me a goofy smile. His eyes are droopy and glazed. "Hottest Girl Ever Turns Out To Be *Coolest* Girl Ever." He makes another checkmark in the air with his finger. "And she says we're gonna be happy, happy, happy *florebblaaaaaaaaaaaaaaah.*"

73

KAT

My phone beeps with a text just as I'm walking through the front door of my apartment. I put down a stack of mail on my kitchen counter and check my phone.

"Hey, PG," Josh writes.

My heart explodes the same way it does every time I see the name "Josh Faraday" land on my screen.

"Hey, PB," I write back, grinning broadly.

Oh my God, being away from Josh this past week has been torture—I've literally been counting the hours until he lands in Seattle to visit me and meet my family. Just forty-eight more to go. Gah.

"Are you home from work yet?" Josh writes.

"Just got home this very second."

"Cool. A package is being delivered to your apartment in exactly five minutes. You'll have to sign for it personally. Wanted to make sure you'll be there."

"Five minutes? Lucky I'm here."

"I'm a lucky guy."

"Are you hiding in the bushes outside my apartment watching me?"

"No. But that's a good idea. Note to self."

"Why not bring this package with you when you come on Saturday?"

"Nope. This particular package had to be delivered to you TODAY."

"Ooooooh! Is it youuuuuuuuuuuuuuuuuuuuuuuuuuu?!!" I write.

"LOL," he writes. "No. Sorry."

"Derby Field," I reply. "Darn."

"I gotta go. Just wanted to make sure you'll be there for my package. T-minus four minutes."

"So mysterious! Gimme a hint, PB."

"Okay, one hint: good things come in very large packages."

"OMG!!!"

"Namibia!!! What?"

"It's youuuuuuuuuuuuuuuuuuuuuuuu!!!!!"

"Nope."

"Darn. I thought I was so smart. Waaaaah."

"LOL."

"Derby Field."

"Haha. Bye, PG. See you in two days. Can't wait. Enjoy your package."

My heart melts. "Bye, PB. Can't wait." I add a heart emoji and a kissing emoji.

I stand and stare at my phone for a minute.

Oh my God. I'm a smitten kitten. A fish on a line. Done-zo, as Sarah would say. And the amazing thing is that Josh seems to feel the same way about me. Of course, I still don't know where I stand with the guy beyond next week. There are no labels allowed, no relationship-status updates, no declarations of serious feelings—ha!—nothing ever assumed, planned, or implicitly promised more than ten days out (it's kind of hard to put *florrebblaaaaaah* on the calendar). But still, as long as I stay in the moment and don't wonder what might happen a month from now, everything's fantastic. Better than fantastic.

But damn. Not looking to the future is easier said than done when you've fallen in love with someone as amazing as Josh. In fact, that's all I seem to want to do—fantasize about the future—about one day living in the same city, sleeping every night in the same bed, maybe even planning a trip to Europe for next summer with a little of my finder's fee money. But in what world can a woman be the first one to say "I want you to be mine and only mine forever and ever until the end of time" and not have everything implode after that? And that's especially true when the man you wanna say it to is the raging commitment-phobe, Joshua William Faraday. And so, I've made a pact with myself to keep my big mouth shut and just enjoy the ride.

The doorbell rings. I look at my watch. Damn. Josh's deliveryman is freaking prompt. I lope to the front door and open it—and, lo and behold, The Terminator is standing on my doorstep in a T-shirt and jeans, his hand in his pocket.

"Jonas?" I look past him into the walkway. "What are you doing here? Is Sarah here, too?"

Jonas holds up a poker chip.

"No way!" I shriek, instantly elated. It doesn't matter what specific fantasy Jonas is here to kick off—all that matters is what that poker chip clearly implies about Josh's current geographical location: that boy is here in Seattle!

Jonas hands me the poker chip and rolls his eyes. "Hi, Kat. I'm *Blane*," he says, his tone oozing with complete disdain. "Great to finally meet you. You look even more beautiful than in your online profile."

I throw my hands over my blushing face with embarrassment and glee. Just from these few words, I know exactly what imaginary-porno Josh and I are about to act out and how I'm supposed to play along. Oh my freaking God.

Jonas makes a face like he's being tortured. "Is any of what I'm saying making *any* sense to you? Josh gave me the exact script, but if this isn't making any sense to you—"

"No." I laugh. "It makes perfect sense. I know exactly what this is."

In fact, I've got zero doubt about what's on the fantasy-fulfillment docket for tonight: we're gonna do my "slut who ditches her boring date to have sex with the hot bartender in the bathroom" fantasy—a scenario I explained to Josh in detail during our last night together in Las Vegas (along with my other fantasies, too). "And in *this* fantasy," I explained to Josh that night, "I'm on a first date with some random guy—like, some accountant I met on Match dot com or whatever—and it turns out he's The Most Boring Man in the World. He'd probably be named *Blane*."

"Blane?" Josh said. And then he quoted the exact line from *Pretty in Pink* I was referring to—about Blane being an appliance, rather than a name.

"Oh my God!" I squealed. "I guarantee no other man on the planet could quote Ducky from *Pretty in Pink*."

"I'm wise and powerful, babe," Josh said. "I keep telling you."

I laughed.

"So what happens next in this particular fantasy?" Josh asked. "Something tells me it doesn't end well for poor Blane."

"No, it doesn't. I'm on my date with *Blane* and he's talking my ear off about taxes or politics or whatever, and I keep locking eyes with the hot bartender. So, after a bit, I excuse myself to go to the restroom. And on my way, I slip the bartender a note on a napkin that says, 'Bathroom in five.'"

"Whoa," Josh said. "You little minx.'

"Hot, right?"

"Definitely."

"So then I fuck the bartender in the bathroom and when we're done, I go right back to my sweet but boring date like nothing ever happened. When Blane and I leave the bar, the bartender winks at me as I pass by—but we don't exchange phone numbers or anything like that—we both just know it was a one-time thing. Blane takes me home and I kiss him on the cheek and thank him for a lovely evening like the proper young lady I am. And then I never see him again."

"Where the fuck do you get this shit?" Josh asked.

"Well, this particular fantasy came about as a total 'what if' on a real-life boring date."

Josh laughed.

"But that's the thing, I have these little pornos playing in my head all the time, but I'd never actually *do* them. Believe it or not, I'm actually not as big a slut as I seem."

"I don't think you're a slut," he said earnestly. "Not at all. Well, not any more than I'm a slut. Am I a slut?"

"Yeah, a little bit."

Josh laughed. "No, I'm not. Not nearly as much as I seem."

"Then we're even."

Jonas clears his throat, drawing my attention back to my present-day doorstep. He looks remarkably uncomfortable. "So you ready to head out?" he asks. "I've been given strict instructions to take you for cocktails and to be extremely *boring*." He rolls his eyes again.

"What did Josh tell you about tonight?" I ask, my cheeks suddenly feeling warm. God help me if Josh told Jonas everything about my imaginary-pornos.

"Josh didn't tell me a thing," Jonas says.

I exhale with relief.

"All he said was, 'Kat's got, like, a thousand crazy pornos playing in her head at all times and I need your help setting the stage for one of them so we can act it out tonight.'" He shrugs.

I cover my face. "Gah! Josh said all that? Jonas, that's not exactly 'not a thing.' Oh my God, I'm completely mortified. *Jesus*."

"Aw, don't worry about it, Kat. That's literally all Josh said. He didn't give me any details. He just told me to show up here and be 'super-duper boring'—which, he said 'should be like falling off a log' for me. I told him to go fuck himself, but then he went ballistic on me, screaming about every fucking favor he's ever done for me through the history of time—which is a lot, I must admit—so I was like, 'Fine, motherfucker! Stop acting like me! I'll do it—if only to make you stop screaming at me like a fucking lunatic.' And then he laughed his ass off and was like, 'Ha! Welcome to my world, motherfucker.'"

I laugh. "So you're here to ply me with alcohol and bore me to tears, then?" I ask.

Jonas shrugs. "Yeah, talk about asking two fishies to swim, huh? You get to drink and I get to be boring."

I giggle.

"Wait, you do drink, right?" Jonas asks.

I give him a perplexed look.

"Kat, I'm *Blane*, remember? I don't already know you're a total lush."

I snort. "Oh yeah. Well, yes, Blane, on occasion, I do indeed imbibe."

"Okay, that's fine. I don't drink at all—I hope that's okay. I'm a professional baseball player and I don't drink a drop during the season."

I burst out laughing.

"Okay good. I'm glad that means something to you. Josh gave me explicit instructions to say that exact line, but I have no idea why." Jonas leans forward like he's telling a secret. "But actually I'll totally have a drink with you—you know that, right?" He winks.

"Awesome. Will Sarah be joining us? I bet she could use a break from studying. She seemed really stressed about finals when I talked to her the other day."

"Who's Sarah? I told you, my name is *Blane*." He leans forward like he's telling me another secret. "Actually, I tried to pull her away from her books for the night, but she's totally freaking out about her exams next week. She said she can't afford to go out two nights in a row so she'll just see everyone tomorrow night."

"What? We're going out tomorrow night?" I shriek happily. "I had no idea." I clap my hands and jump up and down. "Will it be all four of us?"

Jonas suddenly looks like he's been caught with his hand in the cookie jar. "Uh." His face turns bright red. "Fuck. Josh is gonna kill me. That's supposed to be a surprise." He runs his hand through his hair. "Just pretend I never said anything. My name is Blane. You look even better than your online profile. I don't drink. I'm a professional baseball player. I'm boring."

I squeal. "Josh is so sneaky-freaky-deaky. I thought he was coming into town on *Saturday*, did he tell you that? He's meeting my family." I squeal again, overwhelmed with excitement. "He's such a sneaky little fucker."

"Shit. Kat. Stop it. He's gonna kill me. I'm Blane. I'm boring. You look better than your online profile. Gah."

I put out my hand, laughing. "Nice to meet you, Blane. I'm super-duper excited about our boring date. Let's go." I step outside and lock my door and we begin walking down the pathway toward the front of my building. Well, actually, Jonas is walking—I'm careening down the walkway a good five paces ahead of him, my heart exploding with joy.

"Hey, Kat. Real quick. Hang on."

I stop sprinting.

"Before I'm stuck being Boring Blane for the rest of the night," Jonas says, "can I be Boring Jonas for a minute? There's something I wanna ask you about."

"Sure, Boring Jonas—bore away."

Boring Jonas takes a deep breath and pulls a ring box out of his pocket. "Do you think Sarah's gonna like this?" He opens the ring box and I'm blinded by the most spectacular rock I've ever seen. "Or should I have gotten bigger?" he asks.

My knees literally buckle. "Holy shitballs, Jonas. It's flippin' gorgeous!"

"You think she'll like it?"

"*Like* it? She's gonna sob like a baby with overflowing *love* for it! It's jaw-dropping. Glorious. Fabulous. *Beyond*."

"But would you go so far as to call it '*magnificent*'?"

I laugh. "Absolutely. That's exactly what it is. *Magnificent*."

"Phew. It's big enough?"

"Jonas, any bigger and her knuckles would drag on the ground."

He exhales in obvious relief and shuts the box. "Okay. Thank you." He runs his hand through his hair again. "I've been losing my mind lately, thinking about getting this right. Josh says this is the story Sarah will be telling her grandchildren one day so I'd better not fuck it up."

"Josh said that?"

"Yeah."

"Josh said, 'This is the story Sarah will tell her *grandchildren*'?" I ask, my chest tight.

"Yep. That's exactly what he said."

"Wow," I say. "That's an incredibly romantic thing to say." I clutch my chest, trying to get ahold of myself. "I didn't know Josh was capable of saying something so... *epic*." My heart is suddenly slamming against my chest bone, banging mercilessly, trying to lurch out of its cage. I can't fathom Josh assuming children and grandchildren for Jonas and Sarah. That's so... *futuristic* of him. "Well, yeah, Josh is right," I manage. "Sarah will most definitely be telling your future grandchildren about your proposal one day."

Jonas grimaces.

"But the good news is that you can't fuck it up no matter what you do. As long as you speak from your heart, whatever you say will be grandchildren-worthy, I promise."

We begin walking down the pathway toward the street again.

"God, I hope you're right," Jonas says. "I've been making myself sick, planning this whole elaborate speech in my head, trying to get it exactly right."

I wave my hand in the air. "You're overthinking it. Just tell her how you feel and she'll be thrilled. All that matters at times like these is that you tell the one you love how you feel, straight from your heart. Keep it simple."

We've reached Jonas' car on the street in front of my building. He opens my door for me and I settle myself inside the car.

"Thanks, Kat," Jonas says. "I think you're right. I'll keep it simple and straight from the heart. Nothing too elaborate."

"There you go. That's all any girl could ever hope for in a marriage proposal —a simple declaration of love from the man of her dreams."

Jonas shoots me an adorable look that clearly says, "*Oh my God, I'm really gonna do this.*"

"You'll do great," I say.

He shuts my door and walks around the car to the driver's side.

I think this is the first time I've ever chatted with Jonas alone, just him and me, with no one else around. No, wait. That's not true. This is the *second* time. The first was at Jonas' house the morning after The Club broke into my apartment—the morning after I first laid eyes on Jonas' sexy-as-sin brother. Wow, that feels like a lifetime ago. What did I say to Jonas that morning, standing in his kitchen? "Sarah thinks you're in love with her, Jonas. *Don't crush her.*" I roll my eyes at myself. Yet another whiz-bang example of my amazing ability to sense a man's true intentions.

Jonas settles into his car seat and turns on the engine.

"So, I gotta tell you, *Blane*," I say. "I don't have high hopes for a second date.

It's a really bad sign when a guy asks for advice on how to propose to another girl on a first date."

Jonas laughs. "Sorry. From here on out, I promise to focus all my energy on boring you to tears."

"Thank you. I really appreciate that."

Jonas pulls his car into traffic. "In fact, you know what I'll do?" he says, grinning. "*I'll bore the pants off you.*" He snickers.

My stomach clenches. "Josh told you everything, didn't he?" I choke out.

Jonas laughs gleefully. "Nope. Josh gave me absolutely no details, just like I said. But I'm not a complete idiot, Kat, despite appearances. If me showing up at your apartment and handing you a fucking *poker chip* doesn't somehow lead to you and Josh fucking in the bathroom, then I don't know what would be the fucking point."

I cover my face with my hands.

Jonas laughs again. "Aw, come on, Kat. It's just me—and I'm a huge fan of bathroom fuckery, believe me. Besides, what do you care what I think? I'm *Blane*. I'm the boring guy you'll never see again."

I laugh and look out my car window for a long moment, letting the blush in my cheeks subside. "So where are we going, Blane?"

"A bar near my house called The Pine Box. Are you familiar with it?" He's got a wicked grin on his face.

"Yeah, as a matter of fact, I am. My best friend and I once went to The Pine Box to spy on this guy she really liked."

"You *spied* on him, huh? What was he doing?"

"Hitting on another girl."

"Ooph. Sounds like an asshole."

"Yeah, that's what I thought. But I've since learned he's a total sweetheart. Best guy, ever. And a perfect match for my best friend, too. I couldn't be happier for them."

I look over at Jonas and he's absolutely beaming with joy. God, he's such a cutie, I can't stand it. I wanna roll him in glitter and glue and hang him on my fridge.

He looks at me, his face bursting with happiness. "You're definitely way cooler than your online profile, Kat."

74

JOSH

I don't know what to do with myself, so I pick up a dishrag and wipe off the top of the bar for a long minute. I'm so amped to finally see Kat again, I can barely breathe. A week has never felt so long. Fuck. I look at my watch. Jonas should be here with her any minute now. *Fuck.* I'm leaping out of my skin. *Fuck.* I haven't been able to get that woman out of my head all fucking week, despite how busy I've been with work. The smell of her. The softness of her skin. The way she laughs like a dude. That electricity that courses between us when we have sex, nice and slow. What the fuck *is* that? It's gonna be the death of me.

"Hey, bartender," a guy in a charcoal three-piece suit calls to me.

I nod to the guy. It's been a long time since anyone's called me "bartender" in an actual bar. Sure, I'm always "bartender" at parties with my friends, but there's a special kind of jolt to being the guy who's large and in charge in an actual bar. I'd forgotten how much I love that feeling.

I glance at Tim to my left, the actual bartender at The Pine Box, seeking permission to assist the guy in the suit and Tim motions for me to go right ahead. He's not just being nice, of course—I've paid him and his boss (the owner of the bar) handsomely for the privilege. But, still, I can't help feeling giddy to be doing this again after all these years.

"Hey there, man." I say to the dude in the suit, sauntering to him. "What can I do you for, sir?"

"A Manhattan," the guy says. He motions to a cute brunette standing just behind him. "And a Chardonnay."

"Absolutely. Guess what? Great news. Tonight just so happens to be Dudes In Charcoal Suits Drink For Free Night." I slide two cocktail napkins onto the bar in front of him. "Your drinks are on the house, man."

The guy looks surprised. "Really?"

"Yep. They're on me." I flash him a huge smile. "Tip included."

When I contacted The Pine Box (at Jonas' recommendation) and asked the owner if I might help tend bar for an hour tonight (because, I said, I was trying to decide if I wanted to quit my fancy job and go back to my college job), he wasn't the least bit open to the idea. As usual, though, money made the guy change his mind and decide to help a brother out. "But you can't handle any customers' money," the owner warned. "Leave that to Tim." "No problem," I assured him. "How about this: I'll pay for every single drink in the place, all night long. And I'll serve all premium liquor the whole time I'm there—you'll make a mint, bro."

"Whoa," the guy in the charcoal suit says, stuffing his wallet back into his pocket. "A random act of kindness. Thanks."

"Something like that," I say. "So check this out, bro. I'm gonna make your Manhattan with a little extra kick, okay? I'm gonna use a premium rye whiskey—maybe Overholt?—plus, I'm gonna go off the rails and use orange bitters."

The guy raises his eyebrows. "You're going rogue, huh?"

I laugh. "I know what you're thinking—is he mad? Just roll with it. If you don't absolutely love it, I'll make you one the traditional way. But you'll see. The rye whiskey's gonna really offset the flavor of the bitters nicely."

"Okay. Cool. Thanks, man. Awesome."

I look at the adorable brunette behind the guy. "Are you in the mood to try something besides Chardonnay tonight? I've got a Purple Rain recipe I'm dying to make for a lucky lady tonight. Also completely on me, of course. If you like gin, you'll love it."

"I love gin," she says, her face lighting up. "I'll give it a whirl."

I glance at the door. Jonas should have been here already. Maybe Kat kept him waiting when he came to pick her up. Kat didn't know Jonas was coming, after all. She probably made him sit and wait while she put on makeup or changed her clothes. That girl is never fucking on time for a goddamned thing. I smile broadly. And she's always worth the fucking wait.

I push the drinks across the bar to the dude and his date.

"Whoa," the guy says. "Best Manhattan I've ever had."

"Love it," his date says. "What's in it besides gin?"

I tell her and she praises me for being fucking amazing, which, I must admit when it comes to making drinks, I am. "When you're ready for round two, lemme know. I'll keep my tab open for you all night long."

"Thanks. Wow. You're the man."

Damn, I should totally do this once a week, just for kicks. This is fun.

A smoking hot brunette comes into the place alone, sits at the bar, and motions to me that she wants to order something. I glance at Tim on the other end of the bar and he motions to me like, "She's all yours, man."

I saunter down to her. "Hey, beautiful," I say. "What can I do for you?"

She raises her eyebrow. "Answering that question with a drink order seems like such a shame."

Oh. Well. I glance at the door. I'd forgotten about how much women hit on the bartender. That was always one of the best perks of tending bar.

I smile at her. "You here alone, sweetheart?"

"Waiting for a friend. She just texted she's running late." She makes a sad face.

"Well, no one gets lonely when I'm tending bar. That's the rule. What can I get you? It's on me."

Her eyes blaze. "Oh, thank you. That's awfully sweet of you."

I look at the door. No Jonas. No Kat.

"Um," she says. "Do you have a recommendation for me? I feel like going outside my usual tonight. Maybe taking a walk on the wild side." She levels her dark eyes at me.

Oh man. This woman's not fucking around.

"Hmm. Well, would you like a screaming orgasm, perhaps?"

"You read my mind."

"Coming right up." I flash her my most lascivious look.

"And what do you recommend to *drink*?" she adds.

I laugh. "What's your name, beautiful?" I ask.

"Lucy." She puts out her hand and I shake it.

"Hi, Lucy. Love the name. I'm Josh. Pleased to meet you."

"You're new here?"

"Yeah. Just on a trial basis. Just for tonight."

"Oh, well, lucky I came in tonight, then. I'd be happy to tell the owner to hire you. You're the best bartender, ever."

"I haven't made your drink yet."

She flashes a flirtatious smile. "It doesn't matter." She licks her lips.

I run my hand through my hair. Shit, have women gotten more aggressive since I used to do this in college? "Well, Lucy. Thanks for the vote of—" I glance down at the other end of the bar and I'm met with two eyes of blue steel boring holes into the back of my skull like a fucking Gamma Ray. *Kat.* In full Jealous Bitch mode. My heart and dick both leap at the sight of her. How is it possible she's even more beautiful than she was last week?

I wink at her and her eyes flicker.

She grits her teeth.

It's all I can do not to burst out laughing. Fuck, I love Jealous Kat. She's never sexier than when she's plotting a murder.

I quickly turn my attention back to my new brunette admirer. My gut tells me letting Jealous Kat simmer for a little while longer will only make this porno hotter in the end. Plus, I'm not one hundred percent sure how this particular porno's supposed to play itself out. I know Kat's on a date with Boring Blane and I'm the hot bartender who catches her eye. That part is clear. But the rest is kind of nebulous. I'm pretty sure she's gonna slip me a note. Yeah, that's it.

She's supposed to slip me a napkin with a note scribbled on it. And then we fuck in the bathroom. And then she returns to her date like nothing even happened. Fucking hot.

"Sorry, Lucy," I say. "I got distracted there for a second. Thanks for the vote of confidence. Yeah, if you could tell the owner you want me to get the job, I'd be grateful. Seems like a cool place."

"Sure, Josh. My friends and I come in here about once a week after work. You'd be a sight for sore eyes after a long day, that's for sure."

I flash her my most charming smile. "Thanks. You're a sweetheart."

She throws her head back and laughs. "Oh, my. You're adorable." She bites her lip. "Absolutely adorable." She leans in. "How late are you working tonight?"

I lean in. "I'm not sure yet."

"Well, let me know when you find out," she whispers.

I grin. "First things first, lemme get you that screaming orgasm."

"If I get my way, that'll be first things first. Second things second. And third things third."

Oh shit. This woman is a fucking carnivore. Were women this savage when I was tending bar at twenty-two? Shit, if they were, I don't remember it quite this way. If I weren't here to deliver a porno-fantasy to the woman of my dreams tonight, I'd no doubt be banging this woman to within an inch of her life an hour from now. Jesus God.

"Just a second, Lucy. I've got a customer flagging me down at the other end of the bar. Your screaming orgasm will be coming right up." I wink.

As I walk the length of the bar toward Kat, I feel like a man walking a gang-plank. She looks literally homicidal. Damn, she's gorgeous. Especially when she's in terrorist mode. I have the sudden impulse to leap over the bar and take her into my arms and kiss the hell out of her, but this slow burn is way too hot to fuck with. Kat's got fantasy-pornos playing in her head? Well, I guess it turns out I do, too. She's jealous of the man-eater down at the other end of the bar? Well, good. It'll only make sex in the bathroom that much better.

I come to a halt immediately across the bar from Jonas and Kat. My brother looks like he wants to throttle me and Kat looks like she wants to filet me and cut off my balls.

"Hey, guys," I say. "Welcome to The Pine Box." I push two napkins in front of them, my eyes fixed on Kat. "Hey, beautiful," I whisper. "Man, are you a sight for lonely eyes. I haven't stopped thinking about you all week, babe."

Kat bites her lip. Her chest is rising and falling visibly. (And, damn, what a fine looking chest it is, especially in the cleavage-baring blouse she's got on.)

"Hey, bartender," Kat says, her voice tight. She clenches her jaw. "I've been dying to see you, too." Her cheeks flush. "Surprised to see you working the crowd so well."

I shrug. "It's what bartenders do, babe. Can't keep a fish from swimming."

She practically snarls.

"So, you two on a date tonight? Lemme guess. Did you two kids meet online?"

Jonas rolls his eyes, clearly not willing to play along.

I laugh. "What can I get you? Drinks are on me."

"What are you having, Jonas?" Kat asks.

"I'd like the most complicated and annoying drink you can possibly imagine. Something that literally *pains* you to make because it's so fucking involved. I don't normally drink because I'm a professional baseball player and I'm highly disciplined during the season, mind you, but for some reason now that I'm seeing you here, acting like a total douchebag"—he motions to the other end of the bar—"all I wanna do is cause you maximum *pain.*"

I glance down the bar in the direction Jonas has indicated. Lucy is biting her fingertip, watching me, her eyes burning like hot coals.

I clear my throat. "Hey, bro. No *problemo.* I know exactly what to make you. I've got the perfect drink for you." I look at Kat. "And you, miss? What can I do for you? My wish is your command."

I can almost hear Kat's heart beating from here.

She's so fucking gorgeous, she's causing me pain.

I shouldn't do it—I know I shouldn't—it's obviously not part of the role-play —but I can't resist. I've missed her too much not to feed my addiction right fucking now.

I reach across the bar and touch that hot little cleft in her chin.

At my touch, Kat parts her lips and exhales a shaky breath.

And just like that, I'm rock hard.

"What can I get you?" I breathe. "Name it. It's yours. Anything at all, babe."

She swallows hard. "*I want a douchebag,*" she says.

There's a long beat. I can't decide if that's a drink order or if she's referring to me.

"Crown Royal and a splash of Coke," she clarifies, solving the mystery for me.

"Really? Is that really a thing?"

She nods. "Look it up. It's a real thing. And I want one—I want one bad."

I smirk. "Okay, then. A douchebag it is. With pleasure." I look at Jonas. "And for you, sir, I'll be making something called The Dork. White rum, Pisang Ambon, Licor 43, lemon juice and pineapple juice—served in a highball glass. Hope you enjoy it."

Jonas makes a face of pure disgust.

I laugh and slide a Heineken across the bar.

He grins despite himself.

My eyes flicker back to Kat. "I'll be right back to serve up your douchebag, gorgeous. I gotta go give that brunette down there a screaming orgasm first." I motion to my admirer down at the other end of the bar. "While I'm gone, enjoy your date. This guy seems super interesting. Have fun, you two."

Kat's eyes flash wickedly at me, but I turn my back on her and traipse on down to the other end of the bar, my cock tingling.

"Sorry for the delay, Lucy. Got to chatting with a couple down there. They're on a blind date. Cutest couple ever."

"No problem. Tim came over and offered to give me a screaming orgasm, but I told him I only want one from *you*."

"Aw, shucks, Lucy. That's awfully sweet of you. That makes me feel so special." I glance at Kat on the other end of the bar. Her eyes are trained on me like a sniper. She looks ready to jump on top of the bar and leap on this woman like a cheetah downing an impala. "Well, then, I guess I'd better get moving, huh? Don't worry, it only takes me a couple minutes to give most women the best screaming orgasm of their life. You're only minutes away from complete satisfaction, sweetheart."

She shifts in her chair and makes a sexual sound.

I steal a quick look at Kat—and she's about to lose her fucking mind.

I turn around and grab the ingredients I need for Lucy's drink, laughing to myself about what a stroke of luck it was to unexpectedly have this hot little tamale on my tip right in front of Kat. I couldn't have planned it better if I'd tried.

I serve up Lucy's drink to her and she takes a greedy sip.

"*Orgasmic*. Thank you. And thank you for buying it for me."

"My pleasure," I say.

"Excuse me," Kat's voice says from behind Lucy's shoulder. She's standing literally right behind Lucy, her hands on her hips, her nostrils flaring. I straighten up to get an unimpeded view and I'm met with Kat's blazing face in full Jealous Bitch mode.

"Oh, hey, miss," I say, trying not to grin too broadly. "Your douchebag is coming right up. I'm sorry I'm kinda slow. I'm new. I was just giving Lucy here a screaming orgasm."

"Forget about making me a *drink*," she says. "I want a *douchebag*." She elbows her way to the edge of the bar, right next to Lucy, completely invading the other woman's personal space. Much to my surprise, she turns her head and smiles with full teeth at Lucy, the way a great white shark smiles at a sea lion. Oh shit. I've never seen her look more like a murderer than right now. "I'm on a blind date with that guy down there," she says breezily. She points to Jonas.

Lucy cranes her neck and catches sight of my brother in all his magical glory—and, not unexpectedly, the woman's eyes pop out of her head. "Oh my God, honey. You're on a *blind* date with *him*? Jackpot."

"Yeah. His name is *Blane*." Kat rolls her eyes.

Lucy squints at Jonas and then looks at me. "He looks a lot like you, actually. Are you two related?"

I crane my neck and look at Jonas. "Hey, yeah, he does kinda look like me. Huh." I shake my head. "Nope, never seen that guy before in my life."

"Wow. He's your doppelgänger."

"You think?"

Kat leans in and whispers. "He's so boring I wanna gouge my eyes out. He's a professional baseball player and he keeps talking about *Plato*." Kat makes a sound like she's snoring.

I laugh.

"He's a professional baseball player?" Lucy steals another look. "Honey, if it were me, I'd let that man talk about anything he wanted to, whether it's Plato or Play-Doh. Good lord, girl. You better get back over there. Don't let some other woman swoop in and make a move on him." She cranes her neck to look at Jonas again—a move I've seen women in bars perform more times than I can count. "Holy hot damn. *Go*."

Kat sniffs and trains her eyes on me. Oh man, she's absolutely on fire. "Eh. He's okay, I guess. The problem is, while I was sitting over there with *that* guy, I kept getting distracted by *another* guy—a smoking hot bartender to be exact." Kat leans over the bar, notably edging Lucy out of the pocket (and giving me a fabulous view of her pretty titties in her low-cut blouse). She lowers her voice to barely above a whisper. "This bartender I've been watching all night has so much swagger, I figure it can only mean one thing."

I lean forward, my pulse pounding in my ears. "And what would that be?"

She licks her lips. "I figure it means he's gotta have a *really* big dick."

Lucy's face turns bright red.

Oh my God, she's ruthless. "What's your name, sweetheart?" I ask, leaning into Kat even closer, my dick lurching in my pants.

"Kat."

"Nice to meet you, Kat," I say, putting out my hand. "I'm Josh."

"*Josh*. Sexy name, *Josh*. That's the name of a guy with a really big dick if I've ever heard one." She wets her lower lip slowly like she's licking barbeque sauce off a rack of ribs. "Please believe me, I've never done this before, and I know I'm on a date with *Blane* down there—and I know I'm probably coming off like a world-class slut—but I don't give a crap. You're so hot, I can't stop myself." She lowers her voice again. "If I leave here tonight without knowing if I'm right about what your *swagger* means, I'm gonna regret it for the rest of my life."

Lucy physically jolts on her barstool like she's been stuck with a cattle prod —and I'm right there with her, jerking like Kat just gripped my dick.

I lean into Kat's ear, right next to poor Lucy, like we're having a conversation about how Kat and I are gonna rob a bank, right in front of Lucy the Bank Teller. I feel vaguely guilty Lucy's become an unwitting pawn in our little game, but it can't be helped—having another woman as part of this conversation is turning me on too much to spare the odd-woman-out from discomfort. "Well, gosh, Kat," I say. "What do you propose to do about your date? He seems like a nice enough guy—pretty damned good-looking, too. And a professional baseball player to boot. Maybe you ought to give him a chance."

I crane my neck to look down the length of the bar at Jonas. He flashes me a look that can only be described as utter contempt for making him sit through this.

Kat glances down the bar at Jonas. "Oh, I'm not gonna ditch him. I'm going home with him and I'm gonna make him fall in love with me—he's a professional ball player, after all. But that doesn't mean I don't wanna know if I'm right about your *swagger*—I won't be able to sleep tonight if I don't find out." She straightens up and winks. "Bathroom in five, bartender."

She leaves.

I look at Lucy. Her mouth is hanging open. Her eyes are wide.

If I weren't so fucking turned on right now, I'd throw my head back and howl with laughter at the expression on Lucy's face. Damn, Kat's the best. Never a dull moment with that woman.

But I don't laugh. No way. This porno is too fucking hot.

I lean across the bar toward Lucy, my dick pulsing in my pants. "Well, that was unexpected, to say the least," I say, smirking. I reach down and shift my hard-on to the side, trying to get relief from the persistent throbbing.

"Wow," Lucy says, obviously at a loss for words.

"Hey, hon!" a female voice calls from behind Lucy's back.

Lucy turns her head—and as she does, I steal a quick look at Kat. She's sitting with Jonas, chatting, flipping her hair as Tim serves them a second round of drinks. Oh my God, she's a fucking sociopath. She really is. How is she looking so light-hearted and happy right now when I'm about ready to blow a fucking gasket, I'm so turned on?

"Josh?" Lucy says.

I hear my name, but I can't peel my eyes off Kat. She's a fucking force of nature, that woman. A tsunami. God help anyone who stands in the way of something she wants. She's a fucking beast.

"Josh?" Lucy says again.

I force my eyes to look at Lucy, though it pains me to do it.

"This is my friend Christine."

"Hi, Christine," I say, my voice lacking its usual charm. I glance down the bar at Kat again. She's throwing her head back, laughing. Diabolical.

"Hi," Lucy's friend says.

I peel my eyes off Kat and look at the new woman. She's a short redhead with freckles and an adorable smile.

"Hi," I say. "What can I get you? It's on me. Whatever you want."

Christine's about to reply, but Lucy hijacks the conversation.

"Hang on, honey. Josh, what the *fuck* are you gonna... do... about her?" She crinkles her nose and tilts her head toward Kat's end of the bar. "Are you actually gonna... meet her?" She makes a face like that's a patently ridiculous notion. "She just said she's gonna do two guys in one night." She grimaces.

I look stealthily to my right and then left, and then I lean over the bar toward Lucy like I'm about to tell her a scandalous secret.

Lucy leans in and licks her lips with anticipation.

"Fuck yeah, I'm gonna meet her," I whisper. "I'm not proud of it, Lucy, I'm really not. But I'm only a man. And I can't resist showing that woman she's *exactly* right about what my swagger means."

Lucy's eyes pop out of her head and roll around on the floor.

I glance down the bar at Kat again and this time, her blue eyes are trained on mine, too. She smiles wickedly and I shoot her a look of pure arousal. "I'm gonna meet that diabolical woman in the bathroom and fuck the living shit out of her with my huge dick and give her a screaming orgasm that has absolutely nothing whatsoever to do with vodka." My eyes shift to Lucy. "And then, don't you worry, beautiful, I'll come right back out here and make you whatever drink you desire."

I've clearly rendered Lucy speechless.

"Hey, Tim," I call to the real bartender, straightening up. "Get these two spectacularly gorgeous women whatever they want, on me. Food, drinks, whatever it may be—a bottle of your finest champagne. They can name it. I'm gonna take a short break."

With that, I throw down the dishrag in my hand, stride to the opposite end of the bar from where Jonas and Kat are sitting, slip around the end, and waltz toward the bathroom, my throbbing hard-on leading the mighty way.

75

JOSH

I have to wait a couple minutes outside the bathroom door for someone to come out, but once they do, I slip inside, my breathing ragged. Holy shit, I'm so turned on, I can barely breathe.

Kat was supposed to slip me a note on a napkin—that's what she said when she described this particular mini-porno that night in Las Vegas—she wasn't supposed to proposition me right in front of another woman. But my jealous little terrorist went for the fucking jugular, didn't she? There's no controlling that woman when her eyes turn a blazing shade of green.

Fuck, she turns me on.

Damn, that was hot.

Goddamn, I can't wait to fuck her.

There's a soft rap on the bathroom door. I open it slightly and Kat word-lessly slips inside, already breathless with obvious arousal. I've barely locked the door behind her when Kat's mouth is on my lips, her tongue in my mouth, her body pressed into mine.

"Kat," I say, wrapping my arms around her and kissing her deeply. "Oh my God, I've missed you."

Our kiss is instantly blazing with passion. I feel like I'm drinking water after a long slog across Saudi Arabia wearing nothing but a Speedo. How is it possible I'd forgotten how good this woman tastes in one short week? I grind my hard-on into her. How have I lasted seven days without tasting these delicious lips? Touching this soft skin? Smelling this glorious mane of golden hair?

"Are you wet for me?" I ask, furiously unbuttoning her jeans.

"Dripping wet," she breathes.

"That got you going, huh? Watching that brunette make the moves on me?"

"She would have left with you in a heartbeat if you'd asked her."

I kiss Kat's neck while sliding my fingers inside her jeans. "Yeah, she made that clear."

My fingers find Kat's wetness. She moans and so do I.

"You sure didn't discourage her," Kat says.

"All part of the role-play, baby—I'm the hot bartender all the women wanna fuck, right?" I unbutton my jeans and pull down my briefs, freeing my cock.

"You like making me jealous," Kat says, gripping my shaft.

I exhale sharply at her touch. "You know I do. So hot." I maneuver her to the sink, push her belly up against it, and press myself into her back, staring over her shoulder at us in the mirror. "Making you jealous turns me on," I say. I move her hair off her neck and kiss her hidden Scorpio tattoo.

She shudders.

"I like it when you're a terrorist." I yank her jeans down farther and slide my fingers into her wetness from behind. Oh yeah, she's dripping wet. I slide my fingers up to her clit and shudder at the texture of it. It's swollen and hard, slick against my fingertip. I swirl it around and around and she groans with excitement. I lean into her ear. "I like knowing you want me all to yourself."

I bend my knees and slide my cock inside her slowly, ever so slowly, my gaze fixed on hers in the mirror as I enter her, and we both exhale audibly with relief and pleasure at the fucking awesome sensation.

She grips the sink with white knuckles as I begin thrusting in and out of her, my eyes locked onto hers as I do.

"You feel so good," I whisper, fondling her breast under her blouse. "You've got a magic pussy, baby."

Her nipples are rock hard. I pinch them greedily and she yelps.

"Say you want me all to yourself," I command. I trail my hand down from her breast to her clit and she presses herself into my hand. "Tell me you were so fucking jealous you couldn't stand it."

She's staring at me in the mirror with ice-blue eyes.

My hips are rocking with hers. We've found the perfect rhythm. It's slow and sensual.

"I was so fucking jealous I couldn't stand it," she breathes, moving her hips with mine. "You're *mine*."

"Oh, I like that," I whisper in her ear, my eyes still locked on hers in the mirror. "Say it again." I bite her earlobe.

"*Mine*," she says, gritting her teeth. She reaches her arm up and around my neck.

I suck her earlobe like it's her clit. "You feel so good," I say. "You always feel so fucking good."

"You make me so wet," she whispers. "No one's ever made me wet like this."

"You like the way I fuck you, babe?"

She makes a sound like she just got burned with hot coffee.

"Yeah, baby. Here we go. Give it to me. This is the money right here—what I've been craving all fucking week."

She whimpers. "*Fuck.*"

"Yeah, baby. Come on."

"It's a big one." Her eyes darken.

"Yeah, baby. Let it go." Our bodies have picked up speed. Sweat is beading on her face. Her cheeks are flushed. My fingers are working her hard clit furiously. This is so fucking good, I'm about to blow.

"I missed you so much, babe," I whisper in her ear, my gaze never leaving hers in the mirror. "Had to come see you early, I missed you so fucking bad."

Her eyes flutter and roll back into her head briefly. She lets out a loud groan and I clamp my free hand over her mouth.

"Let it go, baby," I purr into her ear, gyrating into her, fingering her like I own her. I lick her neck, nibble her ear. "Let it go for me."

Her entire body heaves and jolts and spasms. She arches her back, a pained sound pooling in her throat. I clamp my hand over her mouth again, trying to muffle the sounds coming out of her.

"Yeah, baby," I whisper into her ear. "Here we go."

She bites my finger. "*Fuck.* Oh, Josh. Oh my God."

She buckles, almost like she's dry heaving, and then every bit of warm, wet flesh surrounding my cock suddenly squeezes and clenches around me, like a glorious dam breaking. It feels so good, I release into her like a tsunami, slamming myself into her as I do.

The minute I've got my equilibrium back, I turn her around, grab her face and kiss her deeply. "I missed you, baby," I say. "I couldn't wait 'til Saturday to see you."

She kisses my lips, cheeks, neck. "I've been going crazy all week. It's been torture."

I wrap my arms around her, bury my nose in her hair, and inhale. "I wish I could bottle this smell so I could sniff it whenever I'm lonely in L.A."

"Bumble and Bumble Crème de Coco Shampoo and Conditioner," she says. "Seventeen ninety-nine per bottle."

I laugh.

I pull back from our embrace and zip up. "Okay 'slut who ditches her boring date at a bar to fuck the hot bartender in the bathroom.' What happens next? I do believe you're supposed to slip out of the bathroom, rejoin your boring date, and never look back, right?"

Kat shrugs. "Yeah, that's what the script says." She tilts her head. "But there's no fucking way I'm letting you go back in there and serve that bitch another drink."

I laugh. "So I take it we're changing the script?" I say.

"Damn straight we are," she says.

I smirk. "How 'bout this? What if the bartender goes out there and quits his job because he can't stand the thought of you leaving here to fuck that other guy? And what if he does it right in front of the woman who was hitting on him all night?"

Her face lights up. "Oh, I like that ending to the porno a whole lot better."

"Yeah, except now it's not a porno—it's a fucking rom-com."

She smiles. "*When Josh Met Kat*."

I return her smile. "So, hey, I should tell you. Jonas and I are waking up at chicken-thirty tomorrow morning to go climbing for the day. I'll take you home, see your place—but then I'm gonna stay at Jonas' tonight since we're heading out before sunrise, okay?"

"That's cool with me. I've got to work tomorrow, anyway."

"When are you gonna quit your job already, you puss? I told you I'll help you."

She makes a face.

"What are you waiting for, PG?"

She considers for a beat and then nods decisively. "You know what? You're right. Fuck it. I'll quit tomorrow."

"Really?"

"Yeah. YOLO, right?"

"Damn straight."

"Starting my own business can't be that hard, right? I'm smart. I can do it. If I fail, I'll just pick myself back up."

"Atta girl."

There's a beat.

Damn, she's gorgeous.

"Hey, Jonas' house is really close, right?" she asks.

"Just a few blocks."

"Yeah, that's what I thought. In that case, it doesn't make sense for you to take me all the way to my apartment when you're staying at Jonas' tonight. I'm sure Sarah will give me a ride home later. Let's walk to Jonas' house from here and—" She gasps. "Oh my God. I just had an idea. You, me, and Jonas should leave the bar together. That'd be so frickin' funny."

I chuckle. "And just like that, our movie's back to being a porno again."

Kat laughs.

"Do you really gotta do that to the poor woman? She already hates you enough to hire a hit on you."

"Hell yeah, I gotta. It's just too freaking hilarious. How much you wanna bet that tiger-woman is out there hitting on Jonas right now?"

"I'm not stupid enough to take that bet. I've been in far too many bars with Jonas over the years."

Kat laughs and throws her arms around my neck. "God, I missed you."

"I missed you, too, babe." I wrap my arms around her and kiss her.

"I'm so glad you came to Seattle early," she says into my chest, squeezing me tight. "This long-distance thing is killing me, Josh. It's brutal."

My chest constricts. If ever there was a cue for me to tell Kat about my upcoming move to Seattle that was just it. But I'm not ready to tell her. I can't. It's definitely happening—I've just made an offer on the perfect place a few miles from Jonas'. But now's not the time. We're in a fucking bathroom, for Chrissakes, and there's probably a line of people waiting outside the door. And, anyway, my move is happening a whole two months from now, maybe even three. I should probably wait another month or so before I tell her and we start making plans.

"Come on, PG," I say. "Let's go see if Lucy's torn Jonas limb from limb yet, or if she's at least left the poor guy with a stump to stand on."

Kat pulls herself together and smooths down her blouse. "Oh my God, I can't wait to see that woman's face when I suggest we three leave together." She does a little shimmy. "This is gonna be the best porno *ever*."

76

KAT

"Thanks again for the ride, Sarah," I say, flopping onto my couch. "Sorry if I pulled you away from valuable study time."

"No, I needed a break," Sarah says, plopping herself down next to me. "There's only so much a girl can read about *mens rea* and *caveat emptor* before she starts to go a little cuckoo for Cocoa Puffs."

"Well, thanks. It's awesome to see you. You've been studying like a banshee lately."

"I love how adding 'like a banshee' to anything makes it totally next level," Sarah says, laughing. "I don't even know what a banshee is or what the hell one does in real life."

"Hell if I know. I think they scream?"

"And study for law exams, apparently."

"Well, whatever they do, those damned banshees put their entire heart and soul into it, every time, that's for sure."

We both laugh.

"So when do exams finally start? Seems like you've been studying every minute since Vegas."

"Next week," Sarah says. " I've got exams Monday through Thursday. And then on Friday Jonas is whisking me away to an undisclosed location. He says he's taking me somewhere really special, but he won't tell me where."

My heart swoons vicariously for her. She's gonna flip out.

"So things are good between you two?" I ask.

Sarah absently touches the platinum bracelet around her wrist. "Things couldn't be better. I didn't know I could love someone this much. It physically *hurts*—like I'm literally straining my heart muscle."

I bite my lip. "I'm so happy for you."

Sarah smiles sheepishly. "Thank you. I'm happy for me, too. So tell me about you and Josh. You guys were on fire in Las Vegas. Like, kerzoinks. Whenever we were all together, I kept looking around for fire extinguishers, just in case."

I laugh.

"You like him?"

"Yeah, I'm gone—*Gone, Baby, Gone*. I'm Ben *and* Casey Afflecked."

Sarah squeals. "And Josh? Is he *Gone, Baby, Gone*, too?"

"Well, all signs point to yes. Not all *words*, mind you, but all signs. I've definitely gotta read the tea leaves a bit when it comes to Joshua William Faraday."

Sarah rolls her eyes. "Those Faraday boys sure weren't raised to talk about their 'fucking feelings.'"

I sigh wistfully. "You can say that again."

"Aw, sounds like you're a smitten kitten," Sarah says.

I twist my mouth. "Sarah, I'm not smitten. I'm head over heels in love with him."

Sarah's eyes widen. "Holy crappola, girl. I've never heard you say that before."

"I've never said it before. But I am."

"Have you told him?"

I shake my head. "I've told him he's the sexiest man alive. And that I think he's awesome and I'm addicted. But we certainly haven't traded the magic words—we haven't even called each other boyfriend and girlfriend yet." I roll my eyes. "It's the weirdest thing. We're so intimate on the one hand—so close and open and honest and connected—it's insane how connected—and yet we're so closed off in some ways. Like there are these unwritten rules." I shrug. "I don't know how to explain it."

"I get it—believe me—more than you know. Well, have you had the whole 'let's not date other people' conversation, at least?"

"Yeah. But not in the usual way. It came up through this weird back door."

Sarah grimaces.

"Oh, Sarah. You and your fear of anal." I laugh. "I wasn't being literal. I meant it came up because we were talking about doing all sorts of freaky sex-stuff and we decided to be exclusive for that. It wasn't like, 'Oh, darling, my heart simply can't beat without you. I'm ready to take our intimate and budding romance to the next level.'"

Sarah makes a commiserating face. "Same with Jonas. He invited me to be the 'sole member of The Jonas Faraday Club.' He never said, 'Let's be exclusive.' Everything's always in code with that guy. But, really, is there some official way a guy's supposed to ask to be exclusive? It all gets you to the same place in the end, right?"

I shrug. "Yeah, that's true. And he did say he doesn't want anyone touching me. He said it makes him crazy to think of someone else with me."

"Well, see? There you go. He's telling you. And he flew you down to L.A.

for a long weekend, and now he's up here to see you the very next weekend. That sure screams 'girlfriend' to me."

"Under normal circumstances, I'd agree. But I don't know for sure."

Sarah grabs my hand. "Kat, you're overthinking it. I saw you two in Vegas. The chemistry is through the roof. He's totally into you."

"I know he is. He's made that clear. I'm not blind. It's just that our relationship is so sexual—which is fan-fucking-tastic, don't get me wrong. But I just can't tell if it's all about the sex and excitement and here-and-now for him or if he wants something more. You know, something a bit more permanent."

"Here's a crazy idea: just ask him. Talk like adults."

"Pfft. Yeah, because that's what *you* did, right? I seem to recall Jonas not saying the three magic words after Belize and you were like, 'I don't need no stinkin' magic words. He told me in a super-secret code and that's just great with me.'"

Sarah makes a face. "That's true. I did say that."

I motion like she's just made my point.

"Okay, I get it," Sarah says. "Well, then. Here's a different approach. How about you get yourself stabbed in a bathroom at U Dub? That'll jumpstart a conversation about your fucking feelings in a New York minute."

"Hey, there's an idea. Why didn't I think of that?"

"God only knows if Jonas ever would have told me he loves me if external forces hadn't intervened."

"Well, I'm gonna pass on getting stabbed, thank you very much. But how about this as an 'intervening external force': Josh is meeting my family on Saturday night."

Sarah squeals. "No way. Really? You're sicking the Morgan clan on the guy? Holy hell, now that's a frickin' 'intervening external force' every bit as powerful as a hitman in a bathroom. Holy hell, the guy doesn't stand a chance coming out of that night all in one piece. By the end of the night, he'll be like, 'Just tell me what you want me to say! Please! I'm sorry!'"

I laugh. "I know, right?"

Sarah looks thoughtful for a minute. "You know, I really wouldn't get too hung up on expecting Josh to say certain words or make conventional promises to you. If Josh is anything like his brother, then he's way more fucked up than you even realize. I think their childhood was just utterly crippling in a way we can't completely understand. I've got my own issues, for sure, as you know, and they *pale* in comparison to what Jonas has had to overcome in his life."

A vision of Josh's "overcome" tattoo suddenly leaps into my mind.

"Even with all my fucked up stuff, I always had my mom, teaching me how to love," Sarah continues. "Who did Jonas and Josh have? I don't think either of them has ever learned the first thing about how to express emotion or love in a healthy way. They literally don't know how to love or be loved."

I process that for a moment. "When we were talking about my mom, he said, 'I've never actually witnessed a wife roaming in its natural habitat.'"

Sarah laughs. "Josh said that?"

I nod.

"Poor Josh." Sarah touches her platinum bracelet again. "Same with Jonas. He doesn't understand conventional, fairytale commitment. We never talk about the future or make any long-term plans. He's just not *capable*. He'll never, you know, ask me to marry him or anything like that—and I totally accept that."

I can barely keep a straight face.

"I just take what I can get in the here and now and that's enough for me. But I trust him with my life and I've learned to just let go and enjoy what we have. Jonas has already promised me forever the way he knows how," Sarah continues. "He gave me this engraved bracelet and he's got a matching one— and he got tattoos in my honor—one in Spanish and one in English." She chokes up. "The most beautiful and poignant words you ever saw." Her eyes are brimming with tears. "And that's enough for me. More than enough." She wipes her eyes and smiles.

I squeeze Sarah's hand, smiling to myself. Of all the tattoos I babbled off-the-cuff about being "lame" and "prohibited" to Josh, the "girlfriend" tattoo is by far the one I regret the most. It's absolutely awesome—whether the relationship winds up working out long-term or not. I was such a fool. "You can't get much more 'forever' than a guy getting a tattoo for you," I say. "Florebblaaaaaah," I add.

"Floreblaaaaaah?" Sarah asks.

"That's as close as Josh comes to saying that word."

Sarah laughs and wipes her tears again. "Maybe you can just decide to 'hear' what Josh is telling you with his actions, and not get too bogged down in needing particular words or assurances?" she suggests. "Maybe he'll never give them to you, Kitty Kat. Maybe he just *can't*." She wipes her eyes again. "I'm a firm believer that actions speak louder than words, anyway. And from what I can see, Josh has been screaming about his feelings for you from the rooftops."

"Thank you, Sarah." I exhale. "You're right. I'll do my best to just be happy about right now and not look forward. Unfortunately, I'm not nearly as patient or kind as you are."

"Well, you might not be as *patient* as me but—"

"I'm not."

Sarah laughs. "But you're every bit as kind. You've got a heart of gold, my sweet. Just tap into that golden heart and cut Josh a bit of slack. He's damaged, you know—just totally fucked up—but he's also a sweetheart. Just listen to his actions and forget about ever hearing the words. He's a freaking Faraday, after all. Normal rules don't apply."

My cheeks flush. "Thanks, Sarah."

We stare at each other for a moment, smiling.

"So, I gotta know," Sarah finally says. "What the *eff* was the dealio with tonight? Jonas left, saying he was taking you for drinks because Josh wanted to act out an imaginary-porno with you? What the fuck?"

I blush. "That's how Jonas described it?"

"Yeah. I was studying so I was like, 'Have fun, dear.' And then after he left, I looked up from my book and I was like, 'Wait. Did I just hear that right?'"

I laugh. "Yeah, Josh and I like to get a little freaky-deaky. But don't worry, Jonas was just our ignorant pawn—an unwitting extra in our movie. No Jonas Faradays were harmed in the making of our imaginary porno."

"So what was the plot of this imaginary porno? And what was Jonas' part in it, if you don't mind me asking? Did he 'come to fix the kitchen sink' wearing a huge tool belt?"

I giggle. "No. Jonas' part was *very* G-rated, I assure you."

"You're making me very intrigued—and very uncomfortable."

"No, I swear. It was harmless." I laugh. "I have this fantasy—well, I *had* this fantasy—I've now officially checked it off the list—that I'm on a date with some boring guy, like, you know, a guy I met online named *Blane* or whatever, and—"

"*Blane?*" Sarah says, aghast. "Blane's not a *name*—that's an appliance!"

"Exactly!"

We share a long laugh.

"I love Ducky," Sarah says.

"So, anyway, *Blane* and I are at a bar, and while poor Blane is babbling about something excruciatingly boring, I catch eyes with the hot bartender and it's like ka-boom."

"It's on like Donkey Kong."

"Exactly. So I excuse myself to go to the restroom and on my way I slip a note to the bartender—you know, total slut move—"

"Total."

"He meets me in the bathroom and fucks the crap out of me and then I return to my date like nothing happened."

"Oh my God. *Hawt.*"

"Isn't it?" I shudder. "So hawt. Gah."

"And extremely freaky-deaky."

"This coming from a girl who processed sex club applications?"

"People weren't nearly that creative in their applications, believe me. You'd be shocked how same-same people are. Most people aren't hankering to star in imaginary-pornos. They just want their dick sucked by a pretty girl."

I laugh. "Sarah," I say. "So unlike you to talk like that."

Sarah bats her eyelashes. "Jonas is bringing out my dirty girl lately. I'm spinning out of control."

"Good. It's about time."

"So my sweet Jonas was Boring *Blane,* huh?" She makes a frownie face. "That's so mean—you guys are such meanies."

"I didn't do it to him. Josh arranged everything. Jonas just showed up on my doorstep and handed me a poker chip."

"A poker chip?"

"Oh. Yeah. That's Josh's code for 'Let the imaginary-porno begin.'"

"Oh my gosh. You guys are crazy."

I shrug. "I told you. We're freaky-deaky."

"Well, I'll have you know Jonas isn't boring," Sarah says, sniffing the air. "He's really funny and smart and very, very interesting. In fact, Jonas is the most interesting person I've ever met."

I laugh. "I believe you. It wasn't me who cast Jonas as Blane—it was his mean brother." I make an apologetic face. "Are you mad?"

"*Mad?* No! I'd much rather you cast my boyfriend as the date you ditch than the hot bartender you screw in a bathroom."

We both laugh.

"Speaking of which, did you snag your hot bartender or what?"

"Of course. He didn't exactly play hard to get."

"Was he actually tending bar or just sort of standing near the bar, pretending?"

My eyes blaze. "Oh, he was actually tending bar, all right."

"Really? Wow."

"I don't know how he arranged it—the guy's a magician—but when Jonas and I got there, Josh was behind the bar serving drinks like effing Tom Cruise in *Cocktail*. In fact, there was one woman who was just about ready to jump his bones."

"Oh. You made mincemeat out of her, I imagine."

"Of course."

"Oh, Kitty Kat."

"Meow."

Sarah giggles. "What bar was it?"

"Oh, you're gonna laugh. *The Pine Box*."

Sarah throws her hands over her face. "No!"

"*Yes.* The whole time I was having flashbacks to when you and I watched Jonas with that bitch."

Sarah shakes her head. "Why would Jonas take you *there?*"

"Actually, it was really sweet. While we sat there on our date, he gave me a detailed play-by-play of when he first saw you behind that stupid menu."

"He did? Aw." Sarah visibly swoons. "Jonas is so sweet."

"Well, yeah, he might be sweet, but he's a date from hell. What guy goes out on a date and babbles the whole time about falling in love, sight unseen, with another girl? What a jerk. Who could blame me for screwing the hot bartender in the bathroom?"

Sarah makes a truly ridiculous face. "I can't believe you had sex in the bathroom at The Pine Box."

"Aw, come on now. Don't be a Judgy McJudgy-pants, girl. I thought you said Jonas has been helping you find your dirty girl. Trust me, there's nothing wrong with engaging in a little bathroom sex on occasion. You should try it some time, little Miss Goody Two-shoes. You might like it."

She snickers. "Well, gosh, thanks for the tip, Kitty Kat. Maybe I will. One day. If I can muster the courage."

There's a beat. Sarah's the absolute worst at playing it cool. She looks like a cartoon character with a secret.

I smirk. "So I take it from that ridiculous expression on your face you and Jonas have already had some über-hot bathroom-sex, huh?"

Sarah bursts into hearty, snorting laughter and her face turns bright red. "At The Pine Box!"

77

KAT

I'm absolutely screaming with laughter.

Henn and Hannah are onstage right now, delivering a straight-up *redonk* karaoke version of "You're the One That I Want" from *Grease*. I knew these two would be magic if I could get them together, I just knew it, but even I couldn't have predicted how truly destined for each other they'd be. John Travolta and Olivia Newton-John have absolutely nothing on these two in the made-for-each-other department. They're utter perfection.

I hear Sarah squeal with laughter to my right and I glance at her. She's dancing in her chair and singing along as she watches Henn and Hannah onstage.

God, this is the best night ever. Better than any fantasy.

Yes, being Josh's million-dollar whore was pretty damned exciting; and, yes, having him pick me over a supermodel felt pretty damned good; and, of course, being bound and fucked in a sex dungeon was freaking hot, too; and yesterday's tryst in the bathroom with that Hottie McHottie-pants bartender was ridiculously scorching, not to mention the look on that woman's face when I emerged from the bathroom and left with two hot guys. But, as titillating and sexy and hilarious as all that stuff has been, none of it is what I thought about while missing Josh and getting down with my battery-operated boyfriend this week. Nope. When I crawled into my empty bed at the end of each long and lonely day this past week, aching for Josh a thousand miles away in Los Angeles, I fantasized about one thing and one thing only: Josh making love to me to that James Bay song.

And today at work, whenever my mind meandered to daydreams of Josh (as it so often did), what did I dream about (besides the way he made love to me last week to that James Bay song)? Sex dungeons? Bartenders? Ski masks? Nope. I thought about how excited I am to introduce him to my family tomorrow night. And to sing the "Fish Heads" song at the fish market—an activity we've planned for tomorrow, perhaps after a leisurely brunch (after we've spent our first night together in *my* bed).

I lean into Josh's shoulder and breathe in his scent and he wraps his arm around me. I look up at him and grin and he beams a heart-stopping smile at me.

When Josh picked me up at my apartment two hours ago, dressed to kill in a trim black Armani suit and sunglasses, I immediately checked out his palms, expecting to see him carrying a poker chip. But, nope.

"No poker chip?" I asked as we waltzed down the walkway hand-in-hand toward his car.

"Not right now. But you never know when a sneaky guy might whip one out, so you better keep on your toes, Party Girl."

I peel my attention off Josh's striking face and watch Henn and Hannah singing the final lines of their song. Man, they're killing it. They're milk and cookies. Bert and Ernie. Macaroni and cheese. *Peanut butter and jelly*. I lean into Josh's shoulder again and squeeze his hand and he squeezes right back.

Maybe Sarah was right. This is enough. I've been overthinking. I don't need promises. All I need is the way I feel right now.

Henn and Hannah traipse happily off the stage toward our table, getting high-fives and cheers from everyone they pass, while a large guy with a bushy beard assumes the stage to belt out "Living on a Prayer."

"Utter brilliance," Josh says when Henn and Hannah plop themselves down.

"You're definitely tied for best of the night with Josh and Kat," Sarah agrees. "You both can actually sing."

"As opposed to *me*, is that what you're saying?" Josh says, laughing.

"No, that's not what I'm saying. Your performance was brilliant, Joshy Woshy. You didn't just *sing* your parts, you told the truth with every goddamned word."

Josh laughs and re-enacts his repeated "turn around" refrain from "Total Eclipse of the Heart," which Josh and I performed together earlier in the night to raucous applause from the entire bar.

"Hey, at least I'm a better singer than Jonas," Josh says.

"Josh," Jonas pipes in. "Don't congratulate yourself on being a better singer than me. I'm literally tone deaf—hence the reason you'll never catch me doing karaoke."

"Love, what you lack in actual singing ability, you make up for with the heart of a lion," Sarah says. "But yeah, the lead singer of our group's boy-band is definitely Henny. I didn't know you could sing, Henn."

"Yeah, I sang in an *a cappella* group at UCLA."

I exchange a smile with Josh. Why am I not surprised about that? That's so damned Henn.

"But I'm chopped liver compared to Hannah," Henn continues. "I sing like a choir boy, but she's got true *soul*. You should hear her singing Beyoncé in the shower. Sexy."

Hannah pushes up her glasses and busts out the chorus of "Say My Name." "Queen Bey better watch her back, that's all I'm sayin'," she says. And then she snorts.

"I love it when you sing," Henn gushes. "You're *amazing*."

I exchange a smiling look with Sarah. Oh man, that boy's in love.

Hannah giggles. "Henn. You think everything I do is *amazing*. I made you buttered toast the other day and you said it was the best toast you'd ever had."

"Well, it was—just the perfect amount of butter. It was even better than amazing—it was *schmamazing*."

We all laugh, though I personally have no idea what the hell that means.

Henn looks at all of us with puppy-dog eyes. "And you should see how well she draws *anime*, too. And she makes the best chocolate chip cookies you've ever had. They melt in your mouth."

Oh my God. It's all I can do not to leap across the table, grab Henn's lapels and shake him like you're not supposed to shake a baby. The boy's *in love*! It makes me feel as gooey as a fresh-baked chocolate chip cookie.

"Chocolate chip cookies, computer coding. Same-same," Hannah says. "Both take equal amounts of genius."

"You can't eat *code*, baby. I'll take the cookies. *Hey*. There's a hacker-pun in there somewhere, I'm sure of it." He snickers. "So, anyhoo, we've already seen Josh and Kat's spectacular rendition of 'Total Eclipse of the Heart,' which was legendary, by the way, guys, and now Banana and I have stopped the earth rotating on its axis for approximately four and a half minutes with what can only be described as sob-inducing spectacularity—so what are you two planning for our delight and entertainment?" Henn says, looking at Jonas and Sarah. "I'll die a happy man if I get to witness you sing karaoke, big guy."

"I don't do karaoke, like I said," Jonas says evenly, swigging his Scotch. "I can't sing for shit. I'm not in the business of embarrassing myself—at least not on purpose."

"Oh, baby," Sarah purrs, stroking his forearm. "You have a beautiful voice." She leans in and whispers something to Jonas and he grins broadly. He looks up and quickly catches the attention of the waitress across the room.

I lean into Josh. "The countdown clock just started on Jonas singing tonight."

Josh leans his lips right into my ear. "What's the over-under on how long it takes Sarah to get him up there?"

Josh's hand is on my bare thigh, making my skin buzz with every touch of his fingertips. His cologne smells divine. His eyes are a scorching blue. I feel intoxicated, though I've barely had a sip of alcohol. I feel drunk on Josh.

"Come on, PG. Give me your prediction."

"I'm not gonna say an amount of time," I say. "I'm gonna go with the number of Scotches, instead."

"Ooh, good call. How many?"

"Two more tops, and then he's gonna be singing like a tone-deaf canary."

"Two *on the outside*, huh? That's pretty ambitious."

I shrug. "That's the over-under. So you're betting *over*, then?"

Josh grins broadly and runs his hand up my thigh, right up to the hem of my mini-dress, making my skin erupt in goose bumps. "I've learned my lesson, babe. I'll never bet against you as long as I live. If you say two Scotches is all it's gonna take to get my brother up there, then that's what it'll take."

The "Living on a Prayer" guy leaves the stage and we're treated to three adorably silly women launching into a heartfelt rendition of Wilson Phillips' "Hold On."

The waitress approaches our table. "Hey, folks," she says. "Another round?"

Josh looks pointedly at everyone, gathering drink orders, and I shake my head, signaling I'm good. For some strange reason, alcohol just isn't hitting the spot tonight.

But Josh doesn't seem to understand my headshake. "Yeah, sure," Josh says absently to the waitress. "Another round. Plus Patron shots for everyone, too, please. With limes."

"And a club soda," I add. "Please."

"And a couple bottles of champagne, too," Jonas adds. "We're celebrating tonight."

"Oh yeah?" the waitress asks. "What are we celebrating?"

"Oh, just, you know," Jonas says, pulling Sarah into him, his face bursting with pure happiness. "*Life*."

Oh, jeez, those two. I've never seen two people more madly in love. I wish so badly I could watch Jonas pop the question to Sarah next week in Greece. I'd bet dollars to doughnuts she's gonna lose functionality in all four limbs and flop on the ground like a freshly caught trout.

The waitress leaves and Josh leans back in his chair, adjusting his dick in his pants. God, he's a sexy dude. Gotta love a man in a designer suit whose dick is so big, it won't fit comfortably inside his pants.

"Well, Jonas might be celebrating *life*," Josh says, "but I've actually got a few specific things I'd like to celebrate tonight." He raises his old-fashioned and the rest of us follow suit, holding up our various drinks. "First," Josh begins, "I wanna celebrate Hannah officially joining our *Ocean's Eleven* crew. Welcome, Hannah. You fit right in."

"Thank you," she says, pushing up her glasses.

"We all have our roles to play, Hannah," Josh continues. "So now that you're officially part of the crew, I'd like to christen you our cookie-baking Olivia Newton-John."

Hannah nods. "Wow. Thank you. I accept my role with humble gratitude. What's everyone else's roles?"

"Well, he's the asshole," Josh says breezily, motioning to Jonas. "And also the comic relief, though hardly ever intentionally."

Sarah laughs.

"Sarah's our George Clooney—our fearless leader—and also Jonas' handler. Without Sarah, Jonas becomes very, very cranky—so I'd like to take this moment to expressly thank Sarah Cruz for coming into my brother's life. By doing so, you've made mine immeasurably better." Josh beams a huge smile at his brother, and, much to my surprise, Jonas laughs heartily.

"Thank you," Sarah says, blushing. Jonas kisses her cheek and I swoon.

"Henn's our fucking genius, of course," Josh continues. "I'm sure that's not news to you, Hannah—plus, the guy's heart has a ten-terabyte storage capacity." He flashes Henn an adoring look.

"Yes, I'm well aware of that," Hannah says.

The look on Henn's face is priceless. Oh my effing God. He's adorable.

"And you and Kat?" Hannah asks. "What are your roles in the crew?"

"Well, unfortunately, I'm nothing but a playboy—just coasting on everyone's coattails, pretty much—not particularly useful or smart—just the eye candy of the group."

We all laugh.

"Don't listen to him. He's wise and powerful beyond measure," I say.

"Oh, well that's true," Josh agrees. "Hannah, you might as well learn it now: I'm wise and powerful beyond anything your feeble mind could possibly comprehend. Let me just say, in advance of whatever pearls of wisdom I'll bestow upon you one day in the near future: you're very welcome."

Hannah laughs. "Okay. Thank you, Josh, in advance. Wow, I'm honored to be in your presence."

"As you should be. Thank you. And Kat here—well, the list is too long to say it all right now, but I'll give you the Cliff's Notes version. She's our secret weapon. The Party Girl with a Hyphen who also happens to be The Party Girl with the Heart of Gold. Plus, she's a suicide bomber, a terrorist, and, sometimes, if you really rile her up, a very stubborn cat."

I giggle.

Josh chuckles and squeezes my hand. "And, she's got the best laugh you ever heard, as I'm sure you already know. The girl laughs like a dude."

"I'm well aware."

I giggle again.

"Hey, I have an item for the toast," Jonas says.

"Hang on, bro," Josh says. "I'm not done with Kat." He looks into my eyes. "She's loyal. And honest. A force of nature when she wants something. She loves her family. And her hair smells incredible."

I can't breathe.

Josh holds my gaze for a long beat. "There's more, but we'd be here all night," he says softly. He kisses me tenderly on the lips and my heart bursts out my chest cavity and zings around the bar.

"I wanna salute Sarah for making it through her first year of law school..." Jonas is saying. But I'm only half-listening. I'm caught in an alternate universe with Josh. Yes, Sarah was absolutely right. He's screaming his feelings for me from every mountaintop the best way he knows how. And that's enough for me.

"Well, jeez, don't jinx me. I gotta get through my exams before I'm toast-worthy," Sarah says.

I manage to peel my eyes off Josh's face and look at Jonas and Sarah, clasping Josh's hand.

"But you finished your classes yesterday," Jonas says. "No reason not to celebrate that." He grabs her hand and kisses the top of it and she melts.

"Can I add an item to the toast-list, too?" Sarah asks. "I wanna toast Henn and Kat for officially becoming *mill-i-on-aires* this week. Congrats, guys."

"Didn't you get your finder's fee money this week, too?" Henn asks.

"Yeah." Sarah beams a smile at Jonas. "But I can't even think what to do with it—I want for absolutely nothing these days."

Henn and I shoot a look at each other like that's the stupidest thing either of us has ever heard. I'm glad Sarah's googley-eyed in love and all, but who couldn't use an extra million bucks, for crying out loud?

"Yeah, congrats to all three of you," Josh says. He grabs my hand and kisses it the way Jonas just kissed Sarah's hand, making me swoon, and raises his drink to me. "Which reminds me of a biggie. To Kat. She officially took a leap of faith today and quit her job to start her own PR firm. Congrats, babe. Sky's the limit."

Everyone expresses congratulations and excitement.

"I'm so excited for you," Hannah says. "Even though I'll miss you terribly." She sticks out her lower lip.

Of course, I'm not blindsiding Hannah with this news—I told her about my plans earlier today at lunch, and she was full of congratulations and excitement then, too, but she also cried. "Working with you has been the best part of my job," she said.

"Well, like I said at lunch," I say to Hannah, "the master plan is to bring you on as soon as humanly possible, Hannah Banana Montana Milliken," I say. "As soon as I know what I'm doing, you'll be my right-hand woman."

Hannah raises her drink. "Cheers to that. Just call me and I'll come running, girl. Whatever you touch turns to gold, Kitty Kat—I have no doubt your new company will be golden, too."

"Thank you, honey."

The waitress returns with our new round of drinks, plus the shots and bottles of champagne, and we pour bubbly all around.

"What are you gonna call your new company?" Henn asks.

"PGPR?" I say without confidence—but even as I say it, it sounds pretty lame. "Short for Party Girl PR," I add, hoping that clarification makes the name more palatable.

Sarah scrunches her nose.

"You don't like it?" I ask.

"Kinda stodgy, don't you think? A little boring—and you're anything but boring."

I twist my mouth, considering. She's got a point.

"It's not an accounting firm, right?" Sarah asks. "It's publicity. It's gotta have some pizzazz."

"Yeah, at first I thought maybe Party Girl PR—but that sounds too much like an event planner."

"Yeah, you're right—it kinda does. Hey, but you're the Party Girl *with the Heart of Gold*, right? Hannah just said everything you touch turns to *gold*. Why not Golden PR? You could have a sexy golden-blonde avatar of yourself as your logo. That'd be adorable. Or, hey, better yet, maybe even Golden Kat PR and make your logo a sexy golden cat with long eyelashes."

I look at Josh and he nods enthusiastically. "Either one. Probably have more luck securing Golden Kat for trademark purposes."

"Great idea, Sarah," I say. "I'll look into that."

Sarah smiles. "You bet, baby. I got a million ideas." She taps her temple. "I'm at your service, baby."

"Thank you."

We grin at each other.

"Okay, everyone, get 'em up," Josh says—and we all raise our glasses of champagne. "To Hannah and Henn, and to Sarah for finishing her first year of law school, and to three newly minted *mill-i-on-aires*, and, last but not least, to Kat and her new baby." Josh looks at me, his blue eyes sparkling. "YOLO, Kat—I'm glad you've decided to go for it. May you climb and conquer."

"Hear, hear!" we all shout, bringing our champagne to our lips.

"Wait!" Sarah blurts and we all stop. "*Duh*. We gotta toast Climb & Conquer!" She raises her shot of tequila. "This one we gotta do with Patron, in Joshy-Woshy's honor."

Everyone raises a shot glass.

"To Climb & Conquer," Sarah says. "I can't wait to watch the Faraday twins 'climb and conquer' every peak of their dreamscape."

Jonas and Josh share a look of unmistakable excitement.

"Hear, hear," everyone says, clinking glasses.

"Please hire me soon, Kat," Hannah adds and everyone laughs.

"I'm so proud of you," I whisper to Josh, squeezing his hand.

"Thanks," he says, his blue eyes sparkling. "I've never been so excited about anything in my life."

As everyone throws back his or her shots, I put my glass down, untouched. Just the smell of the tequila is making me kinda queasy. Maybe it's something I ate?

Josh kisses my cheek. "To new beginnings," he says softly into my ear. He grabs my tequila and downs it for me, seemingly unfazed by my disinterest in it.

"And to giant leaps of faith." He kisses my lips and rubs my cheek with his thumb. "I missed you this week, PG. I was going out of my mind."

Boom.

That's it.

Put a fork in me.

My body can't physically contain these feelings any longer. This sexy beast of a man's got me hook, line, and sinker. I'm gonna tell him how I feel when we're alone later tonight. I can't take it anymore. I love him and I've got to tell him so, come what may.

Sarah leaps up suddenly, pulling gently on Jonas' muscled arm. "You ready, hunky monkey boyfriend?" she asks. "The alcohol has started to kick in—it's time for you to pay your debt."

Jonas grimaces—but Sarah's persistent. She pulls on his arm again, flashing a seductive smile. "Come on, love," she purrs. "You lost fair and square and you know it." She leans into Jonas' ear again and whispers something, and Jonas begrudgingly stands and lets her lead him toward the stage.

Josh flashes me a look of pure astonishment. "You were right."

"Of course, I was. I'm always right when it comes to two things," I say.

Josh chuckles. "Men and PR, I know, Party Girl." He gazes at his brother for a beat. "Look at him," he says, motioning toward Jonas and Sarah taking the stage. "God, he must really love that girl."

78

JOSH

This is officially the most entertaining thing I've witnessed in my entire life.

Jonas and Sarah are doing a God-awful rendition of "I Got You Babe" by Sonny and Cher. Sarah's actually pretty good—she really comes alive up there. But Jonas is so fucking terrible, the entire bar is on its feet, cheering him on. But why am I surprised? Even when Jonas sucks at something, people love him for it. In fact, now that I think about it, I'm pretty sure people love Jonas *especially* when he sucks at something, not despite it.

How Sarah gets my brother to do any of the shit she gets him to do is beyond me. But there he is, standing in front of strangers, singing this ridiculous song to her at the top of his off-key lungs. And, by God, he actually looks like he's having fun. Well, fun mixed with pain—utter, tortured, unthinkable pain. But with Jonas, that's just about the best anyone could ever hope for.

I put my hand into my pocket and finger the edges of the poker chip sitting there. Now would be a fantastic time methinks. We're all nice and loose. I look at my watch. We're not due at the laser tag emporium for another hour. All is going perfectly according to plan.

"Excuse me for a second," I say, unclasping my hand from Kat's. She doesn't bat an eyelash—apparently too enthralled with the train wreck unfurling onstage to care about where the heck I'm going.

I move across the room to the karaoke DJ, wading through clapping, screaming, hooting people, all of them hurling love with both arms at Jonas and Sarah, and make my way to the DJ.

"Hey, man," I say. "You ready to do that thing we talked about?"

"Whenever you are, bro."

"Okay. How about you do one song after Sonny and Cher for whoever else and then we launch into my thing?"

The DJ grabs the piece of paper I slipped him earlier (along with a fat tip that ensured there'd be no waiting all night long for anyone in our group). "This still what you want me to say?" he asks, looking at the short script I gave him.

"Yeah. Hey, can you hand me that scarf I stashed earlier?"

"Sure." He grabs the scarf behind him. "Fucking hilarious, man," he says, handing it to me covertly. "You think she's gonna ham it up? Or will she chicken out?"

"Oh, my girlfriend never chickens out about anything—it's not in her DNA. Did you see her doing 'Total Eclipse of the Heart'? She'll ham it up for sure."

"Cool. Okay. One more song after Sonny and Cher and then we'll do it."

"Thanks." I stick the scarf in the waistband of my pants, hidden by my jacket.

The guy looks up at Jonas and Sarah, singing their adorkable hearts out, and chuckles. "Man, this guy's *horrible*—absolutely atrocious. Pretty much the worst I've ever heard and I've been doing this a really long time."

I look at my brother and grin. He's totally outside his comfort zone right now—sweating bullets, moving across the stage like a gorilla with hemorrhoids. God, he's awesome.

Out of nowhere, my stomach clenches vicariously to think about what he's about to do next week. He's taking a huge fucking step—the hugest step known to mankind—but, damn, he sure looks happy. Hard to argue a guy off doing anything that makes him smile that fucking big.

"Yeah, he's terrible, huh?" I say. "Gotta love him."

I head back to our table, my fingertips toying with the poker chip in my pocket, and sit back down next to Kat. She's clutching Henn's forearm, tears of laughter streaming down her cheeks.

Jonas and Sarah reach the slow finale of their song and the entire place erupts into a standing ovation.

When the song is done, Jonas dips Sarah dramatically, kissing her like no one else is in the room, and she comes back up red-faced and giggling.

The waitress pays another visit to our table. "Another round?"

"Yeah," I say absently. "Why the fuck not?"

Jonas and Sarah make their way back toward our table while two young, toker-looking guys get up onstage and start singing "American Pie."

"Awesome, bro," I say to Jonas when they return to our table and plop themselves down. "I can die a happy man now."

"Never again," Jonas says. "That memory's gonna have to last you your whole life long."

"How the fuck did you get him up there, Sarah Cruz?" I ask.

Sarah shrugs. "I'm magic, Josh Faraday."

"Sarah and I had a little bet and I lost," Jonas says. "I'll never bet against her again, I swear to God."

I look at Kat and she flashes me a smart-ass grin, obviously telling me, "See? Never bet against a woman."

"What was the bet?" Kat asks.

"Oh, the details aren't important," Sarah says. "But let's just say I held onto my title in the underwater breath-holding Olympics."

We all look at each other and make a face. Clearly, this is a sexual innuendo of some sort, and God knows we don't wanna know.

"Well, you were awe-inspiring, big guy," Henn says.

"Hey, Kitty Kat, you haven't gone in a while," Hannah says. "What are you gonna sing next?"

"Oh, I dunno. You wanna do another duet, Josh? A little 'Islands in the Stream,' perhaps? Or am I flying solo?"

"Yeah, a duet for sure," I say, the hair on the back of my neck standing up. I can't let Kat go up there again and ruin my little plan. "But let's give it another song or two, okay? I've got drinks coming for us."

Kat leans back. "Sure. So, hey, Henny, how long are you in town? You and Hannah wanna do dinner with Josh and me Sunday night before Josh heads to the airport?"

"Sorry, leaving tomorrow. I've got a job in Munich, actually." He looks at Hannah. "But after that I'll be home in L.A. for a good long stretch. Maybe you and Hannah can come visit Josh and me together and we can all go out in La La Land?"

Kat looks at Hannah for confirmation. "Great," she says.

"Hey, maybe you should think about opening Golden PR in Los Angeles instead of Seattle," Hannah suggests. "Maybe you could do PR for the entertainment industry."

"Well, that'd be pretty stupid," Jonas pipes in, sipping his Scotch.

"What would be stupid?" Henn asks, clearly feeling defensive on behalf of Hannah. "Sounds like a great idea to me."

"No, I mean, it'd be stupid for Kat to move to L.A.," Jonas clarifies. "What would be the point of Kat moving to L.A. right when Josh is moving back home to Seattle in a couple months?"

Fuck me. My stomach lurches into my throat and my eyes bug out. This isn't the way I'd intended to tell Kat about my upcoming move. Shit. I didn't even think to warn Jonas I hadn't told Kat about the move.

"What?" Kat asks, her eyes blazing with instant excitement. She whips her head to look at me. "Is he serious?" She clutches her chest, obviously overcome. "*You're moving to Seattle?*" She's practically shrieking with joy.

I open my mouth to speak, but nothing comes out.

"For good? You're moving here... for good? To *live*?" Yep, full on shrieking. She's acting like she just won the showcase showdown on *The Price is Right*.

"Yeah. Um. I'm moving home. Just got a place."

She's bouncing happily in her seat. "When? This is *awesome*. A dream come true."

"In a two or three months, probably."

"Really? Oh my God. Why didn't you tell me? Did you just decide today? Why didn't you tell me? This is incredible news. Oh my God. I'm elated."

"You didn't know?" Jonas asks, his face etched with obvious confusion.

Kat takes in the expression on Jonas' face and her entire demeanor changes on a dime. *Boom.* She knows something's up. Just like that. Thanks, Jonas.

"No, he didn't mention it to me," she says slowly, her eyes drifting warily to mine. "Why didn't you mention it to me, Josh?" she asks, her tone edged with obvious apprehension. "Were you planning to... surprise me?"

Oh shit. This isn't good. This is really, really bad. "Uh..." I begin.

"How long have you known?" she asks quietly, understanding dawning on her. "You said you already found a place?"

Shit. I've totally fucked up here. I've really, really fucked up.

"I've known for just a little while," I say. "Let's talk about it later, okay?"

She swallows hard. "How long have you known, Josh?" Her lip trembles.

I look at the group. They're all staring at me.

"Did you know when I said that thing about the long distance thing being brutal? Did you know then?"

Shit. "Let's talk about it later, babe," I say, trying to sound charming and smooth. "Don't get all worked up about it. I was just waiting until it was for sure."

A strange cocktail of emotions flashes across her face in response to that comment—like she's not sure whether to be extremely disappointed or relieved. "Oh, it's not for sure? That's why you didn't tell me?"

"Well, no. Actually." I swallow hard. "It's for sure. I'm moving."

"Oh." She shifts in her seat. Her cheeks flush. "That's great. So you've already made... plans? You've got a place?"

"Let's talk about it later. What's everyone planning to sing next?"

The entire bar is boisterously singing along to the final chorus of "American Pie." But I feel anything but festive. My stomach is churning. My chest is tight.

"Have you put your house on the market yet?" Kat asks, her chin wobbling.

Oh shit. This is a catastrophe. Why didn't I foresee how badly this would go down?

"Uh. Yeah, actually, it sold last week."

"It already *sold?*" Her face turns bright red and her eyes prick with tears. "How long was it on the market?"

"Can we talk about this later. In private?"

"How long was it on the market?" she asks between gritted teeth.

"About three weeks."

The two "American Pie" guys depart the stage to raucous applause.

"And now," the DJ says into his microphone, reading from the piece of paper I gave him earlier. "I have a very special treat for you."

"Kat, we'll talk about it later, okay? Here." I pull the poker chip out of my pocket and plunk it into her palm. "Please. I'll explain everything to you later. Right now, I've got a surprise for you."

She looks down at the poker chip, her eyes filling with tears, and I know I just made matters worse, not better. Much, much worse. Oh Jesus. I'm an idiot.

I stand and motion to the DJ to tell him to stop, but he doesn't see me because he's looking at the fucking piece of paper in his hand—the paper I gave him and asked him to read into his goddamned microphone.

"We unexpectedly have a superstar among us tonight, folks," the DJ says, reading from my script. "The one and only *Rachel Marron.*"

People at nearby tables are looking at each other quizzically, clearly not recognizing the name.

"Poor Rachel's endured some death threats recently, so she's here with her devoted and stoic *bodyguard* Frank Farmer—former Secret Services detail for the President of the United States."

There's a tittering in the crowd. People are starting to get it.

I look at Kat and my heart squeezes. "Babe," I say. "Please don't leap to conclusions. It's not what you think. Just enjoy the poker chip."

"Under Frank's watchful eye, Rachel's agreed to sing her signature song for us. A heartfelt rendition that's sure to make you weep."

The place is going crazy all around us.

"I don't understand why you didn't tell me. You already sold your house. You didn't want me to know you were moving here?"

"So let's hear it for Rachel Marron everyone!"

Everyone in the bar hoots and screams.

"You're not excited to live in the same city with me? To see each other every day? You don't wanna go to the dry cleaners and the fish market?"

"Looks like she's feeling shy, folks. Let's get her up here, huh? To perform her classic hit, 'I Will Always Love You!'"

The place explodes with excitement.

But Kat looks like a wounded deer in headlights right now.

My heart is breaking. What have I done?

"Babe, you're totally misunderstanding the situation," I say. "I'll tell you all about it later. Right now it's poker chip time. Enjoy it. This is your biggest fantasy."

"Come on, Rachel!" the DJ calls. "Come on up here with your bodyguard!"

Kat looks down at the poker chip in her palm, a pained look in her eyes, and it's abundantly clear acting out her bodyguard fantasy is the last thing on her mind.

I pull the scarf out of my pants and hold it up, trying to make her smile. My heart is beating a mile a minute. I've fucked up. Oh, fuck me, I've royally fucked up. I've got to get control of the situation. Make it better. I've got to charm her back to being Happy Kat.

"Remember the last scene of the movie—when Whitney wears the scarf on her head?" I coo. "I brought the scarf for you, babe. So you could look just like her."

Kat's dumbstruck. She looks at the poker chip in her hand again, tears filling her eyes.

"Kat, come on—be my Whitney, baby. I've got it all planned. We're doing the song here and then I rented an entire laser tag place for the six of us. It'll be everyone else against you and me, baby, all night long—I'll protect you. *I'll be your bodyguard.*"

"Rachel?" the DJ says. "Are you coming or not? Your fans are waiting. Last chance."

"Sing here, then laser tag, and then I'll take you home and let my feelings override my stoic sense of duty." I smile, trying my damnedest to charm her.

"Rachel? Last call."

She abruptly snatches the scarf out of my hand, wraps it around her head a la Whitney, and marches in a huff toward the stage, determined.

Thank God. She's playing along. This is gonna be okay. That's my girl. She'll understand when I explain it to her. She'll totally understand. I let out a huge sigh of relief, slide my sunglasses on, and follow my beautiful Whitney to the stage, my heart pounding in my ears.

79

KAT

Everyone in the place is cheering and banging on their tables. But I'm in a daze. I can't think straight. Josh is moving to Seattle? That's incredibly awesome news. I'm ecstatic about it. *But why didn't he tell me about it?* Was he planning to surprise me—the way he burst into his bathroom wearing a ski mask?

Josh places a chair at center stage for me—and I position myself onto it exactly the way Whitney sits on a chair in the snow in the music video—and then Josh fusses with the scarf around my head, making it Whitney-with-a-broken-heart-on-the-private-airplane-perfect, and everyone in the place laughs and hoots, totally loving the set-up. When he's done with me, Josh turns to the audience and makes a big point of sweeping the crowd for snipers and wack-jobs—and everyone slurps him up like a tray of Jell-O shots.

The music starts.

I'm in automatic pilot. I've heard this song ten million times. I don't even need to think to sing it.

There's got to be a logical explanation why Josh didn't tell me about his move that has nothing to do with him intending to break up with me when he moves here. He had to have his reasons. Good reasons. The fact that he didn't tell me doesn't mean he doesn't want to be with me. There's got to be another logical reason. But I can't think what it could be. What other reason could there possibly be except that Josh doesn't want to be with me when he moves to Seattle?

Tears fill my eyes. Why doesn't he want to be with me? I want to be with him more than anything. More than I want literally anything else. I think it's fair to say I want to be with Josh more than I want to breathe.

I pick up the microphone.

Maybe he was just gonna surprise me with the news—and Jonas let the cat out of the bag? But, no. I saw Josh's face when Jonas spilled the beans. He didn't look like a guy whose happy surprise got unwittingly spilled by his brother. He looked like a guy who just got busted on something—a guy whose cover just got blown.

The teleprompter begins scrolling the words to the song, and, even though I have no desire to sing it right now, my mouth begins half-heartedly mumble-singing the first lines. But the words are slaying me. They're too close to home. They're about Whitney having no choice but to leave her lover. She loves him, but she's got to go. It's just the way it is.

Everyone's cheering uproariously. As far as they're concerned, I'm giving the performance of a lifetime—an emotion-packed Whitney-tribute.

I yank the scarf off my head. Fucking scarf. Why the fuck am I doing this? I don't want to role-play a freakin' fantasy right now. I wanna talk to Josh in real-life. I wanna know why he didn't tell me.

The teleprompter reaches the words of the chorus—the words I've been singing at the top of my lungs in the shower since I was ten years old.

I look at Josh. He's standing stock-still, no longer playing his part. He's looking at me with the same expression he had when I opened my door to him in Las Vegas after reading his application.

My eyes drift to the teleprompter again, though I certainly don't need it to know the lyrics.

I can't sing these words to Josh. Not like this. These are sacred words—magic words. The words I'd planned to say to Josh later tonight when we were all alone in my bed.

The words I'd planned to say when I thought Josh loved me, too, but just didn't know how to say it. And now, suddenly, I realize he doesn't feel the way I do.

Without conscious thought, I toss the scarf into the air, letting it flutter to the ground, bolt out of my chair, and sprint out the front doors of the bar, ugly tears streaming down my face.

80

JOSH

"Kat!" I yell. She doesn't turn around. The night air is chilly, but my skin is blazing hot. This is a fucking catastrophe. "Kat!" I yell again, my voice strained.

She whips around to face me, heat wafting off her skin. "Why didn't you tell me?" she blurts, tears streaming down her cheeks.

My heart is physically pained at the sight of her. I grab her shoulders, desperate to make her understand. "You're blowing this way out of proportion. Just listen to me, okay?"

"You put your house on the market three weeks ago—you've obviously known for a while."

I exhale. "I only decided for sure about a month ago."

She throws up her hands.

"But I'm not moving for two or three months," I say. "I can't move until I've got everything squared away with Faraday & Sons."

Her expression is a wicked combination of devastation and fury.

"I didn't wanna say anything until it was closer," I say soothingly. "That's all. I was gonna tell you. Just *later*."

She clenches her jaw. "Why?"

"Why what?"

"Why wait 'til later to tell me?"

"Because I didn't want you to get your hopes up if..." I stop. I can already tell this isn't gonna go over well. Oh shit. I'm fucked.

"If what?"

I pause.

"If *what*?"

"If things didn't work out. Between. Us."

There's an excruciating silence.

"Let me see if I understand this," she says. "Standing here right now you're not one hundred percent sure you wanna be with me *two months* from now?"

I throw up my hands. "Well, shit. When you say it like that, it sounds horrible. But, yeah, I just wanted to wait until I was sure I wasn't gonna get your hopes up and then somehow, you know, disappoint you."

She blinks and huge, fat tears streak out her eyes and down her beautiful cheeks.

"Kat, please," I say, my voice quavering. My eyes are burning. I close them and compose myself for a beat. "It's no reflection on how I feel about you. I think you're amazing. And gorgeous. Funny. Smart. Sweet. I think about you night and day—that's why I came to Seattle early. I've never had so much fun in my life as I have with you."

Oh shit. Something I just said lit her fuse—and not in a good way.

"*Fun?*" she spits out, utterly enraged.

I roll my eyes. "Did you hear anything else I said? *Fun* was the very last thing I said—*after* saying a bunch of other really awesome things. And, by the way, saying you're fun is a huge compliment."

"Oh, thanks for the compliment. Makes me feel *great*. You can always count on Kat for a little *fun*." She wipes her eyes, but it's pointless—tears are streaming out.

I look up to the night sky and roll my entire head in frustration. This is so fucking horrific. I can't believe she's overreacting like this. She's so fucking temperamental, I swear to God. "This is spiraling way out of control," I say. "How much have you had to drink? Are you drunk?"

"No, I'm not drunk. I've hardly had a drop."

"Well, you're acting drunk."

"I'm not drunk. I'm pissed. And hurt. Deeply hurt."

"Why the fuck are you 'deeply hurt'? I'm sorry I didn't tell you I'm moving, but I'm not gonna apologize for saying I'm having *fun* with you—because I am."

"I was gonna bring you home to meet my family, Josh," she says, her eyes watering and her voice cracking. "I obviously can't do that if all we're doing is having *fun*."

"What the fuck? You're not gonna let me come meet your family now? You're *uninviting* me from the birthday party?" Now I'm pissed. That goddamned party is the whole reason I flew the fuck up to Seattle in the first place.

She's in full terrorist mode. "I've brought a grand total of three guys home to meet my family, Josh. *Three*. And the last one didn't work out so well. Colby sniffed Garrett out like a St. Bernard tracking a lost skier. Colby knew Garrett was with me for nothing but *fun* while I was in it for a whole lot more. I'm not gonna subject myself to that ever again."

I'm speechless. She's comparing me to Garrett Bennett? She thinks I'm *using* her? Could she possibly believe that, after everything we've been through together? After everything I've said and done to make my feelings clear?

"That was such a low blow," I say between gritted teeth.

"Why is that a low blow? You can't imagine dating me eight measly weeks from now," she seethes. "Fifty-two *days*. My family would know you're not in it for the long-haul—especially Colby—and they'd eat you for breakfast."

"Shit, Kat. Motherfucker. I fucked up, okay?" My voice cracks. I press my lips together, regaining my composure. I wait. My eyes are stinging. I take a deep breath and push everything down. "I should have told you, okay? I'm sorry. But you're reading way too much into this. I'm not Garrett-Bennetting you. You can't seriously believe that."

She shrugs.

"What did that fucker say to you, again?"

"He said I'm *fun*."

"No, the other thing."

"He basically called me a slut."

"But what were his exact words?"

She shifts her weight. "He said I'm not 'marriage material.'"

I close my eyes and shake my head. I'm an idiot. This is Kat's Achilles' heel —her Kryptonite—and I've served it up to her on a silver platter.

"Listen to me, babe." I grab her shoulders and look into her eyes. "I never said I don't wanna be with you eight weeks from now. All I said was I can't make promises about the future. But that's only because nothing's for sure *in life*—it has nothing to do with you, personally. That's a factual statement. Anything can happen. But right now do I *want* to be with you? Yes. So bad it hurts—that's why I came to Seattle early."

Yet another battery of tears springs into her beautiful blue eyes.

"Kat, please, trust me. I'm crazy about you. It's just that, except when it comes to business, I take things a day at a time. It's all I can handle—" I have to stop. If I say anymore, I'm gonna lose it. My eyes are burning.

"I don't wanna be some kind of glorified booty call," she says softly.

"*What?* Did you hear a word I said? I think maybe you're clinically insane. Or maybe you're PMSing or something because that's the furthest thing—"

She makes a sound that can only be described as prehistoric, making me stop dead in my tracks.

"I'm *not* PMSing! I'm crying because you hurt my frickin' *feelings*—not because I have ovaries. You're the one who can't imagine dating me fifty-two freakin' days from now, so don't try to worm out of your assholery by playing the PMS card!"

Her nostrils are flaring. Her eyes are wild. She looks like a fucking dragon.

"Oh my fucking God," I say. "You're overreacting. Again."

"No, I'm not overreacting. You didn't tell the girl you're supposedly 'addicted to' you're moving to her frickin' city in eight weeks! How'd you expect me to find out? By bumping into you at Whole Foods?"

I look up to the sky, biting my lip. She's pissing me off. I should have told her, yes, but she's making mountains out of molehills. "Yes, Kat. You guessed it," I say. "I was gonna wait to tell you until after we'd bumped into each other at Whole Foods."

She abruptly turns around and marches away from me. "I'm going home," she says.

I roll my eyes at her backside. Her purse and phone are inside the bar and I'm the one who drove her here. How the fuck does she plan to go home? *Déjà fucking vu.* We might as well be in another hotel hallway right now. For a split second, the image of her dripping wet ass cheeks stomping down the hallway after Reed's party flashes across my mind and I smile. She's a handful, this one —never a dull moment.

"Wait," I command.

She doesn't wait.

"*Wait.*"

"Enjoy living in Seattle," she tosses back to me over her shoulder. "Hope you have *fun.*"

"Oh my God. The drama," I say. In five easy strides, I've caught up to her. I grab her shoulders and turn her around and kiss her. Without hesitation, she presses herself into me, throws her arms around my neck, and surrenders to me.

I always say, when it comes to women, especially angry ones, there's very little that can't be fixed with a fucking awesome kiss.

We stand together, kissing like crazy for several minutes, both of us bursting with desire and emotion and arousal.

"I just don't understand why you didn't tell me," she whispers, abruptly pulling away from me. "I would have been bursting at the seams to tell you if the situation were reversed. You would have been the first person I would have called."

My heart drops into my toes. When she puts it like that, I suddenly understand why she's so upset. "Babe," I say. "I'm just not wired to make promises about the future, that's all. My brain doesn't work like a normal person's."

"I'm not asking for promises about the *future*—you think eight weeks from now is 'the future'?" Kat shakes her head and steps back from our embrace. "I'm not thinking clearly. You kiss me and I lose my mind. That's always been my problem around you. I'm so physically attracted to you, I can't think." She rubs her forehead. "I think we need to take a step back. Slow things down. I think we need to find out if we actually like each other in real life. Obviously, you're scared shitless this thing between us won't translate to living in the same city— and maybe you're right." She swallows hard. "Maybe we should trust your gut."

"*What?*"

"We've been living in a weird sort of fantasy from day one," she continues. "First we were in Las Vegas doing our *Ocean's Eleven* thing and now we fly to see each other on weekends so we can role-play imaginary-pornos and get stoned. Everything with us is nonstop excitement—*fantasy.* We never do

normal, real-life stuff like play a board game or go to the freakin' grocery store."
She shrugs. "Maybe you're just addicted to excitement, and not to me, specifically. Maybe none of this is real."

My blood is pulsing in my ears. "Kat, no. Everything I've ever said or done
when I'm with you is real. Always. Even our fantasies are real—that's what's so
awesome about us—real life is a fantasy when it comes to you and me."

"Your move to Seattle is for sure?" she asks softly.

"Yeah. I made a cash offer on a place yesterday. It's ten minutes away from
Jonas' place."

Kat's face contorts. "I just can't believe you didn't mention that to me—
especially after how many times I've said the long distance thing is killing me or
I wish we lived in the same city."

"I'm sorry. I was just... " I don't finish my sentence. There's really no
adequate way to explain why I didn't tell her. I'm suddenly realizing I'm a
complete idiot.

She sniffles. "I get it. Sarah told me to listen to your actions and not your
words. Well, I guess I just heard you loud and clear. From here on out, I'll
expect nothing from you. We'll continue to have *fun* with no expectations
and no promise of a future. We can date other people, whatever. We'll start
from scratch. Get to know each other outside all the excitement and
fantasy."

"You wanna date other people?" I blurt, my heart exploding with panic.

"No," she says quickly. "Not at all. I don't want anyone but you." Tears
flood her eyes. "That's what I've been trying to tell you."

"Well, I don't want anyone but you, either," I say. I clutch her to me, relief
flooding me. If she'd said she wanted anyone but me, I would have lost my shit.
"Kat, we both feel exactly the same way." I kiss her temple. "Please don't read
into me not telling you. It doesn't mean anything—we feel the same way."

"I don't think we do, Josh. I don't think you realize how much... " Her
words catch in her throat. Tears spill out of her eyes. "If I'd bought a house in
L.A.," she says, "I would have been *thrilled* to tell you about it. I would have
talked your ear off about it."

"Kat," I choke out. "You're breaking my heart. I feel the way you do. I'm
just not good at... saying certain things. I'm not good at committing to certain
things. But that doesn't mean I don't *feel*. Please, Kat. I just need time, that's
all."

Kat wipes her eyes again. "I get it. Take as much time as you need. You're
not ready for a commitment of any kind. Good for me to know—better I learned
it now than later." She wipes her eyes and sets her jaw. "Obviously, I can't take
you home to meet my family tomorrow. I'm sure you understand."

"No, I don't understand. I really wanna meet your family—I'm *dying* to
meet your family."

"I'm sorry. It's not possible—not when my heart is on the line like this."

A little voice inside my head is screaming at me to tell her my heart is on the line, too, but the words don't come. I swallow hard, forcing down the lump in my throat again.

There's an awkward silence.

Her eyes are glistening with obvious hurt.

"Kat," I finally say. "Maybe I should have mentioned it. I just... Please believe me—you're my fantasy sprung to life."

Her jaw tightens. "Yeah, I'm the fantasy you don't want 'tainting' your real life when you move back home."

Shit. That was a not-so-subtle reference to my application to The Club, wasn't it? Yeah, it was. *Because I don't want this shit to taint my real life,* I wrote in my application. Oh, God, this is a complete disaster.

"Kat, no," I say. "You're not a Mickey Mouse Rollercoaster. Now you're just being crazy. Please don't do this. You're spinning out of control."

"I'm not doing anything but agreeing with you. From here on out, we're gonna do things Josh-Faraday-style. The future doesn't exist. There are no expectations, no commitments. All we have is right now. *YOLO.*" Her lip is trembling. "If I wanna stay, I'll stay. If I wanna go, I'll go. There'll be nothing to keep us tied to each other but however the wind blows on any given day. *Just the way you like it.*"

81

JOSH

I flip on the TV in my hotel room and quickly turn it off again.

What's wrong with me? Am I really *this* fucked up?

I told Emma the magic words, didn't I? Which means I'm capable of saying them. But Emma gave me a lot more time than this—ten times more time than this.

But what am I thinking? There's no comparison between Kat and Emma. I never felt this white-hot passion with Emma—this *electricity*. How the hell does Kat expect me not to fuck up when I constantly feel like I'm gripping a goddamned electric fence around her?

I get up and look out the window of my hotel room, a glass of Jack Daniels from the mini-bar in my hand. I've got a perfect view of the Space Needle from my room. It's lit up like a Roman candle at night.

I could have stayed at Jonas' house tonight, of course, but I was too embarrassed not to be staying with Kat to ask him. Plus, Jonas looked so happy tonight, I didn't have the heart to bring him down with my pathetic sob story. Jonas is the one who's supposed to cry like a big fat baby to *me*—our relationship doesn't work the other way around.

"Let's take a break for a couple days—see how we're feeling then," Kat said when I walked her to her door earlier tonight. "Maybe I'll realize I'm overreacting; maybe not. I'm just too hurt to think straight right now. I think I need some time to regroup and figure out what I'm feeling."

I take a swig of my whiskey, shaking my head. How did things go so wrong? I was on top of the world when I picked Kat up tonight. I couldn't wait to see her—the same way I always feel when I'm away from her. I couldn't wait to take her to the fish market tomorrow morning to sing the "Fish Heads" song with her like a couple of dorks. And I was losing my mind about meeting her family tomorrow night, too. And, most of all, I was chomping at the bit to fuck her on her Hello Kitty sheets.

And now it's all gone. *Poof.* And here I am, yet again, where I always am, sitting in yet another hotel room, another drink in my hand, looking out at yet another lonely cityscape.

I turn on the TV and flip the channels. Sports. Local news. I flip around and around and finally land on a music station. Lenny Kravitz is singing "Fly Away." Hey, at least something's going right for me tonight.

I sit down in an armchair in the corner, lean back with my whiskey, and listen to the song. Yeah, Lenny, I agree: let's fly away to anywhere but here—you and me, bro—to a place without stress and responsibility and worry. A place where I won't have this thousand-pound weight on my chest at all times—a place where I won't feel so fucking *lonely* all the time. And so fucking *guilty.* To a place where I'm not constantly being crushed by shit I can't control and feelings I can't express and memories that haunt me.

I run my hands through my hair. I've never thought of this song as sad before, but, motherfucker, it's making me wanna cry. Fuck this shit. I turn the channel to the next music station, only to run smack into "Little Lion Man" by Mumford & Sons. They're in the midst of singing the chorus and it's like they've written the words for me. Kat told me her heart is on the line tonight, didn't she?—and I really, *really* fucked it up.

Jesus.

I take another huge guzzle of my whiskey and stare at the Space Needle.

The torturous song ends, thank God—but there ain't no rest for the wicked: the next song is Adele. She's wailing her heart out in "Someone Like You." And kicking me square in the balls.

I take a gigantic gulp of my whiskey.

No, Adele, I'll never find another woman like Kat. Fuck you. She's a fucking unicorn, Adele. One of a kind.

I rub my forehead and look out the window with burning eyes.

Goddammit, I fucked up—maybe even irreversibly. I didn't realize it at the time, but tonight was a fork in the road for Kat and me and I took the wrong path. I should have told Kat about my move to Seattle in the first place, for sure, but even more than that, I should have handled things differently tonight when the shit hit the fan. I should have said all the right things—the things Kat was dying to hear.

But I didn't.

I imagine myself saying, "My heart's on the line, too, Kat." Damn, I should have said that to her. Or, at the very least, "Mine, too."

But who am I kidding? Kat didn't want to hear me say my heart's on the line—she wanted more than that. She wanted the magic words—the whole nine yards. And I let her down.

I drain the rest of my drink and pour myself another tall one.

Jesus. Adele's voice is cutting me like a thousand razors dragged across my heart.

Kat wanted a promise of forever from me tonight. It was written all over her face. But what she doesn't understand is there's no such thing as forever—I mean, shit, there's no such thing as *next week*. Anything could happen. Nothing's guaranteed. A guys' life can change in a single afternoon. I mean, hell, a guy might go out to a football game with his dad in the morning and come back later that day to find out no one will ever sing "You Are My Sunshine" to him again. Or call him Little Fishy. Or, worst of all, say the words, "I love you."

I take a long swig of my drink.

"No, son, they don't let kids go to the morgue," my father said. "You'll just have to say goodbye to her in your prayers, son."

"But I wanna say goodbye to her face and kiss her lips and tell her I love her. Not like in a prayer. For real."

"You can't do it to her face—you have to do it in a prayer."

"But I wanna see her face when I say it. Not like talking on the phone."

"Fine. Shit. I dunno. Then say it to her photo, then."

"But I don't have a photo of her."

"Well, Jesus Fucking Christ, Joshua William. Fine... Take this one. Your mother always loved this photo of the three of you. Say everything to her face in the photo and stop talking about it. I've got my own goodbyes to say, son—we're all hurting, not just you. I'm sorry but I can't talk about this anymore."

My eyes are stinging. I rub them and take another long gulp of my whiskey.

Kat wants me to promise her fifty-two days? Shit. I can't even promise her tomorrow.

Because a guy might go to school one morning and then return home that afternoon to find out his dad had shipped his brother off to a "treatment center" without even letting him say goodbye. And just to add insult to injury, the guy's dad might even say his brother will "never come home again" because "that boy's fucking crazy" and "we're better off without him" and "you need to stop crying about him like a little fucking baby."

Motherfucker.

I drain the last of my drink, refill my glass, and settle into my chair again.

What's the point in putting anything on the calendar at all when a guy could get called at a football game because his dad's brains have unexpectedly exploded all over the carpet in the study? And not only that, his brother's lying in a hospital bed, not talking or responding to anyone, after driving himself off a fucking bridge? When a guy could sit in his big, empty house in the dark, right after the cleaning crew's finished scraping his dad's brains off the ceiling, and fight tooth and nail to convince himself that marching into his father's bathroom and taking every fucking pill in the medicine cabinet is a terrible idea rather than the best fucking idea he's ever had?

I swallow hard, keeping my emotions at bay, and take another long sip of my whiskey.

Kat wanted to hear those three little words tonight—I know she did. But those are words I simply can't deliver to her. Not yet, anyway. If only she'd give me more time. If only she'd understand. I said those loaded words to Emma and look what happened—the relief of saying them for the first time lulled me into saying other things, too—things I shouldn't have said—and only a month after I'd first said the magic words, Emma was long gone. *I love you,* I told her. *Please don't leave me. Please.*

But she left.

I bought myself a fucking Lamborghini after Emma left me—so what am I gonna buy myself this time when the girl doing the leaving is my fantasy sprung to life? A jumbo jet?

Fuck me.

I look down at the glass of whiskey in my hand and, suddenly, a rage wells up inside me like a fucking tsunami. Fuck *overcoming.* Fuck this shit.

Fuck me.

Without a conscious thought in my head, I hurl my glass against the wall, shattering it into a million tiny pieces and spraying glass and whiskey all over the white fluffy bed.

My chest is heaving. My eyes are stinging. I rub them and force down my emotion. Fuck you, Adele, you fucking bitch. No, I won't find someone like Kat. I'll never find someone like her again as long as I fucking live. I'll be alone and lonely and fucked up and worthless—just like I've always been. Just like I'll always be.

Forever.

82

KAT

Whitney's sitting in her private jet, a scarf wrapped demurely around her head, looking out the airplane window at Kevin standing out on the tarmac, his arm in a sling.

Why is Kevin's arm in a sling? Because he took a bullet for Whitney. *Because he loves her.* And she loves him, too. But the horrible tragedy is that, despite their love, even though he took a freaking bullet for her, they simply can't be together. And they both know it. Because they're from different worlds, after all. And life isn't always fair, motherfucker. But the injustice of it all only makes their love more intense—harder to give up.

Whitney yells to the pilot to stop.

The jet engines abruptly stop and the airplane-steps come down. Whitney runs out of the private plane to Kevin and throws her arms around him. They kiss passionately.

And the most gigantic ugly cry ever released in the history of ugly cries leaves my mouth. "Josh!" I sob, throwing my head back onto the throw pillow on my couch. "Jooooosssssshhhhhh!"

Oh, I talked such a good game in front of the karaoke bar, didn't I? "From here on out," I said, "we're gonna do things Josh-Faraday-style. The future doesn't exist. There are no expectations, no commitments."

But I was full of shit.

I love him. With all my heart and soul. I don't want anyone but him.

I know he's 'crazy about me.' And that he's done a million amazing things for me, just like Richard did for Julia in *Pretty Woman.* Yes, just like Julia, I've been showered with gifts and money and offers to help me in countless ways —and, I suppose, for most women, all of that would be more than enough. But I'm not most women. I'm just like Julia—I want it all. I want a commitment. I want true love. I want a knight in shining armor on a white horse. Goddammit, I want more than *florebblaaaaah*. And I simply can't pretend I don't.

I clutch my stomach and put the pint of Ben & Jerry's I've been scarfing down onto the coffee table. I'm so worked up about all this, I feel physically ill. Queasy. And my nipples are sore, too, by the way, which is really weird. I know Josh pinched my nipples pretty hard yesterday when he fucked me in the bathroom at The Pine Box, but did he really pinch them *that* hard? Jeez. They still hurt.

Whitney's glowing face appears onscreen in close-up, her teeth a spectacular shade of computer-paper-white, her mocha skin flawless.

She begins singing The Song—the most famous song in the world.

Oh, God, she's an angel. My beautiful Whitney.

And I'm a sobbing mess. *Again.*

This song was written for Josh and me and no one else. I love him and he doesn't love me back. He's crazy about me, sure—addicted to me. But he can't promise me tomorrow, he says. Which is a telltale sign he's not in love with me. Because when you love someone, you're willing to promise forever, even though you intellectually know you can't make that promise. You don't *not* promise forever to the one you love simply because we're objectively mortal— you promise it, regardless, and hope forever turns out to be more than fifty-two days.

No one knows what life might bring or what might happen two months from now, I get that, but the point is that when you're in love, you're stupid enough to think you can promise forever. You wanna believe it so badly, you're willing to tell that little white lie. And if you're not willing to tell it, well then, that's the surest way to know you're not really in love, after all.

Whitney's done singing.

I grab the remote control, and just that sudden movement makes my stomach flip over violently, almost like I'm gonna barf. But that's ridiculous. I hardly drank a drop tonight.

Out of nowhere, my body dry heaves.

What the hell? I cock my head to the side, totally perplexed. What the heck was that? My body heaves again—only this time, holy shit, fluid has gushed into my mouth.

I sprint off the couch into the bathroom, my palm clamped over my mouth, and only semi-make it to the toilet before another, violent heave makes me vomit up every drop of fluid and Cherry Garcia in my stomach, not to mention the chicken wings and guacamole I ate at the bar.

Oh, jeez. Not pretty. Not pretty at all.

What the hell? I barely drank tonight.

I barf again.

Damn, I feel horrible.

Were the chicken wings bad? I wonder if anyone else is feeling sick, too?

I rinse out my mouth and clean the barf off the toilet seat and floor and shuffle back to my couch.

Damn, my nipples are hurting.

I can't imagine bad chicken wings would make my nipples extra sensitive.

I begin to nestle back onto the couch and grab the remote, but then all of a sudden, I sit up, tilting my head like a cockatiel. An alarming thought just skittered across my brain like a cockroach after the kitchen lights have been turned on.

No.

It couldn't be *that.*

I took a pregnancy test ten days ago and it was negative—and I haven't missed any pills since then. Have I? I don't think so. I didn't take them at the exact same time every day like you're supposed to, granted, but close enough.

I sprint back into my bathroom. The box of pregnancy tests I bought the other day had three pee-sticks in it, and I've only used one.

I pull out one of the unused pee-sticks, sit on the toilet, and pee on it, my heart racing. There's no effing way. That would be ridiculous. Unthinkable. I just quit my job with medical benefits *today.* Ha! No. God doesn't have that mean a sense of humor.

I sit and stare at the stick, waiting. One line means I'm in the clear. Two lines means I'm fucked six ways from Sunday.

I sit and wait.

I thought it was weird I almost barfed in the sex dungeon, but when I Googled "vomiting from intense orgasm," the Internet was littered with countless women who'd experienced the exact same thing. So I didn't sweat it.

"Don't you dare let me catch either of you *ever* making an accidental Faraday with a woman unworthy of our name or I'll get the last laugh on that gold digger's ass and disown the fuck out of you faster than she can demand a paternity test." That's what Josh said his father told him when he was barely a teenager.

The faintest second pink line begins to appear on the pee stick and my eyes pop out of my head.

"No," I say out loud. "Go away. Go away!"

The line is getting darker.

"No," I say, pulling at my hair. "Please, God, no."

This has to be a mistake. A false positive. Yes, that's what it is. A false positive. Of course. I run into the living room and grab my laptop. I Google "false positive pregnancy test" and it turns out there's no such thing, basically—except in cases of certain medication (no), defective test (maybe?), or, rarely, certain kinds of cancer. Is it wrong to be wishing I have cancer right now?

Okay, maybe the test was defective. That's my only hope.

I drink a couple glasses of water and sit on the couch, Googling like a madwoman for at least thirty minutes, trying to find a reasonable explanation for those two pink lines that doesn't involve a little Faraday growing inside me, and when I feel the tiniest hint of pee in my bladder, I run back into the bathroom and pee on the third pee-stick.

I would never try to trap you, I assured Josh. *I'm a millionaire now, Josh—I don't need your stinkin' Faraday money.*

Oh, I know you'd never do that to me, he assured me. *Of course, not.*

I look up at the ceiling, another massive wave of nausea slamming into me.

Within a minute, a second pink line appears on the new pee-stick. I stare at the two positive pregnancy tests lined up on my counter, my eyes bugging out of my head, my recent conversation with Josh echoing in my head. Oh God, Josh is gonna shit. He's gonna kill me, and then he's gonna shit.

And then he's gonna call me a gold digger.

And then he's gonna run away, his arms flailing.

And then he's gonna shit again.

My heart is aching.

This is a complete disaster.

Worst-case scenario.

"Shit," I say out loud.

I amble into my living room in a daze, clutching the two positive pregnancy tests.

I sit down on my couch, my eyes wide, my head spinning.

"Shit," I say again.

From the minute I laid eyes on Josh, I felt like I'd hopped aboard a bullet train.

Well, it looks like our train just jumped the tracks.

And now there's only one possible outcome.

Crash.

consummation

USA Today and International Bestselling Author

Lauren Rowe

83

JOSH

I stumble out of Walmart (the only place open at eleven-forty-five that sells electronics) and cross the parking lot toward my waiting town car. I open the door of the black Sedan and hurl myself into the backseat. "Thanks for waiting, man," I mumble.

"Did they have what you were looking for?" the driver asks.

I hold up a plastic Walmart bag containing my new purchases.

"Where to now?"

I give the guy the address of Kat's apartment and he starts the engine.

As the car pulls out of the parking lot, I surreptitiously dig into my plastic bag and pull out one of my three Walmart-purchases: a bottle of Jack.

The driver's eyes flicker at me in the rearview mirror, but, thankfully, the guy doesn't say jack about my Jack. I lean back in my seat, the bottle of booze perched against my lips.

Man, I fucked up tonight. I had no idea not telling Kat about my upcoming move to Seattle would play out like fucking Armageddon. Watching Kat cry big ol' soggy tears, especially on account of something I did (or, technically, didn't do), ripped my heart the fuck out of my chest. Each tear that streamed down Kat's beautiful face felt like a knife stabbing me in the heart.

"I would have been bursting at the seams to tell you if the situation were reversed," Kat said in front of the karaoke bar, her eyes glistening. "You would have been the first person I would have called."

Up until that moment, I'd been thinking my tempestuous little terrorist was simply overreacting—letting her emotions and temper run wild, as she's been known to do a time or two. But the minute those daggers left Kat's mouth, I knew they were cutting me so deep because they were the God's truth—and that if Kat were to buy a house in L.A. and not bother to mention it to me, I'd be crushed.

Which is exactly how Kat seems to be feeling right now: *crushed*. In fact, it seems like Kat might be thinking she's done with me for good, though that's not what she said when I dropped her off at her apartment. All she said before slipping inside her place was that she "needed a couple days to think and regroup" so she could "figure out if she was overreacting or not"—but the look on Kat's face as she closed her door made it clear she wasn't even close to deciding she'd overreacted.

"Okay," I said softly, even though all I wanted to do was plant a deep kiss on her mouth that would somehow erase her short-term memory from her brain. "Take your time," I said. "I'll call you in a few days." And I wasn't bull-shitting her when I said that—I really wasn't—I truly planned to leave her alone. I mean, shit, God knows groveling never has been my style. But, fuck me, after only an hour alone in my hotel room, drinking whiskey and staring at the Space Needle—not to mention getting my ass chewed by fucking Adele—I just couldn't sit there like a flop-dick anymore. I had to do *something* to make her forgive me.

So I texted Kat a couple times, asking her to call me—but she didn't respond. So I bit the bullet and called her—let the groveling begin!—but my call went straight to voicemail. So, finally, I tucked my dick and balls firmly between my legs and left Kat a rambling voicemail that can only be described as "vaginal." But, still, I didn't hear a goddamned peep from her. Which is when a panic started descending upon me, a thumping need to make Kat understand I'm genuinely crazy about her, addicted, insatiable. *And that's when I got my brilliant idea.*

I pull my new portable CD player out of my Walmart bag and remove it from its packaging. It's quite a bit smaller and way more modern looking than the old-school boom box I'd envisioned when I stumbled into the electronics aisle at Walmart, but I suppose beggars can't be choosers, especially at just before midnight on a Friday night.

The sedan pulls up to the front of Kat's apartment complex.

"Just park in the driveway," I say to the driver. I hand him my phone. "Connect this to your stereo—I've got a song all cued up."

"Huh?"

"Blast the song I've got cued up on my phone."

The driver looks incredulous, not to mention annoyed. "It's past midnight, sir. We can't be blasting music in a residential area."

I shove a couple hundred bucks at the guy. "Come on, man, I've got a girl to win back. I fucked up and now I gotta make her forgive me."

The driver takes my cash. "The song's cued up?"

"Yep. Just press play at my signal—and then blast the motherfucker at full volume, as high as your speakers will go."

"Full volume? Sir, I really can't—"

I throw a bunch more bills at the guy. "Just do it," I bark. "I'll handle any complaints."

Without waiting for the driver's reply, I stagger out of the car with my CD player in one hand and my brand new Walmart-issued trench coat in the other.

I can't believe I'm doing this. Was there an exact moment when I handed Kat my dick and balls, or did I give her my manhood in bite-sized pieces, the same way I fed her a peanut butter and jelly sandwich in the sex dungeon? Well, either way, the woman's definitely got my crown jewels in a Ziploc baggie now.

I place the CD player on the ground so I can put on my spiffy new trench coat, and when I'm positive I'm sufficiently John-Cusack-ified, I take a deep breath, lift my makeshift boom box over my head, and signal to the driver to start the music.

Peter Gabriel's song "In Your Eyes" begins blaring loudly from the car.

I stand stock still, holding the boom box over my head. And I wait.

But no Kat. What the hell? Surely, she can hear the loud music—her apartment is one of the units closest to the street.

I continue waiting, holding the CD player over my head.

But, still, no Kat.

Shit.

A feeling of pure desperation floods me. Is she really gonna ignore me out here? I'm putting my fucking heart on the line for her. But wait. What if Kat hears the song but doesn't put two and two together? What if she thinks it's just some drunken asshole, passed out in his car, playing the oldies station much too loud? I quickly stride back to the sedan and bend down to the driver.

"Hand me my phone," I say. "I'm gonna send my girl a text."

"You want me to disconnect it from the stereo?"

"No," I reply. "Keep the song going. I'll just reach over you real quick." The driver pulls my phone toward me, as far as it will go with the connection cord attached, and I lean over him and tap out a text to Kat: "Come out to the street, Kitty Kat. There's a hound dog out here with his tail between his legs." I press send on my message and quickly reposition myself with the boom box again.

A few seconds later, a shirtless guy with a beer belly marches out of the apartment building, a lit cigarette in one hand, a beer can in the other.

"What the *fuck*, man?" the guy shouts. "I've got a baby trying to sleep in there."

"I'm doing *Say Anything* for my girl, man," I say. "I'm in the doghouse."

The guy makes a face like I've just blurted I have no penis.

"Dude, I got no choice," I continue. "My girl's a fucking unicorn."

The guy nods and takes a long drag off his cigarette. "She likes that movie, huh? The one with the boom box?"

I roll my eyes. "She thinks it's 'romantic.'"

The dude laughs heartily and takes a few steps back, apparently ceding center-stage to me. "This I gotta see," he mumbles.

A brunette woman comes out of one of the apartments, a look of complete annoyance etched onto her face—but when she catches sight of me, her face melts. She quickly disappears into the apartment building and returns with another woman in tow, and when the second woman sees me, her face melts, too. Well, shit. I'm glad these two women think I'm so fucking adorable, but they're not my intended audience. Where the fuck is Kat? Could she be asleep already? Or maybe in the shower? Did she not see my text?

My arms are getting tired. I didn't expect to have to do this for so long.

I shift my weight. Shit. In the movie, the girl looked out her window right away, didn't she? What the fuck is taking Kat so goddamned long to come out here and put me out of my misery?

A guy's face appears in the window of the front apartment. He turns to say something to someone behind him and an instant later, a second face appears in the window, laughing at me.

Well, let them laugh. As long as Kat comes out here and sees me and forgives me for crushing her, I don't care if the whole world laughs at me tonight. All I care about is setting things right with Kat—making her understand my failure to tell her about Seattle had nothing to do with her and everything to do with me.

"Hey, sir," the driver says to me above the music. "You just got a text. I don't think she's coming out."

I lower my boom box and turn around to face him, my heart beating like a steel drum.

"She replied to your text," the driver continues. He motions to my phone.

I lurch over to the car and grab my phone, my eyes bugging out of my head.

"I'm not playing hard to get or being a terrorist," Kat's text says. "I can't see or talk to you tonight. Please just give me a couple days to think and regroup and figure a few things out."

84

KAT

"Happy birthday to youuu!" everyone at the table sings and Colby blows out the thirty candles on his carrot cake.

"Thanks, everyone," Colby says. "The cake looks great, Dax."

Mom begins taking the candles off Colby's cake and cutting slices for everyone while Dax assumes ice-cream-scooping duties.

"None for me," I say when Mom offers me a thick slice.

"Are you feeling okay, honey?" Mom asks. "You look a bit peaked." She hands Ryan the piece of cake she'd offered to me.

"I'm fine. I just went a little crazy at the karaoke bar with friends last night," I say. "Shouldn't have had that last martini."

Mom shoots me a scolding look. "You weren't driving, I hope?" she asks. She hands a huge slice of cake to Keane.

"Nope," I say.

"And whoever was driving wasn't drinking?"

"Correct," I say.

"Never drink and drive," Mom says firmly. She slides a noticeably slim piece of cake to Dad. "Just get that Uber-thingy on your phone and they'll pick you right up."

"You mean the Uber *app*, Mom?" Dax asks, shooting me an amused look.

"Yep. It's called Uber. They'll pick you right up."

"Wow. Sounds neat-o, Mom," I say, returning Dax's smile. She's so cute.

"Did you hit 'em with your karaoke-specialty last night?" Keane asks. He puts his hand on his heart and breaks into a full-throated chorus of "Total Eclipse of the Heart."

"Of course," I say. I toss my hair over my shoulder. "And I *nailed* it, too."

"Aw, you cheated on me, Baby-Gravy?" Ryan asks. "I'm devastated."

"Sorry, Ry," I say. "The opportunity presented itself and I had to take it. I thought you'd understand."

"Well, I *don't* understand," Ryan says. "That's *our* thing, Kum Shot."

"Stop with the semen-nicknames," Mom says. "You know I hate that."

"Sorry, Mom," Ryan says. "But I think your disciplinary efforts would be better spent telling Ebenezer Splooge over there not to stab me in the heart with a rusty blade."

"Aw, come on," I say. "I couldn't let the moment pass me by. *YOLO*, brah. That's how I dooz it."

Ryan scoffs, utterly miffed.

"*YOLO*," Dax mutters with disdain. "I wanna strangle the genius who came up with that."

"What's 'YOLO'?" Dad asks, happily chomping on his little morsel of cake.

"'You only live once,'" Dax answers, practically holding his nose.

"Oh, *carpe diem* isn't cool enough for the kids these days, huh?" Dad says.

"That's too long to text," Mom says, taking a bite of ice cream. "They shorten everything these days, honey. 'LOL! OMG!'" She throws up her hands, apparently imitating a spazzoid-teenager at a mall.

Derby Field! Namibia!, I think to myself, my heart panging.

"So who sang my part for you last night?" Ryan asks. "Whoever the bastard was, I guarantee he didn't even come close to doing *this*." He breaks into singing the 'Turn around, Bright Eyes' part of the song with hilarious gusto.

I laugh despite myself. Ryan can always make me laugh, no matter how dark my mood. "You're right. The guy who sang it didn't even come close to doing *that*."

"So who was this douchebag who deigned to poach on my sacred karaoke-territory?" Ryan asks, stuffing a huge forkful of cake into his mouth.

"Language, Ry," Mom says. "Please, honey."

"Just this guy I've been seeing," I say. "Sarah's boyfriend's twin brother."

"Whoa. That's a lot of possessive nouns," Keane says.

"The twin brother of Sarah's new boyfriend," I clarify.

"Yeah, I got it, Protein Shake. I was kidding," Keane says. He rolls his eyes. "I'm dumb but I'm not *that* dumb."

"Sorry," I say.

Keane winks at me, apparently not genuinely offended.

"You've been seeing someone?" Ryan asks.

I nod.

"What's his name?"

"Josh Faraday," I say.

"Also known as the one and only porn king 'Sir J.W. Faraday,'" Dax says reverently, and I swiftly glare at him, nonverbally telling him to shut the fuck up.

"What?" Mom asks. "You're dating a porn king?"

"*No.*" I shoot bullets at Dax, the little fucker. "Dax is just being a little shit."

"*Kat,*" Mom says, rolling her eyes. "*Language.* Come on, guys. Not at the table. *Please.* Can we just pretend to be civilized through one birthday meal?"

"Sorry, Mom." I bat my eyelashes. "Dax is just being a little *pill.*"

"Thank you," Mom says. "That's my little lady. Keep it clean, people."

"Always, Mommy," I say sweetly.

"Always," my brothers chime in with mock solemnity.

"Hey, no porn kings, Kitty," Dad says. "You know that."

"Yes, dearest patriarch," I say. "I know the rules. We all do. No dating porn kings, porn stars, pimps, hoes, felons, junkies, or *strippers.*" On that last word, I shoot Keane a snarky look and he smiles broadly. We kids all know Keane's recently been raking in the cash (one dollar bill at a time) as the Morgan Family's answer to Magic Mike, but our parents certainly don't know that. "Don't worry, Pops," I continue. "This Josh guy isn't a porn king or a pimp. He runs an investment-something-or-other with his brother and uncle. He's a respected member of society, I assure you."

"Oh, is this the boy from Las Vegas you were telling me about?" Mom asks.

"Yeah," I say. "But he's not from Las Vegas, Mom—he's actually from Seattle, though he lives in L.A. now."

"Wasn't that guy supposed to come to dinner tonight?" Colby asks.

"Oh, that's right," Mom says. "I forgot about that. Why didn't he come?"

"Something unexpectedly came up at work and he had to fly home to L.A." Heat flashes into my cheeks at my lie. "He told me to tell Colby 'Happy Birthday' and that he's sorry to miss the party. He was especially sorry to miss out on your spaghetti, Mom—I told him it's legendary."

Mom smiles.

"Don't worry. I'm sure you'll meet Josh one of these days soon," I say breezily, smiling at Mom, even though my stomach is turning over. *Considering he's gonna be the father of your grandchild.*

"Damn," Dax says. "I was looking forward to seeing if J.W. Faraday is as pretty as his picture." Dax addresses the group. "I saw a photo of this guy the other day and he's even prettier than Ry, if you can believe it."

Keane scoffs. "Pfft. Nobody out-pretties our Pretty Boy."

"Fuck you, Peen," Ryan says. "I keep telling you: I'm not pretty, I'm 'ruggedly handsome.'"

"*Language,*" Mom says. "Good lord, guys. You're a bunch of sailors. Where did I go wrong? And don't call Keane that name. It's disgusting."

"Sorry, Mom," Ryan says. He addresses Keane again. "*Eff* you, *Peen*elope Cruz. How's that, Mom?"

Dad belly laughs and Mom shoots him a scolding look.

"It's funny," Dad says sheepishly, still laughing.

"Well, I'm sorry Josh couldn't make it this time," Mom says, peeling her scolding eyes off Dad. "Please tell him he's always welcome here. I'll make my 'legendary' spaghetti for him whenever he's able to come."

"Thanks, I'll tell him." *Right after I tell him I'm pregnant with your grandchild.*

My eyes drift aimlessly around the table and finally land squarely on Colby's ruggedly handsome face. He's staring right at me with flickering eyes, looking at me like he can see right through me—and the moment our eyes connect, my cheeks burst into flames.

"Sorry Josh couldn't make it tonight," Colby says evenly. "I know you were excited to introduce him."

"Oh, it's okay," I manage to say, tears pricking my eyes. "Maybe another time."

Colby holds my gaze for a long beat until finally shifting his attention to Dax.

"This cake is great, Dax," Colby says. He rests one of his muscled forearms on the table. "Thanks for making it."

"Actually, I was hoping the cake would put you in such a great mood, you'd let me borrow your truck tomorrow? I gotta haul some gear."

Colby chuckles. "Sure. But only for a couple hours. I've got stuff to do tomorrow."

"Thanks, bro."

"And thanks for the spaghetti, Mom," Colby says. "It was fantastic, as always."

"You're welcome, honey. I made extra sauce so you can take some home with you and put it in your freezer. The birthday boy always gets extras."

"Thanks, Mom."

"Can I have extras, too, Mom?" Keane says. "I've been living on Taco Bell."

Mom laughs. "Yes, I made extras for you, too, Keaney—and also for Kitty Kat. It's in the fridge with your names on it."

"What about me?" Ryan says. "You're not gonna give extras to your favorite kid?"

"You got extras last time," Mom says. "I'll make extras for you and Daxy next time. And, by the way, you're *all* my favorite kid."

"Keane got extras last time," Dax says. "He shouldn't get 'em this time."

"Hey, that's right," Ryan says. "And the time before that, too. Why does Keane always get extras?"

Mom grabs Keane's hand. "Because Keane always *needs* them."

We all roll our eyes and Keane shoots us a "fuck you" look. "Thank you for understanding that, dearest mother," Keane says, flashing a mega-watt smile. "You're an exceptional caregiver to us all."

We all roll our eyes again, even Dad.

Mom has obviously caught wind of all the eye-rolls going on around her. "Stop it, guys," she says. "I know Keane's a brown-noser—I'm not an idiot."

Everyone bursts out laughing, even Keane.

"But it doesn't matter. The boy needs extras. He can't even boil water."

"And who's fault is that?" Dax says. "Whatever happened to personal responsibility?"

"You're an enabler, Mom," Ryan says. "Plain and simple."

"Don't listen to 'em, Mom. You're doing great," Keane says.

Mom squeezes Keane's hand again. "Look, I'll be the first to admit I parent each of you guys differently. For each and every one of you, I'm the mother you specifically *need*." She looks at Keane adoringly. "And when it comes to extras, Keane needs them."

The table erupts.

"Enough," Mom says firmly. "No arguing about extras, guys."

We all grumble quietly for another long moment, especially Ryan.

"Hey, Ry, you can have my extras," I say. "I don't need 'em."

"Nah, it's okay," Ryan says. "I'll happily steal extras from *Pee*nelope Cruz with a clear conscience, but I won't steal 'em from Spunky Brewster. I'll wait my turn."

Mom's face lights up. "*Spunky Brewster?* Finally, a sweet one. Now was that so hard?"

Ryan's expression is absolutely priceless right now. "No, Mother Dear," he says piously. "It wasn't. In fact, it was really quite easy."

Mom looks at me lovingly. "I love it. It sure fits our Kitty Kat. I can't think of a better word to describe her than *spunky*."

My brothers are absolutely dying right now.

"Yep," Ryan says, his nostrils flaring. "That's our Kitty Kat for you: full of *spunk*."

Everyone at the table bursts into raucous, tear-filled laughter except for poor, clueless, adorable Mom who's obviously never heard that particular slang term for cum before.

"What?" Mom asks, her eyes wide. "What's so funny? Am I being dumb?"

"I'll tell you later," Dad says, laughing his ass off.

"Am I being dumb?"

Dad shakes his head. "I'll tell you later, Louise."

But we all know he won't tell Mom a goddamned thing. Not a single one of us, including Dad, would ever dream of throwing our hilarious Captain Morgan under the Mom-bus—he's just too goddamned entertaining.

"So when's your next gig, Dax?" Dad asks, obviously trying to change the subject. "Anything I might be able to catch?"

Dax wipes his eyes from laughing. "Uh, sure, Pops. Friday we're playing at that Irish pub downtown, and Saturday we're playing at a street fair in Bremerton..."

Normally, I love hearing every last detail about Dax's upcoming gigs, but at the moment I can't concentrate on what Dax is saying—not when my oldest brother is staring me down, drawing my attention like a magnet.

When my eyes lock onto Colby's, he makes a sympathetic face—and, just like that, my eyes water. I look away, my lower lip trembling. Damn, that Colby —even when Josh isn't here, Colby can sniff him out.

As if on cue, my phone buzzes with a text from Josh.

"Are you at Colby's birthday dinner?" Josh writes.

It's all I can do not to scream in frustration. For crying out loud, it was only last night I told Josh I needed a few days to think and regroup after being blind-sided at the karaoke bar. What does he think has changed in twenty-four little hours? (Okay, yes, in point of fact, every goddamned thing in my life has changed in twenty-four little hours, thank you very much—but Josh doesn't know that. And, anyway, discovering I'm pregnant with Josh's accidental spawn has only made me feel *less* prepared to talk to him any time soon, not *more*.) Gah. If only I could talk to Sarah. She always helps me find clarity in the midst of any shit storm. Unfortunately, though, talking to Sarah isn't an option, at least not for a few weeks. She's starting her final exams on Monday and right after that, she's heading off to Greece to get engaged (unbeknownst to her).

I tune back into the conversation at the dinner table. Ryan and Colby are talking about the second season of *True Detective*.

"I agree it isn't as good as the first season," Colby says. "But I don't know why people are trashing it. It's still one of the best shows on TV."

"It's just that the first season was so *epic*," Ryan says. "Everyone's expecta-tions were just so high after that."

Under-promise and over-perform. That's what Josh once said is one of his many life mottos. Is that what Josh was doing by not telling me about Seattle? Under-promising? I'm guessing yes. So, hey, maybe I should take a page out of Josh's under-promising playbook and hold off telling him about the accidental Faraday gestating inside me for a bit? Given the timing of when we were in Las Vegas together, there's no way I'm out of my first trimester yet, which means my chances of miscarriage are still relatively high (especially, I'd think, in light of my boozing and weed-smoking and Sybian-riding).

If nature winds up taking its course and this pregnancy doesn't stick, then I'd be awfully bummed if I'd stupidly told Josh about the situation early on. And on the other hand, if this pregnancy *does* wind up sticking—if I actually do wind up giving birth to Josh Faraday's lovechild—oh my fucking God—well, then, there'd still be no *rush* in telling Josh about it, right? Because if we're ulti-mately gonna have a kid together some time this year, there's no reason Josh needs to know about it tomorrow versus, say, in a month... right?

I suppose if I thought Josh would ask me to get an abortion, there might be a different analysis about timing, but I already know (based on a surprisingly deep conversation we had about religion and spirituality one night on the phone) that Catholic-raised Josh wouldn't ask me to do that; and, for myself, I've already seriously considered and rejected that option, anyway. Which means, under any scenario, it makes no difference if I tell Josh about my acci-dental bun in the oven now or a month from now.

A feeling of relative calm washes over me.

I think I just made a decision: I'll wait a month to tell Josh about the baby, just in case natural selection takes care of things between now and then. And in the meantime, I'll just try not to think about it (other than taking pre-natal vitamins and picking up *What To Expect When You're Expecting*).

Yep. That's the plan.

Okay.

Whew.

I take a deep breath and tune into the conversation at the table again, feeling oddly relieved.

"So it turned out it was just a little brush fire," Colby's saying. "And yet there we all were, geared up for the Apocalypse."

Everyone laughs.

"I always get so nervous every time you go out on a call," Mom says to Colby.

"I know, Mom. But I wouldn't wanna be doing anything else with my life. I love it."

"I know you do, honey. We're so proud of you."

I look down at my phone and stare at Josh's text, the one asking if I'm at Colby's birthday dinner. I suppose I should answer the guy.

"Yeah, I'm at the party," I write. "Sitting at the dinner table with everyone right now, as a matter of fact. We're eating Dax's carrot cake, which is utterly DELICIOUS, bee tee dubs. Too bad you had to miss it." I press send on my text and look up from my phone. "Hey, Mom, can you cut me a little slice of cake, after all?"

"Sure," Mom says. "Does that mean you're feeling a bit better?"

"Mmm hmm."

My phone buzzes with Josh's reply: "I wanted to be there, but you UNINVITED me." He attaches a sad-face emoji.

"Are you in L.A.?" I write.

"Yeah. I took the first flight home this morning." Another sad-face. "Did you tell your family why I'm not there?"

"No. I told them you had to return to L.A. for work."

"Why didn't you tell them I'm a total asshole?"

"Because it's none of their business you're a total asshole," I write. "WHICH YOU ARE."

Everyone at the table laughs uproariously about something Keane is saying.

I glance up from my phone to find Colby staring at me, his eyes full of sympathy.

Damn, that Colby.

"Excuse me," I say, leaping up from the table. I sprint across the house toward my mom's office, intending to close the door behind me and continue texting with Josh, but my sudden movement has made me feel horrendously queasy all of a sudden, so I hang a sharp right and bolt into the bathroom.

Gah. Thar she blows.

Bye-bye, carrot cake.

Lovely.

So far, being a mommy is super-duper fun.

I rinse out my mouth and run cold water over my face and then sit on the edge of the tub, my head in my hands. I can't believe this is my life. I quit my job yesterday, thinking I was gonna spend the next year building a business—but, instead, it turns out I'm gonna spend the next *eighteen* years unexpectedly raising a *kid*. Without any desire to do so, I've trapped Josh exactly the way he's always feared some gold digger would do—and at a time when he's so unsure about our potential future as a couple, he didn't even tell me about his impending move to my city.

I put my hands over my face. This is a freaking nightmare.

My phone buzzes with an incoming text.

I wipe my eyes and look down at my phone, my vision blurred by tears.

"This 'total asshole' just booked you a first-class flight to L.A. on Thursday," Josh writes. "I get why me not telling you about Seattle hurt your feelings. You're entitled to that. But I'm not gonna let you torture me with it forever. Go ahead and 'think and regroup' all you want for exactly five motherfucking days, but that's all you get, Madame Terrorist. After that, I'm gonna fly your tight little ass down here and give you no choice but to forgive me."

85

JOSH

I crane my neck, scrutinizing the passengers filing through the gate, my skin buzzing with anticipation, my heart clanging in my chest. Not her. Not her. Not her. Did the entire city of Seattle board Kat's flight to L.A.? Jesus.

I can't wait another minute to see her. I'm wrecked. Out of my mind. These past five days, I haven't been able to sleep. Think. Eat. Laugh. I fully expected Kat to break down and call me at some point this past week—or at least *text* me —especially in light of all the ridiculously expensive flowers I've sent her every day—but she didn't. Nope. I didn't hear a goddamned peep out of Kat (unless, of course, you count texts that said: "Thank you for the beautiful flowers and for continuing to give me time to think and regroup."). Fucking terrorist. I've been physically sick with loneliness and yearning and regret all fucking week. If she wanted me to know what my life would feel like without her in it, well, now I know: it's fucking torture.

Not her. Not her. Not her. I'm dying here. I shove the bouquet of red roses I'm holding under my nose and inhale deeply, trying to calm myself down with a little aromatherapy. Where the fuck is she? She was seated in the first-class cabin on the plane—so she should be one of the first people off the flight. Is she waiting to de-board just to prolong my torture a bit more? Motherfucker, I'm *dying* here.

Oh, good God, no—I just had a horrible thought: could Kat possibly have missed her flight? Or worse, did she decide not to come to visit me, after all? Oh God, that would crush me. In all honesty, it might even kill me at this point— I'm just that desperate to see her.

All I did this past week was play and replay our post-karaoke conversation in my head—only not the real conversation as it truly happened, but a revised, fantasy-version in which Kat said, "My heart's on the line, Josh," and I smoothly took her into my arms and replied, "My heart's on the line, too, babe." If only I'd said that, maybe things would be different now.

My heart stops. Oh, thank God. There she is. *Katherine Ulla Morgan.* The one and only. My unicorn. Long legs. Golden mane. Head held high. Just the sight of her jumpstarts my aching heart and makes me feel half-alive for the first time in five days.

"Kat!" I yell. I wave at her. "Kat!"

She looks toward the sound of my voice and her eyes light up when she spots me. Oh my God, I feel euphoric. She's here. Thank God. She didn't leave me for good. My heart can beat again. Everything's gonna be okay.

"Kat," I say when she reaches me.

But she looks upset. She's pressing her lips together. Her face is tight. Her eyes are moist.

I hand her the flower bouquet, wrap her in my arms, and kiss her deeply, crushing the flowers between us. Oh my fuck, she tastes like heaven. Minty. Like she just brushed her teeth. I press myself into her and devour her lips, feeling like a junkie who's finally, blissfully, *blessedly* getting his next fix.

When we finally pull away from each other, Kat's eyes are dark with desire and I'm hard as a rock.

"Josh," Kat breathes, her cheeks flushed. She licks her lips and tilts her face up like she wants another kiss.

I put my fingertip under her chin. "I know we've got a shit-ton to talk about, but *please* give me one night to—"

"We have nothing to talk about," Kat says curtly, cutting me off.

I shoot her a look of blatant skepticism.

"I'm serious, Josh," Kat says. "From this day forward, all I wanna do is be in the moment with you. No talking about the future. No talking about our feelings. Just kiss me and let's pretend this past week never happened."

"**S**crabble?" I ask. "Not quite what I was expecting as our first activity of the weekend."

Josh puts the game box on his dining room table and crosses his arms over his muscled chest—and much to my surprise, he's not flashing a smart-ass smirk. In fact, he looks completely earnest. "You were upset we never do normal, real-life stuff like play board games—so that's what we're gonna do. *All. Weekend. Long.* You want real life? You think I'm addicted to excitement, and not to you, personally? Fine. This entire weekend, I'm gonna be every bit as boring as Boring Blane or Cameron Fucking Schulz. No booze. No weed. No poker chips. No 'numbing the pain of my tortured soul.'"

Ah, there it is—he flashes the smart-ass smirk I was expecting a moment ago.

"From here on out," Josh continues, "I'm all about Scrabble and Monopoly and adamantly *not* trying to escape the pain of reality in any way."

My mind is racing with a thousand emotions all at once, but the one that seems to be rising to the top of the heap is *relief*. The entire plane ride to Los Angeles, I was stressed out, wondering how the heck I was gonna deflect attention away from my newfound aversion to alcohol—I *am* the Party Girl with a Hyphen, after all—and now, in an unexpected turn of events, Josh has just made club soda this weekend's beverage of mutual choice.

"But... we're seriously gonna play *Scrabble?*" I ask, dumbfounded.

"Yeah," Josh says, spreading the game tiles onto the table. "We're gonna find out if we're every bit as addicted to each other when we're playing a board game as when we're saving the world or smoking weed or drinking martinis or fucking in a sex dungeon. I'm willing to bet anything we will be—but, apparently, you're not convinced. So, here we go."

"*I'm* not convinced? Are you on crack? You're the one who didn't want me to know you're moving to Seattle."

"Oh my shit. *Really?* That's the story you're telling yourself inside your head? That I 'didn't *want* you to know' I'm moving to Seattle? That's an interesting spin on reality—and when I say 'interesting,' what I mean is 'completely *delusional.*'"

I open my mouth to protest. Is he seriously picking a fight with me? We just walked into his house from the airport not five minutes ago and he's already laying into me? Why the hell did I come all the way down here to L.A. if he's just gonna 'dick it up' and not even *try* to convince me he's sorry for—

"Babe," Josh says emphatically, cutting off my internal rant. "I didn't *tell* you I was moving to Seattle, which is a whole lot different than me 'not *wanting* you to know,' because I'm a total flop-dick who's scared shitless about the intensity of my feelings for you."

My heart skips a beat.

A sexy smile dances on his lips. "I didn't *tell* you because I'm having a hard time believing feelings this intense could possibly lead to anything but a gigantic fireball in the sky that burns out as quickly as it ignites," he continues. "But, I'll be damned, no matter what happens, my feelings don't seem to burn out—not at all—they just keep on blazing hotter and hotter." He bites his lip. "And *hotter.*"

If I were a cartoon character, I'd be saying, "Hummanah-hummanah-hummanah" right now. But since I'm a flesh-and-blood human, I just stare at Josh, my chest rising and falling with my sudden arousal.

Josh grins. "So don't say I didn't *want* you to find out. Big difference. Okay?"

I nod, my eyes wide. I want to tackle him. Lick him. Kiss him from head to toe. *Suck his dick.* But I don't move a muscle.

Josh settles into a chair and moves the Scrabble pieces around on the table. "Now pick your fucking tiles so we can play the game." He picks up the directions sheet from the box and studies it while I continue staring at him like a wide-mouth bass. "It says here each player picks seven tiles," he says.

My crotch is burning. My nipples are hard. That was the most incredible speech any man has ever given me—and he wasn't even buzzed or high or enacting some sort of fantasy role-play when he said it.

"We're *seriously* gonna play *Scrabble* right now?" I manage to say. My cheeks feel hot. My clit is buzzing. All I want to do is fuck the crap out of him.

"Yup. Sit the fuck down, Party Girl. We're gonna test my theory that you and I can have fun doing literally anything. Since playing Scrabble is my idea of the seventh circle of hell, I figure if we can have fun doing this, then I'll have empirically proven once and for all we can have fun doing *anything*. And if we can have fun doing *anything*, then I *also* will have empirically proven I'm not Garrett Bennetting you." He rolls his eyes with disdain. "Which, by the way, still pisses me off that you'd even think that for a minute."

I open my mouth to speak, but close it again.

Josh claps his hands like he's commanding a puppy. "Now, come on, Party Girl, sit down and pick your fucking tiles. Time to get your tight little ass whooped."

I sit down across the table from him and stare at him blankly.

"Pick seven tiles," Josh says, motioning to the scattered game pieces on the table.

I make a face like he's a total dork, but I do as I'm told.

After I've got my tiles lined up on my rack, I look up, blankly. "Okay," I say.

Josh's gorgeous blue eyes are fixed on me intensely. "Go ahead," he says, motioning to the table. "Play Scrabble."

"'Play Scrabble'?" I say. "I've never played this game before. I have no idea what to do."

"You've *never* played Scrabble?" he says, incredulous.

"We always played cards and video games at my house—not board games. You go ahead and I'll just do whatever you do."

Josh grabs the directions sheet off the table in a huff. "Well, shit. I dunno what the fuck to do—I've never played Scrabble, either. I thought you'd know, growing up in a real family, and all."

I bite my lip, trying not to smile.

Josh scans the directions for a moment, obviously completely annoyed. "Jesus, Kat, I figured you'd played *all* the board games." He reads again for a long moment. "Okay, well, it looks ridiculously simple. Seems like we just lay tiles on the board to spell words and rack up points for the letters. Nothing to it."

"Okay. You go first," I say.

Josh pauses briefly, considering the tiles on his rack, and then lays down three letters: *D-U-M.*

"Dum?"

He shrugs sheepishly. "I don't have 'B-S-H-I-T' on my rack," he says. His eyes flicker with apology. "I was a total *dumbshit* for not telling you about Seattle," he says softly.

I nod emphatically. "Yeah, you were."

"I know—I just said that," he says. "Okay, that's six points for me. It's your turn."

I assess the seven tiles on my rack and lay down three: *A-S-S.* "I don't have 'H-O-L-E,'" I say, smirking. "How many points does that get me?"

Josh is clearly stifling a smile.

"Come on," I say. "How many points?"

Josh looks at the directions again. "Three. But I think you should be awarded triple points for being one hundred percent right."

"Agreed. Okay, your turn," I say, jutting my chin at him. "Play Scrabble, Josh."

"I think I'm supposed to pick three more tiles to replace the ones I already played," he says. He picks up the directions sheet again. "Yeah. It says here we both pick tiles to replace the ones we've played."

We each pick three additional tiles and, after brief consideration, Josh lays his new word onto the board: *W-O-O*.

"Woo?" I ask. "Like 'woo-hoo!'?"

"No. Like, '*woo*,'" he says. "Like 'I'm gonna *woo* you, Miss Katherine'—like, you know, old timey *wooing*." He flashes a charming smile. "As in, 'You better brace yourself, Miss Katherine, because I'm gonna *woo* the fucking shit out of you.'"

"Oh my goodness, sir. You're gonna *woo* me *shitless*?"

"Yes, I am, m'lady."

"Well, sir, I'm not completely sure I'm ready to be wooed shitless, to be perfectly honest. What would people say?"

"You don't get to decide. You're gettin' wooed shitless whether you like it or not."

My pulse is pounding in my ears.

"Okay. Quit stalling," Josh says. He motions to the game board again. "It's your turn. Play Scrabble, Kat."

I bite my lip and look at my tiles, considering my move. But none of the letters on my rack are calling to me, so I begin rearranging the tiles Josh used to spell W-O-O.

"No, babe, you're supposed to use new tiles from your—" Josh begins, but he abruptly stops talking when he sees the word I've spelled with his tiles.

"Ow," I say softly, reading the new word I've created.

Josh's face twists with what appears to be sincere remorse.

"You *really* hurt my feelings, Josh," I say. "I felt totally rejected—like I'm in this relationship all by myself."

Josh opens his mouth to speak but apparently thinks the better of it. He begins furiously peeking at the down-facing tiles on the table, apparently looking for something specific, and when he's found his desired tiles, he lays a word onto the game board: *S-O-R-R-A*.

"Sorra?" I ask.

Josh shrugs. "I couldn't find a 'Y.'"

I bite my lower lip, simultaneously amused and touched.

"I'm sorry, Kat," Josh says softly. "I didn't tell you about Seattle because there's something wrong with *me*—not because there's something wrong with *you*. You're perfect in every way. I just... " He looks up at the ceiling, apparently searching for the right words. "I just fucked up, that's all," he finally says matter-of-factly. "Because *I'm* fucked up—more than you know." He pauses. "More than I even realized."

I bite my lip and nod.

"And, in the interest of full disclosure, this probably won't be the last time I fuck up, either. I'm not sure exactly how or when I'll do it again, but I most certainly will. And when I do, please, just try to be patient with me. I'm trying my damnedest to 'overcome' every single day—I swear I am—and, mostly, I succeed. But sometimes, I can't seem to get out of my own way."

I swallow hard, stuffing down the fierce emotion rising up inside me.

Josh exhales. "I'm really, really sorry, Kat," he says, his blue eyes begging for forgiveness.

Oh, his eyes. I could get lost in those beautiful blue eyes forever. I begin hurriedly peeking at the undersides of tiles spread out on the table, looking for specific letters. Finally, when I've gathered almost everything needed, I lay my tiles down on the table: *I-F-O-R-G-V-U.*

Josh cocks his head to the side, looking at my tiles.

"I forgive you, Josh," I say. "But I'm too impatient to keep looking for the rest of the tiles."

Josh lets out a long, relieved exhale, and before I can say another word, he swipes the game board off the table, scattering tiles all over the floor, pulls me out of my chair, and proceeds to maul me.

"I'm so sorry," he breathes between voracious kisses.

"I forgive you," I say, my body exploding with desire.

"I'm not Garrett Bennetting you."

"I know. I'm sorry I said that."

"Never," he murmurs.

In a frenzy of heat, he pulls off my clothes and guides me onto the table on my back and begins covering my body with greedy kisses. He's everywhere, all at once. His lips are on my neck, and then my breast; my nipple's in his hungry mouth; his fingers are brushing lightly against my thigh and then across my hipbone. I arch my back with pleasure at the urgency of his touch, his mouth, his lips.

"I've been wrecked without you," he whispers.

"Me, too," I say. I breathe in his intoxicating scent and shudder with desire. "I was miserable."

"I wanna be with you when I move every fucking day," he says, and my clit zings like Josh just sucked on it.

I moan loudly, already on the edge of ecstasy.

"I can't stand being away from you, Kat. It *hurts.*"

My clit flutters and ripples wildly with anticipation.

"Please, please don't ever shut me out again," he breathes.

"Josh," I blurt, my excitement beginning to boil over.

His tongue finds my clit and I arch my back, shoving myself into him urgently. He groans loudly, obviously enjoying my reaction, and the sound of his pleasure sends me over the edge. I let out a low growl as my body begins clenching and rippling ferociously into his mouth, and he responds with noises that quite clearly convey his excitement.

When I'm done climaxing, Josh begins working his way from my crotch toward my face with his tongue and lips. I'm writhing, moaning, out of my head with desire—his for the taking, in every conceivable way. When I feel his hard-on slide inside me and fill me up to the brim, I explode and melt at the same time. I reach around him and pull him into me by his muscled ass, attacking him with deep and passionate kisses. I throw my legs around his waist and lift my pelvis, synchronizing my movement with his, moaning like a cat in heat as he fucks me.

Josh presses his lips against my ear. "My heart is on the line, too," he whispers as his body rocks with mine.

I gasp and claw at his back, pulling him into me as deeply as I can, my heart and body bursting simultaneously.

"I was wrecked without you, babe. Don't do that to me again."

He pulls out of me, turns my twitching, trembling body around, and bends me over the table. In a flash, he's inside me again, pumping into me while kissing the back of my neck.

My body's on fire. My heart's racing. For the first time since I peed on that goddamned stick, I feel like me again.

"Don't leave me," he whispers hoarsely in my ear.

"I'm not going anywhere," I say, gasping for air.

"Don't cut me off again."

"I won't," I grit out, just as another orgasm rips through me. "I'm all yours, Josh. Oh my God. I'm all yours. *Fuck.*"

He comes behind me, clutching me fiercely as he does, his fingers digging deeply into my flesh, and then we both collapse onto the table into a mangled, crumpled heap, mutually gasping for air.

When we've quieted down, he slides into his chair, his chest still heaving, and pulls me into his lap.

My chest is pressed against his.

My arms are wrapped around his neck.

I rest my cheek on his shoulder, breathing deeply, fighting to quell my sudden urge to bawl and/or barf all over him.

Finally, when I'm pretty sure I'm not gonna cry or hurl, I lift my cheek and look into his sparkling blue eyes. "Was that one of our boring 'real life' activities, Josh?" I ask.

Josh laughs and makes a face like I'm a total smart-ass.

"So what other boring 'real life' activities are on tap for the weekend, babe?" I ask.

Josh strokes my hair for a moment. "Well, tomorrow we're going hiking in Runyon Canyon and then I thought maybe we'd do a little grocery shopping and stop at the dry cleaners on the way home." He smirks. "And then I thought maybe we'd play some late-night backgammon while guzzling club soda—and then maybe binge watch *The Walking Dead.* You know, just normal, real-life stuff boring people in normal relationships do. No saving the world, no cocktails, no poker chips." He shrugs nonchalantly, but there's a wicked gleam in his eye.

Clearly, he's daring me to say, "Never mind what I said in front of the karaoke bar—gimme more of the Playboy Razzle-Dazzle, baby!" But, obviously, I can't say any such thing without Josh hopping up to make me a stiff drink. "Hmm," I say. "That all sounds super fun. I'm totally on board. I especially like this no-booze idea—good thinking. Maybe Boring Cameron Schulz was onto something."

Josh scowls.

"But *maybe* we don't have to be *so* disciplined about experiencing real life," I continue. "Maybe it wouldn't hurt if we mixed a tiny bit of *fantasy* in with our real-life activities?"

Josh raises an eyebrow. "Well, gosh, PG, I wouldn't want you to compromise your core values or anything."

I narrow my eyes and flare my nostrils at him.

He smirks.

"What about this?" I say. "What if we skip any and all mind-altering substances for, oh, I dunno, let's say a month, just for kicks—*but* we also continue fulfilling items on our fantasy-list? Kind of a nice middle-ground-approach, don't you think?"

Josh considers. "Kind of arbitrary cherry-picking of what we can and can't do, I'd say. If we're gonna do fantasies, why not have a cocktail while we do 'em? I've got a great recipe for a basil and lime margarita—"

"No," I blurt.

Josh looks at me quizzically.

Damn. How the heck am I going to convince Josh it's completely normal I don't want to drink? It's so unlike me as to be worrisome, I'm sure. "Absolutely no booze," I say. "As a fun challenge—to prove we don't need it to have a great time. Doesn't that sound fun?"

"No. Not at all."

"Well, I think it would be good for us."

Josh makes a face. "Why, exactly? I'm not sure I understand your thinking on this."

I scoff like it's totally self-explanatory, even though I'm shitting a brick. "So we know we can generate fun and excitement all by our little selves, Joshy Woshy. So we know we're addicted to *each other*, organically, with or without having beer goggles on."

"Beer goggles?" Josh says, incredulous. "You seriously think I'm attracted to you because I'm wearing *beer goggles*? Are you mad?"

I giggle. "Well, no. I don't think that."

"That's utterly ridiculous," he says emphatically. He touches the cleft on my chin with his fingertip. "But, okay, my batshit-crazy little terrorist. Your wish is my command, no matter how bizarre. No more booze for either of us for a month. Happy?"

"Yes, thank you," I say, exhaling with relief. Wow, I really am diabolical.

"But poker chips are okay, right?" he asks.

I smile. "Yes. I think we should *definitely* reintroduce poker chips into our fun."

"Well, all righty, then. Thank goodness for small mercies." Without hesitation, he stands up from his chair, taking my naked body along with him, and carries me like a baby monkey across the house, making me squeal. In the middle of the hallway, he stops at a closet and bends down to rummage for something (still holding my body wrapped around his), and when he stands upright again, he's got a poker chip trapped between his teeth.

I giggle and extract the poker chip from his mouth with my teeth.

"Come on, my little sex slave," Josh says, licking his lips. "I predict you'll be wearing a pair of soft cuffs in your immediate future."

87

KAT

.

"Who are all the guys who'll be playing?" I ask. "Will Reed be there?"
It's Saturday morning and Josh and I are zooming down the
freeway in his Lamborghini, en route to a park where Josh is
meeting his buddies for their regular Saturday-morning game of flag football—
another in a long line of "this-is-what-real-life-would-be-like-if-we-lived-in-the-
same-city" activities Josh has planned for us this weekend.

"No, Reed won't be there," Josh says, steering his car onto an exit ramp.
"He's in London with one of his bands. But Henn will be there, plus a bunch of
our old fraternity brothers. And lots of guys bring random buddies or brothers
to round out the teams."

"I'm excited to see Henny," I say.

"He said the same about you. You sure you won't get bored?"

"Are you kidding? It's gonna be real life, right? *Exciting*."

Josh chuckles. "Well, if you change your mind and get bored out of your
skull, you can always jog around the field and get in a workout. I won't be
offended."

"Great," I say, even though I have no intention of jogging around the field.
If I did, I'd almost certainly have to dart behind a bush to barf my lungs out by
the second lap. "I'm sure I won't get bored, though," I add.

Josh slows the car and makes a right turn, and then another, and, all of a
sudden, we're in the empty parking lot of a massive football stadium.

"Hey, I know this place," I say. I've never been to this particular stadium in
person, but I've watched enough college football on TV to know it's the famed
Rose Bowl—the legendary football stadium where UCLA plays its games. "You
and your friends are playing flag football at the freaking *Rose Bowl*?" I ask,
incredulous. "How? Are we gonna climb the fence and sneak in?"

Josh chuckles. "No, we're not gonna sneak in—I rented the place." He pulls his car into a parking spot and kills the engine.

"You *rented* the *Rose Bowl*?" I ask, my jaw hanging open.

"Yup."

I can't believe my ears. "Do you regularly rent the Rose Bowl for friendly games of flag football?"

"Nope. First time." He grins. "Actually, I rented the place specifically for *you*, Party Girl."

"For *me*?" I look at him dumbly.

Josh reaches across my body, opens his glove box, and pulls out a laminated ID badge attached to a lanyard. "How else am I gonna play in the Super Bowl?" he asks.

I touch the edge of the badge dangling from Josh's hand to stop it from twirling and gasp when I'm able to read the card. It's a press badge identifying me as "Heidi Kumquat, Reporter for ESPN," bearing the photo from my Oksana passport.

"Oh my God!" I squeal, my cheeks flushing. Just from this press badge alone, I know exactly what imaginary-porno Josh and I are about to act out.

But just in case I had a sliver of a doubt, Josh promptly lays a poker chip in my palm. "Hey, Heidi Kumquat. Guess what?" Josh says, a naughty smile dancing on his lips. "I hear the MVP of the Super Bowl has a thing for blondes —and a *really* big dick."

"**G**od, they're manly, aren't they?" Henn asks, surveying the action on the field. "Neanderthals, all of them."

"You sure you don't wanna play with them?" I ask, linking my arm in Henn's. "It looks pretty fun."

"You think *that* looks fun? Ha! No, I came to this barbaric game just to see you, Kitty Kat." Henn beams a smile at me that melts my heart like butter in a microwave.

"Aw, thanks, Henn."

Josh races past us on the field, cradling the football in his muscular arm. He evades a potential tackler, and then another, progressing at least twenty yards before being stopped.

Henn and I cheer like crazy and Josh looks over at us, pumping his fist.

"So what's new, Henny?" I ask. "You been working a lot?"

"Yeah, I just got back from D.C., working on our little case with the feds." He snickers. "Agent Eric asked me if you're single, bee tee dubs."

"What'd you tell him?"

Henn motions to Josh on the field. "Well, duh—I told you you're madly in love with the greatest guy ever."

I bite my lip but I don't deny it.

Henn grabs the "press badge" hanging around my neck. "Speaking of which, what the heck is this? 'Heidi Kumquat, Reporter for ESPN'? Josh asked me for your Oksana photo but he didn't tell me why he wanted it. Are you two crazy kids finding new and creative ways to take ol' one-eye to the optometrist or what?"

I decide to ignore his question. "Speaking of people falling madly in love, how's it going with Hannah Banana Montana Milliken?" I ask.

Henn's face lights up. "Oh my God, she's incredible. She keeps doing this bizarre thing no other woman has ever done in the history of time—she's genuinely *nice* to me. Like, all the time."

"Wow. Cray," I say.

"Un-sane," Henn agrees, smiling adorably. "Did Hannah say anything to you about how things are going between us?"

"Yeah, she said you're the man of her dreams."

"Are you teasing me right now? Kat, please don't tease me."

"Henn, I swear on a stack of bibles. That's exactly what she said. 'The man of her dreams.'"

Henn looks like he could keel over with joy.

"Aw, you so deserve this, Henny," I say. "I'm so happy for you."

"Motherfucker!" Josh yells on the field after unsuccessfully trying to catch a long pass in the end zone. "That was my fault, bro," Josh shouts to his quarterback, patting his chest. He begins jogging back toward the line of scrimmage, but makes a sudden, lurching detour toward me on the sideline. With a loud growl, Josh throws his arms around my waist and twirls me around, making me shriek. "Hey there, Heidi Kumquat," Josh bellows. He lays an abrupt kiss on my mouth. "You know I'm trying to impress you, right?"

"You are?" I ask demurely.

"Is it working?"

"Definitely."

Josh laughs and trots away, leaving me swooning in his wake. Or, wait, maybe I'm not *swooning*—maybe I'm just queasy from being unexpectedly twirled around. I clamp my hand over my mouth, suddenly feeling the urge to heave.

"Hey, you okay?" Henn asks.

I take several deep breaths, trying to calm my churning stomach. "Yeah, I'm fine," I squeak out.

"You look like you feel sick," Henn says.

I swallow hard. "I'm just a little hung over, that's all."

"Ah, gotcha." Henn returns his attention to the action on the field, apparently completely convinced by my explanation.

For the next thirty minutes, Henn and I watch the action on the field, cheering and screaming as Josh and his friends play flag football as fiercely as any gladiators in ancient Rome, and when the game is finally done, Josh jogs over to Henn and me on the sideline. I'm expecting Josh to pick me up and whirl me around like he did earlier, but, instead, he whispers something to Henn, winks at me, and silently heads toward a tunnel on the opposite side of the field.

"Where's he going?" I ask Henn, admiring Josh's supremely bitable ass as he jogs away.

"To the locker room," Henn says. "He asked me to bring you there in five minutes."

"Oh, okay," I say, trying my best to sound nonchalant.

Henn shoots me a snarky look. "Josh had a message for you, bee tee dubs. He told me to tell Heidi Kumquat he's such a huge fan of your reporting for ESPN, he's decided to grant you an *exclusive* post-game interview.'"

89

KAT

"Bye, Henn," I say, hugging him outside the locker room.

"Enjoy your optometry appointment," Henn says, snickering.

"Hey, man," I say. "Regular eye exams are critical to maintaining peak visual health."

Henn laughs. "Oh my God. You truly are the male version of Josh, you know that?"

"You think?" I ask.

"Indubitably." He hugs me again. "Bye, Kitty Kat."

I watch Henn walk away, sighing with my love for him, and when he turns the corner and disappears from sight, I open the locker room door and step inside, my skin buzzing with excitement. "Sports Reporter Bangs Super Bowl MVP in Locker Room After the Big Game" has been one of my top fantasies for a very long time—a go-to scenario I've thought about many, many times while pleasuring myself. I can't believe Josh has gone to such lengths to deliver it to me.

I begin walking slowly into the spacious locker room, my stomach bursting with butterflies, my crotch swelling with each step I take. I turn a corner around a bank of lockers, and—*boom*—there he is: the Super Bowl MVP himself, bending down to put something into a locker, his back to me.

Holy Beefcake, Batman. Josh is dressed in nothing but shoulder pads and tight football pants. His skin is gleaming with grime and sweat. Good lord, he's hot as hell—testosterone on a stick.

My phone buzzes in my pocket but I ignore it. Whoever it is can wait.

"Excuse me," I say softly. "Josh?"

Josh turns around and my heart palpitates—he's raw masculinity in its purest form.

"Yes?" Josh asks.

"Do you have time for an interview?" I hold up my badge to him. "Heidi Kumquat, ESPN."

Josh smiles and runs his hand through his sweaty hair, flashing me his "THE GUN SHOW" underarm-tattoo as he does. "Sure thing, Heidi. It would be my pleasure."

I motion behind me to my imaginary cameraman. "This is my cameraman, Brad."

Josh's eyes sparkle with obvious amusement. He looks over my shoulder to where I've indicated. "Hey, Brad," he says. He runs his hands over his muscled chest like he's lathering himself in the shower. "Ask me anything you want, Heidi—I'm all yours."

Oh, man, my body's having a physical, chemical reaction to this muscled, tattooed, sweaty man. My brain knows this is make-believe, of course, but my body apparently didn't get the memo.

My phone buzzes with another text but I ignore it.

"All mine, huh?" I say. "I like the sound of that."

"*And* I'll do the interview for you, too," Josh adds, his smile widening.

I return his smile. "Lemme just do my intro for the segment."

I turn away from Josh and look into the imaginary camera behind me, holding a pretend-microphone up to my mouth. "Hey, everyone. Heidi Kumquat for ESPN. I'm in the locker room with Josh Faraday, the star wide receiver for the Seahawks and the MVP of this year's Super Bowl. If you watched the game, then you know Josh well deserved his MVP honors—he was utterly brilliant out there today. Every man watching him wanted to be him, and every woman wanted to fuck the living hell out of him." I turn around and face Josh. "Ready?"

Josh's eyes are burning. "Why don't you start by asking me why I missed that one easy pass in the end zone?"

"Why'd you miss that one easy pass in the end zone, Josh?"

"'Cause I was looking at you. As it turns out, it's awfully hard to concentrate on catching a ball when you're thinking about fucking the smokin' hot blonde standing on the sideline a few yards away." He snaps the waistband of his tight football pants and my eyes are drawn to the hard bulge straining just below his hand.

I primly clear my throat. "Well, that's sweet of you to say. But I'd really better get to my interview."

"Of course. You're a professional—I admire that. Ask me anything, Heidi. I'm all yours."

My phone buzzes with another text. Hastily, I pull my phone out of my pocket, silence it, and shove it back into my pocket.

"Sorry about that," I say. "Well, first off, let me say congratulations on being named MVP of the game."

Josh flashes perfect, white teeth. "Thanks. But, you know, it was a total team effort." He runs his palm across his chiseled abs. "Damn, girl, you're something to look at, you know that? You're the kind of woman makes an MVP wanna *fuck*."

"Oh my goodness, thank you," I say demurely. "I'm flattered, but I really can't flirt with you, Josh. I've got a job to do."

"*Flirt* with me?" He smiles lasciviously. "You think I'm hard like this because I wanna *flirt* with you?" He makes an extremely sexual noise. "'Flirt' isn't the 'f' word I wanna do with you, Heidi."

I take a shaky breath and hold my imaginary microphone to my mouth. "Um." I swallow hard. "To what do you think you owe your success this season?"

Josh begins stroking the hard bulge straining behind his tight pants, his eyes smoldering. "I'd say the key to my success this season was just taking it one game at a time." His voice suddenly drops to a husky growl. "Shit, baby, you're making me hard as a rock. I can't even think straight, looking at you." He takes a step toward me and snakes his arm around my waist. "You've got beautiful eyes, you know that? I can't wait to watch 'em roll back into your head when I'm fucking you to within an inch of your life."

"Thank you. You have beautiful eyes, too."

Josh presses his hard-on into me. "Ever fucked the MVP of the Super Bowl, Heidi?"

I pretend to put my microphone to my lips again. "The Patriots definitely fought hard—"

Josh abruptly grabs my imaginary microphone and throws it forcefully across the room, making me laugh. "Interview over, Heidi," Josh says. "Time for the Super Bowl MVP to fuck you."

There's a beat.

I glance over my shoulder at my imaginary cameraman. "Beat it, Brad." I wait a moment to allow my imaginary cameraman to exit the locker room and then turn back to Josh. "You were saying?" I whisper.

Josh skims his lips against mine slowly. "I was saying I'm the MVP of the fucking Super Bowl, which means I can fuck any woman I want in the entire fucking world—and, baby, I want you. *Right fucking now*."

My heart is pounding like crazy. "Oh, you think I'm gonna spread my legs and fuck you for no other reason than you're the Super Bowl MVP?" I whisper.

Josh presses his hard-on into me and levels me with blazing blue eyes. "No, baby, you're gonna spread your legs and fuck me because you're gonna enjoy sucking my dick so goddamned much."

Oh, he's good. He's very, very good.

Without further ado, Josh grips my hair and forcefully pushes me down to my knees—damn, the Super Bowl MVP's a bossy motherfucker—and a grand total of two seconds later, I'm on my knees, voraciously sucking the Super Bowl MVP's dick, making myself come like a freight train. Shortly after that, I'm dangling from a pull-up bar, my thighs resting on the Super Bowl MVP's shoulder pads, my pussy deep in his mouth, my flesh rippling against his lips and tongue. And after that, yep, the arrogant but sexy bastard called it—I'm spreading my legs for the Super Bowl MVP while getting fucked *hard*, until my eyes are rolling back into my head.

"Good times," Josh says after we're both done and completely spent. He spanks my ass playfully. "You wanna join me in the shower, Heidi?"

"I'll be right there. I'm gonna check my phone real quick. I got a couple texts."

"Okeedoke," Josh says. He turns around, flashing me his YOLO'd ass, and practically skips toward the showers. "Hey, a bunch of guys went for burgers and beers nearby. You wanna meet up with them?"

"Sounds great," I say. I bend down to grab my phone out of my jeans on the floor.

"All my friends thought you were awesome, by the way," Josh calls over his shoulder. "A couple of them said before today they were already on the cusp of hating my guts, and now, after meeting you, they absolutely do." He laughs heartily.

But I'm not listening to Josh any more. I'm looking at my phone, reeling, trying desperately not to freak out that every single member of my family except Colby has been furiously trying to reach me for the past thirty minutes. What on earth has happened? And why everyone *except Colby?*

"Oh my God! Josh!" I shriek, clutching my throat. "I think something's happened to Colby!"

90

JOSH

"I'm here to see my brother Colby Morgan," Kat says to the woman sitting behind the desk in the hospital lobby.

Poor Kat. When she called her mom and found out what had happened to Colby, I had to physically hold her up so she wouldn't crumple onto the cement floor of the locker room.

"Oh, the firefighter," the woman at the desk says, clicking on her computer keyboard. She looks at Kat sympathetically. "I saw what your brother did on the news. He's a real hero. We're all praying for him and that little baby he saved."

Kat lets out a little yelp.

"He's in the burn unit, room 402. Do you know where that is?"

Kat shakes her head and a pained sound escapes her throat.

"Just go down this hall and take the elevators to the fourth floor," the nurse continues. "When you get off the elevator, check in at the nurses' station there and someone will show you to his room. It's a restricted area."

Kat nods, apparently unable to speak.

"Thank you," I say, answering for Kat. I put my arm around her shoulders and usher her toward the elevators. "Come on, babe."

Kat nuzzles her nose into my shoulder as I lead her limp body down the hallway—and by the time Kat and I reach the fourth floor, I'm just about carrying Kat's full body weight in my arms.

"We're here to see Colby Morgan," I say to the nurse at the fourth-floor desk, my arm around Kat's shoulders.

"Are you family?" the nurse asks.

"Yes, this is Colby's sister," I say.

"And you?" the nurse asks me. "Are you family, too—are you her husband?"

For some reason, I feel like this nurse just punched me in the balls. "No," I say, my throat tight.

"He's my boyfriend, " Kat chokes out.

I nod and pull her closer to me. That was the first time Kat's called me her boyfriend—but it's hardly the time or place for me to feel excitement about that milestone.

"I'm sorry," the nurse says. "Only immediate family is allowed in the room for now. There've been a lot of people wanting to see your brother—reporters, other firefighters, well wishers—even the Mayor came by. We're gonna have to stick to the rules, at least until we get clearance from the doctor."

Kat looks stricken. "But," she begins, "Josh is my *boyfriend*." She grips my arm.

The nurse shakes her head. "I'm sorry. Your boyfriend will have to wait out here until I get clearance for non-family members. There are a lot of people already in the room—you've got a big family."

When the nurse uses the word "family," Kat looks toward the hallway with undisguised longing.

"Go ahead," I say, squeezing Kat's shoulders. "Go be with your family, babe. I'll wait out here."

Kat looks like a deer in headlights.

"Go on," I say, stroking Kat's golden hair. "I'll be right here." The truth is I don't want to leave Kat's side—I want to go with her and hold her through whatever awaits her in that room. But, obviously, my only job in this horrible situation is to make this as easy on Kat as possible. "Go on," I say softly.

Kat hugs me and I breathe her in for a moment.

"I'll be right here if you need me," I whisper.

Kat nods and the nurse wordlessly guides her down the hallway through swinging doors marked "Authorized Personnel Only." I watch her through glass panes in the doors as long as possible, until, finally, she and the nurse turn a corner and disappear.

With a deep sigh, I wander down the hall and take a seat in the waiting room. Shit. I feel like I've let Kat down somehow. When the nurse asked if I was family—if I'm her husband—should I have lied and said yes? I really don't think I was imagining the pained look in Kat's eyes when I said no. Why the fuck do I feel like I've somehow fucked up?

An older gentleman with a young woman and toddler are seated across from me in the waiting room. The trio's got the exact same features—same eyes, noses, dark hair. They're like generational Russian nesting dolls—even a casual onlooker would know instantly the three of them are family.

Family.

The nurse asked me if I'm Kat's family and I said no.

I put my head in my hands.

I've got the distinct feeling I've fucked up somehow, but I'm not sure how.

Are you her family? Are you her husband?

I really don't think I was imagining the look of utter disappointment on Kat's face at that moment.

A tidal wave of loneliness rises up inside me—an all-too familiar emotion for me. My eyes water but I swallow hard and stuff it down like I always do. Fuck. This isn't about me. This is about Colby and Kat and her family.

What I need to do is make myself useful, however I can.

I bow my head, close my eyes, and clasp my hands.

Dear Heavenly Father...

I take a deep breath.

Dear Heavenly Father...

I lift my head and open my eyes.

Fuck me.

The only prayer that's coming into my mind is so full of motherfucking expletives, I can't imagine it would help Colby at all.

91

JOSH

For the past hour, Kat's been in Colby's hospital room with her family while I've been sitting out here in this waiting room, listening to "Hold Back the River" by James Bay on my phone, trying my damnedest not to cry or, worse, catch Spanish Influenza from the cocksucker who sat down two seats away from me in an almost-empty waiting room and proceeded to cough up his goddamned lung.

From what I've gathered, Typhoid Joe was deemed "too sick" to go into the room of whatever patient he came to visit in the hospital, but rather than go home and take some fucking Nyquil, he decided to sit two feet away from me and try to take me down with him. Motherfucker. Of course, I moved as far away from him as I could in the tiny room, but just the sound of his constant hacking is making me feel like I'm hurtling to my premature demise on a bullet train.

Or maybe I'm just losing my mind.

I pull my earphones out of my ears and, for the second time since sitting down in this waiting room, bow my head in prayer. *Heavenly Father who art in heaven, please, I beg you, stop fucking with everyone I—*

My phone buzzes with a text that makes me open my eyes.

It's Jonas. "I CAN'T SLEEP!" he writes.

"Why, hello, Jonas," I write, smiling at the screen. "Why can't you sleep, bro? Could it be... SARAH?"

"YES!!!!! Today's finally the day!!!!" he writes—and, of course, I know he's referring to the fact that today he's finally gonna take his "Magnificent Sarah" to the top of Mount Olympus, push the poor girl off the edge of it, and ask her to be his wife.

"What time is it over there?" I type.

"Almost 4:00 a.m."

I look at my watch and do a quick calculation. They're ten hours ahead.

"Are you just getting to bed or just waking up?" I write.

"Been lying here wide awake for hours while Sarah's been sleeping next to me, blissfully unaware my every happiness hangs in the fucking balance today. FUCK ME! I can't stop thinking about my big speech."

"Your big speech?" I write, chuckling to myself. "WTF. No big speech required, bro. Just say, 'Will you marry me, Sarah Cruz?' Easy-peasy."

"No, you DUMBSHIT. Any man who says 'Will you marry me?' and nothing more when asking the woman of his dreams to be his wife is a DUMB-SHIT of epic proportions. Either that, or he fundamentally doesn't understand what makes women tick."

"Jonas," I write, rolling my eyes. "Don't make poor Sarah listen to a long, drawn-out speech or she's gonna jump off the mountain before you push her off just to get the fuck away from you." I laugh out loud as I press send.

"I don't need your advice this time, Josh. I got this," Jonas replies. "I can't ask Sarah to marry me without telling her WHY I'm asking her to be my wife or I'd never be able to look myself in the fucking mirror ever again. She's the goddess and the muse, Josh. She deserves to know that—and to understand WHY."

"Dude. First off, the all-caps are totally unnecessary. You're hurting my ears. Second off, you're overthinking this. Make it memorable, sure. Sweep her off her feet, absolutely. But too much talking and poetry and babbling about 'goddess and muse' shit and she's gonna think you've got a fucking vagina."

"Josh, please trust me, just this once I know more about something than you do. SO FUCK OFF."

"Testy, testy," I write. "Okay, okay. I'm hereby officially fucking off. Hey, can you talk instead of texting? My fingers are getting tired."

"No. Sarah's lying on my chest, fast asleep. I don't wanna wake her. So enough about me and my soon-to-be-fiancée (I HOPE AND PRAY)." He attaches a praying-hands emoji. "How's everything with you?"

I sigh, considering my reply. On our flight to Seattle earlier, Kat and I agreed not to mention the Colby situation to Sarah (and therefore not to Jonas, either).

"Knowing Sarah, she'd drop everything and immediately fly back to Seattle to be with me," Kat said during our conversation on the plane. "I'd never do that to her—or to poor Jonas. He's been planning this proposal for weeks."

"Agreed," I replied to Kat. "We'll tell them both what's going on when they get home. Hopefully, by then, Colby will be up and around and feeling like himself again."

Kat looked out the window of the airplane, her beautiful face etched with anxiety. "I pray that's true, Josh."

I quickly tap out my reply to Jonas' question: "Everything's good here." I give him a quick update on the refurb-job I'm overseeing for our twenty gyms and also regarding the buy-out of our shares of Faraday & Sons. "Oh, and escrow closed on my Seattle house yesterday," I type. "I'm officially your neighbor. I clocked it the other day and it takes exactly eleven minutes to drive from my house to yours."

"Awesome," Jonas writes. "So when do you think you'll move in?"

"Three or four weeks at most," I write. "Don't forget to send me a housewarming gift. Patron is greatly appreciated."

"Pretty weird you didn't tell Kat you're moving," Jonas writes. "She looked really upset about it at the karaoke bar."

My stomach twists at the memory of that horrible night. "Yeah, thanks for blabbing about that, motherfucker. That was super awesome."

"How the fuck was I supposed to know you hadn't told Kat you're moving? And why exactly didn't you mention it to her, btw? I'm still not sure I understand your thinking on that."

"I just didn't wanna get her hopes up," I write, but even as I tap out the words, I know they're douchey.

"Well, mission accomplished, huh? I'd say Kat's hopes are definitely way, way down."

I roll my eyes. Does my brother really need to remind me how badly I fucked up with Kat? That's *my* job—to remind Jonas when *he* fucks up with women.

"Was Kat really pissed at you?" Jonas writes.

"Worse than pissed. Crushed," I write, my heart squeezing.

"Poor Kat," Jonas writes. "The Faraday brothers strike again."

"More like DAD strikes again," I write. "He's the gift that keeps on giving."

"No shit," Jonas writes. "I don't know how either of us is ever supposed to know what's normal behavior when it comes to women. You, especially. He fucked with your head the most."

"My head? No way," I write. "You got it way worse than me, bro. Ten times worse."

"I don't think so. He hated my guts, but he loved you. Is it better to be told you're worthless every fucking day of your life or that you're better than everyone else? Either way, you're fucked. At least I got to escape to the 'treatment center' for months at a time over the years. You were stuck there with him, day after fucking day."

I stare at my phone. I've never thought about it that way. Holy shit. I think Jonas might have a point. I was Dad's golden boy, his heir to the Faraday throne, and Jonas and I both knew it. All these years I've felt guilty to have garnered so much of Dad's favor and attention—but did I actually draw the short straw, after all?

"You might have a point," I write. "I never thought about it like that."

"I've got more than a point. I'm right as rain. I'm the smart twin, remember? Never doubt me."

"You wish."

"Hey, I'm not the one who didn't tell my hot girlfriend I'm moving to her city," Jonas writes. "DUMBSHIT."

I scowl at my phone. Jonas knows I've got no comeback to that. "Yeah, I fucked up," I write.

"So did Kat break up with you when she found out?" Jonas writes.

"No, but almost," I write. "I salvaged it. I made her play Scrabble with me until she forgave me."

"Scrabble?" Jonas writes.

"Fun game, as it turns out, if you get creative with your words."

"Hmm. I see what you mean. I'm already thinking about all sorts of four-letter words I could play."

"There you go."

"So everything's good now?" Jonas writes. "Kat's happy again?"

Typhoid Joe coughs violently across the waiting room and I momentarily look up from my phone. Fuck me. I hate not telling Jonas what's going on with Colby. I never hide stuff from Jonas. But there's no fucking way I'm gonna throw a dark cloud over the biggest day of my brother's life.

"Everything's great," I write.

"Good. Don't fuck it up again, Josh. Kat's a great girl."

"I'll do my best. The question is whether I can avoid fucking it up when I don't realize I'm fucking it up?"

"I feel you. Just think, 'What Would Dad Do?' and then do the opposite," Jonas writes. "That's pretty much my true north."

"Good advice."

"Hey, so what's up with the MacKenzie deal for F&S?" Jonas writes. "Last loose end. Dying to make that fucker go away."

"Dude. I don't give a shit about the MacKenzie deal or anything else relating to F&S," I write. "That place can burn to the ground as far as I'm concerned. Sayonara, fucker."

"I'd agree if it weren't for Uncle William. We can't leave him hanging. Plus, the payday on the buy-out's gonna be sweet if we set it up right."

I pause. Jonas is right. The MacKenzie deal itself isn't that rich, but we each stand to net close to half a billion in cash in the buy-out of Faraday & Sons by a huge conglomerate if we leave the company on strong legs, everything in place. "Okay," I tap out. "I'll work up the MacKenzie deal this week and put it to bed."

"Thanks," Jonas writes. "I'd do it myself but Sarah would kill me if I worked while we're in Greece."

"No. Don't do a fucking thing. Just get engaged and bang your new fiancée every which way for the rest of the trip. I'll handle it."

"Roger that. Thanks, Josh."

"Now get some sleep, bro. You've got a big day tomorrow."

"Today, actually. I'm ten hours ahead."

"Oh yeah. Well, get some sleep, either way," I write.

"I don't sleep, remember? Sarah says I'm a droid."

"Man, she's got you pegged."

"In more ways than one." He attaches a smiley-face emoji.

I roll my eyes. "Try to sleep for a bit, Jonas. You gotta be bright-eyed and bushy-tailed when you bore Sarah to fucking tears at the top of Mount Olympus."

"I'm not gonna bore Sarah to fucking tears at the top of Mount Olympus, motherfucker—I'm gonna bore her to fucking tears on the shore of the Aegean down below."

"Either way, you need to rest up so you can bore her to fucking tears EXCELLENTLY, wherever the fuck you do it."

"I sense mockery in that all-caps word."

"Correct, sir."

"Oh man, I'm so excited," Jonas writes. "I'm about to become the happiest asshole-motherfucker alive."

"So you keep telling me, Jonas. Over and over and over."

"Sorry. I'm just so happy. It's a new feeling for me. I don't quite know how to handle it."

I grin broadly at that. "I'm happy for you, Jonas. It's pretty crazy. I never thought I'd see the day when either of the Faraday boys would ask a woman to be his wife. You're shocking the hell out of me, actually."

"I'm shocking the hell out of myself. It's awesome! Hey, you think maybe you'll shock the hell out of us, too? And maybe soon?" He adds a winking emoji and a cat.

"Hell no. Asking any woman to be my wife isn't in my life plan, dude—even a woman as awesome as Kat. You'll just have to represent for both of us."

"With pleasure," Jonas writes. "I can't wait to call Sarah my wife."

I roll my eyes again. "Good night, Jonas. Have fun tomorrow (today). Text me right after you ask her. I'll drink a shot of Patron in your honor."

"I will. Well, actually, I won't text you RIGHT after I ask her, if you know what I mean." He attaches another winking emoji and a muscled-arm emoji.

I chuckle. My brother is such a dork. "Hey, Casanova," I type. "What's with all the emojis? I didn't know you even knew what emojis were."

"I didn't until recently, but Sarah uses them all the time. Funny, right?"

I chuckle. What has this woman done to my dorky-ass brother? Jesus God. She's made him even dorkier than ever.

"Get some sleep, Mr. Emoji," I write.

He sends me a thumbs-up emoji in reply and I laugh.

"Josh."

I look up from my phone to find Kat walking into the waiting room, her face stained with tears. I leap up from my chair, instantly twitching with dread. Oh fuck, please God, don't let Kat be here to tell me Colby's dead.

Kat beelines to me and, without saying a word, throws her arms around my neck, presses her body into mine, and loses herself to wracking sobs.

92

JOSH

I wrap Kat in a tight embrace and hold her to me for several minutes, kissing her hair, rubbing her back, my heart pounding in my ears, dreading whatever's about to come out of her mouth.

Finally, Kat breaks away from me, wiping her eyes. "Sorry," she says. She pulls me down to sitting. "I've been holding it together pretty well for my mom, but seeing your face made me lose—" She suddenly clamps her hand over her mouth.

"Kat?" Holy shit. She seriously looks like she's about to hurl. "*Kat?*" I ask again, my skin prickling. I've never seen someone react to grief by throwing up before.

Kat takes a few deep breaths and groans like she's eaten a piece of rancid meat.

"Are you okay?" I ask, the hairs on my arms standing on end.

Kat makes a face I can't interpret and takes another deep breath. "I'm okay," she mumbles.

Typhoid Joe across the room lets out a hacking cough and Kat grimaces.

"How's Colby?"

"The tests came back and it was pretty much all good news, relatively speaking. Broken leg, ribs, and collarbone. Ruptured spleen. Smoke inhalation —but not too bad, thank God. He suffered some burns to his left side where the beam was crushing him, but his turnout gear protected him pretty well. Could have been a whole lot worse. No head trauma at all, thank God." She takes a deep breath. "It's gonna be a long road to recovery—lots of physical therapy. But he's gonna pull through."

I exhale with relief.

"But the baby Colby went back in to save?" Kat says, tears flooding her eyes. "She just died in her mother's arms in the pediatric unit."

"Oh no," I say softly, my heart dropping into my toes.

"Her parents came to Colby's room to thank him for what he did to try to save her. He wasn't conscious so they thanked my parents." Tears are streaming out of Kat's eyes and down her cheeks. "They said they were grateful to my brother for giving them the chance to hold their little angel one last time and say goodbye. Oh my God, it ripped everyone's heart out, Josh. All of us were crying, even Ryan, and he never cries."

I nod, incapable of speaking.

Kat inhales sharply again and suddenly clamps her hand to her mouth. "Shit," she mumbles. She leaps out of her chair and sprints to the bathroom across the hall, her body jerking with loud heaves as she runs.

What the fuck? Kat's puking *again*? I've never seen someone react to grief by puking before—and this is the second time today (the first time being in the locker room immediately after Kat talked to her mom about Colby). Does she have food poisoning?

Typhoid Joe coughs loudly again on the far side of the waiting room, jerking me out of my thoughts, and I share a "this guy's gonna infect us all" look with the young woman sitting across from me.

After a few minutes, Kat returns from the bathroom, her face pale. "Sorry about that," she says.

"Do you always react this way to extreme stress?" I ask.

"What way—by crying?"

"No, by barfing."

Kat twists her mouth.

"Do you think maybe you have the stomach flu or something?" I ask.

There's a long beat. Kat takes a deep breath and flaps her lips on her exhale.

"Shit," she says. She shakes her head like she knows she's about to say something highly regrettable. "Life is so funny. Before today, I thought I had the weight of the world on my shoulders—I really did—or, I guess, on my *uterus*." She snorts to herself. "And now, all of a sudden, my supposedly huge problem doesn't seem like that big a deal."

Wait. Did Kat just say she thought she had the weight of the world on her *uterus*? I open and close my mouth, but I'm too freaked out to link coherent words together. Does that mean . . ?

Kat levels me with a firm gaze. "Yeah, I'm pregnant, Josh," she says evenly.

The room warps. I can't breathe. *No.* Blood rushes into my ears in a loud whoosh.

"I'm sorry to tell you so bluntly, but there's really no other way." She clears her throat. "I'm pregnant with your accidental Faraday." She shakes both fists in the air in mocking celebration. "*Yay.*"

There's got to be some mistake. Kat said she was on the pill. *Holy fucking shit, Kat said she was on the fucking pill!*

"I didn't do it on purpose," Kat continues calmly. "I swear to God, Josh, this isn't a case of a 'gold digger' trying to 'trap' you. It was a complete accident—an honest mistake."

My heart is palpitating wildly. I clutch my chest. I feel like I'm having a heart attack.

"I missed a pill one of the days we were in Vegas," she continues, "but only because the days and nights blurred together so much while we were there—remember that? And the minute I realized I'd messed up, I immediately took the missing pill. And I really thought everything was okay—I really did, Josh—but just to be sure, I took a pregnancy test a few days after I got home and it was negative, so I figured we were in the clear." She grimaces. "But then I started feeling sick and my nipples were sore and then I barfed out of nowhere so I took another test, and lo and behold..." She exhales loudly and shrugs. "I'm rambling—sorry. The bottom line is I'm pregnant with your mighty spawn and I didn't do it on purpose—I swear to God on a stack of bibles—and I'm really, really sorry."

I feel like I'm gonna hurl. This seriously can't be happening.

"I'm not looking to trap you into anything," Kat says, her blue eyes flickering with obvious anxiety. "Nothing needs to change between us. We'll just, you know, keep doing what we're doing—and, at some point, we'll, you know, happen to have a baby together."

I open and shut my mouth, willing myself to speak, but nothing comes out. That was the stupidest thing I've ever heard anyone say in my life. *Nothing needs to change? We'll just keep doing what we're doing and one day we'll happen to have a baby?* Did she really just say that to me? Is she high?

Typhoid Joe begins coughing and sniffling loudly and I look at the guy, willing him to keel over and fucking die.

Shit. This can't be happening.

I stare at the toddler sitting across from me for a moment. Kat's growing one of *those* inside her body—and it's a *Faraday*? I run my hands through my hair. This is a fucking nightmare—the one thing I was never supposed to do. Oh my God. How many times did Dad tell me not to make a Faraday unworthy of my name and bank account? A Faraday has to be *planned*. A Faraday has to be on *purpose*. "If you're not careful, you'll wind up having a crazy-ass kid like Jonas with some gold digger you don't give two shits about," my father used to say.

Kat clears her throat. "So are you gonna say something or what?"

The room is closing in on me. I can't breathe. I open my mouth and close it, yet again. *Fuck.* How many times did my dad make me *swear* I'd never bring an accidental Faraday into the world? How many times did he fill me with the fear of God about some scheming gold digger using a baby to trap me into making her a part of our "empire"?

Kat shakes her head, obviously annoyed by my silence. "Say something," she says softly. But when I don't speak, her entire body stiffens with defiance. "I'm not gonna get an abortion, if that's what you're thinking."

I don't know what in my facial expression made Kat think I was about to ask her for an abortion—because I wasn't. I went to St. Francis Academy growing up, for fuck's sake. Some things are just too deeply ingrained to change.

"Say something, Josh," Kat pleads, her eyes glistening. "You're killing me, Smalls."

"I..." I stammer. "I would never ask you to... get rid of it. That's not at all what I'm thinking."

"Then what are you thinking?"

Fuck me. I have no idea what I'm thinking, other than "How the fuck did this happen to me?" Every single fuck of my life, without exception, from minute one, I've practiced safe sex. Kat's the first woman I've ever fucked without a rubber—*ever*—and now she's *pregnant?*

"Hey, look on the bright side," Kat says. "It's still early yet. The pregnancy might not stick."

"What do you mean?" I ask dumbly.

"There's a relatively high chance of miscarriage during the first trimester," she says, shrugging her drooping shoulders. "Especially, I'd assume, when you ply the poor little thing with booze, pot, and blinding orgasms on a Sybian."

I put my head in my hands. Holy shit. This is a nightmare. I can't believe she forgot to take her pill. I trusted her and she totally blew it. All of a sudden, I can hear my dad's voice as surely as if he were standing an inch away from me, pressing his lips against my ear. *I'll get the last laugh on that gold digger's ass and disown you faster than she can demand a paternity test.*

"You're sure it's mine?" I blurt.

Kat clenches her jaw. "I'm sure."

"I'm sorry," I say. "I just meant... how far along are you? That's what I meant to ask. I know you were with Cameron the week before me, so..." I abruptly shut my mouth. Oh shit. She looks like she's about to stab me.

"It's yours, Josh." Her eye twitches. "That was a low blow."

"I'm sorry," I say, my heart exploding. "That came out wrong." I cover my ears with my palms. I can't stop hearing my father's voice screaming at me.

The toddler in the waiting room shouts something to his mother about wanting a box of raisins and she gently shushes him. Oh shit. I'm gonna have a kid who screams about raisins in a hospital waiting room?

When my gaze returns to Kat, she's looking at me with steely eyes. "Your father really did a number on you, didn't he?" she says.

I can't reply.

"So are you gonna say something besides asking me if it's yours?" Kat asks. "Because if not, I'm gonna head back into Colby's room and be with my family."

I swallow hard. "How far along are you?" I ask. "That's all I meant to ask, Kat. I wasn't implying..." I trail off.

"I'm about seven weeks, I think," she says. "Maybe eight. But the whole counting thing is kind of confusing—the minute you miss your period, you're already considered four or five weeks pregnant—but since I haven't been having periods, I'm not completely sure yet. I'll know more when I have a sonogram, probably next week."

A nurse walks by in the hallway, her shoes squeaking on the linoleum and we both look toward the noise for a moment.

"Cameron and I used a condom," Kat continues, sounding like she's ordering a hit. "And I was with Cameron way before the timeframe, anyway. I'm one hundred percent positive it's yours. But I'd be happy to take a paternity test if you have a shred of doubt. Actually, fuck it, I'll take one, anyway, just so you never have room to doubt." Oh man, she sounds like a cold-blooded killer right now.

"I know it's mine," I say. "I'm sorry. I didn't mean to ask that. It just slipped out."

Kat sniffs the air, utterly pissed. "You're entitled to ask. But I'm telling you there's no doubt in my mind whatsoever. You're the only man I've been with." She grits her teeth. "We're exclusive and I don't cheat. But, like I say, I'll get a paternity test. No problem."

I've got goose bumps. She looks really scary right now, like she's sharpening her blade to cut off my balls and smash them between graham crackers.

"I don't doubt you," I say. "I know you've only been with me. I've only been with you, too."

"I guess you're thinking I'm some sort of gold digger who's trying to trick you into marriage, just like your father warned you against." She rolls her eyes. "But I swear to God that's the furthest thing from my—"

"We should get married," I blurt suddenly.

Kat stops talking and stares at me, her blue eyes wide.

There's a long beat during which we could hear a pin drop if it weren't for the loud hacking noises coming from Typhoid Joe on the other side of the room.

"What?" Kat says. She looks at me like I've screamed, "I'm a merman!"

"We should get married," I say softly, my heart pounding in my ears, my stomach churning. Oh my God. I can't believe I just said those words. I feel like I'm gonna throw up. I wait for a moment, fully expecting Kat to burst into happy tears and shout, "Yes!" But she doesn't. She just glares at me silently, her blue eyes on icy fire. "Well?" I ask, unable to keep the testiness out of my voice. Why does she look like she wants to clobber me instead of kiss me? Honestly, she should be crying with gratitude and relief right now—she's the one who forgot to take her goddamned fucking pill, not me, so she's got no right to be thinking up ways to detach my balls from my body. "I just asked you to marry me, Kat," I say, my tone impatient. "I'm doing the noble thing here. I think you should at least do me the courtesy of a reply."

Kat smiles thinly—but it's clearly a "fuck you" kind of a smile.

There's a long, silent, excruciating beat.

To be perfectly honest, Kat's starting to piss me off. For fuck's sake, I'm a fucking *Faraday* and I just offered to marry her—how the fuck is she not leaping at the chance? I'm doing the right thing, without hesitation or waffling, despite the fact that, as I've mentioned to her *quite clearly*, marriage isn't something I've *ever* contemplated doing before this very moment *and* despite the fact that she's the one who fucked up here, not me. I'd say I deserve a fucking medal, not the daggers Kat's throwing at me with her eyes. If my dad were here watching this exchange, I can only imagine how that vein in his neck would be bulging with fury.

"You want me to reply?" Kat says coldly.

I nod—but by the tone of Kat's voice, I'm not so sure.

"Okay, then I will." She shifts her weight in her chair, obviously gearing up to decimate me. "Thank you for your *noble* proposal of marriage, good sir. That was an *admirable* thing to do. You really should feel quite *proud* of yourself for displaying such unimpeachable *integrity* and *bravery* in the face of such horrific and victimizing circumstances."

Jesus fucking Christ. Only Kat could make a whole bunch of words generally regarded as complimentary sound like a string of curse words.

"I didn't expect you to ask me to marry you," she continues. "Not in a million years. I'm genuinely impressed with how quickly you rose to what you perceive to be your *obligation*. Thank you for that, good sir."

I nod. That's right. I rose to my obligation. But I'm confused. Kat's words and body language are completely at odds. It feels like she's doing that licking-and-punching-my-balls-thing she always does. And why the fuck does she keep talking like she's in a miniseries on fucking PBS?

"*But,*" Kat adds, her voice prim, "although I'm infinitely *grateful* to you for swooping in to *save* me from this incredible cluster-fuck of a situation that will surely heap shame and disgrace upon my family's good name, I think I'll have to politely decline your *kind* and *generous* offer, good sir." Kat grits her teeth again. "I think I'd rather take my chances, however slim, that there might be a man out there who'll one day ask me to marry him simply because he's fallen head over heels in *love* with me to the point of actually *wanting* to marry me, the crazy son of a bitch, despite the fact that, by that time, I'll be the mother of *another man's goddamned kid.*"

I blink quickly. What the fuck did Kat just say to me? Motherfucker! Did Kat just break up with me to marry some other hypothetical guy—*and with my fucking kid in tow?*

"Excuse me?" I say, suddenly enraged.

"You heard me," Kat says, jutting her chin at me. "I said *no.*"

"What the fuck, Kat!" I bark, rising out of my seat. I know I'm talking way too loudly for this small waiting room but I can't control myself. "You can't say something like that to me—I'm a fucking Faraday!"

Kat looks around the waiting room, obviously embarrassed. "Sit down, Josh. Jesus."

I glower over her for a moment longer, but then I sit, clenching my jaw.

"You can't say shit like that to me," I grit out in a hoarse whisper. "Now's not the time to be a terrorist, Kat. You're pregnant with my kid—so don't talk to me about running off into the sunset with some other guy. You're *my* Party Girl with a Hyphen and you're not marrying some other guy with my goddamned kid in tow." I take a deep breath. "Now I'm gonna ask you one more fucking time—and this is the last time I'm gonna ask you, so don't blow it." My nostrils flare. "Will. You. *Fucking*. Marry. Me?"

Kat's lip curls with blatant disgust. "*Nooooooo*," she says, forming the long "O" sound like she's falling down a thirty-foot well.

"What the fuck?" I say. I still can't believe I'm hearing her right. "*No?*"

"*No.*" She squints her eyes like she's taking aim with a shotgun. "*Nooooooooooooooooooo*," she says again, this time emphasizing the "O" sound like she's falling down a *fifty*-foot well. "Thank you very much for being such a duty-bound gentleman, good sir," she says through gritted teeth. "Believe me, I know you're doing me a *huge* frickin' favor—a *massive fucking favor*—especially since you're a *Faraday* and my family is but an assemblage of lowly commoners without a noble title to our shameful name. Goodness, I really, really appreciate your infinite *generosity* good sir." She rolls her eyes. "But no fucking thank you, Sir J.W. Faraday. This isn't 1815. I'd rather just figure my shit out on my own and roll the dice that even a harlot from a simple family of *serfs* might one day get to marry for *love* instead of motherfucking *obligation*."

I make a face registering my disbelief. "You're kidding, right?"

Kat shakes her head. "No, sir. I am not."

I leap up again, pulling at my hair in frustration, and immediately sit back down. Goddamn, this woman. When that nurse said I couldn't accompany Kat to Colby's room because I'm not fucking *family*, Kat looked at me in that moment like she would have given *anything* in the world to call me her husband—I'm positive I didn't imagine those puppy-dog eyes she flashed at me —and now that I've asked her to marry me only sixty minutes later, she's turning me the fuck down? The woman's deranged. What *sane* woman would ever dream of turning me down?

For fuck's sake, I'm a thirty-year-old with over six hundred million dollars to my personal name—I'm talking *personally* here—and that's not even including unvested shares in Faraday & Sons that will soon be coming my way to the tune of half a billion bucks if we play our cards right—or the eight hundred million bucks my uncle has told Jonas and me he's earmarked for us in his will. And on top of all that, I'm not exactly Quasimodo to look at, either, let's just be real—not to mention the fact that I've got a magic cock and I make the woman come like a fucking freight train every time I fucking *glance* at her. *And she's turning me the fuck down?*

"Kat, don't be a fucking terrorist right now," I say, my voice filled with barely contained rage. "Think about what you're doing."

"Oh, you want me to *think*?" she says. "Am I having trouble *thinking—* perhaps due to the pregnancy hormones, good sir?"

I throw up my hands. "Would you stop calling me 'good sir'? You're annoying the shit out of me. Look, the bottom line is you're having my baby, Kat, and it should have my name."

Kat crosses her arms and leans back in her chair. "Fine. The baby can have your name. Happy?"

I'm stunned. "Well, no. I mean the baby should have my name and so should you—the mother of my child. We should be, you know, a unit—a legal unit."

"Aw, you think so? You think 'the mother' should take your name because that's the way we 'should' do it so we can be a 'legal unit'?" She scoffs. "How sweet."

I nod, not understanding her reaction in the slightest. "That's right."

"You really think so?"

I nod again. Why the fuck is she reacting like this? If anyone should be mad it's *me*. Kat's the one who didn't take her goddamned pill. And now we both have to pay for her mistake for the rest of our lives. Under the circumstances, I think I'm behaving exceedingly well.

"You think we *should*, Josh?" She glares at me like she's laced my iced tea with arsenic and she's waiting for me to keel over. "Golly gosh, Joshua, I truly appreciate your incredible sense of *duty*. You're a man of endless integrity, through and through (and, actually, I'm serious about that, even though I'm pissed at you—you really *are* a man of integrity). But I'm not gonna marry any man out of sheer obligation, not even my filthy-rich-hot-as-fucking-sin-baby-daddy." Her eyes prick with tears. "Not even if he's you."

"Kat," I say, rolling my eyes. "Stop acting like a fucking lunatic. I'm the one who should be pissed, not you."

Kat raises an eyebrow. "Why should you be *pissed*?"

"Because you're the one who fucked up and didn't take your pill."

Kat doesn't speak for a long beat. "I'm really sorry about that," she finally says. "You're right—I totally fucked up." Her eyes catch fire. "But I'm sure as hell not gonna compound one mistake with another. I'll be your baby-momma, Josh, and I'll certainly expect you to step up and be a father to this kid, financially and otherwise (which, by the way, I have no doubt you'll do—again, I know you're a man of integrity). But I'm most certainly not gonna *marry* you for no other reason than I'm gestating your accidental Faraday. Now, if you actually *want* to marry me, that's a different story..." She pauses, her eyebrows raised, obviously expecting me to say something. "If that's something you *want*, regardless of the baby...?"

I stare at her blankly. She's got to be kidding. Why the fuck would I want to get married, other than the fact that she's gestating my accidental Faraday? She knows I have no interest in marriage—I've told her so, as plain as day. There's literally no other circumstance when I'd even *think* of asking Kat, or any woman, to be my wife, sorry-not-sorry. "Kat," I say, emotion suddenly rising up inside me. "You're asking too much of me. Stop being a terrorist and be rational."

Kat's eyes soften with sudden and surprising sympathy. "Josh, I'm not being a terrorist, though if I were, you'd certainly deserve it. I'm being kind to you in the long run, though you obviously can't see it now. This baby was an accident, plain and simple. We both made it, but you're right, I'm the one who flubbed taking my pill. You were relying on me to have my shit together and I blew it—so I hereby release you. You've made it clear how you feel about marriage—you don't see the point in it." She adopts a deep voice obviously intended as an impression of mine: "'If you wanna go, go—if you wanna stay, stay.' I haven't forgotten what you said. Just because I've got an accidental Faraday in my uterus doesn't mean you suddenly want to marry me in your heart. And I deserve to marry a man who loves me—not a guy who's asking me to marry him to appease the ghost of his asshole-father."

A lump rises in my throat. Is Kat right? Is my father *still* controlling me, even after all these years, even from the grave?

There's a long beat, during which Typhoid Joe hacks up his tenth lung of the night.

"Josh," Kat says softly after Typhoid Joe quiets down. She puts her hand on mine in a gesture of tenderness, making my heart pang. "If it weren't for this baby growing inside me, you wouldn't even be *thinking* of asking me to marry you. Today when you introduced me to your friends at flag football was the first time you ever called me your girlfriend—which I really liked, by the way."

"Kat, please just say yes," I whisper, despair overtaking me. She's pregnant and I'm proposing. Why won't she say yes?

"Thank you, Josh. I really appreciate the offer," Kat says, her tone surprisingly sweet. "But how are you gonna vow to be my husband 'til death do us part when you haven't even told me something as simple as 'I love you'?" She looks at me pointedly, like she's willing those three words to come out of my mouth right this very minute.

I run my hand through my hair. Shit. I should say it. I've never felt this way about any woman before. I'm addicted to her in every way. I'm ninety-nine percent sure what I'm feeling for Kat is what normal people call love—which means I should say the goddamned words. I open my mouth and close it again. Fuck.

Kat scoffs. "I know turnabout is fair play and all, but please don't barf on me."

"What?"

"You look like you're about to barf."

I exhale.

Kat waves her hand dismissively, anger once again rising in her face.

"Forget it. I'm not gonna be the gold-digging whore who proves your asshole-father right and traps you into marital bondage. I don't want your fucking money or your goddamned name and I certainly don't wanna force you to say something you're not genuinely feeling. Give me whatever to sign and I'll sign it, saying I don't want your freaking money and that you're only obligated to take care of your kid and nothing more." Tears prick her eyes.

"Kat, I don't think you're a gold digger," I say softly. "I've never thought that about you, not for a minute. I know you forgot to take your pill by accident."

"It's okay, Josh. Here's what we're gonna do. We'll keep going the way we are and see where this thing leads—which, if I were placing bets after this conversation, looks to be nowhere—but who knows? And when the baby comes, we'll see where things stand between us—if we're even talking to each other by then—and we'll figure our shit out from there, one day at a time." She glares at me with glistening eyes.

"Kat, listen to me. Just gimme a minute to absorb the situation. Maybe I'm not saying all the right words, but my heart's in the right place."

"No, you're *heart* isn't remotely involved in this conversation—that's the problem."

"Kat," I say softly. If my heart's not involved in this conversation, like she says, then why does it feel like it's shattering?

"It's okay, Josh," Kat says. "I've had a lot more time to process the situation than you have—a full week. Take your time. Think and regroup."

"You've known for a week?" I ask.

"Yeah, I barfed right after I got home from the karaoke bar, so I took a pregnancy test."

"You found out the night of the karaoke bar?"

She nods.

"Shit." I shake my head, remembering myself holding a goddamned boom box over my head in front of her apartment building. "I came over that night—I wanted to apologize to you."

"Yeah. I got your text," Kat says softly. "I couldn't come out. I was too much of a wreck."

My heart is aching. Kat obviously has no idea I stood out in front of her apartment with a boom box, ready to hand her my dick and balls in a baggie.

"Kat," I say. "Fuck what I said about marriage being pointless, okay? All bets are off. You're pregnant with my baby. We should get married. *Please.*"

Kat shakes her head.

I throw up my hands, suddenly exasperated with her. "Goddammit. I don't know what you expect from me. You've totally blindsided me here, Kat." I look up at the ceiling, begging God for patience, and then level her with pleading eyes. "Kat, think about what you're doing. You're turning down an offer of marriage from the father of your child—who, lucky for you, happens to be *me.*"

Kat scoffs. "Oh, now I'm the 'lucky one'?"

I throw up my hands. What the hell is she holding out for? Some sort of fairytale? Some knight on a white horse, whisking her off into the sunset? "I'm sorry my proposal isn't fulfilling your girlhood fantasies," I say caustically. "But maybe it's time to stop dreaming about being Cinderella and get real. This is as good as it's gonna get under the circumstances."

Kat glares at me for a long beat, her eyes full of homicidal rage. "Fuck you," she finally spits out. "'Get real'? 'As good as it's gonna get'? Fuck you, you arrogant little prick. I deserve the fairytale, whether I'm knocked up or not, you motherfucking asshole-douche-prick-fuckwad." She glares at me and flips her golden hair behind her shoulder. "I'm Julia Roberts in *Pretty Woman*," she says. "And I'm not gonna settle for, 'Oh, fuck it, we might as well get married,' simply because I *happen* to be a street-walker in thigh-high boots and you *happen* to be Mr. Darcy." She juts her chin at me. "Let me be really clear about something, Josh: I. Don't. Care. About. Your. Freaking. Money."

I blink rapidly, completely floored.

"Yes, I'm impregnated with your mighty Faraday spawn," Kat continues, still seething, "which, according to you, is a huge *win* for me—from an *evolutionary* standpoint, I suppose." She scoffs. "But I'm here to tell you, Joshua, evolution is no reason for me to marry a man who doesn't actually *want* to marry me."

We stare at each other for a long, angry beat. Yet again, she's obviously waiting for me to say something very specific. But she can wait for-fucking-ever as far as I'm concerned. She's crossed a fucking line and I'm fucking done. I ask her to marry me and she calls me a fuckwad? Fuck this shit. She's right. This is a horrible idea. We're obviously fundamentally incompatible. God help me if I were to marry this batshit crazy woman and be stuck with her for eternity—I'd quite literally go insane.

"Well," Kat says primly, filling the excruciating silence. "I just wanted to come out here and tell you about Colby. I didn't intend to tell you about the pregnancy. Sorry. It just slipped out."

I suppress an eye-roll.

Kat narrows her eyes, shooting daggers at me. "Let's just take some time and regroup," she says stiffly. "*Starting right now.*"

I exhale with exasperation. "Have you told your family yet?"

"No. They've got enough to worry about with Colby. Probably won't tell them for a few months—for however long I'm not showing."

"Have you told Sarah?"

"No. She had her finals last week and now she's in Greece, getting engaged to the man of her dreams—a guy who actually *wants* to marry her more than he wants to breathe, by the way." She glares at me like I just flicked her in the forehead.

"Kat, let's play the honesty-game here for one cotton-pickin' minute, okay?" I grit out.

"Yes, please, good sir. I thought that's what we were doing already, but I guess that was just me."

God, she's annoying. "Let's talk about the pink elephant in the room, shall we?" I say.

"I have no idea what the pink elephant in the room is, Josh. I'm pregnant and you're a dick. Those are pretty much the only pink elephants I see, and I just talked about both of them."

I make a noise of frustration.

"But, please, good sir, enlighten me about the pink elephant you see in the room," she continues.

"Would you stop with the 'good sir' crap? I don't even understand the reference."

"Because you're an idiot."

I close my eyes for a moment, once again asking God for patience, and when I feel ready to speak without wringing Kat's pretty little neck, I open my eyes. "The pink elephant is this: my family is worth a shit-ton of money. You don't need to know exactly how much, but trust me, it's more than you think. Now I don't think for one nanosecond you were trying to *intentionally* trick or trap me—okay? But you definitely fucked up here, let's call a spade a spade, and now you're *definitely* coming out on top in The Game of Life. Under the circumstances, it's not outlandish for me to point out that through an honest *mistake* you'll wind up doing quite well for yourself for the rest of your fucking life."

Well, that did it. I just lit the fuse on a gigantic stick of dynamite. She pops up out of her chair and wiggles her body around like she's suddenly possessed by a demon.

I recoil in my seat, genuinely scared of her flailing movement. "Jesus, Kat," I say. "Are you gonna barf on me or dive to the ground and start speaking in tongues?"

Kat abruptly leans into my face. "Go back to L.A. before I do grave bodily harm to you, Josh," she seethes.

"Kat, you're misunderstanding me. What I'm saying to you is that—"

"I know exactly what you're saying to me. And here's what I'm saying to you in reply: Fuck you and the horse you rode in on, you arrogant little rich-boy-prick. My answer to your romantic proposal of marriage is 'no thank you.' And not only that, in the interest of the honesty-game, I should also tell you that I wouldn't marry you if you were the last goddamned man on earth." With that, she turns on her heel and marches away, just like she did after Reed's party—just like she always does.

I follow her, rolling my eyes. Obviously, what I've said came out wrong. Horribly wrong. I just meant that she's pregnant and the best outcome for her would be marriage to the father of her child, especially when he can support her and the baby in ways she's never even dreamed of. She was out of her head about getting a million bucks for taking down The Club? Well, how's she gonna feel about snagging a husband who could buy her a million-dollar diamond necklace on a fucking whim?

"Kat, *wait*," I say.

But Kat keeps stomping away.

I follow her as far as I'm allowed to go, but there's only so far a guy can chase a girl in this particular hospital when he's not a part of her fucking *family.*

Kat bursts through the swinging doors leading into the Hallowed Land of Family Members, leaving me decidedly behind in her pissy, dramatic, tempestuous wake.

"Fine!" I yell toward the doors. "Have yet *another* tantrum, Kat. See if I care."

"Fine! I will!" she shouts, continuing to stomp away.

Goddamn her. Who does Kat think she is, turning me down? Who's she planning to marry, if not me? Cameron Fucking Schulz? Well, I hope she *really* likes Shirley Temples and watching motherfucking *baseball*. I hope when her initials are KUS, she'll appreciate the irony of her name being synonymous with "curse word."

I turn around in a huff and take two angry steps away from her and then abruptly stop dead in my tracks.

Oh shit.

Kat could marry Cameron Schulz—or any other guy in the entire fucking world. Kat could literally have *any* guy she wants—it's the God's truth. All she has to do is crook her index finger at any man, rich or poor, young or old, professional athlete or accountant, and he'd come running, engagement ring in hand —*and she knows it.*

Oh my God. *Kat's gonna give birth to my child and then marry someone else!*

"Kat!" I shout, loping back toward the double doors. "*Wait!*"

Kat stops dead in her tracks. She turns around slowly and stares at me with burning eyes.

"Come back," I say. "Please. I have something I need to say to you."

She bites the inside of her cheek for a moment, but then slowly saunters back toward the swinging doors, her eyes as sharp as knives. When she reaches the doors, she pokes her head out, raises her eyebrows and exhales, deigning to give me a moment of her time. "*Yes, Mr. Darcy?*"

I exhale. I have no idea why she keeps calling me that. "Just think about what you're doing," I say. "You're being a suicide-bomber."

Kat squints at me. "*That's* what you called me back here to say?"

I shift my weight. "No. That just slipped out. I called you back to ask you to *please* marry me." I pause. "It's the right thing to do all around. For everyone. And it's... what ... I... want."

"*It's the right thing to do?*" she says slowly. "All around?"

I nod, but I can already tell this isn't going my way.

Kat crosses her arms over her chest, keeping the double-doors open with her shoulder. "*No thank you,*" she says, cold as a fucking sniper.

"Think of the baby," I say earnestly. "Let's not be selfish, either of us. Let's do the right thing. Now's not the time to be a terrorist, Kat."

Without warning, Kat pushes completely through the swinging doors toward me—to the "non-family members" side, as it were—and glowers over me with such ferocity, I leap back, surprised. "I guess you didn't pay very close attention in Las Vegas when I taught Henn how to bag a babe." She leans into my face, her eyes on fire. "Remember what I told him?"

I shake my head.

"Then I'll refresh your memory. 'Every time you're about to say something to a woman, ask yourself: is this more or less likely to get me a blowjob? If the answer is yes, then say it. If the answer is no, then *shut the fuck up!*'"

"What are you talking about? I just asked you to marry me, and you're acting like I spit on you."

"Because you *did*," she says, her eyes flooding with tears.

I throw up my hands, at a total loss.

"Oh for crying out loud," she says. "Let me spell it out for you, plain and simple." She wipes her eyes and takes a deep breath, gearing up. "Whoever I wind up marrying one day—whether I'm the mother of his accidental spawn *or not*—" She gives that last phrase "or not" exaggerated emphasis. "It'll be for no other reason than he desperately wants *me* and only *me* to be his *wife*, forever and *ever*, as long as we both shall live." She glares at me for a beat, tears streaming down her cheeks. "It'll be because he couldn't stand the thought of living his life without me in it—couldn't stand the thought of me being with any other man—because he loves me more than the air he breathes—more than life itself." She wipes her eyes again. "And it sure as hell won't be because he felt some begrudging sense of obligation toward the unwitting incubator of his accidental spawn." Without letting me respond, she literally harrumphs at me, turns on her heel, and marches down the hallway, her arms swinging wildly with sudden fury.

I watch Kat striding away through the panes of glass in the doors, feeling like I've just been kicked in the balls with a steel boot. When she's gone, I swallow hard and shake my head, the full enormity of the situation descending upon me.

I've got quite the track record with the ladies, don't I? I told Emma I loved her and she said, "Me, too" and promptly ran off with Ascot Man on a polo pony. And now, a year later, I've asked the mother of my impending child to pretty-please marry me, and Kat basically flipped me the bird and told me she wouldn't marry me if I were the last man on earth. Talk about winning in The Game of Life. *Yahtzee.*

I swallow hard again. Fuck this shit. I'm done begging a woman to love me, even if that woman's a unicorn and the most incredible woman I've ever been with. And most of all I'm done handing Katherine Ulla Fucking Morgan my motherfucking dick and balls in a motherfucking Ziploc baggie and letting her throw them into a fucking meat grinder at her bitchy little whim. Clearly, she's always gotten everything she's ever wanted from every other motherfucking man she's ever run across, but not anymore. I'm done.

I wipe my eyes on my sleeve, leaving a surprising streak of wetness on the fabric. And then I flip off the swinging doors with both hands, turn the fuck around, and march out of the hospital without looking the fuck back.

"Do you wanna wait for your friend before being seated or go to your table now?" the restaurant hostess asks me.

"I think I'll be seated now. My friend texted she's running a bit late."

"Of course." The woman picks up two menus. "Right this way."

She leads me to a small table in the back and I immediately set down the thick stack of bridal magazines in my arms. "Thank you."

"Can I get you something to drink while you wait?"

"Ginger ale? Extra ice, please," I ask, taking a chair. I pull a Saltine from a baggie in my purse and take a little nibble. Gah. This round-the-clock nausea is getting really old.

A busboy brings a ginger ale to the table along with a basket of bread, and I take a greedy bite of a roll, hoping it'll calm my churning stomach.

My phone buzzes and I glance down, expecting to see a text from Sarah.

"Hello, Stubborn Kat," Josh writes.

My heart instantly leaps at the sight of Josh's name displayed on my screen, just like it always does—but then I remember the current iciness between us, and my heart pangs with an overwhelming sense of hurt and regret. Why'd Josh have to look like his balls were being fed through a wood-chipper when he asked me to marry him at the hospital a week ago? And why'd he have to act like such a spoiled, rich-boy-prick, too? If only he'd looked even the teensiest bit like he actually *wanted* me to be his wife, if only he'd flashed a fraction of his usual down-to-earth, irresistible charm, I surely would have thrown my arms around his neck and screamed, "Yes!" despite myself.

"Hello, Mr. Darcy," I reply to Josh's text.

"Why do you keep calling me that?"

"Google it," I write.

"I did. He's the guy from Pride and Prejudice. But since I haven't seen that movie (a fact I've already mentioned to you, by the way—thanks so much for listening intently to everything I say), I have no idea what you're talking about."

Jeez, I guess being fed a weeklong diet of cold-shoulder by your pregnant girlfriend (or am I his pregnant *ex*-girlfriend?) is enough to make a guy a big ol' grouch.

"Well, Mr. Grouchy Pants," I type, "I'd never dream of spoiling Pride and Prejudice for you by explaining why I keep calling you that name. You'll just have to watch it and find out."

"Go ahead and spoil it," Josh replies. "I'm positive I'll NEVER see that movie."

"Never say never," I write.

"NEVER. Because I don't have a VAGINA."

"You never know."

"I KNOW."

"So is that why you've texted me (in all caps, no less)? To argue about whether you're ever gonna watch Pride and Prejudice?"

"No. Sorry. That just slipped out. I'm texting to ask how Colby's doing and also to find out if you're feeling a bit better today?"

These are the same two questions Josh has politely asked me via text every single day this week. And in return, I've politely responded to him (via text) each and every time, as smoothly and impersonally as Elizabeth Bennett (the well-mannered heroine of *Pride and Prejudice*) would do, assuming she'd lived in the age of smartphones.

I'll admit it's taken quite a bit of willpower on my part not to instigate contact with Josh at all this week. So many times, I've wanted to call him and scream into the phone, "Even if you're an arrogant prick, I still love you! Ask me again!" But I've somehow managed to maintain full control and stuff down the raging, clanging, almost desperate swell of emotion I've felt nearly every moment since I marched away from Josh at the hospital.

And it's not just memories of Josh's so-called marriage proposal that have been plaguing me all week. Even more so, it's the way Josh has been treating me ever since that horrible night—like he's done with me for good. His behavior this past week has been a complete one-eighty compared to the week after the karaoke bar. Back then, there were daily flowers, texts begging for my forgiveness, late-night, drunken voicemails telling me he was hard as a rock and couldn't stop thinking about me. But this week? Nope. There's been none of that. Just polite texts asking after my brother and my health, exactly as the ever-polite Mr. Darcy would do—only signs of his perceived obligation and nothing more. And it's damn-near broken my heart.

Goddammit. I truly thought I was doing the right thing when I turned Josh down at the hospital—I really did—and I guess I still do, intellectually—I mean, jeez, he was such a little prick, oh my God. But, shoot, I just don't know anymore. I can't even think straight these days, I miss him so freaking much. If it weren't for how busy I've been this past week visiting Colby and gathering ideas and information for Sarah's wedding, I'd have hopped a flight to L.A. days ago to fling myself upon Josh's arrogant mercy and beg him to ask me again.

"Colby's doing well," I text to Josh in reply to his polite query. "Thank you for asking." (I refrain from adding, "good sir" to the end of my sentence, though I'm dying to do it.) I tap out a lengthy (and exceedingly polite) status report about Colby, just as I've done every day this past week in reply to Josh's texts. "All in all, great progress," I conclude. "At least regarding Colby's physical healing," I add. "Mentally, Colby's not doing quite as well. When I saw him this morning, he was convinced he'd somehow cost that baby her life. He thinks he should have taken a different route out of the building or something."

"Oh, man. Poor guy. You told him that's crazy, right? He's a hero."

"I told him. But he wouldn't listen."

"Well, he's lucky to have you," Josh writes. "If anyone can put a smile on a man's face, it's you."

My heart leaps. That's the first time Josh has texted anything remotely personal to me in a full week—let alone something so lovely. "Thank you," I write, my heart suddenly gushing with relief and yearning. Oh my effing God, I'm fighting back tears. Oh, how I want to write, "I miss you, Josh! I loooooooooove you. Ask me again and I'll say yes this time, even though I know you don't really want to marry me!" But I can't do that. I know full well Josh doesn't want a wife any more than he wants a baby, and I'll be damned if I'm gonna be the woman who's trapped Josh Faraday into having *two* items of baggage he never bargained for. "It means a lot to me that you'd say that about me," I type, my heart pounding. "Especially now. Just knowing you still feel that way about me is making me want to sob like a baby."

I've no sooner pressed send on my text than my phone rings with an incoming call.

"Hi," I say softly into the phone, holding back tears.

"Hi," Josh says.

Oh God, just hearing his sexy voice for the first time in a week is making my heart explode. "I miss you so much," I blurt. "Josh, I *miss* you."

Josh pauses, just long enough to make my stomach drop into my toes.

"I miss you, too," he finally says, his voice cracking. "So, so much, babe."

"I thought you hated me," I whisper.

"Of course, not. *Never.*" He pauses, apparently collecting himself. "Are you feeling any better today?"

My heart is physically aching. I want to reach through the phone line and kiss him and tell him I love him desperately. "Yeah," I manage to reply. "I figured out Saltines and ice-cold ginger ale take the edge off my nausea a little bit."

"Good." He pauses. "So what are you up to today?" he asks softly.

Oh. We're gonna have a routine conversation? We're not gonna talk about his proposal or this past week? No talking about our feelings? Okay. I can do that. I clear my throat. "Well, I visited Colby in the hospital all morning. And now I'm meeting Sarah for lunch to go over wedding stuff. She and Jonas got back from Greece yesterday—oh, duh—you probably heard that from Jonas. But, anyway, since the wedding's happening so soon—in just twenty-six little days, courtesy of your impatient brother—I pulled together some ideas for Sarah these past few days while she was finishing up her trip."

"Yeah, I heard about that quick turnaround thing. Classic Jonas."

"I guess some people in this world just, you know, really *want* to get married."

Josh exhales.

Shit. I shouldn't have said that. That was a decidedly terroristic thing to say. Shoot. "So, anyway," I continue, trying to deflect attention from my apparently pathological need to strap bombs to my chest. "So now I'm sitting in a restaurant with a stack of bridal magazines, waiting for Sarah to arrive."

"Are you gonna tell her about the pregnancy?"

"No. I think we should wait to tell Jonas and Sarah until after the wedding. They've got plenty to think about 'til then."

"I agree."

"Plus, you never know. It still might not stick. So, anyway, continuing with my exciting agenda for the day, after lunch, I've got a doctor's appointment."

"A doctor's appointment? You mean for the baby?"

"Yeah."

"Why didn't you tell me? I would have flown up for it."

"Flown up for a doctor's appointment?"

"It's my kid, right?"

I bristle.

"Shit. That came out wrong. Kat, please don't freak out. I meant, 'Hey, it's my kid, right?' *Not,* 'It's my kid... *right?*'"

I can't help but smile. "I know exactly what you meant. It's okay. But, bee tee dubs, it's your kid, Josh."

"Yeah, I know that." He pauses. "Well, the point I'm making is that I plan to be there for my kid, right from the start. Doctors appointments and everything. I'm gonna be a real father—not just a wallet. So tell me about appointments, please, and I'll always try to make them."

"Okay. I'm sorry. It didn't occur to me to tell you about today's appointment —we haven't exactly been chatting each other's ears off this week." I clear my throat. "But I'll be sure to tell you next time."

"Please do."

"I will." There's a beat. "So how's your day going, Josh?"

"Fine. I'm just trying to finish this huge report. It's the last thing I've got to do for Faraday & Sons and then I'm free at last, free at last, thank God almighty, I'm free at last. And the other thing I'm doing is sitting here watching moving guys put all my shit into a humongous truck."

"What?"

"Yeah, considering what's going on with you and the baby and everything, I decided to move into my new house a couple weeks early," Josh says.

My heart leaps. "Really? When will you be up here?"

"Really soon. A matter of days. I'll let you know when I get the moving schedule confirmed." He lets out a pained exhale. "Shit. Fuck this, Kat—I can't take it anymore. I've been going out of my head this whole week, dying to tell you—"

"Kitty Kat!" It's Sarah, standing at the edge of the table, holding out her arms for a big hug. "I'm so sorry I'm late."

94

KAT

"Hang on, Josh—Sarah's here," I say into the phone, cutting him off. I leap up from the table and give Sarah a huge hug. "Welcome home! Ooooph, I missed you, girl. Let's see it."

Sarah shows me the humongous diamond on her hand.

"Oh my God!" I shriek, ogling Sarah's rock. "It's so huge! And sparkly! Oh, Sarah! That's the most gorgeous ring I've ever seen. To die for! What girl wouldn't kill to get a ring like that?"

We take our seats, both of us giggling and glowing and cooing at each other like we haven't seen each other in twenty years.

"Hello?" a compressed voice says through my phone on the table.

"Oh my God," I gasp, picking up the phone. "I'm so sorry, Josh," I say. "I totally forgot you were there."

"Mmm hmmm. Gosh, it sure sounds like Sarah's ring is big and sparkly, Kat."

I smile demonically to myself. "Oh, you heard all that? I'm sorry. Yeah. It's gorgeous." Sarah smiles at me, oblivious to what's been going on between Josh and me this past week. "You should see Sarah," I say to Josh. "She looks so *happy*. Hang on." I hold the phone out to Sarah. "Say hi to Josh, Sarah—tell him how happy you are."

Sarah giggles and takes the phone from me. "Hi, Joshy Woshy. Thank you... . Hey, that's right, *brother*." She squeals. "Hellz yeah, I will, you silly goose... Yep. Smart thinking... I love you, Joshy Woshy." She giggles again. "I will. Bye." She hands the phone back. "Here you go."

I put the phone to my ear, but Josh is gone. "He hung up," I say, feeling deflated.

"He told me to tell you goodbye. He said he'll talk to you later."

I stare at Sarah, stunned. "You told Josh you love him."

"I sure did, because I do. I loooooove him. Josh is gonna be my *brother*—isn't that awesome? I've always wanted a brother."

"And what did Josh say in reply when you said that?" I ask.

"He said, 'I feel the same way about you, my dearest sister.'" Sarah giggles. "Oh, the Faraday men. Gotta love 'em."

"Yeah. Gotta love 'em."

Oh my God, that should have been *me* saying "I love you" to Josh. I love him more than I knew I could love. I love every part of him, even the douchey parts. *And I'm dying to tell him so.* I already knew it, of course, but this week without him has made me realize I truly can't be happy without him.

"Hello, ladies," the waitress says, standing at the edge of our table. "Can I answer any questions about the menu for you?"

"Oh, gosh. I haven't even looked at the menu yet," Sarah says. "I'm sorry."

"There's no rush. Let me just tell you about our specials today." The waitress rattles off several specials, all of which sound like they'd make me hurl. "What can I get you to drink while you decide?" the waitress asks.

"I'd love a glass of white wine," Sarah says. "Maybe a Pinot Griggio?"

The waitress nods. "And another ginger ale for you, Miss?"

"Thank you."

Sarah looks at me funny. "I've never seen you drink ginger ale before," she says. "Does it have tequila in it?"

I shake my head. "I was feeling a little queasy for some reason—thought ginger ale might help."

"Oh, I'm sorry, Kat. Are you sick?"

"No, I'm fine. Although I must admit I'm totally jealous you just told Josh the exact three words I'm *dying* to say to him."

"You two *still* haven't said 'I love you'?"

I shake my head.

"Why don't you just tell him, Kat?"

"Sarah, please. I'd never say it first in a relationship. Come on. I'm lovesick, but I've still got at least a shred of self-respect."

"Well, *I* just said it first to Josh and he seemed quite receptive."

"Not quite the same thing, honey."

"I know." She giggles. "So you're in luuuurve, huh?"

"Completely-totally-I'm-in-physical-pain-lurve."

"Aw, just tell him. I'm sure he feels the same way. How could he not?"

I sigh loudly. "Things are a bit complicated right now."

"Well, I think everyone should tell everyone else in the whole wide world 'I love you' all the livelong day," Sarah says effusively, glancing down at her huge rock.

"It's like you're high on crystal meth," I say.

"That's how I feel—or so I'd imagine—I've never done crystal meth, of course."

"No offense, but you're the last person's advice I should be following about saying 'I love you' to anyone. You're so high on Jonas-crack right now, you'd swear your undying love to the bag lady on the corner."

Sarah giggles. "As a matter of fact, I believe I did exactly that on my way into the restaurant. I grabbed that bag lady by her *Iron Man* T-shirt and I said, 'I love you, bag lady!' And then I French-kissed her."

I laugh. "You're so freaking weird, Sarah."

"I'm just so happy, I can't contain myself." Sarah giggles for the millionth time since she waltzed into the restaurant. "Once I started saying 'I love you' all the time to Jonas, I can't seem to stop saying it to everyone. I'm addicted. I-love-you-I-love-you-I-love-you. See? I can't stop. I love you, Kat!"

The waitress approaches our table with Sarah's wine and another ginger ale for me. "Are we ready to order?" she asks.

"I love you!" Sarah says to the waitress.

"Oh, wow. Thank you. I love you, too."

"See, Kat?" Sarah says. "Easy peasy."

"Forgive my silly friend," I say to the waitress. "She just got engaged. She's out of her head."

"Oh, congratulations. Did you get a—*whoa!* Oh my god. Look at that ring. *Wow.*"

Sarah giggles and puts her hand down.

"That's quite a ring," the waitress says, her cheeks flushed. "Spectacular."

"Thank you. But it's not nearly as spectacular as the man who gave it to me."

The waitress and I exchange a look like, "Lucky bitch."

Sarah picks up her menu. "I still haven't looked at the menu. I'm sorry. I'm a babbling fool."

The waitress laughs. "Understandable." She flashes me another "lucky bitch" look. "Take your time. Sounds like you've got a lot to celebrate." She walks away.

"So, hey, what did Josh ask you?" I ask.

"When?"

"On the phone just now. When you said, 'Hellz yeah, I will'?"

"Oh. He asked if I'll be taking Jonas' name. He said if I take the Faraday name then I'll 'single-handedly increase the number of Faradays roaming the earth by 33.33 percent.'" She smiles. "So I told him, 'Hellz yeah, I will, you silly goose!'" She squeals with unadulterated joy.

"It's like you've been sucking on nitrous oxide."

Sarah laughs.

"And what did Josh say in response to that?" I ask.

"He said, 'Good. I think it's best for everyone in our family to have the same last name—that way we'll never be turned away when visiting each other in the hospital.'"

My stomach flips over. "So enough about Josh," I say. "I'm dying to hear everything about Greece."

"Oh my God, I can't wait to tell you. But lemme figure out my order first so the waitress doesn't kill me when she comes back."

I watch Sarah study her menu for a moment, my heart going pitter-pat with love for her. She's so damned cute. And so damned *happy*. God, I'm thrilled for her—I really am—but I'd be lying if I didn't say I wish I were in her same shoes, wearing a rock on my finger from Josh. Actually, no, on second thought, I don't even care about the marriage part so much as I just want Josh to *want* me, totally and completely, without reservation, the way Jonas so obviously wants Sarah.

Sarah looks up. "Salmon burger with a spinach salad. *Boom.*"

"Sounds good," I say, even though the thought of anything fishy turns my stomach. "Okay, now *spill*, honey."

Sarah launches into telling me every swoon-inducing detail about Jonas popping the question, stopping only to chomp on her salmon burger when our food arrives. And when Sarah's done telling me every last thing about Jonas' incredible proposal, we begin poring over the huge stack of bridal magazines I've brought, formulating ideas for the wedding of the century a mere twenty-six days from now (oh my God!).

"Okay," I finally say after almost an hour of brainstorming. I look down at the lengthy list of questions and ideas scrawled on my notepad. "Do you want me to go with you to your meeting with the wedding planner tomorrow?"

"No, I know you're busy getting your new business up and running—I'll handle everything from here on out."

My stomach clenches. God, I hate keeping anything from Sarah. It makes me feel even more like throwing up than I already do. "Sarah, I'm the Party Girl, remember?" I say. "I live for parties—and weddings are just the grand-daddy of all parties. Plus, I'm the maid of honor, after all—let me help you pull it all together."

Sarah beams a huge smile at me. "Really?"

"Of course."

"I must admit I'm a bit overwhelmed. Jonas says he'll pay for everything and show up, so I'm kind of on my own here."

"I'm thrilled to do it. Anything you need, whatever it is, I'm your girl."

"Thanks so much, Kat. You're the absolute best," Sarah says. She emphatically closes the bridal magazine in front of her on the table. "So enough about me, me, me. I've talked your ear off this whole lunch. Tell me what's going on with you, you, you? How's Golden Kat PR coming? When's the launch date, you think?"

"Um," I say. I bite my lip. "Hmm."

"I've been thinking," Sarah says. "What do you think about 'Kitty Kat PR'? Too juvenile? It's certainly memorable."

I don't reply.

"Yeah, you're right. Probably too juvenile," Sarah says. "So how's the planning going? Are you having fun?"

I take a small sip of ginger ale, trying to figure out how best to answer Sarah's seemingly innocuous questions without unleashing the kraken on her. Shit. I suppose I should tell Sarah about Colby, but I'm certainly not gonna tell her about my accidental Faraday, not when she's in the throes of planning her dream wedding—plus, the sonogram at my doctor's appointment later today might reveal the accidental spawn is smoking and losing altitude, you never know. And if I'm not gonna tell Sarah about my accidental bun in the oven, then I sure as heck won't be telling her about Josh's so-called marriage proposal, either, or about how I've been crying my eyes out ever since.

"So, come on—tell me everything," Sarah says, sipping her wine.

"Well..." I begin slowly, my stomach in knots. "Um." My lower lip begins to tremble. My eyes water.

Shoot.

I take a deep breath, trying to quell the despair rising up inside me—and then I burst into big, soggy tears.

95

KAT

"The doctor will be in shortly," the nurse says, taking the blood-pressure cuff off my arm.

I shift my weight, eliciting a crinkling sound from the wax paper underneath me. "I'm nervous," I say softly.

"About what?" Sarah asks. "A sonogram doesn't hurt, does it?"

"I'm not nervous the sonogram will *hurt*," I say. "I'm nervous about, you know, what it might show—that something might be wrong."

Honestly, I'm shocked at how anxious I am that something might be wrong with my little accidental Faraday. Two weeks ago, when I first peed on those pregnancy tests, the baby going bye-bye on its own was all I kept praying for. But with each passing day since then, I've surprisingly found myself more and more attached to the idea of having a baby of my own—perhaps a little boy who looks just like Josh? Despite myself, I keep imagining a dark-haired boy sitting at the Morgan Family Thanksgiving table in a little blue suit to match his sapphire eyes, or maybe throwing a football in the backyard with Colby, or learning how to play guitar with Dax? Or, craziest of all, I keep finding myself imagining Josh and me cuddled up in a warm bed with our cute little guy, giggling and whispering about how happy we are. It's crazy, I know, but I can't stop thinking about it.

Sarah juts her lip with sympathy as only she can do. "Aw, don't be nervous, honey." She opens my dog-eared copy of *What To Expect When You're Expecting* and flips to a marked page. "I was just reading in your fascinating little book here that being a barf-o-matic is generally regarded as a great sign— that it typically indicates your hormones are at high levels, which is good."

"Thanks, Sarah," I say. "And thanks for coming to this appointment with me. I didn't realize it would be so comforting to have someone here."

"Are you kidding? I wanna come to everything. I wish you'd told me sooner —I would have hopped the next flight home from Greece to hold your hand."

"That's exactly why I didn't tell you," I say. "So, are you gonna tell Jonas?"

Sarah shakes her head. "I think Josh should be the one to tell Jonas he's gonna be an uncle."

"Yeah, probably."

"Just make sure Josh spills the beans really soon, okay? I don't like keeping secrets from Jonas."

I nod.

Sarah buries her nose in my pregnancy book again, but after a moment, lifts her head, smiling. "Hey, you wanna hear something crazy? I think with the time difference, Josh proposed to you *before* Jonas proposed to me." She laughs. "Who would have predicted *that*?"

"Yeah, but Josh's proposal doesn't really count—he was just fulfilling an obligation. It wasn't even in the same universe as what Jonas did for you. That's like comparing a hamster to a racehorse."

Sarah's smile vanishes. "Aw, I'm sorry, Kat."

I rub my face. "I keep thinking maybe I should have said yes—that maybe when I said no I was being selfish and not looking out for the bean."

"What? No frickin' way. You did the right thing—one hundred percent."

"You think?"

"Absolutely. Regardless of marriage, Josh is gonna step up and take care of his kid—there's no doubt about that."

"True."

"And it's not like you need to get married to get onto Josh's medical insurance or something—Josh can well afford to make sure you have the best medical care."

"Also true. In fact, he's already told me he'll pay for all my expenses, medical and otherwise."

"Of course, he will. Which means there were no *practical* decisions to make in response to Josh's proposal—only emotional ones. And in that case, you did exactly the right thing: you followed your heart. Because, Kat, we both know you'd never be happy being married out of obligation. You're a diehard romantic, through and through—and you need the fairytale."

"*Me?*"

Sarah scoffs. "Yes, *you*. You've watched *The Bodyguard* and *Pretty Woman* like ten times each, for Pete's sake."

"Twenty."

Sarah motions like I just proved her case.

"Yeah, you're probably right." I rub my forehead and sigh. "The funny thing is I totally would have said yes if Josh's proposal had been even the slightest bit from his heart—just the teeniest, tiniest bit."

"I gotta be honest, Kat, from what you've told me, I don't really understand what was so horrible about it. I mean, you said he acted like he was doing you a huge favor, but maybe you just misinterpreted him? I'm sure he was just freaking out."

I pause, choosing my words. "Remember Mr. Darcy's first proposal in *Pride and Prejudice?* When he was like, 'Oh, you're so beneath me, Miss Elizabeth and I really shouldn't do this because you're from a disgraceful family and wanting to marry you goes against all reason and logic and will *besmirch* my good name—but, hey, will you marry me?'"

Sarah chuckles. "Yes, I remember it well because you've made me watch that movie, like, three times with you."

"Well, it was just like that. 'Oh, Kat. I have no desire to marry you whatsoever and I'm doing you a *huge* favor and I don't want our child *at all* and you're so *lucky* I'm asking you because I'm *so* rich and amazing, but, hey, will you marry me?'" I wave my hands in the air. "It totally sucked donkey balls."

Sarah nods. "Sounds pretty shitty."

"And not only that, he had the audacity to ask me if the baby is his." My cheeks turn hot at the memory.

Sarah shrugs. "Okay, you just lost me. Why was that such a dastardly thing to ask?"

I'm appalled. "Sarah, he was basically calling me a slut."

"Uh, *no*, he was asking if the baby is his. Not quite the same thing as calling you a slut."

"Josh is the only guy I've been with and he knows it," I say, full of indignation.

"Oh, well, then, you're absolutely right: Josh should never have double-checked the baby he was about to support for the rest of his life, financially and otherwise, is definitely his." Sarah shoots me a scolding look. "Cut him a little slack, honey—I'm sure Josh was just totally blindsided. Plus, you'd be the first to admit you're no virgin. I don't blame Josh for at least asking the question, Kat. I really don't."

I open my mouth to refute her, but then I shut it. God, I hate it when it turns out I've been wrong about something. "Why are you *always* so damned nice, Sarah?" I ask. "It's really annoying."

"I'm not that nice."

"Please don't say that. Because if you're not really, really nice, then that means I'm really, really bitchy."

Sarah laughs. "Okay, I'm really, really nice."

The door opens and my doctor, a slender woman with brown skin and salt and pepper hair, enters the room.

"Hi, Doctor Gupta," I say, shaking her hand. "This is my best friend, Sarah —soon to be Auntie Sarah."

The doctor shakes Sarah's hand and smiles at me. "Are you ready to see your baby, Kat?"

"Heck yeah. How about you Auntie Sarah? You ready to see your niece or nephew?"

Sarah squeals and claps.

After spreading some gel on my stomach, the doctor runs the wand of the sonogram machine over my stomach, and a swirling image of what might as well be outer space comes up onscreen.

"What's that?" I ask, pointing.

"One moment," the doctor says, maneuvering. "Okay. This is your uterus, Kat. And right there? That's your baby."

"Wow," Sarah says, putting her hand to her mouth.

"That's my *baby*?" I ask.

"Yep. He or she is just about the size of a grape."

I look at Sarah. "My baby's a grape."

"Grape Ape," Sarah says.

I bite my lip, too overwhelmed to speak further.

"And do you see that bit of flickering right there?" the doctor continues. "That's the baby's heartbeat. Oh, it's nice and strong—exactly what we like to see."

Sarah makes a sound of wonderment. "Hey, we should take a video of this for Josh."

"Oh, good idea," I say. "My phone's in my purse."

Sarah pulls out my phone and aims it at the screen. "Okay, *action*. Doctor, will you explain what's onscreen for the baby's father?"

"Of course." The doctor motions to the screen and explains everything, and when she's done, Sarah pans the camera to me.

"Hi, Josh," I say, waving. "Well, it looks like our accidental Faraday is a stubborn little thing—surprise, surprise! I guess he or she's decided they're not going anywhere, after all." I try to smile but tears unexpectedly prick my eyes. Goddammit. Josh must hate me. I'm the one who missed my pill, after all, not him. He trusted me to protect him from the one thing that freaked him out the most and I let him down. I wipe my eyes. "I'm really sorry, Josh," I squeak out.

Sarah turns off the video recorder. "I'm gonna edit that last part out. You have nothing to apologize for, Kat. It takes two to tango."

"No. Leave it in. I forgot to take my pill—and now I've totally ruined his life. I owe him an apology."

"You haven't ruined his life," the doctor interjects, her tone firm. "You've *blessed* it immeasurably. He just doesn't know it yet."

Tears fill my eyes at these unexpectedly kind words from the doctor. "Thank you," I say softly.

Sarah squeezes my hand. "Listen to the doctor. She went to medical school and everything."

Doctor Gupta smiles warmly. "Kat, I've seen many women in your shoes. If you had a crystal ball and could see yourself a year from now, I think you'd be surprised in a good way."

I manage a smile. "Thank you."

The doctor turns back to the machine. "Now. Based on what I'm seeing here, you're about nine weeks along, which makes your due date... December second, give or take two weeks on either side."

"*Oh*," I say, my mood instantly getting a lift. "December second is *Sagittarius*," I say.

"Is that good?" Sarah asks.

I nod. "Same as Henny."

"Oh, that *is* good."

"It's a fire sign. A Sag is adventurous, creative, and passionate. Loves to travel. Makes friends easily. Funny as hell. But also can be bossy and impulsive as hell—especially a female Sagittarius. A female Sag can be hell on wheels."

Sarah raises an eyebrow. "Sounds like the grape isn't gonna fall far from the vine." She addresses the doctor. "Can you tell if the grape is a boy or girl?"

"Not yet. We'll probably be able to determine gender at around twenty weeks."

"Okay, I'm calling it right now," Sarah says, putting up her hand. "You're having a girl."

"You think?"

"I *know*. And do you know *how* I know? Because I believe in God—and if there's one person in this world who karmically deserves to wind up with a hell-on-wheels daughter, it's you, Kat."

"Hey, did you just insult me?" I ask.

Sarah laughs. "Not at all."

The doctor takes the sonogram wand off my belly and cleans up the gel on my skin. "Do you have any questions, Kat?"

"A couple." I take a deep breath, gathering my nerve. "Before I found out I was pregnant, I drank some booze—quite a bit, actually. I was in Las Vegas. When will I know if I gave the baby alcohol-fetus-whatever-whatever?"

"Fetal alcohol syndrome?"

"Yeah, that."

"There's no way to know for sure until later, but the odds are low. In the vast majority of unplanned pregnancies, the mother has consumed alcohol and there's absolutely no ill effect. We'll keep an eye on things, and if there's any sign of a problem, we'll do more testing later."

"Okay," I say, exhaling.

"At this point, I'd put it out of your mind and not worry at all—although, of course, I want you to abstain from alcohol for the remainder of your pregnancy."

"And is it the same answer if I smoked pot once, too?"

Sarah looks surprised.

"Well," the doctor says, doing a much better job of keeping a poker face than Bugs Bunny to my left. "There are no guarantees, yet again, but the chances of a problem are still low. We'll know more at the twenty-week sonogram. Of course, you should swear off all controlled substances for the remainder of your pregnancy."

"Yes, of course." I clear my throat. "It was a one-time thing."

"Any other questions?" the doctor asks.

"Yes. One more. I've had some pretty insane orgasms lately—like, really, really intense orgasms—some of them while sitting on an orgasm machine with the power of a jet engine, and—"

Sarah gasps. *"What?"*

"Long story," I say. "But, anyway, is it possible I scrambled the baby's brain or, you know, made it implode or something?"

The doctor lets out a surprised chuckle but then quickly pulls herself together. "Generally speaking, sex and orgasms aren't harmful to the fetus during pregnancy—and, in fact, orgasms arguably provide a benefit because they're stress-relieving for the mother."

I shoot Sarah a smart-ass grin. "See? I was just being a selfless mother when I sat on that jet engine and almost passed out from sexual pleasure."

Sarah blushes. "Just as all selfless mothers have done throughout the history of time, Kitty Kat."

The doctor smiles. "At this stage, you need not limit your sexual activity with yourself or a monogamous partner, although I'd definitely advise staying off that jet engine for the remainder of your pregnancy, just to be on the safe side."

"Okay," I say, pouting. "Well, that's a bummer—I like my jet engine."

"Well, then here's some good news to cheer you up," the doctor says. "As soon as your morning sickness subsides, which I predict will happen in the next few weeks, you might very well experience a dramatic increase in your sex drive."

"Whachoo talkin' about, Willis?" I say. "An *increase* in my sex drive?"

"A *dramatic* increase?" Sarah adds, her eyes wide. "Is there a level of sex drive in existence above 'Katherine Morgan'?"

Sarah and I share a laugh and the doctor can't help but giggle with us.

"And here's something else: when you do engage in sexual activity, you might also experience heightened pleasure," Doctor Gupta adds, raising her eyebrow.

I throw my hands up. "Thank you, Baby Jesus in a Wicker Basket," I say. "Finally, some fantastic news in all this. Thank you so much, Doctor."

The doctor chuckles. "So, do you have any other questions?"

"Nope. I'm good. Thank you so much."

The doctor touches my forearm. "You're going to be fine, Kat. You'll see."

96

KAT

Sarah and I settle into her car and fasten our seatbelts.

"You wanna swing by Starbucks before I take you back to your car?" Sarah asks, starting her engine.

"Great," I say. I look at my watch. "After that, I think I'll head back to the hospital to check on Colby again."

"Can I join you?" Sarah asks. "I'd love to give Colby a big hug."

"I'm sorry. I think you should visit Colby after he's home. Honestly, he's been pretty depressed lately—he doesn't really wanna see anyone but family."

"Poor Colby," Sarah says. She pulls her car out of the parking lot and heads toward the restaurant where my car is parked. "Hey, don't forget," Sarah says, "before you send that video to Josh, delete your apology at the end."

I don't reply.

"Kat. You don't owe Josh an apology for being pregnant with his child—he made that baby right along with you."

"I know he made the baby with me, but he didn't intend to take the heightened risk he did. If a girl tells a guy, 'Yes, I'm on the pill,' then she'd better be on the frickin' pill to the best of her ability." I shake my head. "Plus, I was pretty harsh with him in the hospital. You know how I get when my panties are in a twist."

Sarah makes a face that tells me she's well aware of how I get when my panties are in a twist.

"But now I realize Josh was just doing his best in a difficult situation," I say. "Oh, Sarah, I want him so much. I don't care about marriage. I don't care about the magic words. I just want Josh to be mine—I want us to love each other completely." I let out a long, tortured exhale and put my face in my hands. "Sarah, I think I might have lost him forever."

Sarah scoffs. "*No.*"

"*Yes.* He's totally pulled away from me this past week. I think he might be done with me for good."

"No, honey. Josh isn't done with you—not even close."

I look at her, tears in my eyes. "I love him, Sarah. I love him like I've never loved anyone before. I'm so scared I've lost him."

"Aw, honey."

"I want to give him everything but he's always holding back. He's always got his guard up. He never lets me in completely."

"Sounds like the Faraday twins are more alike than meets the eye." She smiles sympathetically and touches my hand. "Jonas was the same way and look at him now. He couldn't be more 'all-in.' Just be patient. Josh just needs time."

"I don't know how to be patient."

"I know, honey—but maybe it's time you learned." She purses her lips. "It's really too bad you can't get yourself stabbed by a Ukrainian hitman in a bathroom at U Dub. I really think that would do the trick."

"Damned grape spoils everything," I say. "I'd totally get myself stabbed if it weren't for the damned grape."

Sarah laughs.

"And Josh meeting my family is off the table, too, at least for a while. At this point, that would be a recipe for disaster."

Sarah makes a sympathetic face.

"So other than those two ideas, what other 'external event' could I arrange to make Josh realize he loves me and finally wants to go 'all-in'?" I ask. "Obviously, me being pregnant with his spawn didn't do the trick."

"I dunno," Sarah says. "It's gotta be something that makes Josh realize you love him completely—like, you know, *unconditionally*. If you can convince him he's completely safe with you, no matter what, then maybe he'll feel like he can finally let go and love you the same way in return."

"Good idea in concept," I say. "But I have no idea what that 'something' would be." I bite the inside of my cheek and look out the car window. "Hmm."

"Hmm," Sarah agrees. "Can you think of something that would make him feel—"

"I've got it." I sit up in my seat, adrenaline flooding me. "I know exactly what to do."

"Well, that was fast. What is it?" Sarah asks.

A demonic smile spreads across my face.

"*What?*" Sarah asks. "Oh my God—*what?*"

"I can't tell you," I say. "It's too personal. But trust me, it's something that's gonna make Josh realize I'm one hundred percent all-in—and also that I'm the woman of his dreams."

"You're smiling devilishly," Sarah says.

"Because I'm thinking something *devilish.*"

"Gimme a hint," Sarah says.

"Oh, little Miss Sarah Cruz, you couldn't handle it, trust me—your head would explode."

Sarah makes an adorable face. "God, you scare me," she says.

I look out the window of Sarah's car again, my skin sizzling and popping with electricity, a happy smile dancing on my lips for the first time in a week. *Yes.* I know exactly what to do to coax Joshua Faraday to finally let go completely. I've just got to make him see he's absolutely safe with me, in every conceivable way—that I love every little molecule of him, no matter how perverted.

My smile broadens.

They say the way to a man's heart is through his stomach. But in the case of my beloved sick fuck, Joshua William Faraday, I'm quite certain the entry point into his tortured heart is through an organ just a tad bit lower on his anatomy.

97

JOSH

I think Kat was put on this earth to torture me.

Goddammit, I don't just want her. I don't just miss her. I *crave* her like a drug.

I look up from the report I'm writing on my laptop and rub my forehead. Fuck, I can't concentrate worth a shit. I should have finished this stupid report three days ago, but I can't seem to trudge through it. I peer at my screen, just to see if whatever the fuck I've been writing for the past hour makes a lick of sense. For all I know, I've been writing, "Goobledoobledabbah" over and over. Fuck me.

I lean back in my chair.

Why'd I have to give in to my addiction and call Kat two hours ago? I thought hearing her voice would make me feel better, maybe take the edge off the pain I've been feeling all week, but all it did was torture me and make me crave her even more.

I blame 3 Doors Down, the bastards. "Here Without You" came on just as I was texting with Kat about how depressed Colby is, and the next thing I knew, I was texting Kat she could bring a smile to any man's face, and then, right after that, hastily pressing the button to call her, stupidly throwing an entire week's worth of self-imposed Kat-rehab out the fucking window.

"Theresa," I say, looking at my longtime personal assistant across the room. She's standing in my kitchen, cataloging a bunch of stuff that's about to be loaded onto the moving truck out front. "You got any Ibuprofen?"

"Of course." Theresa rummages into her purse and hands me a couple pills and a bottle of water from the fridge.

"Make it four," I say.

She hands me two additional pills.

"Thanks." I swallow the pills and look down at my computer.

"You've got a headache?" Theresa asks.

"I'm fine," I say. But I'm a liar. I'm not fine. In fact, I'm a wreck. And I've been a fucking wreck all week long, ever since I dragged my sorry, rejected, confused ass out of the hospital and onto the next flight back to L.A. I was so shattered by Kat's rejection of me that night, so overwhelmed at the bomb she'd dropped on me, I made a decision that very night to quit her once and for all. *If she's my addiction,* I thought, *then I'll just send myself to motherfucking rehab.*

Of course, I knew it'd be hard to quit a fucking unicorn, especially a unicorn tinged with a delicious streak of evil—a unicorn who happens to be the most exciting and incredible woman I've ever been with—a unicorn who sets the gold standard for turning me on—a unicorn who laughs like a dude and thinks like a terrorist and has a sexy little indentation in her chin that drives me wild. But I truly thought I could do it. I'm a fucking Faraday, after all, and, as my dad always used to drill into me, "Faradays never fucking quit." (Other than when they blow their brains out or drive off a bridge, I guess).

"Josh, sorry to bug you," Theresa says. A couple movers walk between us holding one of my black leather couches, and she pauses to let them pass before speaking. "The interior designer asked if we could move our consultation at the new house from Wednesday to the following Monday? She's got a family emergency."

After six years of running my life, Theresa surely must know what I'm going to say in response to her question. But, okay, I'll say it anyway. "If I happen to be in town on Monday, I'll be there," I reply. "If not, handle it for me. Just make the house look the way I like it—masculine, sleek, expensive, and in good taste—like it popped out of a glossy magazine."

"Okeedoke," Theresa says. "Gotcha."

I look down at my laptop again.

"Just one more thing," Theresa says.

I look up, annoyed.

"Your cars won't arrive at the new house until Tuesday at the earliest. So I went ahead and rented you a Ferrari 458 until then. It'll be sitting in your garage when you arrive in Seattle. Keys on your kitchen counter. I've arranged a limo to pick you up from the airport."

I nod and look back down at my laptop. I have no idea what Theresa just said. I think she said she rented me a Ferrari, but I'm not sure. I can't think. I can't track. Shit. I can't eat or sleep or breathe. I'm losing my fucking mind. *Kat, Kat, Kat.* She's all I can think about. I'm drowning in an all-consuming ache. I need to see her. Touch her. Fuck her. Smell her. Bite her. Spank her. I'm dying. I actually think I might literally be dying. This week has been goddamned fucking hell.

"Hey, Miss Rodriguez?" one of the moving guys asks. "Sorry to bug ya, but is this painting—"

"Yes, that's one of the items that was purchased by the new owner and will stay with the house," Theresa says, hopping up from her stool with obvious exasperation. "Put that painting down and come with me. I'm gonna show you which artwork stays and which goes *again*."

My phone buzzes with an incoming text and I look down.

Kat.

My heart leaps. This is the first time all week Kat's instigated contact with me.

"Hi, Josh," Kat writes. "Just finished my doctor's appointment. Attaching a video of the sonogram. XOXO Kat. P.S. I told Sarah about the baby at lunch and she went to the appointment with me. Sorry. It just slipped out." She attaches a blushing-face emoji. "P.P.S. I'd strongly advise you NEVER send me into war with any classified information. Oh, and Sarah says she won't tell Jonas about the baby—she'll leave that to you. But she says you better tell your brother he's going to be an uncle soon—because even though Sarah's not nearly as big a blabbermouth as me (but who is?), she's still only human."

I shake my head. It's so *Kat* to insist we hold off telling Jonas and Sarah about the pregnancy until after their wedding and then go right ahead and blab about it to Sarah not five minutes later. I press play on the video, still shaking my head, completely annoyed.

"Doctor," Sarah's voice says, "will you explain what's onscreen for the baby's father?"

My entire body jolts at Sarah's use of the word "father." Holy fuck. Sarah's referring to *me*.

The doctor explains what's onscreen, including pointing out a flicker she says is the baby's heartbeat—what the fuck?—the baby's got a *heartbeat* already?—and when the doctor's finished talking, the camera pans to Kat.

Kat.

Oh my God.

My heart wrenches at the sight of her. She's lying on an examination table, her blouse pulled up, her golden hair splayed around her head—and her eyes looking as sad and lackluster as I've ever seen them. Oh my God. My heart's absolutely breaking at the pitiful, lonely, *tortured* look in Kat's beautiful blue eyes.

Instantly, all the anger I've been feeling toward Kat this week evaporates into thin air. I can't get over how unhappy my gorgeous Party Girl looks—and utterly exhausted, too. Clearly, she's not well. She's still hot as hell, of course—she's Katherine Ulla Morgan, after all—but I've never seen Kat look quite so ragged. So *vulnerable*. So fucking *miserable*. Even when she was hung-over and functioning on three hours of sleep in Vegas, even when she was scared to death to walk into a bank and impersonate a Ukrainian pimpstress, *even when she found out I didn't tell her about my move to Seattle*, Kat never looked quite the way she does in this video.

"Hi, Josh," Kat says toward the camera, waving half-heartedly. "Well, it looks like our accidental Faraday is a stubborn little thing—surprise, surprise! I guess he or she's decided they're not going anywhere, after all." Emotion overwhelms her all of a sudden. She wipes her eyes. "I'm really sorry, Josh," Kat says, her voice wobbling.

The video abruptly ends.

I lean back in my chair, my heart exploding with yearning and regret and sympathy. Oh my God. *Kat.* My Party Girl with a Hyphen. My beautiful unicorn.

The woman I love.

Oh my God, yes. It's suddenly as obvious to me as the nose on my face: *I love Kat.* I don't know why it's taken me so long to realize it. I love Katherine Ulla Morgan and I can't live another day without her. I can't fucking *breathe* without her. Jesus Fucking Christ. What the fuck have I been doing this whole past week, staying away from the woman I love? I should have been comforting her—taking care of her—telling her we're in this cluster-fuck of a situation together. I should have been strong enough—compassionate enough—*man enough*—to tell the voices in my head to shut the fuck up.

I feel like the earth has suddenly broken off its axis and hurtled uncontrollably into space. Oh my God. *I love Kat*—and I should have been there for her this whole past week while she was dealing with Colby's injuries and the shit-storm her life's become, rather than sitting around moping and wallowing in self-pity and fear. Oh my God. I'm such a prick. An immature, self-involved, pussy-ass of a little prick.

I pick up my phone, adrenaline coursing through my body.

"Hi," Kat says softly, answering after one ring.

"Hi," I reply. "I got your video, Kat—I saw the grape."

Kat exhales. "I'm so sorry, Josh." She lets out a little yelp.

My heart squeezes. "You have nothing to apologize for," I say, emotion overwhelming me. "I'm the one who's sorry."

"You? But I'm the one who forgot to take my pill."

"Kat, so what? Birth control pills aren't one hundred percent effective in the best-case scenario. So we took a *slightly* higher risk than I'd originally realized. It was a fucking *accident.*"

"But you trusted me and I screwed up."

I scoff. "Who could remember to take a pill with the schedule we were keeping in Vegas? Seriously, Kat, if the situation were reversed, I would have missed a whole *week's* worth of pills, I guarantee it."

Kat lets out a little whimper.

"Whatever the increased odds were after missing one pill, I'm sure I would have taken them in advance, I just wanted to fuck you so goddamned much."

Kat laughs through tears.

"I'm sorry I've been a prick this week—I guess I had some shit to work out."

"You haven't been a prick—you've just been extremely *polite.*"

"I made you feel like you're alone in this, and you're not."

Kat sniffles loudly but doesn't say anything for a long beat. "I thought maybe you were done with me, Josh. I was scared you didn't want me anymore."

"Done with you? Are you mad? No fucking way."

Kat breathes a huge sigh of relief.

"Are you done with *me*?" I ask, holding my breath.

"No fucking way," she says. "I'll never be done with you, Josh. *Never.*"

My heart lurches like a guard dog on a leash. "So, hey, how 'bout that grape," I say. "Pretty crazy, huh?"

"Crazy corn chowder," Kat replies.

"That's a total Henn-ism, you know."

"I think that's where I got it." She sniffles again.

"Seeing the baby's heartbeat made everything seem so *real*," I say softly.

"Totally," she agrees. "This shit is real, man."

"Crazy."

"You know, it's so weird," she says quietly, "but when I saw the heartbeat, I started feeling protective about the grape—like I don't want anything to happen to it, after all."

"Immortality through reproduction, remember? It's evolution, baby."

"But I've never wanted a baby. I don't even think babies are cute. They just look like tiny old men."

"Your heart's answering the call of the wild, babe."

"But it's so unlike me."

"Yeah, I guess we're both doing things we never thought we'd do, huh?" I pause, hoping Kat will address her soul-crushing rejection of me in the hospital, but she doesn't. "So, hey, PG," I say, clearing my throat. "It turns out I'm moving on Wednesday."

"Yay," she says.

"I've got to see you," I say, my heart racing. Fuck me. That's the understatement of the century.

"Shoot," Kat says. "Wednesday's not good for me. Colby's getting out of the hospital and my entire family's gonna hang out with him. Can we do Thursday?"

"Thursday it is. I'll text you my new address. Seven o'clock?"

"Great. I can't wait to see your new house." She pauses. "I can't wait to see *you*."

"Same here. I've missed you," I say. I clutch my chest. Jesus, I can barely breathe.

"Josh, I've missed you so much," she whispers. "I've been feeling like I'm *dying*."

"Me, too, babe. Exactly. I've been in physical pain without you. You have no idea."

I can hear her smiling over the phone line, even as she sniffles. "Really?"

"Hell yes. I've been miserable."

"Me, too," she says softly. She sniffles again. "I'll be counting the minutes until Thursday. And maybe Friday, too? Because... you'll be living here, so . . ?"

"Yep. Absolutely," I say, breathing a sigh of relief. "You'll be seeing me so much, you'll get sick of me. I promise."

Kat sniffles again. "Impossible. I could never get sick of you. *Ever*."

My heart squeezes.

"Okay. Well. I gotta go," Kat says. "I'm gonna hang up and sob my eyes out now."

"Okay, babe. Have fun. Call me later."

"I will," Kat says. "I can't wait to see you."

"I can't wait to see you, too. I miss you so much, babe."

"I miss you, too—so, so, so, so much."

"Don't be sad anymore, Kat. I'm here now—and I'm not going anywhere."

She starts bawling on the other end of the line and my heart shatters at the sound of her wails.

"It's okay, baby," I coo. "I'm right here. Don't cry, beautiful. I'll see you really soon."

"Okay. I gotta go," she murmurs, obviously still crying. "I'll call you later after I pull myself together."

"Wait, baby. Don't go," I say. "Don't leave like this. You're crying."

"No, I'm okay. I gotta go. I wanna have an ugly cry on my own."

"Okay, baby," I say. "But call me again soon."

We hang up and I sit, staring at my phone for a long moment. Oh my fucking God. I love her. I love Kat with all my heart and soul. And I'm gonna tell her so on Thursday—the way I should have told her at the hospital if I'd had an ounce of sense.

Kat was absolutely right to turn me down at the hospital. Actually, I never should have proposed in the first place—I know that now. I have no genuine desire to get married—I was just trying to appease the ghost of my father—get his absolution from the grave. But fuck that. My father's not here to disown me anymore, and even if he were, I'd tell him to fuck off. Okay, fine, I've got a hot baby-momma-girlfriend. So fucking what? It's not the end of the world. We'll figure it out. The most important thing is that I love her—I know that now. *I love Kat*. And when I see her on Thursday, I'm gonna tell her exactly how I feel, no holds barred—and I don't need a fucking ring and the promise of a stupid piece of paper from the government to do it. I'll tell her straight from my heart and soul. Oh shit. I've suddenly got a brilliant idea. Oh my God, I'm a fucking genius. I close my laptop and leap up from the table, a surge of adrenaline flooding me. "I'm going out, T-Rod!" I call to Theresa in the back of the house.

"Hang on," Theresa's voice calls from another room.

"Gotta go!" I yell, bounding toward the front door. "I've got something important to do!"

"Hang on a sec," Theresa says, entering the room breathlessly. She's holding a cardboard box.

"Sorry, T-Rod," I say, striding toward the front door. "I've got something I've got to do."

"Just take a quick peek at this stuff, Josh." She holds up the box. "The movers were about to load this stuff onto the truck and I thought you might want to pull a few things out to take with you on Wednesday."

"No. Whatever that stuff is, they can load it onto the truck."

"But the truck's gonna take four or five days to get to Seattle. Is there anything here you want to have with you the first night in your new house—you know, something to make it feel like home on your first night there?"

I'm exasperated. A house is just a house, for fuck's sake—there's no such thing as a home. But, fine. Anything to make Theresa happy. I peek inside the box and half-heartedly rummage through its contents for half a second. "Nope. Nothing I care—" I shut my mouth. Oh. Yep. There's one thing I care about. A whole lot, in fact. I pull it out reverently. "Just this," I say. I run my fingertip over the three smiling faces gazing back at me from the framed photo. "Don't let them load this onto the truck—I'll take it with me in my bag."

Theresa nods. "I'll put it into your carry-on—inside pocket. Don't forget it's there, okay? You don't want it to break."

"Thanks."

"Of course."

I turn toward the front door again. "Hey, T-Rod," I say, turning back around to face her. Why don't you give yourself a raise? Maybe, I dunno, twenty-five percent?"

Theresa smiles. "Thank you. Very generous of you."

"And, hey, can you do something for me?"

"It's my reason for living, Josh."

"Arrange a romantic dinner-for-two at my new place in Seattle for Thursday night. Seven o'clock. I'm talking a top-rated chef, a waiter in a tux, flowers everywhere, candles all over the place—the whole nine yards. You know, a five-star-dining experience, but right in my own dining room."

"No problem. But the truck won't be there with your furniture until Saturday. I'll have to rent some furniture for the night—at least a table and chairs."

"Great. And as long as you're renting stuff, would you rent me a pool table for a couple nights? I might wanna play pool before my table arrives—it always helps me relax."

"Sure."

"Oh, and rent me a really comfortable bed for Thursday night—a *really* nice one. Pillow-top mattress. Silk sheets. You know, the whole nine yards."

"Josh, just a little tip: you never need to say the phrase 'the whole nine yards' to me. I know when it comes to you there are only two gears in everything you do: zero and 'the whole nine yards.'"

I laugh.

"Speaking of which, what do you think about a violinist to play during dinner?"

"Ooh. I like that. Do it."

"I'll set it up," Theresa says.

"Just do whatever you have to do to make me look really good, T."

"Don't I always, Josh? Speaking of which, I just bought you three new Anthony Franco suits from his new collection, already tailored to fit you to a tee. Do you want them loaded onto the truck or sent in a garment bag with you on the plane?"

"Is one of them blue, by any chance?"

She grins. "Of course. Sapphire blue to match your eyes."

"Garment bag for the blue one, truck for the others. I'll wear the blue one Thursday night." I wink. "Gotta look sharp for my big night."

"Oh, it's a big night?"

"It sure is. I'm finally gonna talk about my fucking feelings—to a *girl*."

"To a *girl*? Ooooh. Wow. That *is* big." She beams a huge smile at me. "Lucky girl."

"That's what I told her."

Theresa laughs.

"I'm not kidding, unfortunately. That's exactly what I told her."

Theresa grimaces.

"Yeah. So now I've got my work cut out for me to get myself out of the doghouse."

"Ooph. I think we'd better add a cellist. Sounds like an emergency."

My smile broadens. "Thanks, T."

"You're very welcome, Josh."

"I mean, you know, thanks for everything."

"Just doing my job."

"Hey, how about we make that raise thirty percent? Sound good?"

Theresa makes a "meh" face. "Well, thirty percent is certainly *good*. Nothing to sneeze at—believe me, I'm grateful for your generosity. But you only live once, right? Why not 'go big or go home,' I always say?"

"Ah, you want 'the whole nine yards,' huh, T?"

Theresa laughs. "You've rubbed off on me, I guess."

"Okay. Forty percent. But that's my final offer."

Theresa nods. "I think that sounds about right." She winks.

I laugh. "Okay. Forty it is—until the next time you squeeze me, that is." With that, I turn around and waltz out my front door, a spring in my step and a gleam in my eye for the first time in an entire fucking week.

98

JOSH

"Six-ball in the side pocket," I say. I bend over the pool table and sink my shot with a loud clack.

"Kat turned you *down?*" Jonas says, incredulous.

"Third worst day of my entire life," I say. "She hit me with a mean left cross followed by a crushing right hook. *Bam!* Right on the chin."

"I can only imagine. Sounds horrible, Josh."

"Four-ball off the bumper, ricochet off the seven-ball into the corner pocket, " I say. I line up my shot carefully, whack the white cue ball with confidence, and sink the four, exactly as described. "Damn, I'm good," I say.

"Pretty impressive."

"My life may be falling down around my ears, but I can still sink a goddamned billiard ball, motherfucker."

"Sorry I wasn't here for you when all this shit was happening. Sounds like you took it pretty hard."

"No worries, bro. 'Twas merely a flesh wound. I'm over it now—back in the saddle. Two-ball in the far corner—straight shot." I bend down over the table and take my shot, but I've miscalculated the angle by a hair and the ball rebounds off the bumper. "Shit," I say. "Goddammit. I always miss the easy ones." I motion to Jonas. "Okay, go ahead and run the table now, bro. I'll just sit down for the rest of the game."

"You never know," Jonas says, rubbing chalk on the end of his stick. "I haven't played in months—I might be rusty."

"Mmm hmm," I say, leaning against the wall. "You've never been rusty at anything in your life."

Jonas walks around the table, surveying his first shot. "I'm thinking the seven-ball off the bumper right here and then off your two-ball into the side pocket," Jonas says.

"Pfft. Good luck with that—tough angle, bro. Just do the three. The three's a clean shot."

"No, the three's a red herring. If I sink the seven first, then I'll have my whole table set up for me like clockwork."

"If you say so."

"Oh, I do." Jonas bends over, takes his complicated shot, and sinks it with ease.

"Goddamn, you." I roll my eyes. "I hate playing against you. Against everyone else, I'm a fucking beast."

"I'm sure you are. So how far along is she?"

"Almost ten weeks."

Jonas whistles. "Wow."

"Last week, the baby was the size of a grape. This week, it's already the size of a kumquat." I can't help smiling to myself. *The Kumquat's carrying a kumquat.*

"Good to see you smiling about it."

I pause, surprised. "It's actually kind of amazing how fast a guy can adjust to a new reality when there's no other option," I say.

"Happiness depends upon ourselves,'" Jonas says.

"Gosh, thanks, Plato."

"Aristotle. You want Plato?"

"No," I say.

"'There are two things a person should never be angry at: what they can help, and what they cannot.'"

"Incredibly profound," I say. "I feel magically better now. Hey, you wanna see something wild?" I pull out my phone and show Jonas the sonogram video Kat sent me the other day.

"Sarah was there?" Jonas asks at the sound of Sarah's voice asking the doctor to explain the image on the sonogram screen.

"Yeah. Kat blabbed to her at lunch right before her doctor's appointment. I guess Sarah didn't wanna steal my thunder by telling you—she thought I should break the news to you." I put my hands out like ta-da! "'Hey, Jonas—you're gonna be an uncle!'" I say with faux excitement. "There, I told you."

Jonas shakes his head. "I'm impressed Sarah was able to keep such a big secret."

"Kat couldn't keep a secret to save her life," I say, rolling my eyes. "Actually, I wouldn't have minded Sarah telling you. I wish I could crawl under a rock and not have to tell anyone, to be honest."

"You're not jumping for joy about your impending fatherhood, I take it?"

"Pretty much shitting a brick."

"So when's the baby due?" Jonas asks. He calls another shot and sinks it with ease, yet again, and I place my stick on a rack in the corner in utter resignation.

"December second," I reply. "Sagittarius."

"Sagittarius?"

"Just like Henn."

Jonas laughs. "Oh, shit. That'd be funny if you had a kid just like Henn."

I can't help but join Jonas laughing. That really would be funny.

"So do you believe all that astrology stuff?" Jonas asks.

I shrug. "Sort of. Kat's kind of made a believer out of me, actually."

Jonas surveys the table, lining up his next shot. "I can't believe you're gonna be a father, Josh."

"So I'm told."

Jonas stands upright from the table and assesses me for a long beat. "You're gonna be a fantastic father."

My cheeks feel hot all of a sudden. "You really think so?"

"I *know* so. You were born to be a father, Josh—more than anyone I know. It's in your DNA—you got it from Mom. You take care of people—it's who you are—who you've always been."

"Wow. Thank you."

"It's the God's truth. That's one lucky kid."

I bite my lip. "Thanks, Jonas."

Jonas leans over the pool table again, assessing his next shot. "Can you even imagine what Dad would be saying right now? 'I'll disown you faster than that gold-digger can demand a paternity test!'"

"Dude, stop, please. I don't have to imagine it—I've been hearing Dad's voice screaming in my ear since Kat dropped the baby-bomb on me."

Jonas calls his next shot and sinks it with ease.

"Mr. Faraday?"

I look toward the door. It's the violinist Theresa hired for me, a petite Asian woman in a black dress.

"The cellist and I are all set up in the dining room," the woman says. "Do you want us to stay hidden in the kitchen until your signal, or... how do you wanna play this?"

I look at my watch. Kat should be here in just under thirty minutes. "I think you should start playing the minute my girlfriend walks through the front door —you know, set the mood right away that this is gonna be a magical night for her."

"Okay, great," the violinist says. "We'll just stand in position and wait for your signal, then."

"Why don't you start playing the minute the doorbell rings? That can be your signal."

"Perfect. Oh, and the chef wanted me to tell you he's all ready, too. He has a few questions."

"Great. Will you tell him I'll be right out? I'm about to get my ass whooped. Shouldn't take too long."

She chuckles and leaves.

"Wow, you're really going balls to the wall here," Jonas says. "Flowers. Candles. Chef. Violin. Cello. I gotta get everyone's contact info from you—Sarah would go nuts for something like this."

"Email T-Rod and ask her for the info—she set everything up for me."

Jonas leans down and lines up his next shot. "Well, yeah, I figured."

"She just gouged me for a forty percent raise, by the way. The woman's a shark."

"She deserves every penny."

I laugh. "True."

"Oh, which reminds me—thanks for the bottle of champagne and fruit basket you sent to Sarah and me in Mykonos to congratulate us on our engagement. So thoughtful of you."

We both burst out laughing.

"You're so welcome," I say. "It was the least I could do."

"I ought to chip in for half of Theresa's raise. Half the shit you do for me is probably her."

"I'm not gonna dignify that with a response," I say, though he's one hundred percent right.

"One-ball in the side pocket," Jonas says, just before sinking the shot. "So did Theresa help you pick out Kat's ring, too? Something that'll 'sear her corneas'—I believe was the phrase you used when you nagged me about it?"

"Oh, no," I say, scoffing. "I'm not *proposing* to Kat tonight. I'm not a fucking masochist. I already asked her once and she practically flipped me the bird. Getting disemboweled once by Kat was plenty, thank you very much."

"What the fuck did you say to Kat when you asked her? I don't understand why she said no."

"Actually, I think her exact words were, 'I wouldn't marry you if you were the last goddamned man on earth.'"

Jonas grimaces. "Wow, that's pretty harsh."

"That's Kat for you—you never wonder where you stand with her."

"Josh, seriously. Why'd she turn you down? I don't understand. You love each other, right? And she's carrying your baby. So it should be a no-brainer—you two should get married."

I shrug. "I pissed her off. It's not hard to do—trust me. And now she doesn't wanna marry me. Which is fine because I don't wanna get married." I motion to the pool table. "Take your shot, bro. Kat will be here soon."

"But if you're not gonna ask Kat to marry you tonight, then what the fuck are you doing with the violin and the chef?"

I grin. "Tonight's gonna be even better than a marriage proposal. I'm giving Kat a once-in-a-lifetime gift—and then I'm finally gonna tell her the three little words."

Jonas raises his eyebrows, clearly surprised. "You haven't already told her you love her?"

My stomach clenches. He's making me feel insecure. "No. I'm gonna tell her tonight. Plus, like I said, I'm gonna give her a gift she'll never forget."

"But you already asked her to marry you."

"Correct."

"I'm totally confused. You proposed *marriage* to Kat without telling her you *love* her?"

I nod, suddenly feeling sick to my stomach. It sounds so wrong when he says it in that holier-than-thou tone of voice.

Jonas scowls at me. "You said 'Will you marry me, Kat?' but you didn't also say 'I love you more than the air I breathe, Kat'?"

I nod. I wish he'd drop it already.

"Josh, what the fuck did you say to Kat when you asked her to marry you? I can't for the life of me fathom what you said if it didn't include the words 'I love you more than life itself and I can't live without you.'"

I shift my weight. I feel my cheeks flushing. "I just told her, you know..."

Jonas waits for me to finish my sentence, and when I don't, he shakes his head at me, bends over the table, and lines up his next shot. "Nine-ball off the ten, then off the side, and then into the side pocket." He sinks his shot in one fluid, confident motion.

"Why do I even bother playing pool with you?" I say. "If I don't run the table out of the gate, I might as well just sit the fuck down. It's pointless."

"Three in the far corner." He bends over and sinks his shot. "How could you possibly propose marriage to a woman and *not* tell her you love her in the same breath?"

I roll my eyes. "Jonas, come on. I'd just found out Kat's pregnant with my accidental spawn. I was a deer in headlights. Love was the furthest thing from my mind. I was just trying to do the right thing."

Jonas grimaces. "Well, shit. No wonder Kat turned you down—rightfully so, you dumbshit." He calls his next shot and sinks it with startling ease.

"Yeah, fuck it—it doesn't matter. It all worked out for the best," I say, feeling defensive. "Kat really did me a big favor by saying no. I didn't know it then, of course—at the time, it felt like Kat was kicking me in the teeth—but now I see she was the only one thinking clearly. Holy shit, I can't believe I just said that about *Kat*."

Jonas stands completely upright and rests his hands on the end of his pool cue, staring at me intensely. "Do you love her?" he asks.

"Yeah. I do. Without a doubt."

"And she's carrying your baby?"

I nod. "Yeah, we've already established that fact. I showed you the video, remember?"

"Then *marry* the girl, for fuck's sake, Josh. It's not that complicated."

I exhale in exasperation.

"Josh, Kat obviously turned you down because you were asking her out of obligation, not love. If you ask her again, but this time tell her you love her, she'll say yes—I guarantee it."

I wave Jonas off. "I'm not gonna ask Kat again. Once was enough. The truth is I have no interest in getting married, not even to Kat. If I wanna be with someone, I'll be with them. And if I wanna go, then I'll go. And it's the same for her. I think it's more satisfying to know the other person's there because they *want* to be—not because they *have* to be based on some stupid piece of paper from the government."

Jonas shakes his head but he doesn't speak. After a moment, he surveys the table again. "Eight-ball, rebounding off your two, and then into the far right corner." He sinks his shot and wins the game.

"Goddammit, Jonas. I hate playing against you."

Jonas puts his stick on the rack, his jaw muscles tight.

"What?" I ask.

"Nothing."

"Dude, I can tell you've got something to say. Just say it."

"Nope. I've got nothing to say. Congratulations on telling Kat you love her tonight. Big step. I'm sure she'll be thrilled to hear it."

"Jonas," I say, exhaling. "You don't understand. I'm gonna support my kid, okay? I'm gonna be the best father I can be. That's a given. And I'm hopefully gonna raise the kid with Kat because I love her and wanna be with her. She's the most incredible woman I've ever been with and I can't imagine finding anyone better, ever. But I'm not the marrying kind of guy. I don't need a piece of paper *forcing* me to be with Kat—I'm gonna be with her because I *want* to be."

There's a long beat.

"Cool," Jonas says, clearly brushing me off. "Congrats. Come on. The chef wanted to talk to you, remember?"

"Yeah, and you gotta get the fuck out before Kat gets here." I look at my watch. "Kat's supposed to be here in ten minutes—which means she'll be here in thirty."

We start walking toward the dining area.

I keep expecting Jonas to say something, but he doesn't.

"What?" I finally say. "Just say it."

Jonas presses his lips together.

"Fuck, Jonas. I know what you're thinking."

"You do? What am I thinking?"

"You're thinking I should propose to Kat again. And, yeah, I know that's the way we were raised—you get a girl pregnant, you marry her. No other option. I know that's what Dad would demand of me. But I'm not beholden to Dad anymore. He's gone—he made his choice—and I'm a grown-ass man. I've decided I'm not gonna ask Kat to marry me and that's final. It's my choice. I love her, I really do, and that's enough. I've decided I'm gonna love Kat with all my heart and be committed to her and help her raise our baby and we'll just see what happens between her and me. If she wants to go, she can. Same for me." I'm breathing heavily. My chest is tight. "*What?* Stop looking at me like that."

"Mr. Faraday?" It's the chef, accompanied by a guy in a tux. "How are you this evening, sir? This is Gregory. He'll be serving you tonight."

The four of us shake hands.

"Is this your guest for the evening?" The chef asks, motioning to Jonas.

Jonas and I look at each other and laugh.

"No. This is my brother. He's just leaving. My guest will be arriving in a few minutes."

"But I'd love to get your card," Jonas says. "I'm thinking about hiring you guys as a surprise for my fiancée."

I smile at the exuberant tone of Jonas' voice when he says the word "fiancée."

"When's the wedding?" the chef asks.

"Exactly three weeks from today."

"Oh. Congratulations."

"World's shortest engagement," Jonas says, laughing. "And she's not even pregnant."

I glare at him. Low blow.

Jonas winks at me.

"So, Mr. Faraday," the chef says, addressing me. "I just had a few questions..." He runs through his menu items, making sure I'm happy with each course as he plans to prepare it, and I give him approval on everything.

"Wonderful. We'll start with a light appetizer and drink pairing when she arrives."

"Oh, I should have told you: my girlfriend's pregnant," I say. "No alcohol this evening for either of us."

"Oh. No problem. Thanks for letting me know. Congratulations."

The chef and waiter head back into the kitchen.

"Well, have fun," Jonas says, slapping my back. "I'd better get home. Sarah just sent me a text saying she misses me—always a good sign." He snickers.

"Hang on a second," I say. "We're not done." I motion to a loveseat (rented for me by Theresa), and we sit.

"What?" Jonas asks, obviously anxious to leave.

"I just... " I exhale. "I need you to understand something."

Jonas waits.

"I have no desire to get married, not even to Kat. From here on out, just don't give me a hard time about it, okay? It is what it is. I know Kat's pregnant and I know we were raised to—"

"I don't think you should ask Kat to marry you," Jonas says, interrupting me. He levels me with his startling blue eyes.

"You don't?"

"No."

"But *you're* getting married."

"Yeah, and that's exactly why I don't think you should marry Kat."

"I'm confused."

Jonas sighs. "Josh, I'm marrying Sarah in twenty-one days because I can't wait a day longer than necessary to call her my wife. I'm marrying Sarah because I can't wait to declare my undying love for her in front of God and everyone we know. I'm marrying Sarah because she's the air I breathe, the embodiment of my hopes and dreams and my every drop of happiness. Because I want Sarah to be mine, all mine, in every possible way 'til the end of time. Because I never want another man to touch her, ever again—because even the *thought* of another man touching her makes me homicidal. Because I want to be there for her, for better or worse, for richer or poorer, in sickness and in health, until death do us part—and I want to promise that to her in the most sacred way possible. I'm marrying Sarah because I don't want there to be any doubt in her mind how I feel about her, not even for a moment, for the rest of her life." He scowls at me. *"And not because I think I need a motherfucking piece of paper to tell me my love is real or official."*

I swallow hard, rendered completely speechless.

"So if you don't feel exactly the same way about Kat," Jonas continues, his eyes burning like hot coals, "if you don't want to make that woman your wife for all the reasons I just described, then she didn't just do *you* a favor by turning down your proposal—she did *herself* a favor, too."

99

JOSH

My heart is pulsing in my ears. I open my mouth and close it, but Jonas has stunned me into complete silence.

The doorbell rings and, instantly, the violin and cello begin playing.

"Oh shit," I say. "You're not supposed to be here, Jonas. You gotta get the fuck out."

"I'll go in the kitchen and slip out when you and Kat head into the dining room."

"No. That's stupid." I sigh. "Why don't you just say hi to her—you can congratulate her on the kumquat."

We move to the front door together, my head spinning. I've never been kicked so fucking hard in the teeth by Jonas in my entire life. What the fuck just happened? I feel like I'm walking through molasses with cement blocks strapped to my ankles as I trudge to the front door. I smile at the violinist and cellist as I pass them on my way to the front door, but my smile is a façade. I seriously can't breathe.

When I reach the door with Jonas a few feet behind me, I take a deep breath, gathering myself. I'm gonna give Kat an amazing gift tonight—a truly once-in-a-lifetime gift—and then I'm gonna tell her I love her. And that's a pretty big fucking deal. I just need to shake off what Jonas said—the man's clearly pussy-whipped beyond anything I could have fathomed. I just need to shake it off.

I exhale and open my front door, my heart pounding at the thought of seeing Kat after this past long, torturous week apart. This is gonna be an epic night for both of us. A new beginning. But when I swing open the door, it's not

Kat—it's the male version of her, holding a motorcycle helmet in his arm and dressed in a black leather jacket, a pair of dark jeans, and an *Rx Bandits* T-shirt.

The male version of Kat puts out his hand. "Sir J.W. Faraday, I presume?"

I shake the guy's hand.

"Hey, Josh." The guy smiles. "I'm Dax, Kat's brother?"

"Oh." I clear my throat. "Yeah. Hey, Dax. Kat's told me a lot about you. Glad to finally meet you."

Dax peeks behind me into the house. "Wow. Violin and cello. Oh, hey, do you mind if I get the musicians' contact info? I'm recording an album next week and I could totally use violin and cello on a couple of my songs."

"Uh. Sure. Yeah. Come on in." I open the door wide and Dax bounds into my house like he owns the place. "So where's Kat?" I ask.

"Oh." Dax turns around. "Sorry. I got so excited about the violin and cello, I forgot why I'm here. Kat asked me to give you this."

He hands me a sealed envelope and my heart instantly drops into my toes. *Shit.*

Kat's not coming.

I look at Jonas and he looks as crestfallen as I feel.

Kat sent her baby brother to hand me a "Dear John" letter? Is she really *that* heartless? Yes, she is, unfortunately, and I've always known it—deep down inside, I've always known this day was coming. Maybe that's why I've been holding back all this time with Kat—because I knew deep down in my bones this thing with her was just too good to last—that she'd eventually slip past my borders with a bomb strapped to her chest and blow me to fucking bits.

"Uh. This is my brother, Jonas," I manage to say, my cheeks hot.

"Hey, Dax," Jonas says, shaking Dax's hand. "Nice T-shirt. Rx Bandits is my all-time favorite band."

"Hey, mine, too. Ever seen 'em live?"

"Yup. Lots of times. Best live band ever."

I'm literally shaking. I feel like crying like a pussy-ass little bitch, but I swallow it down.

"So it's okay if I talk to your musicians real quick?" Dax says.

"Go ahead," I say, my throat tight. I call over to the violinist and cellist. "Hey, ladies, you can stop playing. It's not my girlfriend."

The music ceases.

"Well, are you gonna open the card?" Jonas asks.

I swallow hard. Part of me doesn't want to open the envelope. If Kat's decided she's done with me—*even though she's carrying my goddamned kid*—I'm not gonna bounce back any time soon. In fact, I'm gonna be in a world of fucking hurt for the rest of my fucking life, to be honest. Visions of Kat dragging my kid to baseball games with her new boyfriend flood me—images of Kat fucking another man while my baby's fast asleep in a crib in the other room. Fuck me. Based on the way I handled the whole thing with Emma, I can't even begin to imagine the human pile of rubble I'm about to become after I read this note. I absent-mindedly touch my left bicep and instantly feel an avalanche of anticipatory regret. Oh my God. I can't believe I got a fucking girlfriend tattoo mere days before my girlfriend decided to break up with me. Oh, irony of ironies—please, God, no. I shake my head at my own stupidity. Kat warned me, didn't she? "Johnny Depp had to change 'Winona Forever' to 'Wino Forever,'" Kat told me way back when. *"Don't do it."* But did I listen to her? Fuck no—of course, not. *Dumbshit.*

"Josh," Jonas says emphatically, drawing me out of my rambling thoughts. "Open the fucking envelope."

I stare at Jonas dumbly.

"Open it, for fuck's sake."

I open the envelope slowly and pull out the card—and as I do, something falls onto the floor.

Jonas bends down and picks it up—and when he straightens up, glory be, he's holding a poker chip in his palm, his eyebrow raised.

Relief and excitement flood me. Thank you, God. Kat's not a heartless terrorist—well, yeah, she is—*but she's also the woman of my dreams!*

I hastily open the notecard and read, my heart racing, my dick tingling.

"Hello there, my darling, beloved Playboy," the card reads. "The doctor said my sex drive might increase *dramatically* due to pregnancy hormones. Well, guess what? *She was right!* I'm excited to see your new house one of these days, I really am, and I sure hope you didn't go to too much trouble with dinner tonight—because there's been a change of plans, baby! Tonight, my beloved, sexy, beautiful Playboy, we're going to fulfill one of your all-time sick-fuck fantasies. That's right, honey—I hope you like windows—*wink!*—because you're about to fuck one any which way you please." Kat writes the name and address of a nearby five-star luxury hotel plus a room number. "Hurry up, my gorgeous, well-hung Playboy. Your window's waiting for you—along with her selected window dressing (*another wink!*). I guarantee you're gonna *love* how dripping wet this window is you when you get here, baby. XOXO Kat."

I look up from the note, my eyes bugging out. I'm rock hard. Oh my God.

"Good news?" Jonas asks.

"Call Sarah," I say abruptly. I grab my suit jacket off the back of the loveseat. "A romantic dinner for two just fell into your lap, bro. Enjoy." I call out to Dax over by the musicians. "Hey, Dax. Nice to meet you, man. I've gotta go—I've got an unexpected dinner date with your diabolical sister. Hopefully, we'll have a chance to talk another time."

Dax waves. "Oh, I'm sure we'll have a chance to talk one of these days, Josh —maybe at the hospital when Kat gives birth to your baby?"

I stop dead in my tracks and turn around to face him, my cheeks instantly burning.

Dax shoots me an evil smile that reminds me so much of his heinous sister, it freaks me the fuck out. "Don't worry, Sir Faraday," Dax says, still smiling. "Kat didn't tell anyone else in our family about your little 'oops'—it's just impossible for her to keep a secret from me." He winks.

I swallow hard, words failing me.

"I won't say a word to anyone," Dax adds. "I promise."

"Thanks," I manage to say.

"I'm actually gonna enjoy watching you guys tell the fam." He chuckles. "Ought to be extremely entertaining."

My stomach flips over. "Yeah. Should be a real blast."

"So, yeah, looks like we'll be seeing a lot of each other in the future, huh? Assuming, of course, you're planning to do more than write checks and attend your kid's birthday parties once a year?"

"Hey, Dax," Jonas says stepping forward, his muscles visibly tensing. "Josh would never—"

"I got this, bro," I say, putting up my hand. "Dax, I'm gonna do a whole lot more for this kid than write checks and attend birthday parties. I'm gonna be this baby's father in every sense of the word—every single day for the rest of my life. You can count on it."

Dax's face softens. "Good." He shifts his weight. "Sorry. Just looking out for my sister."

"Understandably," I say. "I'd do the same."

Dax beams me a genuine smile this time, without even a hint of evil. "You better go, man," he says. "My sister's not exactly patient."

I chuckle. "That's an understatement. She's hell on wheels, bro. But I wouldn't have her any other way."

Dax nods, seemingly pleased with that answer. "You better go."

I hug my brother goodbye—nice to know he was ready to beat the shit out of Kat's little brother for me, if necessary—gotta love Jonas—and stride into the kitchen.

"Change of plans," I say to the chef. "My brother and his fiancée will be dining tonight—so let the booze flow, after all."

The chef says something but I don't catch it. I'm too busy grabbing the keys to my rented Ferrari off the counter and racing out of the kitchen.

"Wait, Josh," Jonas yells at my back, just before I make my escape through the front door of my house. "Hang on just a sec."

I stop, though it pains me to do it.

I turn around to face my brother. "Jonas, please, I gotta go. Kat's waiting, man."

"Hang the fuck on," Jonas says. He saunters up to me slowly, clearly enjoying torturing me, and when he finally reaches me, he opens my palm and lays the poker chip inside it. "You can't meet Kat without your ticket to ride."

"Oh yeah. Thanks." I turn on my heel.

"Wait," Jonas says.

I exhale and turn around to face him again. "*What?*"

Jonas leans in and lowers his voice. "I don't know what this poker chip buys you this time, Josh, but, whatever it is, don't even *think* about calling me and asking me to play Boring Blane ever again."

Always the hooker, never the john? Is that how that old saying goes? Or maybe that's bridesmaids? Well, whatever. Either way, I just paid a woman for sex—and when I did, my clit buzzed like a bumblebee trapped inside a windowsill.

"Thank you," Bridgette says, stuffing the wad of bills I just handed her into her Fendi bag. "I sure hope this means you're gonna follow through this time."

"I already told you, Bridgette, last time Josh and I were just too early in our relationship—honestly, I was just too insecure. I gave Josh mixed signals and I think he felt the need to reassure me. But this time, I'm rarin' to go. And if *I'm* rarin' to go, Josh will be, too."

Bridgette sniffs, apparently not completely convinced.

"I wouldn't have flown you all the way up to Seattle and paid you a shitload of cash if we weren't gonna do it this time."

Bridgette narrows her eyes. "My time is valuable, you know. I'm giving you the benefit of the doubt only because you're so damned fuckable." She runs her fingertip up my arm. "Otherwise, I wouldn't have bothered."

"I give you my word. Now, stop stressing me out, Bridgette. I've never done this before and I need to relax."

Bridgette's eyes flicker. "I thought you said you'd done this once before in college?"

"Well, yeah, sort of, but it was amateur-hour. Second base only and I didn't even have an orgasm."

Bridgette's aghast. "No *orgasm?* Aw, poor little pussycat. Don't worry, I'll be sure to get you off this time." She bites her lower lip. "How about a drink to calm your nerves?"

I shake my head. "No, thanks. I'm good." I look at my watch. "Will you do me a favor and take off your clothes? Josh will be here any minute and I want to give him an insta-boner when I open the door."

Apparently, I don't have to ask Bridgette twice. I've barely gotten the words out and she's already peeling off her clothes, revealing her world-famous body underneath. "You want my bra and panties off, too, *häschen*?"

"Not yet. I'll take them off you later. We'll make a show of it."

"Ooh. Fun." She tosses her clothes on a chair and stands before me, her hands on her hips. "How's this?" She poses like the supermodel she is, jutting her hip and pushing out her breasts, and, instantly, every hair on my body stands on end.

Holy crap, Bridgette's incredible. I can't imagine any human, man or woman, straight or gay or otherwise, who wouldn't feel insanely turned-on by the sight of her almost-naked body, especially when she's posing like the super-star she is.

Bridgette tosses her blonde hair behind her shoulder. "And you?" she asks. "Let's see what you're hiding under that dress, shall we?"

"Um." I slide my hands down the front of my dress nervously. "I think I'll wait until Josh gets here to—"

There's a loud knock at the door.

"Eep!" I say, clamping my hand to my mouth.

Bridgette chuckles.

I sprint to the door and look through the peephole. "Holy shitballs, it's Josh."

"Were you expecting someone else?"

"Oh my God," I say, nervously shaking out my hands.

"What's gotten into you? You had ice in your veins last time and now you're acting like a mouse."

I take a deep breath, trying to calm myself. "Well, yeah. This time, I'm actu-ally gonna do it. Plus, I haven't seen Josh all week—it's been a bit of a rough week. He's somehow gotten hotter since I last saw him, if that's possible." I peep through the door again. "Oh my god, he looks amazing. He's wearing this incredible blue suit that fits him perfectly. Really brings out his eyes. Gah."

Bridgette laughs. "Pull yourself together, Kat. I think I liked you better when you were Heidi Kumquat."

Josh bangs on the door. "Kat?"

"Hang on!" I call through the door. "I'll be right there!"

"Take off your clothes," Bridgette says. "We're gonna give him a show, remember?"

"Oh yeah. I almost forgot." I peel off my clothes, revealing a hot pink lace bra and G-string underneath.

"Very nice," Bridgette says, blatantly ogling me.

Josh knocks again.

"Hang on!" I call through the door.

Shit. I'm suddenly wracked with nerves. I've arranged this threesome to prove to Josh I'm the anti-Emma—that I truly love him—*all of him*—even the parts that make him a sick fuck. But what if he unexpectedly pulls some caveman shit on me and declares, "Nobody touches my Party Girl with a Hyphen but me!"? A counter-move like that would undeniably stroke my ego (just like it did last time), but it certainly wouldn't get me any closer to my mission of *owning* Josh in a way no other woman ever has. By God, if it's the last thing I do, I'm gonna worm my way into Josh's damaged heart—even if I have to sneak in through a hidden trap door marked "Sick Fuck."

Josh knocks again. "Kat?" he yells through the door.

"Hang on!" I yell. "Don't forget," I say to Bridgette. "You're only allowed to touch yourself and me, but—"

"Not Josh," Bridgette interrupts. "Yes, yes, you've made that perfectly clear. I'm a hooker, you're my client, and Josh is *your* client—you've already told me all that. Trust me, I have no desire to touch that asshole ever again. I'm here for no other reason than I want to fuck you, plain and simple—so let that kinky bastard in so I can finally get my hands on you."

"Before I let him in the room, I'm gonna talk to him at the door for a minute, just me and him."

Bridgette looks at me suspiciously.

"We're not gonna ditch you, I promise."

"I'll give you five minutes, and if you don't come back into the room by then, I'm outta here."

I open the door and quickly slip my body in front of it, keeping it open just a tad with my backside.

Josh's eyes instantly blaze at the sight of me. "Please answer the door dressed like this every fucking time." He sweeps me into his arms and devours me with a passionate kiss. "Oh God, I've missed you. I was such a prick to you this week—forgive me." He takes my face in his palms and kisses me again. "I felt like I was dying without you all week long."

Oh God, I wanna tell him I love him. I'm aching to say the words, physically aching. "I've been in pain without you," I mumble into his lips, my heart racing.

"I can't live without you, baby," he replies, kissing me furiously. "I..." He pauses and every hair on my body stands on end. "I..."

I hold my breath. This is it. I can *feel* it.

"I can't live without you," he finally says.

Oh, well, not what I was hoping for, but I can't complain. I run my hands through his hair and kiss him passionately, pushing my pelvis into his hard-on.

Josh breaks away from kissing me and cranes his neck, obviously trying to look through the small gap in the door. "Why are we standing at the door?" he asks.

Oh yeah. *Bridgette.* When all the blood in my brain whooshed into my crotch, I instantly forgot all about the supermodel on the other side of the door.

"We're standing at the door because I have a surprise for you," I reply.

Josh cranes his neck to look past me again, but the crack in the door is too narrow for him to see inside. "I got your note," he breathes, his voice brimming with excitement. "You said you're gonna be my *window* tonight?" Josh looks like he's literally holding his breath.

"Yeah," I say. "I'm your window—and I've invited someone quite lovely to be our window dressing."

Josh's eyes blaze.

Oh, wow. The look of arousal on his face is making my clit zing.

"Tonight's all about you, babe," I purr, pulling away from him and stroking the hard bulge in his pants. "You've delivered all my fantasies to me, one after another on a silver platter, and now it's time for me to return the favor." Josh's erection jolts under the fabric of his pants. "Tonight, I'm gonna give you what turns you on the most, baby—no holds barred."

"*You're* what turns me on the most," he says softly, kissing my neck.

Damn, he's good. "Well, then," I say, "I'm gonna give you what turns you on the *second* most." I press the entire length of my body against his. "I wanna do it this time, babe—I really do. This isn't reverse psychology, I promise. All I wanna do is turn you on and let your sick fuck run amok."

Josh eyes me, obviously not completely convinced of my sincerity.

"I'm serious, babe. I want you to enjoy this without reservation—and so will I. Whatever gets you off, whatever it is, you can always tell me and show me and do it to me or with me, and I promise I'll never ride off on a polo pony with a guy wearing an ascot."

The look on Josh's face is priceless. I can't imagine he'd look any more touched if I'd just said, "I love you."

"As long as you don't touch her—same as before," I caution. "That's the only rule."

Josh nods, his eyes smoldering.

"So is that a yes? Are you in, my beautiful sick fuck?" I ask.

Josh nods. "I'm in."

"Excellent." I grab Josh's hand and begin pulling him through the door.

"Wait a sec," he says, dropping my hand.

I stop and stare at him, but he doesn't speak further. "What?" I finally ask.

"I... " he begins.

Oh my God, my Scooby Doo senses tell me he's about to tell me he loves me. It's on the tip of his luscious tongue—I know it. I can practically hear the words rattling around in his head like gumballs in a chute.

"What?" I whisper fiercely. "Whatever it is, just say it." I pinch the width of Josh's face between my fingers and thumb and squeeze, making his lips pucker like he's a blowfish. "Say it," I say, squeezing Josh's cheeks, trying to physically coax the words out of him.

Josh bats my hand away, chuckling. "What the fuck are you doing?"

But I'm not laughing. I feel like a woman possessed. "Say it," I coax. "*Please*, Josh."

Josh's eyes drift to the gap in the door. "Now's not the time for chitchat." He kisses me, pressing his hard bulge into me again. "I can't think straight right now, babe—you've got me too wound up, talking about windows and shit." He grins. "All I wanna do is fuck my beautiful window and make her come."

"Well, who doesn't?" I say. "The line forms behind the hot blonde inside the suite."

Josh's eyes flicker. "Is she a hooker?"

I bite my lower lip. "It's Bridgette again."

"*What?* Bridgette? Fuck, Kat. *No.*"

"Yeah, she graciously flew up to Seattle to fuck me for your viewing pleasure."

"Are you fucking kidding me? Come on, Kat."

I shrug.

"Kat, not *Bridgette.*" Josh takes a step back. "How the fuck did you even convince her to—"

"I paid her."

"*What?*"

"A shitload of money, too. But it's okay because I'm a mill-i-on-aire, so I can afford it—money well spent."

"You're joking, right?"

"No."

"*Bridgette?*" He scowls. "Kat, she's not human. She's got no heart."

"Which makes her perfect for the job of being our window dressing. I'm not gonna bring some wonderful woman with a heart of gold into our bed who's gonna make you fall head over heels in love with her."

Josh rolls his eyes in complete exasperation. "There's no danger of me falling in love with anyone else, Kat." He opens and closes his mouth in rapid succession, apparently contemplating saying more, but nothing comes out.

Oh my effing God. *Because I'm in love with you.* That's what Josh was about to say—there's no doubt in my mind. *Come on, Josh,* I think. *Just say it.*

But Josh remains mute.

I exhale, resigned. I'm obviously gonna need a lot of lube to extract those damned words from Josh's vocal cords—lube in the form of a certain lesbo-fantasy. "So you wanna watch me get it on with Bridgette or not?" I ask. "Should I ask the poor girl to leave?"

"You sure about this?" Josh asks.

"I'm positive. *YOLO.*" I wink.

Josh grins. "You're seriously the perfect woman."

"Yeah, I know." I look at my watch. "Well, if we're gonna do this, then we'd better get in there. Bridgette said if we don't come back within five minutes, she's leaving and it's already been six minutes."

"You're not actually trying to manipulate me into 'absconding' with you, are you?"

"No, I told you—I'm being sincere. I want you to let your inner sick fuck out—no holds barred."

"And you're feeling up to it?" He gently touches my stomach, making my entire body twitch with excitement.

"Yeah. I'm feeling much better these days. Still sick now and again, but a lot better."

"And it's safe?"

I nod. "The doctor said sex is just fine." I press myself into him. "So, it's decision time. Are you in or out, Playboy?"

Josh touches the indentation in my chin with his fingertip and then licks it with a sensuous flicker of his tongue. "I'm all-in, Party Girl. Let's do it."

101

JOSH

"Here you go," Bridgette says, handing me a glass filled with tequila and an opened bottle of Patron.

"Thanks," I say. I put the bottle on a little table next to me, lean back in my armchair, and shift my dick in my pants, my eyes fixed on Kat. She's sitting on the edge of the bed in her bra and panties, her body visibly trembling, her skin covered in goose bumps.

"Can I put some music on?" Bridgette asks.

I nod and Bridgette leaves the room, striding away confidently on her impossibly long legs.

Kat and I stare at each other, both our chests heaving.

Have Kat's tits always been this perfect? And that belly ring of hers—damn, it slays me. The way her blonde hair falls around her shoulders... I can't get enough of her. I swig the tequila in my glass and shift my dick in my pants again.

"Sugar" by Maroon Five begins blaring—not at all what I would have picked—this song's the musical equivalent of a fucking chick flick. But Kat's exuberant face makes it clear she's thrilled with the song choice and that's good enough for me.

Bridgette re-enters the room, shaking her ass to the song.

"I love this song," Kat says.

Bridgette joins Kat on the end of the bed. "Me, too, pussycat." She places her hand on Kat's knee and Kat jolts at Bridgette's touch.

My cock twitches at the sight of them sitting together, both of them barely clothed. Oh shit. This is really happening. I've done this multiple times, of course, *but never like this*. Never with a woman I love—wait, no—not *a* woman I love—*the* woman I love—the *only* one. Oh my God, it's true. Kat's the only woman I've ever truly loved, heart and soul—and, holy fuck, she's really doing this for me. Or so she says. God help me, if this is a test—if Kat's actually hoping I'll stop everything, the same way she expected me to stop her from kissing Henn in Vegas, the same way she expected me to whisk her away from Bridgette the last time. Because, if so, she's gonna be sorely disappointed—I'm not stopping shit this time around.

I take another swig of my drink.

Bridgette runs her hand up and down Kat's arm. "Relax," she coos. "Ssh, pussycat—just relax." She strokes the full length of Kat's thigh. "Take a deep breath."

I smirk. This is so fucking awesome.

Kat takes a deep breath and her breasts visibly strain in her pink pushup bra.

Oh my God, I feel like my dick's gonna explode, this is so fucking hot. Is this normal? Shouldn't I be sweeping Kat into my arms and making love to her, showing her my new tattoo and saying the magic words? Because that's exactly what I'm gonna do—I swear to God—*right after this.*

Bridgette leans in and whispers something into Kat's ear, and Kat nods and whispers something back.

"Could you ladies speak up, please?" I say.

Both women turn their heads and look at me.

"I'd like to hear what you say to each other," I say. "Please."

Kat's blue eyes are trained on me like lasers. "Your wish is my command," she says, one side of her mouth hitching up. "Bridgette said she had a sex dream about me the night we first met."

"I did," Bridgette says. "It made me come in my sleep."

My cock jolts.

"And what I said to Bridgette in reply was, 'That makes me so wet, honey—my clit is throbbing.'"

My chest constricts. Jesus Christ. I gulp down the rest of my tequila and put the glass down on the table.

"Enough talking, pussycat," Bridgette says. She leans in slowly and lays a soft, closed-mouth kiss on Kat's lips.

"Hang on," Kat says softly. She turns her head and gazes at me, clearly asking for permission to continue.

I nod. Fuck yeah, I do.

Kat's eyes darken and burn. She turns her face toward Bridgette again. "I'm ready, baby."

I can barely breathe.

Bridgette cups Kat's face in her hands, leans in, and kisses her lips gently, and, much to my shock, Kat leans into Bridgette, slides her palm onto Bridgette's smooth cheek, cupping her jawline, and shoots her glistening tongue straight into Bridgette's gorgeous mouth.

Oh my fuck.

I quickly unzip the front of my pants and pull down my briefs, freeing my hard-on from its bondage, breathing like I'm on a fucking treadmill. Oh my fuck. Well, it's official. Emma was right—I really am a sick fuck. I'm supposed to be at my new house right now, telling Kat I love her for the first time to the dulcet sounds of fucking Mozart, but instead, I'm watching the woman I love play tonsil-hockey with an almost-nude bisexual supermodel, my hand stroking my hard dick. Am I really this depraved? Well, apparently so, because I'm finding this hot as fuck.

The two women are kissing passionately now—and, from Kat's body language, it's clear to me she's not pretending to be turned on. Holy fuck, she's genuinely on fire. She's so fucking sexy, it's like she's another species of woman altogether. I've never seen anything like her, paid or otherwise.

I grasp my shaft and work myself with more urgency. Every little arch of Kat's back, every shudder of her tight little body, every soft lapping noise of her tongue and lips is making my cock jolt and throb in my hand. Oh, fuck, I love this woman. I thought I knew what love was with Emma, but I was an idiot. This is love. Right here. *This.* There's no one else like Kat Morgan in the world. She's perfect.

Kat reaches behind Bridgette's back and unclasps her bra, and Bridgette's bountiful breasts bounce free. Bridgette quickly finishes the job and tosses her bra off and then returns the favor, unclasping Kat's bra and practically ripping it off her body.

Both women are topless now. Their nipples are erect, straining toward the other's. They're moaning softly, breathing hard—both of them obviously turned-on.

And so am I. Oh my fuck, so am I.

Bridgette stands and pulls off her undies, revealing her fully waxed pussy underneath, and even from here, I can see goose bumps rise up on Kat's skin at the sight of her naked body.

Bridgette pulls Kat to standing, whispering something into her ear again. Motherfucker, I wanna tell Bridgette to speak the fuck up, but I couldn't talk right now if the hotel were burning down around us.

The women are standing nose to nose. Breast to breast. Nipple to nipple. Bridgette leans forward and her nipples brush gently against Kat's.

An involuntary groan escapes me. Oh, shit.

Bridgette kneels and begins pulling Kat's G-string down slowly—kissing her hipbone as she does it.

My cock lurches. I can't breathe. I feel dizzy.

As Kat's panties reach her knees, she turns her head and looks straight at me, her eyes drunk with arousal, her chest rising and falling visibly. Her eyes drift down to my hand pumping up and down my hard shaft, and then back up to my face. She licks her lips. "Yes?" she asks, her breathing ragged.

I nod, incapable of speaking.

Bridgette lays a kiss on the inside of Kat's thigh, drawing Kat's attention away from me. She reaches between her legs and runs her fingers over the top of Bridgette's blonde head, and then rakes her fingers passionately through Bridgette's thick, shiny hair.

Bridgette lets out a low moan of excitement and Kat replies with a moan of her own.

Holy fuck, I'm gonna blow.

Kat's undies are completely off. She's nude with a head of long, blonde hair bobbing and moving between her legs—a blonde head attached to perfect fucking tits and an un-fucking-believable ass and perfectly curved hips and toned thighs, and oh my fucking God I'm about to fucking blow.

Bridgette's lips trail up from Kat's thigh toward her pussy. She's an inch away from the money and obviously going in for the kill.

"Wait," I choke out, shocking myself. "Stop."

Both women freeze and look at me. They're panting, heaving, trembling with arousal—and so am I.

"Don't touch her pussy," I say. "Her pussy's all mine."

Bridgette looks up at Kat, incredulous, but Kat's looking at me, her mouth hanging open in shock.

"Kat's pussy's all mine," I murmur, gaining my equilibrium. "She's got a magic pussy and it's all mine."

"Are you fucking kidding me?" Bridgette bellows, clearly on the verge of losing her shit.

"Ssh." Kat puts her slender hand on Bridgette's head, signaling her to stay put and cool her jets. Kat begins stroking Bridgette's hair like she's a kitten. "My pussy's all yours, baby," Kat coos to me, still stroking Bridgette's hair. "But *just this once* Bridgette's gonna lick my pussy and make me come really, really hard, solely for your pleasure." Her eyes flicker. "She's our Mickey Mouse roller coaster, babe—just this once. And then never again."

Kat brushes her fingertips against her own erect nipples and bites her lower lip and it's suddenly crystal clear to me Kat's not doing this for me at all. Maybe it started out that way for her—in fact, I'm sure it did—but now, in an unexpected turn of events, doing this is getting Kat off more than she ever expected. I thought I'd caught a tiger tonight, but I'm suddenly realizing I'm the asshole gripping the tiger by its fucking tail. And for some reason, this realization turns me the fuck on.

I nod slowly, my pulse pounding in my ears.

Kat smiles devilishly and looks down at Bridgette kneeling on the floor. "Eat me like you're a world class whore who charges a million bucks a night and your only job is to give me my money's worth. Can you do that for me?"

Bridgette shoots me a steely look that quite clearly says, "Fuck you, asshole," and then she leans with exaggerated flourish into Kat's waxed pussy and begins lapping at her clit with outrageously enthusiastic swirls of her glistening tongue.

At the touch of Bridgette's effusive tongue, Kat throws her head back, grips Bridgette's hair, and releases a guttural growl.

And what am I doing? Oh, nothing much. Just jolting in my chair like I'm being electrocuted by a thousand electric eels. Oh my fucking shit. With each and every energetic swipe of Bridgette's glistening, wet tongue against Kat's beautiful pussy, every movement of Bridgette's jaws, every bob of Bridgette's head, my dick twitches like Bridgette's sucking my tip. Or would that be punching me in the balls? Oh my fuck. I'm turned on and jealous as hell all at the same time. Oh God, that should be *me* and my flickering tongue tasting Kat's slippery sweetness. That's *my* magic pussy and no one else's, goddammit —my juices to lap up. But oh my holy fuck—this is the hottest thing I've ever seen in my fucking life by a long mile. I love it. I hate it. I'm dying. I'm in pain. *I'm gonna come so fucking hard.*

I stand, rip my pants and briefs completely off, and begin quickly unbuttoning my shirt—but just as I'm about to pull my shirt off my shoulders, I remember my new girlfriend-tattoo on my left bicep, and I stop. There's no way I'm giving Kat her first ever glimpse of my once-in-a-lifetime gift to her while she's fucking Bridgette.

I leave my unbuttoned shirt on and move behind Kat, pressing my hard-on into her ass and kissing her smooth shoulder as Bridgette continues lapping at her pussy from her knees.

The instant my lips touch Kat's skin, goose bumps visibly erupt on her skin. She lets out a low moan and begins jerking her hips in a phantom humping movement, obviously so overwhelmed with arousal at my unexpected touch, her body's going suddenly haywire.

I reach around Kat's torso and stroke her erect nipples as my mouth trails the length of her shoulder to her neck and then to her jawline.

Kat lets out a loud groan of pleasure and gyrates her pelvis back and forth from Bridgette's mouth in the front of her to my erection poking her in her ass.

I swipe Kat's blonde hair off the back of her neck and kiss her hidden Scorpio tattoo and she reaches up and grips my hair, her entire body jolting.

I press my lips against her ear and pinch her nipples, grinding my hard-on into her with urgency. "Let your inner sick fuck out to play, Party Girl," I coo into Kat's ear, my voice low and intense. My palms explore the smooth skin of Kat's belly, and when my fingertips unexpectedly brush the soft hair atop Bridgette's bobbing head, my cock jolts. "Enjoy every minute, baby," I growl, letting my fingertips float back up to Kat's breasts. "Because after tonight, no one but me is gonna touch your magic pussy again."

Kat inhales sharply and her body stiffens. A guttural roar emerges from her throat, followed by a string of expletives, followed by a pained wail. I slide my finger between her ass cheeks and press my fingertip against her anus just in time to feel her orgasm ripple against my finger, and my cock throbs at the delicious sensation.

Even before Kat's orgasm is over, Bridgette leaps to standing and clutches

Kat's shoulders like she's going to kiss her full on the mouth, but I rip Kat's shuddering body away from Bridgette's grasp and drag her to the bed. In one fell swoop, I push Kat down forcefully onto her hands and knees on the bed, grip her hips from behind, and enter her, letting her feel every inch of me as I slide my cock into her tight wetness. "Tell me you were aching for my cock when she was licking you," I command, pumping in and out of her all the way, pulling her hips into me.

"Yes."

Bridgette crawls slowly onto the bed like a cat, her ass in the air, and positions herself shoulder to shoulder with Kat like the two of them are the bottoms in a naked-cheerleader pyramid. As I continue fucking Kat, Bridgette spreads her legs slightly, her ass in the air, giving me an unimpeded view of every inch of her ass crack and pussy all at once, gyrating her hips like she's inviting me to fuck her in any hole.

Bridgette's hot, I'll give her that, but I force myself to look away and focus on Kat. "You have a magic pussy," I growl to Kat—but it's actually a message for Bridgette. She can shove her pussy and asshole at me all night long, but I'll never take the bait. I've got my unicorn right here and she's all I need.

I rub Kat's smooth back with my palms and shift the angle of my entry on my next thrust, trying to find the exact spot inside Kat that's gonna push her into ecstasy, and at the shift of my body, Kat inhales sharply—always a good sign—and suddenly begins gyrating her body in synchronicity with my thrusts.

"Get it, baby," I say. "Let's make it rain."

As I continue sliding in and out of Kat's sweet pussy with strong, deliberate strokes, Bridgette runs her fingertips down the length of Kat's back and licks at her shoulder. In reply, Kat turns her head and kisses Bridgette, lapping at her with languid swirls of her tongue.

Bridgette reaches out and runs her hand down the full length of Kat's back, continuing to kiss her as she does, and Kat lets out a loud moan that makes me physically shudder with excitement. Thank you, God. If I ever doubted your existence, I take it all back.

I change the angle of my dick yet again, and, holy shit, that's the magic bullet. Instantly, Kat breaks away from her kiss with Bridgette, gasping and whimpering.

"Oh my God," she growls. "Oh, *fuck.* That's it. *Yes.*"

I grip Kat's hair and pull her head back forcefully and that's all she needs: her pussy begins clenching around my cock in rolling ripples.

Bridgette exhales—perhaps realizing she's not getting fucked tonight—and flips onto her back next to Kat. "You're so sexy, honey," Bridgette purrs. She reaches out and fondles Kat's dangling, swinging breast. "I love watching you get fucked, pussycat."

At Bridgette's touch, Kat arches her back like a cat on a hot tin roof and then forcefully slams her spine down in the opposite direction, over and over, like her body's trying to expel a demon.

"Kiss me, pussycat," Bridgette purrs. "Come down here."

Bridgette grabs Kat's face with her slender hands and gently pulls on her head, coaxing Kat to lie with her on the bed, and, in response, Kat slowly lowers herself, taking me and my thrusting cock with her, until Kat's lying on her right side, kissing Bridgette passionately, while I'm spooning Kat and fucking her from behind.

Holy fuck, this is literally the hottest thing I've ever experienced—way hotter than anything I did in The Club by a long mile. I'm fucking the woman I love—the woman who gets me off like no one ever has—while watching her French kiss one of the most beautiful females on the planet.

I let my eyes drift down the length of Bridgette's long, ridiculous body. She's lying on her back, her legs spread, her fingers working her own clit.

"Touch her, Kat," I whisper into her ear. "Make her come for me."

I reach around and massage Kat's clit and she moans into Bridgette's mouth.

"Touch her and make her come," I command, working Kat's clit with authority.

Kat's jerking with pleasure at my touch, but she nonetheless follows orders. Her hand trails down Bridgette's torso slowly and slides straight into her pussy, taking over the job from Bridgette's fingers. Oh my God, I'm right on the edge. I bite Kat's shoulder and increase the speed and depth of my thrusts, groaning loudly. Oh yeah, I'm about to boil over.

I press my lips against Kat's ear. "You're a sick fuck, baby," I whisper.

Kat moans. "*Yes.*"

"Lick her tits for me," I say. "Make her come."

Without hesitation, Kat bends over Bridgette and begins sucking and licking her erect nipples, all the while continuing to stroke Bridgette's pussy— and all while getting fucked by me—and within thirty seconds, Bridgette arches her back, blurts something in German, and comes completely undone.

It's quite plain to see Bridgette's orgasm is doing wonders for Kat—she's clearly on the very brink of an epic climax herself.

I press my lips against Kat's ear. "Enjoy this, baby, because after tonight, your pussy's all mine."

Kat lets out a pained wail, arches her back, and squirts, gushing warm liquid all over my dick and balls in a torrent.

I jerk out of Kat, my hard-on straining, guide her quivering body onto her hands and knees, and enthusiastically suckle her pussy from behind, sucking and lapping up every drop of sweet cum off her lips like I'm licking the cream filling out of an Oreo. By the time I've got Kat's pussy all cleaned up, I'm in a frenzy—completely out of my mind. I flip Kat onto her back, rest her calves on my shoulders and plunge myself balls-deep into her wetness.

Holy fuck, I'm enraptured. Kat's never felt *this* good, has she? It's like we were designed for each other, like we're the last two pieces of a celestial jigsaw puzzle, just now snapped into place. Oh my fucking God, Kat's the answer to every question I didn't even know I had.

Kat lets out a mangled cry and I join her, groaning and growling like a man possessed as I continue fucking her with all my might.

Bridgette, apparently recovered from her orgasm, reaches out and runs her slender fingers over the smooth skin of Kat's thigh, even as Kat's legs are wrapped around me.

"No," I bark at Bridgette, slapping at her hand. "She's mine. Fuck off."

"Josh," Kat breathes, her blue eyes blazing. "*Yes.*" She runs her hands into my hair and yanks on it roughly. "*Yes.*"

I can't breathe. The room is warping and spinning. Kat's as hot as sin and as depraved as fucking hell. She's an angel and the devil all rolled into one. *And I love her more than life itself.* I lean my face into Kat's, intending to kiss her passionately, but Madame Terrorist has her own ideas. Even as I'm pumping in and out of her, Kat turns her head and levels her foe with an icy glare.

"He's mine," Kat hisses, her beautiful face an inch away from Bridgette's.

Bridgette chuckles. "Oh, go fuck yourself, bitch—I don't even want him."

"Good, because you can't have him," Kat spits out.

I grab Kat's face roughly, wrenching her attention away from Bridgette. "This isn't about her," I growl. I pull Kat's arms above her head and pin her wrists together. "This is about you and me."

Kat's eyes ignite at my rough touch. "*Yes,*" she purrs.

"Just you and me, baby," I say, thrusting with all my might. "No one else."

Kat's eyes are absolutely blazing with rabid excitement. She lifts her pelvis to receive me even more deeply, her breathing ragged, and I respond by slamming her even harder with my full length.

I lace my fingers tightly into Kat's. "You're all mine," I growl, my body on the brink of release.

"Yes," Kat breathes. "*Harder.*"

My thrusts are becoming savage. I'm on the very cusp of losing myself completely. I grip Kat's hands in mine and stare into her blue eyes, willing myself to hang on as long as possible. Oh my God, this feels so good, I want it to last forever.

"Yes," Kat groans, her blue eyes leveling me, her fingers entwined in mine, her heart beating wildly against my chest.

"You feel so good, baby," I growl. "You always feel so fucking good."

Kat's eyelids flutter. Her eyes roll back into her head. And she's gone. Her muscles surrounding my cock begin clenching and rippling fiercely, sending shockwaves of pleasure throughout my entire body.

"Get it, baby," I choke out. "Get it."

As I thrust into her, I kiss Kat voraciously and she returns my hungry kiss, enthusiastically swirling her tongue inside my mouth and devouring my lips.

Out of nowhere, I feel fingers grip my swinging balls... followed by a wet, warm tongue lapping at them furiously... and then, holy fuck, a warm, wet mouth envelops my entire ball sack. With a loud growl, my body hurtles into a brutal release that leaves me gasping for air and certain I'm dying an extremely pleasurable death.

Several moments later, when Kat and I have both stopped quaking, I lie on top of Kat, the most sexual and sensual and beautiful creature I've ever encountered—sweat pouring out every inch of my flesh, my breathing ragged, my hands still clasped tightly in hers—and I try my mighty fucking best to understand what the *fuck* just happened to me.

I realize my brain is likely short-circuiting right now and my thought processes probably aren't particularly trustworthy, but the more I ponder the situation, the more I think I know exactly what happened. In fact, yep, there's only one *sane* conclusion to be reached: my magical, mystical unicorn *momentarily* transformed into a magical, mystical *octopus* with a supernatural mouth. Yep, that's got to be it—or, at least, that's my story and I'm sticking to it.

Because when a guy's got a smokin' hot baby-momma-girlfriend with a white-hot temper, a woman undoubtedly capable of committing double-murder if properly provoked (and that was before pregnancy hormones began coursing through her blood stream, making her even crazier)—and when the guy's absolutely certain his smokin' hot future-murderess of a baby-momma-girlfriend would, indeed, feel provoked to kill if she were to believe her firm "no touch" rule had been violated by a certain bisexual supermodel (through no fault of the boyfriend, mind you)—well, then the boyfriend can't help but conclude it's most prudent for everyone involved if he conjures a paranormal unicorn-turned-octopus rather than try too hard to come up with any other plausible explanation.

But, hey, the magical-unicorn-turned-octopus theory isn't really *that* far-fetched, is it? No, I really don't think so. Because if there's one woman in the entire world who could pull off grabbing and licking a man's balls, and then tea-bagging his entire ball sack like a fucking champ, all while simultaneously getting plowed with her hands firmly pinned above her head and her mouth otherwise engaged in a passionate kiss, then that woman would have to be the one and only magical, mystical unicorn, Katherine Ulla Morgan.

102

JOSH

"God, I thought she'd never leave," I say, pulling Kat away from the door and onto my lap on a nearby couch.

"You were pretty rude to her just now," Kat says, throwing her arms around my neck and pressing her forehead against mine.

"Fuck Bridgette. I couldn't wait to be alone with you." I press my nose against Kat's until she appears to have one big, blue eye. "Mike Wazowski," I say.

Kat giggles.

"I can't believe you *paid* her to fuck you," I say. "You're a savage beast, Kat."

"She said I had to pay her money as 'collateral' to ensure I'd actually go through with it."

"How much did you pay her?" I ask.

Kat tells me the number with wide eyes like it's some astronomical sum, and I can barely keep from laughing.

"Babe, Bridgette earns that amount of money per *minute* as a model."

"Oh."

"Clearly, she didn't come here for the money. In fact, I'm one hundred percent sure she would have paid *you* for the pleasure of fucking you. Anyone would. Just look at you. You're a fucking unicorn." I stroke her hair. "A kinky little unicorn." I bite her naked shoulder and she squeals.

"I didn't even know I was *that* kinky, to be honest," Kat says. "I thought I'd chicken out after second base, just like I did in college."

"Well, hot damn, you certainly didn't chicken out tonight, baby. You rounded third like a pro and slid headfirst right into home."

Kat giggles. "I guess you bring out the sick fuck in me, Playboy."

"Oh no, don't you dare pin your sick-fuckeduppedness on me. You out sick-fucked me by a long mile tonight, baby. I'm the one who said 'no pussy' and you *begged* me to let her keep eating you."

Kat grins gleefully. "Oh, yeah. I did, didn't I?"

"You sure did."

We share a smile.

"I almost passed out at one point. I was seeing pink and yellow flashes of light."

The hairs on the back of my neck stand up. "Do you think it's safe for the kumquat for you to come that hard? Maybe we should be taking it easy?"

"No, the doctor said sex and orgasms are fine. I'm just not allowed to sit on a jet engine, that's the only limitation."

"You asked the doctor if you could ride your Sybian?" I chuckle. "Oh, Jesus. I can only imagine the dinner conversation your poor doctor had that night with her husband when he asked about her day."

We both laugh.

"You know she was Googling that shit the minute you left her office," I add.

"Probably."

I roll my eyes. "Oh, Kat."

"Oh, Kat," she agrees.

"Sorry you can't ride your toy for a while."

"Just one of the many sacrifices we mothers make for our children," she says piously.

I grin. She's so damned cute. If I didn't already love this woman, I would have just fallen in love with her.

"Actually, I don't even need my Sybian anymore," Kat says matter-of-factly. "Now that you and I finally live in the same city, you'll be my one-and-only orgasm machine every single night."

"Amen," I say. I stroke her golden hair. "Hey, you think when I was fucking you really deep at the end the kumquat was like, 'Eek! An anaconda!'?"

Kat giggles. "Or maybe the kumquat was like, 'A little to the left. *Lower.* Aaaah."

I grimace. "Ew, Kat. *No.* That's disgusting. Don't say that."

Kat looks stricken. "No, I meant like a baby-back-scratcher—you know, like your dick was scratching an itch on the kumquat's back." She makes a face. "I didn't mean anything *sexual*, for cryin' out loud."

I put my hands over my ears. "Stop. Please. Either way, I don't want to think about my *dick* touching our baby. You're totally traumatizing me."

"Oh. I'm sorry. I just meant—"

"*Stop.* Please. I might never be able to get a hard-on again if I'm thinking about my dick scratching our baby's back."

Kat's face bursts into a huge smile.

"You're charmed by the thought of me becoming impotent?" I ask.

"You just said 'our baby.'"

I look at her blankly.

"'Our baby's back,'" she says. "That's what you said."

"Yeah. Because I don't want my dick to become a baby-back-scratcher. Duh."

"*Our baby*," she says reverently. "You called the kumquat our baby." She grins.

"I did, didn't I?" I tilt my head, trying to figure out what I'm feeling right now—and, honestly, I'm feeling *happy* and nothing else. "Our baby," I repeat.

Kat visibly swoons.

"Our wee little baaaaaybaaaaaaaaaaaay," I say.

Kat giggles.

"You know what?" I say. "I just realized I'm not freaked out anymore."

"Me, either."

"Well, actually, I'm still a little freaked out, don't get me wrong, but not nearly like I was when you first told me."

Kat smiles. "Onward and upward."

"Indubitably."

"Hey, bee tee dubs, it's anatomically impossible for anyone's dick to become a baby-back-scratcher, even a dick as huge as yours."

"Really?" I ask.

Kat nods. "I researched it. The cervix is in the way. Impossible, no matter how big the donkey-dick."

"You're *sure?*"

"Look it up for yourself, Anaconda-boy. Literally impossible."

"When did you look that up?"

"A couple days ago."

"Why?"

She shrugs. "You're huge—I was worried about the wee little baaaybaaay."

"Aw. Check out the momma-Kumquat looking out for the baby-kumquat. That was a very motherly thing for you to do. Well, I assume it was motherly. I haven't seen an actual mother in the wild any more than I've seen an actual wife. But I *think* you're having what the anthropologists call 'maternal instincts.'"

The look on Kat's face is utterly adorable. It's the same look I'd expect from her if I'd just asked her to go steady.

"So, hey, hot momma," I say, pulling her close. "Are you hungry?"

"*Famished*," Kat says.

"Room service or dine out?"

"Room service."

"Burgers and fries or five-star?"

"Burgers and fries," Kat says. "And milkshakes. Oh, and will you see if they have split pea soup? I have a weird craving for split pea soup—oh, and cantaloupe—or any kind of melon, really, except honeydew—oh, and maybe some blueberry yogurt?"

"Wow, I guess that whole pregnancy-cravings thing is real, huh?"

Kat pats her belly. "The kumquat wants what the kumquat wants. I guess the little guy (or gal) burned lots of calories dodging that big ol' anaconda who's been trying to scratch his back all night long."

"Well, then, by all means, let's feed the kumquat—not to mention get it a therapist. Lemme up, babe. I'll make the call." I pat her thigh and she hops off my lap. I stride across the room and pick up the hotel phone. "Room service, please."

"Yes, sir. One moment, please."

While I'm waiting for the call to connect, Kat grabs her purse and pulls out a package of crackers.

"You feeling sick?" I ask, still holding the phone to my ear.

Kat nods. "It mostly hits me these days when I'm hungry. Or tired. And late at night, too—and early morning. Oh, and in the car." She rolls her eyes. "It still hits me a lot, I guess."

I make a sad face.

"Thank you for waiting," a male voice says into my ear. "What would you like to order, Mr. Faraday?"

I place our ridiculously bizarre order. "How long will it take?" I ask. "I've got a pregnant woman here who needs to eat right away."

"About forty-five minutes."

"They say about forty-five minutes, hot momma," I say to Kat. "Are you gonna be okay for that long?"

"Yeah, I'll be okay," Kat says, holding up her Saltines. "I'll just go lie down until the food arrives."

"Yeah, go rest, Party Girl. I'll let you know when the food is here."

She disappears into the bedroom.

"Okay, let me make sure I've got your order right, Mr. Faraday..." the voice on the phone says.

But I'm not listening. I can't concentrate. Kat only left me to go into the next room and my heart's suddenly yearning for her like she's a thousand miles away.

"Is that correct?" the guy asks.

"Yes. Thanks," I reply.

After I hang up the phone, I stand for a moment, looking around like a lost puppy, not sure what to do with myself. I'm physically aching for her *and she's only in the next fucking room.* What's happening to me? Who am I? I lived across the country from Emma for three fucking years and that was just fine by me. And now I can't stand to be more than fifty feet away from Kat?

There's a mirror hanging on the wall a few feet away, and I stare at my reflection for a moment, marveling that I still look like me on the outside, despite the fact that I've apparently turned into my pussy-whipped brother on the inside. That's my Anthony Franco suit on my body. That's my dark hair. And those are my blue eyes. Ah, but my eyes. They look slightly deranged, don't they? They give me away. I'm definitely a man possessed—a man who's head-over-heels in love with the perfect woman. Or, perhaps, more accurately, a *sick fuck* who's head-over-heels in love with the perfect *sick fuck*. I smirk. Damn, I'm a lucky bastard.

I stride toward the bedroom, my heartbeat pulsing in my ears. *It's time.* I'm gonna tell Kat I love her right now. It's not perfect timing, I know—she's not feeling well, plus our food's on the way—and it'd probably be best for me to wait for a time when I can tell her while making love to her, slowly and gently. But fuck it. I can't wait another minute to tell that woman how I feel about her.

I burst through the door of the bedroom, my heart bursting... and... *Oh.*

My heart wilts.

Kat's fast asleep in the bed, a half-eaten package of Saltines lying in her opened palm.

I smile wistfully to myself.

Now there's a woman I wouldn't kick out of bed for eating crackers.

I shake my head—oh, life—and head back into the main room.

"Yes, Mr. Faraday?" the front-desk guy asks when he picks up my call.

"I just ordered a bunch of food from room service and I need to change my order," I say into the phone.

"Of course. One moment, please." There's a long pause while the call connects. "Yes, Mr. Faraday? How can I help you?"

"On that room service I just ordered, cancel everything except the melon and yogurt, plus add a couple cold turkey sandwiches and maybe five or six other cold-food items to choose from—stuff that'll keep for hours. My girl-friend's the one who wanted all that stuff I ordered earlier and now she's fallen asleep. The new plan is for there to be a bunch of food ready for her whenever she wakes up."

"Yes, sir. Not a problem."

"And do me a favor, don't knock when you bring the food. Enter the main room of the suite and load everything into the refrigerator behind the bar. We'll be in the bedroom with the door closed. And please be extra quiet. My girl-friend's pregnant and needs her rest—she hasn't been feeling all that well." Why is my heart racing like this? My entire body is buzzing and I don't under-stand why.

"Yes, sir. We'll be very quiet. Any requests on the food items for the new order?"

"Nope. Surprise me. Just give her lots of options. She eats like a truck driver these days. Go crazy."

The guy laughs. "Yes, sir."

"Thanks."

I hang up the phone and lay my palm on my chest. My heart's racing a mile a minute and I don't understand why. All I did was order food for Kat—so why is my skin suddenly feeling electrified? I take a deep breath, trying to calm myself. Wow, I feel like I just ran a hundred-yard dash. Why is my heart thumping like this?

I grab a cold water bottle from the refrigerator behind the bar, creep into the bedroom, and close the door behind me. Gently, I lift the package of Saltines out of Kat's open palm and place the crackers on the nightstand along with the bottle of water—and then I stand over Kat's sleeping body, transfixed by her beautiful face.

I've never felt the way I do, standing here right now. Not once in my whole goddamned life. Something new is coursing through my veins—something that wasn't there when I first knocked on the door to the suite tonight. What Kat did for me tonight—and how she so obviously got turned on doing it—was the final piece of a puzzle I didn't even know I was trying to solve. Kat didn't just *participate* in tonight's depraved little fuck-fest, and she didn't need to be *coaxed* into doing it with me, either—she *arranged* it and then *begged* me to keep going when I tried to throw on the brakes midway through—proving once and for all she's an even bigger sick fuck than I am.

Which makes me love this woman more than I ever thought possible.

And, now, out of nowhere, I suddenly feel a primal desire to take care of Kat's every need, to make sure her every desire, big or small, is fulfilled—and not just sexually. In every conceivable way, top to bottom.

I gaze in wonder at Kat's sleeping face, my heart straining for her. God, even without animation, Kat's features are spectacular. Her lips slay me. Her high cheekbones. Her bold eyebrows. That little cleft in her chin. If the kumquat-inside-the-Kumquat pops out looking anything at all like its freakishly beautiful mother, the kid's gonna fucking rule the world.

I pull off all my clothes, flip off the lamp next to Kat, and quietly slide underneath the sheet behind her.

Her breathing is rhythmic and slow. Her hair is soft against my nose.

I scoot right up against Kat's naked backside and wrap my arm around her —and then I lay my palm flush against her flat belly and cradle our little baby-to-be, the kumquat I didn't even know I wanted until this very moment.

I lie still for a long time, breathing in her scent, pressing my hand against her flat stomach as it moves with her breathing—thinking about the words I'm gonna say to her when she wakes up. After a while, I hear the main door to the suite open, followed by a soft clatter—and then the sound of the main door opening and closing again. Silence. Nothing but the sound of Kat breathing and the beating of my heart against her back.

"I love you, Kat," I whisper softly. I shift my palm on Kat's belly, spreading my fingers out, trying to cradle every inch of it. "And I love you, too," I say softly.

And that's the last thing I do before surrendering to serene and blissful sleep.

103

KAT

I wake up with a start. Josh's arm is around me.

I'm in a warm bed.

I glance around the moonlit room, momentarily confused about my whereabouts.

Oh, yeah—now I remember. The hotel room where Josh and I let our sick fucks run amok with Bridgette.

Delicious.

But I've no sooner had that highly pleasant thought than bile rises in my throat and my mouth waters. Shit.

In a flash, I disentangle myself from Josh's muscular arm and bolt out of bed, straight into the bathroom—where I proceed to hurl every Saltines cracker and drop of fluid out of my body with loud, ghastly heaves. Oh, God. I'm so gross. Gah.

I flush the toilet and whimper. I feel like I'm made of cardboard, not flesh and blood. *I need to eat something right now or else I'm gonna die.*

I wash out my mouth, rinse my face, and hobble back into the bedroom, expecting to find Josh sitting up in bed and staring at me, aghast at the horrendous noises I just made in the bathroom. But, somehow, Josh is still fast asleep, completely oblivious to the T-Rex I just wrestled in the toilet.

I stand over Josh's beautiful sleeping body for a moment, looking at his peaceful face in the moonlight. Normally, when I think of Josh, the first word that pops into my mind is *sexy*. Typically followed by *funny*. And *generous* soon thereafter. But right now, standing over his striking features in the moonlight, the only word coming to my mind is *beautiful*.

I sigh.

I love him.

With all my heart and soul.

More than I ever thought possible.

And I'm aching to exchange the words with him—to finally give full voice to my overwhelming feelings for him.

My stomach clenches hungrily, drawing me out of my Josh-induced stupor, so I pad carefully out of the darkened room to the main room of the suite, desperate to find something to eat.

I flip on a lamp and instantly spot a room-service tray on a table, so I head over there like a starving hyena looking for a carcass.

Along with utensils and tiny salt-and-pepper shakers, there's a handwritten note on the tray: "Mr. Faraday, per your request, an assortment of cold-food selections are in the refrigerator. Please let us know if you require anything further."

I make a "yay" face to myself and happily beeline over to the refrigerator.

Sweet Baby Jesus, I've hit the mother lode. If I didn't already love Josh, I would have just fallen in love with him. How'd he know to have food waiting for me when I woke up? Is he some sort of pregnant-woman whisperer?

For a solid fifteen minutes, I'm a ravenous animal, stuffing food into my mouth with both fists and making "nom nom nom" sounds in the quiet room like Homer Simpson at a doughnut shop—and when I'm done eating and feeling fan-fucking-tastic again, a steely determination suddenly washes over me: *It's time to get my man.*

I head back into the dark bedroom and fumble around in the moonlight until I find my laptop. I scroll into my music and stop when I see Audra Mae, my new obsession. "Addicted to You" with Aviici leaps out at me from my song list. Oh, how I want to make love to Josh to this redonkulously awesome song— but I'll just have to wait. Josh and I have already confessed we're *addicted* to each other—now it's time for us to take our words to the next level. But to get Josh over the line, I'm thinking I'm gonna need a song that'll beat Josh over the head with an "I love you" sledge hammer—a song that leaves absolutely no room for misunderstanding.

As I scroll through my music, I realize I've got lots of options—the lyrics "I love you" aren't exactly a rare commodity when it comes to pop music—but I stop scrolling when I see "1234" by the Plain White T's. I absolutely love this sweet little song—and the lyrics are so literal, Josh would have to be a pill bug not to catch their meaning.

I set the song to play on a loop, tiptoe slowly to the bed, and, as the song begins, slip naked under the covers onto my left side, facing Josh.

When I slide my arm over Josh's sleeping body, his skin is warm and smooth. Delectable. I nuzzle Josh's nose with mine and kiss his soft lips and run my fingertips over the ridges in his abs. Gently, ever so gently, I stroke his dick from his balls to his tip, and then stroke his shaft with the barest of touches, and the sensation of him hardening in my hand, even before he's fully awakened, ignites me.

I throw my leg over Josh's hip and slip his full length inside me and ride him slowly, reaching between my legs to feel him slipping in and out of me as I do, and in no time at all, Josh's lips find my neck, his warm hands find my breasts and belly and hips and clit, his tongue slips inside my moaning mouth, and his movement inside me deepens and intensifies. And all the while, the Plain White T's sing those three little words repeatedly, telling Josh exactly how I feel—and more importantly, instructing him there's only one thing to do: say "I love you."

"Kat," Josh breathes. "I missed you."

Not the words I'm hoping for, but this feels so damned good, I don't even care. I gyrate my hips passionately, coaxing Josh to his release, but, much to my surprise, Josh pulls out of me, pushes me onto my back, and begins pleasuring me in every conceivable way. He kisses my breasts and neck and face and runs his hands over my thighs and sucks on my fingers and toes and kisses my inner thighs, and, finally, laps at me with his warm, wet tongue, licking my clit with particular fervor. A warm and delicious orgasm rolls through me, almost lazily, like it's taking its time on a quiet Sunday afternoon. Finally, Josh slips inside me again and gyrates on top of me until he comes, too, just as the Plain White T's are telling him, as explicitly as song lyrics can possibly do, it's time for him to freaking tell me he loves me already.

When we're done, we lie nose to nose for a long moment, stroking each other's warm skin in the dark.

"Did you choose this song or was it the next song on your playlist?" he asks.

"I chose it. Because of its lyrics. Specifically. For you."

There's a beat.

Josh takes a deep breath. "I love you, Kat."

Every hair on my body stands on end. Thank you, Baby Jesus in the Manger.

"I love you more than the air I breathe," Josh continues. "More than life itself. I love you so, so much, Kat." He lets out a shaky breath. "I love you, I love you, I love you."

Thank you, God. I throw my arms around Josh's neck and kiss the hell out of him. "I love you, too," I blurt. "I love you, Josh. Oh my God. I love you, I love you, I love you."

Josh clutches me fiercely. "I love you with all my heart and soul, Kat."

"I love you to the moon and back again," I say.

Josh is trembling, covering my face and neck with kisses. "I love you more than I knew was even possible," he says.

"I love you, I love you, I love you," I reply.

"No one's ever said those words to me before," he whispers. "Thank you. Oh my God, thank you."

"What?" I say, but my words are muffled by his furious lips.

"I love you," he says, over and over, kissing me without reprieve.

I laugh and cry at the same time, I'm so completely flooded with joy. "I can't live without you," I murmur into his lips. "I can't breathe without you. I can't—"

Josh pulls away from kissing me. "Move in with me, Kat," he blurts.

My heart leaps. I don't even need to think about it. "Yes."

"Yes?"

"*Yes.*"

He kisses me voraciously, yet again.

Damn, I wish I could see Josh's beautiful blue eyes right now, but the room is too dark. "Are you sure?" I ask, and immediately regret it. Why am I giving Josh a chance to worm out of his offer? Stupid Kat!

But my worry is for nothing—Josh thrills me with his immediate and confident reply: "I'm sure," he says. "I can't live without you. I love you more than life itself."

I exhale and hug him fervently. "I love you," I gasp. "I love you, I love you, I love you."

"I can't stand being away from you," he says. "I want to sleep with you every night. I want to wake up to the sight of you every morning. I want to take care of you—to make all your dreams come true."

"Oh my God. I'm gonna explode," I say, tears rising in my eyes.

"When can you move in?"

"Right away."

"Oh my God," he says. He's panting. "This is gonna be awesome."

He's shaking like a leaf. Is that anxiety or joy coursing through his veins? I wish I could see his face.

"I haven't even met with the interior designer for my house yet," Josh says breathlessly. "We'll decorate the place together. It'll be *our* house, Kat—with *our* baby—yeah, and we'll make one of the rooms a nursery, and you can decorate it however you like and we'll live together and raise our kid and we'll be *happy.*" He's rambling maniacally, practically gasping for air, stroking my face feverishly. It's like the Hoover Dam has broken inside him and a pent-up reservoir of words and feelings is gushing out of him all at once. "We'll be together because we *want* to be," Josh continues, his words pouring out of him like a torrent. "Because we *love* each other. We won't need a piece of paper to make our commitment official." He abruptly stops talking. His voice quavers. "Right? We love each other and that's all we need?" He swallows audibly. "Right?"

"I don't need a piece of paper," I say soothingly. "All I need is you, Josh. If you promise to love me and our baby the best way you know how, that's enough for me."

He exhales a huge breath. "I promise. I'll love you and our baby. That's what I can give you."

"Then that's enough."

He's panting now. "I want you to live with me, babe—I want you to be all mine."

"I will be. I am."

"Promise?" He's trembling against me.

"I promise."

His chest is heaving against mine. He's literally twitching and jerking next to me. I touch his face. His cheeks are wet.

I'm flabbergasted. "Josh? Oh my God. Are you okay?"

Josh grips me to him. "I love you more than I ever thought possible. I didn't know I could love like this. I didn't know I was *capable*."

Wetness is streaming across my fingertips.

"I love you, too," I say, trying to calm him. "More than I thought possible. Baby, what's wrong?"

Josh takes a shuddering breath, obviously trying to collect himself.

"Josh, honey, calm down. *Breathe*. You're going off the deep end all of a sudden. This is a happy thing—nothing to cry about."

Josh suddenly sits up in the bed, shaking, and I rub his back, trying to soothe him. This isn't how I expected this to go. I thought I'd coax the magic words out of him and we'd hug and kiss and make love and then nuzzle noses. I don't understand. It's almost like he's having some sort of panic attack. What the hell is happening to him?

"When I asked you to marry me at the hospital, you were right to say no," he says, panting. "I was just doing the right thing. I was acting out of obligation —trying to appease my father's ghost—or maybe flip him the bird, I dunno. But I shouldn't have asked that—I realize now I can't deliver on that."

The hairs on the arms are standing up. "Sssh," I soothe. "I don't care about getting married. I just want *you*. We're having a baby together—that's plenty for us to deal with. Our love is enough."

There's a very long silence between us. I have no idea what to say or do, so I continue rubbing his back. He's quiet for so long, I'm beginning to feel like maybe he's regretting telling me he loves me.

"Josh?" I ask, my stomach clenching. "I don't understand why you're freaking out."

Josh pauses. "My dad blew his brains out onto her wedding dress, Kat," he says softly, barely above a whisper.

My heart is pulsing in my ears. I wait but he doesn't elaborate. "I don't understand," I finally say.

"If you were my wife," he continues, "and if I lost you, I'm scared I'd do the same fucking thing. He always said I'm just like him."

My heart lurches into my throat. "Josh," I whisper. "Why are you... ? I don't understand." I sit up next to him and put my cheek on his shoulder, still rubbing his back. "Please explain what you're feeling right now."

"I've lost everyone I love, my whole life," he says, barely above a whisper. "Every single time I love someone, they wind up leaving me—or trying their damnedest to leave me. That's what I'm always trying to 'overcome.' And now that I love you, now that I'm not holding anything back... Kat, I couldn't overcome it if I lost you."

"Well, then, that's easy. You won't lose me. Simple."

Josh scoffs. "No, you don't understand."

I wait.

"What if it's not your choice?" he finally says. "It wasn't my mother's choice."

I take a deep breath. "Well, sorry to be blunt about it," I say, "but that's just the gamble of life, honey. Life can be a bitch and a half and there's nothing we can do about it. Look what just happened to Colby. But I'm telling you I'm not going anywhere, if I can help it. Wild horses couldn't drag me away and that's all I can promise you. And that's got to be enough, babe—I'm only human."

Josh makes a sound I can't interpret.

"What?" I ask.

"What if I fuck up? What then? Will you leave me then?"

"Just don't fuck up."

Josh scoffs. "*Kat.*"

I smile in the dark. "What?"

"I'm serious."

"So am I."

"Kat, I'm gonna fuck up—we both know that. How could I not? I told you—I don't know what love looks like up close. I'm a blind man feeling my way in the dark with my hands tied behind my back. I'll fuck it up and then you'll leave me and then my brains will be splattered on the ceiling."

"Well, first off, that's just dumb," I say. "You're not giving yourself enough credit for your awesomeness. You're covered in Teflon, baby, remember? But second off, I've got an easy fix for the whole situation." I touch his face and I'm shocked to find his cheeks are still wet. "Oh, Josh," I breathe.

Josh abruptly turns his face away from my touch. "What's your easy fix?"

I kiss his broad shoulder and turn his face toward mine in the dark. "I'll teach you what to do, honey. Problem solved. Slowly but surely, I'll teach you how to do this love-thing. And so will my family. And so will our baby. And whenever you fuck up, I'll forgive you and you'll get better and better at it until you hardly fuck up at all."

He doesn't reply. And in the silence, I suddenly realize the Plain White T's song on constant repeat is starting to annoy the shit out of me. I reach over to my laptop and flip my playlist onto shuffle, and "Mirrors" by Justin Timberlake randomly begins to play.

I scoot back to Josh in bed, smashing my breasts against his broad back. "Babe," I say. "Listen to me. You can totally do this. Remember when you started the L.A. branch of Faraday & Sons? You didn't know a goddamned thing about running a business, but you learned on the job and kicked ass and now you're a freaking beast. Well, same thing here."

Josh lets out a long exhale.

"Plus, it won't even be possible for you to blow your brains out onto my wedding dress because there won't *be* a wedding dress. Ever. Easy peasy pumpkin squeezy. Problem solved."

Josh doesn't reply.

Shit, this man is a tough nut to crack.

"Hello?" I say. "You've gone completely mute on me, boy. At least gimme a hint about what you're thinking."

"I'll give you more than a hint," he says, his voice soft but intense. "I'm thinking I love you. I'm thinking I'm so lucky I found you. And I'm thinking I hate myself for crying like a little bitch right now."

"I love you, too," I say, sighing with relief. "And you're not crying like a little bitch. You're crying like a normal human. *Finally.*"

Josh kisses me passionately. He's obviously calmed down and returned to his usual form. His panic attack, or whatever the heck it was, seems to be over.

"Okay?" I ask, stroking his hair. "All better?"

"Yeah," he says, sounding like the weight of the world has just been lifted off him. "I'm good."

"Honey, slowly but surely, you'll learn how to do the love-thing and you'll become wise and powerful and unstoppable. Okay?"

"Well, I'm already wise and powerful. I've told you that a hundred times. Damn, you're a horrible listener."

"Oh, yeah," I coo. I touch his cheeks in the dark. They're dry now. Sticky with his dried tears, but dry. "I know you're wise and powerful," I whisper. "I was just seeing if you were listening."

"I love you, Kat," Josh whispers.

"I love you, too—I love you, I love you, I love you."

Josh's breathing hitches. "Thank you for saying 'I love you' and not 'me, too.' I had no idea how awesome it would feel to hear you say those *actual* words to me."

"I love you, I love you, I love you," I say. "*Forever.*"

Josh kisses me—but he doesn't say that last word back to me, I notice.

Well, damn. I knew I was pushing my luck hoping for a promise of "forever" from Josh Faraday, but, hey, it didn't hurt to try. Really, I should have known "forever" simply isn't in the man's vocabulary. It's okay, though—I'm content. Josh has promised to be mine—to love me and make a home with me and to be a father for our child. Considering what he's been through in his life, and how fucked up he is underneath all that glitter, I'm pretty sure that's the most I could ever hope to squeeze out of this particular turnip.

I pull on his shoulder and guide him to lie back down in the bed with me, nose to nose, just as the song on my laptop flips to the next random song on my computer: "The Distance" by Cake.

"Oh, God, I love Cake," Josh says.

"Me, too. I saw them last year. They were fantastic."

"You did? In Seattle?"

"Yeah."

"I saw them in L.A. last year," Josh says.

"Oh my God, the dude with the trumpet—"

"I know," Josh says cutting me off enthusiastically. "I couldn't take my eyes off him the whole time. He was singing backup-vocals and playing keys and trumpet, all at the same time. Incredible."

"Incredible," I agree. I sing the chorus to "Sheep Go To Heaven, Goats Go To Hell," one of my favorite Cake songs, and Josh laughs.

"I love that song," he says, nuzzling his nose into mine in the dark.

"Well, I love you," I reply.

He presses his body against mine. "That Plain White T's song was a stroke of genius—utterly diabolical," Josh says. "Thank you for that."

"I've been dying to tell you," I say. "I thought I was gonna explode if I didn't finally tell you. I figured if that song plus the thing with Bridgette didn't finally make you break down and say the magic words to me, then nothing ever would."

"What do you mean the thing with Bridgette?"

"Yeah. The thing with Bridgette. You know. I figured the way to unlock your tortured heart once and for all was through a trap door marked 'Sick Fuck.'" I smile smugly in the dark. "And I was right, of course."

Josh laughs. "Oh my God. You think you *manipulated* me into saying 'I love you' tonight?"

"No. Not *manipulated* you—more like made a *safe place* for you to say it. I'd say I 'set the stage' for you to say it."

"Well, guess what, Madame Terrorist? I was gonna say it tonight no matter what. So there."

I scoff.

"It's true. I had everything planned. I had a romantic dinner lined up at my house and I was gonna tell you tonight."

"Mmm hmm. Sure thing, Playboy."

"Babe. I had a violinist and a cellist—a chef and waiter. Five-star meal. *Candles.* I was gonna do this whole romantic thing."

"Oh, that's so sweet. I had no idea. Thank you. But you wouldn't have said it unless I masterfully *unlocked* you—I guarantee it."

Josh chuckles. "Nope. I was already gonna say it."

"Hmmph," I say, completely unconvinced.

"Hmmph?"

"Yes. Hmmph."

"You don't believe me?"

"Nope."

"You wanna bet?"

"We can't *bet* because there's no way to objectively prove it."

"Oh, yes, there is."

"Prove it, then."

"What do I get when I do?"

"I dunno. If you prove it, then I'll decide after the fact what you win. You'll just have to take a leap of faith." I roll my eyes, even in the dark. "But just because you had a violinist doesn't *prove* you would have taken the next step and told me you love me. In fact, I think it's highly unlikely you would have said it with a violinist standing there breathing down your neck."

Josh pauses. "Hmm. You might be right about that part. But I still would have said it—maybe after dinner, when we were alone in bed."

"I highly doubt that," I say. "You needed an expert push from a woman who knows you better than you know yourself."

"No, I didn't—I was gonna do it all by myself."

"Nope," I say.

"Ha!" he says. "Get ready to eat crow, Madame Terrorist." Josh sits up, turns on the lamp next to him, and lies back down next to me on his side, smiling devilishly.

"Well?" I ask. "Why are you smiling like that? All you've proved is that you know how to turn on a lamp. That proves absolutely nothing."

"Look at my arm," he whispers softly.

"Hmm?"

"Look at my arm, babe."

I sit up and peer at Josh's muscled arm in the dim light and instantly gasp.

Holy shitballs. Josh has a brand new tattoo on the outside of his left bicep— a golden cat with big blue eyes, long lashes, and a mischievous feline-smile on her sleek face. Wow. She looks just like me if I were reincarnated as a cartoon cat.

For a long moment, I study Josh's tattoo in detail, marveling at it's amazingness. The cartoon-cat version of me is wearing a pink collar adorned with a dangling "PG" charm at its center and she's holding a martini glass filled with two olives in her slender paw. And, best of all, her bottom legs are entangled in a swirl of barbed wire that trails from her tail and wraps clear around Josh's bicep.

"Josh," I gasp. "You got a girlfriend-barbed-wire-double-social-suicide-tattoo!"

"Yep," Josh says, his face bursting with excitement.

I laugh gleefully.

Josh puts his finger under my chin, his eyes smoldering. "I know I've gotten some questionable tattoos in my life, babe, but do you really think I'd have committed *double social suicide* if I wasn't planning to tell you I love you?"

I can't speak. It's taking all my energy not to pass out, cry, or climax. This is the most incredible gift Josh could have given me—way better than a big, fat diamond any day. (Well, okay, not way better than a big, fat diamond, let's not get too carried away here—but pretty damned close.) Certainly, in the land of Joshua William Faraday, this barbed-wire-girlfriend tattoo is the closest thing to a promise of forever I could ever hope to receive. And that's good enough for me.

I nuzzle my nose into Josh's. "You do realize you're gonna have this thing *florebblaaaaaah?*" I say.

"That's the idea, baby. I'm gonna love you *florebblaaaah.*" He laughs. "I promise."

I laugh with him. "I was wondering why you didn't take your shirt off during the Bridgette thing—I just thought you were being extra careful not to piss me off."

Josh laughs. "Well, yeah, that, too."

"Thank you so much," I say, running my fingers through Josh's hair. "The tattoo is incredible. I love it."

"My supreme pleasure." He kisses me.

Damn, my clit is throbbing like crazy. I do believe this man's about to get lucky again.

"So, Madame Terrorist," Josh says, pulling away from our kiss. "Do you concede?"

I raise an eyebrow. "*Concede?*"

"Yeah. Do you admit my tattoo empirically proves I was gonna tell you I love you, whether or not you arranged the Bridgette thing?"

I squint at him.

"Well?" he asks, a smug smile dancing on his lips.

My nostrils involuntarily flare.

"You're seriously gonna be Stubborn Kat about this?" he asks.

I smash my lips together and narrow my eyes further.

Josh shakes his head. "You're such a little terrorist. You know full well this tattoo proves I would have—"

I place my fingertip on Josh's lips, shushing him. "*Josh,*" I whisper seductively.

He abruptly stops talking.

"In the big picture, it really doesn't matter who's right and who's wrong, now does it?"

"*It doesn't matter?* Ha! I've finally got Stubborn Kat dead to rights for once in my life."

"*Josh,*" I coo quietly, shushing him again.

He shoots me a wicked smirk. "*What?*"

I lick my lips. "What's the cardinal rule for bagging a babe?" I ask, reaching underneath the sheet and sliding my fingers down his abs to his penis. "What's the most important thing I taught you and Henn about bagging a babe?"

Josh's cock instantly responds to my touch. A lascivious smile spreads across his gorgeous face. "Oh," he says.

"What's the rule, Playboy?" I whisper, skimming my lips against his, sliding my hand up and down his thickening shaft.

Josh smiles into my lips. "Ask yourself, 'Is what I'm about to say more or less likely to get me a blowjob?'" He presses his pelvis forward and his hard-on presses emphatically into my palm. "'If the answer's yes, then proceed—and if not, then shut the fuck up.'"

I nod slowly. "So, based on that one simple rule, what do you think you should do right now?"

Josh smiles. "Shut the fuck up."

"Give that man a salami," I say. I touch the tip of his erection and swirl my finger around and around. "And to answer your question," I whisper. "Yes, I'm gonna be Stubborn Kat about this. Surprise, surprise." I shoot him a naughty smile. "But I truly don't think you'll mind."

Josh nods, but, smartly, doesn't say a word.

"Congratulations, baby," I whisper, biting my lip. "I do believe you just bagged yourself a babe."

Josh's hard-on twitches in my hand.

With a happy giggle, I lift the sheet and begin kissing my way from Josh's muscled chest all the way down to his massive hard-on. After sucking on his tip like a lollipop for a brief moment, the anticipation is too much for me to bear—I gotta have him. I slide his full length into my mouth, all the frickin' way—eliciting an excited sound from the other side of the sheet—and then I proceed to give the love of my life the most enthusiastic and heartfelt Katherine Ulla Morgan Ultimate Blowjob Experience the world has ever seen.

104

KAT

"Wow, it's nice," Josh says, pulling his Lamborghini to a stop in front of my parents' house.

I've always been proud of my childhood home—it's the place everyone always wanted to hang out when I was growing up—but now that I'm looking at it through Josh's eyes, I'm realizing the entire house probably would fit inside the *garage* of Josh's childhood home.

"This house is right out of a movie," Josh says.

"What movie would that be, babe?" I ask.

"You know, every movie where a suburban high-schooler throws a raging kegger when his parents go out of town."

"Oh, I think I've seen that one," I say. "Does everyone get trashed and start jumping into the pool, fully clothed?"

"Yeah. And then hijinks ensues."

I giggle. "That's right. I'm pretty sure Ryan was in that movie at least ten times in high school, always playing the guy throwing the party."

"I think I'm gonna love Ryan."

"Oh, you will—he's your spirit animal."

Josh chuckles. "Ryan Morgan's my spirit animal?"

I laugh. "Yes."

"Is he gonna be here tonight?"

"Yep. Everyone but Keane—he had to work. Oh, and by the way, don't mention the whole male-stripper thing to my parents. They have no idea Keane's become Seattle's answer to *Magic Mike*."

"Would they care if they knew?"

I shrug. "Keane seems to think my dad would be really disappointed in him. But I told him, 'No, Peen, Dad would have to have actual *expectations* in the first place in order to be *disappointed*.'" I snort.

"Well, that wasn't a very nice thing to say."

I chuckle. "When you meet Keane, you'll understand. He's just... *Keane*." I touch Josh's arm. "So are you ready to go in and face the firing squad?"

"Why you gotta say that?" Josh asks. "I'm nervous enough, babe."

"Aw, I'm sorry. Just teasing. They're gonna love you."

"Just do me a favor. Don't let it slip about the baby tonight, okay? Just like we agreed. First time out, I want your family to get to know me as Josh, not as The Guy Who Knocked Up Their Precious Baby Girl."

"Babe, we already agreed to keep mum—my lips are sealed."

"Kat, your lips are never sealed—you're the biggest blabbermouth I know, bar none."

I'm genuinely aghast at Josh's characterization of me. "No, I'm not—I'm a steel safe."

Josh hoots with laughter. "Kat, you blabbed to Sarah not five minutes after you said we should wait 'til after the wedding to say anything, and then you told Dax right after you said we were gonna wait to tell your family until after you're showing."

"Well, yeah, but Sarah doesn't count as *blabbing*—telling Sarah's the same thing as telling myself. And Dax doesn't count as telling my *family*—because he's *Dax*." I roll my eyes. "Trust me, I'm a steel safe, babe—a locked vault."

"Oh really? Well, guess who called me this afternoon out of the blue to congratulate me on our 'little Cinnabon in the oven'?"

I bite my lip, too afraid to give myself away by venturing a guess—but I'm pretty sure there's only one person in the world who'd ever refer to a baby as a "little Cinnabon in the oven."

"*Henn*," Josh says, confirming what I'm thinking. "He called to congratulate me and ask why the hell I didn't tell him myself."

I make a face that says, "Oops."

"When did you tell Hannah?" Josh asks, scowling at me.

I flash Josh my most charming smile. "Okay, now, see, telling Hannah wasn't my fault. Hannah and I went to lunch today and she was asking me about Golden Kat PR, hinting about how much she wants to be a part of it, and I didn't want to string her along into thinking I was gonna be starting my company any time soon as originally planned. So I told her, 'Hey, I can only handle birthing one baby at a time—and this year, my one-and-only baby's gonna be the accidental Faraday that's currently growing inside my uterus.'"

Josh shakes his head. I can't read his expression well enough to gauge if he's genuinely upset with me.

"Was Henny pissed he heard the news from Hannah and not you?" I ask.

"No, you know Henn. He's always chill. I told him I didn't tell him about the baby because you and I had solemnly agreed to keep it quiet until you're showing." He glares at me, but his eyes are sparkling. "Little did I know the 'steel safe' was out blabbing to everyone and their uncle about our little 'Cinnabon in the oven.'"

"Oh, speaking of which, have you told your uncle?"

"Uh, *no*. Because we'd agreed to keep things quiet, you blabbermouth."

I laugh. "So what did Henn say?"

"He said every time he sees our kid he's gonna wonder if he personally witnessed it being conceived."

I groan. "God, that was so embarrassing."

Josh laughs. "He also said he predicts an entire minivan filled with screaming kids in my near future."

My entire body jolts at the thought. "Slow down, High Speed," I say, my heart in my throat.

"Oh, and he said I'm the luckiest bastard in the whole wide world." He touches the cleft in my chin. "Which is the truth."

I blush like a schoolgirl on a first date.

"And, hey, Miss Steel Safe, guess who called me right after Henn?" Josh asks, mock-glaring at me.

I hold my breath, trying to remember if there's anyone else I've blabbed to besides Sarah, Dax, and Hannah. Nope. Not a soul. Only the girls at my yoga class, but they don't really count. Oh, and the UPS guy—but only because I'd ordered a bunch of maternity leggings and he mentioned his wife is pregnant— so what was I supposed to do—*not* tell him? Oh, and the barista at my favorite Starbucks, of course—but that was only because I'm no longer drinking caffeine and my usual barista noticed I'd ordered a decaf, so that one's not my fault, either. Oh, and Sarah's mom. But that was only because I went to see the new additions she's making to Gloria's House (thanks to the finder's fee money she received after we took down The Club), and Gloria said I looked "awfully pretty"—so what was I supposed to do then—*not* tell her I'm pregnant? I scour my memory, trying to think if I've told anyone else—but, nope, I think that's it.

Oh, Josh is staring at me, apparently expecting me to guess who called him after Henn.

I shrug. "I have no idea who called you," I say. "I haven't told anyone else."

"*Reed*," Josh says. "Because, apparently, Henn called Reed right after Hannah told him the news."

"He did? Oh."

"Yeah, he did. Which is so unlike Henn, I was shocked—if you wanna see what a *real* steel safe looks like, look no further than Peter Hennessey—so I asked Reed what Henn had said to him, *and do you know what Reed said?*"

I shake my head.

"He told me that when you told Hannah our baby news, Hannah asked if you were keeping things on the down-low for a while—*because she was fully prepared to keep our secret and respect our privacy*—but *you* said, and I quote, 'Not at all! I don't care who knows about it! Blab away, Hannah Banana Montana Milliken! I'm bursting at the seams for the whole world to know!'"

I bite my lip. "I said that? I don't think I said *that*."

"Well, either you said it or Hannah's lying. Which is it?"

"Hannah's lying. Definitely. She's a big, fat liar. Actually, there's something you should know about Hannah: she's a pathological liar. Poor thing truly can't discern the difference between truth and fiction. It's such a shame. She's a really sweet girl otherwise."

Josh is clearly suppressing a smile. "Huh. Pretty weird you set Henn up with a known pathological liar. That wasn't very nice of you."

I shrug, trying to suppress my smirk.

"And even weirder you wanted her to be your right-hand-woman at Golden Kat PR. That sounds like horrible judgment on your part, PG."

"Well, you know, I was hoping to rehabilitate her—kill her with kindness until she saw the error of her ways."

Josh chuckles.

"So you're not mad at me for being a blabbermouth?" I ask.

"No, if you wanna blab, go ahead. All I ask is that you *tell* me first so my best friends aren't calling me up, congratulating me on my forthcoming *child*, and I'm sitting there like a flop-dick with my thumb up my ass."

"I'm sorry. I just couldn't keep it to myself. Now that I'm finally through the first trimester and feeling so much better, I'm bursting to tell people."

Josh grabs my hand. "You're so fucking adorable, Kat."

I grin. "So what did Reed say? Was he shocked?"

"To put it mildly," Josh says. "But when I told him I'm starting to get sort of excited about our little kumquat, he was really happy for me—for us."

"*Lime*."

"Huh?"

"The baby's the size of a *lime* now." I pat my stomach. "No longer a kumquat."

Josh makes a face that melts me. He touches my stomach. "No matter how big the baby gets, it will always be the-kumquat-inside-the-Kumquat to me."

My heart leaps. "You told Reed you're getting sort of excited about the kumquat?"

Josh beams a beautiful smile at me. "Yeah."

"And are you?"

"Babe, what the hell have I been doing this whole past week with you, shopping for cribs and diaper changing tables and fucking onesies and maternity leggings if I'm not starting to get at least a little bit excited about the-kumquat-inside-the-Kumquat?"

I shrug. "It still feels nice to hear you say it."

Josh grabs my hand, his eyes sparkling. "Well that settles it, babe—you've definitely got a vagina."

"I sure hope so," I say. "Because pushing a baby out my peen would *really* hurt."

"Oh my God. Gah." He shudders with phantom pain and puts his forehead on his steering wheel. "Don't say that. Just the thought."

I giggle. "Okay, Playboy. You ready to go into Morgan Manor now?" I look at my watch. "Oh, we're still a bit early—it's ten to seven. My mom said to come between seven and seven-thirty."

Josh takes a deep breath. "Good. That gives me a little more time to prepare mentally."

"Prepare mentally? To meet my family? Babe, they're gonna love you. Don't worry, they're predisposed to love you because *I* love you and I told them so. I told them I love you, I love you, I love you—and I do."

"But you said the same thing about Garrett-Asswipe-Bennett and Colby hated that fucker."

I roll my eyes. "No, Colby hated Garrett-Asswipe-Bennett because he was an asswipe, and you're not. Plus, I didn't actually love Garrett—I just *thought* I did because I was young and stupid and blinded by hormones. And, anyway, regardless, I never told Garrett I loved him and I certainly never, ever told my family 'I love him, I love him, I love him,' the way I've told them about you." I touch Josh's thigh. "Because I've never love, love, *loved* anyone before you—and my family will easily be able to see that."

Josh's smile could light the night sky. "I love you, Kat."

I sigh happily. "It'll never get old hearing you say that."

"Hey, you know what I just realized?" Josh says. "After all your blabbing, I bet someone's gonna say something about the baby to your parents at Jonas and Sarah's wedding—definitely not the way we'd want them to find out."

"Oh, shit," I say. "Good point." I twist my mouth. "Shoot. I guess that means I'd better tell them before the wedding." I grimace. "Which means I gotta tell them this week." My stomach flips over at the thought.

"Yeah, but just don't do it tonight, okay?" Josh says. "And let's not tell them you've moved in with me, either. After they get to know me a bit, that's when we'll hit them with all our fantastic news. No sense making them hate me the first time they meet me."

"They're not gonna hate you when they find out we're shacking up—and they're not gonna hate you when they find out you knocked me up, either. They'll handle all of it with grace."

Intellectually, I know I'm telling Josh the truth and not just placating him—my parents will most certainly deal with whatever I throw at them, like they always do. But that doesn't mean my stomach's not clenched tightly right now, imagining myself telling them I'm pregnant. The truth is, no matter how much my family has always treated me like one of the guys in some ways, I'm still my parents' baby girl and my brothers' Kum Shot—and there's no doubt me becoming an unintentional mother isn't the future my family members envisioned for me.

I look out the window of the Lamborghini for a moment, gazing at my parents' house, lost in my thoughts.

"Hey," Josh says softly, touching my arm. "You want me to be there when you tell your parents about the baby this week?"

"Nope. It should be just me and them." I let out a slow exhale, suddenly wracked with anxiety. "It'll be fine."

Josh takes a deep breath and mimics my slow and anxious exhale.

"Wow, the two of us are really not living up to our nicknames right now," I say. "Come on. Let's pull ourselves together, Playboy—time to get this party started."

Josh lets out a loud puff of air. "Maybe I should have driven the Beemer instead of the Lamborghini? You know, gone for something a little less ostentatious?"

"Babe, first of all, your Beemer's not exactly a low-key car. I didn't even know they made Beemers that fancy. Second, Ryan would have *killed* me if he found out you drive a Lamborghini and he didn't get to see it."

"Oh yeah? Well, Ryan can do more than see it—he can test drive it tonight if he wants. Shit, I'll let him borrow the damned thing for a week."

I grimace. "Josh. Pull yourself together."

Josh makes a face. "Too much? Douchey?"

"Not douchey, honey—sweet. But a tad bit *desperate*. Next thing you know, you'll be standing with a boom box over your head on my parents' front lawn." I snort, but Josh grimaces. "What?" I ask.

Josh shakes his head. "Nothing."

"I was just kidding, babe. I know you'd never do something that 'desperate.'" I wink.

"So, okay," Josh says, rolling his eyes. "I shouldn't hand my Lamborghini keys over to Ryan. Any other tips for tonight?"

"Yes. Madame Professor says: 'The best way to bag a family is to be your awesome self—and the rest will take care of itself.'"

"Excellent advice. Thank you, Madame Professor."

"You're so cute," I say. "I've never seen you nervous like this."

"I've never tried to bag a family before. Babes, I can bag by the dozens in my sleep—families not so much."

"Haven't you ever met a girl's family before?"

Josh shakes his head. "Not really. I've met parents before—lots of times—but only incidentally. That tends to happen in the circles I move in—lots of black-tie galas and bumping into people on the slopes or at birthday parties—or maybe I was fucking some girl at her parents' vacation house in wherever and her parents unexpectedly dropped by to say hi." He laughs. "But I've never been invited for 'next level' spaghetti with a girl's parents and brothers on a quiet suburban street in Seattle. And I've certainly never brought *pie*." He motions to the pie box sitting on his lap. "I feel like I'm in a movie."

"Babe, you've got it backwards. Going to black-tie galas or staying at Gabrielle LeMonde's vacation home in Aspen is the thing that's like a movie. Pie is real life."

"Not to me. This is amazing. I don't wanna fuck it up." He looks down at his black button-down shirt and jeans. "I'm so damned glad I dressed like Jonas tonight. Thanks for the heads up about that."

"You look great."

Josh nods decisively. "Okay. Let's do this, Party Girl." He grabs the bouquet of flowers off my lap and the pie off his. "Can you hand me the wine and Scotch?"

I grab the booze bottles down by my feet. "You can't carry everything plus the pie," I say. "Let me carry something."

"Okay. You take the Scotch," Josh says. "I can handle everything else." He reaches for his door handle. "Stay put, babe. I'll let you out."

I sit primly with my hands in my lap as Josh moves around the back of the car and opens my door.

"Thank you, sir," I say as Josh helps me out of the car and escorts me toward my parents' front door. "Glenfarclas 1955," I say, reading the label on the box of Scotch in my hand. "I know nothing about Scotch. Is that a good one?"

Josh lets out a little puff of air. "Yeah."

I stop short. That little air-puff raised the hair on the nape of my neck. "Hang on," I say.

Josh stops. "What?"

"How good?" I ask.

"How good what?"

"How good a bottle of Scotch is this?"

"Good. You said your dad loves Scotch, so I got him something I was sure he'd really like."

"Oh, jeez."

"What?"

"Josh. *Honey.* Your idea of a 'good' Scotch is gonna be different than the average person's."

Josh looks at me blankly.

"Josh, how much did this bottle of Scotch cost?"

He opens his mouth and closes it.

"Josh?"

"It cost me nothing. My uncle gave it to me from his private collection."

"Your uncle . . ? Oh, shit. Josh, what's it *worth*?"

Josh winces. "Well, okay, it's a *little* on the extravagant side, I'll admit that— but not too bad. Not, like, *crazy.* I just wanted to be sure it'd be something your dad would really like."

"How much is a *little* extravagant, honey? Gimme a number."

"Don't forget this is a special occasion. I'll never again meet your parents for the first time. I just wanted to make a good impression."

My heart's racing. "Josh, you're freaking me out. How much is it worth?"

"Eight."

I inhale sharply. "Eight hundred dollars?"

Josh looks as guilty as sin.

"Eight *hundred* bucks for a bottle of Scotch?" I ask again slowly, incredulous.

Josh doesn't reply, but he looks like he just confessed to murder.

"Josh, you can't give my father an eight-hundred-dollar bottle of Scotch—especially not the first time you meet him."

Josh grimaces.

"It was such a sweet thought, honey, but you're gonna freak him out and make him think you're some sort of eccentric tycoon or something—like, who's that hermit-guy with airplanes?"

"Howard Hughes."

"*Yes.* My dad's gonna think you're Howard Hughes—or, worse, he's gonna think you're trying to buy his affection."

Josh winces like I've punched him in the stomach. "Shit. I just wanted to give your dad something he'd really, really like."

"I know, babe, but it's too extravagant. I'm sorry."

Josh exhales. "Well, shit." He looks crestfallen. "If an eight-*hundred*-dollar bottle of Scotch is too extravagant to give your dad, then I *really* screwed the pooch here."

I pause, processing what Josh is trying to say. "It's not an eight-hundred-dollar bottle?" I ask.

Josh shakes his head.

"Oh, Josh," I say gasping. "Eight *thousand?*"

He nods. "I called my uncle to ask for a recommendation and he insisted on sending me a bottle of the good stuff from his private collection."

"Oh my God. *Josh.* If my dad knew how much that bottle was worth, he'd never open it. He'd sell it and finally take my mom to Hawaii, instead."

Josh's face lights up. "Your parents have never been to Hawaii? What about your brothers? Do you think they'd like to go, too?"

"Josh, focus. You're not taking the entire Morgan clan to Hawaii. We're talking about Scotch."

Josh laughs. "You read my mind."

"I know I did."

"It'd be fun, though, wouldn't it?"

I laugh. "You're crazy."

"I know I am. But that doesn't mean it wouldn't be fun."

"Oh, it'd definitely be fun," I say.

"Maybe after Colby's feeling better and the baby's born we could take a big family trip to celebrate both?"

I smile. This is the first time I've heard Josh make future plans. "Maybe." I bite my lip, my heart bursting. "That would be incredible."

"Then we'll do it. It's a plan."

"I love you, Josh."

I've never seen Josh smile quite so big. "God, I love it when you say that," he says. "I love you, too."

My entire body's tingling. "Well, you've artfully distracted me, my darling Playboy. I was telling you to put the Scotch in the car."

Josh's facial expression morphs from elation to disappointment. "I'd hate to meet your dad empty-handed."

"You're not empty-handed, babe—you've got pie and wine and flowers. That's plenty. Maybe you can give my Dad an eight-thousand-dollar bottle of Scotch to celebrate him becoming a grandfather when the baby comes. You know, once he already loves you and knows you're not a hermit-tycoon-weirdo."

Josh's shoulders droop. "Okay."

I hand Josh the Scotch and he hands me the wine bottle to hold in return. "I'll be right back," he says, turning around and heading toward the car.

"Hang on," I say, the hair on my neck standing up again.

Josh stops and looks at me expectantly.

"What about this, Playboy?" I ask, holding up the wine bottle.

Josh waves me off. "Oh, that's just, you know, a Cabernet."

"Mmm hmm. Just a Cabernet?"

"Yep."

He's not fooling me for a minute—he looks guilty as hell. "Like, you mean the kind of Cabernet someone could pick up at Whole Foods for twenty bucks?" I ask. "Or, maybe if they *really* wanna splurge, for like, fifty?"

Josh looks like I've just tweaked his nipple. Hard.

"Joshua?" I coax. "What kind of Cabernet are we talking about here, babe?"

Josh purses his lips. "Goddammit, Kat. I can't be expected to follow your stupid rules. I am what I am."

I laugh. "Did you buy it or get it from your uncle?"

"I bought it. And it didn't cost even *close* to eight thousand bucks, I promise. We're good."

"If it's more than a hundred bucks, it's too much, baby. I'm sorry."

Josh makes a face but doesn't speak.

"It's more than a hundred bucks, isn't it?"

He nods. "But only slightly. How 'bout we give it to her and not mention its pedigree? We'll just let her think it's some Australian red I got at Whole Foods on the way here."

"How much, Josh?"

He shrugs. "Four."

I squint. "*Hundred*?"

He shakes his head.

"Josh!"

Josh makes an absolutely adorable face.

I point at his car. "Put it in the Lamborghini with the Scotch," I say. "Jesus God, man. Have you no common sense?" But even as the words come out of my mouth, I glance at his ridiculous car that probably cost as much as a condo and feel like I just answered my own question.

Josh laughs. "Babe, but this particular Cabernet's a *really* great vintage."

I shake my head. "Oh my God, you're so out of touch, it's scary. You can't give my mom a four-thousand-dollar bottle of wine, honey. I'm sorry. You're a sweetheart, you really are, but you're insane."

"Shit," Josh says, looking bummed. "Fine." He grabs the wine from me and hands me the pie, and then traipses to his car, exhaling in resignation as he goes. "Sorry," he says when he returns to me on the walkway again. "I was just trying to..." He trails off and doesn't finish his sentence. He shrugs.

"I know what you were trying to do," I say. "But it's too much."

Josh twists his mouth. "Douchey?"

I kiss him. "Not at all. *Sweet*." I kiss him again. "God, I love you."

Josh grins into my lips. "Say that again."

"I love you," I whisper.

Josh nuzzles my nose. "One more time."

"I love you," I coo. "I love you, I love you, I love you. Infinity."

"I love you, too," he says. He takes a deep breath. "Okay. I'm good now. Momentary blip. I'm ready to get in there and give 'em the Playboy Razzle-Dazzle."

"They won't know what hit 'em, baby," I whisper.

"That's right," he says. He glances toward the house, unmistakable anxiety flickering across his face. "The Josh Faraday charm-bomb's about to go off all over your family's unsuspecting asses." He swallows hard. "*Ka-boom*, baby. Let's do this shit."

105

KAT

I was wrong. Ryan's not Josh's spirit animal—he's his soul mate. Watching them meet was like watching one of those movies where the hero and heroine see each other across a crowded room and everyone else instantly fades away. It was insta-love of the highest order. But, just in case anyone hadn't caught on to the immediate connection, there was no missing it when, not twenty minutes after Josh and I had entered the house, Ryan invited Josh to play foosball in the garage.

The way it went down was like this: We were all gabbing amiably in the family room, talking about I don't know what. And even Colby, laid out with his leg in a cast and his arm in a sling and his dog Ralph by his side, was chatting Josh up. And that's when my Dad asked Josh how a Seattle boy wound up living in L.A.

"I went to UCLA and wound up staying down there after graduation to open a satellite branch of my family's business," Josh answered.

"Were you in a fraternity at UCLA?" Ryan asked.

"Yeah," Josh answered. "I lived in the house my first two years. I didn't get a whole lot of studying done, but I got *really* good at foosball."

And that was it. Cupid's arrow had struck. Ryan lifted his head like a meerkat on the African plains, little red and pink hearts twinkling where his pupils should have been.

"Oh-no-he-di'n't," I said.

"Here we go," Dad said.

"Oh, it's on," Dax agreed.

Poor Josh looked perplexed, clearly not aware of the Pandora's Box he'd just opened.

"We have a foosball table in our garage," I explained. "It was a Christmas gift from Ryan to my parents years ago—"

"Which was actually a present to *himself*," Dax added.

"And now our family's sort of obsessed with it," I said. "It's kind of our family's *thing*."

"*Oh*," Josh said. "Well, I haven't actually played foosball in forever."

"No excuses," Ryan said, leaping up from the couch. "You and me, Josh." He motioned to Dax and me. "We're gonna kick the Wonder Twins' asses."

"Aw, come on," Dax said. "Don't make me play with Jizz."

"Hey now," I said. But that's all I could muster. I'm the worst foosball player in our family (other than Mom, of course), and everyone knows it, including me.

"Don't worry, we'll play a second game and switch up the teams," Ryan assured Dax. "If need be, I'll get stuck with Jizz the second game."

"*Hey*," I said again.

But Ryan just laughed.

"You need help, Mom?" Dax called to Mom in the kitchen.

"Nope! Dinner will be on the table in thirty!" Mom called back, prompting the four of us to grab our drinks and barrel into the garage, leaving Dad and Colby on the couch, semi-watching a baseball game.

As it turned out, Ryan and Josh soundly kicked the Wonder Twins' asses in the first game, and, in the second game, after poor Josh was saddled with me (because Dax shoved me at him and screamed "You take her, for the love of God!"), my team lost *again*.

"Are you starting to see a pattern here, Kum Shot?" Ryan teased after my second loss. "Now let's think. Who was the common player on *both* losing teams?"

"Hardy har," I replied, feigning annoyance. But I wasn't annoyed. Not even a little bit. In fact, I was walking on air, despite my two foosball losses. Because despite how much I typically abhor losing at anything, I felt like I'd just gained something a whole lot better than a couple of stinkin' foosball victories: I'd gained my brothers' approval of the man I love.

Holy shitballs, Ryan must have slapped Josh on the back at least *five* times during our first game and high-fived him another *ten*. And in the second game, when Ryan and Josh were on opposing teams, Ryan floored me by doing the one thing that conveys matriculation into the Morgan clan more than anything else: he christened Josh with a stupid nickname.

"Aw, come on, *Lambo*," Ryan teased when Josh failed to guard against one of Ryan's many goals. "You can do better than *that*."

"Eh, you got lucky, Captain," Josh shot back easily.

My heart stopped. I looked at Dax, ready to share a look of pure elation, but Dax's gaze was fixed squarely on Josh.

"I thought you said you actually knew how to *play* this game, Hollywood," Dax zinged at Josh. "Pfft."

Josh laughed. "You best not be talking any smack, Whippersnapper—or else it's gonna come back to bite you in your rock-star ass."

And that was that. My brothers had made their feelings about Josh crystal clear—and Josh had returned their affection in no uncertain terms. Just like that, it was two Morgans down, four to go (or, rather, two Morgans down, *three* to go, since we all know Keane's vote doesn't matter).

And now, having finished our two foosball games, the four of us are walking into the family room, laughing and teasing each other as we go, joining Dad and Colby (and Colby's boxer Ralph) on seats around the TV.

"Oh, yeah!" Colby shouts at the television. "Come on, baby! Come on!"

I settle myself onto Josh's lap in a big armchair and glance at the TV, just in time to see the center fielder for the Twins run back, back, back—and then watch helplessly as a long-ball disappears over the center-field fence.

"*And that ball is gone, baby,*" Ryan says.

Colby and Dad shout with glee and the camera cuts to... *Cameron Schulz,* the All-Star shortstop for the Mariners, rounding second-base and fist-pumping the air.

At the sight of Cameron, I stiffen on Josh's lap and look down, hoping against hope he's somehow, through the grace of God, not looking at the TV right now.

"And *Cameron Schulz* smashes a three-run homer to put the Mariners ahead of the Twins three-two in the bottom of the third," the TV announcer says, just in case Josh isn't paying attention to what's happening onscreen. "That was *Cameron Schulz's* twelfth homer of the season after a ten-game drought."

At the mention of Cameron's name on the TV, I glance at Josh to find him shooting me a look that can only be described as *homicidal.*

I bite my lip.

"Schulz is sucking ass this season," Dax says. He flashes me a snarky look, clearly reminding me he knows Cameron's penis was once lodged deep inside me.

I shoot Dax a look in reply that unequivocally warns him not to say or do a goddamned thing to give my secret away or else I will cut him.

"Yeah," Ryan says. "The guy's having a shitty-ass year. Glad he finally did *something* to earn his big, fat paycheck."

Dax opens his mouth to say something but I shoot him daggers again, and he shuts it—for a nanosecond, that is—and then he opens it again. "I heard the guy's juiced up," Dax says, smirking at me. "I bet he's got a tiny little peepee."

I squint at him.

"Well, if that guy's on 'roids, he should fire his dealer," Ryan says, swigging his beer. "Because they're definitely not working."

Josh laughs.

"Totally," Dax says. "The Mariners should trade him."

"They're not gonna *trade* Cameron Schulz," Colby says. "He's a franchise player."

"Poor guy's just having a bad year," Dad pipes in. "It happens to the best of 'em. Give him a break."

Josh's face is mere inches from mine. His eyes are smoldering. He touches the cleft in my chin, a gesture I interpret to mean I'm his and only his (and definitely not that asswipe Cameron Schulz's)—and goose bumps erupt all over my body.

Josh licks his lips and I know he wants to kiss me, but he doesn't—a show of restraint around my family, I suppose. Instead, he leans back in his armchair, his eyes burning holes into my face, wraps his arms around me, and pulls me into him.

"So how's the album coming, Dax?" Josh asks, stroking my hair. "You were about to start recording when we first met at my house."

"Oh, it's going great," Dax says. "We've already got three songs in the can."

"You've got three songs finished?" Dad says. "Wow, that was fast."

"Yeah, we still might tweak the mixes, I'm not sure," Dax clarifies. "But, yeah, all the instrumentation is recorded."

"Did you wind up using the violinist and cellist you met at my house?" Josh asks.

"Yeah, and they slayed it. Total game-changers on the songs."

"Well, let's hear what you've got," Dad says.

Dax looks at me for nonverbal guidance.

Normally, Dax would reply to Dad's question by saying, "Not 'til the songs are one hundred percent finished, Dad"—because that's just the way Dax is. I'm the only one Dax ever lets hear his works in progress (and, in fact, he emailed me MP3s of his three new songs last night, swearing me to secrecy). But Dax refusing to play his new songs right now with Josh sitting right here would be a felony-stupid thing for my brother to do. What if Josh loves the songs (and there's no doubt in my mind he will)? Josh might very well offer to forward them to his best friend Reed, without me ever saying a word about it.

I nod encouragingly at Dax, telling him he should play the songs.

"You can listen to 'em right now, Dad," Dax says. "I've got 'em on my laptop in the back room." He hops up and disappears into the hallway.

"Louise!" Dad calls excitedly to Mom in the kitchen. "Get in here! Daxy's gonna play three songs from his new album."

There's a clatter in the kitchen. "Oh my gosh! I'm coming!" Mom calls—and in a heartbeat, she appears in the family room, her eyes sparkling, her cheeks flushed, a glass of red wine in her hand. "I'm so excited." She plops herself down on the couch next to Dad and puts her head on his shoulder (her patented move), and Dad clasps her free hand in his.

I glance at Josh and I'm not surprised to observe he's absolutely transfixed by my parents and their easy show of affection. *That's right, Playboy*, I think, warmth gurgling at my core like molten lava. *Watch and learn how it's done.*

Dax returns with his laptop and hooks it up to the sound system and a few seconds later, his first song fills the room.

"Oh, your voice is gorgeous, honey," Mom coos. "Smooth as silk." She pauses, listening. "Oh, and that guitar—I *love* it." She pauses again. "Oh my gosh, those lyrics—so clever. Beautiful. Oh, Daxy."

"Ssh, honey," Dad says gently, stroking Mom's arm. "*Listen.*"

I glance at Josh again to find him still mesmerized by my parents. Damn, I wish I could read his thoughts.

The song ends and everyone enthusiastically praises it.

"How do you record a full song like that with all those instruments?" Colby asks, scratching his beloved dog's head. "Did everyone in the band stand in a room and play the song together?"

"No, recording a song's not like playing it live," Dax says, and then he goes on to explain in detail how songs are recorded in a studio, each instrument and vocal methodically recorded one at a time onto separate tracks, and then layered, one on top of the other. "It's like putting together a giant Jenga tower," Dax explains.

"That's so cool," Colby says. "Well, however you did it, the song turned out great."

I shoot Mom a relieved look about Colby and she returns it. Colby's been staying at my parents' house to recuperate, and this is by far the most engaged and upbeat I've seen him in all the times I've come over to hang out with him.

Dax plays his second song, and when it's over, we all agree it's a great song, no doubt about it. But when Dax plays his third song, the room catches fire. And I'm not surprised. When I heard Dax's third song on my computer last night, I instantly became obsessed with it. And hearing it today over a nice sound system has only heightened my love affair with it. The song is ear candy and soul candy all rolled into one, one of those songs you hear to the end and immediately play again.

After everyone in the room has praised the song up and down, Dax tells Josh that all those stringed instruments we just heard on the track were nothing more than those two musicians Dax met at Josh's house, each woman playing on about ten separate tracks to simulate an orchestra.

"Oh my gosh, those violins absolutely make the song," Mom gushes. "I was mesmerized."

"I guess it was kismet I met those ladies at Josh's house when I did," Dax says. He looks at Mom and Dad. "Kat asked me to deliver a dinner invitation to Josh at his house—she'd planned a surprise dinner for him at a restaurant, even though, unbeknownst to her, Josh had planned a romantic dinner for *her* at his house on the same night. When I got there, Josh had a violinist and cellist all set up to play for them during dinner, so I got the musicians' phone numbers."

I shoot a grateful smile at my baby brother, nonverbally thanking him for calling my note to Josh a "dinner invitation" in front of our parents.

"Well, that was sweet of you, Josh," Mom says, putting her hand over her heart. "What a shame you put in all that effort and Kat never saw any of it." She shoots me a scolding look like I somehow *purposefully* fucked up Josh's big plans.

"How was I supposed to know he'd planned a romantic dinner?" I ask.

Josh laughs. "It's okay. My brother Jonas and Sarah wound up enjoying the dinner I'd arranged, and Kat and I had a lovely meal elsewhere."

I force myself not to snicker at Josh's use of the phrase "lovely meal" to describe what we wound up doing with Bridgette that night.

"And, anyway," Josh continues, his eyes shifting to me, "I'd only planned all of that stuff so I could tell Kat I love her for the first time—which I did that night, regardless."

My heart stops. *Oh my God.*

"Because I realized," Josh continues, his eyes darkening, "'Hey, I don't need violins and a private chef to tell Kat I love her—I can do that anywhere, anytime.' So that's exactly what I did."

Oh my effing God. I just had an orgasm, right here in front of my parents. And, apparently, so did my mother—she literally just made an unmistakable "O" sound, God bless her.

For a brief moment, there's an awkward pause in the conversation as Mom and I flutter and twitch and coo and then giggle uproariously at how much we're completely embarrassing ourselves—all while the male members of my family exchange looks that say, *They've definitely got vaginas.*

In the midst of my momentary meltdown, I glance at Dad. He's smiling at me—a full smile that reaches his eyes.

I glance quickly at Colby and he's looking at me with twinkling eyes—the first time I've seen light dance in his eyes since the accident.

And then I look into Josh's beautiful eyes mere inches from mine—the eyes of the man who just declared his love for me in front of my entire family (minus Keane, but he doesn't count), and I'm instantly home—even more so than inside the physical walls of my beloved childhood house. This beautiful man is my safe place. He's where I belong. Always.

"I love you," I whisper.

"I love you, too," Josh whispers back, almost inaudibly.

I kiss him on the cheek, my crotch burning, my heart fluttering, my very soul soaring around the room.

Mom clears her throat. "Well, that was very sweet of you, Josh." Oh, man, her cheeks are flushed. Get that woman a cigarette. "Very, very sweet."

There's another awkward silence, which Colby rescues by redirecting the conversation back to Dax. "That third song blew me away, Dax. By the end, it sounded like you had an entire orchestra playing behind you."

"That third song's my favorite of anything you've ever done," Mom says.

"Mine, too," I say. "And you know how much I love everything you've ever done."

"Hey, I don't know if Kat's mentioned it to you," Josh says to Dax, "but my best friend from college owns an independent record label. I'd be happy to forward your songs to him if you'd like. He's always scouting new talent."

Holy fuckburgers. *Jackpot.*

Dax's eyes immediately dart to mine, and there's no mistaking the elation in them. And I'm right there with him. I'm literally jiggling on top of Josh's lap, unable to contain my excitement. Not only will Dax's songs find their way to Reed, exactly as we'd hoped and schemed, but *Josh,* not me, is gonna give them to him. *And,* best of all, it was completely Josh's idea, with no prompting by me. This is truly the absolute best-case scenario.

"Wow," Dax says, somehow managing to keep his composure (sort of). "That'd be amazing, Josh. Thank you." Oh my God, he's practically hyperventilating. "You think I should wait 'til I have all ten songs recorded on the album or send these three now?"

Oh God, I can see Dax's chest constricting from here.

"It's up to you," Josh says calmly. "I'll forward whatever you want, whenever. Just lemme know."

Dax looks at me, obviously trying to keep his eyes from bugging out. "What do you think, sis?"

"Send these three now," I say definitively. "Reed won't need ten songs to know you're amazing. Strike while the iron is hot."

Dax's face lights up. "Awesome. Thanks, Josh. I'll send you all three MP3s now. What's your email address?"

Josh gives Dax his email address, just as a timer goes off in the kitchen.

"Oh," Mom says, hopping up. "Everyone up, up, up. It's time to eat!"

"Kat didn't exaggerate, Mrs. Morgan," Josh says. "This is the best spaghetti sauce I've ever had."

Mom's face bursts with joy. "Thank you, Josh. I simmer for ten hours and put red wine in the sauce—oh, and a little dash of nutmeg, that's the secret. And, please, call me Louise."

Josh's smile is absolutely adorable.

"Mom, Josh has been to Italy, so if he says it's the best sauce ever, that's a huge compliment," I say.

Mom is positively beaming. "Well, thank you. Where in Italy have you been?"

Josh shifts in his chair. "Pretty much all over."

"Oh, how nice. I've always wanted to go to Italy. I think I was Italian in a past life." She grins. "So Kat tells us you've just moved back home to Seattle?"

Josh has just taken a huge bite of spaghetti, so he simply nods in reply.

"Josh came home to start a new company with his brother Jonas," I say. "Rock climbing gyms."

"Wow, cool," Ryan says. He asks Josh several questions about Climb & Conquer, which prompts Dad and Colby to chime in and ask a few, too, and Josh answers every question with obvious enthusiasm.

"How wonderful to start a business with your brother," Mom says. "Is Jonas older or younger?"

But, once again, Josh is scarfing down a big bite of spaghetti just as Mom asks her question.

"Jonas and Josh are twins," I say. "Fraternal."

"Oh. Sorry, Josh. I keep asking you questions right after you've taken a bite."

Josh swallows his food. "No, I'm sorry. I'm acting like a caveman. I can't control myself. This is the best spaghetti I've ever had."

Ryan chuckles. "Oh, man, Josh. You just bumped Keane out of the number one spot."

"I don't have a number one spot," Mom says defensively. "You're all in the number one spot—except for you, Ryan, for saying that." She scowls at him.

"And if she did have a number one spot, it certainly wouldn't be occupied by *Keane*, for crying out loud," Dad adds.

We all burst out laughing—Dad never joins in on razzing Keane.

"Nice one, Dad," Ryan says.

Mom wags her finger at Dad. "That's not funny, Thomas. Don't encourage them." She addresses all of us kids. "You guys stop picking on Keane all the time. He's more sensitive than he lets on."

We kids all roll our eyes.

"He *is*," Mom insists. "He used to write me poetry when he was little."

Ryan laughs. "What was it? 'Roses are red, violets are blue, but enough about flowers and shit, Mommy, let's talk about me?'"

Everyone laughs, including Mom.

"'And, by the way, can I borrow twenty bucks?'" Dax adds to the poem.

Everyone laughs again.

"Mom, Peen asks for it and you know it," Ryan says. "A guy can't act like he does and not expect to get razzed for it. He's made his choice."

Mom's expression is noncommittal, which is tantamount to admitting Keane deserves every bit of razzing he gets.

"Mom," Dax says, "I love our penile brother more than anyone in this family, probably, and I still think he's an idiot."

Oh, now he's crossed a line—but not because he called Keane an idiot. "You don't love Keane more than anyone," Mom says, scowling. "I'm his *mother* —which means *I* love him more than anyone. That's the very definition of 'mother.' 'She who loves the most.'"

I put my hand on Josh's thigh under the table.

"Really?" Ryan asks. "That's what 'mother' means? You mean, like, in Latin or something?"

"No. That's *my* definition—I made it up." Mom sighs reverently. "She who loves the most."

Ryan chuckles.

"And just to be clear, I love *all* my kids the most, not just your penile brother."

Everyone laughs, even Dad. Mom's never called Keane a penis before. Could it be my darling mother's already well into her third glass of wine?

Mom shoots Ryan a scolding look. "See what you did? You dragged me into the muck with you. No more referring to penises at the dinner table for anyone —and that includes me. It's just not nice."

We all laugh again.

"So anyway, Josh," Mom says, pushing a lock of her blonde hair away from her face like she's just kicked someone's ass in a street fight. "Sorry about that. We're a bunch of hoodlums in this family—completely out of control." She takes a sip of her wine. "So Kat says you're originally from Seattle?"

Josh is smiling from ear to ear. "Yes."

"What part?"

Josh's smile vanishes. He clears his throat. "Medina," he says evenly, apparently trying to make that word sound as ho-hum as humanly possible.

I glance around, gauging everyone's reactions to the revelation of Josh's hometown—and it's immediately clear everyone fully understands the implication: it means Josh Faraday could use hundred-dollar bills to wipe his ass every day for the rest of his life and still afford to buy himself mansions all over the world. Surely, my family must have at least suspected Josh has cash to burn when he drove up in a freaking Lamborghini—but now they know Josh could buy an entire *fleet* of Lamborghinis if he wanted.

"Oh, Medina's very nice," Mom says politely, but it's plain to see she's flustered. "Some of the homes there are spectacular."

"Was Bill Gates your next-door neighbor growing up?" Dax asks, going straight for the jugular as only my baby brother can do.

My stomach clenches. Shoot. It didn't even occur to me to tell everyone to refrain from asking Josh questions about his childhood.

"No. Bill Gates lives about three miles from where I grew up," Josh says.

"Where did you go to school?" Mom asks.

"St. Francis Academy."

"Oh," Mom says, obviously surprised. "Catholic school?"

Josh nods. "Yeah. I went there from grade school all the way through high school. Sixty-two people in my entire graduating class. After that, I couldn't wait to get to UCLA. A student population of thirty-five-thousand sounded awfully good to me."

"Oh, I bet," Ryan says.

"I had total anonymity for the first time in my life—I absolutely loved it."

Of course, I know Josh landed at UCLA immediately after the death of his father and institutionalization of his brother—which means it might not have been the best of times for him, despite the way he's portraying it right now. But my family certainly doesn't need to know about any of that.

"Are you a practicing Catholic?" Mom asks.

Josh smiles from ear-to-ear like Mom's said something highly amusing. "No," he says simply without elaboration. He takes a huge bite of his food. "This is so good, Mrs. Morgan."

"Louise."

"Louise. Thank you. This is delicious."

Mom beams a huge smile at him. "Thank you. Actually, feel free to call me *Lou*."

My heart stops. Only family and very close friends call my mom Lou. I rub Josh's thigh under the table. *Three down, two to go,* I think.

"So before you decided to open rock-climbing gyms with your brother, what did you do for work?" Dad asks.

Josh proceeds to politely tell everyone about Faraday & Sons—a topic I'm sure he has no interest in, since he's never once talked about it with me. As I listen to him, I learn a lot I didn't know, actually—and also realize, hey, Josh is pretty damned smart. But my attention span quickly evaporates and, while Josh is explaining something horrendously boring, no offense, I steal a glance at Colby. He's studying Josh intently, listening to every word he says, nodding occasionally. There's color in Colby's cheeks, I notice—a sparkle in his eyes. In fact, Colby looks remarkably close to his former self—as good as he's looked since the roof so horribly caved in on him, literally and figuratively, four weeks ago.

"So your father started the business, then?" Mom asks. "He's the 'Faraday' in 'Faraday & Sons'?"

Josh's thigh tenses under my palm. "That's right."

"And do your parents still live in Medina?" Mom asks.

Josh's thigh twitches under the table and I squeeze it.

"Mom, Josh doesn't wanna talk about that," I intervene.

"No, it's fine," Josh says, patting my hand under the table. He clears his throat. "My parents have both passed away."

There's a palpable shift of energy in the room. Instantly, the air is thicker—heavier—and every member of my family, without exception, suddenly looks some variation of ashen, somber, or flat-out devastated.

"I'm so sorry," Mom says.

Everyone follows Mom's lead and mumbles some form of condolence.

"It's okay," Josh says. "It's been a long time."

"How old were you?" Mom asks. "Did they die together in some sort of accident?"

"Uh, no, not together. My mom died when I was seven. She was murdered in our home by an intruder. And my dad died when I was seventeen."

Josh's last sentence hangs in the air. Clearly, everyone is waiting for Josh to identify the cause of his father's death the way he identified his mother's—but Josh doesn't say another word.

"What happened to your father?" Dax asks after a moment.

Mom puts her hand on Dax's shoulder as if to quiet him. "Unless you don't want to talk about it, honey," she says, her voice awash in tenderness. "We totally understand."

"No, it's fine," Josh says. "Uh. My father suffered from severe depression after the death of my mother." Josh bites his lip. "He never got over losing her." He presses his lips together and leaves it at that.

For the first time, I'm seeing exactly why Josh once told me he hates telling people his life's story. *Everyone suddenly looks at me funny when I tell them,* he said. *Like they think I'm "laughing through the pain."*

And now I see exactly what Josh meant. Of course, I know my family members are looking at Josh with nothing but deep sympathy, but I'd shut the hell up over time, too, if people constantly looked at me the way my family's looking at Josh right now.

"Well," Mom says definitively. "I'm very sorry for your losses, Josh."

"Thank you," Josh says. "Like I said, it's been a long time."

"Please know you're always welcome here. Any time."

"Thank you," Josh says. His cheeks are red.

There's an awkward silence. Mom looks like she's gonna cry.

Josh shifts in his chair and then, almost like a turtle burrowing himself into his shell, he takes a huge, conversation-ending bite of spaghetti. "This really is the best sauce I've ever had," he mumbles between chews, filling the awkward silence.

Mom's face is bursting with compassion. "I'm glad you like it—especially since it's your turn for extras."

We all exchange looks, nonverbally acknowledging our shock.

From the look on his face, it's clear Josh doesn't understand the gift Mom's just bestowed upon him.

"Whenever Mom makes her spaghetti sauce or chili or lasagna," I explain, "two or three of us get to take home a huge portion of leftovers to put in our freezer. We call it getting extras."

"It's always Keane plus someone else," Ryan adds.

"It's not *always* Keane and someone else," Mom says defensively. "Sometimes, I don't give extras to Keane."

"Mom, it's always Keane and someone else," Dax says.

Mom looks to Colby for support, but Colby nods in solidarity with Dax.

"Well, Keane's not here tonight, is he?" Mom sniffs. "So that means he doesn't get extras this time." She pauses, smirking. "If your penile brother would rather dance in his underwear for a bunch of screaming women at a bachelorette party than eat dinner with his dear mother, well, then, that's his choice, isn't it?"

Every single person at the table, including Mom and Dad, simultaneously lose their shit.

"You think I don't know what Keane's been up to?" Mom says, laughing hysterically.

But Colby, Ryan, Dax, and I can't compose ourselves enough to reply to her. We're like flopping fish on a riverbank, incapacitated by our laughter.

Mom shrugs and takes a long sip of her wine, her eyes full of pure evil. "Let this be a lesson to all of you kids: in the age of smartphones, don't even try to get away with something devious—your mother will always find out."

My brothers and I can't stop screaming with laughter.

"Who ratted him out?" Ryan finally asks, clutching his stomach.

"One of my friends from Bunco. Her daughter Deanna went to a bachelorette party the other night, and apparently a certain male stripper showed up to entertain the ladies with some gyrating dance moves." Mom rolls her eyes. "I must say the photo I've got of Keane dancing around in his underwear is definitely one for my memory book—I'm gonna put it right next to the one I have of Keane dancing around in his diapers."

Everyone laughs again.

"Oh my God," Dax says, holding his sides. "Best day ever."

"So, anyway," Mom continues, "the point is you guys gotta actually show up for dinner in order to get extras—it's how I bribe you to come home occasionally. Which means Keane's extras are now Josh's." She smiles sweetly at Josh and takes a long sip of her wine.

"Oh, no, I couldn't take Keane's extras," Josh says politely, but even I can hear how much he's hoping she'll insist.

"I *insist*," Mom says, right on cue, much to my joy and relief.

Josh's thigh jiggles under my palm.

"I coddle Keaney way too much, anyway," Mom continues. "It's time for that boy to get off the teat."

We all burst out laughing, yet again. Oh my God, when Mom gets a little tipsy, she's truly hysterical.

Mom leans toward Josh, her eyes sparkling. "You're in the line-up now, honey, whether you like it or not. Ask the other kids—when it comes to extras, what I say goes."

"Yup," Ryan says. "And not just about extras. Mom runs a tight ship all around. Don't let that pretty face fool you—she's a barracuda." He winks at Mom.

Josh beams a huge smile at Mom. "I think I see where Kat gets her backbone."

Dad and all three of my brothers simultaneously express agreement with that statement.

"Thank you very much," Josh says. "I'm thrilled and honored to be in the extras line-up."

"We're thrilled to have you," Mom says—and my heart skips a beat at the smile she flashes him.

Oh my God, this night is going better than I could have dreamed. I rub Josh's thigh under the table and I swear I can feel an electric current buzzing just underneath the denim of his jeans.

Mom turns her iron-butterfly gaze on Ryan. "You get extras tonight, too, Rum Cake."

"Yesssss," Ryan says, fist-pumping the air. "Thank you, dearest Mother."

"Enjoy, honey. Thank you for coming to dinner—I know you're busy." She takes a deep breath and wipes her eyes, betraying the emotion she's actually feeling, despite her outward swagger. "So, it's settled: Josh and Ryan get extras; Josh is welcome here any time; and Keaney's a male stripper. New topic. How's the planning for Sarah's wedding coming along, Kitty? Seems like you've been running all over town like a chicken with your head cut off."

It takes a moment for me to regroup—I kinda feel like Mom just gave me mental whiplash—but I somehow manage to reply coherently—sort of—about everything I've been doing to help Sarah pull off the wedding of the century in such a short amount of time. But, honestly, though I'm speaking coherently—sort of—my mind is engaged elsewhere—namely, with Josh and his beautiful, damaged heart. Not to mention the palpable electricity I feel buzzing underneath my fingertips as my hand rests on his muscular thigh.

"Well, it sounds like you've been an exceptional maid of honor," Mom says. "Sarah's lucky to have you."

"You've been doing all that stuff for Sarah and still coming to help me every day, too?" Colby asks. "I had no idea, Kat. I'm sorry."

"Colby," I say. "I've *wanted* to help you. I wouldn't have had it any other way."

"Thank you—I just didn't realize you were so busy."

"It's no big deal. I'm unemployed, remember? I've had all the time in the world to help my two favorite people."

"Hey," Dax says. "I thought *I* was your favorite person."

"Ssh," I say. "Let Colby feel special just this once—the dude's got broken bones, after all."

"No need to make me feel special," Colby says. "I've been feeling a lot better."

"Yeah, but you're still on the mend, Colby," I say. "It's a slow climb—you can't overdo."

"How much longer 'til the wedding?" Colby asks.

"Six days," I say.

"Okay, then, in six days, you're officially gonna be done with *both* your maid-of-honor *and* Florence-Nightingale duties. Starting a new company's hard work, Kumquat. If you're gonna get your PR company off the ground, you're gonna need to focus all your time and energy on that. I'll be fine."

My stomach somersaults. Ooph. I feel sick all of a sudden. I hate letting Colby (and my entire family) think I'm still chomping at the bit to start my own PR company when, in actuality, I put that sucker on the backburner the minute I saw those two little pink lines.

Now don't get me wrong, I'm no stranger to lying to my family—I've told them plenty of whoppers throughout the years. But telling lies to my family about how many martinis I've had or whether I've studied for an Algebra test or saying I spent a hundred bucks on a pair fringed boots when I actually paid two isn't quite the same thing as sitting here impliedly telling every member of my family (except Keane, of course, but he doesn't count) that I'm planning to launch a new PR company when in fact I've got *What To Expect When You're Expecting* sitting on my nightstand at home—oh, and, by the way—fun fact!—my "home" these days is actually Josh's gorgeous new house.

"Just go on your trip with Josh and have fun," Colby continues, "and when you get back home, start focusing on your own life for a while."

"You and Josh are taking a trip?" Mom asks. "Where to? You haven't told me about any trip."

"Oh, I didn't tell you about that?" I ask.

"No," Mom says. "Where are you going?"

Josh's palm lands firmly on my thigh under the table and I place my hand on top of his.

"Oh. I thought I told you. Yeah, Sarah's gonna surprise Jonas during their honeymoon by taking a short detour to Venezuela to see Jonas and Josh's childhood nanny, Mariela. Josh and I are gonna meet them there."

"In *Venezuela?*" Mom says. "Wow. I've never even thought of going there. How exciting. Is it safe?"

"Yes, Mom." I look at Josh. "Josh and Jonas haven't seen their nanny since they were seven, since right after their mother died. This is gonna be a really special reunion for them both."

Color rises in Josh's cheeks. He nods.

"Wow," Dad says. "Where in Venezuela?"

Josh clears his throat. "Just outside Caracas. Mariela just bought a new house there, and I figured as long as Kat and I are gonna be in South America, I might as well take Kat to Brazil and Argentina, too."

Mom and Dad look at each other, their faces bursting with excitement.

"That sounds fantastic," Dad says. "Wow, guys. How fun."

"How come Colby knew about this trip and Daddy and I didn't?" Mom asks, pouting.

"Because, Mom," Colby says, "you two were at work when Kat was here, yacking my ear off about it." Colby shoots me a smile that melts me. "I'd gladly switch places with either of you, trust me—these days, the girl never stops talking to me and I can't get up and walk away."

Mom and I share yet another elated look. Yep. It truly seems our beloved Colby is back (or, at least, well on his way)—which means the rest of us Morgans can finally exhale the anxious breath we've been holding for four long weeks.

Everyone at the table peppers Josh and me with questions about our itinerary for the trip, as well as about Mariela, and Josh answers each and every question smoothly.

"Jonas and I decided to launch Climb & Conquer right after Jonas gets back from his honeymoon," Josh says, "so I thought I might as well travel at the same time. I figure this trip with Kat will be a nice little vacation before I start putting in eighteen-hour days."

"Well, it sounds like perfect timing," Dad says. "Because Kat will be putting in long hours when she gets home, too, launching her new company." He shoots me a proud smile that makes my stomach twist.

"You know, Kitty Kat, that reminds me," Mom says. "I just got some new billing software that's super easy to use on a Mac. When you come to walk Ralph tomorrow morning, I'll sit you down and show you how it works. I think it would work well for you, at least to start with. And don't worry—it's not complicated. If *I* can figure it out, *you* certainly can."

I can't reply. My tongue feels thick in my mouth.

"And if you'd like to talk to the guy at my bank about setting up a commercial account—you know, so your business can take credit card payments—I can take you over there and introduce you."

I nod. Sort of. Oh, God, I feel like I'm gonna barf.

"Kitty, what's wrong?" Mom asks.

I look at Josh, swallowing hard. Oh my God. I gotta tell my family about the-kumquat-inside-the-Kumquat. I can't lie like this anymore. It's time to come clean.

Josh squeezes my thigh under the table and I look at him, pleading with him to let me spill the beans. Josh's jaw muscles pulse for a moment, and then he nods.

I shift my gaze to my parents, my breathing shallow.

"What is it?" Mom asks, her face awash in anxiety. "Is everything okay, honey?"

I scan the faces at the table. Dax's eyes are full of sympathy—he knows what's coming and, clearly, he's taking no pleasure in what I'm about to do. Ryan looks mildly concerned. But Colby's blue eyes are killing me—he's genuinely worried.

I look at Mom and Dad again. "Mom. Dad," I begin. I take a huge breath and squeeze Josh's hand under the table. "I'm pregnant with Josh's baby."

107

JOSH

There's a pause, like that moment just before a tidal wave crashes onto the shore. Kat's parents inhale sharply—and then nothing. No exhale. No words. No sounds. Just silence for what feels like forever, though it's probably only a nanosecond.

Kat squeezes my leg under the table.

"Oh, Kat," her mom says. "*Honey.*"

I look around the table at Kat's brothers and their facial expressions all convey the same exact sentiment: *Holy fucking shit.*

"It's okay, Mom," Kat says, coming off as much more composed than I'd be able to manage. "It was definitely an accident, that's for sure—and I totally freaked out when I first found out—but Josh and I are both starting to adjust to the idea pretty well. In fact, I think we're both starting to get kind of excited." She looks at me and half-smiles and I nod in solidarity.

I steal a quick glance at Kat's parents and my cheeks blaze. The way they're looking at me, I'm positive they're both imagining me boning their daughter right this very minute. I clear my throat. "Please be assured I'm fully committed to Kat and our baby. I'm gonna take care of them both."

Kat's mom breathes a visible sigh of relief. "How far along are you?" she asks.

"Twelve weeks."

"Oh my gosh."

"I know—end of the first trimester. The baby's the size of a lime."

"A lime? Ohmigosh."

Kat's father clears his throat but doesn't speak.

"Yeah, but no matter how big the baby gets, Josh says it's still the-kumquat-inside-the-Kumquat. Isn't that cute?"

Colby can't keep himself from smiling at that and Kat's mom shoots me an adoring look—but Ryan and Kat's dad both still seem to be processing things.

"Oh, honey," Kat's mom says. She rubs her forehead. "How are you feeling? Have you been to the doctor? Is the baby healthy?"

"I'm good, Mom. Yes, I went to the doctor—I saw the baby's heartbeat. So far, so good—knock on wood." Kat shoots me an anxious look, and I'm pretty sure she's thinking about the booze and weed she ingested before we knew—something I've thought a lot about, too. "I was throwing up nonstop for a while," Kat continues, "but that's tapered off a bit. Now it's mostly late at night and early morning." Kat squeezes my hand again. "I'm good, Mom. The baby's good. Josh is good."

Kat's mom sighs with relief, yet again. Wow. If I'm not mistaken, I'm beginning to see a glimmer of excitement in Louise's eyes—just that fast.

"So what are your plans?" Kat's father asks evenly, breaking his silence. My eyes shift away from Louise's beautiful face—damn, that woman looks so much like her gorgeous daughter it's truly freaky—and I'm met with two blue chips of steel. Oh, boy. There's not a hint of excitement on Kat's father's face. It's all fierce protectiveness.

My stomach clenches.

Kat squeezes my hand under the table. "The plan?" she says, replying to her father. "The plan is I'm gonna move in with Josh—er, actually, okay, to be honest, I already did. Got the last of my stuff moved in yesterday."

Kat's father glances at his wife and his face quite clearly conveys deep concern.

"So, you know, we're gonna live together," Kat continues. "And have a little tiny human that's made up of both our DNA. And we'll raise it together. And be happy. The End."

"I meant what are your *plans*? For the child? For the future?" He motions to Kat and me. "For the two of you?"

"*Oh*," Kat says, like she totally understands—but then after a beat she cocks her head to the side, apparently perplexed. "What do you mean? I just told you. We're gonna live together and raise our kid. The End."

I gently extricate my hand from Kat's steel claw and wrap my arm around her shoulders. "Mr. Morgan, as far as I'm concerned, the plan is for me to take care of your daughter and our baby in every conceivable way," I say evenly. "You don't have to worry about either of them, I promise. They'll want for nothing. I give you my word on that. I'll always take care of my baby and the mother of my child, no matter what happens." I clear my throat. "And not just out of obligation. Because I love Kat, Mr. Morgan. I love your daughter with all my heart and soul."

Kat twitches against me and I squeeze tighter.

There's a brief beat of silence during which Kat's mom visibly swoons and then bursts into tears.

"Mom," Kat says, holding up her arms.

Kat's mom leaps out of her chair and lopes around the table to her daughter, sounds of femaleness gurgling out of her as she goes.

"Everything's gonna be okay, Mom," Kat says into her mom's blonde bob.

Kat's mom sniffles. "*I* should be reassuring *you*, honey. I'll help you—you know that, right? We'll do this together." She kisses Kat's cheek twenty times, making Kat giggle through her tears.

"Come here, Josh," Kat's mom says, breaking away from her daughter and reaching for me. She hugs me. "Welcome to the family, honey," she murmurs into my chest, squeezing me tight.

"Thank you," I say, my heart racing.

When Kat's mom pulls away from our hug, Ryan and Dax are standing behind her, offering handshakes and hugs—but Kat's father is still sitting in his chair, his face unreadable to me.

"Daddy?" Kat says when it's clear he doesn't plan to get up and join the hug-fest.

The look on the man's face makes my hair stand on end.

"So you're not planning to marry Kat?" he asks me evenly.

"*Thomas*," Kat's mom says, obviously mortified. "They're adults. It's none of our business."

Kat's father steeples his fingers under his chin and exhales. "Josh, I really appreciate everything you just said, believe me—it's good to hear. And I'm glad you two are in love. That's great. But what about ten years from now? Are you gonna draft some sort of support agreement, in case things don't work out between the two of you—or is this just, you know, we'll see how it goes and *whatever?*"

I feel like he just punched me in the balls.

"*Dad*," Kat says, sounding exactly like her mother did a moment ago.

Kat's father shrugs. "It has to be said, honey. If no one else is gonna say it on your behalf, then I sure will. You need some form of commitment about the future, one way or another."

I swallow hard. "I'd be happy to sign a support agreement," I say, my blood whooshing into my ears. "I'll have my lawyer draft it up. As I say, I'm making a commitment to be a father in every way. My word is my bond, every bit as binding as any written agreement. I have no qualms about memorializing my verbal promise in writing."

Kat looks utterly appalled. "Jeez, this isn't some kind of corporate acquisition, Dad. I'm not *chattel.*" She turns her gaze on me, her eyes blazing. "You don't need to call your *lawyer*, Josh—our relationship is between you and me. We don't need legal documentation."

"I'm not talking about your *relationship*—I'm talking about the child," Kat's dad says. "I'm talking about securing my grandchild's future and therefore yours."

Kat shoots an icy glare at her father. "With all due respect, it's none of your

business, Dad. Josh has promised to take care of the baby and that's his only obligation as far as I'm concerned. He owes me absolutely nothing. Our relationship will
rise or fall, just like anyone else's, whether we have a piece of paper making us official in the eyes of the government or not." Oh man, she's ramping up into full terror-
ist-mode. "You and mom don't realize how unique you are. Saying marriage vows
doesn't guarantee anyone a happily ever after, Dad. Fifty percent of marriages end
in divorce—did you know that? The piece of paper doesn't guarantee a damned
thing. In fact, the divorce rate's the highest among couples who married for no other
reason than an accidental pregnancy." She sniffs. "So no thanks to that."

"Kat, don't get all riled up—" Kat's father begins. But, surely, he must know
his words are pointless. Kat's already riled up and she's not even close to
coming down.

"Josh and I have talked about it, Dad. We don't believe in marriage for the
sake of marriage. All that matters is that Josh is gonna be a father to this baby—
which he's promised to be," she continues, her head held high. "The rest will
take care of itself. We'll just live in the moment and do our best, which is all
anyone can do, anyway, whether they've got a piece of paper or not. I don't
even want to get married, to tell you the truth. The idea of it freaks me out. I'd
much rather stay because I want to stay and go if I want to go." She's practically
panting. Damn, apparently her father hit a nerve. Jesus. The lady doth protest
too much, methinks.

"Kat, you're flying off the handle. I was just—"

"No, I'm not. You're butting in where you don't belong, Dad. I'm twenty-
four. And Josh is *thirty.*"

I don't particularly like the way Kat just said my age. She said it like I'm
older than the hills.

"And we've decided, after discussing it like reasonable adults, that we don't
want to get married. It's just not for us. In fact, I wouldn't even say yes if Josh
proposed this very minute at this table—I really wouldn't."

I make a face of surprise. Is she serious?

"And do you know why?" Kat asks, forging right ahead, breathing hard.
"Because I don't want to get married for the sake of a kid and nothing more.
That's just a recipe for unhappiness and I'm not about to—"

"*Kitty,*" Kat's mom says sharply, shutting Kat up. "Honey, you need to stop
now. *Please.*"

Kat's mouth is hanging open. Her chest is heaving. Her eyes are bugging
out.

Kat's mom strokes Kat's cheek, obviously trying to calm her batshit crazy
daughter down. "Honey, your father and I support you, one hundred percent.
Don't we, Thomas?"

"Of course."

"Now see?" Louise exhales loudly. "Good lord, Kat."

Kat takes a seat and so do I.

"Goodness gracious," Louise says, moving back to her chair on the other side of the table. "You get so riled up sometimes, honey."

Ryan chuckles.

"I'm sorry," Kat's dad says. "You're right. You're both adults. It's none of my business. I was just looking out for you. But it's your life. I'm sorry." He sighs and puts his hand on his forehead. "I was just trying to help."

Kat lurches around the table and into her father's arms and he hugs her.

"You're sure you're okay, honey?" he whispers.

Kat nods into his chest. "I was scared at first but now I'm happy and excited. And Josh is amazing, Dad. You'll see. I love him so much, Dad."

"I was just looking out for you because I love you so much."

"I know, Daddy. I know."

I clutch my chest. I've never seen a father behave like this with his kid. This is straight out of a movie. He told her he loves her—even after she told him she royally fucked up. And now he's hugging her and kissing her cheek, showering her with fatherly affection? Wow. *This is the kind of father I'm gonna be,* I think. *Just like this.*

"Okay," Kat's father says. He kisses his daughter's cheek again. "I'm glad you're happy. Just wait. You're gonna love this baby more than you ever thought possible—and so will we." He looks at me. "I'm sorry, Josh. I didn't mean to butt in where I'm not wanted and I certainly didn't mean to imply you were gonna shirk your obligations as a father. I'm just not used to this new way of doing things, I guess." He smiles ruefully at his wife and she flashes him a sympathetic face. "I'm too old-fashioned for my own good sometimes."

"You don't have to worry about Josh's intentions," Kat says. "Babe, show my dad your arm." She addresses her dad. "Josh got a girlfriend-tattoo in my honor."

I know Kat means well, but, at this particular moment, hearing Kat call my permanent declaration of love for her a "girlfriend-tattoo" feels like she just called me a flop-dick.

"Show 'em," Kat says. "Wait 'til you see this, Dad—then you'll understand how much Josh loves me."

I have zero desire to bare my Kat-inspired tattoo to her family, but I obviously can't leave her hanging. Begrudgingly, I roll up my sleeve to display the full expanse of my bicep—and everyone instantly expresses amazement and amusement all at once.

"What's 'PG' on her collar?" Ryan asks, leaning in to get a closer look.

"Party Girl," I say. "The first night I met Kat, I asked her how a magazine article would label her if they were writing an oversimplified article about her, and she said, 'They'd call me a Party Girl with a Heart of Gold.'"

Kat's entire family expresses agreement with that assessment.

"I wanted to put K-U-M on the collar, but I figured Kat would kill me if I told the entire world her initials."

"Ha!" Ryan says, looking at Kat. "You don't want the world to know you're name is semen, Jizz? You see what you did to your poor daughter, Mom? You've scarred her for life. She'd rather be known as a party girl than get called Kum Shot everywhere she goes."

Kat's mom rolls her eyes. "Only you guys would even *think* to call her that. Katherine Ulla is a beautiful name."

"Sure it is, Mom," Ryan retorts. "That wasn't a cruel thing to do to your one and only daughter at all—was it Kum Shot?"

"Stop it," Kat's mom snaps. "You won't be able to say that in front of your niece or nephew, you know, so you'd better start cleaning up your act now."

"Not gonna happen, Mom," Ryan says breezily. "That baby will think Kum Shot is Mommy's given name."

Kat's mom covers her face with her hands.

"I like the two olives in the martini glass," Dax says, scrutinizing my arm. "Nice touch."

Kat kisses her dad on his cheek. "See, Dad? A man doesn't get a tattoo for his girlfriend lightly." She smiles broadly. "I'd say it's pretty serious."

Shit. Yet again, I know Kat means well, but every time she uses the word "girlfriend" I feel like she's calling me flop-dick.

"Hey, Kumquat," Colby says, breaking his silence. "What's a guy with a broken leg gotta do around here to get a hug from his pregnant sister?"

Kat breaks away from her dad and bounds to the end of the table where Colby's marooned with his leg in a cast. Gingerly, Kat takes Colby's face in her hands and kisses him on the cheek and the two of them hug for a long minute.

"What the hell is 'chattel,' by the way?" Colby asks softly into Kat's hair. "And why the hell do you know that word?"

Kat laughs. "Sarah always says it. I think it just means, you know, like when a woman used to be a man's property?"

"Ah. I see." Colby locks eyes with me. "Welcome to the family, Josh," he says. "I think you'll find it's a pretty fucking awesome family—excuse my language, Mom."

"Oh, well, shit, that's okay," Kat's mom says. "If ever there was an appropriate time to drop an f-bomb, this is it. Speaking of which—holy fuck—I'm gonna be a grandma."

Everyone laughs.

"Welcome to our fucking awesome family, Josh," Kat's mom continues. "I for one already love you."

My heart explodes in my chest. "Thank you, Lou."

"So what do you say we dig into that pie you brought, huh?" Louise says. "I feel the sudden need to eat a very big slice."

108

JOSH

I peek through a crack in the door and peer out into the courtyard, scanning the faces of Jonas and Sarah's wedding guests, all of them seated and patiently awaiting the start of the ceremony. Obviously, ninety percent of the attendees at this wedding are Sarah's friends and family—which doesn't surprise me. Jonas and I have no family other than Uncle William—and if Jonas has made any close friends over the years, he's certainly never introduced them to me.

"Wow, those flowers are incredible," I say, surveying the virtual explosion of flowers in the courtyard. "I've never seen anything like that. It's like a gingerbread house made of flowers."

"Sarah saw this 'wall of flowers' in some celebrity magazine and lost her shit," Jonas says behind my back. "So I told her to do whatever her little heart desired."

"It's amazing. Hey, are those the violinist and cellist from my house the other night?" I ask, spotting the two women playing a symphonic piece, along with a third woman playing a large harp.

"Yeah," Jonas says from behind me. "Sarah had originally planned to have just the harpist, but when she heard the violin and cello at your house during our 'romantic dinner for two'—thanks again for that, by the way—she flipped out and hired them for the ceremony on the spot."

I chuckle. "Those ladies ought to give me a commission for all the work I've indirectly sent their way. Kat's brother Dax hired them to play on his album, too."

"Yeah, I know. I met Dax, remember?"

"Oh yeah. I forgot."

"Have you heard his album?" Jonas asks.

"Just the first three songs. They're really good—I sent them to Reed and he absolutely loved them. He's probably gonna sign Dax's band. He just wants to watch them play live first."

"Awesome," Jonas says. "I'd love to hear them."

"Stay still, Jonas," Uncle William says from behind me. "Joshua says I have to retie the knot to make it *perfect*. Stand still, Jonas, for the love of God."

"Sorry. I'm bouncing off the walls."

"Really? I hadn't noticed," Uncle William says, chuckling.

I continue scanning the faces of the guests, looking for anyone I recognize.

Well, I see Henn and Hannah in the third row, sitting with their hands clasped tightly together. And there's Uncle William's longtime housekeeper (and longtime lover?), Katya, sitting next to my uncle's vacant chair. I see a handful of familiar faces from Faraday & Sons—the CFO, Jonas' assistant and her husband, a few people on Jonas' team. There's Sarah's mom Gloria in the front row wearing a corsage and Jonas' friend Georgia with her boyfriend and son Trey, all of whom I met last night at the rehearsal dinner.

My eyes lock onto T-Rod in the back, standing in front of a mammoth wall of white flowers, talking to a woman in black holding a clipboard. I smile to myself. Six years ago, when I decided to dive headfirst into launching the L.A. branch of Faraday & Sons, I hired Theresa through a temp agency, thinking I was gonna need someone a few hours a week (at most) to organize my life and possibly run a few errands for me. I never in a million years thought, six years later, Theresa would be my faithful 'woman behind the curtain' for the Wise and Powerful Oz.

Holy shit. There's Miss Westbrook—Mrs. Santorini now—sitting with three kids, including a teenage boy who must be her son Jonas, the one she named after my brother. I smile to myself. Sarah Fucking Cruz is a force to be reckoned with, I swear to God. Apparently, she's hell-bent on "healing" my brother's tattered soul, through any means (and people) necessary, God love her.

My eyes continue drifting over the faces in the crowd and finally lock onto Kat's parents, seated in the farthest row. Kat's mom is in the process of whispering something into her husband's ear and he's smiling and nodding. Man, they're a handsome couple. Especially Kat's mom. Damn. She's a knockout, even at fifty-something, especially in that sparkling gold dress. Holy shit, it blows me away how much Kat looks like her mother. It's like Louise is a crystal ball, showing me exactly what her hot twenty-something-year-old daughter's gonna look like thirty years from now: a hot fifty-something-year-old.

As I'm spying on her, Louise rests her cheek lovingly on her husband's shoulder—the exact same move Kat always uses on me—and all of a sudden, I feel the world warp and buckle around me, like I've slipped through a gap in the space-time-continuum. Suddenly, I'm no longer looking at Kat's parents awaiting Jonas and Sarah's wedding, I'm seeing Kat and me, awaiting our son or daughter's wedding, thirty years from now.

Whoa.

I quickly shut the door, my heart pounding in my ears, and turn around.

Uncle William's just finishing tying the knot on Jonas' tie.

"There we go," he says, patting Jonas' chest. He grabs Jonas' shoulders and turns him toward me like he's a preschooler on picture day. "I used a Windsor knot the second time. Does that meet with your approval, Master Joshua?"

I survey my brother from head to toe. "Yeah, he looks absolutely perfect now. Good job."

Jonas beams a huge smile at me. "I'm right here—you can compliment me directly."

"You look absolutely perfect, Jonas."

"Thank you."

"I'm gonna take my seat now," Uncle William says. He hugs Jonas and pats him on the cheek. "I'm happy for you, son. Sarah's a great girl. Be good to her."

"I will. Always."

"I know you will. You're an exceptionally kind-hearted person, Jonas. Always have been." He pats the side of Jonas' neck. "She's a lucky girl."

"I'm the lucky one."

"Be happy, Jonas," Uncle William says softly, emotion warping his voice. "That's all I've ever wished for you, son." His voice cracks.

Jonas swallows hard. "I will be. I already am."

The emotion on Uncle William's face is making my eyes water—I've never seen him look quite like this before.

Uncle William turns to go.

"Hey, Uncle William?" Jonas says.

Uncle William stops and turns around.

"Thank you for letting Sarah wear Sadie's necklace. It means a lot to me that you did that for her. Sarah was absolutely thrilled. Thank you."

"Oh, I'm glad you mentioned that," Uncle William says. "When I gave the necklace to Sarah last night, she seemed so excited to make it *both* her 'something old' *and* her 'something borrowed' for the big day, I didn't have the heart to tell her I was *giving* her the necklace and not just loaning it to her." He chuckles. "I figured I'd tell her after the ceremony. So when I drink way too much Scotch at the reception and forget to tell Sarah the necklace is hers, will you make sure to tell her for me?"

"Oh, wow," Jonas says. He looks at me, astonished—but since I've never seen the necklace they're talking about, I can't return his expression. "Sarah's gonna be shocked as hell. Are you sure? She's not expecting that *at all*."

"Of course. It's my wedding gift to Sarah—my way of welcoming her into our family." He looks wistful. "Sarah reminds me of Sadie, you know. Same spirit. Sadie would have been thrilled to know her favorite necklace will be worn again, especially by someone as beautiful as Sarah, rather than sitting and collecting dust in a vault for another thirty years."

"Thank you so much. Sarah will be thrilled. I'll be sure to tell her."

Uncle William grins. "Now go get married to your dream girl, son."

"Yes, sir. With pleasure."

When Uncle William is gone, I take a good, long look at my brother from head to toe and marvel at the joy wafting off him. I've never seen him look so damned *happy* before. Hell, I don't know if I've ever seen Jonas look happy at all before Sarah came along. Maybe every smile and laugh before Sarah was nothing but a dress rehearsal, a dry run preparing him for true happiness.

"You ready?" I ask my brother.

"I've never been more ready for anything in my entire life," Jonas replies.

I hug Jonas and kiss his cheek, and as I do, my eyes tear up. I pull back from our embrace, wiping my eyes, intending to turn my back on him, but Jonas grabs my neck and forces me to stay put.

"Josh," Jonas says softly, his palm on my neck, his forehead against mine. "You're the best brother a guy could ask for. I thank God for you every single day."

My body twitches with the emotion I'm stuffing down. What the fuck is happening to me? I'm a fucking wreck. I swallow hard, successfully forcing down the huge lump in my throat.

A woman with a clipboard pokes her head into the room and saves me from myself. "You gentlemen ready?" she asks.

Jonas nods. "Just give us a minute."

"Okay. Take your positions in the courtyard whenever you're ready. We'll cue off you."

"Thanks." Jonas takes a deep breath and smiles at me. "You need a minute?"

I nod.

"Take your time, Josh," my brother says, grinning. "They can't start this shindig without me."

I look up at the ceiling for a moment, and once I've got complete control of my emotions again, I fix my eyes on Jonas' face. "Jonas, I'd be lost without you," I say quietly. I rest my palm on his broad shoulder and take a big gulp of air. "Seeing you happy is the best thing that's ever happened to me." I swallow hard. "I love you."

Jonas' lip trembles and his face contorts like he's trying to keep himself from crying. But it's no use. His eyes fill with water. "Fuck, Josh," Jonas says, sounding pissed. He wipes his eyes. "What are you trying to do to me, motherfucker?"

"Sorry."

"I was fully prepared to cry like a baby at the sight of Sarah walking down the aisle—that's to be expected—but I wasn't prepared to cry with *you*, just standing here, talking about our fucking feelings, for Chrissakes. Come on, man, leave me a shred of dignity on my wedding day, would you?"

"Sorry, bro. How's this? 'Hey, fucker. Congrats on bagging an awesome babe. Hope you have a fucking awesome life, you cocksucker—now fuck off.'"

"That's much better. Jesus. You scared me. For a minute there, I thought you were going soft on me."

"No chance of that," I say. "I'm the emotionally stunted asshole of the two of us—you know that."

Jonas grins, his eyes sparkling.

"Okay, motherfucker," I say warmly. "Time to bag yourself a wife and me a sister."

"Fuck yeah, it is."

"Fuck yeah."

We smile at each other.

"I'm so happy for you, Jonas," I say softly.

"I'm so happy for me, too," he says. He takes a deep breath. "Okay. Enough yapping—it's time for me to get married to the divine original form of womanness, the goddess and the muse, the magnificent Sarah Cruz."

109

JOSH

Jonas and I take our positions in front of the audience, standing to the left of the wedding officiant. The distinctive scent of gardenias—my mom's favorite flower—blasts me all of a sudden. I turn around to glance at the spectacular wall of white flowers towering behind us—and, yes, although there are certainly roses and lilies and all sorts of other unidentifiable white flowers comprising the blooming wall, gardenias are by far the most prominent. Did Sarah do that on purpose? Did Jonas tell her how Dad always said Mom loved gardenias?

I look at Jonas and he's gazing anxiously toward the back of the room, his cheeks flushed, his breathing labored. I can almost hear his heart beating from here. Or maybe that's my own heartbeat pounding forcefully in my ears. Why the fuck am I nervous? I'm not the one getting married.

The music shifts to a Mozart-Beethoven-type thing, a pleasant piece of elegant music I've heard a thousand times at various black-tie events, and Kat appears at the back of the center aisle.

My heart skips a beat at the sight of her. Holy fuck, she's absolutely stunning.

"I'm getting fat," Kat said yesterday when she tried on her bridesmaid dress to make sure it still fit. "I should have had the tailor leave a little extra room through the midsection—my belly's totally pooching out."

I laughed. There was literally no hint of a pooch in the dress—which makes sense because, despite our kumquat in the oven, there still hasn't been even the slightest change in Kat's figure since the day I first laid eyes on her in Jonas' living room.

"Babe," I said to her yesterday. "You're not showing at all. Like, literally, not at all."

"You're blind, babe," Kat said. "*Look.*" She pointed at the perfectly smooth midsection of her dress. "It's like I'm hiding a volleyball under there."

"Do you have body dysmorphic disorder?" I asked.

I grabbed her shoulders and moved her in front of the full-length mirror on the other side of our bedroom, and then I stood behind her, staring at both our reflections in the mirror, my palms resting on her smooth, bare shoulders.

And that's when I completely forgot whatever the fuck I was gonna say. I'd meant to drag Kat in front of the mirror to prove my point she's not showing yet (and that she's batshit crazy, too, which certainly isn't news to me), but for some reason, staring at us together in the mirror, looking at her in that blue dress—even with her hair in a ponytail and her face completely bare of makeup—she took my breath away.

So, of course, I proceeded to get my Party Girl with a Hyphen the fuck out of that dress and myself inside of her.

But that was yesterday.

Today, Kat in that same blue dress isn't merely taking my breath away—she's stopping my heart, too. The dress fits Kat the same way it did yesterday, of course—like a glove. But, today, she's not just *wearing* her bridesmaid dress as she glides down the aisle, she's *strutting* in it like a peacock—or, rather, I suppose, like a pea*hen* graced with a pea*cock's* tail. (Thank you, Jonas.) And Kat has every reason to strut like she's on a catwalk—lord almighty, does she ever. Her golden hair is falling around her shoulders in perfectly formed tendrils. Her skin peeking out of her sweetheart neckline is glowing. Her sky-high heels accentuate the glorious length of her lithe frame. And, oh my God, Kat's gorgeous face, always radiant, always mesmerizing, is downright spectacular today. It's the face that could launch a thousand ships, bring a grown man to his knees, make a man believe in God. And at this moment, lucky me, the blazing eyes lighting up that supernaturally beautiful face are trained on *me.*

By the time Kat reaches the end of the aisle and takes her position to the officiant's right, my heart's bursting, my cock is tingling, and my brain is utterly scrambled. I beam a huge smile at Kat and she winks.

The musical selection changes and everyone in the audience stands.

For a moment, I can't identify the song the musicians are playing. I know the melody, but it's not a song normally played by a harp, cello, and violin, so I'm having a hard time placing it. Oh, wait. I've got it. It's "Melt With You" by Modern English. Great song—cool arrangement. I glance at my brother. He's about to burst into a trillion tiny molecules and scatter into the sky.

I fix my gaze at the end of the aisle, my heart in my throat, and there she is —our beautiful bride for the occasion. Our George Clooney. Jonas' handler. My brand new little sister. The great love of my brother's life. *Sarah Fucking Cruz.*

I glance at Kat to find her lower lip trembling and her eyes filled with tears. I look at my brother again and my breathing hitches at the unabashed demonstration of joy and love on his face. Oh my God, Jonas is clearly on the verge of crying.

Keep it together, man, I think.

But, really, I should be using all my keep-it-together mojo on myself. For fuck's sake, I'm shaking like a leaf as I try to contain the emotion welling up inside me.

I take a deep breath and successfully force it down.

Sarah glides down the aisle slowly, her eyes fixed on Jonas, her smile as wide as I've ever seen it. Wow, she's beautiful. Simply stunning. Glowing from the inside-out. And not only that, she's a sexy little thing, isn't she? Hot damn. I knew my brand new sister was a hot tamale and all, but Jesus Fucking Christ— she's scorching hot. Are brides supposed to be this *sexy*? Good lord. Sarah's strapless, white gown hugs every curve of her body leaving absolutely nothing to the imagination, and then fans out mid-thigh, accentuating her hips to full effect. Holy hot damn, that's quite a dress. I'm guessing Sarah picked it espe-cially for Jonas—my brother always has been an ass-man.

For a fleeting moment, my deranged brain actually forms the thought: *I wonder what kind of wedding dress Kat would wear for me?*

My heart squeezes. What the fuck am I thinking? Have I gone insane?

A loud sob lurches from the front of the audience, grabbing my attention. It's Sarah's mother, crying her eyes out at the sight of her beautiful daughter. I can't help but smile. I only met Gloria last night and I already love her—it seems Jonas definitely lucked out there.

I steal another look at Kat, thinking I'll catch her giggling about Gloria's meltdown, but, nope—Kat's crying her eyes out every bit as much as Gloria, completely lost in her own Cinderella-fied world. Wow. Is Kat crying like that because she's so happy for Sarah—or because she's despairing she'll never get to be the one wearing the white dress?

I peel my eyes off Kat and gaze at Sarah Fucking Cruz walking toward us. She's almost at the end of the aisle—and now that she's closer, I can plainly see why Jonas shot me that look of astonishment about Uncle William's gift. Holy shit, the necklace encircling Sarah's elegant neck is fit for a queen. I mean, I'm no expert on diamonds, but that's got to be half a million bucks worth of them, if not more.

It makes no sense, and I know I should be ashamed of myself for thinking it, but for a fleeting moment, jealousy rises up inside me that Uncle William gave that thing to Sarah, and not to Kat. Kat deserves to have the crown jewels around her neck, too.

Wait. What the fuck am I thinking? If it wouldn't be a totally weird thing to do in front of all these people, I'd slap the shit out of myself right now for my rambling and bizarre thoughts.

Sarah glides up to the officiant and Jonas lurches over to her. He grabs both her hands and leans in to whisper something into her ear. Sarah nods and smiles and Jonas kisses Sarah full on the mouth like they've just been pronounced husband and wife.

"Not quite yet, Jonas," the officiant says, and everyone laughs.

Jonas laughs and pulls away, but then quickly leans in and pecks Sarah's lips one more time, like he's literally stealing a kiss.

Everyone laughs again.

"Oh, Jonas," Sarah says, beaming at him.

"You look beautiful," Jonas says softly.

"So do you, love. You've got *happy* eyes."

"Very happy eyes," Jonas whispers. "I love you, Sarah."

"I love you, too, *mi amor. Te amo.*"

"I can't wait to call you my wife."

The officiant clears his throat comically. "Excuse me," he says. "Would you two lovebirds mind if I cut in?"

Everyone in the audience laughs, yet again.

"Would you two like to get married, or . . ?"

"Yes, please," Sarah says.

"As quickly as humanly possible," Jonas adds.

Again, the entire place collectively chuckles.

I steal a look at Kat and she beams at me through her tears.

"I'm thrilled to welcome everyone to this happy occasion—the marriage of Jonas Faraday and Sarah Cruz," the officiant begins. "Both Jonas and Sarah have told me, separately, that they believe finding the other was their life's sacred destiny, their soul's mission—that the other is the missing piece to their soul's sacred puzzle."

Normally, this kind of you-complete-me marriage-speak at weddings doesn't affect me any more than a speech about global warming, but this time, for the first time ever, the officiant's words are making my heart palpitate and the hair on my neck stand up.

After a few opening remarks and a prayer, the officiant reads from Corinthians about the nature of love. "Love is kind and not jealous," he says— and when he says the word "jealous," I can't help but shoot a pointed look at Kat. She flares her nostrils and narrows her eyes in reply, making me smile. I love it when Kat gives me her dragon-lady look.

"Love doesn't brag and is not arrogant," the officiant continues solemnly— and at the word "arrogant," Kat shoots me a snarky look that tells me in no uncertain terms the guy's talking about *me*.

I bite my lip and look away from Kat so I won't burst out laughing at her expression.

"But love rejoices with the *truth*," the officiant concludes—a statement prompting Kat and me to simultaneously grin at each other.

"Honesty-game," Kat mouths to me, making me bite my lip. The woman just read my mind.

"For love bears all things, believes all things, hopes all things, and endures all things, but above all, love never fails."

The snarky smile dancing on my lips a moment ago vanishes. I look at Kat and the earnest expression of love and tenderness on her beautiful face is like a mirror reflecting my own feelings back to me.

"And now, Jonas and Sarah have prepared vows they wish to say to each other under God, to be witnessed by you, their dearest family and friends," the officiant says. He turns to Sarah. "Sarah?"

Sarah grabs both of Jonas' hands and looks deeply into his eyes. She smiles a truly lovely smile. "Jonas," she says softly. "My sweet Jonas—*mi amor*. When I look into your beautiful, kind eyes, I see the man of my dreams—my destiny. With you, I'm completely safe for the first time in my life. With you, I know who I am and who I hope to become. With you, I'm finally *me*. Thank you for showing me what true love is, my sweet Jonas—for teaching me how to love with all my heart and soul. And, even more, for teaching me how to be loved. I love you, my beautiful, sweet, generous, devoted Jonas, and I promise to be your loving and loyal wife from this day forward, forever and ever, 'til the day I die and long after that when I hold you in my arms in heaven."

The courtyard is filled with nothing but muffled sniffles and sighs as everyone, especially Jonas, processes everything Sarah's just said. After a beat, Jonas takes Sarah's face into his palms and kisses her so fervently, the entire audience collectively sighs. And even though Jonas is obviously jumping the gun by planting that kiss on Sarah at this point in the proceedings, the officiant apparently doesn't have the heart to stop him.

As Jonas kisses Sarah, my eyes drift to Kat, my heart clanging wildly in my chest. What would Kat vow to me before God, in front of all our family and friends? And what would I say to her in return?

Kat's eyes are glistening as she returns my gaze. Oh my God. She's looking at me the exact same way Sarah always looks at Jonas—like I'm the answer to her prayers. My skin prickles with goose bumps.

A titter rustles through the crowd and I peel my eyes off Kat. Jonas and Sarah's kiss is finished.

"Thank you, Sarah," the officiant says. "Jonas?"

Jonas sheepishly takes a folded piece paper out of his pocket.

I look at Kat again, my pulse raging in my ears. Oh my God. She's still doing it—looking at me the way no one's ever looked at me before.

"Sarah," Jonas begins, drawing my attention away from Kat. He looks down at his paper, his hands visibly shaking. "My Magnificent, Beautiful, Loving Sarah. My precious baby. My life. Plato says at the touch of love, every man becomes a poet. So I sat down and tried to write you an epic poem rivaling *The Odyssey* that would adequately convey how I feel about you, baby—but, unfortunately, when I tried to rhyme about my feelings for you, I sounded like Dr. Seuss."

Everyone chuckles.

Wow, I think. *Intentional humor by Jonas Patrick Faraday.*

"So I've decided to speak to you from the depths of my heart and soul, instead." Jonas takes a deep breath. "Sarah Cruz, you're the goddess and the muse. You're The One, my love—the heart that sings my heart's song back to me. I was lost and you led me to the light outside the dark cave—to my destiny." Jonas shifts his weight, his chest heaving. "Sarah, our love is the wonder of the wise, the joy of the good, the amazement of the gods. We're the greatest love story ever told, baby—the divine original form of love. You're the air I breathe— the blood coursing through my veins—my very heart and soul. And I vow from this moment forward to dedicate my life to your eternal happiness—to love and protect you always and forever, to the very best of my ability—to strive every day to lead you to the top of your personal mountaintop and rejoice with you when you get there." Jonas takes a deep breath, puts his paper away, and cups Sarah's face in his palms. "Sarah, my beloved, the greatest joy in this life will always be the honor and privilege of calling you my wife."

"Oh, Jonas," Sarah breathes, clearly overcome with emotion. "That was beautiful."

Jonas kisses Sarah, yet again—I guess normal marriage-ceremony rules don't apply to him?—and everyone watching laughs.

Everyone, that is, except for me.

I can't laugh.

I can't move.

Jesus Fucking Christ, I can't breathe.

I feel like I've suddenly been struck by a lightning bolt. *My greatest joy in this life will always be the honor and privilege of calling you my wife.* Oh my God. I've got goose bumps. My chest is tight. My heart is pounding in my ears. *My greatest joy in this life will always be the honor and privilege of calling you my wife.*

I look at Kat, every hair on my body standing up. She's staring at Jonas and Sarah, a look of unadulterated love on her face.

Holy shit.

Kat's The One.

Of course, she is. I don't just *love* Kat. I don't just *want* her. *I want the honor and privilege of calling Kat my wife.*

She's the air I breathe.

The blood coursing through my veins.

My very heart and soul.

I can't live without her. I *need* her like a plant needs water and sunshine and soil. Oh my God. I love Kat and I always will, forever and ever, 'til the day I die—and, holy fuck, Kat deserves to hear me say it in front of God and everyone we love. *Yes.* Kat deserves to be the one gliding down the center aisle wearing a white dress—not to mention a shit-ton of diamonds, too.

I want Kat to be my bride.

Fuck my father.

Fuck the past.

Fuck being scared of what tragedy tomorrow might bring.

Whatever might happen tomorrow—*whatever it is*—I want Kat by my side to experience it with me, good or bad.

"Repeat after me, Sarah," the officiant is saying.

I steal another look at Kat. She's still watching Jonas and Sarah, completely unaware that my head and heart and body and soul are all exploding simultaneously like fireworks on the Fourth of July.

"Jonas, with this ring, I promise to be your faithful and loving wife..." Sarah is saying.

Yes, I want to declare my eternal love to Kat in front of our family and friends and God and I want her to take my name. I want to make a life with that demonic-devil-woman. I want to be her husband—her *family*. "This is my beautiful wife," I want to say when I'm introducing Kat at a party. "Oh, you haven't met my wife yet? Well, here she is—Katherine Faraday."

Sarah slips a ring onto Jonas' finger and he exhales a loud, shaky breath.

"And now it's your turn, Jonas," the officiant says. "Repeat after me."

I look at Kat again to find her blue eyes trained on me.

"Sarah, with this ring, I promise to be your faithful and loving husband..." Jonas is saying.

My eyes are locked with Kat's.

My chest is tight.

Jonas slides a sparkling ring onto Sarah's shaking hand and she squeals with glee, making everyone in the audience chuckle, yet again.

"And now, by the authority of the state of Washington, I pronounce you husband and wife," the officiant declares. "Jonas, you can now *officially* kiss your lovely bride."

Jonas swoops Sarah into his arms and plants a passionate kiss on her lips to raucous applause.

"Ladies and gentlemen, may I present to you—for the very first time—Mr. and Mrs. Jonas Faraday."

The place erupts with cheers.

I clap and cheer, too—of course—but I'm distracted.

My eyes are still locked onto Kat's.

My heart is pounding in my ears.

There's no doubt in my mind—I want to make that beautiful terrorist my wife.

Jonas and Sarah link arms and bound happily down the aisle together, waving and fist-pumping as they go, and Kat and I link arms and follow them, exactly as we were instructed to do during last night's rehearsal. But tonight's walk down the aisle with Kat feels completely different than last night's dry run. Because tonight, for the first time in my entire life, I finally know what I need to be truly happy in this one and only life: I need to make Katherine Ulla Morgan mine, all mine. *Forever.*

110

JOSH

"Go Henny! Go Henny!" Kat shouts, and the crowd around Henn on the dance floor joins in on the chant, goading him on.

How much has Henn had to drink tonight? He's always entertaining, but this right here is a gift from the comedy gods. I can't tell if he's trying to break dance or if he's going into cardiac arrest; but either way, I'll never forget the sight of him as long as I live.

I look up at the band as I dance with Kat. The horns players are swiveling in synch as they play. Two women in fringed dresses and go-go boots are shaking their asses and singing their hearts out at center stage. And the guitarist is totally laying it down. I don't know who was responsible for finding this awesome band, whether it was Jonas or Sarah or Kat—but whoever it was, they deserve a medal. I've never had so much fun dancing in all my life. Even Jonas has been dancing all night long.

The band begins playing a new song—"Uptown Funk" by Bruno Mars— what else would a wedding band play these days?—and Uncle William grabs Kat's hand and steals her away from me, twirling her around.

Kat doesn't know this, but during dinner, while Kat was chatting with Sarah, I pulled my uncle aside and told him the news about my impending fatherhood—and also about my nascent plan to ask Kat to marry me. It was the first time I'd told anyone my intention to make Kat my wife, having only formed the idea two hours earlier—and my uncle's reaction was better than I could have imagined.

"Hallelujah! The Faradays are multiplying!" Uncle William exclaimed, hugging me enthusiastically and patting me on the back. "This is the second best day of my life." And then he poured me a tall glass of fifty-year-old Scotch from the bottle he'd brought with him from New York—a bottle of

Glenfarclas 1955, exactly like the one he'd given me for Kat's dad—and we clinked glasses.

"You got yourself a knockout with that one," Uncle William said, looking at Kat across the room. "She looks just like your mother."

I swigged my Scotch rather than reply.

"And don't you worry, Joshua," Uncle William continued, taking a long sip of his pricey liquor. "I'll make sure Kat's dripping in diamonds for you every bit as much as Sarah was for Jonas today—you can be sure of that." He winked and leaned into me like he was telling me something confidential. "Like I *always* say, we Faraday men *always* keep our women dripping in diamonds."

It was a truly bizarre statement, given that, one, I'd never heard Uncle William say a damned thing about women and/or diamonds before, and, two, I have no idea who "our women" would be in relation to "we Faraday men." But, still, the fact that my uncle was so effusive about my news and immediately wanted to spoil my future bride every bit as much as he'd spoiled Sarah today sent electricity shooting through my every nerve ending.

"Fuck yeah, Uncle William," I said, clinking his glass. "Cheers to that. That's how we Faraday men keep our women—*dripping* in the biggest fucking diamonds the world has ever seen."

"Fuck yeah," Uncle William replied, making me laugh.

It was an unexpected (and supremely ridiculous) conversation, to say the least, and so fucking awesome, I'll never forget it as long as I live. And now, on top of all that awesomeness, Uncle William's dancing with Kat like a madman, laughing with her and throwing his hands up every time the singer in the band commands everyone to "hit their hallelujah." Best night ever.

I look to my left on the dance floor, and there's Jonas, sweating like a pig, smiling from ear to ear, dancing with Sarah like he doesn't have a care in the world. I'm not sure I've ever seen Jonas dance before tonight—but if I have, I've certainly never seen him dance like *this*. He's the epitome of that old saying, "Dance like no one's watching."

Through the dancing bodies on the dance floor, I glimpse Kat's parents at the back of the restaurant, sitting all alone at an otherwise empty table, and I realize now's my chance to steal a private moment with them. I glance over my shoulder at Kat, and she's still happily cutting a rug with Uncle William, so I move quickly off the dance floor toward the back of the restaurant, taking a brief detour at my uncle's table to pour two tall glasses of his rare Scotch.

"Hey, Mr. and Mrs. Morgan," I say, sauntering up to their table. "Can I hang out with you for a bit?"

"Thomas and Lou, remember?" Kat's mom says warmly. "And, *of course*."

Louise pats the chair next to her and I take a seat.

"I brought you a present, Thomas," I say, putting one of the glasses of Scotch in front of him. "It's a Glenfarclas 1955 from my uncle's private collection. Fifty years old."

"Oh my God," Thomas says. "Really?"

"You want to try it, Lou?" I hold up the second glass to her.

Louise crinkles her nose. "No, thank you. I'm not a big Scotch drinker. I'll just take a little sip of Thomas'."

"How about some more champagne, then?"

Louise's face lights up. "Ah, now *that* I'll happily accept. We're staying at the hotel across the street, so I'm really letting loose tonight."

I flag down one of the roving waiters and grab Louise a flute of champagne and she takes a greedy sip.

"Okay, Thomas. Ready to have your taste buds ruined for any other Scotch?"

Thomas lifts his Scotch in reply and we both take sips at the same time.

"Oh my God," Thomas says, his eyes bugging out.

"Amazing, right?" I say.

"*Damn.* That stuff should be illegal."

"My uncle's somewhat of a connoisseur," I say. "He's got an amazing collection."

Thomas takes another sip. "Wow. So smooth."

I'm about to tell Thomas I've actually got a bottle of this exact stuff for him at my house—the bottle Kat wouldn't let me give to him a week ago—but in light of what I'm about to ask the guy, I refrain. Now's definitely not the time to make Kat's father think I'm trying to buy his affection.

I take a deep breath. "I wanted to talk to you both privately," I say. I look over my shoulder to make sure Kat's not nearby and quickly spot her on the dance floor, still whooping it up. "I want you to know I love your daughter— she's the best thing that's ever happened to me."

Louise makes an adorable face.

"And now that I've met the two of you and your incredible family, I'm realizing what marriage and family can be." I take a deep breath. "So, what I'm trying to say is I'm planning to ask Kat to marry me and I'm hoping you'll give me your blessing."

Kat's mom throws her arms around my neck, exactly the way Kat always does, and kisses me on the cheek. "*Of course*, you have our blessing, Josh. Oh my gosh, we're thrilled. Absolutely *thrilled.*"

When she pulls away from me, she's got tears in her eyes.

I look at Thomas, hoping for a similar reaction, but he's stoic.

There's a short beat that feels like an eternity.

Finally, Thomas lifts his Scotch in the air, inviting me to clink his glass, which I gratefully do. "Welcome to the Morgan family, Josh," he says calmly. "We're thrilled to have you."

I let out a huge sigh of relief. "Oh, thank God," I say, laughing.

Kat's mom giggles—and, suddenly, it's clear to me she's pretty damned tipsy.

"So when are you gonna ask her?" Louise asks, leaning into my face and batting her eyelashes. "And *how* are you gonna ask her, hmm? What you got up your sleeve, Joshy-baby?"

I chuckle. "Um. I don't know yet. I've got to get a ring first, make a plan. I'll do it as soon as possible after we get back from our trip—I won't have time to get a ring before we leave."

"When do you leave?"

"Tomorrow night."

"Oh. Well, if you need help shopping for a ring when you get back, I'd be happy to go with you," Louise says. "I know Kat's taste like the back of my hand."

"Thank you, Lou. I'll definitely take you up on that. We can make a day of it. I'll take you to a nice lunch, too." I motion to her champagne flute. "With plenty of champagne."

Louise squeals—oh yeah, she's definitely looped—and leans forward excitedly. "From now on, you can call me Mom if you want, honey. I mean you don't have to, of course, but you can. Or Momma? Or, hey, maybe Momma Lou?" She giggles again.

"*Momma Lou?*" Thomas asks, incredulous. "Louise, Josh isn't gonna call you *Momma Lou*. Do you think you run a soup kitchen in the South, for cryin' out loud?"

Kat's Mom throws her head back and laughs like a dude. "Sorry. I was thinking about what I want the baby to call me and I thought maybe Gramma Lou? Wouldn't that be *adorable*? So then I guess my mind just wandered to Momma Lou." She takes a swig of her champagne, giggling happily to herself. "Gramma Lou—isn't that darling? Or maybe Grammy Lou?" She sighs. "Gah. I can't wait."

"Slow down, Gramma Lou," Thomas says, rolling his eyes. "You're spinning out of control, honey. First things first—let the boy ask her."

Louise laughs heartily. "Well, anyway," she says, poking her fingertip into the top of my hand. "The point is, Josh, as far as I'm concerned, I just now birthed my fifth son." She guzzles down the rest of her champagne.

"*Louise.*"

Louise giggles. "Oh, Josh knows what I mean. All I'm saying is Josh is now one of my sons, every bit as much as the others. That's all I meant. What's your full name, honey?"

"Joshua William Faraday."

"*Joshua William,*" Louise says reverently. She makes a trumpet sound. "Doo doo doo doo! Birth announcement! The Morgan Family has just adopted a fifth son. There's Colby Edwin, Ryan Ulysses, Keane Elijah, David Jackson, and now *Joshua William*. You're now officially a member of the Morgan family, honey. Welcome."

Thomas rolls his eyes. "Maybe slow down on the champagne, honey."

Louise giggles and waves him off. "Oh, you'll benefit later, old man, so hush up." She puts her hand on my forearm. "We couldn't be more thrilled, Josh."

"Thank you," I manage to say, my heart leaping.

Louise flashes me a truly lovely smile. "No, thank *you*. You obviously make our Kitty Kat *very* happy."

Speak of the she-devil, Kat sidles up to our table, a bottle of water in her hand, her face covered in a light sheen of perspiration. "You guys look like you're plotting the invasion of a small country," she says. "What's shakin', bacon?"

I leap up and give Kat a kiss on her rosy cheek and guide her to the seat next to mine. "Hey, babe. I was just giving your dad a taste of my uncle's Glenfarclas 1955."

Kat shoots me a look of chastisement. "You just couldn't resist, could you, Playboy?" She looks at her parents. "Josh always says *I'm* the blabbermouth who can't keep a secret but look who's the blabbermouth now. Ha!" She snorts and swigs her water. "I told him it was too extravagant, but I guess the Playboy just couldn't control himself."

Kat's mom and dad look utterly confused.

"What are you talking about?" Thomas asks.

There's a beat as Kat realizes she's just blabbed yet another secret. "Oh. You... didn't give my dad the bottle?" she asks.

I shake my head.

"Damn," Kat says. "Whoops." She grins sheepishly. "Well, Dad, surprise! Josh is *giving* you that bottle of that Glenfarkity-fuckity-fuck-whatever. Do you like it?"

I shake my head again. "Kat, no. My uncle brought his *own* bottle of Glenfarclas tonight—he has several bottles of it in his collection. I just brought your dad a *glass* to *taste* from my *uncle's* bottle. I've still got your dad's bottle—*which I didn't tell him about and was still planning to give him later as a surprise.*"

Kat's face turns bright red. "Oh. Well, oops again." She snorts. "Well, Dad, Josh got a bottle of the stuff for you but I wouldn't let him give it to you because I said it was too extravagant a gift."

"Oh, wow," Thomas says. "Really? Thank you, Josh. But Kat's right, that really is too extravagant."

"Can I get all the single ladies onto the dance floor?" the lead singer of the band calls over the microphone on the far side of the restaurant. "It's time for the bouquet toss!"

"No, Thomas, I insist," I say. "I'll have the bottle delivered to your house this week." I shoot Kat a scolding look. "There's no sense in waiting now, is there?"

Thomas looks elated, but he nonetheless says the polite thing. "No, I really can't accept."

"Too late. It's yours. If you feel too weird about it, then open it for a special occasion—maybe when the baby's born?"

Thomas beams a wide smile at me. "All right. Thank you. I accept, but only if we're gonna open it together to celebrate the birth of my grandbaby."

"Deal," I say.

"And, Mom, don't feel left out," Kat says. "Josh got some fancy Cabernet for you, too. Some hoity-toity vintage."

"Oh, Josh. You're so sweet," Louise says. "But I really wouldn't know the difference. I'm happy with a twelve-dollar bottle of merlot."

Beyoncé's "Single Ladies" starts blaring over the sound system.

"Last call for all the single ladies to try to catch Sarah's bouquet!" the band-leader calls out.

"Too late," I say. "I already got it for you, Lou. I guess you'll have to grin and bear it."

"Well, thank you, Josh. You're so sweet." Louise glances at the commotion happening on the dance floor. "Honey, aren't you gonna get over there?" she says to Kat.

Thomas touches Louise's forearm, obviously signaling his wife to shut the fuck up and she clamps her lips together, apparently realizing she's treading into dangerous territory.

"Mom, *please*," Kat says, her tone suddenly indignant. "Like I told you guys last week, Josh and I aren't gonna get married. Deal with it. We've talked about it like adults and made our decision. Please respect that."

"Oh, we do, honey," Thomas says, pacifying his little stick of dynamite. "We completely respect that."

"Here we go!" the bandleader says behind us on the dance floor. "Are you ready, Sarah?"

Kat looks longingly toward the dance floor for a beat and then back at us, setting her jaw. "I can understand how being at this wedding has probably made you guys dream about watching me walk down the aisle in a white dress. Dad, seeing as how I'm your only daughter, I'm sure you can't help imagining yourself walking me down the aisle on your arm. But it's just not gonna happen, okay? You've got to let it go. I certainly have. One hundred percent."

Thomas, Louise, and I trade a long, skeptical look, all of us nonverbally acknowledging this girl's full of shit.

Louise throws up her hands. "Well, jeez. I'm sorry I mentioned it. I certainly didn't know I was opening a big ol' bottle of whoop-ass on myself."

Kat laughs. "It's a big ol' *can* of whoop-ass, Mom—not a bottle."

"Well, you know what I meant—I'm just saying I didn't mean to make you mad. Your father and I will never bring up the topic of marriage ever again. I swear. You two kids do whatever's right for you and we'll support you. Our lips are sealed. In fact, please don't get married. Blech. Marriage. Ew. Horrible idea." She mock-shudders.

Thomas touches his wife's arm again, glaring at her.

"Sorry," Lou says, giggling. "I've had a little bit to drink. I won't bring up marriage again—that's all I'm saying." She locks her mouth and throws away the key.

Thomas glares at his wife for a long beat. "As your mother said, we support you kids, whatever you decide."

Kat nods. "Thank you. Josh and I really appreciate that." Kat smiles at me and my heart aches at the blatant expression of longing reflected in her eyes.

How, before tonight, did I not understand how much Kat wants the fairy-tale? And how the fuck did I not want to give it to her?

There's a loud cheer from the dance floor.

"Let's hear it for *Hannah!*" the bandleader shouts into her microphone, and everyone on the dance floor cheers.

Kat glances over her shoulder toward the commotion behind us, and when she sees Hannah triumphantly holding up Sarah's bouquet, her face falls for the briefest moment. "Like I said, all this hoopla just isn't for us," she says, her jaw setting with resignation.

Kat's parents and I share another look.

"We completely understand," Thomas says evenly.

Louise nods like a bobble head doll. "We sure do. We all know how much you hate *hoopla*, Kitty Kat." She snorts.

"*Louise.*"

Kat's mom laughs like a dude and clamps her hand over her mouth again. "Sorry."

I put my arm around Kat's shoulder, demonstrating my faux solidarity with her. "Thanks for understanding," I say to Kat's parents. "As Kat said, we've talked about it and marriage just isn't for us."

"We understand," Thomas says.

"Good," Kat says, jutting her chin. "Now enough about that. Let's celebrate Jonas and Sarah's happy day—and never speak of the whole marriage-thing again."

111

JOSH

"Looks really good," Jonas says, looking at the spreadsheet displayed on my laptop screen. "I'd like to get our costs down by two percent over the course of the first year, ideally—especially as we start funding our designated charities—but as initial operating costs, I think these numbers crunch pretty well."

Sarah and Kat burst into a collective sob in the other room and Jonas and I exchange a smile. Just over an hour ago, the girls went into one of the bedrooms of our shared hotel suite to watch a chick flick on my iPad while Jonas and I got a little work done in the main room, and it seems the walls of this Venezuelan hotel are paper-thin.

"Anything else you need me to look at?" Jonas asks.

"No, I think Kelly and Colten have things well under control until we get back," I say, referring to the two regional managers we've hired to manage day-to-day operations of our initial twenty gyms. "I'll send them your notes and set up a meeting for the week we get back."

"Good. Thank you. And how about the grand opening?"

"I've got T-Rod overseeing the final details with an event planner. We were originally gonna have a DJ, but the band at your wedding was so awesome, I hired them to play the event. Go big or go home, right?"

"Well, cost-wise, I'm not sure if we really need to—"

"Jonas, I'll cover the band personally if you think the cost is excessive. I wanna kick things off with a bang—you know how much I love a good bang."

Jonas smirks. "Yeah, I'm well aware, Josh. Okay, thanks. Now what about the conference call with the sales team? We should get their numbers in advance of the call so we can—"

I shut my laptop with gusto. "Nope. No more work allowed for you for the rest of your trip."

Jonas opens his mouth to protest.

"If anything else comes up this week, I'll handle it. You're on your honeymoon, bro—erase work from your mind."

"Well, yeah, but you're on vacation, too."

"A honeymoon trumps a pre-baby vacation every time. Besides, Kat's been sleeping a ton lately—she gets pretty wiped out these days—so I'll have plenty of downtime in Argentina whenever she's napping to address anything that might come up."

Jonas exhales with relief. "Okay, cool. Thanks, Josh."

"Just enjoy your honeymoon, man."

"I plan to. We're going to Belize next."

"Ah, back to the scene of the original crime, huh?"

Jonas' face lights up. "Yup. A tree house in the middle of the jungle, surrounded by howler monkeys—my idea of heaven on earth."

"Sounds awesome."

"So how's Kat doing? Is she still puking?"

"Yeah, but not as much. She's mostly just really tired. Apparently, it takes a lot of energy to incubate a mighty Faraday spawn. The good news for me is that, when Kat's not sleeping or puking, her pregnancy hormones are through the roof." I snicker. "It's like my unicorn permanently strapped a jet engine between her legs."

Jonas laughs. "Excellent."

"Oh, yeah. I highly recommend pregnancy hormones." I kiss the tips of my fingers like a French chef blessing his masterpiece.

"Good to know. Hopefully, Sarah will have the same experience when it's her turn to incubate a mighty Faraday spawn."

"Oh, you and Sarah are thinking about having kids?"

"Definitely. Not any time soon—but yeah."

"Well, don't wait too long," I say. "My mighty Faraday spawn's gonna need another mighty Faraday spawn to boss around sooner rather than later."

"Oh, please. Your spawn's gonna be my spawn's little bitch," Jonas says.

I laugh. "Bullshit, motherfucker. My spawn's gonna kick your spawn's tiny ass."

"Ha! My spawn's gonna make your spawn cry like a little baby."

We both laugh.

"So how was New Zealand?" I ask.

"Fucking amazing," Jonas says, leaning back in his chair. He gives me a summary of his and Sarah's exciting Kiwi-adventures over the past week. "We stayed at the coolest place," he says. "I'll get you the info so you can take Kat."

I scoff. "I think it'll be a while before I take Kat rappelling down cliffs and bungee jumping off bridges."

"Oh yeah." Jonas grins. "I guess you'll be laying low for a while on stuff like that, huh? How far along is she?"

"Fourteen weeks."

"When the fuck will she actually look pregnant, by the way? She looks exactly the same as she always has."

I shrug. "Hell if I know. I've never done this before."

The girls let out a tortured wail in the other room—and then immediately giggle together—and Jonas and I laugh.

"I think there's a good chance the two humans in that bedroom have vaginas," I say.

Jonas nods his agreement. "God, I hope so, or else I've been seriously duped. So how was Brazil?" he asks.

"Un-fucking-believable." I give him a brief synopsis of Kat's and my travels through Brazil and show him a few photos on my phone. "In Rio, we stayed at this bungalow right on the beach. This is the view from the deck out front."

"Whoa," Jonas says, looking at my photo. "Send me the info on that place, would you? Maybe I'll take Sarah to Rio later this year."

"Oh, you should take Sarah for *Carnival*," I say.

"Oh, good idea," Jonas says. "Yeah, I'll do that."

I tap out a quick text to Theresa on my phone. "I'm texting T-Rod to send you the info on where we stayed in Rio. She'll hook you right up."

"Thanks," Jonas says. He gets up and ambles to the bar in the corner of the suite. "You wanna beer?"

"Yeah. Hit me with some Venezuelan *cerveza* I've never heard of before, bro."

Jonas opens the fridge. "Hmm. Looks like we've got something called *Cardenal*?"

"*Perfecto, mi hermano.*"

Jonas hands me an opened beer and sits back down.

"*Gracias,*" I say.

"*De nada,*" Jonas says, swigging his beer. "*Con mucho gusto, mi hermano estupido.*"

"You did really well talking to Mariela today," I say. "I was impressed."

"Yeah, Sarah speaks Spanish to me all the time," Jonas says, grinning. "She's so fucking sexy." He sighs happily. "But my Spanish was already pretty good before Sarah came along. I guess it's just burned into the deep recesses of my brain from when Mariela used to talk to us as kids."

"Well, maybe it's burned into the deep recesses of your brain, but it's certainly not burned into mine. I couldn't understand a fucking word Mariela was saying all day besides *gracias* and *mi hijo* and *amor*."

Jonas chuckles. "You didn't need to understand Mariela's words—I think she made herself pretty damned clear with her body language."

"Definitely," I agree. "It was pretty hard to misunderstand all that hugging and kissing and crying."

The girls squeal loudly in the other room and Jonas glances toward the source of the sound.

"Damn, these walls are thin," Jonas says. "Maybe I should have gotten a separate suite for Sarah and me?"

"Meh, it's fine," I say. "It's only for two nights. Plus, the four of us will be out all day tomorrow exploring Caracas—we'll hardly be in the suite together except to sleep at night."

"Well, maybe you and Kat plan to *sleep*. But I'm on my honeymoon, man—sleeping's not on the agenda." Jonas snickers. "And Sarah's a *screamer*."

"Dude, why you always gotta go there? I know you love screwing your beautiful wife, okay? I got it." I roll my eyes. "I don't need that visual of you."

"What the fuck?" Jonas says, laughing. "You just told me your unicorn has a jet engine permanently strapped between her legs, and I'm not allowed to—"

"Blah, blah, blah," I say, cutting Jonas off, making him laugh again. "All I'm saying is if you've got a problem with all of us sharing a suite, then you'll have to be the one to move, not me. Theresa said this is the only hotel in Caracas that's up to my standards—and there's only one penthouse suite in the whole goddamned hotel. So if you wanna move to a ghetto room on a lower floor be my guest, motherfucker, but I'm staying right here where the streets are paved with gold."

"You're such a snob, you know that?"

I shrug and take a sip of my beer. "I make no apologies—I like what I like."

"Eh, Sarah won't want to switch rooms, anyway," Jonas says. "She insisted on staying with Kat our two nights here. She's been going through some sort of Kat withdrawal this past week."

I laugh. "Same with Kat. Every little thing we did in Brazil, Kat was like, 'Oh my God, Sarah would love this.'"

We grin at each other for a long beat.

"How'd we get so fucking lucky?" I ask.

Jonas shrugs. "I have no idea. A broken clock is right twice a day, I guess."

"Sarah's really sweet," I say. "I can't believe she even *thought* to arrange a reunion with Mariela, let alone pull it all together on the sly like that."

"That's Sarah," Jonas says. "She's the sweetest person I've ever met. Just genuinely *kind*."

"She's the sweetest person I've ever met, too," I agree.

"What about Kat? She's not the sweetest person you've ever met?"

I snort. "Hell no."

Jonas laughs. "Well, that's not a very nice thing to say."

"Aw, come on," I say. "Kat's *sweet*—really sweet. Heart of gold. But it's buried underneath a thick outer shell of evil. The woman's a demon spawn of the highest order." Once again, I kiss my fingertips like a chef.

Jonas chuckles. "You always did like 'em evil."

I mock-shudder like the very mention of evil excites me. "And, even better, *crazy*-evil."

"Well, Sarah doesn't have an evil bone in her body," Jonas says. "Does she have a crazy-bone? Hell yes. A bossy-bone? Fuck yes. But an evil-bone? Not even in her little toe."

"Like I said, Sarah's the sweetest person I know," I say, swigging my beer. "Which is perfect for you—you've always liked 'em sweet."

Jonas shrugs. "I don't think that's a particularly weird thing to like, Josh."

"Bah," I say. "Gotta have a little evil to brighten your day, I always say."

Jonas chuckles. "Sicko."

"I am what I am. So were you shocked when you got off the plane and saw Kat and me standing there—or did you already have a hunch?"

"I was completely shocked—and then I was even more shocked when we drove up to that big ol' house and Mariela came out. I couldn't believe my eyes."

"Dude, me, too—I thought I was gonna keel over in shock."

"For so long, I always thought, 'If Mariela passed me on the street, would I recognize her?'" Jonas says. "All through the years, whenever I'd see a Latina woman of the right age walking by, I'd think, 'Could that be Mariela?' But then, the minute I actually saw the real thing, there was no doubt it was her—a thousand memories instantly came rushing back to me."

"I didn't recognize her *physically* so much as I recognized her..." I trail off, searching for the right word. "Her *soul*? Is that a totally Jonas Faraday thing to say?"

Jonas chuckles. "I hate to break it to you, but you're actually referencing Plato's theory of forms without realizing it. Plato said when we see something in the physical realm with our eyes, we're seeing the imperfect form of it—because nothing's perfect in the physical world—but your *soul* is nonetheless able to recognize it, despite its imperfections, because it innately knows the thing's divine original form from the *ideal* realm." He pauses briefly. "I think for both of us, Mariela was our divine original form of nurturing—an ideal form of safety and affection and love—and our souls recognized her instantly, even if our eyes didn't."

I smile at Jonas. There's just no one like my brother. "Makes perfect sense to me," I say.

Jonas smiles.

"Hey, did you catch her *scent*?" I say, taking in a deep breath through my nose. "I didn't even know I remembered that scent, but the minute Mariela hugged me, I instantly remembered how she used to rock us to sleep in that big rocking chair—remember that?—and I'd nuzzle my nose into her neck and breathe in that flowery scent."

Jonas shakes his head in apparent awe. "It's amazing what the brain retains that we don't even realize on a conscious level." He drinks his beer. "When Mariela hugged me and called me Jonasito today, I felt like I'd traveled back in a time machine to when I was seven years old."

I sip my beer and consider that concept for a minute. "Dude," I say. "I'm thinking deep thoughts about the illusion of time and the infinite nature of love. Make it stop, Jonas. Please. My head hurts."

"Jesus, Josh. You can't be thinking deep thoughts like that—you'll fuck up the entire world order."

I smirk. "Okay. Phew. I'm thinking about motorboating pretty titties now. I'm good."

Jonas laughs. "That was a close call. God help us if you created some sort of butterfly effect and fucked us all."

"Seriously. That was truly scary."

"Don't do anything like that again," Jonas warns. "You've still got five days in Argentina with your pregnant girlfriend after this—for fuck's sake, don't injure yourself, man, especially if your unicorn's on a hot streak."

"Hey, that reminds me," I say. I peek toward the bedroom. This is the first time I've been alone with Jonas since the wedding—and his use of the word "girlfriend" just reminded me I haven't told him about my plan to ask Kat to marry me. I glance toward the bedroom again to make sure Kat's not coming out. "Hey, at your wedding, I had this epiphany that slammed me like a ton of bricks, man," I begin.

The girls let out a collective sigh followed by a cheer in the other room and I glance at the door again.

"When we get home," I say, "I'm gonna ask Kat to—"

Sarah and Kat burst out of the bedroom, both of them sobbing, and I abruptly shut my mouth.

"Oh my gawd," Sarah bawls, wiping her eyes. "Best movie *ever*."

"Ever, ever, ever!" Kat agrees, tears streaming down her beautiful face. She hands my iPad to me. "Thank you, babe. Oh my gawd. I *loved* it."

"One of my all-time faves," Sarah says.

"Me, too. Top ten for sure. Maybe even top five."

"Fo shizzle pops." Sarah plops herself onto Jonas' lap. "Hello, hunky monkey husband."

"Hello, wife."

Kat follows suit and plops herself down onto my lap, too. "Hey, PB," she says

"Hey, PG," I reply, my heart panging. Shit. If ever there was a time when our Playboy-Party-Girl nicknames felt woefully insufficient, it's right now. Ever since Jonas and Sarah's wedding, I've been chomping at the bit to call Kat my wife, and with each passing day, my desire becomes more and more urgent. "What movie were you two watching in there?" I ask. "It sounded like you were watching *Schindler's List*."

"Oh, no, it was a romantic comedy."

Jonas and I share a chuckle.

"*About Time*," Sarah says reverently. "Oh my *gawd*. Have you seen it?"

"Never heard of it," I say.

"You gotta see it," Kat says. "The girl from *The Notebook* is in it. Have you seen *The Notebook*?"

I shake my head.

"Oh. Well, did you see *Love Actually*? You know the rock-star-British guy in that one?"

"Dude, unless Seth Rogan or Will Ferrell or Adam Sandler is in a movie, it's a good bet I haven't seen it."

Kat rolls her eyes. "Do you know the red-haired guy from the *Harry Potter* movies?" Kat asks.

"Well, of course," I say. "Now you're speaking my language."

"But not the one who played Ron Weasley," Sarah interjects. "The redheaded guy who played his older brother."

Kat swats my arm. "The guy in *Ex Machina*."

"Oh," I say. "Yeah?"

"He's the main guy in this one and he's so cute—"

"*So* cute," Sarah agrees.

"And he figures out he can time-travel by going into a closet and then he meets *The Notebook* girl and—what's her name, Sarah?"

"Rachel McAdams. She's so cute."

"*So* cute. So, anyway, I won't spoil it for you, in case you ever wanna watch it but it's *so* good." Kat lets out a long, swooning sigh.

Sarah mimics Kat's swooning sigh. "So good," she agrees.

Jonas and I exchange a look. Honestly, I don't know what the fuck either of these two women have said for the past three minutes—I pretty much tuned out after Kat said the words *The Notebook*—but, damn, both of these girls are fucking adorable.

Clearly, Jonas agrees with my assessment because he's begun nuzzling Sarah's neck and whispering to her.

Sarah makes a sound of sheer happiness. "Oh, how I love you, hubster," she breathes.

"Oh, how I love you, *Mrs. Faraday*," Jonas replies.

Sarah runs her hand through Jonas' hair. "I'll never forget the look on your face when you saw Mariela today. You were beautiful, love."

"Thank you for arranging that for me. I'll never forget it."

"Yeah, thank you, Sarah Cruz," I say. "I'll never forget today as long as I live. It was amazing."

"It was my pleasure. It warmed my heart to see the Faraday boys looking so happy."

"Mariela had quite a house, didn't she?" Kat says. "I'd say Mariela's livin' large in the ol' Vee-Zee, baby."

"Half a million bucks goes a really long way here," Jonas says, referring to the finder's fee money we secured for Mariela (along with equal shares for Sarah's mom, Jonas' friend Georgia, and Miss Westbrook).

Sarah whispers something into Jonas' ear and he kisses her tenderly.

I look away from them and I'm met with Kat's intense gaze. *Oh.* I know that look—it means my unicorn's feeling frisky.

Kat runs her fingertip over my bottom lip. "Are you all done with your work, honey pot pie?" she whispers.

I chuckle. "Someone's been hanging out with Sarah Weirdo Cruz today."

Kat giggles. "Yeah, that was extremely Sarah-Cruz-ish, wasn't it?"

"Yes, it was. And, yes, I'm all done with my work." I stick out my tongue and lick the tip of Kat's finger. "I'm all yours for the rest of the night, hot momma."

Kat presses her forehead against mine. "Mike Wazowski," she whispers.

I grin.

Kat presses her lips against my ear and whispers softly, "I'm so frickin' horny, I'm gonna blow."

"God, I love pregnancy hormones," I whisper back.

Kat smiles.

Out of nowhere, Jonas makes a kind of growling noise and abruptly stands with Sarah in his arms, lifting her like a rag doll. "Good night, guys," he says. "It seems Mrs. Faraday and I have a date with a Venezuelan mattress. Come on, wife." Without waiting for our reply, Jonas barrels away like the gorilla he is, happily carrying his love-monkey-bride in his protective arms.

"Good night, guys!" Sarah calls to us, just before their bedroom door closes with an emphatic thud.

"Those two are so freaking cute," Kat says.

My stomach clenches with envy. Fuck me. I want to say, "Come on, wife!" to Kat, exactly the way Jonas just said that to Sarah. And, fuck me, I want to say "Mrs. Faraday and I have a date with a Venezuelan mattress!" too, even if, yes, that's a supremely cheesy thing to say. Shit. At least fifty times this past week in Brazil, I almost blurted, "Will you marry me, Kat?" But I refrained every time— of course, I did—because the sane part of my brain knows I've already asked Kat to marry me without a ring or ironclad plan in place and that she replied, "I wouldn't marry you if you were the last man on earth." So, obviously, another spontaneous (flop-dick) proposal ain't gonna cut it a second time around.

Kat skims her lips against mine, yanking me out of my thoughts, and I slip my tongue eagerly into her mouth. In reply, she presses herself into my hard-on.

"How are you feeling, beautiful?" I ask, kissing her softly.

"Good," she says. "I didn't barf *once* today."

"Wow," I whisper. "Sexy. You know I can't resist a woman who doesn't barf."

"One might even say it's your Achilles' heel, although I seem to recall you're also quite willing to fuck a woman who barfs on your shoes."

"Not 'a woman' who barfs on my shoes," I say. "Only *you.*"

"Sweet-talker."

"Okay. Enough chitty-chat," I declare suddenly. I stand and swoop Kat into my arms, and Kat practically growls with excitement. "It's time to put those pregnancy hormones of yours to maximum use, Party Girl."

"I've got a present for you," I coo as Josh lays me down on the bed.

"Oh yeah?" Josh pulls off his shirt, revealing his gloriously muscled and tattooed torso.

"Oh my God," I say, ogling him.

Josh pulls down his pants and briefs, letting his straining donkey-dick spring free.

"Sweet Baby Jesus," I blurt. "I feel like my clit's a lawnmower and you just yanked its starter-cord."

Josh smiles wickedly. "Oh, the things I'm gonna do to you, hot momma." He advances on me like a panther.

"Wait. Close your eyes."

Josh exhales like I've asked him to stop and change the oil in my car. "You're killing me, Smalls," he says.

"Close 'em, Playboy. I've got a surprise for you. It'll take five seconds and then you can do whatever you please to me."

Josh settles onto his knees next to me, his naked body taut, his erection massive. "You've got twenty seconds and then I can't be held responsible for what this dick might do to you."

I pull my sundress off, revealing my leopard-print-electric-blue bra and undies underneath, and carefully cover my hipbone with my palm.

"Okay," I say. "Open."

Josh opens his eyes. "Great surprise. You're gorgeous. Now lie back." He pushes me back gently.

"No, you fool," I say. "I haven't shown you the surprise yet."

Josh exhales again.

"You ready?" I ask.

Josh motions to his straining dick in reply.

I bite my lip and remove my hand, revealing the temporary "tattoo" Sarah drew on my hip with a Sharpie pen while we watched *About Time* in the other room. "For you, Playboy," I say, unveiling the famous Playboy-rabbit-head-logo drawn onto my hip. "I can't get a tattoo while pregnant—apparently, there's a risk of infection or whatever—but I finally figured out what I'm gonna do for my second tattoo after the baby's born."

Josh's hard-on visibly twitches. "Aw, you're gonna get a *boyfriend* tattoo?"

I nod.

Josh's sapphire eyes smolder. "Sounds pretty serious, babe."

"Oh, it is—as serious as it can be."

Josh advances on me slowly, his taut muscles flexing, his hard-on huge, and slowly pushes me onto my back. He deftly removes my bra and, the minute my breasts bounce free, he buries his face into my cleavage and motorboats my boobs, making me giggle.

"I'll be damned, your pretty titties might actually be getting a little bit bigger, babe," he says.

I look down at myself. "Really?"

"Maybe. Lemme double check." He takes my left nipple into his mouth, swirling his tongue around and around.

I let out a soft moan.

"Yeah, definitely," he says. He runs his palm over my belly. "And you're a tiny bit rounder here, too, I think."

My heart lurches into my mouth with excitement. "You really think so?" I sit up, completely distracted from our imminent fuckery. "Do you think I'm finally pooching?" I look down and poke myself with my fingertip.

"Lie back down, babe," Josh says, pushing me back. "I'll examine you and let you know for sure."

I stare down at myself. "I think you might be right. *Look.*" I poke my belly again and there's definitely a little pooch under my fingertip. "I put on my favorite skirt this morning and it didn't fit quite right but I thought I was imagining it."

Josh pushes gently on my shoulders again. "Lie back, beautiful."

"By the end of this trip, nothing I packed is gonna fit right," I say, my skin buzzing. "I'm probably gonna need maternity clothes any day now, babe, and I didn't pack any."

"Lie back, hot momma," Josh persists. "We'll go shopping in Buenos Aires if we need to—surely, there are pregnant women there, too. *Relax.*" He peels off my undies while licking my neck and firmly pushes me back onto the bed.

"Do you really think I'm showing?" I breathe.

"Oh yeah." He licks my ear and slides his fingers between my legs. "Definitely. What fruit is the baby now?"

"A lemon."

"A *lemon?*" He shudders like I just said a dirty word. "God-*damn*, I've got a pregnant-woman fetish these days." His fingers are massaging me. His lips are on mine. His tongue is in my mouth. "My sexy little baby-momma," he whispers.

He begins trailing kisses down my body, heading slowly toward my bull's-eye—and when his warm, wet tongue finally reaches my clit, I arch my back and exhale, settling in for what's surely going to be a delicious ride. But just as Josh's mouth begins devouring me in earnest, the unmistakable sound of Sarah having an orgasm in the other bedroom wafts into our room. The sound is muffled, and oddly restrained, like Sarah's trying her damnedest to be quiet but utterly failing.

Josh lifts his head and looks at me, a smirk on his gorgeous face, and we both giggle. "Sounds like they're having fun."

I snort.

Josh sits up, his eyes dark with desire. "You wanna play a game, Party Girl?"

I bite my lip. "What kind of game?"

Josh lies alongside me, grabs a pillow, and places it under his head. He licks his lips. "Have a seat, babe." He waggles his tongue at me, making my clit flutter.

"That's the game?" I ask. "I sit on your face?"

"No, the game is you sit on my face and try not to scream the way Sarah just did. If you scream, I win—if you don't, you win."

I smirk. "Am I trying not to *come*—or trying not to *scream* when I do?"

"Oh, you're gonna come—there's no doubt about that." He licks his lips with an exaggerated motion. "In fact, I'm gonna eat your pussy 'til I make it rain." He snickers. "And good fucking luck not screaming through *that*."

"Babe, the walls are so thin. I have no desire for Jonas and Sarah to hear me climaxing."

Josh shrugs. "So does that mean you accept my challenge?"

"Of course. And I assure you, I'm gonna win. I'm a sniper, baby—total control."

"We'll see about that."

"What do I get when I win?"

"If you can squirt without waking half of Caracas, then I'll be your sex slave for the rest of the night. Command me as you please, hot momma." He begins stroking his erection, a pervy gleam in his eye. "But if I make you scream louder than Sarah just did, then you're all mine, every fucking inch of you, for the rest of the trip."

I giggle. "Sounds like I'm gonna come out a winner in this game either way."

Josh adjusts the angle of the pillow under his head and makes a loud smacking sound like he's calling a horse. "Come on, m'lady—hop aboard your valiant steed. I'm thirsty for some lemonade."

"Oh my God, Josh. That's disgusting."

He laughs and continues stroking his hard-on.

"You really are a sick fuck, you know that?" I say, crawling over his face.

"Yes, I am."

After positioning myself carefully over Josh's beautiful mouth, I lower myself onto his lips and immediately sigh with pleasure at the sensation of his warm tongue penetrating me. "Oh, God," I say. "That's so good, babe."

Josh growls underneath me and slides his finger into my ass and I jerk my pelvis against him like I'm slowly fucking his face. Within minutes, my skin pricks with goose bumps and my toes curl—and it's quite clear to me I'm gonna lose this goddamned bet. Oh, God, yes, I'm gonna lose this motherfucking bet by a landslide—*which means, of course, I'm gonna win.*

"I love you," I breathe, my pleasure ramping up. "Oh my God, yes, babe— oh, my fucking-motherfucker-fuck. *Yes.*" I bite the tip of my finger, trying to relieve the pressure rising inside me, but it's no use. This is just too freaking good. Oh my God, *yes.*

Josh growls underneath me again and slips his finger right up my ass and the wall of my vagina contracts sharply. Josh's lips and tongue continue voraciously eating me and my body tightens again, and then again, ratcheting itself up for what promises to be an outrageous release.

"*I love you so much,*" I choke out, fondling my breasts. "Oh, God, I love you." But those are the last coherent words I utter before letting out a scream that's not only sure to be heard by Jonas and Sarah in the next room, it's no doubt going to awaken the entire continent of South America, too.

113

JOSH

I've been lying here in the dark, spooning Kat's sleeping body, for over an hour—but sleep won't come, no matter how many Venezuelan sheep I try to count.

Fuck.

I carefully extricate myself from Kat's long limbs, slip quietly out of the bed, and pad into the moonlit suite. After grabbing a water bottle from the fridge, I head out to a large balcony overlooking pre-dawn Caracas, expecting to grab a few minutes of insomnia-laden solitude. But I'm surprised to find I'm not alone out on the balcony.

"Jonas?"

My brother turns around in his chair. "Hey," he says softly.

"What are you doing out here, bro?"

"Same as you, I'm sure," he says. "I can't sleep."

"You want something from the fridge?" I ask, holding up my water bottle.

Jonas holds up a glass in his hand.

I sit in a wicker chair next to my brother and look out at the skyline. "Why can't you sleep?" I ask.

Jonas shrugs. "I've had chronic insomnia my whole life. This time, luckily, I've got *happy* insomnia—I can't stop thinking about how *happy* I am." He smiles. "You?"

I run my hand through my hair and exhale. "I've been wanting to tell you about this, actually. I've decided to pop the question to Kat—and I can't figure out how the fuck to do it."

"Really? Congrats. That's great. When are you gonna do it?"

"As soon as I can get a ring and figure out how the fuck to do it right this time. There's no margin for error—failure isn't an option."

Jonas looks genuinely elated. "Well, do you have any ideas? Bounce 'em off me—I'll help you figure it out."

"Dude, I have no idea how to do it—that's why I've got insomnia. I can't just, you know, take her to dinner and pull out a ring or take her to a basketball game and ask her on the fucking Jumbotron. Whatever I do, it's gotta be *big*." My stomach clenches. "Honestly, I'm kind of freaking out about it, bro. I asked Kat once and totally fucked it up. I gotta do it right this time or I dunno if she'll give me a third bite at the apple." I rub my forehead. "Kat didn't just turn me down the first time—she got *pissed*. And even worse than that, she got her feelings hurt. I'm the first man in the history of the world to ask a woman to marry him and make her feel *shitty* about it."

Jonas grimaces. "How'd you manage that?"

I shrug. "I have no fucking idea."

"Come on. You must have an idea what you did wrong. How'd you ask her? You never told me any details. All I know is your proposal *didn't* include the words 'I love you.'"

I shake my head, not wanting to relive it.

"Tell me, Josh. We gotta figure this out."

I begrudgingly tell Jonas every detail of how that night at the hospital went down. "And then the whole next week, I felt so rejected and bummed and confused, I actually told myself I was done with her," I say, rolling my eyes at the absurd thought. "And the most aggravating part was she kept calling me 'Mr. Darcy,' and I have no idea why."

"You mean from *Pride and Prejudice*?" Jonas asks.

"Why the fuck do you know that? I had to Google that shit to figure it out."

Jonas shrugs.

"You amaze and appall me," I say. "But we're off track here. The point is, I fucked it up and Kat said no and I've never felt so rejected in all my life. For both our sakes, I couldn't handle a repeat performance. I have to do it right this time."

"Yeah, well, proposing in a hospital waiting room when the girl's sitting vigil for her brother definitely doesn't sound like a story Kat would wanna 'tell her grandchildren one day'—unless, of course, you want her to tell her future grandchildren 'The Story of How Grandpa was a Dumbshit.'"

"The scary thing is I truly didn't realize I was fucking up at the time—I thought I deserved a fucking medal for being so honorable."

"Well, that's the problem right there. Women don't want honorable—they want love."

"Yeah, I know that now. Duh. *Now* I realize Kat just wanted to hear me say 'I love you' and 'you're the woman of my dreams' and all that—okay, I get it—but at the time I was too freaked out to say any of that. But still, I'm not sure why she punched me so fucking hard in the balls. She could have just said 'no thanks'—that would have been sufficient, thank you very much. But not Kat. Of course, not. She was *livid*, man—and, honestly, I still don't fully understand why. Which means I could totally piss her off again and fuck it up completely and not even realize I'm doing it."

"Well, duh, Josh. You seriously don't know why?"

I shrug.

"Josh, you made Kat feel like you were doing her a fucking favor by marrying her—like *she* was the lucky one. No woman wants to feel like that, especially when a man's proposing to her—she wants to feel like a princess out of a fairytale. She wants to feel like the grand prize."

"Holy fuck, Jonas. That's exactly what she said. *Exactly*." I close my eyes, chastising myself. "How is it possible you know more about this than I do?"

"Because I've watched *Pride and Prejudice* and *Fools Rush In* and a bunch of other chick flicks—and those movies tell a guy everything he needs to know about the female psychology, you dumbshit."

"Well, I fully realize I'm the lucky one now, believe me—I'd be the luckiest bastard in the world to call Kat Morgan my wife."

"Well, just tell her that, then. Perfect."

"No, that ship has sailed man," I say. "I've gotta bring out the big guns now—this is round two, bro. I need a whole lot more than a good proposal—I need a shit-ton more than 'I love you'—I need *redemption*."

"Yeah, I guess you're right," Jonas says. He squints, clearly thinking hard about something. I've seen this look on my brother's face a thousand times when he's poring over an acquisition report and crunching numbers in his head. "Okay. If you wanna crack Kat's secret code, you gotta figure out what makes her tick. For Sarah, it was overcoming her lifelong fears and finally letting go completely. That was the key with her—making her *surrender* and let go. So, first off, I took Sarah to the top of a thirty-foot, underground waterfall in Belize and made her jump off. That was stage one. And, then, when I finally proposed to her, I took her to the highest mountaintop in Greece and made her jump off and paraglide down to the beach." He chuckles, apparently at some memory. "I made Sarah face her fears and let go and, man, it was fucking epic. You've just gotta figure out how to do the same for Kat. Unlock her. Figure out her secret code and crack her. And that's how you'll deliver her unto pure *ecstasy* in the way the ancient Greeks defined that word—'the culmination of human possibility.'"

I roll my eyes. My brother is such a fucking freak. "Well, Kat's not afraid of a goddamned thing," I say. "I could take her to the top of a waterfall and she'd cannonball off it, honking her boobs as she plummeted down."

Jonas laughs. "Well, then, fine—overcoming fear clearly isn't the ticket with Kat. But there's got to be *something* that will unlock Kat's deepest desires—something her soul is desperately yearning for."

I'm silent.

"Well?" Jonas says.

"I'm thinking," I say.

"Don't strain yourself."

I laugh.

"Hey, you're wise and powerful, remember?" Jonas says. "Even if Kat's not scared of a damned thing, she's gotta be *scarred* by something—or maybe secretly *yearning* for something. *Think.* What's buried deep, deep, deep inside that woman's heart and soul? Figure it out, unlock it, and deliver it to her on a silver platter—bigger and better than she'd ever imagine—and that's how you'll give her a proposal she'll 'tell her grandchildren about.'"

I wince. "When I said that to you at Uncle William's house, I never thought in a million years it would come back to bite me in the ass."

"Well, it has. So take your own advice. Your exact words were, 'If you're gonna surprise the girl, then make sure you blow her socks off. This is the story she's gonna be telling her grandkids one day. So don't fuck it up,'" Jonas says. "That's *exactly* what you said to me." He brings his glass to his lips and surveys the twinkling Caracas skyline. "So now it's time to walk the walk, motherfucker."

I lean back in my chair, my mind reeling. "Shit," I say. "I seriously have no idea what to do."

"Well, whatever it is, you've got to pull out all the stops."

"Fuck," I say, feeling suddenly panicked. "Kat said she wouldn't marry me if I were the last man on earth, Jonas. Help me, man. I need to trick that demon-woman into saying yes."

Jonas laughs. "You've tricked her pretty well so far."

I scowl at him.

"Don't worry, Josh," Jonas says soothingly. "We'll figure this out. She's but a mortal woman and you're a wise and powerful demi-god. We'll topple her."

"Thank you, Jonas," I say, feeling mildly comforted. "So where do I start?"

"Well, let's start with the basics," Jonas says. "You gotta tell her you love her this time."

"Thank you, Einstein."

"And you gotta get her a ring so big it sears her fucking corneas."

I nod. "Yet again, not rocket science."

"You say that but you weren't already planning to do that, were you?" Jonas says.

"Yes, I was. *Duh.* I'm gonna get Kat a ring so big, she's gonna need a fucking *crane* to carry it around."

Jonas laughs. "Good boy."

I swig my water, my mind reeling. Fuck me. I've got to get this exactly right.

"So what else are you thinking?" Jonas says. "'Whatever you do, it's gotta be rock solid, man—it's got to be a homerun. There's absolutely no room for failure.'"

Obviously, he's quoting me from Uncle William's dining room. Who knew my own words would come back to put the fear of God into me a mere two months later? Back then, I truly thought I'd never get married—a thought that's absolutely laughable to me now.

"Okay, okay," I say. "I get it. I talk a good game when it's not me stepping up to home plate." I swig my water again. "Stop razzing me and help me, Jonas. Please. I'm desperate."

Jonas chuckles. "Finally, the Kung Fu master begs Grasshopper for help."

"Jesus, are you gonna berate me or help me? I need your help, Jonas. I already asked her once and she said no. If she turns me down again, especially now that I love her like I do, I'd seriously never recover, man. I'm not exaggerating. I'd be a broken man, forever." I clutch my stomach, suddenly feeling ill.

Jonas looks sympathetic. "Aw, Josh. She won't say no. She loves you."

"You don't know Kat," I say. "She's capable of anything. She's a demon spawn, like I said. She'd cut off my balls and make s'mores out of 'em without batting an eyelash."

Jonas grimaces. "Jesus."

"Welcome to my world."

"Well, she won't say no—because you won't fuck it up this time."

"But what if I can't help myself? What if I'm just so clueless I'm incapable of getting it right?"

"You can't fuck it up, Josh."

"Well, that's obviously not true."

"No, I mean, you can't fuck it up this time. All you have to do is follow Kat's own advice."

I look at my brother blankly.

"When I was Boring Blane for you—which by the way gave me a mild case of post-traumatic stress disorder—thanks so much for that—I asked Kat's advice about proposing to Sarah. And you wanna know what she told me?"

"No, Jonas. Please keep that little nugget to yourself."

"She told me to keep it simple. She said as long as I spoke from my heart, whatever I said would be grandchildren-worthy."

I sigh. "Kinda vague to be helpful, bro."

"Not really. Just speak from your heart. Tell her you love her. Tell her all the reasons *why* you love her. That right there will be epic enough."

"Says the guy who shoved his fiancée off Mount Olympus and made her paraglide to the Aegean before he'd kneel and give her the ring."

Jonas laughs.

I look out at the city. The sky behind the faraway buildings is beginning to lighten with the faintest glow of orange.

"Jonas, I need something more concrete than 'speak from your heart,'" I say. "*Please.*"

"Well, I don't know, man. I don't know Kat like you do. You just gotta think about what makes her tick and deliver it to her."

I think about that for a minute. "Fantasies. Mini pornos," I say. "She's got the most active imagination of anyone I've ever met."

"Okay. Good start," Jonas says.

"She loves shit like *The Bodyguard* and *Pretty Woman*," I continue. "She's seen her favorite movies like twenty times each."

Jonas laughs. "Well, there you go."

"In the beginning I thought Kat was a total dude—I kept asking her if she was hiding a dick and balls under her dress—but now that I know her really well, it turns out she's a chick through and through. A diehard romantic."

"Well, you just answered your own question. Make Kat feel like *Pretty Woman*. Give Kat the modern-day fairytale she obviously yearns for."

I swig my water, thinking about that. It makes perfect sense, actually. "I've never seen *Pretty Woman*," I confess.

"What? Are you kidding me?"

"You've seen it?"

"Of course."

I shake my head. "Jesus, Jonas. Have some pride, man."

"Josh, you're an idiot. Why do you think romantic comedies are so successful? *Because women absolutely love them.* So why the *fuck* wouldn't you want to know *why*?" He shakes his head at me like he's explaining something ridiculously basic to me. "If you know *why* women love that stuff, then you gain invaluable insight into what makes them tick—which you can then use to your benefit in countless glorious ways."

I must admit, he's got my attention. "I'm listening," I say.

"God, it always freaks me out when you're the dumb one," Jonas says. He shakes his head at me again. "Josh, the movies Kat watches over and over, the movies she so obviously loves, are the most obvious roadmap to her deepest desires. If she loves *Pretty Woman,* then watch it and give it to her."

My pulse is pounding in my ears. "You know what, bro? You're absolutely right. *The Bodyguard, Pretty Woman, Say Anything, Magic Mike.* She loves 'em all."

"There you go. Whatever floats her boat and gets her going, watch it, learn it, and deliver it to her. She's telling you as plain as day how to hack her. So do it—*hack the shit out of her.*"

"Oh my fuck, yes," I say. I'm suddenly so excited, I can barely sit still. "This is brilliant, bro. I'm gonna hack the fuck into Katherine Ulla Morgan and give her what she's always wanted."

"There you go." Jonas takes a sip of his drink. "Sounds like you've got some research to do."

"Fuck yeah, I do. I'll watch all her stupid movies on the sly whenever she's asleep—which is a lot these days."

"Hey, you should watch that movie the girls watched tonight, too," Jonas says. He snaps his fingers like he's trying to come up with the title.

"Shit. You're right," I say. "What was that thing called? I was only half listening."

"I dunno. I was only half-listening, too," Jonas says. "*The Notebook*?"

"No, that wasn't it—but I'd better watch that one, too."

"Yeah, good idea. That one's pretty sappy. Have a barf bag ready when you watch that one."

I laugh. "You've seen that one, too?"

"Of course."

I shake my head. "You're better at this woman-thing than I gave you credit for, Jonas."

"Thank you. Finally, you understand my brilliance."

"Okay, so back to the task at hand. What the fuck was the movie the girls watched tonight? Kat said the woman from *The Notebook* was in it. That's when I tuned out."

Jonas pulls out his phone. "The girls said a red-haired guy's in it, too, right?"

"Yeah. That's right. The guy from *Harry Potter* and *Ex Machina*."

"Boom," Jonas says, looking at his phone. "*About Time*."

"That doesn't even remotely ring a bell," I say.

"Well, not for me, either. I must have tuned out, too. But it's gotta be it. It's Rachel McAdams and some redheaded guy." He shows me his phone, upon which a decidedly vaginal movie poster is being displayed.

"Yep. That's definitely it. Can't get much more chick-flick than that. Hey, I just thought of another movie I gotta watch," I say. "*Pride and Prejudice*."

"Oh, definitely. She's been calling you Mr. Darcy, you better figure out why."

"I can't believe you've seen that one," I say. "Have you no pride?"

"No, I don't—but you obviously do—hence the reason Kat kept calling you Mr. Darcy." He rolls his eyes. "I can't believe Kat called you that and you didn't even bother to watch the movie and find out why. Clearly, she was giving you a coded message."

"It didn't even occur to me."

"Well, watch it, you dumbshit. Mr. Darcy proposes twice in that movie and the heroine turns him down the first time." A light bulb clearly goes off in Jonas head. "Oh shit," he says, sitting up in his chair. "And do you know what the woman says when she turns Mr. Darcy down the first time?"

I shrug. "Fucketh you-eth?"

"Holy shit, Josh. *No*. She says, 'I wouldn't marry you if you were the last man on earth.'"

"Oh my fuck." I slap my forehead. "Kat's diabolical."

"No, you're just a dumbshit of epic proportions."

"Apparently," I agree.

"Watch it and pay careful attention to the difference between the first and second proposals. That'll tell you everything you need to know about what she wants the second time around."

I exhale. "Shit. I'm an idiot."

"You really are."

"Damn. I've got a lot of homework to do."

"I'll grab my hotspot out of my room so you can download all the movies onto your iPad. The hotel Wi-Fi is for shit."

"Thanks, bro."

Jonas gets up and moves toward the French doors.

"Hey, Jonas?"

Jonas stops and turns around, his eyebrows raised.

"I don't know what I would have done without your help on this. I was really stressed out and now I feel like I've got a plan of attack. Thank you."

"No thanks required," Jonas says. "I'm not doing this for you—I'm doing it for me."

"Oh, really?"

"Yes. If you marry Kat, then Sarah will be insanely happy, which will make *me* insanely happy. Happy wife, happy life." He smiles from ear to ear. "Very, very happy life."

"Ah. Well, you're a selfish bastard, then."

Jonas laughs and turns toward the French doors, but before he leaves, he turns back around. "Hey, by the way. What the fuck did you do to poor Kat earlier? I thought *Sarah* was a screamer. Holy fuck, Josh."

I grin and take a long sip of my water—I'm a gentleman, after all.

"So I take it you found the books I sent you helpful?" Jonas asks.

My smile broadens. "Yeah. Definitely. Although what I did to Kat earlier was all me—no research required." I snicker.

Jonas' white teeth are glowing in the pre-dawn light. "Hey, whatever works—just as long as you keep your unicorn well fed, right?"

"Fuck yeah," I say.

"Fuck yeah," Jonas replies. He pauses. "Hey, if I didn't happen to be out here on the balcony when you had insomnia, would you have asked me for help?"

I don't reply.

"You can lean on me, Josh," Jonas says earnestly. "It doesn't always have to be you carrying me on your back all the time. I'm right here. I can help you sometimes, too."

"Dude, are you on crack? I lean on you all the time," I say. "You're the man, Jonas—a fucking beast."

Jonas flashes me a look of such unadulterated love and kindness, my heart squeezes in my chest.

"Now go get me that hotspot, cocksucker," I say. "Or any second now you're gonna make me wanna slap my own fucking face—I can feel it coming on now—and it's way too early in the morning for me to be doing that shit."

114

JOSH

The band onstage behind Jonas and me finishes playing a cover of Pharrell William's "Happy" and the partygoers packed into Climb & Conquer's flagship Seattle gym applaud uproariously.

"Welcome to our grand opening," I say to the crowd, speaking into the microphone in my hand. "I know you're all chomping at the bit to keep climbing and conquering our rock walls for the first time ever today—so we're gonna keep the talking to a minimum. We just wanted to thank you all for coming out to the gym today to celebrate the birth of our baby."

Everyone claps and cheers.

"For those of you who don't already know," I continue, "I'm Josh Faraday and this is my brother, Jonas—and we're the founders of Climb & Conquer." The band behind us breaks into a spontaneous riff of "For He's the Jolly Good Fellow" and everyone laughs. "Wow, could you guys follow me around wherever I go?" I say.

Everyone in the room chuckles.

"Although, if you're gonna follow me around playing my own personal theme music, I think it'd have to be 'The Joker.'"

The band instantly breaks into a few bars of that song, and everyone in the entire building, including me, bursts out laughing.

"Wow, you're good," I say, pointing at the bandleader, and she points back at me, a huge smile on her face. I address the crowd again. "Jonas and I have worked hard to bring Climb & Conquer to life—but it's really Jonas who first had the vision—so I'm gonna turn the microphone over to my brother and let him tell you what Climb & Conquer is all about. Jonas?"

Everyone applauds and I hand the microphone to my brother.

"Hi, everyone. Thanks, Josh." Jonas flashes his most charming smile and

begins telling the rapt audience about what climbing has meant to him personally during his life and how he's always dreamed of sharing his passion with the
world.

Wow. For a guy who despises public speaking as much as Jonas does, I'm
duly impressed with how well Jonas is pulling this off—especially since, when
we were planning our speeches for this event a few days ago, Jonas practically
begged me to do all the speaking. "How about I stand onstage next to you and
nod while you talk?" he said. "I'll be the 'something shiny'—remember that?"

"Sorry, bro," I told him, much to his obvious chagrin. "Your 'something
shiny' days are officially over—you're our frontman now, baby. And, anyway,
C&C has been your dream from day one—you gotta be the one to explain it."

He looked totally bummed.

"Plus, as a practical matter," I continued, "a bunch of local news stations
are gonna be covering the grand opening. If one of our faces is gonna be plastered all over the news talking about our company's mission, it's gotta be yours,
Pretty Boy."

Jonas groaned.

"Oh, just nut up, Jonas. It's not my fault you're the pretty one."

"But that's the thing, Josh," Jonas replied. "You always say I'm the pretty
one—that I've got the looks and you've got the personality—but in all seriousness—and believe me, I hate to stroke your ego about this—I truly think you're
better looking than I am."

"Well, yeah, *duh*, I'm better looking than you are, numnuts—of course, I
am," I said. "It's just that, for some reason, no one else seems to recognize that
obvious fact."

Jonas laughed.

"It is what it is, bro—embrace it. You're the pretty one, which means you've
got to do the pretty-brother-speech." I patted him on his pretty cheek. "Just
pretend everyone in the audience is naked. Isn't that what they always say you
should do for public speaking?"

"Yeah," Jonas sighed, resigned to his fate.

"Except for Kat—don't pretend Kat's naked or I'll have to punch you in
your pretty face."

"Isn't Henn gonna be there?" Jonas asked.

"Good point." I grimaced. "Don't picture Henn naked, either, or you might
give yourself an aneurysm."

"And Sarah's mom? And Kat's parents? Because I'd rather cut off my arm
than imagine any of them naked," Jonas said.

"Okay, fine. Shit," I replied. "I wasn't being literal. I was just saying don't
stress about the speech—you'll be great."

Jonas laughed. "Don't worry—I'll be fine. I'll *hate* to do it, but I'll manage it.
I'll just look at Sarah the whole time and I'll be fine."

The audience in front of me laughs at something Jonas is saying and my
brain tunes back into the present moment.

"... . our initial twenty gyms in five states," Jonas is saying into the microphone, "and we're just getting started."

My eyes scan the crowd and land on Kat's gorgeous face—and then immediately drift down to the adorable baby bump that's only recently popped out of her slender frame. Damn, Kat's hot as hell. I can't get enough of that terrorist under normal circumstances, but nowadays, with her cute little belly and blossoming tits and raging pregnancy hormones, my Kat-addiction is now officially completely out of control. If Kat were a drug, there'd be no choice but for my loved ones to stage an intervention.

"How's our avocado today?" I asked Kat just this morning in our bed, running my hands over her naked belly, pressing my hard-on into her side, licking her nipple, inhaling her scent.

"Oh, no, babe," she said, sighing with pleasure when my fingertips migrated south and began gently stroking her tip. "The kumquat was an avocado a couple weeks ago—the kumquat's a freaking bell pepper now."

"A bell pepper?" I said, running my fingertips lightly over her slick tip, coaxing her into delicious hardness. "Whoa, this kid's unstoppable."

Kat shuddered with pleasure and arched her back as my fingers began massaging her in earnest, and that was all the dangling carrot I needed to stop talking and get serious about pleasuring her. With a loud growl, I opened her thighs, burrowed my head between them, and begin licking my hot little momma into a delicious frenzy.

"... and that's why the Climb & Conquer brand embodies adventure, fitness, and, most of all, the pursuit of excellence," Jonas is saying. "Each person's individual but universal quest to find the *ideal* version of himself."

I smile to myself. Jonas had originally planned to say "each person's individual quest to find the *divine original* form of himself," but I told him no fucking way. "Mark my words, the news stations will run that one sound-bite out of context, and all anyone will remember is the word 'divine,'" I said.

"And what's wrong with that?" Jonas asked.

"Dude, they'll think we're some sort of religious cult, not a rock-climbing gym. It's off-brand. Tell Plato he's gotta stay the fuck away from my grand opening. He's cramping my style."

"Fine," Jonas said begrudgingly. "I'll kick Plato to the curb just this once and dumb it down, Josh Faraday style. Happy?"

"Yes. Happy as a clam," I said.

"So what should I say if not 'divine original'?"

"I dunno. What would Josh Faraday say? That ought to lead you to the right level of dumb."

"... all about reaching higher than you ever thought you could reach—literally and metaphorically..." Jonas is saying—and I have to force myself not to roll my eyes at that last bit. *That's* Jonas' idea of pretending he's a dumbshit like me—saying our company's all about reaching one's highest peak 'literally and metaphorically'? It's true, of course—that's what we're all about—

but Josh Faraday would never say that particular phrase in a million fucking years.

"... and becoming better than you ever thought you could be," Jonas says.

Everyone claps enthusiastically.

"And as part of our genuine commitment to extraordinary aspiration," Jonas says, yet again making me want to roll my eyes at his word choice, "Climb & Conquer has identified certain designated charities we'll be supporting with a portion of our proceeds."

I look at Sarah in the crowd. She's standing next to Kat and Henn and Hannah, staring up at her new husband like he's a golden god. Just as I'm about to look away from Sarah, she pushes a lock of dark hair away from her face and her rock sparkles at me all the way up onstage. Shit. I hate seeing Sarah's big-ass diamond—no offense to her. As happy as I am for Mr. and Mrs. Jonas Faraday, that goddamned ring only serves to remind me how much I'm physically *aching* to slip a big-ass ring onto Kat's finger, too.

The good news is that, last night, after watching *Pride and Prejudice*, the last of the movies on my "Kat's all-time favorites" list, I *finally* figured out exactly how to propose to Kat. Actually, the gist of my plan came to me weeks ago in Argentina while watching *Pretty Woman*—specifically, the scene where Julia Roberts goes into that ritzy store in Beverly Hills, all dressed up in her brand new clothes, and tells the bitchy store clerk she made a "huge" mistake the prior day by refusing to help her—but, last night, every last detail of my entire plan finally came together in my mind.

Everyone claps at something Jonas has said, so I clap, too, not wanting to look like I'm not listening (which I'm not).

"So, without further ado," Jonas says, "let's let the band play while you guys climb and conquer our rock walls and have a great time."

Everyone claps and cheers.

I grab the microphone from Jonas. "Thanks for coming, everyone—Happy Birthday, Climb & Conquer!"

Everyone cheers again.

I motion to the band and they launch into a rousing rendition of "Shout" that has everyone instantly throwing up their hands and singing along.

Jonas and I stand for a moment, smiling together in front of a "Climb & Conquer Grand Opening!" banner as a photographer takes a hundred shots. When we finally make our way offstage, Sarah and Kat greet us, both of them sporting huge smiles.

"I'm so proud of you," Kat coos into my ear, throwing her arms around my neck. "Watching you up there made me wanna attack you, babe—you're a freakin' rock star. Gorgeous. Funny. Charismatic. The sexiest man alive." She literally growls and presses her body into mine, making my dick open its single eye and say, "Did I just hear a cock-a-doodle-doo?" "Oh my God, you make me horny," Kat whispers, pressing her body into mine. "I feel like I've got a vibrator permanently pressed against my clit these days."

"Babe," I whisper. "You can't say that to me right now. You're making me rock hard."

"Oh my God. Press it against me."

I do.

"Ooph. I can't resist you," Kat says. "I wanna give you a blowjob right now."

I don't hesitate. "Bathroom in my office in twenty," I whisper.

"It's a date." She makes a sexual sound. "God *damn* you turn me on, Joshua."

"You're killing me, Katherine," I whisper. "I still gotta say hi to your fucking parents, for Chrissakes."

"Sucks to be you, I guess," she says. "Except that it's about to be freaking *awesome* to be you, baby." She winks.

"You're killing me," I whisper.

"What a way to go," she whispers back.

"Come on, Kitty Kat," Sarah says. "Dance with me."

"Great," Kat says, letting Sarah pull her to the dance floor. But just before she disappears into the crowd, Kat flashes me a look that's so naughty, I have to put my hands in front of my crotch to hide my arousal.

Damn. Who knew pregnancy could be this fucking awesome? It started out rough, I'll admit that, but these days, it's nothing but fun. The woman's been on fire lately, even for her.

"Can I ask you a few questions?" a female reporter asks Jonas to my left, her cameraman in tow—and for a split second, I'm reminded of Heidi Kumquat, who I seem to recall asked the Super Bowl MVP that very question. *Kat.* There's never a dull moment with her. I'm so fucking head over heels in love with that girl, so obsessed with the idea of making her my wife, so *addicted* to her, mind, body, and soul, I can barely function these days. I can't even remember how it felt not to love her and sleep with her every night and fuck her at every opportunity. I truly never knew I could love someone this way—so completely. So *honestly.* It's like Kat's unlocked something that was hidden deep inside me, and every day I become more and more fully *me,* as ridiculous as that sounds.

"Sure," Jonas says to the reporter, but then he looks at me with desperation in his eyes, clearly hoping for some backup.

But he's shit out of luck. For once, Jonas' ever-reliable brother is going rogue.

I smile and wave at Jonas and, much to his obvious shock and annoyance, quickly slip into the crowd. Deserting him is a chicken-shit thing to do, probably, especially today—but I've got some important personal business to take care of before my bathroom date and only a limited opportunity while Kat's distracted on the dance floor. Plus, there's no doubt Jonas can handle that reporter on his own—she's a woman, after all—which means all he needs to do is smile at her and she'll throw her panties at him and offer him the lead-off spot on the six o'clock news.

I scan the crowd looking for Louise, and quickly locate her standing next to Thomas, Ryan and Colby (who's leaning on crutches), all of them watching the band and looking festive.

"Hey, everyone," I say when I reach the group. "Thanks for coming."

"Lambo!" Ryan says. He bro-hugs me. "Congrats. This is awesome."

"Thank you."

"Congratulations, Josh," Colby adds, shaking my hand. "Really impressive."

"Thanks. You've all got lifetime memberships, if you want 'em," I say. I motion to Colby's leg. "Standing offer for you, Colby, whenever you're up to it."

"Thanks," Colby says. "Gimme three more months and I'll definitely take you up on that."

"Fantastic. I'll personally climb with you whenever you want."

"I'll join you guys," Ryan says. "Best work-out, ever. Hey, Dad, you should try it with us. I think you'd like it."

"Maybe I will."

"You've never climbed a rock wall?" I ask Thomas.

Thomas shakes his head.

"Gimme a call. I'll give you a private lesson."

"Thanks. That sounds fun," Thomas says.

"Sure thing." I glance across the room, making sure Kat is still dancing. "Hey, Louise, can I talk to you for a second?"

Louise's face lights up. "You bet, honey. Excuse us, fellas."

Kat's mom and I move several yards away from the group, both of us looking furtively toward Kat on the other side of the large room. The band is playing "Brown Eyed Girl" and Kat's twirling Sarah around and singing the song to her.

"Did you get it?" I whisper. "Hey, that just sounded like we're doing a drug deal, huh?"

Louise giggles and looks covertly across the room at her daughter. "It came in yesterday—and it's *gorgeous*." She fishes into her purse and pulls out a ring box and then palms it to me like she's handing me a kilo of hashish. "It's sized and polished and ready to go."

"Thanks for picking it up for me. I've been crazy-busy this past week."

"Oh, honey, it was my pleasure. Plus, it was safer this way—it would have been terrible if Miss Busy-Body somehow intercepted the delivery at your house." Louise glances at Kat across the room again. "Just a little warning for you—Kat's peeked at every single Christmas present I've ever gotten for her. She unwraps the gift and then rewraps it and puts it back under the tree." Louise rolls her eyes. "Kat doesn't know I know she does that, by the way, so don't tell her I know. This year, I'm gonna beat her at her own game and put a wrapped box of hemorrhoid cream under the tree for her to peek at—that ought to teach her a lesson about peeking."

I chuckle. "Now I see where she gets that little dash of evil I love so much." I slip the box into my pocket. "Thank you again."

"Aren't you gonna look at it? It's beautiful, Josh. Gives me chills every time I look at it."

Carefully, taking great care not to let anyone around me see what I'm doing, I open the box a tiny crack, just enough to confirm it contains the engagement ring Louise and I picked out for Kat on our highly enjoyable shopping trip together last week.

"Wow," I say. "It's incredible."

"Just be prepared—Kat's gonna lose her mind when you give this to her. Like, seriously, honey, she's going to go completely ballistic on you. Just be ready to scrape her off the floor."

"Oh, God, I pray you're right," I say. "If Kat says anything but hell yes, you'll have to scrape *me* off the floor, and not in a good way."

Louise touches my forearm. "Why on earth would Kat say no? She loves you."

I shrug. "Unexpected things have happened to me before, Lou. Bad things. I'm kind of used to getting blindsided by life."

Louise's face melts. "Oh, honey. No. Kat loves you. She's having your baby. For God's sake, she'll say yes."

"But you heard her: 'Marriage just isn't in the cards for us.'"

Louise snorts. "Oh, please. Kat's full of it and we both know it."

I grin. "I sure hope so."

"Josh, I know so. I'm her mother. Trust me."

I give Louise a quick hug. "Thank you again." I pause. "*Momma Lou.*"

Louise blushes. "Oh my gosh, I *love* the sound of that!" She giggles. "Although, I must admit, Thomas is right—it does sound a bit like I run a soup kitchen in the South, doesn't it?" She giggles again, reminding me of Kat for the millionth time. "Don't tell Thomas I said he's right, by the way—I wouldn't want him to get a big head."

"I'll never tell."

"Josh."

I turn around. It's Theresa.

"Jonas asked me to come get you. He wants you to join the interview. He says *please.*" She motions across the room to where Jonas is still talking to that same reporter. He's feigning comfort quite well from the looks of him, but I know him well enough to know he's dying on the inside.

I chuckle. "Okay. Josh to the rescue. Bye, Louise. Thanks again."

"My pleasure. Keep us posted."

"Will do."

I cross the room quickly and help Jonas finish up his interview, much to his obvious relief, and when that's over, Jonas disappears into the crowd to find Sarah.

I scan the room looking for Kat and spot her talking to her family—looks like I've still got some time—so I survey the place, searching for Henn. *Boom.* He's talking with Hannah and Sarah, and when I catch his eye, I motion for him to meet me in a quiet corner behind one of the rock walls.

"Hey, man," I say, bro-hugging Henn when he reaches me. "Thanks for coming today. You didn't have to do that."

"I wouldn't have missed it," Henn says. "Plus, it gave me an excuse to come see Hannah."

"So, hey, man, do you think you could do me a favor? I need to find someone—get me dialed in."

"Sure. Who is it this time, boss?"

I tell him the name of the person I want him to locate and everything I know, which isn't much.

"Okay. Shouldn't be hard. I'll see what I can find out."

"Thanks, man. As soon as possible, please."

"Yeah, I figured. When have you ever asked me to find someone 'whenever it's convenient for you, Henn'?"

I chuckle. "Sorry."

"No worries. Whatever you need. Always."

"Thanks, bro. So what's been shaking with you?" I ask. "Work good?"

"Yeah, finally finished working with the feds on our sitch. They've got enough to put the pimpstress extraordinaire into an orange jumpsuit forever, probably. Bye-bye, Oksana. Nice knowing you."

"That's a relief. Any sense there's anyone else left in The Club organization we should be keeping an eye on?"

"There are definitely some heavy hitters in Russia and Ukraine who ran a big part of the show from there, but no one stateside with any real power—and certainly nobody who'd know about us."

"Keep an eye on things, though, would you? Just so we know if there's ever something we should be concerned about. Jonas is already starting to doubt his decision to leave Oksana standing—we should probably give him periodic assurances that everything's still quiet."

"No problem."

"So what are you working on now that The Club stuff is all done?" I ask.

"Oh, I just did a really fun job." He tells me about a large department store chain that recently hired Henn to try his mighty best to breach their own computer system for the purpose of testing their security. "It was awesome," Henn says. "They truly believed they were impervious to hacking. They'd supposedly hired 'the best cyber-security team money could buy' to protect their data, but I dug around and broke 'em wide open in less than a day. I waltzed into my first meeting with their supposedly 'expert cyber-security team —'" He snorts loudly with glee. "And I was like, 'So, hey, folks, great to meetcha. Oh, by the way, I got into your piddly-diddly system four different ways from Sunday in about six hours—here, here, here, and here,' and they totally shit their Depends." He sighs happily. "God, I love my life."

I chuckle. "And how's everything else? Things with Hannah good?"

"Better than good. *Awesome.* She's moving to L.A. next month."

"Really? Wow. That's fantastic."

"Yeah, the long distance thing is killing us, man. And since Kat's decided to put her PR company on the back burner for a while to become a mommy, Hannah's decided to look for a PR job in the entertainment industry."

"Awesome. Hey, you should ask Reed if he knows someone who might be able to help her with her job search. Reed knows everyone."

"Yeah, I already talked to him. He's on it."

"Good."

"So how are things with Kat? Have you two been nesting, getting ready for baby?"

I glance at Kat across the room. She's dancing with Sarah again, wiggling like she's got ants in her pants, throwing her tiny belly around with abandon. "I'm gonna ask Kat to marry me." I pat my pocket. "Got the ring right here."

"No shit?" Henn hugs me. "Awesome. When are you gonna do it?"

"As soon as you get me that info."

"Ah. Interesting. What does one thing have to do with the other?"

I briefly explain how I'm planning to propose to Kat, using the information Henn's gonna get for me.

"Very cool," Henn says. "Okay. I'll put a rush on it, boss." He grins. "Wow. I never thought I'd see the day Josh 'YOLO' Faraday would get married and settle down."

"I never thought I'd see the day, either. And now it's all I want." I bite my lip. "Let's just hope Kat says yes."

Henn waves his hand dismissively at me. "Bah. Just dick it up and she won't be able to resist you."

I laugh. "Yeah, well, I've recently learned the whole dick-it-up-strategy might not be *quite* as effective as I originally thought." I steal another look at Kat. "At least not with Madame Terrorist."

"I'm really happy for you, Josh," Henn says.

"Thanks, man."

"You've definitely come a long way from the dude who got YOLO inked onto his ass-cheek over a quote from *Happy Gilmore.*"

"God, I hope so. Hey, what was that quote we were arguing about, by the way? I can never remember what it was."

"Oh, it was really deep and profound. Grandma in the nursing home asks Ben Stiller if she can trouble him for a warm glass of milk because it helps her sleep. And he goes, 'You could trouble me for a warm glass of shut the hell up!'"

I laugh. "Oh, shit. Really? No."

"Yes."

"Really?" I ask.

"Yes."

"I got YOLO stamped on my ass over *that?*"

Henn nods, laughing. "You were *positive* Ben Stiller says, 'You could trouble me for a *tall* glass of shut the *fuck* up.'"

I shake my head. "God, I was such a little punk. Please tell me I'm not that big a tool anymore."

Henn puts his hand on my shoulder. "You were never a tool, Josh—you've always been the greatest guy ever, right from day one. And you've only gotten better with age. You're a fine wine, man."

My heart pangs. "Thanks, Henn. Back at you."

He smiles.

"Okay, well, this fine wine had better get back to his adoring public," I say. "Thanks again for coming—and thanks for the favor."

"Any time," Henn replies.

We bro-hug again and then Henn slips into the crowd, saluting me as he goes.

My eyes drift to where Kat was dancing with Sarah a moment ago—but she's not there. I reflexively look at my watch. Oh shit—it's been way longer than twenty minutes since Kat and I made our "date."

I practically sprint toward my office in the back of the gym, getting stopped at least ten times along the way by well-wishers, and finally manage to slip unnoticed through a door marked "Authorized Personnel Only." Once inside my darkened office, I beeline to the bathroom in the back and rap softly on the door. "Kat?" I whisper.

The door opens a crack and in one fluid movement, Kat grabs a fistful of my shirt and yanks me forcefully into the bathroom.

"I just made myself come while waiting on you, Playboy," she whispers, furiously unbuckling my belt, her eyes on fire. "You're such a naughty boy for making me wait."

"Oh, yeah?" I ask, my dick throbbing with anticipation. "My pregnant whore is feeling horny, huh?'

She reaches into my pants and strokes my hard-on furiously. "Oh, yeah," she says. "Heidi Kumquat's on fire. She's aching to give you your money's worth, baby."

"God, I love you," I growl, my body jerking as she works me with her hands.

"I love you, too," Kat says. "I love you, I love you, I love you." She fondles my balls. "*And I love your dick.*"

Without further ado, Kat kneels down and swirls her tongue on the tip of my cock—right into my little hole—making me jolt. "Oh my fuck, Kat."

She looks up at me from under my straining cock and smiles. "I never knew I could love someone the way I love you, Joshua William Faraday," she purrs— and then she takes the full length of my cock into her mouth and proceeds to deliver a blowjob so intense, it makes me grip the sink ledge to keep from falling to my knees.

"Oh, God, I love you," I growl, trying to hang on. I grip her hair and press myself farther into her open throat. "You're worth every fucking penny, baby," I choke out, my passion reaching its boiling point. But even as I'm saying those words—because, of course, those are the magic words Kat loves best when she's giving me head—what I'm actually thinking is something new for me while in the midst of receiving a mind-blowing blowjob: *If a guy needs more than this to be eternally happy with one woman, then he's either crazy or just a greedy-ass motherfucker.*

115

KAT

"Blood pressure looks good," the nurse says, removing the cuff from my arm. "Sit tight for a bit and Dr. Gupta will be right in."

"Thank you," I say. I exhale and squeeze Josh's hand. "I'm nervous."

Josh kisses my forehead. "The kumquat's gonna be fine," he says softly. "Hey, Sarah Cruz. Hit us with some 'Would You Rather?' questions. Kat's nervous—we gotta distract her."

"Okay, Josh Faraday," Sarah says. "But under the circumstances, I'm gonna keep it family-friendly."

"Boo!" I shout.

"Yes, Kat," Sarah says sternly. "Playing X-rated 'Would You Rather?' in this crowd would hurtle us into TMI territory on a bullet train."

I laugh. "Probably true."

"Okay, then," Sarah says. "Would you rather be hideously ugly but extremely wealthy, or spectacularly good looking but dirt poor?"

We all ponder that for a moment.

"Jonas?" Sarah asks. "What say you, love?'

"In which of these scenarios do I have a better shot at snagging you?" Jonas asks.

"Doesn't matter. I'd love you rich or poor, gorgeous or hideous."

Jonas shrugs. "Then I don't care. You pick. As long as I have you, I'm good."

Josh shoots me an annoyed expression, and, in reply, I pretend to stick my finger down my throat.

"Is it your life's mission to make me look like a prick?" Josh asks Jonas. "Because I was about to say rich and ugly."

"Aw, come on, babe," I say. "Good looking and poor, all the way."

"No, babe. If I'm rich and ugly, I can wine and dine you, which means I'd still bag you. Best of both worlds—I'd still be rich *and* I'd still have you."

"You'd bag me even more if you were dirt poor but looked the way you do, I assure you." I wink. " If you wanna wine me and dine me when you're dirt poor, just make me one of your orgasm-inducing PB&Js."

"*Kat,*" Sarah chastises, putting her hands over her ears. "Family friendly, remember?"

"Okay, okay," I say. "Ask another one, Sarah."

"But this time don't lob a softball at your husband that makes me look like a total prick, Sarah Cruz," Josh adds.

"I don't think it was Sarah's question that made you look like a total prick," Jonas says.

I look at my watch and shift on the examination table, making the wax paper crinkle underneath me. "Where's the doctor?"

"Okay, Kat. Listen up," Sarah says. "Would you rather have balls hanging from your chin or a two foot tail that wags every time you feel excited?"

We all laugh at the ridiculousness of the question.

"Hey, I thought these were supposed to be *hypothetical,*" Josh says, and we all laugh again.

"Okay, okay," Sarah says. "That was a dumb one. Here's a good one: would you rather be a wildly successful artist who makes totally uninspired crap you abhor creating, or a starving but brilliant artist who makes art that feeds your soul?"

"Wildly successful artist who makes total crap," Josh says without hesitation.

"Yeah, baby!" I shout, high-fiving Josh. "Me, too. Totally."

Sarah and Jonas look at each other, absolutely dumbfounded.

"Are you joking?" Jonas asks. "You've only got one *soul,* for fuck's sake."

Sarah high-fives Jonas. "You tell 'em, baby."

"There you go again, making me look like a prick," Josh says.

"Aw, screw them," I say. "Let Jonas and Sarah be soulful *arteests* while you and I make oodles of cash off our bottle-cap-pipe-cleaner sculptures. And while they're eating Kraft Macaroni & Cheese in their rat-infested hovel in SoHo, surrounded by their frickin' art, we'll head to Cabo on our private jet and 'feed our souls' while making love on a white-sand beach."

"You're a fucking genius, babe," Josh says.

"You truly can't keep it family-friendly if your life depended on it, can you, Kat?" Sarah says.

"Oh, come on, Cruz. That was PG-rated at worst," I say. I look toward the door. "Where the heck is Dr. Gupta? She doesn't normally take this long."

"Okay, listen up, Party Girl," Josh says. "Would you rather be the star player on a football team that loses every game of the season or warm the bench on a team that wins the Super Bowl?"

"Hmm," Sarah says. "Play on the losing team, I think. What do you think, my love?"

"I think I'd rather sit the bench on the winning team," Jonas says. "Because, ultimately, I'd aspire to become the head coach—so this way, I'd have the opportunity to watch and learn from the best."

We all burst out laughing.

"What?" Jonas asks. "That's my honest answer."

"Oh, Jonas," Sarah says. She touches his cheek tenderly and her diamond rings sparkle under the lights of the examination room. "I love you."

"Okay, I've got one," I say. "Would you rather be stuck on a desert island for the rest of your life all alone or with someone who talks incessantly?"

"I'd rather be stuck on a desert island with *you*, babe," Josh says sweetly.

"Aw, that's lovely, honey—but you gotta pick one of the choices."

Josh raises an eyebrow. "Oh, I *did* pick one of the choices."

Everyone bursts out laughing, even me, just as the door to the examination room opens.

"Oh, wow," Dr. Gupta says. "There's a party going on in here."

"Hi, Doctor," I say. "You remember Josh—my baby-daddy?"

Josh blanches. He hates it when I call him that, which is why I keep doing it.

"And this is my best friend, Auntie Sarah, whom you've met before," I continue. "And Sarah's husband, Uncle Jonas, who also happens to be Josh's brother."

Dr. Gupta shakes everyone's hand and introduces us to the technician who'll be conducting the sonogram. "So are you ready to see your baby?" Dr. Gupta asks.

We all respond enthusiastically.

I lie back on the examination table and the technician spreads some gel on my baby bump. "My heart is racing," I say, putting my hand on my heart. "I'm really nervous."

Josh leans down and kisses my forehead. "The kumquat's gonna be fine."

The tech puts the wand on my belly and moves it around and, suddenly, we're met with the unmistakable image of an actual *baby*.

"Holy crap," I say. "That's a *baybay*!"

"Oh my God," Josh says. "Definitely not a kumquat."

"Quite different than the first sonogram, isn't it?" the doctor says. She begins pointing out various body parts, all of which, she says, look perfectly formed and right on track.

"Oh, thank God," I say, sighing with relief. "I was really worried I'd hurt the poor thing with too much partying before I knew."

"Well, this should put you at ease, then," the doctor says, patting my hand. "So, do you want to know the baby's gender?"

"Heck yeah," Josh says. "That's the dangling carrot we used to lure Uncle Jo Jo and Auntie Sarah to this shindig."

"Do you already know?" I ask.

"I sure do. The baby's legs are spread wide and I've got an unimpeded view." The doctor pauses for effect. "Any guesses?"

"Girl," Sarah says calmly.

The doctor nods. "Yep. Congratulations. You're having a baby girl."

Tears spring into my eyes.

"Oh my God," Josh breathes. He leans down and kisses me. "I love you, Kat."

"I love you, too," I whisper into his lips.

"I was hoping for a girl so much," Josh says.

I'm shocked to hear Josh say that—don't all big, athletic men secretly hope for a boy who'll grow up to play on the Seahawks one day? But when I look at Josh and see the moment he's sharing with Jonas, I suddenly understand completely—this baby's a tribute to their late mother in heaven, a baby girl to keep their mother's memory alive.

Josh and I haven't discussed baby names yet—in fact, several times I've told Josh I was too freaked out about the booze and pot thing to think about baby names until I was sure everything was okay—but now that I've seen our baby girl growing inside me—and especially now that I'm witnessing the expressions of emotion on both Josh and Jonas' faces, there's only one name I'd even consider.

"Grace," I blurt.

Josh's face lights up. "Grace," Josh repeats reverently, nodding. He bends down to kiss me. "Thank you."

I mumble "of course" into Josh's lips, but my words are incomprehensible.

"Grace Louise?" Josh asks, pulling away suddenly from my mouth.

"Perfect," I say, smiling.

"Aw," Sarah says. "That's so sweet. Gracie Louise Faraday."

"Hey, Doctor," Jonas says, putting his arm around Sarah. "Are you sure? I've heard stories of people painting a room pink based on the sonogram and then giving birth to a boy."

"Oh, I'm positive," Dr. Gupta says. She points to the sonogram screen. "See between her legs there? Definitely no penis. The baby's made it really easy for us by spreading her legs wide."

Josh snickers.

"*Don't say it*," I warn sharply, slapping his arm.

"Don't say what?" Josh says, grinning.

"You know what."

Josh chuckles and kisses me tenderly. "Babe," he says. "I would never make a crass joke about my baby girl making it easy just like her hot momma does for me every night—because that would be rude and inappropriate. But, just so you know, if I ever do compare our beautiful daughter to her gorgeous mommy in any way, shape or form, I'll *always* mean it as the highest compliment, no matter what."

116

KAT

"So where do you guys want to go for lunch?" I ask, floating happily through the parking lot outside my doctor's office, my hand caressing my baby bump. But when I realize nobody's walking alongside me, I stop and turn around. "Guys?" I ask. "Any ideas on where we should go for lunch to celebrate little Gracie Louise?"

"I'm sorry, honey," Sarah says. "I can't do lunch. I promised to help my mom today."

"Oh," I say, deflated.

"There's only two more weeks before school starts back up, so I promised I'd help down at Gloria's House every day 'til then."

"Oh, no problem," I say, trying my best to sound sincere. Of course, I know intellectually that helping victims of domestic abuse is far more important than celebrating my baby's gender—and, of course, I know we can celebrate any time, not just today—but I still can't help feeling disappointed, nonetheless.

"No worries," Josh says breezily. "The four of us will go out another time. How about a celebratory dinner later this week?"

"Great," Sarah says. She gives me an enthusiastic hug. "Bye, sweetie. Congratulations again." She pats my bump. "Bye-bye, Gracie Louise. I can't wait to meet you, boo."

Jonas hugs me goodbye and then shocks the hell out of me by tenderly placing his palm on my belly—a move so full of affection—and so unlike him—it catches me off guard. "I can't wait to meet you, Gracie Faraday," Jonas whispers.

I exchange a swooning look with Sarah.

Josh follows suit, putting his hand on my belly when Jonas pulls his hand away.

"I can already tell you're gonna own me, Gracie Louise," Josh says. He bends down and kisses my belly, making me swoon. "I already love you, Little G," he whispers.

Oh my God, I can barely stand, I'm so overcome by this beautiful moment. "Josh," I say, barely above a whisper.

Josh stands. "Good God, I'm gonna be surrounded by a shit-ton of estrogen in my own house," he blurts, completely shattering the fairytale-nature of the moment. "I'm officially fucked."

We all laugh.

"Yep. You're definitely gonna hone your *listening* skills," Jonas says.

"Oh, you know you'll love it," I say. I look at Jonas and Sarah. "Okay, guys, I love you truly, madly, deeply, but the kumquat's hangry—so if you're not coming with us to eat, then you best get out of my freakin' way so I don't start barfing all over you."

"You're *still* barfing?" Sarah asks.

"Not nearly as much, but, yeah, on occasion, especially when I get really hungry."

Sarah grimaces. "You poor thing."

I pat my belly. "It's okay. Seeing Gracie today made it all worth it."

Josh and I wave to Jonas and Sarah as they drive off in their car, and then, since we'd hitched a ride with Jonas and Sarah to get here in the first place, we grab a taxi.

"Hotel 1000," Josh instructs the driver as we settle into the backseat of the cab. "Okay with you, babe? There's a new restaurant in the hotel I wanna try."

"Great," I say. "What kind of food do they—*Oh.*" I abruptly stop talking, my hand on my belly.

"What?" Josh asks, his eyes wide.

I hold up a finger, holding my breath—and there it is again: a teeny-tiny jabbing sensation in my lower abdomen, poking me from the *inside*. "Oh my gosh," I say. "I think I just felt the baby *move*."

"Really?" Josh asks, his eyes lighting up.

I place Josh's hand on my bump, right where I just felt movement, and it happens again. "Did you feel that?" I ask.

Josh shakes his head, his eyes on fire. "What did it feel like?"

"It felt like someone poking me—like *this*." I touch the top of Josh's hand with my fingertip. "Only imagine feeling that little jab from *inside* your body— like a little alien wanting to get out."

"That's so cool," Josh says. He places both palms on my bump, squinting like he's concentrating on complex calculus—and for the rest of the taxi ride, he forbids me to speak while he silently touches every inch of my tiny bump, trying with all his might to feel movement. But it's no use. Every time I feel a little jab, Josh can't feel it with me.

"I guess the kumquat's just too small for you to feel her yet," I finally conclude. "I'm sorry, babe."

"Damn. Tell me every time you feel her move, okay? I'm dying to give her a high-five with my fingertip."

I swoon for the twentieth time today. Who is this adorable man sitting next to me in this taxi? I can't believe the man touching my baby bump with such tenderness and enthusiasm is the same commitment-phobic playboy who not too long ago said he planned to wait until eighty to have a baby so he could simultaneously have the kid and forget he was ever born.

"I love you so much, Josh," I say softly, touching his cheek.

"I love you, I love you, I love you, Kat—more than I ever thought possible," Josh replies, just before planting a kiss on me that makes me forget where I am.

After a moment, the driver clears his throat. "Um. Excuse me. We're here," he says.

Josh brushes my cheek with his thumb, and then touches my chin with the tip of his finger, and finally, slowly, tears himself away from me to pay the man.

We float inside the hotel together, Josh's arm around my shoulders, but, much to my surprise, Josh steers us away from the restaurant in the lobby and toward the elevator bank.

"Hey, isn't that the restaurant?" I ask, pointing behind me.

Josh stops walking and pulls me into him, a huge smile on his face. "We're not going to the restaurant, my love—I only told you that to lure you here."

My love? Did Josh just call me "my love"? He's never called me that before.

"Why aren't we going to the restaurant?" I manage to ask.

"Because we're going to our room," Josh replies simply—and before I can say another word, he fishes into his pocket, pulls out a poker chip, and places it in my palm, a wicked smile dancing on his lips. "Let the mini-porno begin, baby."

"Ooh!" I squeal. "Yay! Which fantasy are we doing, babe?"

"Actually, today we're doing one of *my* fantasies—a fantasy I've never told anyone about, not even you." Josh wraps me into his arms and smashes his hard body into mine. "It's my top fantasy, actually—something I've only recently discovered I want to do."

"You didn't write about it in your application?"

"Nope. I've never told a single soul about this particular fantasy—didn't even know I had it until recently. But today, for the first and only time, I wanna do it with you, Party Girl." A huge smile spreads across his face. "*My love.*"

117

KAT

"Oh, that was good—the artichoke was hangry as hell," I say, putting my napkin onto the table and patting my belly. I've just devoured a huge spread of food Josh had waiting for us in our hotel suite, and I'm feeling fine as wine and ready to role-play.

"So you're feeling good now?" Josh asks.

"Yup. I'm feeling *great*. Heidi Kumquat reporting for duty, sir, any which way you please. So what's your pleasure, sir? Whips? Chains? Donkeys?"

Josh shoots me a sly smile. "You'll see. The outfit I want you to wear for me is laid out on the bed in there." He indicates the master bedroom of the suite.

"Oh," I say, raising my eyebrow. "French maid costume, maybe? Latex? Rabbit suit? Damsel in distress?"

"You'll see soon enough. I packed your makeup and toiletries, by the way—they're in the bathroom." He stands, his eyes blazing. "Meet me back out here in forty-five minutes. I'll get dressed in the other bedroom."

"*Oh*. We're doing his and hers costumes, huh?" I say. "What on earth have you been fantasizing about on the sly, you naughty Playboy?"

"No questions. Just do as your told. This is *my* fantasy—not yours—you're just my plaything today."

"Oooh, I like the sound of that. But, seriously, babe. I want to be sure you get your fantasy, whatever it is. What if I don't know what to do?"

"Oh, you'll know." He pulls me to him and plants a kiss on my lips that's so passionate, I'm certain he's about to bend me over the table and fuck me senseless right here and now. But, nope, he doesn't. Instead, he pulls away and slaps my ass. "Now get showered and dressed, Party Girl. You've got exactly forty-five minutes—don't keep me waiting."

"Yes, sir," I say.

I head into the bedroom, as directed, and gasp when I see what Josh has laid out for me to wear: a formal red gown, red lace bra and undies, black strappy heels, and a small clutch covered in sparkling Swarovski crystals. I look at the label on the gorgeous dress. *Carolina Herrera.* Oh my God. I can't even imagine how much this beautiful creation must have cost. Quickly, I throw off my clothes and slip the gown on, even before showering, just to make sure it fits—and, man, oh man, does it ever—like a glove, baby bump and all.

"Wow," I say out loud, staring at myself in the mirror. "Hello, *Pretty Woman.*"

It's actually astonishing how much this dress looks like a modern update of the iconic red dress Julia Roberts wore in that movie. Of course, Josh wouldn't know that since he's the only human in the Western Hemisphere who's never seen *Pretty Woman,* but, truly, this gown is a dead ringer for that famous dress. I giggle to myself. This is such classic Josh Faraday—even without knowing it, he's managed to fulfill one of my top fantasies.

I slip out of the dress and hop into the shower, singing "Pretty Woman" at the top of my lungs—and just over an hour later (oops, I'm little late), I emerge from the master bedroom wearing my beautiful Julia-dress and gorgeous, strappy heels.

Josh is sitting across the room, looking down at his phone, dressed to perfection in a classic, tailored tux. At the sound of my entrance into the room, he looks up from his phone and his handsome face bursts into immediate flames.

"Wow," Josh says. He hops up and strides toward me. "Look at *you*. Wow."

I twirl. "You like?"

"I *love*." He kisses my cheek and I'm treated to the scent of his delicious cologne. "You're absolutely stunning, Kat," he adds.

"So are you," I say. "You look amazing."

Josh furrows his brow, apparently considering something. He blatantly looks me up and down. "Hmm."

"What?" I ask, suddenly feeling insecure.

"Something's missing."

"Huh?" I look down at myself. "There was nothing else laid out on the bed," I say.

Josh purses his lips. "Ah. I know. Hang on."

He strides with great purpose across the room and grabs a flat velvet box off the bar—and the minute I see that damned box in Josh's hand, I know exactly what's up. *Red gown. Tux. Flat velvet jewelry box.* Holy Julia Roberts, Batman —Josh is re-enacting *Pretty Woman*!

I clamp my palm over my mouth. "Oh my God!" I gasp.

Josh holds up the velvet box, a huge smile on his face, but before he can say a word, I begin jumping up and down and shrieking like a monkey escaping from the zoo.

"Oh my God, I *love* this movie," I shriek excitedly. I take a deep breath and shake out my arms. "You're incredible-amazing-wow-I'm-so-excited-thank-you!"

Josh laughs. "Are you okay? Do you need a minute?"

I giggle like a hyena. "I can't believe you did this! When did you watch it? Oh my God!"

"Are you okay? Are you gonna pass out?"

"I'm good. Oh my God. Go ahead. Holy shit. Okay, I can totally do this—I swear. Do it. Gah! Okay. *Go.*" I bite my tongue to keep myself from babbling further.

Josh smiles. "Ready?"

I nod, still biting my tongue.

Josh slowly opens the box... to reveal the most redonkulous diamond necklace I've ever seen in my entire freakin' life. It's even more spectacular than the one Sarah wore on her wedding day—something I didn't think was possible.

Of course, I know this necklace is just a rental—I've seen the movie twenty times, after all, so I know how this scene goes—but, still, this is so freaking exciting, so *unexpected*, I can barely stand. I can't believe Josh even *thought* to arrange a *Pretty Woman* fantasy for me! I can't fathom how that's even possible.

Josh is grinning wickedly, holding the box open, inviting me to enact what comes next in this scene—and, of course, I'd never, ever disappoint him.

"Can I touch it?" I breathe.

Josh nods, smiling from ear to ear. "I was hoping you'd ask me that."

I shudder with excitement.

"Go on," Josh coaxes. "If you dare."

I giggle. "I'm nervous."

"Dig deep, baby—be brave."

"Whew. Okay." I reach slowly into the box, my Julia-Roberts belly laugh all cued up—oh my God, this is so freakin' *awesome!*—and, as expected, even before my fingers have touched the sparkling necklace, Josh clamps the lid down on my fingers. And even though I had my Julia Roberts impression ready to rip, I surprise myself by bursting into authentic Kat-Morgan, dude-like guffaws, sending Josh into a fit of hysterical laughter along with me.

When both of us have calmed down a bit, Josh removes the dazzling necklace from the box. "Turn around, hot momma," he says. "Let's get this bad boy on you."

I turn around and I'm rewarded with the sensation of my hair being pushed off my neck and Josh's soft lips against my Scorpio tattoo—followed by Josh securing the outrageous necklace around my neck.

I touch the dazzling rocks against my skin, trembling. "Oh my freaking God," I breathe.

"Lemme see you," Josh says softly. "Turn around."

I do.

"Gorgeous," Josh says, his eyes blazing. "Wow."

I touch the necklace again, feeling slightly faint. "Josh?"

"Yes, my love?"

"If I forget to tell you later: I had a really good time tonight."

Josh laughs. "Thank you." He leans forward like he's going to kiss me, but, instead, he presses his lips against my ear. "It's all yours, baby," he whispers, his voice low and sexy.

I stand stock still, holding my breath, positive I've misunderstood him. It sounded like Josh said, "It's all yours, baby." But what would the "it" in that sentence be? That's what my brain isn't comprehending. Josh's heart? The dress? I pull back and stare at Josh with wide eyes. "Huh?"

Josh cups my face in his large palms. "The *necklace* is all yours, my love— my gift to you—because I love you with all my heart and soul."

My entire body jolts. "*What?*" I shriek.

The look on Josh's face is utterly priceless—he's a kid in a candy shop, as excited as I've ever seen him. He moves his hands to my shoulders. "My beautiful Kat, marriage isn't in the cards for us, as you know." He strokes my hair. "So I'm hoping you'll accept this necklace as a symbol of my eternal love for you."

My heart has truly stopped beating. Oh my God, no, wait, now it's exploding. And, now, holy fuck, it's bursting out of my chest and hurtling against the hotel wall.

"*What?*" I say, this time in a hoarse whisper, my eyes bugging out of my head.

Surely, I'm misunderstanding this conversation. The strange words coming out of Josh's mouth sound remarkably like English, but they're being strung together in a nonsensical way.

"You're the great love of my life, Kat," Josh says, still stroking my hair, gazing into my eyes. "I choose you, baby. That's what this necklace means. Not because of a piece of paper, not because of the kumquat, but because I want you and no one else. I choose you, Kat, and I hope you choose me, too. *Forever.*"

I clutch my throat like I'm choking on a big-ass diamond. "Forever?" I blurt. "You choose me *forever*?"

Josh nods.

"You're promising to love me *forever*?"

He nods again.

"And this necklace is *mine*?"

Josh nods again.

"To *keep*?"

"Yes."

I throw my arms around his neck. "I love you, too," I shriek, tears of joy springing from my eyes. "I choose you, too, forever and ever and ever! Yes, yes, yes. I choose you, too, baby! *Yes!*"

And just like that, even before I can say, "Well, color me happy!"—(which I was totally gonna say, by the way, but how the *fuck* could I possibly remember to say my line now?)—my beautiful gown is hiked up, my pretty lace panties are on the floor, and Josh's donkey-dick is sliding in and out of me, filling me to the brim and making me scream. Oh, God, this is insanity. I'm not only screaming with pleasure, I'm crying and howling, too. I'm either thoroughly enraptured or possessed by a freaking demon, it's not clear which.

After several minutes of fuckery that can only be described as "a mini-porno-version of *The Exorcist*," Josh lays me down on my back on a table in the suite and fucks me with breathtaking fervor, whispering into my ear as he does about how much he loves me and how hot I am with my little baby bump and how good and wet and tight I always feel for him—and, within minutes, I'm convulsing with an orgasm that curls my effing toes and blurs my vision (and also makes my green head spin round and round on my shoulders).

When we're both done, Josh hulks over me on the table for a long moment, catching his breath. "Holy fuck," he says, his breathing ragged. "That wasn't according to plan."

I breathe deeply, trying to calm my racing heart. "Are we gonna be late now?" I gasp.

Josh straightens up, his eyebrows raised. "Late for what?"

"For the opera?"

Josh chuckles. "Oh, Kat." He pulls me off the table and wraps me in his strong arms.

"What? That's where Richard took Julia in the red dress—to the opera in San Francisco."

"Yeah, I know—I've seen the movie," Josh says, rolling his eyes. "But this is *my* fantasy, remember?—and I'd rather poke needles in my eyes than go to the fucking opera."

I giggle. "Oh, thank God. I was gonna be a good sport about it, of course, but I'd rather poke needles in my eyes than go to the fucking opera, too."

Josh kisses my forehead. "Don't you worry, PG. You're with *me*, remember? The Playboy—and where I'm taking you today is gonna curl your toes and soak your panties a thousand times more than any stinkin' *opera* ever could." He winks. "I guarantee it."

118

KAT

Our limo pulls up to a small airport displaying a sign at the entrance that says, "Boeing Field."

"Are we flying to San Francisco?" I ask.

Josh grabs my hand. "No questions. Your only job today is to *react*—not to try to figure things out."

"Richard took Julia to San Francisco," I say.

"We're not going to the opera, and we're not going to San Francisco," Josh says. "No more questions."

I survey the long line of small jets lined up on the tarmac. "But we're flying somewhere?"

Josh puts his finger to his lips.

The limo winds its way through a gate and stops at a hangar about fifty yards from a small jet with its door opened wide and retractable staircase down.

"Are we going somewhere on that plane there?" I ask, pointing.

"God, you're a terrible listener," Josh says.

"Sorry. But are we going somewhere on a private plane? I've never been on a private plane. Oh my God."

"Ssh."

The limo driver opens our door and Josh gets out first.

"Don't forget our bags in the trunk, please," Josh instructs the driver. He bends down and peeks at me in the backseat. "You ready to make my hottest fantasy come true, Party Girl?"

I shoot Josh a look that says I don't believe for a second we're here to fulfill *his* fantasy. So far today, Josh has dressed me like Julia Roberts, slapped a beachside condo around my neck, and told me he'll love me forever and ever. It really doesn't take a brain surgeon to realize he's fulfilling *my* top fantasies today, no matter what he says. "If you say so, PB," I say, looking at him sideways.

"Oh, I do." Josh pulls me out of the car and threads my arm into his. "You look incredible in that dress," he whispers. He begins escorting me toward the nearby jet.

"Thank you. I absolutely love it. And the *necklace*—oh my God, Josh, it's beyond my wildest dreams." I touch the dazzling rocks encircling my neck, still not able to comprehend they're mine.

"That's good. Because *you're* beyond my wildest dreams, babe."

I abruptly stop walking. "Okay, that's it," I say. "What the heck is going on?"

Josh furrows his brow. "What do you mean?"

"I mean I had to lesbo-out with a bisexual supermodel and hypnotize you with a devious song to trick you into saying 'I love you' not too long ago, and now, suddenly, you're watching *Pretty Woman* and acting like Michael Bublé on steroids?"

Josh laughs and touches my belly. "Kat, just roll with it, baby. Don't overthink it. Your job is to *react*. Nothing more."

"At first I thought maybe you'd arranged all this because you're so happy to be having a daughter named after your mom, but then I realized you had to have arranged all this before we found out the kumquat's gender."

"Don't think, babe. *React*."

"But, Josh, you watched *Pretty Woman*, for cryin' out loud. Have you gone completely mad?"

Josh brushes the hair out of my face and gazes into my eyes. "Yes, I have. Completely and utterly insane." He smiles. "And I've never been happier."

I bite my lip.

"Now come on, baby—we've got a private plane to catch."

When we reach the jet on the tarmac, a pilot in full uniform descends the retractable stairs and greets us. Josh leads me up the stairs and directs me to a window seat.

"You need anything?" Josh asks as I settle into my seat. "Club soda? A barf bag?"

I shake my head. "Nope. I'm good. I haven't barfed in a few days, actually."

"Hey, give that girl a salami," Josh says, grinning. "Will you do me a favor and hang out here for a minute, PG? I've got to talk briefly to the pilot about the flight plan."

"Is it okay if I send Sarah a photo of my necklace?"

"Of course," Josh says. "It's yours, after all."

"Oh my God," I breathe. "You just made my heart skip a beat."

Josh grins. "I'll be right back, baby." He winks and disappears down the stairs.

I pull my phone out of my clutch bag, take a quick selfie (making sure my dazzling necklace is front and center), and shoot the photo off to Sarah, tapping out a quick message along with it. "OMFG," I write. "I'm sitting on a PRIVATE PLANE wearing THIS!"

"Really? Wow! Amaaaaazing!" Sarah writes back instantly. "Where are you going?"

"I have no freaking clue!!!!!!" I write. "Josh dressed me in a Pretty Woman red dress and gave me this ridicky diamond necklace—TO KEEP!!!!!!—and told me he's gonna love me 'FOREVER' and called me 'MY LOVE'! And he didn't pass out or hurl during any of it! And now we're on a private jet heading to I DON'T CARE WHERE!"

"No way! That's so exciting! WOWZERCATS!"

Even in text, something about Sarah's reply feels canned to me. I shoot a snarky look at my display screen. "Oh, Sarah Cruz," I write. "You're the worst liar ever, even in text. I hope when you're a lawyer you wind up defending only innocent people because, otherwise, your guilty clients are all going straight to prison."

"LOL," Sarah writes. "First off, I'm not gonna practice criminal law—I'll be working for Gloria's House helping women get restraining orders and stuff. Second off, I like the fact that I'm a horrible liar. It's one of my best qualities." She attaches a scared-face emoji to the end of her message.

"You already knew about the necklace, didn't you?" I write.

"Of course. Do you really think I would have chosen working with my mom today over celebrating the big reveal of Gracie Louise Faraday? Come on, girl!"

"Yeah, I thought it was weird you were turning down an opportunity to drink champagne," I write. "So, hey, will you go shopping with me when I get back? I'm suddenly feeling the urge to buy lots and lots of PINK!!!!! Woohoooooooo!"

"Hellz yeah!!!" Sarah writes. "I'm already planning to buy my sweet little niece a pair of her very own pink, sparkly boots! Yeehaw!"

I laugh out loud and begin tapping out a reply, but before I can finish my message, a text notification comes in from Josh.

"Raise the blind on your window and look outside," Josh's text says.

"Gotta go," I quickly type to Sarah. "The director of our mini-porno just told me to take my mark. Teehee. I'll give you a full report later, girlio."

"You better," Sarah writes. "Have fun, Kitty Kat!" She attaches a cat emoji and a heart.

"Meow," I write, followed by a salsa dancer (the emoji I always use to symbolize Sarah), plus a heart of my own.

I put my phone back into my sparkling clutch and then, as instructed, slowly raise the window blind and peek outside.

No.

Impossible.

Joshua William Faraday has just killed me. I'm officially dead. RIP Katherine Ulla Morgan. It's been a great life.

Josh is standing below me on the tarmac in his perfectly tailored tuxedo, staring up with a smoldering expression on his handsome face—*and with his arm in a freakin' sling!*

"Stop!" I yell toward the cockpit, even though the airplane isn't moving (and the engines aren't even on). "Stop!" I shriek again, leaping dramatically up from my chair. My brain isn't processing coherent thought right now, it's true, but I don't need conscious thought to know what I'm supposed to do in this scene—I've seen it in *The Bodyguard* twenty times, after all.

I burst down the stairs of the plane as fast as I can manage in my tight-fitting dress and towering heels and sprint (sort of) to Josh. And when I reach him, I throw my arms around his neck, hyperventilating. "Josh," I gasp. "I love you, I love you, I love—"

Josh's tongue slides into my mouth, shutting me up, while his free hand caresses my back—and when he pulls away from our kiss, his eyes are on fire. "Katherine Ulla Morgan," he says, his voice intense. "I. Will. Always. Love. You."

I squeal loudly, completely enthralled.

"I know marriage isn't in the cards for us," Josh says, "since neither of us wants that kind of *hoopla*, as we've discussed." One side of his mouth hitches up. "But I hope you'll accept this gift as a symbol of my eternal love for you." He pulls a skinny, rectangular jewelry box out of his pocket.

"Oh my effing God," I blurt, even before Josh has opened the box. "No, Josh. *No.* Whatever that is, it's too much, honey. *No.*"

"There's no such thing as 'too much' when it comes to you, babe," Josh says.

"No," I breathe. "Baby, no. You can't. Too much."

"Ssh. You can forbid me to give extravagant gifts to your parents," Josh says. "But when it comes to giving gifts to you, I'll do whatever the fuck I want."

I clutch my stomach. "Oh God, I feel like I'm gonna hurl," I say.

Josh flinches. "Not quite the reaction I was going for, babe."

I feel myself turning green.

"Well, shit," Josh says, crinkling his nose. "Maybe take a deep breath? Fuck, Kat. Seriously?"

I take a deep breath, but my nausea doesn't subside.

Josh's scowl intensifies. "I haven't even opened the box yet, Kat."

"Sorry."

Josh exhales in frustration. "Maybe bend over and breathe deeply? I'll hold onto you so you don't fall over."

I bend over and breathe for a long moment as Josh holds me and rubs my back and, soon, thankfully, I've regained my equilibrium. "Okay," I say, standing upright again. "I'm good."

"You sure?"

"Yep. I'm fine. I'm ready."

"You gonna barf if I open this box?"

I shake my head.

"I really like these shoes, Kat," Josh warns. "These are Stefano Bemer shoes, babe—*please* don't barf on them."

"Ooh la la—Stefano Bemers," I say, even though I've never heard that name in my entire life. "I'd never barf on *Stefano Bemer* shoes, baby. I respect Mr. Bemer too freaking much."

Josh laughs. "Okay. Here we go." He opens the box, and, instantly, I'm a goddamned fucking wreck. If my necklace is a beachside condo, then the behemoth of a diamond bracelet sitting inside that velvet box is at *least* a convertible Porsche.

"Oh my *God!*" I shriek, tears pricking my eyes.

Josh pulls the bracelet out of the box and clasps it to my wrist. "I love you, Kat," he whispers. He wraps me in a huge hug and kisses my tear-soaked cheeks.

"It's too much," I mumble into Josh's lips. "Oh my God, Josh. You can't do this. I'm not worthy."

Josh pulls back sharply from me, his eyes on fire. "Don't say that," he grits out, his voice spiking with sudden intensity. "Never, ever say that—do you understand me?"

My breath catches in my throat. I'd only meant that phrase as a figure of speech, kind of like from *Wayne's World*—"We're not worthy! We're not worthy!" Although, of course, I'm truly *not* worthy. Who could *possibly* be worthy of this kind of extravagance?

Josh cups my face in his large hands, heat wafting off him, his eyes burning. "You're my Pretty Woman and I'm your Bodyguard, Kat. You're the great love of my life and the mother of my future daughter." He presses himself into me and the hard bulge between us feels like it was forged in a steel factory. "Babe, have you been listening to me *at all*? You're *mine* now. *Forever*. Mine, all mine. And I'm not just some normal, boring guy—I'm *Josh Fucking Faraday*. And that means you gotta be *dripping* in fucking diamonds when you're on my arm." He slaps my ass, making me jump. "Now, come on, babe. Time to get your tight little ass onto that plane. I'm hard as a rock and ready to initiate my Party Girl with a Hyphen into the mile-high club."

119

JOSH

"Ooooh, a *white* limo," Kat says, settling herself into the backseat. She shoots me a snarky smile. "Just like in the final scene of *Pretty Woman.*"

"Ssh," I say, pulling the skirt of Kat's gown out from under my thigh as I scoot closer to her in the back seat. "This is *my* top fantasy—not yours, baby. You're here to *react,* not to try to figure things out."

"Okay, well, my *reaction* is, 'Hey, you arranged a white limo just like that awesome final scene in *Pretty Woman.*'"

I roll my eyes. "Smart-ass."

Kat grins.

I glance through the rear window of the limo just in time to see our driver closing the trunk. My stomach somersaults with excitement. *This is it.*

The driver walks along the length of the limo and settles into his seat up front.

"You got everything into the trunk?" I ask, referring to more than just our overnight bags.

"Yes, sir," the driver says. "Everything's there." He winks.

"Fantastic," I say. "Let's blow this popsicle stand."

The limo begins to pull away.

"Where are we going?" Kat asks, looking out the car window at the small airport we're leaving behind.

"Are you hungry, Party Girl?" I ask, completely ignoring her question. "There's a platter here—fruit, cheese, tapenade, crackers, prosciutto."

"Oh, God, yes. Thank you. I'm *starving.*" Kat begins literally stuffing food into her mouth like her very life depends on it. After a moment, she giggles at herself. "Dude, I'm in full Homer-Simpson mode," she says. "Nom nom nom. I can't control myself."

"The kumquat's really hungry, huh?" I ask.

"Pretty much all the time these days. She's a demanding little thing."

I open my mouth to make a snarky comment but Kat holds up her hand.

"Don't say it," she says, mock-glaring at me.

I smash my lips together and we both laugh.

"You know, the two of us are really not behaving in a way becoming of people dressed in formalwear," Kat says, chomping on a piece of cheese.

"Thank God," I say.

"Yeah, sure, it's all fun and games for *us*, but definitely not for the flight attendant," Kat says. "It really wasn't *that* big a plane, poor thing."

"Oh, she'll survive. We can't possibly be the first people to fuck like rabbits on a private plane."

"I wouldn't be so sure," Kat says. She giggles. "Surely other people fuck, but not like *that*—that was pretty *enthusiastic*, even for us, Josh. Dressed in a gown like this, I really should have acted much more like a proper young lady on that plane. Tsk, tsk."

I lean forward and touch Kat's chin. "Promise me something, babe," I say.

"Anything, my love."

"Promise me, no matter what, you'll never, ever act like a proper young lady as long as we both shall live."

A lovely smile spreads across Kat's face. "I promise."

"Thank you."

A few minutes later, after Kat's finished eating like a truck driver suffering from mad cow disease, she scoots closer to me on the car seat and rests her head on my shoulder. "Thank you for this amazing day, Josh," she says. "This is the best day of my life." She clasps her fingers in mine.

"That's sweet," I say nonchalantly. "But your feelings are completely irrelevant, since today is for my benefit and not yours."

Kat giggles. "You're so full of shit."

We silently watch the passing scenery through the car window for several minutes, the Southern California ocean glimmering in the late-afternoon light. "I've never been to San Diego," Kat says. "It's beautiful here."

"Yeah, I love it here," I say. "I usually make it down here a couple times a year during racing season. I've got several good friends who own racehorses."

"Of course, you do. I'm shocked you don't own a couple yourself."

"Meh. I did a few years ago. But it turns out racehorses are fucking money pits to own—a lot more fun when someone else is paying the bills."

"God, ain't that the truth," Kat says, squeezing my hand. "It's what I *always* say."

We look out at the passing scenery again, our hands clasped comfortably.

"I love the ocean," Kat says. "Especially at this time of day when the light is soft and golden."

Just like your hair, I think, stroking the full length of her soft, golden mane —but, of course, I keep that thought to myself. There's only so much poetic babbling a guy can do in one day and I've got to rest up for all the poetic babbling that lies ahead. I stare at the passing scenery for a long minute, stroking Kat's glorious hair, breathing in the scent of her, thinking about what I'm gonna say to her when we reach our destination.

"Staring at the ocean always makes me feel small, but in a good way," Kat says quietly, looking out the window.

"Me, too," I say. "Like my problems don't matter in the grand scheme of things."

"You have problems?" she asks.

I kiss the top of her head. "Not anymore."

Kat nuzzles into me. "I wish I had something amazing to give you—the male equivalent of a Carolina Herrera gown and diamonds, whatever that would be—so you could feel the way I do right now."

"Well, the male equivalent of a Carolina Herrera dress and diamonds would be an Italian sports car—which I already have. But, don't worry, you've already given me something ten times better than that."

Kat lifts her head, apparently about to say something, but yawns, instead.

"Damn, you're hard to impress," I say.

She giggles. "Sorry. It's been an exciting day. I'm duly impressed, I assure you."

I open my arms to her and pat my heart. "Lay your cheek right here, beautiful. Close your eyes for a bit."

Kat nuzzles into my chest. "Where are we headed?" she asks groggily.

"God, you're a terrible listener," I say, stroking her hair.

Kat purrs like a kitten against my chest and in less than a minute, her head droops like a dead weight. I shift in my seat, trying to make her more comfortable, but, inadvertently startle her awake, instead.

"Oh, I'm sorry," I say. "I was trying to make you more comfortable. Go back to sleep, babe. I won't move."

"How long 'til we get wherever we're going?" she asks, her voice thick with drowsiness. "Do I have time to sleep?"

"How much longer 'til we reach our destination?" I ask the limo driver.

"About thirty minutes, sir, depending on traffic," the driver says.

"Plenty of time for a little nap, hot momma," I say. "Go for it."

Kat rests her cheek against me again. "I think I will, if that's okay—just for a few minutes."

Twenty seconds later, Kat's out like a light, passed out with her cheek against my heart, her little belly underneath her red gown rising and falling evenly with every breath she takes. When I'm sure Kat's deeply asleep, I tilt her face up to mine and stare at her stunning features, marveling at God's handiwork. I trace the line of one of her bold eyebrows with my fingertip, brush the back of my hand against her cheekbone, stare for a long moment at her perfectly formed lips.

As evil as Kat's startling beauty is when she's awake, her face is actually quite angelic when she sleeps. This isn't the face of a woman who'd blindside me, is it? After everything that's passed between Kat and me since my first god-awful proposal, Kat wouldn't shatter me by turning me down for a second time, would she?

My stomach flips over. If by some shocking turn of events Kat was actually telling the truth when she said she wouldn't marry me if I were the last man on earth, if she truly doesn't want all the "hoopla" of a wedding, if marriage truly isn't something she yearns for in the depths of her soul—or, at least, not marriage with *me*—then I truly don't think I'd survive the rejection.

My phone buzzes with an incoming text and I pull it out of my pocket.

"The eagle has landed," Henn writes. "The fucker's at his house. Go straight there. No Plan B required."

"Well, how considerate of him to be home in time for my visit," I write.

"Can you talk?" Henn writes.

I look down at Kat. Her mouth is hanging open and she's drooling. "Calling now," I write.

"Yo," Henn says when he picks up my call.

"Nice of the bastard to be sitting at home, waiting for me," I reply softly.

"He's always home at this time of day after a round of golf at the country club. But just to make double-damn sure he was gonna be there for you today, he *might* have received a VIP-invitation to a live chat with his favorite porn star. *Wink.*"

"Fucking genius."

"So I've been told. How close are you?"

I glance at Kat, making sure she's not overhearing any of this, and she's snoozing like she's been cold-cocked. "We're in the limo now," I say quietly. "I'd say we're about fifteen minutes out."

"Cool. The dude's not going anywhere. He's watching a gangbang-*bukkake*-porno on his iPad while simultaneously live-chatting with a porn star on his laptop."

"He's double-fisting porn?" I ask.

Henn laughs. "I think he *might* have an addiction."

"Ya think?" I say.

"So, hey, I went through the dude's computer like you asked me to," Henn says. "You were right—he's totally cheating on his wife. Like, compulsively."

"Yeah, I figured. A leopard doesn't change his spots."

"The guy's a scumbag," Henn says. "I literally *hate* him."

"Welcome to the club," I say.

"I went through his wife's phone and laptop just to get the lay of the land and she's a total sweetheart—a genuinely good person. Clearly, she's got no idea who she's married to."

"Not surprised at all."

"So are you gonna rat him out?"

"I wish I could so badly—but, no, I wasn't planning to, for the sake of the wife."

"Yeah, I guess that's the right call. It's not really our place to ruin her life. But it kills me. They're trying to have a baby—doing hard-core fertility treatments. I hope one way or another she finds out she's married to a cheating scumbag before she gets pregnant with the guy's kid."

"So you think we should rat him out, after all?" I ask.

"No," Henn says. "It's really not our place, man. That's not the mission."

I sigh. "Damn. I would have loved to decimate that cocksucker in every conceivable way."

"Oh, well. I guess even a guy as awesome as you can't have everything, Josh."

I look down at Kat's beautiful, sleeping face. "Actually, I'm beginning to think he can."

"Wait. So you *do* wanna tell the wife about his extracurricular activities?"

"No, sorry. I wasn't referring to ratting him out. Kat's asleep on me. I was looking at her face when I said that."

"Oh, well, I can see why you'd say that, then."

"Kat's totally drooling right now," I say, chuckling.

Henn laughs. "Yeah, but I bet it's really *pretty* drool."

"Actually, it is." I smile to myself. "Okay, yeah, I agree," I say. "We don't tell the wife she's married to the world's biggest scumbag."

"Not today, anyway. I might not be able to control myself tomorrow. I make no promises."

"Hey, you gotta follow your conscience, baby," I say. "I trust you. But just not today."

"Okay. Got it, boss."

"So can we somehow make sure the wife's not there when Kat and I arrive?"

"You should be good. Her iPhone says she's got an appointment at a hair salon ten miles from their house. She left about fifteen minutes ago. Don't women's hair appointments at hoity-toity salons take at least an hour or so? Her appointment's at one of those really fancy places where they give you cucumber water and wash your hair, so she should be gone a while."

"That's your definition of a fancy salon?" I say. "They give you water and a shampoo?"

"Hey, I go to Supercuts, man. What do I know?"

"You do? Oh, I totally couldn't tell that from looking at you, Henn."

Henn laughs. "So, here's the sitch, man. When you get there, the name 'Frank Farmer' is on the approved visitors' list at the guard station. Just text me when you're there and I'll go in and freeze the bastard's hard drive."

"Will do. We're almost there. Sit tight and wait for my signal, okay?"

"Yup. No worries. I'll just be sitting here, watching him watch porn," Henn says. "Don't you worry about a thing except bagging that babe."

"I'll do my mighty best."

"Is that a note of *anxiety* I detect in your voice, boss?"

"Yeah, this is life or death, man—I don't wanna fuck it up."

"Aw, come on. You can't fail. Just dick it up and the babe will be eating out the palm of your hand."

"Gee, thanks for the tip."

"No prob."

"I'll text you when we're there."

"Roger that."

Ten minutes later, the limo pulls up to an exclusive gated community in Del Mar, California—a wealthy seaside enclave north of San Diego—and our driver tells the security guard at the gate the name of the resident we're here to see.

"And what's the visitor's name?" the guard asks.

"Frank Farmer," the driver says, motioning to me in the back seat. "He should be on your list."

"Wait here."

The guard disappears into his guardhouse, presumably to look at his approved visitors' list, and my stomach clenches sharply. But when the guy comes back out, he's all smiles.

"Do you know how to get there?" the guard asks my driver.

"We have the address," the driver replies.

"Well, lemme just tell you: follow the main road here for two miles and then take the third right. Mr. Bennett's house is on the left."

"Okay, thanks," the driver says.

As we cruise slowly down the main drag of the complex, I survey the McMansions lining the street, my stomach bursting with butterflies. In just a few minutes, my life will be forever changed. *And I can't wait.*

My eyes drift down to Kat, still asleep against my chest.

It feels like a lifetime ago that Kat waltzed out of the bathroom at Jonas' house and straight up to me like she owned me—which she did, of course, right from the start. I fought her on it, for sure, but now in retrospect it's clear this very moment with Kat was unavoidable. My fate. A beautiful brick wall I've been barreling toward my whole fucking life.

I nudge Kat gently. "Babe," I whisper. "Time to wake up, beautiful."

Kat's dead to the world.

"Party Girl," I whisper. "It's time to party, sweetheart." I nudge her again and she rustles.

"Hmm?" Kat says. She lifts her head and looks around with dazed eyes.

"It's time to party, honey," I say softly.

Kat wipes the drool off her chin and gazes out the car window, just as the limo turns right onto a street lined with the same cookie-cutter mansions on the main drag.

"Where are we?" Kat asks, stretching her long arms and looking around.

The limo comes to a stop in front of our destination.

"It's a surprise," I say. "Stay here, baby. I'm gonna set something up for us—it'll just take a minute. While I'm doing that, you freshen up—put on some lip gloss, wipe your chin, whatever—and when you hear blaring music, come out of the limo and stand next to me, okay?"

"What?" she asks. "Come stand next to you?"

"Yeah, baby, when you hear blaring music, that's your cue to come out of the limo and stand next to me." I stroke her hair. "Freshen up your makeup, babe—make yourself extra pretty—I want you looking like a man-eater when you step out of the car, okay? And the minute you hear the music, come out and stand next to me."

"Okay," she says. She grabs her makeup bag out of her duffel. "Your wish is my command, sir."

I grab Kat's face and kiss her. "See you soon, my love," I say.

"Josh?"

"Yeah?"

"Um. I'm really sorry, but I have to pee—like, really, really bad. Is this gonna take long, whatever it is? I'm about to explode."

I chuckle. Damn. I didn't think about Kat's constant need to pee these days when I planned this mini-porno-rom-com. I peek out the window of the car. There are definitely plenty of bushes in The Asshole's manicured landscaping, including some fairly large bushes along the side of the house.

"Okay, Party Girl—come with me," I say. "We'll find a place for you to pop a squat."

Kat laughs. "I'm dressed in a Carolina Herrera gown, diamonds, and Manolo Blahniks—and you're asking me to 'pop a squat' behind a bush?"

"Do you have a better plan?"

"Well, no. I just didn't want you to think I'm low-class."

"Babe, you're the classiest broad I know. Now, come on. Let's go take a classy piss behind a bush."

120

JOSH

"Sir, do you want—?" the driver begins when Kat and I emerge from the backseat of the limo looking for a place to relieve Kat's bursting bladder. The driver's standing at the back of the car, exactly as instructed, getting ready to set up two speakers currently nestled in the trunk of the car.

"Hang on," I say, putting up my hand and cutting him off. "My baby-momma needs to take a quick piss before we begin. Await further instruction."

The driver smirks. "Yes, sir."

Kat and I creep around the side of the large house and quickly find a suitable bush—and while I keep a lookout, she hikes up her red dress around her hips, squats her tight little ass down, and pisses like a racehorse.

"Ah," she says as a loud stream of urine blasts out of her. "Delicious."

I laugh. "*Delicious?*"

"Yes, *delicious*. When I have to pee really, really bad and finally get to go, it feels semi-orgasmic. Same muscles releasing, actually. *Delicious.*"

"Only you, Kat," I say, zipping down my fly and taking a quick whiz myself.

"Wow, we're a classy pair, aren't we?" she says. She stands almost upright, still hiking her elegant gown up, and shakes her pelvis furiously like a wet dog after a bath.

"What the fuck are you doing?" I ask.

"Shaking the extra pee off my cooch. That's what I do when I don't have toilet paper—the pee-pee-shake. It's not just me, trust me—every girl who's ever gone on a pub crawl or painted her fingernails and then realized she has to pee has resorted to the pee-pee-shake." She straightens up.

"You good now?"

"Oh yeah, I'm gooood." She shoots me two thumbs up.

"Okay, then get your tight little ass back into the limo. Freshen up your makeup—I want you looking like you could eat a douche for breakfast, okay?—and then come out the minute you hear blaring music."

"And stand next to you. I got it, Playboy." She smiles and looks around. "Where are we, by the way? Who lives here?"

"No questions. Now *go*."

Kat shoots me an adorable smile and traipses back to the limo—and the minute she closes the car door behind her, I powwow with the driver at the opened trunk.

"You want both speakers aimed at the house?" the driver asks.

"Yep," I say. "The song's all cued up on my phone and connected to the speakers via Blue Tooth. Just point the speakers at the house and press play on the song at my signal."

"Yes, sir." He holds his hand out for my phone.

"Hang on," I say. I tap out a quick text to Henn. "In exactly three minutes, do your thing," I write.

"You got it," Henn replies.

"Here you go," I say, handing my phone to the driver. "The song's all cued up."

Three minutes later, I grab my trusty Walmart boom box out of the trunk of the car, position myself on the porch of our host's McMansion, make quadruple sure the ring box is still in my pocket (it is), raise the boom box over my head, and, finally, with a curt nod, cue the driver.

Here we go.

Whitney Houston begins belting out "I Will Always Love You" at full volume—so fucking loud, in fact, my molars feel like they're one high-note away from popping out of my head.

My pulse is pounding in my ears.

My hands are shaking.

This is it. Oh my God. The love of my life is about to come out of that white limo and, hopefully, make me the luckiest man in the world.

The door to the limo opens. And there she is. *Kat*—my fantasy sprung to life, looking as gorgeous as ever... and utterly confused. But when Kat's eyes land on me and she sees the CD player over my head, her face contorts with instant glee. She sprints toward me as fast as her heels will allow, her eyes glistening, her cheeks flushed. Just before she reaches me, I put my makeshift boom box on the ground and open my arms to her.

"I love you," Kat cries, barreling into my arms. "I love you so much."

I kiss her passionately, devouring her, lost in her—until the sound of an aggravated male voice behind us, shouting over the music, breaks us apart.

"What the fuck is this?" the voice shouts behind us. "Turn that music off and get your shit off my—"

"Garrett?" Kat blurts, obviously floored. She looks at me, her mouth agape, apparently trying to make sense of this incomprehensible ghost from her past. "This is *your* house?"

"Kat?" Garrett yells above the blaring music, obviously as shocked to see Kat as she is to see him. "What are you doing here?"

I motion to the driver to cut the music and he does.

"Hey, Garrett Asshole Bennett," I say smoothly, my voice cutting through the sudden silence. "Sorry for the interruption—I know you were busy inside wacking off to gangbang-*bukkake*-porn, but Kat and I have some important business to attend to and it requires your participation. Shouldn't take more than fifteen minutes at the outside."

Garrett looks absolutely blindsided. "*What?*" he chokes out. "Who are you?"

"My name's Frank Farmer," I say.

Kat's face lights up at the mention of my code name. (It should, for fuck's sake—the woman's only seen *The Bodyguard* twenty fucking times.)

"I believe you're acquainted with my baby-momma, Kat?" I continue.

Garrett stares at me dumbly.

"We came here today because there's something important I want to ask Kat—and I thought it'd be extra special for her if I asked her this particular question in front of you."

Kat lets out a little yelp, perhaps realizing where this thing is headed.

"So I'd really appreciate it if you'd stay put and listen carefully to everything I'm about to say to her," I continue. "And when I'm done asking Kat my important question, we'll leave you alone so you can continue watching your hardcore porn and cheating on your wife with hookers and the bookkeeper at your church and the waitress at your country club."

"Who *are* you?" Garrett blurts, his face ashen.

"I told you, I'm Frank Farmer," I say. "And you're gonna stay put and listen to everything I'm about to say to this gorgeous woman, or I'm gonna make your life a living fucking hell." I look at my watch. "We'd better get started, Garrett. We don't have that much time before your wife gets home from her hair appointment and I have no desire for her to hear any of this."

"Fuck you," Garrett blurts. "Get off my property or I'll call the police."

I take a menacing step forward, my fists clenched, and Garrett flinches.

"You're not in any position to *fuck* me, cocksucker," I say. "If anyone's getting *fucked* today, trust me, it's gonna be you. Now I want you to listen patiently to every word I have to say to this gorgeous creature, especially the grand finale at the end, because if you don't, a certain photo that's frozen on your laptop screen right now will be blasted to every single person on the email lists for your church and country club, not to mention your senator-daddy's campaign-donor list, too. Feel free to run inside and check out the image on your laptop right now if you don't believe me. We'll wait."

Garrett's face twists in shock. He opens his mouth and shuts it again, but he doesn't move from his spot on his doorstep.

"Good boy." I look at Kat and smile. She looks like her head's about to pop off. I take her hands in mine. "Kat, this motherfucker here once said you're not 'marriage material.' But I'm here to tell you that you are. In fact, you're not just 'marriage material' in general for *some* lucky guy, my love—you're specifically marriage material for *me*."

Kat lets out a little yelp and literally wobbles in place.

I grasp her arm and steady her. "You okay?"

Kat shakes her head. She's totally losing it. She clamps her hand over her mouth.

"You gonna barf?" I ask.

She shakes her head again. "Keep going. I'm fine. Oh my God. Keep going, babe. Holy fuck."

I look at Garrett. "Don't go anywhere, fuckwad."

Garrett crosses his arms over his chest, but he doesn't move.

"Katherine Ulla Morgan," I say. "You're the great love of my life. I'll never want anyone besides you, ever, 'til the end of time, forever and ever, and I'm one hundred percent sure of that fact. You're The One, babe. The one and only. It's literally impossible for me to want someone else, ever, because you're sheer perfection in every way." I glare at Garrett. "The reasons I love you are too numerous to count, but let me tell you just a few of them while we've got Garrett's undivided attention."

Kat whimpers.

"You're hysterically funny, baby. Sweet and kind. Caring and compassionate. You take care of those you love with a fierceness I've never witnessed before. Babe, I *admire* you."

She gasps.

"You're a sassy little thing," I continue. "Good lord are you sassy. A fucking terrorist. A demon spawn. A force of nature. To call you *determined* is like calling a pit bull *assertive*."

Kat laughs.

"You're honest, Kat. Oh my fuck, do you call me on my shit. The way you *don't* kiss my YOLO'd ass is one of the best things about you. You're smart, baby. Intuitive. Clever. Bold. When I'm with you, there's no place I'd rather be, no matter what we're doing, even if we're just peeing in a fucking bush."

Kat laughs heartily through her tears.

"You're hell on wheels, Kat Morgan. Totally unpredictable. A heart of gold hidden beneath a layer of pure evil. *And I love all of it.*"

Kat laughs again and wipes her eyes.

"I'll never get bored with you. It's impossible. Never a dull moment." I glare at Garrett. "I'm one hundred percent positive I'll never feel the need to watch gangbang-*bukkake*-porn as long as you're by my side because you're better than any porno—better than any fantasy. With you, life *is* a fantasy. Every single day."

Kat makes a weird chortling sound, a combination of a cry and a laugh.

I shoot daggers at Garrett again and then return my gaze to Kat. "Garrett here didn't think you were marriage material because you're so sexual. Let's talk about that, shall we? Because, my love—my beautiful, sexy, feisty, funny, kinky, perverted, wonderful sick fuck—the way your motor runs so fucking hot is definitely one of the best things about you. You're highly sexual because you're so fucking passionate, Kat—because you're relentlessly honest and raw and a fucking beast in every way. You should never, ever be ashamed of your amazing sexuality. It's your superpower, baby." I glare at Garrett again, and, for some reason, a rage rises up and boils over inside me. "Hang on a second, my love," I say to Kat. I drop her hands and take a menacing step toward Garrett, pointing at Kat behind me. "This woman right here is a fucking unicorn," I seethe. "She fucks like a dude and sucks a dick like nobody else."

Kat squeals with glee behind my shoulder.

"In fact, she's quite literally the best dick-sucker the world has ever seen. If there were an Olympic event in the sport of dick-sucking, Katherine Morgan would take the gold, silver, and fucking bronze."

Kat makes a sound of pure joy.

"And the way she fucks? Oh my God. When it comes to fucking, this woman right here is truly gifted. If fucking were *thinking*, Kat Morgan would have a genius-level IQ."

Kat bursts out laughing and so do I.

But Garrett isn't laughing. Not at all. "I'm calling the cops," he seethes.

"Oh, shut the fuck up, Garrett. No, you're not. Because we both know I'm in your computer right now—and what information I've got access to. But, for what it's worth, I promise I'm not here to harm you today. Actually, I'm here to *thank* you—from the bottom of my heart. If you hadn't been such a slut-shaming prick who was more concerned about what Mommy and Daddy would think than letting yourself be truly happy in this one fucking life, if you'd rather secretly beat off while watching porn on your computer than fuck a woman who looks like Kat every day of your life—then all I can say is, you're my new best friend. Because, thanks to you and your tiny dick and even smaller balls, this gorgeous woman is all mine 'til the end of fucking time, praise be to God."

Kat makes a strangled sound.

"Which brings me to that question I've got for you, Kat."

I turn away from Garrett, pull the closed ring box out of my pocket, and kneel down. "Katherine Ulla Morgan," I begin, holding up the box, a huge smile on my face.

"Oh my God, oh my God, oh my God!" Kat shrieks.

I pause, thinking Kat's gonna calm down and let me get a word in edgewise, but, instead, she lets out a pained wail like she's a spider and her eight legs are being simultaneously ripped off her body.

"Babe," I say. "Are you okay?"

She nods, but she looks like she's about to keel over.

"Put your hands on my shoulders," I say. "I guarantee you, when I open this box, your knees are gonna buckle, babe."

Kat puts her hands on my shoulders, squealing and trembling.

I take a deep breath. "Katherine Ulla Morgan," I begin again, beaming up at her—but before I can say another word, Kat pivots, buckles over, and barfs all over Garrett's shoes.

"What the fuck!" Garrett yells, jumping back.

I burst out laughing. Oh my God. This is the best day of my life.

"You people are fucking crazy!" Garrett shouts. "Get the fuck off my property!"

I stand, howling with laughter. "You okay, babe?" I choke out, completely ignoring Garrett.

Kat's laughing hysterically right along with me. "Yeah, I'm great." She wipes her mouth. "Oh my God. Now *that's* a story for the grandchildren."

"I'm not gonna say it again," Garrett says. "I don't know who the fuck you think you are, but—"

I've suddenly got anti-freeze in my veins. In a flash, I've got a fistful of Garrett's shirt in my palm and I'm slamming his backside against his front door. "My hacker's in complete control of your computer right now, motherfucker," I growl, "which means he's in complete control of your *life*. Now, if you don't believe me, go check your screen right now—your screen-saver is that selfie you took when you were getting blown by that hooker in Vegas."

Garrett's jaw drops.

"Go look at your laptop if you don't believe me, cocksucker," I grit out. "I'll wait."

Garrett waffles briefly and then slams the door in our faces.

"You need some water, PG?" I ask.

Kat nods. "Sorry. That was so gross." She looks down at herself. "Did I get puke on my pretty dress?"

"Nope. Not a drop. Just all over Garrett." I chuckle. "So fucking hilarious."

Kat giggles.

"You're sure you're okay?"

"I'm great." Her face is positively glowing. "Better than great."

"Hang on. I'll get some water and your toothbrush out of your duffel bag." I sprint to the car, grab a couple bottles of water, Kat's toothbrush, and a tube of toothpaste out of her bag, and race back to her. "Here you go, PG. Do your thing. I'll wait." I wink.

She smiles sheepishly and walks toward the side of the house, but before turning the corner, she stops and turns around. "Josh, please, while I'm gone, for the love of God, don't change your mind about what you're planning to ask me. *Please*."

"Are you gonna say yes?" I ask.

She clutches her heart. "Of course."

I breathe a sigh of relief. "Thank God."

"Was there ever a doubt?"

"Babe, when it comes to you, I'm never completely sure what the fuck you're gonna do."

We beam massive, excited smiles at each other.

"Now go brush your teeth, hot momma," I say. "I'm gonna wanna kiss you after you say yes."

"Oh. Right. Okay. I'll be right back." She sprints around the side of the house, giggling, and disappears.

I pull out my phone and text Henn. "The Asshole's inside his house, looking at his computer. He was threatening to call the police. Send him a message loud and clear, would you? Make sure he knows he's at my fucking mercy."

"Gotcha, boss. When he comes back out, the tiger will be nothing more than a pussy cat—I promise."

Kat returns from around the corner looking fresh as the morning dew at the same time Garrett opens his front door, his face bright red.

"Motherfucker," Garrett says. "So this is blackmail? You want money?"

I scoff. "No, not at all. This is twenty minutes of payback for you being a total asshole to the love of my life for eight long months. I'm gonna make your life miserable for mere minutes and then leave you alone to cheat on your wife as much as you please. Of course, you deserve to have me fuck up your life irreparably, but by all accounts, your wife is a really sweet lady and totally clueless about you. So I'm not gonna do a damn thing to you, just to spare her from embarrassment. Plus, as a side note, blackmailing a guy worth a mere fraction of my net worth would be a pretty stupid thing to do, don't you think? Yeah, that's right, Garrett, I've seen your bank statements. I could buy you at least a hundred times over, fucker." I point to Kat's necklace. "See that? *Real.*" I hold up Kat's arm like she's a rag doll and point to her sparkling bracelet. "And this? *Real.* Both gifts from me—and that's just *today.* Who the fuck knows what tokens of my affection I might give her for Christmas and her birthday and maybe after she sucks my dick extra nice. And do you wanna know why? Because this woman's gonna be my *wife.*"

Kat lets out a loud wail and throws her arms around me.

I hug her to me, still looking at Garrett Asshole Bennett, my eyes burning with near-homicidal rage. "Make no mistake about it, motherfucker, any wife of mine is gonna be *dripping* in motherfucking diamonds, cocksucker—I promise you that."

Kat makes a very, very bizarre sound—a sound I couldn't categorize if I tried—and presses her body fervently into mine, kissing my cheeks frenetically.

"So," I say, dodging Kat's furious lips, "like I said, if you want us to leave and never come back, then all you've got to do is stand here and watch me pop the question and we'll be on our merry way, off to fuck like rabbits for the third (but not final) time today, never to think about your pathetic, hypocritical, miserable ass ever again as long as we both shall live." I look at Kat. "You ready, my love? It's time for me to ask you to be my wife."

Kat nods, her eyes blazing. "Oh my God."

"But, wait. You know what? One more thing before I do that."

Kat throws up her hands and exhales loudly, flapping her lips together.

I wink at her. "Patience, my love." I look at Garrett and my jaw sets. "Apologize to my future wife for what you did to her, asshole."

Garrett looks flabbergasted.

"It's okay," Kat says, putting her hand on my forearm. "Let's not waste our time on—"

"Ssh. I told you, baby. This is *my* fantasy, not yours." I look at Garrett again, my eyes burning. "Tell my future wife and mother of my child you're sorry for what you did to her. For using her. Lying to her. Slut-shaming her. You gave my future wife a complex about her superpower and now you're gonna tell her you're sorry."

Garrett's nostrils flair. His jaw muscles pulse. He looks at Kat, not a hint of apology in his eyes. "Kat, I think you took things between us *way* too hard. I don't even remember saying you weren't 'marriage material'—"

"Are you calling my future wife a *liar*?" I bellow.

"No," Garrett says quickly, recoiling.

I take a deep, shaky breath. It's taking all my willpower not to beat this little prick to within an inch of his life. "Now apologize to my future wife. Last fucking chance."

Garrett looks like he's gonna cry. "Kat, *if* I said that to you—which I honestly don't even remember—"

I lunge at Garrett and he immediately throws up his hands defensively, cowering. "Wait! Wait! If I said that, which I don't remember—but it's definitely *possible*—then all I meant was that you weren't 'marriage material' for *me* personally. That's all I meant, Kat."

Kat squints. Her nostrils flare. She's turning into the dragon-lady before my eyes.

"That sure didn't sound like an apology, Garrett," Kat says evenly. "I didn't even hear the word 'sorry' pass your lips." Kat grits her teeth. "Did you not hear my future husband? Apologize to me—and make me believe it—so this sexy man can ask me to marry him and I can say 'hell yes.'"

Garrett exhales a shaky breath. "I'm sorry, Kat. You were great and I was an asshole and I'm sorry. I shouldn't have said that to you."

"And not only that, you shouldn't have used me to cheat on your virgin-girl-friend in the first place, asshole," Kat says.

Garrett clenches his jaw. "Yeah, I'm genuinely sorry about that."

Kat's face magically transforms into pure sweetness. "I forgive you, Garrett. But only because I don't give the slightest fuck about you." Kat flashes me a truly angelic smile. "Go ahead, my darling beloved. You were saying?"

I smile broadly. "You're pleased with his apology?"

"Quite pleased."

"All right, then. Let's proceed." I clear my throat. "'My dearest Katherine, if your feelings are the same as you described to me that horrible night in the hospital, then tell me now—one word from you will silence me forever.'"

Kat's face lights up with instant recognition of the scene I'm portraying. She puts her hand on her heart, her face aglow. "Mr. Darcy," she whispers, her eyes watering. "Oh, Josh."

I kneel down slowly, my eyes fixed on hers, and open the ring box.

Kat gasps at the sight of the spectacular rock. "*Josh!* Oh my God! *Josh!*"

I hold the ring up and beam a huge smile at her. "Katherine Ulla Morgan, the love of my life, the mother of my future baby girl, the Party Girl with a Hyphen *and* Heart of Gold: 'You have bewitched me, body and soul, and I love, I love, I *love* you.'"

"Oh my God," Kat breathes.

I take a deep breath. My heart is racing. I'm shaking like a leaf as adrenaline suddenly floods me. "Kat, my love, will you *please* make me the luckiest man in the world and say yes to marrying me?"

"Yes!" Kat shrieks, tears springing into her eyes.

I stand and slip the ring on Kat's finger—and she shrieks at the sight of the massive rock on her hand. She throws herself into my arms, crying and cooing and purring and basically losing her shit completely.

"Can I go now?" Garrett says dryly.

I break free from Kat and wipe my eyes. "Almost, Garrett. We're really close. There's just one more thing."

"For fuck's sake," Garrett says, rolling his eyes. "My wife's gonna be home any minute." He looks at his watch. "Whatever it is, say it already and get the fuck off my property and the fuck out of my computer."

I take Kat's hand and squeeze it. "Kat wanted you and you rejected her," I say. "Big mistake. *Big*." I motion to Kat like I'm giving her the floor but, much to my surprise, she looks at me with wide, blank eyes, not catching my meaning. "*Big mistake. Big*," I repeat. I motion to Kat again. But she's still clueless. I throw up my hands, totally annoyed. "Aw, come on, babe," I say. "You're totally fucking this up, babe."

"I am? What am I supposed to do?"

"You really don't know?"

She shakes her head.

"Babe. Duh. I'm doing the thing when Julia goes back to the ritzy clothing store in Beverly Hills after the store clerk wouldn't help her the day before?"

"Oh my God!" Kat slaps her palm on her forehead. "I can't believe I didn't get that. My brain's not even functioning right now." She holds up her hand, displaying her massive rock. "Who could blame me—holy shitballs, honey—this thing is causing me brain damage." She giggles. "Okay, cue me again, honey. I'll nail it this time."

"You two are fucking crazy," Garrett says.

"Ssh," I say to Garrett. "Listen up, fucker." I clear my throat, clearly cuing up the script. "Garrett, she wanted you and you rejected her," I say. I motion to Kat, yet again.

A huge smile spreads across Kat's face. "Big mistake," she says enthusiastically. "Big. *Huge.* Now I gotta go do some shopping."

"Are you people *insane?*" Garrett asks. "You show up at my house in fucking formal wear, blast Whitney Houston at me, and hack into my computer —and then you fucking *barf* on me and tell me to—*oh shit.*" Garrett's eyes suddenly bug out of his head. "My wife. Oh, fuck. You gotta get the fuck out of here. Oh, God, no."

We all turn toward the end of the long driveway, just as a sleek black Mercedes pulls in.

"Oh, shit," Garrett blurts, suddenly looking panicked. "Please. I'm begging you. Don't you dare—"

"We won't say a word," I say. "Chill the fuck out, fucktard. I told you. I have no desire to hurt your wife."

A demure brunette walks up to us, a quizzical look on her face, looking every bit the nice girl Kat described, right down to her sweater set and the large cross around her neck.

"What's going on, sweetheart?" the woman asks. She nods at Kat and me. "Who are your friends?"

I put out my hand. "Hi, I'm Kevin. And this is my wife, Whitney. Garrett and I went to school together—we played on the golf team together. Whitney and I were visiting a friend in your neighborhood on our way to a benefit gala so we thought we'd pop by and say a quick hello."

"Oh," the woman says. "Hello."

"I was excited to tell Garrett about our little bun in the oven." I pat Kat's stomach.

An unmistakable shadow passes across the woman's face. "Oh, congratulations. How wonderful. When are you due?"

"Early December," Kat says quietly, clearly picking up on the shift in the woman's demeanor.

There's an awkward beat.

"Oh, gosh. Where are my manners?" the woman says. She extends her hand and shoots daggers at Garrett, clearly chastising him for failing to introduce her. "I'm Maggie Bennett, Garrett's wife. I don't think we've met before?"

"We haven't," I say, shaking her hand. "I was a senior when Garrett was a sophomore, so our paths didn't cross for long. Lovely to meet you, Maggie."

"Would you like to come inside?" she asks. "I baked brownies today."

"No, thank you. Whitney and I have that gala to attend. We just wanted to stop by and say a quick hello and, you know, reminisce about old times for a minute." I shake Garrett's hand. "Great to see you again, buddy. Like I was saying, man, I owe you big. *Huge.* I'll never forget the favor you did for me. Thanks again."

"Oh my goodness," Maggie says, putting her hand on her heart. "What on earth did Garrett do for you?"

"Oh. He gave me some life-changing advice," I say.

"Life-changing advice? Really? What was it if you don't mind me asking?" She looks at her husband like he's got three eyes.

"I don't mind at all," I say. "Garrett told me, 'When you find The One, hold onto her and never let her go. Because all great happiness in a man's life comes from finding his one true love. I should know.'"

"Wow," Maggie says, obviously completely shocked. "*Garrett* told you that? *My* Garrett?"

"He sure did."

Kat pats Maggie's shoulder like she's petting a German Shepherd. "It was so nice to meet you, Maggie. Garrett was just telling us how wonderful you are —and now I see what he was talking about."

"He was?" Maggie says, seemingly dazed.

"Bye, Garrett," Kat says. "Thank you so much for what you did for Kevin. It sure worked out well for me."

Garrett shifts his weight.

"Well," I say, "I guess I'd better tell my buddy we're on our way—he's waiting for us at the gala. Excuse me." I pull out my phone and text Henn: "I bagged the babe. She said YES. Fuck yeah! Exit The Asshole's system now."

"Congratulations!" Henn writes back. "I'll leave without a trace."

I look up at Garrett. "Okay, my buddy says he's gonna quit working now." I look at Maggie. "A mutual friend of ours from school. Great guy. A computer specialist. He says he's leaving work right now to meet us at the gala."

There's a very awkward silence. Clearly, Maggie doesn't know why the fuck I'm telling her this bit of information.

"Okay," she says awkwardly.

"Well, we've definitely taken up enough of your time," I say, grabbing Kat's hand and pulling her toward the limo. "Come on, Whitney—time to party, honey." I kiss Kat's cheek. "Have I ever told you you're really *fun?*"

Kat giggles. "Yes, you have."

"Well, you are. And as far as I'm concerned, that's one of the greatest qualities any man could ever ask for in a wife."

121

KAT

I lean back from the table as our private butler clears our plates from dinner and then disappears through French doors leading back into our suite.

"Are you chilly?" Josh asks. He stands, obviously intending to remove his tuxedo jacket for me.

"No. I'm good. It's still pretty nice out. Great idea to eat out here on the patio."

"I wanted to take full advantage of the view in the moonlight."

I look out at the dark Pacific Ocean glimmering in the moonlight beyond the cliffs. "Yeah, this view is absolutely spectacular."

"I was talking about you."

"Aw." I bat my eyelashes. "Sweet-talker."

"You really are gorgeous, Kat. You take my breath away."

"I guess complete happiness looks good on me, huh?"

"You sure you're not cold?" Josh asks. "It's getting a bit chilly out here. I don't want you to catch cold."

"I'm fine. The kumquat must be some kind of internal furnace—I'm never cold these days." I look down at the sparkling rock on my finger and the convertible Porsche on my wrist and touch the beachside condo around my neck. "Plus, it's amazing how lots and lots of ice keeps a girl toasty warm," I add.

Josh laughs.

The butler approaches the table. "Are we ready for dessert?" he asks.

"Yes, that'd be great," Josh says. "Just bring us a sampling of your best stuff. And I'll have some Sambuca, too."

"Very good, sir. Madame?"

I touch my belly. "No Sambuca for me. Just a decaffeinated cappuccino would be great."

"Very good," the butler says, and leaves.

"This is so fun," I say, giggling. "I guarantee you, if Sarah were here, she'd be calling that poor guy Jeeves all night long."

Josh smiles. "And singing that Iggy Azalea song."

I sing the chorus from "Fancy."

"Yep. That's the one," Josh says. "I'll send Jonas the info about this hotel so he can bring Sarah here for a weekend of relaxation."

"Awesome. Maybe the four of us could come here together—a last hurrah before the baby comes?"

"Sure, but only if we get separate suites. No more listening to each other having sex through paper-thin walls ever again, thank you very much."

"Babe, this suite is massive—bigger than my parents' entire house. I'm pretty sure we could share it with Jonas and Sarah and not hear each other having sex."

Josh shakes his head. "Not if you're gonna scream the way you did in Caracas. Jesus, woman, that was the shriek heard 'round the world—or at least throughout South America." He snickers.

I smile. "Yeah, that was a good one."

"Good times," Josh agrees. "I'm getting hard just remembering it. Do you see what you do to me? I can't get enough of you."

"Well, that's good, because you're stuck with me now." I hold up my hand with my engagement ring on it. "No refunds or exchanges."

Josh laughs.

I look at my ring for a long moment, dazzled. "How the heck did this happen? I'm not trying to talk you out of the whole will-you-marry-me-thing, believe me, but what the fuckity happened to the guy who not too long ago didn't even mention he was moving to Seattle?"

Josh shrugs. "It's not a *thinking* thing—it's a *feeling* thing. You're The One and I know it and nothing will ever change that fact as long as I draw breath into this body."

I swoon.

Josh leans forward. "But enough talking about our fucking feelings. Let's talk about the wedding. You wanna marry me before or after Gracie makes her screaming entrance?"

"Oh, before, definitely," I say. "I wanna be Mrs. Faraday when I check into that hospital. Is that okay with you?"

"Whatever you say, hot momma. I'd marry you tomorrow."

I know Josh is saying that as a figure of speech, but, for a brief moment, I actually consider marrying Josh tomorrow down at City Hall and calling it a day. "No, tomorrow's no good," I finally conclude, scrunching up my face. "I want to wear a pretty white dress and I definitely want my entire family there. And not just my parents and brothers—the whole Morgan-enchilada. I've got a pretty big extended family—I should warn you—lots of aunts and uncles and cousins—and some of them pretty effing crazy—and I'd want them all there. Fasten your seatbelt."

Josh purses his lips, thinking. "Hmm. Well, if we're aiming to do this before Gracie arrives, we'd better not wait too long. We definitely don't want you going into labor while we're saying our vows. That would totally fuck everything up for me."

"Fuck everything up for *you*?" I say, laughing.

"Yeah, it'd fuck up my dream wedding." He shoots me a snarky smile. "I've been dreaming of my perfect wedding since I was a little boy."

I burst out laughing and we giggle together for a long time.

"Okay, let's get serious for a second, Party Girl," Josh says. "If we're gonna do this wedding thing before Gracie comes, we really don't have that much time to pull our shit together." He looks up, apparently calculating something. "I'm thinking we've got, what, three months tops before we're potentially butting up against your water possibly breaking as you say 'I do'?"

"Yeah. Sounds about right. Actually, I'd rather we aim for two months, just to be on the safe side. I'd like to have a little extra time after the wedding to relax before the kumquat shows up and fucks everything up."

"Okay. Two months. How many people are we talking about here? I've probably got, oh, I dunno, twenty people I genuinely care about being there? Give 'em all a plus-one and let's say forty."

"For me it's about fifty people, plus give everyone a guest. So a hundred?"

"Okay, so we're talking a hundred-fifty people max, right? Sixty days from now?"

I shrug. "When you say it like that, it sounds impossible."

He waves me off. "Bah. Totally doable."

"You think?"

"Oh, yeah. Easy peasy. You forget—I've got T-Rod in my back pocket. She can hire a wedding planner and throw gobs of money at the whole thing and it'll happen like magic. No worries. Will you still be allowed to travel in eight weeks?"

"Yeah, I've got twelve weeks—I'm supposed to stay put beginning at thirty-two weeks."

"Okay, perfect. Why don't we do a destination wedding in eight weeks? Plus a two-week honeymoon after that? Then we'll come home and hunker down and get ready for the arrival of Mademoiselle Terrorist."

My heart skips a beat. "A destination wedding? Where?"

"I dunno. A medieval castle in France? A vineyard in Tuscany? The beach in Bora Bora? Bali? Fiji? You pick."

"Oh my God, Josh. Slow down."

"Why? Any of those would be a blast."

I place my hand on my racing heart. "I'm overwhelmed. Gimme a minute."

"Please don't barf, Kat. I love you, I really do, but I'm not sure my love can withstand watching you barf more than once a day."

I squint at him. "Don't tempt me."

He laughs.

"But, seriously, I might hurl if you keep talking about flying a hundred-fifty people to France or Bora Bora in eight weeks. I'm sorry to be Debbie Downer here, but some of my peeps probably don't even have passports. Not everyone is used to gallivanting all over the world on a moment's notice to party with Gabrielle LeMonde's daughter."

He rolls his eyes.

"And, even if my peeps have passports, they wouldn't be able to afford taking off work and getting themselves to France or Bora Bora just to watch me get married."

Josh waves his hand dismissively. "Babe, *duh*. Whatever we do, I'll pick up the tab for everyone, all expenses paid. We'll fly them to wherever and show 'em a great time. We'll take over some resort for an entire week."

"Are you serious?"

"Of course."

"Holy shitballs, I'm crapping my pants," I say. I put my hand on my heart again. "You would do that?"

"Kat, it's our *wedding*. I'm only doing this once. YOLO, baby. Go big or go home. Work hard, play hard. We can sleep when we're dead." He grins. "I'm sure there's another spiffy little catch-phrase that would be even more *apropos* than all those, but you get the gist."

"My family's gonna lose their freaking minds."

"Good. Shit-stained pants and psychotic breaks are what we're going for here."

"But I still think something international is too ambitious," I say. "Just too many logistics. Plus, from here on out, I wanna stay in the U.S. 'til after Gracie's born—just in case she decides to make an early appearance."

"Yeah, probably a good idea. I didn't think about that. Hmm. Well, that really limits our choices for the 'destination' part of our 'destination wedding,' doesn't it?" He pouts.

"Sorry to rain on your parade, Groomzilla." I assess Josh's beautiful, pouting face for a moment. "You know what? Let's just do it in Seattle, babe. It'd be so much easier for everyone."

Josh looks aghast. "Seattle? Fuck no. Jonas just did that. I'm *Josh*. I gotta show that bastard up. Plus, it's my duty to show everyone the Playboy Razzle-Dazzle."

I roll my eyes. "Okay, so how about here in Del Mar, then?" I say. "This resort's spectacular."

"Yeah, we could do that." He shrugs. "Or maybe Hawaii?"

My eyes light up.

"Oh, I see that little gleam in your eye, PG. The idea of Hawaii floats your boat, huh?" He snickers. "You dreaming of doing a little wedding-night hula-dance on my face?"

"Yes, Josh. That's precisely what I was thinking just now."

He laughs.

"Really, we should just do Seattle, babe," I say. "It'll be easier. I have a huge extended family—lots and lots of batshit-crazy aunts and uncles and cousins. Plus, my mom and dad have longtime friends who are like family to me, and I really want them there—"

"Babe, we're not going for easy here—we're going for *awesome*. Case closed. Decision made. I saw the look in your eye when I said Hawaii, and I'm in the fantasy-fulfillment business, remember? Hawaii it is."

I open my mouth to protest.

"It's settled. It's an easy five-hour flight from the west coast; it's still the U.S. but it feels like a faraway tropical paradise; and you said your family's never been. Just give me your list and we'll make it happen. Easy peasy."

I pause. "Seriously?"

"Yeah."

"And you really think we can pull this off just eight weeks from now?"

"Of course. This is exactly why I pay T-Rod an ungodly amount of money. I get the crazy ideas and she makes 'em happen. She'll find us a venue—you really can't go wrong anywhere in Hawaii, so we'll let her pick which island and resort depending on availability. And if we have to do it mid-week or some-thing to book a good place on such short notice, we'll do it. Bada-bing-bada-boom."

I squeal. "Okay. If you really think we can pull it off. Wow. That's exciting. Done." I clap my hands together.

"Shit, that was easy," Josh says. "That was like planning a wedding with a dude."

"I told you right from the start—I'm an honorary dude."

Josh snorts. "Yeah, yet another big ol' steaming pile of bullshit brought to you by Katherine Ulla Morgan." He snorts again. "You *said* that, but it didn't turn out to be *quite* as true as the brochure promised."

I want to be pissed, but it's impossible. I laugh heartily.

"So you got any must-haves?" Josh asks. "Speak now or forever hold your peace. Time's already tickin'."

I think for a minute. "Well, I definitely wanna wear a pretty white dress. I don't care if I'm pregnant, I'm still your virgin-bride, right?"

"Absolutely. I've never fucked you as Mrs. Faraday before. That's virgin enough for me."

"And I want my family and best friends there, of course." I twist my mouth, considering. "If we're doing this in Hawaii, then I'd like to get married on a beach at sunset, right on the sand. And I don't wanna wear shoes. I think it'd be hilarious if I were barefoot and pregnant."

Josh laughs. "Awesome."

"You like that idea?" I ask.

"Of course. I love it. Why wouldn't I?"

"Because if we're gonna do a beach-on-the-sand-thing, you can't really wear one of your fancy suits."

"Whoa, whoa, whoa. Them's fighting words, babe. Why the fuck not? I'm wearing a tux to my wedding, no matter where it is. If it's on the beach, I won't wear shoes—but I'm wearing a goddamned tuxedo to my own wedding. I'm the *groom*."

I giggle. "Sorry, Playboy. Momentary insanity on my part."

"Jesus," Josh says, mock-glaring at me. "Don't even joke about me not getting my dream wedding."

I laugh.

"We gotta look like the bride and groom on top of a wedding cake."

I laugh again. "Wow, you've actually thought about this, haven't you?"

"Hey, I know," Josh says, his eyes lighting up. "Why don't we have everyone go barefoot? The theme can be black-tie barefoot-and-pregnant."

"Dude, you should be a party planner. It's brillz."

"Yeah, I'm liking this," Josh says, his eyes sparkling. "What else, Party Girl?"

"I'd like to have a kick-ass band at the reception. Dancing is definitely one of my bridezilla demands."

"I'll put Reed in charge of getting us a kick-ass band. He'll get someone awesome for us, I'm sure."

My heart is beginning to race with excitement. "Oh, and a fully-stocked, open bar all night long so everyone but me can get shit-faced drunk."

Josh rolls his eyes. "You really feel the need to say that explicitly to me? Do you also feel the need to tell me you want *food* at our wedding? How about toilet paper in the bathroom?"

I get up from my chair and fling myself onto Josh's lap. "Thank you so much. This is the best day of my life."

"From this day forward, my goal is to make you say that every day of your life."

I kiss him. "Thank you. This is amazing."

"Hang on," Josh says, pulling out his phone. "Lemme shoot T-Rod a quick text. If I tell her the gist tonight, by tomorrow she'll have a list of potential venues for us, I guarantee it. And then you can work with her and whatever wedding planners she hires to get everything exactly the way you want it."

I purse my lips. "It's funny," I say. "After all the wedding planning I helped Sarah with, I really don't have any thumping desire to do it all again, even if it's for me this time. I think I just wanna show up, basically."

"Hey, maybe you are a dude, after all," Josh says. He pokes his fingertip into my crotch. "Are you sure you don't have a dick and balls under there?"

"Nope. Definitely a vagina and uterus." I pat my belly.

"Okay, I'll tell Theresa to talk to you about basic vision and whatever's on your wish list and she'll take it from there. Sound good? We'll both show up and look fucking gorgeous and enjoy whatever treats Theresa's lined up for us."

"That sounds really nice."

"It does, doesn't it? That's how I run pretty much my whole life—I just show up looking fucking gorgeous and enjoy the treats."

I nuzzle my nose into his. "You do that really well, Playboy." I kiss Josh's soft lips and I'm instantly aroused. "You know," I purr. "I thanked you for my diamond necklace and bracelet, but I never thanked you for my beautiful ring."

"Oh," Josh says, raising an eyebrow. "Well, shit, we'd better remedy that situation right away."

"Here we are," the butler says, out of nowhere, making us both flinch. He lays down a platter of desserts on the table.

"Change of plans," Josh says abruptly. "Sorry, Jeeves. We've decided we'd prefer privacy for the rest of the night."

"Yes, sir."

"Just bring the desserts inside. I'm sure we'll nibble them later."

"Yes, sir."

The butler picks up the platter of scrumptious looking desserts and quickly disappears into the suite.

The moment we hear the front door open and close, Josh smirks wickedly. "Guess what, my lovely fiancée?"

"What?"

He reaches into his pocket and tosses a poker chip onto the table. "It's time for your bachelorette party."

122

KAT

I'm sitting on the edge of the bed in our hotel bedroom, completely naked except for the startling array of diamonds decorating me, while Josh stands before me, still fully dressed in his immaculate tuxedo, looking like Richard Gere *wishes* he looked in *Pretty Woman*. Holy hell, he's an utterly gorgeous man.

"It turns me on seeing you naked and dripping in diamonds," Josh says, reaching out to caress one of my erect nipples. "Now I wanna see you naked and dripping down your thighs."

"I'm already well on my way," I manage to say. But I can barely speak. I've suddenly got the delicious idea that Josh's reference to my "bachelorette party" means I'm about to behold the sexiest man alive re-enacting *Magic Mike* just for me, and I can barely keep it together at the mere thought.

Josh heads over to his laptop and "Kiss Me" by Lil Wayne begins playing.

Immediately, I giggle with nostalgia. This is the song Josh taunted me with (and brought me to orgasm with) on the dance floor during our first night out together in Las Vegas. "A walk down memory lane," I say. "God, that feels like a lifetime ago."

Josh grins mischievously. "That night was when I first realized you're not like anyone else."

I smile from ear to ear. "Are you gonna dance for me the way you did on the dance floor that night—only this time with a lot less clothes on, hopefully?"

"Ssh. No questions. That poker chip gets me *my* fantasy, not yours."

I giggle. "Sure, Playboy. This whole day has been about *your* fantasies."

"It has been." He looks me up and down lasciviously and bites his lip. "And if it hasn't been, then it sure as fuck is now. Hot damn, woman, you're giving me a raging boner. Look at you. *Fuck*, you're hot."

I flash him a naughty smile. "Well, send that raging boner my way—I know just what to do with it."

"That's not how this bachelorette party works."

"No?"

"Nope." He trails his fingertip over my necklace. "If you want a show, you gotta earn it. Touch yourself for me—turn yourself on. The more turned-on you get, the more articles of clothing come off. Reach orgasm, and you'll get the fully monty."

"Oh," I say. "So you're a *Magic Mike* wind-up doll, powered by sexual arousal—like how in *Monster's, Inc.* they powered the city with little-kid-screams?"

"Exactly." He bends down like he's gonna kiss me, but instead, he gently licks the cleft in my chin. "Guys in strip clubs work for dollar bills—the Playboy works for orgasms."

I giggle.

"Now come on. No more chitty-chat. It's time to play my game." Josh squares himself in front of me and lowers his chin. "Power me up, baby."

"Yes, sir," I purr. I reach between my legs, my eyes fixed on his gorgeous face.

"Other hand," he commands. "I wanna see my rock sparkling between your legs."

Wordlessly, I switch hands, never looking away from his smoldering eyes.

A few moments later, a soft moan escapes my mouth that seems to flip the "on" switch on my *Magic Mike* wind-up doll. Josh begins swiveling his hips and singing along to the song, his eyes instantly on fire.

"Oh," I say. "Work it, baby. You're so sexy, you should be illegal," I purr.

Damn, this boy can *move.*

Another moan involuntarily escapes my mouth, and, in response, Josh removes his jacket with a sexy flourish.

"Oh yeah, take it off," I growl.

I let out a long, loud moan and Josh immediately begins unbuttoning his shirt, revealing taut muscles, sexy tattoos, and sexy nipples standing on end.

"Oh, Jesus," I say. "You're so freaking hot, babe."

Josh peels off his shirt and throws it across the room, his body gyrating, his eyes devouring me. "Kiss me," Josh sings along to the song, a devilish gleam in his eyes. "Kiss me."

"Oh my God," I sputter. "Come here and kiss me. I can't stand it."

"Make yourself come first."

"Get the hell over here and kiss me," I coo, "and I guarantee I will."

Much to my happy surprise, Josh complies with my request, gyrating his body an inch away from my face to the bass-heavy beat of the music.

Like a woman possessed, I pull him into my face and devour his abs with my lips and tongue, my fingers fumbling frantically with his belt and zipper.

Oh God, I'm hyperventilating with desire. He's truly the sexiest man alive, especially when he dances.

When I've loosened Josh's belt and pants, I yank his pants down, desperate for him—and I'm met with the unexpected sight of his huge bulge straining behind briefs emblazoned with... a large Batman logo right on his bull's-eye.

"Holy... *Batman*, Batman!" I breathe.

Josh laughs. "A little present for you, baby," he says. "Happy Bachelorette Party, Party Girl." He leaps back and does a sexy little dance for me, rocking his hips, flexing every muscle on his body, kissing his own biceps—and when I shudder with a little orgasm, he attacks me, sliding his fingers into my wetness and his mouth on my breast.

I stroke the outside of his briefs, grasping frantically at his Batman-bulge—my body boiling over with desire. "Holy Fuck Me Now, Batman," I breathe, pulling down his briefs and letting his hard-on spring out. "Holy I'm Gonna Get Fucked by Batman, Batman. Holy Batman's Got a Donkey-Dick, Batman. Holy... Fuck..."

"Okay, you can stop now," he whispers.

He slides his briefs completely off and hurls them across the room and I lick the side of his enormous shaft like it's a melting popsicle on a sunny day, and then greedily take his glistening mushroom-tip into my mouth like it's liquid chocolate.

When Josh's balls begin rippling against my palm, ramping up for ejaculation, he pulls his donkey-dick out of my mouth, turns me around, bends me forcefully over the edge of the bed, and shocks the living hell out of me by slapping my ass *hard*.

I gasp, paralyzed with shock. Not What I Was Expecting at This Particular Moment, Batman. For the love of all things holy, I'm sitting here covered in sparkling diamonds. The man has asked me to be his *bride*. I'm gonna be this man's beloved *wife*—the saintly mother of his *child*—which is currently growing inside me as surely as Jesus grew inside the Madonna—*and he just spanked the motherfucking shit out of me like a two-dollar whore?*

But Josh is in the zone, apparently bound and determined to show his fiancée just how much he owns her. He spanks me again—this time even harder—and every nerve ending in my body explodes with sudden, outrageous pleasure.

Josh blasts me one more time and I'm gone, hurtling into an orgasm that sends me reeling with vision-blurring pleasure. When my orgasm finishes, Josh grabs my hair, pulls my head back roughly, and enters my wetness powerfully, like a wild stallion mounting a defenseless mare in a freaking pasture. Holy shit-balls, he's claiming me as his property—there's no doubt about it. *And I love it.*

Oh, God, yes. This is good. How the hell does this man always know the shortcut into my deepest desires? *Yes, yes, yes.* Before Josh, the men I've been with have treated me with kid gloves—like a very pretty and fragile trophy—

and I guess I thought once Josh asked me to be his wife, he'd fuck me differently somehow—with some sort of newfound reverence and awe. But I should have known better. Josh always knows what's gonna get me off hardest at any given moment—and right now is no exception.

Oh, God, *yes*. Delicious. The diamonds around my neck are slapping my skin with each pounding thrust of Josh's muscled body into mine. I reach down and fondle his balls behind me—God, I love the sensation of those suckers slapping my ass as he fucks the crap out of me.

I slowly move my fingertips from Josh's balls to the place where his hard donkey-dick is pounding into me, and my body shudders with indescribable pleasure. This man is all mine. *Forever.*

"I wanna call you Mrs. Faraday," Josh growls out. "I'm gonna make you my *wife*."

I shriek as another orgasm powers through me, twisting my insides violently.

At the sound of my orgasm, Josh pulls out of me, bends down behind me, and begins eating me through the back door, lapping at me, sucking me, gnawing on me—all the while fingering-fucking me, too—and my body responds with complete and utter rapture. Where the fuck did this man learn the stuff he does to me? It's like he's some sort of sexual Jedi. Oh, Holy... Oh, shit. I'm on the cusp of truly losing my mind.

A strangled cry lurches out of my throat. Oh my God.

Josh shifts his fingers inside me and begins flicking at me in a way he's never done before, and it's more than I can bear. I'm seeing pink. Then yellow. Oh, shit.

He does it again and then again—and it's like he's turned a key to a secret room inside me. My skin pricks with goose bumps. My toes curl. I feel like I'm being jolted with an electric current.

Josh flicks inside me again on that same weird spot and, all of a sudden, I feel my entire body unlock for him in a whole new way—a dam bursting inside me—and not figuratively. A shocking torrent of warm fluid absolutely gushes out of me, more than ever before... and pours right into Josh's waiting mouth.

"Oh my God," I sputter, my entire body warping and flailing.

Josh laps at me feverishly for several more minutes, cleaning me like he's licking icing off a cupcake, and finally turns my limp body over onto my back on the bed, slides his massive dick inside me, and thrusts powerfully into me again from this new position. His mouth lands on mine. His warm skin brushes against my breasts and baby bump. Oh God, I'm absolutely enraptured.

This man is my master. I'm his slave—and not as part of a freakin' role-play. I genuinely have no free will left. I'm his to command—mind, body and soul.

"I'm gonna make you my wife," Josh growls into my ear. "I'm gonna give you my name." He kisses me passionately.

"Yes," I choke out.

Josh grips my face, covering me in kisses. His lips find my ear. "Don't leave me, Kat," he says, his muscled body moving against mine, his voice tight. "I need you. Don't leave me."

I grab his muscled ass, urging him to burrow into me even more deeply. "I'll never leave you. I love you. *Forever.*"

He comes inside me, quite forcefully, growling and shuddering as he does—and when he's done, he grabs my face again, his eyes blazing with an intensity I've never seen from him before. "I can't live without you. I can't breathe without you, can't smile or laugh." He doesn't even sound like himself. "I love you. Oh, God, baby, I love you so much, it hurts. I've never risked this much before—I'm risking *everything.* Please, God, don't leave me, Kat. It would destroy me." He clutches me to him fiercely, his chest rising and falling violently, his breathing ragged, his skin drenched in sweat. "I've never loved like this, Kat. *Please.*" His words are tumbling out. He's trembling. He buries his nose into my neck and I stroke his hair, soothing him. "Please, Kat," he chokes out. "Don't leave me. I couldn't overcome it."

"It's okay, baby," I say calmly, stroking his hair. "I'll never leave you. *Never.*" I rub his back, coaxing him to calmness. "You're okay, baby. Ssh. We're gonna be happy, honey. We're gonna have a beautiful family, you and me and a pretty baby makes three. And whenever you don't know what to do, it'll be okay because I'll teach you."

He's shaking. "I love you, Kat."

"I love you, too, baby. Don't you worry about a thing. We're gonna be happy forever and ever. You'll see. We're gonna be a family—a *happy* family. It's gonna be better than your wildest dreams. I promise."

He's calm now. His breathing is regular. He's stopped shaking.

"Okay?" I ask.

He nods into the crook of my neck. "Okay."

I kiss his cheek and continue stroking his back. "I love you, honey. I'm not going anywhere, I promise. If you fuck up, so what? I'll be patient. And when I'm insane, you'll be patient with me. And if you don't know what to do, then I'll teach you. No big whoop. Okay?"

"Okay."

I kiss his cheek again. "I'm gonna love you and take care of you forever, baby. You'll see. You won't need to overcome a goddamned thing. Those days are over, baby. I got you. I promise."

123

JOSH

"Hey, Uncle William, will you tie Henn's bowtie?" I ask. "I'd do it, but I'm so nervous my fingers won't function."

Uncle William laughs. "Sure thing. Come here, Peter."

"If this bowtie were a motherboard," Henn says, "I swear it'd be my bitch."

"It's hard to tie a bowtie," Uncle William reassures Henn. "Much harder than it looks."

"See, Reed?" Henn says. "It's not me that's the problem—it's the bowtie."

Reed laughs. "Keep telling yourself that, man."

"All the chairs are filled," Jonas murmurs quietly. He's peeking out a crack in the bungalow door toward the beach. "Everyone looks really excited."

"Gah. Don't tell me that," I say. "I'm nervous enough already."

"What do you have to be nervous about, Faraday?" Reed asks. "You're marrying the greatest girl, ever."

"Which is exactly why I'm nervous. I don't wanna fuck this up for her. Hey, Jonas," I call to him at the door. "Were you nervous right before you went out to marry Sarah?"

Jonas shuts the door. "Oh, yeah, I was shitting." He glides toward the group, absently twirling his wedding ring around his finger. "I wasn't nervous about getting married—I was just freaking out I was gonna fuck up my vows."

"*Exactly*," I say. "What if I spontaneously start spewing gibberish up there? Or pass out? Or, worst-case scenario, what if I spontaneously shart in front of everyone?"

Everyone bursts out laughing, except Uncle William.

"What's *sharting*?" Uncle William asks.

"When you think you're gonna fart, but you unexpectedly shit instead," Henn explains.

Uncle William laughs and shakes his head. "*Joshua.*"

"Well, let's look at this logically," Reed says. "When was the last time you sharted?"

"Hmm," I say. "Maybe when I was ten?"

"Okay, then, realistically, the odds are extremely low it will happen within the next thirty minutes for the first time in twenty years," Reed says.

"God willing," I say.

"Unless, of course, it's been so long, you're now statistically *overdue*," Henn says.

"Not helpful, Henn," I say. "In what universe would you ever think that's a helpful thing to say?"

"Sorry."

Jonas puts his hand on my shoulder. "Josh, you got this. If *I* can say my vows without sharting, then you most certainly can." He flashes me a warm smile and I'm struck, as I often am these days, by how genuinely happy my brother seems.

"You know what, Jonas?" I say. "You should wear black-tie more often, bro —it suits you. You've got this Thor-meets-James-Bond thing going on."

Jonas scoffs. "I feel more like I've got an Idiot-Brother-meets-Dancing-Monkey-thing going on."

"All done," Uncle William says, patting Henn on his shoulder. He turns Henn to face me. "Acceptable, Joshua?"

"Suave perfection," I say. "You're Cary-Grant-meets-Steve-Jobs, Henn."

Reed sidles up to me with a bottle of Patron. "A little something to calm the jitters, Faraday?"

"Just a little sip," I say, grabbing the bottle. "Any more than that and I might spontaneously shart from being too relaxed." I take a quick sip and then pass the bottle around.

"Pretty good," Uncle William says when the bottle makes its way to him. "But at the reception, we're all drinking my Scotch."

"Did you bring the good stuff?" I ask.

"Of course. I brought several different bottles to be shared at the party, plus I've got bottles of some forty-year-old stuff for each of you boys to take home."

"Bottles of what now?" Henn asks, his face perking up.

"Scotch," I answer. "From my uncle's private stash. Whatever it is, it'll change your life, I guarantee it."

"Well, don't mind if I do," Henn says. "Thanks, Uncs." He pats my Uncle on the back.

Uncle William laughs. "You're very welcome, Peter. Do you boys know anything about Scotch?" he asks, and when Henn and Reed both admit they're fairly clueless, my uncle proceeds to school both of them on the topic.

"Hey, Jonas?" I say. "Can I talk to you for a second?"

We move to the corner of the bungalow.

"You okay?" Jonas asks.

I nod. "Just a lot more nervous than I expected to be." I shake out my arms. "It's taken me a lifetime to get here. I don't wanna fuck it up."

Jonas looks at me sympathetically. "Just take a deep breath. It'll be over soon."

"No, not the ceremony. The *marriage*. I don't wanna fuck it up."

"You won't. You never fuck anything up."

I scoff. "We both know that's a load of complete bullshit. Got any advice for me?"

"Just imagine everyone naked," Jonas says. "Except Sarah. Definitely don't picture Sarah naked or I'll have to punch you in your pretty face."

"No, don't give me advice about saying my vows—gimme your best advice for a happy marriage. You're the happiest married guy I know."

Jonas shrugs. "Well, I haven't been married all that long—but, yeah, I guess I already know the secret. Put her happiness ahead of your own every single day and it'll come back to you ten-fold."

"You sound like a fortune cookie."

He laughs. "Yeah, just add 'in bed' to anything I say."

"Thank you, Jonas," I say. "That's exactly what I'll do. I'll worship her every fucking day."

"In bed," Jonas says. Emotion washes over his face and he hugs me. "I'm so happy for you, Josh. You've been my rock my whole life, and I don't know what I would have done—"

"Whoa, whoa, whoa," I say, pushing him away. "Bro, we just did this exact thing mere *months* ago at your wedding. Do we really need to talk about our fucking feelings *again* so fucking soon?"

Jonas laughs. "But, Josh—talking lets the feelings out."

We both laugh.

"Honestly," I say, "I love you, bro, I really do, but I don't have a pressing need to articulate every warm and gooey feeling I have about you more than, say, once a year?"

"Fine by me," Jonas says, shrugging. "Once a year sounds good. And, by the way, I love you, too."

"Gah. Stop. What'd I just say? Once a year, bro. How 'bout we do it on our birthday?"

"Great. I'll mark it on my calendar: 'Remember to tell Josh I love him today and that he's the best brother a guy could ever hope for.'"

"I think you just did an end-run around that one-year thing," I say.

Jonas winks. "I'm smart like that. Remember? I'm the smart one, and you're the good-looking one."

"No, I don't think that's how things got divvied up. You're the smart one *and* good-looking one, Jonas. I'm the *charming* one."

"And we're both the *happy* ones," Jonas says.

We share a huge smile.

"Did you ever think life would turn out like this for us?" Jonas asks, shaking his head.

I join him in shaking my head. "Never. Like, literally, *never*. Things weren't looking too good for the Faraday brothers for a while, but we've pulled victory out of the jaws of defeat, haven't we?"

"Definitely."

The wedding planner pokes her head into the bungalow. "We're ready for you gentlemen now. Time to take your positions on the beach." She looks at her watch. "We have to time this with the sunset, so you've got to be in position in five."

"Thanks," I say to her.

Jonas and I hug.

"Congratulations, Josh," he says.

"Couldn't have done it without you, bro—you showed me how to do it."

Jonas flashes a huge smile.

"Thank you, Jonas."

Jonas nods. "My pleasure."

I take a deep breath and turn toward the rest of the guys. "Ready, men?"

Everyone says they're ready and raring to go.

"Reed, hand me that tequila one more time."

Reed hands me the bottle of Patron and I take another huge swig—and everyone does the same thing right after me.

I put my hand on Jonas' shoulder. "Hey, bro, you got a Plato quote for me to think about when I'm up there, just in case I suddenly feel like I'm gonna spontaneously shart?"

"Of course. 'Courage is knowing what *not* to fear.' And the one thing *never* to fear is spontaneous sharting."

Everyone laughs.

"Perfect. Thank you. You're a beast of a best-man, Jonas Faraday." I take a deep breath. "Now let's get out there and get me a smokin' hot wife, shall we?"

Everyone expresses enthusiastic agreement with that plan of action.

"Wife on three," I say, putting my hand into the huddle.

Everyone covers my hand with theirs. "One, two, three. *Wife!*" we all shout together, and then throw our hands up.

"I love you, Josh," Jonas says, slapping me on the back.

"No. Stop it."

"I love you, too, Joshy," Henn says, laying his cheek on my shoulder and side-hugging me.

"Me, too," Reed says, laying his cheek on my other shoulder.

"So do I," Uncle William says, patting my cheek.

"Look what you started, motherfucker," I say to Jonas. I shake Reed and Henn off me and they laugh hysterically. "I love you all, too. You're the best guys I know and I'd be lost without each and every one of you. Now, come on, guys. Quit making me say all this shit. I swear to God if I shart up there, I'm blaming all of you."

Everyone laughs and high-fives and passes the tequila around one final time.

"All right. Enough fucking around. My fantasy-girl awaits. Let's get out there and bag me a goddamned gorgeous wife."

124

JOSH

The girl walking toward me on her father's arm is literally the most spectacularly beautiful creature I've ever laid eyes on in my entire life, without exception. She's the precise sum of parts I'd order at the Build-a-Wife store if there were such a thing. Her dress is simple and white—the bottom half of the dress cascading over her round belly and floating like a soft cloud down to the sand.

She's glowing from the inside-out, shining brighter than any diamond—which maybe explains why, despite all the ice I've recently showered her with, she's opted to wear only two items of jewelry for her once-in-a-lifetime walk down the aisle: the ring I slipped onto her finger when I asked her to be my wife and the fucking amazing tear-drop sapphire-and-diamond earrings Uncle William gifted her from his late wife's jaw-dropping collection. "Something old and something blue," Uncle William said to Kat when he gave them to her last week. "But definitely *not* something borrowed—they're all yours, sweetheart. Welcome to the Faraday family."

She's gliding down the aisle with her father, floating like a glorious feather, smiling at people in the audience, and beaming at her father.

And then she locks eyes with me—and every bit of nerves I've been feeling vanishes. Why? Because my future wife is looking at me the exact way Sarah did when she walked down the aisle toward Jonas—the exact way I've longed for someone to look at me my whole fucking life, not even realizing it's what I yearned for most.

Thomas and Kat reach me on the sand, and after kissing Kat's cheek, Thomas gently guides his daughter toward me.

"Make her happy," Thomas whispers to me, shaking my hand.

"Forever," I murmur, taking Kat's slender hand.

I kiss Kat's cheek and whisper to her: "I'm the luckiest man alive."

"I love you," she replies.

"I love you, too."

The officiant—a large Hawaiian guy in a white linen suit, sunglasses, and a lei—welcomes everyone and leads us through our very simple marriage ceremony. Or, at least, that's what I presume he's doing—I'm only half-listening. Because, seriously, what mortal man could possibly concentrate on what a Hawaiian dude in a white suit is saying while looking straight into the face of God's most heavenly creation?

"And now, Josh and Kat have prepared vows for each other," the officiant prompts—grabbing my full attention. "Kat?"

Kat takes a deep breath and squeezes my hand. "Josh," she begins. "*Joshua*. You once asked me if I believe in fate—and I said, no, that I believe in kicking ass."

I laugh and so does everyone in the audience.

"But now I know I was wrong about that. You're my fate, my love—my destiny. I truly believe that every minute of my life up 'til now was engineered by a greater power to bring me to this moment—to *you*—so that I could become your devoted wife." She smiles and her eyes twinkle. "One of the things I love about you most is how you take care of everyone you love. As your wife, I vow to be the one who takes care of *you*, Josh. I promise to love you forever, always making sure your needs and greatest desires are satisfied beyond your wildest dreams. Every single day, I vow to make sure you wake up thinking, 'Damn, I'm a lucky bastard,' and every single night fall asleep thinking, 'I can't wait for tomorrow.'"

We share a huge smile.

"I'll love you forever, Joshua William Faraday," Kat continues. "I promise to love and honor you in good times and in bad, in sickness and in health, all the days of my life and never, ever leave your side as long as I'm drawing breath into my body."

"I love you," I whisper to her. "Thank you."

"I love you forever and ever, my love," Kat whispers. "I promise."

Kat looks at the officiant, signaling she's all done speaking.

"Josh?" the officiant prompts.

Those nerves I felt before the ceremony slam into me again. I take a deep breath and take Kat's beautiful face in my palms. "My beloved Kat." I take another deep breath. "Good God, you're *evil*."

She laughs in obvious surprise.

I take her hands in mine. "And not just evil. Stubborn as hell, too." I flash her a huge smile. "But you're also hilarious. Compassionate. Honest. *Passionate*. Baby, you're hell on wheels. And, most of all, you're loving and kind and beautiful." I stroke her golden hair. "*And I love it all—every single thing about you.*"

The bottoms of her eyes fill with tears.

"When I first laid eyes on you at Jonas' house, you waltzed into the living room and marched straight up to me like I'd ordered you out of a catalog—and right then, I knew I was totally screwed."

Kat laughs along with everyone else.

"But a man has never been so happy or *lucky* to be totally screwed in the history of time."

Kat's face contorts with pure joy.

I take a deep breath. "Katherine Ulla Morgan, you've single-handedly taught me how to love—how to be a man in every sense of the word. You're the answer to a prayer I didn't even know I had. And I vow to you, in front of God and all these witnesses, to cherish you every single day—all parts of you, even the heinously diabolical parts—*especially* the heinously diabolical parts—to make your happiness my mission in this life. If someone hurts you, I'll kick their ass, baby. If you're sad, then I'll make you laugh—unless, of course (for some reason only women can possibly understand), you don't *want* to laugh, in which case I'll simply hold you and let you cry on my shoulder."

She sniffles and laughs.

"Kat, I vow to love you and take care of you and our precious baby." I touch her belly gently. "*All* our babies, in fact, because now that I've become a part of your awesome family, I'm hoping God will gift us with an entire minivan full of them."

Kat's eyes pop out of her head and plop into the sand.

Oh, shit. I don't know where that came from. I haven't mentioned my recently discovered desire for a big family to Kat before this moment. Perhaps during our wedding ceremony wasn't the optimal time for me to lay that idea on her for the first time? Oh, well, fuck it. I am what I am.

I clear my throat and barrel ahead.

"And, most of all, my beloved Kat, I vow to you, right here and now, in front of God and all the people we love, which includes Keane, by the way, just to be clear—"

Every Morgan in attendance bursts out laughing along with Kat and me.

When the Morgans have finally quieted down, I continue speaking again, holding her hands in mine. "Like I was saying, I solemnly vow to you, in front of God and all the people we love, that when I'm eighty, I won't have a baby with a trampy twenty-six-year-old gold digger, even though she'll be at optimal child-bearing age."

Kat hoots with laughter and so do I—and so does everyone watching us, even though, surely, no one but Kat and me fully understands the joke.

I cup Kat's jawline in my palm. "YOLO, Kat," I whisper. "Damn, I'm a lucky bastard that I get to live my one and only life with you." I touch the cleft in her chin. "I. Will. Always. Love. You." I reach into my pocket, pull out a poker chip, and covertly place it into Kat's palm. "I promise to make every day of our life together better than any fantasy, baby. *Forever.*"

125

JOSH

"When Josh asked me to be his best man," Jonas says, speaking into the microphone in his hand, "the first thing I thought was, 'Oh, shit.'"

Everyone seated in the reception room laughs.

"Because I immediately realized I'd have to give this fucking speech—excuse my language—and anyone who knows me will tell you I absolutely *hate* giving speeches, almost as much as I hate hip-hop and One Direction and talking about my fucking feelings—excuse my language again." He grins at Sarah and she beams an adorable smile at him. "So I'm gonna try to keep this short and sweet." Jonas raises his champagne flute and everyone follows suit. "Aristotle says love is composed of a single soul inhabiting two bodies. Well, Josh and Kat, when I look at you two together, and the way you fit together like two halves of a divinely designed puzzle, I know in my bones Aristotle's words remain true to this very day. My wish for you both is that you find eternal light outside the cave together. Welcome to the Faraday family, Kat—and thank you for taking my constantly *emoting* brother off my hands." Jonas raises his glass. "To Josh and Kat. Hear, hear."

"Hear, hear," everyone says, taking a sip of champagne.

"Damn, we Faradays rock," Kat whispers into my ear.

Jonas lurches over to Kat and me and hugs us fervently, and then hands the microphone to his adorable wife.

"Kitty Kat," Sarah begins, smiling. "My best friend and now my *sister*—oh, I just gave myself goose bumps saying that." She giggles and everyone joins her. "Anyone can see how beautiful you are on the outside—it's actually quite unfair how truly gorgeous you are, Kat—but the amazing thing about you, the unexpected thing, is that you're as beautiful on the *inside*, too." Sarah's voice wobbles. "Most people can only dream of having a best friend like you, Kitty Kat—and I'm the lucky bitch who actually does."

Everyone in the reception room laughs.

"I love you so much, Kat," Sarah says.

"I love you, too," Kat mouths, her hand on her heart.

Sarah looks at me, seated next to Kat at the end of our table. "Joshy Woshy. You're quite a beast of a man, you know that?"

Everyone in the reception chuckles and cheers in agreement with that statement.

"Josh, I marvel at your sheer amazingness every day," Sarah continues. "I'm so lucky to be your sister. Thank you for embracing me as part of your family. I love you with all my heart."

"I love you, too," I mouth.

"And to Josh and Kat together—the Playboy and The Party Girl with a Hyphen—the unstoppable duo. The poet Kahlil Gibran said, 'Marriage is the golden ring in a chain whose beginning is a glance and whose ending is Eternity.' It's been thrilling to watch your first glance at Jonas' house turn into the beautiful eternity of today."

Kat rests her cheek on my shoulder and I squeeze her hand.

"But I'd be lying if I didn't admit you two scare the bajeezus out of me," Sarah continues, and everyone in the room chuckles. "Seriously, every time I'm in an enclosed space with you two, I find myself immediately scanning for emergency exits and fire extinguishers."

Everyone laughs again.

Sarah raises her glass. "To Josh and Kat. May you always inspire everyone around you to scan for emergency exits and fire extinguishers. Hear, hear."

"Aw," Kat says next to me, raising her sparkling apple cider.

"Hear, hear," everyone in the room says.

I get up and kiss Sarah's cheek and take the microphone from her.

"Thank you, Sarah. Thank you, Jonas. We love you guys so much. We Faradays are pretty effing cool, I gotta say." I turn toward the smiling faces in the room. "I want to thank you all for joining us, not just for today's celebration, but for this whole past week in paradise. I know you all have busy lives so we thank you for taking so much time to celebrate and party with us this whole week. It's been incredible, hasn't it?"

Everyone claps and cheers.

I glance at Kat and the sight of her makes me completely forget what I was about to say. "Hello, Mrs. Faraday," I say softly, not into the microphone.

Kat blushes. "Hello, Mr. Faraday."

We stare at each other for a beat.

"Better give your speech, honey," she prompts. "People are waiting."

I chuckle and put the microphone to my lips again. "Thank you, dear."

Everyone laughs.

"First off, I'd like to say my first ever toast to Mrs. Katherine Faraday. You rock my world, baby. My greatest joy in this life is the honor and privilege of calling you my wife."

Kat blushes and bats her eyelashes.

"To you, babe. The Party Girl with the Heart of Gold."

Everyone in the room toasts and drinks.

"Oh!" Kat suddenly blurts, her hand on her belly. "Wowza. That was a biggie!"

I lurch toward Kat and she grabs my hand and places it on the side of her belly, and, instantly, I feel someone throwing an upper cut against my hand.

"Whoa!" I shout. This isn't the first time I'm feeling my baby kick, of course —I finally managed to give Little G her first-ever high-five a few weeks ago—but this is by far the strongest movement I've felt. "So cool," I say when Gracie punches me forcefully again. I give Gracie a high-five with my fingertip and she kicks the crap out of my finger, right on cue. I put the microphone to my mouth again. "Sorry about that, folks. Gracie wanted to join the toast to her mommy, I guess. I think she's inside her mommy's belly shouting, 'Hear, hear!'"

Kat pulls the microphone in my hand to her mouth. "We're starting her young," she says, and everyone laughs. Kat hands the microphone back to me. "Come on, babe. These people wanna dance. Wrap it up." She makes a swirling motion with her index finger.

"Okay, just a few more words," I say. "The missus says I gotta wrap it up. I'd like to say a special thanks to my great friend Reed for that incredible surprise earlier. Wasn't that amazing?"

Everyone claps and cheers wildly.

"When Reed asked me what song Kat and I wanted for our first dance, I thought he was gonna arrange for the cover band to play it for us. I truly had no idea he was gonna fly James Bay to Maui." I laugh heartily, thinking about how shocked Kat and I were when James Bay himself waltzed into our reception hall two hours ago and started serenading us on acoustic guitar. I raise my champagne flute to Reed. "Thank you, bro. We'll never forget that moment as long as we live."

Reed points his glass at me and winks.

I guide Kat out of her chair, snake my arm around her ever-growing waist, and pull her to me as I address the room again. "And one last thing. With my beautiful wife by my side, I wanna say a few words of thanks to my new family, The Morgans. There's been a lot of talk about Kat becoming a Faraday today, but, trust me, I got the better end of the bargain. You know that expression 'The apple doesn't fall far from the tree'? Well, that's especially true when it comes to Kat." I raise my glass to Kat's immediate family at their nearby table, and they all return the gesture. "To Tom Tom Club, Momma Lou, Cheese, Captain, Peen, and Baby Brother—and all the Morgans I've met this past week, too—" I raise my glass to the various Morgans seated at tables in the large room. "Thank you for your part in making Kat the incredible woman she is today and for letting me be part of your hilarious and fucking awesome family. Hear, hear."

"Hear, hear," everyone in the room says in unison.

Kat throws her arms around my neck and squeezes me tightly.

"You wanna say a few words?" I whisper to her.

Kat shakes her head. "Hell no. I just wanna *dance.*"

"So, okay," I say into the microphone as Kat squeezes the life out of me. "Mrs. Faraday says enough talking about our fucking feelings—it's time to *dance.*"

126

JOSH

"Fucking motherfucker!" Kat shrieks, squeezing my hand. "Jesus Christ Superstar!"

I lean into Kat's sweaty face. "Do your breathing, babe. Breathe in through your nose and out through your mouth."

"Fuck that shit. *You* breathe in through your nose and out your mouth, motherfucker—I want a fucking epidural!"

"Babe, you heard the doctor—everything happened way too fast for an epidural. We missed the window. Just *breathe.* Like this." I lean into Kat's face and model the breathing we learned at our getting-ready-for-childbirth class at the hospital.

Kat's eyes turn unequivocally homicidal. "If you breathe like that again, I swear I'll cut off your balls and make s'mores out of 'em," she growls.

I bite my lip and cease all breathing.

The monitor attached to Kat tells me she's in the throes of another huge contraction.

"Push now, Kat," the doctor says. "Right now."

"I can't."

"Sure you can," I say. "You're a beast—you can do anything."

"Just gimme a second—fuck!" She lets out a blood-curdling scream. "Motherfucker!"

I look at the doctor, my heart racing. "Is something wrong?"

"Nothing's wrong," the doctor says. "Kat's just *expressing* herself. Isn't that right, Kat?"

Kat whimpers. "December second's not for eleven more days—I needed more time to mentally prepare to do this."

"Sorry, Kat. She's decided to come today," the doctor says. "In about three minutes, I'd estimate."

"But she wasn't supposed to be a *Scorpio*," Kat whines. "She's supposed to be a *Sagittarius*." She lets out a truly pathetic sound. "Please, God, I'll be good and nice from here on out. I'll never lose my temper. I'll be patient. *Saintly*. Just, please, don't give me a goddamned fucking female *Scorpio*." She grips my hand fiercely. "Babe, listen to me. Tell them to stuff her back in for another twenty-four hours. *Please*. Tomorrow, she'll be a sweet little Sagittarius. Please. *Pay them, Josh*. Make them listen."

The monitor hooked up to Kat indicates another huge contraction is hitting her—which is something I'd have surmised without the monitor, based on the string of expletives suddenly spewing from her mouth.

"Push now," the doctor says. "Push with the contraction, Kat. You can do it."

Kat bears down and pushes, as instructed, growling and whimpering as she does.

When the contraction is over, I lean into Kat's sweaty face. "Good job, baby. You're doing great."

"Okay, Kat," Dr. Gupta says. "Two more big pushes and the baby will be out."

"I can't," Kat says, her tone pathetic.

I touch Kat's beautiful, sweaty face. "You can do this, babe." I squeeze her hand. "We're so close."

"What do you mean 'we'? Are you gonna do this? Are you gonna pass a fucking bowling ball?"

"Push now, Kat," the doctor instructs. "*Right now*."

Kat takes a huge breath and bears down, her face turning bright red.

"Good. That's good," Dr. Gupta says. "You're doing great, Kat. Okay. Rest for a moment and then we'll do it one more time."

Kat grips my hand. She's shaking violently. "I'm done," she says meekly. "I can't do any more. Knock me out, Doc. Stuff her back up inside me and cut her out. I don't care. Do whatever you have to do. I quit."

I stroke Kat's beautiful cheek. "You don't know the meaning of the word 'quit.'"

"Yes, I do," Kat whimpers. "I'm not a beast—I want my mommy." She bursts into tears.

"Your mommy's coming as fast as she can. Everyone's on their way, baby. It just happened too fast for them to get here in time."

"I've change my mind. I don't want a baby, after all. Stuff her back in!" she cries. "Make her go away!"

I laugh, even though I shouldn't.

"Here we go," Dr. Gupta says calmly, looking at the monitor next to Kat. "You're gonna push with this next contraction, Kat—one more big push and this baby will be out and you'll be a mommy. Come on."

Kat whimpers pathetically again.

I squeeze Kat's hand. "Come on, baby. Dig deep."

"*You* dig deep, motherfucker," she says, making me chuckle, but, immediately, she bears down, as instructed, grunting loudly with her effort, and not more than twenty seconds later, a tiny, pink angel pops out from between my wife's legs, shrieking like I just woke her up from an afternoon nap in front of the TV by shouting "Boo!"

And, just like that, my heart is no longer inside my body.

My cheeks are absolutely soaking wet.

And I'm exactly the man—the husband and father—I was always meant to be.

127

JOSH

"**B**abe! Get in here!" Kat shrieks. "They just introduced him!"

I throw on a pair of briefs, race out of the bathroom still wet from my shower, and leap onto the bed next to Kat, careful not to crush Gracie's blonde head as she sleeps at Kat's breast.

"There he is!" Kat shrieks, pointing with excitement at the TV.

I look at the television screen and, I'll be damned, yep, there he is: Will "2Real" Riley, holding a microphone and launching into a beastly performance of his monster hip-hop hit, "Crash" on *Saturday Night Live*. "Oh my God!" Kat shrieks. "Look at him! He's *killing* it!"

"I feel electrified just *watching* him," I say. "I can't imagine how he must feel."

"Did you know Will was *this* amazing?"

"I had no idea," I say. "He was so funny and chill when we hung out with him. Who knew?"

"I guess we were hanging out with *Will*, not '2Real,' huh?" Kat says.

"Indubitably," I say.

We sit and watch Will's entire performance, completely mesmerized, and when it's over, we cheer and clap like we're sitting in the live audience.

I grab my phone off the nightstand and quickly shoot a text to Reed. "Just watched your boy on SNL," I write. "HE KILLED IT. Tell him congrats from Mr. and Mrs. Faraday and Little G." I put my phone back on the nightstand. "Jesus, between 2Real and Red Card Riot this past year, Reed's absolutely slaying it."

"God, I sure hope his streak continues into next year when Daxy's album comes out," Kat says.

"Reed sure thinks it will. He told me just the other day he smells a smash hit."

"Which song?"

"Reed predicts 'People Like You and Me' will be the break-out first single."

"That's my favorite, too," Kat says.

Out of nowhere, Gracie busts out with an ear-piercing wail.

"Oh my goodness, little lady," Kat says, opening a flap on her nursing night-gown and pulling out her engorged boob. "No need to scream, for crying out loud. I'm right here." She sticks Gracie on her nipple and Gracie immediately latches on and starts gulping down milk in hungry swallows. "Wowza, can this kid eat," Kat says, looking down at Gracie's little face.

I lay my palm on the top of Gracie's soft head as she suckles and stroke her white-blonde peach fuzz. "She's passionate about eating, that's for sure," I say softly. "Aren't you, my little angel?"

Kat rolls her eyes. "Don't kid yourself by calling her an angel. We both know she's a demon spawn *disguised* as an angel."

"No. She's just *passionate*, like I say—she simply knows what she wants. Nothing wrong with that." I continue gently stroking Gracie's soft head. "Isn't that right, Mademoiselle Terrorist? You're just *assertive,* that's all."

Kat looks down at Gracie's face as she nurses. "Mark my words, she's a wolf in sheep's clothing, I'm telling you, babe. She's gonna be bossing you around in no time."

"Good. I've always liked 'em sassy," I say. "Don't worry, I know just how to handle her."

We share a smile.

"So what do you wanna do for your birthday in a couple weeks, honey?" Kat asks. "After three months of being marooned in Babyville, are you in the mood to break out of our baby-bondage and paint the town red?"

I lean down and nuzzle my nose into Gracie's soft hair for a long moment, breathing in her scent. "Not really," I say softly. "I'm happy to stay home this year. Why don't we do the romantic-dinner-thing I'd originally planned for the night you poker-chipped me with Bridgette?"

"You sure? Thirty-one's a biggie."

I chuckle. "Thirty-one is meaningless."

"Bite your tongue. You didn't think you'd make it to thirty, remember? And now you're gonna be thirty-*one*. That's a big deal."

I make a face like maybe she's got a point.

"You sure you don't wanna get freaky-deaky and do something really wild and crazy to celebrate your unexpected old age?"

I touch Gracie's hand as she continues to eat and she curls her little fingers around my index finger. "No. I had a huge party for my thirtieth. Jay-Z played, actually."

"Oh, well that wasn't excessive or anything."

"So this year I'm ready to have a quiet celebration, just my wife, my baby, and me—a romantic dinner for two-and-a-half—followed by you and me getting freaky-deaky on the carpet in the nursery again after Little G falls asleep." I wink. "I really like the way that carpet feels on my balls."

Without warning, Gracie pulls sharply away from Kat's breast, milk dripping down her chin, and glares at me like she understood every word of what I just said.

We both burst out laughing at the hilariously pissed expression on Gracie's face—and the sound of our laughter makes Gracie break into gurgling peals of adorable laughter, too.

"Take a video of her giggling, babe," Kat says. "Oh my God. She's hilarious!"

I grab my phone and take the video, followed by a whole bunch of photos of Kat and Gracie together. But after a moment, Gracie begins fussing so Kat tries to get her to feed off her other boob.

"Aw, come on, Gracie-cakes," Kat says. "Don't you want my other boob? You're gonna leave me lopsided, baby."

Gracie breaks into a pterodactyl scream.

"What the heck?" Kat says. "She gets riled up so freaking fast, I swear to God."

"Gee," I say. "I wonder where she gets *that*?"

"Definitely not from me," Kat sniffs—and much to my surprise, she sounds completely serious. But before I can reply to her and tell her she's a delusional loon, my phone buzzes with an incoming call from Reed.

"Oh, it's Reed—I wanna take this." I leap out of bed and sprint out of the bedroom, far away from Gracie's loud shrieks, to take the call.

"Tell him congrats from me!" Kat calls to my back.

"Reed!" I shout into the phone. "Congrats, man! Your boy *killed* it!"

"Oh my God. Didn't he? He hit a fucking homerun, man."

"A grand slam in the bottom of the ninth," I say. "We were screaming at the TV like we were right there in the audience. Was he loving it?"

"Yeah, afterwards, for sure. But beforehand, he was so nervous, he puked into a trashcan. Oh my God—you should have seen him, worse than you were right before your wedding." He laughs. "This is the first major performance Will's given since the whole Carmen thing. She's normally the one who calms him down when he gets really amped."

"What 'whole Carmen thing'?"

"Oh, shit. I didn't tell you? Oh. Yeah. They broke up."

"Oh, really? Aw, she seemed like a sweetheart."

"She is—a total sweetheart. You know how it goes. He's twenty-four. He fucked it up. It's to be expected under normal circumstances, but he's also adjusting to the whole fame thing, you know—women throwing themselves at him wherever he goes. Pretty tall order not to fuck up at least once."

"Too bad."

"Believe me, he regrets it."

"So when are you gonna be on the West Coast, bro?" I ask. "You gotta swing by and see Little G. She's gotten so big since you saw her."

"Not for a while, man. I'm hopping a flight to Thailand first thing in the morning with Will. We recorded a song with this Thai hip-hop group, and—"

"A *Thai* hip-hop group?" I interject. "I didn't realize there was such a thing."

"Yeah. *Thai*me's Up. They're huge in Thailand."

I laugh. "Are you serious?"

"Yeah, they're massive and so is American hip-hop—this song's gonna make me a fucking mint, mark my words. So, anyway, we're shooting the music video with the Thai boys in Phuket for a week and then we're doing a promotional appearance the following week at a nightclub in Bangkok."

"Ah, Bangkok," I say, chuckling. "The scene of the original crime."

"Ah, yes. I remember it well. If you weren't such an old man these days, I'd have invited you to join me for a little walk down memory lane."

"Oh, fuck. No thanks. I'm too old and too happy to do any of that shit now. Almost killed me at eighteen—God only knows what that shit would do to me at thirty-one."

"Oh, yeah. Happy almost-birthday, old man."

"Thanks. So what dates are you gonna be in Bangkok?"

He tells me.

"I think Jonas and Sarah are actually gonna be there during those dates," I say.

"Really? No way."

"Yeah. Jonas is taking the missus climbing in Mae Do for four days—poor, poor Sarah—and then I'm pretty sure he said they're gonna hit Bangkok for a few days after that."

"Well, if the timing works out, tell 'em to come to the promotional thing at the nightclub. I'll put 'em on the VIP list. Will and the Thai boys are gonna perform their new song, plus they'll all do 'Crash' together. The crowd's gonna go apeshit—'Crash' is number one in Thailand right now."

"Where *isn't* 'Crash' number one?"

"In countries filled with stupid people."

I laugh. "Yeah, put Jonas and Sarah on your VIP list, for sure. Sarah loves hip-hop. She'll freak out."

"Okay, cool. I'll text you the details when I have 'em. You can forward the info to your brother."

"Awesome. Thanks. Just be warned, though, Jonas might try to break your pretty face for torturing him—as much as Sarah loves hip-hop, Jonas absolutely abhors it. Plus, Jonas hates nightclubs—so he'll be extra grouchy for you."

"Eh, I'll be okay. If Jonas tries to attack me, I'll sic Barry on him."

"Oh, Barry will be there? Say hi to him for me. I love that guy."

"Will do. So, hey, I gotta go—we're at the after-party with the *SNL* cast—I just stepped outside for a smoke."

"You're already partying? Will just performed a few minutes ago."

"Three-hour-tape-delay for the West Coast, numnuts."

"Oh, yeah. Duh. Well, have fun, man—enjoy every minute of your success. You deserve it. You're totally winning at The Game of Life, man. It's awesome to watch."

"Hey, that's the idea, man—as you well know. Win, win, win, as much as humanly possible—and then die taking none of it with you. Speaking of winning at The Game of Life, say hi to Stubborn Kat for me and tell Little G her Über-Cool Uncle Reed loves her like crazy."

"I will. Text me the info about Bangkok when you have it."

"Sure thing. Bye, bro. Enjoy changing shitty diapers. Peace."

I hang up my phone and walk back into my bedroom—and I'm met with Arma-fucking-geddon currently in progress: Mademoiselle Terrorist is wailing her head off and Kat is leaping desperately around the room like a kangaroo, bouncing Gracie up and down frantically, obviously trying her mighty best (and failing miserably) to quiet our mini-beast. When Kat sees me, she flashes me a look of such desperation, I almost laugh out loud.

"I don't know what's pissing her off so much," Kat whimpers. "I've tried everything."

"Give her to me, babe." I hold out my arms. "I'll hit her with the Playboy Razzle-Dazzle."

"It won't work," Kat whines. "I fed her. I changed her. I burped her. I sang to her. She just cries and cries and *cries*. Oh my *God*."

"Give her to me, babe. She likes the smell of my skin." I take Gracie's writhing, shrieking body from Kat and hold her against my bare chest—and not four seconds later, Gracie's head does three complete revolutions on her neck and she pukes breast milk all over me.

"Gah!" I shout.

"Whoa, that's a lot of puke," Kat says, laughing.

I look down at my puked-covered chest, grimacing. "Fuck."

"Poor baby worked herself up into a puking frenzy," Kat says.

"Gee, I wonder where she gets that?" I ask.

Kat laughs. "Give her to me so you can shower, babe." She puts out her arms.

"No, just grab me a towel. I'll shower after I get her calmed down."

"Nothing will calm her down, like I said," Kat says, throwing me a burping towel. "I've tried everything, trust me."

"Not everything—you haven't *playboyed* her." I gently wipe the puke off Gracie's chin, right off the little cleft I love so much, and then off the "G-R-A" in my "GRACE" tattoo, and bring Gracie to the makeshift diaper-changing table on top of our dresser. I gently lay Gracie down on her back, stroking her screaming face with my fingertip. "I'm sure my baby just needs a fresh diaper, that's all," I say soothingly.

"No, I just changed it," Kat says. "It's something else."

"Is your diaper bothering you, little one?" I coo to Gracie, ignoring Kat's skepticism. I lean over Gracie's face, shooting her my most serene and soothing smile—and, instantly, Gracie stops crying on a dime, even before I've opened her diaper, and stares at my face, completely transfixed.

"That's right, my little Scorpio," I soothe. "Look into my eyes. That's it, baby girl."

Gracie reaches up and touches my nose and I kiss her little fingertips, eliciting dove-like coos from her.

"No freaking way," Kat says. "I tried *everything*—and one smile from her handsome daddy and she's blissfully happy?"

I touch the teeny-tiny indentation on Gracie's chin and stroke the soft, blonde peach fuzz on top of her head. "She's just a daddy's girl, that's all," I say softly, my voice low and calm. "Isn't that right, Little G?" Gracie gurgles at me and pulls on the scruff on my chin and I rub my nose against hers. "My baby girl just needed a little Playboy Razzle-Dazzle, that's all," I say quietly. "Isn't that right, angel?" I shoot a snarky look at Kat. "It's the same tactic I use to soothe another Scorpio I know when she goes off the rails and starts acting like a demon spawn."

I smile, expecting Kat to shoot me a snarky expression to match my own, but she doesn't. To the contrary, she's looking at me the same way she did when she walked down the aisle toward me on our wedding day—like I'm the answer to her most fervent prayer.

"I love you," Kat says softly, her eyes wide and sparkling.

"And I love you," I say. I begin changing my serene daughter's diaper. "I love you forever and ever and ever, Mrs. Faraday."

Kat's face melts.

"I tell you what, Party Girl," I say. "How about you get yourself into a nice, hot tub in the bathroom while I rock our little terrorist to sleep, and then I'll join you in the bath and let you wash the baby-puke off me?"

"Oh," Kat says. "That sounds lovely." Without hesitation, she pulls her nightgown over her head and throws it onto the bed, revealing her new, sexy curves and dark, erect nipples. "Maybe while we're in the tub together, I'll imagine I'm a mermaid who's recently sprouted legs—and maybe if you're *really* sweet to me, I'll let you teach me what my newfangled *vagina* is for."

I laugh. "So, we're gonna do a porno version of *The Little Mermaid?*"

Kat giggles and winks. "See you soon, Prince Eric. Don't keep me waiting too long." She honks her delectable boobs and sashays into our bathroom, singing "Part of Your World" at the top of her lungs, her ass cheeks swishing to and fro as she moves.

I look down at Gracie. "Damn, you're mommy's sexy," I say. "And very, very silly, too."

I scoop Gracie off the dresser, change her into her Hello Kitty footy-pajamas, and bring her over to the rocking chair that's now a permanent fixture in the far corner of our large bedroom. After settling into the chair with Gracie in my arms, I rock her slowly, looking deeply into her big, blue eyes—the beautiful blue eyes that make me want to be a better man—and I begin to sing my favorite lullaby to her: "You Are My Sunshine."

"You are my sunshine," I sing softly, rocking rhythmically in my chair, staring into my daughter's ocean-blue eyes—and, as always happens in moments like this, I begin thinking about Gracie's namesake, the supernaturally beautiful woman who long ago sang this same, simple song of love to me.

When I reach the end of the song, Gracie's still staring at me with wide eyes, so I sing it again from the top, rocking my sweet little baby slowly, calmly, breathing deeply as I do—until, finally, Gracie's lovely eyelids flutter and shut.

"Gracie Louise Faraday," I whisper softly when my song is over and her breathing has turned deep and rhythmic. "I love you, Little G." I close my eyes, sending a little prayer to heaven to the other Grace Faraday, the one surely watching over us at this very moment. "I love you, Mom," I whisper.

Gracie's rosebud lips part and hang open in complete relaxation. Her body's a tiny sack of potatoes in my arms. I get up from the glider and carefully lay her down on the center of our large bed, and then I head toward my bathroom, my cock tingling with anticipation.

I enter the bathroom and there she is—my beautiful mermaid, soaking in a hot tub, her skin pink, her eyes closed.

"Hey, Ariel," I say softly. "Our little fishy's out like a light."

Kat opens her eyes and smiles. "Thank you, Baby Whisperer. Now take off those briefs and get your YOLO'd ass in here."

I do as I'm told, of course—and, as I'm lowering myself into the warm water, Kat points at my crotch with cartoon-like, wide eyes.

"What's *that*?" Kat asks.

I look down at my naked body. "What?"

"*That*." She points right at my hard dick. "That ding-a-ling thing."

"Oh *that*?" I smile from ear to ear. "It's my *thingamabob*."

Kat giggles. "You've seen *The Little Mermaid*?"

"I told you I was a very nice boy." I stroke her smooth thighs under the warm water.

"You *were* a very nice boy?"

"That's right. Past tense. I'm a very *bad* boy now—a *beast* with a raging boner."

"Ooh, that gives me a faboosh idea," Kat says. "How about you and me do a porno version of *Beauty and the Beast* tomorrow night?"

I chuckle. "So we're gonna do the entire Disney catalog, huh?"

Kat giggles. "Why not? I'd love to see how you'd pull off *Snow White and the Seven Dwarfs*."

"Pfft. Child's play," I say, running my palms over her curves under the warm water. "Six dildos and an apple. Easy peasy."

Kat laughs.

"Okay, Little Mermaid," I say. "We've got probably three hours 'til our little fishy wakes up, screaming and demanding to be fed—so let's use our free time wisely, shall we?"

"Yes, sir." Kat grabs my dick and strokes it with authority. "Let *The Little Mermaid* mini-porno begin."

"You know what?" I say, licking my hungry lips. "I've suddenly got an inexplicable craving for sushi."

I begin lowering my face into the water, but Kat grips my hair, stopping my movement.

"Ariel is mute when she's human remember?" she says. "Her voice is trapped in that necklace thing. So let me say this now: I had a really great time tonight, my love. I love you so much—and, oh, you fucked me brilliantly."

"I love you, too," I say. "Now quit your yapping, Ariel. It's time for me to show you what that *whatzit* between your legs can do."

EPILOGUE

JOSH

I pull my brand new, cherry-red Ferrari FF into my driveway and sit for a moment, singing along to the song blaring through my speakers. It's my current theme song: "All I Do Is Win" by DJ Khaled. When the fucking awesome song finishes, I kill the engine of my fucking awesome car and lovingly caress my steering wheel.

"I love you, baby," I say softly to my beautiful car—my thirty-first birthday present to myself. It's just a little something to celebrate how fucking hard I'm *winning* at The Game of Fucking Life. God-*damn*, I'm a fucking beast. All I do is win, win, win, baby. Fuck yeah, I do. No matter what. Because I'm a *winner*. Truth.

I run my hands tenderly over my steering wheel again, exhaling with near-sexual pleasure as I do. God-*damn*, this is a beautiful fucking car. I get a hard-on every time I get behind the wheel. Fuck yeah, I do. I've got a beautiful fucking Ferrari to match my beautiful fucking Ferrari of a wife and my sweet little baby girl and fucking awesome house ten minutes away from my fucking awesome brother.

And not only that, Climb and Conquer is absolutely slaying it these days—we've already shattered our mid-year revenue projections and we're planning major expansion in seven more markets later this year—plus, our designated charities are all flourishing, too. As it turns out, Jonas' entire business model was pure fucking genius. Surprise, surprise.

And, on top of all *that*, when I got home from work last night, I'd no sooner taken two steps through my front door than my beautiful sick fuck of a wife silently greeted me at the door by unzipping my pants, kneeling before me, and sucking my big ol' dick 'til I exploded into her waiting mouth. God-*damn*, I'm crushing life. Winner, winner, chicken fucking dinner, baby. Boo-fucking-yah.

I pull my phone out of my glove box and quickly scan my texts, and, as expected, there's a message from good ol' fucking awesome and reliable T-Rod, confirming everything's set for my romantic-stay-at-home birthday dinner with my two favorite blondes. "Everyone's already at your house, setting up," Theresa writes. "Chef, waiter, violin, cello. Oh, and I added a viola just for yucks. Have fun, Birthday Boy!"

I shoot off a quick reply. "Thanks a million, T. Just got home. Gonna be a great night."

I tilt my rearview mirror toward my face and survey my reflection. Handsome motherfucker. Lucky bastard. *Winner.* I run my hand through my hair, carefully smoothing a stray, and straighten the knot on my Roberto Cavalli necktie.

I pick up the bouquet of gardenias and the velvet jewelry box sitting on the passenger seat of my fucking awesome car—what better way to celebrate my birthday than giving my wife more ice for her ever-growing collection?—and then I bound happily toward the front door of my fucking awesome house, clicking the heels of my Stefano Bemer shoes, singing the DJ Khaled song under my breath as I go.

But when I get inside my house, it's perfectly quiet. No hustle-bustle; no signs of preparations for a birthday dinner; no wife dropping to her knees as she greets me in the doorway.

I peek into the kitchen. No chef. I check the dining area. No violinist, cellist or viola-ist. (What the fuck do you call someone who plays a viola?)

"Kat?" I call.

But my smokin' hot wife is nowhere to be found.

I head into the nursery and, lo and behold, there's my mother-in-law, sitting in a glider with Gracie, quietly reading her a book about farm animals.

Louise looks up from the book in her hands and her face lights up. "Happy birthday!" she says. "Look, Gracie. Daddy-the-birthday-boy is here!" Louise gets up from the glider, toting Gracie in her arms.

"Hi, Gramma Lou," I say, kissing Louise on her cheek. "Where's my wife?"

"Oh, she went out," Louise says.

"What? We were supposed to have a romantic dinner-for-two-and-a-half here at the house. I had everything all set up."

"Yes. And, I must say, everything you arranged looked *very* romantic, indeed—absolutely stunning. The chef was a real sweetheart, too. He took it *very* well when Kat sent him and the musicians to Colby's house, instead." Louise leans in like she's telling me a secret. "Colby's got a hot date with his physical therapist tonight, so I'm sure he'll greatly appreciate everything you had planned."

I stare at Louise dumbly. "Kat sent everyone *away?*"

"Mmm hmm. She left a note explaining the new plan. It's in the kitchen. I've got a few birthday presents waiting for you in there, too. Come on." She hands Gracie to me and the three of us make our way into the kitchen. When we arrive, Louise hands me a rectangular box off the counter, wrapped in bright yellow paper and a bow.

"Thank you," I say. I hand her Gracie and unwrap the box to find a genuine treasure awaiting me. "Wow. 'Barrique de Ponciano de Parfidio,'" I say, reading the label on the elegant—and rare—bottle of tequila. "Lou, this stuff is *really* hard to come by—a total collector's item. How on earth did you get it?"

She shrugs. "Oh, just a little something called the Interwebs."

"Thank you so much. I've tasted this stuff once before a long time ago and it was fantastic. Thank you." I kiss her on the cheek, and as I do, Gracie reaches for the scruff on my chin so I take her back from Louise.

"It's from the whole family—the boys, too—we all chipped in. Even Keane."

"Even Keane?" I ask, laughing.

"Even Keane. So that tells you where you rank in this family's pecking order. Pretty darned high."

"Wow, I'm totally honored. I'll call everyone and thank them tomorrow—but will you tell them I got it and loved it?"

"I sure will. Ryan said you better save him a couple shots of that stuff, by the way, or he'll never forgive you."

"That goes without saying—not just for Ry, for everyone. Maybe we can do a foosball-tournament-tequila-tasting-dinner later this week?"

"Great. It'll be your belated birthday party. What would you like me to make?"

"Oh, everything you make is great."

"It's your birthday, honey. Pick what you want."

"Spaghetti, then," I say definitively. "My favorite."

Louise smiles. "You got it. Plus extras for the birthday boy."

"Hot damn. You know I love my extras."

Louise giggles and hands me another box. "This one is from Ryan, specifically."

I open the box and it's a crystal shot glass, etched with the name "Lambo."

"Ry got himself one engraved with 'Captain' so you two can sit out on the patio like lovebirds, watch the sunset together, and drink your new tequila." She rolls her eyes. "Ryan's truly talented at giving gifts to others which actually turn out to be gifts to himself, isn't he?" She grabs a gift bag off the counter. "And this one is from me. Just a little trinket."

"This is all too much, Lou," I say. "Really."

"Oh, no. This is just a little nothing. Hardly anything at all. I saw it and thought of you."

Gracie bats me in the face so I shift her in my arms and pull out the contents of the gift bag. A lump rises in my throat at the sight of my gift—a coffee mug, emblazoned with the phrase, "World's Greatest Son-in-Law."

"Thank you," I say, hugging Louise with my free arm.

"Whenever you have a cup of coffee, you'll be reminded how much you're loved, honey."

I bite my lip. "Thank you."

Louise waves her hand. "You're impossible to buy presents for, you know that, Josh? What do you get the guy who has everything?"

I motion to everything I just opened. "All this."

"We all just wanted you to know how much you're loved, that's all."

"Thank you. I feel it. I love all of you, too."

Louise wipes her eyes. "So, enough of that. You never intended to spend your birthday hanging out with your boring mother-in-law. Gimme that baby." She grabs Gracie from me and hands me an envelope off the counter. "Here you go. Kat asked me to deliver this to you exactly at six."

I look at the clock on the kitchen wall. Six on the button.

I open the sealed envelope and immediately smile from ear to ear. There's a poker chip inside—and a typewritten note: "Happy Birthday, my darling, beloved Playboy with a Heart of Gold!" the note reads. "Sorry-not-sorry, but our romantic dinner-for-two-and-a-half has been cancelled and donated to a very good cause (namely, getting Colby laid by the hot physical therapist he's been drooling over for the past two months). The Playboy and The Party Girl with a Hyphen can't stay home like old farts on the Playboy's thirty-fucking-first birthday! Hell no, old man! We can sleep when we're dead! Go big or go home! YOLO! It's time to party like it's 1999! (Well, until about midnight, that is, since that's when Gracie's been waking up lately for a feeding.) So get into your fancy new Ferrari and get your YOLO'd ass to this address, PB." It's an address in nearby Kent. "Because, Playboy, I feel the need—the need for speed! XOXOXOXOX Mrs. Katherine Ulla Faraday. P.S. I've always wanted to fuck the winner of the Indy 500!"

I look up from reading the note, my cheeks hot, my dick tingling.

"Well?" Louise asks. "Good news?"

"Great news." I pull my phone out of my pocket and Google the address on the note and quickly discover it's a professional-grade racetrack about forty minutes outside of Seattle, exactly as I figured. "*Fantastic* news," I say. I kiss Louise and Gracie on their cheeks and gather my car keys off the counter. "Thanks for watching Gracie. We'll be home around midnight, if not before."

"Don't rush home. Kat pumped before she left—we've got plenty of milk to tide us over."

"Thank you so much." I kiss Gracie again. "Bye, Little G. I love you, honey."

"Guh," Gracie says.

I sprint toward the exit of the kitchen.

"Hey, wait, honey," Louise calls to my back. "Aren't you hungry? Maybe you should take a little something to nibble on?"

"Good point." I say. Quickly, I make a couple orgasm-inducing peanut butter and jelly sandwiches—one for me and one for my wife—and throw them into a bag with some apples and chips and bottles of water. "A meal fit for a king and queen," I say. I wink at Louise. "Thanks again for watching Little G."

"Have fun, honey," Louise calls to my back.

"Oh, I will," I yell back.

I race outside, hop into my fucking awesome new car, and peel out of the driveway of my fucking awesome house, my dick throbbing, my heart racing, my skin buzzing; and, once I'm driving smoothly on the highway, I press the button to call Kat through my wireless connection.

"Hey, Playboy," Kat purrs into the phone. "Did you get my note?"

"I sure did," I say. "I'm on my way."

"Are you mad about dinner being cancelled?"

"Hell no. This is a much better offer. YOLO, right, babe?"

"Words to live by."

"Especially for a guy who happens to have 'em stamped on his ass."

"Amen." Kat laughs. "Drive safe, my love. I can't wait to celebrate your birthday in a manner befitting the one and only Playboy with the Heart of Gold. I've got a whole bunch of surprises waiting for you." She snickers. "I sure hope you're well rested."

"Thanks, baby. You're the best. I think you might know me better than I know myself sometimes."

"*Might? Sometimes?* Of course, I do—and don't you ever forget it. If there are two things I know in this life, it's PR and Joshua William Faraday."

I chuckle. "Truer words were never spoken, PG."

"Okay, get off the phone, honey. Concentrate on your driving—I need you here in one piece or else you'll fuck everything up." She makes a sexual sound. "Oh, baby, I'm gonna give you a birthday present you'll never, ever forget."

"Oh, yeah, Party Girl?" I ask.

"Oh, yeah, Playboy," she replies. "It's gonna be so gooooood."

I laugh. "So that's how this story ends, huh?"

"You don't know how this story ends?" Kat asks.

"Well, yeah, I do—we fuck like rabbits."

"Oh. Well, that's a pretty damned good ending, I'd say."

"And then we live happily ever after," I add.

"Aw, amen, baby," she says softly. "The best ending of all."

"I love you, Kat," I say quietly, my heart soaring. "I love you, I love you, I love you."

"I love you, too, my beloved Joshua. With all my heart and soul." She sighs on the other end of the line. "*Forever.*"

Josh and Kat's story is over, but you can find out more of their story while reading about the Morgans!

Start reading the Standalone Morgan Brothers Series today with *Hero..*

The story of heroic firefighter, **Colby Morgan**. When catastrophe strikes Colby Morgan, will physical therapist Lydia save him . . . or will he save her?

Or maybe you're in the mood to read a love story about another wealthy, hot dude with demons? Then read about Josh's fraternal twin, **Jonas Faraday**, who becomes obsessed with an anonymous woman he "meets" online. Start THE CLUB TRILOGY today!

Continue reading for a full list of Lauren's books.

BOOKS BY LAUREN ROWE

Standalone Novels

Smitten

When aspiring singer-songwriter, Alessandra, meets Fish, the funny, adorable bass player of 22 Goats, sparks fly between the awkward pair. Fish tells Alessandra he's a "Goat called Fish who's hung like a bull. But not really. I'm actually really average." And Alessandra tells Fish, "There's nothing like a girl's first love." Alessandra thinks she's talking about a song when she makes her comment to Fish—the first song she'd ever heard by 22 Goats, in fact. As she'll later find out, though, her "first love" was

actually Fish. The Goat called Fish who, after that night, vowed to do anything to win her heart.

SMITTEN is a **true standalone** romance.

Swoon

When Colin Beretta, the drummer of 22 Goats, is a groomsman at the wedding of his childhood best friend, Logan, he discovers Logan's kid sister, Amy, is all grown up. Colin tries to resist his attraction to Amy, but after a drunken kiss at the wedding reception, that's easier said than done.

Swoon is a **true standalone** romance.

Hate Love Duet

An addicting enemies to lovers romance with humor, heat, angst, and banter. Music artists Savage of Fugitive Summer and Laila Fitzgerald are stuck together on tour. And convinced they can't stand each other. What they don't know is that they're absolutely made for each other, whether they realize it or not. The books of this duet are to be read in order:

Falling Out Of Hate With You

Falling Into Love With You

The Reed Rivers Trilogy

Reed Rivers has met his match in the most unlikely of women—aspiring journalist and spitfire, Georgina Ricci. She's much younger than the women Reed normally pursues, but he can't resist her fiery personality and drop-dead gorgeous looks. But in this game of cat and mouse, who's chasing whom? With each passing day of this wild ride, Reed's not so sure. The books of this trilogy are to be read in order:

Bad Liar

Beautiful Liar

Beloved Liar

The Club Trilogy

Romantic. Scorching hot. Suspenseful. Witty. The Club is your new addiction—a sexy and suspenseful thriller about two wealthy brothers and the sassy women who bring them to their knees . . . all while the foursome bands together to protect one of their own. *The Club Trilogy* is to be read in order, as follows:

The Club: Obsession

The Club: Reclamation

The Club: Redemption

The Club: Culmination

The fourth book for Jonas and Sarah is a full-length epilogue with incredible heart-stopping twists and turns and feels. Read *The Club: Culmination (A Full-Length Epilogue Novel)* after finishing *The Club Trilogy* or, if you prefer, after reading *The Josh and Kat Trilogy*.

The Josh and Kat Trilogy

It's a war of wills between stubborn and sexy Josh Faraday and Kat Morgan. A fight to the bed. Arrogant, wealthy playboy Josh is used to getting what he wants. *And what he wants is Kat Morgan.* The books are to be read in order:

Infatuation

Revelation

Consummation

The Morgan Brothers

Read these **standalones** in any order about the brothers of Kat Morgan. Chronological reading order is below, but they are all complete stories. Note: you do *not* need to read any other books or series before jumping straight into reading about the Morgan boys.

Hero

The story of heroic firefighter, **Colby Morgan**. When catastrophe strikes Colby Morgan, will physical therapist Lydia save him . . . or will he save her?

Captain

The insta-love-to-enemies-to-lovers story of tattooed sex god, **Ryan Morgan**, and the woman he'd move heaven and earth to claim.

Ball Peen Hammer

A steamy, hilarious, friends-to-lovers romantic comedy about cocky-as-hell male stripper, **Keane Morgan**, and the sassy, smart young woman who brings him to his knees during a road trip.

Mister Bodyguard

The Morgans' beloved honorary brother, **Zander Shaw**, meets his match in the feisty pop star he's assigned to protect on tour.

ROCKSTAR

When the youngest Morgan brother, **Dax Morgan,** meets a mysterious woman who rocks his world, he must decide if pursuing her is worth risking it all. Be sure to check out four of Dax's original songs from *ROCKSTAR*, written and produced by Lauren, along with full music videos for the songs, on her website (www.laurenrowebooks.com) under the tab MUSIC FROM ROCKSTAR.

Misadventures

Lauren's *Misadventures* titles are page-turning, steamy, swoony standalones, to be read in any order.

- *Misadventures on the Night Shift* –A hotel night shift clerk encounters her teenage fantasy: rock star Lucas Ford. And combustion ensues.

- *Misadventures of a College Girl*—A spunky, virginal theater major meets a cocky football player at her first college party . . . and absolutely nothing goes according to plan for either of them.

- *Misadventures on the Rebound*—A spunky woman on the rebound meets a hot, mysterious stranger in a bar on her way to her five-year high school reunion in Las Vegas and what follows is a misadventure neither of them ever imagined.

Standalone Psychological Thriller/Dark Comedy

Countdown to Killing Kurtis

A young woman with big dreams and skeletons in her closet decides her porno-king husband must die in exactly a year. This is *not* a traditional romance, but it *will* most definitely keep you turning the pages and saying "WTF?"

Short Stories

The Secret Note

Looking for a quickie? Try this scorching-hot short story from Lauren Rowe in ebook FOR FREE or in audiobook: He's a hot Aussie. I'm a girl who isn't shy about getting what she wants. The problem? Ben is my little brother's best friend. An exchange student who's heading back Down Under any day now. But I can't help myself. He's too hot to resist.

All books by Lauren Rowe are available in ebook, paperback, and audiobook formats.

AUTHOR BIOGRAPHY

Lauren Rowe is the USA Today and international #1 best-selling author of newly released Reed Rivers Trilogy, as well as The Club Trilogy, The Josh & Kat Trilogy, The Morgan Brothers Series, Countdown to Killing Kurtis, and select standalone Misadventures.

Lauren's books are full of feels, humor, heat, and heart. Besides writing novels, Lauren is the singer in a party/wedding band in her hometown of San Diego, an audio book narrator, and award-winning songwriter. She is thrilled to connect with readers all over the world.

To find out about Lauren's upcoming releases and giveaways, sign up for Lauren's emails here!

Lauren loves to hear from readers! Send Lauren an email from her website, say hi on Twitter, Instagram, or Facebook.

Find out more and check out lots of free bonus material at www.LaurenRoweBooks.com.

Lightning Source UK Ltd.
Milton Keynes UK
UKHW010101021221
394930UK00003B/1042

The Effects of the Draw

by Graham Wheldon

Published by *Raceform* Ltd., Compton, Newbury, Berkshire RG20 6NL

Tel 01635 578080   Fax 01635 578101

WEB: www.*raceform*.co.uk   Email: *raceform*@*raceform*.co.uk

Typeset by Graham Wheldon for *Raceform*

Photographs by Alan Johnson

Printed by Greenshires, Telford Way Industrial Estate, Kettering, Northants

Acknowledgements: Thanks to Paul 'Each-Way' Maguire,
Chris Broom, Peter Howes, Ashley Rumney and Richard Lowther

Front cover: Rudi's Pet wins the Doncaster
Writers Stakes in October 1997 (Steve Cargill)

CONTENTS

3

INTRODUCTION

On many British racecourses, the draw has more influence on the outcome of the races than any other single factor. In fact, it is possible to make a healthy profit simply by backing well-drawn horses. This can not be said for any other feature of horse races, including the suitability of the going, ability of the jockey or trainer, or any type of performance rating system. Although it may seem that I am overstating the importance of the draw, personally I do not believe this is possible, and race results year after year support this view. In this book I will attempt to convert any 'draw sceptics' and show how a profit can be made from this most crucial factor.

National Hunt racing has never appealed to me in quite the same way that flat racing does, as I could never find any way of getting an edge. Your horse could lose twenty lengths at the start or gain the same margin, but there is rarely any way of knowing which is more likely beforehand, unless A. P. McCoy has a ride. Your horse could fall, unseat, be pulled up, run out, slip up, be brought down, so on, so on. A good friend of mine reckons that only 10% of runners in jump races fail to finish, but I have always found that very hard to believe. It may well be true in novice hurdles and the like, but surely not 3½ mile handicap chases in the mud at Haydock. Somehow, I would rather know from what position my horse will start, where he is likely to be at an early stage of the race, and that he is 99.9% certain to complete. I would rather have a horse I back beaten a head into second than be twenty lengths clear and cantering when coming down at the last.

As with any system, it is vital to watch as much racing as possible, something that has become easier since Sky's involvement began. Draw-bias races are likely to pop up at any point, thanks to the variable nature of British courses and the erratic manner in which they are watered, and they are not necessarily confined to events run on straight courses.

Significant draw advantages are prevalent on about half our racecourses, and races that are affected by a bias obviously have to be treated differently afterwards to races run on a level playing field. In draw-bias races, some horses will have been flattered by racing on the best ground and others will have seemed to run way below form because they are racing on the worst ground. This will obviously affect where each horse finishes within the race and how far it is beaten, which in turn has other implications. Horses that run in bias races can be split into three distinct categories, those favoured by the draw, those unaffected by it and those hindered by it, and it is this evaluation that pinpoints future

5

punts. 'He is a winner without a penalty' is a comment frequently attached to horses beaten a short-head in a handicap, but that is not strictly true since he is likely to be put up a good few pounds in the weights. However, a horse finishing in front on his side when the field splits into two groups but only finishing fifth overall is unlikely to go up in the weights, and may even come down a bit. Now that IS a winner without a penalty. How a draw-bias race can affect handicapping is looked at in more detail in Chapter 4.

As with any system, other factors still have to be taken into consideration when contemplating a bet. Computer-based systems which take into account trainer statistics, trainer form, jockey, course, ground, distance, weight, handicap mark, time of the year, class of race, type of race etc. are all very well, but where is the edge over the bookmaker? If you can balance the importance of each category correctly then you may find a system that throws up more than the average quota of winners, but many of them will start favourite. What do bookmakers take into consideration when pricing up a race? Basically all of the above, but very rarely, if at all, do they consider the draw from previous races.

I would say that the draw accounts for about three-quarters of the thinking behind my selections. Only then will I look at the other factors likely to affect its performance. How many punters, apart from the likes of the Frankie Dettori accumulator merchants, would be so bullish about only one factor. I hope to convince you to think the same way.

CHAPTER 1

THE EFFECT OF THE DRAW

Rules of Racing No.28(v): The Starter shall call the names of the runners and, for Flat races, assign the horses to the places drawn by lot, all horses taking their place at the start in the order drawn for them. The rider who has drawn No. 1 must always be placed on the left (as from behind the stalls) and the other riders must take their places in consecutive numbers from the left.

Presuming the Stands are on the outside of the course, on right-handed courses, low numbers will be towards the stands' rail at the start of the race. On left-handed courses, high numbers will be towards the stands' rail.

This Chapter deals with the effect of the draw at each course, and how it varies depending on the ground. The official going reports in this country still have to be taken with a pinch of salt and it is surely time to introduce the penetrometer to replace 'a stick'. Many times throughout a season, the official going will vary a good deal from the *Raceform* going allowance* and probably the best way to ascertain the actual going is to compare the two. For example, at Newcastle on March 25th 1997, the official going was returned as good, but whilst the *Raceform* going allowance on the round course (minus 0.03 seconds per furlong) suggested that the surface was as near to good ground as you can get, a figure of 0.29 seconds per furlong was given to straight course events, suggesting that the ground there was verging on being good to soft.

---

*   *The Raceform going allowance is a figure based on the race times at the course that day, and is published in Raceform, the Official Form Book and in the results section of Raceform Update. The figure, expressed as seconds per furlong, is the time each furlong took under/over what it would have on good ground, according to Raceform standard times. A plus figure means that the ground was on the soft side of good, whilst a minus figure would mean it was faster than good.*

Many courses change the position of the stalls from meeting to meeting, so it is vital to check the racing press to see where they are placed, although even they get it wrong sometimes (there were at least two cases in 1997 of the stalls' positioning being different to that advertised). On particularly bad ground, stalls can sometimes be dispensed with and flip starts used to start races.

ASCOT (R-H) - *When the ground rides soft, runners invariably tack over towards the outside rail down the side of the course in races of beyond 1m. This part of the course is partially covered by overhanging trees and the ground is definitely at its quickest there, presumably as it is sheltered, but this seems common knowledge among the jockeys (Willie Carson brought Bahri wide all the way in the 1995 Queen Elizabeth Stakes). Low numbers have the advantage on the straight course when fields are at their biggest, irrespective of the ground. The draw does not seem to make much difference on the round course, apart from on soft.*

The straight course seems to have more of a pronounced draw effect these days, but the bias has switched noticeably within the last three years and low numbers (towards the stands'-side rail) now seem to hold sway. This was not the case in 1994 at the Royal meeting, when the three big-field handicaps on the straight course were all taken by runners drawn very high, with Face North winning the Royal Hunt Cup from stall 30, Venture Capitalist taking the Wokingham from the same stall and Wizard King running away with the Britannia from 28 (all on good to firm ground). 1995 saw the draw bias start to even out and possibly swing towards those drawn low, although Realities took the Royal Hunt Cup to be yet another winner from stall 30. The Royal meeting of 1996 was a bumper week for tricast punters. Although the draw seemed to have little effect on the Tuesday, the ground was probably a bit firmer then than for the following three days (a theory backed up by the race times) and the softening ground saw a swing in favour of those drawn low. In the nine straight races from Wednesday onwards, the winners were drawn 2 of 16, 2 of 13, 3 of 31, 11 of 10 (one non-runner), 2 of 17, 4 of 12, 11 of 10 (one non-runner), 7 of 29 and 7 of 17. Yeast led home a 1-2-3 for horses drawn 1, 2 and 3 in the Royal Hunt Cup, producing a tricast in excess of £1,000 and a trio of £344. Donna Viola from stall 4 finished fourth. In the Wokingham, Emerging Market from stall 7 led home another 1-2-3-4 for horses drawn in the bottom quarter of the draw.

Best Examples*		5f-6f	7f + st
	Firm	2114 *(1996)*	2053 *(1996)*
	Good	2105	4423
	Soft	4677	

* The Best Example races are 1997 Raceform numbers unless specified

Subsequent Record of runners 'winning their side*' in the Wokingham and Royal Hunt Cup at Royal Ascot (1992-7)					
1992	**Marine Diver**	(6th Hunt Cup)	next time	Unp	33/1
	No Qualifiers**	(Wokingham)			
1993	No Qualifiers**	(Hunt Cup)			
	Hard to Figure	(6th Wokingham)	next time	Unp	16/1
1994	**Kayvee**	(5th Hunt Cup)	next time	2nd	4/1

8

	No Extras	(3rd Wokingham)	next time	Unp	9/1
1995	Billy Bushwhacker	(4th Hunt Cup)	next time	Unp	13/2
	No Qualifiers**	(Wokingham)			
1996	No Qualifiers**	(Hunt Cup)			
	Sir Joey	(5th Wokingham)	next time	3rd	6/4
1997	Lonely Leader	(6th Hunt Cup)	next time	Unp	16/1
	To The Roof	(6th Wokingham)	next time	Unp	7/2

* 'winning their side' - In big-field handicaps, the tendency is for runners to form two or three distinct groups. The runner listed will normally be the first one home on the unfavoured rail.

** No obvious pattern to the draw

AYR (L-H) - *It used to be considered vital to be drawn low to middle in the Ayr Gold Cup, with a stall between 5 and 15 looking ideal when the ground was good or softer. However, in the past three years and particularly in 1995 and 1996, a high draw has been critical in both the Gold and newly introduced Silver Cups, with runners drawn low rarely getting a look in. On the round course, low numbers enjoy a decent advantage when the fields are fairly big, and runners who normally race prominently are likely to find a high draw a difficult hurdle to overcome.*

The effect of the draw seems to have switched in the past few years and a high draw now looks vital when the Ayr Silver and Gold Cups are run on fast ground. Cool Jazz in 1995 was the perfect case in point. Drawn on the far side (low), he came home a never-dangerous fifth overall, but he comfortably 'won' the race on his side of the course. The impression left that this was an improved effort was confirmed when he went on to win the Group Three Diadem Stakes at Ascot at 33/1 next time, although time was to prove that the most important factor for Cool Jazz was to have a left-hand rail to race against. He was first home against the far rail in the 1995 Ayr Gold Cup, won the 1995 Ascot Group Three Diadem from stall 1, against the stands' rail, and won the 1996 Group Three Palace House at Newmarket from stall 1, against the stands' rail. 1996 saw a huge draw bias in both the Silver and Gold Cups. In fields of 28, Cretan Gift from stall 27 led home Thwaab from 25 and La Petite Fusee from 22 in the former. An hour and a half later, Coastal Bluff from stall 28 led home Mr Bergerac from stall 29 and Prince Babar from stall 27 to complete a 1-2-3 for runners drawn in the top three stalls. With the ground probably just on the soft side of good in 1997, the high-drawn horses did not enjoy a complete monopoly, but both the Silver and Gold Cup winners were drawn high, Perryston View, from stall 28 of 29, and Wildwood Flower from stall 24 of 29. Wildwood Flower had already shown that she liked Ayr in 1996 when she was first home on the far side in the Gold Cup, and fifth overall. The ground was good to soft when Daring Destiny (stall 29 of 29), who had been well backed in the build-up, won the Ayr Gold Cup in 1994. This was after low numbers had looked favoured in the Silver Cup, but Daring Destiny's trainer Karl Burke felt that there was a faster strip up the stands' rail and the filly proved him right.

Best Examples		5f-6f	7f +	1m-1m 2f
	Firm	4314 *(1996)*		
	Good	4280	4270	4283
	Soft	4707		

Subsequent Record of runners winning their side in Ayr Silver & Gold Cups (1992-7)				
1992	Prenonamoss	(6th Silver Cup)	next time 4th	20/1
	Echo-Logical	(2nd Gold Cup)	not run again	
1993	Jigsaw Boy	(9th Silver Cup)	next time 2nd	8/1
	Castlerea Lad	(10th Gold Cup)	next time Unp	25/1
1994	Bayin	(9th Silver Cup)	next time 3rd	6/1
	Alzianah	(2nd Gold Cup)	next time Unp	5/1
1995	Selhurstpark Flyer	(7th Silver Cup)	next time Unp	16/1
	Cool Jazz	(5th Gold Cup)	next time WON	33/1
1996	Wardara	(4th Silver Cup)	next time Unp	France
	Wildwood Flower	(5th Gold Cup)	next time Unp	8/1
1997	Hard to Figure	(3rd Silver Cup)	not run again	
	Double Action	(2nd Gold Cup)	next time 4th	5/1

On the whole, the subsequent outing record of runners first home on their side in the Silver and Gold Cups is good, with Cool Jazz winning at 33/1 and half the others being placed. The temptation at this late stage of the season seems to be for trainers to run in-form sprint handicappers from the top end of the scale in listed or group races. Cool Jazz and Wardara went on to run in Group threes, while Wildwood Flower ran in a listed event.

BATH (L-H) - *Low numbers have been slightly favoured over sprint distances by virtue of a left-hand turn about a furlong from the line, but this is to be straightened out for 1998. Low numbers are also favoured in races of a mile as the start is on a chute and the course turns left most of the way, but the advantage is minimal.*

BEVERLEY (R-H) - *High numbers are usually favoured in races over the straight five furlongs and also on the round course in races at up to 1m 100y. In sprint races, the runners have to negotiate a right-handed jink not long after the start and it seems harder here than at probably any course for runners drawn low to get over to the favoured rail, so Beverley has to be of interest to followers of the draw. High numbers are particularly favoured on firm and soft ground and, when conditions are testing, there is a strip of ground by the far rail that is significantly quicker than the middle of the course. Runners drawn high on the round course, especially in races over 7f 100y, are favoured as the course turns right soon after the start.*

It is worth checking whether the stalls are being used when the ground is heavy, since flip starts (which are used to start most jump races and some long distance races on the Flat) were not uncommon here in 1997 over sprint distances. In such circumstances, runners do not always line up strictly in stall order, with shrewder jockeys able to improve their position.

When there are more than 13 or 14 runners in a Beverley sprint and the ground is soft, runners drawn low can make use of a strip of decent ground under the stands' rail.

Best Examples		5f	7f 100y-1m 100y
	Firm	3761	
	Good	3481	571
	Soft	1119, 2467	2463

BRIGHTON (L-H) - *When the ground is soft or worse, runners invariably tack across to the stands' rail in the straight. When this is the case, high numbers hold a slight edge. Otherwise, low numbers have a minimal advantage in sprint races.*

CARLISLE (R-H) - *High numbers fare marginally better in sprints, although when the ground rides soft low numbers seem to enjoy the advantage. Genuinely soft ground at Carlisle is something of a rarity though and has not been seen there for any meeting during the past two seasons, possibly because they do not race after August.*

CATTERICK (L-H) - *When the ground is testing, the stands' rail is definitely the place to be, which suits high numbers in five-furlong races. However, when the ground is good or firmer, horses drawn on the far side (low) hold the distinct edge. Low numbers are marginally preferred in races run on the round course on all surfaces, particularly so over 5f 212y as runners have to take a left-handed bend into the straight. When the ground is soft, horses switched to race on the stands' rail are benefited.*

Best Examples	5f	5f 212y-7f
Good	3287	4285
Soft	4770	4773

CHEPSTOW (L-H) - *High numbers used to be favoured on the straight course in races at up to 1m 14y, but these days the draw seems of little account.*

CHESTER (L-H) - *Low numbers have an advantage, especially in races at up to 7f 122y, where a slow start from a high draw can be virtually impossible to overcome, given the constantly turning nature of the course. Soft ground seems to accentuate the advantage enjoyed by runners drawn low, until it has been raced on a few times, when a higher draw becomes less of a disadvantage as the ground on the inside becomes chewed up.*

Best Examples	5f-6f 18y	7f-7f 122y
Good	4365	4362
Soft	2211	1017

DONCASTER (L-H) - *The draw is only really an issue here during Lincoln weekend, when maximum fields are guaranteed in the Spring Mile and the Lincoln itself, but which side is likely to be favoured is almost impossible to predict from year to year. Neither side was conclusively favoured in 1995, low numbers were well on top in 1996, and the centre strip of ground looked best in 1997. Low numbers are best in big fields on the round course.*

The question of what will be the best draw seems to come up more in the Press during Lincoln weekend than at any other meeting of the year, and it is probably the most difficult to predict. The best idea is probably to see what happens in the Spring Mile and then decide whether it is likely to have any effect on the Lincoln. In 1995 on good ground, the stands'-side rail (high) seemed favoured in the Spring Mile but in the following day's Lincoln, those drawn low to middle seemed favoured, so it was probably down to where the pace was. On much softer ground in 1996, the far rail seemed to be favoured in the Spring Mile, when all those drawn 7 and above in a field of 22 elected to switch towards the stands' side. With hindsight, Cool Edge was a cracking bet at 20/1. Drawn 2, so racing on what turned out to be the best ground, and on his favoured soft surface, he led home runners drawn in stalls 1, 7 and 3. Interestingly, the draw seemed less biased in the following event, a six-furlong handicap, when the first one home on the far side managed only fifth. The extra two furlongs of the Spring Mile and Lincoln seems to make all the difference and the longer trip certainly encourages a more positive splitting of those racing on opposite rails. As in the Spring Mile the previous day, those drawn low in the 1996 Lincoln (Race 455) held a significant advantage, with the winner and runner-up coming from stalls 6 and 7 in a field of 24.

The next time the Spring Mile and Lincoln are run on soft ground at Doncaster, there is no reason why low numbers should not again dominate.

At the time of going to press, permission had just been given by the BHB for trainers to pick their own draw for their runners in the Lincoln. This system, already successfully employed in America for the Kentucky Derby, works by all the runner's names going into a hat, with the first one out being given the choice of where to be drawn. If successful, it could prove popular with all 48-hour declaration showpiece races in the future.

Best Examples		5f-6f	7f + st	1m-1m 2f 60y
	Good	1760		
	Soft	2313	5050	450, 455 *(1996)*

Subsequent Record of runners 'winning their side' in the Spring Mile and Lincoln at Doncaster (1992-7)					
1992	No Qualifiers	(Lincoln)			
1993	**Indian Slave**	(4th Spring Mile)	next time	3rd	14/1
	Buzzards Bellbuoy	(7th Lincoln)	next time	Unp	7/2
1994	No Qualifiers	(Spring Mile)			
	Missed Flight	(3rd Lincoln, disq)	next time	**WON**	**6/1**
1995	No Qualifiers	(Spring Mile)			
	Mr Martini	(3rd Lincoln)	next time	4th	10/1
1996	**Dances With Hooves**	(3rd Spring Mile)	next time	2nd	4/1
	Barbaroja	(3rd Lincoln)	next time	Unp	8/1
1997	**Sandmoor Chambray**	(4th Spring Mile)	next time	Unp	7/1
	No Qualifiers	(Lincoln)			

Only Missed Flight managed to win on his next outing, but Indian Slave, Buzzards Bellbuoy and Mr Martini won at good prices two runs subsequently.

EPSOM (L-H) - *When the ground is on the soft side, jockeys tack over to the stands' side in races of six furlongs and beyond to look for the better ground. The ground is better here in such conditions as the course cambers away from the stands' rail towards the far side, keeping it drier. In five-furlong races, the stalls are invariably placed on the stands' side, so when the going is soft the majority of the runners are on the best ground from the* *outset. Horses drawn low in round-course races are able to take the shortest route around Tattenham Corner, and on faster ground have a decisive edge over six and seven furlongs and 1m 114y, particularly so front-runners and those that race prominently in their races. Over five furlongs, high numbers used to hold quite an advantage, but this did not seem the case in 1997. Stall number 10 had a remarkable record in the Derby between 1989 and 1991, accounting for three straight winners in Nashwan, Quest For Fame and Generous, but this was a pure fluke.*

Best Examples	5f	6f-7f
Good	1766	
Soft		2390

FOLKESTONE (R-H) - *High numbers have a slight edge on the round course, and low numbers are marginally preferred in sprint events, but neither advantage is that great. However, when the ground is soft, there has looked to be a decent strip of ground towards the far rail on the straight course, which would suit high numbers.*

GOODWOOD (R-H) & (L-H) - *High numbers are favoured on the round course, particularly over seven furlongs, except in very wet conditions when jockeys tend to tack over to the stands' side. For the past two seasons, low numbers have looked to do best in sprints when the stalls were on the stands' side (low) and the field did not stretch right across the course. In big-field races such as the Stewards' Cup though, high numbers still seem to just about hold sway.*

Best Examples	5f-6f	7f-1m
Firm	3115	
Good	3217	3150

Sprint Handicaps with between 10 and 15 runners at Goodwood (stalls low) (1996-7)						
Year	Race No	Going	Winner	Draw		Runners
1996	1334	Soft	Montserrat (5/1)	12	of	13
1996	1715	Good	Don Pepe (8/1)	13	of	13
1996	1777	Good	Sally Slade (9/1)	2	of	12
1996	1958	Good	Friendly Brave (5/1)	2	of	10
1996	2129	Good	Scissor Ridge (10/1)	11	of	12
1996	3128	G-F	Young Bigwig (13/2)	1	of	13
1996	3145	G-F	Youdontsay (20/1)	6	of	13
1996	3160	G-F	Frederik T'Fierce (8/1)	2	of	11
1997	1742	G-F	Polly Golightly (100/30)	5	of	12
1997	2115	Soft	Arnie (33/1)	2	of	11
1997	3113	G-F	Halmahera (11/4)	2	of	11
1997	3152	G-F	Mislead (12/1)	4	of	11
1997	3194	G-F	Tear White (15/2)	2	of	10

Backing the bottom three in the draw in fields of between 10 and 15 would have produced a level-stakes profit of £39.75 for a £1 stake (39 bets, 7 winners). Below 10 runners, it is hard to rule out any runners and above 15 the inclination is for runners to form two groups. 33/1 winner Arnie obviously had a big effect on the profit, but even without him it would still have been good. When the ground becomes softer, runners towards the centre seem to have a better chance, although several of the above winners drawn high on soft ground switched over to the stands' rail.

Subsequent Record of runners 'winning their side' in Stewards' Cup (1992-7)					
1992	Master Planner	(6th)	next time	WON	16/1
1993	No Qualifiers				
1994	No Qualifiers				
1995	Jayannpee	(3rd)	next time	unp	15/8
1996	Wildwood Flower	(5th)	next time	WON	8/1
1997	No Qualifiers				

It is unusual to see one flank completely dominate in the Stewards' Cup, but the three times that it has happened in the last six years has seen the winner on the unfavoured side go on to score next time on two occasions.

HAMILTON (R-H) - *On ground good or softer, it used to be essential to be drawn middle to high in sprints, although the advantage did not always seem quite so great in 1997. A high draw is also a real advantage in races over 1m 65y as there is a tight right-hand loop into the home straight. It is not uncommon for the ground to become too bad for the use of stalls here.*

Best Examples		5f-6f 5y	1m 65y
	Firm	1613	
	Good	610	4471
	Soft	956, 2384	

HAYDOCK (L-H) - *When soft ground prevailed in the past, jockeys often used to bring their mounts over to the stands' side in races run on the round course as the ground always used to be widely recognised as being better there. However, in 1997, this did not appear to be the case. High numbers used to be favoured in sprint races when the ground was good or softer, but there now appears to be a faster strip of ground towards the far rail (low).*

Best Examples		5f-6f
	Firm	3410
	Good	4012
	Soft	4733

KEMPTON (R-H) - *On the separate sprint track, when the stalls are on the stands' side and the ground is soft, a low draw is a great advantage. When the stalls are placed on the far side, high numbers are favoured, but when the runners stretch right across the track, low numbers just about hold the edge.*

The Teal Handicap, formerly the Syringa Handicap, run in April, and The Underwriting Handicap in May, used to show up a draw bias most years, with big-priced, well-drawn runners often making the frame. The stalls were usually placed on the far rail (high).

Kempton, April 20, 1992, good to soft:-

480 TEAL H'CAP (0-90)
4-10 (4-13) 5f £2,872.00 (£856.00: £408.00: £184.00) Stalls: Centre GOING: 0.20 sec per fur (G)

			SP	RR	SF
344[14] **Olifantsfontein (68)** (RSimpson) 4-8-11b[1] WRyan(8) (racd far side: mde virtually all: clr 2f out: r.o wl) ....—	1	20/1	81	73
236[9] **Ski Captain (60)** (PHowling) 8-8-3 NCarlisle(10) (racd far side: chsd wnr: rdn over 2f out: unable qckn)..........6	2	16/1	55	41
414[8] **Greetland Rock (53)** (PHowling) 4-7-7[(3)ow1] FNorton(11) (swtg: racd far side: lost pl over 3f out: hdwy over 1f out: r.o)..................................1½	3	33/1	43	25
414[2] **Across the Bay (69)** (SDow) 5-8-12v WCarson(5) (outpcd: gd hdwy over 1f out: r.o)..................¾	4	9/2[2]	56	41
455[8] **Gondo (71)** (EJAlston) 5-9-0v LPiggott(6) (a.p: one pce fnl 2f) ....s.h	5	7/1	58	42
344[4] **Baysham (USA) (80)** (BRMillman) 6-9-9b GBaxter(3) (lw: dwlt: nvr nr to chal) ....½	6	5/1[3]	65	49
349[0] **Wanda (72)** (KRBurke) 5-9-1 DHolland(1) (b.off hind: gd spd over 3f) ....s.h	7	4/1[1]	57	—
Cash a Million (FR) (55) (PDCundell) 4-7-12 EJohnson(4) (a bhd)...	8	25/1	35	—
386[7] **Miami Banker (79)** (WRMuir) 6-9-8b MRoberts(7) (racd far side: prom 3f)...........................¾	9	7/1	56	—
386[4] **Touch of White (85)** (JEBanks) 6-9-9[(5)] LNewton(2) (gd spd 3f) ....½	10	5/1[3]	60	—
Forlorn Diver (56) (BGubby) 4-7-13 JQuinn(9) (swtg: racd far side: a bhd)..................................3½	11	33/1	20	—

(SP 116.9%) **11 Rn**

61.21 secs (2.11) CT £9,012.95 TOTE £25.60: £4.20 £2.90 £6.50 (£105.50) OWNER Mr Trevor Painting (WENDOVER) BRED Whitsbury Manor Stud

Best Examples	**5f-6f**	
Good	520, 3686	

LEICESTER (R-H) - *It used to be considered that low numbers had an advantage on the straight course, particularly on soft ground. In recent seasons though, the advantage has been with runners drawn closest to the pace, and most races now seem to end up being run down the centre of the course. However, the odd meeting still seems to pop up where either high or low numbers are favoured, but there is little consistency.*

Best Examples	**5f-5f 218y**	**7f 9y-1m 8y**
Firm	4328	
Good		3691

LINGFIELD Turf (L-H) - *The draw advantage depends entirely upon the ground. When it is good to firm or firmer, high numbers have an advantage on the straight course. On good ground, the draw seems to have little effect, but when it is good to soft or softer, those drawn low (towards the far rail) seem to enjoy the edge. The one factor that can have a massive effect on the draw here is heavy rain falling onto firm ground. Presumably because of the undulating nature of the track and the fact that the far rail on the straight course is towards the bottom of a slope where it joins the round course, rainfall seems to make the middle and far side of the straight course ride a lot slower. In these conditions, runners drawn right up against the stands' rail, often only the top three or four stalls, have a massive edge. The advantage does not seem to be anything like as great over sprint distances as it is over seven furlongs and 7f 140y under any conditions.*

Lingfield, May 30, 1992, good, morning rain:-

1133 DAILY MAIL DREAM COTTAGE GAME H'CAP (0-110)
2-30 (2-33) 7f £9,240.00 (£2,760.00: £1,320.00: £600.00) Stalls: High GOING: 0.00 sec per fur (G)

			SP	RR	SF
941[3] **Cheveux Mitchell (70)** (MRChannon) 5-8-7v RHills(15) (mde virtually all: drvn out) ....—	1	7/1[1]	79	72

15

					SP	RR	SF
860[4]	**Kimberley Park** (66) (DWPArbuthnot) 4-8-3 MHills(13) (a.p: ev ch fnl f: r.o)	½	2	8/1 [3]	74	66
887*	**Bold Angel** (79) (MHEasterby) 5-9-2 MBirch(11) (a.p: ev ch ins fnl f: unable qckn)	1½	3	15/2 [2]	84	74
610[3]	**Mango Manila** (89) (CAHorgan) 7-9-12 AMcGlone(12) (b: lw: hdwy over 1f out: one pce)	4	4	8/1 [3]	86	72
935[3]	**Hard to Figure** (91) (RJHodges) 6-10-0 RCochrane(9) (a.p: rdn over 1f out: wknd fnl f)	¾	5	10/1	86	72
1013[8]	**Darakah** (60) (CJHill) 5-7-11 JQuinn(4) (nvr nr to chal)	1½	6	12/1	52	36
898*	**Rocky Waters** (USA) (86) (GLewis) 3-8-12 BRouse(10) (hdwy 2f out: one pce)	1	7	9/1	78	—
860[9]	**Superoo** (74) (JSutcliffe) 6-8-11 DeanMcKeown(8) (a mid div)	2	8	14/1	60	—
997[8]	**Candle King** (IRE) (59) (MJFetherston-Godley) 4-7-5b [5]ow3 DHarrison(6) (a mid div)	hd	9	25/1	44	—
	Wild and Loose (86) (DRCElsworth) 4-9-9 SCauthen(14) (bit bkwd: a bhd)	6	10	14/1	58	—
930[4]	**Merlins Wish** (USA) (89) (RHannon) 3-9-1 LPiggott(7) (bhd fnl 3f)	5	11	8/1 [3]	52	—
853[6]	**Baysham** (USA) (83) (BRMillman) 6-9-6b SWhitworth(2) (bhd fnl 3f)	4	12	20/1	36	—
692[6]	**Domicksky** (75) (MJRyan) 4-8-12 WCarson(3) (prom over 3f)	2	13	9/1	24	—
858[7]	**Fair American** (USA) (78) (MRStoute) 3-8-4 PaulEddery(1) (lw: bhd fnl 4f)	2½	14	25/1	24	—

(SP 120.2%) **14 Rn**

1m 22.72 (1.52) CT £391.13 TOTE £6.50: £2.30 £2.80 2.00 (£20.80) OWNER Chitty Ltd (UPPER LAMBOURN) BRED Colby Bloodstock
WEIGHT FOR AGE 3yo-11lb

Lingfield, June 17, 1995, good to firm, showers:-

1785 GSP (S) H'CAP (0-60) (3-Y.O+) (Class G)
7-00 (7-07) 7f £2,870.20 (£797.20: £382.60) Stalls: High GOING minus 0.40 sec per fur (F)

					SP	RR	SF
1629[2]	**Four of Spades** (48) (WSCunningham) 4-9-8b AMcGlone(15) (a.p: led over 1f out: sn clr: comf)	—	1	4/1 [1]	53	41
	Legend Dulac (IRE) (43) (JohnHarris) 6-8-12 [5] PMcCabe(13) (led: hdd over 1f out: unable qckn)	3½	2	12/1	40	28
882[13]	**Glen Miller** (40) (JWPayne) 5-9-0v MTebbutt(14) (a.p: rdn 2f out: one pce)	7	3	12/1	21	9
882[7]	**Finjan** (53) (AGFoster) 8-9-13 TSprake(11) (mid div: hdwy over 2f out: rdn over 1f out: one pce)	2½	4	9/1	28	16
1521[5]	**Sandra Dee** (IRE) (54) (BAPearce) 3-9-5 SWhitworth(16) (a.p: rdn over 2f out: one pce)	s.h	5	16/1	29	8
1355[15]	**Beware of Agents** (49) (MJohnston) 6-9-9 NAdams(12) (chsd ldrs: rdn over 2f out: one pce fnl 2f)	1½	6	8/1 [3]	21	9
1472[8]	**King Parrot** (IRE) (46) (LordHuntingdon) 7-9-1v [5] AWhelan(9) (prom tl rdn & wknd over 1f out)	1¾	7	7/1 [2]	14	2
1509[4]	**Doodies Pool** (IRE) (51) (GLMoore) 5-9-4 [7] LSuthern(6) (rr: hdwy over 1f out: nvr nrr)	½	8	8/1 [3]	18	6
1321[9]	**Splash of Salt** (IRE) (49) (TJNaughton) 5-9-9b DBiggs(10) (prom over 4f)	2½	9	20/1	10	—
1276[7]	**Apollo Red** (51) (AMoore) 6-9-11 CandyMorris(3) (prom over 4f)	½	10	16/1	11	—
1323[16]	**Tiddy Oggie** (44) (NAGraham) 4-9-4b [1] RMimmer(4) (mid div: rdn over 3f out: wknd 2f out)	1¼	11	10/1	1	—
1499[10]	**Waders Dream** (IRE) (45) (PatMitchell) 6-9-5b SO'Gorman(8) (chsd ldrs 5f)	2	12	20/1	—	—
	Ain'tlifelikethat (40) (TJNaughton) 8-9-0 GBardwell(7) (a bhd)	9	13	25/1	—	—
1403[5]	**Assignment** (49) (JFfitch-Heyes) 9-9-9 GDuffield(1) (a bhd)	4	14	16/1	—	—
1334[6]	**It's So Easy** (40) (APJames) 4-8-11 [3] DWright(2) (a bhd)	¾	15	25/1	—	—
1501[9]	**Lord Alfie** (40) (BJMeehan) 6-9-0b JQuinn(5) (a bhd)	4	16	25/1	—	—

(SP 127.9%) **16 Rn**

1m 23.06 (1.86) CSF £49.33 CT £486.82 TOTE £3.80: £1.30 £2.60 3.60 £4.80 (£21.00) Trio £325.10 OWNER Mr B. L. Cassidy (YARM) BRED Hesmonds Stud Ltd
WEIGHT FOR AGE 3yo-9lb
No bid

To my knowledge, these were the only two 7f-7f 140y races to be run on recently rain-softened good or better ground at Lingfield in the past five years (to be fair they had to meet a very strict set of conditions). The result of the effect of the draw on both occasions was very conclusive.

Best Examples		5f-6f	7f-7f 140y
	Firm	1236	1965
	Good		1785 *(1995)*
	Soft		3677 *(1995)*

LINGFIELD all-weather (L-H) - *Low numbers are slightly favoured, an advantage which can be accentuated by a fast break.*

MUSSELBURGH (R-H) - *High numbers are favoured over seven furlongs and a mile. Over five furlongs, low numbers have a considerable advantage, particularly on soft ground, irrespective of the size of the field. On the rare occasions that the stalls stretch right across the track, low numbers still do best, although the far rail (high) seems to ride quicker than the centre.*

Best Examples	5f
Good	2540
Soft	494

NEWBURY (L-H) - *When the ground is genuinely soft, it is not uncommon to see runners race wide down the back straight and the side of the course in events of between 1m 3f 56y and 2 miles. It is particularly the case in races of 1m 5f 61y, which start on a chute at the far end of the back straight. In such circumstances, a high draw becomes a huge advantage. Many consider a low draw to be an advantage in big-field races over the round 7f 64y and 1m 7y courses, since there is a sharpish left-hand bend into the home straight not long after the starts. Whilst this is pretty much the case when the ground is good or firmer, it is definitely not true when the ground becomes soft. After a few races, the ground on the rail becomes chewed up and horses that are drawn high are able to race on the better ground (often only four or five horse widths off the rail) and swing onto the better ground in the straight, so while they are travelling that bit further, the surface is that much better. In races run on the straight course, a high draw is always an advantage and it becomes a necessity on soft ground. When the ground is good or firmer, low-drawn horses have more of a chance, especially over the straight seven furlongs and mile as runners tend to split into two distinct groups or all bunch over towards the stands' rail. In sprints here though, runners often seem to race where they are drawn and, on soft ground, it is worth ruling out any horse drawn below halfway and concentrating on the five or six drawn closest to the stands' rail.*

Best Examples	5f 34y-6f	7f-1m st	rnd 7f 64y +
Soft	1240	1190 *(1996)*	1193, 1194 *(1996)*

NEWCASTLE (L-H) - *On the straight course, high numbers are favoured when the ground is good or firmer, but low numbers have a marked advantage when the ground rides good to soft or softer. On good ground, runners that race down the centre do not look to be at any disadvantage.*

Best Examples	5f-6f	7f-1m 8y st
Firm	993	
Good	4842	3802
Soft	2326	

NEWMARKET July Course (R-H) - *It is rare for the draw to play any part, but the occasional meeting will be affected. High numbers seemed to just have the edge at the 1997 July Meeting when the stalls were mostly on the stands' side.*

NEWMARKET Rowley Mile (R-H) - *It is not uncommon to see fields of 30+, and when this is the case, runners up against either rail can have the advantage. When the going is soft, runners right up against the far rail hold sway, but soft ground at Newmarket is not a common occurrence. In late season, it has been known for the stands' rail to be moved to unveil virgin ground up against the stands' side. In these circumstances, runners drawn* *low can have a big advantage. As on the July Course, the odd meeting seems to pop up where one rail is favoured and there were quite a few examples of this in 1997. In fields of around 15, stalls in the middle (between about 8 and 10) seem to do quite well, presumably because they can get covered up on such an open course. Over longer trips, when the fields are large, high numbers enjoy a slight advantage, as long as the runners stick to the far rail (they came across to race against the stands' rail in the 1997 Cesarewitch).*

> The stands' rail is sometimes moved at Newmarket's Rowley Mile course to accommodate large fields and horses racing on the fresh ground enjoy a decisive advantage. When the rail is moved, runners drawn above 20 are faced with a real struggle.

Best Examples		**5f-6f**	**7f-1m 1f**	**1m 2f +**
	Firm		4558	4971
	Good	942	4781	

Newmarket, October 6, 1990, good to firm:-

3589 WILLIAM HILL CAMBRIDGESHIRE H'CAP (0-115)
3-35 (3-41) **1m 1f (Rowley)** £61,607.50 (£18,610.00: £9,055.00: £4,277.50) Stalls: High GOING: minus 0.30 sec per fur (F)

				SP	RR	SF
3220*	**Risen Moon (USA)** (BWHills) **3-8-9** SCauthen**(2)** (stdd s: gd hdwy over 1f out: str run to ld wl ins fnl f)	—	**1**	7/1[1]	—	73
3282*	**Mellottie** (MrsMReveley) **5-7-11** JLowe**(4)** (hdwy over 3f out: led over 1f out: hdd wl ins fnl f)	1½	**2**	10/1[2]	—	56
3448[6]	**Line of Vision (USA)** (MrsJRRamsden) **3-7-7**(5) DHolland**(6)** (a.p: led 3f out to over 1f out: one pce)	3	**3**	25/1	—	43
3463[5]	**Operation Wolf** (CEBrittain) **4-9-4** TQuinn**(18)** (gd hdwy 2f out: ev ch 1f out: no ex)	hd	**4**	20/1	—	67
2868[16]	**Chase the Door** (JSutcliffe) **5-8-8b** MWigham**(5)** (a.p: ev ch over 2f out: wknd wl over 1f out)	1½	**5**	50/1	—	52
3233[3]	**Dashing Senor** (ACStewart) **3-8-10** DeanMcKeown**(19)** (hdwy 3f out: one pce fnl 2f)	2	**6**	33/1	—	48
3476[17]	**Dawn Success** (CEBrittain) **4-8-5**(7) BDoyle**(7)** (prom: no hdwy fnl 2f)	s.h	**7**	50/1	—	—
3248[5]	**Gilderdale** (JWHills) **8-8-9** AClark**(35)** (hdwy 3f out: nvr able to chal)	2	**8**	50/1	—	—
3398[3]	**Re-Release** (MCPipe) **5-8-2v**(5) SO'Gorman**(32)** (lw: hdwy 4f out: styd on fnl 2f)	1½	**9**	20/1	—	—
3476*	**Pontenuovo** (DRCElsworth) **5-9-3** JBleasdale**(34)** (led far side: no ch over 1f out)	½	**10**	25/1	—	—
3311[2]	**Bottles (USA)** (GAHuffer) **3-8-0**(7) LNewton**(30)** (chsd ldr far side: no ch fnl 2f)	4	**11**	33/1	—	—
2868[3]	**Usa Dollar** (BGubby) **3-8-5b** GDuffield**(8)** (nvr nrr)	½	**12**	20/1	—	—
3481[4]	**Halkopous** (MHTompkins) **4-8-2** RFox**(1)** (lw: dwlt: n.d)	hd	**13**	33/1	—	—
3399*	**Lord of Tusmore** (BWHills) **3-8-12** MHills**(15)** (lw: n.d)	2½	**14**	12/1[3]	—	—
3399[4]	**Parador** (GHarwood) **4-8-11**(7) DStather**(9)** (prom 6f)	½	**15**	33/1	—	—
3476[5]	**You Missed Me** (DWPArbuthnot) **4-9-3** BRaymond**(33)** (n.d)	¾	**16**	50/1	—	—
3469[4]	**Hawwam** (CJBenstead) **4-7-10** DMcKay**(26)** (lw: hdwy 3f out: wknd wl over 1f out)	s.h	**17**	66/1	—	—
2974*	**Gulmarg** (HCandy) **3-8-4** CRutter**(21)**	1½	**18**	13/1	—	—
3359[3]	**Karazan** (JGFitzGerald) **3-8-11b[1]** KFallon**(10)** (n.d)	½	**19**	20/1	—	—
3311*	**Red Toto** (ACStewart) **3-9-9** MRoberts**(22)** (n.d)	1½	**20**	20/1	—	—
3470[7]	**Clear Light** (GAHuffer) **3-7-10v[1]** GBardwell**(24)** (n.d)	½	**21**	66/1	—	—
3357*	**Arany** (MHTompkins) **3-8-12** RHills**(14)** (w ldrs over 5f)	s.h	**22**	16/1	—	—
3193[4]	**Silver Ore (FR)** (WAO'Gorman) **3-8-12** AMunro**(3)** (led 6f)	½	**23**	33/1	—	—
3344*	**Ned's Aura** (RMWhitaker) **5-8-13** WRyan**(13)** (n.d)	2	**24**	14/1	—	—
3360[8]	**At Peace** (RCharlton) **4-8-4v[1]** WNewnes**(23)** (n.d)	hd	**25**	33/1	—	—
3141[4]	**Gran Alba (USA)** (RHannon) **4-9-4b[1]** KDarley**(29)** (prom over 6f)	hd	**26**	50/1	—	—
3463[10]	**Kiya (USA)** (LordHuntingdon) **4-7-11**(3) DaleGibson**(17)** (n.d)	¾	**27**	50/1	—	—
3470[2]	**Minimize** (LMCumani) **3-8-6** LDettori**(20)** (n.d)	hd	**28**	20/1	—	—
3399[10]	**Monastery** (MrsLPiggott) **4-9-2** BCrossley**(28)** (n.d)	½	**29**	66/1	—	—
3463[7]	**Lost Innocence (USA)** (MRStoute) **3-8-11v[1]** WRSwinburn**(11)** (n.d)	hd	**30**	33/1	—	—
3553[12]	**Genair (FR)** (GMMoore) **5-7-6**(3) SWood**(27)** (n.d)	nk	**31**	100/1	—	—
3488a[7]	**Waki Gold (USA)** (PAKelleway) **3-8-2** AMackay**(12)** (w ldrs 6f)	3	**32**	66/1	—	—
3143[9]	**Vague Shot** (CEBrittain) **7-9-10** JCarroll**(40)** (lw: n.d)		**33**	66/1	—	—
3223[6]	**Well Furnished** (AAScott) **3-8-8** NDay**(37)** (lw: n.d)		**34**	66/1	—	—
3399[2]	**Unknown Quantity** (LordHuntingdon) **5-9-5** GCarter**(38)** (prom far side 6f)		**35**	20/1	—	—
2123[4]	**Nakora Bistraya (USA)** (GAPritchard-Gordon) **3-7-11** JQuinn**(36)** (swtg: n.d)		**36**	66/1	—	—
3463[6]	**Western Wolf** (WCarter) **5-7-11**(5) NGwilliams**(39)** (n.d)		**37**	66/1	—	—
3513[4]	**Gordons Dream** (CNAllen) **3-7-12** NCarlisle**(31)** (chsd ldrs far side 5f)		**38**	100/1	—	—

2755* **Vilanika (FR)** (CEBrittain) 4-7-12(3) RonHillis(16) (swtg: n.d) .... 39 66/1 — —
34683 **Breezed Well** (CNAllen) 4-9-3 MTebbutt(25) (n.d) .... 40 66/1 — —
(SP 139.3%) **40 Rn**

1m 49.4 (-1.10) CT £1,565.06 TOTE £8.10: £3.30 £2.60 £10.80 £5.60 (£29.90) OWNER Mr R. E. Sangster (LAMBOURN)
WEIGHT FOR AGE 3yo-4lb

NOTTINGHAM (L-H) - *On the straight course, it used to be a case of low numbers being favoured when the stalls were on the far rail and high numbers when they were on the stands' rail, but these days the advantage does not seem that great. On several occasions in 1997, high numbers looked to be favoured, but low numbers held sway too often to be bullish about any advantage. Low numbers are slightly favoured over 1m 54y, but not by as much as in the past.*

Best Examples	5f-6f 15y
Good	649, 759, 4169

PONTEFRACT (L-H) - *Low numbers are considered best here for the same reason as at Chester, in that the course has several distinct left-hand turns with a short home straight, but the advantage is not that great. A high draw can be a big setback on fast ground, since it forces runners to race wide or drop in behind and onto the rail, but on soft ground a high draw becomes a distinct advantage. When the ground becomes really wet, jockeys tend to head for the outside rail and runners drawn low can have little chance when the stalls are placed on the inside. However, the ground can become so bad that the stalls are moved to the outside of the course, negating any advantage in being drawn high.*

Best Examples	5f-6f	1m 4y+
Soft	4805, 4807	4802, 4806

REDCAR (L-H) - *It is not unusual to see fields verging on 30 in straight-course races several times throughout a season, and high numbers (stands' side) are usually favoured. However, a majority of the runners seem to race towards that side in these events and, considering how few go for the far rail, low numbers have held their own.*

Best Examples	5f-6f	7f-1m
Firm	3431	4994
Good	4790	

RIPON (R-H) - *High numbers are slightly favoured on the round course. However, the draw has a massive effect in sprint races and, as shown by the table on page 20, any runner drawn in the centre stalls can be completely ignored. The optimum conditions for low numbers seems to be when the ground is good or faster and there are 16 runners or below. When the stalls stretch far enough across the course though, in races of 16 or more runners, there is a fast strip of ground towards the far rail which horses drawn very high can utilise.*

Best Examples	5f-6f
Firm	2891
Good	3812
Soft	3937 *(1996)*

Sprint Handicaps with 10 plus runners at Ripon (stalls low) (1996-7)						
Only three sprint handicaps have attracted fewer than 10 runners in the last two years						
Year	Race No	Going	Winner	Draw		Runners
1996	610	Good	Super Benz (6/1)	21	of	24
1996	704	G-F	Chadwell Hall (5/1)	3	of	13
1996	824	Good	Antonias Melody (6/1)	1	of	16
1996	1199	Good	Portend (10/1)	3	of	10
1996	1527	Good	Finisterre (25/1)	21	of	21
1996	2064	G-F	Insider Trader (7/2)	3	of	11
1996	2902	G-F	Camionneur (11/10)	2	of	12
1996	3296	G-F	Bollin Joanne (11/1)	10	of	16
1996	3622	Good	Samwar (15/2)	2	of	17
1996	3844	G-S	Naissant (10/1)	17	of	18
1996	3937	Soft	Another Nightmare (9/1)	19	of	20
1997	596	G-F	French Grit (10/1)	2	of	18
1997	702	G-F	Johayro (7/1)	1	of	19
1997	845	Good	Denton Lad (14/1)	2	of	18
1997	1269	G-S	Canovas Heart (6/1)	7	of	11
1997	1496	G-F	Swift (7/1)	8	of	16
1997	2044	Good	Double Action (6/4)	2	of	10
1997	2061	Good	Blessingindisguise (9/1)	14	of	14
1997	2891	G-F	Aquatic Queen (9/2)	1	of	17
1997	3271	G-F	Bashful Brave (12/1)	3	of	15
1997	3273	G-F	So Intrepid (3/1)	5	of	15
1997	3604	G-F	Tadeo (12/1)	19	of	21
1997	3812	G-F	Samsung Spirit (12/1)	2	of	16
1997	3823	G-F	Folklore (5/1)	16	of	16
1997	3910	Good	Bowlers Boy (10/1)	24	of	24

Incredibly, backing stalls 1, 2 and 3 blind in all Ripon sprint handicaps with 10 or more runners would have made a £1 level-stakes profit of £32.10 over the past two years. Equally amazing is that backing the top 3 stalls (Blessingindisguise fortuitous in that he raced up the stands' rail) in the same races would have posted a level-stakes profit of £12.00. Covering the top 3 and bottom 3 stalls in every race (backing 6 horses in all per race) would have made a level-stakes profit of £44.10. All of the above level-stakes figures are based on backing blind without allowing for other factors, such as ignoring runners not suited by the ground.

Only 5 winners in 25 races shown in the above table came from any other stall than the bottom or top 3 and some of those must have turned in outstanding performances to score. Super Benz was only 4 off the far rail in a field of 24, so was probably drawn high enough. Bollin Joanne did very well to win from stall 10 in a field of 16, and subsequently showed herself to be pattern class. Canovas Heart was winning first time out for the third season in a row, but it was still a very good effort. Swift missed the break and was able to race on the best ground, but this was still a remarkable effort in the light of every other Ripon result in the past two years. His handicap mark was slipping down again at the end of the 1997 season and he remains one to watch. Blessingindisguise, although drawn 14 of 14, actually raced towards the stands' rail, making this an incredible performance. He went on to win three of his next four outings (see pages 104-5). So Intrepid was drawn just about low enough in stall 5 of 15.

SALISBURY (R-H) - *High numbers have the advantage on the straight course when the ground is on the soft side of good.*

Best Examples	5f-6f	6f 212y-1m
Good	3698 *(1996)*	
Soft		3979

SANDOWN (R-H) - *There is little or no draw advantage on the round course, but on the separate sprint track, the advantage is among the greatest of any course in the country. When the going is on the soft side of good and the stalls are placed on the far side (high), high numbers have a massive advantage. When the stalls are placed on the stands' side, low numbers enjoy a slight advantage when all the runners stay towards the stands' rail, but when a few break off and go to the far side, as in Raceform Race 3898 1997, high numbers comfortably hold the upper hand again. The far rail is without doubt much faster than the stands' rail, which in turn is much faster than the centre of the course over five furlongs. The softer the ground, the bigger the advantage seems to be.*

Best Examples	5f
Good	834

Sandown, April 26, 1996, good:-

812 SURREY RACING H'CAP (0-90) (3-Y.O+) (Class C)
4-45 (4-47) **5f 6y** £5,784.00 (£1,752.00: £856.00: £408.00) Stalls: High GOING minus 0.15 sec per fur (GF)

		SP	RR	SF
582 4 Mister Jolson (70) (RJHodges) 7-8-8 RCochrane(18) (b.nr fore: lw: hdwy 2f out: led 1f out: pushed out)	—	1 100/30 1	73	55
582 11 Sir Joey (USA) (77) (PGMurphy) 7-8-12(3) SDrowne(17) (hld up: rdn over 1f out: r.o one pce)	2	2 8/1 2	74	56
Glorious Aragon (80) (RFJohnsonHoughton) 4-9-4 ACulhane(1) (swtg: rdn & hdwy over 1f out: r.o)	s.h	3 33/1	77++	59
Master of Passion (85) (JMPEustace) 7-9-9 MTebbutt(15) (bit bkwd: led 3f out tl over 1f out: one pce fnl f) ...½		4 8/1 2	80	62
Gone Savage (60) (WJMusson) 8-7-12 FNorton(13) (bkwd: a.p: led over 1f out: sn hdd: one pce)	s.h	5 9/1 3	55	37
Rock Symphony (87) (WJHaggas) 6-9-4(7) ElizabethTurner(14) (s.s: hdwy over 1f out: nvr nrr)	1¼	6 25/1	78	60
692* Galine (76) (WAO'Gorman) 3-8-4 6x SSanders(16) (a.p: rdn over 2f out: wknd fnl f)	¾	7 100/30 1	64	36
601 14 Followmegirls (58) (MrsALMKing) 7-7-10 JQuinn(11) (s.s: nvr nr to chal)	1¾	8 33/1	41	23
749 16 Our Shadee (USA) (58) (KTIvory) 6-7-10v NAdams(10) (lw: prom over 3f)	nk	9 33/1	40	22
577 17 Multan (61) (GLMoore) 4-7-13ow1 WCarson(8) (b: nvr nrr)	1	10 33/1	40	21
582 12 Tinker Osmaston (71) (MSSaunders) 5-8-9 JFEgan(5) (lw: bhd fnl 2f)	½	11 20/1	48	30
711 7 Lennox Lewis (90) (APJarvis) 4-9-7(7) KHopkins(12) (prom over 3f)	¾	12 20/1	65	47
582 18 Sally Slade (77) (CACyzer) 4-9-1 JReid(2) (a bhd)	s.h	13 33/1	52	34
632 7 Tart and a Half (77) (BJMeehan) 4-8-8(7) GHannon(3) (lw: a bhd)	nk	14 33/1	51	33
Twice as Sharp (84) (PWHarris) 4-9-8 GHind(6) (prom over 3f)	2	15 12/1	57	39
Ashtina (72) (BAPearce) 11-8-10 PatEddery(7) (led 2f: wknd over 2f out)	hd	16 20/1	38	20
632 9 Halbert (65) (PBurgoyne) 7-8-0v(3) DRMcCabe(4) (bhd fnl 2f)		17 33/1	31	13

61.3 secs (0.60) CSF £26.82 CT £682.40 TOTE £3.90: £1.40 £2.50 £5.10 £2.80 (£7.60) Trio £399.60 OWNER Mr Bob Froome (SOMERTON) (SP 124.8%) **17 Rn**
BRED Mrs D. D. Scott
LONG HANDICAP Our Shadee (USA) 7-2 Followmegirls 7-2
WEIGHT FOR AGE 3yo-10lb

582 Mister Jolson had the plum draw here and took full advantage. Beginning his effort a quarter of a mile from home, he swooped into the lead a furlong out and needed only to be nudged along for a decisive victory. (100/30)
Sir Joey (USA) chased the leaders and stayed on up the hill to snatch second prize. (8/1)
Glorious Aragon ran a tremendous race from her poor draw. Picking up ground from below the distance, she kept on really well up the hill, and only just failed to take second prize. She should be followed. (33/1)
Master of Passion, with something left to work on, hit the front three furlongs from home but, headed below the distance, failed to summon up another gear. (8/1: 6/1-9/1)

21

Sprint Handicaps with 10 plus runners at Sandown (stalls HIGH) (1996-7)						
Year	Race No	Going	Winner	Draw		Runners
1996	812	Good	Mister Jolson (100/30)	18	of	17
1996	2787	G-F	Magic Mail (14/1)	10	of	12
1996	2976	G-F	Squire Corrie (12/1)	7	of	11
1996	3506	G-F	Half Tone (5/2)	12	of	12
1996	3930	Good	Squire Corrie (11/2)	14	of	15
1996	3946	Good	Crowded Avenue (7/1)	10	of	13
1997	834	G-F	Gone Savage (6/1)	13	of	17
1997	854	Good	Hattab (16/1)	11	of	10
1997	2481	G-S	Sally Green (2/1)	9	of	10
1997	2529	G-S	My Best Valentine (20/1)	6	of	13
1997	3500	Good	Half Tone (3/1)	16	of	14

No horse bar one has won from the bottom half of the draw in the past two seasons, with the exception being My Best Valentine who went on to show he was better than ever. Backing the top 3 stalls in each of the above races would have posted a £1 level-stakes profit of £18.33.

Sprint Handicaps with 10 plus runners at Sandown (stalls LOW) (1996-7)						
Year	Race No	Going	Winner	Draw		Runners
1996	2500	G-F	Clan Chief (2/1)	2	of	10
1996	4234	G-F	Polish Warrior (7/2)	6	of	12
1997	2769	G-F	Faith Alone (100/30)	5	of	11
1997	2964	G-F	Shalstayholy (7/1)	5	of	11
1997	3892	G-S	High Carry (7/1)	11	of	11
1997	3898	G-S	Sweet Magic (11/2)	11	of	12

SOUTHWELL all-weather (R-H) - *Low numbers seem slightly favoured since the course has been resurfaced. Before this, low numbers had looked well favoured over five furlongs, particularly after a frost.*

THIRSK (L-H) - *In sprints, high numbers are usually favoured when the stalls are placed on the stands' side (high) and the runners race centre to stands' rail on fast ground. However, there is a strip of decent ground towards the far rail which is not far off being as quick as the stands' rail. Runners that switch to race there from a low draw often reach the frame (see Ziggy's Dancer page 111). When the going is on the soft side, low numbers have the advantage as the far rail becomes the place to be. In races run on the round course, low numbers are favoured over 6f 216y and a mile.*

On more than one occasion in the recent past, David Chapman-trained sprinters drawn low have switched straight over to race on the far rail when most thought that the stands' rail would be much quicker. His representatives are always worth noting under such conditions.

Perhaps the best known of all draw-affected races is the six-furlong Dick Peacock Sprint Handicap, run at Thirsk towards the middle of May, normally on the second day of the two-day meeting. There used to be another handicap sprint on the first day (the Friday) to give punters the chance to evaluate what part the draw was playing, although it was run over five furlongs, at which trip the draw is not so vital. Unfortunately, the Dick Peacock was moved in 1995 from its traditional Saturday home to the Friday, thus taking away the chance for punters to view a dry run.

Thirsk, May 19, 1990, good to firm:-

945 DICK PEACOCK SPRINT H'CAP (0-80)
4-15 (4-18) **6f** £3,158.00 (£944.00: £452.00: £206.00) Stalls: High GOING: minus 0.30 sec per fur (F)

				SP	RR	SF
714[11]	**Cumbrian Express** (MHEasterby) **5-9-12** MBirch**(18)** (mde virtually all: r.o wl fnl 2f)	—	**1**	11/1	—	28
522[8]	**Gods Solution** (TDBarron) **9-8-10**(5) AlexGreaves**(19)** (lw: chsd ldrs: effrt over 1f out: r.o: nt rch wnr)	1½	**2**	9/1	—	6
593[12]	**Bernstein Bette** (PSFelgate) **4-9-3** SPerks**(16)** (gd hdwy over 1f out: n.m.r: r.o wl nr fin)	3	**3**	14/1	—	1
819[4]	**So Careful** (JBerry) **7-9-12** JCarroll**(17)** (lw: chsd ldrs: effrt u.p over 1f out: unable qckn)	¾	**4**	9/2[1]	—	7
818[*]	**Amigo Menor** (KMBrassey) **4-10-0b** SWhitworth**(6)** (w wnr tl wknd wl over 1f out)	1½	**5**	8/1	—	3
	Whipper In (JEtherington) **6-8-9** NDay**(9)** (lw: hdwy over 2f out: styd on same pce fnl f)	1½	**6**	25/1	—	—
818[7]	**Like Amber** (CEBrittain) **4-8-10** MRoberts**(8)** (effrt u.p over 2f out: nt rch ldrs)	¾	**7**	7/1[3]	—	—
655[15]	**Saladan Knight** (JGFitzGerald) **5-9-12** KFallon**(11)** (swtg: hdwy ½-wy: wknd wl over 1f out)	1	**8**	10/1	—	—
936[5]	**Waverley Star** (JSWainwright) **5-7-7b** LCharnock**(3)** (racd far side: swtchd rt ½-wy: n.d)	1½	**9**	20/1	—	—
508[3]	**Singing Star** (JBalding) **4-8-5** SWebster**(4)** (b: sn drvn along: n.d)	¾	**10**	12/1	—	—
739[8]	**Priestgate** (JWharton) **5-9-5** TWilliams**(15)** (hld up: effrt & n.m.r 2f out: hung lft & wknd appr fnl f)	hd	**11**	7/1[3]	—	—
636[5]	**Spittin Mick** (GMMoore) **6-7-8** JLowe**(10)** (lw: chsd ldrs over 3f: sn wknd)	3	**12**	13/2[2]	—	—
	Daleside Ladybird (TFairhurst) **4-7-12**(7) KBrownsword**(14)** (bit bkwd: w ldr over 3f: sn wknd)	½	**13**	25/1	—	—
713[9]	**Doris Girl** (WJPearce) **3-7-2**(5) SWood**(1)** (racd far side: bhd fnl 2f)	1½	**14**	50/1	—	—
691[13]	**Master Ofthe House** (DWChapman) **4-8-8** KDarley**(7)** (outpcd fr ½-wy)	hd	**15**	25/1	—	—
	The Singing Man (JBalding) **4-7-7**(7) ClaireBalding**(12)** (bit bkwd: sn outpcd)	1½	**16**	50/1	—	—

(SP 129.6%) **16 Rn**
1m 12.4 (2.70) CT £1,287.29 TOTE £12.70: £2.50 £2.70 £4.20 £1.50 (£34.00) OWNER Cumbrian Industrials Ltd (MALTON) BRED Heathavon Stables Ltd
WEIGHT FOR AGE 3yo-9lb

Thirsk, May 18, 1991, good to firm:-

952 DICK PEACOCK SPRINT H'CAP (0-90)
4-30 (4-31) **6f** £3,406.50 (£1,017.00: £486.00: £220.50) Stalls: High GOING: 0.15 sec per fur (G)

				SP	RR	SF
416[6]	**Premier Touch (89)** (TDBarron) **4-9-11**(3) AlexGreaves**(11)** (lw: a in tch: hdwy to ld over 1f out: all out)	—	**1**	10/1	92	67
	Quatre Femme (73) (MJohnston) **4-8-12** RPElliott**(9)** (chsd ldrs: hdwy 2f out: r.o wl nr fin)	s.h	**2**	16/1	76	53
	She's Smart (84) (MHEasterby) **3-9-0** MBirch**(12)** (bit bkwd: led tl hdd over 1f out: no ex)	1½	**3**	10/1	85	49
625[3]	**Norfolkiev (FR) (73)** (MMoubarak) **5-8-12** ACruz**(8)** (lw: w ldrs tl rdn & btn appr fnl f)	3	**4**	6/4[1]	62	35
	Belfort Ruler (75) (BGubby) **4-9-0** JQuinn**(1)** (bhd tl hdwy over 1f out: r.o)	nk	**5**	25/1	63	36
	Valley Mills (54) (TDBarron) **11-7-4**(3) SWood**(7)** (b: bkwd: outpcd & bhd tl styd on wl fnl f)	¾	**6**	50/1	40	13
564[14]	**Macs Maharanee (75)** (PSFelgate) **4-8-9**(5) JFanning**(3)** (lw: disp ld: sn pushed along: btn wl over 1f out)	2½	**7**	11/1	—	22
679[14]	**Amron (74)** (JBerry) **4-8-13** JCarroll**(2)** (lw: nvr wnt pce)	nk	**8**	9/2[2]	—	—
670[6]	**Darika Lad (71)** (AHarrison) **3-8-1** KFallon**(4)** (lw: s.i.s: nvr trbld ldrs)	½	**9**	11/2[3]	—	—
625[19]	**Madeley's Pet (56)** (DenysSmith) **4-7-9** LCharnock**(6)** (chsd ldrs to ½-wy: sn rdn & wknd)	5	**10**	50/1	—	—
866[7]	**Stamford Bridge (72)** (MBrittain) **3-8-2** PSedgwick**(5)** (b.hind: prom over 2f: sn outpcd)	2	**11**	20/1	—	—

(SP 118.5%) **11 Rn**
1m 13.1 (3.40) CT £1,476.28 TOTE£12.70: £3.20 £4.00 £2.30 (£34.70) OWNER Mrs Michael Watt (THIRSK)
WEIGHT FOR AGE 3yo-9lb

For the third year in succession, including 1989, high numbers dominated with those drawn against the stands' rail filling the first four places, and for the third year in succession I landed returns on forecast and tricast punts. It is surprising just how few £13,000 tricast dividends (1989) it takes to turn a season profitable, and I heard of at least one 'draw punter' at the time who took his bookmakers to their quarter-of-a-million limit. Obviously, these races were a thrice-in-a-lifetime opportunity, but it is surprising just how many other races have shown up big draw biases year after year in the past.

Best Examples		**5f-6f**	**6f 216y-1m**
	Good	1225, 3240	2019

Subsequent Record of runners 'winning their side' in Dick Peacock H'cap (1989-97)				
1988	No Qualifiers			
1989	**Nagem**	(6th)	next time	unp	7/1
1990	**Amigo Menor**	(5th)	next time	2nd	33/1
1991	**Belfort Ruler**	(5th)	next time	unp	12/1
1992-97	No Qualifiers			

During the peak of high numbers dominating, there was a hard-luck story in the shape of Amigo Menor. He showed excellent early pace from stall six to get towards the stands' rail (although never quite on it), and gave tricast punters quite a scare before gradually weakening to finish fifth. Amigo Menor went on to finish third in the Stewards' Cup and was sent off third-favourite for the Ayr Gold Cup, before winning a 0-110 handicap at Newbury. Although he doubtless improved throughout the season, the Thirsk run was an indication as to what was to come, as I believed at the time that he probably would have won from a better draw.

WARWICK (L-H) - *Low numbers on good or faster ground are slightly favoured only because the course turns left-handed at some point over all distances. However, when the ground is genuinely soft, high numbers have the edge over most distances as the stands' rail rides much faster.*

Best Examples		5f-6f	7f-1m
	Soft	2491	2492

WINDSOR (Fig. 8) - *It is not uncommon to see large fields right throughout the summer at Windsor, particularly over sprint distances and in the 1m 67y events. Over the latter distance, runners drawn high enjoy the edge since the start is set on a chute and the course follows a tight right-handed loop to the point where it joins the sprint track. In sprints, high numbers seem to hold a slight advantage when the ground is good or faster, when a very low draw can become a difficult hurdle to overcome in big fields. When the ground becomes soft, low numbers seem to have a better chance.*

Best Examples		5f-5f 217y	1m 67y
	Firm	2917	
	Good		1297
	Soft	1141	

WOLVERHAMPTON all-weather (L-H) - *It used to be considered that the going was at its slowest towards the inside rail and very few jockeys ever raced there, most preferring to come down the centre. However, the going has seemed to level out and it apparently rides much faster now than before.*

YARMOUTH (L-H) - *High numbers have a big advantage when the ground is firm and the fields are large. Fortunately, that is often the case at Yarmouth and there are plenty of handicaps run on the straight course that attract maximum fields though the season, even when the ground is very fast. In straight-course races with 15 or more runners, it is not*

24

unusual to see one or two runners drawn low make the frame, but rarely do they manage to win overall. Part of the reason for high numbers enjoying such an advantage is that the off-shore breeze blows away from the stands' rail, making it difficult for the watering to be even.

Best Examples

	5f-6f 3y	7f 3y-1m 3y
Firm	4248	4951

Straight-course fast-ground handicaps with 15 plus runners at Yarmouth (1996-7)

Year	Race No	Going	Winner	Draw		Runners
1996	1691	Firm	Irrepressible (20/1)	12	of	18
1996	4240	G-F	Don Pepe (8/1)	11	of	17
1996	4259	G-F	Corniche Quest (10/1)	18	of	18
1996	4263	G-F	Night of Glass (7/2)	18	of	18
1997	1501	Firm	Safey Ana (9/1)	13	of	15
1997	1689	Firm	Mr Rough (7/2)	13	of	20
1997	2922	G-F	Mezzoramio (4/1)	11	of	16
1997	4228	Firm	Lunch Party (3/1)	17	of	19
1997	4243	Firm	Shark (16/1)	2	of	19
1997	4248	Firm	Gay Breeze (5/1)	20	of	18
1997	4951	Firm	Speedy Classic (14/1)	20	of	20

Only one horse has won from a single-figure stall in the past two seasons under these conditions. Backing the top 3 stalls in each of the above races would have posted a £1 level-stakes profit of £27.50.

YORK (L-H) - The draw at York has been thoroughly unpredictable in the past few seasons and neither side of the track seems to have that much of an edge. Very high draws and very low draws look worst off in big-field sprints, but the main requirement seems to be to race with the main bunch and thus closer to the pace. The last time that the draw played a major role was at the 1991 Ebor meeting, when the ground had been watered in the run-up, only for significant rainfall to follow. That week, low numbers were favoured on the round course as trainers and jockeys complained of false ground.

Best Examples

	5f-6f
Good	3649, 4636

CHAPTER 2

RACECOURSE DETAILS AND MAPS

Distances open to change when 'dolling out' occurs are shown in **bold**, as are the amended safety figures. 'Dolling out', or moving the inside rail, can cause the actual race distance to vary from the distance shown. Such races are advertised in the racing press prefixed by the word 'about'.

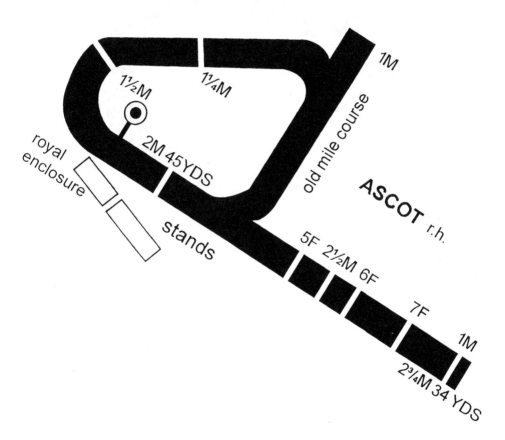

Ascot put the stalls on the stands' side (low) nine times out of ten in races run on the straight course, but they can occasionally go on the far side or down the centre. Both rails on the straight course, which is about 30 metres wide, are permanent.

Maximum runners: 5f (28), 6f (30), 7f (30), 1m (st) (32), 1m (rnd) (30), **1m 2f** (18), 1m 4f (20), **2m 45y** (20), **2m 4f** (29), **2m 6f 34y** (32)

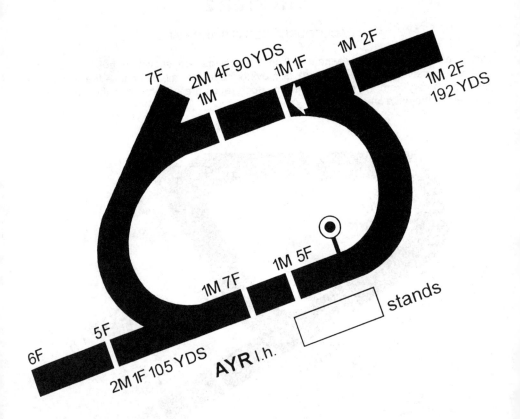

Ayr normally put the stalls on the stands' rail (high) in races at up to six furlongs, although they are occasionally put on the far rail (low) to preserve the ground up the stands' side. For a trial period here (and at many other courses), the stalls were placed in the centre of the course, but apparently this move proved unpopular with trainers. No drainage work has been carried out on the flat course in recent times, although some was done on the jumps course. Ayr is generally a free-draining course with two clay belts running through. Both rails in the straight can be moved and are frequently, with the inside rail being moved every meeting, gradually shifting outwards (for as much as 3 metres) and then going back to the inside. The stands' rail is not moved as often, but both rails have to be moved out as far as they go to accommodate the 29 runners of the Gold and Silver Cups. The straight course is about 30 metres wide.

Maximum runners: 5f (20, 27 at Western Meeting), 6f (20, 29 at Western Meeting),
    7f (18), **1m** (20), **1m 1f** (20), **1m 2f** (20), **1m 2f 192y** (20),
    1m 5f 13y (20), **1m 7f** (20), **2m 1f 105y** (20)

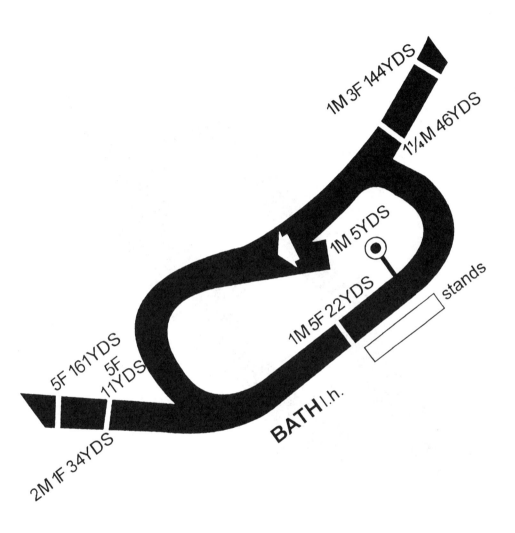

Bath invariably put the stalls on the inside rail (low) over all distances. Realignment work was carried out on the home turn in 1994/5 and the rail is movable there. Both rails are permanent in the straight, although the far rail was moved slightly in 1997 in a bid to resolve bunching which was occurring in sprints due to the slight kink in the course. The 5f 11y start is about 34 metres wide, considerably wider than the 5f 161y start which is only 19 metres across.

Maximum runners: **5f 11y** (20), **5f 161y** (19), **1m 5y** (18), **1m 2f 46y** (20), **1m 3f 144y** (20), **1m 5f 22y** (15), **2m 1f 34y** (20)

29

Beverley always put the stalls on the inside rail (high). Flip starts are not uncommon in five-furlong events, since it is difficult for the stalls to be moved across the centre of the course to the starting point when the ground is wet. Drainage work was carried out in the autumn of 1997 at two points, just after the winning post and on the bend by the 1m 1f 207y start. Neither rail in the straight is moveable. The safety figures were reduced from 25 to 20 at the start of the 1996 season, to aid stalls' accessibility. The straight course is about 30 metres wide.

Maximum runners: **5f** (20), **7f 100y** (17), **1m 100y** (19), **1m 1f 207y** (19), **1m 3f 216y** (15), **2m 35y** (20)

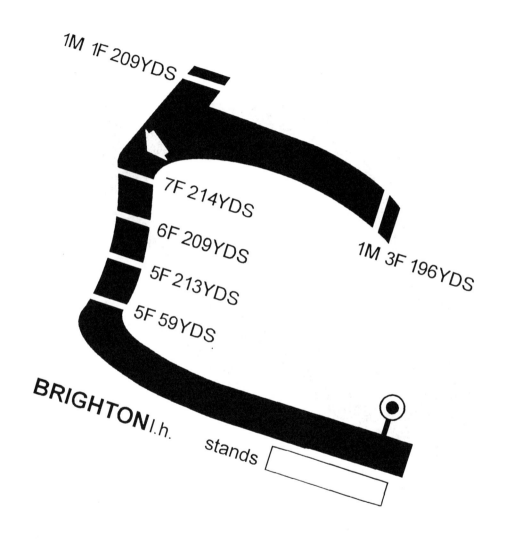

Brighton - No information available

Maximum runners: **5f 59y** (16, **14**), **5f 213y** (18, **16**), **6f 209y** (18, **16**), **7f 214y** (15),
1m 1f 209y (20), **1m 3f 196y** (18)

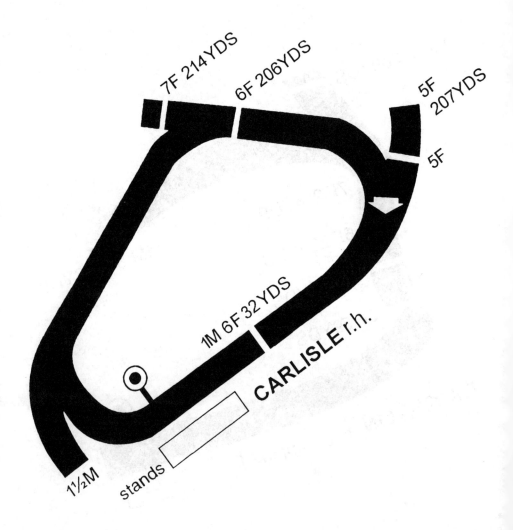

Carlisle normally put the stalls on the inside (high) at all distances, although they sometimes go down the centre in sprints. The sprint course is about 22 metres wide.

Maximum runners: **5f** (20), **5f 207y** (20), **6f 206y** (15), **7f 214y** (18), **1m 1f 61y** (16), **1m 4f** (20), **1m 6f 32y** (14), **2m 1f 52y** (18)

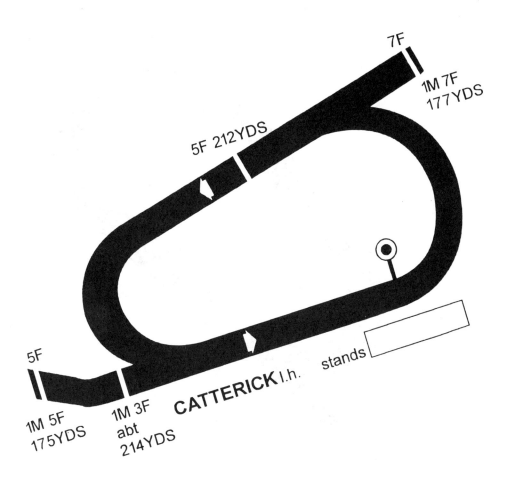

Catterick usually put the stalls on the far rail (low) for five-furlong races and at every other distance apart from 5f 212y, where they are often placed on the outside (high). Drainage work took place on the home turn in 1994. The inside rail can be moved by as much as 3 metres and on the home bend by as much as 4-5 metres, but the stands' rail is permanent.

Maximum runners: **5f** (20), **5f 212y** (normally 14, temporarily 12), **7f** (norm 20, temp 17), **1m 3f 214y** (norm 20, temp 18), **1m 5f 175y** (20), **1m 7f 177y** (norm 20, temp 17)

33

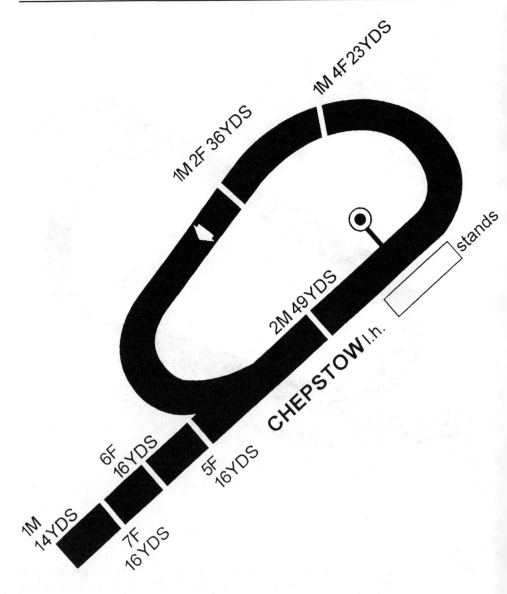

1M 4F 23YDS

1M 2F 36YDS

stands

2M 49YDS

CHEPSTOW l.h.

6F 16YDS

5F 16YDS

1M 14YDS

7F 16YDS

Chepstow always put the stalls on the stands' side (high) on the straight course, where both rails are permanent. The straight course is about 24 metres wide.

Maximum runners: 5f 16y (20), 6f 16y (20), 7f 16y (20), 1m 14y (20), **1m 2f 36y** (16), **1m 4f 23y** (19), **2m 49y** (flip start) (20), **2m 2f** (18)

34

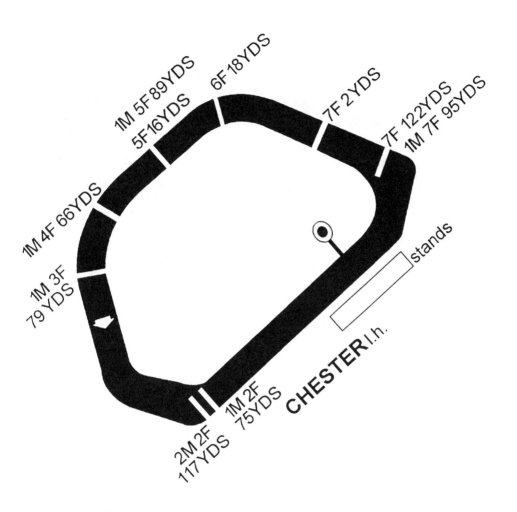

Chester always have the stalls on the inside (low), except for races run over 1m 2f 75y and 2m 2f 117y (same starting points) where they are put on the outside (high). Flip starts were used at one meeting in 1997 and the ground can often become wet enough for their use to be necessary. The inside rail can be moved, from the 5½-furlong from home point to the furlong pole, going out by as much as 4 metres at the furthest point. It is usually moved on the Thursday of the May meeting, and often in August and September.

Maximum runners: **5f 16y** (16), **6f 18y** (16), **7f 2y** (16), **7f 122y** (16), **1m 2f 75y** (17), **1m 4f 66y** (16), **1m 5f 89y** (16), **1m 7f 95y** (16), **2m 2f 147y** (18)

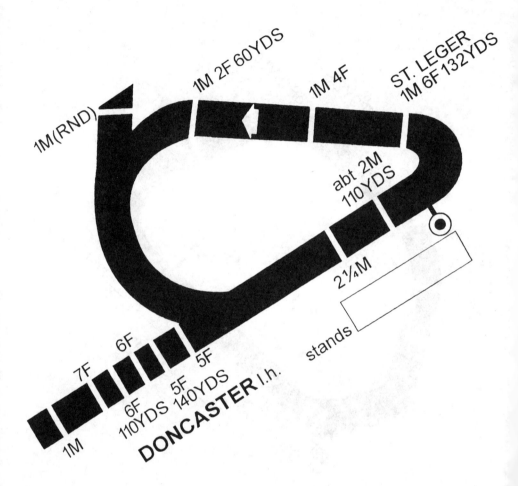

Doncaster normally put the stalls on the stands' rail (high) in the straight, and on the inside rail (low) at distances of 1m 2f 60y and beyond. Over the round mile, they are now placed on the outside, since during a trial period in 1996 when they were placed on the inside it was found that jockeys on runners drawn high were inclined to chop off those on the inner. The straight course is about 25 metres wide.

Maximum runners: 5f (22), 5f 140y (22), 6f (22), **6f 110y (22)**, 7f (22), 1m (straight) (24), **1m (round) (25*)**, **1m 2f 60y (20)**, **1m 4f (24*)**, **1m 6f 132y (24*)**, **2m 110y (18)**, **2m 2f (20)**

* Safety figures only apply to Lincoln meeting, Leger meeting and November Handicap

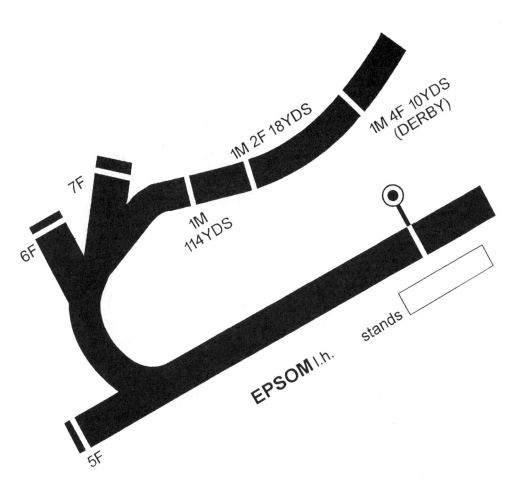

Epsom invariably put the stalls high (stands' side) over five furlongs and over six furlongs (which starts on a chute). The number of races run on the five-furlong course, the fastest in the world but one which is difficult to set up, has been scaled right down in recent times, and in 1997 only two events were staged on it. There are no plans to vary the position of the stalls in the future, apart from at the Derby start where they can be put on the outside when the fields are on the small side. The inside rail is dolled out from the mile point down to the winning post for the Spring meeting before being pulled right back to the inside for the Derby meeting. However, it is pushed back out slightly from the five-furlong point to the line until Derby Day itself to save a strip of ground on the inside. The stands' rail on the straight course, which is about 35 metres wide, is permanent.

Maximum runners: 5f (20), **6f** (17), **7f** (17), **1m 114y** (20), **1m 2f 18y** (30), **1m 4f 10y** (30)

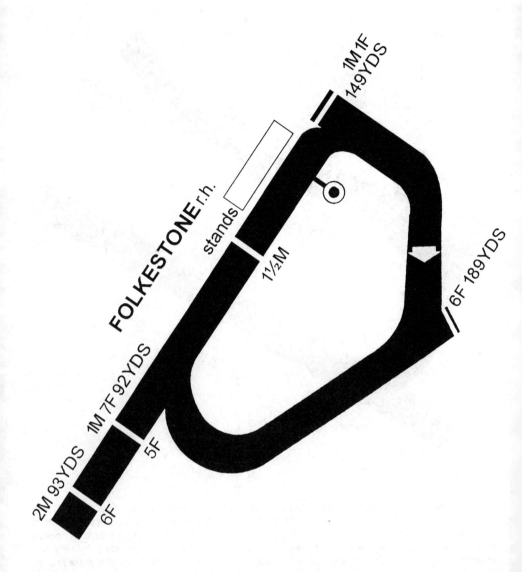

Folkestone usually put the stalls on the stands' rail (low) for sprint races. The rails in the straight course, which is about 24 metres wide, are never moved.

Maximum runners: 5f (16), 6f (16), **6f 189y** (16), **1m 1f 149y** (15), **1m 4f** (18), **1m 7f 92y** (16), **2m 93y** (16)

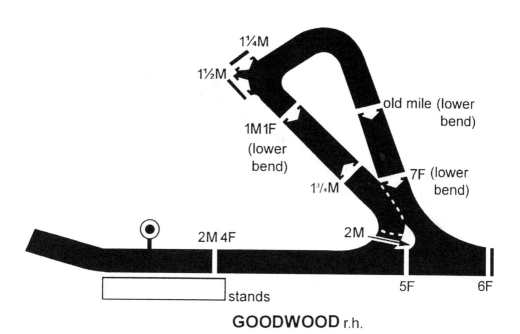

GOODWOOD r.h.

Goodwood try to put the stalls on the stands' side (low) wherever possible on the straight course and only switch them to the far rail in exceptional circumstances. There has been no drainage work done since the winter of 1995. The stands' rail is permanent but the far rail can be moved, right the way down to the winning post by as much as 5 metres. The straight course is about 31 metres wide.

Maximum runners: 5f (30), 6f (30), **7f** (20), **1m** (22), **1m 1f** (22), **1m 2f** (22), **1m 4f** (16), **1m 6f** (17), **2m** (16), **2m 4f** (22)

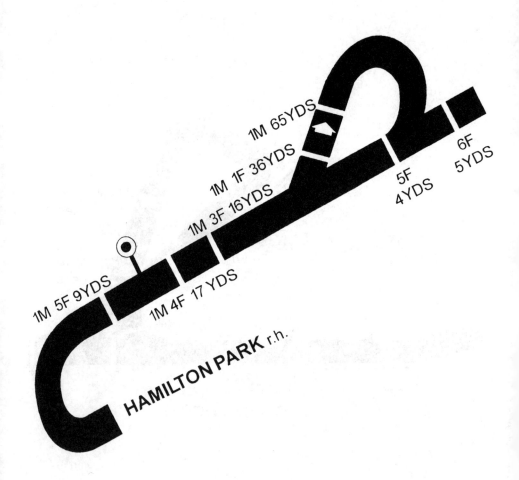

Hamilton normally put the stalls on the far side (high) on the straight course if the ground looks like being good to soft or softer and on the stands' side (low) if the prediction is for the ground to be good or faster. There has been ongoing drainage work over the past decade, which has improved conditions in wet weather. The inside rail on the 'loop' can be moved by up to 10 metres, but both rails in the straight are permanent. The straight course is about 22 metres wide.

Maximum runners: 5f 4y (18), 6f 5y (18), **1m 65y** (16), **1m 1f 36y** (18), **1m 3f 16y** (18), **1m 4f 17y** (18), **1m 5f 9y** (18)

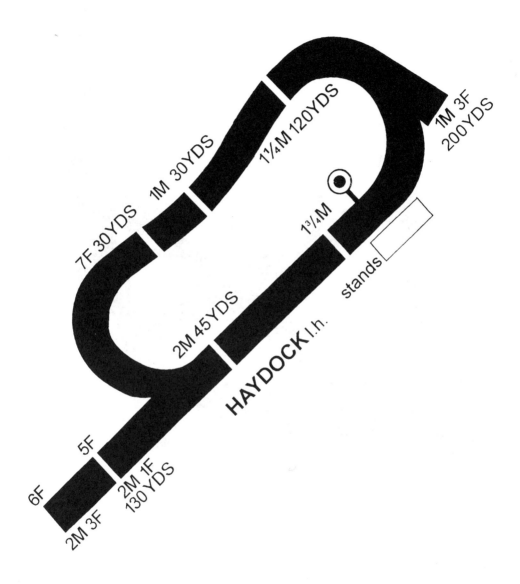

Haydock put the stalls on the stands' side (high) on the straight course, unless there is a good reason not to. Both rails in the straight course, which is about 26 metres wide, are permanent.

Maximum runners: 5f (24), 6f (24), **7f 30y** (16), **1m 30y** (18), **1m 2f 120y** (20), **1m 3f 200y** (20), **1m 6f** (20), **2m 45y** (20)

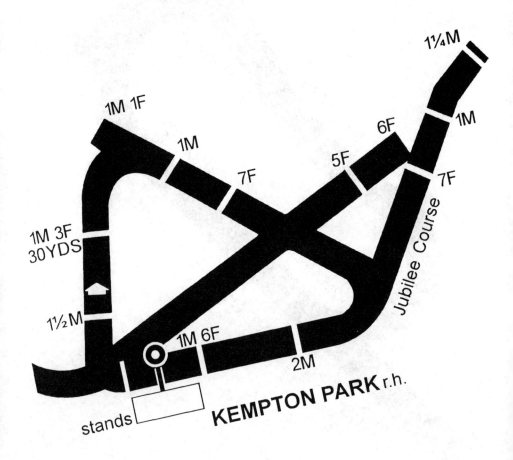

Kempton alternate the stalls between the far rail (high) and the stands' rail (low) over sprint distances. The road which used to cross the sprint course has been removed, and plans are in place to resurface the road that crosses the Jubilee course before the 1998 season. The home turn can be moved outwards by up to 3-4 metres. Both rails on the sprint course, which is 28 metres wide, are permanent.

Maximum runners: 5f (26), 6f (26), **7f** (Jubilee) (17), **7f** (round) (17), **1m** (Jubilee) (20), **1m** (round) (18), **1m 1f** (20), **1m 2f** (Jubilee) (20), **1m 3f 30y** (20), **1m 4f** (20), **1m 6f 92y** (14), **2m** (18)

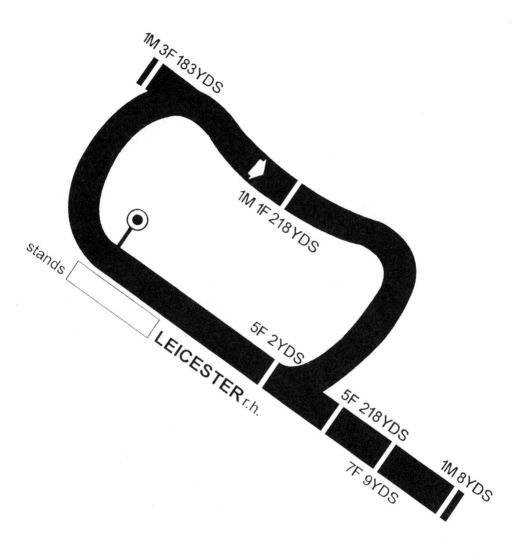

1M 3F 183YDS

1M 1F 218YDS

stands

5F 2YDS

LEICESTER r.h.

5F 218YDS

7F 9YDS

1M 8YDS

Leicester normally put the stalls on the stands' rail (low) on the straight course. A pop-up sprinkler system (staggered on both rails) has improved the watering of the centre of the course, which used to get watered less. Both rails in the straight course, which is about 25 metres wide, are permanent.

Maximum runners: 5f 2y (25), 5f 218y (22), 7f 9y (20), 1m 8y (20), **1m 1f 218y** (19),
1m 3f 183y (22)

LINGFIELD PARK

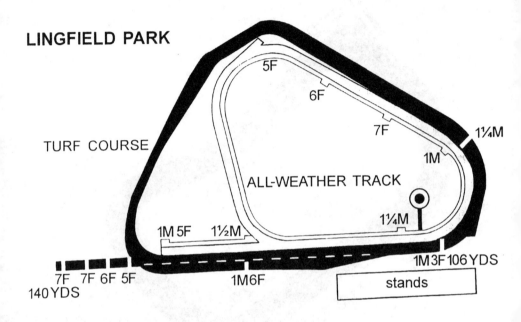

Lingfield (turf) usually put the stalls on the stands' rail (high) for races between five and seven furlongs, but down the centre for races over the straight 7f 140y. Whilst it is rare for them to be placed on the far rail (low), that was the case at the meeting on October 3rd, when they had been advertised as high. The reason for the switch was that the stands' rail had been moved 5 metres in to doll off a patch of ground yet to recover from recent drainage work. Flip starts are rare, but are possible early season since the course lies on clay soil and can become wet. The stands' rail can be moved by as much as 3 metres inwards and, when that is the case, the safety figure (maximum number of runners) for five and six-furlong races can drop to 18.

Lingfield (awt) put the stalls on the inside (low) for every distance bar five furlongs, when they are invariably on the stands' rail (high). The entire course is 20 metres wide.

Maximum runners: (turf) 5f (norm 20, temp 16), 6f (norm 20, temp 16), 7f (norm 18, temp 16), 7f 140y (norm 18, temp 16), **1m 2f** (norm 20, temp 16), **1m 3f 106y** (norm 20, temp 16), **1m 6f** (norm 20, temp 12), **2m** (norm 20, temp 16)
(awt) **5f** (10), **6f** (14), **7f** (16), **1m** (12), **1m 2f** (14), **1m 4f** (18), **1m 5f** (18), **2m** (14)

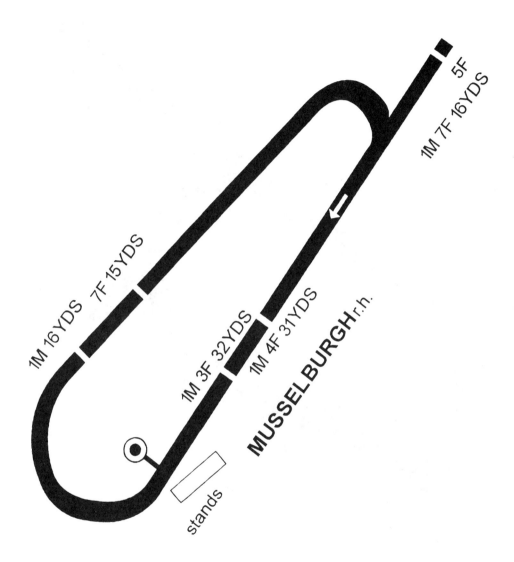

Musselburgh vary the stalls' position on the five-furlong course. Flip starts are always unlikely since the ground rarely becomes wet enough, and Musselburgh soft ground is never too bad. The home turn was re-cambered for the start of the 1997 season, but otherwise neither the stands' rail nor the far rail are ever moved. The straight course is about 19 metres wide.

Maximum runners: **5f** (17), **7f 30y** (14), **1m** (14), **1m 1f** (14), **1m 4f** (16), **1m 5f** (16),
1m 6f (12), **1m 7f** (16), **2m** (17)

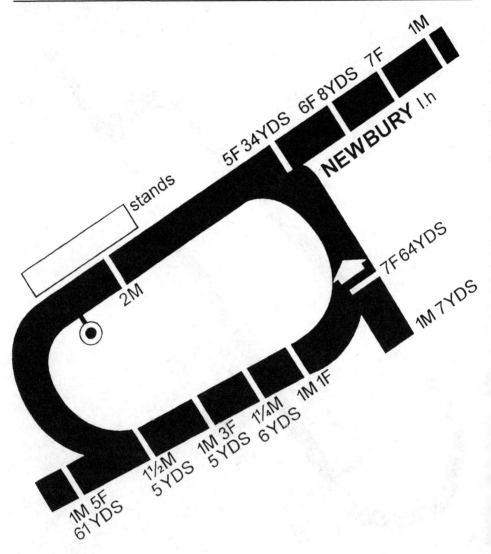

Newbury normally put the stalls down the centre in straight-course races. Sometimes they are placed on the stands' rail (high) but never on the far side (low). The stands' rail was replaced at the start of the 1997 season, but it was put in the same place as the old one and is never moved, a comment that also applies to the inside rail. The straight course is about 27 metres wide.

Maximum runners: 5f 34y (27), 6f 8y (27), 7f (straight) (27), **7f 64y (round)** (20), 1m (straight) (27), **1m 7y (round)** (20), **1m 1f** (18), **1m 2f 6y** (22), **1m 3f 5y** (22), **1m 4f 5y** (22), **1m 5f 61y** (20), 2m (19)

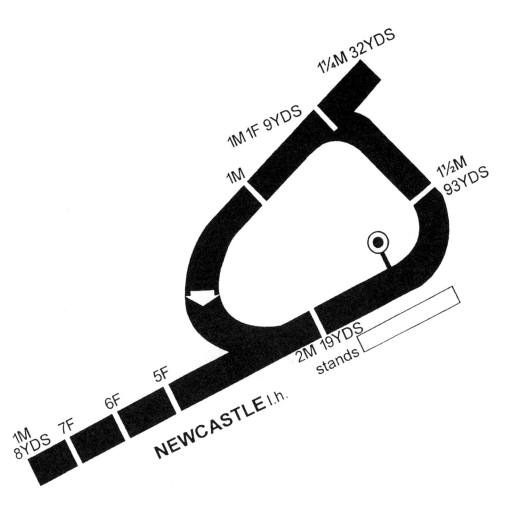

Newcastle normally place the stalls on the stands' side (high) on the straight course, but for two days in 1997 they were placed on the far rail because the ground between the 1m 8y start and the four-furlong point on that side is never otherwise used. This will be repeated in the 1998 season, but only for two or three meetings. A new watering system was implemented in June 1996 after extensive drainage work had been carried out in October/November 1995. The inside rail has not been moved since the drainage work and the stands' rail is permanent. The straight course is about 21 metres wide.

Maximum runners: 5f (20), 6f (20), 7f (20), **1m (round)** (20), 1m 8y (straight) (20),
1m 1f 9y (20), **1m 2f 32y** (20), **1m 4f 93y** (20), **2m 19y** (20)

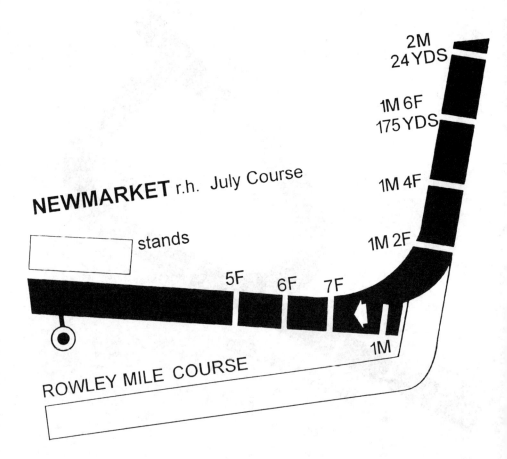

Newmarket July Course vary the stalls' position fairly equally between the stands' rail (high), the far rail (low) and the centre of the course. There is a permanent dividing rail down the centre of the course, which effectively creates two different tracks and racing is divided up pretty much equally between the two. All the rails are permanent from the 7½-furlong point.

Maximum runners: 5f (20), 6f (20), 7f (20), 1m (20), **1m 2f (36)**, **1m 4f** (36), **1m 6f 175y (36)**, **2m 24y (36)**

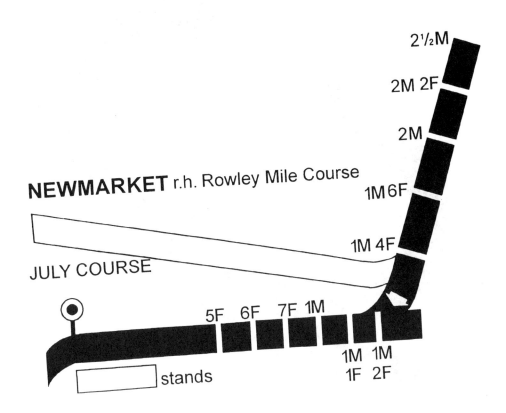

Newmarket Rowley Mile vary the stalls' position, similarly to the July Course. The course is 176 feet wide and the middle strip gets used more than any other part. During the spring, racing is done on the stands' side two-thirds of the course bottle-necking down to the stands' side half of the course at the winning post. In the autumn, the far side two-thirds of the course is used, narrowing down to the far side half at the line. This means that there is a triangular shaped piece of ground down the centre which is in use all the time. Both the stands' rail and the far rail are moveable. The straight course narrows from being 53 metres wide at the mile start down to 36 metres at the five-furlong start.

Maximum runners: 5f (30), 6f (30), 7f (30), 1m (30, Autumn H'cap 35),
1m 1f (30, Cambs 40), 1m 2f (30), **1m 4f** (36), **1m 6f** (36), **2m** (36),
2m 2f (36)

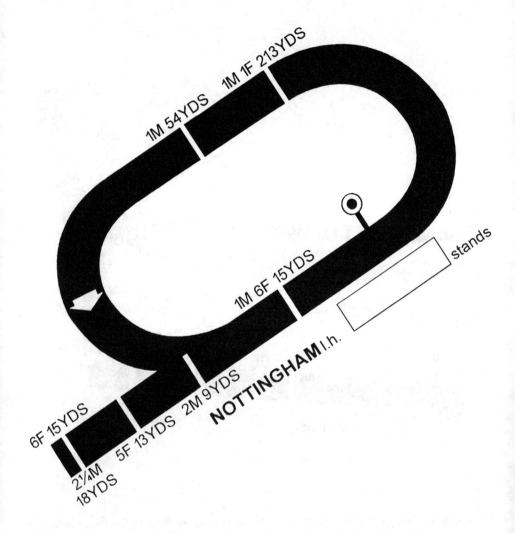

Nottingham prefer to keep the stalls on the stands' side (high) in straight races, but they can sometimes go on the far rail (low). Drainage and re-cambering work on the home turn was completed at the end of 1996, but it was not raced on until June 1997 and the old hurdle course was employed in the interim. The inside rail can be moved all the way up to the winning post, but the stands' rail is permanent.

Maximum runners: 5f 13y (norm 24, temp 20), 6f 15y (norm 24, temp 20),
      1m 54y (norm 20, temp 18), **1m 1f 213y** (norm 23, temp 18),
      1m 6f 15y (norm 20, temp 16), **2m 9y** (norm 20, temp 17),
      2m 1f 188y (norm 20, temp 18)

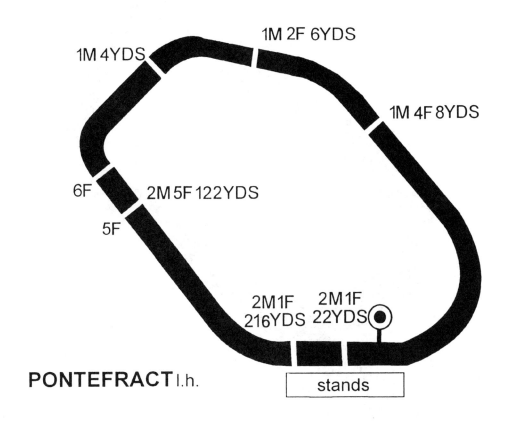

PONTEFRACT l.h.

Pontefract put the stalls on the inside rail (low), unless the ground becomes soft, when they are sometimes moved to the outside. Some drainage work was done at the three-furlong point in December 1997, but nothing major. A temporary rail is erected from the six-furlong pole down to the winning post 4 metres outside the permanent rail before the fourth meeting of the season to make use of fresh ground and is taken down before the Friday meeting in mid-July.

Maximum runners: **5f** (18), **6f** (18), **1m 4y** (20), **1m 2f 6y** (19), **1m 4f 8y** (18), **2m 1f 22y** (20), **2m 1f 216y** (20), **2m 5f 122y** (20)

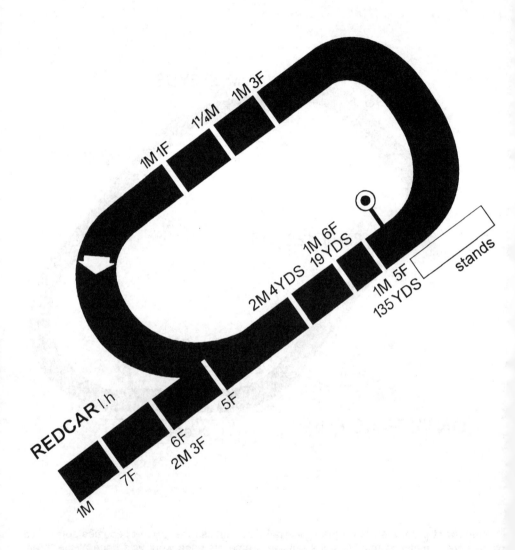

Redcar put the stalls close to the stands' rail (high) for the majority of 1997 meetings, but not right on it because of the shape of the course towards that side. Both rails on the straight course are permanent. The straight course narrows from being 33 metres wide at the mile start down to 24 metres at the five-furlong start.

Maximum runners: 5f (23), 6f (26), 7f (30), 1m (30), **1m 1f** (16), **1m 2f** (17), **1m 3f** (17), **1m 5f 135y** (15), **1m 6f 19y** (16), **2m 4y** (18), **2m 3f** (18)

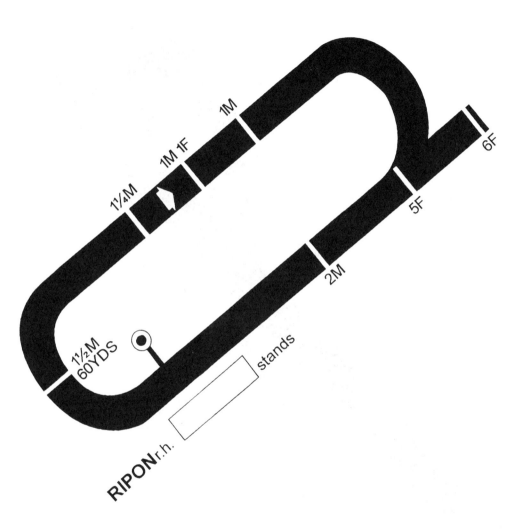

Ripon try to keep the stalls on the stands' rail (low) in sprint races wherever possible. A new pop-up sprinkler system was implemented in August 1997 covering both rails in the straight, but the westerly wind which tends to prevail blows away from the stands' rail could prove to make even watering difficult. The inside rail is movable between the mile and five-furlong points, but both rails in the straight are permanent. The straight course is about 24 metres wide.

Maximum runners: 5f (23), 6f (23), **1m** (20), **1m 1f** (25), **1m 2f** (25), **1m 4f 60y** (20), **2m** (20), **2m 1f 203y** (23)

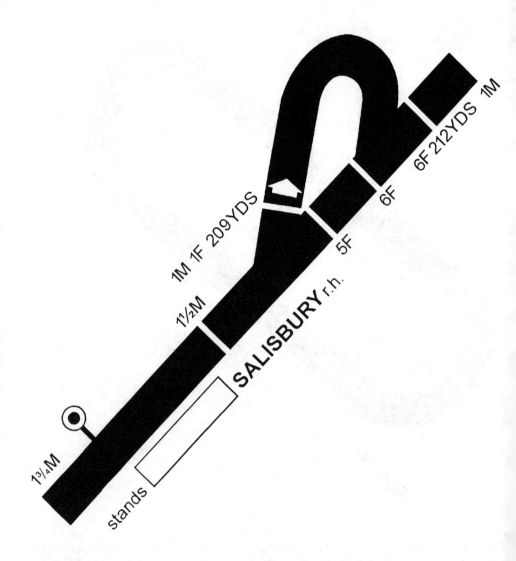

Salisbury try to keep the stalls high (far side) whenever possible, but they can be put on the stands' side if the ground gets cut up. The straight course widens from being about 19 metres wide at the mile start up to about 29 metres at the five-furlong start.

Maximum runners: 5f (20), **6f** (20), **6f 212y** (20), **1m** (18), **1m 1f 209y** (18), **1m 4f** (20), **1m 6f** (flip start) (20)

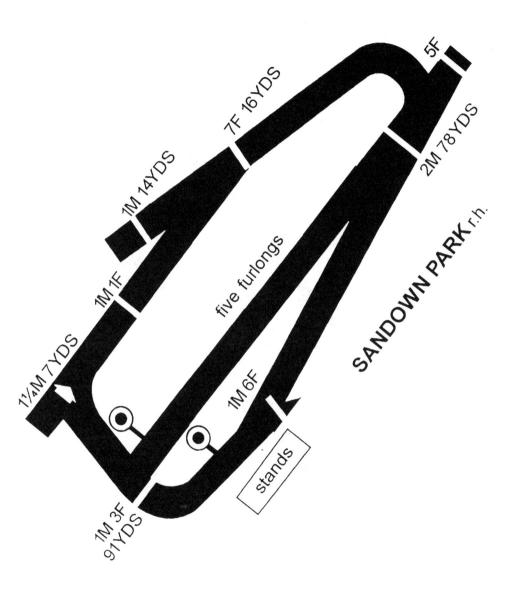

Sandown alternate the position of the stalls on the straight five-furlong course between either rail. The whole inside rail on the round course can be moved, but both rails on the separate sprint course are permanent. The sprint course is about 34 metres wide.

Maximum runners: 5f 6y (20), **7f 16y** (16), **1m 14y** (18), **1m 1f** (16), **1m 2f 7y** (20), **1m 3f 91y** (14), **1m 6f** (18), **2m 78y** (20)

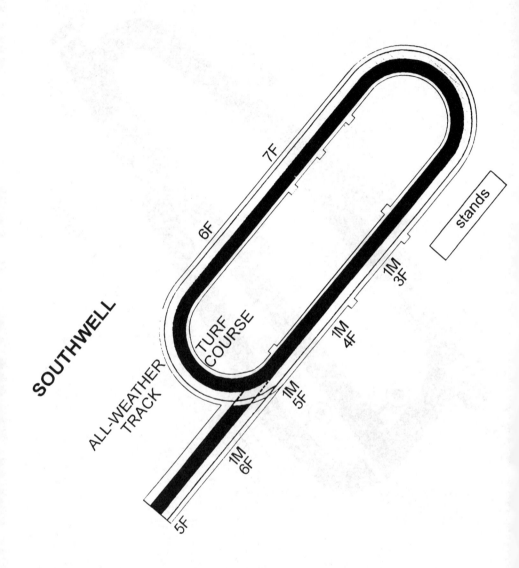

Southwell (awt) re-laid the entire track before the meeting on October 20th, 1997 and the jockeys reported it to be riding much quicker than before. Amateurs and apprentices do not race over six furlongs. The straight course is about 18 metres wide.

Maximum runners: 5f (17), **6f** (16), **7f** (16), **1m** (16), **1m 3f** (16), **1m 4f** (17), **1m 5f** (17), **1m 6f** (17), **2m** (16), **2m 2f** (16)

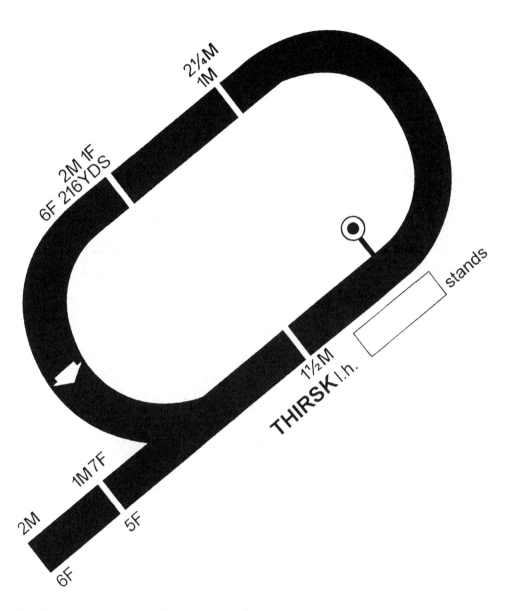

Thirsk invariably put the stalls on the stands' side (high) over sprint distances and at a mile and a half, which starts in the straight. Both rails in the straight, which is about 26 metres wide, are permanent.

Maximum runners: 5f (24), 6f (24), **7f** (16), **1m** (18), **1m 4f** (19), **2m** (24)

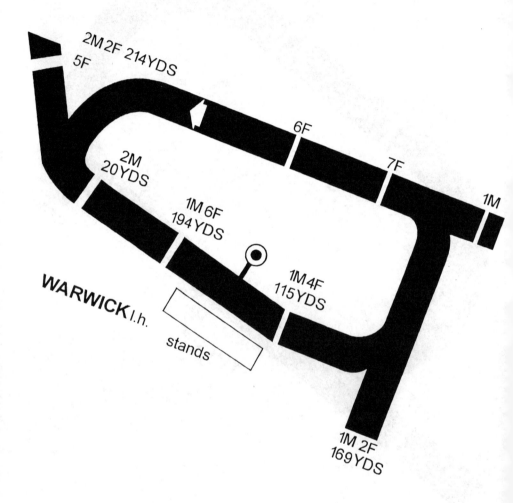

Warwick put the stalls on the inside rail (low) at all distances. The home turn can be moved outwards for up to 3 yards, but both rails on the straight course are permanent. The five-furlong course is about 30 metres wide.

Maximum runners: **5f** (20), **6f** (17), **7f** (20), **1m** (20), **1m 2f 169y** (20), **1m 4f 115y** (13), **1m 6f 194y** (14), **2m 20y** (19), **2m 2f 214y** (20)

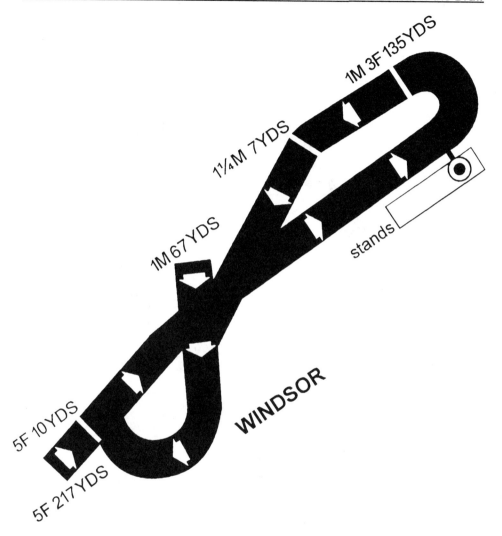

Windsor invariably put the stalls on the inside rail. Work is due to start in February 1998 to level out the ground and it should be completed by the time of the first meeting on May 11th. Repairs were deemed necessary because the ground became uneven and worn as a result of the consistently dry weather in recent times drying up underground water. The re-levelling should allow more scope for rails to be moved, something that has been difficult in the past due to the unique configuration of the course. The straight course is about 36 metres wide.

Maximum runners: 5f 10y (30), 5f 217y (30), **1m 67y** (18), 1m 2f 7y (25), **1m 3f 135y** (20)

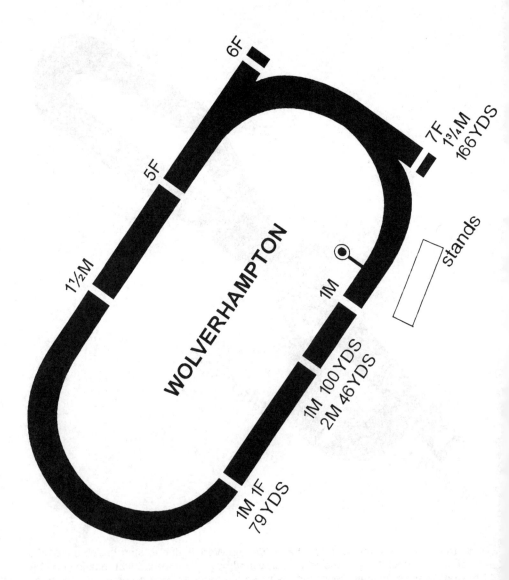

Wolverhampton (awt) seem to vary the position of the stalls frequently. Amateurs and apprentices do not race over seven furlongs.

Maximum runners: **5f** (13), **6f** (13), **7f** (12), **1m 100y** (13), **1m 1f 79y** (13), **1m 4f** (12), **1m 6f 166y** (12), **2m 46y** (13)

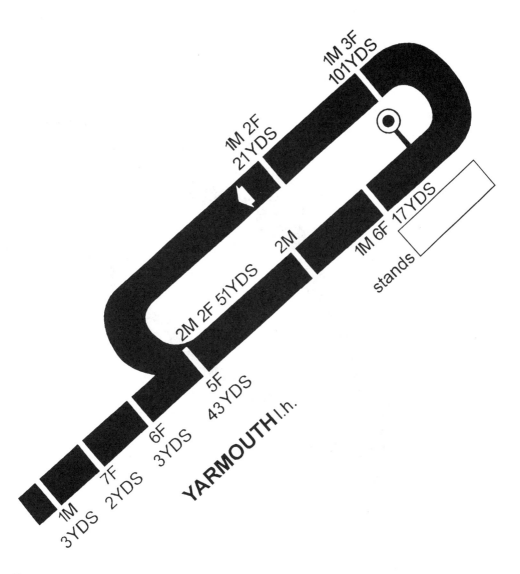

Yarmouth try to rotate the stalls position on the straight course as much as possible, placing them either on the stands' rail (high) or the far rail (low). The ground often rides firm due to the course being based on sand under between 4 and 8 inches of topsoil. Both rails in the straight are permanent. The straight course is about 22 metres wide.

Maximum runners: 5f 43y (20), 6f 3y (20), 7f 3y (20), 1m 3y (20), **1m 2f 21y** (17), **1m 3f 101y** (17), **1m 6f 17y** (20), **2m** (20), **2m 2f 51y** (20)

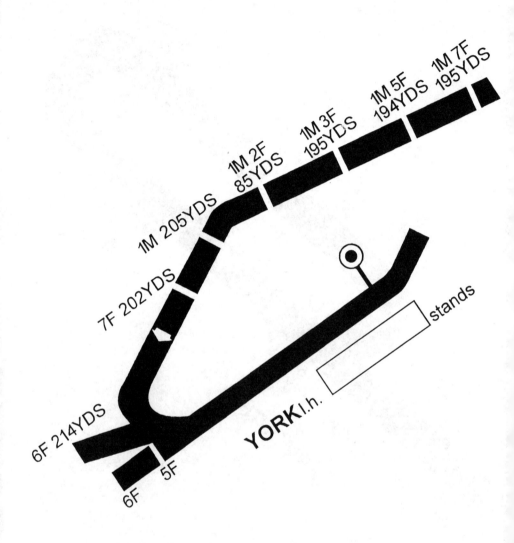

York usually put the stalls on the stands' side (high) on the straight course, but sometimes on the far rail (low). Both rails in the straight, which is about 24 metres wide, are permanent.

Maximum runners: 5f (23), 6f (23), **6f 214y** (24), **7f 202y** (26), **1m 205y** (27),
1m 2f 85y (22), **1m 3f 195y** (22), **1m 5f 194y** (22), **1m 7f 195y** (22)

CHAPTER 3

DIARY OF 1997

This Chapter is a daily account of the 1997 season and, as my betting patterns indicate, the busiest time tends to be from early May until mid-September. Whenever possible, example races have been included as they appeared in *Raceform* Annual for 1998. Otherwise the corresponding *Raceform* number is shown, since it should prove a useful reference in determining why each selection was considered worth following.

Horses I felt at the time should be followed are shown in **bold** type and alongside each of them is a line to show how they fared on their next outing. Whether and why I considered backing them or not is covered in the next Chapter. Backing these selections blind would have made a £1 level-stakes profit of over £36 at a 33.3% strike-rate by the end of the season, but as with every system, backing blind is not the best way to go. I have found it necessary to ensure that each potential selection meets with the following main criterion before making an investment:-

1) **The ground is suitable** - the selection must have won or at least shown very good form on the prevailing ground.
2) **The trip is suitable** - the selection is not stepping up to seven furlongs for the first time having caught the eye over a sprint trip, unless he seems likely to be suited by it.
3) **The handicapper has not raised the rating a ridiculous amount** - the selection is not asked to race off a much higher mark than when it was picked. Anything more than a 3 or 4lb rise is pushing the limits.
4) **The race is similar in class to the time before** - the selection has not raised from, for example, a Class F handicap to a Class C handicap.
5) **The selection has not been off the course for any length of time** - any longer than a two-month absence may suggest some sort of problem.
6) **Most importantly, the selection has a reasonable draw** - if the draw is again against the selection, he may again run above expectations, but is likely to be facing another impossible task.

63

It is also worth looking for other less obvious performance-affecting factors, such as the form of the trainer, previous course form, the jockey (look for jockeys who have shown in the past that they know where the best ground is - see Chapter 5, and jockeys who do not), and any other factors that you may consider important in making a selection.

As an example, Refuse To Lose was marked down as a horse to follow after his second at Newmarket at the Craven Meeting in April, but he did not reappear until late July and had presumably had some sort of problem. So, despite the impression he made on me that day, I did not back him when he next came out.

Also, Garnock Valley was marked down as one to follow after his run at the opening Doncaster meeting, but I chose not to follow him next time, and probably never would back him, because he is moody and needs everything to go his way. Nevertheless, a friend of mine chose to back him next time, the time after, the time after that and for every one of his runs for the rest of the season. That is not the way to make money, or keep friends. On another occasion, Mezzoramio seemed ready to strike next time after an excellent reappearance run at Yarmouth, but the ground was good to soft when he came out again, and he had never won on softer than good to firm. He was beaten. However, next time back on a fast surface and coming out of a high stall at Yarmouth over the same course and distance, he won easily at 4/1. As with any system, selectivity is the key. Some may like to back a horse they have picked out for his next run only; his next two runs; until he wins; or most sensibly when he next has conditions in his favour. Try to adopt the latter approach.

Sea-Deer (stripes) was high in the weights after a successful 1996, but continued to run well

Thursday, March 20

Doncaster - Proper racing returned with Jimmy Fortune looking as though he should probably have won on Bishops Court (*Raceform* Race 434, stalls high), but only managing third. Fortune, an extremely confident pilot in handicap sprints, often seems to wait for a gap to come up the rail if stuck behind a wall of horses, sometimes for a painfully long time. When it pays off and he gets the better ground close to the fence, he rightly receives the plaudits, but when it doesn't, it does look very bad.

Friday, March 21

Doncaster - The 22-runner six-furlong handicap (Race 443, high) gave a big clue as to where the best strip of ground lay. Five of the first six home came from stalls numbered between 8 and 13. Four of those five, with the exception of the runner-up Safio, raced down the centre of the course. Safio, together with the third Sea-Deer, raced centre to stands' side. The impression left was that **Sea-Deer** (stall 17), the gamble of the race, would have finished much closer to the winner given a better draw, although he was high enough in the handicap after such a good 1996. Garnock Valley (stall 16), a very quirky character, ran a promising race towards the stands' side to finish seventh.

The problem that arises with the best ground being down the centre of the course is that even when they line up right across the track, very few can be counted out of calculations as they are likely to bunch into one group down the middle. This was pretty much the case in the Spring Mile (Race 444, low), where Michael Roberts took his record on Artful Dane to three wins from four rides. As usual Roberts knew where the best ground was before most others, switching his mount towards the centre. Five of the first seven home in a field of 23 came from towards the centre of the course. The two that did not were the third and fourth, Sharp Shuffle (far side from 5) and Sandmoor Chambray (stands' side, 17). **Sandmoor Chambray** ran well under such a big weight.

Follow	**Sea-Deer**	next time	2nd	5/1
	Sandmoor Chambray	next time	Unp	7/1

Saturday, March 22

Doncaster - On a day that is often a good one for any follower of the draw, not a great deal went right. Six of the seven races were run on the straight course, including the Lincoln (Race 450, high), but the jockeys had latched on to where the best ground was by now, this being the third day in a row on the course. *Raceform*'s Lee McKenzie, commenting on the Lincoln for Radio Five Live said, "I have never seen anything like this, the whole field are coming down the centre strip of the track". The fact that they were all on the best ground negated any advantage from being drawn down the centre in the first place, the first four home being drawn 21, 6, 4, and 10.

Tuesday, March 25

Newcastle - This card is often a useful guide to the Easter Monday meeting as far as concerns the draw, but the only race with enough runners to be able to make a judgement was the five-furlong handicap (Race 464, high). A group of five went to race on the far rail, with the remainder racing centre to stands' side. Amron, indisputably well handicapped on his old form, won by 3½ lengths out of stall 1 of 14 (drawn 1 in a field of 14), with Kalar, from stall 3, just sneaking second ahead of 3/1 favourite **Surprise Mission** (11), who was comfortably first home of the stands'-side group.

Surprise Mission enjoyed a successful campaign

In previous seasons, the far rail was only favoured when the ground was on the soft side, but the official going returned here was good. However, a look at the *Raceform* going allowance suggested otherwise. A figure of 0.29 seconds per furlong was given to the straight-course events, suggesting that the ground there was verging on being good to soft. Therefore, those drawn low would have been entitled to finish in front, so Surprise Mission may well have run better than it looked, for he beat the rest of his group easily enough. He was racing off a mark of 71 here, just 1lb higher than the mark off which he recorded his only victory in 1996.

Follow   **Surprise Mission**   next time   **WON   15/8**

Wednesday, March 26
Folkestone - It was at the corresponding meeting the previous year that John Stack switched Lloc to race alone on the far side in the handicap sprint, and the pair came home 5-length winners. Although the ground was faster here - it had been good to soft in 1996 - it still came as something of a surprise that nobody tried to repeat the tactics in the equivalent event (Race 473, low), especially as several horses raced down the centre.

66

Thursday, March 27
Musselburgh (Soft) - Soft ground at Edinburgh in the spring, with 14 runners in a sprint handicap (Race 494, high) always has to be of interest, especially with the fairer Scottish bookmakers betting to only 123.1%, offering all bar the first three in the betting at double-figure prices. Runners drawn close to the stands' rail hold sway in soft ground and, with the intended runner from stall 2 being withdrawn and those coming out of stalls 4 and 5 looking moderate, things looked very good for Chemcast (stall 1) and Tropical Beach (3).

494   BRUNTON HALL H'CAP (0-70) (3-Y.O+) (Class E)
3-20 (3-24) **5f** £3,168.00 (£954.00: £462.00: £216.00) Stalls: High GOING: 0.18 sec per fur (G)

			SP	RR	SF
397[5]	Chemcast (68) (JLEyre) 4-10-0b RLappin(1) (lw: racd stands' side: mde all: all out) .... —	1	6/1 [2]	68?	19
406[3]	Gi La High (60) (MartynMeade) 4-9-1[5] DSweeney(12) (hdwy far side ½-wy: r.o fnl f: nrst fin) .... ½	2	7/1 [3]	58	9
	Tropical Beach (63) (JBerry) 4-9-2[7] CLowther(3) (dwlt: hdwy & edgd rt over 1f out: r.o) 1¼	3	7/1 [3]	57	8
	Goretski (IRE) (59) (NTinkler) 4-9-5 JCarroll(13) (cl up far side: ev ch ½-wy: no ex fnl f)................. 1¼	4	9/2 [1]	49	—
	Queens Check (49) (MissJFCraze) 4-8-9b SWebster(8) (b: sme hdwy 2f out: nvr rchd ldrs).............. 6	5	10/1	20	—
	Johayro (54) (JSGoldie) 4-9-0 ACulhane(6) (cl up stands' side tl wknd wl over 1f out) 3½	6	10/1	14	—
423[8]	Another Nightmare (IRE) (48) (RMMcKellar) 5-8-8 TWilliams(14) (lw: led far side to ½-wy: sn outpcd) ...... ½	7	12/1	6	—
	Leading Princess (IRE) (50) (MissLAPerratt) 6-8-5b[5] JBramhill(11) (racd far side: n.d)................. ½	8	20/1	7	—
	Red Romance (60) (DenysSmith) 3-8-8 LCharnock(5) (sn outpcd) 1½	9	20/1	12	—
	Lunch Party (53) (DNicholls) 5-8-13 DaleGibson(9) (dwlt: a bhd)... 1	10	16/1	2	—
	Sunset Harbour (IRE) (47) (SEKettlewell) 4-8-7 JFortune(7) (racd far side: n.d) .... nk	11	16/1	—	—
	Sarabi (64) (JPearce) 3-8-9[3] CTeague(4) (chsd ldrs stands' side 3f: wknd)................................ hd	12	16/1	12	—
	Zain Dancer (55) (DNicholls) 5-9-1 AlexGreaves(10) (sn outpcd) 3	13	16/1	—	—
	Swan At Whalley (65) (RAFahey) 5-9-4[7] RWinston(2) (Withdrawn not under Starter's orders: ref to ent stalls)	W	14/1	—	—

64.0 secs (6.30) CSF £40.41 CT £243.36 TOTE £6.80: £2.40 £2.30 £3.60 (£13.30) Trio £68.60 OWNER Clayton Bigley Partnership Ltd (HAMBLETON) BRED C. R. and V. M. Withers
WEIGHT FOR AGE 3yo-12lb
406 Gi La High ran a smashing race from a poor draw, and would surely have won had she been up the stands' side. (7/1: op 9/2)

However, **Gi La High**, supposedly an all-weather specialist, ruined the day for forecast backers by finishing second from stall 12. Racing towards the far side, she was only half a length down at the line on what was definitely the worst ground. She was racing off a mark of 60 here, which was 6lb lower than her all-weather mark at the time, and looked to have improved through the winter.

Follow   **Gi La High**   next time   3rd   5/2

Saturday, March 29
Haydock - Soft ground at Haydock has in the past meant a big advantage for anything drawn up against the stands' rail (high) as any follower of Lord High Admiral over the years will know. Neither race on the straight course really attracted enough runners to be of interest, with 11 in the two-year-old maiden (Race 500, high) and eight in the Field Marshal Stakes (501, high), which looked very trappy and full of potential 'not-trained-ons' beforehand. However, there was still enough evidence to suggest that the draw bias was as big as ever in the juvenile event, with runners from stalls 8 and 9 of 11 finishing in the frame. **Pacifica**, who was a handful before the start on this debut and not the type to handle soft ground according to *Raceform*'s Ivor Markham, was the one who really caught the eye though, finishing second from stall 6.

Looking at the bare result of the race and seeing that stall 8 beat 6 beat 9 does not tell the full story here and again illustrates the importance of actually watching races whenever possible, as results sections will rarely tell you where each runner raced. Pacifica, unlike the winner and third, was towards the centre of the course in the final couple of furlongs and never really got close to the rail when leading earlier, so the fact that she was finishing as well as anything whilst racing on the worst ground made this effort all the more meritorious.

Kempton - The three-year-old handicap (Race 506), which is usually a useful draw guide to the Teal Handicap on Easter Monday, attracted a slightly disappointing field of 11. The stalls were placed on the far side (high) as usual, so high numbers should again have been favoured, but the finish was fought out by a couple of outsiders drawn low to middle.

Follow   **Pacifica**   next time   **WON 5/1**

Monday, March 31
Kempton - The Teal Handicap (Race 520, high) is often productive for followers of the draw and that again looked possible given what had happened in the previous event (Race 519 where stall 11 of 11 beat 9), especially when a group of six went to race on the far rail soon after the start, with the remainder coming towards the centre. Eastern Prophets (17) made it all to win at 20/1 (a look at *Raceform Racehorse Record* would have revealed that he finished about 4 lengths behind champion sprinter Anabaa this time the previous year, clearly making him a certainty!). However, the other five to race on the far side failed to reach the frame, re-enforcing the opinion formed two days earlier that the advantage in being drawn high might not actually be that great any more. Therefore, it could have been worth making the assumption that the two best horses finished one-two in the previous race (Monaassib (11) and Oh Nellie (9)).

Newcastle - The going at this meeting was given as good to firm, compared with the return of good six days earlier, and the race times also suggested that the ground was quite a bit faster, although again the straight track was riding slower than the round course. The recently reopened straight mile course (1m 8y rather than the round course which is exactly a mile) staged a selling handicap (Race 526, high) with 20 runners but, although the far side had been favoured at the previous meeting, the faster surface meant that those drawn high should have come out on top. This was indeed the case as Gadge, from stall 17, beat Sandmoor Denim (18) and Seconds Away (16), with the next three home also being drawn over 12. The other two straight-course races run on the card were not quite so conclusive.

Nottingham - This was the first meeting here of the season, and rather like Doncaster for the Lincoln meeting it was a case of taking a watching brief to see if the draw bias was the same as before. The stalls were placed on the stands' side for the only decent-sized race on the straight course (Race 532), but all the action was centre to far side, the first three being drawn 8, 9 and 11 of 18. Treasure Touch was landing a gamble for David Nicholls in winning, so the fact that he made all and set a good pace for those drawn around him meant that this race was likely to prove untrustworthy as a guide to the draw.

Tuesday, April 8
Nottingham - There was only one race with a decent-sized field on the straight course (Race 585, high) and, unlike the week before, a draw advantage seemed much in evidence. Meranti left the impression that he was probably very well handicapped, as he switched over from stall 1 (on the far side) to what looked the favoured stands' rail and won by 4 lengths. Switching from one side of the course to the other would have cost him a couple of lengths at least, so this was a good effort. He led home runners drawn in the centre.

Wednesday, April 9

Ripon - The first meeting here saw two well-subscribed races being staged on the straight course and both left the impression that the advantage of being drawn low was as great as ever. In the two-year-old maiden (Race 594, low), Out Like Magic had already had a run in the Brocklesby and looked as solid a favourite as you get at this stage of the season, being drawn in stall 3. He led home runners from stall 10 and 11, with the first three finishing 2½ lengths clear of the rest. The two placed horses, **Happy Days** (10) and **Quiz Master** (11), were both making their debuts and left the impression that they should pay to follow in the future. In the sprint handicap (Race 596, low), there looked to be plenty of pacey horses drawn low, but the well-handicapped **Kira** (12), who had run away with a more competitive event at Doncaster's opening meeting, headed them all off from a moderate draw and was very unlucky not to win. French Grit and Maiteamia, drawn 2 and 1 respectively, finished first and third, but all the others drawn low did not figure and looked worth opposing in the short term.

Follow	**Happy Days**	next time	Unp	7/4
	Quiz Master	next time	2nd	10/1
	Kira	next time	WON	3/1

Thursday, April 10

Hamilton - The advance going reports again suggested the likelihood of soft ground, but this was a drying day with a fresh wind, so the surface was probably good at worst. The opening 1m 65y apprentice handicap (Race 608, high) was a muddling affair, with none of the horses drawn high taking advantage of their good position, so Rambo Waltzer (14 of 16) probably won on merit. However, in the six-furlong handicap (Race 610, high), where the professional jockeys doubtless possessed the knowledge the apprentices didn't, a high stall was absolutely crucial, with the top seven in the draw filling seven of the first eight places in a field of 18. The first two pulled a long way clear of the rest, with the second Return of Amin looking a bit unlucky to come up against such a well-handicapped rival. Nothing drawn low finished within 12 lengths of the winner Foist.

Friday, April 11

Beverley - Most of the ten runners in the juvenile seller (Race 631, high) had already had a previous outing and the draw looked to play a large part on the outcome with high numbers favoured. With the ground on the fast side of good, stall 8 beat 10 of 10, with the favourite Captain Bliss, who ran green, third from stall 2.

Nottingham (Good to firm) - Given that the stands' rail had looked favoured at the previous meeting here, it was slightly strange to see both straight-course races being dominated by runners drawn low, especially as the going was very similar. In Race 649, stalls high, Treasure Touch (5) made most of the running from a low draw as he had done at the previous meeting, effectively off the same mark, with Iona Wands knocking off the 7lb penalty, and he was again pursued by runners drawn near to him. He was probably just very well handicapped. **Jupiter**, drawn 17 of 17, finished exactly the same distance behind Treasure Touch as he had done the time before and on exactly the same terms, but this time he was racing apart from the winner and actually won the race up the stands' rail. He was nibbled at in the betting and was the only one from a double-figure draw to finish in the first seven, so he looked like he could be worth following.

Follow	**Jupiter**	next time	Unp	7/2

649 NEW BASFORD H'CAP (0-70) (3-Y.O) (Class E)
4-40 (4-42) **6f 15y** £3,356.25 (£1,005.00: £482.50: £221.25) Stalls: High GOING minus 0.17 sec per fur (GF)

			SP	RR	SF
532*	**Treasure Touch (IRE)** (70) (DNicholls) 3-9-0(7) 7x IonaWands(5) (a.p: led 2f out: clr fnl f).............................—	1	100/30 1	78+	57
483⁹	**Always Alight** (60) (KRBurke) 3-8-11 RPainter(3) (chsd ldrs: rdn 2f out: kpt on fnl f: no ch w wnr) 3½	2	33/1	59	38
532²	**Master Foley** (55) (NPLittmoden) 3-8-6 TGMcLaughlin(2) (led 4f: rdn & one pce appr fnl f) ....hd	3	10/1	54	33
532⁵	**Jupiter (IRE)** (70) (GCBravery) 3-9-7 MRimmer(17) (lw: chsd ldrs stands' side: rdn 2f out: one pce) ....¾	4	5/1 2	67	46
532³	**Mike's Double (IRE)** (52) (GLewis) 3-8-3b PaulEddery(1) (trckd ldrs: hrd rdn appr fnl f: eased whn btn cl home)..¾	5	7/1 3	47	26
458²	**Chasetown Flyer (USA)** (55) (NEBerry) 3-8-6 RPerham(7) (w ldrs: rdn & lost pl over 2f out: rallied u.p fnl f) ..¾	6	16/1	48	27
532⁴	**Distinctive Dream (IRE)** (47) (KTIvory) 3-7-12b GBardwell(6) (hdwy 2f out: nt rch ldrs) 3	7	14/1	32	11
	Cairn Dhu (55) (MrsJRRamsden) 3-8-6b1 JFortune(12) (wnt lft s: nvr nrr)...nk	8	14/1	39	18
466⁷	**William's Well** (52) (MWEasterby) 3-8-3 JFEgan(13) (bit bkwd: nvr nr to chal).......................................hd	9	16/1	36	15
489*	**Eager To Please** (67) (MissGayKelleway) 3-9-4b DHolland(11) (spd over 4f)......................................hd	10	10/1	50	29
287⁶	**Supercharmer** (67) (DNicholls) 3-9-4 FNorton(4) (a in rr)...nk	11	10/1	50	29
546⁴	**Jack Says** (50) (DShaw) 3-8-1 DWright(15) (outpcd)..1½	12	33/1	29	8
506¹⁰	**Forgotten Times (USA)** (69) (TMJones) 3-9-6 NCarlisle(16) (b: prom over 3f).................................1½	13	14/1	44	23
	Ludo (67) (RHannon) 3-9-4 PatEddery(14) (bit bkwd: a bhd)..½	14	9/1	40	19
	Fan of Vent-Axia (54) (DJSCosgrove) 3-8-2(3) MBaird(8) (bkwd: outpcd).......................................4	15	20/1	17	—
473¹¹	**Keen Waters** (58) (JRArnold) 3-8-9 MRoberts(10) (bit bkwd: outpcd).......................................1¾	16	25/1	16	—
	Parijazz (IRE) (70) (MartynMeade) 3-9-4(3) RHavlin(9) (bit bkwd: s.s: a bhd: t.o) 11	17	14/1	—	—

(SP 142.4%) **17 Rn**

1m 13.9 (2.40) CSF £135.06 CT £737.83 TOTE £3.80: £1.20 £15.40 £3.70 £1.60 (£147.70) Trio £705.60 OWNER Mr N. Honeyman (THIRSK)
BRED St Simon Foundation

532 Jupiter (IRE) had little chance of turning the tables on the winner on identical terms, and he finished exactly the same distance behind as he had done last month. (5/1: op 8/1)

Thursday, April 17
Newmarket Rowley Mile - The three-year-old six-furlong handicap (Race 694, high) looked an interesting race beforehand and so it proved. Ray Cochrane, a jockey who usually seems to know where the best ground is, was drawn 20 of 20 on **Refuse To Lose**, and he elected to race alone by the far rail. Cochrane has employed this policy before at Newmarket, as he successfully chose to race Yeast by himself down the centre of the course while the remainder went up the stands' rail at a previous meeting here in 1996. This time, however, it did not quite come off, and there was no evidence from the remainder of the meeting that the ground was notably faster on the far side. Even so, he managed to finish second when all the pace had been set by runners drawn low to middle, including by the winner Treasure Touch (10), who had not actually been able to lead the way, such was the tempo.

Ripon - River Tern (Race 702, low), despite a slipping saddle and getting well behind, stuck to the stands' rail and managed to get up for second. The first three were drawn 1, 4 and 6 of 19 and the rest of the positions had a nice symmetry about them as concerned the draw. Kalar (16), rated much higher on the all-weather and not the force of old on turf, showed that the fast strip of ground down the far side was still there as he finished a good fifth. The interesting one here though was **Meranti** (11), who had recently returned to form, and his effort in finishing fourth having raced down the centre looked highly meritorious.

Follow	**Refuse To Lose**	next time	Unp	11/2
	Meranti	next time	WON	2/1

Saturday, April 19
Thirsk - It had looked the previous day as though the stands' rail was quicker than the centre, but this was the first chance of the season to see how the far rail compared. Diamond Steve was a successful punt in the claimer (Race 743, high) and had all the makings of being such, being visored for the first time and running from stall 12 of 12. Ellenbrook (10) chased him home. In the 20-runner handicap (Race 744, high), it looked

as though there was nothing between the two sides of the course, although George Duffield took **Ziggy's Dancer** (1) to race alone on the far rail and he had to be considered unlucky. It is no surprise that Sir Mark Prescott refuses to look at another jockey, as Duffield is as shrewd as his guv'nor and can always be relied upon to find the best ground. **Squire Corrie** (11), who finished fourth, has always been under-rated in my book. He seems to run really well from poor draws, but rarely manages to win when he has the best of the draw and remains a nightmare to predict, although he ran a cracker here from a centre stall. Admittedly he did get across to the stands' rail thanks to his early pace, but history shows that any horse that does that has to do a lot of racing early on (memorably Amigo Menor in 1990, see page 24, but many others along the years).

Follow	**Ziggy's Dancer**	next time	2nd	7/4	
	Squire Corrie	next time	4th	5/1	saddle slipped

Monday, April 21
Nottingham - Low numbers had looked to hold the edge in sprint races at recent meetings, but that was turned upside down here (Race 759, high), as the well-handicapped Grey Kingdom (17) made all up the stands' rail (high). The placed horses were all drawn high, but were probably flattered as they had raced with the pace. Napoleon Star (7), in good form coming here, ran very well to finish fifth overall and comfortably first down the far side. He would normally have gone down as a horse to follow but, given that his draw should have been an advantage, the chances are that he just ran a fair race.

Thursday, April 24
Beverley - Cathedral (12 of 14) was sent off the 2/5 favourite to beat a field of average-looking maidens in Race 792, high, and had the required high stall. The rest were beaten 6 lengths and over and, in the circumstances, nothing from a low stall ran well enough to warrant being noted.

Friday, April 25
Sandown (Good to firm) - Daunting Lady was the subject of encouraging reports (Race 828) and looked very backable at 100/30, given that she was drawn 15 of 15 with the stalls on the far side. The only worry was that Miss Hit and Fayrana, the 5/1 second and 6/1 third favourites, were also drawn fairly high. Those two both ran poorly though and looked like they would be worth opposing next time, as high numbers did dominate on the whole.

834 BOW STREET H'CAP (0-90) (3-Y.O+) (Class C)
5-20 (5-22) **5f 6y** £5,129.25 (£1,554.00: £759.50: £362.25) Stalls: High GOING: 0.13 sec per fur (G)

		SP	RR	SF
698²	**Gone Savage (75)** (WJMusson) 9-9-0 RCochrane(13) (b.nr fore: hdwy on ins 2f out: nt clr run over 1f out: led ins fnl f: r.o wl) ....— 1	6/1³	79	67
	Literary Society (USA) (69) (JARToller) 4-8-8 SSanders(17) (a.p: led 1f out tl ins fnl f: unable qckn) 1¼ 2	9/1	69	57
527²	**Broadstairs Beauty (IRE) (72)** (DShaw) 7-8-11b KFallon(15) (b: lw: led: rdn 2f out: hdd 1f out: one pce) ....¾ 3	5/1²	70	58
726³	**Eastern Prophets (85)** (GLewis) 4-9-10 PaulEddery(10) (lw: a.p: rdn over 2f out: ev ch 1f out: one pce) 1½ 4	7/1	78	66
585⁴	**Pointer (57)** (MrsPNDutfield) 5-7-10 JQuinn(14) (a.p: rdn over 2f out: one pce)..¾ 5	12/1	48	36
694⁵	**Ellens Lad (IRE) (85)** (RHannon) 3-9-0 PatEddery(16) (lw: rdn & hdwy 2f out: 7th & btn whn hmpd ins fnl f).1¼ 6	4/1¹	72	50
520¹⁷	**Longwick Lad (74)** (WRMuir) 4-8-13 JReid(11) (a.p: hdwy fnl 2f) ....¾ 7	16/1	58	46
520⁴	**Cim Bom Bom (IRE) (75)** (MBell) 5-8-9v⁽⁵⁾ GFaulkner(4) (a.p: rdn over 2f out: wknd fnl f) ....nk 8	11/1	58	46
	High Domain (IRE) (68) (JLSpearing) 6-8-7 SDrowne(2) (prom 2f)..1¾ 9	20/1	46	34
	Half Tone (57) (RMFlower) 5-7-10b JLowe(9) (nvr nrr) ....hd 10	14/1	34	22
731⁸	**Sweet Magic (75)** (PHowling) 6-9-0 FNorton(7) (outpcd) ....nk 11	25/1	51	39
744¹⁰	**Dande Flyer (70)** (DWPArbuthnot) 4-8-9 SWhitworth(3) (a bhd)...½ 12	33/1	45	33

726′ **Mr Bergerac (IRE) (82)** (BPalling) 6-9-7 I Sprake(6) (a bhd)..3 **13** 14/1   47   35
364⁵ **Rififi (66)** (RIngram) 4-8-5 AMcGlone(8) (b: a bhd) ....hd **14** 16/1   31   19
        Splicing (70) (WJHaggas) 4-8-9 MHills(12) (lw: a bhd) ....½ **15** 12/1   33   21
443¹⁶ **Lord High Admiral (CAN) (89)** (MJHeaton-Ellis) 9-10-0 MRoberts(5) (spd over 3f)......................s.h **16** 16/1   52   40
541⁹ **Mindrace (64)** (KTIvory) 4-8-0(3) MartinDwyer(1) (prom over 2f)...3 **17** 33/1   18   6
                                                                                                                           (SP 142.6%) **17 Rn**

62.33 secs (1.63) CSF £60.90 CT £226.97 TOTE £5.80: £1.80 £4.50 £1.60 £2.00 (£65.80) Trio £43.90 OWNER The Square Table (NEWMAR-KET) BRED Mrs C. F. Van Straubenzee and R. Mead
WEIGHT FOR AGE 3yo-10lb
IN-FOCUS: **At this first Flat meeting of the year, this event once again illustrated the importance of a high draw, when the stalls are on the far side on the straight course.**

The sprint handicap (Race 834, high) looked tailor-made for tricast punters with a good mix of front-runners and hold-up horses drawn high. In a 17-runner race, the first six home came from stalls 13, 17, 15, 10, 14 and 16, with the first one home from a single-number stall coming just eighth overall. Sandown probably has the biggest draw bias of any course in the country (Ripon would push it close though) irrespective of the ground, although it is better still with some cut, but bookmakers do seem now to be accounting for this in the prices. Even so, backing tricasts here is close to buying money (although you will be buying less money than before the tricast reduction formula was brought in a couple of years ago - see page 129-130).

Saturday, April 26
Leicester - The draw advantage at Leicester seems to vary a good deal and it probably depends mostly on where the pace lies. Even so, it is still well worth following any outliers* as in the handicap here (Race 835, low). The first six home were drawn 14, 16, 17, 4, 13 and 15 of 17, with 5 lengths back to the seventh horse, and it was **Weetman's Weigh** from stall 4, who performed with credit to come fourth.

* An outlier is any runner that finishes up the field from what turns out to be an unfavoured draw. For example, in a field of 20, if a horse drawn 19 finishes third when every other runner to finish in the first six or seven comes from a single-figure stall, he would be the 'outlier'.

Ripon - 18 runners in a sprint handicap (Race 845, low) on good ground looked ideal for tricasts, even given that three-year-old only events are less likely to work out as well as all-aged races so early in the season, because so few of them are fully exposed. They finished well strung out here, but the draw seemed to play as big a part as always with big-priced horses from stalls 2 and 3 of 18 filling first and third spot. However, there was a fly in the ointment in **Always Alight** (13), who ran an amazing race to finish second. The first three finished 5 lengths clear of **Return of Amin**, who looked as though he could be capable of better after veering left off the faster strip of ground on the far side to end up on the stands' side from stall 18.
Sandown - **Bishops Court** again ran a race full of promise (Race 854, high), finishing third from stall 4 behind horses drawn 10 and 11 in an 11-runner race.

Follow	**Weetman's Weigh**	next time	WON	5/1
	Always Alight	next time	Unp	5/1
	Return of Amin	next time	Unp	6/1
	Bishops Court	next time	WON	5/2

Tuesday, April 29
Nottingham (Good) - There were three races over sprint distances and they produced the usual mixed bag of results as far as concerned the draw. However, one who did catch the

eye was **Prince Foley** (Race 884, high). Sent off favourite, he raced alone down the centre from stall 2 and finished a close third, 2½ lengths clear of the fourth. The comment-in-running "raced alone" should always be of interest to draw pundits, especially when they run so well. He may well have won this had he raced with the pack, but the fact that he didn't meant he was able to compete in similar events without further penalty.

884 PORCHESTER NOVICE MEDIAN AUCTION STKS (2-Y.O) (Class F)
3-15 (3-18) 5f 13y £2,277.00 (£627.00: £297.00) Stalls: High GOING: 0.23 sec per fur (G)

		SP	RR	SF
5577 Rusty Babe (IRE) (JJQuinn) 2-8-12 JQuinn(7) (chsd ldrs: led over 1f out: r.o wl)............— 1		10/1	81	23
684* Young Ibnr (IRE) (PDEvans) 2-9-4 JFEgan(8) (w ldr: led ½-wy tl over 1f out: rdn & no ex fnl f)...........2½ 2		7/1	79	21
6372 Prince Foley (WGMTurner) 2-8-9(7) DMcGaffin(2) (racd alone centre: a.p: rdn over 1f out: kpt on)...........nk 3		7/2 1	76	18
Santa Faye (IRE) (BPalling) 2-8-7 TSprake(3) (w'like: bit bkwd: chsd ldrs: outpcd ½-wy: kpt on ins fnl f)......2½ 4		4/1 2	59	1
583* Blushing Victoria (MartynMeade) 2-8-10(5) DSweeney(4) (w ldrs tl outpcd 2f out: n.d after).............nk 5		4/1 2	66	8
Sweet Reward (JGSmyth-Osbourne) 2-8-12 DHarrison(12) (leggy: unf: bhd tl styd on appr fnl f)...........¾ 6		33/1	61	3
5369 Swift Time (MRBosley) 2-8-7 CRutter(10) (unruly: led to ½-wy: wknd wl over 1f out) ....¾ 7		25/1	54	—
53611 Fey Rouge (IRE) (RHollinshead) 2-8-4(3) FLynch(1) (sn rdn along: a outpcd: t.o)...........8 8		20/1	28	—
Kantone (IRE) (JMPEustace) 2-8-12 RCochrane(9) (str: cmpt: bkwd: s.i.s: a bhd: t.o) ....¾ 9		10/1	31	—
55710 O' Higgins (IRE) (BBoss) 2-8-12 KFallon(6) (in tch tl ½-wy: sn wknd: t.o).............¾ 10		5/1 3	29	—
Captain Jones (IRE) (BJMeehan) 2-8-12 RHughes(11) (w'like: cmpt: bit bkwd: a bhd & outpcd: t.o).............3 11		6/1	19	—
		(SP 135.4%) **11 Rn**		

64.4 secs (5.50) CSF £80.53 TOTE £12.60: £3.60 £4.80 £1.60 (£81.60) Trio £55.80 OWNER Mrs K. Mapp (MALTON) BRED Rathasker Stud
637 Prince Foley ploughed a lone furrow up the centre of the track and was in the firing line all the way but, like the runner-up, had to admit he had met his match when the winner got down to business. (7/2)

Follow **Prince Foley** next time **WON 2/1**

Wednesday, April 30
Ascot - The two races on the straight course, the Victoria Cup (Race 892, low) and the White Rose Handicap (Race 895, low) often attract capacity fields. The White Rose used to be a Derby Trial over ten furlongs, but fell foul of the growing trend of replacing everything with big-field handicaps (at least they kept White Rose in the title). Long may the trend continue. These races are particularly reliable as they are invariably run at a true pace, and for draw purposes they can be treated as two or three separate races, depending upon how many groups they split. The best ground seemed to be on the far side at this meeting and, while the Victoria Cup seemed pretty straightforward, the White Rose looked a very interesting heat, with **King of Tunes** (1) coming from an unpromising position up the stands' rail.

Follow **King of Tunes** next time **Unp 5/1**

Thursday, May 1
Redcar - As is usually the case in very big fields on the straight course, both rails looked to be quicker than the centre of the course (Race 896, centre), Dispol Diamond (2 of 24) leading home runners drawn 21, 20 and 23.

Friday, May 2
Musselburgh - In a field of ten for the sprint handicap (Race 924, low), only one runner, 50/1 outsider Take Notice (1) chose to race up the favoured stands' side. Given this scenario, the winner Southern Dominion (10) ended up being drawn best of all. Either this was a case of the other amateurs following the experienced Diana Jones in expectation of her knowing best, in which case they were outwitted, or none of them knowing where best to go.

Saturday, May 3
Newmarket Rowley Mile - The six-furlong handicap (Race 942, centre) split into two distinct groups and those on the stands' side came out well on top. Low numbers being

favoured is becoming a trend at this meeting, as there were plenty (myself included) prepared to argue that Alhaarth had only lost the previous year's Guineas because of his high draw with the stalls placed on the stands' rail (time showed that not to be true). The first seven home here were drawn 5, 3, 17, 7, 1, 6 and 9, the outlier being **Blue Goblin** (17) who came home third overall and well clear of his group. He had previously looked a bit one-paced over seven furlongs, but this showed him to be on the upgrade.

Thirsk - The first three home in the five-furlong handicap (Race 949, high) were drawn 15, 16 and 17 of 17 runners, highlighting again that high numbers still dominate on the whole. Nothing caught the eye in behind, with the fourth and fifth (drawn 2 and 1) making the most of the fast strip of ground close to the far rail.

Follow	**Blue Goblin**	next time	**WON 8/13**

Monday, May 5
Newcastle - In both sprint races, some of the runners went to race on the far side, three in Race 993, centre, and nine in Race 995, high. **Sandside** (4) finished less than 2 lengths off the winner and 6 lengths clear of his nearest pursuer on the far side to be fourth on this debut, and he left the impression that he should win races. **Levelled** (2) seemed to show much-improved form in the latter race, travelling well for most of the way and beating his group by 2 lengths. He was sent off at 16/1 for this and looked capable of winning in the future.

Follow	**Sandside**	next time	**WON 10/11**
	Levelled	next time	**WON 9/2**

Tuesday, May 6
Chester - The going at the May meeting started off soft and low numbers fared best in the earlier races, particularly so in Race 1018, low, when the bottom four in the draw filled the first four places in a field of 14, all at decent prices, and in Race 1029, low. However, after midweek rain, the ground had become desperate come Thursday, when finding a horse who could handle the conditions became more important than finding one drawn low.

Friday, May 9
Lingfield - The official going was returned as good, good to soft patches, but the race times suggested it was at least on the fast side of good and, after showers had fallen in the early morning, conditions were perfect for high numbers to dominate. In the five-furlong handicap (Race 1083, high), the pacey Runs in the Family was always likely to get the stands' rail from stall 13 of 13 and she led home runners drawn 14, 6, 12, 10 and 11. The outlier was **Polly Golightly** (6), who did very well to reach the frame on the evidence of the remaining races run on the straight course, won by runners drawn 8 of 9, 5 of 7, 12 of 12 and 10 of 12. By the Saturday, further rain had fallen and the ground was on the soft side, although Friday's going report was kept until after the first race. Surely it is time that punters did not have to wait for jockeys' confirmation of the ground before being giving an accurate report mid-meeting.

Follow	**Polly Golightly**	next time	2nd	7/1

Saturday, May 10
Beverley - On what looked genuinely good ground, high numbers fared best in the sprint handicap (Race 1098, high), with the first five being drawn 16, 12, 1, 13 and 19 of 18. **Sue**

Me (1) would have had the option to have raced wide, towards the stands' side, along with Insider Trader (3) and Ned's Bonanza (2), but Alex Greaves chose to work her way over towards the main group, making finishing third a highly-commendable effort.

Follow **Sue Me** next time 3rd 7/2

Sunday, May 11
Beverley - After heavy rain, the going became soft and got worse as the afternoon went on, which meant that low numbers were favoured in the 19-runner five-furlong maiden (Race 1119, high). Nifty Norman (1) made it all and had his field well strung out at the line.

Friday, May 16
Newmarket Rowley Mile - Michael Roberts again showed himself a jockey to trust when it comes to finding the best ground (Race 1219, centre), as he took Purchasing Power (2) to race by himself against the stands' rail, even though the stalls were placed in the centre. Assuming that he got the best of the ground on this occasion would have made him one to avoid on his next outing.

Thirsk (Good) - The ground was not as fast as at the previous meeting, which was a shame as the Dick Peacock (Race 1225, high) attracted 24 runners with some likely-looking outsiders drawn high. The signs had looked good here two weeks earlier, when stalls 15, 16 and 17 of 17 filled the first three positions on a good to firm surface, but in the other sprint handicap this time (Race 1223, high), Squire Corrie managed to win from stall 5 of 13. To be fair, three of the top five in the draw, Oatey (9), Chadwell Hall (11) and Present 'n Correct (13) were brought down in a melee after halfway, but Squire Corrie would have been placed at least anyway.

1223 KILBURN H'CAP (0-80) (3-Y.O+) (Class D)
3-50 (3-51) 5f £4,406.00 (£1,328.00: £644.00: £302.00) Stalls: High GOING minus 0.14 sec per fur (G)

					SP	RR	SF
1098[4]	Squire Corrie (69) (DWChapman) 5-9-3 ACulhane(5) (chsd ldrs: led ½-wy: all out)	——	1	12/1	70	44
834[3]	Broadstairs Beauty (IRE) (73) (DShaw) 7-9-4b[3] CTeague(12) (lw: b: a chsng ldrs: ev ch over 1f out: kpt on)	¾	2	9/2[1]	72	46
1037*	Impish (IRE) (56) (TJEtherington) 3-7-5[5] [7x] JBramhill(1) (lw: racd alone far side: cl up: nt qckn fnl f)	2½	3	12/1	47	13
949[3]	Captain Carat (60) (DNicholls) 6-8-8b DaleGibson(3) (sn drvn along: hdwy 2f out: styd on: nrst fin)	nk	4	9/1	50	24
702[19]	Dominelle (55) (TDEasterby) 5-8-3 GDuffield(4) (racd centre: w ldrs tl btn appr fnl f)	1½	5	20/1	40	14
905[3]	Malibu Man (77) (EAWheeler) 5-9-11 JCarroll(8) (lw: cl up tl wknd over 1f out)	1¾	6	7/1	56	30
949[4]	Johayro (64) (JSGoldie) 4-8-5[7] JMcAuley(10) (disp ld to ½-wy: wknd)	5	7	11/2[2]	27	1
	U-No-Harry (IRE) (70) (RHollinshead) 4-9-1[3] FLynch(2) (sn outpcd & bhd)	hd	8	20/1	33	7
357[8]	Master of Passion (70) (JMPEustace) 8-9-4 JTate(7) (dwlt: outpcd & bhd: bdly hmpd 2f out: eased)	dist	9	20/1	——	——
772[2]	Able Sheriff (63) (MWEasterby) 5-8-6b[5] GParkin(6) (chsd ldrs tl b.d 2f out: dead)		B	15/2	——	——
901[7]	Oatey (64) (MrsJRRamsden) 4-8-12 JFortune(9) (hld up: effrt whn b.d 2f out)		B	6/1[3]	——	——
772[8]	Chadwell Hall (67) (SRBowring) 6-8-8b[7] PBoyle(11) (disp ld to ½-wy: cl up whn fell 2f out: dead)		F	9/1	——	——
956[7]	Present 'n Correct (48) (CBBBooth) 4-7-10 LChamock(13) (chsd ldrs tl bdly hmpd & uns rdr 2f out)		U	9/1	——	——

(SP 131.8%) **13 Rn**

60.2 secs (2.20) CSF £63.85 CT £640.79 TOTE £14.50: £4.10 £1.90 £3.90 (£28.40) Trio £611.40; £51.67 to Newbury 17/5/97 OWNER Miss N. F. Thesiger (YORK) BRED Whitsbury Manor Stud
LONG HANDICAP Impish (IRE) 6-10
WEIGHT FOR AGE 3yo-8lb

In the Dick Peacock itself, followers of runners drawn high never looked like collecting and, with hindsight, the ground was probably too soft to back them in forecasts and tricasts. Even so, it was difficult not to get involved having seen what had happened in previous years. The thought "what if stalls 22, 23 and 24 finish first, second and third" enters your mind and when you see them go off at 16/1, 25/1 and 8/1, tricast slips almost write themselves.

When the ground here rides softer than good, runners drawn towards the far rail have an advantage and that looked the case here.

The Effects of the Draw

Saturday, May 17
Newbury (Soft) - For the first time this season, the ground was genuinely soft (it had looked as though it was cutting up the day before when First Island won the Lockinge but the race times suggested otherwise) and the first race run on the straight course confirmed the importance of a high draw. The first three home in the six-furlong maiden (Race 1240, high) were drawn 12, 13 and 14 of 14, but the one who really took the eye was **Lady In Waiting** from stall 6. She was making her debut and was weak in the market, but finished less than 3 lengths behind the winner and 9 lengths clear of the fifth, despite racing down the centre of the course. As *Raceform*'s Anthony Kemp highlighted in his *Note-Book* comment, the ground was undoubtedly slower down the centre, and this looked an amazing effort.

1240   KINGWOOD STUD MAIDEN STKS (2-Y.O F) (Class D)
2-30 (2-31) **6f 8y** £3,808.00 (£1,144.00: £552.00: £256.00) Stalls: High GOING: 0.36 sec per fur (GS)

			SP	RR	SF
	Dance Trick (USA) (PWChapple-Hyam) 2-8-11 JReid(12) (leggy: unf: lw: a.p: led over 2f out tl over 1f out: rallied nr fin: led last stride) ....—	1	5/4 [1]	93	40
	Ajig Dancer (MRChannon) 2-8-11 RPerham(13) (leggy: unf: hld up: led over 1f out: hrd rdn ins fnl f: hdd last stride)..s.h	2	16/1	93	40
	Tadwiga (RHannon) 2-8-11 DaneO'Neill(14) (neat: rdn over 3f out: hdwy over 1f out: r.o wl ins fnl f)............1	3	11/1	90	37
	Lady In Waiting (PFICole) 2-8-11 TQuinn(6) (w'like: w ldr: led 3f out tl over 2f out: unable qckn) 1½	4	11/2 [2]	86	33
739 [6]	Face-Off (RHannon) 2-8-11 PatEddery(4) (led 3f: wknd wl over 1f out) 9	5	9/1 [3]	62	9
965 [5]	Princess Londis (AGFoster) 2-8-11 DHolland(2) (hld up: rdn over 2f out: sn wknd) ....hd	6	14/1	62	9
722 [7]	Distinctly Lillie (IRE) (JSMoore) 2-8-11 WJO'Connor(3) (s.s: nvr nrr) 1½	7	50/1	58	5
	Gipsy Moth (BJMeehan) 2-8-11 OPeslier(10) (w'like: bit bkwd: s.s: hld up: rdn over 2f out: wknd wl over 1f out) 1¾	8	11/1	54	1
	Respond (GLMoore) 2-8-11 CandyMorris(11) (leggy: prom over 2f)..1	9	50/1	51	—
	Primavera (MJHaynes) 2-8-11 RCochrane(7) (unf: bit bkwd: bhd fnl 3f)..............................8	10	40/1	30	—
	Miss Muffett (IRE) (PMooney) 2-8-11 DeclanO'Shea(5) (unf: s.s: a wl bhd)..........................nk	11	50/1	29	—
	No Shame (JGSmyth-Osbourne) 2-8-11 DHarrison(8) (str: bkwd: bhd fnl 3f) 10	12	50/1	2	—
739 [9]	Burning Love (JSMoore) 2-8-11 KFallon(9) (cmpt: bkwd: bhd fnl 3f).................................½	13	16/1	1	—
	Miss Chief Maker (WRMuir) 2-8-11 KFallon(9) (cmpt: bkwd: bhd fnl 3f)................................12	14	25/1	—	—

(SP 119.1%) **14 Rn**

1m 17.93 (6.13) CSF £20.66 TOTE £2.00: £1.30 £5.00 £3.30 (£20.50) Trio £58.10 OWNER Mr R. E. Sangster (MARLBOROUGH) BRED Swettenham Stud
Lady In Waiting, a medium-sized filly, came down the centre of the track where the ground was undoubtedly slower. (11/2: 3/1-6/1)

In the other race run on the straight course (Race 1243, high), the first three were drawn 13, 12 and 10 of 13. None of those drawn low took the eye as the unplaced horses finished well strung out.

Thirsk - The ground started off good but became softer after a storm between the first and second races. In such conditions, you would normally expect to see low numbers do best in the straight races, but the four sprints on the card only attracted 12, 11, 10 and 11 runners, so the stalls only stretched halfway across the course and they all raced centre to stands' side. Under these circumstances, runners drawn high tend to fare just the better without being completely dominant and that was true here.

Follow   **Lady In Waiting**   next time   **WON 6/5**

Sunday, May 18
Newbury - It was at this meeting in 1996 that I almost landed my biggest payout on a placepot, let down by one race for a £10,500 dividend. The ground was riding very soft that day and, after plenty of weekend rain, it was soft again, but nothing like as bad. There were two races run on the straight course and both attracted decent fields. Middle to high numbers held the advantage in the mile handicap (Race 1262, high) with the first four coming from stalls 9, 11, 19 and 17 of 17. However, in the two-year-old maiden (Race

1263, high), **Bold Edge** won from stall 2 of 12. This looked a very good effort to beat some better-drawn fancied runners.

Ripon - Both sprint events looked likely to be dominated by runners drawn low, but Alconleigh managed to win Race 1267, low, from stall 11 of 14, and Canovas Heart took the handicap (Race 1269, low) from stall 7 of 11, both of them having got across to the stands' rail. None of the fancied runners from low stalls performed that well, making them opposable next time.

Follow   **Bold Edge**   next time   Unp   4/1

Wednesday, May 21

Goodwood - The draw at Goodwood has always been unpredictable in big fields and that again looked the case here (Race 1317, low), as they finished in a heap as usual. Sea-Deer (18) seemed to run yet another good race from an unlikely draw, but the chances were that the ground was as good where he was racing as it was on the stands' side.

Friday, May 23

Nottingham - A group of six went to race on the far side in Race 1385, high, and the one that took them along there, Alfahaal (2), did well to finish fifth overall and second on that side. However, it was **Almasi** (3) who caught the eye, coming home almost 6 lengths in front of Alfahaal in second, having only passed him inside the final furlong before sprinting clear.

Follow   **Almasi**   next time   **WON   6/5**

Croft Pool (No.3) won the 1997 Temple Stakes, but Bolshoi (right) caught the eye from a bad draw

Monday, May 26

Sandown - The Group Two Temple Stakes (Race 1455, high) attracted a field of just 10, but as usual what should have been an informative race was distorted by a huge draw bias, even though the ground was riding faster than ideal. Croft Pool (stall 9), making his reappearance having missed his intended run at Newmarket, and Brave Edge (10) were drawn in the top two stalls and returned at odds of 20/1 and 25/1 respectively. The result? Croft Pool beat Brave Edge for a straight forecast of £375.46. The one to catch the eye was **Bolshoi** from stall 1. Although the field was not that large, the top four in the draw filled four of the first six places, with a gap to the seventh, so Bolshoi did remarkably well to make the frame. In the maiden (Race 1457, high) **Sada** (1 of 10) did well to make the frame behind two much better-fancied rivals from high stalls, especially finishing 3 lengths clear of the rest.

Follow	**Bolshoi**	next time	3rd	100/30
	Sada	next time	Unp	8/1

Wednesday, May 28

Ripon - This was another of those rare meetings where it was not imperative to be drawn either very low or very high in the sprints, although runners from centre stalls had fared quite well at the previous meeting as well. May must have just been an off-month.

Yarmouth (Firm) - The first meeting of the season here saw firm ground (hard according to the race times) and a biggish field lining up for the seven-furlong handicap (Race 1501, low) allowing a chance to see if high numbers still held sway. Yarmouth never used to be of much interest, but several results in 1996 pointed to the ground being much faster towards the stands' rail and that again appeared to be the case. A group of six stayed to race on the far side and it was **Mezzoramio** (2) who came home clear on that flank and second overall. Safey Ana (13) and Ertlon (14) dominated the high numbers, coming home first and third, and they finished nicely clear of the fourth. The result had a balanced look to it.

Mezzoramio, who won two amateur races in 1996, always seems to be particularly reliable when in form, although he has never handled ground softer than good.

Follow	**Mezzoramio**	next time	Unp	9/2

1501 DAVID STOTT H'CAP (0-70) (3-Y.O+) (Class E)
3-45 (3-47) 7f 3y £3,122.25 (£933.00: £446.50: £203.25) Stalls: Low GOING minus 0.65 sec per fur (HD)

		SP	RR	SF
1219[12] **Safey Ana (USA) (61)** (BHanbury) 6-9-5 WRyan(13) (b: racd stands' side: led ins fnl f: r.o wl) ....— 1		9/1	67	58
1128[2] **Mezzoramio (46)** (KAMorgan) 5-7-11v[7] JoHunnam(2) (b: overall ldr far side: hrd rdn & ct cl home)..............¾ 2		6/1[3]	50	41
1154[2] **Ertlon (70)** (CEBrittain) 7-10-0 BDoyle(14) (a.p stands' side: led after 3f tl hdd & no ex ins fnl f)...............½ 3		9/2[2]	73	64
838[16] **Gain Line (USA) (58)** (BobJones) 4-9-2 NDay(5) (racd far side: hdwy over 2f out: nrst fin)........................3 4		9/1	54	45
1248[5] **Godmersham Park (62)** (PSFelgate) 5-9-6 LDettori(7) (w ldr far side: rdn 2f out: sn btn)...........................1¾ 5		6/1[3]	54	45
1292[7] **Jibereen (70)** (PHowling) 5-10-0 PaulEddery(3) (chsd ldrs far side: hrd drvn 2f out: one pce)....................4 6		12/1	53	44
1131* **Gymcrak Flyer (64)** (GHolmes) 6-9-8 KFallon(1) (b.hind: lw: hld up far side: hdwy over 2f out: sn rdn: nvr able to chal)...3 7		5/2[1]	40	31
1135[10] **Hadadabble (38)** (PatMitchell) 4-7-5[5] APolli(4) (racd far side: bhd tl sme late hdwy)...............................nk 8		50/1	14	5
1116[13] **Persephone (38)** (JLHarris) 4-7-10b JLowe(10) (nvr plcd to chal)..1¾ 9		66/1	10	1
1011[7] **Dia Georgy (38)** (CADwyer) 6-7-10 JQuinn(9) (b: a in rr)..2 10		50/1	5	—
1225[13] **Melodic Drive (57)** (JAGlover) 7-9-1b GCarter(12) (bit bkwd: s.s: racd stands' side: a bhd)........................1 11		14/1	22	13
686[10] **On The Green (47)** (AHide) 4-8-5 DBiggs(6) (s.i.s: a bhd)..2 12		33/1	10	1
Bear To Dance (40) (PHowling) 4-7-7[5] RMullen(8) (bit bkwd: bhd fr ½-wy)...2 13		50/1	—	—
1134[7] **Spanish Stripper (USA) (38)** (MCChapman) 6-7-10 GBardwell(15) (led stands' side 3f: sn lost tch) ....¾ 14		50/1	—	—
1219[11] **Watch The Fire (67)** (JEBanks) 4-9-11 JStack(11) (lw: hld up: hdwy u.p over 3f out: wknd fnl 2f) ....s.h 15		14/1	23	14

(SP 128.6%) **15 Rn**

1m 23.4 (1.50 under best) (-0.20) CSF £58.63 CT £266.06 TOTE £11.20: £2.60 £2.10 £1.90 (£33.10) Trio £59.90 OWNER The Optimists Racing Partnership (NEWMARKET) BRED Robert N. Clay
1128 Mezzoramio made a brave attempt to make it all and he did finish clear on the far side but the winner, under the stands' rail, beat him to the punch in the final 50 yards. Losses are only lent. (6/1)

Monday, June 2nd

Hamilton - 16 lined up for the six-furlong apprentice handicap (Race 1613, low) and the first three home came from stalls 15, 14 and 13. The prevailing good to firm ground would not have encouraged tricast punters to invest, as the advantage of a high draw is nowhere near as great on fast ground as it is on soft, but there is still a slight bias.

Season after season, a few unexpected tricasts pop up at courses where there is undoubtedly a draw bias, but at times when you least expect it, with the above race at Hamilton being the perfect example. The ground did not look soft enough on that occasion, but high numbers dominated. Similarly, Leicester and Nottingham often seem to throw up one or two handicap sprints a season where stalls 1, 2 and 3 finish first, second and third, so even when the conditions do not look ideal for the draw bias to work, it is always worth looking through the favoured stalls in a bid to find the winner, especially when the pace is on that side.

Thursday, June 5th

Yarmouth - Given what had happened at the opening meeting here a week earlier, everything looked in the favour of those drawn high in the straight-mile selling handicap (Race 1689, low). In a field of 20, Mr Rough was sent off quite a warm favourite for his first venture into the lowest grade in four years and seemed fairly drawn in stall 13. After tracking the leader towards the stands' rail, he came through to lead home horses drawn 5, 19 and 20. The clear outlier, **Clytha Hill Lad**, from stall 5, ran a cracker to finish 3 lengths clear of the third having raced up the unfavoured far side.

Follow   **Clytha Hill Lad**   next time Unp   7/2

Friday, June 6

Catterick - Low numbers should have been favoured in the sprint handicap (Race 1730, low), but all the principals were drawn high, leaving question marks about the low-drawn runners.

Goodwood - In a field of 12 for the sprint handicap (Race 1743, low) the first four home all came from the bottom half of the draw.

Saturday, June 7

Epsom - Ya Malak (10) confirmed the impression that he had run well when badly drawn at Sandown the time before with a very impressive performance (Race 1766, high). He led home runners from stalls 11 and 13 in a 12-runner affair, but the ground up the stands' rail did not appear to be noticeably faster.

Wednesday, June 11

Beverley - The official going report was changed several times before settling on good becoming soft, but the race times suggested the ground was fast. Royston Ffrench had clearly decided that the far rail was the place to be (Race 1828, high) and switched Sunset Harbour across from stall 1 of 17 after the start. As it turned out, there was probably little to choose between the two sides.

Hamilton - Squire Corrie (2 of 17) again defied the odds, making all the running against the far rail having been drawn against the stands' rail (Race 1835, low). Sprint handicaps at Hamilton remain thoroughly unpredictable affairs, with runners often switching and racing where least expected, and placed and winning horses often returning at big prices.

Saturday, June 14

Lingfield - Richard Perham showed with this ride that he is a jockey to watch for (Race 1965, high), switching Abtaal (1) over to race onto what looked the best ground and beating Silver Harrow (18). The first two home raced up the stands' rail and came home comfortably clear of the third **Roy Boy** (4), who finished nicely in front on the far side.

York - High numbers had just about held the call the previous day when the stalls were placed on the stands' rail, although the fields were not nearly large enough to make any firm conclusions. The two sprint handicaps here attracted fields of 23 and 19 and the signs after the first of them (Race 1977, high) were that high numbers were indeed well favoured on this occasion. **Grey Kingdom** (9) must have given away a good deal of ground to get over to the stands' rail, so it was a very good effort to win. He beat home horses drawn 19, 21, 23, 18 and 14, so the chances were that he was still ahead of the handicapper. In the William Hill Trophy (Race 1980, high), runners drawn high never looked like challenging those drawn middle to low. Presumably, the first four were a class apart.

| Follow | **Roy Boy** | next time | Did not race again |
| | **Grey Kingdom** | next time | 3rd   4/1 |

Tuesday, June 17

Royal Ascot - As always, the Britannia Handicap (Race 2013, low) produced a good turnout, but the ground looked to be pretty even. Although the latter part of the week was marred by adverse weather, the rain did not seem to get into the ground until the Friday when the going eventually became soft. On the Wednesday and Thursday the draw seemed to play little part in any of the big-field races, although the stands' rail did look marginally quicker than the rest of the course.

Thirsk (Good) - While Royal Ascot was attracting all the attention, two horses caught my eye at Thirsk. There were two sprints on the card and high numbers looked to hold sway in both, with stalls 13, 2, 16, 18 and 17 of 17 filling the first five places in Race 2016, high, and stalls 12, 11, 10 and 1 of 12 filling the first four positions in Race 2017, high.

2016 GROSVENOR CASINOS NORTH EAST REGION (S) STKS (2-Y.O) (Class G)
2-50 (2-54) 6f £2,442.50 (£680.00: £327.50) Stalls: High GOING minus 0.51 sec per fur (F)

			SP	RR	SF
1829[11] **Tancred Times** (DWBarker) 2-8-6 TWilliams(13) (chsd ldrs: led 2f out: r.o) ....—	1	33/1	64	—
1829[5] **Inchalong** (MBrittain) 2-8-6 JCarroll(2) (a.p: ev ch over 1f out: kpt on wl)............................1	2	5/1[2]	61	—
1438[4] **Tremonnow** (JMBradley) 2-8-6 LCharnock(16) (a chsng ldrs: kpt on fnl f)...............................1	3	5/1[2]	59	—
1758* **Figawin** (GLewis) 2-9-4 NDay(18) (a chsng ldrs: kpt on one pce fnl 2f)...................................½	4	7/1	69	—
1600[2] **Newhargen (IRE)** (PDEvans) 2-8-11 GDuffield(17) (led tl hdd 2f out: kpt on same pce) ....½	5	12/1	61	—
1815[7] **Toll's Times** (MWEasterby) 2-8-6[5] GParkin(11) (drvn along & hdwy after 2f: kpt on: nvr able to chal) 1¾	6	33/1	56	—
1789[2] **Edna's Gift (IRE)** (JBerry) 2-8-6[7] CLowther(5) (prom: hung lft over 2f out: r.o one pce)............½	7	6/1[3]	57	—
1298[7] **Adrenalin** (MrsJRRamsden) 2-8-11 ACulhane(10) (s.s & swtchd rt s: hdwy ½-wy: no imp)............½	8	25/1	54	—
1581[3] **Hopefully** (MRChannon) 2-8-6 RPerham(7) (a.p: outpcd over 2f out: no imp after).......................¾	9	11/1	47	—
Son of Skelton (JWharton) 2-8-11 JFanning(1) (leggy: scope: s.i.s: stdy hdwy over 1f out: nvr nr to chal).....nk	10	50/1	51+	—
1581[2] **Final Claim** (JGFitzGerald) 2-8-11 DHolland(12) (b: lw: chsd ldrs: outpcd ½-wy: sn btn) 3	11	3/1[1]	43	—
1614[5] **Docklands Dispatch (IRE)** (NTinkler) 2-8-8[3] PMcCabe(8) (a bhd)......................................hd	12	12/1	43	—
1819[13] **Eager Hero** (MBrittain) 2-8-4[7] DMernagh(9) (sn outpcd & bhd).......................................nk	13	100/1	42	—
1626[4] **Dispol Lass** (PCalver) 2-8-3[3] DarrenMoffatt(15) (chsd ldrs 4f: wknd)...............................2	14	20/1	32	—
1290[5] **General Joey** (MDods) 2-8-8[3] CTeague(14) (lw: s.s: a bhd)..2	15	100/1	31	—
1815[6] **Sunshine Pet (IRE)** (JJO'Neill) 2-8-6b[1] RLappin(4) (nvr wnt pce)......................................2	16	50/1	21	—
1253[7] **Sixth Avenue (IRE)** (RMWhitaker) 2-8-3[3] RHavlin(6) (a bhd) 7	17	20/1	2	—

(SP 134.0%) **17 Rn**

1m 13.6 (3.90) CSF £179.11 TOTE £58.90: £8.40 £3.00 £2.30 (£305.10) Trio £329.60; £417.83 to Ascot 18/6/97 OWNER The Ebor Partnership (RICHMOND) BRED W. L. Barker
No bid
1829 Inchalong put in a tremendous effort from a very poor draw, and will surely find a suitable event before long. (5/1)

Inchalong (2), who had been on the go for a long time already, was the only runner from a single-figure stall to get anywhere near the principals, and to finish second was, as *Raceform*'s Alan Amies noted, a tremendous effort. **Rum Lad** had little chance of making the frame in the following race from stall 1, but did well to finish fourth overall.

Follow	**Inchalong**	next time	WON	12/1
	Rum Lad	next time	WON	7/2

Thursday, June 19
Ripon - History has shown it to be just about impossible to win a sprint handicap at Ripon from stall 14 when the whole field race up against the stands' rail, but **Blessingindisguise** managed it here (Race 2061, low). This was an exceptional effort and he looked to be improving.

Follow	**Blessingindisguise**	next time	2nd	10/1

Friday, June 20
Royal Ascot - Soft ground led to low numbers holding the upper hand in straight races, notably in the King's Stand (Race 2106, low), but also in the Wokingham (Race 2105, low). Selhurstpark Flyer, from stall 5 of 30, beat Danetime (19), who had been switched after only a furlong to race under the stands' rail, and Bollin Joanne (4). Runners drawn 4, 2 and 3 of 18 filled the first three positions in the King's Stand and the result had a symmetrical look to it.

Unfortunately, I missed the gloomy weather at Royal Ascot this year, as I was in Las Vegas for the week, pursuing my less successful roulette system (high numbers aren't favoured at Caesar's Palace after all) at the bigger casinos. I managed to get hold of a racing paper in Bally's Sports Book and found a Royal Ascot report tucked away on about page 10. The only British runner to warrant a mention was Bosra Sham, while the rest of it was made up of how Gary Stevens had made history, how Gary Stevens had ridden a winner and how Gary Stevens had picked up a whip ban for his ride on Danetime. The whip ban was just about deserved but Danetime would have to have gone down as an unlucky loser, as the ground he forfeited by being switched from the centre of the track would have cost him at least a length or two. Neville Callaghan, regarded by most as one of the shrewder trainers, seems to know his stuff when it comes to the draw.

Saturday, June 28
Newcastle - With the ground coming up unseasonally heavy, low numbers were favoured in the first three races on the card (Races 2324-2326, high), which attracted 10, 16 and 18 runners respectively. In the first, stall 3 led home 4 and 2, in the second 4 beat 13 (Tertium who edged left and ended up on the best ground centre to far side), and 7, and in the third Cretan Gift (4) led home Return of Amin (6) and **Grey Kingdom** (15). Grey Kingdom was the only runner from a double-figure stall to finish in the first seven and, on his tenth outing of the season here, he clearly enjoyed the testing ground.

Follow	**Grey Kingdom**	next time	WON	3/1

Thursday, July 3
Catterick (Soft) - As is usually the case when the ground rides on the soft side, most of the jockeys elected to race up the stands' rail in the sprint (Race 2412), even though the

81

stalls were placed on the far side (low). However, almost half the field chose to stay and race centre to far side and **Beechwood Quest** (4) came home miles clear of the far-side group and second overall, the first four home being drawn 15, 4, 14 and 11 of 13. The second horse home up the far side came seventh overall and was some 14 lengths behind Beechwood Quest, who clearly turned in a fine effort.

Follow   **Beechwood Quest**   next time   **WON 7/4**

2412   SAINT-CLOUD (S) STKS (2-Y.O) (Class G)
2-20 (2-23) 5f £2,302.50 (£640.00: £307.50) Stalls: Low GOING: 0.29 sec per fur (G)

		SP	RR	SF
2165[3] Oriel Girl (PDEvans) 2-8-6v[1] JFEgan(15) (lw: led stands' side: led overall ins fnl f: r.o u.p) ....— 1		7/4[1]	65	24
2288[7] Beechwood Quest (IRE) (BSRothwell) 2-8-6be LCharnock(4) (led far side: clr ½-wy: hdd ins fnl f: kpt on) ..1¾ 2		6/1[3]	59	18
2288[10] Hayburner (MWEasterby) 2-8-11 TLucas(14) (prom stands' side: rdn ½-wy: kpt on: no imp) 6 3		14/1	45	4
2186[5] Angry Albert (CSmith) 2-8-4v[1(7)] CLowther(11) (lw: outpcd tl styd on fnl 2f)...........................2 4		12/1	39	—
1860[6] Candy Twist (RonaldThompson) 2-8-1[(5)] JBramhill(7) (a chsng ldrs: rdn & no imp fr ½-wy)............½ 5		20/1	32	—
2042[5] Dispol Emerald (SEKettlewell) 2-8-6 JFortune(13) (w wnr stands' side tl wknd fnl 2f) 5 6		5/1[2]	16	—
767[7] Sea Imp (IRE) (MartynMeade) 2-7-13[(7)] RBrisland(2) (chsd ldrs far side to ½-wy: sn outpcd)...............½ 7		8/1	15	—
1124[5] Wilfred Sherman (IRE) (JBerry) 2-8-8[(3)] PFessey(12) (lw: s.i.s: bhd tl sme late hdwy).....................1 8		8/1	16	—
2233[7] E B Treasure (NBycroft) 2-8-6 DHolland(10) (nvr trbld ldrs)...2½ 9		66/1	3	—
1791[5] Boccolino (TDBarron) 2-8-11 RLappin(1) (chsd ldrs centre 3f: wknd)..3 10		5/1[2]	—	—
1124[8] Sharp Pet (DMcCain) 2-8-6b[1] GDuffield(3) (bolted 3f gng to post: n.d) 1½ 11		66/1	—	—
2288[14] Shirleys Girl (IRE) (WStorey) 2-8-6 NKennedy(8) (s.i.s: a bhd)...................................1¾ 12		50/1	—	—
2233[4] General Joey (MDods) 2-8-6b[(5)] PRoberts(6) (cl up far side 3f: sn wknd).......................hd 13		25/1	—	—
		(SP 134.1%)	**13 Rn**	

63.0 secs (0.10 under 2y best) (5.50) CSF £12.66 TOTE ₤1.70: £1.40 £2.30 £4.20 (£20.90) Trio £131.00 OWNER Mr D. Maloney (WELSHPOOL) BRED Mrs F. A. Veasey
No bid
1137 Beechwood Quest (IRE) ran a super race up the far side, showing blistering speed, and a similar event would seem to be on the cards. (6/1)

Friday, July 4
Beverley - The ground got so bad after all the rain that the stalls had to be done away with for the five-furlong and middle-distance races, and those races had flip starts. In the opening race over 7f 100y (Race 2463), high numbers dominated with stall 12 beating 14 and 15 of 14, the first three home all racing prominently on the best strip towards the far side. It is hard enough for horses to quicken from behind in races run on this type of surface as it is, but when they have to come off the best strip of ground to mount a challenge, it makes the job nearly impossible.
Sandown - The five-furlong handicap (Race 2481, high) attracted a field of 10 with all the fancied runners drawn high, thus racing on the far rail. The outcome was predictable enough with Sally Green (9) leading home runners drawn in stalls 10 and 7, with 8 fourth. This race again illustrated the importance of being drawn in the top few stalls in sprint races here.
Warwick - On soft going, three of the 20 runners chose to race wide in Race 2487, low, and they finished first, second and seventh (50/1). The ground on the outside appeared far and away the quickest throughout the afternoon and, in the big-field races, the winners were drawn 17 of 20, 15 of 20, 9 of 13 and 15 of 17, with nothing drawn low getting a look in and none of them catching the eye. Warwick is of no interest as far as concerns the draw unless the ground is soft, but when there is cut, it seems to act very similarly to Newbury. The starts of races of six furlongs and upwards are on the round course (five-furlong races start on a chute) and runners that race towards the outer in the back straight and then up the stands' side in the home straight are on the best ground all the way.

Saturday, July 5
Beverley - On desperate ground, the stalls were again dispensed with for races started at the five-furlong gate (including the race run over 2m 35y) and flip starts again employed.

82

Jockeys canny enough are able in these circumstances to improve their position at the start and Dean McKeown took full advantage on Dona Filipa (Race 2496). He had been due to start from stall 5 of 13, but started from a position akin to about stall 10 and made a beeline towards the far side, finishing third at 25/1. Mary Magdalene, who was to have gone from stall 12, made no mistake and also headed for the far rail (trainer Michael Bell and protegé Michael Fenton invariably know where the best ground is). McKeown later repeated the dose aboard High Domain (Race 2497), due to start from stall 7 of 9, but who actually lined up right on the outside.

Sandown (Good to soft) - **Cathedral** (Race 2526, high) turned in an amazing effort to get up for third from stall 1 of 14. The ground looked to have a bit of cut in it, so high numbers should have completely dominated, which they largely did, with the runners from the top four stalls finishing first, second, fourth and fifth, including reliable yardstick Struggler (11) in second. The fact that Cathedral was outpaced and stuck to the slower strip of ground towards the centre of the course before running on at the end made this performance extraordinary. In Race 2529, high, My Best Valentine followed Cathedral's lead and sprung a surprise at 20/1, but in slightly different circumstances. He took the 'Gone Savage route' in dropping in and switching straight towards the far rail, a tactic suited only to horses who enjoy being messed around and barged a bit, as it is not easy to break through the tightly-packed group that always tends to accumulate on the far rail. Even so, this effort showed My Best Valentine to be in top form.

Follow **Cathedral** next time 2nd 12/1

2526 SANDOWN PARK SPRINT STKS (Listed) (3-Y.O+) (Class A)
3-20 (3-22) 5f 6y £11,522.50 (£3,490.00: £1,705.00: £812.50) Stalls: High GOING: 0.05 sec per fur (G)

				SP	RR	SF
2106¹⁰ **Ya Malak** (113) (DNicholls) 6-9-7 AlexGreaves(12) (lw: nt clr run over 2f out: stdy hdwy over 1f out: rdn fnl f: led nr fin)	—	1		11/2²	111	77
2106⁶ **Struggler** (112) (DRLoder) 5-9-3 LDettori(11) (a.p: rdn over 2f out: led ins fnl f: hdd nr fin)	nk	2		7/2¹	106	72
2106¹³ **Cathedral (IRE)** (98) (BJMeehan) 3-8-12 JWeaver(1) (outpcd: gd hdwy over 1f out: r.o one pce)	2½	3		33/1	98+	59
679⁸ **Proud Native (IRE)** (112) (APJarvis) 3-8-12 MJKinane(13) (lw: rdn over 2f out: hdwy over 1f out: one pce)	....½	4		12/1	97	58
2105⁶ **To the Roof (IRE)** (105) (PWHarris) 5-9-3 MHills(14) (lw: led to 1f out: sn wknd)	hd	5		7/2¹	96	62
2056¹⁰ **Tedburrow** (102) (EJAlston) 5-9-3 ACulhane(9) (outpcd: hdwy over 1f out: nvr nrr)	s.h	6		11/1	96	62
2023⁹ **Omaha City (IRE)** (95) (BGubby) 3-8-12 AClark(2) (rdn over 2f out: hdwy over 1f out: one pce)	1¼	7		40/1	92	53
Eveningperformance (116) (HCandy) 6-9-5 CRutter(3) (chsd ldrs over 3f)	1¼	8		11/1	90	56
2277³ **Sally Slade** (67) (CACyzer) 5-8-12 GDuffield(8) (outpcd)	1¼	9		100/1	79	45
2106¹⁶ **Brave Edge** (106) (RHannon) 6-9-3 DaneO'Neill(5) (spd over 3f)	s.h	10		20/1	84	50
2106⁸ **Bolshoi (IRE)** (106) (JBerry) 5-9-3b KDarley(4) (lw: a.p: rdn over 2f out: wknd fnl f)	s.h	11		10/1³	84	50
2106¹⁸ **Sylva Paradise (IRE)** (103) (CEBrittain) 4-9-3 BDoyle(10) (bhd fnl 2f)	s.h	12		20/1	84	50
2105²³ **Astrac (IRE)** (103) (MissGayKelleway) 6-9-7b¹ KFallon(6) (spd over 3f)	4	13		20/1	75	41
1975* **Johnny Staccato** (93) (JMPEustace) 3-8-12 JTate(7) (squeezed out s: a bhd: virtually p.u fnl 2f: sddle slipped)	dist	14		20/1	—	—

(SP 118.7%) **14 Rn**
61.69 secs (0.99) CSF £20.25 TOTE £5.60: £2.60 £1.80 £3.90 (£7.40) Trio £184.20 OWNER Contrac Promotions Ltd (THIRSK) BRED Mrs R. B. Kennard
WEIGHT FOR AGE 3yo-5lb
OFFICIAL EXPLANATION Johnny Staccato: saddle slipped after one furlong.
792* Cathedral (IRE) did not appear to have a prayer from his low draw, which makes this performance most commendable. Unable to go the early pace, he made giant strides below the distance, and stayed on for third. (33/1)

Monday, July 7

Musselburgh - Low numbers were completely dominant in the five-furlong handicap (Race 2540, high) with the first three home coming from stalls 2, 4, and 1 in a field of 17. Two rank outsiders finished fourth and fifth from stalls 3 and 7, showing just how much faster the stands' rail is on any ground. Lynda Ramsden trained the winner, and Lillibella had the look of a likely type beforehand, stepping back in trip so certain to race prominently and also never likely to leave the rail (Ollie Pears probably had his instructions to stick to the fence all the way). Mrs Ramsden seems to tell any jockey riding for her to stay on the best ground almost come what may and this can cause problems for her runners that have to be held up, such as Bishops Court (Race 434) and Storyteller

(Race 3812), who would both have gone closer had they been switched. That is not to say it does not pay off more often than it fails. As usual, the Scottish bookmakers showed themselves less tight than their English counterparts, betting to a very fair 128.6% in a large field. It was hard not to think that the first three would all have been a point or two shorter had the race been run at Sandown, so the tricast dividend of £202.31 had to be considered good.

Ripon - Three of the first four in the market for the five-furlong maiden (Race 2545, high) were drawn in the bottom five stalls in a field of 18. Predictably, they finished first, second and third, with a 4-length gap to the rest. In the sprint handicap (Race 2547), the stalls were placed on the far rail (high) due to a heavy patch of ground on the stands' rail between the five and six-furlong starts and high numbers predictably just about held the call, since the field was not really big enough for any runners to come over to the stands' rail. It is rare for the stalls to be high in sprints at Ripon.

Tuesday, July 8
Newmarket July Course - Low numbers looked to be at a slight disadvantage in the big-field races at the July meeting when the stalls were high. No horse from a single-figure stall managed to finish in the first six in Race 2557, high, when Ben Gunn flew through right against the stands' rail.

Tuesday, July 15
Beverley - The ultra-shrewd partnership of Mick Easterby-Dale Gibson teamed up for Miss Eliminator (Race 2736, high). Drawn 3 of 11, she did not seem to run extraordinarily well, but so many times when runners from shrewd stables appear to have a poor draw, they are switched in behind and a comment-in-running like 'dwelt, headway to chase leaders halfway, not clear run over one furlong out, stayed on under pressure' is often seen. The sprint handicap (Race 2738, high) was dominated by high numbers with the first five drawn 12, 18, 17, 1 and 19 of 20, the outlier being **Superfrills** (1), who seemed to run very well from her low draw.

Follow   **Superfrills**   next time   Unp   12/1

Wednesday, July 16
Sandown - Even though the stalls were placed on the stands' rail (low) in the sprint handicap (Race 2769), there were 11 runners and it came as something of a surprise that nobody chose to switch over to the far side. Russell Price would have had that option on **Taoiste** (9) since he bounced out and made the running, but he elected to switch towards the stands' side, so the combination did well to finish third.

Yarmouth - Four of the races run on the straight course attracted fields big enough to see a draw advantage and, after the first of them, it was clear that the stands' rail was again well favoured. However, in the following races, some jockeys amazingly chose to race out towards the centre.

Follow   **Taoiste**   next time   Unp   10/1

Friday, July 18
Musselburgh - Although the stalls were placed on the far side and there were only six runners (Race 2826), two jockeys (both connected to Jack Berry's stable) chose to bring their mounts right over to the stands' rail and they finished first and second.

Saturday, July 19
Ripon (Good to firm) - A low draw was essential in the sprint nandicap (Race 2891, low) as the first four were drawn 1, 2, 5 and 4 of 17, with only two runners electing to race up the far side. Ted Durcan, after successfully bringing Palacegate Jack over to race on the stands' rail at Musselburgh the previous day, continued his run on Aquatic Queen (1) and never left the fence.

2891 LEEDS CORN EXCHANGE SHOPS MAIDEN H'CAP (0-70) (3-Y.O+) (Class E)
5-10 (5-13) 6f £3,210.00 (£960.00: £460.00: £210.00) Stalls: Low GOING minus 0.42 sec per fur (F)

				SP	RR	SF
2177[2]	**Aquatic Queen (50)** (CADwyer) 3-8-8[5] TEDurcan(1) (lw: trckd ldr: led over 1f out: r.o wl)	—	1	9/2[2]	55	33
2313[2]	**Gay Breeze (38)** (PSFelgate) 4-8-6 DWright(2) (led tl over 1f out: kpt on same pce)	2	2	9/4[1]	38	21
2510[4]	**Presentiment (51)** (MartynWane) 3-9-0 SWebster(5) (s.i.s: hrd rdn & styd on appr fnl f)	2	3	10/1	45	23
1963[13]	**Madam Zando (29)** (JBalding) 4-7-11[ow1] NCarlisle(4) (lw: bhd tl styd on wl appr fnl f)	½	4	33/1	22	4
2732[7]	**Dona Filipa (39)** (MissLCSiddall) 4-8-4[3] DarrenMoffatt(9) (bhd tl styd on wl appr fnl f)	nk	5	14/1	31	14
2788[12]	**Ohnonotagain (33)** (LRLloyd-James) 5-8-1 KimTinkler(8) (a chsng ldrs: rdn over 2f out: one pce)	1	6	20/1	23	6
2169[8]	**Mill End Boy (53)** (MWEasterby) 3-9-2v[1] TLucas(11) (bhd: hdwy over 1f out: nvr nr ldrs)	4	7	11/1	32	10
2121[3]	**Gain Line (USA) (54)** (BobJones) 4-9-8 AMcGlone(15) (mid div: rdn over 2f out: no imp)	nk	8	7/1[3]	32	15
2540[5]	**Maydoro (44)** (MDods) 4-8-12 MGallagher(6) (swtg: s.i.s: bhd: hdwy & hung rt 2f out: n.d)	4	9	14/1	11	—
2313[21]	**Colonel's Pride (45)** (RMWhitaker) 3-8-8 VHalliday(17) (swtg: racd far side: n.d)	s.h	10	33/1	12	—
2313[20]	**In Good Nick (60)** (MWEasterby) 3-9-6b[3] GParkin(13) (in tch: rdn & outpcd ½-wy: sn lost pl)	1½	11	10/1	23	1
2657[2]	**Belbay Star (31)** (JLEyre) 4-7-13b TWilliams(14) (hdwy u.p over 2f out: sn wknd)	6	12	7/1[3]	—	—
2354[6]	**Tom Pladdey (34)** (RBastiman) 3-7-11b JQuinn(7) (a bhd)	¾	13	20/1	—	—
2235[3]	**Star of The Road (44)** (JMCarr) 3-8-7 LCharnock(10) (chsd ldrs tl lost pl over 2f out)	¾	14	9/1	—	—
2659[2]	**Fisiostar (44)** (MDods) 4-8-12b DaleGibson(3) (a bhd)	¾	15	8/1	—	—
2547[9]	**Tom Mi Dah (61)** (MDHammond) 3-9-3[7] NHorrocks(12) (a bhd)	3½	16	25/1	—	—
2704[11]	**Petsong (40)** (VSoane) 3-8-3 JFanning(16) (racd far side: bhd fnl 2f)	3½	17	33/1	—	—

(SP 157.1%) **17 Rn**

1m 12.5 (2.00) CSF £16.64 CT £104.23 TOTE £5.10: £1.80 £1.60 £4.50 £9.50 (£6.50) Trio £85.80 OWNER Mr J. Johnston (NEWMARKET) BRED Joseph H. Johnston
LONG HANDICAP Madam Zando 7-8
WEIGHT FOR AGE 3yo-5lb
IN-FOCUS: A low draw seemed a big advantage. The first two were drawn one and two and only those two horses ever got into contention.

The mystery of the race was why Stuart Webster on **Presentiment** (5) chose to drift off the rail from a good draw and bring him through the pack towards the centre.

Follow   **Presentiment**   next time   Unp   5/1

Monday, July 21
Beverley - **Quiz Master** (2) not for the first time ran a very good race from an impossible-looking draw. With the ground riding firm (Race 2904, high), the first five home in the five-furlong maiden were drawn 14, 2, 12, 10 and 15 of 15.

Follow   **Quiz Master**   next time   Unp   7/1

Wednesday, July 23
Catterick - With the stalls placed on the far side, low numbers looked sure to be favoured on the good ground in Race 2934 and Cross The Border looked a solid favourite from the best draw in stall 1 of 16. However, it was **Imp Express** (17) who caught the eye, finishing third having raced up the stands' side. He beat the rest of his group easily enough to show he was in good form.

Follow   **Imp Express**   next time   2nd   9/4

Friday, July 25
Thirsk - The official going was returned as good, but the race times suggested that it was at least on the fast side and high numbers should have dominated in the sprint handicap (Race 3034, high). However, **Grand Chapeau** (2 of 16) came home well clear on the far

rail in second overall and should have won, but Dale Gibson dropped his hands close home and was caught by Benzoe (15) on the opposite flank. The front two finished well clear and the result had a balanced look to it.

Follow   **Grand Chapeau**   next time   **WON 5/2**

Tuesday, July 29
Goodwood - Low numbers again did best in sprints at Glorious Goodwood when the fields stayed in one group towards the stands' rail and the stalls were low.

Friday, August 1
Newmarket July - With the ground being good, there seemed no reason why the draw should have had any effect, but on this occasion the going looked to be better towards the far rail (low), which is where the stalls were placed. In Race 3198, the field split into just about two, with five of the first six home coming from stalls 1, 2, 3, 4 and 5. The outlier was **Mr Bergerac** (12) who came home well clear towards the stands' side and second overall.

Mr Bergerac (right) was a rare selection from a Newmarket race

Thirsk - As at the previous meeting, the ground was returned as good but the race times suggested it was a touch quicker. Grand Chapeau made no mistake this time from stall 15

of 14 (Race 3208, high) as he led home runners from 3, 12 and 14. **Camionneur** did very well to finish second from a low draw, especially as he did not switch to race on the far side and instead tracked the main bunch having missed the break.

Follow	**Mr Bergerac**	next time	**WON**	11/4
	Camionneur	next time	Unp	9/2

Saturday, August 2

Goodwood - Danetime (5 of 30) did very well to win considering he had no company from quite a way out after taking over on the stands' rail in the Stewards' Cup (Race 3217, low). He just held rivals racing towards what looked the favoured far rail. The one to catch the eye though was **Faraway Lass**, who despite being drawn 2, ended up finishing best of all down the slower centre of the track. She had to be switched after meeting trouble and may well have won granted a clear run.

Newmarket July Course - With the jockeys having learned from the meeting the previous evening, most of the runners elected to race centre to far side.

Thirsk - The first three races on the card were sprints with the stalls placed on the stands' side (high), and high numbers had the advantage in all three. Perfect Peach looked a solid favourite drawn 12 of 13 in Race 3239 and once more Ted Durcan never left the stands' rail, but it was **Happy Days** (1) who again caught the eye, finishing second having started towards the centre of the course and racing prominently all the way. In the 24-runner handicap (Race 3240), Another Nightmare (20) gave the perfect indication as to how much quicker the stands' rail was compared with the far rail. She was always clear of her group and had to compete hard with a decent-sized group on the opposite flank before coming home 2½ lengths clear.

Follow	**Faraway Lass**	next time	Unp	7/2
	Happy Days	next time	Unp	9/2

Monday, August 4

Ripon - Low numbers were again favoured in the sprints, although not by as much as at recent meetings. In Race 3271, low, Bashful Brave (3) led home runners from 8, 6 and 5 of 15. Good To Talk, from stall 14, was the only one to switch across to race on the far side and he ran a fair race to finish fifth. **Faith Alone** was the one to catch the eye in Race 3273, low, finishing third of 15 from stall 12, behind runners drawn 5 and 3, having raced towards the stands' side.

Follow	**Faith Alone**	next time	Unp	4/1

Tuesday, August 5

Catterick (Good to firm) - **Johayro**, the perfect example of a sprint handicapper who has defined periods of being in and out of form, showed he was coming back to form in Race 3287, low.

3287 'YORK KNAVESMIRE' H'CAP (0-65) (3-Y.O+) (Class F)
4-45 (4-49) 5f £2,973.00 (£828.00: £399.00) Stalls: Low GOING minus 0.10 sec per fur (G)

		SP	RR	SF
3126² **Double Oscar (IRE) (62)** (DNicholls) 4-9-11b AlexGreaves(7) (lw: in tch: hdwy to ld ins fnl f: r.o) ....—	1	2/1¹	69	55
Lady Caroline Lamb (IRE) (60) (RBastiman) 4-9-4⁽⁵⁾ HBastiman(9) (in tch: hdwy over 1f out: nt qckn ins fnl f) 1½	2	33/1	62	48
3208⁴ **Johayro (58)** (JSGoldie) 4-9-7v KDarley(19) (racd stands' side: a chsng ldr: kpt on wl) 1	3	10/1	57	43

3121⁶ **William's Well (60)** (MWEasterby) 3-9-3b⁽³⁾ GParkin(5) (b.nr fore: in tch: hrd rdn over 1f out: styd on)............1 **4** 20/1 56 39
2703⁴ **Sotonian (HOL) (44)** (PSFelgate) 4-8-0⁽⁷⁾ RWinston(6) (a chsng ldrs: ev ch ins fnl f: no ex) 1½ **5** 7/1² 35 21
3271² **Imp Express (IRE) (38)** (GMMoore) 4-8-1 NCarlisle(12) (in tch: hdwy ½-wy: nt qckn ins fnl f)......................hd **6** 11/1 29 15
3034⁷ **Panther (IRE) (62)** (PDEvans) 7-9-11v JFEgan(8) (lw: styd on fnl 2f: nrst fin) 1 **7** 25/1 50 36
2759² **Southern Dominion (43)** (MissJFCraze) 5-8-6b SWebster(2) (prom tl rdn & btn over 1f out).....................½ **8** 7/1² 29 15
2540* **Lillibella (56)** (MrsJRRamsden) 4-9-5 JFortune(18) (prom tl lost pl appr fnl f) ....s.h **9** 8/1³ 42 28
2754⁶ **Bowcliffe Grange (IRE) (49)** (DWChapman) 5-8-12 ACulhane(10) (led & sn clr: hdd & wknd ins fnl f) ....½ **10** 12/1 33 19
2759⁷ **Chemcast (65)** (JLEyre) 4-9-7b⁽⁷⁾ SBuckley(1) (chsd ldrs over 3f) ....½ **11** 12/1 48 34
2934⁶ **Blazing Imp (USA) (47)** (MrsJJordan) 4-8-10 MFenton(15) (wnt rt s: a bhd)...hd **12** 20/1 29 15
2759¹⁰ **Hamilton Gold (36)** (MGMeagher) 4-7-13 FNorton(11) (chsd ldrs 3f: sn lost pl)...2 **13** 66/1 12 —
2061⁹ **Time To Tango (57)** (GMMoore) 4-9-6 JWeaver(20) (a bhd) ....nk **14** 20/1 32 18
2895³ **Windrush Boy (52)** (MRBosley) 7-8-10⁽⁵⁾ AimeeCook(3) (in tch 3f: wknd) ....hd **15** 12/1 27 13
2721⁴ **Tymeera (44)** (BPalling) 4-8-7 TSprake(16) (lw: s.i.s: n.d) 1 **16** 16/1 15 1
3077⁸ **Stolen Kiss (IRE) (57)** (MWEasterby) 5-9-6b TLucas(13) (unruly s: a bhd)..1¾ **17** 17/1 24 10
2674² **Amy Leigh (IRE) (48)** (CaptJWilson) 4-8-4b⁽⁷⁾ AngelaHartley(17) (s.i.s: a bhd) ....¾ **18** 40/1 13 —
Brawling Springs (45) (JJO'Neill) 3-8-5 JCarroll(4) (dwlt: a bhd) ....1¾ **19** 66/1 4 —
(SP 147.1%) **19 Rn**

60.3 secs (2.80) CSF £94.52 CT £602.06 TOTE £3.80: £1.40 £7.00 £1.60 £4.30 (£61.70) Trio £632.20 OWNER Trilby Racing (THIRSK) BRED
Tasia Limited
WEIGHT FOR AGE 3yo-3lb
OFFICIAL EXPLANATION Stolen Kiss (IRE): the trainer reported that the ground was too firm for the filly.
3208 Johayro is certainly coming back to form, and this was a fine effort from his draw. (10/1)

The finish was dominated by runners drawn low to middle, but Johayro finished third of 19 from stall 19 having raced on the unfavoured stands' side.

Follow **Johayro** next time 2nd 4/1

Wednesday, August 6
Newcastle - With the ground riding good to firm, high numbers should have been favoured on the straight course, but there appeared to be nothing between the stands' rail and the far rail in the six-furlong maiden (Race 3306, low), where they raced in two distinct groups. In the next event, a group of four went to race up the centre, including runners ridden by George Duffield and Jason Weaver who finished first and third. If Duffield and Weaver chose to race there, it is safe to assume that the ground there was at least as fast as any other part of the course.
Yarmouth - The stalls were placed on the far side (low) for the three races run on the straight course, but most of the runners elected to tack over towards the stands' rail. When this is the case, the jockey often becomes more important than the draw, since the rider most anxious to reach the stands' rail tends to reach it. Ollie Pears set the trend for the afternoon by bringing Shark (Race 3321) across from stall 2 of 14, with the rest following him. It was surprising to see Michael Roberts aboard Polly Golightly (Race 3323) race on what looked the slower ground towards the centre.

Wednesday, August 13
Beverley - On a day when the going description looked a touch inaccurate to say the least - it was given as good becoming good to soft, but did not rain after racing got underway and was actually drying out by the end - one factor remained stable in that high numbers dominated the sprint handicap (Race 3481, high). Stall 11 beat 12 and 13 of 14 with nothing drawn low catching the eye.
Sandown - The stalls were on the far side for both sprints and a high draw was again essential. Raise A King (9 of 9), who had run well from a not-ideal low draw at Windsor to be third in a big field on his debut, was a well-backed favourite and led home the market second-choice Storm Fromthe East (8), with the pair 4 lengths clear (Race 3497, high). In the handicap (Race 3500, high), previous course and distance winner Half Tone (16 of 14) had the best draw and Dane O'Neill was unlikely to fail to capitalise. He led home runners drawn 13, 7, 15 and 14, with Bright Paragon (7) the outlier. Bright Paragon was

running above himself from a poor draw for the second time during the campaign (he won at Lingfield from a low draw when the rest of the principals were drawn high) and had not been ideally berthed on several other prior occasions. With this effort he confirmed himself a spot in the 'Squire Corrie' enigma category of horses who seem to perform best from poor draws.

Saturday, August 16

Ripon - Tadeo (19 of 21) (Race 3604, low) made the best possible use of the fast strip up the far rail and his undoubted speed to get to the front of that group. He led home three runners drawn towards the stands' rail in 5, 4 and 7, with Golden Pound (17) second home of the far-side bunch and fifth overall. The only surprise was that the field did not split into two more even groups, given that the best strip of ground is so narrow up both rails, as only seven went to the far side. Nigel Day aboard Canovas Heart (14) and John Egan on Ziggy's Dancer (13) would certainly have had the option to switch there. In the maiden (Race 3606, low), the first three in the market were drawn 1, 3 and 10 of 12, with Jimmy Fortune drawn wide on Archello (10), so it was inevitable that all three would head straight for the rail. They went on to fill the first three positions.

Wednesday, August 20

Kempton - This was the first chance since the amendments at Kempton to assess the draw advantage on the sprint course and the 23-runner maiden (Race 3686, high) looked perfect. The first three home, from stalls 3, 5 and 6, all raced up the stands' rail and came home 5 lengths and more clear of the remainder. There were some fancied runners drawn high, so it looked as though low numbers were again well favoured.
Leicester - The middle strip of ground looked far and away the quickest part of the course, but there had been no indication before the meeting that this was likely to be the case. The stalls were placed on the far side all evening, but the jockeys soon realised and started bringing their mounts over, so negating any advantage in being drawn towards the centre in the first place. Indeed, in the last heat (Race 3696, high), a high draw was an advantage as Maraud (10 of 12) brought them all across so quickly.

Saturday, August 23

Beverley (Good) - The ground looked to be riding very fast and high numbers looked sure to hold sway in the sprint handicap (Race 3761, high), especially with the in-form, front-running favourite Cross The Border being drawn 16 of 17. He led home runners drawn 15, 17, 6 and 13 in a straightforward race where there looked to be no hard-luck stories. The outlier **Suedoro** (6), who was dropping back to five furlongs, missed the break but, rather than switching across in behind the main bunch on the far rail, John Lowe kept towards the middle. This made their effort of finishing fourth all the more commendable.

▶Follow   **Suedoro**   next time   Unp   25/1

3761   SNOWY GRAY MEMORIAL H'CAP (0-75) (3-Y.O+) (Class D)
4-30 (4-33) 5f £3,990.00 (£1,200.00: £580.00: £270.00) Stalls: High GOING minus 0.63 sec per fur (F)

		SP	RR	SF
3756* **Cross The Border (62)** (DNicholls) 4-9-1 AlexGreaves(16) (mde all: clr appr fnl f: pushed out)............— 1	11/8 1	68	34
3566⁴ **Captain Carat (56)** (DNicholls) 6-8-9b JFanning(15) (hdwy over 1f out: fin wl)................1 2	14/1	59	25
3481³ **Brecongill Lad (65)** (MissSEHall) 5-9-4 LCharnock(17) (b.nr hind: a.p: hrd drvn appr fnl f: unable qckn) 1¼ 3	11/2 2	64	30
3484¹⁵ **Suedoro (43)** (JSGoldie) 7-7-10 JLowe(6) (dwlt: hdwy 2f out: r.o wl ins fnl f) ....½ 4	25/1	40	6
3481⁶ **Bowlers Boy (70)** (JJQuinn) 4-9-9 DaleGibson(13) (chsd ldrs: rdn appr fnl f: r.o one pce) 1¼ 5	14/1	63	29
3625¹¹ **Pathaze (43)** (NBycroft) 4-7-3⁽⁷⁾ JennyBenson(7) (lw: hdwy over 1f out: nvr nrr) 1½ 6	30/1	31	—

				SP	RR	SF
3481[13] **U-No-Harry (IRE) (60)** (RHollinshead) 4-8-13 JFEgan(11) (chsd ldrs: rdn over 1f out: nt pce to chal) ....hd	7	20/1	48	14		
3625[12] **Middle East (60)** (TDBarron) 4-8-13 KDarley(9) (trckd ldrs: effrt & rdn over 2f out: no imp) ....s.h	8	16/1	48	14		
3625[3] **Soaked (43)** (DWChapman) 4-7-3b[7] JMcAuley(3) (racd wd: prom tl outpcd appr fnl f)................................	9	16/1	30	—		
3224* **Ballard Lady (IRE) (48)** (JSWainwright) 5-8-1 TWilliams(18) (hdwy on ins over 1f out: sn rdn: outpcd fnl f)....nk	10	14/1	34	—		
3649[21] **Royal Dome (IRE) (73)** (MartynWane) 5-9-9[3] RHavlin(8) (lw: gd spd over 3f).....................................s.h	11	14/1	59	25		
3399[3] *Time To Fly (46)* (BWMurray) 4-7-6b[7]ow1 RWinston(14) (w ldrs over 3f)...½	12	16/1	30	—		
3481[2] **Dominelle (48)** (TDEasterby) 5-8-1 DWright(2) (lw: nvr gng pce of ldrs)...½	13	10/1[3]	31	—		
3075[15] **Maiteamia (65)** (SRBowring) 4-9-1b[5] CTeague(10) (b.off hind: w ldrs: rdn 2f out: sn wknd) 1½	14	20/1	43	9		
3698* **Dona Filipa (46)** (MissLCSiddall) 4-7-13[7x] EJohnson(4) (outpcd)..½	15	16/1	22	—		
3484[8] **Pageboy (59)** (PCHaslam) 8-8-7[5] PRoberts(5) (hld up: effrt over 1f out: sn rdn: wknd ins fnl f) 1¾	16	20/1	30	—		
3566[2] **The Happy Fox (IRE) (58)** (BAMcMahon) 5-9-7b LNewton(1) (prom: pushed along ½-wy: sn outpcd)............½	17	14/1	37	3		
2480[4] **My Abbey (49)** (ABailey) 8-8-2 RLappin(12) (Withdrawn not under Starter's orders: veterinary advice) .... W		14/1	—	—		

(SP 151.2%) **17 Rn**

62.67 secs (0.87) CSF £23.93 CT £98.89 TOTE £2.30: £1.30 £2.60 £1.60 £5.90 (£29.50) Trio £17.70 OWNER Mr P. D. Savill (THIRSK) BRED Brook Stud Ltd

LONG HANDICAP Pathaze 7-6 Suedoro 7-7 Soaked 7-2

Monday, August 25

Newcastle - As at the previous meeting, the ground up the centre of the straight course looked as fast as anywhere.

Ripon (Good to firm) - Storyteller (3 of 16) was sent off favourite for the sprint handicap (Race 3812, low) and would have looked a solid choice but for the fact that Michael Fenton would probably have been told not to leave the stands' rail and to hold the horse up. As it turned out, he never got a run and had to sit and suffer as slightly higher-drawn prominent-racing horses dominated proceedings ahead of him, so this run could be safely ignored.

3812 SUMMER BRIDGE H'CAP (0-80) (3-Y.O) (Class D)
4-15 (4-15) 6f £3,663.75 (£1,110.00: £542.50: £258.75) Stalls: Low GOING minus 0.09 sec per fur (G)

		SP	RR	SF
3119[12] **Samsung Spirit (70)** (EWeymes) 3-8-13 JFanning(2) (swtg: mde all: styd on wl fnl f)..............................— 1	12/1	72	47	
3269[3] **Hi Mujtahid (IRE) (53)** (SEKettlewell) 3-7-10b NKennedy(7) (chsd ldrs: ev ch 1f.out: kpt on same pce towards fin)..1 2	11/1	52	27	
3621[2] **Style Dancer (IRE) (74)** (RMWhitaker) 3-9-3v MTebbutt(4) (swtg: trckd ldrs: nt clr run 1f out: kpt on wl towards fin)..hd 3	11/2[3]	73	48	
3565[4] **Gipsy Princess (57)** (MWEasterby) 3-8-0b FNorton(9) (a chsng ldrs: nt qckn fnl f) ....½ 4	8/1	55	30	
3460[5] **Mouche (63)** (MrsJRRamsden) 3-8-3v[1[3]] DSweeney(13) (sltly hmpd s: sn trckng ldrs: ev ch 1f out: wknd towards fin)..hd 5	14/1	61	36	
3443[3] **Colway Ritz (72)** (JWWatts) 3-9-1b[1] GHind(1) (trckd ldrs: shkn up over 2f out: kpt on same pce)...................1 6	13/2	67	42	
3334[3] **Storyteller (59)** (MrsJRRamsden) 3-8-2v MFenton(3) (lw: bhd: hdwy over 2f out: n.m.r: kpt on: nvr rchd ldrs)..2½ 7	9/2[1]	47	22	
3273[13] **Just Visiting (77)** (CaptJWilson) 3-8-7[7] AngelaHartley(11) (a chsng ldrs: rdn 2f out: one pce)...................1¾ 8	50/1	61	36	
2326[14] **Night Flight (74)** (JJO'Neill) 3-8-12[5] GCowther(12) (chsd ldrs: rdn & outpcd 2f out: n.d) ....s.h 9	12/1	57	32	
3399[10] **Master Foley (56)** (NPLittmoden) 3-7-13[7]ow1 DRMcCabe(5) (sn bhd: sme late hdwy)....................2½ 10	14/1	33	7	
3410[15] **Cauda Equina (78)** (MRChannon) 3-9-7 AColhane(16) (prom rdn over 2f out: wknd over 1f out)...................hd 11	10/1	54	29	
3621[7] **Two On The Bridge (58)** (DenysSmith) 3-7-8b[7]ow1 RWinston(15) (racd wd: outpcd fr ½-wy)...................½ 12	16/1	33	7	
2847[10] **Showgirl (54)** (CaptJWilson) 3-7-11[ow1] DWright(8) (sn outpcd & drvn along) ....¾ 13	33/1	27	1	
3130[14] **Mumkin (74)** (MrsLStubbs) 3-8-10[7] GMcDonald(6) (swvd rt s: swtchd lft & a wl bhd)...................1 14	33/1	44	19	
3710* **John Emms (IRE) (72)** (MBell) 3-9-1 MRoberts(14) (lw: racd wd: mid div: effrt over 2f out: sn wknd)...................1½ 15	5/1[2]	38	13	
2891[14] **Star of The Road (53)** (JMCarr) 3-7-10 JLowe(10) (in tch: outpcd ½-wy: sn lost pl)...................15 16	100/1	—	—	

(SP 135.5%) **16 Rn**

1m 13.5 (3.00) CSF £137.29 CT £764.10 TOTE £19.60: £3.60 £2.20 £1.80 £2.20 (£176.30) Trio £373.10 OWNER Mr T. A. Scothern (MIDDLEHAM) BRED Red House Stud

LONG HANDICAP Showgirl 7-9 Hi Mujtahid (IRE) 7-9 Star of The Road 7-0

3334 Storyteller (IRE) found it hard to come from behind when the leading group were determined to race as close as possible to the favoured stands' side rail. (9/2)

Samsung Spirit (2) led home runners from 7 and 4, with Gipsy Princess (9) fourth ahead of Mouche (11) in fifth. The latter had raced with the pace from her outside stall and paid the penalty for racing on the worst ground by weakening in the closing stages. Nothing looked to run outstandingly well though.

Tuesday, August 26

Ripon - Folklore (16 of 16) finally had the best of the draw and, having been beaten three times previously as an odds-on favourite, was actually made second best in the market

(Race 3823, low). She led a group of just four runners to the far rail - although they were joined by another one near the finish - and beat Far Removed (stands' rail, 1) and Angel Hill (far rail, 14). The one to catch the eye though was **Mighty Sure** (11), who finished fourth and was not beaten far. Having raced with the pace after being brought across to the stands'-side group from her centre stall, she veered back across the slower ground down the centre to join the leaders on the far side before actually managing to keep on again towards the line.

Follow   **Mighty Sure**   next time   **WON 3/1**

Folklore finally had the best of the draw at Ripon when odds-against for the first time

Friday, August 29

Sandown - **High Carry** turned in a good effort to win the nursery (Race 3892, low) from stall 11 of 11 with the whole field having raced towards the stands' rail - it was surprising that nobody went to race on the far side as the ground looked genuinely soft. She did well enough to win, but to win by 6 lengths was impressive. In the handicap (Race 3898, low) the two runners in the top stalls did go to race on the far rail, with Sweet Magic (Michael Roberts, 11 of 12) leading home Tinker Osmaston (Jimmy Quinn, 12), but **At Large**, from stall 4, ran better than it looked in finishing third. Only half a length and a head down on the front two on the opposite side of the track, he beat the other nine in his group comfortably enough.

Follow   **High Carry**   next time   2nd   9/2
           At Large   next time   2nd   7/2

Saturday, August 30
Ripon - Handicaps are always better mediums for employing the likely effect of the draw than maidens, with most of the runners already exposed and few jokers in the pack, especially at courses such as Ripon. However, occasionally something will pop up and win a maiden so impressively from an impossible draw that it has to leave a mark. One such example was **Ring Dancer** (Race 3905, low). Drawn 13 in a field of 20, Darryll Holland chose not to go over to the far rail but instead edged towards the stands'-side group, and he went on to beat well-touted favourite Cease Fire (10) and Thistle Park (12) by 3 lengths and 6 lengths. Without the winner, the favourite would have seemed to have won well from a poor draw, and without the first two, Thistle Park would have seemed to have done well to scrape home from a poor draw. So the fact that Ring Dancer blew away two fancied rivals who had both seemingly run as well as possible made this victory all the more impressive. In the 24-runner handicap (Race 3910, low), everything was back in order with the first five being drawn 24, 21, 19, 1 and 15 (switched far rail). Opening Range (1) would have finished closer had she not edged right, off the rail.
Sandown - The stalls for the sprint handicap (Race 3914) were advertised in some places as being low, but were actually placed on the far rail (high).
Curragh - In big fields, runners drawn on the Curragh side (low) used to be massively favoured in sprints, but the stalls were repositioned in 1997 to give high numbers a chance, and the ploy was successful.

Follow   **Ring Dancer**   next time   2nd   11/4

Tuesday, September 2
Pontefract - The ground looked to be soft and was certainly cutting up - although the race times were not too bad - and jockeys on high-drawn runners chose to race wide from the second race onwards (the apprentices only came wide in the later stages). Nothing that stayed on the inside rail from a low draw looked like making the frame.

Thursday, September 4
Salisbury - On good to soft ground, runners drawn in the top half of the draw had the edge throughout the afternoon. In the opening event (Race 3979, high) more than half the field came towards the stands' side and they all finished well behind.

Friday, September 5
Haydock - With the ground riding on the soft side of good, runners drawn high should have had the edge, but as at recent meetings, low numbers looked to be favoured, racing towards the far side. In the maiden (Race 4012, high) bookmakers found it difficult to separate Escudo (8 of 22) and Sarah Stokes (12) and there would probably not have been much to separate them on the course without the draw bias, but the former raced on the far side and came home nicely clear of her rival racing on the opposite wing. The money was down on Halmanerror (Race 4016, high) who looked to have the plum draw in stall 1 of 22, but he was caught by his stablemate, King Uno (17). Nothing else looked to run well above expectations.
    Draw advantages seem to come and go at some courses, with Haydock and Nottingham prime examples. Both courses would have figured among my top five draw-effect courses three or four years ago, but now the draw does not seem to matter much at either.

Wednesday, September 10

Kempton - Conversely to the recent meeting here, low numbers did not look in control in the sprint maiden (Race 4103, high) although the first two would probably have been first and second from any draw. After course amendments, it is worth holding judgement on draw advantages until a big field of handicappers have raced.

Thursday, September 11

Doncaster - With the ground riding fast, there seemed no reason as to why low numbers should have been favoured in the 21-runner mile nursery (Race 4116, high) but that appeared to be the case. It was probably just that all the pace (including the top-class Lend A Hand) was on that side. In the other handicap run on the straight course (Race 4121, high) five of the first six home in a field of 21 raced on the stands' side, reiterating the uncertainty of the Doncaster draw.

Monday, September 15

Musselburgh - The runners finished in a heap in the maiden (Race 4159, high), but the first two, Take A Risk (10 of 11) and **Love Again** (11) would probably have finished a couple of lengths clear granted better draws. The latter was particularly unlucky, racing prominently from the start and never really getting the best ground. She should have won, but at least this kept her maiden status intact.

Follow	**Love Again**	next time	2nd	6/1

Tuesday, September 16

Sandown - The going on the sprint track looked softer than on the round course and high numbers dominated both races run on it. In the claimer (Race 4179, high) Rapid Reliance (9 of 13) beat runners drawn 15 and 14, but it was **Rita's Rock Ape** (3) and **Legal Lark** (1) who caught the eye, finishing fourth and fifth respectively from impossible draws. The former had shown nothing at all in two previous outings and was sent off at 50/1 but, after racing prominently, managed to hit the front until inside the final furlong before keeping on well enough.

Yarmouth (Good to firm) - A high draw on the straight course was absolutely crucial and nothing drawn low got a look in.

Follow	**Rita's Rock Ape**	next time	2nd	12/1
	Legal Lark	next time	WON	3/1

4183 BRIAN TAYLOR H'CAP (0-90) (3-Y.O+) (Class C)
3-40 (3-41) 5f 43y £5,677.50 (£1,695.00: £810.00: £367.50) Stalls: High GOING minus 0.45˙sec per fur (F)

			SP	RR	SF
3984 12 **Spender** (77) (PWHarris) 8-9-5 DHolland(12) (lw: a.p: rdn to ld ins fnl f: hld on gamely) .... — 1			14/1	82	59
3198 12 **Literary Society** (USA) (80) (JARToller) 4-9-8 SSanders(10) (lw: hdwy 2f out: chal ins fnl f: unable qckn nr fin)					
3410 17 **That Man Again** (83) (SCWilliams) 5-9-11b KDarley(9) (led tl ins fnl f)................... nk 2			12/1	84	61
3217 30 **Kilcullen Lad** (IRE) (82) (PMooney) 3-9-9v RCochrane(8) (lw: s.i.s: hdwy & nt clr run 2f out: r.o wl ins fnl f) .1¾ 4			10/1	84	61
3765 7 **Levelled** (72) (MRChannon) 3-8-13 MHills(4) (s.i.s: hdwy 2f out: sn rdn: nt pce to chal)................... nk 3			16/1	79	55
4137 8 **Cross The Border** (76) (DNicholls) 4-9-4 AlexGreaves(5) (lw: w ldrs tl wknd & eased ent fnl f)................... 1¾ 5			9/1 3	64	40
4048 10 **Ivory's Grab Hire** (67) (KTIvory) 4-8-9b MartinDwyer(1) (lw: w ldrs tl wknd & eased ent fnl f)................... nk 6			3/1 2	67	44
3761 11 **Royal Dome** (IRE) (70) (MartynWane) 5-8-9(3) AWhelan(6) (trckd ldrs over 3f)................... nk 7			16/1	57	34
4048 18 **Just Dissident** (IRE) (59) (RMWhitaker) 5-8-1 FNorton(1) (prom tl rdn & wknd over 1f out)................... ¾ 8			16/1	59	36
4013 3 **Bahamian Beauty** (USA) (85) (DRLoder) 3-9-12 KFallon(13) (sn pushed along: a bhd & outpcd)........... 1¾ 9			25/1	46	23
3851 7 **Anokato** (63) (KTIvory) 3-8-4b GBardwell(11) (outpcd: a bhd)................... 1¾ 10			9/4 1	6b	42
			33/1	43	19

The Effects of the Draw

3065[8] **Meliksah (IRE) (87)** (MBell) 3-9-9[5] GFaulkner(3) (chsd ldrs 3f: sn lost tch) 2 12 14/1 61 37
3600[13] **Rushcutter Bay (81)** (PLGilligan) 4-9-9 WRyan(7) (a bhd & outpcd) ....¾ 13 33/1 52 29
(SP 123.3%) **13 Rn**
61.3 secs (0.10 under best) (0.60) CSF £158.57 CT £1,044.98 TOTE £16.10: £3.50 £3.50 £3.30 (£52.60) Trio £219.30 OWNER The Entrepreneurs (BERKHAMSTED) BRED The Mount Coote Partnership
WEIGHT FOR AGE 3yo-1lb

4184 CAISTER (S) STKS (3-Y.O+) (Class G)
4-15 (4-17) 7f 3y £2,763.00 (£768.00: £369.00) Stalls: High GOING minus 0.45 sec per fur (F)

				SP	RR	SF
3921[7]	Gymcrak Premiere (68) (GHolmes) 9-9-5v KFallon(16) (hld up: hdwy to ld wl over 1f out: rdn out)	—	1	13/8[1]	69	43
4016[8]	Shontaine (56) (MJohnston) 4-9-5 DHolland(19) (hdwy 2f out: str chal fnl f: r.o)	nk	2	10/1[3]	68	42
3855[8]	Shashi (IRE) (47) (PatMitchell) 5-9-0 PBloomfield(20) (in tch stands' side: r.o appr fnl f: nvr nrr)	5	3	14/1	52	26
3968[2]	Petite Danseuse (60) (CADwyer) 3-8-11 SSanders(11) (a chsng ldrs: rdn & one pce ins fnl f)	s.h	4	11/4[2]	52	23
3969[7]	Gunners Glory (51) (MrsLStubbs) 3-8-11v[1] RCochrane(13) (hdwy fnl 2f: nrst fin)	nk	5	12/1	51	22
3855[9]	Waders Dream (IRE) (36) (PatMitchell) 8-8-9v[5] AmandaSanders(9) (trckd ldrs stands' side: rdn 2f out: sn btn)	2½	6	40/1	45	19
3297[7]	Aegean Sound (53) (KTIvory) 3-8-6 MartinDwyer(14) (led stands' side over 5f: sn rdn & wknd)	1½	7	33/1	37	8
3261[5]	Sir Tasker (46) (JLHarris) 9-9-5 AlexGreaves(17) (chsd ldrs over 5f)	1½	8	33/1	44	18
4059[13]	Birchwood Sun (53) (MDods) 7-9-5b AClark(10) (chsd ldrs: rdn 2f out: grad wknd)	¾	9	33/1	42	16
3910[16]	Axeman (IRE) (36) (MartynWane) 5-8-11[3] AWhelan(6) (racd far side: rdn & drifted rt over 1f out: eased whn btn)	¾	10	40/1	35	9
3966[6]	Glen Ogil (MRChannon) 3-8-11 RPerham(8) (b: nvr trbld ldrs)	¾	11	16/1	33	4
2922[13]	Hopeful Bid (IRE) (44) (PHowling) 8-9-0b KDarley(18) (b.hind: s.s: a in rr)	¾	12	33/1	32	6
3749[4]	Gresatre (48) (CADwyer) 3-9-2 WRyan(1) (racd far side: bhd fnl 3f)	½	13	14/1	36	7
3565[13]	Persephone (17) (JLHarris) 4-8-4b[5] RMullen(4) (prom far side over 4f)	nk	14	50/1	25	—
4114[11]	Move Smartly (IRE) (42) (MrsLStubbs) 7-8-7b[7] GMcDonald(3) (led far side over 4f: sn outpcd)	5	15	40/1	19	—
3933[12]	Old Roma (IRE) (45) (JohnBerry) 4-8-9b[1] MFenton(12) (prom stands' side 4f: t.o)	7	16	40/1	—	—
1991[4]	Time of Night (USA) (55) (JLEyre) 4-8-9 MGallagher(5) (racd far side: rdn along ½-wy: a bhd: t.o)	3½	17	12/1	—	—
424[14]	Wahab (25) (RFMarvin) 4-9-0v[1] TGMcLaughlin(2) (b.hind: bit bkwd: racd far side: a bhd: t.o)	5	18	40/1	—	—
3321[14]	Emmas Breeze (36) (GGMargarson) 3-8-6 GBardwell(15) (prom to ½-wy: wknd qckly: t.o)	13	19	50/1	—	—

(SP 136.3%) **19 Rn**
1m 26.1 (2.50) CSF £17.90 TOTE £2.60: £1.90 £3.30 £5.60 (£12.40) Trio £45.90 OWNER The Gymcrak Thoroughbred Racing Club (PICKERING) BRED Cheveley Park Stud Ltd
WEIGHT FOR AGE 3yo-3lb
No bid

4185 JACK LEADER CHALLENGE TROPHY NURSERY H'CAP (0-85) (2-Y.O F) (Class D)
4-45 (4-55) 7f 3y £3,947.50 (£1,180.00: £565.00: £257.50) Stalls: High GOING minus 0.45 sec per fur (F)

				SP	RR	SF
4097[9]	Belle de Nuit (IRE) (72) (BJMeehan) 2-8-9 KFallon(9) (a.p: led over 2f out: hrd rdn: hld on wl)	—	1	14/1	73	36
3411[2]	Chocolate (IRE) (81) (JLDunlop) 2-9-4 KDarley(11) (trckd ldrs: hdwy over 1f out: rdn to chal ins fnl f: unable qckn)	nk	2	9/2[2]	81	44
3387[6]	Summer Deal (USA) (77) (PFICole) 2-9-0 SSanders(12) (led over 4f out tl over 2f out: rdn & unable qckn fnl f)	1	3	14/1	75	38
3638[3]	Ratiyya (IRE) (78) (BHanbury) 2-9-1 RHills(10) (hdwy 3f out: ev ch over 1f out: sn rdn: no ex)	1¾	4	9/1	72	35
3924[6]	Sassy (IRE) (63) (APJarvis) 2-8-0 NVarley(4) (hdwy 4f out: rdn & wknd 2f out)	5	5	16/1	46	9
3799[6]	Miss Muffett (IRE) (59) (PMooney) 2-7-10 JLowe(2) (dwlt: swtchd rt sn after s: rdn 3f out: n.d)	3	6	50/1	35	—
3911[10]	Jato Dancer (IRE) (59) (JRArnold) 2-7-10 MartinDwyer(13) (led 3f: rdn & wknd over 2f out)	5	7	33/1	23	—
3861[3]	Risada (IRE) (73) (DRLoder) 2-8-10 RCochrane(8) (led 4f out tl over 2f out: sn rdn & wknd)	8	8	5/1[3]	33	—
3927*	Up At The Top (IRE) (84) (BWHills) 2-9-7 MHills(7) (a bhd: rdn over 2f out: no imp)	1½	9	13/8[1]	40	3
3924[15]	Mrs Middle (67) (NACallaghan) 2-8-4 GBardwell(1) (trckd ldrs on outside 4f)	3	10	33/1	17	—
4065[5]	Deva Lady (70) (CNAllen) 2-8-4[3] JDSmith(3) (hld up: in tch whn clipped rival's heels & uns rdr after 2f)	U		14/1	—	—

(SP 116.7%) **11 Rn**
1m 25.9 (4.60 under 2y best) (2.30) CSF £67.85 CT £832.38 TOTE £15.30: £2.60 £1.30 £3.50 (£22.90) Trio £46.50 OWNER Mr Richard Withers (UPPER LAMBOURN) BRED Lodge Park Stud
LONG HANDICAP Jato Dancer (IRE) 7-7 Miss Muffett (IRE) 7-5
OFFICIAL EXPLANATION Up At The Top (IRE): unsuited by the fast ground.

Wednesday, September 17

Beverley - With the race times suggesting the ground was riding very fast, it was no surprise to see high numbers well favoured over five furlongs. In the juvenile maiden (Race 4211, high) **Surprised** (3 of 16) continued his education with a promising fourth, and he was the only one from the bottom half of the draw to finish in the first nine. An hour and a half later, a group of five finished nicely clear of the remainder in a field of 18 (Race 4214, high), a group containing the three market leaders drawn 14, 19 and 18 plus **At Large** (4) and **Nobalino** (2), who both raced prominently throughout, making their efforts all the more impressive.

94

Sandown - **Bandbox** (2 of 14) turned in an excellent effort to finish second (Race 4216, high) having raced down the centre of the course for most of the way, a move which would have cost him in the region of between 4 and 6 lengths with the winner, who beat him by ¾ length.

Sandicliffe (No.4) ran inexplicably poorly at Newmarket after catching the eye at Yarmouth

Yarmouth (Firm) - Man of the moment Kieren Fallon, enjoying a late-season purple patch, worked the oracle on Gymcrak Flyer (Race 4225, high) who had looked to have a difficult draw in stall 3 of 14. Every other race on the straight course was dominated by runners drawn high, with the winners drawn 5 of 6, 7 of 8, 17 of 19 and 5 of 9. **Sandicliffe** (2) finished best of all from an impossible draw in the 19-runner handicap (Race 4228, high).

Follow				
	Surprised	next time	2nd	9/4
	At Large	next time	**WON**	**5/1**
	Nobalino	next time	2nd	10/1
	Bandbox	next time	2nd	15/8
	Sandicliffe	next time	Unp	6/1

4228 SHADWELL STUD SERIES APPRENTICE H'CAP (0-70) (3-Y.O+) (Class E)
4-45 (4-46) 7f 3y £3,191.00 (£968.00: £474.00: £227.00) Stalls: High GOING minus 0.62 sec per fur (F)

				SP	RR	SF
3143[11] **Lunch Party (38)** (DNicholls) 5-8-0 IonaWands(17) (led after 3f: clr 2f out: jst hld on)	—	1		3/1 [1]	42	30
4184[10] **Axeman (IRE) (38)** (MartynWane) 5-8-0ow2 PPMurphy(20) (trckd ldrs: rdn 2f out: str chal fnl f: jst failed)	hd	2		20/1	42	28
3718[5] **Mezzoramio (51)** (KAMorgan) 5-8-13v JoHunnam(15) (b: lw: led 3f: rdn appr fnl f: r.o wl)	nk	3		7/1 [2]	54	42
3421* **Sandicliffe (USA) (57)** (JARToller) 4-9-5 RFfrench(2) (a chsng ldrs: outpcd 2f out: str run fnl f: fin fast)	s.h	4		3/1 [1]	60	48
3718[10] **Flying Pennant (IRE) (49)** (JMBradley) 4-8-6b[1](5) DarrenWilliams(18) (hdwy over 1f out: sn rdn: unable qckn fnl f)	1	5		33/1	50	38
3854[2] **May Queen Megan (43)** (MrsALMKing) 4-8-5 GMilligan(13) (s.s: hdwy 2f out: fin wl)	1½	6		12/1	40	28
3966[5] **Racing Telegraph (40)** (CNAllen) 7-8-2 CLowther(11) (hdwy over 2f out: kpt on ins fnl f)	1½	7		20/1	34	22
3936[2] **Plum First (53)** (JLEyre) 7-8-10(5) SBuckley(3) (hdwy over 1f out: nvr nrr)	¾	8		14/1	45	33
4184[6] **Waders Dream (36)** (PatMitchell) 8-7-12v AmandaSanders(9) (nvr nrr)	hd	9		33/1	28	16
3868* **Warrior King (IRE) (53)** (CADwyer) 3-8-9(3) AMcCarthy(14) (nvr bttr than mid div)	s.h	10		8/1 [3]	45	30
4059[4] **Allinson's Mate (IRE) (61)** (TDBarron) 9-9-9b KimberleyHart(12) (nvr trbld ldrs)	¾	11		10/1	51	39
3787[7] **Delight of Dawn (49)** (EAWheeler) 5-8-11 ADaly(10) (nvr nr to chal)	nk	12		12/1	38	26
3852[7] **Chaluz (42)** (KRBurke) 3-8-1 DSweeney(8) (a in rr)	s.h	13		25/1	31	16
3746[7] **Don Pepe (61)** (RBoss) 6-9-6(3) NHorrocks(19) (nvr plcd to chal)	hd	14		9/1	50	38
3787[11] **Blowing Away (IRE) (65)** (MHTompkins) 3-9-3(7) JSavage(6) (lw: mid div: effrt over 2f out: wknd wl over 1f out)	½	15		25/1	53	38
4181[8] **Karinska (59)** (MCChapman) 7-9-4(3) SCarson(4) (trckd ldrs 5f: sn rdn & outpcd)	2	16		20/1	42	30
3718[8] **On The Green (38)** (AHide) 4-8-0v PDoe(1) (racd alone far side: bhd fnl 3f)	½	17		16/1	20	8
4043[2] **Silver Harrow (56)** (AGNewcombe) 4-9-4 DGriffiths(7) (a in rr)	2½	18		14/1	33	21
3565[16] **Meranti (59)** (JMBradley) 4-9-2(5) JFowle(5) (lw: prom centre 5f)	1	19		25/1	33	21
				(SP 159.0%)		**19 Rn**

1m 24.5 (0.40 under best) (0.90) CSF £81.80 CT £336.60 TOTE £8.50: £2.50 £3.60 £2.40 £1.90 (£87.70) Trio £239.70 OWNER Mr S. Aitken (THIRSK) BRED Aston Park Stud
WEIGHT FOR AGE 3yo-3lb
3421* **Sandicliffe (USA)** was beaten by the draw for she was in front two yards past the post and she must be considered a most unfortunate loser. (3/1: tchd 9/2)

Thursday, September 18

Ayr - An almost capacity field for the five-furlong handicap (Race 4233, high) gave punters the chance of a dry run before the weekend's Silver and Gold Cups. With good to soft ground prevailing, conditions were similar to those of 1994 when Daring Destiny won the Gold Cup racing up a fast strip of ground on the stands' rail while most of the action was centre to far side, and the result here suggested that nothing had changed. The first three all raced on the far side from stalls 6, 8 and 3 of 25, with Gold Edge (24) first home up the stands' rail in fourth.

Yarmouth - **Suite Factors** (2 of 18) ran a cracking race up the far rail (Race 4249, high) to win comfortably on his side.

Follow   **Suite Factors**   next time   Unp   10/1

Saturday, September 20

Ayr - As had looked likely, the top third and the bottom third in the draw enjoyed a big advantage over runners stuck down the middle - admittedly only ruling 10 or so out, but again on good to soft ground both winners of Ayr's principal races came from the top half a dozen stalls, Perryston View (24 of 28) taking the Silver Cup and Wildwood Flower (28 of 29) taking the Gold Cup. Of those to race towards the centre of the track on the outside of their groups, nothing ran eyecatchingly well.

Monday, September 22

Leicester - There were four races run on the straight course, all attracting big fields, and high numbers enjoyed the advantage in all of them. There had seemed no reason why this should have been the case, since the ground was good to firm.

Saturday, September 27

Ascot - Low numbers held a big advantage in the 25-runner seven-furlong handicap (Race 4423, high), the first six home all being drawn in the bottom ten. About half the field went to race on the far side and they were all 8 lengths and more down at the line. High numbers again had little chance in the straight mile handicap the following day (Race 4441, low). Although nothing went to the far rail, the centre of the course was still appreciably slower than the stands' rail.

Wildwood Flower made amends for an unlucky defeat in the 1996 Ayr Gold Cup

Monday, September 29

Hamilton - High numbers dominated in the 1m 65y handicap (Race 4471, high), with runners from stalls 10, 15, 2, 4, 12 and 13 of 16 filling the first six positions. The two outliers were **Winston** (2), who did well to finish third since he raced towards the pace and was always being forced wide, and Raindeer Quest (4) who probably just ran her race since she was held up and able to race on the best ground by the rail. Winston, only beaten half a length, may have won from a better draw and finished nicely clear of the fourth.

Follow   **Winston**   next time   3rd   8/1

From October onwards, few horses that catch the eye reappear during the same season. The likes of Indian Missile (Race 4670, low - ran well up the slower centre of the course), who would normally have been included, are not shown unless they appeared again in 1997.

Friday, October 3

Lingfield - The stalls, advertised in the racing press as due to be placed on the stands' rail (high) were in fact placed on the far rail (low) as a result of recent drainage work. Firm ground should have meant no decisive draw advantage, but low numbers looked slightly favoured when the fields split into two groups on the straight course.

Saturday, October 4
Newmarket Rowley Mile - Runners drawn in the top dozen stalls again looked at a disadvantage in the Cambridgeshire (Race 4558, low).

Saturday, October 11
Ascot - The stalls were positioned on the stands' rail for the straight-course races and low numbers held the edge in desperate ground, with the exception of the mile handicap (Race 4680, low)

Wednesday, October 15
Haydock - On very soft ground, there again appeared to be a faster strip of ground centre to far side in the sprint handicap (Race 4733, high) with runners drawn 5 and 1 of 22 leading home two runners drawn high.

Friday, October 17
Catterick (Soft) - As at the previous meeting here when soft ground prevailed, high numbers were well favoured in the five-furlong races. Odette ran another very sound race to finish second from stall 3 of 13 (Race 4769, low) and retain her maiden status in an event where Ted Durcan yet again got the best ground on the winner. In the sprint handicap (Race 4770, low) the first four home all came from the top half of the draw. Palacegate Touch did quite well to finish fifth from stall 3 having raced on the far side, but he was beaten quite a way and all those that were drawn towards the centre finished well beaten.

4770 CROW HOLE BANK H'CAP (0-85) (3-Y.O+) (Class D)
3-55 (3-57) 5f £4,003.00 (£1,204.00: £582.00: £271.00) Stalls: Low GOING: 0.28 sec per fur (G)

		SP	RR	SF
4636[2] Polly Golightly (54) (MBlanshard) 4-7-11b DaleGibson(19) (chsd ldrs: styd on wl to ld ins fnl f) .... — 1		4/1[1]	60	54
4512[3] Squire Corrie (81) (DWChapman) 5-9-10 ACulhane(12) (lw: w ldrs: led 2f out tl ins fnl f: no ex) 1¼ 2		8/1[3]	83	77
4527[3] Passionatti (62) (SGollings) 3-8-5 TWilliams(11) (led to 2f out: nt qckn appr fnl f) 2½ 3		9/1	56	50
4527* Dominant Air (84) (SirMarkPrescott) 3-9-13 GDuffield(16) (a chsng ldrs: rdn 2f out: kpt on same pce)........1¼ 4		11/2[2]	74	68
4414[7] Palacegate Touch (74) (JBerry) 7-8-12b[5] CLowther(3) (chsd ldr far side: kpt on wl appr fnl f) ....s.h 5		20/1	64	58
4707[5] Pallium (IRE) (53) (DANolan) 9-7-10b NKennedy(20) (a in tch: kpt on wl appr fnl f)..............................nk 6		14/1	42	36
4636[3] Pleasure Time (62) (CSmith) 4-8-5v JTate(13) (a chsng ldrs: kpt on same pce fnl 2f) ....nk 7		9/1	50	44
4580[6] Flying Harold (54) (MRChannon) 4-7-11ow[1] FNorton(1) (swtchd rt s: hdwy over 1f out: styd on towards fin)...¾ 8		33/1	40	33
4636[11] White Emir (72) (BJMeehan) 4-9-1b MTebbutt(15) (a in tch: one pce fnl 2f) ....¾ 9		16/1	55	49
4636[9] Just Bob (77) (SEKettlewell) 8-9-6 JFortune(5) (lw: dwlt: sn wl bhd: hdwy & edgd lft over 1f out: nvr nr ldrs) ...1 10		9/1	57	51
4414[16] Lennox Lewis (55) (DNicholls) 5-7-5[7] ANicholls(14) (bhd: hdwy u.p over 1f out: n.d) 1 11		40/1	32	26
4482[7] Pride of Brixton (72) (CWThornton) 4-9-1 PaulEddery(18) (outpcd ½-wy: sme hdwy over 1f out: n.d) 1 12		16/1	46	40
4512[8] Goretski (IRE) (79) (NTinkler) 4-9-8 LCharnock(17) (mid div: drvn along ½-wy: n.d) 2½ 13		9/1	45	39
4434[4] Kira (81) (JLEyre) 7-9-10 OPears(7) (b: led far side over 3f: sn wknd)......................................nk 14		14/1	46	40
4512[9] Lady Sheriff (83) (MWEasterby) 6-9-12b TLucas(9) (bhd fr ½-wy)...½ 15		16/1	46	40
473[4] Miletrian Refurb (IRE) (58) (MRChannon) 4-8-1 AMackay(8) (a in rr)...5 16		25/1	5	—
4270[12] Treasure Touch (IRE) (85) (DNicholls) 3-10-0 AlexGreaves(10) (bhd fr ½-wy)..............................1½ 17		33/1	27	21
2354[7] Keen To Please (53) (JParkes) 3-7-10 GBardwell(2) (racd far side: a outpcd)..............................1¼ 18		100/1	—	—
4512[14] Ballymote (73) (JBerry) 3-8-13[3] PFessey(4) (mid div: rdn ½-wy: sn bhd)..................................nk 19		25/1	10	4
		(SP 137.8%)	**19 Rn**	

60.7 secs (3.20) CSF £33.61 CT £276.27 TOTE £5.60: £1.30 £3.60 £3.30 £2.20 (£49.30) Trio £148.70 OWNER Mr David Sykes (UPPER LAMBOURN) BRED Aston Park Stud and T. R. Lock
LONG HANDICAP Pallium (IRE) 7-9 Flying Harold 7-3 Keen To Please 7-0

Saturday, October 18
Newmarket Rowley Mile - The stands' rail was moved closer towards the stands to reveal a fresh strip of ground, something that often happens on the Rowley Mile late in the season (often for the Cambridgeshire meeting) and the runners that raced there enjoyed a big advantage in the mile handicap (Race 4781, low). In a field of 30, the first six home

were drawn 3, 2, 12, 4, 5 and 27. The third horse Bowcliffe (12) was held up and got onto the favoured strip and it was **Prince of Denial** (27) who caught the eye, finishing sixth from an impossible draw towards the far side.

Follow **Prince of Denial** next time **WON 4/1**

Monday, October 20
Pontefract - On ground described as good to soft but which cut up quite a bit, high numbers again held a definite advantage.

Wednesday, October 22
Newcastle - Both sprint handicaps attracted 20 runners and the majority chose to race towards the stands' rail. Unlike the recent meeting staged here, high numbers did look to have the edge to the tune of something like 3-4 lengths. Double Bounce (5 of 20) finished first home on the far rail and fifth overall in Race 4842, high, and Southern Dominion led the far-side group in Race 4844, high, but neither looked must-punt material for next time.

Wednesday, October 29
Yarmouth (Firm) - On unseasonably firm ground, high numbers finished off the Yarmouth season as they had started it, with the first two home in the seven-furlong handicap (Race 4951, high) being drawn 20 and 19 of 20. A decent-sized group went to race on the far rail and they finished in a heap, the leaders being around 2 lengths down on the first two at the line.

4951 CALIFORNIA H'CAP (0-70) (3-Y.O+) (Class E)
4-10 (4-12) 7f 3y £3,659.75 (£1,097.00: £527.50: £242.75) Stalls: High GOING minus 0.44 sec per fur (F)

			SP	RR	SF
4404⁵	Speedy Classic (USA) (53) (MJHeaton-Ellis) 8-8-12 AClark(20) (a.p stands' side: led 2f out: all out) ....— 1		14/1	60	43
4451*	Lord Olivier (IRE) (69) (WJarvis) 7-10-0 JReid(19) (chsd ldrs stands' side: rdn & r.o wl fnl f) ....nk 2		8/1³	75	58
4738⁶	Mybotye (59) (RBastiman) 4-9-4 WRyan(6) (racd far side: led wl over 1f out: rdn & r.o) 2 3		5/1¹	61	44
4404⁷	Lunch Party (40) (DNicholls) 5-7-8⁽⁵⁾ IonaWands(5) (led far side after 2f: wknd over 1f out) ..nk 4		7/1²	41	24
4601⁴	Kosevo (IRE) (42) (MGMeagher) 3-7-10⁽³⁾ PFessey(2) (chsd ldrs far side: ev ch 1f out: unable qckn) ....nk 5		12/1	42	23
4741⁹	Mr Speaker (IRE) (55) (CFWall) 4-8-9⁽⁵⁾ RMullen(8) (trckd ldrs far side: styd on ins fnl f) ....s.h 6		20/1	55	38
4561²⁰	Gain Line (USA) (54) (BobJones) 4-8-13 NDay(14) (nvr nrr) ....¾ 7		14/1	53	36
3910⁷	Lachesis (45) (MrsSLamyman) 4-8-4 JQuinn(18) (hdwy stands' side over 1f out: nrst fin) ....nk 8		25/1	43	26
4629¹²	Mezzoramio (50) (KAMorgan) 5-8-4v⁽⁵⁾ JoHunnam(7) (led far side 2f: rdn 2f out: wknd appr fnl f) .....nk 9		8/1³	47	30
4333⁵	Shining Cloud (55) (MBell) 4-9-0b¹ MFenton(13) (led stands' side 5f: sn rdn & grad wknd) 1¼ 10		8/1³	49	25
4695⁵	Tael of Silver (43) (ABailey) 5-8-2 DWright(16) (in tch stands' side over 4f) ....s.h 11		9/1	37	20
4738¹⁵	Mazeed (IRE) (58) (PDEvans) 4-9-3 KFallon(4) (s.s: hdwy 5f out: rdn & wknd over 2f out) 1 12		20/1	50	33
4404⁶	Dark Menace (45) (EAWheeler) 5-7-11b⁽⁷⁾ SCarson(1) (racd far side: nvr nr to chal) 1½ 13		25/1	34	17
4798⁵	Be Warned (50) (JPearce) 6-8-9 GBardwell(3) (nvr nr ldrs) ....s.h 14		8/1³	38	21
4872¹⁶	Court House (58) (MCChapman) 3-9-1 LNewton(9) (nvr trbld ldrs) ....¾ 15		25/1	45	26
3476⁷	Super Park (38) (JPearce) 5-7-6⁽⁵⁾ APolli(17) (bkwd: a bhd) 2 16		33/1	20	3
4773¹⁴	Finarts Bay (57) (MrsJCecil) 3-9-0 JWeaver(15) (chsd ldrs stands' side over 4f) 5 17		20/1	28	9
4333¹²	Aegean Sound (46) (KTIvory) 3-8-3 MartinDwyer(12) (trckd ldrs over 4f) ....nk 18		33/1	16	—
4606²	May Queen Megan (43) (MrsALMKing) 4-8-2 NAdams(11) (prom: rdn along ½-wy: sn lost tch) ....hd 19		9/1	13	—
	Absolutely Abstone (45) (PDEvans) 3-8-2ow¹ JFEgan(10) (t.o) 18 20		33/1	—	—

1m 25.6 (2.00) CSF £117.61 CT £623.74 TOTE £14.20: £3.20 £2.10 £1.70 £5.20 (£58.40) Trio £167.80 OWNER South Wales Shower S
Faucets (WROUGHTON) BRED Lagrange Chance Partnership & Overbrook Farm
WEIGHT FOR AGE 3yo-2lb
(SP 149.3%) **20 Rn**

Bath, Brighton, Carlisle, Chepstow, Southwell, Windsor and Wolverhampton all failed to produce a meeting with a definite draw advantage in 1997. Perhaps the most surprising of these were Carlisle, where the soft ground required to show a draw advantage was never seen, Chepstow, which now seems fairly even, and Windsor, where neither side ever dominated. It will interesting to see how the upcoming drainage work to be done at Windsor affects the draw, since both flanks looked slightly slower than the centre in 1997.

CHAPTER 4

BEATING THE BOOKMAKER

Sprint handicappers seem to go through much more clearly defined periods of being in and out of form than other racehorses, possibly because a majority of the races in which they compete are truly-run, which leads to fewer hard-luck stories. Since most sprint handicaps are run on straight courses, the effect of the draw is likely to provide big clues as to into which category they fall. A friend of mine used to swear by backing sprint handicappers with form figures along the lines of 000042, based on the theory that they have been out of form but are coming back, and are likely to have slipped down the handicap in the meantime. He enjoyed a fair measure of success using this method, but such form figures will never tell the full story, since the 4 may have come in a field of five and the 2 in a straight match, or the 4 when he was last of a group of 4 racing up the favoured rail in a field of 20. Herein lies another way of employing the effect of the draw, by effectively cancelling it and simulating how the result would have looked given a level playing field. A horse with form figures 88755 who had raced on the unfavoured side for his last three runs would go off a falsely large price compared to the same horse with the figures 88422 next to his name. On the other side of the coin you have the horse flattered by having raced on the best ground. Form figures of 00001 are not that unusual in the world of sprint handicaps, but if the win came when he had the best of the draw and you assume that he would not have been in the frame from a poorer stall, then you can adjust your personal form figures to 00000. When he goes off favourite for his next run under a penalty, your set of figures will suggest that you have a favourite to oppose.

Both of the above sets of circumstances affect the handicapping of a horse, since the handicapper can only rate races and the horses that ran in them on the bare result (although allowing for jockeys easing down) and can not allow for the effect of the draw, which is doubtless considered a subject open to conjecture. According to David Dickinson, author of How to Compile your own Handicap, 8 lengths in a sprint handicap is worth somewhere in the region of 20lb. Courses such as Ripon and Sandown often provide races where the draw has that much of an effect. So while the overall winner will be put up in the handicap, the 'winner' of the group on the unfavoured side of the course could be left with an unchanged handicap mark, or even be dropped a pound or two.

A perfect example of this scenario came in the sprint handicap at Newbury in May 1996. On very soft ground, high numbers were favoured and most of the runners came towards the stands' rail, including the winner Thatcherella (drawn 14 of 14), but Ray Cochrane kept Bowden Rose (7) towards the slower ground down the centre of the course. This was surprising not just because she was drawn high enough to join the stands'-side group, but also because Cochrane is not usually slow to find the best ground. Racing down the centre would have cost her, in my opinion, somewhere in the region of 8-10 lengths, so the fact that she was keeping on so well at the end was particularly commendable. Adding 8-10 lengths to Bowden Rose's finishing position would have seen her going very close to winning, and this on ground which was not supposed to suit her (although she showed at Chester a year later that she handled it).

As a consequence of this result, the handicapper raised Thatcherella from a rating of 68 at Newbury to 75 for her next outing. One did not win again that season.

1178 WINCHESTER H'CAP (0-90) (3-Y.O+) (Class C)
3-30 (3-32) 6f 8y £5,614.50 (£1,686.00: £813.00: £376.50) Stalls: Centre GOING: 0.33 sec per fur (G)

		SP	RR	SF
928[16] Thatcherella (68) (MajorDNChappell) 5-8-10 BThomson(14) (a.p: led over 2f out: clr over 1f out: drvn out) ..— 1		10/1	77	49
692[4] Domak Amaam (IRE) (76) (JHMGosden) 3-8-9 MJKinane(10) (hld up: hdwy over 2f out: hrd rdn over 1f out: r.o ins fnl f)..............¾ 2		13/2 [2]	83	46
896* Intiaash (IRE) (74) (DHaydnJones) 4-8-11[5] MartinDwyer(9) (a.p: rdn over 1f out: one pce)..............4 3		16/1	70	42
928[8] Bowden Rose (85) (MBlanshard) 4-9-13b RCochrane(7) (w ldrs: one pce fnl 2f)..............3½ 4		20/1	72	44
1064[10] Louisville Belle (IRE) (54) (MDIUsher) 7-7-10 NAdams(8) (hld up: edgd rt over 1f out: nvr nr to chal)..........nk 5		50/1	40	12
1078[6] Golden Pound (USA) (83) (MissGayKelleway) 4-9-8b[3] DaneO'Neill(13) (lw: racd alone stands' side: led 4f out tl over 2f out: wknd over 1f out)..............½ 6		14/1	68	40
1073[2] How's Yer Father (79) (RJHodges) 10-9-7 PatEddery(6) (rdn over 3f out: no hdwy fnl 2f)..............hd 7		6/1 [1]	64	36
928[20] Bayin (USA) (73) (MDIUsher) 7-9-1 RStreet(5) (hld up: nvr nr to chal)..............nk 8		14/1	57	29
648[4] Persian Butterfly (68) (ICampbell) 4-8-10 SSanders(11) (s.i.s: a bhd)..............2½ 9		12/1	45	17
1064[2] Tart and a Half (79) (BJMeehan) 4-9-7b BDoyle(3) (prom over 3f)..............s.h 10		10/1	56	28
846* Latching (IRE) (85) (RFJohnsonHoughton) 4-9-13 JReid(4) (w ldrs over 3f)..............1½ 11		10/1	58	30
1064[5] Sir Joey (USA) (82) (PGMurphy) 7-9-7[3] SDrowne(1) (a bhd) 5 12		9/1	42	14
893[10] Oggi (64) (PJMakin) 5-8-6b PaulEddery(12) (hrd rdn over 2f out: no rspnse)..............½ 13		7/1 [3]	23	—
814[11] Sailormaite (80) (SRBowring) 5-9-8 RPrice(2) (led 2f: wknd over 2f out)..............1 14		12/1	36	8

(SP 118.7%) **14 Rn**

1m 17.0 (5.20) CSF £67.28 CT £951.41 TOTE £12.20: £3.10 £2.40 £4.80 (£37.70) Trio £331.40 OWNER Mr J. H. Widdows (PULBOROUGH) BRED M. L. Page
LONG HANDICAP Louisville Belle (IRE) 7-5
WEIGHT FOR AGE 3yo-9lb

Conversely, Bowden Rose, who ran off 85 at Newbury, was actually dropped 2lb to 83. Had she won that race, which she may well have done had she raced up the stands' rail, her rating would have gone up around 5-7lb, so adjusting out the draw disadvantage, she was 7-9lb better off than she should have been when next seen out at Newmarket. This led to her being maximum-bet material (11/1 was available in the morning and she opened at 9/1 on course before being backed down to 7s).

Back on her favoured fast ground at Newmarket and dropped to five furlongs (the trip at which she had gained her most recent win), she looked likely to be suited by the uphill finish having stuck on well over six at Newbury, and everything else was in her favour:-

1) **The ground was suitable** — (all wins had come on good or faster)
2) **The trip was suitable** — (her last win was over five furlongs)
3) **Her rating had not gone up 3lb+** — (dropped 2lb to 83)
4) **The race was similar in class to last run** — (Class C again)
5) **She had not been off the course for long** — (14 days)
6) **She had a reasonable draw** — (9 of 12, stalls centre)

102

Bowden Rose (blinkered) showed she was improving at Newbury in 1996

Unfortunately, although she ran her race at Newmarket, Bowden Rose was again beaten by a runner drawn wide apart from her - this time Top Banana, who finished best of all towards the stands' rail on her blind side. She had to be considered unlucky and it was a serious reversal from my point of view, but it does not take many 11/1 winners to make a profit over the course of a year, and 1996 still turned out to be a very profitable season. Bowden Rose went on to win once among several other good runs and finished the season on a mark of 90.

Southern Dominion was an example of a horse who was particularly unlucky with the draw several times throughout 1997 and consequently he ended the campaign better handicapped for the future than he would have been had all his races been run on courses without a draw bias. Of the sixteen races he ran during the turf season, he had the draw against him on no fewer than five occasions, but consistently caught the eye, especially towards the back-end of the campaign. His **actual** form figures for 1997 were:-

7190453287442141

Knocking out the effect of the draw, his figures would have been something along the lines of:-

7195453287142121

103

His final six runs were especially noteworthy, since with better draws he would have won three, and possibly four of them, rather than two. His fourth at Musselburgh, behind the much in-form Cross The Border in late August, kicked off his late-season run of form. Drawn in stall 12 in a field of 16, he raced on the far side (the only one in the first six home to do so) and edged across the slower ground down the centre. He would arguably have won from a low draw, but as a result of finishing fourth, he was dropped 1lb in the handicap from a mark of 42 to 41, meaning he could run next time from a lower mark. Had he had the best of the draw at Musselburgh and won, his rating would have been put up somewhere in the region of 5-7lb, so he was effectively 6-8lb better off for having run well from a bad draw. Southern Dominion looked to have a good chance of exploiting his generous mark next time at Yarmouth, being drawn 18 of 18 on firm ground, but the race was over six furlongs - he had always looked best blasting off over the minimum trip. He ran a strange sort of race, finishing best of all into fourth after being held up, which at least showed he was still in good form. Stuart Webster obviously had his orders, but holding up a confirmed front-runner when you have the best of the draw is not the soundest tactic of all time. As a result of this effort, his handicap mark was left unchanged on 41 compared to a mark in the low 50s that he would have been on had he won both races.

Next time at Leicester, again over six furlongs, front-running tactics were re-adopted and he was desperately unlucky to be caught by Magic Lake (who had herself run well from a moderate draw the time before). His draw of 11 of 21 here was decent enough and he would have been an impressive winner over five furlongs, but at least getting beat stopped him picking up a penalty for his surely-imminent return to the minimum trip, and indeed his mark was only raised a fair 4lb. Finally back over five furlongs for his fourteenth run of the season, he finally did what he been threatening to do all year and blasted apart a field of 20. Running off a mark of 45, he was around 10lb lower than he would have been had he had everything in his favour for his previous three runs.

Under a 7lb penalty, but still well in on my reckoning off a mark of 52, he showed he was still on a winning mark by finishing first home on the far side at Newcastle next time, even after missing the break and not being able to lead. With a better draw, this might have been his fifth success on the bounce, but he had still only won once, and was thus dropped 1lb for his final outing, where he made all the running to lead home a field of 22 at Doncaster.

Southern Dominion's final success of the season (at odds of 9/1) came off a mark of 51, so he will probably start the next campaign rated around the mid-50s, having started 1997 on 40. It would be no surprise to see him continue to improve, since he looked to have no trouble living with the speedsters that contest 0-80 handicaps when successful at Doncaster and it would not be amazing to see him finish up rated in the 70s. He could even turn out to be the 1998 answer to Blessingindisguise.

Blessingindisguise himself finished 1997 with five victories to his name and was another horse who consistently belied bad draws throughout the season. He finished up with the form figures:-

80022101211133U83

After three runs he started to come into form, but on more than one occasion after that he was unfavoured by the draw and my draw-adjusted opinion of his figures were:-

80022101211121U83

Therefore, with any luck at all, he would have finished up with six or maybe seven wins rather than five, although connections will have settled for that number, especially as one of the victories came when he was drawn 14 of 14 at Ripon. Going into his fifteenth run of the season, he had recently followed up his hat-trick with two third positions and most would have thought that the handicapper had got a grip on him. However, both those thirds came from bad draws, from a stands' rail position at Haydock (which would have been the place to race in the past but not in the 1997 season) and after racing alone right up against the slightly unfavoured stands' rail at York. My thoughts were that he would have been second in the former and won the latter from better draws, so he had a better chance than his odds of 11/1 suggested for the listed Scarbrough Stakes at Doncaster. I was neither proved right nor wrong since he unseated his jockey in the stalls (a very harsh way to lose money), although to be fair his two subsequent runs suggested his form was on a downward spiral.

Southern Dominion and Blessingindisguise were two genuine examples of horses that were unlucky with the draw on more than one occasion, but ran well because they were in-form and/or well handicapped. However, some horses are notorious for only running well when conditions are *not* in their favour and these are best categorised as horses to be wary of, rather than horses to follow. Some thoroughbreds seem to enjoy being messed around and hampered, and run best when they can get involved in a barging match before weaving their way through. Similarly, and of more interest to followers of the draw, some only put it all in when they race alone.

Squire Corrie (No.4) ran several good races from poor draws

The majority of jockeys in any race are going to try to ensure that their mounts run on the best ground, so poorly-drawn horses will often get left alone or in a group containing just a few runners on their side. It is when the same horse seems to come out best of an unfavoured group of runners time and again that he shows himself to possibly be of questionable temperament. One such enigma in 1997 was Squire Corrie, who probably returned the most misleading set of form figures in the history of racing during the turf season. The form book will show the following:-

4441611112570732083320

It is very hard to question the willingness of a sprint handicapper who won four times during the season and showed blistering speed right through, especially as he was deemed by the handicapper to have improved a stone during the campaign, rising from 70 to 84. However, on too many occasions he seemed to run below-par when well drawn and he may have been keeping something to himself, a view enhanced by the fact that trainer David Chapman tried him in a visor just after his winning spell. Other horses to fall into the 'questionable outlook' category during 1997 were two-year-olds Quiz Master and Happy Days. This type of horse always give the impression that facing difficult tasks above the grade in which they would normally race may be the answer.

It stands to reason that if some horses are going to run unexpectedly well from poor draws, others are going to run poorly from good draws. Runners that fall into this category are usually worth opposing in the immediate future, since it is a sure sign of an out-of-form sprinter. On the handicapping front, it also stands to reason that while the handicapper will struggle to raise a horse who runs into an unexpectedly high position from a bad draw without winning or being placed, he can not fail to raise a horse that wins a race or is placed from a good draw. These horses are effectively being put up in the weights for running just fair races.

A perfect example of this in 1997 was French Grit, who won the sprint handicap at Ripon's opening meeting when perfectly drawn in stall 2 of 18. He was racing off a mark of 72 but was lucky to win (Kira should have won but had the worst of the draw in stall 12), and consequently had his rating raised 7lb to 79, while Kira was only put up 2lb. Predictably, French Grit finished well beaten on his next three outings and he was easily opposable every time, simply because he had been penalised for achieving what he was entitled to achieve from the best draw. His seasonal form figures were completely typical of a sprint handicapper:-

Fin Pos		Ran	Off Rating	Draw
1	of	18	72	excellent
13	of	29	79	good
8	of	11	77	fair
9	of	10	74	fair
1	of	14	71	fair
9	of	10	78	fair
14	of	14	78	fair
7	of	7	78	fair
13	of	13	74	fair
4	of	17	70	fair
20	of	20	71	v.good

Formerly a high-class handicapper who competed in the top handicaps for his age division as a three-year-old, French Grit had probably stopped improving by the end of that season and was winless throughout 1996. As a result, he had slipped to a mark of 72 for the Ripon race. When he finally slipped back to a mark of 71, he won again, albeit not as impressively as at Ripon and off a lower mark. He then went on to struggle again off ratings between 74 and 78 before slipping down the weights again towards the end of the campaign. His season was typical of a sprint handicapper, with him turning in good efforts when conditions were in his favour and running poorly when they weren't, although his final outing was disappointing.

1997 Bets (horses to follow from Chapter 3)

Several of the runners that were picked out as horses to follow early in the 1997 season would not have been selected later in the season, since the effect of the draw seemed to change a good deal at some courses throughout the year. A perfect example was Pacifica, who was picked out after running well towards the centre of the course at Haydock on soft ground. The centre strip later showed itself to be just about favoured over the stands' rail, so Pacifica would then have been deemed to have run an ordinary race, although in this case it would have cost backing a 5/1 winner. Jupiter was picked out as a horse to follow after winning on his side in a big field at Nottingham, but Nottingham became a course of no interest to followers of the draw as the season went on, having shown one of the largest biases of all in years gone by.

Clearly, not all selections will turn in equally meritorious performances and I have found it best to grade them on a scale of one to five (stars). For example, Sea-Deer at Doncaster (Race 443) merited one star in my opinion, while Cathedral at Sandown (Race 2526) was awarded five. It is this assessment, which is open to change on the day the selection next runs, that decides the level of investment. For example, Sue Me was noted as having turned in a three-star performance, but he did not have everything in his favour next time at Hamilton and was scaled down to two. The table later on pages 127-8 shows how stakes were amended for selections that did not have everything in their favour.

MARCH

Sea-Deer * (selected in Race 443, next ran in Race 520), who was selected after his performance in Race 443, had everything bar the draw in his favour at Kempton (the most important of the following six factors), so this resulted in no bet.

As long as a selection has five or more of the following factors (four or more in the case of non-handicaps) in his favour for his next run, he should be backed, but factors 1, 3 and 6 must all be among them.

1) **The ground was suitable**	(had won several times on fast ground)
2) **The trip was suitable**	(had won several times at six furlongs)
3) **His rating had not gone up 3lb+**	(same mark of 81)
4) **The race was similar in class to last run**	(down one to Class D)
5) **He had not been off the course for long**	(10 days)
6) He DID NOT have a reasonable draw	(8 of 18, stalls high)

Next time   2nd 5/1   No Bet   Running total £0.00

The prices shown throughout are starting prices, although better odds were often available in the mornings.

Sea-Deer did not meet with all the requirements again through the rest of the season, since he was put up 4lb for finishing second at Kempton, so he was a rare example of a selected runner not being worthy of support at any time after catching the eye.

Surprise Mission ** (selected in Race 464, next ran in Race 527) had all six requirements in his favour for his next run, also at Newcastle, and won cleverly. He finished the season rated in the mid-80s.

1) **The ground was suitable**	(had won before on good to firm)
2) **The trip was suitable**	(all previous wins were five furlongs)
3) **His rating had not gone up 3lb+**	(same mark of 71)
4) **The race was similar class to last run**	(Class D again)
5) **He had not been off the course for long**	(6 days)
6) **He had a reasonable draw**	(6 of 11, stalls high)

Next time   WON 15/8   Running total +£1.87

Gi La High ***** (Race 494, Race 541) would have been maximum bet material at Warwick, but there was a slight doubt about the ground and bets had to be scaled down. Her excellent Musselburgh run came on a soft surface - like so many all-weather specialists she looked better on a surface with some cut in it on turf - but at Warwick it was good to firm.

1) **The ground was suitable ?**	(form on good to firm, but best on soft)
2) **The trip was suitable**	(all previous wins were five furlongs)
3) **Her rating had not gone up 3lb+**	(same mark of 60)
4) **The race was similar class to last run**	(Class E again)
5) **She had not been off the course for long**	(4 days)
6) **She had a reasonable draw**	(2 of 13, stalls low)

Next time   3rd 5/2   Running total +£0.87

APRIL

Pacifica ** (Race 500, Race 682), being an early-season two-year-old, was relatively unexposed, as were the runners that she was racing against. Her effort at Haydock was still fresh in the memory when she next came out at Newmarket and the 5/1 starting price came as a welcome bonus, particularly as she would probably not have been picked out had the Haydock race been run later in the season, since a middle draw looked more of an advantage than a disadvantage as the season progressed. However, it is only possible to base selections on what has previously happened at a course, and she did look overpriced anyway as the only runner to have raced before that had shown decent form, with Frankie Dettori booked. 5/1 tax-free got my Newmarket season off to the best possible start (I only missed two meetings all season at Newmarket, my local track, but unfortunately one without much of a draw bias).

1) The ground was suitable	Not applicable
2) The trip was suitable	Not applicable
3) Her rating had not gone up 3lb+	Not applicable

4) The race was similar class to last run   (up one to Class D)
5) She had not been off the course for long (18 days)
6) She had a reasonable draw   (5 of 9, stalls high)

Next time   WON 5/1   Running total +£5.87

Although only three requirements were applicable to Pacifica as an early-season juvenile, none of the three were against her.

Meranti ***** (702, 734) caught the eye racing down the centre at Ripon, receiving the comment in running 'looked well, swerved right start, soon chasing leaders centre, kept on well final furlong' over an inadequate five furlongs. He was not surprisingly sent out to run again two days later at Thirsk before the handicapper had a chance to put his rating up after his previous win - he ran at both Ripon and Thirsk under a penalty. Indeed, he was actually running off a lower mark at Thirsk because of the different race conditions, so 2/1 looked a very fair price. He had been finishing well over sprint trips before, so the easy Thirsk seven looked likely to suit.

1) The ground was suitable   (previous win was on good to firm)
2) The trip was suitable   (easy seven furlongs)
3) His rating had not gone up 3lb+   (down 1lb to 49)
4) The race was similar class to last run (Class E again)
5) He had not been off the course for long (2 days)
6) He did have a reasonable draw   (4 of 16, stalls low)

Next time   WON 2/1   Running total +£7.87

Squire Corrie *** (744, 772) had everything in his favour next time at Pontefract. He only finished fourth, but his performance had to be considered unlucky, since his saddle was slipping from soon after the start.

Next time   Unp 5/1   Running total +£6.87

Quiz Master *** (594, 836) ran well from a poor draw at the same Ripon meeting as Kira and, as he had seemed unfancied in the market that day, he looked a possible punt next time. Early-season juveniles that run well on their debuts for smaller stables are never going to go off comparably short in price next time as similar types from the Cecil or Johnston stables. Quiz Master had everything in his favour at Leicester and was actually dropped from a Class D to a Class F. He finished a creditable second at 10/1, a very generous starting price and one surely only returned as a result of him being trained in the north.

Next time   2nd 10/1   Running total +£5.87

MAY

Kira ***** (596, 901) had already won at the opening Doncaster meeting and showed at Ripon that she was still handicapped to win, running an amazing race up the centre of the track. Next time at Redcar, she met all six requirements and made it two out of two for the season for five-star selections.

Kira looked a good thing at Redcar following her excellent Ripon effort

1) **The ground was suitable** (most previous wins were on firm)
2) **The trip was suitable** (most previous wins were 5 furlongs)
3) **Her rating had not gone up 3lb+** (up 2lb to 77)
4) **The race was similar class to last run** (down one to Class D)
5) **She had not been off the course for long** (23 days)
6) **She had a reasonable draw** (8 of 10, stalls centre)

Next time   WON 3/1   Running total +£8.87

Ziggy's Dancer * (744, *905*) was one to keep an eye on after Thirsk rather than one that had to be backed next time. As it turned out, his next outing was on the all-weather, which immediately made him a no-bet. Even when a horse shows itself to be in-form/well handicapped by running an eyecatching race on turf, there is no guarantee that he will carry forward the improvement onto the all-weather, since he will have a different handicap rating for that surface. All horses that compete on both turf and the all-weather have two handicap ratings, one for each surface. In this case, Ziggy's Dancer ran off a mark of 81 at Thirsk, but was asked to run off 84 next time at Wolverhampton, which would have made him a no-bet anyway (3lb higher mark).

Ziggy's Dancer (black armlets) became a no-bet as a result of switching from turf to all-weather

There is no cast-iron guarantee that any horse that improves on turf will improve when it returns to the all-weather, just as there is no guarantee that any horse that improves on the all-weather through the winter months will translate the improvement to turf.

The next time Ziggy's Dancer raced on turf, he was rated 86, a rise of 5lb on his Thirsk mark, so he again fell into the no-bet category.

Next time   2nd 7/4   No bet   Running total +£8.87

Weetman's Weigh * (835, 946) was a rare selection from a Leicester event, but his effort to finish fourth in an otherwise balanced race was an obvious outlier. Whilst draw outliers at courses without a huge bias are never as good a punting proposition as the likes of the Ripon and Sandown selections, they can still be of interest. Weetman's Weigh was stepping up to seven furlongs at Thirsk which looked likely to suit, as he had previous form at the trip. He went on to complete a hat-trick.

1) **The ground was suitable**	(previously won on firm)
2) **The trip was suitable**	(easy seven furlongs)
3) **His rating had not gone up 3lb+**	(down 1lb to 73)
4) **The race was similar class to last run**	(up one to Class C)
5) **He had not been off the course for long**	(7 days)
6) **He had a reasonable draw**	(5 of 10, stalls low)

Next time   WON 5/1   Running total +£13.87

Sandmoor Chambray * (444, 947) ran well enough at Doncaster without looking must-punt material. He met with all six requirements at Thirsk and, although beaten, went on to win three times in a highly successful season, finishing with a handicap rating of over 100.

Sandmoor Chambray (rail) showed at Doncaster that he was set for a good season

1) **The ground was suitable**	(good to firm again)
2) **The trip was suitable**	(one mile again)
3) **His rating had not gone up 3lb+**	(same mark of 81)

4) The race was similar class to last run   (down one to Class C)
5) He had not been off the course for long   (40 days)
6) He had a reasonable draw   (6 of 17, stalls low)

Next time   Unp 7/1   Running total +£12.87

Happy Days *** (594, 954) ran equally as well as Quiz Master on his debut at Ripon and went off a fair-looking 7/4 favourite for his next outing, but only managed to finish fourth of eight.

Next time   Unp 7/4   Running total +£11.87

Jupiter ** (649, 1000) had to be considered unlucky at Warwick. Backed down from 11/2 to 7/2, he never got a run in the final quarter-mile and was only beaten around 2½ lengths into sixth. Although he was stepping up to seven furlongs having caught the eye over six, he had looked likely to be suited by the extra distance, so was not ruled out by the trip not being suitable. As with any other system, a degree of opinion has to be incorporated, so if you feel that the selection is likely to be suited by a step up/down in trip, or his sire's progeny have shown that they can handle an extreme surface which he is facing for the first time, then there is no reason to desert him.

1) The ground was suitable   (same as previous run)
2) The trip was suitable   (looked likely to be)
3) His rating had not gone up 3lb+   (down 2lb to 68)
4) The race was similar class to last run   (up one class to Class D)
5) He had not been off the course for long   (25 days)
6) He had a reasonable draw   (2 of 15, stalls low)

Next time   Unp 7/2   Running total +£10.87

Return of Amin * (845, 1017) was again hopelessly drawn at Chester (15 of 16), so became a no-bet. However, he had been dropped 1lb to 67 there and showed enough to remain of interest for his next run, but was then raised 6lb to 73, making him a no-bet again. He went on to win the valuable William Hill Trophy at York and ran his final race of the season off a mark of 85.

Next time   Unp 6/1   No bet   Running total +£10.87

Bishops Court ** (854, 1029) had everything in his favour next time, bar the imponderable about the ground which was very soft. He had not raced on anything like it before, so while there was no way of guaranteeing that he would not handle it, bets had to be scaled down - if only his brother Surprise Mission had bolted in at the same meeting the day before rather than the day after.

1) The ground was suitable ?   (heavy)
2) The trip was suitable   (looked likely to be)
3) His rating had not gone up 3lb+   (same mark of 83)

4) The race was similar class to last run   (down one to Class C)
5) He had not been off the course for long   (12 days)
6) He had a reasonable draw   (6 of 13, stalls low)

Next time   WON 5/2   Running total +£13.37

Prince Foley ** (884, 1084) was able to race without further penalty for the race he should have won the time before.

Next time   WON 2/1   Running total +£15.37

Prince Foley had the best of the draw next time when winning at Lingfield

Always Alight ***** (845, 1090) was dropped into a maiden after catching the eye in a handicap but, whilst many would consider this a step down in grade, I am inclined to disagree when the maiden is competed for by older runners with experience. Similarly, I do not feel that the step up from top handicap company to listed or Group three class is as difficult to make as many seem to.

Always Alight met with all five requirements for which he was eligible at Nottingham and the booking of Warren O'Connor, a jockey with a good record of knowing where to race on well-drawn horses, looked a bonus.

114

1) **The ground was suitable** (good again)
2) **The trip was suitable** (six furlongs again)
3) His rating had not gone up 3lb+ Not applicable
4) **The race was similar class to last run** (down one to Class E)
5) **He had not been off the course for long** (13 days)
6) **He had a reasonable draw** (1 of 13, stalls low)

Next time   Unp 5/1   Running total +£14.37

With hindsight, low numbers (racing on the far rail) did seem to have the worst of the deal at this meeting and Always Alight set off far too quickly. He went on to win three decent handicaps during the season and ran his final race off a mark of 80, some 20lb higher than the mark off which he raced at Ripon.

The winner of the Ripon race Denton Lad finished the season with typical figures for a horse that had won when racing from the best of the draw, 1000754700. Raised a harsh 7lb from 64 to 71 for the win, he was in the frame just once afterwards, although to be fair his mark was back down to its original point after four runs. His remaining runs showed just how lucky he was to win.

Sue Me *** (1098, 1227) did not have any factors against him next time, but did not have everything going completely for him. He had been put up 2lb and was in an apprentice handicap (not ideal for a horse of his nature with such a poor wins-to-runs ratio). He was given a bit too much to do, but still showed himself to be in good form, only then to be put up another 1lb for a much better race at Ripon, where he was again poorly drawn.

Next time   3rd 7/2   Running total +£13.37

Blue Goblin *** (942, 1237) had the look of a certainty at Lingfield and had everything in his favour, but this was reflected in his starting price of 8/13. The fact that he ended up competing in the top sprints showed just how unlucky he had been at Newmarket of a mark of 90.

Next time   WON 8/13   Running total +£13.99

Polly Golightly **** (1083, 1250) was extremely unlucky next time at Nottingham, being beaten a short-head by a runner racing wide apart from her, but Michael Roberts was on board so she was probably on the best ground. Polly Golightly went on to win her next two races off marks of 54 and 59.

1) **The ground was suitable** (previously won on good)
2) **The trip was suitable** (both previous wins were 5 furlongs)
3) **Her rating had not gone up 3lb+** (down 2lb to 51)
4) **The race was similar class to last run** (Class E again)
5) **She had not been off the course for long** (8 days)
6) **She had a reasonable draw** (9 of 18, stalls high)

Next time   2nd 7/1   Running total +£12.99

115

Sandside ** (993, 1280)

Next time   WON 10/11   Running total +£13.90

King of Tunes *** (895, 1308) was picked out after finishing third in a big field on the straight course at Ascot from stall 1, but would not normally have been, since that is often the best draw. However, at that meeting, the ground looked distinctly faster down the middle to far side and he was selected for a number of reasons. Firstly and most importantly because he had the worst of the draw, but also because he was carrying topweight on his first run for a long time. However, although he met with all six requirements next time, few things were completely in his favour and bets were scaled down. He could not have been a no-bet though.

1) **The ground was suitable**   (previously won on soft)
2) **The trip was suitable**   (previously won over a mile)
3) **His rating had not gone up 3lb+**   (up 1lb to 77)
4) **The race was similar class to last run**   (up one to Class C)
5) **He had not been off the course for long** (20 days)
6) **He had a reasonable draw**   (9 of 11, stalls high)

Next time   Unp 5/1   Running total +£12.90

The biggest factor against King of Tunes at Goodwood was that he was having his second run back after a long break. He went on to win the time after at Newmarket, and ran his final race of the season off a mark of 85.

JUNE

Lady In Waiting ***** (1240, 1619) scrambled home next time on completely different ground. The firm surface was the only factor that stopped her from being a maximum bet, but that is always going to be the way next time out with two-year-olds that have caught the eye on their debut on either very firm or very soft going.

Next time   WON 6/5   Running total +£14.10

Bolshoi *** (1455, 1881a)

Next time   3rd 100/30   Running total +£13.10

Sada ** (1457, 1653) was taking a big step up in class at Beverley next time and again had the draw against her, so she became a no-bet.

Next time   Unp 8/1   No bet   Running total +£13.10

Almasi ** (1385, 1765) was stepped up from a Class F to a Class D for her next outing, but she had gained her most recent win in a Class D handicap in 1996, so the fact that she had been dropped 1lb in the weights cancelled out the rise in class.

Next time   WON 6/5   Running total +£14.30

King of Tunes (right), selected at Ascot, went on to perform well in big handicaps

Lady in Waiting (No.2) turned in a remarkable effort down the centre at Newbury

117

Levelled ** (995, 1989) had everything in his favour at Brighton, over an easier six furlongs. The one potential off-putter was that he had been off the course for six weeks, longer than probably ideal for an in-form sprint handicapper.

Next time   WON 9/2   Running total +£18.80

Bold Edge *** (1263, 2012) was stepped up to a Group race next time (Class A) having caught the eye in a Class D maiden. To be fair, most two-year-olds that race at Royal Ascot are likely to be taking a step up in class, but this jump negates any advantage that may have been prevalent from previous races, and bets have to be scaled down.

Next time   Unp 4/1   Running total +£17.80

Mezzoramio *** (1501, 2121) almost became a no-bet purely because of the ground next time at Newmarket. Not only had he never won on going worse than good to firm before, but he had only ever raced on good to soft once previously, when pulled up over hurdles at Market Rasen. Kevin Morgan is a trainer who tries wherever possible to run his horses only when conditions are perfect for them and presumably Mezzoramio was only sent here because he had won the big ladies' race at the July Course the season before. There are not many other apprentice races at Newmarket throughout the season.

1) The ground was NOT suitable   (both previous wins on good to firm)
2) **The trip was suitable**   (previously won over a mile)
3) **His rating had not gone up 3lb+**   (up 1lb to 47)
4) **The race was similar class to last run** (Class E again)
5) **He had not been off the course for long** (23 days)
6) **He had a reasonable draw**   (6 of 11, stalls high)

Next time   Unp 9/2   Running total +£16.80

Mezzoramio won his following race, back on good to firm ground and with the best of the draw at Yarmouth.

Grey Kingdom * (1977, 2124) was one of only three runners during the season to catch the eye when actually winning a race (the others being Blessingindisguise and Ring Dancer). A little more leeway has to be allowed when accounting for a previous winner's handicap mark next time, since they are sure to be raised more than 3lb. In the event, Grey Kingdom was raised 5lb, which looked fair.

Next time   3rd 4/1   Running total +£15.80

Clytha Hill Lad *** (1689, 2152) was put up 5lb from a mark of 29 to a mark of 34 for his next outing. The first time he slipped back down to a weight less than 3lb above his eyecatching effort was at Redcar in July when he ran off a mark of 31. He won that race and went on to take three of his next four outings, and ran his final race of the season off a mark of 56.

Next time   Unp 7/2   No bet   Running total +£15.80

Mezzoramio again failed to handle cut in the ground, but made amends at Yarmouth

Rum Lad * (2017, 2235) would not normally have been considered to have met all six requirements at Carlisle since he had been raised from a Class G to a Class E. However, the only reason for the Thirsk race being awarded Class G status was because it was for lady amateurs only. Both events were 0-70 for three-year-olds only and were effectively identical.

1) The ground was suitable	(good again)
2) The trip was suitable	(good form over five furlongs)
3) His rating had not gone up 3lb+	(same mark of 56)
4) The race was similar class to last run	(up two to Class E - Not applicable)
5) He had not been off the course for long	(9 days)
6) He had a reasonable draw	(6 of 8, stalls high)

Next time   WON 7/2   Running total +£19.30

Inchalong ** (2016, 2288) was allowed to go off at a surprisingly big price for her next outing, in the valuable Newcastle seller, especially considering that none of the other runners looked anything out of the ordinary for such an event. The one slight doubt was that she had been upped two grades in class, but she had everything else in her favour.

1) The ground was suitable	(good again)
2) The trip was suitable	(six furlongs again)
3) Her rating had not gone up 3lb+	Not applicable

4) The race was similar class to last run ?   (up two to Class E)
5) **She had not been off the course for long** (10 days)
6) **She had a reasonable draw**   (9 of 14, stalls high)

Next time   WON 12/1   Running total +£31.30

Blessingindisguise ***** (2061, 2289) almost made it a tremendous evening's punting after Inchalong had won the opening race of the evening on the same card, although bets had been scaled right down since Blessingindisguise was running from 8lb out of the handicap (although still only 8lb higher than when he won at Ripon). He was also up two steps in class to a Class B Handicap, a type of race that I always think requires a certain type of horse (for some reason few horses seem able to win two Class B handicaps in a season).

Next time   2nd 10/1   Running total +£30.30

JULY

Grey Kingdom *** (2326, 2390) had everything in his favour next time at Epsom. The only potential problem was his draw in stall 1, which would have been ideal had the ground been on the fast side, but the going was soft and the chances were that the field would switch over to the stands' side in the straight. However, horses such as Grey Kingdom that race prominently are not inconvenienced, since they can take up a good position before reaching the straight.

Next time   WON 3/1   Running total +£33.30

Grey Kingdom ran 22 times in 1997 and showed great improvement

Beechwood Quest **** (2412, *2606*) was switched to the all-weather next time after catching the eye on turf, similarly to Ziggy's Dancer earlier in the season, but such a move is not as much of a drawback with horses competing in non-handicaps, since having two different handicap marks is not applicable. Beechwood Quest had already gained experience on the all-weather on her debut and, as she was still a lightly-raced juvenile, the chances were that she was just improving.

Next time   WON 7/4   Running total +£35.05

Refuse To Lose *** (694, 2925) did not see the course again for another three months after catching the eye at Newmarket and it was hard not to get the impression that he must have had some sort of hiccup. Having performed so promisingly, connections would surely have wanted to run him again quickly before the handicapper had a chance to reassess the Treasure Touch form, but he did not get back until mid-July, by which time he had gone up 3lb in the weights. He was made 11/2 third-favourite with a poor draw from stall 4 of 11 at Yarmouth (stalls low so there was a chance the field would come across to the stands' rail) and he predictably finished down the field.

1) **The ground was suitable**   (same as previous run)
2) **The trip was suitable**   (same as previous run)
3) His rating HAD gone up 3lb+   (up 3lb to 77)
4) **The race was similar class to last run** (Class C again)
5) He HAD been off the course for long   (97 days)
6) He did have a reasonable draw ?   (4 of 11, stalls low)

Next time   Unp 11/2   No bet   Running total +£35.05

Superfrills *** (2738, 3086) was stepped up from a 0-60 Class F handicap to a competitive Class D maiden and bets were scaled down. She was clearly still fancied to run well though, being backed down from 20/1 to 12/1.

Next time   Unp 12/1   Running total +£34.05

Presentiment * (2891, 3088)

Next time   Unp 5/1   Running total +£33.05

Cathedral ***** (2526, 3111) would have been a maximum bet next time at Goodwood had he had a better draw, since there is probably not a great deal of difference between listed and Group three sprints - they are usually contested by the same bunch. Cathedral was a desperately unlucky loser, beaten by a horse who flew home up the best ground towards the stands' rail and got a charmed run throughout.

1) **The ground was suitable**   (previous win on good to firm)
2) **The trip was suitable**   (five furlongs again)
3) His rating had not gone up 3lb+   Not applicable
4) **The race was similar class to last run** (up from listed to Group three)
5) **He had not been off the course for long** (24 days)
6) He had a reasonable draw ?   (10 of 15, stalls low)

Next time   2nd 12/1   Running total +£32.05

AUGUST

Taoiste ** (2769, 3198) was raised 2lb for his next run in better grade and turned out to be badly drawn, although that had not looked the case beforehand. However, he would not have won wherever he had been drawn, as he failed to live with the equally badly-drawn runner-up Mr Bergerac towards the stands' side.

Next time   Unp 10/1   Running total +£31.05

Grand Chapeau **** (3034, 3208) had the best of the draw next time back at Thirsk and made no mistake.

1) **The ground was suitable**	(good again)
2) **The trip was suitable**	(six furlongs again)
3) **His rating had not gone up 3lb+**	(up 1lb to 51)
4) **The race was similar class to last run**	(Class D again)
5) **He had not been off the course for long**	(7 days)
6) **He had a reasonable draw**	(15 of 14, stalls high)

Next time   WON 5/2   Running total +£33.55

Quiz Master ** (2904, 3265) was running in a visor for the first time when catching the eye and it was always unlikely that the blinds would work as well second time round on a dubious character such as he. He was also stepped up from a claimer to a maiden and almost became a no-bet.

Next time   Unp 7/1   Running total +£32.55

Imp Express ** (2934, 3271) was dropped 2lb for his next run, which came in a seller, and he would have been something to bet on, but he was again drawn out of it in stall 8 of 15 at Ripon.

Next time   2nd 9/4   No bet   Running total +£32.55

Camionneur * (3208, 3334) enjoyed absolutely no luck at Pontefract on his next outing, never getting a clear run.

Next time   Unp 9/2   Running total +£31.55

Mr Bergerac ** (3198, 3385)

Next time   WON 11/4   Running total +£34.30

Johayro ** (3287, 3406) was stepped up from a Class F to a Class D and was also going up to six furlongs having shown his best form over the minimum trip, so bets were scaled down.

Next time   2nd 4/1   Running total +£33.30

Happy Days * (3239, 3571)

Next time   Unp 9/2   Running total +£32.30

Faith Alone *** (3273, 3600) looked likely to find the shorter trip against her at Newbury and bets were reduced.

Next time   Unp 4/1   Running total +£31.30

Oggi (near side) was remarkably consistent in 1997 when often faced with poor draws

Faraway Lass **** (3217, 3765) was a huge disappointment back at Goodwood, since she looked to have everything in her favour and Frankie Dettori had been booked for the ride. The only slight question mark was that she had been raised 3lb for her fourth in the Stewards' Cup, but that looked fair enough in the context of her finishing so close to the well-handicapped Danetime.

1) **The ground was suitable**   (good to firm again)
2) **The trip was suitable**   (six furlongs again)
3) Her rating had not gone up 3lb+ ?   (up 3lb to 85)

4) The race was similar class to last run (down one to Class C)
5) She had not been off the course for long (21 days)
6) She had a reasonable draw (1 of 20, stalls low)

Next time Unp 7/2 Running total +£30.30

There were 20 runners (pushing the limit for low numbers to be favoured) and the danger that some of the runners would race on the favoured far side materialised. Even so, Faraway Lass, backed down from 6/1 to 7/2, still finished behind Oggi (stall 3, stands' side) on similar terms and probably just had an off-day.

Suedoro *** (3761, 3856) had been put up 5lb from 43 to 48 at Carlisle and also had the draw against her.

Next time Unp 25/1 No bet Running total +£30.30

SEPTEMBER

High Carry ** (3892, 4006) was raised a fair-looking 5lb for winning over the stiff five furlongs at Sandown and the easy Epsom six furlongs looked likely to suit.

Next time 2nd 9/2 Running total +£29.30

At Large **** (3898, 4214) had another impossible draw at Beverley and, although given a four-star rating from Sandown, had to become a no-bet. He drifted from 2/1 out to 7/2, but again caught the eye, finishing second, a head in front of the perfectly-drawn John Gosden-trained favourite Dark Mile.

Next time 2nd 7/2 No bet Running total +£29.30

Legal Lark * (4178, 4401)

Next time WON 3/1 Running total +£32.30

Suite Factors ** (4249, 4404) was stepped up to seven furlongs at Folkestone, which did not look likely to suit as he had always shown plenty of pace in previous outings. He had also been raised 2lb and was stepping up to a Class E event, so bets were scaled down.

Next time Unp 10/1 Running total +£31.30

Mighty Sure ***** (3823, 4419) would have been a maximum bet at Redcar, but she had been wearing first-time blinkers when catching the eye at Ripon, and they had been removed. The only doubt was that the application of headgear had improved her and that she would not perform as well without them, but otherwise she had everything in her favour.

1) The ground was suitable (good to firm again)
2) The trip was suitable (five furlongs again)
3) Her rating had not gone up 3lb+ (down 1lb to 61)

124

4) **The race was similar class to last run**   (down two to Class E)
5) **She had not been off the course for long** (31 days)
6) **She had a reasonable draw**   (4 of 8, stalls high)

Next time   WON 3/1   Running total +£34.30

**Surprised ** (4211, 4428)

Next time   2nd 9/4   Running total +£33.30

Love Again * (4159, *4479*) was making her debut on the all-weather at Wolverhampton and could not be backed as a result.

Next time   2nd 6/1   No bet   Running total +£33.30

OCTOBER

Sandicliffe **** (4228, 4561) did not have any factor against her at Newmarket, but she had been raised 2lb and was up in class from a Class E to a Class C. Her draw looked fine beforehand, as Pasternak had not been stopped by racing up the centre in the Cambridgeshire earlier in the afternoon.

Pasternak (near side) was twice a thorn in the side of bookmakers

1) **The ground was suitable**   (both previous wins on good to firm)
2) **The trip was suitable**   (seven furlongs again)
3) **Her rating had not gone up 3lb+**   (up 2lb to 59)
4) **The race was similar class to last run** (up two to Class C)
5) **She had not been off the course for long** (17 days)
6) **She had a reasonable draw**   (15 of 24, stalls low)

Next time   Unp 6/1   Running total +£32.30

Nobalino ** (4214, 4563)

Next time   2nd 10/1   Running total +£31.30

At Large *** (4214, 4565) had seemed likely to be suited by the step up to six furlongs at Nottingham and had everything else in his favour. Some considered him lucky to win, since all the placed horses had little luck in running, but he was only as lucky to win as Polly Golightly had been unlucky not to win at the same course earlier in the season.

1) **The ground was suitable**   (good to firm again)
2) **The trip was suitable**   (good form over six furlongs)
3) **His rating had not gone up 3lb+**   (down 1lb to 74)
4) **The race was similar class to last run**   (Class D again)
5) **He had not been off the course for long**   (17 days)
6) **He had a reasonable draw**   (9 of 14, stalls high)

Next time   WON 5/1   Running total +£36.30

Rita's Rock Ape *** (4178, 4566) was running in a handicap for the first time at Nottingham having caught the eye in a claimer and looked to be off a fair enough mark - the handicapper being able to rate her only on the bare form of her three runs - and had everything else in her favour.

Next time   2nd 12/1   Running total +£35.30

Bandbox *** (4216, 4602)

Next time   2nd 15/8   Running total +£34.30

Winston ** (4471, 4629)

Next time   3rd 8/1   Running total +£33.30

Prince of Denial ** (4893, 4781) had everything in his favour at Newbury, having faced two impossible tasks at Newmarket in his two previous outings.

1) **The ground was suitable**   (previous win on good to soft)
2) **The trip was suitable**   (previous win over nine furlongs)
3) **His rating had not gone up 3lb+**   (same mark of 89)
4) **The race was similar class to last run**   (Class B again)
5) **He had not been off the course for long**   (8 days)
6) **He had a reasonable draw**   (11 of 15, stalls low)

Next time   WON 4/1   Running total +£37.30

Ring Dancer **** (3905, 4955) drifted alarmingly in the betting at Nottingham and had a 6lb penalty to contend with, so probably turned in a commendable performance.

Next time   2nd 11/4   Running total +£36.30

Roy Boy ** (1965, did not race again)

Final £1 level-stake profit **+£36.30**

Employing a typical 'bank system'

Starting with a bank of £1,000, a one-star selection becomes a £25 bet and a five-star selection a £125 bet. Every time the bank doubles, the bets are also doubled, so when the bank gets up above £2,000, a one-star selection becomes a £50 bet and so on. Similarly, every time the bank halves, bets halve.

Selection and Revised Rating	Next Ran	Revised Bet	Profit	Running Bank
Sea-Deer	31 March	No bet		£1,000
Surprise Mission **	31 March	£50 at 15/8	£93.75	£1,093.75
Gi La High ****	31 March	£100 at 5/2	Loser	£993.75
Pacifica **	16 April	£50 at 5/1	£250	£1,243.75
Meranti *****	18 April	£125 at 2/1	£250	£1,493.75
Squire Corrie ***	22 April	£75 at 5/1	Loser	£1,418.75
Quiz Master ***	26 April	£75 at 10/1	Loser	£1,343.75
Kira *****	1 May	£125 at 3/1	£375	£1,718.75
Ziggy's Dancer	1 May (awt)	No bet		£1,718.75
Weetman's Weigh *	3 May	£25 at 5/1	£125	£1,843.75
Sandmoor Chambray *	3 May	£25 at 7/1	Loser	£1,818.75
Happy Days ***	4 May	£75 at 7/4	Loser	£1,743.75
Jupiter **	5 May	£50 at 7/2	Loser	£1,693.75
Return of Amin	6 May	No bet		£1,693.75
Bishops Court **	7 May	£50 at 5/2	£125	£1,818.75
Prince Foley **	9 May	£50 at 2/1	£100	£1,918.75
Always Alight ****	9 May	£100 at 5/1	Loser	£1,818.75
Sue Me **	17 May	£50 at 7/2	Loser	£1,768.75
Blue Goblin ***	17 May	£75 at 8/13	£46.15	£1,814.90
Polly Golightly ****	17 May	£100 at 7/1	Loser	£1,714.90
Sandside **	19 May	£50 at 10/11	£45.45	£1,760.35
King of Tunes **	20 May	£50 at 5/1	Loser	£1,710.35
Lady In Waiting ****	2 June	£100 at 6/5	£120	£1,830.35
Bolshoi ***	2 June	£75 at 100/30	Loser	£1,755.35
Sada	4 June	No bet		£1,755.35
Almasi **	7 June	£50 at 6/5	£60	£1,815.35
Levelled **	16 June	£50 at 9/2	£225	£2,040.35, double
Bold Edge **	17 June	£100 at 4/1	Loser	£1,940.35, halve
Mezzoramio *	20 June	£25 at 9/2	Loser	£1,915.35
Grey Kingdom *	20 June	£25 at 4/1	Loser	£1,890.35
Clytha Hill Lad	21 June	No bet		£1,890.35
Rum Lad ***	26 June	£75 at 7/2	£262.50	£2,152.85, double
Inchalong ***	27 June	£150 at 12/1	£1,800	£3,952.85
Blessingindisguise **	27 June	£100 at 10/1	Loser	£3,852.85

Grey Kingdom ***	2 July	£150 at 3/1	£450	£4,302.85, double
Beechwood Quest ***	10 July *(awt)*	£300 at 7/4	£525	£4,827.85
Refuse To Lose	22 July	No bet		£4,827.85
Superfrills *	28 July	£100 at 12/1	Loser	£4,727.85
Presentiment *	28 July	£100 at 5/1	Loser	£4,627.85
Cathedral ****	29 July	£400 at 12/1	Loser	£4,227.85
Taoiste **	1 August	£200 at 10/1	Loser	£4,027.85
Grand Chapeau ****	1 August	£400 at 5/2	£1,000	£5,027.85
Quiz Master *	4 August	£100 at 7/1	Loser	£4,927.85
Imp Express	4 August	No bet		£4,927.85
Camionneur *	7 August	£100 at 9/2	Loser	£4,827.85
Mr Bergerac **	8 August	£200 at 11/4	£550	£5,377.85
Johayro *	9 August	£100 at 4/1	Loser	£5,277.85
Happy Days *	15 August	£100 at 9/2	Loser	£5,177.85
Faith Alone **	16 August	£200 at 4/1	Loser	£4,977.85
Faraway Lass ***	23 August	£300 at 7/2	Loser	£4,677.85
Suedoro	27 August	No bet		£4,677.85
High Carry **	5 Sept	£200 at 9/2	Loser	£4,477.85
At Large	17 Sept	No bet		£4,477.85
Legal Lark *	26 Sept	£100 at 3/1	£300	£4,777.85
Suite Factors *	26 Sept	£100 at 10/1	Loser	£4,677.85
Mighty Sure ****	26 Sept	£400 at 3/1	£1,200	£5,877.85
Surprised **	27 Sept	£200 at 9/4	Loser	£5,677.85
Love Again	30 Sept	No bet		£5,677.85
Sandicliffe ***	4 Oct	£300 at 6/1	Loser	£5,377.85
Nobalino **	4 Oct	£200 at 10/1	Loser	£5,177.85
At Large ***	4 Oct	£300 at 5/1	£1,500	£6,677.85
Rita's Rock Ape ***	4 Oct	£300 at 12/1	Loser	£6,377.85
Bandbox ***	7 Oct	£300 at 15/8	Loser	£6,077.85
Winston **	8 Oct	£200 at 8/1	Loser	£5,877.85
Prince of Denial **	25 Oct	£200 at 4/1	£800	£6,677.85
Ring Dancer **	30 Oct	£200 at 11/4	Loser	£6,477.85

(66 selections - 22 winners, 34 losers and 10 No bets)   39.3% strike-rate

Inchalong's win at Newcastle came at a particularly opportune time, since bets had just been doubled with the bank having broken £2,000. Then again had Polly Golightly won, and she was most unlucky not to, bets would have been doubled a month earlier. May and July were not as successful as usual, but the £1,000 bank had still grown to £6,477.85 by the end of the season.

BOLA Report

In early 1996, it was decided by BOLA (the Betting Office Licensees' Association) that there was a need to change the formula used for calculating tricast, and later forecast, dividends to eradicate the effect of the draw.

A press release dated February 1st 1996 stated:

'A new horserace tricast designed to eliminate problems associated with the stalls draw in certain races is to be introduced from 5th February (1996). The new formula, which is the result of extensive research, will produce returns which are increased, reduced or remain unaltered according to the stalls position of the placed horses.........

Overall, there will be lower returns when placed horses are drawn together, but higher returns in the majority of cases. The new formula will more accurately reflect the true chances of any combination of runners in a race..........

In these races, the stall position (draw) of the runners may impact the result favouring one side of the course or the other. This may be aggravated by other factors such as the state of the going, watering methods and a horse following the pace of a race.'

This 33-page report showed that the days of bookmakers offering 25 and 33% bonuses on correct tricasts are gone. In any instance where the first three horses in a tricast race (8+ runner handicaps) are drawn together, substantial reductions now take place, with slight increases being made in cases where the runners come from different positions. This not only affects races at courses where draw biases are prevalent, but also races where all the pace is on one side.

Basically, reductions are now made when the first three home come from the same third in the draw (i.e. in an 18 runner race, the first three all come from stalls 1-6 or all from stalls 13-18 - it was decided that the middle segment of runners could not realistically be favoured by the draw). Without going into too much detail about the very complicated formula (which is worked out by calculating the 'Stall Difference Parity') a few examples of how the new formula affects tricasts dividends are shown below (based on an 18-runner straight-course handicap):-

Stalls of Placed Runners	Starting Prices	Old dividend	New dividend	% +/-
1-2-3	12/1 25/1 6/1	£1,791.31	£1,142.38	- 36.23%
2-4-6	25/1 50/1 20/1	£20,212.10	£9,621.56	- 52.4%
2-8-17	25/1 10/1 7/1	£1,767.76	£1,811.74	+ 2.49%
1-14-18	12/1 14/1 20/1	£2,998.57	£3,073.17	+ 2.49%

The bigger the prices of the placed horses, the greater the percentage of the old dividend is knocked off the revised figure when they are drawn together. The reductions go well over 50%, a figure not compensated for by the increases for the times that the runners are drawn apart, normally only 1 or 2%. Although the report shows that in an 11-runner handicap, where there are 165 different possible three-horse combinations, 38 tricasts would remain the same, 119 would show an increase and only 8 would result in a decrease, the increases are minimal while the reductions potentially huge.

Therefore, tricasts are no longer a viable option for draw punters and since the introduction of the BOLA formula, many have switched to backing Tote trios.

The Tote trio has only been in operation for a few years, but its popularity has grown recently, thanks no doubt in part to the fact that all the carry-forwards from the previous day get carried into the same race, often the day's most competitive handicap. As opposed to the tricast, the Tote trio requires selections to finish first, second and third in any order, so a £1 trio on 3 horses costs £1, while a £1 combination tricast costs £6 (covering the permutations A-B-C, A-C-B, B-A-C, B-C-A, C-A-B and C-B-A). Therefore, a trio which pays more than a sixth of the tricast dividend would be the better dividend of the two. However, the more draw punters that latch onto backing the Tote trio, the lower the dividend will become in the races where the effect of the draw works out, since it is a pool bet.

Computer straight forecasts (Csf's) are also open to reductions, since the formula to calculate them now incorporates such factors as the bookmakers' betting margin and the numbers of 'rags'. The formula is again very complicated to laymen such as myself and an algebra degree is probably needed to crack it.

It used to be that a rough way to work out the likely straight forecast dividend in decent-sized fields was to add a point onto the starting price of the runner-up, multiply it by the winner's price and then knock one point back off (as in win doubles), i.e. if the winner was returned 5/1 and the runner-up 7/2, multiplying 5 by 4½ would give 22½, minus 1, so the likely Csf would have been around £21.00.

1995	Talented Ting (11/2) beat Sarmatian (10/1) in a field of 12 at Hamilton where the favourite was returned at 2/1. The straight forecast paid £60.69.
	It should have been approximately 5½ (11/2) x 11 (10/1 + 1) = £60.50 - 1 = £59.50, so the dividend was good.
1995	Pallium (7/2 Fav) beat Arc Lamp (5/1) in a field of 10 at Ripon. The straight forecast paid £19.73.
	It should have been approximately 3½ x 6 - 1 = £20.00, so the dividend was good.
1995	Sharp Prospect (8/1) beat Set Table (9/1) in a field of 23 at Doncaster. The straight forecast paid £73.45.
	It should have been approximately 8 x 10 - 1 = £79.00, so the dividend was fair.

However,

1997	Artful Dane (10/1) beat Shinerolla (8/1 Fav) in a field of 23 at Doncaster (Spring Mile). The straight forecast paid £71.78.
	It should have been approximately 10 x 9 - 1 = £89.00, so the dividend was poor.

The straight forecasts returned for the 1997 Doncaster Spring Mile and the Lincoln (£66.75 for an 11/1 shot beating a 7/1 shot) were the subject of several letters of complaint in the racing press at the time and it was hardly surprising. Bookmakers were betting to 131.4% in the Spring Mile, a very competitive heat, so the odds were already shorter than they should have been. To then knock off around 20% of what the Csf would have been was a little unfair.

Races with fewer runners than the likes of the Spring Mile do not seem to have been affected quite so badly by the new formula, since there tend to be fewer 'rags'. The more competitive the race seems to be (i.e. the lesser the range between the favourite and the outsiders in the prices) the better the straight forecast dividend now seems to become. However, a better option now for draw punters is another Tote bet, the dual forecast, a pool bet and unfortunately one which rarely involves carry-forwards. The dual forecast, which involves selecting the first and second in a race in either order (Computer straight forecasts require getting the selections in the correct order) are always worth looking into, particularly at the bigger meetings, where there is a larger proportion of 'Holiday Punter' money going into the pool blind on the better-known jockeys' and trainers' representatives.

Bookmakers are never slow on the uptake if they feel that money is being given away unnecessarily, but the new formulae have effectively made both tricasts and straight forecasts, formerly the life-blood bets of the draw punter, unproductive.

Double Draw

Spread Betting Bookmakers I.G. Index at one time introduced a Double Draw bet, but it was discontinued in May 1997 due to an apparent lack of interest. It seems strange that spread bettors will gamble on the number of corners in a football match and the combined shirt numbers of touchdown scorers in American football, but will not take up the challenge of the Double Draw at a race meeting. The bet involved doubling the draw of every winner at a given meeting, so if the winners of a six-race meeting were drawn 2, 13, 8, 8, 7 and 1, the Double Draw figure would have been 78 (4 + 26 + 16 + 16 + 14 + 2). At courses such as Newbury when the ground was soft, this bet should have been of interest to punters, with such a bias favouring runners drawn high. If the Double Draw were to be reintroduced, and it would probably only require a decent level of interest to see it brought back, then it should be a bet that appeals to those wealthy enough to play what is essentially a rich-man's game. Particularly so when a lot of the fancied runners are unfavoured by the draw, since where the fancied runners are drawn is no doubt considered when the spread is being set.

131

CHAPTER 5

CONCLUSIONS

Implementing the system

As has already been stressed on more than one occasion, it is imperative to watch as much racing as possible, and also to have access to either a daily or weekly results section. I have found that the best way is to calculate selections is to cross out all races which do not have any sign of a draw bias in the weekly results section of the *Raceform Update* (any other results section would do, daily or weekly) and then start sifting through looking for outliers. Write down the selections on a 'rolling' list and award them a rating on a scale of one to five. It is unlikely that this list will ever contain more than about ten selections, and each selection should be scratched after being backed once.

Watch For

* *Any horse that wins his side or runs exceptionally well when the field splits into more than one group.*
* *Any horse that runs well when racing alone.*

Beware Of

* *Any horse that seems to run well on the unfavoured side on more than one occasion during a season.*
* *Handicappers switching from turf to all-weather or vice versa.*
* *Any horse that runs unexpectedly poorly from a good draw. These are always worth opposing next time.*

When to scratch selections

If a selection goes on to win next time, it should then almost always come off the list, but what to do if he does not have everything in his favour next time is a matter of opinion. If the selection does not have the ground in his favour for his next run, or he has gone up 3lb or more in the weights, he will probably become a no-bet and a decision then has to be made whether or not to still keep him on the list.

Even if he does not have his ideal conditions for that run, you should still be looking for him to run well in order to show that he remains in the sort of form that led to him being chosen in the first place. If he runs a poor race without having a valid excuse, it is probably best to delete him.

How and where to back selections

Once a selection has been made and given a revised rating on the day of his next outing, all that remains (other than to actually race) is where and how to back him. Fortunately, my lifestyle allows me to back on-course most of the time, and knocking the 9% tax-deduction out of the equation obviously helps, as does being able to shop around for the best price. Failing this, the best idea is to take early prices.

A majority of draw-based selections come from, and go on to run next time in, sprint handicaps, races that off-course bookmakers tend to price up in the mornings. Shopping around for the best morning prices is the most advisable way to go rather than to take starting price, as most of the value is to be found early, since the bigger firms have to be seen to be competitive in the Racing Post's Pricewise and similar columns, normally betting to around 125% in larger-field races. So many times in the past, races that started off as 8/1 or 10/1 the field in the morning ended up with a favourite at 7/2 and a second-favourite at 6/1, as the 'Magic Sign' and others moved in to shorten them up. To this end, it helps to be able to bet with as many different bookmakers as possible.

Very few bookmakers these days price up every race, including maidens and two-year-old events, but there are some Independents around that still do. My local firm, Reg Allen of Bedford, price up every race and they tend to be more accommodating with all their prices, and more customer-friendly than bigger bookmakers.

Another option is to back on the Tote, but this would only apply to certain runners. If the selection hails from a big Newmarket stable and/or is ridden by a top jockey, the chances are that the Tote dividend will be comparably shorter than the starting price as more public money will go on him. However, if he comes from a less well-known yard (often the case in sprint handicaps) and is ridden by a jockey not familiar to the public, the Tote can be of interest, especially at the bigger meetings.

Try to stick to just backing win singles though. Any bookmaker will tell you that the bet they least like to lay is the win single, since it gives them the lowest percentage profit of any bet on offer. To my mind, backing each-way, and receiving just a quarter or a fifth the odds a place, is not a viable option.

Implementing a bank system

Keeping discipline as a punter is very important, since it is so easy to start punting on every event when on a racecourse, so employing a bank system, as shown on pages 127-128, can be very useful. Start with an amount that suits you and decide how much a maximum bet will be. So if your starting bank is £1,000 and you decide that a maximum bet (or five-start bet) will become £80, then a one-star bet will become £16 and so on. Bets will then halve if the bank halves, double if the bank doubles and quadruple *when* it reaches £4,000.

1997 Racecourse conclusions

The effect of the draw changed at several courses during the 1997 season, some as a result of new watering systems and other because of course amendments. My idea of the top ten draw-effect courses under optimum conditions now would be:-

1)   Sandown   (soft)
2)   Ripon
3)   Yarmouth   (firm)
4)   Newbury   (soft)
5)   Thirsk   (fast)
6)   Beverley   (fast)
7)   Musselburgh
8)   Lingfield   (firm)
9)   Goodwood
10) Catterick

Ascot - The draw advantage was not as pronounced in 1997 as in the recent past, although again the far rail rarely looked the place to be. Outliers in well-subscribed straight-course handicaps are always of interest here, since the tendency is for fields to split into two, or sometimes three, groups.
*Watch For (Straight races only) **(During racing)** either rail being favoured at festival meetings at up to a mile. **(After racing)** outliers in big-field handicaps.*

Ayr - High numbers were again favoured in the Silver and Ayr Gold Cups, although not as dominant as in the previous two years. At other meetings, Ayr remained of little interest.
*Watch For **(After)** outliers in the Silver and Gold cups.*

Bath - No real interest.

Beverley - High numbers were again dominant in five-furlong races and a vast majority of the winners came from the top six stalls.
*Watch For **(Before)** any runner drawn in the top six stalls in five-furlong races (very few winners come from positions further from the far rail). **(During)** flip starts. **(After)** outliers from low draws that raced towards the far side.*

Brighton - No real interest.
*Watch For **(During)** runners switching towards the stands' side on soft ground.*

Carlisle - No real interest.
*Watch For **(Before)** low numbers in sprints when the ground is soft.*

Catterick - High numbers were favoured over five furlongs when the ground was soft, and low numbers did best when it was fast.
*Watch For **(During**) runners racing towards the outside and then towards the stands' side when the ground is soft in races run on the round course. **(After)** outliers in five-furlong races.*

Chepstow - High numbers, unlike in the past, seemed at a disadvantage over sprint distances.

Chester - Low numbers again enjoyed a decisive advantage on soft ground until the course had been raced on a few times.
*Watch For **(Before)** the bottom six or so stalls in early-in-the-meeting races at up to 7f 122y when the ground is soft and **(After)** outliers in such races.*

Doncaster - The draw remained difficult to predict.
Watch For (Before) the bottom six or seven stalls in the Spring Mile and Lincoln when the ground is soft. Now that the plan for trainers to pick stalls out of a hat for the Lincoln has been given the go-ahead, it will interesting to see how each trainer interprets the likely effect of the draw. *(After)* outliers in big fields when one side is clearly favoured.

Epsom - Low numbers again looked to have the edge in races run on the round course up to 1m 114y.
Watch For (During) runners switching towards the stands' side on soft ground.

Folkestone - Low numbers continued to hold sway in sprints.
Watch For (During) runners switching towards the far side in sprints.

Goodwood - The centre of the course looked way slower than the stands' rail in sprints, but the far rail again looked slightly faster than the stands' rail. Low numbers in big-field seven-furlong races again struggled.
Watch For (Before) low numbers in sprints with between 10 and 15 runners.

Hamilton - Unlike previous years, the draw became difficult to predict in sprints, although high numbers were again favoured in races of 1m 65y.
Watch For (After) outliers in sprints when one side was clearly favoured, and over 1m 65y.

Haydock - High numbers used to be massively favoured in sprints when the ground was soft or worse, but the advantage seemed to switch to favour low numbers as the season progressed.
Watch For (During) runners switching to the stands' side in round-course races on soft ground, although this may no longer happen. *(After)* outliers in soft-ground sprints.

Kempton - It is hard to be certain about the draw advantage on the sprint course as a result of the amendments, although only a small part of the course was affected.
Watch For (After) outliers in sprints.

Leicester - On more than one occasion, as in the past, one part of the course occasionally proved much faster than the remainder, but it was as difficult to predict as usual and probably down to the prevailing wind during watering.
Watch For (After) outliers when one side of the course was clearly favoured.

Lingfield all-weather - No real interest.
Lingfield turf - There was just one meeting in 1997 when conditions were right for high numbers to be favoured (May 9th) and they were again completely dominant.
Watch For (Before) the top three or four stalls on recently rained-on fast ground and *(After)* outliers in such races.

Musselburgh - Low numbers were again well favoured in sprints, particularly on soft ground.

Watch For (Before) low numbers in sprints when the stalls are low, and for the possibility of a few runners from the bottom stalls coming across to the stands' rail when the stalls are on the far side. (After) outliers in sprints.

Newbury - High numbers again did best on soft ground, although the surface never became as bad as it was in 1996.
Watch For (Before) any runner drawn in the top four of five stalls in straight-course races when the ground is soft and (After) outliers in such races.

Newcastle - The effect of the draw seemed to balance out during 1997 and Newcastle is no longer of as much interest as in the past. The centre of the course now seems just as fast as both rails.

Newmarket July Course - No real interest.
Watch For (After) outliers when one side seemed favoured.

Newmarket Rowley Mile - Runners drawn very high in big fields in races at up to 1m 1f again looked at a disadvantage.
Watch For (Before) low numbers when the stands' rail is pushed towards the stands. (After) outliers from high stalls.

Nottingham - On some occasions, high numbers looked favoured, yet on others low numbers looked to have the edge. When either side held sway, they tended to have complete control, but it looked to be largely a case of where the pace in the race was rather than any faster strip of ground. This was certainly not the case in the past, when the far rail was clearly favoured.
Watch For (After) outliers when all the pace was on one side.

Pontefract - High numbers had a massive advantage on soft ground.
Watch For (Before) the top four or five stalls in races over trips up to middle-distances when the ground is soft.

Redcar - High numbers looked favoured in straight-course races.

Ripon - Low numbers were hugely favoured in sprints with up to about 16 runners, above which figure runners drawn very high had an equally good chance.
Watch for (Before) the bottom three stalls in sprints with less than 16 runners. The bottom three and the top three stalls in sprints with 16 or more runners. (After) outliers in sprints.

Salisbury - High numbers enjoyed a marginal advantage when there was cut in the ground.

Sandown - High numbers were again massively favoured in sprints when the stalls were high on any ground, but particularly so when it was soft. The stands' rail was still quicker than the centre of the course though.
Watch For (Sprint Course) (Before) high numbers when the stalls are on the far side. (During) runners switching to race on the far rail when the stalls are low. (After) outliers.

Southwell all-weather - No real interest.
Watch For (Before) the bottom three stalls in five-furlong races after a frost.

Thirsk - High numbers continued to dominate in sprints when the ground was riding on the fast side.
Watch For (Before) the top four or five stalls in sprints when the ground is fast. The bottom three stalls when the ground is soft. (After) outliers.

Warwick - High numbers were favoured on soft ground.
Watch For (Before) the top four or five stalls on soft ground at most distances.

Windsor - No real interest.

Wolverhampton all-weather - Runners that raced on the inside did not seem to do as badly as in the past.

Yarmouth - Yarmouth only came to prominence as a draw-affect course in 1996 and continued to show a huge bias in 1997 for runners drawn high on fast-ground straight-course events.
Watch For (Before) the top four or five stalls up to 1m 3y on fast ground. (After) outliers.

York - Runners drawn middle to high just about held sway in big-field sprints, but the effect of the draw was never conclusive.
Watch For (After) outliers in sprints when one side was clearly favoured.

Jockeys to follow

Jimmy Fortune caught my eye as a young apprentice riding for Mike O'Neill a good few years ago, and since he started his time with the Ramsden stable he has gone from strength to strength. Armed these days with the knowledge of where the best ground is at every course, he has become a very accomplished pilot in sprint handicaps, never getting flustered and always being prepared to wait for a gap up the favoured rail. It can be pretty much guaranteed that when he has the best of the draw at courses like Thirsk or Ripon, he will never leave the fence and, while he can sometimes find traffic problems employing such tactics, the ploy pays off more often than it fails. Fortune has produced memorable rides on Benzoe, among others, over the past few years.

Michael Roberts surprised a few people, myself included, when becoming champion jockey in 1992, but he has since shown himself to be among the elite when it comes to exploiting a good draw. I would bracket him in a group with Fortune, Ray Cochrane, George Duffield, Dean McKeown, Richard Perham, Warren O'Connor, Ted Durcan, Dale Gibson, Michael Fenton and Robert Winston (already) of jockeys guaranteed to find the best ground. Although Roberts no longer gets as many rides or enjoys as many winners as the year in which he was crowned, to my mind he is riding better than ever, and his performances aboard Artful Dane, Purchasing Power and Sweet Magic were just a few of his 1997 highlights.

George Duffield, half of probably the shrewdest duo in Flat racing along with Sir Mark Prescott, started the 1993 season with a real flourish and attracted a few bets at fancy prices about claiming a first jockeys' championship. Although he was not likely to win that prize, simply because he could never compete numerically with the likes of Pat Eddery, all the rides he got were given the best possible chance, a comment that still applies. With years of experience behind him, Duffield knows all the courses on which he rides, and no doubt all the fastest strips of ground on them.

Of the 'lesser' jockeys, Dean McKeown showed on more than one occasion in 1997 that he is one to watch for in draw-bias races; Ted Durcan struck up an excellent partnership with Palacegate Jack, making the most of the best ground on more than one occasion to squeeze more success from a totally-exposed gelding; much-touted apprentice Robert Winston showed that he had already learned the importance of the draw with his ride on Tarxien at Pontefract among others. He will be a jockey to follow. Dale Gibson, in his role as jockeys' safety officer, always puts his hands-on experience to the best possible use, especially when riding lower-class handicappers for Mick Easterby. His win on the very-moderate Mill End Lady at Thirsk in 1996, where he never left the stands' rail, dug me out of a hole on a day where losses were incurred at Newmarket. Michael Fenton rarely makes a mistake when well-drawn and he and Michael Bell are always worth following.

Of the top jockeys, I would favour the likes of Jason Weaver and Kieren Fallon over Frankie Dettori and Pat Eddery. Fallon spent his formative years in Britain attached to the Ramsden stable and doubtless picked up some good habits there. His riding of Averti in the King George at Glorious Goodwood, where he never came off the favoured stands' rail (and beat Cathedral) was most impressive. Jason Weaver has plied his trade for a good few years around the Ripons and Beverleys for Mark Johnston and doubtless picked up plenty of tips from his guv'nor. Dettori and Eddery, whilst not falling into the category of jockeys 'failing to find the best ground' have never conclusively proved that they go off in search of it as much as the likes of Roberts or Cochrane.

Trainers to follow

Whomever the jockey that takes a ride for the Ramsden stable may be, they seem to be given a very definite game-plan in races likely to effected by the draw. Be it Joe Fanning, Kieren Fallon or currently Jimmy Fortune, the instructions seem to be stick to the rail on both prominently-racing horses and those that need holding up.

Mick Easterby, as shrewd a trainer as you could wish to find, has never been averse to running more than one horse in potential draw-affect races, particularly nurseries, no doubt in the hope that one or more will be well-drawn. His representatives are always worthy of consideration in such events. Other trainers that I consider worth following would be found in most lists of 'shrewd' handlers, and include Sir Mark Prescott, Jack Berry, Michael Bell, Neville Callaghan, David Chapman and less familiar names such as Ron Hodges, Paul Howling and Karl Burke.

Ten to follow

The following list of horses all ran well at some point in 1997 when faced with a difficult draw. They are all consequently fairly handicapped as a result and some fortuitously remain maidens.

Bright Paragon is completely exposed after several seasons racing, but more than once in 1997 he ran well enough from poor draws to show he is still handicapped to win more races. K Ivory

Cathedral turned in an unforgettable effort to finish third at Sandown from an impossible draw and his two later runs did nothing to suggest that he does not remain one to follow in 1998. Unlucky to be caught by Averti in the Group Three King George at Goodwood before just being touched off in a conditions event at Lingfield, he should more than pay his way in pattern sprints at four and could be open to further improvement. **B. Meehan**

Cathedral should enjoy plenty of success in 1998

Johayro is a typical sprint handicapper, in that he can be relied upon to run to give his running when he has things in his favour. He finished the season on a handicap rating of 64 having started on 54, but some of his efforts from poor draws suggested he could still have enough improvement in him to be able to win off marks higher still. **J. Goldie**

Odette amazingly finished 1997 a maiden after making the frame four times from four runs. Every time though she showed good speed from difficult draws and she should win her maiden at the very least, despite pessimism from her trainer. **Sir Mark Prescott**

Return of Amin was unlucky with the draw on more than one occasion in 1997 and may be capable of winning further decent handicaps off what could still be a fair mark. The early-season target could be the Victoria Cup followed by other valuable six and seven-furlong handicaps, but a mile would probably be beyond him. He looks the sort that will improve as he gets older and faster ground should not be a hindrance. **J. Bethell**

Return of Amin won the William Hill Trophy and should continue to pay his way

Ring Dancer made a deep impression when winning down the centre at Ripon and did nothing wrong when stepped up in class for his only other run at two. He has had a trouble-free build-up to his three-year-old campaign and should pay to follow. **P. Makin**

Rita's Rock Ape was an extremely speedy youngster and goes into 1998 at the right end of the handicap. The plan is to stick to five-furlong handicaps on easy tracks and, when she finally gets a plum draw, she will take some catching. **R. Brotherton**

Southern Dominion finished the 1997 season with a flourish and may well be able to continue his improvement into next season, given that he had no problems living with better rivals once stepped up in class. The plan is to run once on the all-weather before returning to turf for the start of the season, and he could take some pegging back in 0-70 handicaps. **Miss J. Craze**

Surprised hails from a stable that specialises in placing unexposed horses to maximum effect, and he could run up a sequence in handicaps, for which he will be eligible straight away after three runs as a juvenile. His first 1997 outing did not come until September when he ran promisingly, and he then had the worst of the draw in two further good runs. **Mrs J. Ramsden**

Swift had the draw against him more than once in 1997 when running well and will be one to keep on the right side for some of the better seven-furlong/mile handicaps. The plan is to have two runs on the all-weather before the Spring Mile, and his turn of foot will always hold him in good stead. **M. Polglase**

By backing these horses throughout 1998, I feel sure you will make a profit, but only when they have the draw in their favour!